THE DRIVEN SERIES

Driven

Fueled

Crashed

Raced

Aced

K. BROMBERG

Cover art created by: Tugboat Design

Formatting by: Champagne Book Design

PRAISE FOR THE NOVELS OF K. BROMBERG

"An irresistibly hot romance that stays with you long after you finish the book."

—# 1 *New York Times* bestselling author Jennifer L. Armentrout

"Captivating, emotional, and sizzling hot!"

—#1 *New York Times* bestselling author S. C. Stephens

"Bromberg is a master at turning up the heat!"

—*New York Times* bestselling author Katy Evans

"K. Bromberg is the master of making hearts race and pulses pound. Colton and Rylee will forever be one of romances sexiest and most passionate couples."

—New York Times bestselling author Jay Crownover

"Romance and connection explode from K. Bromberg's books and every story is full of love, emotion, and true life that makes the fantasy even more poignant. Plus she has the most delicious heroes in the book world! A master storyteller!!"

—*New York Times* bestselling author Pepper Winters

"Colton and Rylee are back - hotter, sweeter, and more passionate than ever. I loved this new chapter in their epic romance. K. Bromberg writes the perfect romance, packed with steam, sizzle, and soul.

—*USA Today* bestselling author Ella James

"The more I read, the more I want. . . . Your emotions will be taken on one hell of an angst-filled, heartbreaking, gut-wrenching, mind-blowing, and wickedly sexy, beautiful journey."

—Book Crush

"[A] highly emotional yet satisfying series, oh, and let me not leave out SEXY."

—Guilty Pleasures Book Reviews

"An emotionally charged, adrenaline-filled, steamy, and passionate read. . . . K. Bromberg deliver[s]."

—TotallyBookedBlog

"This series is *everything* a true fan of romance would want or need."

—Sinfully Sexy Book Reviews

"An intense, emotional, riveting ride [that's] sexy, romantic, heartbreaking, and uplifting. This is the kind of book you don't want to put down."

—Aestas Book Blog

"K. Bromberg has created wonderful characters that you just can't help but fall in love with . . . beautifully written and a very emotional read."

—Ramblings from This Chick

"K. Bromberg is nothing short of an absolute genius . . . so real and raw that you truly feel every single emotion."

—Romance Addiction

Also by K. Bromberg

Driven
Fueled
Crashed
Raced
Aced
Slow Burn
Sweet Ache
Hard Beat
Down Shift
UnRaveled
Sweet Cheeks
Sweet Rivalry
The Player
The Catch
Cuffed
Combust
Cockpit
Control
Faking It
Resist
Reveal
Then You Happened
Hard to Handle
Flirting with 40
Hard to Hold

Foreward

To My Readers:

This boxed set contains almost everything I have ever written in regards to the Driven series. With that said, there are a few things to keep in mind while reading:

If you are new to the series, welcome. I truly hope you enjoy the journey into Rylee and Colton's world. I look forward to watching you feel every emotion as you become lost in the roller coaster ride of ups and downs and sighs and screams that this series takes you on.

The Driven Series consists of nine books. Of those nine books, four are complete standalones (*Slow Burn, Sweet Ache, Hard Beat, Down Shift*) and five are a true series that must be read in order (*Driven, Fueled, Crashed, Aced,* and a novella, *Raced*). This boxed set contains the five read-in-order books, bonus scenes from those books, and then extras from the standalone books.

Raced is a unique book—let me explain why. After writing *Driven, Fueled,* and Crashed, readers often asked what Colton was thinking in certain scenes of those books. After much thought, I decided to write a collection of chapters from the trilogy told in his point of view. This is the novella titled *Raced*. It's not pertinent to read to understand the series, but it does add extra insight to the ever-complicated Colton Donavan.

After *Raced* was released, readers started telling me that they hated having to flip between books (i.e. reading *Driven* then switching to Raced to read Colton's point of view and then back to *Driven*). It was a common request that I combine all of the books and add the Raced chapters in the appropriate locations in the series.

That is what I did in this boxed set.

It's important to understand this since each chapter that that has been integrated into the series from *Raced* is an add-on. That means that there might be two of the same chapter numbers but the second one will say 'Colton-Raced' under the chapter heading (because it's the same chapter told in Colton's point of view) or the chapter might be a half (i.e. Chapter 3 ½) because the chapter encompasses a Colton point of view in between the two chapters of the original books. There are even a couple that say 'Bonus scene' and that is just what it sounds like, an extra scene I wrote that fits right in that location.

When reading this new collection, sometimes readers feel like these added chapters end abruptly without a smooth segue to the next chapter. I apologize for that, but these added chapters were never intended to be blended with the original books so please know that if a chapter ends and flows oddly (or not at all) into the next chapter, this is why.

In addition to combining *Driven, Fueled, Crashed, Raced,* and *Aced* in one giant boxed set, I've also added extras at the end of the book. Deleted scenes between Colton and Rylee as well as some bonus content from the standalones in the series (*Slow Burn, Sweet Ache, Hard Beat, Down Shift*) that previously could only be read if you purchased the paperback.

I hope this helps to clear up any confusion on, but more than anything, I truly hope you enjoy taking the ride with Colton, Rylee, and the rest of the gang!

Happy reading and I race you!
Kristy

To my readers …

It's been over seven years since you all met Rylee and Colton. It's been a wild, chaotic, and incredible ride since then and I owe so very much of it to you!
Thank you for your unending support and endless love for these characters.

—Kristy

Driven

To B, B & C-

May you always follow your dreams.
The path will never be easy and you might have to chase them for years.
There will be obstacles to overcome and criticisms to ignore.
There will be periods of doubt and moments of insecurity.

But you will reach them.

And when you finally touch those dreams,
No matter how old you are or where life has taken you,
Hold on tight—savor that feeling of accomplishment—and never let go.
Ever.

Chapter One

I sigh into the welcoming silence, grateful for the chance to escape—even if only momentarily—from the mindsuck of meaningless conversations on the other side of the door. For all intents and purposes, the people holding these conversations are my guests, but that doesn't mean I have to like or even be comfortable around them. Fortunately, Dane was sympathetic enough to my need for a reprieve that he let me do this chore for him.

The clicking of my high heels is the only other sound accompanying my categorically scattered thoughts, as I navigate the vacant backstage corridors of the old theater that I've rented for tonight's event. I quickly reach the old dressing room and collect the lists that Dane forgot in our chaotic, pre-party rush to clean up. As I start to head back, I run over my mental checklist for tonight's highly anticipated date auction. The niggling in the back of my mind tells me that I'm forgetting something. Reflexively, I reach for my hip, where my cell phone with my always-compiled task list lives, but instead, I come up with a handful of my cocktail dress's copper-colored silk organza.

"Shit," I mutter to myself as I stop momentarily, trying to pinpoint what exactly it is that I'm overlooking. I sag against the wall, the ruched bodice of my dress hindering my ability to inhale a deep sigh of frustration. Even though it looks incredible, the damn dress should've come with a warning: breathing optional.

Think, Rylee, think! With my shoulder blades pressed against the wall, I shift inelegantly back and forth to try and alleviate the pressure on my toes, which are painfully crammed into my four-inch heels.

Auction paddles! I need the auction paddles. I smile widely at my brain's ability to remember, considering I've been so overwhelmed lately as the sole coordinator of tonight's event. Relieved, I push myself off of the wall and take about ten steps.

And that's when I hear them.

The flirty, feminine giggle floats through the air, followed by the deep timbre of a masculine moan. I freeze instantly, shocked at the audacity of our party's attendees, when I hear the unmistakable sound of a zipper, followed by a breathless but *familiar* feminine gasp of, *"Oh yes!"* in the darkened alcove a few feet in front of me. As my eyes adjust to the shadows, I become aware of a man's black dinner jacket lying carelessly across an old chair shoved askew and a pair of strappy heels haphazardly discarded on the floor beneath it.

You couldn't pay me enough money to do something like that in public. My thoughts are interrupted when I hear a hiss of breath followed by a masculine, exhaled, *"Sweet Jesus!"*

I squeeze my eyes shut in a moment of indecision. I really need the auction paddles that sit in the storage closet at the end of the intersecting hallway. Unfortunately, the only way to reach that hallway is to walk past Lover's Lane alcove. I have no choice but to go for it. I send up a silent yet ludicrous prayer, hoping that I can skate past unnoticed.

I scurry forward, keeping my blush-stained face angled to the wall opposite them while I walk on my toes to keep my heels from clicking on the hardwood floor. The last thing I need right now is to draw attention to myself and come face to face with someone I know. I breathe a silent sigh of relief when my clandestine tiptoe is successful.

I'm still trying to place the woman's voice when I reach the storage closet. I fumble clumsily with the handle, having to aggressively tug on it before finally yanking it open and flicking on the light. I spot the bag of auction paddles on the far shelf as I walk inside the closet, forgetting to prop the door open. As I grab the handles of the bag, the door at my back slams shut with such force that the cheap shelving units in the closet rattle. Startled, I whip around to reopen the door and notice that the arm on the self-closing hinge has disconnected.

I immediately drop the bag. The sound of the paddles hitting the concrete floor and spilling out causes an eruption of sound. When I reach for the handle, it turns but the door doesn't budge an inch. Panic licks at my subconscious, but I suppress it as I push again on the door with all of my strength. *It does not move.*

"Shit!" I chastise myself. "Shit, shit, shit!" I take a deep breath and shake my head in frustration. I have so much to do before the auction starts. And of course I don't have my cell phone to call Dane to get me out of here either.

When I close my eyes, my nemesis suddenly makes its move. The long, all-consuming fingers of claustrophobia slowly begin to claw their way up my body and wrap themselves around my throat.

Squeezing. Tormenting. Stifling.

The walls of the small room seem to be gradually sliding closer to each other, closing in on me. Surrounding me. Suffocating me. I struggle to breathe.

My heart beats erratically as I push back the panic rising in my throat. My breath—shallow and rapid—echoes in my ears. Consuming me. Zapping my ability to suppress my haunted memories.

I pound on the door, fear overwhelming the small hold I have left on my control. On reality. A rivulet of sweat trickles down my back. The walls keep moving in on me. My need to escape is the only thing I can focus on. I pound on the door again, yelling frantically, hoping someone roaming these back corridors can hear me.

I lean my back against the wall, close my eyes, and try to catch my breath; it's not coming quickly enough and dizziness surfaces. Becoming nauseous, I start to slide down the wall and accidentally hit the light switch. I'm submerged in pitch-black darkness. I cry out, frantically searching for the switch with my trembling hands. I flick it on, relieved to have pushed the monsters back into hiding.

But when I look down, blood covers my hands. I blink to try and snap out of my reverie, but I can't shake it. I'm in a different place. A different time.

All around me, I smell the acrid stench of destruction. Of desperation. Of death.

In my ears, his thready breathing is agonizing. He's gasping. Dying.

I feel the intense, blazing pain that twists so deep in your soul, you fear you'll never escape it. Even in death. My screams shake me out of the memory, and I'm so disoriented that I'm not sure if they're from the past or the present.

Get a grip, Rylee! I rub the tears off my cheeks with the backs of my hands and think back to my previous year in therapy to try to keep my claustrophobia at bay. I concentrate on a mark on the wall across from me, try to regulate my breathing, and slowly count. I focus on pushing the walls out, pushing the unbearable memories away.

I count to ten, gaining a scrap of composure, yet desperation still clings to me. I know Dane will come looking for me shortly. He knows where I went, but the thought does nothing to alleviate my surmounting panic.

Finally, I surrender to my intense need to escape and start pounding on the door with the heels of my hands. Shouting loudly. Cursing sporadically. Begging for someone to hear me and open the door. *For someone to save me again.*

In my ragged state of mind, seconds feel like minutes and minutes feel like hours. I feel like I've been locked in this ever-shrinking closet forever. Feeling defeated, I yell out once more and rest my forearms on the door in front of me. Bracing my weight on my forearms, I lay my head on them and succumb to my tears. Large, ragged sobs shake violently through me.

And suddenly, I have the feeling of falling.

Falling forward as I stumble into the solid body of a man in my path. My arms encircle a firm torso while my legs lie awkwardly bent behind me. The man instinctively brings his arms up and wraps them around me, catching me, holding my weight and absorbing my impact.

I look up, quickly registering the shock of dark hair spiked haphazardly, bronzed skin, the slight shadow of stubble … and then I meet his eyes. A jolt of electricity—an almost palpable energy—crackles when I meet those guarded, translucent green irises. Surprise flashes through them fleetingly, but the intrigue and intensity with which he regards me is unnerving, despite my body's immediate reaction to him. Needs and desires long forgotten inundate me with this one, simple meeting of eyes.

How can this man I've never met make me forget the panic and desperation I felt only moments before?

I make the mistake of breaking eye contact and glancing down at his mouth. Full, sculpted lips purse as he studies me intently, and then very slowly, they spread into a lopsided, roguish grin.

Oh, how I want that mouth on me—anywhere and everywhere all at once. What in the hell am I thinking? This man is way out of my league. Like light years away out of my league.

I draw my gaze back up to see amusement in his eyes, as if he knows what I'm thinking. I can feel a flush slowly spread over my face as embarrassment for both my predicament and my salacious thoughts registers in my brain. I tighten my grip around muscular biceps as I lower my gaze to avoid his assessing eyes and try to regain my composure. Bringing my feet back under me, I accidentally stumble farther into him, my balance compromised by my inexperience with sky-high heels. I jump back from him as my breasts brush against his firm chest, setting my nerve endings ablaze. Tiny detonations of desire tickle deep in my belly.

"Oh ... um ... I'm so sorry." I hold my hands up in a flustered apology. The man is even more disarming now that I'm able to drink in the whole length of him. Imperfectly perfect and sexy as hell with a smirk suggesting arrogance and an air exuding trouble.

He raises an eyebrow, noticing my slow inspection of him. "No apologies needed," he responds in a cultured rasp with just a hint of edge. His voice evokes images of rebellion and sex. *"I'm used to women falling at my feet."*

My head snaps up. I can only hope he's joking, but his enigmatic expression gives nothing away. He watches my response, bemusement in his eyes, and that cocksure smile widening, causing a single dimple to deepen in his defined jaw.

Despite having taken a step back, *I am still close to him*. Too close for me to gather my wits, but close enough for me to feel his breath over my cheek. To smell the clean scent of soap mixed with his subtle, earthy cologne.

"Thanks. Thank you," I respond breathlessly. I see the muscle in his clenched jaw pulse as he watches me. Why is this man making me nervous and feeling like I have to justify my situation? "The-the door shut behind me. It jammed. I panicked—"

"Are you okay? Miss—?"

My response falters as his hand cups the back of my neck, pulling me closer and holding me still. He runs his free hand up and down my bare arm in what I assume is an attempt to make sure that I'm not physically harmed. My body registers the trail of sparks his fingertips blaze on my naked flesh while my mind becomes acutely aware that his sensuous mouth is only a whisper away from mine. My lips part and my breath hitches as he moves his hand up the line of my neck and then uses the back of it to run his knuckles softly down my cheek.

I have no time to register the confusion mingled with a heavy dose of desire that surges through me when I hear him mutter, *"Oh fuck it,"* seconds before his mouth is on mine. I gasp in utter shock, my lips parting a fraction as his mouth absorbs the sound, giving him an opening to caress his tongue over my lips and dart slowly between them.

I push my hands against his chest, trying to resist the uninvited kiss from this stranger. Trying to do what logic tells me is right. Trying to deny what my body is telling me it wants. To abandon inhibition and let myself enjoy this one moment with him.

Common sense wins my internal feud between lust and prudence, and I manage to push him back a fraction. His mouth breaks from mine, our breaths panting over each other's faces. His eyes, wild with lust, hold steady to mine. I find it hard to ignore the seed of desire that's blooming deep in my belly. The vehement protest that's screaming in my mind dies silently on my lips as I succumb to the notion that I *want* this kiss. I want to *feel* what I have been so devoid of—what I have purposely denied myself. I want to act recklessly and have "that kiss"—the one that books are written about, love is found in, and virtue is lost with.

"Decide, sweetheart," he commands. "A man only has so much restraint."

His warning, the insane notion that *simple me* can make a man *like him* lose control, bewilders me, confusing my thoughts so that the denial on my tongue never crosses my lips. He takes advantage of my silence, a lascivious smile curling the corners of his mouth before tightening the hold he has on the nape of my neck. From one breath to the next, he crushes his mouth to mine. Probing. Tasting. Demanding.

My resistance is futile and lasts only seconds before I surrender to him. I instinctively move my hands over his unshaven jaw to the back of his neck and tug my fingers in the hair that curls over the top of his collar. A low moan comes from the back of his throat, bolstering my confidence, allowing me to part my lips and take more of him. My tongue entwines and dances intimately with his. A slow, seductive ballet highlighted with breathy moans and panted whimpers.

He tastes of whiskey. His confidence exudes rebellion. His body evokes a straight punch of lust to my sex. A heady combination hinting he's a bad boy that this good girl should stay clear of. His urgency and adept skill hint at what could come. Images flash through my mind of back-arching, toe-pointing, sheet-gripping sex that no doubt would be as dominating as his kiss.

Despite my submission, I know this is wrong. I can hear my conscience telling me to stop. That I don't do *these* kinds of things. That I'm not *that* kind of girl. That I'm betraying Max with each caress.

But God, it feels so incredibly good. I bury all rationality under the surmounting desire that rages through my every nerve. My every breath.

His fingers stroke the back of my neck while his other hand travels down to my hip, igniting sparks with every touch. He splays it on my lower back and presses me into him. Laying claim to me. I can feel his erection thickening against my midsection, sending an electric charge to my groin, making me damp with need and desire. His leg slightly shifts and presses between mine, adding pressure to the apex of my thighs and creating an intense ache of pleasure. I push farther into him, softly mewling as I crave more.

I am drowning in the sensation of him, and yet I'm not willing to come up for the air I so desperately need.

He nips my lower lip as his hand moves down to knead my backside, pleasure spiraling through me. My nails scrape the back of his neck in reaction as I stake my claim.

"Christ, I want you right now," his husky voice pants between kisses, intensifying the ache in the muscles coiling below my waist. He moves the hand from the back of my neck and traces it down my ribcage and over until it cups my breast. I cry out a soft moan at the sensation of his fingers rubbing over my hardened peak through the soft material of my dress.

My body is ready to consent to his request because I want this man too. I want to feel his weight on me, his bare skin sliding on mine, and his length moving rhythmically in me.

Our entangled bodies bump up against the small alcove in the hallway. He presses me against the wall, our bodies frantically grabbing, groping, and tasting. He skims his hand down to the hem of my cocktail dress, finding purchase when he touches the lace tops of my thigh-high stockings.

"Sweet Jesus," he murmurs against my mouth as he runs his hand at a painstakingly slow pace up my outer thigh to the small triangle of lace that serves more as decoration than as panties.

What? Those words. When they finally register, I recoil as if whiplashed and push on his chest trying to shove him away from me. Those are the same words that I'd heard earlier in the darkened alcove. They hit me like cold water to my libido. *What the hell? And what in the hell am I doing anyway, making out with some random guy?* And more importantly, why pick now to do this while I'm in the midst of one of my most important events of the year?

"No. No—I can't do this." Staggering back, I bring a trembling hand up to my mouth to cover my swollen lips. . His eyes snap up to mine, the emerald color darkened by desire. Anger flashes through them fleetingly.

"It's a little late, sweetheart. It looks as if you already have."

Fury flashes through me at his sardonic comment. I'm intelligent enough to infer that I've just become another in the line of his evening's conquests. I look back at him, and the smug look on his face makes me want to hurl insults at him.

"Who the hell do you think you are? Touching me like that? Taking advantage of me that way?" I spit at him, using anger to ward off the hurt I feel. I'm not sure if I'm more upset at myself for my willing submission or the fact that he took advantage of me in my frenetic state. Or is it that I feel ashamed because I succumbed to his mind blowing kiss and skilled fingers without even knowing his name?

He continues to observe me, his anger simmering, eyes glowering. "Really?" he scoffs at me, cocking his head to the side and rubbing a hand over his condescending smirk. I can hear the rasp of his stubble as his hand chafes over it. "That's how you're going to play this? Were you not participating just now? Were you not just coming apart in my arms?" He laughs snidely. "Don't fool your *prim* little self into thinking that you didn't enjoy that. That you don't want more."

He takes a step closer to me, amusement and something darker blazing in the depths of his eyes. Raising a hand, he traces a finger down the line of my jaw. Despite flinching, the heat from his touch reignites the smoldering craving deep in my belly. I silently castigate my body for its betrayal. "Let's get one thing clear," he growls at me. "I. Do. Not. Take. What's. Not. Offered. And we both know, *sweetheart*, you offered." He smirks. "*Willingly*."

I jerk my chin away from his fingertips, wishing that I were one of those people who can say all the right things at all the right times. But I'm not. Instead, I think of them hours later and only wish that I'd said them. I know that I'll be doing that later, for I can't think of a single way to rebuke this overconfident yet completely correct man. He has reduced me to a mass of overstimulated nerves craving him to touch me again.

"That poor defenseless crap may work with your boyfriend who treats you like china on a shelf, fragile and nice to look at. Rarely used..." he shrugs "...but admit it, sweetheart, that's boring."

"My boy—" I stutter, "I'm not fragile!"

"Really?" he chides, reaching up to hold my chin in place as he looks in my eyes. "You sure act that way."

"Screw you!" I jerk my chin from his grasp.

"Ooooh, you're a feisty little thing." His arrogant smirk is irritating. "*I like feisty, sweetheart.* It only makes me want you that much more."

Prick! I'm just about to make a retort about what a manwhore he obviously is. That I know about his "getting acquainted" with someone else down the hall not too long ago before moving onto me. I stare at him, the thought rattling around in the back of my head that he vaguely reminds me of someone, but I push it away. I'm flustered, that's all.

As I'm about to open my mouth, I hear Dane's voice calling my name. Relief floods me as I turn to see him standing at the end of the hallway, looking at me oddly. Most likely perplexed by my disheveled state.

"Rylee? I really need those lists. Did you get them?"

"I got sidetracked," I mumble. I glance back at Mr. Arrogant behind me. "I'm coming. I just … wait for me, okay?"

Dane nods at me as I turn to the open door of the storage closet and quickly grab the scattered paddles off of the floor as gracefully as possible and shove them in the bag. I exit the closet and avoid meeting *his* eyes as I start to walk toward Dane. I exhale silently, glad to be heading toward more familiar ground when I hear his voice behind me. "This conversation isn't over, *Rylee*."

"Like hell it isn't, *A.C.E.*," I toss over my shoulder, the thought at how perfect the acronym fits him passes through my mind before I continue hastily down the hall, keeping my shoulders squared and head held high in an attempt to keep my pride intact.

I quickly reach Dane, my closest confidant and friend at work. Concern etches his boyish face as I loop my arm through his, tugging him back toward the party. Once we're through the backstage door, I release the breath I didn't know I was holding and lean back against the wall.

"What the hell happened to you, Rylee? You look like a hot mess!" He eyes me up and down. "And does it have anything to do with that Adonis back there?"

It has everything to do with the Adonis, I want to confide but for some reason hold back. "Don't laugh," I say, eyeing him warily. "The closet door jammed shut, and I was stuck inside."

He stifles a laugh and looks toward the ceiling to contain it. "That would only happen to you!"

I playfully push his shoulder. "Really, it's not funny. I got panicked. Claustrophobic. The lights went out and it brought me back to the accident." Concern flashes in his eyes. "I freaked out, and that guy heard me yelling and let me out. That's all."

"That's all?" he questions with a raise of his eyebrow as if he doesn't believe me.

I nod. "Yes. I just really lost it for a minute." I hate lying to him, but for now it's my best course of action. The more adamant I am, the quicker he'll drop the subject.

"Well, that's too bad because *damn*, girl, he's fine." I laugh as he wraps his arm around me in a quick hug. "Go on and freshen up. Take a breather. Then we need you back out to mingle and schmooze. We're about thirty minutes out from the start of the date auction."

I stare at myself in the bathroom mirror. Dane's right. I look like hell. I've ruined the hair and makeup my roommate, Haddie, helped me with. I take a paper towel and try to blot at my makeup to repair the damage. The tears have left my amethyst eyes rimmed red, and I need not wonder why my lipstick is no longer perfectly lining my lips. Pieces of my chestnut color hair are falling out of its clip, and the seam of my dress is horribly askew.

I can hear the dull bass of the music on the other side of the wall. It plays background to the hundreds of voices—all potential donors. I take a deep breath and lean against the sink for a moment.

I can see why Dane questioned what had really happened and if Mr. Arrogant had anything to do with it. I look completely disheveled!

I shift my dress so its sweetheart neckline and my more-than-ample *girls* sit properly. I smooth my hands over my hips where the fabric clings to my curves. I start to put the wisps of hair that have escaped back into my clip but stop myself. The tendrils have returned to their naturally wavy state, and I decide that I like the softened effect the curls have on my overall look.

I reach into my purse, which Dane has brought me, and freshen up my make-up. I add some mascara to my naturally thick lashes and reapply my smudged eyeliner. My eyes look better. Not great—but better. I pucker my lips, tracing my lipstick over the full M shape of them, rub them together, and then blot.

Not as good as Haddie, but good enough. I'm ready to rejoin the festivities.

Chapter One

Colton—Raced

What. The. Fuck?

My body jolts with the impact as she slams into me. Fingernails dig into my biceps. A pile of wild, brown curls is all I see when I look down at the top of her head. Her shoulders shudder with each hyperventilated breath—a sound that goes hand in hand with the earsplitting scream that will inevitably happen next.

Thank you social media! You can take your goddamn tweets and stalker.com posts and shove them up your asses. Thanks for helping another faceless, frantic, fangirl find me.

What the fuck is it with women attacking me in this place? First the auburn piranha in the alcove and now this.

Seriously? The damsel in distress route? Like I haven't seen that one before. *You're one of millions, sweetheart.* You want me to notice you, baby, you've got to have less clothes on. Well, unless you count thigh highs and heels. And *nothing else*. That'd sure as hell catch my attention.

I shift my feet but she doesn't move. Okay, *stalker girl*, time's up. Let the fuck go so I don't have to be a dick and pry you off of—

Fuck me running.

The air punches from my lungs when her eyes—fucking magnificent eyes—look up at me from beneath dark lashes. Her head is still angled down so my only focal point is their unique bluish-purple color. Even with that crap smudged under them, the way she looks at me—shocked, terrified, relieved, all at once—stops the crass send-off from spewing out of my mouth.

What the fuck is wrong with me? Hysterics plus female equals crazy. A surefire sign to get the fuck away from her. Lesson learned a long ass time ago. She smells damn good, though. Focus Donavan, remember rule number one: *Don't ever dip the wick in the pool of crazies.*

Her eyes break from mine, gaze slowly descending, and stop on my lips again, silently staring. Her body stiffens, fingers tensing on my arms, breath stopping momentarily before shuddering out in a fortifying sigh.

Wait for it. Wait for it. It's coming. Her inevitable offer. The scripted rush of air and waste of breath where she tempts me with the wicked things she'll let me do to her body in exchange for the bragging rights of spending a few hours with me.

Been there done that, sweetheart. *Hence, rule number one.* Shit—she can toss the salad any way she wants, it doesn't mean that I'm gonna like the dressing.

She shifts onto her heels and stumbles further into me, firm tits pushing against my chest before jumping back like she's touched a livewire.

That's right, sweetheart, I'm electric.

It's the first time I get a glimpse of all of her, and she's definitely worth a second glance. She's got more curves than I'm used to but fuck if she doesn't wear them well. My eyes devour and take in the come-fuck-me heels, long, shapely legs, and the full, more than a handful-sized tits. And I've got big hands. I can't help the quickening of my pulse. She might be crazy, *but shit*, fangirl has one smoking hot body.

I don't hear the apology she fumbles through—her lame excuse why she was *trapped*—because my eyes travel further up and fixate on her mouth. *Sweet Christ*—perfect fucking lips. Now *those lips* I can picture just how perfect they'd look wrapped around my cock. It takes everything I have to not groan aloud at the image in my head of fangirl kneeling before me, *those* eyes looking up at me, and her cheeks hollowing as my dick slides in and out of her mouth.

Fuck this. Since when have I ever followed the goddamn rules?

Ha. Rule breaker, heartbreaker. I'll gladly take the title in exchange for a moment of fun with her.

Buh-bye rule number one.

I force myself to look away from her mouth and drag my gaze up to gauge the intention in hers. So she wants a wild night with the notorious bad boy? After the self-imagined porno I've just created in my head with her as the star, fuck if I won't give it to her.

But I'm going to make her work for it. Shit, what I've got is too good to give away for free. Fangirls are a dime a dozen, but I'm a fucking two dollar bill.

She averts her eyes again, and I watch them wander. *Yeah, she likes what she sees all right* … I don't think she has any idea who she's up against.

Undoubtedly like a good a stalker should, she's read the rags and thinks this is going to be easy—that I sleep with anyone who spreads their legs for me. *She so wants to play*. Little does she know, I'm in the mood for a good game of hardball.

She just keeps staring, and I can't help the smile that curls one side of my mouth. Her eyes widen and her breath hitches. *Oh yeah*, she's definitely game. Talk about swinging for the fences.

After a beat, she drags her eyes back up to mine. Dilated pupils, parted lips, a flush creeping into her cheeks. *Fuck*, I bet that's how she looks when she's coming. My dick stirs at the thought of being the one to put that look on her face as I slide into the prize between her thighs.

Then walk away from her. What is it they say? Easy come, easy go.

"No apologies needed," I tell her, smirking at how this boring event just became a helluva lot more interesting. *Batter up*. "I'm used to women falling at my feet."

Her head snaps up and confusion mixed with what I'm guessing is disgust flashes through those extraordinary eyes of hers.

Welcome to the big leagues, sweetheart!

She opens her mouth again. Flustered. Stumbling over her words.

I make her nervous. *Good*.

"Thanks. Thank you. The-the door shut behind me. It jammed. I panicked—"

When she speaks this time, I actually *hear* her voice. The telephone-sex operator rasp of it. *Shit*. My dick's doing more than stirring now. The sex-kitten purr is enough to make a monk hard. "Are you okay? Miss—?"

She just stares at me. Frozen. Indecision and confusion warring across her incredible features. She's questioning her resolve already? *Not a chance in hell*. She's not going anywhere. I always finish what I start, and this—the chance to hear her screaming my name while I'm buried in her later—is by no means over.

Game. On.

I reach out, cup the back of her neck, and pull her closer to me. That's all I plan on doing. A little touch to up the ante—force her to place her cards on the table or call her bluff. I pull her close enough to touch her lips, tease her a bit to let her know the stakes behind this unexpected game we're playing.

But fuck if I know what it is about her—something different, challenge or not—that's got me reaching my free hand out and running it up her arm, across the curve of her neck, and over her cheek.

I don't want to want her. Don't need her. Shit, a simple text will have Raquel in my bed in a heartbeat for a nightcap. Fuck, she's probably already there. Our arrangement may be nearing its end, but she's still game.

And she has mad skills.

But there's something about crazy fangirl that has me looking twice, has me forgetting this is a game.

Those eyes. Those curls, wild and fallen from her clip, looking like they've been fucked loose. Those plump, perfectly parted lips. *Sweet Christ*. I just might have to let her win this game because damn, she's not playing fair.

Options of how to play her flicker through my head. Dive right in and consider the consequences later or draw this out and have some fun with her?

Then she sucks in a ragged breath that let's me know she's affected. Let's me know she's bitten off more than she can chew. Hints at that little bit of vulnerability I see flicker in her eyes. And that sound—the subtle shudder telling me her body wants to betray her mind's warning to steer clear of me—is such a fucking turn on.

And desire overwhelms all logic.

Testosterone wins.

Just a little taste.

"Oh fuck it!" I slant my mouth over hers and use her surprised gasp to slip my tongue between her now parted lips. To taste what she's offering. *Holy shit!* Talk about knocking me off of my stride. The woman tastes like nothing I've ever had before. You hear addicts say that their first line of coke is what hooks them, causes them to do irrational things for the next fix. I finally get it.

Sweet. Innocent. Sexy. Willing.

Fuckin' A.

And before I can take more of what I suddenly want very badly, game be damned, she struggles and breaks her lips from mine.

Only one thought fills my head. Clouds my resolve.

More.

Her pulse quickens beneath my palm. Her panted breaths mix with mine. Her eyes flash with confusion and fear. And desire.

More.

"Decide, sweetheart," I demand, an unbidden ache settling deep in my balls and taking hold. "A man only has so much restraint."

Her eyes, so much contradiction flashes through them; they say "come fuck me" and "stay the fuck away" at the same time. Her lips part and then close. Her hands fist my lapel, indecision warring across her stunning features. Why the sudden resistance when she's getting exactly what she came here looking for? Did the stakes just become too real for her? *Ah* ... a boyfriend then. How can she not have one when she looks like that?

She just stares at me, eyes blank but body still responding, as every nerve within me shouts to drag her against me and take until I get my fill of her addictive taste. Time's up, sweetheart. Decision's mine now. I'll show her what she wants. Give her what the boyfriend doesn't. She had her chance to walk away and she didn't. I sure as hell am not. I always get what I want.

And right now, I want her.

I tighten my fingers on her neck, unable to hold back the smile on my lips as I think about pressing into her soft curves and wet pussy. And then I move. She resists as I claim her mouth. I'm skilled but far from gentle as I coax her trembling lips open and take my next fix.

One more taste.

That's all I want. I lick my tongue against hers. Probing. Tasting. Demanding.

Sweet fucking Jesus. That's the only thought I can manage when she begins to respond, our bodies connecting, her tongue playing with mine. Her hands move, fingernails scrape along my jaw, and fist in my hair. A fucking inferno burns its way down my spine and into my gut, a groan falling from my mouth as her body moves against my rock hard dick. Her soft yielding to my steel.

Every primal urge in my body begs to touch her, to claim her as mine. I drag one hand down the curved lines of her hips, our bodies vibrating with adrenaline and desire. I put one hand on her back pressing her into me, my cock against her stomach, my knee wedging between hers. She responds instantly, the Holy Grail between her thighs rubbing against my leg so I can feel her wet and wanting pussy through my slacks.

So fucking responsive. Her body just complies with the subtlest hints from mine, reacts to the slightest touch. Takes selflessly. Submits willingly.

God, I want to corrupt her.

And then she makes the softest, most erotic fucking sound I've ever heard. A gentle moan that begs and pleads and offers all at the same time.

And I'm decided. Consumed. Determined.

Fuck the game.

Mine.

I want her. Have to have her. I'm calling the shots now. Adrenaline hits me, coursing through me like the wave of the green flag.

I need to make her mine.

I nip her lower lip then lick away the sting. *Pleasure to bury the pain.* "Christ, I want you right now." I murmur against her lips between kisses, my dick throbbing at the thought of slamming into her. My hands move to possess now. Desire fueling my fire. Fingers rub over hardened nipples just begging to be tasted as we crash against the wall. My hands roam to connect with naked flesh. I reach the silk of her nylons and skim my way up until I trace the lace tops of her thigh-high stockings. I groan into her mouth.

Motherfucking perfection. Silk, lace, and skin. If it's possible to get any harder, I just did.

I guess fangirl doesn't want to be considered a dime a dozen.

As she gains confidence, her tongue taunts mine in a dizzying barrage of maneuvers. My fingertips snake up the bare skin of her inner thigh—smooth softness just pleading for me to lick, suck, and nip. I reach the swatch of lace at my awaiting heaven just begging to be ripped off.

"Sweet Jesus," I murmur as I feel how wet the material is, how ready she already is for me.

"No. No—I can't do this!" She pushes me back a step, and I watch her bring a trembling hand to her mouth. Her eyes tell me no, but her body? Her treacherous body vibrates with anticipation: chest heaving, lips swollen, nipples pebbled.

I force myself to swallow. To breathe. To regain the equilibrium she just shook and pulled out from under my always steady feet. I've had more women than any guy could ever ask for, but she just rocked my fucking world with her lips alone.

She's not going anywhere.

Mine.

"It's a little late, sweetheart. It looks as if you already have." *Like you have any fucking choice now.* You started this, fangirl, and I'll say when it's finished.

Fire leaps into her eyes and she lifts her chin in insolence. *My God,* that look alone gives new meaning to the word sexy.

"Who the hell do you think you are?" she spits at me. "Touching me like that? Taking advantage of me that way?"

We're back to the damsel in distress thing again? "Really?" I scoff at her, running my hand over my jaw as I ponder what to say next.

It's a little late for self-preservation, sweetheart.

"That's how you want to play this? Were you not participating just now? Were you not just coming apart in my arms?" I can't help the sliver of a laugh that escapes. "Don't fool your prim little self into thinking that you didn't enjoy that. That you don't want more."

I take a step closer and I can see a mixture of emotions flicker in her eyes. But most of all I see fear and denial. Resistance. Is she going to ignore what just happened between us? *Fangirl just might be crazy after all.* But fuck-all if I don't already crave my next taste of her.

And I have every intention of having it.

She watches as I lift my hand and trace a finger along the line of her cheek. Despite the hard set of her jaw, she instinctively moves her face ever so subtly in response to my touch. *Oh yeah.* She's definitely still interested, so why is she fighting it so hard?

"Let's get one thing clear," I warn through gritted teeth, trying to mask my irritation at having to fight for something that all of a sudden became complicated. "I. Do. Not. Take. What's. Not. Offered. And we both know, sweetheart, you offered. *Willingly.*"

She jerks her chin from my fingertips. Who knew defiance could be so goddamn arousing? And irritating. I can't remember the last time I had to work to get a woman beneath me.

Her body vibrates with anger. Or desire. Of which I can't tell. I step back into her personal space, pissed at myself that I've allowed her to affect me this much.

"That poor defenseless crap may work with your boyfriend who treats you like china on a shelf, fragile and nice to look at. Rarely used." I shrug as if I don't care, but all I want is a reaction out of her. Anything to tell me what she's thinking behind her stoic façade. "But admit it, sweetheart, that's boring."

"My boy—" she stutters, hurt flashing in her eyes. Hmm. She must have just broken up with him. Perfect time for a pump and dump, then. "I'm not fragile!"

Bingo!

"Really?" I want to push more buttons. Get her to admit she wants me. I reach out and grip her chin with my thumb and forefinger to make sure she can't hide from my stare. "*You sure act that way.*"

She jerks her chin from my hand as "Screw you!" grates from between her beautiful lips. The heat in her eyes holds me captive.

And to think I was going to pass up fangirl without a second thought.

"Oh, you're a feisty little thing!" I can't help the smirk on my lips. If she's this lively now, I can only image how wild she'll be between the sheets. "*I like feisty, sweetheart.* It only makes me want you that much more."

So many emotions pass over her face that I can't begin to comprehend them. She steps to the side of me, putting distance between us in our silent stand-off. Just as I think she's about to speak, the door down the hallway opens, flooding the quiet corridor with noise from the party beyond. Right before fangirl whirls around at the sound, I see a flicker of relief on her face.

I glance around her to see an average-sized guy standing with his back to the door, eying us with blatant curiosity. For a second I can't place him, but then realize I saw him earlier with some of the Corporate Care bigwigs. "Rylee? I really need those lists. Did you get them?"

Rylee? What the fuck?

"I got sidetracked," she mumbles to the guy as she glances back at me, her expression a mix of relief, regret, and disappointment. *She works with him? For Corporate Cares?* She says something else to the guy that I don't hear because I'm trying to wrap my head around the fact that crazy fangirl isn't a fangirl at all.

Or crazy.

Rylee. It sounds vaguely familiar. I mentally roll her name around on my tongue, liking the way it sounds, the way it feels.

She skirts past me and avoids making eye contact before stepping into the storage closet. I stop myself from reaching out for her because we're far from finished here. I follow her, hold the door open, and watch her jerky movements as she hurriedly shoves auction paddles into a bag. I can feel her co-worker's eyes boring holes in my back as he tries to assess the situation. Guaranteed he's telling me to *step off*.

The same way that I feel about him. Step off buddy so we can finish what we started here. I glance back to Rylee and she straightens up with the bag in hand, squares her shoulders, and walks past me without a second glance.

Anger fires in my veins. I do not get dismissed. "This conversation isn't over, Rylee."

"Like hell it isn't, Ace." She throws the words over her shoulder as she stalks down the corridor.

I watch her walk away. Hips swaying with purpose. Curves begging to be touched. Heels—heels I want left on with nothing else but those fucking lace top stockings—clicking against the floor.

Since when have I ever considered a woman walking away to be one of the hottest fucking sights I've ever seen?

The door closes behind them, and it's silent once again. I run a hand through my hair and lean back against the wall, trying to wrap my head around the past twenty minutes. I blow out a loud breath, confused as to why I'm pissed.

You must be losing your touch, Donavan.

Shit, when they walk away, it's supposed to be a good thing. Lessens the chance of complications. I don't chase. It's not my thing—never has been, never will be. There are too many willing women; why bother wasting my time on the ones that make things difficult? Why work for it when life's complicated enough as it is? I fuck who I want, when I want. My pick. On my terms. To my benefit. Rules two through six.

But shit ... that ... her ... how can I just let her—*Fuck me!*

Nobody walks away until I say I'm done. And I have every intention of finishing what I started with her. Checkered flag's mine. I'll definitely be crossing that finish line.

Here's to a night of firsts.

First a brunette.

Next a pursuit.

Bring it on.

Wave that checkered flag, sweetie, because I'm gonna claim it.

Chapter Two

Jewels, designer gowns, and name-dropping are prevalent among the celebrities, socialites, and philanthropists who fill the old theater. Tonight is the culmination of much of my efforts over the past year—an event to raise the majority of the funds needed to break ground on the new facilities.

And I am way out of my comfort zone.

Dane discreetly rolls his eyes at me from across the room; he knows I would much rather be back at The House with the boys in jeans and my hair pulled back into a ponytail. I allow a ghost of a smile to grace my lips as I nod my head, before taking a sip of champagne.

I am still trying to wrap my head around what I willingly allowed to happen backstage and the sting of knowing I wasn't the first person Mr. Arrogant had made his moves on tonight. I'm dumbfounded at both my uncharacteristic actions and confused by how hurt I feel. Surely, I can't expect a man looking for a quick romp to have any intention but to boost his already-inflated ego.

"There you are, Rylee," a voice interrupts my thoughts.

I turn to find my boss—a bear of a man standing close to six and half feet tall with a heart bigger than that of anyone I've ever met. Appropriately enough, he looks like a big teddy bear.

"Teddy," I say affectionately as I lean into the arm he's placed on my shoulders in a quick hug. "Looks like it's turning out well, don't you think?"

"Thanks to all your hard effort. From what I hear, the checks are coming in." His lips curve, the smile causing his eyebrows to wiggle. "And even before the auction begins."

"Just because it's a successful way to raise money, doesn't mean I have to agree with it," I reluctantly admit, trying to not sound like a prude. It's a debate we've had countless times over the past couple of months. Even though it's for charity, I just don't understand why women are willing to sell themselves to the highest bidder. I can't help but think the bidders are going to want more than just a date in return for the fifteen-thousand dollar starting bid.

"It's not like we're running a brothel, Rylee," Teddy admonishes. He looks over my right shoulder as a guest catches his attention. "Oh, there's someone I want you to meet. This is a cause very near and dear to him. He's one of our chairpeople's sons who—" he stops his explanation as whoever it is approaches nearby. "Donavan! Good to see you," he says heartily as he shakes hands with the person at my back.

I turn around, willing to make a new acquaintance, but instead I meet the bemused eyes of Mr. Arrogant.

Well, shit! How is it that despite being twenty-six years old, I suddenly feel like a prepubescent, awkward teenager? The half an hour away from him has done nothing to dampen his scorching good looks or the forbidden pull he has on my libido. His six-foot-plus frame is covered in a perfectly tailored black tuxedo that screams affluence, and my knowledge that beneath the jacket lies an obviously toned torso makes me bite my lower lip in unwanted need. And yet despite his magnetism, I'm still furious.

I think again about how he looks familiar, how he resembles someone I know, but the shock of seeing him again overrides the thought.

He smirks at me, his mirth apparent, and all I can think about is how those lips felt on mine. How his fingers, holding a tumbler now, felt traveling over my bare skin. About the length of his body pressed against mine.

And how he had licentiously *acquainted himself* with another woman moments before moving on to debase me.

Plastering a fake smile on my face, my eyes glare at Donavan as an unaware Teddy addresses him. "There's someone I'd like you to meet. She's the driving force behind what you see tonight." Teddy turns to me, placing a hand on my lower back. "Rylee Thomas, please meet—"

"We've already met," I say, interrupting him, saccharine oozing from my words as I smile at them. Teddy looks at me oddly; it's rare for me to be insincere. "Thank you for the introduction, though," I continue, looking from Teddy to Donavan, reaching out to shake his hand as if he were just another potential benefactor.

Dragging his eyes from me and my abnormal behavior, Teddy focuses back on Mr. Arrogant. "Are you enjoying yourself?"

"Immensely," he muses, releasing his too-long hold on my hand. I have to refrain from derisively snorting. How can he not be enjoying himself? *Arrogant bastard.* Maybe I should get on the stage and take a schoolyard poll of women here tonight to see whom he has not debauched already.

"Were you able to get some food? Rylee was able to get one of the hottest chefs in Hollywood to donate his services," Teddy explains, always trying to be the consummate host.

Donavan looks at me, humor crinkling the corners of his eyes. "I had a little taste of something while I was wandering around backstage." I suck in my breath, catching his innuendo as he moves his eyes back to Teddy. "It was rather unexpected but quite exquisite," he murmurs. "Thank you."

I hear someone call Teddy's name, and he eyes me again with curiosity before apologizing. "If you'll excuse me, I'm needed elsewhere for a moment." He turns toward Donavan. "It's great seeing you again. Thank you for coming."

We both nod in assent as Teddy leaves. Scowling, I turn on my heel to walk away from Donavan. I want to erase him and his memory from my evening.

His hand hastily closes over my bare arm, tugging me so my backside lands against the steeled length of his body. My breath hitches in response. I glance around, glad that everyone seems to be so absorbed in their own conversations that we've not drawn their attention.

I can feel Donavan's chin brush against my shoulder as his mouth nears my ear. "Why are you so pissed, *Ms. Thomas?*" There is a biting chill to his voice that warns me he's not a man to be messed with. "Is it because you can't let go of your highbrow ways and admit that despite what your head says, your body wants more of this rebel from the wrong side of the tracks?" He releases a low, patronizing growl in my ear. "Or are you so practiced at being frigid that you always deprive yourself of what you want? What you need? *What you feel?*"

I bristle, trying unsuccessfully to pull my arm out of his firm grip. Talk about a wolf in sheep's clothing. I still as another couple walks past us, eyeing us closely. Trying to figure out the situation between us. Donavan releases my arm, and rubs his hand over it instead, giving the impression of a lover's touch. And despite my fury, or maybe because of it, his touch triggers a myriad of sensation everywhere his fingers trace. Goose bumps ripple in their wake.

I can feel his breath rake over my cheek again. "It's very arousing, Rylee, knowing that you're so *responsive* to my touch. Very intoxicating," he whispers as he trails a finger across my bare shoulder. "You know you want to explore why your body reacted the way it did to me. You think I didn't see you undressing me with your eyes, enjoy you fucking me with your mouth?"

I gasp as he puts his hand on my stomach and pulls me tightly back against him so I can feel the evidence of his arousal pressing into my lower back.

Despite my anger, it's a heady feeling to know that I can make this man react in such a way. But then again, he probably reacts this way to the numerous women who, without a doubt, throw themselves at his feet on a regular basis.

"You're lucky I don't drag you back in that storage closet I found you in and take what you offered. Make you cry out my name." He nips softly at my ear, and I have to stifle the uncontrollable moan of desire that threatens to escape. "To fuck you and get you out of my system. Then move on," he finishes.

I've never been spoken to this way—would never have thought I'd allow someone to—but his words, and the vigor with which he speaks them, unexpectedly turn me on.

I'm mad at my body for its unbidden reaction to this pompous man. He obviously knows the hold he can have over a woman's body, and unfortunately, it is mine at the moment.

I turn slowly to face him and narrow my eyes. My voice is cold as ice. "Presumptuous, aren't you, Ace? No doubt your typical MO is to fuck 'em and chuck 'em?" His eyes widen in response to my unexpected vulgarity. Or maybe he's just surprised that I have him figured out so quickly. I hold his stare, my body vibrating with anger. "How many woman have you tried to seduce tonight?" I raise my eyebrows in disgust as guilt flickers fleetingly across his face. "What? Didn't you know that I happened upon you and your first conquest of the evening in the little alcove backstage?" Donavan's eyes widen. I continue, enjoying the surprised look on his face. "Did she play you at your own game, Ace, and leave you wanting for more? Aching to prove what a *man* you are since you couldn't fulfill her? That you had to pick a frantic woman locked in a closet to take advantage of? I mean, really, how many women have you used your bullshit lines on tonight? How many have you tried to leave your mark on?"

"Jealous, sweetheart?" He raises his eyebrows as his grin flashes arrogantly. "We can always finish what we started, and you can mark me any way you'd like."

I gently shove my hand against his chest, pushing him back. I'd love to wipe that smirk off of his face. *Leave my mark that way.* "Sorry, I don't waste my time on misogynist jerks like you. Go find someone—"

"Careful, Rylee," he warns as he grips my wrist, looking every bit as dangerous as his voice threatens. "I don't take kindly to insults."

I try to yank my wrist away but his hold remains. To anyone in the room, it looks as if I'm laying my hand on his heart in affection. They can't feel the overpowering strength of his grip.

"Then hear this," I snap, tired of this game and my warring emotions. Anger takes hold. "You only want me because I'm the first female who's said no to your gorgeous face and come-fuck-me body. You're so used to every female falling at your feet, *pun intended,* that you see a challenge—someone immune to your charm—and you're unsure how to react."

Despite his nonchalant shrug, I can see his underlying irritation as he releases my wrist. "When I like what I see, I go after it," he states unapologetically.

Shaking my head, I roll my eyes. "No, you need to prove to yourself that you can, in fact, get any girl who crosses your path. Your ego's bruised. I understand," I patronize, patting his arm. "Well, don't sweat it, Ace, I forfeit this race."

He raises an eyebrow, a ghost of a smile appears on his lips. The muscle in his clenched jaw tics as he regards me momentarily. "Let's get something straight." He leans in, inches from my mouth, the gleam in his eyes warning me I've gone too far. "If I want you, I can and will have you, at anytime and in anyplace, sweetheart."

I snort in the most unladylike way, astonished at his audacity, yet trying to ignore the quickening of my pulse at the thought. "Don't bet on it," I sneer as I hastily try to skirt past.

His hand whips out and grabs hold of my arm again, spinning me back toward him, so I'm standing intimately close. I can see his pulse beat in the line beneath his jaw. I can feel the fabric of his jacket hit my arm as his chest rises and falls. I glance down at his hand on my arm and glare back at him in warning, yet his hold remains. He leans his face in to mine so I can feel his breath feather across my cheek. I angle my head up to his, not sure if I'm raising my chin in defiance or in anticipation of his kiss.

"Lucky you, I'm a gambling man, Rylee," his resonating voice is just a whisper. "I do, in fact, like a good challenge now and again," he provokes, a mischievous smile playing at the corners of his mouth. He releases my arm, but runs his finger lazily down the rest of it. The soft scrape of his finger on my exposed skin sends shivers down my back.

"So let's make a bet." He stops and nods at a passing acquaintance, bringing me to the here and now as I've forgotten that we're in a room full of people.

"Didn't your mother teach you when a lady says no, she really means no, Ace?" I raise my eyebrow, a look of disdain on my face.

That smarmy smirk of his is back in full force as he nods in acknowledgement at my comment. "She also taught me that when I want something, I need to keep after it until I get it."

Great, so now I've acquired a stalker. A handsome, sexy, very annoying stalker.

He reaches out and toys with a loose curl on the side of my neck. I try to remain impassive despite my urge to close my eyes and sink into the soft touch of his fingers across my skin. His smirk tells me that he knows exactly what his effect is on me. "So, like I said, Ryles, a bet?

I bristle at his proposition, or maybe his effect on me. "This is asinine—"

"I bet by the end of the night," he cuts me off, holding a hand up to stop me, "I have a date with you."

I laugh out loud, stepping back from him. "Not a chance in hell, Ace!"

He takes a long swallow of his drink, his expression guarded. "What are you scared of then? That you can't resist me?" He flashes a wicked grin when I roll my eyes. "Agree then. What do you have to lose?"

"So you get a date with me and your bruised ego is restored." I shrug indifferently, wanting no part of this contest. "What will I get out if it?"

"If you win—"

"You mean if I can resist your *dazzling* charm," I retort sarcastically.

"Let me rephrase. If you can resist my dazzling charm by the end of the night, then I'll donate." He flickers his fingers through the air in a gesture of irrelevance. "Let's say, twenty thousand dollars to your cause."

I catch my breath and look at him in bewilderment, for this I can agree to. I know that there's no way in hell I'll succumb to Donavan or his captivating wiles, the *arrogant bastard.* Agreed, I was caught in his tantalizing web for a few moments, but it was just because it's been so long since I've felt like that. Since I've been kissed like that. Been touched like that.

Come to think of it, I don't think that I have ever been made to feel like that. But then again, I know that a man has never kissed me while his lips were still warm from another woman's.

I regard him impassively, trying to figure out the catch. Maybe there isn't one. Maybe he's just so cocky that he really thinks he's that irresistible. All I know is that I'm going to increase our contribution total tonight by twenty thousand.

"Isn't this bet going to put a damper on your evening's pursuit of other possible bedside companions?" I pause, taking a survey of the room. "It's not looking too promising, Ace, considering you're oh for two right now."

"I think I'll manage." He laughs out loud. "Don't worry about me. I'm good at multitasking," he quips, trying to beat me at my own game. "Besides, the night's still young, and by my count the score is oh for one so far. The second score has yet to be settled." He arches his eyebrows at me. "Don't over think it, Rylee. It's a bet. Plain and simple."

I cross my arms over my chest. The decision is easy. *Anything for my boys.* "Better get your checkbook ready, Ace. There's nothing I like better than proving arrogant bastards like you wrong."

He takes another sip of his drink, his eyes never leaving mine. "You sure are certain of yourself."

"Let's just say that my self-control is something that I pride myself on."

Donavan steps closer to me again. "Self-control, huh?" he murmurs, challenge dancing in his eyes. "Seems we've already tested that theory, Rylee, and it didn't seem to hold true. I'd be glad to test it again, though ..."

The muscles in my core clench at the possible promise, the ache burning there, begging for relief. Why am I acting like a girl who has never felt a man's touch before? *Maybe because it has never been this man's touch.*

"Okay," I tell him, sticking out my hand to shake his, "It's a bet. But I'll warn you, I don't lose."

He reaches out to take my hand, a broad smile lighting up his features, eyes sparkling a bold emerald. "Neither do I, Rylee," he murmurs. "Neither do I."

"Rylee, sorry to interrupt but we need you right now," says a voice behind me.

I turn to find Stella, with a look of panic on her face. I look toward Donavan, "If you'll excuse me, I'm needed elsewhere." I feel awkward, unsure of what else I should say or do.

He nods his head at me. "We'll talk more later."

As I walk away, I realize I'm not sure if his response is a threat or a promise.

Chapter Three

I am sitting backstage in the chaotic aftermath of the auction, but my mind is still reeling from it. The last hour and a half has been a blur. A successful blur in fact, but one that has come at a very high cost—*my dignity*.

At the last minute, one of our "date" auction participants had become ill. With no one else willing to partake, and programs pre-printed with a set number of participants, I begged, bribed, and pleaded with every member of my staff to step in and fill the role. Of all of the available people who were not physically needed for the facilitation of the auction, those left were either married or seriously attached to someone.

Everyone that was, except for me.

I whined, cajoled, pleaded even, but in an ironic twist that many of the staff took pleasure in, I became auction block Item Number Twenty-Two. So I had to suck it up and take one for the team, all the while ignoring a hunch that something wasn't quite right, but I couldn't put my finger on it.

And believe me, I hated every fucking minute of it! From the beauty-pageant-style introduction, to the parading around on a stage like a trophy, to the whistling catcalls of the audience, to the vapid calling of bidders' dollar amounts by the announcer. The lights were so blinding I couldn't see the audience, just a vague outline of figures. My time in the spotlight was consumed by embarrassment, the sound of my heartbeat rushing in my ears, the fear that my sweating from the heat of the stage lights would leave dark marks on the underarms of my dress.

I'm sure if I'd been on the other side of the stage, I would have found the auctioneer's comments entertaining, the participation of the audience endearing, and the silly antics of some of the women on stage trying to increase their bids amusing. I would've watched the contribution total rise and would have been proud of my staff for the successful outcome.

Instead, I'm sitting in the backstage area, taking a deep breath, and wrapping my head around what the hell just happened.

"Way to go, Ry!" I hear Dane's amusement at my predicament as he makes his way backstage toward me through the twenty-four other women who were willing participants in the auction. They're all exiting off the stage, gathering their bags of swag that we provided to thank them for their participation.

I glare at him, my annoyance evident. He gives me a wide, toothy grin as he grabs me in an unreciprocated hug. I'm beyond grumpy. I'm downright bitchy. I mean what a fucking night! First locked in the closet, then playing unknown sloppy seconds on the conquest list of Mr. Arrogant, and then enduring the humiliation of being purchased like prime beef at a meat market.

I cannot believe the giddiness of the women around me. They are chatting animatedly about their moment in the spotlight and bragging at how much they went for. I'm grateful for their participation, ecstatic at the outcome, but just simply bewildered by their enthusiasm.

His earlier accusation of being prim comes back to my mind, and I shake it off.

"That was fucking horrible!" I whine, shaking my head in incredulity as he laughs sympathetically at me. "All I want is a large glass—no screw that, a bottle of wine, some form of chocolate, and to get this damn dress and heels off, in no particular order."

"If that's all it takes to get you naked, I'd have brought you wine and chocolate a long time ago."

I glare at him, finding no amusement in his comment. "Too bad I don't have the right equipment to keep you satisfied."

"Meow!" he responds, biting his lip to suppress his laugh. "Oh, sweetie, that had to have been horrible for you, Ms. Keep-me-out-of-the-spotlight-at-all-costs! Look at you ..." He sits in the chair next to me, putting his arm around my shoulder and pulling me to him. I rest my head on his shoulder, enjoying the comforting feeling of friendship. "At least you sold for above the asking price."

"You asshole!" I pull away from him as he laughs childishly at me, rubbing in what he knows is a sore spot. To be honest, I still have no idea what amount my 'winning bid' was because I was too busy listening to the frantic pounding of my heartbeat fill my head.

To say that my ego doesn't care how much I was auctioned for is a mild understatement. Even though I detested the process, what female wouldn't want to know that someone thinks she is worthy enough to be bid money on for a date? Especially after my experience earlier in the evening.

"What are friends for? I mean between the bidding war and the ensuing brawl over your potential suitor..." he blows out a large breath, humor in his eyes "...and the all-out melee that ensued—"

"Oh, be quiet will you!" I laugh, relaxing for the first time at his ribbing. "No really, how much did I raise?"

"Listen to you! Most women would first say 'How much did I go for?'" he mocks in a high-pitch, pretentious voice, making me giggle, "and then the next question would be 'How hot is my date?'"

I turn to him and arch my eyebrows in the manner that always has the boys at The House answering quickly—or taking cover. "Well?" When he doesn't respond, but rather stares at me in mock horror for wondering, I allow myself to become one of the whiney voiced women around me. "Dane, give me the details!"

"Well, my dear, you sold ... " I shiver in mock horror at his words. He continues, "Excuse me, your future date spent twenty-five thousand dollars for an evening with you."

What? Holy shit! I'm dumbfounded. I know the starting bid was fifteen thousand for all entrants, but someone actually paid ten thousand more than that? Pride and a feeling of worth soars within me, repairing part of the damage Donavan inflicted earlier.

I try to rationalize someone I don't know spending that kind of money on a date with me, and I can't. It had to have been one of the chair people who worked closely on the board with me. This was the only plausible explanation. Most of the other women on the stage had been part of the elite Hollywood charity circle—they had friends and family in the audience to bid on them. I didn't.

I sigh and relax a bit with the knowledge that I will probably have to go on a date with a widowed elderly gentleman or possibly none at all. Maybe the person just wants to donate to us and will let me off the hook. What a relief! I was worried about the date part. Some loser expecting something in return for his generous donation—ugh!

"So did you see who won the auction?"

"Sorry, sweetie," he says as he pats my knee. "The guy was off to the side. I was in the back. I couldn't see him."

"Oh—okay." Disappointment fills my voice as I begin to worry again.

"Don't worry. I'm sure it is one of the old guys from the board—" he stops, realizing he's just implied that those are the only men willing to bid on me. He continues cautiously, knowing full well that I'm in bitch-mode right now. "You know what I meant, Ry. They all love you! They'll do anything to support you." He eyes me carefully and realizes he should stop while he is ahead.

I sigh loudly, relaxing from the realization that I'm uber-sensitive right now. I take note that most of the participants have cleared out of the backstage area. "Well, my friend, I should be getting back to the soiree." I stand, smoothing my dress down and wincing as my feet bunch back down into my shoes. "I, for one, am more than done with my duties for the evening. I'm ready to go home and devour that chocolate and wine in the comfort of my fluffy robe and comfy couch."

"You don't want to wait and see what the tally is for the night?" he asks, rising from the seat to follow behind me.

We walk past the alcove that Donavan and I had occupied earlier, and I blush, keeping my head down so Dane won't question me. "I asked Stella to text me later when it's added up." I push open the door to enter the party again. "I don't need to be here for that—" I falter as I walk through the door and see Donavan leaning a shoulder casually against the wall, surveying the crowd.

He's a man who is obviously at ease with who he is, regardless of his surroundings. He exudes an aura of raw power mixed with something deeper, something darker that I can't seem to put my finger on. Rogue. Rebel. Reckless. All three descriptions fit him, and despite this man's refined look, he screams trouble.

Dane bumps into me from behind as I stop abruptly when Donavan's scanning eyes connect with mine. "Rylee—" Dane complains until he realizes why I've stopped. "*Well, shit*, if it isn't Mr. Brooding. What's going on here, Ry?"

I roll my eyes at the thought of Donavan's stupid bet. "Arrogance run amuck," I mutter to him. "I have to take care of something." I toss over my shoulder, "Be right back."

I stalk toward Donavan, more than aware that his eyes track my every movement and at the same time annoyed at having to deal with this now. Our banter has been an amusing way to pass the evening's time, but the night's over and I'm ready to go home. Game over. He pushes his shoulder off the wall, straightening the long length of his lean body as I walk toward him. The corners of his mouth turn up slightly as he attempts to gauge my mood.

I reach him and hold up a hand to stop him before he even begins to speak. "Look, Ace, I'm tired and in a really shitty mood right now. It's time for me to call it a night—"

"And just when I was going to offer to take you places you didn't even know existed before," he says dryly with just a ghost of a smile and an arch of an eyebrow. "You don't know what you're missing, sweetheart."

I snort loudly, all propriety out the window. "You're fucking kidding me, right? You actually get women with lines like that?"

"I'm wounded." He smirks, his eyes full of humor as he holds his hand to his heart in false pain. "*You'd be surprised what my mouth gets with those lines.*"

I just stare at him. The man has absolutely no humility. "I don't have time for your childish games right now. I just had to endure humiliation beyond my worst nightmare, and I'm more pissed off than you can imagine. I *especially* don't want to deal with *you* right now."

If he is shocked at my rant, he hides it well. His face remains impassive except for the muscle pulsing with his clenched jaw. "I do love a woman who tells it like it is," he murmurs quietly to himself.

I place my hands on my hips and continue, "So I'm going home in about ten minutes. Night's over. I win our idiotic bet, so you better get your check and fill it out because you're going home with lighter pockets tonight."

His lips quirk up in an amused smirk. "Twenty-five thousand lighter, in fact," he deadpans.

"No, we agreed on twen—" I stop as a smile spreads across his lips, realization slowly dawning on me. *Oh fuck!* He bid on me. Not only did he bid on me, but he bid on me and won. He *officially* has a date with me.

I grit my teeth and raise my head toward the ceiling, inhaling slowly, trying to calm myself. "No—uh-uh. This is bullshit and you know it!" I glare at him as he starts to speak. "That wasn't the deal. I didn't agree to this!" I'm flustered and exasperated, so furious that I'm beyond reason.

"A bet's a bet, Ryles."

"It's Rylee, you asshole!" I spit at him. Who the hell does he think he is? First he buys me and then he thinks he can give me a *nickname*? I know that the irrational female in me has reared her Medusa-like head, but I really don't care at this point.

"Last time I checked, sweetheart, my name wasn't *Ace*," he retorts with some justification. The rasp of his voice grates over me like sandpaper. He casually leans back against the wall, as if this is a conversation he has every day.

His nonchalance fuels my ire. "You cheated. You-you-aaarrgh!" My frustration is stifling my ability to form coherent thoughts.

"We never had time to outline any rules or stipulations." He raises his eyebrows and shrugs. "You were pulled away. That left everything as fair game." His smile is irritating. The humor in his intoxicating green eyes is infuriating.

Oh shit! I try to argue cleverly with him and I just end up looking like a guppy, opening and closing my mouth several times without a word falling from my lips.

He pushes off the wall and steps in closer to me. His signature scent envelops me. "I guess I just proved you do, in fact, lose sometimes, *Ryles*." He reaches up to move a tendril that has fallen over my face, his lone dimple deepening with his victorious smirk. I recoil at his touch but he holds my jaw firm in his hands. "I'm looking forward to our date, Rylee." He grazes a thumb over my cheek and angles his head to the side while he considers his next statement. "In fact, more than any other date I've had in a while."

I close my eyes momentarily, leaning my head back as "Oh God!" slips from my lips in a sigh. *What an unbelievable night!*

"So that's what it will sound like?"

I open my eyes, confused by his comment, to see him regarding me with a bemused look on his face. "What?" I bark, my response harsh like a curse.

"Those words, *Oh God*," he mimics me, reaching out and running a finger down the side of my face. "Now I know exactly how you'll sound when you say that while I'm buried deep inside of you."

I open my mouth in shock at his audacity, the overconfidence of his words astounding me. His haughty smile grates on my last nerve. *The arrogant prick.* Luckily I'm able to voice an articulate thought. "Wow! You sure think a lot of yourself, don't you, Ace?"

He slips his hands into his pockets, his smirk dominating his magnificent face. He leans in, a salacious look in his eyes and his voice a daunting whisper. "Oh, sweetheart, *there is definitely a lot of me to think about.*" His quiet laugh sends a chill up my spine. "I'll be in touch."

And with that, Mr. Arrogant turns on his heels and walks away without a backwards glance. I watch his broad shoulders until he disappears into the throng of people and finally exhale the breath I didn't know I was holding.

Screw him and his sexy mouth and his gorgeous green eyes framed with thick lashes and his dexterous hands and his … his … *just his everything*! Ugh! I'm shaking I'm so furious with him.

And at myself. Donavan is confident and sure of himself and more than comfortable with being the alpha male. For me, there is nothing more attractive in a man than that. But right now, I'm irritated with him. He's gotten under my skin. And I'm not sure if that's a good thing or not, but I know that places inside of me that died that horrific day two years ago showed some signs of life tonight.

Starting the moment he touched me.

I stand there trying to comprehend the night's unexpected events, and after a few moments, I'm certain of two things. First, there is absolutely no way I am honoring this agreement. And second, deep down, despite my staunch resolve, I know this will not be the last time I'll be seeing Donavan.

Chapter Three Bonus Scene

Colton—Raced

FUCK MY RULES.

Addictive.

Fuck her defiance.

She's mine.

She just doesn't know it yet.

My eyes collide with hers as she steps out of the backstage door. The sneer on her face and fire in her eyes tells me *she knows*.

But that's not possible.

She couldn't have figured it out yet. But I'll be damned if she's not pissed off by the way she's stalking those sexy-as-fuck curves toward me right now. I can't help my eyes as they drag over every inch of her body, wanting more than just the taste I got earlier. I want the whole fucking meal.

And I want it now.

Patience is definitely not my virtue.

And I'm sure as fuck going to steal hers.

I can't help the smile that threatens the corners of my lips as I push myself off of the wall when she nears. A freight train of anger and she doesn't even have a clue that I'm her fucking fuel.

What I wouldn't give to push her up against the wall and taste her again—crowd around us be damned—so long as I get my fix. She reaches up and holds her hand to stop me before I speak. Fuck! The woman does everything to try and turn me off, and all it does is spur me further the opposite way, arousing me like she wouldn't fucking believe.

"Look, Ace, I'm tired and in a really shitty mood right now. It's time for me to call it a night—"

"And just when I was going to offer to take you to places you didn't even know existed before." I can't help pushing her buttons. The words are out of my mouth before I can stop them. *But fuck if it's not true.* I have no doubt we'd set the sheets—if not the fucking bed or floor or couch or wherever we crash—on fire. Those luscious lips of hers fall lax at my comment, and I figure I'll keep her on her toes. Keep pushing those buttons. It's just too much goddamn fun. "You don't know what you're missing, sweetheart."

She snorts. She actually snorts at me standing here in her elegant dress, and fuck me if that too isn't a mix of sexy and adorable. "I'm wounded," I say, clutching my heart in mock pain. "*You'd be surprised what my mouth gets with those lines.*"

Let's see what she says to that one. My eyes trace over the outline of those lips that I want wrapped around my cock, those fucking magnificent eyes looking at me with a trace of shock. Even after all of our interactions tonight, she still doesn't know how to take me.

Good. Keep her guessing. Confusion is my advantage.

"I don't have time for your childish games right now. I just had to endure humiliation beyond my worst nightmare, and I'm more pissed off than you can imagine. I *especially* don't want to deal with *you* right now."

"I do love a woman who tells it like it is," I murmur to myself, unable to tear my eyes from hers. Or comprehend being told no. That's a new one.

"So I'm going home in about ten minutes. Night's over. I win our idiotic bet, so you better get your check and fill it out because you're going home with lighter pockets tonight," she rants and places her hands on her hips.

Fuck, there's that defiance again that makes my balls tighten in anticipation. In unfettered lust. And she thinks I'm just going to write her a check and let her walk out of my life without having her? She's sadly mistaken. I'm a take it or leave it kind of guy.

And I'm definitely taking this one. Too bad she doesn't know it yet.

I don't fight my smirk this time. *Game on, baby.* "Twenty-five thousand lighter, in fact."

"No, we agreed on twen—" Her voice fades and I watch as it slowly hits her. The realization crashes like a tornado across her features and storms through her eyes. I can see her trying to fight it. Trying to resist the urge to throttle me.

And shit, if I thought defiance made her sexy, then anger makes her motherfucking breathtaking.

"No—uh-uh. This is bullshit and you know it!" She glares at me with every ounce of hatred I think she can muster, and it only makes me more determined to have her. "That wasn't the deal. I didn't agree to this!"

I tuck my tongue in my cheek, trying to bite back the grin tugging at the corners of my mouth. "A bet's a bet, Ryles."

"It's Rylee, you asshole!" she hisses at me.

Testy. Testy. *Ryles it is, then.*

"Last time I checked, sweetheart, my name wasn't *Ace*." *But when you're screaming my name later, it can be anything you want it to be.* I lean back against the wall and watch the emotions play over her face.

She's so frustrated. Mission accomplished, buttons pushed. And now I have one feisty hellcat on my hands, and I bet sure as fuck she's going to be fun to try and tame. Then again, why tame her? A few scratches never hurt anyone.

"You cheated. You-you-aaarrgh!"

"We never had time to outline any rules or stipulations," I explain with a raise of my eyebrows and a shrug of my shoulders. "You were pulled away. That left everything as fair game."

Those lips of hers that I want to taste fall open and then close again to only fall back apart. I pull my thoughts from what else I'd like them to open and close around. *Sweet Christ!* I force my mind to focus on the here and now and away from what exactly is under that dress. I push myself off the wall and step toward her.

I can't resist.

"I guess I just proved you do in fact lose sometimes, *Ryles*."

I have to touch her.

Irresistible.

Mine.

"I'm looking forward to our date, Rylee."

I watch her eyes follow my fingers as they move a loose curl of hair from her cheek. I catch the slight hitch in her breath, and I know I've got her. Know it's only a matter of time now.

The pull is just too great. Resistance is futile. I graze a thumb over her cheek, wanting to feel her skin. Needing to feel that spark of current that vibrates between us. "In fact, more than any other date I've had in a while."

She leans her head back, my thumb still on her cheek, and "Oh God!" falls from her mouth in exasperation.

The sound of her sex-kitten voice turns my insides, calls to some part deep within me, and I don't like it one bit. The only part of me that should be affected should be my dick and my mind counting the minutes until she's beneath me.

Or on top of me. Beggars can't be choosers and fuck if reverse cowgirl isn't a mighty nice position.

See, Donavan? It's the alcohol twisting things around making you think that feeling deep down is more than just the ache in your balls. C'mon, all you want is a quick, uncomplicated fuck and an attempt to tame the wildcat.

That's it. Nothing else.

I swear.

Unease creeps through me at the thought of only having her once, and I force myself to stop thinking this fucking nonsense and grab the control back my dick has hijacked. I hear those words of hers echo through my mind, and I know exactly how to do it.

"Those words, *oh God*," I mimic her and give in one last time to my need to touch her by running a finger down the side of her face. "Now I know exactly how you'll sound when you say that while I'm buried deep inside of you."

I love the look of shock that flashes across her face. Love the insolence in her expression as she lifts her chin and glares at me. Such a fucking turn on.

"Wow! You sure think a lot of yourself, don't you, Ace?"

Shit! She walked right into that one and I can't resist. Just can't fucking stop myself from pushing those buttons of hers one last time before I walk away and leave her wondering whose court the ball is really in. I slip my hands in my pocket and lean into her, the smile on my face suggesting exactly what I want to do with her. To her. For her.

"Oh, sweetheart, *there is definitely a lot of me to think about*." I laugh softly, loving the look I've just put on her face. "I'll be in touch."

I forgo the urge to touch her one last time. Taste her one last time. And I force myself to turn around and walk away. To put one foot in front of the other when I'd much rather be dragging her back to that damn storage closet and taking exactly what I want.

The chance to claim her.

Game fucking on.

I walk out into the parking lot and thank fuck Sammy is already there or else I might be tempted to walk back inside. Because fuck yes her playing hard to get is a turn on, but experience has me wagering that given ten more minutes either I wouldn't be going home alone or that storage closet just might have gotten some use.

Can't say I have a losing track record.

I pull my phone from my pocket and laugh when I see the notifications blaring across my screen. Case in fucking point. I thumb through the ten texts from Raquel. Each one dirtier than the first.

Sweet Jesus I could use a good fuck tonight after all of that verbal foreplay and by the suggestions she's sent to my phone, it's gonna be a long, sweaty, sleepless night.

"Hey, Wood. Good night?" Sammy asks as I climb into the back of the Range Rover, fingers already untying my bowtie and undoing the noose of buttons closing my collar on my neck.

"You have no idea, Sammy," I tell him and then laugh when my thoughts veer to how my evening has turned into the beginning of a good joke—*so a redhead, a brunette, and a blonde walk in a bar*—when I think of Bailey, Rylee, and Raquel.

He laughs and shakes his head, having been with me long enough that he knows how my life goes. Women willing for whatever I'm game for. Well except for the unexpected Ms. Thomas tonight.

Knowing what was beneath that dress has made it ten times harder to walk away without having her. Since when do I care what a woman's wearing so long as it's piled on the floor?

Normally I'd say she's not worth my time, but I can't remember the last time I had a challenge. Shit, women say the word no to me about as often as they keep their legs together at the knees. *Never.*

Christ, I should let it go. Write the check, Donavan. Leave her alone.

Don't touch complicated—that's my default. So why in the fuck do I want to play with fire? Light the match to her flame and see how hot she gets.

Damn it to Hell.

I'm just horny. Pump primed and turned on from her defiance. I'll lose myself in Raquel tonight—every tight fucking inch of her—and realize I'm being stupid. That I shouldn't opt for complicated when I can have easy.

Decision made. Mind-numbing sex. That fixes everything.

I'm just about to text Raquel back when my phone rings. I look down to see her name. Well, can't get much easier than that.

Damn, I'm good. All that's missing is the snap of my fingers

"Hey." I smirk at Sammy meeting my eyes in the rearview mirror.

"I'm naked. I'm wet. And my mouth is ready to suck your cock 'til you're dry. I sure hope you're coming home soon because my mouth is kind of empty and, baby, I'd love for you to fill it."

My dick is already stirring to life, balls tightening. The need to come front and center. What red-blooded male wouldn't be with that greeting? Shit.

"Fuck, baby, that sounds like Heaven ... but I need to take a rain check." My own words shock me. *What the fuck are you doing, Donavan? What is wrong with you?* I hear myself yelling, my dick begging, but my mouth has a mind of its own.

"What?" Her voice is soft, disappointment evident.

"I'm sorry. My mom needs me to stay here and wrap up some of the charity shit for her. I'll make it up to you, though. I was invited to some launch party for the new sponsor, Merit Rum. It'd be good exposure for you—media and big wigs and shit, okay? You know I wouldn't pass up the chance to fuck you unless it was unavoidable."

I just used my mother to get out of fucking Raquel. There is something extremely pathetic about my state of mind right now. Is the Apocalypse coming? Is Hell freezing over?

What. The. Fuck?

She accepts reluctantly, I apologize again, lie about being busy, and end the call. Sammy catches my eyes and just raises his eyebrows. "I take it I should drive to Broadbeach instead, now?"

I scrub a hand through my hair and sigh. "Yeah." I shake my head trying to figure out what in the fuck I just did. "Sammy, did I just pass up pussy?"

"Yep. Sounded like it. You feeling okay? Dick still attached? It didn't fall off with all of the hobnobbing at the event?"

Fucking Sammy. Dude's funny as hell. I grab my dick and adjust it. "Still there, Sam. Still there." My voice trails off as my thoughts wander.

Rylee Thomas. It's gotta be because of her. How could three fucking hours of defiance make me look at wet and willing and think it's too damn easy? That working for a piece of ass might be fun for a change.

It's her fucking fault I'm headed home to my hand and some lube. And even I know it's fucked up so I start to tell Sammy to head to the Palisades but nothing comes out of my mouth. Because as hot as Raquel is and as good as she can ride me, my interest is elsewhere.

Back at the benefit. With curves and class and holy fuck that ass of hers. And that's just scratching the surface of everything I plan on touching.

My phone rings again and I'm immediately irritated. Raquel needs to drop it and leave me the hell alone. "What?" I bark the word into the phone, Sammy's shoulders moving as he laughs at my self-inflicted misery.

"Wow. Someone needs to get laid. Relieve stress and shit." Shit. Guess I should have looked at the screen. I was so lost in what I can't have right now that I assumed it was Raquel and not Becks.

"Sorry," I tell him. "I thought you were Raquel."

"Damn, dude." He laughs. "I guess she's holding out on you tonight by the pissiness in your tone. She make other plans or something besides being at your beck and call?"

Fucker. I grunt out a laugh. "Hardly. Just not on the menu tonight."

Becks chokes out a cough on the other end of the line. *Fuck,* I just left him an open door to walk right through. "Well considering your menu is usually pussy pie, I guess you're looking for a new diner to eat it out of besides Raquel."

The smile is wide on my face but my silence tells him volumes.

"Who'd you meet, Wood?" I can hear the *here we go again* in his voice and just shake my head because he's right. "What woman has made you look at Raquel like she's an inconsequential notch in that belt of yours?"

The only belt notch I'm thinking of is mine coming undone so I can take Rylee beneath me and hear that *oh God* fall from her mouth. My head fills of lace-top thigh-highs, her smart-assed mouth, and violet eyes filled with contempt. Two of the three should turn me off but fuck if it doesn't make my dick jerk thinking of the whole fucking package.

"Nobody." I lie to protect myself from the one thing I fear the most.

That Rylee just might be the somebody I told myself I'll never allow myself to have.

She's a forever kind of girl and I'm a just for the night kind of guy.

But fuck if it's not going to be fun to see just how far we'll each bend to break our own rules.

Chapter Four

I strum my fingers on my desk as I peruse our parent company's website. I have so many other things I need to be doing right now, but I find myself looking at pictures of all of the chairpersons on our board, as well as the members of the organizing committee.

I can't place which member's son is Donavan, and it's really starting to annoy me. I don't have his last name to help the puzzle pieces fit into place. I wish I hadn't told my staff that they could wait a few days on getting me the paperwork. I was just trying to be nice after all of the hard work they had put in. If I had it though, I'd have the answer. I know I could just call up Stella or Dane and ask the name of my future date, but then they'd know something is up because something like that wouldn't be important to me. And with those two gossipers, I don't want to open *that* floodgate.

More importantly, I'm irritated at myself for even caring who he is. "Manwhore," I grumble under my breath.

I rub my tired eyes and run my fingers through my hair, pulling it back off my shoulders. I exhale loudly. It's been a long, tiring weekend, and I'm exhausted.

I glance at the clock. I have fifteen minutes before I have to leave to get to The House for my twenty-four hour shift.

My computer pings and I click on my mailbox to see an incoming email. I don't recognize the address but can assume the person's identity. *Here we go again*. I click on it because the subject line has piqued my curiosity.

To: Rylee Thomas
From: Ace
Subject: Backstage Liaisons

Ryles—
Would you have opened the email if the subject line simply stated, "Date the Highest Bidder"?
Didn't think so.
You owe me a date.
Let me know your availability so I can make plans.
You have twenty-four hours to respond. Or else.
—Ace

I sigh heavily in confused relief. I'm irritated at his ridiculous ultimatum. More so though, I'm irritated at myself. Why, even if I don't want to go out with him, do I feel like a giddy schoolgirl excited that he's emailed me? That the cool, popular kid has acknowledged the awkward, ordinary girl.
After he's made out with the head cheerleader behind the bleachers, that is. *God, he is annoying!* I check the clock to make sure that I have time for a response.

To: Ace
From: Rylee Thomas
Subject: Cat Got Your Tongue?

Ace—
Demanding, aren't we?
You never addressed your subject line. Should I worry about how many other emails you sent out with the same title to your other conquests from Saturday night trying to get a follow-up date?
-Ryl-E-E

I smile as I hit send, picturing his face in my mind. His smile. His emerald eyes. The devastation he had over my control. It's only been two days since the auction, and yet I wonder if my memory is making Donavan out to be more than he really is. Making his transgressions seem less offensive than they really were. Before I can ponder it further, my inbox alerts me.

To: Rylee Thomas
From: Ace
Subject: Chivalry isn't dead

Ryl-E-E—
A gentleman never kisses and tells, Ryles. You should know that.
When you think about me, make sure to note that my demands will only result in your pleasure.
And you never answered my question. A bet's a bet. Time to pay up, sweetheart.
—Ace

I laugh out loud to his response. Maybe if I ignore his question, he'll just go away. Good luck with that! Despite detesting the game he's playing, I find myself smiling as I type my reply. I'm a challenge to him, plain and simple. If I'd acquiesced to his request for a date, or maybe even if I had continued kissing him in the hallway without backing away, he'd never have given me a second thought. He would have had his wicked way with me and walked away without a backwards glance.

To: Ace
From: Rylee Thomas
Subject: Fat ladies and yellow birds

Ace—
I read somewhere that a boy needs the adulation from many girls to be satisfied, whereas a gentleman needs the adoration from just one woman to be fulfilled. By that definition alone, you are definitely not a gentleman. That means you should be singing like a canary, then.
Besides, a date is WAY ABOVE my pay grade.
—Rylee
P.S. Oh, and don't worry, I don't think of you. At all.

Take that! I think, proud of myself for my wit despite the blatant lie in the last comment. I stand and pack up my stuff, straightening my desk. As I reach to turn my computer off, my inbox alerts me again.

To: Rylee Thomas
From: Ace
Subject: You need a raise

Rylee—
I may be a man, but I'm nowhere near gentle. In fact, I think you're a little curious just how I like it. Step over the edge with me, Ryles—I'll hold your hand and revel in making you lose that self-control you pride yourself on. I'll be anything and everything but gentle.
I promise. You'll never know your limits until you push yourself to them.
If you refuse to give me availability, I may have to take matters in my own hands. Maybe someone taking control is exactly what you want? What you need?
—Ace

"Egotistical asshole," I mutter as I switch off my computer, refusing to respond. Like he knows what I want or need. But despite my anger, his words reverberate through me more than they should.

My phone rings as I drive to The House. I'm in a foul mood for some reason, and I can only blame it on Donavan and his damn emails. Damn him for filling me with wants and needs and desires again. I glance at the screen on my phone and groan.

It's Haddie, my best friend and roommate. I've successfully avoided her and one of her notorious inquisitions since the event on Saturday night. Luckily, she'd had plans that kept her out of the house because one round of her questions and she would've known something had happened.

"Hey, Had!"

"Ry! Where've you been? You're avoiding me!" she reprimands.

Geesh, five words into the conversation and she's already starting in on me. "No, I'm not. We've just both been busy with—"

"Bullshit," she argues. "I talked to Dane and know the story! Why didn't you wake me up and tell me when you got home?"

I blanch, wondering what Dane told her, and then I realize that she is probably talking about the auction. "Because nothing happened but absolute humiliation. It was awful."

"Oh, it couldn't have been that bad!" she says sarcastically. "At least you got a hot date out of it. Who is he?"

I roll my eyes at her as I turn my car into the driveway of The House. "Some guy—"

"Well, obviously. I'm glad it wasn't *some* girl because that would put a whole different spin on this." She laughs, and I can't help but smile. "So spill it, sister!"

"Really, Haddie, there's nothing to tell." I can hear her guffaw. "Oh, will you look at that? I just pulled up to The House. I gotta go."

"Likely story, Ry. Don't worry, I'll get the scoop out of you when you get home tomorrow from work." I cringe at the Haddie Montgomery promise to dig deeper. She never forgets.

"Look, I don't know the guy," I relent, hoping if I give her some information she'll be satisfied and not pry any further. "Teddy introduced me to him before I was pulled into being a *contestant*. His name is Donavan something, and he's the son of one of the chairpersons. That's all I know." I cringe at my blatant omission.

I hear her hum of approval on the end of the line and know the exact expression that is on her flawless face. Her button nose is scrunched up in disbelief while her heart-shaped lips purse as she tries to figure out if I'm telling the truth. "I really am at work now, Had. I have to go. Love ya, bye," I sign off with our usual parting words.

"Love ya, bye."

There is chaos in The House as usual when I walk in the door. I step over six book bags that lay haphazardly in the entryway. I can hear Top 40 music coming from one bedroom and the beginning of an argument coming from another as I pass the hallway on my way to the core of the house.

I hear the pop of a baseball mitt coming through the open windows at the rear of the house, and I know that Kyle and Ricky are in the midst of their frequent bout of catch. Any minute, one of them will be complaining that the other one has horrible aim. They'll argue and then move to the next activity, playing with their Bakugan or competing at baseball on the Wii.

I walk into the great room to hear Scooter giggling as he sits next to my fellow counselor, Jackson, on the couch, arguing the merits of Spiderman versus Batman.

The great room is a common area of the house, combining the kitchen with a large open living area. Large windows open up to the backyard where I can see the boys playing catch. The room has couches on one end that form a U-shape around a small media center, while the other end houses a big wooden table, currently covered with what appears to be incomplete homework. The earth tone furniture is neither new nor shabby but gently worn and well used.

"Hey, guys," I say as I place my bag on the kitchen island, appraising the state of dinner in two large Crock-Pots on the counter.

I hear various versions of "Hi, Rylee" in response.

Jackson looks up from the couch, his brown eyes full of humor over his debate with eight-year-old Scooter, and smiles. "We were just taking a break from homework. They'll have it finished before dinner is ready."

I lift the lid off a Crock-Pot and stir what appears to be pot roast and vegetables. My stomach grumbles, reminding me that I'd worked through lunch today at the corporate office.

"Smells good," I say, smacking Shane's hand as he reaches to pinch a piece of the freshly baked loaves of bread that sit on cookie sheets on top of the stove. "Hands off. That's for dinner. Go get a piece of fruit if you're hungry."

He rolls his eyes at me as only a fifteen-year-old boy can. "Hey, can't blame a guy for trying," he counters, his prepubescent voice cracking as he skirts around me, brushing his shaggy blonde hair off his forehead.

"You need a haircut, bud." He shrugs at me, his lopsided grin stealing my heart as it does regularly. "Did you finish your paper yet so I can review it?"

He turns around to face me, walking backwards. "Yes, *Mom!*" he replies, the term of endearment not lost on me. For that, in fact, is what the staff here is to these boys; we are the parents they no longer have. And in most instances, the chance of adoption above a certain age diminishes drastically. The state has turned over their guardianship to my company.

I work mostly in the corporate office several miles away, but require that all of my trained staff work at least one twenty-four hour shift per week. This time allows them to connect with the boys, and to never forget whom exactly we are fighting on behalf of on a daily basis.

These boys and my staff are my second family. They fuel me emotionally and challenge me mentally. At times they try my patience and push my limits, but I love them with all my heart. I'd do anything for them.

Connor comes flying through the kitchen, running to the back door with something under his arm, while Aiden is chasing after him. "Hey, guys, calm down," I reprimand as I hear Aiden shout that he's going to get it back and make him pay.

"Cool it, boys," Jackson says in his deep baritone, rising from the couch to watch the interaction. Those two have a habit of antagonizing each other, sometimes to the point of becoming physical.

I feel small hands wrap around my thigh, and I look down into the angelic eyes of Scooter. "Hey, bud." I smile, taking slow and deliberate movements to reciprocate the hug. I can see him steel himself for my touch, but he does not flinch. It has taken me sixteen months to elicit this reaction from an eight-year-old whose only physical contact with his mother was through fists or objects. I squat down to his eye level and kiss him softly on the cheek. Trusting, chocolate-brown eyes look at me. "I agree with you. Spiderman is *way cooler* than Batman. He's got that spidey-sense that Batman only wishes he had." He smiles at me, nodding his head enthusiastically. "Why don't you go pick up your mess? It's almost time for dinner."

He nods, flashing me a shy smile, and I watch him walk back to the family room where his beloved comic books are sprawled haphazardly across the floor. I move my gaze from Scooter to the figure huddled on the other couch.

Zander is static. He is in the same mute state he's been in for the past three months he's been in my care. He is curled into himself, an impassive expression on his face, as he watches the muted television with large, haunted eyes. He has his beloved stuffed dog, ratty and coming apart at the seams, a lifeline held tightly against his chest. His wavy brown hair curls softly at the nape of his neck. He desperately needs a haircut, but I can still hear his terrified shrieks from a month ago when he caught sight of the scissors as I approached him for a trim.

"No change, Jax?" I murmur to Jackson who has walked up beside me, keeping my eyes on Zander.

"Nope." He sighs loudly, empathy rolling off him in waves. He continues in a muted tone, "His appointment with Dr. Delaney was the same. She said he just stared at her while she tried to get him to participate in the play therapy."

"Something is going to trigger him. Something will snap him out of his shock. Hopefully it will be sooner rather than later so we can limit damage to his subconscious..." I hold back my sorrow for the lost little boy "...and help the police figure out what happened."

Zander had come to us after the police found him covered in blood in his house. He had been trying to use a box of Band-Aids to stop the bleeding from the stab wounds that covered his mother. A neighbor walking her dog had overheard his mother's strangled cries for help and called the police. She died before they arrived. It is assumed that Zander's father committed the murder, but without Zander's statement, the events that led up to the actual act are a mystery. With his father missing, he's the only one who knows what happened that night.

Zander has not uttered a word in the three months since his mother's murder. It's my job to make sure we provide for him in every way possible so he can dig his way out of the catatonic, repressed state he's in. Then we can help him begin the lengthy process of healing.

I turn from the heartbreak that is Zander and work with Jackson to get dinner finished. We work in sync, side by side, like an old married couple; we've had this shift together for the past two years and can now anticipate each other's movements.

We both work in silence, listening to the flurry of activity in The House.

"So I heard the benefit was a success—with an unexpected entrant in the auction." He wiggles his eyebrows at me, and I roll my eyes in response before turning back to the sink. "And one hot and heavy make-out session backstage."

I drop the knife I'm washing. It clatters loudly against the stainless steel basin. I'm grateful that my back is to Jackson so he can't see the stunned look on my face. *What the hell?* Someone must have seen me with Donavan. I have to remind myself to breathe as I panic, trying to figure out how to respond. I don't need my staff gossiping about my backstage encounter.

"What—what do you mean?" I try to sound casual, but I hope I am the only one who can hear the distress in my voice. I turn the water off, waiting for the response.

Jackson laughs his deep, hearty laugh. "I would have loved to see you in action, Ry."

Shit, shit, shit! My heart races. How am I going to explain this one? I feel warmth on my cheeks as my flush spreads. I open my mouth to answer him when he continues.

"Parading around on stage at the event you so desperately fought against." I can hear the amusement in his voice. "My God, you must have been pissed!"

"You have no idea." My response is almost a whisper. I have nothing left to wash, but I keep my back to him, afraid the questions will start if he sees my face.

"And then Bailey told me she met this hot guy—her words, not mine—and lured him backstage in typical Bailey fashion and had a hot and heavy make-out session with him."

I release the breath I'm holding, grateful that it was our intern Bailey bragging about her exploits rather than gossiping about her boss's. And then I realize that sexy siren Bailey, whom all the guys at work want to date, was most likely Donavan's first conquest on Saturday night.

If that were the case, why would he want to go from the leggy, auburn-haired bombshell to me? Talk about reinforcing my feeling of being second choice.

I blow my hair up out of my face. "Well, you know Bailey," I counter, trying to phrase my next words carefully. "She definitely likes to have her fun."

Jax laughs, patting my back as he walks by. "That was a nice way of putting it," he says as he starts to make the boys' school lunches for the next day. "She's a great girl, works hard, the kids love her ... just not a girl I'd want my son to date."

I murmur an agreement thinking about our beguilingly sweet intern, who is only five years my junior, and her *free* ways. A part of me has always been jealous of girls like her. Girls who throw caution to the wind and live their life without regrets, kiss random boys recklessly, take spur of the moment road trips, and are always the life of the party. I often worry that one day I'll look back on my life and feel like I haven't lived. That I haven't taken enough chances, sown my wild oats, or ventured outside my comfort zone.

My life is safe, predictable, controlled, and always in order. I like it that way most of the time. It's not that I'm not jealous of her because she kissed Donavan first—well maybe a little—but rather that she lives without regrets.

I shake myself out of my thoughts, ones that I have been having more frequently with *the anniversary* approaching. If anything, I should have learned that life is short and I need to *really* live it, not stay in my safe corner as it passes me by. I pull myself from my thoughts and refocus on the task at hand.

"Boys," I shout over the chaos, "it's time to come finish your homework." I hear groans coming from various rooms because I've said the dreaded "H" word. Six boys, varying from eight to fifteen years old, sullenly walk toward the table, grumbling as they go.

I look over toward the couch where Zander remains curled into himself, rocking back and forth for comfort.

I slowly walk toward him and kneel in front of him. "Zander, do you want to join us? I can read you a book if you'd like?" I speak softly to him, slowly reaching my hand out, holding it still for him to see my intention, and rest it on his hand that rests on his knee. He continues rocking, but his blue eyes flicker over to hold mine.

I see so many things in the depths of his eyes that shake me to the core. I smile softly at him and squeeze his hand. "We'd love for you to join us." He remains silent but his eyes are still fused on mine. A small sliver of hope springs within me since he normally looks at me and glances away after a few seconds. "Come on, Zander, take my hand, I won't let go if you don't want me to."

He continues to stare at me for some time as I remain stock still, a reassuring smile on my face. His tiny hand moves, and he closes his fingers around my palm. He stands slowly, and we move to join the rest of the boys at the table.

Chapter Five

I'm dragging big time. I've hit the last hour of my shift at The House, and the long hours of the past couple of days have caught up with me. The boys were a handful today.

Kellen, my co-counselor, is playing tag with the boys outside. I can hear their laughter and squeals through the open windows.

I'm in the kitchen getting everything together for dinner for the next shift when the house phone rings.

"Hello?"

"Oh, good! You're still there." I hear relief tinged with excitement.

"Just barely." I laugh. "I have about fifteen minutes left. What can I do for you, Teddy?"

"I know you're probably exhausted, but is it possible for you to stop by the office on the way home?"

It's the last thing I want to do, as much as I love him. I just want to go home, crawl into bed, and sleep until tomorrow. "Um, okay. Sure. Is something wrong?"

"Just the opposite! I think we found the solution to find the rest of the funding for the new facilities." He says enthusiastically. "I'll tell you about it when you get here. We're just hammering out all of the details now."

"Wow! Are you serious?" My hopes start to rise. Even with the charity event and the numerous other donations we have already received, we are still shy of our goal by several million dollars. "I—I will be there as soon as I can, depending on traffic."

I hang up the phone, excitement bubbling inside me. All my hard work over the past two years to get the approvals, the board's backing, the plans, the funding—it all might finally come to fruition.

I finish preparing the dinner so all that the next shift has to do is put it in the oven. I grab my purse and overnight bag and start to gather my things. I glance at my cell phone and begrudgingly decide to check my email. Maybe I can tackle a few phone calls from them while I am in traffic.

I scan my inbox and notice an email I'd received earlier in the day from Donavan. I contemplate just deleting it, but curiosity gets the best of me and I open it up.

To: Rylee Thomas
From: Ace
Subject: Dexterous Fingers

Rylee—
You've left me no choice. Your lack of response has left me to take matters into my own hands. You remember how those felt, don't you?
—Ace

Arrogant ass. I delete the email. What's he going to do? I'm even more indifferent to him now that I know about his and Bailey's tryst in the dressing room. Or at least I am trying to be. Come to think about it, they probably fit each other perfectly. *Manwhore and maneater*.

I smile at the thought as I finish collecting my things and say goodbye to the troops.

Traffic is unusually light as I drive toward the office. I take this as a sign that good things are going to happen. It's a beautiful, sunny California day, unusually warm for the ending of January. What I would give to grab a towel, head to the beach and lie there, letting the sun's warmth rejuvenate me.

In no time at all, I pull into the parking lot of Corporate Cares. I walk quickly up to the building's lobby, checking my reflection in the mirrored windows. I have on my favorite blue jeans that sit low on my waist and a snug, red V-neck T-shirt. Luckily I had an extra one in my bag because I don't think Teddy would enjoy my original one that's now splattered with Ricky's vomit. I fuss with my hair a moment, pulling the clip from it and letting my curls fall down my back.

After a short elevator ride, where I'm able to touch up my lip-gloss and pinch my cheeks for color, I arrive on the floor of the main office. I walk past my office, nod to several people, and exchange pleasantries on my way to Teddy's receptionist. I note that the shutters on the conference room windows are closed and wonder what's going on in there.

"Hi, Sandy."

"Hey, Rylee. I'll let him know you're here. He's expecting you."

I smile. "Thanks." I walk toward the wall of windows that extends throughout the office and watch a line of cars on the freeway heading home. *The ants go marching one by one.*

"That was quick!" I turn to face my boss, a broad grin on his face. "I can't wait to bring you up to speed."

"I can't wait to hear what's going on," I say as I follow him into his office.

I sit down across from him in the black leather chair, happy to be off my feet.

Teddy sits across from me, unable to contain his enthusiasm. "I got a call earlier today and have been in a meeting all afternoon hammering out a deal. Get this," he says as he leans toward me, placing his hands on his desk, "CD Enterprises has come forward wanting to put up half of the remaining cash for the facilities as well as raise the remainder of the money by getting other companies to match or sponsor them." His words come out in a rush of air, excitement in his eyes.

I process his words, trying to formulate a coherent thought. I can't believe this is really happening. "What? How? Wow!" I laugh, caught up in Teddy's whirlwind.

"I am still fine-tuning the finishing details of it. Colton's in the conference room right now." He motions with his hand toward the hallway. "I'll bring you in there in a second to reintroduce you."

"We've met?"

"Yes, I introduced you to him on Saturday at the benefit."

"You introduced me to a lot of people at the benefit," I tell him, laughing. "So many I couldn't keep their names and faces straight. Let's hope I remember what conversation I had with him so I don't look like an ass."

He laughs at me, the reassuring sound booming off the walls of his office. "I'm sure you'll be fine! Anyway, this could be it, kid! All your hard work finally coming to fruition!"

"This is so great, Teddy!" Relief overtakes me. We'd been told earlier in the week that without the complete funding, the project might be delayed for another eight months to a year.

"Almost too good to be true, really." He shakes his head. "I have to tell you though, Ry, I'm gonna have to depend on you to help me with this. They want a dedicated person from our office to work side-by-side with theirs, and they requested you."

I nod despite being confused by why or how the company knows me. It doesn't matter. What matters is getting the funding. "Sure, I'll do anything. You know that." I put my hand up to my chest, covering my heart. "I can't believe it! Whatever you need, I'll do, to get this funding—to keep this ball rolling."

"That's my girl! I knew I could count on you!" He rises from his desk. "C'mon, I can't wait for you and Colton to reacquaint yourselves and go over the fine print on the agreement."

I follow him down the hallway, feeling a little insecure about my attire. I'm underdressed for a business meeting, but if Teddy doesn't care, neither should I.

"Here she is, Colton," Teddy announces as he enters the conference room ahead of me.

I turn the corner, walk through the doorway and come to a dead stop. Donavan is sitting in a chair at the other end of the conference table, a stack of papers in front of him. His arms are crossed casually over his chest, and his biceps pull noticeably at the sleeves of his polo shirt. His eyes meet mine and his mouth spreads into a slow, smug smile.

What the hell? I stop in the doorway looking at Teddy and back to Donavan. "I—I don't under—understand?" I stammer.

The appalled look on Teddy's face tells me that I've made a serious blunder in my reaction. "Rylee?" he questions as he looks at Donavan quickly, making sure I haven't offended him, and then back at me, a warning on his face. "Rylee, what are you talking about? This is Colton Donavan, among other things, the CEO of CD Enterprises—I introduced you to him the other night?"

All at once, my world turns and tilts on its axis. My head is reeling from the fact that the man across from me—the man who reduced me to a puddle of sensation the other night—is none other than Colton Donavan. *The* Colton Donavan—hot and upcoming racecar driver extraordinaire, son of a mega-Hollywood-movie director, and the serial philanderer who provides the tabloids constant fodder for their gossip columns.

The Colton Donavan who left me with salacious dreams and a carnal, unrequited craving since last Saturday. *Fuck me!*

I can't believe that I didn't put it together sooner. I knew he seemed familiar when I met him, but I realize I wasn't thinking rationally either. I'm having a hard time wrapping my head around this. All of the air has been punched out of my lungs.

My head swivels from Teddy to Dona-er-Colton and back to Teddy. From the way Teddy is staring at me, the look on my face must be quite unpleasant. I look down, take a deep breath, and try to compose myself and quiet the emotions rioting through my head. I can't screw up this donation regardless of my feelings—there is too much at stake.

"Um—I apologize," I say softly, "I just—I thought your name was Donavan." I walk further into the room, gaining confidence, telling myself I can do this. "I misunderstood when we met the other night ..." The quick flash of Colton's grin stops me cold.

You can do this, I repeat to myself like a mantra. I refuse to let him know that he has this effect on me.

I hold my head up and walk with purpose to where he sits, holding out my hand and plastering a smile to my face. "Nice to see you again, Mr. Donavan."

I can hear the deep breath Teddy has been holding—afraid my reaction has possibly hampered this deal—release. The tension in his face ebbs.

"Colton, please," Donavan says as he unfolds himself gracefully from his chair and rises, taking my hand in his, holding it a beat longer than necessary. "Nice to see you again too." A spark flashes through his emerald eyes.

"Please, let's all sit," Teddy says enthusiastically. "Colton, I'll let you fill Rylee in on your company's proposal."

"I'd be glad to, Teddy." Colton says professionally, all business, as he shifts his chair to face me, placing a packet of paper in front of me. "CD Enterprises is invested in giving back to our community. On a yearly basis, my team and I choose an organization and devote time, connections, and funds to create awareness for their cause. After unexpectedly attending your function last weekend in my mother's place when she fell ill, I found your organization to be inspiring."

I observe him while he continues on with facts and figures of past organizations that CD Enterprises has supported. I'm having a hard time understanding how this professional, put-together man is the same person who reduced me to tremors and whimpers.

This is the type of man I usually fall for. Black and white, no grey area. Knowledgeable and passionate. This is what I find sexy. Not the arrogant, self-serving bastard from the other night who was reckless and uninhibited. Thank goodness I know the truth so I won't fall for his act.

At least this is what I'm telling myself when I hear my name pass from his lips.

"What?" I ask as I shake myself from my thoughts.

"Do you have any questions?" Colton asks, cocking his head to the side thoughfully. I can tell he knows exactly what I'm thinking about—*him*.

"First of all, let me say that I hope your mother is feeling better," I say, letting my manners override my contempt for him. When he nods, I continue, "What exactly does CD Enterprises do, Mr. Donavan?" I ask.

"My mother is doing better, thank you. As for CDE, the company's primary function is ownership and management of a race team. My race team," he says, exuding pride. "Among other things, our biggest venture is a cutting edge technology that will help increase the safety quotient for drivers. It is currently patent pending."

"Hmmmm," I contemplate, trying to figure out how this can all tie in. "And how exactly are you going to tie a race car or team, per se, into raising funds for orphaned kids and Corporate Cares?" I am back in business mode, my intellect unaffected by his charm. *For the most part.* But I have a feeling there's a catch here.

Once bitten, twice shy.

"Thank you for the segue," he says. "On Monday, I brought your organization to my team's attention. After some research, discussions, and brainstorming, we created the following proposal." He flips open the packet in front of me and looks at me, pleasure softening his hard features as he announces, "CD Enterprises proposes that up front, we donate one and a half million dollars to Corporate Cares."

Holy shit! I try to stifle the words from tumbling out of my mouth. Pride is evident in his eyes as he watches me pensively, quietly gauging my reaction before continuing.

"In addition to the immediate funds, we plan to devote a portion of my car's graphics in the upcoming season to promote your cause or mission, if you will." He sees the confusion on my face and puts his hand up so he can finish. "We plan on using this advertising spot to entice other companies and race teams to add to the sponsorship. My team will get them to commit to paying a set dollar amount per lap that my car completes or a blanket sponsorship."

I widen my eyes in disbelief; this could bring in a staggering amount of money for the company. I glance over to Teddy, who is so excited he is fidgeting, a huge grin on his face. I look back to Colton and my eyes meet his, emerald to amethyst, warring between gratitude and confusion. Why us? Why our company?

He smiles softly at me as if he knows what I'm thinking and acknowledges my dilemma. Accepting the donation means I have to accept his date. He continues, "We're still figuring out whether we offer the sponsorship per race or over the whole season. My team is working on that as we speak, seeing as we only have a little under three months until the first race to get as many corporate sponsors as possible."

"Isn't that unbelievable?" Teddy bellows from beside me.

I turn to him and smile sincerely before turning back to face Colton. "It's very generous of you and your company; I'm just a little baffled about why. Why Corporate Cares?"

The corners of his mouth turn up. "Let's just say that you can be very persuasive, Ms. Thomas." He holds my stare as I inhale a sharp breath. "I think I'll enjoy working with someone as passionate and..." he looks away, finding the word before bringing his eyes back to mine "...*responsive* as I found you to be on Saturday night." He keeps his face impassive, although his eyes are anything but, as his tongue darts out to lick his lower lip.

Despite the blood draining from my head at his words, I can feel a flush spread over my cheeks and down my neck. The corners of his eyes crinkle. I squirm under his gaze, wishing to be anywhere but here.

Like in his bed, under him, with his fingers dancing across my skin and his lips possessing mine. What the fuck? It's bad enough he's in my face, now he's corrupting my thoughts. This is not good. *Definitely not good.*

I suppress my anger at the nerve of Colton. I can't believe he's just said this. Is referring to my indiscretion in front of my boss really that necessary? How dare he come in my office and provoke me, remind me of something I'm not proud of. Something I'm not going to forget anytime soon.

"Responsive," Teddy says, rolling the word over his tongue in thought. "That is a great way to describe my Rylee here!" He pats me on the back and pride fills his voice. He is completely oblivious. "Always going above and beyond."

Colton shifts his eyes to Teddy, who is unaware of our sexual tension. "It is, indeed. And a very hard quality to find in someone." He nods, agreeing with Teddy. "I watched her in *action* on Saturday night and was quite impressed."

I've had enough of this, yet I don't want to give him the satisfaction of knowing he's agitated me. I don't want to work with this man, but let's face it, Corporate Cares has no other option to make all my blood, sweat, and tears over the past two years come to fruition. He's stepping up to the plate, even if his motives aren't completely wholesome.

I have to think of this collaboration as *a means to an end*. My boys and the many others who can benefit from this new facility.

"So Mr. Donavan—"

"Colton, please," he reiterates.

"Colton, I understand the premise," I state primly, wanting to get this conversation back on track. "What exactly is my involvement in this collaboration?"

"Well, Ms. Thomas, I won't need much from you from a business standpoint. I have a team that is very experienced in this type of thing. Obviously though, I'll need you to be the point of contact for their questions and other miscellaneous things."

These "other miscellaneous things" have me worried. "So why—"

Colton holds up a hand again, and I am getting rather annoyed by this habit. "As I discussed with Teddy, the contract between our companies for the donation is contingent on several factors." He pauses, organizing the papers on the table before him. He looks up, his attention focused solely on me. "For the next several months and into the season, I will need a representative of Corporate Cares with me for numerous occasions."

He stops as I purse my lips, my eyes growing large as I hope my assumptions are incorrect. "Me?" I question, already knowing the answer.

"Yes. You." He mouths. I watch his eyes narrow as I lick my lips. All of a sudden, I feel hot. His lips part just a bit as he watches me, and I have to shake the inappropriate thoughts of them out of my head as he continues. "In conjunction with the announcement of our joining forces, there will be several events—some locally, some out of town—black tie affairs, press junkets, et cetera," he says, casually waving his fingers, "that I will need you to escort me to."

"What?" I stand up, pushing my chair back with force and look between Colton and Teddy in bewilderment. How dare he? I turn down a date, turn down going beyond second base backstage, and he schemes up a way to tie me to him with a contract? What an immature prick! His ego must really be bruised from my rejection.

I'm dumbfounded. *No way*. This is not happening. Words I'd love to say to him, to call him, run through my head as I seethe with anger.

"Is there something the matter, Rylee?" Teddy asks, breaking through my haze of frustration. "I think it's a brilliant idea." I turn my head to him, opening my mouth to respond but nothing comes out. "If Colton's willing to use his name, his *connections*, and popularity by standing beside you at a press filled event to get the word out about Corporate Cares, then—"

"Why not take advantage of it?" Colton finishes for him, a smug smile spreading across his face.

I'm starting to feel dizzy, my head spinning from the turn of events. I place my hand on the table to brace myself as I slowly sink into the chair, my eyes focusing on an imaginary spot on the papers in front of me.

"Ry? You okay?" Teddy asks, concerned.

"Huh?" I raise my head up to meet his empathetic eyes.

"You look a little flushed. Are you feeling okay?"

"Yeah. Yes," I answer, taking a deep breath. "I'm just—it was a long shift. That's all," I say, gathering myself. *It's a means to an end.* "Sorry," I apologize. "I'm just overwhelmed that the new project is going to be a reality." Colton sits silently, analyzing me. I shift uncomfortably under his scrutiny.

"Look, Rylee," Teddy says, "I know you have a lot on your plate right now and this is just adding to it, but it's so close now we can taste it. There is no one I'd rather have be the face of this organization. You're the one, kiddo."

His high praise warms me despite the panic I feel from being trapped. From being forced into a situation that I know will be beneficial for Corporate Cares but no doubt devastating for me.

Teddy glances at his watch and reaches over to pat my hand. "I have a conference call in five minutes." He rises from his seat as does Colton. "I trust that I can leave you two in here to fine-tune the remaining details."

He reaches his hand out to Colton, sealing the agreement with a handshake. "Thank you, for your unexpected generosity. You have no idea how many lives you are helping to change with this gift."

An unexplained darkness flickers across Colton's face. "I understand more than most people might think," he says before releasing Teddy's hand. "Thank you for your warm reception to the idea. My lawyer will be contacting you in the morning to draw up the paperwork."

With that, Teddy nods and exits the conference room. I stand watching the empty doorway, my back toward Colton as I contemplate my next move.

I'm overwhelmed by his generosity. At his attempt to make *my dreams* come true, so why can I not feel gratitude toward him? Why do I just want to turn around and throttle him? I hate being forced into anything. It's not that I have to be in control—well, maybe just a little bit. But at least I want to make my own decisions, not be treated like some compliant woman who submits without question.

Why does he irritate me so much? Is it because every time I look at his lips or watch his fingers rub over his jaw, my body tightens in anticipation of how they felt on me? Or is it because I can hear his rasp of a voice in my dreams telling me how much he wants me? *Shit*! My life was perfectly fine until last weekend. And then I meet him and now I'm a flustered mess.

I shouldn't care that he was making out and doing God knows what with Bailey, but I do. I'm embarrassed that he probably thinks I let any guy I meet put his hands on me. I'm irritated that I know the only reason for his pursuit is because I'm not falling for his smooth lines and eloquent bullshit. I'm confused why a man who is like a Pied Piper to women much prettier, sexier—everything—than me is even glancing twice in my direction.

My life is not some Hollywood romance movie where boring girl meets famous boy and they fall madly in love. I'm not naïve enough to believe that this is going to happen to me.

And then, my feelings for Max further confuse things. I feel guilty that, despite loving him, I never felt as alive with him as I did with Colton.

I sigh loudly, my body aware of his proximity.

He chuckles, fueling my irritation, as I turn to face him. He is leaning back in his chair, an ankle resting on the opposing knee, his arms casually resting on the armrests. We stare at each other, observing and scrutinizing each other for the first time without observers. His eyes lazily wander over my body, pausing at my cleavage. I watch his smile widen in what I can assume is an appreciation of the feminine form in general, not just mine, before they travel further down.

His beauty really is magnificent. Thick, dark lashes starkly contrast his green eyes. His strong nose has a slight curve, as if it had been broken. This imperfection in an otherwise perfect face adds to his overwhelming sex appeal. I take in his full lips, the top one slightly thinner than the lower, the darkened stubble that shadows his face, and the pulse that beats steadily under the curve of his jaw. I have the sudden urge to kiss him and nuzzle into him, to feel the pulse of this vibrant man beneath my lips. To be enveloped in his clean, earthy scent.

I shake my head, trying to break the trance. He quirks his eyebrows and waits for me to make the first move. We stare for several moments as we measure each other. I finally break the silence. "Is this what you call taking matters in to your own hands?"

"What's wrong? Can't handle the temptation, Ryles?" He flashes a wicked, arrogant grin at me, and as much as I want to roll my eyes, he's all I can think about.

"Hardly," I snort.

He shrugs indifferently. "A man's gotta do what a man's gotta do, Ry," he says. "You left me no choice."

"No choice? Really?" I scoff, throwing my hands up in disgust. "What are you, fifteen years old throwing a tantrum because you didn't get your way?"

"You owe me a date."

"All this for a frickin' date, Ace? Or is it because I denied your sexual ministrations after I came to my senses?" Ugh, he is so frustrating!

"Oh, you would've come all right," he rebuts sardonically, raising an eyebrow, "and from what I recall, your senses? Those were strewn all over the backstage floor."

Smartass! How can he get me so fuming mad when it takes so much more to get me to this point with other people?

"So because I said no, you offer up tons of money and bind me to a contract? Forcing me to *have* to spend time with you? Money in exchange for a date? I'm not a *whore*, Colton," I rant, waltzing to the window trying to abate my anger. "Especially not *yours*!"

I can hear him shuffling behind me as he rises and walks toward the window. He looks at me through his reflection in the glass and holds my stare. My body vibrates.

"Let's get something straight," he growls. "First of all, I have my own reasons for donating the money that have absolutely nothing to do with you. Nothing! Second, I don't *ever* pay for dates, Rylee. *Ever*. I have more class than that." I can feel his fury roll off him in waves.

"You paid for a date with me," I retort.

"Charity. Auction. Does. Not. Equal. Escort. Service." He snarls, taking a step closer, but never breaking our stare. "Lastly," he seethes, grabbing hold of my arm to emphasize his point, "I don't ever want to hear you refer to yourself as a *whore* again."

We stand in silence as his words settle around us. Why the hell does he care what I call myself? He has no claim over me. I know better than to provoke when someone is angry, but I can't help myself. For some reason I want to push his buttons. If I'm going to be forced to do something, then I might as well say my peace.

"Then why the contract? The events that I'm required to be your *escort* for." I yank my arm out of his grip. "Sounds like your ego is bruised because I won't succumb to your dazzling charm, so you need to tie me to you to prove to yourself that you still have that magic *Colton touch*."

"I didn't say anything about bondage," he cuts me off, smirking. "But if that's your thing, Rylee, I'd be more than happy to oblige. I can teach you *the ropes*."

I shake my head in disbelief as the meaning of his words sink in. Blood rushes to my cheeks before I can meet his eyes in the glass again. "I'm ignoring your last comment," I say dryly, trying to recall what my point was since he has scattered my thoughts. *Um—where was I? Oh!* "Your ego's bruised because I won't fall helplessly at your feet and become your compliant sexual plaything, so you come to my job—take the one thing that I really want, the one thing that I've been working toward for over two years—and you serve it up to me on a platter."

"And the problem with that is ...?"

"The problem is that you offer it to me with terms that are self-satisfying to you ..." I falter because I realize I'm rambling now. And at some point I'm afraid that if I keep talking, private thoughts may tumble out—thoughts about him. And if I slip, then ... he'll know I think about him more than I should.

Colton sidles up next to me, leaning his shoulder on the glass, staring at my profile. Our silence extends for several moments, my anxiety ratcheting from his quiet scrutiny.

When he speaks, his voice is demandingly soft, "Why won't you go out on the date with me?"

Whoa, change of subject! A sliver of a laugh escapes my mouth from nerves. I keep my face averted, watching the world outside. "For what reason? You and I come from different worlds, Colton, that have different rules. You want a date so you can add another to the many notches in your bedpost. You said you wanted to fuck me to get me out of your system and move on," I say, repeating his threat. In my periphery, I see him blanch at my words. "You may be used to women declaring their love for you and dropping their panties at *clever* lines such as that but not this one."

Colton starts to speak. I know he's going to drop a witty one-liner about how I'll have no problem dropping mine for him. Using his own tactic, I stop him before he can interrupt by holding up my hand. "Our encounter was a momentary indiscretion on my part. One that will never happen again." I turn my face to look Colton in the eyes. "I'm not that kind of girl, Ace."

He regards me, the muscle in his jaw pulsing. He leans in, the coarseness of his voice making his words resonate with truth. "You know that deep down, a tiny part of that proper, respectable woman that you are wants to visit that reckless, sexy, uninhibited place inside you that's begging to get out. A place I can undoubtedly help you find."

My eyes blaze while I try to reject the truth behind his words. He watches my internal struggle until I turn from him and walk back toward the conference table. I don't want him to see the despair on my eyes. "You play dirty, Colton."

"And your point?" he retorts, turning and leaning his backside against the glass, a lopsided smile flashing. "Sometimes you have to play dirty to get what you want."

"And what exactly is it that you want?" I ask, crossing my arms across my chest as an invisible means of protection against him. As if anything really could protect me.

Colton pushes off the wall and stalks toward me, like a lion about to pounce on his prey. He stops in front of me, closer than necessary, and reaches out, using a finger to lift my chin up so that my eyes meet his. "You," he states simply.

I feel as if all of the air has been vacuumed out of the room; I can't breathe. Incredulity and willingness flood me momentarily as I accept his answer. The warmth is fleeting as I realize that this is how he does it. This is how he gets so many notches on his bedpost. He makes you feel like you're the only one on his radar. He's good. He's really good. But I'm not going to fall for it.

I walk away from him, creating some distance so I can think clearly. "So why a contract? What are you trying to achieve?" I toss over my shoulder as I circle the conference room table. When I'm across it, I turn to face him. "Are you going to threaten my job if I don't *fuck* you?"

"No..." a wry smile turns up the corners of his mouth "...but there's always that option."

"Well, why don't we just save us both the time and effort and get it over with?" I rebuff, exhausted by this game we're playing. "Then we can move on to what really matters. Hell, we can even use the conference table if you're that desperate."

"We could," he says, laughing, a sincere smile on his face. He presses both hands on the table, testing its stability. "It's sturdy enough." He shrugs. "Although it's not exactly what I had in mind." His eyes express the lascivious thoughts he's left unspoken. "And believe me, sweetheart, I'm far from desperate."

His look sends shivers down my spine. I try to change tactics. Obviously the avenue I've taken is not working to deter him. "We both know you don't need an escort to these functions. Why not have one of your girlfriends escort you?" I continue moving, knowing that if I stand still, I risk the chance of coming into contact with him. And the pull he has over my body is too strong to resist his touch. And if he touches me, then I think my resolve will crumble. "I'm sure that you have a bevy of beauties waiting for you to snap your fingers."

"I don't do the girlfriend thing," he deadpans, stopping me in my tracks.

"Oh, I see. *The casual fucking thing is more your style then?*" I see anger flash in his eyes before he reins it in, covering it with a diminutive smirk. "I guess I was right to not expect too much from you."

"Why tie myself to just one woman when there are so many out there vying for my attention?" he goads, trying to push more of my buttons.

"Do you actually believe your own bullshit lines?" My God, the man is relentless and exasperating at the same time. He just flashes me a smarmy smile and folds his arms across his chest. I try to not focus on the play of muscles beneath his shirt. Try not to imagine what he looks like with his shirt off. "You sure are full of yourself, aren't you, Ace?"

He cocks his head and looks at me. "I can arrange for you to be full of me instead, if you'd like?"

Again, I stop at his words. Regardless of how forward and crass his comment is, all of the muscles south of my waist clench with desire. I can feel the flush of heat creep up my cheeks, staring at a non-existent spot on the wall for a moment, hoping he doesn't notice. He chuckles softly at my reaction, and my eyes flash up to meet his, my expression belying how dumbstruck I am from his words. It's only when I stare at him incredulously for a few moments, my mouth opening and closing trying to form words to berate him for his arrogance, that I see the crack in his game. A smile graces his lips, causing the lines around his eyes to crinkle.

"C'mon," he teases, taking a step closer to me. "You walked right into that one. I couldn't resist."

I know the feeling. I stare at him, shaking my head. "Okay," I concede. "I'm going to pretend that you didn't just say that. But seriously, why don't you do the girlfriend thing?"

He shrugs casually. "Not my thing. I don't like strings attaching me to anything. Relationships equal drama."

A guy with commitment issues, like that's something new.

"So I was right?" I mutter more to myself than to him, astounded by his brutal honesty.

"About what?" he asks, angling his head to the side as he approaches me slowly. My heart beats faster. The tone of his voice and his aura have changed. I can sense raw desire as he nears. The danger. My body clenches in anticipation, while my brain tells me to retreat quickly.

"What I told you on Saturday—you do like to just *fuck 'em and chuck 'em.*" My voice is quiet. The temerity behind my words fades with every step he takes in my direction.

"I told you once I don't take kindly to insults. You just did it again. For that alone you deserve to be taken over my knee." My thighs clench in expectant desire. I'm not into that type of thing. And yet that type of thing with Colton, his hands on me, possessing me, pushing me to ride that fine line bordering between pleasure and pain arouses me beyond coherence.

I part my lips as he comes within inches of mine. My body is attuned to him. His scent. The intake of his breath. My back arches as he lifts a hand to my cheek. "It sucks, doesn't it?" he asks as he trails a finger along my jaw line, stopping, then brushing against my bottom lip.

"What does?" I sigh softly as his finger leaves my skin.

"When you have to stick to your guns out of principal rather than giving into the temptation right in front of you," he whispers, turning the tables on me. "There is no shame, Rylee, in letting your body have what it craves."

We stand, inches from each other, letting the weight of his words settle in my psyche. I know he is right. My body's deepening ache tells me so. That I want exactly what he is offering.

"It's hard to deny it, sweetheart, when it's written all over your body."

I jerk back from him as if I've been bitten. His words fuel my ire and irritate me. "No! I—"

"Shhh," he murmurs, stepping back toward me, pressing a finger to my lips, his eyes ablaze with salacious intensity. "Just know, Rylee, the best sex you will ever have ... will be with me," he says in a low, hypnotizing voice that seems to knock all of the air from my lungs and reason from my usually sensible head.

I jump back, needing space from his carnal words and unending arrogance. He's so forward, so cocksure it's almost unattractive. *Almost.* The man can definitely talk a good game. Too bad I'll never know if it's true or not, if for no other reason than to teach his oversized ego a lesson.

"I'll comply with the damn agreement, Colton," I huff. "For my boys. For the many kids to come." I stalk toward the table to collect my things. "Not for you. Or your stupid machinations behind it." I forcefully square up the papers on the table, paper hitting wood is the only sound in the room. I look up, my steely eyes pinning his. "I will not sleep with you, Ace."

"Yes, you will." He smiles smugly.

Despite the vicious bang his words spark between my legs, I manage a single chuckle. "Don't even think for a single minute—"

"Colton!" A sexy voice purrs at the door to the conference room, interrupting me.

I snap my head up to see the svelte Bailey smiling seductively, all wide eyes and batting eyelashes. My insecurities rise to the surface as I swallow loudly, looking to see Colton's reaction. My eyes meet his because, despite the interruption, his eyes have never left mine. I am unsure what to make of this. He purses his lips, the unresolved issues left hanging between us.

All of the sudden, I'm not feeling well and want desperately to escape from this room. From this man. From witnessing the familiarity between Bailey and Colton. From being jealous despite expressing that I don't want him.

Oblivious to the tension, Bailey sashays into the room, heading toward Colton, finger twirling her perfectly straight, perfectly bottle-dyed auburn hair.

Regret flashes across Colton's eyes as he glances toward her and smiles a warm hello, ever the consummate gentleman. I turn abruptly to leave, knocking into my chair so it scrapes loudly against the hardwood floor.

"I didn't realize you'd snapped your fingers," I mutter as I try again to get around my chair.

From behind me, Colton releases a hearty, sincere laugh at my comment that, despite my frustration, makes me smile. As I exit the room, I hear him call my name. I keep walking, wanting to distance myself from him.

"This is by no means over, Rylee," he yells out.

I continue without responding, right past my office and straight to the elevator doors. I ignore Stella's call, the blinking voicemail light on my phone, and luck out when the elevator door opens as I approach. I need fresh air to clear my head.

I am a confident woman and not afraid to speak up, so why do I feel like one of those blubbering girls I can't stand? Why is it that Colton reduces me to a mass of hormones—angry one minute and wanting his lips on mine the next?

I sag against the wall of the elevator in frustration. He gets me so worked up. So angry. I can't figure out what I want to do more, punch him or fuck him.

Chapter Six

The California sun relaxes me as I drink in its warmth in my backyard. I recline in the chaise, tilting my head to catch the last rays before they sink and fade to dusk. The leaves of several palm trees that line our backyard fence rustle from the light breeze, calming me.

The day's events have taken their toll on me. And with Josie down with the flu, I'll be back at the house in less than twenty-four hours to cover her shift. Despite it being early evening, I really should be getting ready for bed and sleeping off some of my exhaustion. But I've let Haddie talk me into a glass of wine and some pizza that she's making in the house.

I close my eyes, leaning my head back, sighing as I allow myself to believe that the new facilities will become a reality. That our new approach for treating orphaned children can expand and hopefully become the pioneering protocol for change in our foster system. We can strengthen our case that creating small groups of kids under one roof—where they consistently have guardians, rules, school, counseling—will lead to well-adjusted adults. They will have a place where they belong.

A shiver of pride runs through me as I think of all of the possibilities and all of the hope that we can create with the completion of this project.

And then I suddenly feel sick from thinking about him. I still can't figure out what to make of his comment that he doesn't do the "girlfriend thing." Why do I still keep thinking about him if there's nothing there? *Because there is*. I can't deny that he's more than easy on the eyes. And I definitely can't act as if the sparks that shoot up my arm when he touches me are imaginary. But I don't want to get involved with him and his womanizing ways, especially now that I have to because of work.

I sigh heavily when I hear the sliding door open and Haddie walks out with a bottle of wine, two glasses, and a pizza box stacked with plates and napkins on top. I suddenly realize how hungry I am. She walks toward me, the sun framing her tall figure, setting her blonde hair alight like a halo around her head. Long, lean legs stretch from short khaki shorts, and her oversized bosom is covered in an orange camisole. As usual, she is accessorized perfectly and styled flawlessly. And despite her tireless perfection that makes me feel inadequate in so many ways, I love her like the sister I never had.

"I'm starving," I announce, sitting up from the chair to help Haddie place everything on the table.

"And I'm starving for information on what's going on with you. On why you're out here so deep in thought," she prods as she pours red wine into the glasses, and I serve the pizza.

"Just like in our dorm room," I say nodding at our meal, laughing at the memory .

She was my freshman year roommate. I could have never of guessed that first week of college orientation that the Barbie doll I roomed with would turn out to be my best friend. She waltzed into our dorm room looking like a model out of a Ralph Lauren ad campaign, so confident and sure of herself, her picture-perfect family following behind her. She slowly took in our meager surroundings, the painted brick walls and small closet space. My gawky self watched her, cringing at the thought of having to be reminded every morning of how inferior I was to this beautiful creature.

I sat picking at the hem of my dress as her parents left for good. She shut the door, turned to me, a huge grin on her heart-shaped lips, and said, "Thank God they're finally gone!" I watched her out of the corner of my eye as she sagged against the door in relief. She angled her head, studying me, sizing me up. "I think it's time to celebrate!" she said, hurrying over to her suitcase.

Within moments, she produced a bottle of tequila hidden deep in her belongings. She then flopped on my bed next to me. She unscrewed the cap and held the bottle up in the air between us. "To Freshman year!" she toasted, "To friendship, freedom, cute boys, and having each other's backs." She winced as she took a swig of the strong alcohol and then handed the bottle over to me. I looked nervously back and forth between her and the bottle, and then wanting desperately to be liked by her, took a swallow, the burn bringing tears to my eyes.

"My God, we were so naïve then. And young!" she reminisces. "We've been through so much since freshman orientation!"

"All we need is that cheap tequila to bring us back." I laugh and then fall silent as the impending night starts to eat the sun's rays. "Eight years is a long time, Had," I say, taking a long drink of the tart wine, letting it soothe the anxiety gnawing at the edges of my mind.

"Long enough," she says, taking a seat, looking at me, "that I know something is bugging you. What's going on, Ry?"

I smile, so grateful to have a friend like her and feeling cursed at the same time because I can't hide anything from her. I feel tears burn my eyes, the sudden onset of emotions surprising me.

Haddie leans forward, her perfectly tanned legs bending beneath her as she reaches out and places a hand on my leg. "What is it, Rylee? What has you so twisted up?"

I take a moment to find my voice, wanting to tell her everything, to get her opinion on whether I'm being obtuse about Colton. Maybe I know what she is going to tell me if I confess, and that's why I find myself holding back. Not wanting to hear that it's okay to let go and feel again. That being with someone else does nothing to tarnish Max, his memory, or what we had together.

"There are too many things. I don't even know where to start," I confess, trying to sift through my mental baggage. "I'm exhausted from work—worried about Zander's lack of progress, wrapping up all of the details from the benefit last Saturday night," I say, running my hands through my hair, "and the fact that I'm back to the house tomorrow to cover Josie's shift because she's sick …"

"Can't someone else cover it?" she asks, taking a bite of pizza. "You've worked way too many hours this week. I've barely seen you."

"No one can. Not this week. Everyone's hours are maxed out because of all the extra time I had them put in for the benefit … and since I'm on salary … it's left to me," I explain.

"I understand why you do it, Ry—why you love it—but don't let it kill you, sweetie."

"I know. I know. You sound like my mother!" I take a bite of my pizza and chew it slowly. "The good news though, is that I think we secured the rest of the funding for the facility."

"What?" she sputters, sitting up quickly. "Why didn't you tell me? This calls for a celebration," she says, clinking her glass with mine. "What happened? How? Details!"

"We're still ironing out the final details before making anything public," I say, trying to hide my contempt for how we secured the funding, "and then we'll make an announcement." I hope that my answer will be enough to keep her questions at bay.

"Okay," she says slowly, eyeing me, wondering why I'm not being more forthcoming. "So then what's up with your auction date thing that Dane was telling me about?"

I look down, twisting the ring that sits on my right ring finger. I worry it around and around out of habit. "Not sure yet," I say, looking up, noticing her watching me twist my ring.

She looks up, tears in her eyes. "It's because the anniversary is coming up soon isn't it? That's why you seem so overwhelmed?" She scoots out of her chair and sits next to me, wrapping her arms around me.

For a brief moment, I allow myself to give in to the memories and to the thoughts that surround the approaching date. I haven't really put the two together, my sudden sentimentality and my scattered emotional state over the possibility of acting on the nonexistent connection with Colton. I guess I'm subconsciously ignoring the traumatic date, wanting to close my eyes to the grief that will forever exist in the depths of my soul.

I wipe a tear from my cheek and withdraw from the warmth of Haddie's embrace. "Yeah." I shrug. "Just too much all at once." This is the truth, but I feel guilty about not telling Haddie the whole of it.

"Well, sister," she says, handing back my glass of wine, "let's drink a bunch more wine, wallow in pity, and laugh at our stupid selves." Her sincere smile lifts my mood.

I clink my glass to hers, thankful for her friendship. "Cheers, my dear!"

Chapter Seven

I glance at the clock as I finish helping Ricky with his spelling words and shoo him off to play with the others. I have thirty more minutes on shift and then I'm off for a whole glorious two days. I actually have the elusive, rare weekend off, and despite letting Haddie talk me into being her date for a launch party for the newest rum product her company is promoting, I'm excited to have time to myself.

It's been quite a day to say the least.

Earlier, the school called for me to pick up Aiden because he'd been in yet another fight. I received a lecture from the principal that if this keeps up, other measures might need to be taken for his education. I questioned him about whether the other boys, the ones who keep bullying Aiden, were receiving the same threat. He responded with a non-committal grunt.

I was happy to be able to work one-on-one with Zander while the rest of the boys were in school. Our counseling staff thought it was best to home school him until he started communicating verbally. Trying to teach someone who, for the most part, is unresponsive is a frustrating endeavor to say the least. All I want is for some kind of break through. Something tells me he knows how much I care for him. That I wish he still had his mother to soothe him. To hug him. To tell him she loves him.

The boys are keeping themselves busy while I'm at the table reviewing Shane's paper for school. Jackson's shift ended an hour ago and his replacement, Mike, is at a counseling appointment with Connor.

I'm thoroughly impressed with how well Shane is improving in school, a result of our many one-on-one sessions with him. I glance over to the family room area where Kyle and Ricky have brought their box of baseball cards. They sit down on the floor next to the coffee table and turn their attention to the basketball game on the television. Zander is in his usual place, stuffed animal held to his chest and his eyes staring into space. Scooter is lying on the carpet, coloring in one of his Spiderman coloring books. I listen for the telltale sign of music in the back bedrooms to indicate that Shane is in his room. I finish making comments on Shane's paper and shift my attention toward reviewing the meal and afterschool activity schedules for the next week.

I hear a knock at the front door and before I can even put my pen down, I hear Shane yell, "I got it!" from his bedroom. I smirk because I know he's hoping it's his "girl that is a friend." She came over last week, and Shane is still on cloud nine.

"Look before you open," I tell him as I rise from the table and walk toward the hall. As I reach the corner that leads to the foyer, Shane breezes past me, disappointment on his face. "It's for you," he says, plopping on the couch.

I turn the corner, figuring that there's a delivery. The House is always receiving legal documents via courier, regarding our kids' situations. I reach the doorway and when I step out, I come face to face with Colton. Despite his sunglasses, I know he's looking me up and down. A lazy, lopsided grin on his face that causes his dimple to deepen, spreads across his face.

Damn my breath for catching at the sight of him. As much as I don't want him here, don't want the complication of what he has to offer in my life—a quick fuck that's easily discarded—I am giddy at the sight of him. And this turn of events is not looking good for me.

I stop in the doorway, a smile spreading on my face despite knowing that he's bad news for me. We stand, looking at each other, taking each other in for several moments. He's in a well-worn pair of jeans, and a black T-shirt clings to his muscular torso. The simplicity of his clothing only adds to his devastating looks. His dark hair is windblown, wild, and sexy as hell.

Everything about him screams here comes trouble. And I'm standing right in his path like a deer in the headlights, unable to move. Willpower is only going to last me so long. *I'm seriously screwed*.

"Hello, Rylee." The simple rasp of his voice saying my name has me flashing back to his mouth on mine. His hands on me. His vibrations propelling shockwaves through my body.

I cock my head to the side regarding him. "Hi, Ace," I say guardedly. "Since when did you add stalker to your repertoire of talents?"

I slip my hands into the rear pockets of my jeans as I lean against the doorjamb. He removes his sunglasses, his emerald eyes blazing into mine, and then folds them to hang in the neck of his shirt. Their weight pulls the neckline down so several dark hairs curl out. I drag my eyes from the sight back up to his eyes.

He flashes me a lightning fast grin. "I'd be more than happy to show you my talents, sweetheart."

I roll my eyes. "Womanizing is not a talent."

"True." He draws the word out and slowly nods his head, "but you've yet to see the true depths of my many others." He arches an eyebrow, a roguish smile turning up the corners of his mouth. "And since you keep running, I can't show you and we can't solve our little problem about that date you owe me." He takes a step closer, a playful look in his eyes. I retreat a step back into the foyer, leery of this dance we are engaging in. "Aren't you going to invite me in, Ryles?"

"I don't think that's a good idea, Donavan. I've been warned about guys like you."

He smirks. "You have no idea," he murmurs, eyes locked on mine. His patronizing smile irks me. He takes another step closer, causing my pulse to quicken.

"What do you want? Why are you here?" I huff.

"Because I want my date with you," he says, slowly enunciating every word. "And I always get what I want." He places both hands on the doorjamb, leaning into it, his silhouette blocking the afternoon sun, his dark features haloed by the bright light.

I shake my head at his nerve and boundless conceit. "Not this time," I disagree. I push the front door to shut and turn back on my heel down the hallway.

In less than a heartbeat, Colton grabs my upper arm, whirls me around, and has me pressed up against the doorjamb. "Keep fightin' me, sweetheart. The feistier you are, the harder you make me." There is a dangerous amusement in his tone that scrapes over me and prickles my senses.

Shit! How can he make those words sound like a seductive promise?

He presses his hips against mine, holding me against the hard, unforgiving wood. We're both breathing heavily, and I'm unsure if it is from the physical exertion or from our proximity to each other.

Colton releases my upper arm and brings both of his hands to cradle my face, his thumbs brushing at my jaw line. His translucent eyes burn into mine, and I can sense an internal struggle in him, his jaw tensing in deliberation.

"As much as I'd like to warn you away from me, Rylee—for your own sake," he murmurs, inches from my mouth, "all I crave is the taste of you." His finger trails a line down the side of my neck, lighting my skin on fire. "It's been too long since I've savored you. You. Are. Intoxicating." His words are a staccato that match the quickening of my heart.

Oh fucking my! If that comment didn't make desire flood every inch of my skin, nothing will. The man can seduce me with words alone. He's pulling at me, testing my willpower, and making me want way more than I should. We breathe each other in for a moment as I try to form words in my head. Gain some semblance of coherence. His mere presence makes my synapses misfire.

"Why are you warning me," I breathe, completely immobilized by the intensity of his stare, "when you're going to take what you want anyway?"

He quickly flashes a grin before his lips are on mine, his hands on me, proving my point and then some. This kiss is not gentle by any means. I can sense his hunger, his fiery need as our teeth clash. His lips and tongue move at a frenzied pace against mine while his hand grabs hold of my ponytail and tugs down, holding me in place.

I relish this kiss as much as he does, for all of my pent-up frustration over him explodes within me. I am caught up in the hurricane that is Colton. I take as he is taking. I curl my arms around his torso, running my hands up his back, enjoying the firm delineation of his muscles as he moves with me. I nip at his bottom lip, aroused by the low moan that comes from the back of his throat. We press into each other, unable to get enough of each other's touch—the only thought running through my head is that I want *more*.

I'm suddenly shocked back to reality like an angel losing her wings when I hear the boys cheering loudly in the family room at something to do with the basketball game. I push Colton back with two hands against his chest.

I try to catch my breath and my bearings by placing my hand against the wall and trying to steady myself. What the hell am I thinking? I'm making out in the doorway at work. *For the second time*. What the hell is this guy doing to me? When I'm around him it's as if I've lost all sense of reality. I can't do this. I just can't. I'm shaken. Really shaken. No one has ever elicited such a blatant carnal reaction from me, and it scares me.

Colton stands across from me, calm as can be, keenly watching. Why do I feel as if I have just run a marathon and he looks like an uninterested bystander?

I finally find my voice. "You're right," I say ruefully. "I most definitely should stay away from you." I look back toward the hallway as I catch a slight grimace on his face. "I need to check on the boys. You can see yourself out," I tell him as I turn abruptly and walk back toward my responsibilities. My reality.

I enter the great room trying to plaster a natural smile on my face, but failing miserably. All the boys are where I left them and for that I am thankful—glad that no one ventured into the hallway to see their guardian acting like a teenager filled with raging hormones.

Something in my periphery catches my eye. I turn to see Colton standing at the edge of the hallway, thumbs hanging in the pockets of his jeans, shoulder casually leaning against the wall. His face is expressionless, but those iridescent eyes say so much.

What now? Can't he just leave me alone?

I glare at him, hoping my angst is reflected in my eyes. I see that Shane has taken notice of the stranger standing in his home. He turns his attention to Colton, sizing him up. His face scrunches as he contemplates the stranger, trying to place him.

"What do you want?" I scowl despite trying to keep the contempt out of my voice. The last thing the boys need to witness right now is a confrontation. I notice Kyle and Ricky's heads pop up to look over the table like a pair of meerkats.

Colton glances at the boys and smiles politely, although I can see the tension in his eyes. "I told you, Rylee, I'm here to collect my winnings," he drawls. "To collect what's mine." He smiles insolently at me, waiting for my reaction.

"I beg your pardon?"

"You owe me a date, Ryles."

The boys have all turned their attention to us now. The basketball game has been forgotten. Shane is smirking since he's old enough to sense sexual tension, even if he doesn't quite understand it.

Colton walks toward me, purposely placing his back to our audience, blocking me from their vision so they can't watch our interaction. I am grateful when he stops and stands at a respectful distance.

"Sorry, Ace," I say sweetly so only he can hear me. "Hell hasn't frozen over yet. I'll let you know when it does."

He takes a step closer, his voice just above a whisper. "It seems you know all about being cold, Rylee. Why stay frigid when you know I can heat you up?"

His words take a direct hit at my self-esteem. I see the anger at his arrogance but know I must calm myself down before I cause a scene in front of my kids.

I break my glare from Colton when something over his shoulder catches my attention. I step to the side so I can get a better look at what it is. I stifle a gasp as I watch Zander, holding his stuffed animal tightly, move slowly around the couch toward us. He has a curious look on his usually stoic face as he approaches.

Colton turns around to see what I'm reacting to. He starts to ask me a question, and I raise my hand up forcefully, telling him to be quiet. Fortunately, he complies. The other boys in the room have all turned to watch, expectant expressions on their faces, for this is the first time that Zander has ever purposely taken the initiative to interact with someone.

Zander walks up to us, staring at Colton, his mouth opening slightly and closing several times. His eyes are saucers. I kneel down to eye level with him. I sense Colton next to me trying to understand my reaction.

"Hi there," I hear Colton say gently.

Zander stops and just stares. I fear that something about Colton's looks or something he is wearing has triggered a reaction in Zander. Some negative memory that is forcing him to come see for himself if it's real. I'm waiting for the fallout to start—the screaming, the fighting, and the terror to fill his eyes.

"Zander. It's okay, baby," I croon, wanting to break through his trance, letting him know that a familiar, comforting voice is nearby. I turn my head slightly toward Colton, locking my eyes with his. "You need to leave now!" I order him, afraid of what Zander sees in him.

Against my wish, Colton steps forward and slowly crouches down beside me. I hear his boots squeak on the tile, the house is so quiet. One of the boys must have muted the television.

"Hey, buddy," he soothes, "How ya doin'? You okay?"

Zander takes a step closer to Colton and a smile ghosts his mouth. My eyes widen. He is not scared. He likes Colton. I quickly glance to Colton, afraid to miss anything Zander does, and he holds my gaze, nodding his head. He understands that something is happening. Something important. Something that he needs to be cautious about.

"Zander is it?" Haunted eyes meet Colton's, and then he moves his head in a small, discernible nod. I suck in my breath, tears threatening as I watch a small breakthrough happening. "So Zander, do you like racing?"

I can hear the boys in the family begin murmuring excitedly as they realize who Colton is. The boys get louder until they see me staring intensely at them, and then they become silent.

Colton holds his hand out to Zander. "Nice to meet you, Zander. My name is Colton."

For the second time in three days, I am rendered speechless. My head is reeling from the sight of little Zander slowly reaching out to shake the hand of the man next to me.

I watch the first steps of a little boy breaking free from the devastating grasp of a violent trauma. This is his first time initiating physical contact with someone in over three months.

Colton holds Zander's small hand in his, shaking it gently. When they finish their greeting, Zander keeps his hand there, with no indication that he wants to move it. Colton obliges and holds the tiny hand, a soft smile on his face.

Tears burn my eyes as I struggle to hold them back. I want to jump up and shout in excitement at this breakthrough. I want to grab Zander and hug him and tell him how proud I am of him. I do none of these. The power of this moment is so much greater than any of these things put together.

"I'll tell you what, Zander, if Rylee here agrees to the date with me that she's trying to get out of," Colton says, never breaking eye contact with him, "then I'll take you as my personal guest to the track the next time we test. How's that?"

A ghost of a smile returns to Zander's lips, his eyes lighting up for the first time as he nods his head yes.

I hold my hand over my heart as joy races through me. Finally! And all because Colton followed me in the house. All because he didn't listen to me. All because he's using one of my kids to blackmail me into going out with him. I could kiss him right now! Well, I guess I've already done that, but I could do it again. At this point, I'll do anything Colton asks me to do just to see the smile on Zander's face again.

Colton squeezes Zander's hand again and shakes it. "It's a deal then, buddy." He releases his hand and leans in closer. "I promise," he whispers.

Zander's lips curve into a smile. Small dimples form in his cheeks. Dimples I didn't even know he had. He slowly withdraws his hand from Colton's but continues to look at him expectantly, as if to ask when this will take place. Colton glances over at me for help, and I step up.

"Zander, sweetie?" He moves his eyes from Colton's and looks over to me. "Colton and I are going to go over and sit in the kitchen and plan a time, would you like to join us or would you like to go finish watching the basketball game with the boys?" I ask softly.

Zander's eyes glance rapidly back and forth over the both of us before Colton interrupts. "Hey, buddy, I'm gonna stay right here in the kitchen for a couple of minutes with Rylee. Can you go watch the game for me to let me know what I've missed when we're done?"

Zander nods slightly, locking eyes with Colton, once again gauging if he's being sincere. He must believe him because he clenches his stuffed doggy tighter and heads back to the couch. Shane's eyes catch mine, his face blanketed with disbelief before he picks up the remote and turns the sound back up.

I rise from the floor, noticing that all of the boys except Zander have their attention still focused on Colton. It's not every day that a celebrity is in our house. Colton notices the pairs of eyes on him and gives them a heartfelt smile.

"Don't worry," he says to them, "you can all come too when I take Zander to the track."

A large cacophony of whoops ring out as excitement electrifies the boys. "Okay, okay," I placate. "You guys got what you wanted. Please turn around and pay attention to the game so Colton and I can discuss some things."

They obey, for the most part, as we move to the barstools in the kitchen. I offer Colton a seat, and I walk around the island so I can face him. I notice Shane still observing us though, a protective look on his face, wondering why Colton has upset me.

For the myriad of emotions that Colton has made me feel in the week's time I've known him, the gratitude I have for him at this moment trumps them all.

I look up at him and meet his eyes, trying unsuccessfully to keep the tears from filling mine.

"Thank you," I whisper. It's only two words, but the look on his face tells me that he understands how much is behind them.

He nods. "It's the least I can do." His voice is gruff. "We all have our stories," he says, more to himself than to me.

"You got that right," I say, still overwhelmed by the situation. I look over to Zander and smile. He did it. He really did it today. He took a step out from under the fog. And suddenly I feel filled with hope. I feel impulsive from the possibilities.

"Colton!" I jolt him out of his thoughts. He whips his head up, startled by my urgency. I know I will regret this later, but I decide to go with my instinct. I decide to be impulsive and act in the moment. "I'm off in ten minutes," I say, and he looks at me as if he is not following my train of thought, so I continue. "I owe you a date, so let's go on a date."

He shakes his head as if trying to make sure I said the words he heard. "Oh— okay," he stumbles, and I love the fact that I've taken him by surprise. He starts to rise, the corners of his lips curving. "I don't have any reservations or—"

"Who cares?" I motion with my hands. "I'm not high maintenance. Simplicity is rewarding. I'm good with a burger or anything really." I watch his eyes widen in disbelief. "Besides, you paid enough for the date, who needs to drop a bunch of money on food that we eat anyway?"

He stares at me for a beat, and I sense that he is trying to figure out if I'm being serious or not. When I just look at him like he's being dense, he continues. "You are incredible. You know that right?" His simple words go straight to my heart, I can tell that he is being sincere.

I flash a grin over my shoulder as I head to my quarters to grab my things and freshen up. "I'll be right back."

I return in moments to find Mike staring awestruck, shaking Colton's hand in the kitchen. Colton turns to me when he hears me come in. "You ready?" he asks.

I hold up my finger indicating one second. "I'm outta here," I announce to the boys as they rise to give me hugs goodbye. I think the presence of Colton and my acquaintance with him has suddenly elevated me to rock star status, judging by the way they're hugging me so tightly.

As I'm receiving my hugs, I notice Colton walk over to the couch and squat down in front of Zander. He says something to him, but I can't hear what.

Chapter Eight

As Colton and I stroll out of the house, an odd feeling of calm settles over me. I think this may be the best approach for a date with Colton. I've caught him off guard so he can't do any extensive planning. Extensive planning might equal overstated indulgences and premeditated seduction. Two things that I definitely do not need. It's hard enough to resist him as it is.

"We'll take my car," he says, placing a hand on my back, the warmth comforting me as he steers me toward a sleek, carbon-black convertible parked at the curb. The Aston Martin is beautiful and looks as if it is meticulously taken care of. It looks like it can really fly, and for just an instant, I imagine getting behind the wheel, flooring the pedal, and leaving all my ghosts behind.

"Nice ride," I grant him, although I try not to show any interest. I'm sure he's used to women fawning all over him and his car. Not me. *Let the games begin*, I think.

"Thanks." He opens the passenger door for me, and I slide onto the black leather, admiring the crafted interior and utter opulence. "I thought it was a beautiful day to drive with the top down," he says, rounding the back of the car and sliding in next to me. "I just didn't realize I was also going to be taking you out in it, too. An added bonus!" He says, giving me a megawatt grin as he puts on his sunglasses.

I can't help but flash him a smile back. "Whatever happened to good ol' fashioned pickup trucks?" I ask as he leans forward, opening the glove box, brushing his arm across my thigh and laughing loudly.

His touch is electrifying, even when it is accidental. He pulls out a worn, molded baseball hat with "Firestone" emblazoned across the bridge and puts it on his head, his dark hair curls out from under it at the nape of his neck. He pulls the brim down low enough to touch his sunglasses.

I guess this is his "incognito" look, but all I can think is he looks sexy as hell. All smoldering, edgy bad boy wrapped up in a drool-worthy body. I'm seriously fucked here if I actually think that my willpower will prevent me from giving in to any request from him. He reaches over and gives my thigh a quick squeeze before pressing a button on the dash in the center console.

"Don't worry, I have a truck too." He chuckles before the car roars to life, the vibration of the engine reverberating through my body and sending a thrill through me. "Hold on!" he says as he zooms out of the neighborhood, the excited look of a little boy on his face.

Boys and their toys, I think as I watch him from behind my aviators. I shouldn't be surprised by his skill maneuvering the car—this is how he makes his living—but I am. I shouldn't be turned on by his complete competence as he weaves smoothly in and out of traffic, the car accelerating quickly, but I find myself wanting to reach out and touch him. To connect with him, despite knowing that's a dangerous line for me to cross.

The roar of the engine and the whipping wind are loud enough that talking is not an option. I sit back, enjoying the feeling of freedom as the wind dances through my hair and the sun warms my skin. I lean my head back and give in to the urge to raise my hands over my head as we zip onto Interstate 10 heading west.

I glance over to see him watching me, a curious look on his face. He subtly shakes his head, a diminutive smile on his lips before he looks back toward the road. After a beat, he pushes a button and music pours through the speakers.

The song ends and another begins. I throw my head back, laughing at the song. It's a catchy little pop tune that I have heard on Shane's radio enough times. In my periphery, I notice Colton give me a quizzical look, so despite my average voice, I belt out the chorus, hoping he hears the words.

"You make me feel so right, even if it's so wrong, I wanna scream out loud, boy, I just bite my tongue." I raise my arms over my head again, letting myself go, reveling in the thought that I am telling Colton how I feel without telling him. This is so unlike me—singing out loud, letting loose—but something about being with him, sitting next to him in this flashy sports car, has rid me of my inhibitions. As we exit the freeway, I finish the chorus with gusto. "It feels so good, but you're so bad for me!" Colton hears the words and laughs good-naturedly at them.

I continue singing the song, with less gusto since the car's purring engine is quieter now that we are on Fourth Street. He suddenly swerves abruptly and parks the car with adept precision along the curb.

I glance around trying to figure out where we are as he pushes a button in the sleek dashboard and the sexy purr of the engine ceases. "You okay to sit tight for a sec?" he asks, flashing me an earnest grin that affects me more than I care to admit.

"Sure," I answer, and I know at this moment that I am saying yes to so much more than just sitting patiently in the car. I push the fear out of my mind and vow to embrace the idea of feeling again. Of wanting to feel again. I flick my eyes from his, down to his mouth and back up, salacious thoughts running rampant through my mind. His smile widens.

"I'll be right back!" he announces before unfolding himself gracefully out of the car and standing to give me an incredible view of his ass. I bite my lip to suppress the urges whipping through my body. He glances over his shoulder and laughs, knowing full well the impact of his actions. "Hey, Ryles?"

"Yeah, Ace?"

"I told you you wouldn't be able to resist me." He flashes me a disarming smile before hopping up on the curb and walking briskly down the block, long legs eating up the sidewalk without a look back.

I can't help but grin as I watch him walk away. The man is captivating in every way and the epitome of sexy. From that boyish grin that disarms me in seconds to his sexy swagger that says he knows exactly where he's going and what his intentions are. He exudes virility, evokes desire, and commands attention all with a single look from his stunning eyes. He's edgy and reckless and you want to go along for the ride hoping to get a glimpse of his tender side that breaks through every now and again. The bad boy with a touch of vulnerability who leaves you breathless and steals your heart.

I shake myself from my thoughts to admire the view of Colton's broad shoulders and sexy swagger as he strides down the sidewalk. He tugs down on his baseball cap before he walks past two women. They both turn their heads as he passes by and admire him before turning back to each other and giggling, one mouthing the word, "Wow!"

I know how they feel, multiplied by a hundred. I watch as Colton stops and disappears into a doorway. I can't see the sign above the entrance on the worn down façade.

I pass the time admiring the sleek interior of the vehicle and watching people walk by the car and stare at it. The ring of Colton's cell phone sitting in the console startles me. I glance down to see the name *Tawny* flashing across the screen. A pang of irritation flickers in me before I rein in my jealousy. *Of course he has women calling him*, I tell myself.

Probably *all* the time.

"We're all set," Colton says, startling me as he places a paper grocery bag behind me. He walks around the car and slides into his seat. As he buckles his seatbelt, he notices his phone's missed-call message on the screen and thumbs to it. An enigmatic look crosses his face as he sees the caller's name, and I chastise myself for hoping he would scowl when he saw it.

A girl can dream.

Within moments we are back on the road and headed up the Pacific Coast Highway. I'm admiring the sight of the surf crashing on the beach with the sun in the background slowly ebbing toward the horizon before I realize that we're pulling into a nearly empty parking lot. I'm surprised there are so few people here considering the weather is unusually warm for this time of year.

"We're here," he says, pushing a button that has the top of the car lifting and closing in over us before he turns off the car. I look at him, surprised; I was hoping for a non-romantic "date," and yet he has brought me to my favorite place on earth—a near-empty beach just before sunset. He simply is not playing fair, but then again, he doesn't know me well enough to know my preferences, so I just chock it up to luck on his part.

He grabs the bag behind my seat and exits the car. He then collects a blanket from the trunk before coming around to my side. He opens the door with a playful flair as he reaches for my hand to help me out of the car.

"Come," he demands as he tugs on my hand, a thousand sensations overtake me as he pulls me toward the sand and surf. I am giddy with the fact that he continues to hold my hand in his even though I've followed him. The rough calluses on his palm against my smooth skin are a welcome feeling, almost like being pinched to make sure I'm not dreaming.

We walk out onto the beach past a pile of towels and clothes that I assume belong to the two surfers in the water. We walk in silence, both taking in our surroundings as I try to figure out what to say. Why am I all of the sudden nervous over Colton's intensity? Over his proximity?

When we get about ten feet from the wet sand, Colton finally speaks. "How about right here?"

"Sure, although I would've brought my swim suit if I'd known we were coming to the beach," I say, my nerves giving way to stupid humor as it usually does. If I could roll my eyes at myself right now, I would.

"Who said anything about suits? I'm all for skinny dipping."

I freeze at the comment, eyes wide, and swallow loudly. Odd that the idea of stripping down naked with this ruggedly handsome man unnerves me, despite the fact he's had his hands on me.

His perfection next to my ordinary.

Colton reaches out with his free hand and puts a finger under my chin, raising my head so that I can meet his gentle eyes. "Relax, Rylee. I'm not going to eat you alive. You said you wanted casual, so I'm giving you casual. I thought we could take advantage of the unusually warm weather," he says, releasing my chin and handing me the brown bag so that he can lay a large Pendleton blanket on the sand. "Besides, when I get you naked, it's going to be somewhere a lot more private so I can enjoy every slow and maddening second of it. So I can take my time and show you exactly what that sexy body of yours was made for." He glances up, eyes flashing desire and mouth turning up in a wicked grin.

I sigh and shake my head, unsure of myself, of my reaction to him, and how I should proceed. The man can seduce me with words alone. That's definitely not a good sign. If he keeps it up I'll be handing over my panties to him in no time at all.

I fidget under the intensity of his stare and from the direction my thoughts have taken. "Take a seat, Rylee. I promise, I don't bite." He smirks.

"We'll see about that." I snort, but I oblige him and sit down on the blanket, distracting myself from my nerves by unzipping my ankle boots. I pull off my socks, free my feet, and wiggle my toes, which are painted fire-engine red. I pull my knees up, and wrap my arms around them, hugging them to my chest. "It's beautiful out here. I'm so glad the cloud cover stayed away today."

"Mmm-hmm," he murmurs as he reaches into the brown bag from Fourth Street. "Are you hungry?" he asks, producing two packages wrapped in white deli paper, followed by a loaf of French bread, a bottle of wine, and two paper cups. "Voila," he announces. "A very sophisticated dinner of salami, provolone cheese, French bread, and some wine." The corners of his mouth turn up slightly as if he is testing me. As if he is checking to see if I really am okay with a casual, no-frills dinner in this land of Hollywood glitz, glamour, and pretension.

I eye him warily, not liking games or being tested, but I guess someone in his shoes is probably wary of others. Then again, he's the one begging me for a date, although I'm still not sure why.

"Well, it's not the Ritz," I say dryly, rolling my eyes, "but it'll have to do."

He laughs loudly as he pulls the cork out of the wine, pours it in the paper cups, and hands one to me. "To simplicity!" he toasts good-humoredly.

"To simplicity," I agree, tapping his cup and taking a sip of the sweet, flavorful wine. "Wow, a girl could get used to this." When he eyes me with doubt, I continue, "What more could I ask for? Sun, sand, food—"

"A handsome date?" he jokes as he breaks off a piece of bread, layers it with provolone and thin-sliced salami, and hands it to me on a paper napkin. I accept it graciously, my stomach growling. I've forgotten how hungry I am.

"Thank you," I say. "For the food, for the donation, for Zander …"

"What's the story there?"

I relay the gist of it to him, his face remaining impassive. "And today, with you, is the first time he's purposely interacted with anybody, so thank you. I'm more grateful than you will ever know," I conclude, looking down sheepishly, a blush spreading across my cheeks as I'm suddenly uncomfortable again. I take a bite of the makeshift sandwich and moan appreciatively at the mixture of fresh bread and deli fare. "This is really good!"

He nods in agreement. "I've been going to that deli forever. It's definitely better and more my speed than caviar." He shrugs unapologetically. "So why Corporate Cares?" he asks, his mouth parting slightly as he watches me savor my food.

"So many reasons," I say, finishing my bite. "The ability to make a difference, the chance to be part of a breakthrough such as Zander's today, or the feeling I get when a child left behind is made to feel like he matters again …" I sigh, not having enough words to express the feelings I have. "There are so many things that I can't even begin to explain."

"You are very passionate about it. I admire you for that." His tone is earnest and sincere.

"Thank you," I reply, taking another sip of wine, meeting his eyes. "You were quite impressive yourself today. Almost as if you knew what to do despite me telling you to leave," I admit sheepishly. "You were good with Zander."

"Nah," he denies, grabbing another piece of cheese and folding it in the bread. "I'm not good with kids at all. That's why I'm never having them." His statement is determined, his expression blank.

I'm taken aback. "That's a bold statement for someone so young. I'm sure at some point you'll change your mind," I reply, my eyes narrowing as I watch him, wishing I still had the option to make a choice like his.

"Absolutely not," he states emphatically before averting his eyes from my gaze for the first time since meeting him. I can sense his discomfort with this topic—an oddity for a man so confident and sure of himself in all other areas of life. He looks out toward the tumultuous ocean and is quiet for a few moments, an unreadable look on his rugged features.

I think that my questioning statement will go unanswered, until he breaks the silence. "Not really," he says with what I sense is a resigned sadness in his voice. "I'm sure you experience it first hand every day, Rylee. People use kids as pawns in this world. Too many women try to trap men with them and then hate the kid when the man leaves. People foster kids just to get the monthly government stipend. It goes on and on." He shrugs nonchalantly, belying how affected he is by the hidden truth behind his words. "It happens daily. Kids fucked up and abandoned because of their mothers' selfish choices. I'd never put a child in that kind of position." He shakes his head emphatically, still refusing to meet my eyes, his gaze following the surfer riding a wave in the distance. "Regardless, I'd probably fuck them up as much as I was as a kid." He breathes deeply with his last statement and removes his cap with one hand while running his other hand through his hair.

"What do you mean? I don't understand," I falter as I start to ask without thinking. This conversation has unexpectedly gotten heavy quickly.

Annoyance flashes across his face before I watch him rein it in. "My past is public knowledge," he states, my furrowed brow showing my confusion. "Fame makes people dig out ugly truths."

"Sorry," I say, raising my eyebrows, "I don't make it a habit of researching my dates." I hide the unease I feel with this conversation in the sarcasm of my tone.

His green eyes lock onto mine, his clenched jaw pulsing. "You really should, Rylee," his steely voice warns. "You just never know who's dangerous. Who's going to hurt you when you least expect it."

I'm taken aback. Is he warning me about him? Warning me away from him? I'm confused. Pursue me and then push me away? This is the second time today he's issued a statement like this. What should I make of it?

And what the hell is with his comments about being messed up as a kid? His parents are practically Hollywood royalty. Is he saying that they did something to him? The fixer in me wants to probe, but I can tell how unwelcome that would be.

I cautiously glance over at him to see his attention turned back toward the surf. It is in this moment I can see the pictures painted by the media of him. Dark and brooding, a little rugged with the dark shadow of hair on his jaw, and an intensity to his eyes that makes you feel as if he's unapproachable. Unpredictable. The broad shoulders and sexy swagger. The bad boy who is too handsome for his own good mixed with a whole lot of reckless. The rebel who women swoon over and swear they could tame—if they had the chance.

And he's sitting here. *With me*. It's mind-boggling.

I clear my throat, trying to dispel the awkwardness that has descended on our picnic. "So, how 'bout them Lakers?" I deadpan.

He throws his head back and laughs loudly before turning back to me. All traces of Brooding Colton have been replaced by Relaxed Colton, with eyes full of humor and a megawatt smile. "A little heavy?"

I nod, pursing my lips, as I grab for another piece of cheese. Time for a change in topic. "I know it's an unoriginal question, but what made you get into racing? I mean why hurl yourself around a track at close to two hundred miles an hour for fun?"

He sips from his Dixie cup. "My parents needed a way to channel my teenage rebellion." He shrugs. "They figured why not give me all the safety equipment to go along with it instead of racing down the street and killing myself or someone else. Lucky for me, they had the means to follow through with it."

"So you started as a teenager?"

"At eighteen." He laughs, remembering.

"What's so funny?"

"I got a ticket for reckless driving. I was speeding … out of control really … racing some preppy punk." He glances over at me to see if I have any reaction. I just look at him and raise my eyebrows, prompting him to continue. "I was spared being hauled off to juvie because of my dad's name. *Man, was he pissed.* The next day he thought he'd teach me a lesson. Dropped me off at the track with one of the stunt drivers he knew. Thought he'd have the guy drive me around the track at mach ten and scare the shit out of me."

"Obviously it didn't work," I say dryly.

"No. He scared me some, but afterward I asked him if he could show me some of the stunt moves." He shrugs, a half smirk on his lips, as he looks out toward the water. "He finally agreed, let me drive his car around the track a couple of times. For some reason one of his friends had come with him to the track that day. The guy's name was Beckett. He worked for a local race crew who'd just lost their driver. He asked if I'd ever thought about racing. I laughed at him. First of all, he was my age so how could he be part of a race team, and secondly, how could he watch me take a couple of laps and know that I could drive? When I asked, he said he thought I could handle a car pretty well, and would I like to come back the next day and talk to him some more?"

"Talk about being at the right place at the right moment," I murmur, happy to learn something about him that I couldn't read about by looking on the Internet.

"You're telling me!" He shakes his head. "So I met up with him. Tried out the car on the track, did pretty well and got along with the guys. They asked me to drive the next race. I was decent at it so I kept doing it. Got noticed. Stayed out of trouble." He grins a mischievous grin, raising his eyebrows. "For the most part."

"And after all this time, you still enjoy it?"

"I'm good at it," he says.

"That's not what I asked."

He chews his food, carefully mulling over my question. "Yes, I suppose so. There's no other feeling like it. I'm part of a team, and yet it's just me out there. I have no one to depend on, to blame, but myself if something goes wrong." I can sense the passion in his voice. The reverence he still has for his sport. "On the track, I can escape the paparazzi, the groupies ... my demons. The only fear I have is that which I've created for myself, that I can control with a swerve of the wheel or a press of the pedal ... not any inflicted on me by someone else."

The startled look on his face tells me that he has revealed more than he expected in an answer. That he's surprised by his unanticipated honesty with me. I brush aside his unease at feeling vulnerable, by propping my arms out behind me and raising my face to the sky.

"It's so beautiful here," I say, breathing in the fresh air and digging my toes in the cool sand.

"More wine?" he asks as he shifts to sit closer to me. The brush of his bare arm against mine leaves my senses humming.

I murmur in assent as warning bells go off in my head. I know that I need to create some distance between us, but he's just too damn attractive. Irresistible. *Nothing like I expected and yet everything I anticipated.* I know that I need to clear my head because he is clouding my judgement.

"So is this what you imagined, Ace, when you spent all that money for a date with me?" I turn my head and come face to face with him— hair mussed, lips full, eyes blazing. I hold my breath, frozen in the moment, for all it would take is for me to lean in to feel his lips on mine again. To taste his carnal hunger as I did earlier on the porch.

He flashes a grin at me. "Not exactly," he admits, but I can sense our proximity is affecting him too. I can see the pulse in his throat accelerate. His Adam's apple bobs with a swallow. I bring my eyes back up to his, unspoken words flowing between us. "You really have the most unusually magnificent eyes," he whispers.

It's not as if I haven't heard this before about my unique, violet-colored eyes, but for some reason, hearing it from him has desire spiraling through me. Warning bells clang inside my head.

"Rylee?"

I raise my eyes to meet his, trepidation in my heart. "I'm only going to ask this one time. Do you have a boyfriend?" The gravity in his tone as well as the question itself take me off guard. I didn't expect this. I thought he'd already know the answer after the backstage ministrations from the other night. More surprising than the question itself, is the way he asks it. His demanding tone.

I shake my head "no," swallowing loudly.

"No one you are seeing casually?"

"You just asked twice," I joke, trying to shake the nerves skittering up my spine. When he doesn't smile but rather holds my stare in question, I shake my head again. "No, why?" I respond breathlessly.

"Because I want to know who's standing in my way." He tilts his head and stares at me as my lips part in response. My mouth is suddenly very dry. "Whose ass I have to kick before I can make it official."

"Make what official?" My mind flickers trying to figure out what I'm missing.

"*That you're mine.*" Colton's breath flutters over my face as the look in his eyes swallows me whole. "Once I fuck you, Rylee—it's official, you're mine and only mine."

Oh. Fucking. My. How can those words, so possessive, so dominantly male, make me want him that much more? I'm an independent, self-assured woman, and yet hearing that this man—yes, Colton

Donavan—inform me that he is going to have me without asking, without giving me a choice, makes me weak in the knees.

"It might not be tonight, Rylee. It might not be tomorrow night," he promises, the rumbling timbre of his voice vibrating through my body, "but it will happen." My breath hitches as he pauses to allow me to absorb his words before he continues. "Don't you feel it, Rylee? This..." he gestures a hand between him and me "...this charge we have here? The electricity we have when we're together is way too strong to ignore." I lower my eyes, uncomfortable with his overconfidence yet turned on by his words. He takes a hand and reaches out, the spark he's referring to igniting when his index finger trails up the underside of my neck to my chin. He pushes up to lift my chin so I'm forced to stare into the depths of his eyes. "Aren't you the least bit curious how good it will be? If it's this electrifying with just the brush of our skin against each other, can you imagine what it will be like when I'm buried inside of you?"

The confidence in his words and the intensity of his stare nonpluses me, and I avert my eyes down again to focus on the ring I'm worrying around my right ring finger. The rational part of me knows that once Colton has his way with me, he'll move on. And even though I'd know this going into it, I'd still be devastated in the end.

I just don't want to go through it again. I'm afraid to feel again. Afraid to take a chance, afraid that the consequences will be life-altering for me again. I use my fear to fuel my obstinance; no matter how wild the ride, the inevitable fallout isn't worth it.

"You're so sure of yourself, do I even need to show up for the event?" I ask haughtily, hoping my words cover the deep ache he's responsible for creating in my body. His only response to my question is a heart-stopping smirk. I shake my head at him. "Thanks for the warning, Ace, but no thanks."

"Oh, Rylee," he says with a laugh. "There's that smart mouth that I find so intriguing and sexy. It disappeared for a little while with your nerves. I was getting worried." He reaches over and squeezes my hand. "Oh, and Ryles, just so you know, that wasn't a warning, sweetheart. That was a promise."

And with that he leans back on his elbows, a cocky grin on his face and challenge in his eyes as he stares at me. I travel the length of his lean body with my eyes. My thoughts running through how I should resist this over-the-top, reckless, troubled, and unpredictable man whose continual verbal sparring makes me uncomfortable. Makes me desire. Churns up feelings and thoughts that died that day two years ago. And yet, rather then head the other way as I should, all I want to do is straddle him right here on that blanket, run my hands up the firm muscles of his chest, fist my hands in his hair, and take until I surrender all my rational thoughts.

I brave meeting his eyes again for I know he is watching me appraise his body. I make sure that my eyes reflect none of the desire I'm feeling. "So, what about you, Colton?" I question, turning the tables on him. "You said you don't do the girlfriend thing, and yet you always seem to have a lady on your arm?"

He arches his eyebrows at me. "And how would you know what I always have on my arm?"

How do I know that? Do I admit to him that I occasionally glance through Haddie's subscription of *People* and roll my eyes at the ridiculous commentary? Do I confess that I peruse Perezhilton.com as a distraction when I'm in the office sometimes and that I usually skip over the gossip about self-absorbed Hollywood brat-packers like him, who think they're better than everyone else? "Well, I do stand at the checkout lines in the grocery store," I admit. "And you know how true all of those tabloids are."

"According to them I'm dating an alien with three heads and my photoshopped picture is right next to the caption stating a chupacabra was found in a movie theater in Norman, Oklahoma," he says, animating his expression, eyes wide in a mock stare of horror.

I laugh out loud. Really laugh. So glad that he takes the media in stride. Happy that he's added some levity to the heavy topics of conversation. "Nice change of topic, but it's not going to work. Answer the question, Ace."

"Oh, Rylee—all business," he chides. "What is there to say? I hate the drama, the points system of who is contributing how much, the expectation of the next step to take, trying to figure out if there is an ulterior motive for them being with me ..." He shrugs. "Rather than deal with that bullshit, I come to a mutual agreement with someone, stated rules and requirements are laid out, specifics are negotiated, and expectations are managed way before they even have a chance to begin or get out of hand. It simplifies things."

What? Negotiations? So many things run through my head that I know I'm going to have to think about later, but with his eyes boring into mine, awaiting my reaction, I decide that humor is the best way to mask my surprise at his response.

"So a guy with a commitment issue..." I roll my eyes "...like that's something new!" He remains quiet, still regarding me as I think about him, about *this*, about *everything*. "So what were you hoping for?" I continue sardonically, "that I'd just look into your gorgeous green eyes, drop my panties, and spread my legs when you admit that you like women in your bed but you won't let them in your heart?" Despite my sarcasm, I'm being brutally honest. Does he think that just because he is who he is, it'll negate all my morals? "*And they say romance is dead.*"

"You do have such a way with words, sweetheart," he drawls, shifting onto his side, propping his head on his elbow. A slow, measured smile spreads across his face. "I assure you, romance is not something I actively subscribe to. There's no such thing as happily ever after."

The hopeless romantic in me sighs heavily, allowing me to ignore his comment and the smirk on his face—the one that makes me forget all the thoughts in my head because he is in fact that damn attractive and his eyes are that mesmerizing. "You can't be serious? Why the emotional detachment?" I shake my head. "You seem to be such a passionate person otherwise."

He shifts on the blanket, lying on his back and placing his hands behind his head, exhaling loudly. "Why is anyone the way they are?" he answers vaguely, the silence hanging between us. "Maybe that's how I was born or what I learned in my formative years ... how's one to know? There's a lot about me you don't want to know, Rylee. I promise you."

I look at him, trying to decipher his verbal maze of explanations as he lies quietly for a few minutes before reaching a hand out from behind his head and placing it on mine. I revel in this rare sign of affection. Most of the time when we touch it's explosive, carnal even. Rarely is it simple. Undemanding. Maybe that's why I enjoy the warmth of his hand seeping through the top of mine.

I'm still pondering what he's said despite the distraction of his touch. "I disagree. How can you—"

I'm stopped mid-sentence as he tugs on my arm, and within seconds has me lying on the blanket, looking up at his face hovering over mine. I'm not sure how it's possible, but my breath speeds up and stops at the same time. He very slowly, very deliberately uses one hand to brush an errant hair off of my face while the other rests on the base of my neck just under the crease of my chin.

"Are you trying to change the subject, Mr. Donavan?" I ask coyly, my heart thumping and desire blooming in my belly. His touch leaves electric charges on my skin.

"Is it working?" he breathes, angling his head to study me.

I purse my lips and narrow my eyes in thought. "Hmmm ... no, I still have my questions." A smile plays on my lips as I watch him watch me.

"Then I just might have to do something about that," he murmurs with painstaking slowness as he lowers his head until his lips are a whisper from mine. I fight the urge to arch my back so that my body can press against his. "How about now?"

How is it we are outdoors but I feel as if all of the oxygen has been vacuumed away? Why does he have this effect on me? I try to slowly breathe in and all I smell is him—woodsy, clean, and male— a heady, intoxicating mixture that is pure Colton.

I can't find my voice to answer his question, so I just give him a noncommittal "Hmm-hmmm." I'm oblivious to everything around us: the seagulls squawking, the surf crashing, the sun heading slowly toward the ocean on the horizon.

Due to our proximity, I can't see his lips but I know that he smiles because I see the lines crinkle at the corners of his eyes. "Should I *take* that as a yes or should I *take* that as a no?" he asks. His eyes hold mine, daring me. When all I do is breathe in a shaky breath, he says, "Then I guess I'll just *take*."

And with those words, his mouth is on mine.

He sets a slow, mesmerizing pace, feathering light kisses over my lips. Each time I think he is going to give me what I want—deep, passionate kisses—he pulls back. He leans on one elbow, and then cups the back of my neck. His other hand slowly travels down the side of my body, and stops on the side of my hip. He grabs hold there, gripping my flesh through my jeans and presses my body closer to him.

"Your. Curves. Are. So. Damn. Sexy," he murmurs between kisses. The riot of sensation he is causing within me is both exhilarating and tormenting. I run my hands under his shirt, up the plains up of his torso and then his back, as he continues his languorous assault on my lips.

If I were the intelligent woman that I claim to be, I would step back a moment and rationally assess the situation. I'd realize that Colton is a guy used to getting what he wants without preamble or precaution. And at this time, he wants me. He has tried the direct, get-to-the-point approach and basically had me up against a wall within ten minutes. He's tried coercion, a contract, annoyance, and even admitted he doesn't do girlfriends, commitment, or relationships. The rational part of me would acknowledge these facts and realize he's failed the challenge thus far, so now he is moving onto seduction. I'd argue that he's changing his approach, taking his time by making me feel and making me want him. Letting me think this situation is on my terms now. I'd realize that this has nothing to do with emotions and wanting 'an after' with me, but rather he is trying to get me in his bed any way he can now.

But I'm not listening to my rational self and the snarky doubts she's trying to cast. I vaguely push away the niggling feeling that she's trying to force into my subconscious. My common sense has long been forgotten. It has been overrun, inundated, and is being thoroughly obliterated by my new addiction, otherwise known as Colton's mouth. His mouth worships mine with slow, leisurely licks of tongue, grazes of teeth, and caresses of lips.

"Uh-uh-uh," he teases against my lips as I thread my fingers through his hair at the back of his neck and try to pull him closer so I can give into the blistering need he's built inside of me and take more.

"You're frustrating." I sigh because now his lips have moved steadily up my neck, lacing open mouth kisses to nip at my earlobe, causing little sparks of frisson in their path.

I can feel his smile spread against the hollow spot beneath my ear in response to my words. "Now you know how it feels," he murmurs, "to want something ..." He withdraws from my neck so his face hovers an inch from mine. There is no doubt about the desire that clouds his eyes when they fuse to mine. He repeats himself. "To want something that someone won't give you."

I don't even have a moment to register his words before his mouth crushes down on mine. This time he doesn't hold back. His lips possess mine from the very moment we touch. He commands the kiss with a fiery passion that has my head spinning, my sanity ebbing, and my body craving. He kisses me with such an unrequited hunger, it's as if he'd go crazy if he didn't taste me. I have no choice but to ride the wave that he is controlling because I'm just as caught up as he is.

His tongue darts in my mouth, tasting of wine, before he eases and pulls gently at my bottom lip. I arch my neck, offering him more, wanting him to take more because I can't get enough of his intoxicating taste. He acquiesces, laying a row of feather-light kisses along my jawline before coming back to my mouth. He licks his tongue back in against mine—caressing, possessing, igniting.

I revel in the feeling of him. His hand spanning my hip in ownership. The weight of his leg, which is bent and resting on mine, pressing his evident arousal into my hip. His mouth controlling, taking, and giving all at the same time. The low growls of desire that emanate from deep in his throat in pure appreciation, telling me that I excite him. That he wants me.

I could stay in this state of desire all day with Colton, but the sound of approaching laughter brings me to my senses. Brings me to the realization that we're in public view. Colton brushes my lips gently one more time as we hear the surfers walking several feet away, back to their towels. His hands remain cupped on my face though, and he rests his forehead against mine, both trying to calm our ragged breathing.

He closes his eyes momentarily, and I sense him struggle with his control. He rubs his thumbs back and forth on my cheeks, a gentle caress that calms me.

"Oh, Rylee, what do you do to me?" He sighs, kissing the tip of my nose. "What am I going to do with you? You're such a breath of fresh air."

My heart stops. My body tenses. I flash back to three years prior, Max on one knee, ring in his hand, staring up at me expectantly. His words, chock-full of emotion, ring in my ears like it was yesterday. "Rylee, you are my best friend, my ride off into the sunset, *my breath of fresh air.* Will you marry me?"

I am thinking of Max—bright, open, and carefree—but I am looking at Colton: reserved, unattainable, and inescapable. A sob escapes my throat as the memory takes hold of me, of that day, of the aftermath, and guilt washes over me.

Colton is startled at my reaction. He jolts back away from me, but his hands still cup my face, concern filling his eyes. "Rylee, what is it? Are you okay?"

I put my hands on his chest and push him away as I rise up to sit, pulling my legs to my chest and hugging them. I shake my head for him to give me a minute and take in a deep breath, aware that Colton is watching me very closely, curious about what caused my reaction.

I try to push the words out of my head. His mom yelling at me that I killed him, his dad telling me he wished it had been me instead, and his brother telling me it was my fault. That I don't deserve to ever know that kind of love again.

I shudder at the thoughts, collecting myself, preparing myself for the questions I'm waiting for Colton to ask. But they never come. I look over at him, his face somber as he studies me, and I look back out to the sea. He rubs his hand over my lower back, the only form of solace he gives me.

I shake myself out of my thoughts, upset at what they interrupted. Why can't I just let it all go and enjoy this man—this virile man within my grasp—who for some ridiculous reason wants me? Why can't I just give in to his sordid excuse of a one-night-stand-type relationship just to get me out of this revolving nightmare? Use him, as he wants to use me.

Because that's not you, I whisper to myself. *You are a breath of fresh air.*

I'm thankful to Colton for his silence. I'm not sure if it is a silent understanding, or a detachment from someone else's drama, but regardless, at this point I'm glad that I'm not being asked to explain myself.

I reach back to grab for my plastic cup of wine. Colton hands it to me as he takes his and sips. "Well, I guess it's a good thing we're outside," I say, trying to diffuse the awkwardness with humor.

"Why's that?"

I take a long swallow of my drink before I continue. "To keep us from getting out of hand *in public,*" I respond, turning my head so that I can smile at him.

"What makes you think that being outside would stop me?" He flashes a devilish grin before laughing out loud, throwing his head back when he sees the shocked look on my face. "The danger of being caught only heightens sensation, Rylee. Increases the intensity of your arousal. Your climax." His voice wraps seductively around me, spinning me in his web.

I stare at him, trying to unwrap my thoughts from his snare. Trying to find my wits about me so I can respond and appear to be unaffected by his hypnotic words. "I thought you said you wanted somewhere private the first time?" I smirk, arching an eyebrow at him.

He leans in close to me, his breath feathering over my face and amusement dancing in his eyes. "Well at least I just got you to admit that there's going to be a first time."

My eyes widen as I realize what I'd just willingly walked into. I can't help the smile that breaks across my lips as I take in the mischievously wicked one on his. He shakes his head and as his eyes break from mine he says, "Look at that." He points to the horizon where the bottom of the sun hits the edge of the water, a bright ball sinking and spilling pastels across the sky.

Grateful for the change in topic, I turn my head to look. "Why is it that the sun seems to take forever to reach the horizon and the minute it gets there it sinks so fast?"

"It reflects life, don't you think?" he asks.

"How so?"

"Sometimes our journeys in life seem to take forever to get to the culmination of our efforts—to achieving the goal. And once we do, it goes so fast and then it's over." He shrugs, surprising me with his introspection. "We forget that the journey is the best part. The reason for taking the ride. What we learn the most from."

"Are you trying to tell me something in a round about way, Colton?" I ask.

"Nope," he says, a smile lighting up his features. "Just making an observation. That's all."

I eye him cautiously, still unsure what he's trying to tell me despite his denial. I dig my toes into the sand still warm from the sun's rays. I scrunch my toes back and forth, loving how it feels.

I hear Colton move next to me before I hear the paper bag from the deli rustling. I turn to see him stretched out across the blanket, pulling two Saran-wrapped squares from the bag. He sits back up next to me, crossing his legs like a kid in grade school. He holds a square up between us. "The cure for all woes," he says, handing it to me.

Our fingers brush as I take the brownie from him, his touch welcome. "You thought of everything on this twenty-five thousand dollar date, didn't you?" I tease him, making quick work of the package. He watches me as I take my first bite, the scrumptious chocolate is delectable and has me rolling my eyes in appreciation, and moaning with ecstasy. *This* is the way to get to my heart.

I look from the brownie back up to Colton, a captivated look on his face. "Do you have any idea how fucking sexy you are right now?" His voice is gruff, pained even.

I stop chewing, mid-bite, at his comment. How is it he can make such simple words so spellbinding at the oddest times? The candor on his face throws me off. We just sit there, a few feet apart on a blanket on a beach, and stare at each other. No pretenses. No audience. No expectations. The unspoken words that flow between us are so powerful I'm afraid to blink, afraid to move, afraid to speak for fear of ruining this moment. I'm seeing the true Colton Donavan—the unmasked version with a vulnerability that makes me want to reach over and take away the hurt that often flickers through those green eyes and make it better. To show him that love and commitment are possible without complications. That it is real and pure and much more powerful than ever imagined when it is built and shared between two people.

I feel a phantom ache in my heart as a tiny piece tears off, lost forever to Colton in this moment.

I finally break eye contact, lowering my eyes back to watch my fingers pick at my brownie. I know that I'll never get to express this to him. I'll never get the chance. At some point in the near future I will give my body to him willingly, despite my head telling me it's a mistake. I will revel in that moment with him which will be filled with reverent sighs and entangled bodies, and I'll be devastated when he walks away after having his fill of me. I blink away the tears that burn in my eyes.

It has to be the approaching anniversary, I tell myself. I'm never this emotional—this unstable.

I pick a chunk off the corner of my brownie and push it in my mouth. I look back up at him, a shy smile creeping onto his face, telling me that he felt the moment between us as well. I shiver .

"You cold?" he asks, reaching out with his thumb to wipe a piece of chocolate from the corner of my mouth. He brings his thumb and holds it out to my mouth. I open my lips and suck the chocolate off. A groan rumbles in the back of his throat, and his lips part slightly as he watches me. If I knew it'd be this erotic to watch his reaction, I'd leave a Hansel and Gretel trail of brownie crumbs all over my body and enjoy watching him find them.

I shiver again in response to his question, despite the heat burning within me.

"Since this was so impromptu, I didn't bring a jacket or an extra blanket for you," he says with disappointment in his voice. "We can go somewhere else if you'd like?"

I look up at him, a sincere look on my face. "Thank you, Colton. I really had a good time ..."

"Despite the heavy conversation," he adds when I pause.

I laugh at him. "Yes, despite the heavy topics, but I've had a really long week and I'm exhausted," I apologize, "so I think it's best if we head back." I really don't want to, but I am desperately trying to keep a level head here.

"Ooooh, the blow off!" he teases, pressing a hand to his wounded heart. "That's harsh, but I understand." He laughs.

I help him start to wrap up the left-over food and place it back in the bag. I start putting my socks and shoes back on when he says, "So Teddy signed the deal today with CDE."

"That's great!" I say sincerely. Excited for the opportunity and uncertain about the effect it will have on my personal life—being forced to be with him. "I can't express how thankful I am—"

"Rylee," he says with enough force to stop me short. "That, the donation, has nothing to do with *this*," he says, gesturing between the two of us.

Like hell it doesn't. I wouldn't be here with him if it weren't for that arrangement.

"Sure," I mumble in agreement, and I know that I haven't convinced him.

"That's mine," I point toward my red and white Mini Cooper parked on the street outside of The House. He pulls up behind it, pushing the button to quiet the sexy purr of the engine. The streetlights are on and the one nearest The House keeps flickering on and off. I can hear a dog barking several houses down, and the smell of meat cooking on charcoal hangs in the air. It feels like home, normalcy, just what the seven boys tucked inside the house in front of me deserve.

Colton comes around the side of the car and opens the door, holding a hand out to help me from my seat. I clutch my purse to my chest, suddenly feeling awkward as I make my way to my car with Colton's hand on the small of my back.

I turn to face him, leaning my back against my car. I have my bottom lip between my teeth and worry it back and forth as my nerves seem to be getting the better of me. "Well ... thank you for a nice evening, Colton," I say as I look around the street unable to meet his eyes. Am I afraid that this might be it? Of course not, because I know I'll have to see him for work. Then why do I suddenly feel a mixture of unease and sadness over parting with him? Why am I mentally kicking myself for not taking him up on the offer to go somewhere else?

Colton reaches out and places a finger under my chin, turning my face so I'm forced to meet his eyes. "What is it, Rylee? What has you so afraid to feel? Every time you start to get caught up in the moment and hand yourself over to the sensation, something flashes across your face and has you withdrawing. Pulling back and becoming unavailable. Has you bottling back up all of that potential passion of yours in a matter of seconds." He searches my eyes in question, his fingers firm on my chin so I can't avert my eyes. "Who did this to you, sweetheart? Who hurt you this badly?"

His eyes probe mine looking for answers I'm not willing to give him. The muscle in his jaw tics in frustration at my silence. His features, darkened by the night sky, are tense, awaiting my response. The flickering streetlight creates a stark contrast with his warring emotions.

I can feel my protective wall bristle at his unwanted attention. The only way I know how to deal, how to keep him at arm's length, is to turn the question back on him. "I could ask you the same question, Colton. Who hurt you? What haunts those eyes of yours every so often?"

He quirks his eyebrows at my tactic, his concentrated stare never wavering. "I'm not a very patient man, Rylee," he warns. "I'll only wait so long before—"

"Some things are better left alone," I cut him off, my words coming out barely above a whisper and my breath hitches.

He moves his thumb from my chin and drags it over my bottom lip. "Now that," he whispers back to me, "I can understand." His response surprises me, reaffirming my assumption that he is in fact hiding from something himself. Or running.

He leans in slowly, brushing a reverent, lingering kiss on my lips, and all thoughts in my head vaporize. His tenderness is unexpected, and I want to capture this moment in my mind. Revel in it. I sigh helplessly against his lips, our foreheads touching briefly.

"Goodnight, Colton."

"Goodnight, Rylee." He leans back, grabbing the handle of my door, opening it for me and ushering me in. "Until next time," he murmurs before shutting the door.

I start the engine and pull away from the curb. Instinctively, I reach out and push the stereo on, shuffling for the sixth disc in the changer. I glance in my rearview mirror as I make my way down this street, music flooding the car. I can see his figure as he rocks back on his heels with his hands in his pockets, standing beneath the flickering streetlight. *An angel fighting through the darkness or a devil breaking into the light?* Which, I'm not sure. Regardless, he stands there, my personal heaven and hell, watching me until I turn the corner and am out of his sight.

Chapter Nine

I pull into my driveway and sit in the car for several moments humming to the music pouring out of the speakers, running through my time with Colton. I sing the song out of habit. The words and the rhythm are comforting to me. I place my hands on the top of the steering wheel and rest my head on top of them. It's not like I have been out with many guys in my life, but that was one of the most intense, passionate, and strangely comforting dates of my life. I shake my head as I replay it again.

Holy shit! That's all I can really think about my evening. About Colton's unexpected pursuit. The devil on my shoulder reiterates to me that this is all my fault. That if I'd acted like the *normal* me, I would've never been a willing victim to his deft hands in a backstage alcove. I would've never been in the position to tell him "thanks but no thanks," spurring on this whole chase—this whole challenge—a welcome change in his world of overly eager, willing women.

I scream out, startled by the knock on my car window. I am so deep in thought, I never saw Haddie approach my car. My heartbeat returns to normal as I open the door to her.

"Hi, Had. Just a sec," I say as I reach across my seat to grab my belongings.

I sense Haddie's presence shift into the doorway as her body blocks the garage light, throwing a shadow over the front seat. "Is that Matchbox Twenty?" she questions as she strains to hear the music playing quietly on the stereo system.

Uh-oh, I tell myself, *she knows something is up*. She knows I listen to Matchbox Twenty whenever I'm upset. Haddie knows this all too well from the dark period of my life.

I look over at her, hands on her hips, irritation emanating off of her in waves, and I'm not sure just how much she knows. And depending on what she knows is how hurt she'll be that I've kept it from her.

There is no rationalizing with Haddie when she's angry. When she feels wronged. I silently groan and know my interesting day is about to get longer. She never backs down until she gets the answers she wants. She can fool everyone because behind her innocent beauty is her razor sharp wit—but not me.

I know better.

I turn off the car quickly before she can hear which song I have on repeat, *Bent*. At least it's not *Unwell*. I have my bag in my hand but can't exit the car because she is standing in the way.

"I think we need to have a little chat," she says haughtily. "Don't you?" She moves out of the way, her hands on her hips. All she needs is to tap her foot and I'll be transported back to being in the principal's office in grade school.

I force a cheerful smile on my face. "Sure, Had. What's up? You seem pissed at something?"

"You."

"Me?" I respond, walking to the front door, rolling my eyes.

"Don't roll your eyes at me either, Ry," she demands as we walk through the front door.

I drop my stuff by the tall table that stands against the entry wall. I skulk over to the couch in our front room and sink into it, wishing I could just close my eyes and fall asleep. But I can't because Haddie sits down on the other end of the couch and curls her lithe legs beneath her.

"When were you going to tell me?" Her voice is chillingly quiet. This is not a good sign. The quieter she is, the more pissed she is.

"About?" I prompt, figuring if she gives me what she knows, I can at least get credit for telling her the rest.

"Colton freakin' Donavan?" she sputters, eyes wide, trying to suppress a grin that threatens to break through her implacable façade. "Are you fucking kidding me? And you didn't tell me?" The pitch of her voice escalates with each word. She grabs her glass of wine on the end table next and sips it, never breaking eye contact. "Why?" she says quietly but clearly hurt.

"Oh, Haddie." I blow out, scrubbing my hands over my face, trying to bite back the tears that threaten to break free. I lose the battle and a single tear slips down my cheek. "I'm so confused." I sigh, closing my eyes momentarily to gain control of my slipping emotions.

Haddie's face softens at my confession. "I'm so sorry, Ry—I just—I'm hurt you didn't tell me—I didn't mean to—"

"It's okay," I tell her, slipping my shoes off, the grains of sand stuck to my feet, reminding me that I really was with Colton tonight. As if I need a reminder. The scent of his cologne mixed with the smell of *him* still fresh in my mind. "I didn't mean to hurt you. How did you—"

"You didn't answer your phone … like at all. I was excited to tell you about someone we confirmed for the big launch party tomorrow. I texted and called several times and didn't get a response," she says. "I was concerned. It's not like you to not give me at least a one-word answer if you're busy. I was worried so I called Dane." My eyebrow rises. "I guess he just put two and two together." She shrugs. "So what's going on, Rylee? What are you hiding from me?"

"It's just—I am just so overwhelmed with everything." I continue to tell her the story, every sordid detail despite my embarrassment at our first ten minutes of interaction. Her face remains impassive during my replay of events as she digests everything.

When I'm finished, she is quiet for a few moments, staring at me with unconditional affection on her face. "Well," she says, rising to get more wine and returning with a glass for me, "there are many things to say, to discuss, but first and foremost," she grabs my knee, excitement vibrating off of her, "Holy shit, Rylee! Colton Donavan? Backstage at the theater! Woohoo!" She raises her arms above her head, and I mentally cringe, hoping she won't spill her wine. "I'm so proud you finally got a little crazy. What's gotten into you?"

I feel the deep crimson flush over my face as I bow my head and start twisting the ring around and around my finger. "I know," I mumble. "I don't get it either."

"What?" she shouts at me. "What the hell are you talking about?" She shoves my knee vigorously. "I meant wow in admiration, not wow in why would he pick you. Snap out of it, Ry." She snaps her fingers in front of my face, forcing me to look at her. "He is fucking gorgeous! All rebellious and smoldering bad boy …"

As if I need to be reminded.

Haddie looks back at me. I can see her giddiness rising to the surface. "Is he as good looking in person as he is on TV?"

I try to find the perfect word, but I say the first one that comes to my mind. "He's breathtaking," I say reverently, "and sexy and domineering and frustrating and his eyes are just … and his lips … ugh!" I am caught up in the memory of him, my mind drifting over bits and pieces. When I come back to the here and now, I find Haddie staring at me, a ghost of a smile on her mouth.

"You really like him, don't you?" she asks quietly, sensing what I feel but refuse to say.

Tears pool in my eyes at the thought despite the smile plastered on my face. "It doesn't matter if I do or don't, he made it clear he only wants me for one thing." I shrug, taking a long swallow of my wine. "Besides, I can't do that to M—"

"Whoa, whoa, whoa!" she yells, waving her arms in the air to stop me. "I'm going to take this discussion and break it up into two different parts—compartmentalize it for you and your anal ways, if you will—because both really need to be addressed." She scoots closer to me. "Rylee, honey..." gravity in her voice "...who cares what the future holds when it comes to Colton. If he only wants you for your body and some earth-shattering sex, then so be it. Go for it. Just because it's not what you're expecting doesn't mean it's not everything you might need. And who better to do it with than a fucking Adonis like him?" She swigs another drink, amused. "Shit, I'd take that for a ride in a heartbeat," she murmurs, her lips pursing in thought at what it would be like.

I laugh out loud. "You would," I tease, slowly feeling my body unwind from the tension. "That kind of thing is easy for you."

She shoves at my leg. "Gee, thanks! I'm not a slut!" she contemplates. "Well, unless I want to be." She laughs.

"No," I huff, "I mean you are so carefree and sure of yourself. Everything you do you're sure about. No regrets." I cock my head to the side. "*And you sure are attracted to the bad boys.*" I smirk at her.

"Hmm-hmm, I do love them naughty." She laughs, momentarily lost in her thoughts. "But back to you. No need getting me all twisted up over a man that's into you."

I roll my eyes at her comment.

"Rylee, the guy can have any woman he wants, and he is busy chasing you around, paying thousands for dates, spending millions to make your dream come true, and taking you on impromptu romantic dates to the beach. At sunset."

"According to him, he doesn't do romance."

She snorts loudly. "Well maybe he needs to redefine what romance is," she rebukes, "because all of those things spell out a man in pursuit."

I shake my head and her Haddie frankness. "He just wants me because I told him no. I'm a challenge to him in an otherwise willing world of women."

"You were quite the challenge when he had you up against the wall backstage, huh?" She quirks her mouth, goading me.

"You know that is so not like me, Haddie! I haven't been touched since …" The silence settles and I shake my head to clear it of the memories holding me hostage. "Besides, I came to my senses. It was just the adrenaline from being trapped—"

"You just keep telling yourself that, sweetie, because I'm not sure if you're trying to convince me or yourself that it's just a simple lapse in morality." She shrugs, not breaking eye contact with me. "It's nothing to be ashamed of. It's okay to feel again, Rylee. To live again."

Tears threaten again, and I dash them away with the back of my hands before they can fall. "And even though we aren't done with item number one on our agenda, let's visit item number two." I level my eyes with hers, apprehension filling me. All of a sudden, her expression changes into understanding as the realization hits her. "You didn't want to tell me because you didn't want me to tell you that it's okay to live again. That it's okay to move on." Her questioning voice is soft, soothing.

I nod slowly as I swallow the huge lump in my throat. She scoots close to me, wrapping her arms around me, rocking me slowly and making hushing noises. A huge sob escapes and I succumb to the tears that have threatened me for several days. It feels so good to let them out, cathartic really.

After a few moments I find a semblance of control and am finally able to speak. "I just—I feel like I'm betraying Max. I feel like I don't deserve..." my breath hitches from my sobbing "...I feel guilty—"

"Rylee, honey..." she tucks an errant curl of hair behind my ear "...it's normal to feel that way, but at some point you have to start living again. It is a tragic, horrific thing that happened to you guys. To him. To you. But it's been over two years, Ry..." she grabs my hand "...and I know you don't want to hear it, but at some point you have to move on. You don't have to forget, but you—the wonderful, beautiful woman that you are—needs to live again. You too were once carefree. It's not too late to find that again."

I stare at her, tears blurring my vision, afraid that my next admission will make me a horrible person. I avert my eyes, afraid to look at her when I speak. "Part of the reason I feel guilty … I … the intensity, the desperation, the everything that Colton makes me feel is so much more, so much stronger, than I ever felt with Max." I take a chance and look back at her face, finding the exact opposite expression than what I had expected. I find compassion rather than disappointed disgust. "And I was going to marry Max," I choke out, relieved to have gotten this huge burden off of my chest and off my conscious. "I know it's stupid, but I can't help feeling it. I can't help that it pops into my head in that moment when all I feel, breathe, and want is more of Colton."

"Oh, Ry … why have you been holding all of this in by yourself?" She wipes one of her own tears before pulling me to her and squeezing me again. She rests her cheek on the top of my head. "Rylee, you were a different person then. Your life is different now. Back then, anyone that saw you and Max together—we just knew that you were perfect for each other—just as you knew." I can hear the smile in her voice as she reminisces. "And now," she sighs, "you've been to hell and back in a little over two years. You are not the same person you were. It's natural to feel differently—to love deeper, feel stronger—no one is going to fault you for that. No one has touched you in two years, Rylee. Your reaction is going to be more intense."

We sit there in silence as I absorb the truth in her words. I know she's right, I just hope that I can believe it when the time comes. My contemplative silence is broken when Haddie suddenly starts laughing. She releases me from her hug, and I lean back to look at her perplexed. What in the hell is so funny? *"What?"*

She looks at me and I can see debauchery in her eyes. "He's probably great in bed." She smirks wickedly. "I bet he fucks like he drives—a little reckless, pushing all the limits, and in it until the very last lap." She raises her eyebrows at me, her grin sassy.

Her words make me bite my bottom lip at the thought of him hovering over me, sinking into me, filling me. I relive the feel of his lips on mine, the firm muscles beneath his clothes flexing with me, and his raspy voice telling me he wants me. I break from my thoughts, my core dampening at the thought of him. I look back to Haddie, watching her watch me, her eyebrows still raised, as if she is asking me if I think her assessment is accurate.

Oh boy, do I. *And then some.*

"Since when do you watch racing? Know how he drives?" I shift the focus of the conversation.

"Brody watches it. I pay attention when they say Colton's name," she says of her brother and then smirks devilishly. "It's definitely worth watching when they flash his face on camera."

"The man can kiss," I confess, grinning like a loon. "He can definitely kiss." I nod my head in agreement.

"Don't think about it, Rylee ... just do it! Be reckless. Let your hair down," she urges. "Do you want to wake up twenty years from now with a perfectly ordered life with everything in its proper place but never having really lived? Never really putting yourself out there?"

"Well, I like the everything in order part," I kid as she rolls her eyes at me.

"Of course, that's what you would focus on! Just think of the stories you can tell your grandkids someday—about the sordid affair you had with the hot playboy race car driver."

I take a sip of my wine, contemplating her comments. "I know what you're saying, Haddie, I really do, but the sex without commitment thing. Without the relationship thing ... how do you do that?"

"Well you stick flap A in slot B," she answers wryly.

"It was a rhetorical question, you bitch!" I laugh, throwing a pillow at her.

"Thank God! I was worried it had been so long that I was going to have to give you a sex-ed lesson." She reaches over to the table and uncorks another bottle of wine, topping off both of our glasses. She settles back in the couch, and I can see her mentally choosing her words before she speaks. "Maybe it's best that way?" When all I do is raise my eyebrows in question, she explains. "Maybe for your first guy since Max, maybe it's best that he isn't relationship material. You're bound to have some hiccups—after everything you've been through—so maybe it's best to throw caution to the wind and embrace your inner slut for a little bit. Have some fun and a lot of mind blowing sex!" She wiggles her eyebrows and I giggle at her, my overconsumption of wine slowly taking effect, smoothing over my frayed nerves.

"My inner slut," I reiterate, nodding my head, "I like that, but I think she's lost."

"Oh, we can find her, sister!" she snickers. "She's probably hiding behind the layers of cobwebs covering your crotch."

We both laugh before we start giggling uncontrollably. My overwrought emotions from the week welcome this release. I giggle until tears seep from the corners of my eyes. Just when I think my laughter is going to subside, Haddie shakes her head. "You have to admit, Ry, the man is fucking hot!"

I start giggling again. "Scorching hot!" I confirm. "Man, I can't wait to see him naked!" The words are out before my fuzzy brain has had a chance to filter them.

Haddie stops mid-laugh, a knowing smile playing over her lips. "I knew it!" she yells at me, pointing at my face. "I knew you wanted to fuck him!"

"Well, duh?" I respond before we collapse again in another fit of giggles.

"Let's get you drunk tomorrow night at the event, and then we'll drunk dial his ass for a booty call."

"Oh God, no!" I blanch. *What have I gotten myself into?*

Chapter Ten

The light filling the room is way too bright. The pounding in my head makes me groan out loud and grab my pillow from under my head, pulling it down over my eyes. I curse the numerous glasses of wine that Haddie and I drank last night but smile remembering our tears, and our laughs.

And Colton. Hot, delectable Colton.

Hmmm, I sigh at the memory of yesterday and him. He's going to have to do something to take care of this ache he's churned inside of me. I press my thighs together to abate it without success.

Since I can't get him out of my head, my hopes of falling back asleep are now gone. I reach my hand out blindly and fish around for the cell phone on my nightstand, knocking over an empty bottle of water. It clatters loudly on the hardwood floor, the sound making me cringe. I lift the pillow slightly to glance at the screen of my phone, wanting to know what time it is.

I lift the pillow further when I see my screen. I have numerous missed calls and texts from last night. I scroll through them quickly noting Haddie's texts getting more frantic as time passed. There are several from Dane and as I scroll to the next screen, the very last alert shows me there is a text from an unknown number. It was sent after I'd gotten home last night, during my discussion with Haddie. I open the text, and a smile spreads across my face. The text is from Colton:

> **Ryles—Thanks for the unexpected picnic. Since you seem most comfortable telling me what you think through music, I'll do the same. Luke Bryan, "I Don't Want This Night to End"—take it for what it is. *Ace**

I smile at his words when I realize he heard the words I sang to him yesterday in the car. I'm unaware of the song he's mentioned, so I scramble quickly, ignoring my hangover to grab my MacBook Pro. I pull it off my dresser and plop back on my bed, anxiously waiting for it to power up. I immediately Google the song and am surprised to find that it is country; Colton does not seem like a country music kind of guy to me, more hard rock or something with a thumping bass. I click on the link and within seconds the song is playing.

I lie back on my bed, close my eyes, and listen to the words of the song. A soft smile plays on my lips as the song washes over me. My first peek inside of Colton's head—sure, he verbally tells me he wants me, but the gist of the words is that he enjoyed his time with me last night. That he didn't want the night to end. I enjoy the little boost to my ego and the flutter in my stomach from the thought that Colton wants to *get drunk on my kiss*.

Don't jump to conclusions. I warn myself. This is the same man who warned me off of him. Who tells me I need to research my dates to know who's dangerous and will hurt me when I least expect it.

I sit back up and grab my computer. I immediately replay the song and open up another window to Google "Colton Donavan." The search is immediately populated with page upon page of links referencing him: racing sites, the Speed Channel, fan-created sites, and so many more.

I decide to narrow the search and type in "Colton Donavan Enterprises." I click on the company's website. The opening page is a picture of what I assume is Colton's racecar next to a picture of the office facility. I click through the menu and am led through a corporate mission statement, history, products, media, and race team information. It's all very impressive, but I stop when I click on the tab "drivers" and Colton's face fills the screen. It is a close-up, candid shot of him in his fire suit. He is looking intensely at something off-camera, and his green eyes are clear and intrigued. He has a half-smile on his face as if he is remembering a fond moment, the dimple in his right cheek winking. His hair is in need of a cut and curls over the neck of his suit.

I suck in my breath. My God, the man is sex on a stick.

I bookmark the picture for good measure before I force myself to change the page and search Google Images. I reluctantly type in his name, afraid of what I'll see. The page refreshes and dozens of images of him pop up on the screen, most of them with a gorgeous woman draped on his arm or looking up in obvious adoration of him. I know I have no reason to be jealous—these pictures are dated—but I find myself rolling my shoulders to ease my agitation. Knowing I should close the page, I do just the opposite and find myself clicking on each picture. Staring. Comparing. None of the captions refer to the women as girlfriends, just dates or companions.

I realize that most of his *escorts* are long, leggy blondes, stick thin, with some type of plastic enhancement. And all are drop-dead gorgeous. Much to my chagrin, I realize they look very similar to Haddie, *except hers are real*. Ironically, the pale hair next to his dark features makes him seem more aloof and edgier somehow.

I note that each girl only seemed to exist in his life for a short period of time, except for one. I wonder why that is. Is she an escort? The one he takes when his other *cookie-cutter blondes* have fallen through and he needs a date? Or is she the one he keeps going back to because there is really something there? After clicking on several of their pictures together, I finally get a caption that offers her name. *Tawny Taylor*. The caller on his phone yesterday. What is she to Colton? I know I could dwell on this for hours so I force myself to push it to the back of my head and resolve to think about it at another time, even though I'm afraid to know the answer.

I look like none of them. I may be tall, but I'm definitely not petite like them. I'm thin but I have curves in all the right places, unlike their ruler-straight physiques. I have an athletic body that I'm proud of—that I work hard to maintain—whereas they look like they have no need to even think about exercise. I have rich chocolate brown curly hair that stops midway down my back; it is unruly and a pain, but it suits me. I continue the comparisons until I tell myself that I need to just get off the page before I become depressed. That my hatred toward them has nothing to do with them in particular.

I go back to Google and type in "Colton Donavan childhood." The first few pages reference children's organizations that he is involved with. I quickly scan through the links, looking for one mentioning his childhood.

I finally find an old article written five years ago. Colton was interviewed in connection with a charity he was supporting that benefited new changes speeding up the adoption process.

Q: *It is public knowledge that you were adopted, Colton. At what age?*

CD: *I was eight.*

Q: *How was the adoption process for you? How would you have benefited from these new initiatives that this foundation supports?*

CD: *I was lucky. My dad literally found me on his doorstep, took me in, for lack of a better term, and I was adopted shortly after that. I didn't have to go through the lengthy process that occurs today. A process that makes kids who desperately crave a home, a sense of belonging, wait months to see if an application will be approved. The system needs to stop looking at these kids as cases, as paperwork to be stamped with approval after months of red tape, and start looking at them as delicate children who need to be an integral part of something. A part of a family.*

Q: *So what was your situation, prior to being adopted?*

CD: *Let's focus less on me and more on the passing of these new measures.*

Does he not want to talk about it because it draws attention away from the charity, or was it so bad he just doesn't talk about it? I scan the rest of the article but there is nothing else about his childhood. So he was eight. That leaves a lot of time to be damaged, conditioned as he's said, by whatever situation he was in.

I stare at the screen for a couple of minutes imagining all kinds of things, mostly variations of the kids who have come through my care, and I shudder.

I decide to look up his parents, Andy and Dorothea Westin. The pages are filled with Andy's movie credits, Oscar nominations and wins, and top-grossing movies amongst other things. His family life is referenced here and there. He met Dorothea when she had a bit part in one of his movies. At the time she was Dorothea Donavan. Another piece clicks into place. I wonder why he uses his Mom's surname and not his Dad's. I continue scanning and see the basic Hollywood mogul background, less the tabloid drama or stints in rehab. There are a few mentions of his children, a son and a daughter, but nothing giving me the answers I'm looking for.

I return to search again and scan through the different links that mention Colton's name. I see snippets about a fight in a club, possible altercations with current-generation brat-pack actors, generous donations, and gushing comments from other racers about his skill and the charisma he brings to his sport that had been tinged after the CART and IRL league split years ago.

I sigh loudly, my head filled with too much useless information. After over an hour of research, I still don't know Colton much better than I did before. I don't see anything to validate the warnings he keeps giving me. I can't help myself. I open up the page again for CDE and click on the picture of him. I stare at it for sometime, studying every angle and every nuance of his face. I glance up and sadness fills my heart as the picture on my dresser of Max catches my eye. His earnest smile and blue eyes light up the frame.

"Oh, Max," I sigh, pressing the heel of my palm to my heart where I swear I can still feel the agony. "I will always miss you. Will always love you," I whisper to him, "but it's time I try to find me again." I stare at his picture, remembering when it was taken, the love I felt then. Seconds tick by before I look back at my computer screen.

I close my eyes and breathe deeply, strengthening my resolve as the song on my computer, Colton's song, repeats itself for the umpteenth time. *It's time.* And maybe Haddie is right. Colton may be the perfect person to help me find myself again. For however long he lets me, anyway.

I look back at my phone, suppressing the overwhelming urge to text him back. To connect with him. If I'm going to do this, I at least need to make sure a couple things are on my terms.

And chasing after him is definitely not going to allow me to achieve that.

Chapter Eleven

I barely recognize the girl in the mirror who stares back at me. Once again, Haddie has gone all out with her preparations for the launch party tonight thrown by the public relations company she works for. She spent almost an hour blowing my ringlets out so that my hair hangs in a straight, thick curtain down my back. I keep staring at myself in the mirror, trying to adjust to this different person. My eyes are subtly smoked so the dark smudges have an opalescent quality, reflecting the violet in my irises. My lips are lined with nude liner and lip-gloss, making the slight touches of bronzed blush on my cheeks stand out.

She has talked me into wearing a little black number that shows off more skin than I'm comfortable with. The bust of the dress runs into a deep V, hinting suggestively at my abundant bra-proffered cleavage without being trashy. The straps go over the shoulders and connect the non-existent back with thin gold chains that drape loosely and attach at the swell of my butt. I tug down on the hemline that falls mid-thigh, something I'm not altogether used to.

I look again in the mirror and smile. This is not me, the girl I know. I sigh shakily as I add chandelier earrings to complete the look. This may not be me, I think, but this is the confident girl I want to be again. The new me who's going to go out tonight, let loose, and have fun. The girl who has resolved to have a night of fun and gain some self-assurance before I undertake all that is Colton and his warning-laced pursuits.

"Holy shit!" Haddie walks into my bathroom, a whistle blowing from her lips. "You look hot! I mean—" She stumbles over her words. "I'm at a loss here. I don't think I have ever seen you this smokin' sexy, Ry." I smile widely at her praise. "You're going to have them lining up tonight, baby. Hot damn, this is going to be fun to watch!"

I laugh at her response, my self-esteem bolstered. "Thanks. You're not so bad yourself," I compliment her harlot-red dress that shows off all of her best assets. I slip my heels on, wincing and smirking at the memory of the last time I wore them. "Give me a sec and I'll be ready."

I grab my clutch and stuff my driver's license, money, and keys into it. When I grab my phone to place in the small purse, I realize I never asked Haddie about the voicemails from her that I'd listened to earlier.

"Had? I never asked you what was so exciting about the event tonight. What hot celebrity did you guys secure as a carpet walker?"

She gives me an enigmatic smile. "Oh, it fell through," she dismisses casually. I shake off the feeling that for some reason she is laughing at me. I quirk my head at her and she turns around, "Let's go!"

The entrance to the trendy club downtown is quite the spectacle with criss-crossing searchlights, velvet ropes, and a celebrity ready red carpet complete with a backdrop displaying Merit Rum, the new product being launched. We park in reserved spots for Haddie and her fellow PRX employees at the trendy, upscale hotel that owns and is connected to the club. Haddie flashes her credentials, which allows us to whisk past the hoopla, and within moments we are inside the crowded club, the dull throb of the music pulsing through my body.

It has been years since I've been in a club like this and it takes me a while to acclimate to the dim lighting and loud music and not feel intimidated. I think Haddie realizes my nerves are kicking in and that my confidence is waning despite my sexed-up appearance. Within moments she has pushed us through the throng of people to the bar. With disregard to the numerous bottles of Merit lining the slick countertop, Haddie orders us each two shots of tequila.

"One for luck." She grins at me.

"And one for courage," I finish our old college toast. We clink glasses and toss back the liquid. It burns my throat. It's been so long since I've done a shot of tequila, I wince at the burn and put the back of my hand to my mouth to try and somehow stifle it.

"C'mon, Ryles," Haddie shouts, unfazed by the liquor. "We've got one more to go!"

I raise my glass, an intrepid smile on my face, tap it to hers, and we both toss them back. The sting of the second one isn't as bad, and my body warms from the liquid, but it still tastes like shit.

Haddie gives me a knowing glance and starts to giggle. "Tonight's going to be fun!" She hugs her arm around me and squeezes. "It's been so long since I've had my partner in crime back."

I flash a smile at her as I take in the club's atmosphere. It's a large room with purple, velvet-lined booths around the bottom floor. A glossy bar with a mirror placed behind it fills one whole wall, creating the illusion that the massive space is even larger. In the middle of the main floor is a large dance floor, complete with trussing lined moving head lights that are creating a dizzying array of colors. Stairs rise up from the floor to a raised VIP area where teal booths are sectioned off by velvet stanchions. In one section of the VIP area, a plexiglass partition allows all below to see the DJ spinning the music pumping through the club. Model-worthy waitresses flit around in hot pants and fitted tank tops, purple flowers adorning their hair. The club is swanky class with a touch of sophistication, despite the advertising for Merit Rum around the room.

It's nearing eleven o'clock, and I can see the crowd thickening, feel the pulsating energy. In the VIP area, there is a crowd of people gathered in one corner, and I wonder what trendy celebrity Haddie's team has secured to promote their newest product. I've been to enough of these functions with her to know the drill. Hot celebrities shown taking photos with new product equals big-time press for not only the item but Haddie's company as well.

I take the glass Haddie hands me, my usual Tom Collins, and I sip from the straw as I point to the upper section. I raise my eyes in question rather than shout over the music that is starting to increase in volume as the club becomes more crowded. I figure we have about thirty minutes left until the decibels are so loud that the only way to communicate will be to yell.

She leans over to talk in my ear. "Not sure. We have several people confirmed for tonight." She shrugs a noncommittal answer. "Some surprises are in store as well."

I narrow my eyes at her, wondering why she is being vague. She just smiles broadly and tugs my hand to follow her. We navigate through the mob of people, moving together as one unit. I can feel the alcohol slowly starting to buzz through my body, warming me, easing my tension, and relaxing my nerves. For the first time in longer than I can remember, I feel sexy. I feel beautiful and sensual and at ease with those feelings.

I squeeze Haddie's hand as she pushes through to a purple booth, which is reserved for PRX staff. She looks back and smiles genuinely at me, realizing that I'm starting to relax. We break through the crowd to the booth to find two of Haddie's colleagues there. I smile at them and say a quick hello, having met them before at previous events I've attended. I thank one of them for his compliments on my vamped-up style for the evening. As we sit down there is a large cheer from the other side of the room on the upper level where the crowd had been. I glance up to see what's going on and notice nothing but a number of women showing way too much skin hoping for whatever hot item PRX has invited up there to take notice of them.

I roll my eyes in disgust. "Fame whores," I mouth to Haddie and she bursts out laughing.

I finish my drink as the catchy beat of a Black Eyed Peas song fills the club. I start moving my hips to the tempo, and before I know it, I grab Haddie's hand and drag her through the people out onto the dance floor. The surprised look on her face has me laughing as I close my eyes and let the music take me. We sing the words together, "I gotta feeling, that tonight's gonna be a good night," as we let loose on the dance floor.

I haven't felt this liberated in so long that I just want to suspend this moment in time. I want to capture it in my memory so the next time I start to fall into that dark place, this feeling can help me hold on to the light.

Haddie and I move to the music, working our way through several songs, each one strengthening my confidence and increasing my fluidity on the floor. Several of her co-workers, Grant, Tamara, and Jacob, join us as the song switches to *Too Close*, an old song but one of my favorites. I flirtatiously dance with Grant, acting out the song with him. We laugh, our bodies rubbing innocently up against each other.

I raise my arms over my head, crossing them at the wrists and swivel my hips to the rhythm, the alcohol buzzing through my system. I close my eyes, absorbing the atmosphere around me. A tingling sensation up my spine has me flashing my eyes back open.

I look up, and despite the synchronized unison of the mass on the dance floor, I stop, frozen in place. I see Colton. He is standing on one of the stairways that angles down from the VIP section. He has a drink in one hand and his other arm drapes casually around the shoulder of a statuesque blonde. She is turned into him, her hand rubbing gently through the top unbuttoned portion of his dress shirt. Her face tilts up to him and even from a distance I can see her reverence and adoration, although he has his head turned away from her, laughing with a rakish man on his left. A large daunting man stands behind him, eyes scanning the crowd. His security, maybe? Colton flashes a smile at his male cohort, and it's natural and unguarded, allowing me to momentarily appreciate his absolutely devastating looks. The blonde says something and Colton turns his attention back to her. She lifts her hand from his chest to rest on his cheek and lifts her face up, placing a slow, seductive kiss on his lips in ownership.

My insides churn at the sight, clouding my vision so much that I don't pay enough attention to see if Colton is encouraging and returning the kiss or merely just tolerating it. My mouth is suddenly dry. I am paralyzed as I watch him with her. Numb really. We're not together—my constant refusal of him has not demonstrated that I want otherwise. And despite my intense and unfounded hurt right now, all I want is that to be me he is holding. *Me* he is kissing. In the seconds that all of this swirls within me, my hurt begins to shift to anger. How stupid was I to think a guy like him could actually want a girl like me when he could have a girl like her?

I notice Haddie fall motionless in my periphery, taking notice of what I see. I'm about to turn to say something to her when Colton lifts his chin away from his arm candy, and looks up, his eyes locking onto mine. My heart skips over a beat and lodges itself in my throat. Despite the distance between us, I see shock flash in his eyes.

Even though a fellow dancer jostles me, my eyes hold steadfast to his. I know I need to leave the floor before my emotions get the best of me and my threatening tears begin to fall, but I am riveted in place, unable to break the inescapable, magnetic pull he has over me. He releases his hold on the blonde immediately, discarding her easily. He hands his drink off to his male companion without looking and strides unfaltering down the stairs. His emerald eyes burn into mine, never losing our connection.

As he reaches the dance floor, the music changes to a deep, pulsating throb enveloping Trent Reznor's hypnotic voice. Without a word or a look, the horde of dancers seems to move apart as he stalks onto the floor toward me. His expression is indiscernible, the muscle pulsing at his jaw, the shadows from the lights playing over the angles of his face. His long legs eat up the distance quickly. Numerous people turn their heads in recognition, but the hungry look in his eyes stops them from approaching. Despite the music's volume, I hear Haddie suck in a breath as he reaches me.

All of the things I want to yell at him, all of the hurt I want to spew at him, disappears as he walks up to me, and without preamble grabs my hips in his hands, forcefully yanking me up against him. He holds me there, pressed against him, as his body starts to move, hips begin to grind into mine in sync to the punishing tempo of the song. I have no other option than to move with him, respond to the animalistic rhythm of his body. I slide my hands over his hands on my hips and lace my fingers through his, holding him.

Holding on to the ride that is undeniably coming.

Our eyes remain locked. My head tilts back to look up at him. His lips part slightly, and I can hear him hiss out as my hips respond to him. His eyes darken, glazing with desire, filling with heat—with a predatory need. His scorching look has my nipples tightening and my body becoming a melting mess of need in anticipation of his touch. *Of his undoubted possession of me.*

I bite my bottom lip as he moves our combined hands from my hips to behind my back, kneading my backside through my dress, handcuffing me there. We continue to move as one with the music, the feeling of his firm, defined thighs pressing against mine. His arousal rubs against the lower part of my belly. He leans his face down so we are within inches of each other. I can smell the alcohol on his breath as he sighs.

It is by far one of the most erotically sensual moments of my life. The rest of the world has fallen away. The intoxicating effect he has on my body blocks out the crowd around us, all looking our way, noticing me because of the man I am with. It's just he and I— Moving. Responding. Arousing. Anticipating.

The song comes to an end, but we remain entranced in each other's spell. I breathe for what I feel like is the first time since we've touched, a long shaky breath. I don't realize that the music has stopped, and that the event's emcee is speaking over the microphone about the product of the evening. That except for the small crowd around us, the attention of the club has turned and is focused on the stage.

Colton and I stand there, not moving, feeling like we are barely breathing despite our heaving chests, absorbing each other and the sparks of sexual tension that are igniting between us.

"Colton! Hey, Colton," a voice breaks through our connection, snapping me out of my spellbound state. Colton swivels his head to find one of the PRX staff calling his name. "It's time. We need you on the stage. Now."

He nods curtly before looking back at me, eyes smoldering with an urgency that makes my insides shiver. He unlaces his fingers from mine, releasing his hold on my hands and pulls away slightly. The warmth of his body is gone immediately, but my body is still humming from the connection, aching with need. He gives me a slow, suggestive smile and shakes his head softly. At me? At his own thoughts? At which one I'm not sure.

He reaches up a hand and tugs on my hair, his eyebrows quirk up as if to ask me why the change in my hair. I shrug shyly at him, words escaping me. His name is called again. He turns to go, but not before I watch the transition on his face from the Colton Donavan I know to the public persona. Aloof and untouchable. Sexy and untamable.

We haven't uttered a single word, and yet I feel like we've said so much.

I watch his broad shoulders as he walks through the crowd toward the stage, his bodyguard falling in step beside him, pushing back the swarming people. I watch the spectacle and a little part of me smiles about the fact that I've seen the real Colton. At least, I hope I have.

Before I can finish watching his ascent to the makeshift stage, Haddie has me firmly by the arm and is pulling me from the dance floor. My resistance is futile as she drags me down a corridor, past the line for the bathrooms, and toward a small alcove near the exit. She spins me to face her, an incredulous look on her face.

"Ow, you're hurting me!" I snap at her, yanking my arm away, not exactly thrilled at being taken away from watching Colton.

"What. The. Fuck. Was. That?" she asks, each word a staccato. I don't even know how to answer her. I think I'm still under his spell. "Holy shit, Rylee! You two were basically fucking each other with your eyes. I mean, I felt uncomfortable watching you, like I was peeping into your bedroom," she rambles on as she does when excited, "and you know I never get uncomfortable." She leans back against the wall and tilts her head up to the ceiling, an unbelieving look on her face.

I stand there and stare at her. I don't know how to answer her, so she continues. "I knew you said you guys had made out," she continues, ignoring the childlike snort of laughter that comes from me, "but you never told me that there was … that spark … that chemistry … such intensity … My God! I mean, I was hoping when you saw him that—"

"What?" Her last sentence triggers my brain to function. "What do you mean *you were hoping?*"

She smiles sheepishly at me. "Well …"

What the fuck is going on here? "Quit stalling, Montgomery!"

"Well, I was calling you last night to tell you we had landed him as a guest—Merit's one of his new sponsors. Anyway, I called just because I was excited. I thought we could sit back and lust after him tonight—I didn't know anything about what had happened. I talked to Dane and that was when I found out you were out with him." Her words are tumbling out now. I nod at her to continue, my eyes narrowed, lips pursed. "Then you came home and everything unfolded …"

"And what? You decided not to tell me because …"

"Well," she contemplates, "After you told me everything, I had no idea that you two—your connection—is that magnetic. That captivating. I thought maybe if you saw him here, I could help you—I could push the issue. Help you have some fun."

I blow out a loud breath, silently staring at her. I know she means well, but at the same time, I don't need my hand held like a child. I'm mad at her. Mad at Colton for being here with that bimbo. Mad at him for waltzing up to me and taking hold of me as if I belonged to him. Mad at him for making me want him so badly my insides are burning. Silence settles over us.

"Don't be mad, Ry. I'm sorry. I was doing it from a good place." She bites her bottom lip, pouting at me, knowing I can never stay mad at her. I smile softly, forgiving her.

I sag back against the wall and close my eyes, listening to the cheering of the crowd at something the emcee said. The question rattling around my brain comes to the surface. "Who's his plus one?" I ask, referring to the blonde. Is she one of his *permanent go-to girls that know there is no hope of commitment?* Someone he picked up in the club? Why is he kissing her if he is telling me he wants me? Did he not ask me because I'm not *enough*—pretty enough, sexy enough, glamorous enough—to be on his arm in public?

"Does it matter?" she sputters, "I mean, Jesus, Rylee, you two are—"

"Who?"

"Not sure." She shakes her head. "His people just asked for clearance for ten. No names were given."

I let out a slew of curses that make no sense, it's just something I do when upset. Haddie eyes me cautiously. "Talk to me, Ryles," she urges. "What's going on in that head of yours?"

"I'm not lying to myself, am I?" Haddie looks at me, confusion etched on her face. "I mean, I'm not making it up? The chemistry? Colton?"

"Are you crazy?" she stammers, grabbing me by the shoulder and giving me a little shake. "I thought you two were going to spontaneously combust out there! How can you question it?"

The crowd erupts again, the sound echoing down the hallway. I can hear Colton's voice on the microphone. The rasp of his voice pulls at me. The crowd cheers again at something he says, and I wait for the noise to subside some before I can continue. "If he's that into me. If there is that much chemistry ... then why is he here with that blonde? Kissing her? Why not ask me? Or am I just the girl he wants to fuck on the side?" The confusion and hurt are evident in my voice.

Haddie twists her lips up as she thinks about my comments. "I don't know, Rylee. There are so many scenarios here." I raise my eyebrows as if I don't believe her. "He could have already had her as a date before he met you. Or he could really want you and she could be the piece on the side until you say yes."

I snort again. "Really? Did you see her?"

"Have you seen *you?*" she rebukes. "Have you looked in the mirror, Ry? You're gorgeous on a normal day and you look unbelievable tonight! I'm kind of getting sick of telling you that. When are you going to start believing it?" I roll my eyes at her like a child. She ignores me. "She could be one of his *arrangements?* Or maybe she is a fame whore who met him here? Or maybe she's a friend."

"When's the last time you kissed a friend like that?" I snip. She just stares at me, arms folded across her chest. "What am I supposed to do?"

"I'd say keep doing what you're doing. He obviously likes you, including your stubborn streak and smart mouth."

"But, how do I—what do I?"

"Rylee, if you're mad at him, be mad at him. It hasn't stopped you from saying something to him before, and he still wants you. Just because you've decided to sleep with him doesn't—"

"How do you know I've decided that?"

"Oh, honey, it's written all over your face—and your body for that matter. Besides, anyone watching that display out there already thinks that you have." She laughs sympathetically at me as my eyes widen. "Look, Ry, every girl in this club would fall into line if he snapped his fingers. Everyone, that is, but you. He's the one pursuing you. How many times in his life do you think a woman has said no to him? Has walked away from him? Maybe he likes that. And if he does, don't change it just because you've decided you want to do the deed with him." She wiggles her eyebrows.

"But that's just it," I confess. "Am I a challenge or does he really want me? And if it does happen, then will the challenge be over and then he'll be done with me?"

"Honestly, who the fuck cares?" she castigates me. "You always overthink, overanalyze *everything*, Ry. Just forget your head for once, ignore its sensible warnings, and follow what your body wants. Follow Colton's lead, for God's sake." I let out a shaky sigh, heeding her words. "Be yourself, Rylee. That's what he's liked all along."

I nod my head several times, looking at her. A timid smile forms on my face. "Maybe you're right."

"Well, hallelujah!" she yells, flailing her hands over her head. "You finally listened." She grabs my hand and starts tugging me down the hallway. "Let's get you freshened up, get you some more liquid courage, and see where the evening and Mr. Sexy Colton lead you."

It's been about an hour since Haddie's pep talk, and my confidence, bolstered by my steady intake of alcohol, is back in full force. We have danced and socialized with some of her co-workers and are now sitting at the purple booth, taking a breather before hitting the floor again. I have tried desperately to not search out Colton. Tried to ignore the fact that he is probably kissing *her* somewhere in the vicinity. But I do catch my eyes flitting here and there whenever I see a big mob of people. I also note Haddie watching me as I look for him, so I try to sneak glances and be subtle about it. She assures me that he is probably busy with Merit Rum executives. I appreciate the explanation, her trying to make me feel better, so I just push him out of my head. Or try to, with the aid of Tom Collins.

Haddie's drinks have disappeared at a much slower pace than mine since she is technically "at work" and wants to make sure she has her wits about her. I have a steady buzz, but I'm not drunk. I hate the lack of control that comes with drinking too much alcohol. She is laughing at me as I ask her for the third time to explain a situation with a pretentious A-lister she had to deal with earlier in the week.

"Rylee, my dear, you are—"

"Excuse us ladies, would you mind if we joined you?" I turn to see two attractive gentlemen behind me.

Haddie raises her eyebrows at me in question and looks back at the taller one who'd spoken. "By all means, gentlemen," she answers, a slow, sexy smile growing on her lips. "I'm Haddie and my friend here is Rylee." She nods at me as they slide into the booth with us. The tall, dark haired one sits next to Haddie and the other, a blond haired surfer type, sits next to me in the open-ended booth. He has a kind, nervous smile and takes a long sip of his drink.

"Hi, Rylee, my name's Sam." He holds out his hand to mine, and I shake it, giving him a shy smile. I glance over to see Haddie engaged in conversation with his pal, her giggly, flirty face on. "So uh, I would offer to buy you a drink, but I can see your glass is already full."

"Thanks." I lower my gaze from his and bring my glass to my mouth to take a timid sip through my straw.

"Crazy crowded here tonight."

"Yeah, I know," I shout over the noise.

He says something else to me, but I'm not sure what because a loud cheer erupts from the booth next to us. I hold my hand to my ear, indicating that I can't hear him. He scoots closer, placing his arm behind me on the booth and leans in. "I said that you seem to be having a good time and that I noticed you earlier and am glad I—"

"The lady's with me." I suck in my breath at the sound of Colton's steely voice, the threat in his words clear. My eyes snap up to meet Haddie's, and I see delight flash in them before she gives me a careful, reassuring look. My heart is beating at a frantic pace, my skin laced with goose bumps, and all because I am so damn attuned to him and his body's proximity.

I slowly turn to face him, effectively turning my back to press into Sam's chest, his arm across the back of the booth brushing over my shoulder. I raise my eyes to meet Colton's and try to ignore the pang of lust that shoots straight toward the juncture of my thighs. His hair is a tad mussed, his shirtsleeves are rolled up to the elbow, that muscle I find so damn sexy is pulsing in his jaw, and his eyes smolder with annoyance. I've had just enough alcohol to feel defiant, to test just how irritated Colton really is.

"I'm with you?" I ask, my voice laced with sarcasm. I can feel Sam's body tense behind me and shift nervously, unaware of the chess game he is currently a pawn in, as Colton's eyes narrow at me. "Really? Because I thought you were with her." I shift to the side to look behind him, looking for her. I raise my eyebrows and continue, "You know, the blonde from earlier?"

"Cute, Rylee," he spits out impatiently. I see his eyes shift, lock with Sam's behind me, and deliver the hands-off warning.

I'm irritated that he's been all over the club for the past hour and a half, doing God knows what with the blonde, and yet he thinks he can waltz up and lay claim to me? I don't think so. I reach back and place my hand on Sam's knee and squeeze it gently. "Don't worry, Sam, I'm not with him." I make my voice loud enough that Colton can hear me. I see Haddie's eyes widen as I hear a low growl from Colton. I can feel Sam flinch against me. I turn back to Colton, defiance in my smirk and challenge in my eyes.

"Don't push me, Rylee. I don't like sharing." I can see him clench and unclench his fists. "You. Belong. With. Me."

I quirk my eyebrows up, my insolence mounting. "How so, Ace?" I watch his eyes focus on the hand I've kept on Sam's knee. "Last night you were with me, and tonight you're with her." I shrug calmly at him, although inside I'm anything but—my heart is racing and my breath has quickened. "Seems to me like—She. Belongs. With. You," I mimic childishly.

Colton drags a hand through his hair and gives an exasperated sigh as his eyes flicker over everyone in the booth. I can see him try to rein in his frustration and at having to have this conversation in front our little audience. "Rylee." He blows air out in a sigh. "You—You..." he looks around, out into the crowd and then his eyes finally come back to mine "...you test me on every level. Push me away," he grunts, realizing he is saying this out loud. "What am I supposed to think?"

I look him up and down, my mouth twisting in thought. I'm kind of enjoying toying with him, making the man who is so sure of himself, who always gets what he wants, have to work at something. *"I'm not sure if I want you yet,"* I bait him. I hear Haddie suck in her breath at my flippant comment and the ice clink in Sam's glass as he anxiously drinks what's left. "A girl's allowed to change her mind," I taunt, tilting my head as I regard him. "We're notorious for it."

"Among other things," he says dryly, taking a drink, watching me from over the rim of his glass. "Two can play this game, Ryles," he cautions, "and I think I have a lot more experience at it than you do."

My bravado falters slightly from the warning look in his eyes. I withdraw my hand from Sam's knee and scoot toward the edge of my seat, my eyes never wavering from his. We stay like this for several moments. "You're playing hard to get, Rylee," he admonishes.

I glance over at Haddie who's face is impassive, but her eyes tell me she can't believe what is unfolding. I stand up to face him, squaring my shoulders, defiantly raising my chin. "And your point is?"

He tsks at me, shaking his head, and takes a step closer. "I hope you're enjoying yourself because it's quite a show you're putting on here." He puts a finger under my chin, lifting it so my eyes meet his. "I don't play games, Rylee," he warns, his voice just loud enough for me to hear, "and I won't tolerate them played on me." Sexual tension radiates between us. The air is thick with it.

I breathe in a slow, calculated breath, trying to form an intelligent answer as his proximity clouds my thoughts and heightens my senses. "Well, thanks for the update." I slap a hand on his chest and lean in a little closer, my lips near his ear. "I'll let you in on a little something as well, Ace. I don't like being made to feel like I'm sloppy seconds to your *blonde bevy of babes*." I step back, forcing a confident smirk on my face. "You're developing a pattern of wanting me right after I know you've been with another. That's a habit you're going to need to break or nothing else is going to happen here," I finish, gesturing between the two of us as I raise my eyebrows. "That is, if I want it to at all." His lips curl.

God, he is gorgeous! Even when he is smoldering with anger, he emits a raw sensuality that my body has a hard time ignoring. I turn to glance at Haddie for encouragement as I hear his name being called by a seductive voice. "Colt, baby?"

The words make me want to vomit.

I turn back to him to see a well-manicured hand slide in between his arm and his torso, splaying over his chest. I see him tense at the touch, his eyes guarded in reaction, and he throws back the rest of his drink, hissing at the sting of it between clenched teeth. I proceed to watch as the blonde from earlier slithers up next to him, eyeing me up and down pityingly, trying to stake her claim. I see the spark in her eye when she recognizes that I'm the one he left her for on the stairs. If looks could kill, I'd be dead. But despite it all, Colton's eyes remain steadfast on mine.

I am nauseated by the sight of her hands on him and the thought of him giving any attention to her. I shake my head in condemnation as I cluck my tongue. "Case in point," I say. I glance back at Haddie and the two men sitting with us. "I apologize, but please excuse me." Haddie starts to gather her purse, concern on her face, and I subtly shake my head for her to stay.

I turn back and look at Colton one last time, hoping my eyes portray the message I'm sending. Here's your choice. *Me or her*. You pick. Right now. Last chance.

I avert my eyes, breaking our connection. He stands static with the blonde draped over him like a cheap jacket. I guess he's made his decision. I try to calmly exit the booth. Try to flee from the dangerous path that I undoubtedly know he will lead me down.

Once I feel like I'm clear from view, I blindly push my way through the mass of people, hurt bubbling up inside me. My heart aches from the knowledge that I'll never be able to compete with someone like her. Never. I try to contain it as I push my way to the bar, wanting to numb the feelings I let myself believe were valid. Were reciprocated. Were possible again.

Shit! I swallow back the threatening tears as I squeeze into an open space at the crowded bar and by some miracle the bartender is right in front of me. "What'll you have?" he asks above the noise.

I stare at him a moment, contemplating my options. I opt for quick and numbing. "Shot of tequila please," I request, garnering the attention of the man standing next to me. I can feel him looking me up and down, and I roll my shoulders, bristling at the unwanted attention.

The bartender slides a shot of tequila across the bar to me and I grab it, looking at it for a moment, silently saying our toast. Right now I definitely need the courage portion. *Even if it's false courage*. I toss it back without hesitation and scrunch my face up at the burn. I close my eyes as its warmth slides down my throat and settles in my belly. I sigh deeply before opening my eyes, ignoring the offer of another drink from the man beside me.

I grab my phone out of my purse and text Haddie that I'm fine, to enjoy herself, and I'll see her at home. I know that if she weren't here for work, she'd be at my side taking me home.

I glance up from my phone to look for the bartender. I need another shot. Something to numb the rejection. My eyes flicker down the length of the bar when I see Colton striding purposefully toward me.

Despite the hope surging inside of me, I mutter, "Fuck!" and throw some cash on the bar before turning on my heel and veering toward the closest exit. I find one quickly, and shove open the doors. I find myself in an empty, darkened corridor, relieved when the door shuts behind me, muffling the pulsating music. My moment of solitude is fleeting as the door is thrown open moments later, Colton pushing through. We lock eyes—I can see the anger in his and I hope he can see the hurt in mine—before I turn my back to him and rush down the hallway.

I let out a strangled cry in frustration as Colton catches up to me and grabs my arm, spinning me around to face him. Our ragged breathing is the only sound in the hallway as we glare at each other, tempers flaring.

"What the fuck do you think you're doing?" he growls at me, his grip on my arm holding firm.

"Excuse me?" I sputter.

"You have an annoying little habit of running away from me, Rylee."

"What's it to you, Mr. I-Send-Mixed-Signals?" I throw back at him, wrenching my arm from his grip.

"You're one to talk, sweetheart. Is that guy—is he what you really want, *Rylee?*" He says my name like a curse. "A quick romp with Surfer Joe? You want to fuck him instead of *me?*" I can hear the edge in his voice. The threat. In this dark corridor, his features hidden by shadows, his eyes glistening, he is every bit the intimidating bad boy that the tabloids hint at.

"Isn't that what you want from me, Colton? A quick fuck to boost that fragile ego of yours? It seems you spend an awful lot of time trying to placate that weakness of yours." I hold his glare. "Besides, why do you care what I do? If I recall correctly, you were pretty occupied with the blonde on your arm."

He clenches and unclenches his jaw regarding me, rolling his head back and forth on his shoulder before answering me. "*Raquel? She's inconsequential,*" he states as a simple matter of fact.

I can take that answer so many ways, and all of them paint his opinion of women in a less than stellar light.

"*Inconsequential?*" I question, "Is that what I'd be to you after you fuck me?" I stand my ground, shoulders squared. "*Inconsequential?*"

He stands there seething. At me? At my response? He takes a step toward me and I retreat, my back pressing into the wall behind me. I have nowhere left to run. He reaches out a hand and pulls it back in indecision, the muscles in his jaw clenching, the pulse in his throat pounding. He angles his head to the side, closing his eyes, swearing silently to himself. He looks back at me—frustration, anger, desire, and so much more burning in the depths of his eyes. Their intensity as they look into mine is unnerving, as if he is asking for my consent. I nod my head subtly, giving him the permission to take. The next time he reaches out, there is no hesitation.

Within a beat, his lips are on mine. All of the pent up frustration, irritation, and antagonism of the evening explodes as our lips clash, hands fist, and souls ignite. There is nothing gentle about our union. Rapacious need burns through me as one of his hands snakes around my back, grasps my neck and yanks me against him so his mouth can plunder mine. His other hand slides between the wall and my arching back, splaying against me in ownership. Gone are the gentle sips and the soft caresses from yesterday.

His lips slant over mine and his tongue darts in my mouth, tangling, teasing, and tormenting mine. His hands slide over mine where they're fisted in his shirt. He grabs my wrists and pulls them over my head, presses them to the wall, and handcuffs them with one of his hands. He brings his free hand down and cups my jaw as he breaks from our kiss. He draws his face back and his eyes, darkened and vibrant with arousal, hold mine.

"*Not inconsequential,* Rylee. You could never be inconsequential." He shakes his head subtly, the vibration of his voice resonating in me. He rests his forehead to mine, our noses brushing each other's. "No—you and me—together," he grinds the words out, "that would make you *mine.*" His words feather over my face, enter my soul, and take hold. "*Mine,*" he repeats, making sure that I understand his intentions.

I close my eyes to savor the words. To relish the thought of Colton wanting me to be his *mine*. Our foreheads remain touching as I surrender to the moment, to the feeling, and to the easing of doubts. He steps back from me and gently releases my hands from above my head. Our eyes stay connected and I see what I think is a momentary flash of fear blaze through his.

I reach out tentatively to him and touch his hips, working my hands under his untucked shirt so that I can place my hands on his skin. So that I can feel this vibrant, virile man beneath my fingertips. It's always been his hands on my skin. Him in control. I haven't had the chance to appreciate the feel of him beneath my palms yet.

I find my purchase, my fingers caressing the firm warmth of his defined muscles as they tense at my touch. I slowly run them up the front of his torso, feeling each delineation, each breath he takes in reaction to my touch. It's a heady feeling to hear his response, see his pupils dilate in desire, as I glide my hands from his pecs, smoothing them over ribs and under his arms to scrape my nails up the plains of his back.

He closes his eyes momentarily in rapture, clearly enjoying my slow, teasing assault on his senses. I lean up on my toes and hesitantly lean into him and brush my lips against his. I press my hands into his shoulders, pulling his body into mine. I slant my mouth over his and run the tip of my tongue over his bottom lip.

His fingers slowly brush against my cheeks, his palms resting on the line of my jaw to frame my face as he tenderly deepens the kiss. His lips sipping, his tongue slowly, sweetly parting my lips and melding with mine. His quiet affection touches me in my core, slowly unraveling me and winding me into a ball of need. He takes my breath away with each caress. I sigh into the kiss, my fingers digging into his shoulders, the only sign of my impending impatience at wanting more. At *needing* more.

I can feel Colton's struggle to control his need, his body taut beneath my hands, his impressive erection pressing into my belly. He continues his tender and unrelenting assault on my senses by concentrating solely on my mouth. Seducing my lips. His breath is mine. His action is my reaction.

He stops abruptly, placing his two hands on the wall beside my shoulders and braces himself, letting his forehead drop to my shoulder so that his nose and mouth are buried in the nape of my neck. I feel his chest heaving for air like mine, and I'm relieved that he appears to be as affected by this encounter as I am. I'm a little confused by his actions, but I take the moment to allow him to collect himself while I settle my racing heart. I subconsciously squeeze my knees together to try and quiet the relentless pressure at the delta between by thighs.

I can feel the warmth of his breath as he pants against my neck, struggling for control. "Sweet Jesus, Rylee," he murmurs as he shakes his head, rolling it on my shoulder before scattering innocent kisses along my collarbone. "We need to get out of here before you unman me in the hallway."

He raises his head to look at me as I still from his words. There is no doubt that this is what I want. That he is who I want. But I can't deny the fact that I'm nervous—anxious—afraid I'll disappoint him with my lack of experience in this department.

"Come." He doesn't give me time to speak before he grabs my hand, wraps his arm around my shoulder, pulling me into him, and walks us deeper into the corridor. "I have a room here for the night." His strong arm helps support me, leading me toward my apple in the Garden of Eden.

I follow obediently, trying to quiet the doubt and noise in my mind, for it is actively chattering away now that his mouth is not on mine, blunting my ability to reason. We quickly make it to an elevator at the end of the hallway and within seconds we are stepping in. Colton pulls a key card out of his pocket and inserts it into the panel, effectively unlocking the top floor. The penthouse.

He steps back toward me as the elevator lifts and places a hand on the small of my back. The silence between us is audible and only intensifies the butterflies that are churning in my stomach. "Why the change?" Colton asks as he tugs on my straightened hair, trying to ease my mounting anxiety.

"Just trying to fit the mold," I quip reflexively, referring to the numerous pictures on the Internet of him with straight haired women. His brow furrows, trying to figure out what I mean, when I offer up, "Sometimes change is good."

He uses his hand on my back to turn me toward him. He angles his head down so that we are eye to eye. "I like your curls," he says softly, my ego preening from the compliment. "They suit you." Now that he has me positioned, he raises a hand up to wipe an errant strand off my face. He then places his fingers on the side of my jaw and holds me there, his eyes searching mine. "You have one chance to walk away," he warns me as the elevator alerts us we're at his floor. The husky tone of his voice wreaking havoc on my willpower.

My heart beats erratically. I shake my head in unconvincing acceptance when I can't find the words to speak to him.

He ignores the opening elevator door behind him and continues to look intently into my eyes. "I won't be able to walk away, Rylee," he says as he scrunches up his eyes as if the admission is painful. He blows out a loud breath, releasing me and running his fingers through his hair. He turns his back to me, reaches out, and stabs the door open button, bracing his hands against the elevator wall. His broad shoulders fill the small space. His head hangs down as he mulls over his next words. "I want to take my time with you, Rylee. I want to build you up nice and slow and sweet like you need. Push you to crash over that edge. And then I want to fuck you the way I need to. Fast and hard until you're screaming my name. The way I've wanted to since you fell out of that storage closet and into my life."

I have to bite my lower lip to stifle a groan. I fight the need to sag against the wall for some kind of relief.

"Once we leave this elevator, I don't think I'll have enough control to stop ... to pull away from you, Rylee. I. Can't. Resist. You." His voice is pained, quiet, and chock-full of conviction. He turns back to me, his face filled with emotion. His eyes reflecting a man tinkering on the edge of losing control. "Decide, Rylee. *Yes. Or. No.*"

Chapter Eleven

Colton—Raced

Uh-uh. She's mine, motherfucker.

Over my dead fucking body.

Or most likely *his* if he touches her again.

This club is so packed. So filled with more than willing Grade A pussy. *And sponsorship obligations.* Fucking obligations that have weighed me down like an anchor for the past two hours. Two hours wasted when I could have been with the cause of my shitty mood.

And the source of my current case of raging blue balls.

Sweet Jesus. Dancing with her like that? Pressed against each other from shoulder to knee. Moving in sync. Her body reacting to mine as if she knew each movement I would make before I did. Eyes telling me she's mine for the taking.

The hint of how we'll be together when she finally caves to what her body wants but that her mind keeps fighting. I almost came on the spot. Talk about a tease I can't wait to devour.

And now I have Merit Rum execs in front of me, Raquel plastered to my side making it unmistakable to everyone that she's my date, and Becks, *the bastard*, over their shoulders smirking at me like *it's your fucking fault for asking her to come tonight.*

But more importantly is what I can see through the crowd in interrupted bouts. The man who just sat next to Rylee. Whose arm is around her shoulders. Who is leaning into her, speaking in her ear.

Mine.

The thought snags in my mind and I can't let it go. Let the thought of her go. I can't concentrate on what's being said. I look at the execs from Merit trying to act cool but failing miserably in an element they're obviously uncomfortable in. I glance up at Becks and nod to the side in Rylee's direction hoping he gets my drift and if he doesn't, he will in about five seconds.

"If you'll excuse me," I interrupt the shorter one's spiel about market demographics, "I need to use the restroom." I look again at Beckett, the *greatest fucking wingman ever*, and leave without another word. I just hope they don't realize I'm walking the opposite direction of the head.

What the fuck am I doing? Blowing off a sponsor for a chick? She must have the elusive voodoo pussy or something. *Fucking Christ!* It's like someone has taken over my body—or my dick—because once again I can't get her out of my goddamn system.

And I have to. There's no other option. No other choice. Have to finish the fucking meal I've had just a taste of right before it's cruelly snagged away.

The fucker is touching her. *Again*. Leaning closer.

"The lady's with me." The words are out before I can think. Grated out between my gritted teeth. My voice laced with the obvious threat. All four heads in the booth snap up at my comment and look at me. All except for Rylee. She stares at the blonde who works at PRX sitting across from her for a split second.

And then she turns ever so slowly against the chest of the prick sitting behind her, her posture stiffening with that defiance that causes my balls to tighten with unfiltered lust. Gone is the sexy siren from the dance floor earlier and the vulnerable girl from last night. Right now she's a woman scorned. And when she raises those eyes, I can see it clear as day, but I don't care because they are looking exactly where they need to be.

On me.

The only place I want them to be. But all I can focus on is him. His arm is still on her. His body still beside hers. I clench my jaw. Eyes locked with hers.

"I'm with you?" she asks, those fucking bedroom eyes widening to saucers and her chin jutting out in obstinance. "*Really?* Because I thought you were with her?" she says sarcastically, scrunching up her nose the way she does when she's pissed off—which I've happened to see a lot in the short time we've known each other—and looking behind me. "You know, the blonde from your arm earlier?"

Fucking Raquel. Why'd I invite her again? Her blowjob skills—her best asset frankly, *even if thinking it makes me a prick*—are a distant memory at the sight in front of me. Because right here, right now, all

I can think of is Rylee. Her mouth. Her body. That pussy of hers that I'll bet my life on as being the sweetest fucking thing I'll ever taste. Ever feel.

Might even beg for.

I need to be buried in her so badly right now it's painful. "Cute, Rylee." I spit the words out, not trusting myself to say any more when I see Surfer Joe squeeze her shoulder. My glare shifts to his, my eyes sending the message.

Hands. Off.

I see that my warning's delivered when he tenses as recognition slowly seeps in. *Yeah, that's right, cocksucker. I'm Colton Fuckin' Donavan and she's mine.* And the exaggerations in the tabloids are perfectly accurate. I've got a quick fucking temper and have no qualms getting my hands dirty with a few punches. Touch her again and I'll show you.

Pretty please.

And of course because she always does the opposite of what I want, Rylee turns and puts her hand on the fucker and reassures him that she's not here with me. Then she turns back slowly to me, a derisive smirk on those beautiful lips and challenge in her violet eyes.

So that's how this is going to go?

"Don't push me, Rylee. I don't like sharing," I say, clenching and unclenching my fists to release the anger laced with arousal that's firing through my veins. "You. Belong. With. Me."

Her eyebrows shoot up at my claim. I can see the insolence just beneath her composed exterior. "How so, Ace? Last night you were with me, and tonight you're with *her*." She says *her* like the meanest of slurs, and I can't help but think the same thing. I send a silent thanks to Becks for getting my hint and keeping Raquel occupied right now. "Seems to me like—She. Belongs. With. You." She mimics me.

Sweet Christ! *The woman fucking owns me.* Owns me and I haven't even had her yet. What the fuck is wrong with me? I never chase. Never. But the goddamn woman is constantly pulling me in two opposing extremes. I swear to God she's got some kind of fucking hold on me I can't break from.

I drag my hand through my hair in frustration as I take in the other three sitting in the booth, witness to the stringing of my balls by a singular woman. "Rylee." I sigh, trying to rein in the impatience in my voice. "You—you ..." *She's what, you dumbass?* Grab your balls back firmly and own them. Tell her how it's going to be. "You test me on every level. Push me away. What am I supposed to think?"

Yeah. That was brilliant, Donavan. Fucking brilliant, if you're a pussy.

She eyes me up and down, a little smirk at the corners of her mouth that irritates the fuck out of me. Makes my dick hard. She's playing me once again. Fucking toying with me.

And enjoying it.

"I'm not sure if I want you yet," she antagonizes, startling everyone else at the table, I assume because of my rumored temper and unpredictability. "A girl's allowed to change her mind," she taunts, angling her head and deliberately looking me up and down. "We're notorious for it."

"Among other things." I shoot back instantly and then take a sip of my drink, watching her above the rim all the while. "Two can play this game, Ryles, and I think I have a lot more experience at it than you do."

Her lips part slightly at my words and I want to groan out loud at the fucking image that flickers through my head. Of exactly how I can fill that space between them. I grit my teeth in need as I level my stare at her. She slowly removes her hand from Surfer Joe's knee and scoots toward the edge of the booth.

Toward me.

That's right, sweetheart. Let's end this. Right here. Right now. Come to Daddy.

"You're playing hard to get, Rylee."

She glances over at her girlfriend and then slowly rises from her seat, and all I see are her sweet curves and soft flesh and my head fills with thoughts of how desperately I want her beneath me, naked and coming undone. "And your point is ...?"

Her words force me to focus back to now. To winning her over, despite the combustible sexual chemistry between us that she's constantly fighting. But when I see her—hear her—her shoulders are proud with defiance and her chin, strong.

She wants to go this route? Keep up the charade that she doesn't want me despite her fucking unbelievable body announcing otherwise. I can play this like nobody's business. Run circles around her. I shake my head at her and take a step closer.

Needing to be closer.

She lowers her eyes under my intense scrutiny. "I hope you're enjoying yourself because it's quite a show you're putting on here." I reach out and force her chin up so she has no other option but to look me in the eyes. "I don't like games, Rylee," I warn, my blood thundering through my veins from being so close to her. "... and I won't tolerate them played on me."

The air thickens between us. My breath quickens. My fingers itch to touch.

To possess.

To claim.

She's just as fucking affected as I am. I know it. Can see it. *Fuck me.* The woman turns me inside out, and I can see the moment she tries to deny what's humming between us right now. She takes a slow, calculated breath and steps toward me. "Well, thanks for the update." She slaps her hand to my chest and leans into me, her lips right at my ear.

My senses riot. My restraint tested. The woman needs to back away right now or I'll take her right here on the damn floor. *No holds barred.*

"I'll let you in on a little something as well, Ace. I don't like being made to feel like sloppy seconds to your *blonde bevy of babes.*" Her voice tickles my skin. And she continues to tease as she takes a step back, that smile on her face tempting me to just take without asking. "You're developing a pattern of wanting me right after you've been with another. That's a habit you're going to need to break or nothing else is going to happen here." She gestures back and forth between us, my mind wandering to exactly what else she can do with that perfectly manicured hand. "... That's if I want it to at all."

She smirks at me as she retreats a step. *That smirk* that I'd like to fuck into submission until she's screaming out my name. And I've had enough of this banter. Desire's so strong in me that my balls ache. I'm just about to act on it. To take without asking when I hear "Colt, baby?" followed by a hand sliding up my torso to display ownership. I tense when all I really want to do is shrug Raquel off of me like a hot fucking coal.

The look on Rylee's face—her complete disdain for Raquel—I completely understand. I feel the same way at this exact moment. But what gets me more than anything is the flash of hurt that lingers in those violet eyes a moment too long.

Fuck! I knew it.

She wants this just as bad as I do. There's nothing I can do right now and not look like a dick. Drop Raquel and go after Rylee or leave Rylee after the game I just played and walk away with Raquel. I do the only thing I can do when all my mind and hands want to do is grab Rylee against me and taste her mouth. Sample her body.

I toss back the rest of my drink, the burn of the alcohol not even registering. When I look back toward Rylee, she's saying something to her friend and then picks up her purse. She turns back to face me and my chest tightens. That defiance I find arousing is evident in her posture, but her eyes reflect a myriad of contradictions.

I hate you.

I want you.

How could you?

I should've known.

You're going to break my heart, aren't you?

Your choice: *me or her.*

I clench my jaw. Having answers to all of them. And none of them. She just looks at me one more time, a quiet resignation in her face, and then she turns and pushes her way through the crowd of people. Getting away from me as fast as she can.

I'd run too, sweetheart. That's nothing compared to the poison inside of me.

I look down at the empty glass in my hand while Raquel tugs on my arm, urging me to follow her. I resist the desire to huck it against the wall and hear the crash as the glass splinters into a thousand tiny fucking pieces.

What the fuck are you doing, Donavan? Since when do you care what people think? Fucking voodoo pussy, man. That's got to be it. Got to be the only reason I want to chase the one thing I've never wanted. Never cared to.

Until now.

Fuckin' A.

I look up and meet the blonde friend's eyes. She just arches her eyebrow at me as if to say "*You fucking idiot.*" And she's right. *I am.*

I look over to Raquel. And feel nothing. Absolutely nothing. No buzz. No charge. No ache to take.

I look into the mass of people where Rylee left and I catch a glimpse of her head as she weaves through the crowd. My chest tightens. My fingers rub together. My body craves. And the need humming through me is so strong, all I can do is shake my head at Raquel. My eyes telling her the only words that need to be said.

And then I walk away.

There's not even a choice to be made.

It was made for me. The moment she fell out of that damn storage closet and into my life.

Fucking Rylee.

Fucking voodoo pussy.

The two thoughts are on repeat in my head as I push through the crowd to try and find where in the hell she went.

I'm annoyed I can't find her. Pissed because Colton Donavan does not chase and fuck if this woman hasn't had me on the run since the get-go.

It's easy to tell myself to let her go. Fuck the hassle. So why can't I?

I scan the crowd and through a break I see her at the bar. I push through, tell myself I'm chasing because of the challenge and from the need to show her that she wants this … even if it's just because she's so goddamn nonchalant about rejecting me.

Women aren't blasé when it comes to wanting me. She tried to be but I saw her nipples tighten through her top, her pulse beat in her throat. I know I affected her.

Blasé my ass. She's fucking lying and another shot, another drink, another woman isn't going to convince me otherwise.

I'm used to getting what I want and right now, I want this fucking woman more than any other.

I reach the bar and she catches sight of me, turns, and then hurries to the exit.

Fuckin' A. She's running again and I'm chasing.

And the thing about chasing in racing is sometimes it's a bitch to win a race from behind. But then again, chasing can let you draft, fly beneath the radar, and then slingshot to take the lead and control the race when it matters the most.

Time to slingshot.

I push through the exit moments after her. We're in some type of hallway but I don't take notice because our eyes lock. I see the hurt flash before she turns and keeps going.

Uh-uh. No way. She's not walking away from me again because I may have seen hurt, but I also saw something else. And I need to know what that something else is.

But why, Donavan? Why the fuck do you care when you can have any woman you want? Snap your fingers and another one will replace the current one?

I grit my teeth as I chase, the view of her walking away becoming a familiar one but hell if it's not hot as fuck to watch her ass sway. And therein lies the motherfucking problem. That view is what keeps me coming back for more. And I lie to myself again because I know it's so much more than just the curves that keep me chasing.

Let her go. Let her keep on walking out of the hallway, out of my life.

But I don't want her to. There's just something about her that I can't quite put my finger on. Something about her holds me captive, tempts me, demands that I sit up and pay fucking attention.

I reach out, my hand on her arm, and pull her backwards. Her body turns so we stand face to face, bodies inches apart, and fuck … I'm pissed.

Pissed that she hates me. Pissed that she wants me. Frustrated that I want to just walk away but for some fucking reason I can't.

I was seduced by her kiss and moved by her with her boys yesterday. We basically fucked on the dance floor an hour ago and then she was with Surfer Joe and I swore it was a show. Something to play me like the games so many women use to get my attention. But then when I gave it to her, she left me high and dry without a chance to make the decision her eyes dared me to.

Choose her, pick her, drown in her.

She may not be playing the bullshit games, but it's still her fault. I use the need for her I don't want to feel to feed my anger. I don't want this—complications and estrogen fueled bullshit. I want a quick fuck, that's it. A roll in the sheets to satisfy the craving she's created and move on. I hold onto that lie and give the one reaction I can since the only other option my mind can think of is her beneath me.

And fucking hell, I want that.

"What the fuck do you think you're doing?" My voice is low and spiteful, my hand squeezing tighter on her arm to prevent it from sliding down her side. I yank her against me.

"Excuse me?"

She seems shocked that I'm angry. If I wasn't intimately familiar with the bite to her tongue, her reaction would leave me thinking she's used to being handled with kid gloves. But I know better than that, know she can hold her own.

"You have an annoying little habit of running away from me, Rylee." I watch the shock flicker across her face. Does she not see it? Kisses me and then runs at the benefit. Kisses me and runs at The House. Kisses me until I want so much more than just the small sample I had at the beach. That's a whole lot of tempt and not a lot of take on my part.

It's called blue balls, sweetheart. Something's got to give soon and I sure as fuck hope it's both our zippers.

"What's it to you, Mr. I-Send-Mixed-Signals?" She jerks her arm from my hand. Physical connection broken but fuck if the sexual tension isn't eating us alive.

"You're one to talk, *sweetheart*. Is that guy—is he what you really want, *Rylee?*" My mind flashes back to the fucker's hand on her, body up against hers. I see red then green. Fuck. The red I'm used to, but the jealousy is a whole different ball game I've never even taken a practice swing in. "A quick romp with Surfer Joe? You want to fuck him instead of *me?*"

I clench my jaw to control my need to taste those sexy-as-sin lips of hers she's scowling at me with. I fist my hands, that deep V of her dress calling to my fingers to dip inside and cup those tits she's pushing in my face as her chest heaves up and down from her angered breaths.

I deserve a goddamn medal for fighting this urge. For not touching when every ounce of me screams at me to plunder and pillage that mouth until it's swollen from use. My desire turns to anger because what I see in her eyes, what it makes me feel, isn't something I'm supposed to feel.

Fuck this.

Fuck her.

And fuck me because that's exactly the problem—wanting to fuck her—but newsflash, I know this is too goddamn complicated. A quick fuck is not supposed to be like this. Step away. Back the fuck off and go, Donavan. Turn around and walk the other way because those eyes of hers tell you this is going to be anything but simple.

I take a step closer.

Goddamn woman has me on an invisible line. Like she's cranking the reel and tightening the hook in my mouth before I even have a chance to taste the fucking bait.

We glare at each other, eyes devouring and warning all at the same time.

See? Complicated. Walk the fuck away. Save yourself.

"Isn't that what you want from me, Colton? A quick fuck to boost that fragile ego of yours? It seems you spend an awful lot of time trying to placate that weakness of yours. Besides, why do you care what I do? If I recall correctly, you were pretty occupied with the blonde on your arm."

I ignore the insult she hurls at me because I'm so focused on the tease of her body so tantalizingly close to mine. Tease me and insult me all at once. Contradictions like this are not supposed to be sexy. They are a downright mindfuck that I've learned to keep at restraining order distance. So why the hell do I still want her so fucking bad I can taste it?

I push away the ache to take her right now because she's right. I do just want a quick fuck.

Nice try, Donavan. Keep telling yourself that.

Maybe if I prove to her the asshole that I am, she'll take the reins here and walk the fuck away. Deny me what I want since I'm being such a pussy I can't do it myself and ironically am only thinking with my dick. Game plan in place, time to shift it in gear.

"Raquel? She's inconsequential."

And I mean to sound like a chauvinistic asshole, that I think women are mere blips on my fucking radar, but there's something about *that word*—inconsequential—that is so fitting all of a sudden. It perfectly describes how Rylee made me feel when Raquel was at my side and she, herself, was standing in front of me.

Becks nailed it on the head the other night when I ditched sex with Raquel on the way home from the gala and he never even knew it.

"Inconsequential?" she says, eyes wide and irritation in her voice.

Good. She got the hint. Run baby, run. Let me get a good show as you walk away.

"Is that what I'd be to you after you fuck me? *Inconsequential?*"

Never.

Her words are a verbal backhand. Because as much as I want her to hate me and do what I can to spare me the complications I know she'd bring, when she throws herself in the same category as Raquel, the only word that flickers through my head is *never*.

Fucking hell, Donavan. If I keep this whiplash up—wanting her but not wanting her—I'm going to need to start wearing my HANS device outside of the goddamn car. I just wish I knew what it is about this woman that tells me she's not like the others. And not just because she's kept her legs closed when most others would have theirs spread by now.

Fuck if I know, but I'm done with this game. She just threw out a challenge she didn't even realize when she dared me to prove her different than Raquel.

I want. And I need. And hell if I'm not going to taste her again, fuck her mouth with my tongue to try and show her how badly I want to do the same elsewhere.

Prove to her how she could never be inconsequential even though that's all I really want her to be. The only thing I can allow when the cards fall where they may.

I take a step closer. Her back bumps against the wall, and I lift my hand toward her face but then pull it back.

Somehow I have a conscience and it's just decided to show the hell up. Because this is perfect fucking timing to tell me I can't do this to her, fuck with her to fix me. Like I didn't know already that it's not fair to her, something she doesn't deserve.

Sex without strings is something I've always done so why am I thinking this now? Why didn't I think it earlier when I ditched the Merit execs? I'm not a good guy so why, when all I want is to slide between her thighs and lose myself for a bit, do I suddenly feel like I need to warn her in yet another way?

I stare at her, try to convey my thoughts and hope she gets them.

Run! I want scream at her. Tell her to take the fuck off down the hall and not look back. Explain that I'm a selfish bastard who takes what he wants without worries about collateral damage because I have a feeling that once I have her I'm going to need to destroy some things to prevent me from wanting her again.

Ease the ache. Bury the pain. Fuck her over in the end because she'll hope there's more when I can only give her less.

Can you handle me, Rylee? You fix the broken but there's no hope left here. Can you live with that? Can you handle temporary when your eyes say you're a forever? Do you want me? Can you live with sex and secrets and a selfish son of a bitch who will use you in the end?

Tell me no. Please tell me no because I can't find it in myself to walk the fuck away like I should. Make the choice for me. Push me away. Hurt me.

She holds my gaze and then lifts her chin in a subtle nod.

Fuck! Every part of my body screams the word, each one holding a different meaning to the reaction.

She just said yes, and I swallow the fact that my warnings were all in my head. My excuse to fall back and ease my guilt later when I walk away.

But right now? Right now, I'm taking what she's offering. Restraint obliterated and my dick in command.

Add another demon to the pile within because I sure as fuck don't deserve a quick stop in Heaven before I take the long ride to Hell, but I'm taking it.

Without thought, my hands frame her face and my lips are on hers. I'm hungry for the taste of her, desperate for the feel of her. Smooth skin, gentle moans, soft against hard.

She's like a fix to an addiction. I thought if I had a taste, I'd want it less, but fuck me, all I can think of is more. Take more, want more, feel more, need more.

One hand is on her neck, the other on her back, and I pull her against me, need her against me from chest to knee. My mouth takes, nips, and sips. Her reactions spur me on. The moan in her throat when I suck on her tongue. The arch of her back when I tug on her lip with my teeth. Her body begs for the things her lips refuse to ask me for. And fuck if it's not the hottest thing to know she wants this as desperately as I do, but I need to be in control here. Need to own the situation and the shit I keep pushing out of my head.

Her hands fist my shirt, need burning a hole through me, my dick aching, my body waiting to claim. In reflex, I grab her hands and pin them above the wall over our heads so she's completely open to me.

Mine to control. To set the pace. To prevent her from revealing the shit that needs to stay behind lock and key.

I bring my free hand down to hold her chin so I can brand her lips again. Kiss her senseless so she has no other fucking option than to say yes to the question I so desperately want to ask. But when my fingers hold her there, her eyes flutter up to look into mine, dark lashes framing the most unique of colors. And although my dick is rock hard and wanting to act, I stumble over thoughts I don't mean to say but that fall out of my mouth before I can stop them.

"*Not inconsequential,* Rylee. You could never be inconsequential." I close my eyes and rest my forehead against hers to give myself a moment to try and figure out what the fuck is wrong with me. "No—you and me—together, that would make you *mine. Mine.*"

My confession shocks me. I mean it's one thing to think the words and another fucking thing to say them. Hell yes, they're true, but since when do I say crap like this? Give a woman a drawer for her shit when I only plan on letting her pass through the ever-revolving bedroom door.

My honesty scares the shit out of me. Makes me question when I never second guess myself.

I take a deep breath and step back, releasing her hands still held by mine, our eyes never breaking. And I don't know what it is now that I'm asking her because hell if I know. I'm confused as fuck, desperate to bury myself in her and at the same time trying to figure out what this feeling in the pit of my stomach is.

It's always been pleasure to bury the pain. The sex to quiet my head, override the shame coating my soul, so why the hell is my head screaming right now?

She reaches out to me, her fingers scraping against my abdomen, and fuck if my body doesn't jolt at the connection. I cuffed her hands because I'm used to being in control, used to setting the pace, so why the fuck am I not stopping her. Why do her fingers feel like she's lighting my skin on fire? Like she's burning me with her touch.

I close my eyes, her hands on my back, and my breath labored with the desire that's so strong I feel like I'm ready to snap. To take without asking.

And then her lips touch mine. Soft and sweet. That fucking perfect contradiction against her hands pulling my body into hers. Her tongue teases by tracing my bottom lip and thoughts of how it can trace the line of my cock have me reaching up to touch her face.

I make my hands go there so I can control the need to rip zippers and feast on her flesh, take the usual route when she is anything but my usual, when the situation is so far from my norm that I'm flying solo without a pit crew for back-up. So instead I force myself to part her lips with my tongue, challenge myself to see how long I can last with this tender and soft when all I really want to do is be rough and sate my greed.

I push my limits. Control the desperation. Even when her fingers dig in my shoulders and urge me on, I rein it in. Every time she moves, my dick rubs against her lower belly and I kiss her a little deeper to lose myself for just a moment. To encourage my resistance.

And then she sighs.

Sweet Christ. How can such a simple sound make a man want to lose his fucking control when he's already held out against every other form of her unbeknownst seduction? But that sigh ... fuck, the sound owns me in ways I never thought possible.

I can't take the assault on my senses anymore. I just fucking can't. I press my hands on the wall on either side of her head, my last attempt at restraint. And I'm such a dumbass that I think if my hands are not on her, I can control my urge to take her as I see fit. Take her in ways I don't think by the innocence in her eyes she's experienced yet.

Because shit, she's a soft and slow, make love not just fuck kind of girl and I'm the exact opposite. Physical overriding emotional every day because I can't do emotional. And she deserves so much better than me. I might be a selfish prick but I know this much.

The problem is she's so goddamn addictive that even though I've occupied my hands, I allow myself one small hit. I rest my forehead against the curve of her neck, nose buried. My chest heaves for air. The scent of her perfume and shampoo make my balls tighten and use up my last ounce of control.

"Sweet Jesus, Rylee." I lace kisses along her shoulder while my body aches painfully to have her wrapped around me. "We need to get out of here before you unman me in the hallway."

I raise my head and look into her eyes. Last chance, Ryles. Escape while you can. But she stands her ground, unwavering, accepting of the warning in my eyes and the dominance in my stance.

"Come." God help me because when all is said and done, I think I'm going to need it to walk away from her. She bites her bottom lip to stop it from quivering. Even she knows I'm inviting her into the lion's den.

I give her a soft smile, pretending I can't see the vulnerability in her eyes, ignoring it as I draw her further in … and that makes me even worse of a man than I already thought.

We walk, desire leading us and desperation owning our thoughts. I think I mumble an explanation that I have a room, but I'm not sure because my thoughts are consumed by every single thing about her. Fucking consumed when I've never been this way before.

I usher her into the elevator, unlock the penthouse all the while my dick is begging me to push the red button, halt the elevator right here, right now and take her on the floor. Feed the greed and be done with her.

Return to familiar ground and be the asshole I know that I am.

I reach out to touch her back, begin the process, but I can't bring myself to do it. I can't treat her like she's inconsequential and prove her right. I mutter something about her hair, asking why she's changed the curls I've thought about holding in one hand so I can watch while my cock fucks her mouth. She responds about not fitting a mold but shit my mind is back onto the image of her bobbing her head up and down with hollowed out cheeks and I can't focus.

"Sometimes change is good." She's staring at me when I break from my thoughts.

I mumble a response about liking her curls, sounding so innocent but really being anything but because my mind is thinking about how fucking bad I want her right now. And then her comment breaks into my thoughts … *sometimes change is good.*

Is that what this is? A change from my typical so it's got my dick in a twist?

Gotta be.

The warnings flood my head again. I need to tell her I'm in uncharted territory, that I'm not sure what the hell is going on, but the one thing I do know for certain is that she deserves a chance to leave before I can't turn back.

"You have one chance to walk away." The elevator dings, shattering my concentration that's scattered as it is. I stare at her, need to see her eyes and hear her tell me she wants this without hesitation. "I won't be able to walk away, Rylee."

And that's exactly what I need to do to ease the unsettling I already feel deep down in the parts of me I buried so very long ago. In the dark recesses where the promises I made to myself feel like they are beginning to unseat themselves.

Am I doing the right thing here when I know that fucking her just might hurt … both her and me?

Fuck. That's exactly what all this is. I turn from her, needing a minute myself to decide whether the discorded peace in my soul is worth disturbing.

Snap out of it, Donavan. Quit being such a pussy. You have a woman willing right now. The same one you've passed up Raquel and her blow job skills for twice. You obviously want this. So fucking take it. You know how to walk when the sex turns to emotion so get your shoes and put them by the door for an easy escape.

But fucking hell take what she's offering. Man the fuck up. Tell her how it's going to be and then do it. Give her the option to only say yes because sweet fucking Jesus, if her kiss is that goddamn sweet imagine what the fuck her pussy tastes like.

Problem solved. Everything back on its mental shelf.

I stab the button with my finger for the elevator door and then hang my head as I figure out how to say it all. "I want to take my time with you, Rylee. I want to build you up nice and slow and sweet like you need. Push you to crash over that edge. And then I want to fuck you the way I need to. Fast and hard until you're screaming my name. The way I've wanted to since you fell out of that storage closet and into my life. Once we leave this elevator, I don't think I'll have enough control to stop … to pull away from you, Rylee. I. Can't. Resist. You."

My confession is cathartic. Allows me to fuck her without the guilt because I'm giving her a choice. More steady in my shoes that I momentarily stepped out of, I finally turn back to face her. I need to see her eyes when I give her the only choice I'm going to until after we've come and are panting out of breath and spent.

"Decide, Rylee. *Yes. Or. No.*"

Chapter Twelve

I look up at him through my lashes, my bottom lip between my teeth, and nod in consent. When he continues to look at me, I find my voice and try to push the nerves out of it. "Yes, Colton."

His mouth crushes down on mine instantly, his hunger palpable as he pulls me out of the elevator toward the penthouse. I giggle freely as he tries to insert the key in the door while trying to keep his lips on mine. He finally gets the key in and the door opens as we continue our ungraceful entrance, mouths never leaving each other's. He kicks the door shut and presses me up against it, his hands sandwiched between the door and my butt. His fingers grip my flesh fervently, pressing me into his muscular frame.

I lose myself in him. In his touch, his heat, his quiet words of praise as he rains kisses over my lips and neck and the bare skin in the deep V of my dress. I turn myself over to the moment and experience what it is to feel again. To want again.

I clumsily try to unbutton his shirt, needing to feel his skin against mine but am hindered by his constantly moving arms that are running fervently over every inch of bare skin that his fingers can touch. His lips find my spot just under my jaw line, and I forget the buttons and fist my hands in his shirt as sensation overwhelms me. Consumes me. A strangled cry escapes my mouth, little explosions detonating from my neck down into the pit of my belly.

Colton presses his hands to my backside again, and I wrap my legs around his hips at the same time he lifts me up. One hand supports my back while the other dips beneath the fabric of my dress to palm my breast. I bow into him as his thumb and forefinger rub my pebbled nipple. The electric shock of his touch spreads heat to my sex and wildfire to my senses.

Colton starts to move while holding me, his lips feasting on the ever-sensitive line of my shoulder, his erection pressing between my thighs. With every step he takes, he rubs against me, creating a glorious friction against my clit. I press into him, a ball of tension building, surmounting, and edging toward my need for release.

We enter the bedroom of the suite, and despite the overabundance of sensations surging through me, I'm still nervous. He stops at the edge of the bed, and I lower my legs, dropping my feet to the floor. I resume my attempt to free him of his shirt, and this time I'm successful. He lets go of me, momentarily stepping back as he slips his arms out and lets the shirt fall to the floor.

I get my first glimpse of Colton's naked torso, and he is *utterly magnificent*. His golden skin covers the well-defined muscles of his abdomen. His strong shoulders taper down to a narrowed waist, which give way to that sexy V that sinks below where his slacks hang. On his left flank is a tattoo of some sort, but I am unable to make out what it is. He has a slight sprinkling of hair on his chest and then below his belly button, amidst tightened abs, he has a sexy little trail of hair that disappears beneath his waistband. If my hormones weren't raging already, the sight of him alone would have sent my system into overdrive.

I drag my gaze back up his torso and meet his eyes. He looks back at me, eyes drugged with desire, enflamed with lust. A sexy grin spreads across his mouth as he pushes off his shoes and removes his socks before approaching me again. He raises his hands to my face and frames it, his mouth on mine in a slow, tormenting kiss that has me pressing into him. His hands slide from my face, down my shoulders, and make the slow descent down my torso until fabric gives way to the bare skin of my thighs.

"God, Rylee, I want to feel your skin on mine." His fingers play with the hem of my dress momentarily before grabbing it and slowly lifting. "Feel your body beneath me." His words are hypnotic. Inviting. "My cock buried in you," he murmurs against my lips before he leans back a fraction, his eyes never leaving mine, to pull the dress over my head.

I start to take my high heels off, but Colton reaches down to grab my hand before I can reach my shoe. "Uh-uh," he tells me, smiling lasciviously. "Leave them on."

I suck in my breath, insecurities rearing their ugly head as I stand before him in a bra, a scrap of lace as an excuse for panties, and my stilettos. "I think—"

"Sh-sh-sh," he whispers against my lips. "Don't think, Rylee. The time for thinking is over." He steps us backwards, the back of my knees hitting the bed, and he slowly lays me down, his mouth still lacing me with kisses. "Just feel," his husky voice demands of me. One of his hands cups the back of my neck while the other roams slowly down to the black lace of my bra and over my rib cage before starting the path back up again. A moan escapes my lips. I need his touch like I need my next breath.

"Let me look at you," he whispers, leaning back on his elbow. "God, you are beautiful."

I freeze at the words, wanting to hide the scars that mar my abdomen, wanting to twist away so that I'm not asked, not reminded. I do none of that though. Instead, I remind myself to breathe as his eyes wander down my body. I know the moment he sees them; shock flickers across his face before his eyes flash back to mine, concern etched in his brow.

"Rylee? What—"

"Not now," I tell him before I reach out and grab his neck, yanking him to me in a demanding kiss that obliterates all sense of control. Quiets all questions before they can be asked. A carnal passion ignites within me as I take hold of him—kissing, caressing, digging fingernails into his steeled skin. A feral growl comes from deep within him as his tongue skims a trail down my neck. He palms my breast, slipping the finger beneath the lace and pushing the cup below it. His mouth teases on its descent down before closing over the tight bud of my nipple.

I cry out in ecstasy as he laves my breast, sucking it into his hot, greedy mouth. His hand assaults my other breast, rolling my nipple between his thumb and forefinger—blurring the fine line between pleasure and pain. His acute attention to my sensitive buds mainlines a fire to my sex. It clenches, throbs, and moistens, silently begging him for more to push me over the edge. I shift beneath him to try and ease the intense ache that is building, but the coils of craving are so strong my breath pants out erratically.

I tangle my fingers in his hair as he moves from my chest, sucking, kissing, and nipping his way down my abdomen. I fist my hands in it and grate in a sharp breath as he deliberately lays a row of kisses along my worst scar. "So beautiful," he repeats to me again as he continues his tormenting descent. He stills at the top of my panties, and I can feel the smile form on his lips from his mouth pressed against my skin.

He looks up at me, a mischievous grin lighting his face. "I hope you're not overly fond of these." I don't even have a chance to respond before he rips the panties off of me. A low satisfied purr comes from the back of his throat as he trails a finger down the small strip of curls beneath the material. "I like this," he growls at me, his finger tracing below the strip where I'm void of hair, "and I like this even more."

My breath catches as he slips a finger between my folds, sliding it slowly back and forth. "Oh God," I groan as I grip my hands into the sheets of the bed, ecstasy detonating in sparks of white hot flashes behind my closed eyelids.

Colton sucks in an audible breath as he slips a finger tantalizingly slowly into my passage. "Rylee," he groans, the break in his voice as he says my name betrays his front of control. "Look how wet you are for me, baby. Feel how tight you grip me." I arch my back, shoulders pressing into the mattress as his finger leisurely circles inside of me, grazing over that sweet spot deep along my front wall before deliberately withdrawing, only to start the whole exquisite process again.

"The things I want to do to this tight little pussy of yours," he murmurs as I feel his other hand part me again. His blunt words turn me on. Incite feelings I didn't expect. I writhe beneath him as the cool air of the room hits my swollen folds. "Look at me, Rylee. Open your eyes so I can see you when my mouth takes you."

It takes everything I can to snap out of my pleasure induced coma and open my eyes. He looks up at me through hooded lids from between my thighs. "That's it, baby," he croons as his head drifts down until I feel the warm heat of his mouth as it captures my nerve laden nub at the same time he slips two fingers in me.

I cry out, throwing my head back as a raging inferno blasts through my center—taking, possessing, building. "Look at me!" he growls again. I open my eyes, the eroticism of watching him watch me as he pleasures me is more than I've ever known.

His tongue laves lazily back and forth, over and around as his fingers continue their delicious internal massage. He withdraws and then pushes back in, his fingers leisurely rubbing my walls within. I buck my hips up against him, begging for more pressure as I tinker on the edge of losing my sanity.

"Oh, Rylee, you are so responsive," he praises. "So fucking sexy." As he replaces the warmth of his mouth with the pad of his thumb, the tempo and friction of skin on skin is exactly what I need. He slides up my body as his fingers continue their mind-blowing torture on my sex, his lips kissing, nipping, and licking until he reaches my face. Making me want like I've never wanted before.

"Let go, Rylee," he demands with his erection pressing deliciously into my side. "Feel again, sweetheart," he murmurs as my hands wrap around his shoulders, fingernails scoring his sweat-ridden skin. The ball of tension mounts, begging for release. I buck my hips wildly against him, his fingers increasing their tempo, rubbing, penetrating, driving me into a rapturous oblivion.

"Come for me, Rylee," he growls as I reach the edge and scream out in release as my orgasm explodes within me, crashes around me, and ripples through every nerve and sinew in my body. My muscles flex reactively, clamping down on his fingers, causing him to groan at the sensation. "That's it baby, that's it," he croons as he helps me ride out the rippling waves of my climax.

I feel the bed dip as he leaves it, causing my eyes to fly open. He looks down at me, satisfaction on his face and desire in his eyes, as he slowly unbuckles his pants. "You are breathtaking," he praises as I watch him, struggling to catch my panting breath. "I can't figure out which is hotter, Rylee, watching you come or making you come." His eyes sparkle with his libidinous thoughts. "I guess I'll have to do it again to figure it out." He flashes a wicked grin at me, full of challenge. My muscles coil tightly at his words, and I'm startled that he has me so worked up that my body's churning to come again. I bite my lip as he pulls his pants down with his boxer briefs, his impressive erection springing free.

Holy shit!

He smirks at me as if he can read my thoughts and crawls on the bed with his lean, firm thighs. He grabs one of my splayed feet by the heel of my shoe and laces a row of kisses up my calf, stopping at my knee to caress his fingers at the sensitive underside before continuing the dizzying ascent of his mouth up my thigh. He stops at my apex and kisses me lightly there, swirling his finger gently over my sex, tickling, taunting, testing.

I grip my hand in his hair. "Colton," I pant out, his slight touch on my sensitized flesh almost more that I can bear.

He looks up at me as he plants another kiss on my strip of hair. "I just want to make sure that you're ready, baby," he replies, pulling a wet finger from my core. "I don't want to hurt you."

A dozen things flit through my mind as I watch him slip his finger into his mouth before flashing a devilish grin and humming in approval. He predatorily crawls the rest of the way up my body, his eyes never leaving mine, and covers my mouth with his, his hand palming my trussed up breasts, his cock pressing into the V of my thighs.

Emotions swirl within me as the dizzying pleasure surges again. He parts my legs with his knees and pushes himself up off of me to sit back between my thighs. He leans over toward the edge of the bed and produces a foil packet. My mind buzzes. I've been so overcome with everything in the past week that I haven't even thought about protection. And despite him not knowing about my inability to get pregnant, I am glad he has enough common sense to think of this.

I prop myself up on my elbows as he tears the packet open and watch as he rolls the condom down his iron length. His eyes flash up to mine, desire, lust, and so much more swarming within them. "Tell me what you want, Rylee."

I stare at him until my eyes are drawn down to watch as he runs his fingers over my delta and gradually parts me. I suck in a breath in anticipation. "Tell me, Rylee," he growls, "Tell me you want me to fuck you. I want to hear the words."

I bite my bottom lip, watching as he lays his length against my cleft. He stills, and I look up to meet his eyes. I can see him trying to rein in his control, the vein in his neck prominent as he stares at me, waiting for my words.

"Fuck me, Colton," I whisper as he slowly presses the blunt tip of his cock into my entrance. I tense at the thought of accepting him, at the sensation of him stretching my channel to its limits, at the slight pain from it telling me that I'm alive, that I'm here in this moment with this sublime man.

"Oh God, Rylee," he moans as he pulses slowly in and out. "You feel so good. So damn tight," he hisses, rubbing his fingertips softly up and down my inner thighs. "I need you to relax for me, baby. Let me in, sweetheart."

I close my eyes momentarily as the stretching burn fades to a full feeling. He pushes further, slowly, deliberately, until his cock is sheathed completely root to tip by my velvet walls. He stays motionless, allowing my body to adjust to him as he watches me. I can see his jaw clench as he tries hard to hold onto his control, and it's an invigorating feeling to know that I can push him over the edge.

I clench my muscles around him, gripping him reflexively as I push my torso up to allow me to see where our bodies are now joined as one.

"Sweet Jesus, Rylee," he warns, "you do that again, I'm gonna come right now."

I smile wantonly at him as he slowly starts to move. He pulls out all the way to the tip and then slowly slides his luscious length back in me. The feeling is exquisite and I fall back on the bed, allowing the sensation of my slick walls being penetrated to take over. I wrap my thighs around his hips as he starts to pick up the pace. His muscles ripple beneath his tanned skin as he moves with me. His eyes flick back and forth between mine and watching our union.

I can feel the warmth starting to spread through me again as my body arches into the friction of his length rubbing my patch of nerves inside. My walls bear down on him, tightening and milking his cock as his rhythm quickens.

He leans over me, balancing his weight on his forearms beside my head, and takes my mouth with his in a carnal, no-holds-barred kiss. Teeth nip, lips suck, tongues meld. I hook my arms under his shoulders and tighten my legs around his hips, locking my feet at the ankles. I need to get as close as I can to him. Need him to be as deep as he can be in me. Need to feel his sweat-slicked skin rubbing on mine.

The pressure in me mounts to the point where I can't kiss him anymore because all of my focus is on the insurmountable wave that's about to crash down all around me. He senses my tension, my nearing oblivion, and continues his punishing pace. He reaches a hand down and slides it under my ass, pressing my pelvis further into his, grinding his against mine, causing that slight friction I need on my clit. Before I know it, my world ignites.

I arch off the bed, bucking my hips uncontrollably as the strongest orgasm I've ever had spears through my center. I'm thrown off the cliff and hurled into a never-ending freefall. The pleasure is so strong, bordering on painful, that I sink my teeth into his shoulder trying to stifle it somehow. The wave crashes around me as Colton bucks into me a few more times before I hear him cry my name out. He tenses, his cock pulsing jaggedly within me as he finds his own release. His muscles jerk in torment as he lets his climax tear through him before slowly relaxing. He then buries his head in the curve of my neck, his breathing harsh like mine, his heart pounding against my own.

My orgasm continues to tremble through me, my muscles pulsing around his semi-hard cock still within me. With each tremor, I can feel his body tense from his sensitivity and hear the soft guttural moan from deep within his throat. His weight on me is comforting, reassuring, and I forget what a soothing feeling it can be.

Sex has never been like this for me. This earth shattering. This hedonistic. This unbelievable.

We lie like this for a moment, both silently coming down from our high. He nuzzles my neck, laying a kiss over and over in the same spot, his sated body unable to move. I close my eyes, unable to believe that I'm here. That this gorgeous man is here with me.

I run my fingernails lazily up and down his back, breathing in his earthy male scent. I wince as he grunts and slowly withdraws from me, the empty feeling unwelcome. He ties the condom in a knot and tosses it onto the floor beside the bed before shifting back next to me. He lies on his side and props his head on his hand to watch me while leisurely running a single finger up and down my chest, causing a slow, measured breath to exhale from my lips.

I glance over at him, our eyes holding for a second as we silently reflect on each other and the experience we just shared. I can't decipher the look in his eyes. He's too guarded. I shift my gaze to the ceiling as panic starts to take hold. What now? Colton's had his way with me and now the challenge is over. Crap. I've only ever had sex with Max. We were in a relationship. We made love. It wasn't a casual thing. And although what just happened might have meant a whole lot more to me than it did to Colton, what am I supposed to do now? With Max I didn't have to think about having to leave after. Or the etiquette of if I stay? Does Colton want me to stay? What the hell am I supposed to do? Is this what a one-night stand feels like? *Shit.*

"Stop thinking, Ryles," Colton murmurs. I can sense his eyes trained on me. I still quickly, surprised that he can be so in tune with me despite only knowing me for a short time. How does he know?

"Your whole body tenses up when you're overthinking," he explains, answering my silent question. "Turn that mind of yours off," he warns, reaching out to my hip, pulling me toward and up against him, "or I'll be forced to make you."

I can hear the smile in his voice and I laugh. "Oh, really?"

"I can be very persuasive," he taunts, running his free hand down my rib cage, stopping to idly palm my breast and run his thumb over my peaked nipple. "Don't you think?"

"Didn't you just tell me I'm *not allowed to think?*" I sigh a soft moan, raising my chin as he leans into me to plant kisses in various places.

"I love a woman who obeys," he murmurs softly. I can feel him start to harden against me, and before I can process his ability to recover swiftly, Colton has rolled us over, switching our positions, with me sitting atop his hips.

I sit astride him and stare down at him and his cocky grin. He returns my gaze, trailing his eyes up and down my torso. I can feel his length continuing to thicken against the cleft in my rear end. "My God, Rylee, you are enough to make a man go crazy," he tells me, leaning up and reaching around me to unclasp my bra. My breasts come free, heavy and weighted from desire. Colton groans in appreciation before he lifts himself up to suckle one, my thighs clenching viciously around him in response.

I lift my head up and arch my back so that he has full advantage of my chest. The thoughts I'd had moments before are now pushed away as he continues his barrage of incendiary kisses. I feel his arms wrap around me and fumble near my bottom before I hear the telltale rip of foil. He finishes jacketing himself as he trails kisses with his skillful mouth back up to my lips. He slants his mouth, taking tiny, delirious sips from mine as he brings one hand to my hair and fists it. He whispers gentle praise in between each kiss, each one stoking my craving for him.

"Lift up for me," he whispers as he brings one hand to my hip, helping raise me, while the other positions his turgid cock beneath me.

I bite my lip in anticipation as his eyes hold onto mine, watching as I gently sink down onto the tip of him. I stay suspended momentarily as I let my fluids coat him so it's easier for him to gain entry. It is empowering to watch the desire cloud Colton's eyes while I slowly lower myself inch by delirious inch onto him until he's sheathed entirely. I moan softly as he stretches me to the most incredible feeling of fullness. I'm forced to sit still for several moments so that I can adjust to the entirety of him. Colton closes his eyes, lifting his head back, lips slightly parted as a low rumble comes from deep in his throat.

He brings his hands to my hips, and I start to rock myself on him. I raise myself up to his very tip and then slide back down, leaning back so he rubs the patch of nerves within my walls.

"*Fuck*," he hisses. "You are going to make me lose my mind, Rylee," he moans loudly as he kisses me possessively before lying back on the bed. He starts to piston his hips up in unison with my movements and soon we are moving at a frantic pace. Each needing more from each other. Each driving, pushing, tantalizing each other to the precipice.

I look down at Colton, the tendons in his neck strained, the tip of his tongue peeking through his teeth, eyes darkened by lust—he is sexy as hell. His hands grip my hips, muscles tensing as he holds me, lifts me, and drives into me. I am climbing, spinning dizzily as pleasure washes over me. I grip one of Colton's hands on my hip, our fingers entwining, holding on. He moves his other hand to where we are joined, his thumb stroking my clit, manipulating it expertly.

My body quickens, my muscles clench around Colton, and once again I'm thrown into a staggering oblivion. I cry out his name as a rapturous warmth overtakes me, envelopes me, and pulls me under its all-consuming haze.

"Christ, Rylee," Colton swears, sitting himself up without stopping his voracious tempo, taking control to allow me to lose myself in my orgasm. He wraps his arms around me, strong biceps holding me tight, and brings his lips to mine in a devouring, soul-emptying kiss. The onslaught of sensations pulling at me from every nerve in my body are so overwhelming that all I can comprehend is that I'm drowning in Colton Donavan.

I can feel his body tense, his hips thrust harder, and his arms squeeze tighter with hands splayed wide on my back. Colton buries his face in my neck before yelling out my name, a benediction on his lips, as he crashes over the edge. I feel him convulse wildly as he finds his release.

We stay like this, me sitting astride him, arms wrapped around each other, heads buried into one another for some time, neither of us speaking. I am overcome with emotion as we hold each other.

Oh, shit! How stupid was I to think that I could actually do casual sex? Feelings bubble up inside me. Feelings that I know Colton will never reciprocate, and I find myself struggling to maintain composure. I tell myself to hold it together, that I can wallow and break down once I'm alone.

Colton shifts his legs and leans back. He takes my head in his hands and transfixes me with his intoxicating stare. "You okay?" he whispers to me.

I nod my head, trying to clear the worry from my eyes.

He leans in and kisses me. A kiss so gentle and affectionate that I have to fight back tears because his tenderness disarms me and strips me to the core. When he opens his eyes, he stares at me for some time. I see something flash through them quickly, but can't decipher.

He shakes his head quickly and lifts me off of him before scooting off the bed without a word. He stands hastily, averting my questioning look and runs his hand through his hair, muttering "fuck." I watch his toned, broad shoulders and very appealing ass as he walks to the bathroom. I hear the water run and another muffled swear.

I pull the sheet around me, suddenly feeling alone and uncomfortable. After a few moments, Colton reappears from the bathroom with a pair of black boxer briefs on. He stands in the doorway and looks at me. Gone is all of the warmth and emotion that was in his eyes minutes before. It's been replaced by a cold, aloof appraisal as he looks at me in his bed. He is no longer relaxed. The tension around his eyes and the strain of his jaw is obvious.

"Can I get you anything?" he asks, his voice a curt rasp. "I need a drink."

I shake my head no, afraid that if I speak, the hurt I feel from his sudden detachment will only make matters worse. He turns and walks out to the main room of the suite. I guess I have my answer. I was just a challenge to him.

Challenge conquered, now I'm disposable.

I hold the heel of my hand to my breastbone, trying to stifle the pain inside. Trying to lessen the feeling of being used. I think of Max and the way he used to treat me after we made love as if I was so fragile I'd break. He would caress me and hold me and make me laugh. Make me feel cherished. *My beautiful, idealized Max.* What have I done to him and to our memory by sleeping with someone when I'm technically engaged?

His mother's yells echo in my ears as she tells me it's all my fault his life is over—that I killed him and every hope and dream that went with him. Guilt and shame and humiliation wash over me. I have to get out of here. These thoughts fill my head as I throw the covers off of me and gather all of my discarded clothes before scurrying to the bathroom.

The pressure in my chest is unbearable from trying to hold back my tears as I fumble clumsily to get my bra clasped. I throw my dress over my head, struggling to get my arms in the straps. I don't have any underwear. They're ripped apart somewhere on the floor and aren't worth the hassle of finding. I'm missing an earring, and I don't care. I quickly tug its matching counterpart out as I glance in the mirror, noticing misery mingled with regret heavy in my eyes. I take a tissue and wipe away the smudged eyeliner as I steel myself for my departure. After a few moments of masking my emotions and gathering my thoughts, I'm ready.

I open the door to the bathroom and peek out, relieved and saddened that Colton is not sitting there waiting for me. Then again, what did I expect after how he just acted? For him to be sitting on the bed waiting to profess his undying love for me? "Fuck 'em and chuck 'em," I mutter under my breath as I walk out of the bedroom door to the main room of the suite.

Colton is standing in the suite's kitchenette, his hands pressed against the counter, his head hanging down. I stand for a moment and watch him, admire the lines of his body, and wish for so much more than he can give. Colton shifts and takes a long draw on the amber liquid in his glass. He sets it down harshly, the ice clinking loudly before he turns. His step falters as he sees me standing dressed and ready to go.

"What are—"

"Look, Colton," I begin, trying to control the situation before I can be humiliated further. "I'm a smart girl. I get it now." I shrug, trying to prevent my voice from breaking. He looks at me and I can see the cogs in his head turning as he tries to figure out why I appear to be leaving. "Let's face it, you're not a spend the night kind of guy, and I'm not a one-night stand kind of girl."

"Rylee," he objects, but says nothing more as he takes one step toward me until I hold my hand up to halt him. He stares at me, subtly shaking his head, trying to wrap his mind around my words.

"C'mon, that's probably what this is to you—what you're used to." I take a couple steps toward him, proud of myself for my false bravado, "So I'll just save myself the embarrassment of you asking me to leave and do the walk of shame now instead of in the morning."

Colton stares at me, struggling with some unseen emotion, his jaw clenching tightly. He closes his eyes for a beat before looking back at me. "Rylee, please just listen to me. Don't go," he utters. "It's just that …" He pulls a hand up to grip the back of his neck, confusion and uncertainty etching his remarkable face as he is either unable to find his words or finish his lie.

My heart wants to believe him when he tells me not to go, but my head knows differently. My dignity is all I have left, seeing as my wits have been thoroughly destroyed, scattered, and left on the bed. "Look, Colton." I exhale. "We both know you don't mean that. You don't want me to stay. You got a room here tonight hoping you'd get laid. You just probably thought it would be with Raquel. A nice little suite where there would be no drama and no complications—a place you could leave in the morning without a backward glance at who's still asleep in the bed. Well, I walked into it willingly," I admit, stepping up to him, his eyes never leaving mine as I place a hand on his bare chest. "It was great, Ace, but this girl," I say, motioning toward me and then the bedroom, "this isn't me."

He stares at me, his eyes piercing mine with such intensity that I avert my gaze momentarily. "You're right, this isn't you," he grates out, guarded, as I flick my eyes back to his. He lifts his glass and empties the rest of the glass' contents, pools of emerald continuing to watch my eyes from over the rim of the glass.

When he finishes, he runs his tongue over his lips, angling his head as he thinks something through in his head. "Let me get my keys and drive you home."

"Don't bother," I shake my head, shifting my weight as I figure out how to save face as humiliation seeps through me. "I'll take a cab—it'll make this mistake easier on both of us." It takes everything I have to lean up on my toes and brush a casual, chaste kiss on his cheek. I meet his eyes again and try to feign indifference. "Don't worry, Colton, you crossed the finish line and took the checkered flag," I say over my shoulder as I start to walk toward the door, chin held high despite the trembling of my bottom lip. "I'm just throwing the caution out there before I can be black flagged."

I step through the door and into the elevator. When I turn to push the first floor, I notice Colton standing in the doorway of the penthouse. His mouth twists as he watches me with aloof eyes and a hardened expression.

I continue to stare at him as the doors start to close, a single tear falling down my cheek—the only betrayal my body displays of my sadness and humiliation. I am finally alone. I sag against the wall, allowing the emotions to overcome me, yet fighting the tears swimming in my eyes. I still have to find a way home.

The cab ride is quick but painful. My quiet sobs in the backseat do nothing to alleviate the brutal reality of what just happened. When we pull up to the house a little after three in the morning, I'm glad to see that Haddie is home but asleep because I can't handle her questions right now.

I slip into my room and flip on my IPOD speakers to a barely audible volume, scroll for *Unwell*, and push repeat. As I hear Rob Thomas' familiar words, I shed my clothes and step into the shower. I smell of Colton and of sex, and I scrub obsessively to get his scent off of me. It doesn't matter though. No matter what I do, I can still smell him. I can still taste him. I can still feel him. I allow the water to wash away my torrent of tears, hiding my sobs in its rush.

When I'm waterlogged and the tears have subsided, I pick myself up off the shower floor and make my way into my bedroom. I throw on a camisole and a pair of panties before collapsing into the comforting warmth of my bed and succumb to sleep.

Chapter Thirteen

I can smell fuel and dirt and something pungently metallic. It fills my nostrils, seeps into my head before I feel the pain. In that quiet moment before my other senses are assaulted with the destruction around me, I feel at peace. I feel still and whole. For some reason my consciousness knows I'll look back on this and wish I had this moment back. Wish I could remember what it was like *before*.

The pain comes first. Even before my head can clear the fog away enough so that I can open my eyes, the pain comes. There are no words to describe the agony of feeling like you have a million knives entering you and ripping you apart, just to withdraw and start all over again. And again. Endlessly.

In that second between unconscious and conscious, I feel a jagged pain. My eyes fly open, frantic breaths gulp for air. Each breath hurting, burning, laboring. My eyes see the devastation around me, but my brain doesn't register the shattered glass, smoking engine, and crushed metal. My mind doesn't understand why my arm, bent at so many odd angles, won't move to undo my seatbelt. Why it can't release me.

I feel as if everything is in slow motion. I can see dust particles drift silently through the air. I can feel the trickle of blood run ever so slowly down my neck. I can feel the incremental inching of numbness taking over my legs. I can feel the hopelessness seep into my psyche, take hold of my soul, and dig its malicious fingers into my every fiber.

I can hear him. Can hear Max's gurgled breathing, and even in my shock-induced haze I'm mad at myself for not looking for him more quickly. I turn my head to my left and there he sits. His beautiful wavy blonde hair is tinged red, the gaping gash in his head looks odd. I want to ask him what happened but my mouth isn't working. It can't form the words. Panic and fear fills his eyes, and pain creases his tanned, flawless face. A small trickle of blood is coming from his ear and I think this is a bad thing but I'm not sure why. He coughs. It sounds funny, and little specks of red appear on the shattered window in front of us. I see his hand travel across the car, fumbling over every item between him and me as if he needs touch to guide him, until he finds my hand. I can't feel his fingers grip mine.

"Ry," he gasps. "Ry, look at me." I have to concentrate really hard to raise my head and eyes to meet Max's. I feel the warmth of a tear fall on my cheek, the salt of it on my lips, but I don't remember crying. "Ry, I'm not doing too good here." I watch as he unsuccessfully attempts to take a deep breath, but my attention is drawn elsewhere when I think I hear a baby crying. I swivel my head to look—nothing but pine trees. The sudden movement makes me dizzy.

"Rylee! I need you to concentrate. To look at me," he pants in short bursts of breaths. I swing my head back at him. It's Colton. What's he doing here? Why is he covered in blood? Why is he in Max's seat? In Max's clothes? In Max's place?

"Rylee," he begs, "Please help me. Please save me." He sucks in a labored, ragged breath, his fingers relaxing in mine. His voice is barely a whisper. "Rylee, only you can save me. I'm dying. I need you to save me." His head lolls to the side slowly, his mouth parting as the blood at the corner of it thickens, his beautiful emerald eyes expressionless.

I can hear the screaming. It is loud and piercing and heart wrenching. It continues over and over.

"Rylee! Rylee!" I fight off the hands grabbing me. Shaking me. Pulling me away from Colton when he needs me so desperately. "Damn it, Rylee, wake up!"

I hear Haddie's voice. How did she get down this ravine? Has she come to save us?

"Rylee!" I'm jolted back and forth violently. "Rylee, wake up!"

I bolt up in bed, Haddie's arms wrapping around my shoulders. My throat is dry, pained from screaming, and my hair is plastered to my sweat drenched neck. I heave for breath, strangled gasps mingle with Haddie's pants of exertion. My hands are wrapped protectively around my torso, my arms are tired from straining so hard.

Haddie runs her hands down the sides of my cheeks, her face inches from mine. "You okay, Ry? Breathe deep, sweetie. Just breathe," she soothes, her hands running continuously over me, reassuring me, letting me know I'm in the here and now.

I sigh shakily and put my head in my hands for a moment before scrubbing them over my face. Haddie sits down next to me and wraps her arm around me. "Was it the same one?" she asks, referring to the recurring nightmare that stuck with me for well over a year after the accident.

"Yes and no ..." I shake my head. She doesn't ask for more details. Instead she gives me time to push the nightmare back into hiding. "It was all the same except for when I look back after I hear the baby crying. It's Colton, not Max, who dies."

She startles at my comment, her brow furrowing. "You haven't had a nightmare in forever. Are you okay, Ry? You want to talk about it?" she asks, straining her neck to hear the muted music on the speakers I'd forgotten to turn off before falling asleep. Her eyes narrow as she recognizes the song.

"What did he do to you?" she demands, pulling back so that she can sit cross-legged in front of me. Anger burns her eyes.

"I'm just a mess," I confess, shaking my head. "It's just that it's been so long. I feel like I've forgotten what Max's face looks like, and then I see him so clearly in my dream … and then the suffocating panic hits from being trapped in the car. Maybe I'm just overwhelmed by the emotion of everything." I pick at my comforter, avoiding her questioning gaze. "Maybe it's been so long since I have really *felt* anything that tonight just pushed me over the edge … just overwhelmed me with …"

"With what Rylee?" she prompts when I remain silent.

"Guilt." I say the word quietly and let it hang between us. Haddie reaches out and grabs my hand, squeezing it softly to reassure me. "I feel so guilty and hurt and used and so everything," I gush.

"Used? What the hell happened, Rylee? Do I need to go kick the arrogant bastard's ass right now?" she threatens. "Because I'll switch my tune. I mean, I was impressed when he called earlier to make sure that you'd gotten home all right and that—"

"He what?"

"He called at like 3:30 … somewhere around there. I answered the phone. Didn't even know you were home. Anyway I came in here to check and told him you were home and asleep. He asked me to have you call him. That he needed to explain—that you took something the wrong way."

"Hmmph," is all I can say, mulling over her words. *He actually called?*

"What happened, Rylee?" she asks yet again, but this time I know she won't be ignored easily.

I relay the entire evening to her, from the point I left her, until she woke me up screaming. I include my feelings about comparing "the after" to Max and how hurt and rejected I felt. "I guess I feel guilty because of the whole Max thing. I loved Max. I loved him with every fiber of my being. But sex with him—making love with him—came nowhere near what it felt like with Colton. I mean, I hardly even know Colton and he just turned on every switch and pushed every button from physical to emotional that …" I search for words, overwhelmed by everything. "I don't know. I guess I feel like sex should have been like that with the guy I loved so much I was going to marry rather than someone that couldn't care less about me." I shrug. "Someone who just thinks of me as another notch on his bedpost."

"Well, I can't tell you that you're wrong to feel, Rylee. If Colton made you feel *alive* after years of being dead, then I don't see what's wrong with it." She squeezes my hand again, sincerity deepening the blue in her eyes. "Max is never coming back, Rylee. Do you think he'd want you be numb forever?"

"No." I shake my head, wiping away a silent tear. "I know that. Really, I do. But it doesn't make the guilt go away that I'm here and he's not."

"I know, Ry. I know." We sit in silence for a few moments before she continues, "I know I wasn't there, but maybe you misread Colton. I mean some of the things he said to you …"

"How is that possible, Had? He was swearing under his breath like he'd just made the biggest mistake. One minute he was kissing me so tenderly and looking into my eyes and the next minute he was swearing and walking away from me."

"Maybe he got scared."

"What?" I look at her like she's crazy. "Mr. I-Don't-Do-Girlfriends gets scared of what? That he thinks I'll become attached to him after one night of sex?"

"One night of mind-blowing sex!" Haddie corrects, making me giggle and blush at the memory. "Well, you do wear your emotions on your sleeve. It seems you don't do *casual sex* well."

"Oh, like it's a class I can take over at the Y? I mean, I may be easy to read emotionally, but I'm not in love with him or anything," I defend myself whole-heartedly, despite knowing full well that what I felt between us tonight was more than just full-blown lust. Maybe I did scare him. That final moment between us in the bed, when he held me and stared into my eyes, really got to me. Made me feel hope. Maybe he saw that and had to squelch it before it went any further.

"Of course you're not," Haddie says with a knowing smile, "but that's not what I was talking about. Maybe, just maybe, Mr. I-Don't-Do-Girlfriends … maybe you got to him. Maybe he got scared of what he felt when he was with you?"

"Yeah, right! This isn't a Hollywood romance movie, Haddie. The good girl doesn't get the bad boy to change his ways and fall madly in love with her," I say, sarcasm rich in my voice, as I fall back on my pillow, sighing loudly.

A small part of me relives Colton's words from the night before. *I am his*. I could never be *inconsequential*. He can't control himself around me. That small part knows that maybe Haddie is right. Maybe I scare him on some level. Maybe it's because I am the marrying kind, as I've been told, and he's just not looking for that.

"You're right," Haddie admits. "But that doesn't mean you can't have one hell of a time losing yourself in hours of mindless sex with him." She plops back on the pillow next to me, both of us laughing at the idea. "It could have its merits," she continues. "There's nothing like a good bad boy to make you let go. Remember Dylan?"

"How can I forget?" I reply, remembering the quick fling she had last summer with the gruff and gorgeous Dylan after ending her year-and-a-half-long relationship. "Yum."

"Yum is right!" We both fall silent.

"Maybe Colton is your Dylan. The one to get you over everything that happened with Max."

"Maybe ..." I think. "Oh God," I groan, "What am I supposed to do now?"

"Well, seeing as it's..." she lifts her head to look at my clock "...five in the morning, you should go back to sleep. Maybe give it a day, then call him back. See what he has to say and go from there. Remember our motto. Embrace your inner slut—be reckless with him and try not to think about tomorrow. Just think about the here and now with him."

"Yeah, maybe." We sit in silence for a few moments. Am I just being an overdramatic female reading into things? I don't think so, but deep down I try to justify his actions to myself. I know that I'll do it again if given the chance, and for my sanity I need to rationalize everything to right the world back on its axis. The feelings and sensations he evoked in me were way too intense. Way too *everything*. Maybe it was just the fall from my alcohol buzz that made everything seem so off. Made him seem so detached. I scold myself. I know this isn't the case, but I'm trying desperately to address my inner slut.

I'm way out of my league here. I just hope I can figure out how to play the game without getting burned in the end.

"Do you want me to stay in here tonight?" Haddie asks, breaking the silence. She used to sleep in my bed on the really rough nights to help me get through them nightmare-free.

"Nah. I think I'm okay. Thanks, though. For everything."

She leans over and kisses the top of my head, "What are friends for?" she says as she heads for the door. "Sleep tight, Ry."

"'Night, Had."

She closes the door and I sigh deeply, staring at the ceiling, thoughts running through my mind until sleep pulls me under.

Chapter Fourteen

I'm so exhausted from everything that I'm able to sleep past my usual six-thirty wake up time. It's nine when I get into my exercise gear and head downstairs.

Haddie is sitting at the little table in the kitchen, bare feet with bright pink painted toes propped on the empty chair across from her. She eyes me cautiously from behind her cup of coffee. "Good morning."

"Morning," I mutter, my normal sunny morning self absent. "I'm gonna go for a run," I tell her as I fasten my audio player to my arm.

"I figured," she says, referring to my attire. "Are you grumpy just because you want to be ... or because you are forcing yourself to run after too much alcohol and off-the-charts sex with an Adonis? I'm surprised you can even walk today."

I sneer. "Sounds like someone is a little jealous," I say.

"Damn right I am." She laughs. "I have more cobwebs now than you do." I laugh, my grumpiness subsiding. "Seriously, though ... you okay?"

"Yeah." I sigh. "I'm going to take your advice. Try and live in the moment ... all that stuff." I shrug.

She nods slowly. "Don't try to sound so convincing!" she says as she stands up, knowing I need to work through things myself. "I'm here if you need me. Have a good run."

"Thanks."

The fresh air, pavement beneath my feet, blaring music in my ears, and moving muscles feel masochistically cathartic as I enter my fifth and final mile. I needed this. Needed to get out, clear my mind, and give myself time to think. My muscles, sore from last night's dancing and great sex, are limber and moving on autopilot. As much as I think I should go for an extra mile, my stupidity in overlooking breakfast before my run has my body telling me that I won't last much longer. Pitbull blasts in my ears, the song's constant beat drives my feet and spins my head back to thoughts of last night.

Oh, Colton. My head is still trying to wrap itself around what happened. He's the chance I have been looking for. To be carefree. To live in the moment. To be alive, not just living. I resolve that I can have sex with Colton with emotion. The emotions just have to be fueled by excitement and anticipation and lust rather than love and devotion and the hope of "more." I need to keep being the sassy, smart-mouthed woman I've been all along because the minute he thinks I want more, he'll be out the door. And it—him, me, us—will be over.

I ponder this my last quarter of a mile, recalling how he made me feel physically last night. I guess there's something to be said for lots of experience as I can attest that the man is skilled in the many facets of sexual dexterity. I blush, steeling my resolve that I can be with Colton without falling in love with him. *I hope.* That I'm going to enjoy every second of it because I know he's not the *staying kind*.

Teagan and Sara's *Closer* fills my ears as I turn the corner onto my street, my footsteps faltering when I see a white Range Rover parked in my driveway. The rhythm has been knocked clear out of my stride at the shock of seeing him here. Colton is leaning up against the front fender of the car, his dark figure haloed by its white. A navy blue shirt fits snugly over his torso, hinting at the corded muscles underneath. Muscles I can still feel on my fingertips. A pair of printed board shorts sit low on his hips and his long, lean legs cross casually at the ankles, and he's wearing a pair of flip-flops. Casual suits Colton very well. It lightens the intensity he naturally exudes. His head is bent, concentrating on the phone in his hands, and his unruly hair is spiked with gel to perfection in stylish, messy disarray. The pang of desire that hits my body is so strong, so overwhelming that I almost have to bring a hand to my torso to stifle it. I force myself to remember to breathe as I push my body to start moving again.

To go home. To go to Colton.

Shit. *I'm in serious trouble.* I admire him from afar, looking so unbelievable and attractive, and I realize that everything I thought about on my run—every stipulation, every rationalization, every justification of why it's okay to sleep with him—doesn't matter. Seeing him right here, right now, I know that I'll do anything it takes, whatever the consequences, to be with him again. To repeat how he made me feel last night.

Almost as if on cue, Colton glances up from his phone and locks eyes with me. A slow, smug grin lights up his face as I run my last few steps, turning up my driveway. I slowly pull out my ear buds, laughing to myself that Christina Aguilera's *Your Body* is blasting. I can feel his eyes run up and down the length of my body, taking in my skin-hugging Capri exercise pants and matching razor-back tank top, a V of sweat down the front of my bust.

"Hi," I say breathlessly, my body still huffing from my exertion.

"Hello, Rylee." The rasp of his voice saying my name is an aphrodisiac sending chills down my spine and eliciting a tingling in my belly.

"What are you doing here?" I look at him with confusion, hiding that my insides are privately jumping for joy, shocked that he is here in front of me.

"Well," he says, pushing himself off of the car as I walk in front of him. He exudes a confidence that most people would kill to have. "According to you, I took the checkered flag last night, Rylee..." a provocative smile forms on his lips "...but I seem to have neglected to collect my trophy."

"Trophy?"

He takes my hand, eyes still locked on mine, sparkling with humor, and tugs on it, pulling me forcibly against his chest. "Yes. You."

Oh. Fucking. My. Thoughts run chaotically through my head. How do I respond to that? To him? When all I can think about is the feel of his warm, hard body against mine and the fact that he is here for me *again* after I ran out on him last night? I tell myself to breathe, his mere presence stripping me of the ability to perform the most basic functions. I quickly try to regain my composure, telling myself that I need to keep our interactions on my terms—revert to my sarcastic nature—in order to make sure that I can keep my wits about me.

I hear Haddie's voice in my head telling me to channel my inner slut. To go for it.

I breathe in again before I raise my eyes to meet the challenge in his. His pure male scent, soap mixed with cologne, fills my nose and clouds my head. "Well, Ace, I think you've got your eyes on the wrong prize." I pull my hand from his and put it on his chest, playfully pushing him back, distancing his body from mine. Needing the space to keep a clear head. "If all you're looking for is a trophy, you have your bevy of beauties you can pick from. I'm sure that one of them would be more than willing to be a *trophy* on your arm." I skirt past him toward the front door. I turn back to face him, a smile playing at the corners of my mouth. I shrug as I take a step backwards. "You could probably start by calling Raquel, is it? I'm sure she'll forgive you for last night. I mean, you were..." I turn around and take a step for the door, pretending that I'm searching for a word before shrugging and tossing over my shoulder "*...decent.* She's probably thrilled with *decent.*"

I wish I could see the look on his face for the sharp intake of breath I hear tells me that I made a direct hit. I don't have to wait long to find out because within a breath, Colton grabs my arm and spins me around to him, pressing my body against his.

"*Decent,* huh?" he questions, his eyes boring into mine. I see anger, humor, defiance, all mixed together with desire. His breath flutters over my face, his lips inches from mine—so close that I clench my fists to resist the temptation to kiss him.

It takes all of my composure to keep up my charade of nonchalance. To hide how much he excites me, ignites my insides and shatters my control with just the sound of his voice, the feel of his touch, and the hint of his dominant nature.

I deliberately bite my bottom lip and look up in thought before bringing my eyes back to his. "Hmmm, a smidgen above average, I'd say." Sarcasm drips from each word as I smirk at him, lying through my teeth and then some.

"Maybe I need to show you again. I assure you that *decent* is not an accurate assessment."

He snorts loudly as I push away from him again and provocatively sashay my way up the front walk. "I need to go stretch," I say, sensing his movement behind me. "Are you gonna come?" I ask innocently with a victorious smirk on my face that he can't see.

"If you keep moving your ass like that, I am," he mutters under his breath as he follows me into the house.

I lead him into the family room hoping Haddie is elsewhere and offer him a seat on the couch before I sit on the floor directly in front of him to stretch. I spread my legs out to either side of me as wide as they can go and lower my chest to the ground, hands out in front of me on the floor. With the help of my sports bra and my chest pressing into the floor, my cleavage is pushed up and hedges over the top of my tank. I can see Colton's eyes wander over my body, stopping at my chest and taking in my flexibility. I can hear his hiss of desire, and I see his throat forcefully swallow.

"So, Colton," I say, stretching out over one prone leg, turning my head to look at him. I stifle a smile as I recognize the lust clouding his eyes. "What can I do for you?"

"Christ, Rylee!" He runs a hand haphazardly through his hair, his eyes moving over the cleavage again, before raising up to meet my eyes. He unintentionally wets his bottom lip with his tongue.

"What?" I respond all doe-eyed, as if I have no idea what he's agitated over. I've never played the femme fatale—never had the courage to—but something about Colton allows me to feel daring and bold. It's a very heady feeling to watch him react to me.

"We need to talk about last night." I see his eyes narrow as I switch positions, now lying on my back. I pull my right leg all the way up, pressing it to my chest, my shin inches from my nose. I lift my head up and look through the open V of my legs to encourage him to go on. He clears his throat noisily before continuing, taking a minute to remember his train of thought. "Why you left? Why you ran away? *Again.*"

I switch legs, taking my time to pull my other leg up, and stretch it over my head, making a low moan at how good it feels to elongate my tightened muscles. "Colton—"

"Can you please stop?" he barks out, shifting restlessly on the couch and adjusting the growing bulge that presses against the seam of his shorts. "Christ," he swears again as I roll over into child's pose, my bent rear in his view. "You in those yoga pants all limber and bending in half—you're making me lose my concentration here."

I look over my shoulder from my stretch and coyly bat my eyelashes at him. "Hmmm?" I feign as if I didn't hear him.

Colton sighs in exasperation. "You're gonna make me forget my apologies and take you right here on the floor. Hard and fast, Rylee."

"Oh," is all I can manage for his threat-laced promise sends shock waves through me, my body more than eager for his skilled touch again. My lips part to remind my lungs to breathe. My nipples harden at the thought. I push myself up to a seated position, cross my legs, and adjust my top to try and hide my body's excitement. "Although I'm sure it's me who should be apologizing, Colton."

He ignores my words, his eyes holding mine, various emotions flickering through them. "Why'd you leave, Rylee?"

The command in his tone has me swallowing quickly, my confidence waning. I shrug. "A number of reasons, Colton. I told you, I'm just not *that* kind of girl. I don't do one-night stands."

"Who said it was a one-night stand?"

A bubble of hope sputters inside of me, but I quickly try to stifle it. Not a one-night stand? Then what the hell was it? What the hell is *this?* I try to figure out what he's looking for. What he might think this is between us. I look at his eyes, searching for a clue, but his expression gives nothing away. "What?" Confusion etches my face. "You lost me. I thought commitment wasn't your thing."

"It isn't." He says with a shrug. "I don't believe you." He crosses his arms across his chest, biceps straining against shirtsleeves, and leans back into the couch. He quirks his eyebrows at me and waits for my answer.

"What?" He's lost me.

"Your excuse for running last night. I don't buy it. Why'd you leave, Rylee?"

I guess that's the end of the no-girlfriend discussion. *But what about the not-a-one-night-stand comment?* As for an answer, how do I explain to him how he made me feel last night after he left the bed? Used and ashamed. How do I tell him he hurt me without sounding like I have feelings for him? Feelings mean drama, and he has let me know he doesn't want or tolerate that in his life.

"I just—" I sigh deeply, pulling my hair tie from my ponytail and letting my hair fall down my back, trying to find the right words. I look him in the eyes, figuring honesty is the easiest route. "You made it clear that you were done with me. With us ..." I can feel the heat of my flush spread over my cheeks. Embarrassed that I am going to sound like a needy, whining female. "Cursing adamantly to demonstrate why my presence was no longer needed."

He eyes me cautiously, his eyes blinking rapidly as he contemplates my words. I try to keep my face unexpressive so he can't see the hurt I feel, and yet I see a myriad of emotions fleet across his face as he struggles to gain his footing. "Sweet Jesus, Rylee!" he mutters closing his eyes momentarily, his mouth opening and closing as if he has more to say. Finally he looks back at me. "Do you have any idea ... you made me—" He stops mid-sentence before standing abruptly and walking to the window. I hear him mutter a curse and I blanch at its severity. "I just want to protect you from—" He stops again, and sighs. He puts a hand to the back of his neck and pulls down on it while he rolls his head. He stands there momentarily, looking out at the front yard, both of us silent.

I made him what? Protect me from what? *Finish the sentences,* I plead silently as I watch his tense body framed by the mid-morning light. I just need an ounce of honesty from him. A sign that what happened meant more than just a quick romp. I'd give anything to see his face at this moment. So I can try to read the emotions he's masking from me.

He turns back around and any emotion that was displayed on his face is gone. "I asked you to stay." He says the words as if they're the only apology he's giving for his actions. "That's all I can give you right now, Rylee. All I'm good for." His voice is gruff and laced with what I think is regret. I feel as if he's trying to tell me so much more but I'm not sure what. The words hang between us for a moment, his jaw clenched, eyes intense.

I snort loudly, uncomfortable with the silence, trying not to read too much into his words. "C'mon Colton, we both know you didn't mean it." I rise from the carpet, grabbing my hair and twisting it quickly into a bun.

He takes a couple of steps toward me, his lips twisting as if that action alone will prevent him from saying more. We stand a few feet apart, staring at each other, and each waiting for the other to make the next move. I shrug before looking down and twisting the ring on my right ring finger. I look back up at him, hoping my explanation will stifle any questions he has about having to manage my expectations of a possible future. Baggage equals drama to him, and he's already admitted to me that he hates drama.

"Let's just say I left last night for reasons you don't want to know about." His eyes remain on mine, silently asking for more. I huff loudly. "I've got lots of excess baggage, Ace."

I wait for the deep exhale from him—the impassive expression to glaze over his face reflecting a man distancing himself from complication, but neither happens. Instead, Colton's mouth widens into a cocky smile and his green eyes fill with humor—both of which ease the severity of his countenance.

"Oh, Rylee," he empathizes with a trace of amusement in his voice, "I know all about baggage, sweetheart. I have enough of it to fill up a 747 and then some." Despite his smiling façade, I see the darkness flicker in his eyes momentarily as some unpleasant thought holds his memory.

Holy shit. What can I say to that? How do I respond to him when he's just hinted at a dark, sordid past? What the hell happened to him? I stare at him, eyes wide and my teeth worrying my bottom lip back and forth. Is this why he doesn't do the girlfriend thing? I mean, talk about going from fun, flirty banter to a serious conversation. And why does this seem to be a common occurrence for us?

Because he matters. Because this matters. The words flicker through my head, and I have to push them away, afraid to believe.

He takes a step closer to me, and I lower my eyes momentarily to the visible beat of his pulse at the base of his jaw. My hands want to reach out and touch him. Console him even. To feel the warmth of his skin beneath my palms. I sigh softly before I look back up at him, a suggestive smile turning up the corners of his mouth.

"This could be interesting," he murmurs as he reaches out to play with an errant curl on the side of my face.

His fingers roam to my haphazard bun and tug the self-sustaining knot. My hair tumbles free, falling down my back in a waterfall of curls. He runs a hand through it, stopping at the nape of my neck where my hair is damp with sweat. I cringe at the thought, but he doesn't seem to mind as he fists his hand in it, holding my curls ransom so I can't look away from him.

"How so?" I ask, a charge jolting through me, arousing me, from the possessive nature of his hold. He mesmerizes me—his eyes, the lines of his face, his sensuous mouth, the way his muscles pulse in his jaw when conflicted.

"Well, it seems that your baggage makes you so scared to feel you constantly pull away. Run from me," his voice rasps as he lazily trails a fingertip down my bare shoulder. I struggle to prevent my body from automatically leaning into his addictive touch. But I can't stop myself. He tilts his head to the side, watching my reaction. "Whereas mine? My baggage? It makes me crave the sensory overload of physicality—the stimulating indulgence of skin on skin. Of you beneath me."

And therein lies the problem—when he refers to me, he speaks of feelings and emotions and when he refers to himself he speaks of physical contact. I try to turn my mind off. I try to tell myself that the physical contact is what I want from him too. The only thing that I can have from him. Acknowledge it's the only part he'll share of himself with me.

It's an easy thing to remember because Colton leans forward and brushes his lips tenderly against mine. All conflicting thoughts disappear with his touch. A soft sigh of a kiss that we slowly sink into. I part my lips for him, his tongue slipping inside to stroke gently and meld with mine. Unhurried, lazy strokes of tongue and fingertips as he runs them over my bare shoulders and up the vertebrae on my neck. I could kiss him like this forever in this hazy state of desire. His earthy scent envelopes me, his heady taste consumes me, and his incendiary touch ignites me. He groans with our kiss, the rumble of it caught within me, vibrating through me.

A warm, soothing ache seeps into my chest and spreads throughout the rest of my body. I turn my mind off and allow myself to just feel. To revel in the sensations that he evokes within me. He is my fire on a cold night, the sun warming my skin on a cool spring morning, the wind caressing my face on an autumn day—he is everything that makes me feel alive, and whole, and beautiful.

And desired.

I slide my hands under the hem of his shirt and splay them wide across his lower back. His taut skin heats beneath my touch. I need this connection with him like I need sunlight. For when we touch like this, when I can feel him like this, I have no doubt that I can do this. That I can be what he needs me to be for however long he'll allow it. Because the chance to be with him, to remain under his spell, means I'll push my needs aside and bury them deeply so that I can be who he wants.

Colton cups my face in his hands, the kiss softening, stopping with a brush of lips so gentle that it sends chills up my spine. I sigh softly into him as he wraps his arms around me, strong muscles pulling me into the comfort of his warmth. I rest my head on his chest, smelling clean linen and fresh soap. I can hear his heart beating, strong and steady against my ear. I close my eyes, wanting this moment to last forever.

He rests his chin atop my head. I can hear him inhale a shaky breath before he speaks. "It's unfathomable how much I want you, Rylee." He pulls me tighter into him. "How much I'm drawn to you."

I bask silently in his admission, a small smile on my lips. Maybe I do affect him. I shake the thought from my head, not wanting to overcomplicate, overanalyze, or over think the simplicity and the sweetness of this moment between us.

"Rylee?"

"Hmmm?"

"Go out with me—on a real date." I can feel his body tense against mine, as if it's painful to ask. To admit he wants this from me. "Go out with me, not because I paid for a date with you but because you want to."

Elation soars through me at the thought of getting to see him again. Of spending time with him again.

"Say yes, Ryles," he murmurs with a quiet desperation as he kisses the top of my head. "It's unimaginable how much I want you to say yes."

I lean back, shocked by the vulnerability I hear in his voice and sense in his body language. Why is he afraid I'll say no when everyone else would say yes? I raise my eyes to his, trying to read the emotions flashing through his. I see passion and humor, desire and challenge, promise and fear. Why does this beautifully tormented man want to spend time with ordinary me? I don't have the answer, but I know in this moment, looking at him, I can see so much more in his eyes than I think he wants me to. And what I see, it scares me on so many levels that I have to tuck it away for later when I'm all alone. I can analyze it then. Replay it then.

Hope then.

I raise a hand to run it against the roughness of his slight stubble, liking its coarseness beneath my fingers. The texture tells me that this moment is real. That he is really here with me. I lean up on my tiptoes and place a soft, closed-mouth kiss on his sculpted lips.

"Yes," I breathe, and with my answer, regardless of all of the psychological propaganda I barrage myself with, I know that Colton Donavan has just put the first fissure in the protective wall around my heart.

He nods his head subtly, a shy smile on his face, no words expressed. He pulls me into him one more time. "Tonight?" he asks.

I still, mentally looking over my calendar, knowing that I have no plans but not wanting to seem too eager.

"I'll be here at six to pick you up, Rylee," he decides for me before I have a chance to answer. He releases me and looks me in the eye to make sure that I hear him. All trace of vulnerability is long gone when I meet his eyes. It's been replaced with his trademark confidence.

I bite my bottom lip and nod in agreement, suddenly feeling shy.

He cups my chin, running the pad of his thumb over my bottom lip. "See you then, sweetheart."

"Bye." I exhale, already missing him.

He walks to the front door, opens it, and then turns back to me, "Hey, Ryles?"

"Hmmm-hmmm."

"No more running away from me," he cautions before flashing a quick grin and closing the door behind him. With his departure, I can suddenly breathe again. His presence is so strong, so overpowering, it overwhelms the room. Infiltrates my senses. With him gone, I feel like I can process what just happened. Finally breathe.

I stand facing the door and close my eyes, absorbing everything that has just transpired. Nothing is solved. None of my questions are answered: Why he doesn't do the girlfriend thing? What is this between us since it's not a one-night stand? What was he really going to say when he said I made him, but never finished? What is he trying to protect me from? What kind of baggage fills his 747?

I sigh heavily. So much has been left unanswered, and yet I feel like so much has been expressed without being said. I sit down on the couch, my head reeling from the last week.

"Is he gone?" I hear Haddie's hushed voice from the other side of the wall.

"Yes, nosy girl." I laugh. "Come out here and give me your two cents."

"Holy crap!" she shouts as she hurries around the wall and flops down on the couch next to me. "Hot date tonight!" she sings loudly, raising her arms up in the air. "Whew, I need to take a cold shower after that."

"You watched?" I blush quickly, embarrassed at the thought of having an audience.

"No, no, no, it wasn't like that," she corrects. "I was in the kitchen when you guys came in the house. If I would've left, you'd have seen me and I didn't want to distract from your floor show," she teases, referring to my stretching routine. "I heard only."

I blush at the thought of her listening to our conversation, but find comfort in the notion that she listened. Now I can get an unbiased opinion about our exchange.

"*Ace?* Does he know what that stands for?"

"Nope!" I smirk.

"*Damn, Ry...*" Haddie shakes her head "...the man's got it bad for you."

I falter. Her statement blindsides me. I pick at the cuticle on the side of my nail for a moment, trying not to jump to conclusions. "Nah, it's more like pure, unadulterated lust."

"Not how I see it," Haddie responds, my eyebrows quirk up in question. "Smitten is the word that comes to mind."

"What do you mean?"

"Oh, c'mon, Rylee! Hard and fast?" she sputters.

"That's just sex." I shrug. "Not commitment."

"It's unfathomable how much he wants you?" she tries.

"Sex again," I correct.

"Unimaginable how much he wanted you to say yes to tonight?"

"Because he thinks it will lead to sex," I reply with a smile on my face.

"How about when he said it wasn't a one-night stand?" she tries again, eyes full of humor. Her heart shaped lips form a smile, thinking she's proven me wrong this time.

"Semantics," I answer. "Maybe he wants a thirty-night stand? I mean he only said it wasn't a one-nighter."

"You're incorrigible." She laughs, grabbing my knee and squeezing it lightly. "But hell, at least it'd be thirty days worth of great sex, Rylee!" she gushes, her excitement for me palpable. "You're going out with him again tonight! On a real date!"

"I know." I sigh, shaking my head at the thought of getting to spend more time with Colton. "At least there might be conversation tonight before we have sex," I joke, although a rational part of me knows the truth.

Haddie bursts out laughing. "Oh, Rylee, my sensible friend..." she pats my leg "...this is going to be so much fun to watch you experience."

I quirk my eyebrow at her and shake my head, filled with so much love for her and so much confusion over the situation with Colton. I sigh deeply, leaning my head back on the comfortable couch and angling it to the side so I can look at her. "Did I handle that right, Haddie? I tried so hard to be what he wants and—"

"You are what he wants, Rylee, or he wouldn't have tracked you down to your house." She is exasperated at having to explain this to me. Again. "C'mon, Ry," she says, oblivious to my train of thought. "What you did was brilliant! You walk out on him after sex last night and the next morning he shows up at our doorstep. I mean..." she shakes her head, a knowing smile on her lips "...that's more than just sex, Ry. The man's got it bad for you."

I feel her words take hold, but I'm afraid to believe them. Afraid to hope that there's a chance at anything with Colton. My head tries to shut out the surge from my heart, but it fails miserably. The hopeless romantic in me allows me a moment to daydream. To hope. I close my eyes, sinking in to the glimmer of possibility.

"Shit!" I scrub my hands over my face as panic makes its way through my thoughts.

"What?" Haddie opens her eyes, narrowing them as she looks over at me.

"What if I can't do it?"

"Which part of it are you referring to?" she questions warily. "Because it's a little late, sister, if the it you're referring to is sex."

"*Very funny*." I huff. "I meant what if I can't turn off the emotions. *What if I fall for him, Had?*" I sit up and run my fingers through my hair, and the action makes me think of Colton's fingers there earlier. "I mean he's arrogant and overconfident and he warns me away but tells me he's drawn to me, and he's reckless and he's passionate and sexy as hell and … so, so much more." I press my fingers to my eyes and sit there for a minute, Haddie allowing me the moment to absorb everything. "I know without a doubt that it's a good possibility." I look up at her. "Then what?"

"It seems he's not the only one who's smitten," she says softly before I glare at her. She scoots over next to me and lays her head on my shoulder. "No one can fault you for being afraid, Rylee, but life's about taking chances. About having fun and not always playing it safe. So what if he's a little reckless? The fact that he scares you might be a good thing. Life begins at the end of your comfort zone." She leans back and wriggles her eyebrows. "Have some wild, reckless sex with him. He obviously likes you. Who knows, maybe it will turn into something more. Maybe it won't. But at least you took the chance."

Chapter Fourteen

Colton—Raced

Why the fuck am I here? Seriously, Donavan? Chasing her like a damn chick after last night. After I fucked her and then freaked the hell out and basically pushed her away. Like that doesn't have *douchebag* written all over it.

Walk away, Donavan. Lift the right foot, then the left, and walk around the fucking Rover. Leave the complication alone and ease what-the-fuck-ever is that weird pressure in my chest.

Do it.

Now.

Move your ass.

I look up, conviction in my head but resistance in my soul, and the air punches from my lungs. Lead now weighing down my fucking flip-flopped feet.

My God she's gorgeous. Like knock me to my knees gorgeous. What girl can be sweaty in workout gear, jeans and a T-shirt, or dressed to the hilt like last night and be hot as fuck in all three?

She runs the rest of the way toward me and hell yes I look at the way her tits bounce in her snug little tank thingy. I groan inwardly as I remember the weight of them in my hands. The taste of them on my tongue.

"Hi." She breathes out and although she looks winded I like to think her quickened breath is because of me.

"Hello, Rylee." It's all I can manage to say. Thoughts flicker through my head. How I should apologize. How I should demand to know why she makes me feel like this when I don't even know what *this* is.

"What are you doing here?" Confusion mars her gorgeous face as those eyes of hers search mine for an explanation I can't even give her. One that I know but am not able to put sound to the words because then it would make her … make this too fucking real.

And I don't do real. I do quick. I do easy. I do rules and draw lines that never get crossed.

So why the fuck am I here, then?

I look at her, such a goddamn contradiction in everything she is, and have the urge to tell her the truth but know the truth will push her away. I want to tell her she burned me last night. Fucked me into feeling more than just the physical when I'm so used to being numb. Made me feel raw and vulnerable when I'm always guarded.

And I couldn't handle it. She looked in my eyes so deeply I could see the truths she saw there reflected in her own eyes and it scared the fuck out of me.

Demons best be left untouched or else they destroy. Collateral damage be damned. Been there, done that shit.

She angles her head at me. Her eyes still reflect hurt, but I also see surprise and thank fuck for that because it means I still have a shot. The question is after last night and the goddamn hurricane of emotions that ripped through me during and after we had sex, I'm not quite sure what *the shot* I'm looking for is.

Redemption? Apology? Forgiveness? Another chance?

Pick one, Donavan, because she proved last night she doesn't play the games you're used to so figure out the answer to her question, the one you don't even know the answer to yourself.

"Well, according to you, I took the checkered flag last night, Rylee …" I say as I take a step toward her trying to snap my thoughts in line, make up a reason for being here besides the need to make sure she's okay when I could have just picked up the fucking phone. I resist the urge to reach out and touch her because I know if I do, my dick will rise to the occasion and do the talking for me. And fuck if I know what it will say.

She licks her lips, dick beginning to win the internal thought process, when I suddenly figure out my angle … my in … my stupid-ass excuse for showing up the morning after like some pussy-whipped douchebag. Because Christ, you can't get pussy whipped after just one taste. Shit like that takes time to acquire.

Or so I've heard.

This man might be drawn to the pussy palace but fuck if its queen will hand out orders that I'll obey.

I take another step toward her, still undecided about my excuse for being here when I glance down momentarily and see her nipples harden through her tank. That's always a plus. At least I know she's still attracted to me. Let's see if I can make her like me again. Give me another chance.

Bingo. Truth shall set me free. There's the answer. I just want another chance when I've never wanted one before.

And therein lies the second question, another chance at what though?

I shake the thought, her eyes asking me to finish the question I left hanging. "… but I seem to have neglected to collect my trophy."

"Trophy?"

Hmm. Maybe not such a good idea, now that I think about it. Fix this, Donavan. Fix how you just compared her to something that sits on the shelf and collects dust.

Play, player, play.

"Yes. You." I reach for her hand and pull her into me. Her breath hitches: *check*. Her heart's pounding: *check*.

I've still got my game despite feeling like she knocked it off its field last night. Thank fuck for that.

And then she looks up at me and that damn defiance is back, and I know we're about to go a round. She might be affected but fuck if she's going to back down. Let's see if this gets us where we need to be.

Bring it on, baby.

"Well, Ace, I think you've got your eyes on the wrong prize." She pushes against my chest and steps back, a smirk on her face. "If all you're looking for is a trophy, you have your bevy of beauties you can pick from. I'm sure that one of them would be more than willing to be a *trophy* on your arm." She steps past me and when she turns around, our eyes meet and she holds her ground. "You could probably start by calling Raquel, is it? I'm sure she'll forgive you for last night. I mean, you were … *decent*. She's probably thrilled with *decent*."

Knee-jerk reaction has me grabbing her arm and spinning her around when she goes to walk away again.

Decent? *Decent?* You want to play dirty, huh? I have a whole chest full of toys we can use if you want to go that route, but first things first.

"Decent, huh?" I step in closer to her, wanting so bad to taste the defiance on her lips but refraining. I came here today expecting to find her hurt and all I'm getting is obstinance. I'm confused how the woman who left me last night with tears in her eyes is the same fucking one that stands before me. What has happened in the last ten hours? Shit, I came here to apologize, salvage the chance to have her again so I can figure out what the fuck kind of hold she has over me. Try to see what it is about her that has me coming back for seconds when I prefer my meals to be more varied because shit, if you keep on moving, keep on sampling, no one can get too close.

I'm trying to figure this all out and then she goes and calls my abilities on the carpet when we both know last night was anything but decent. Hell, she blew the doors off the damn bedroom and chiseled away at everything I guard. She wants to pretend I was decent, that she wasn't affected? Go right ahead because I know avoidance when I see it and fuck if she's not using this newfound confidence to cover something up. The question is what?

And that in itself is comical since I'm the king of avoidance.

Interesting.

She stares at me as I try to make sense of this new set of unspoken rules. Her eyes flicker with amusement, her words still hanging in the air between us, still taunting me, still tempting me.

And fuck it. I'm all in. Play me, Ryles, because I'm just getting warmed up. The two of us can pretend we're whole, void of baggage, and see how far that gets us. Objective just went from getting another *chance* at who the fuck knows what to working that sweet spot between her thighs again so she has no option but to admit she's wrong. Admit that her description of decent would be fan-fucking-orgasmic if she were speaking about any other man's skills. And then even though I don't want to care, don't want to fuck with another person's demons, I'm going to figure out what the hell she's hiding.

Decent walks away and doesn't care. Decent gets themselves off without thinking of the other person's needs. Fucking decent, my ass.

She bites her bottom lip deliberately and flutters her lashes like she's innocent. Damn tease. "Hmm, a smidgen above average, I'd say."

I step into her, my mouth close, our chests touching, and just stay there. Taunting her with anticipation until I hear her exhale the breath she's holding. "Maybe I need to show you again. I assure you that *decent* is not an accurate assessment."

She pushes against my chest again because it appears she can't handle the heat. She can talk the talk but she sure as fuck can't walk the walk. Then again, the way she's strutting her ass toward the door right now makes me take the statement back.

Fuck. I know how those curves feel beneath my hands, riding my cock, milking my orgasm. We were so fucking far from decent it's not even funny.

"I need to go stretch. Are you gonna come?"

Sweet Jesus. Seriously? "If you keep moving your ass like that, I am," I mutter under my breath, feet following without a second thought.

I follow her into the house, eyes scanning the interior. Clean, classic, just like I'd expect from her. I sit on the couch wondering where our little charade is going to lead us now. I spot a few possible surfaces that I can more than prove my point on.

But my attention and thoughts are pulled to Ry as she settles on the floor in front of me and proceeds to spread her legs as wide as they go before leaning forward and pressing her chest to the floor. My dick hardens immediately at the sight of her, her impressive flexibility, and the memory of the tight, wet pussy sitting within that V of her thighs.

Shit, she's fighting dirty trying to jog my memory of how she fucks like a sinner and feels like Heaven, as if it wasn't permanently scored into me.

So why am I looking at her eyes and not her tits? Why am I anticipating the next round of verbal sparring when I should be using smooth lines to lure her back so I can prove her wrong?

"So, Colton," she says, breaking through my civil war of thoughts and my absolute focus on her proffered tits and stupendous ass. "What can I do for you?"

Shit, we can start with you on your knees, me on the couch, and your mouth on my cock. The immediate image makes my head spin with need.

"Christ, Rylee!" I bark the words out, trying to stop her stretching, stop my thinking, when I'm the one that's supposed to be taking control of this conversation so I can prove my point in more ways than one. And hell if every ounce of testosterone in my body says "*please don't stop*." Fuck getting the upper hand in the argument because when all is said and done, all that matters is that I get to bury myself in her regardless of how the point is made.

"What?" She bats her eyelashes again. Innocent façade front and center.

"We need to talk about last night." I change the subject. Need to think of rainbows and unicorns and shit to calm my dick the fuck down. Allow me to give my apology for last night. Set one wrong to right before diving right into the next with her because deep down I know we are one of those disasters waiting to happen. Beautiful and devastating all at the same time.

The quick fuck I wanted to ease the ache for her turned out to be so much more than that. It's moved into uncharted territory for me, and no matter which way I look at this, she's added a complication to my simple, fuck-more-care-less lifestyle. She's made me want her more than once, made me pursue when I don't chase, and has me here apologizing when I'm a take-me-as-I-am-or-get-the-hell-out kind of guy.

But fuckin' A, if complicated is flexible like that, I'll take it.

And there she goes again. Making me lose my train of fucking thought as she lies on her back, pulls one leg up, and lifts her head to look at me over the mound of her pussy.

She thinks she can just sit and stretch and she's going to win this little unspoken war we have going? That I'm just going to kowtow because it looks like she can wrap her feet behind her head and makes me think of the positions I can put that body in? That I'd give up the battle of wills here over something that clearly was mind-blowing?

It's time I get some answers myself because if we're both warming up on the same field, then fuck if I'm not ready to go one-on-one with her. I admit that I'm an asshole for treating her like shit last night because I couldn't handle that weird fucking pressure in my chest, but what does that make her? Leave with tears but now flirt with me like she's up for another go?

Goddamn women.

Too compli-fucking-cated is what they are. But if I'm going to test the waters again, I need to get my head wrapped around what's in hers so I can get us back on the sex-without-a-future plan, then I need to know what she's thinking. "Why'd you leave? Why'd you run away? *Again.*"

She switches legs and moans in pleasure, followed by my name. "Colton—"

Just like she fucking did last night.

"Can you please stop?" I can't help it but if she keeps this shit up I'm gonna come in my pants like a goddamn teenager. And there she goes again, rolling over so her ass is in my face. Thoughts of taking her from behind fill my head: hands gripping her hips, dick bottoming out as my pelvis slaps against her ass. "Christ! You in those yoga pants all limber and bending in half—you're making me lose my concentration here."

And something else if you keep it up.

Those violet eyes taunt me as they look over her shoulder. "Hmm?"

Oh, sweetheart, you know exactly what you're doing. And so do I. You can't beat this player at his own game.

"You're gonna make me forget my apologies and take you right here on the floor. Hard and fast, Rylee."

"Oh!" It's all she can say, and I feel a slight thrill of victory for knocking her off stride. But fuck if her lips formed in that little O shape don't have my thoughts drifting back to my couch blowjob fantasy from moments before. "Although I'm sure it's me who should be apologizing, Colton."

And there she goes, fucking up my thoughts of how I don't want to feel anything for her by taking the blame for last night. The selfless saint martyring for the selfish sinner.

I'm starting to get irritated. Don't make me feel. Don't make me think of things outside what I can give you. I'm here trying to be bigger than the man I usually am by making sure she's all right. That's it. Simple and uncomplicated. And she says something like that and knocks me back. Makes me feel like she did last night when I shoved up out of the bed and left her naked body I would have rather lost myself in, long into the early hours of the morning. But no, I can't allow anyone to get close to me and fuck if she's not bringing us right back there with her attempt to apologize.

"Why'd you leave, Rylee?"

The harshness in my tone causes her to stare at me a moment before she answers. "A number of reasons, Colton. I told you, I'm just not *that* kind of girl. I don't do one-night stands."

"Who said it was a one-night stand?" I throw her own excuse for leaving back at her and immediately question myself and the implication I've now left open for interpretation. That's exactly what I need with her to avoid the shit she unknowingly brought to life last night. What the fuck am I doing here besides muddying up the fucking complicated water even more?

"What?" Confusion flickers over her face. "You lost me. I thought commitment wasn't your thing."

I lost me too, sweetheart.

"It isn't." I shrug. Time to turn the subject back to you. Make you explain because fuck if I'm going to delve into my closet of nightmares to explain myself. "I don't believe you."

"*What?*" She's confused. Good, because that makes two of us. Thank fuck, though, I'm the one with the reins now.

"Your excuse for running last night. I don't buy it. Why'd you leave, Rylee?" Give me a real reason. Tell me you got spooked the fuck out too. That it just wasn't me. Tell me you hate me. That you want me. Tell me anything to ease the fucking schizophrenic thoughts owning my head right now because you've turned this man who never needs anything to one who needed to see you. And fuck if I can figure out why.

I need to get this—us—back to where I'm comfortable. A good time with no future.

"I just—" She sighs, fiddling with her ponytail thing, and I can now see her nerves. Can sense her unease. And when she meets my eyes again, she knocks the gas from my tank because they are so full of conflicting emotion. "You made it clear that you were done with me. With us, cursing adamantly to demonstrate why my presence was no longer needed."

No longer needed? That's what she thought? "Sweet Jesus, Rylee!" Why is it with any other woman I'd be ecstatic that she thought that. Would make it easier to have the talk with her that I need to have and lay down the law about the only things I can give her, but hearing the words from Rylee causes a tightness in my chest.

She thought I was done with her. Leave it be, Donavan. Shut your fucking mouth and leave. Apologize for being an ass and walk away.

"Do you have any idea … you made me … I just want to protect you from—" I can't even finish my thought my head's such a mess. *Yeah, the get up and leave idea worked real well there. Fuck me.* I shove up out of the chair and head toward the window, toward an escape.

How do I explain that the way she made me feel caused the demons I'd buried deep down to start to whisper that I don't deserve anything from her? That I saw myself using her—hurting her—like those before her and for the first time ever, I couldn't do it. Knew she didn't deserve it.

Shit just got real—fast. Real when all I want is to go back to our bantering foreplay. I need to get this back on ground I can walk on because right now I'm starting to freak the fuck out.

"I asked you to stay. That's all I can give you right now, Rylee. All I'm good for." I know I sound like an asshole, know that she just said I hurt her and my response was anything but an apology, but at the same time she doesn't have a fucking clue how normally I'd say "my way or the highway" and instead I'm trying to explain a bit of myself when I never have before.

"C'mon, Colton, we both know you didn't mean it. Let's just say I left last night for reasons you don't want to know about," she finally says, eyes lifting to meet mine, and fuck if I can tell what they are trying to say to me that her words aren't. I wonder if these reasons are the cause of her sudden change in demeanor from last night to this morning. "I've got lots of excess baggage, Ace."

A part of me sighs in relief at *the out* she's giving me without another word. The funny thing is that even though my feet itch to walk, I can't bring myself to move because my head has other thoughts.

"Oh, Rylee, I know all about baggage, sweetheart. I have enough of it to fill up a 747 and then some." I say the words without thinking. My immediate instinct is to jump back when I realize the little bit of myself I just gave her. That I'm the pilot of a plane so weighed down with fucking baggage that I might crash at any time. It's not fucking much, but it's a shitload of a confession for me.

I see the shock flicker through her eyes followed by the curiosity. How that comment doesn't scare the hell out of her, I have no clue. She's fearless and I love it. Love that we're standing here in this goddamn minefield of shit and yet she continues to hold my gaze and tempt me, dare me, when the minute the words clear my mouth most would run the other way without so much as a see-ya.

Of course with the exception of those that want something out of being with me. And the way she keeps fighting me, I sure as fuck know she falls into the one percent that doesn't.

"This could be interesting," I say, taking a step toward her, my eyes scraping over her curves and my mind trying to find my footing in this foreign fucking territory. How is it I want to keep this on my terms—keep her at arms' length—and yet at the same time want to figure out why I felt how I felt last night, how I feel right now?

Want my cake and eat her too.

The thought staggers me, fucks with my head, because I don't know how that's going to be possible when all I've thought about since she left the hotel last night was seeing her again. So I do what I came here for, the one thing I know that will settle the war of shit inside of me, quiet my head for just a second, so I can think this through. I reach out to touch her.

I tug her hair out of the bun and fist my hands in the curls as they fall. Her eyes shock open as I pull her head back and parted lips distract my thoughts as I'd hoped.

And just when I'm about to break our stare because she's looking at me again in that way that says she sees more than I intend to give her, she throws out a challenge to my comment.

"How so?" Her voice may be soft, might even reflect a hint of nerves, but she's still asking.

"Well, it seems that your baggage makes you so scared to feel you constantly pull away. Run from me." I trace my finger down her bare arm, the need to touch her consuming me like an addiction. "Whereas mine? My baggage? It makes me crave the sensory overload of physicality—the stimulating indulgence of skin on skin. Of you beneath me."

I mean it as a kind of warning, a simple you're going to fall for me while I just want to fuck you. What a woman wants versus what a man wants. Simple, uncomplicated, right up until she sighs that soft sigh she did last night when I pushed into her for the first time and fuck if I can hold back any longer. I lean in and kiss her, tell myself to slow the fuck down when all I want to do is own her lips.

Her lips, Donavan, not her heart, because I'm trying to keep this on my simple terms.

Because that's *all* I want.

And fuck if I've not kissed a woman like this before—slow and relentless—but something happens with Rylee. Each taste, every sound I coax that hums in her throat begins to seep into parts of me that have been dead for so long. I deepen the kiss. I have no intention of doing this, feeling this way, and I'm sure if my lips weren't drugged by her taste, I'd be pulling away, wanting the end game and not enjoy the fucking journey to get there.

But when she slides her hands up my torso, skin to skin, something happens. It's like the whip of desire snaps and imprints everything about her inside of me.

Fuckin' A was I wrong. Touch her, kiss her to quiet my head? More like set it on fucking fire with thoughts of possibilities I don't want and lust I need to sate. That flutter of panic I had last night flashes through me as I pull back from her lips, needing a minute to settle the shit I don't want to feel but is back with a fucking vengeance.

I pull her into my chest and wrap my arms around her so she can't look into my eyes and see the shit I don't even understand. And I'm trying to process it all, trying to tell myself it's a fucking fluke that it happened again, just the need to fuck her again, that's all. I'm so wrapped up in my thoughts the words are out of my mouth before I can filter them. "It's unfathomable how much I want you, Rylee. How much I'm drawn to you."

An unexpected confession for both her and for me.

"Rylee ..." I'm flustered and I never get flustered. Fuck! I need some time to figure this all out. My reaction to last night, to right now, to how she fits so fucking perfect in my arms. Man, I'm all for turning over a new leaf, trying new shit out, but this is more like shaking the goddamn tree bare.

Breathe, Donavan. Fucking Breathe.

I close my eyes and then she makes a hmm sound as she nuzzles under my neck and I say, "Go out with me—on a real date. Go out with me, not because I paid for a date with you but because you want to. Say yes, Ryles. It's unimaginable how much I want you to say yes."

Where the fuck did that come from, Donavan? I'm freaking the fuck out and want to put it back where I'm comfortable, have a talk to mitigate her expectations of where this can and can't go, but I go and say something like that? How am I ever going be able to fix this now, rein it in before she starts getting too close and I start doing what I do best—shove her away?

She leans back, like she's as shocked as I am from my words, and looks at me. And for some reason I don't break our gaze and let her see just a glimpse of the riot inside of me before I glance away. But she pulls me back to her when she runs a hand against my cheek and then steps on her toes and presses a kiss to my lips.

"Yes," she whispers.

I nod my head at her and pull her back into my chest. "Tonight?"

Rylee, what the fuck are you doing to me?

She falls silent and a part of me freezes while the other part hopes she says yes. I can't give her too much time to think about the shit she's seen in my eyes and the baggage I told her about. She's a smart girl, she'll figure out I'm bad fucking news, a heartbreak waiting to happen, and head for the fucking hills.

And the thought scares the shit out of me. I keep telling myself once I talk with her, I'll set things straight and she'll fall in line like all of the other arrangements I've had. There will be nothing more between us but great sex, a date for an event, and a kick-ass charity partnership. But if that's all I want, why am I here? Why do I care if she says yes or no to another date?

Why do I want her like no fucking tomorrow?

"I'll be here at six to pick you up, Rylee." Time to find out. Test the waters and then jump ship.

Or walk the plank.

She looks back up at me, her bottom lip between her teeth, and hell if I know what I'm doing but fuck if I'm not going to have a good time trying to figure it out.

I lift my thumb and rub it over her bottom lip. "See you then, sweetheart." I walk to the front door as she says goodbye, my dick begging for those lips and my head hoping to make sense of the door I just turned the key in that I have no business unlocking.

I stop and turn to look at her one last time. "Hey, Ryles? No more running away from me."

I flash her a quick grin before I leave and I wonder who I'm talking to about not running away, her or me.

Chapter Fifteen

Life begins at the end of your comfort zone. I think about Haddie's advice as I get ready for my date with Colton. The song in the background makes me smile. It is the song that Colton's earlier text referred to:

Dress casual. Since you still seem to run away rather than talk to me, I'll use your method of communication to relay my message. Taio Cruz, *Fast Car*. See you at six.

Haddie had smiled knowingly when I showed her the text and scrambled for her iPad to play the song for me. We laughed out loud at the song's words. "I want to drive you like a fast car." Perfectly fitting for Colton to send.

We then scrambled to find a song I could send back to him. "Something to make him think about you the rest of the day and knock his socks off," Haddie had said while scrolling through her vast library of music. After several minutes of silence, she yelled, "I've got the perfect song, Rylee!"

"What is it?"

"Just listen," she said as the opening line of the song began. I started laughing out loud, knowing the song and liking the sexiness of it. Before we knew it, Haddie and I were dancing around the living room singing at the top of our lungs. The song was perfect! Sexy, suggestive, and confident—everything I felt but was too shy to be in front of him. So before I lost my nerve, I grabbed my phone and texted Colton back:

Nice song, Ace. It fits you perfectly. Now, I've got one for you that fits me. Mya, *My love is like whoa!* I'll be waiting for you at six.

A few minutes later, I received a response back:

Shit. Now I'm hard. Six o'clock.

I smile at the thought of our earlier exchange, a small thrill running through me that I have such an effect on him. I look in the mirror and scrutinize my outfit, heeding Colton's advice from the text to dress casual. I have my favorite True Religion jeans on with a violet-colored cashmere sweater that has capped sleeves and a sexy but tasteful low V-neckline. I've forgone the Haddie makeover tonight, opting to do my own make-up and hair. My make-up is natural and light: a little blush, some lip-gloss, smudged eyeliner, and thick mascara to highlight my eyes. Despite playing around with my hair for a while, I opt to keep it down, my curls loose on my back. I add simple diamond studs to my ears and some gold bangles to my wrist.

I twist my ring around and around on my finger, contemplating whether I should wear it or not. I take it off and look at it—three thin, wavy, intertwined diamond bands. *Past, present, and future.* I can still hear him whisper those words in my ear as we stared at it on my finger the night he proposed. I close my eyes and smile at the memory, surprised when the tears that usually threaten don't come. I play with it a moment more before hesitantly twisting it off. I stare at it for a beat before I place it in my jewelry box. I pick it back up in indecision, a war of emotions raging inside of me.

Fresh start, I remind myself with a deep, steadying breath, and place it back in the box. I've worn the ring everyday for three years. I feel naked without it, both inside and out. I wiggle my fingers and look at the lighter band of skin that had been protected from the sun. I feel a weight lifting off of me and at the same time a sadness that it's time to move on. I kiss the spot on my finger and say a silent *I love you to Max,* taking a moment to absorb the importance of this moment before turning to do my last minute touch-ups in the mirror.

I'm slipping on my black, heeled boots when the doorbell rings. I press a hand to my belly, finding it oddly strange that I'm nervous. The man has seen me naked, and yet I still have butterflies. Haddie calls out to me that she'll answer the door. I grab my cropped leather jacket and purse, check myself in the mirror one last time, and make my way down the hallway. I nervously run my hands over my sides and hips, smoothing down my shirt, the clicking from the heels of my boots muted by the runner on the hardwood floor. I hear Colton laugh out loud as I turn the corner near the family room.

His back is to me when I enter the room. I suck in my breath when I see him. A pair of dark blue jeans hang low on his hips, hugging his ass and thighs. *The man can fill out denim*, no question about that. His broad shoulders and strong back stretch the cotton of his plain white T-shirt. The back of his hair curls up at the nape of his neck, and I itch to run my fingers through it. He oozes sex appeal, smolders with rebellion, and radiates confidence. One look at him makes me crave and want and fear all at once. *And he's all mine for the night.*

Before Haddie can acknowledge my entrance, Colton stops mid-sentence. My body tightens at the anticipation, and the deep-seated ache he's awakened in me rises to new heights as he looks over his shoulder, his body sensing my presence. I swear I can feel the air crackle with electricity as our eyes meet, our bodies vibrating.

"Rylee." My name comes out in a breath, the single word laced with so much promise for the night.

"Hi, Ace." It's impossible to mask my pleasure at seeing him again. I smile, hoping he sees how much I want to spend time with him and fearing he might read the emotions simmering beneath the excitement.

We step toward each other as he flashes his megawatt grin at me. I fumble with the strap of my purse anxiously as he simply stares at me. "Gorgeous as ever," he murmurs finally after I feel like all of the air has been sucked out of the room. He reaches out and runs his hand up and down my bare arm, the contact casual but powerful. "You ready?"

Two simple words. That's all they are really, but Colton makes those two simple words sound seductive. I nod my head and murmur, "Hmmm-hmmm," and am caught off guard as he leans in and kisses the tip of my nose. Such a simple gesture but so unexpected from someone like him.

"Let's go, then."

I glance over my shoulder and flash a smile at Haddie, my silent goodbye. I catch the quick thumbs up she flashes me before we leave.

Colton places his hand on the small of my back as he walks me toward the Range Rover, the simple placement of his hand a comfort to my unsettled nerves. Before he reaches for the passenger side door handle, Colton moves the hand from my lower back around to my stomach and pulls me into him so his body ghosts mine. I hold my breath, the unexpected contact with him awakening the smoldering burn he's set fire to. He wraps his other arm around my shoulders and lowers his head to nuzzle his face in the crook of my neck. The warmth of his breath, the sandpaper feel of his shadowed beard, the suggested intimacy of the touch, and the rare glimpse at the affectionate side of Colton causes me to close my eyes momentarily to steady myself and quiet the mixture of sensations rioting inside of me.

"Thank you for saying yes, Ryles," he murmurs before kissing the hollow spot just below my ear. "Now, let me show you a good time." I angle my head against his cheek and close my eyes enjoying the firm heat of him against me. And all too soon he's released me from his arms and is opening the car door for me, ushering me in.

By the time Colton has reached the driver's side, his brooding silence has returned. He clicks his seatbelt and glances over at me. Despite the apprehension I see flickering in his eyes, he reaches over and places a hand on my knee, squeezing it in reassurance.

We drive in a comfortable silence as I watch the tree lined street of my neighborhood pass by us. The moon is out, full and bright, lighting up the warm January night sky. I look over at Colton, the dash lights casting a glow on his face. A shock of his dark hair has fallen haphazardly over his forehead, and I watch his eyes, framed by thick lashes, scan the road ahead of us. The line of his profile is stunning with his imperfect nose, strong bone structure, and sensually sculpted lips. My gaze trails down to take in his strong arms and competent hands on the wheel. The combination of dark hair, translucent eyes, and bronzed skin mixed with the potency of his indifferent attitude—an attitude that makes you want to be the one who matters and be the one who can break through that tough exterior—that combination, it should be illegal. He really does take one's breath away.

When I look back at his face, Colton glances over at me and his eyes hold my gaze before flicking back to the road. A shy smile forms on his lips, his only acknowledgement of my quiet observation of him. The car revs, gunning forward on the freeway, and I laugh at him.

"What?" he feigns innocently, squeezing my knee.

"You like to go fast don't you, Ace?" I realize the innuendo the minute I say it.

He looks over at me, a wicked grin on his lips, enunciating every word of his answer. "You have no idea, Rylee."

"Actually, I think I do," I reply wryly. Colton throws his head back in a full-bodied laugh and shakes his head at me. "No, seriously. What is it about speed that's so attractive to you?"

He mulls it over momentarily before answering. "Trying to tame …" He stops to reconsider his answer. "No, rather trying to *control the uncontrollable*, I guess."

"That's a fitting metaphor if I've ever heard one." And I can't help but wonder if he's referring to something deeper.

"Whatever do you mean?" He plays along innocently.

"Someone once told me that I should research my dates." I look over at him, his eyebrows rising at my comment. "Quite the wild child, aren't we?"

Colton gives me his brighter than the sun megawatt smile. "No one can ever claim that I'm boring or predictable," he muses, looking over his shoulder to change lanes. "Besides, outrunning your demons has a way of doing that to you." Before I can even process the words, Colton skillfully changes the subject. "Food or fun first?"

I want to ask questions, figure out what he means by his comment, but I bite my tongue and answer. "Fun. Definitely fun!"

"Good choice," he responds, before muttering a curse when his cell phone rings on the car speaker. "Sorry," he apologizes before tapping a button on the steering wheel.

The screen on the dash says the name Tawny, and I immediately bristle at the sight. Researching my date certainly gave me more information than just his run-ins with trouble. I now know what Tawny looks like, that she's been his date to numerous functions over the years, and this is the second out of the last three times I've been with Colton that she's called him. My sudden pang of jealousy surprises me, but it only gets stronger when I hear Colton's familiarity with her.

"Hey, Tawn. You're on speaker," he warns.

"Oh!" I can't help but find a tiny bit of joy when I hear the surprise in her voice. "I thought that you'd called it off with Raq—"

"I have," he responds in a clipped tone. "What do you need, Tawny?" he says with irritation in his tone.

What a bitchy comment from her. What if I had been Raquel in the car with him? I sense her staking a claim on her territory, Colton.

Silence fills the line. "Oh. Um. I was just calling to tell you that the formal letters went out today for the sponsorship." When he doesn't say a word, she continues, "That's it."

What? She works for him? With him? On a daily basis? That's just what I need filling my head as jealousy rears it's bitchy head. *Fucking lovely.*

"Great. Thanks for letting me know." And with that he pushes a button and the line disconnects abruptly. Colton sighs out loud and a part of me is happy at his impatience.

"Sorry," he says again, and I'm sure he's referencing Tawny's mention of Raquel. *So they were an item.* She just wasn't some chick he found at the club. The catty side of me at least revels in the fact it was me he left with that night. The compassionate side of me winces for I know that Colton isn't someone who would be easy to get over.

"No biggie." I shrug as I take notice of our location. We're heading out of the city, the opposite direction from where I would expect to be going.

We ride in a comfortable silence for a couple of minutes then Colton turns a corner and the bright lights of a Ferris wheel light up the sky. I glance over at him, and my heart tumbles slowly upon seeing the boyish grin on his face. Colton drives between the flagged gates and pulls the car slowly down the bumpy, dirt road.

My eyes widen at the scene before me. The dirt field is crammed with every typical carnival ride one can imagine, complete with a flashing sign for a Midway section with games impossible to win and signs advertising horribly fattening food. I'm so excited.

He parks the car and turns to me. "Is this okay?" he asks, and I swear I can hear nerves tinge his voice, but I know that's not possible. Not from the ultra-confident, always-sure-of-himself Colton Donavan. Or is it?

I nod my head, bottom lip between my teeth as he exits the car and comes around my side to open my door. "I'm excited," I tell him as he takes my hand and helps me out. He shuts the door and turns to me, my back against the car. His eyes blaze with desire as he stares at me, brings his hands up to the side of my neck, and brushes his thumbs over my cheeks.

I can see the muscles in his jaw clenching as he shakes his head softly, silently responding to some internal conflict that causes a ghost of a smile to play on his lips. "Sweetheart, I've wanted to do this since I left your house this morning." He leans in, eyes still connected with mine. "Since I got your text." He raises his eyebrows. "You intoxicate me, Rylee." His words surge into my soul as he closes the distance between us.

His mouth captures mine in a dizzying kiss, tempting me with his addictive taste so I'm left fighting to regain my equilibrium. His mouth possesses mine with a quiet demand, yet the kiss is so full of tenderness, so packed with unnamed emotions, that I don't want it to end.

But it does, and I'm left to grip my fingers onto his biceps to steady myself. He kisses my nose softly before murmuring, "You ready to have some fun?"

I don't know how he expects me to respond since he just stole my breath, but after a moment I manage to say, "Definitely!" as he releases me to open the rear door. He pulls out a black baseball hat, well worn with a threadbare spot on the tip of the bill. The logo is a sewn-on patch of a tire with two wings coming out from the hub, and it's curled up at the edges.

Colton tugs it down on his head, using both hands to adjust the brim properly before turning to me with an embarrassed grimace. "Sorry. It's just easier in the long run if I try to go incognito from the start."

"No problem," I say, reaching up to tug on the lip. "I like it!"

"Oh, really?" He grabs my hand and we begin weaving through the parked cars toward the entrance.

"Yeah, I kinda have a thing for baseball players," I tease, looking over at him and keeping my face straight.

"Not race car drivers?" he asks, tugging on my hand.

"Not particularly," I deadpan.

"I guess I'll have to work a little harder to persuade you then," he says suggestively.

"That might take a lot of persuading." I smile playfully at him, his eyes hidden by the shadow cast from the lid of his cap. I swing our hands back and forth. "Do you think you're up for the challenge, Ace?"

"Oh, Rylee ..." he chides, "Don't ask for something you can't handle. I told you, *I can be very persuasive*. Don't you remember the last time you dared me?" He tugs me closer and puts his arm around my shoulders.

How can I forget? I'm here right now because of that pseudo-dare.

We approach the ticket booth, and Colton releases his hold on me to buy our tickets as well as a wristband giving us complete access to all rides and games at the carnival. We enter through the gates, Colton tugging his hat down low, covering his eyes, before placing his hand on my lower back. The smell of dirt, frying oil, and barbeque fill my nose while my eyes take in the dazzling, blinking lights. I can hear the rush of the small roller coaster to the right of us, along with the screams of its riders as it plunges downwards. Little kids wander around with dazed looks, clutching balloons in one little hand, holding tightly to a parent with the other. Teenagers walk hand in hand, thinking they're so cool that they're here without their parents. I can't help my smile because despite my age, I'm excited—I haven't been to a carnival like this since I was their age.

"Where to first?" Colton asks as we stroll lazily hand in hand down the Midway, smiling and politely refusing the offers to "win a prize" from the game vendors.

"The rides definitely," I tell him as I look around. "Not sure which one yet, though."

"A girl after my own heart!" He pats his free hand against his chest, smiling at me.

"Adrenaline junkie!" I tell him, bumping my hip up against his thigh.

"Damn straight!" he laughs as we approach what appears to be the center of "Ride Alley" as the sign above us advertises. "So which one, Ryles?"

I look around at the rides, noting several different women staring at us. At first I worry that they recognize Colton, but then realize they are probably just looking at the hot guy standing beside me.

"Hmmmm." I contemplate all of the rides, settling on a long-running favorite. I point toward the ride closest to us. "I used to love this as a kid!"

"Good old Tilt-A-Whirl." Colton laughs, tugging me in its direction. "C'mon, let's go." His enthusiasm is endearing. A man who whirls hundreds of miles an hour around a track, rubs elbows with some of the brightest stars in Hollywood, and could be somewhere upscale right now, is excited about going on a simple carnival ride. *With me*. I have to pinch myself.

We get in line to wait our turn. He bumps me softly with his shoulder. "So tell me more about you, Rylee."

"Is this the job interview part of the date?" I tease playfully. "What do you want to know?"

"What's your story? Where you're from? What's your family like? What are your secret vices?" he suggests, grabbing my hand in his again and raising it to his lips. The simple sign of affection sneaks over the protective wall around my heart.

"All the juicy details, huh?"

"Yep!" His grin lights up his face, and he pulls me toward him so he can casually lay his hand over my shoulder. "Tell me everything."

"Well, I grew up in a typical, middle-class family in San Diego. My mom owns an interior design company and my dad restores vintage memorabilia."

"Very cool," Colton exclaims as I reach my hand up to link it with his that's casually resting over my shoulder. "What are they like?"

"My parents?" He nods his head at me. His question surprises me because it's beyond just the superficial. It's as if he really wants to know me. "My dad's a typical Type A, everything in its order, whereas my mom is very creative. Very much a free spirit. Opposites attract, I guess. We're really close. It killed them when I decided to stay in Los Angeles after college." I shrug. "They're great, just worry too much. You know, typical parents." We move ahead in the line as the current set of riders vacate their cars and the next set moves on. "I'm very lucky to have them," I tell him, a little pang of homesickness hitting me. I haven't seen them in a couple of weeks.

"Any siblings?" Colton asks, playing with my fingers as he holds my hand.

"I have an older brother. Tanner." The thought of him makes me smile. Colton hears the reverence in my voice when I speak of my brother and smiles softly back at me. "He travels a lot. I never know where he's going to be one week to the next. He's a foreign correspondent for the Associated Press in the Middle East."

He notes my furrowed brow. "Not exactly the safest job these days. Sounds like you worry a lot."

I lean into him. "Yeah, but he's doing what he loves."

"I can definitely understand that." We start to shuffle forward again. "What do you think? Are we going to make it this time?"

I step in front of him and stand on my tippy-toes and gauge the line. A small thrill moves through me as I feel him place his hands on both sides of my torso, where my waist and hips meet. I look a bit longer than I need to, not wanting him to remove his hands. "Hmmm, I think next time," I respond, lowering my heels to the ground.

Rather than remove his hands, Colton wraps his arms around me and sets his chin on my shoulder. I sink into him, my softness against his steel, and close my eyes momentarily so I can absorb the feeling of him.

"So finish telling me about you," he murmurs in my ear, the coarseness of his whiskered jaw rubbing the crook of my neck as he speaks.

"Not much else to tell really," I shrug my shoulders subtly, not wanting him to move. "Played lots of sports through high school. Went to UCLA. Met Haddie as my roommate freshman year. Four years later, I majored in psychology with a minor in social work. Got my job and have been doing it ever since. Pretty boring really."

"Normal's not boring," he corrects. "*Normal is desirable.*"

I am about to ask him what he means when we move forward and are directed onto the uneven surface of the ride. We slide into the car, lower the safety bar, and wait for the rest of the ride to be loaded. Colton slides his arm around my back before he continues, "So what about vices? *What do you need to have?*"

Besides you? The words almost slip out, but I catch myself before its too late. I look at him, squinting my eyes in thought. "Don't laugh," I warn him.

He laughs loudly. "Now you have me very curious."

"Well, besides the obvious female things, wine, Hershey kisses, mint chocolate chip ice cream." I pause to think, a smile turning up the corners of my mouth. "I'd have to say music." He raises his eyebrows at me. "It's not very scandalous, I know."

"What kind of music?"

I shrug. "All kinds, really. Just depends on my mood."

"When you need it the most, what type do you listen to?"

"I'm embarrassed to say this..." I shield my eyes with my hand in mock shame "...Top 40, cheesy pop music in particular."

"No!" he yells out in mock horror, laughing loudly. "Oh God, please don't tell me you like *boy bands*," he sneers sarcastically. When I just look at him with a smug smile, he starts laughing. "You and my sister will get along just fine. I had to listen to that crap for years growing up."

He plans on me meeting his sister? I quickly wipe the shocked look off of my face and continue. "She must have great taste in music then!" I kid. "Hey, I live in a house full of teenagers, I hear all kinds of Top 40 music, all day long"

"Nice try, but nothing justifies liking boy bands, Rylee."

"Spoken like a true guy!"

"Would you rather I be something else?" he asks, tapping a finger to the tip of my nose as I laugh, shaking my head no. He leans forward and looks around the ride to see when we're going to start. "Here we go."

It's not lost on me that our conversation has been solely about me. I begin to think about this as the ride starts to twist and turn and spin violently in circles. I am thrown against the side of Colton's body, and he clutches his arm around me, holding me tightly to him. He is laughing hysterically at the rush of the ride, and I tell him to close his eyes because it heightens the sensation. I swear I hear him say something about showing me more of that later, but I'm distracted from asking because as soon as it begins, the ride is over.

Colton and I proceed to ride the tea-cups, the swings, sneak a kiss in the Fun House's lover's lane, raise our hands high above our heads as we plummet downward on the roller coaster, and sling back and forth on the dragon ship. We step off of the freefall ride after having our stomachs jolted up into our mouths, and Colton declares his need for a drink.

We stroll over to a food vendor and he buys two drinks and a mammoth funnel of cotton candy. He looks over at me, dead serious. "No carnival is complete without making yourself sick on the pure goodness of spun sugar." He looks at me with the grin of a mischievous little boy, and it melts my heart.

I laugh as we stroll over to a nearby bench. We are almost there when we hear a voice behind us. "Excuse me?"

We both turn to see a middle-aged woman standing behind us. "Yes?" I ask, but it's obvious she couldn't care less about me. Her eyes are completely fixated on Colton.

"Sorry to interrupt, but, my friends and I have a bet going ... are you Colton Donavan?"

I can feel Colton's hand tense in mine, but his face remains impassive. A slow smile spreads across his face as he glances over at me and then back to the woman in front of us. "That's flattering of you to think, ma'am, but I'm sorry to disappoint you. I actually get that a lot." The woman's face falls in disappointment. "Thank you for the compliment, though. My name's Ace Thomas," Colton says as he holds out his hands to shake hers. The mixture of my nickname for him and my last name makes me smile softly at the idea that he is thinking of the two of us as being intertwined. Connected.

She shakes his hand reluctantly, muttering, "Nice to meet you," embarrassed at her intrusion, before she turns quickly and walks back to her friends.

"Nice to meet you too, ma'am." Colton calls after her, the rigidity in his shoulders easing as we turn our backs to her and continue to the bench. He lets out a soft sigh. "I hate doing that. Lying like that," he says. "It's just that once one person realizes, then it's nonstop. Out come the camera phones and the Facebook posts and before you know it, we're surrounded, the paparazzi show up, and I've spent the whole evening tending to strangers and ignoring you."

His reasoning takes me by surprise, and I'm flattered that he's put it in these terms. "This is my life," he explains without apology, "for the most part. I grew up by default with a famous family, but I made the choice to be a public person. I accept the fact that I'm going to be followed and photographed and hounded for autographs. I get it," he says, sitting down on the bench beside me, "and I don't mind it, really. I mean I'm not complaining. I'm usually very accommodating, especially when it comes to kids. But sometimes, like tonight, I just ..." He tugs his hat down further on his head. "I just don't want to be bugged." He leans forward, angling his head so the brim of his hat clears my forehead, and says, "I just want it to be you and me." He leans in, brushing his lips against mine in a brief but tender kiss, emphasizing his last words.

I pull back and smile tentatively at him, raising my hand to toy lazily with the curls flipping over his cap at the back of his neck. We stare at each other for a moment, exchanging unspoken words: lust, desire, enjoyment, playfulness, and compatibility. My grin spreads wider. "Ace Thomas, huh?"

He grins back at me, the lines at the corners of his eyes crinkling. "It was the first thing that came to mind." He shrugs, raising his eyebrows. "If I'd have hesitated, she would've known I was lying."

"True," I concede, taking a pinch of the cotton candy that Colton offers me. "My God, this stuff is over-the-top sweet!"

"I know. Pure sugar." Colton chuckles, widening his eyes at me. "That's why it's so damn good!" He looks out at the rides. "Man, when I was a kid, after—" He pauses quietly. "After I met my parents, they'd spoil me by taking me to baseball games. I'd get so sick eating this crap." The corners of his mouth turn up in a ghost of a smile at the memory. And I can't help but wonder what life was like for him before he met his parents.

We lapse into an easy silence, watching the rides and the people around us, taking small nibbles of cotton candy. I am really enjoying myself. He is attentive and engaging and seems as if he really is interested in me as a person. I guess I was expecting more of a surface get-to-know-you, so being proved wrong is nice.

Colton moves his hand over to squeeze my knee and points over to the only ride left. "You ready to take on the Zipper, Ryles?"

I blanch at the thought of the small enclosed cage tumbling endlessly through the air. Being jolted and shoved backwards and forwards while being confined. I swallow loudly. "Not really." I shake my head.

"C'mon, be a sport," he pressures jokingly.

I can feel the impending claustrophobia of the ride, and I move my shoulders back and forth to ward the phantom feeling away. "Sorry. I can't," I mutter, feeling the heat of embarrassment flush through my system. "I'm super claustrophobic," I tell him, pushing my hair off my face.

"I've noticed," he says wryly. When I raise an eyebrow at him, he continues, "Remember? Storage closet? Backstage?" he says with a suggestive smirk on his face.

"Oh. Yes." I can feel my cheeks burn red, mortified at my, *then*, actions. "How could I forget?"

"Were you always that way or did your brother lock you in the closet and forget about you as a kid?" he chides, laughing with amusement at the thought.

"Uh-uh." I shake my head and quickly shift my eyes away from his, hoping he misses the tears that fill them momentarily at the memory. Although it has been two years, it still hits me like yesterday when old demons resurface. I reach over to twist my ring around my finger and find the spot empty. I exhale shakily, closing my eyes momentarily to control my emotions. I'm angry with myself for reacting so strongly to the suggestion of a damn carnival ride.

His laugh stops immediately when he notices my agitation, and he places an arm around my shoulder, pulling me into him. "Hey look. I'm sorry, Rylee. I didn't mean—"

"No, it's okay." I say, leaning forward out of his grasp, escaping the heat of him and embarrassed at my reaction, "There's no need to apologize. I'm the one who should be sorry." He nods his head in acceptance to me, his eyes imploring me to say more. "I—um, I was in a pretty bad car accident a couple of years back … I was trapped for a while." I shake my head to clear the vivid memories pressing in on me. "Since then, I can't stand being in small places. Feeling trapped."

He places his hand on my back and reassuringly rubs up and down. "The scars?" he asks.

"Uh-huh," I answer, still trying to find my voice.

"But you're all healed now?" The genuine concern that fills his voice makes me look back and smile at him.

"Physically, yes," I tell him as I lean back into the comfort of him, resting my back partially on his torso. His arm instinctively goes around me. "Emotionally..." I sigh "...I have my days. I told you, Colton, excess baggage."

He places a kiss to the side of my head, keeping his lips pressed there. I can feel the questions he wants to ask me in our silence. What happened and how bad was it? Why an accident has baggage that makes me run from him? I don't want to mar the night with sadness so I pinch off a piece of cotton candy and turn my body so that I face him, my bent knee resting on his thigh. I wave the piece of cotton candy in front of his face.

"How sweet do you like it, Ace?" I flirt with him before I lick my bottom lip and then provocatively place the fluff of sugar between them.

He leans into me, need darkening his eyes, a salacious grin playing his lips. "Oh, sweetheart, you taste sweet enough already." He bites at the cotton candy hanging between my lips, purposefully nipping my bottom lip, pulling on it. The quick bite of pain is replaced by a quick lick of his tongue. The low moan of pleasure that comes from the back of his throat turns me on. Makes me want to drink him in. Right here. Right now.

"I definitely like the taste of that," he murmurs against my lips. "We just might have to wrap this up and take this with us for later." He lazily brushes his lips against mine. "In case you need a little sweetener after I dirty you up."

I can feel his mouth curve in a smile against my lips. His suggestive words send a tightening pulse deep down in my belly. The promise of more to come with him dampens my sex and turns my soft ache into a smoldering burn.

I sigh against his lips, completely bewitched and totally enchanted by him. I lean my forehead against his, taking the time to steady myself.

"So," Colton says, pulling back and pressing a soft kiss on my forehead before continuing. "We have two things left that must be done before we leave here."

He rises from the bench, tucking the wrapped bag of cotton candy under his arm, a smirk on his face, and grabs my hand, pulling me to my feet. "Oh, really? And what would those be?"

"We have to ride the Ferris wheel," he says, tapping me on the butt playfully, "and I *have* to win you a stuffed animal."

I laugh out loud as we head for the Ferris wheel. The line is short and we chat, surprised at how many things we have in common despite coming from such different backgrounds. How much our likes and dislikes are similar. How our taste in movies and television are alike.

We are ushered to the car and locked in place with the bar across our laps. We start to move slowly, Colton draping his arm around my shoulder. "So you never finished telling me about you."

"What is this?" I laugh. "Don't think I haven't noticed you haven't been put on the spot yet."

"I'm next," he promises, kissing my temple as I snuggle into the warmth and security of his arms as we climb higher. He points at a vendor juggling balls on the ground below. "Tell me, Rylee. What's your future look like? A nice husband, two point five kids, and a white picket fence?"

"Hmmm, maybe. Someday. But the husband has to be *hot and nice*," I kid, laughing out loud. "No kids, though."

I feel his body tense at my words, his silence deafening, before he responds. "That surprises me. You love kids. Work with them all day. You don't want your own?" I can hear the confusion in his voice and can feel his jaw moving as it rests on the crown of my head.

"I'll see what fate deals me," I tell him, hoping he's satisfied with my answer and that he won't pry any further. "Look!" I point out to the skyline where the top part of the full moon is just rising over the hills, glad that I can change the topic. "It's beautiful."

"Hmm-hmmm," he murmurs as we sit watching its ascent. "You know what the rule is when the Ferris wheel reaches the top, right?"

"No, what?" I ask, pulling away from the warmth of his arms to face him.

"This," he says before closing his mouth over mine and fisting a hand in my hair. The hunger in his kiss is so tangible that I lose myself in him and the moment. His tongue slips past my lips, licking seductively at mine. I feel the gentle whir of the ride; the heated warmth of his fingertips whispering over my cheek; the sweet taste of cotton candy on his tongue; the hush of my name on his lips. The feeling of our marked descent has us pulling back, stepping back from the depths of the fire raging between us.

"Sweet Jesus," Colton mutters, amused, adjusting in the seat so he can shift the seam of denim pressing against his arousal. "I react like a damn teenager around you." He shakes his head, his embarrassment clear.

"C'mon, Ace," I say, my ego inflated, "you owe me a stuffed animal."

Thirty minutes later and several games conquered, my sides hurt from laughing at Colton's playful antics, but I'm the proud owner of an oversized and very lopsided-looking stuffed dog. I lean up against the corner of one of the permanent buildings at the fairgrounds, one leg bent at the knee with my foot flat against the building, and my new treasured prize resting on my hip. I watch Colton play one last game, take the small prize he's won, and hand it off to the little boy standing next to him at the booth. He ruffles the little boy's hair and smiles at his mom before sauntering back to me. Taut muscles bunch beneath his T-shirt as he moves, and his body screams that it was made for sin. It's impossible for me to take my eyes off of him. I can see that I'm not the only one as I watch the mom's eyes follow Colton's back as he leaves, an appreciative look on her face.

"Are you having fun?" he asks, approaching me, tugging on the ear of the stuffed dog.

I grin stupidly at him. As if he even has to ask that question. *I'm with him, aren't I?*

He reaches out and runs a fingertip down my cheek. "I love your smile, Rylee. The one you have right now." He cups my neck, the pad of his thumb running over my lower lip. His translucent eyes look into mine and search inside of me. "You look so carefree and lighthearted. So beautiful."

I angle my head, my lips parting at the touch of his thumb. "As opposed to you?" I question. He quirks his eyebrows in question. "When you smile it screams mischief and trouble." And *heartbreak*, I think. I shake my head when the exact smile I'm talking about graces his lips. I run my free hand up the plane of his chest, liking the hiss of his breath I hear in response to my touch as well as the fire that leaps into his eyes. "And it has '*I'm a stereotypical bad boy*' written all over it."

The grin widens. "*Bad boy*, huh?"

Right now, in this moment, there is no way I'll ever be able to resist him with his tousled hair, emerald eyes, and *that* smile. I look up at him through my lashes, my bottom lip between my teeth.

"Are you one of those girls who like bad boys, Rylee?" he asks, his voice gruff with desire, his lips inches from mine, his eyes glistening with a dare.

"Never," I whisper, barely having enough composure to find my voice.

"Do you know what bad boys like to do?" He takes a hand and places it on my lower back, pressing me forcibly against him. Flash points of pleasure explode every place our bodies connect.

Oh my! His touch. His hard body pressed against mine makes me need things I shouldn't need. Shouldn't need from him. But I don't have the strength to fight it anymore. I suck in a ragged breath, not trusting myself to speak. "No," is all I can manage to say for an answer. Between one breath and the next, Colton crushes his mouth to mine in a heat-searing kiss tinged with near violent desire. He kisses me as if we are in the privacy of his bedroom. His hands run up the length of my torso, flutter over my neck, and cup my face as he slowly eases the intensity of the kiss.

He places his now-signature kiss on the tip of my nose before pulling back, the devilish look still smoldering in his eyes. "Us bad boys?" he continues, while my head still spins. "We like to ..." He leans in, his lips at my ear, the warmth of his breath tickling my skin. I think he is going to tell me something erotic. Something naughty he wants to do to me for his pregnant pause leaves me suspended in thought. "Eat dinner!"

I throw my head back and laugh loudly at him, using my hand on his chest to push him away. He laughs with me, taking the stuffed dog from my arm. "Gotcha!" he says as he grabs my hand, saying goodbye to the carnival.

We make our way to the car, chatting idly as we pull out of the parking lot. Colton turns the radio on and I softly sing along as we drive.

"You really do like music, don't you?"

I smile at him, continuing to sing.

"You've known the words to every song that's played."

"It's my little form of therapy," I answer, adjusting my seatbelt so I can turn and face him.

"The date's that bad you need therapy already?" he jokes.

"Stop!" I laugh at him. "I'm serious. It's therapeutic."

"How's that?" he asks, his face scrunched in concentration as we hit traffic on I-10.

"The music, the words, the feeling behind it, what's not being said." I shrug. "I don't know. Sometimes I think music expresses things better than I can. So maybe vicariously, when I'm singing, everything I'm too chicken to say to someone, I can relay in a song. That's the best way to describe it, I guess." A blush creeps over my cheeks, as I feel stupid for not being able to explain better.

"Don't get embarrassed," he tells me as he reaches out and rests a hand on my knee. "I get it. I understand what you're trying to say."

I pick imaginary lint off of my jeans, a nervous habit I have when I'm put on the spot. I laugh softly. "After the accident ..." I swallow loudly, shocked that he makes me comfortable enough that I'm volunteering this information. Pieces of me that I rarely talk about. "It helped me tremendously. When I came home from the hospital, poor Haddie was so sick of hearing the same songs over and over, she threatened to put my iPod in the garbage disposal." I smile at the memory of how fed up she'd been at hearing Matchbox Twenty. "Even now, I use it with the kids. When they first come to us or if they are having a hard time dealing with their situation, if they can't verbalize how they're feeling, we use music to help them." I shrug. "Sounds lame, I know, but it works."

Colton glances over at me, sincerity in his eyes. "You really love them, don't you?"

I answer without hesitation. "With all my heart."

"They are very lucky to have you fighting for them. It's a brutal road for a kid to have to go down. It easily fucks you up." He shakes his head, lapsing into silence.

I can feel the sadness radiate off of him. I reach down and link my fingers with the hand he has resting on my leg and give it a reassuring squeeze. What happened to this beautiful man who one minute is playful and sexy and the next quiet and reflective? What can put that haunted look in those piercing green eyes? What has given him that roughshod drive to get his way, to succeed at all costs?

"Do you want to talk about it?" I ask softly, afraid to pry but wanting him to share what deep, dark secret has a hold on him.

He sighs loudly, the silence thick in the car. I steal a quick glance over at him and see the stress etched around his mouth. The lights of passing cars cast shadows on his face, making him seem even more untouchable. I regret asking the question, afraid I've pushed him further into his memories.

Colton withdraws his hand from mine and takes his baseball hat off, tossing it in the backseat, and shoves his hand through his hair. He clenches and unclenches his jaw in thought. "Shit, Rylee." And I think that is all I'm going to get as the car descends back into silence. Eventually he continues, "I don't …" He stops as he exits the freeway. I can see him grip the steering wheel tightly with both hands. "I don't need to haunt you with my demons, Ry. Fill your head with the shit that's a psychologist's wet dream. Give you ammunition to dissect and throw back in my face at everything I do—everything I say—when I fuck things up."

I immediately hear the *when* not *if* in his statement. The raw emotions behind his words hit me harder than his insensitivity. My years of experience tell me that he's still hurting—still coping with whatever happened long ago.

We stop at a light and Colton scrubs both hands over his face. "Look, I'm sorry. I—"

"No apologies needed, Colton." I reach out and squeeze his bicep. "Absolutely none."

He hangs his head momentarily, closing his eyes before lifting it back up and opening them. He glances over at me, a reserved smile on his face, sorrow in his eyes before mumbling, "Thanks." He looks back at the road and steps on the accelerator as the light changes.

Chapter Sixteen

Our late dinner is sinfully good. Colton takes me to a small surf-shack type restaurant on Highway One slightly north of Santa Monica. Despite the busy Saturday night crowd, when the hostess sees Colton, she greets him by name and whisks us out to a rather private table on the patio that overlooks the water. The crash of waves serves as soft background music to our evening.

"Come here much?" I ask wryly. "Or do you just use the fact that the hostess is in love with you to get the primo table?"

He flashes a heart-stopping grin at me. "Rachel's a sweet girl. Her dad owns the place. He has a ladder up to the rooftop. Sometimes he and I go up there and throw back a few beers. Shoot the shit. Escape the madness." He leans over and taps the top of my nose with his finger. "I hope this is okay?" he asks.

"Definitely! I like laid back," I tell him. When his grin widens and his eyes darken, I look at him confused, "What?"

He takes a sip of beer from his bottle, amusement filling his face, "I like you laid back too, just not in this environment." His comment causes butterflies in my stomach. I giggle and swat at him playfully. He catches my hand and brings it casually to his lips before setting it on his thigh with his hand closing around it. "No, seriously," he explains, "this is way more my style than the glitz and glamour of my parents' lifestyle and expectations. My sister fits that lifestyle so much better than I do." He rolls his eyes despite the utter adoration on his face when he mentions her.

"How old is she?"

"Quinlan? She's twenty-six and a total pain in the ass!" He laughs. "She's in graduate school at USC right now. She's pushy and overbearing and protective and—"

"And she loves you to death."

A boyish grin blankets his face as he nods in acceptance. "Yes, she does." He mulls it over thoughtfully. "The feeling is completely mutual."

His ability to express his love for his sister is charming in a man otherwise unwilling to express himself emotionally.

The waitress arrives, halting our conversation, and asks me if I am ready to order, although her eyes are fixated on Colton. I want to tell her I understand, I'm under his spell too. I'm still unsure what I want so I look at Colton. "I'll have whatever you're having."

He looks up at me, surprise on his face, "Their burgers are the best. Does that sound okay?"

"Sounds good to me."

"A girl after my own heart," he teases, squeezing my hand. "Can we get two surf burgers with fries and another round of drinks, please," he tells the waitress, and as I try to hand her my menu, I notice how flustered she is by Colton speaking to her.

"So tell me about your parents."

"Uh-oh. Is this the Colton background portion of the night?" he kids.

"You got it, Ace. Now spill it," I tell him, taking a sip of my wine.

He shrugs. "My dad is larger than life in everything he does. *Everything*. He's supportive and always positive and a good friend to me now. And my mom, she's more reserved. More the rock of our family." He smiles softly at the thought, "but she definitely has a temper and a flair for the dramatic when she deems it necessary."

"Is Quinlan adopted too?"

"No." He drains the remainder of his beer, shaking his head. "She's biological. My mom and dad decided one was enough for them with their busy schedules and all of the traveling to onset locations." He raises his eyebrows. "And then my dad found me." The simplicity in that last statement, the rawness behind the words, is profound.

"Was that hard? Her being biological and you adopted?"

He ponders the question, turning his head to look around the restaurant. "At times I think I used it for all it was worth. But when it comes down to it, I realized that my dad didn't have to bring me home with him that day." He plays with the label on his empty beer bottle. "He could have turned me over to social services, and God knows what would have happened since they're not always the most efficient organization. But he didn't." He shrugs. "In time I grew to realize they really loved me, really wanted me, because, they kept me. They made me a part of their family."

I'm a little taken back by Colton's honesty since I expected him to evade my questions. My heart breaks for the struggles of the little boy he was. I know he is glossing over the turmoil he must have experienced joining an already established family. "How was it growing up with parents in the public eye?"

"I guess it really is my turn for the inquisition," he jokes before stretching his arm out, resting his hand on the back of my chair, idly wrapping one of my curls around his finger as he speaks. "They did the best they could to insulate Quin and me from it all. Back then, the media was nothing like it is today." He shrugs. "We had strict rules and mandatory Sunday night family dinners when my dad wasn't on location. To us, the movie stars who came over for barbeques were just Tom and Russell, like any other people you invite to a family function. We didn't know any differently." He smiles broadly. "Man, they spoiled us rotten though, trying to make up for all I had missed out on in my early years."

He stops talking when the food is served. We both thank the waitress and put condiments on our burgers, deep in our thoughts. I'm surprised when Colton speaks again, continuing to talk about growing up.

"God, I was a handful," he admits. "Always creating a mess of one kind or another for them to have to clean up. Defiant. Rebelling against them—against everything really—every chance I had."

I take a bite of my hamburger, moaning at how good it is. He flashes a smile. "I told you they were the best!"

"Heavenly!" I finish my bite. "Sooo good." I wipe the corner of my mouth with a napkin and continue my quest for information on Colton. "So, why Donavan? Why not Westin?"

"So why Ace?" he counters, flashing me a combative grin. "Why not *stud muffin or lover?*"

It takes everything I have not to burst out laughing. Instead, I angle my head, eyes full of humor, as I purse my lips and stare at him. I was curious how long it'd take for him to ask me that question. "Stud muffin just sounds all kinds of wrong coming from you." I finally laugh, setting my elbows on the table and my head in my hands. "*Are you evading my question Ace?*"

"Nope," he leans back in his chair, eyes never leaving mine. "I'll answer your question when you answer mine."

"That's how you're going to play this?" I arch a brow at him. "*Show me yours and I'll show you mine?*"

Colton's eyes light up with challenge and amusement. "*Baby, I've already seen yours,*" he says, flashing me a lightning fast grin before closing the distance and brushing his lips to mine and then pulling away before I get a chance to really sink into the kiss. My body hums in frustration and arousal. "But I'd be more than happy to see the whole package again."

My thoughts cloud and my thigh muscles tense at the thought, sexual tension colliding between the two of us. When I think I can speak without my voice betraying the effect he has on my body, I continue, "What was the question again?" I tease, batting my eyelashes playfully.

"Ace?" He shrugs, darting his tongue out to wet his bottom lip. "Why do you call me that?"

"It's just something that Haddie and I made up a long time ago when we were in college."

Colton raises his eyebrows at me, a silent attempt at prompting me further, but I just smile shyly. "So it stands for something then? And not just pertaining to me in particular?" he asks, working his jaw back and forth in thought as he waits for an answer I'm not going to give him. "And you're not going to tell me *what* though, are you?"

"Nope." I grin at him before taking a sip of my drink, watching his brow furrow as the wheels in his mind turn in thought.

"Hmmmm," he murmurs, his eyes narrowing at me. "Always Charming and Endearing." He smirks, obviously proud of himself for coming up with what he assumes the acronym stands for.

"*Nope*," I repeat myself, a grin tugging at the corners of my mouth.

His smile widens further as he tips his beer at me, "I've got it," he says, scrunching up his nose adorably in thought. "Always Colton Everafter."

The smirk on his face and the charming look in his eyes has me laughing out loud. I reach out and place my hand over his and give it a squeeze. "Not even close, *Ace*," I tease. "Now it's your turn to answer the question."

"You're not going to tell me?" he asks incredulously.

"Uh-uh," I tell him, finding his reaction funny. "Now quit avoiding the question. Why Donavan and not Westin?"

He stares at me for a moment, weighing his options. "I'll get the answer out of you one way or another, Thomas," he says suggestively.

"I'm sure you will," I acquiesce, knowing he'll probably get so much more than just that from me.

He stares at me for a moment, a mix of emotions flickering though pools of emerald before he shrugs nonchalantly and looks out to the ocean, effectively stopping any chance I have of reading what is in them. "At first my parents used Donavan as a way to protect me as a child. When we traveled or had to use an alias, we would use it. But as I got older..." he takes a sip of his beer "...and as I got into racing, I didn't want to be seen as some spoiled Hollywood kid who was just using his name and daddy's money to make it." He looks up at me, snagging a fry off of my plate despite having a plethora himself. "I wanted to earn it. Really earn it." He flashes that grin at me again. "Now it doesn't really matter. I couldn't care less what anybody writes about me. Thinks about me. But back then, I did."

A silence falls between us. I'm having a hard time reconciling the arrogant, sexy troublemaker the media portrays with the man before me. A man comfortable with himself—and yet a part of me still feels like he is striving to find his place in this world. To prove he is worthy of all of the good and bad he has experienced in his life. I have a feeling that the real Colton is a little bit of both *angel and devil.*

"So Colton, how'd you find this place?" I pick up my glass by the stem and swirl the wine around absently in the glass before I take a sip.

"I found it on the way home from surfing one day when I was in college," he muses, wincing at the small shriek from inside the restaurant as a woman recognizes him and calls out his name.

Ignoring the bystanders starting to gather inside to catch a peek at him, I continue. "I don't picture you in college, Ace."

He finishes the bite of food he's chewing before answering. "Well, neither did I." He laughs, taking another swallow of his beer. "I think I broke my parents' heart when I dropped out after two years at Pepperdine, *sans* degree."

"Why didn't you finish?" I flinch when a flash sparks through the dark night from someone's camera.

He casually shifts his chair in a move so fluid it's obviously well practiced. He now has his back more angled to the center of the restaurant so that less of him can be seen. I don't mind. It moves him closer to me so that now we both face the moonlit ocean off of the deck. "I can give you the bullshit answer about being a free spirit, et cetera ..." He flutters his hand through the air in indifference. "It just wasn't my thing." He shrugs. "Concentrated studies, set formats, deadlines, structure ..." He shivers in pseudo-horror at the last word.

I smirk at him and shake my head, leaning back into my chair where Colton's fingers are now lazily running back and forth between my shoulder blades. "Yeah ... I definitely can't see you twiddling your thumbs in class."

"God, my parents were pissed!" He exhales loudly at the memory. "They had spent all kinds of money on tutors to try and get me up to speed after they adopted me..." he shakes his head, smiling "...and then I went and threw it away by dropping out."

I bite off a piece of french fry. "How old were you when ... I mean how did you meet them?" A shadow passes over his face, and I mentally kick myself for asking the question. "Sorry. I didn't mean to pry."

He stares out at the moonlit ocean in thought for a few moments before answering. "No, there's not much to tell." He wipes his hands on the napkin in his lap. "I was—I met my dad outside his trailer on the Universal lot."

"On the set of *Tinder?*" I ask, referring to the movie that I'd learned about during my Google search. It was the movie his dad had won an Academy Award for.

Colton raises his eyebrows, his beer stopping halfway to his lips. "Somebody was doing their homework," he tells me, and I can't tell if he's perturbed or amused.

I offer him a shy smile, embarrassed. "Somebody once told me that it's not safe to go out with someone you haven't researched first," I explain.

"Is that so?" he quips, leaning back in his chair. He crosses his arms across his chest, a beer in one hand, his biceps pressing against the hem of his sleeves.

"Yes," I toy with him, "but then again, I don't think it matters with you."

"Why's that?" he asks, lifting a bottle to his lips. My eyes are glued to the sight of them pursed over the bottle. His tongue darts out to lick them after his sip. I have to drag my mind out of the gutter from imagining those lips on me. Licking me. Tasting me.

"I don't think it matters how much I learn about you," I tell him, leaning into him so my lips graze against his ear and whisper, "I still think you're dangerous." *To me*, I add silently.

He pulls back, eyes fused to mine as he leans in to brush a gentle kiss on my lips before resting his forehead against mine. *"You have no idea,"* he murmurs against my mouth. His words send a shock wave of confusion through me. One minute playful, the next minute guarded. To say he's mercurial is an understatement.

We finish our meal, continuing to talk comfortably, interrupted only once by a fan asking for a picture and an autograph, which Colton gives. Rachel does a good job keeping the rest of his fans at bay, saying that the patio area is closed for a private party.

I can see why women are so taken with him. Why they try and stake their claim to him as Tawny surely had earlier. He leans back in his chair, stretching his torso up before swallowing the last of his beer. He glances over at me and grins as I slowly look over his torso, over his biceps, and up to his face. My belly tightens at the sight of him and the memory of his body pressing me into the mattress.

"See something you like?" he asks, purposefully pulling up the hem of his shirt to scratch an imaginary itch on his washboard abs just above the waistline of his jeans. I breathe in deeply, his hand lazily scratching down to where his happy trail disappears beneath his button fly. *Damn him!*

I pull my eyes back up to his to see amusement laced with desire in his eyes. *Two can play this game.* I think of Haddie and her advice. *Embrace your inner slut,* I repeat like a mantra. Trying to summon my simmering sexuality so that I might somehow fall somewhere in the realm of appeal that Colton has.

I shift in my chair, folding my leg and placing my foot underneath me. I bend forward onto the table, braced on my elbows so my cleavage is on display as I lean into him. I watch Colton's eyes trace over my lips, down the line of my neck, and straight to the curve of my breasts. His tongue darts out and wets his lower lip as they part in concentration. I continue forward until my lips are inches from his.

"*Something I like?*" I reiterate breathlessly as I glance down to his lips and then back up to his eyes. "*Hmmm,*" I whisper as if I'm mulling it over, "I'm still testing the goods to see if they're up to par." My lips are a whisper from his, and when he purses his to kiss mine, I conveniently shift back in my chair, denying him the contact.

Impatience flashes fleetingly in Colton's eyes before the corners of his mouth curl up as he regards me, shaking his head. "That's how you want to play this, Rylee?" His playful question is spoken with a hint of warning. The intensity in his eyes has my body reacting—my pulse, my breath, my nerve endings. "You want to play hard to get, sweetheart?" he asks as he removes his wallet out of his back pocket and pulls a generous amount of bills from it and sets them on the table.

He laughs. The low resonating sound reverberates through me as I continue to watch him silently, a coy smile on my face despite realizing that when it comes to Colton, I'm in way over my head when it comes to playing games. He reaches out and cups the side of my face, running the pad of his thumb over my bottom lip. Desire pools in my belly, aching for him to touch more of me.

Colton leans forward with determination in his eyes. He moves so his mouth is next to my ear. I can feel the warmth of his breath and my skin prickles in anticipation of his touch. "You see, sweetheart, if you want to play hard to get," he whispers, trailing a finger down my neckline, "you've picked the wrong guy to play games with." He closes his lips on my earlobe and sucks on it, the feeling mainlining right down to my sex. I arch my body in response, aware that at our backs is a restaurant full of people. "Didn't your momma ever tell you that playing hard to get is a surefire way to get the man you want?" His voice is seductive, mesmerizing, and sexy as hell. He continues to trace his finger down my shoulder and arm until it reaches my hip. He smoothes the palm of his hand over my thigh and slides it slowly forward until it reaches the apex. His thumb glances over my cleft, conveniently pressing the hard seam of denim against my throbbing clit. I suck in a breath. "You wanna play hardball, sweetheart? Welcome to the big leagues."

I exhale, his words foreplay to my already thrumming libido. He leans back and brushes a teasing kiss on my lips. He pulls back, triumph on his face. He quirks his eyebrows at me, glancing down to my chest and then back up. "Besides, Rylee, your nipples are betraying your ploy to play hard to get."

What? I glance down to note that the tightened buds of my nipples are pressing tautly against my sweater in an all-out announcement of my arousal. *Damn it!*

Colton stands abruptly, smiling brazenly before reaching out his hand to me. "Come," he says, and all I can think is that I hope to very soon, my body yearning with the desire for him to touch me again.

We exit the restaurant from a rear door that Rachel directs us toward to avoid the paparazzi waiting at the front. We make it to his car unscathed, and Colton quickly maneuvers the car onto Highway One. We drive in silence, the air in the car crackling with the unrequited sexual tension between us.

I'm unsure where we're going but I'm smart enough to know that both of us desire the same thing. No words are needed. I can see it in the way Colton grips the steering wheel. In the invisible waves of anticipation and need rolling off of him.

We eventually exit the highway on the outskirts of Pacific Palisades and turn down a street a couple of blocks from the beach. Colton parks in front of a Tuscan-style townhouse and exits the car without saying a word. His home perhaps? By the glow of a streetlight I can see a stucco façade with wrought iron accents and a courtyard enclosed with a rustic gate. It's comfortably charming and not at all what I think I expected of where Colton lives. I guess I figured him for modern architecture, clean lines, monochromatic. He opens the door behind me and gathers our stuff before opening my door to help me out of the car. He grabs my hand to lead me up the cobblestone walkway without speaking or making eye contact.

I wonder if maybe I'm reading into things because suddenly I feel uncomfortable. Why the sudden change in behavior? Did I miss something? Nerves hit me as I realize that when I walk through this door my previous supposition of what I thought was going to happen has now changed. Shifted for some unknown reason. I stop behind Colton in the cozy courtyard where a small swinging bench seat sits amongst hydrangea and plumeria plants.

I hear keys clinking, him swearing at trying the wrong one, and then Colton is pushing open the distressed front door before placing his hand on the small of my back and ushering me in. He enters the alarm code but it continues beeping as he tries the code two more times before the beeping quiets.

The house is painted in soft browns and tans with a few bold splashes of color in pillows and vases. There are little touches here and there, feminine touches, that make me think maybe he had a female interior designer at some point. *Or a female living with him.* I walk hesitantly into the main room, my hands clasped in front of me, unsure what I should do or say. For the first time tonight, I feel awkward in Colton's company. I hear the door close and then I hear Colton's boots on the hardwood floor as he walks behind me and over to the kitchen area.

All the playfulness of earlier is gone, hidden seamlessly away beneath his masked façade. I watch him open a cupboard looking for something and then mutter a curse when it's not there, before opening two more and then he exhales. "What the fuck?"

My sentiments exactly. I can see the tension in his shoulders. In the lines around his mouth. Uncertainty and anxiety fill me as I take a step toward him. "You have a beautiful home." The words squeak out, betraying my uneasiness.

Colton's eyes flash up at my words, meeting mine, gauging me. "That depends," he mutters as I look on perplexed. He shuts the cupboard door and rounds the counter toward me. His eyes are expressionless. Guarded. "I drove here without thinking ..." He shakes his head apologetically. "It was stupid of me to bring you here ..."

His words, the sudden rejection, sting like a slap to my face. I look down at the floor in humiliation and wrap my arms around my torso, a useless form of protection against him. I can feel the threatening tears burn in the back of my throat. This is the second time he has led me down this road and then detached without explanation. One minute he makes me feel like I am the only person in the room he has eyes for and then the next it's like he can't stand the sight of me. I shift my feet, telling myself I will not cry in front of him. Will not give him the satisfaction of knowing the effect he already has on me despite the short time we've known each other.

Sighing deeply, I prepare to make my obvious exit now that I'm suddenly unwelcome here. When I know that I can face him, I look up again to see Colton in front of me tugging his shirt over his head. When the collar clears his face, he throws the shirt onto the couch without looking. His eyes are completely focused on me, his jaw set, hands restless as if he's itching to touch me. The intensity in his stare steals my breath.

Now it's my turn to say it. *What the fuck?* I'm thoroughly confused. Dr. Jekyll has turned into Mr. Hyde and is making a repeat performance. One minute I think he's apologizing for bringing me home with him because he wants to back out, and the next he's deliciously naked from the waist up, staring at me as if he's going to devour me without stopping for so much as a breath.

I break from his stare and run my eyes down the length of his body. His torso flexes under my gaze. His jeans hang low on his hips, the V-cut of his muscles dipping beneath the denim. I find myself thinking how I want to taste him there. How I want to run my lips along that ridge of muscles to where it trails down to the end of the inverted triangle. How I want to take him in my mouth, tempt him with my tongue, and make him lose all control. The ache in my body surges, pulses, and itches to be sated.

"Do you have any clue what you do to me?" he asks softly. I lift my eyes from his body to meet his. The unspoken emotions in his eyes shock me, envelop me, and scare me. "You don't, do you?"

I shake my head no, worrying my bottom lip between my teeth. I only know what he does to me. The power he has over me to make me feel again. To make me forget. How his touch alone can quiet the doubts in my head.

He takes a slow step toward me. "You stand there with that innocent look in those stunning violet eyes. With your hair cascading around you like a fairy. And those lips … hmmm, God … those sexy lips that get swollen and so soft after being kissed. I dream about those lips." His words wrap around me, a slow seduction to my ears. He steps closer, reaching out to take my hand in his. "Your face shows vulnerability, Rylee, but your body? Your curves? They scream sin. They make my mouth water to taste you again. They evoke thoughts in me I'm sure would make you blush." He wets his lower lips with his tongue. "The things I want to do to that body of yours, sweetheart."

I suck in a breath, the stark honesty behind his words stripping me bare. Entrancing me. Emboldening me. Creating another crack in the armor protecting my heart.

"You make me *need*, Rylee," he whispers hoarsely as he takes one more step closer.

Goose bumps run up my arms when he reaches out his other hand and runs it up the flank of my torso, stopping casually so that his thumb can brush over the underside of my breast. I respond instantly to his touch, my nipple pebbling in arousal. He leans into me, his face so close to mine that I can see the dark flecks of green floating in his irises. So that I can understand the unspoken words. "*And I don't ever need anything from anybody.*"

His admission is like a match to my gasoline. His incendiary words stroke that small part of me deep down that hopes there might be more here. I look into his eyes, recalling random comments from our time together, and dare to think of possibilities. He has softened me, worn me down, and built me up all in a single space of time.

"Colton?" My voice waivers, riddled with emotion. "I … Colton—"

I never finish my thought because he yanks me into him and crushes his mouth to mine. All the idle flirtation from the night explodes between us in a torrent of seeking lips and groping hands. The urgency is palpable. Our need to feel our skin on each other's is paramount. Colton releases his grip on my hips and grabs the hem of my sweater, pulling it over my head, and only breaking our kiss when it passes over my head. He tosses it on the floor as his mouth crashes back to mine.

Hunger. That is what his kiss tastes like. What his hands feel like on my body. What I feel inside. I want every inch of him and then some. I want to lose myself in him, get lost in the sensation, and become overwhelmed by his touch alone.

"Christ, Rylee …" he pulls back from me, our chests heaving against each other's, our hearts both beating a frantic rhythm. He cups my face in his hands, the look in his darkened eyes tells me that he understands. He feels the hunger too. "You've stripped me, Rylee. You've teased me all night. *I. Just. Don't. Have. Any. Control. Left.*" He squeezes his eyes shut as I feel his cock pulse against my belly. "I don't think I can be gentle, Rylee—"

"Then don't be," I whisper, my own words surprising me. I don't want to be treated like glass anymore. Like Max treated me. I want to feel that violent passion of his wash over me as he takes me with reckless abandon. I want him to dominate me so that I surge up and crash down without a thought.

His eyes widen at my words, a guttural sigh releases from his throat, and then he is against me, devouring me. Desperation pulses between us. He pushes me backward, our legs shuffling into each other, our hands grabbing at every inch of exposed skin. My backside bumps up against the hard edge of the granite on the kitchen island as Colton's hands fumble with my jeans. He shoves them down over my hips and then easily lifts me onto the countertop.

The chill of the granite slab bites into the bare skin of my heated core, adding a new dimension to the heightened sensation in my sex. Colton tugs my jeans and panties down off of my feet, and then spreads my knees apart. He steps into me, pressing between my legs as he brings his mouth back to mine. His hands run down my chest, cupping my breasts through the thin lace of my bra before continuing their descent to the apex of my thighs. He runs a finger over my cleft before slipping a finger between its seam to find me wet and wanting.

"Oh, Rylee …" he hisses as he slides a finger up and back, coating me with my own dampness and pleasuring me at the same time. His other hand is fumbling with the button fly of his jeans. He looks down to watch his teasing torment of my sex and then brings his lips to mine. "I want to feel you on me, Rylee. Nothing between us," his mouth murmurs against mine. His words deepening the ache I'm drowning in. "Can you trust me when I tell you that I've been tested? That I always use protection. Have never had sex without it. That I'm clean." He kisses me again, his tongue slips between my lips, licking, tasting, tempting. "God, I just want to feel you."

"Yes. Me too. Please—" I gasp out as he slips a finger into me, my mind unable to form a coherent sentence. "On the pill … yes … I trust you," I pant as his finger circles inside of me.

"Lie back," he commands as he frees himself from his jeans and grabs my legs just under my bent knees, raising them up.

The cold stone on my back has me arching up the same minute he parts and thrusts into me. I cry out at the overwhelming sensation of his invasion and the sudden fullness of him. He stills, buried completely within me, allowing the pleasure and pain I feel to subside as my body stretches and adjusts to him.

"Oh fuck, Rylee," he rasps as I see his control slipping. His eyes blaze over my body and up to my eyes. I can see the muscles of his torso strain, his jaw clench, and his eyes glaze over wild with need as he tries to rein it back in. "You feel so damn good wrapped around me. Like velvet gripping me."

I gasp as he pulses inside of me, his control depleted. "Yes, Colton, yes," I cry out as he pulls out and slams back into me. Sensation ripples through me as he grabs my hips and pulls me toward him so that my bottom rests off of the edge of the counter. He sets a punishing pace as he thrusts back into me, over and over. Not breaking rhythm, he leans his torso over me and links his hands with mine, pulling them up over my head. He holds them there with one hand while his other hand slides back down to squeeze my breast. His fingers roll my nipple between them, and he swallows the moan he coaxes from me when he captures my mouth again.

The house is filled with nothing but the sounds of our slick flesh hitting each other, our gasping breaths, impassioned pleas between each other, and cries of ecstasy. I can feel the surge building inside of me, my channel tightening around him as he pistons in and out, each iron-hard inch of him hitting every one of my nerves. But I can also see a man on the verge of losing control and finding release as Colton lets go of my hands and braces himself on his elbows, hovering over me. He thrusts one last time before he yells out my name and then suddenly he pulls out of me.

My body clenches at the unexpected emptiness as Colton buries his head against my chest. His body convulses with his climax. In his hand? I'm confused. He groans from the violent pleasure that is shooting through his body. I can feel the tension ease out of his body and the warm caress of his lips on my bare flesh. His touch makes my body squirm as my nerves tingle with the loss of my anticipated orgasm.

I can feel his smile press against my abdomen and as if he can hear me thinking, he murmurs, "I want you to come for me, Rylee. I want to see how sweet you taste."

Oh! My mind processes the reason for his sudden withdrawal. His mouth. On me. "Colton..."

"Shh-shh-shh," he whispers in my ear, his lips brushing the sensitive spot just below my lobe. I arch my head back, scraping my nails across his back. He hisses at my touch as he lays a row of kisses down my neck and around to the other ear. "You've teased me all night, Rylee," his voice rasps, hoarse with desire. "Now it's my turn to return the favor."

A chill runs down my back and it has nothing to do with the cold granite that I'm laid out on. Colton's body flanks me but I feel his hand stretch out and hear the crinkling of a bag beyond my head. I turn my head up to see what he is doing and Colton's other hand holds steadfast to my jaw. "Uh-uh-uh," he warns. "Keep your head still. I wouldn't want you ruining the surprise."

"Colton?" I furrow my brow, curious at what he's talking about despite my body being on high alert from his words. I'm not exactly good with surprises, especially not when I'm naked and vulnerable.

He chuckles, deep and sexy. "That's going to be hard for you, isn't it?" When I don't respond, he lifts up on an elbow and regards me momentarily. "I think it's time you stopped thinking, Rylee. Stopped trying to figure what's ten steps ahead when we're only just getting started." He presses a chaste kiss to my lips. "Stay here, Rylee. Don't move. Understood?"

The authoritative tone of his voice turns me on. His reasoning behind it unnerves me. His weight lifts off of me, and I can hear him pad out of the kitchen. A drawer opens and closes. Apprehension fills me. For the carefree girl inside of me dying to get out, the anticipation is thrilling. For the control freak in me, the disquiet is unwelcome. Do I trust him? Yes. *Without a doubt.* Why? I'm unsure, and that scares the crap out of me.

I hear him return to the kitchen, and he leans over me, a lascivious smile curling the corners of his lips. "Do you know how gorgeous you look right now?" I don't respond but rather bite my lip as I feel his fingers suddenly at my cleft. They part me and slowly trail up and down. I arch up to meet his touch. He immediately pulls his hand away.

"Colton—"

"Uh-uh, Rylee," he teases. "I'm in control. Right here and right now." I flutter my eyelids as I look up to meet his eyes. My heart hammers in my chest at his words. My nipples tighten at the thought. Fear tingeing the edges of my Colton-induced haze. Handing my control over to someone else is a disconcerting notion. Submitting without a thought even more so.

"Stop thinking, baby," he whispers as he pulls my hands above my head. "I want to take all control from you so that the only thing your mind can do is feel. You won't be able to think five steps in front when you're not the one making the moves now, will you?"

Oh fuck! What is he— My thoughts are obliterated when he crushes his mouth to mine. I wiggle to move my hands and he laughs as we kiss. "Sorry, sweetheart," he murmurs, "you're going to learn that sometimes, not being in control is extremely liberating." He loops something around my wrists and binds them around the faucet at the other end of the island. As I register what he's done, as I start to realize how practiced that move was and how many times before he's done it, my world goes black as he slips a blindfold over my eyes. I gasp. "Time to take your own advice, Rylee."

What? When did I ever say tie me up and take advantage of me?

"You told me to close my eyes on the Tilt-A-Whirl. That it heightens the sensation." The pad of his thumb traces the outline of my lips.

Oh crap! Me and my big mouth.

Something soft but slightly coarse runs over my stomach and up my torso to circle around my nipples. I suck in a breath as whatever he has strokes me lightly down the tops of my legs and then up one inner thigh and down the other. My sex clenches from its touch, desperate for something to help ease the blistering ache. The only thing that touches my body is this object. The only sound I hear is my own breath. The anticipation that builds within me is profound as he continues his slow, tantalizing torture of my senses.

I've never needed a man's touch in my life as much as I do at this moment. My next thought is only where he'll touch me next. There is nothing to do but focus on the sensations. My nerves are on edge awaiting his contact with my body. He has succeeded in making me forget what step ten will be, but rather revel in the step I'm in. I've lost all sense of my surroundings. Nothing else exists in this moment except for him, my desperation for his touch, and my body's craving for release.

Colton is absolutely silent except for the barely audible rush of air I hear escape his mouth in response to my body's reaction to the delicious torment of his sensual sensory deprivation.

Colton stops at my right breast, and before I can place the sensation, he touches me for the first time by capturing my nipple in his mouth. I buck my hips wildly at the warmth of his mouth on my sensitive bud.

"Colton!" I cry out, tugging my hands against my bindings, wanting to touch him. Wanting to thread my fingers in his hair and hold him against me.

He tugs on my nipple with a gentle pull of his teeth and then the warmth of his mouth is gone only to be felt again on my other breast. I feel the strange object circling around it before his mouth closes over it again. He groans softly. "Tasty," he murmurs against me, and I realize he's teasing me about the cotton candy.

I start to speak and am stopped as his mouth closes over mine, the sweet sugary taste on his tongue. It's a soft, tender kiss. A gradual easing of lips and tongue that lacks urgency yet screams of desperation. His lips travel down my exposed neck and back up, nipping at my earlobe. A slow and welcome torture that is making me want like never before.

I can feel the cotton candy slowly move down my torso to my sex. The confection leaves my skin, and I feel his fingers roaming over me, caressing my folds, and catering to my body's addiction to his touch. I gasp as we kiss and Colton takes in my voracious moan of desire. He skillfully teases me with his dexterous fingertips, and I push my pelvis against his hand, wanting more. Needing the friction to inch me closer to the edge.

I hiss out a breath as he parts me, very slowly slipping a finger into my core. Heat flashes through me as I feel my muscles tighten around him, clenching as fire burns through my veins. He cups me, leisurely rocking his hand as his thumb finds and stimulates my nub of nerve endings. He withdraws his finger and then slowly tucks two back into me. He curves them, rubbing against the sensitive spot deep inside, his fingers and tongue mimicking each other as he intensifies his pace. I fist my hands inside my bindings, my nails digging into my palms, as he quickens the rhythm.

I am so gloriously close to crashing into the oblivion and then, all of a sudden, I'm not. Colton has withdrawn from me. I cry out his name in frustration. In desperation. I hear a low, rumbling chuckle from him. "Not yet, sweetheart. Turnabout's fair play," he croons in my ear. "I want to drive you crazy like you do me." I feel a softness tickle my lips and I open them, accepting the sweet bite of cotton candy on my tongue. "I want to drive you to the crest, Rylee. Take you to the brink so that your only thought is of me. So that you cry out my name when your body detonates into a million splinters of pleasure."

His hypnotic words entrance me. Seduce me. And without a hint of what's next, Colton's mouth closes over my clit as he slips two fingers back into me. I call out inarticulately at the exquisite pleasure that pulses through me. He sucks, gently teasing me until my legs tighten impatiently. His fingers slowly press in and out of my channel, rubbing, teasing, and urging me higher. I lift my hips to him, reeling from his manipulation, but still wanting more. I pant in need then moan in ecstasy as I feel the quickening start to build again beneath his touch. I am so close. Within a few grazes of my climax, Colton abruptly withdraws his mouth. His fingers remain, yet stay motionless within me.

Damn him! My chest heaves for air as my body stays wound tight, waiting for the slightest movement to set me off. "Greedy little girl," he admonishes, his breath whispering over my slick flesh. "I may have to rectify this." And before he can finish his last word, he withdraws his fingers and slams into me, burying himself to the hilt in my heated depth.

"Oh God, Colton!" The sudden fullness, the unexpected stroke, makes me writhe against the granite slab.

Colton eases out of me slowly before plunging back in. He continues this slow withdrawal followed by his greedy drive back in, setting a delirious pace that pushes me to the edge. "Come for me, Rylee!" he growls at me.

His words are my undoing. My breath quickens. My pulse races. My muscles tense. My hips grind into him, deepening the burning ache until I am pushed over the edge. I explode like a firecracker. A white-hot heat flits though my body. Sensation shatters around me as the first wave of my orgasm explodes. I incoherently yell out as I pulse around him. He stills, allowing me to absorb the intensity of my climax. I release the breath I've been holding, my taut muscles slowly relaxing before another wave shudders through me.

This wave is more than he can bear. My muscles milk his orgasm out of him. He rears back and pushes into me a few more times, my body gripping his. He yells out my name, his own climax tearing through him, and his hips jerking against me until I can feel his warmth erupt within me.

He collapses on top of me, pressing his face into the curve of my neck. Our chests heave in uneven unison, and I can feel his lips form a smile. My breath shudders as I exhale, the frantic tattoo of my heart beginning to ebb. *That was ... Wow!* I go to remove the blindfold and remember that my hands are still tied.

I wiggle underneath him. He laughs into my neck, the vibration of it seeping into my chest. "I take it you want your hands back?"

"Hmm-hmmm." I don't think I can speak. My body is still processing what has just happened.

He lifts up and I can feel his hands tugging at my bindings. When one hand is free, I reach down and pull off my blindfold, my eyes easily adjusting to the dimmed light in the kitchen. Colton's face is above me, etched in concentration as he works the other knot free. I see the lines ease as my other hand releases from what appears to be a velvet braided rope.

I reach up to run my hands over his cheeks as he looks down at me, an errant lock of hair falling over his forehead. A shy smile lights up his face. I lift my head and brush a soft kiss against his lips, the only way I can express how I feel, how much what just happened meant to me without having him run for the hills.

I lay my head back down, yet Colton's eyes remain closed, the corners of his mouth still smiling. He shakes his head subtly before opening his eyes and easing his weight off of me. "C'mon," he says, pulling me up by my arms, "This can't be all too comfortable for you."

I hop off of the counter, suddenly feeling modest about my nudity. I look around for my clothes as Colton pulls his jeans up over his naked hips. I put my arms through my bra straps as I watch him button up the first four buttons, leaving the top one undone. I have to stifle a sigh as I stare at him naked from the waist up in appreciation.

I hook my bra together and drag my shirt over my head. I start to run my fingers through my disheveled hair but stop when I catch more than just a glimpse of the tattoos that line the side of his torso. I've never really been able to see the whole of them, so I take a moment to look. Four symbols run vertically down his side, all are similar in style. The first three images are solid, the ink filled in completely while the fourth is just an outline. I angle my head, trying to figure out what exactly they are of when Colton looks up and sees my questioning look.

Chapter Seventeen

"What are your tattoos of?"

He turns his body and raises his arm so that I can see the markings. "They're Celtic knots."

"What do they mean?"

"Nothing really," he says gruffly, busying himself by opening the refrigerator, which I notice is almost empty, and grabbing a beer.

"C'mon," I prod, curious about why he is suddenly avoiding the question when he's been so forthcoming all evening. He holds a beer out to me and I shake my head no. "You don't seem like the kind of guy who marks himself permanently without having a reason."

I lean against the counter with my shirt and panties on as he takes a long tug on the beer, his eyes meet mine over the bottom of the bottle. He slides them down the length of my bare legs and back up to my eyes. "The knots mean different things." He lifts his arm again to show me as I move near him. He points to the first one just below his armpit. "This one means to overcome some type of adversity in life." He moves to the next one. "This is the symbol for acceptance. This one is for healing, and the bottom one's for vengeance." He looks up slowly, a darkness in his eyes as they hold mine, waiting for my reaction. Waiting for me to ask why he needs acceptance, healing, and vengeance. We stand silently until he sighs, shaking his head at me, disbelieving that he's said so much.

I step toward him, reach out tentatively, and run my fingers down the four symbols on his body, their meanings resonating in me, telling me somehow, someway they are a marker of his past and where he is in terms of dealing with it. His body shivers at my touch.

"They suit you," I whisper, trying to convey to him that I understand. "Did you get them all at once? Why are three colored in and not the fourth?"

He shrugs away from me, taking another drink from his beer. "No." That's all he gives me, and his tone tells me that that's the end of the conversation.

"You're Irish then?"

"So my Dad tells me."

Mr. Forthcoming. I guess he is done talking about him for the night. The theoretical switch has been flipped, and I'm back trying to catch up to his mercurial mood swings. What now? Does he drive me home? Do I stay the night? Do I get a cab? Unsettled, I pick up my pants and tug them on, struggling to appear coordinated as my ankle gets caught in the cuff. I can feel the heat of his gaze as he watches me although I dare not look up.

"So, Colton ..." I look up as I finish buttoning my jeans to see him watching me as I'd thought, an amused smirk on his face and his eyebrows raised. He may be experienced in the protocol of this type of thing, but I sure am not. My cheeks flush. I search for something to talk about, something that will abate my anxiety until he gives me some kind of indication about what I do from here. "The boys are really looking forward to going to the track when you test the car." He snorts, his head bobbing back and forth, before he stifles a laugh. "What?" I ask, confused by his reaction.

"All business now, are we?" I eye him carefully as he walks toward me, wary of the predatory look in his eyes. "How is it that ten minutes ago you were naked and compliant beneath me and now you're nervous and uncomfortable just being in the same space as me?" *Probably because you dominate any space you occupy*. He reaches out to tug one of my curls. His emerald eyes darken as he watches me. "Am I that scary of a guy, Rylee?"

Shit. I have to work harder at not wearing my emotions on my sleeve. "I'm not nervous." My over-emphatic answer a dead give away that I'm lying.

"Oh, Rylee, it's not exactly polite to lie when some of me is still in you."

My blush darkens. Well, when he puts it that way ... "I'm not lying. I just wanted to—to—uh get the dates so that I can tell the boys."

He raises his eyebrows, a knowing smile on his lips. I'm a horrible liar, and I know he can see right through mine. "What an apropos time to ask." He smirks. "Well..." he reaches out and cups my neck, laying a tender kiss on my lips "...my day planner's at home. I'll have to text you the dates."

I open my eyes from his kiss as I process his words. *What?* I feel his body tense once he's realized what he said. Did I miss something? I snap my eyes up to his and he takes a cautious step back from me. The look on his face is indiscernible.

"Is this not your house?" I shake my head. "What am I missing here?"

Colton runs a hand through his hair, exhaling loudly. "It's my place. I just don't stay here that often." His expression is guarded, tension in the lines around his mouth. His uneasiness unnerves me.

"Oh. Okay. Where else do you …?" And it hits me. The wrong key in the door. The fumbling with the alarm code. The inability to find something in the kitchen cupboards. The empty refrigerator. Colton saying that he shouldn't have brought me here. How could I be so naïve? I raise my eyes to meet Colton's and he knows that I know. The look on his face says it all. I try to swallow the lump in my throat. "So, this is your place, *but not exactly where you live*." I slowly annunciate every word. "It's where you bring all your dates, escorts, whatever you call them, *to fuck*." I choke on the last word. "Right?"

"That's not what this is." His voice is reticent. Rueful.

I snort at his response. "Then what the fuck is this, Colton? I think I need a little clarity here seeing as I still have *some of you in me*, as you so kindly pointed out. Are you referring to the house or as a definition of you and me?"

He just stares at me, green eyes glistening like a hurt puppy dog. "You and me," he breathes.

I walk out of the kitchen, rolling my shoulders, needing some space from him. From that look in his eyes. Why the fuck am I feeling guilty about the look in his eyes when I've done nothing wrong? Ugh! This is bullshit. I walk out into the family room, not wanting him to see the tears of hurt that flood my eyes. I quickly wipe them away with the back of my hand as I focus on the painting, a wash of colors over his fireplace.

"That's not what this is? Then tell me what I'm supposed to think. You tell me you don't do girlfriends, you only *do casual*. Is this where you bring them for a no strings attached good time?"

"Rylee." My name is a one-word plea on his lips. And he is right behind me. I hadn't heard him follow me, my thoughts too loud in my own head. "I keep screwing this up with you," he mumbles to himself.

"You're damn right you do." I turn around to face him. "What? You like me enough to fuck me but not enough to stick around or bring me to your *real house*? Unbelievable!" I huff at him, my confidence at an all time low. Does he really think that I'd be okay with this? Just when I think that I can move on from Max, he makes me jump back as if a rattlesnake has bitten me. *Bastard*! "Maybe you should explain to me a little bit more about your setup here. Make me understand the shit that's in your head." Why am I even asking? It's not like I really want to know the details about his sordid affairs. *To know about what else goes on here on the kitchen counter.* "I mean if that's all I am to you, then I at least deserve to know what's expected of me. *My protocol*." My words drip with anger laced sarcasm. I cross my arms over my chest, a useless form of protection from him.

"Ry? I—uh …" I can see the regret in his eyes. He regards me silently for several moments, an internal struggle warring behind his façade. "Rylee, this is not what I'd planned for me. For us." He pauses, his eyes flooding with emotion. "*You. What you are? What we are? It scares the shit out of me.*"

Whoa! What? Haddie's words come back to me in a rush. I want to melt at his words, at the knowledge that I affect him that much, but a part of me feels like I'm being played here. An easy out for him as an excuse for his actions. Tell me what I want to hear to get me back in his bed, crisis averted, and then drop me at the first chance he gets. He hates drama and I've just caused some. I'm not going to let myself be played by the master player.

"*I scare you?* Shit, Colton, I just let you tie me up, blindfold me, and have your way with me on the kitchen counter. A man I've only known for two weeks when I've only been with one other person before! *And. I. Scare. You?*" His eyes widen, startled by my admission. I raise my hands up, exasperated, wanting to move on before I have to address that little fact about myself. "You told me at the beach that night that you set guidelines, mitigate promises for the future or some bullshit like that … tell me, Colton, do you do that before or after you bring them to this—to here?" I'm on a roll here, anger and humiliation fueling my fire. He just stares at me, eyes wide, arms hanging limply at his sides. "C'mon. Since you didn't have the courtesy to let me know what I was getting in to, I think you should at least tell me now."

"Rylee, that's not what this—"

"I'm waiting, Colton." I lower myself to the edge of the camel-colored leather couch, crossing my arms across my chest. I think I'm going to need to be seated for this one. "How do you set up your *mutual, I'm-only-giving-you-sex-and-nothing-else-arrangements?*"

He sighs loudly, running his hand over his jaw, scrubbing it back and forth before looking back at me. He finally speaks, his voice is soft and hesitant as if he's scared to tell me. "Usually, I hit it off with someone. We figure out we like each other." He shrugs apologetically. "And then I tell her that I enjoy her company, that I would love to spend more time with her, but all I can give her is a few nights a week ... to meet me here..." he gestures at the room we're in "...and have some fun."

I'm not sure if I want to hear this answer. "Go on ..."

He cocks his head to the side and regards me intently, the timid person I'd seen moments before slowly morphing back into the confident man I expect him to be. "The first time we meet here ..." He eyes me cautiously, knowing that I'm thinking this is my first time here. Was this the imminent plan he had laid out for me after screwing me on the counter? I purse my lips, trying hard to keep my face enigmatic. I nod at him to continue, anger unfurling in my belly. "Well, I sit her down and explain that I want to spend time with her, but that there is no happily ever after. Never will be. And if she can accept my terms, my requirements, then I would love to spend time with her here, have her accompany me to functions if need be, and allow her the notoriety and perks of being with me, until our mutual agreement has run its course."

Wow. It takes me a minute to process his words. Talk about taking emotion out of the picture. It sounds more like a business transaction. He stares at me, unashamed.

I look at him wide eyed. "This really works for you?" I sputter, taken aback. "Why not just hire an escort? I mean that's what you're really doing." My head is reeling with this information and yet the masochistic part of me wants to know all the gory details. Wants to hear the words so I heed the warning and walk away unscathed. "Someone to look pretty on your arm and for you *to use* when it suits you."

"I beg to differ," Colton says vehemently. "It's not like that. I never exchange money for sex, Rylee. Never. I've already told you that once. I won't tell you that again."

Like he has any room to be pissy. He just told me he expects me to be his compliant little woman, happy with any scraps he throws my way. Too many thoughts are running through my head to form a coherent, intelligent response. "What—" I finally ask, stumbling for the right words. "You say your arrangement has rules. Do you mind if I ask what exactly those are?"

I'm curious. I'm horrified. I'm floored that this is the path he has chosen when he could obviously have anyone he wants.

I can sense that he's uncomfortable, embarrassed even to respond and this fact gives me a tiny bit of hope. Hope for what though, I'm not exactly sure.

"I know it sounds cold, but I've found that if I lay it all out on the table beforehand, it minimizes complications and lessens expectations further down the line. That way they walk into this willingly after they know the stipulations."

"Not me!" I shout at him. "You didn't tell me!" He starts to speak, and I raise my hand to shut him up. I need a moment to think. I need a minute to wrap my head around his screwy ideals. I lower my head, swallowing loudly. Is this what I am to him? A complication? *God, too much information is sometimes a bad thing*. I chew the inside of my lip in thought. "Why not just say friends with benefits or fuck buddies?"

Irritation flashes through his eyes, and he shifts restlessly, running his fingers through his hair, blatantly ignoring my comment. "You really want to know this, Rylee? The stipulations?" he asks.

I nod, biting down on my bottom lip, worrying it back and forth. "I'm curious," I say, in the back of my head thinking that a psychiatrist would have a field day with this conversation. "I guess I'm just trying to understand this. Trying to understand you. Trying to understand what exactly you *would have* expected from me." His eyebrows shoot up at my comment, and I know that he's heard me. My statement in past tense. That now he knows in no way will I be accepting his self-serving arrangement.

He sits down across from me, his eyes on mine. "What I *would have* expected from you?"

"Yes, your *requirements*," I say sarcastically.

He sighs tentatively, and I nod my head for him to get on with it. "I require monogamy. I require confidentiality, as my reputation as well as my family's is very important to me." He pauses, looking deeply at me, gauging to see if he should continue. "What else?" He breathes in deeply. "I require good hygiene, that she is healthy, drug free, and STD free. Birth control is a deal breaker since as I've told you, children are not now, nor will they ever be an option for me or my future."

He stops and I'm not sure if he's really done, or just thinking of more of his requirements. Ironically enough, I don't think his demands are all that odd. I mean it seems a little much to hammer out on a first date, but if I were to be in a committed relationship with someone, these are things I'd want to know. But then again, to me a committed relationship has the promise of a future, give and take, and the potential for love.

"So...wow!" I say, taking a moment, "that's quite a laundry list of requirements. Are there any more?"

"A few," he admits, "but I think we've exhausted this topic, don't you?"

I silently agree, but I've already delved this far, I might as well get the answers I want from him so I continue. "Oh, you must want to bypass the part where you have your *Pretty Woman* moment and leave the money on the nightstand after you've had your way with her." His eyes whip back up to mine, and I know that I've hit the nail on the head. "I mean, this is all on your terms. Let me guess, you don't actually sleep with her because it's too intimate? Or you buy her clothes and show her off in between bedding her and little do you know, she's using you to further her fledgling modeling career? What exactly is she getting out of this, Ace, besides a quick fuck with a guaranteed prick? And I'm not talking about the one in your pants." My stomach is a bit queasy all of the sudden, and I realize that I don't want to know these details. I don't want to hear what rules and regulations some floozy agrees to so that she can sleep with him and be seen on his arm.

I'm flustered. I'm in way over my head and way out of my element here. I understand that with his usual arrangements, they both use each other. I get that. He gets a companion and she gets the media buzz that might further her career. What I think hurts the most is that I have no intention of using him. I'm not a model or struggling actress. I worry that he dangled the rhetorical carrot in my face with the money for Corporate Cares. That way he can justify using me if he thinks I am using him.

I can feel the tears burn in the back of my throat. I'm so mad right now and oddly it's not at Colton. I'm mad at myself for believing—despite my false bravado that I didn't want anything to progress with Colton—deep down, I still had a touch of hope. Now I know way more than I want to and enough to know that what he's offering is not enough.

"But why, Colton? Why is this all that you'll allow yourself when you deserve so much more?" The look in his eyes tells me that the honesty behind my words affects him.

He puts his head in his hands, his shoulders moving as he sighs. He looks back up at me, a myriad of emotions on his face. "I hate the drama of it, Rylee. The points system of who is contributing how much, the jealousy over my lifestyle and the media surrounding it, the expectation of the next step to take. So many things." He pauses, eyeing me, his tone indifferent. "Relationships are just way too much shit to handle in my crazy life."

I stare into the depths of his eyes and can see right through the bullshit lies he's just tried to feed me. There is something more here. Why is he afraid to get too close to somebody? What happened to get him to this point? "That's a bullshit answer and you know it." He flinches. "I expected more from you."

"Rylee, I'm not one of your troubled kids that needs fixing. I've been fucked up for way too long to be fixed now, so don't get that look in your eye that you know different. Some of the best shrinks in L.A. couldn't do it, so I doubt you'd be able to."

His words sting. The hurt from them sits heavy on my chest as he just sits staring at me. I can see him emotionally pulling away. The cold, detached look on his face tells me he is shutting down. Shutting me out when I'm still fighting for him. But for what?

I rise from the couch, pacing the living room as I try to process everything. The more I think, the angrier I get. "Tell me something, Colton?" I whirl back around. I'm a mix of random emotion. I want to go, to have him leave me alone, and yet I can't stop staring at the train wreck in front of me. Can't stop the part of me that wants to help him. "Is this what I am to you? Is this the type of *relationship*—and I use that term loosely—that you were hoping for between you and me?" I ask him, my voice wavering.

"Rylee, that's not what I—" He shakes his head, running both hands over his face, his emotional struggle being played out before my eyes. "At first, yes," he says, "but after this past week—after tonight—I'm just not sure anymore."

"What? Now I'm not good enough for you?" What the hell am I doing? One minute I'm mad that he thinks of me as a mutual agreement and the next I'm pissed that now he doesn't. *Get your head straight, Rylee!*

"Christ, Rylee!" he hisses as he stands abruptly, shoving a hand through his hair and stalking toward me. He reaches out to touch me, but thinks better of it when I shrug my shoulder back. "I don't know what I want." The muscle in his jaw twitches, and I can see the strain in his neck. He clenches and unclenches his fists, closing his eyes and sighing deeply before opening them up to meet my gaze again. I catch a fleeting glimpse of fear and then resolve before he reins it in. "But whatever this is, *I know I want it with you, Rylee.*"

I have to control the rush of feelings that flood through me from his words. He wants it with me. *What with me, though?* He is so close that I want to reach out and touch him. Calm that fear that I see in his eyes. But I know if I touch him, skin to skin, I will acquiesce to his ridiculous demands. And I know deep down, as much as I want him, I don't think I can be what he wants me to be.

"My way? My *arrangement* as you call it…" he shakes his head "…is all I know how to do, Rylee. Is all I know how to be." He reaches out to grab my hand, and I have to steel myself to not react to his touch. "It's all I can give you right now." The solemnity in his voice touches me deep down and twists in my heart.

I turn from him and walk the length of the room, grabbing his beer without thinking and taking a long swallow. I hate the flavor of beer but I don't even taste it. I'm tired. I'm hurt. And I can't fight the tears anymore. My eyes pool and a single tear falls over and runs down my cheek. My back is to him so I can't see the look on his face when I say, "I don't know if I can do this, Colton." I shake my head, sighing deeply.

"Rylee, don't be ridiculous."

"Ridiculous?" I sputter. "No, ridiculous is me thinking for a second that I *could* do this, Colton." I shrug my shoulders in sadness and resignation. "I walked into this—whatever we have here—telling myself that all you want is a quick fuck from me." I turn back to him as I speak and see him wince at my words. "Maybe a little fling … and I thought I could give that to you. Take that from you. But now that you're actually offering it to me, I don't think I can." Another wayward tear falls, and I see him watch it before bringing his eyes back up to mine.

"What do you mean, Rylee?" His mask slips momentarily, and I see vulnerability and panic flutter over his face. "Why not?"

A small part of me relishes the idea that my threat can make him panic but staying is not going to fix things. I press my fingers to my eyes. I'm sure I look like hell right now: hair frizzed, eyeliner smudged, lipstick gone, but I really don't care. My insides are ten times more devastated than what my outside looks like. "When I tell myself that this is all I am to you—sex without feelings or the possibility of a future—it's one thing."

Without thinking I give into my addiction. I can't resist. I reach out and brush my fingers over his cheek. He starts to turn his cheek into my hand and catches himself before he does. I let my hand fall at his subtle rejection. "But when I hear the words from your lips. When I hear you tell me your *rules and regulations*, it's a whole different thing." I close my eyes momentarily, trying to stop the small tremor in my voice. *"I will not be inconsequential, Colton. To you or anyone else."*

Colton runs a hand through his hair and scrubs his hands over his eyes. "That's not what you are to me, Rylee," he breathes, raising his eyes to me.

I stare at him. I want to believe him. I really do. But I can't sell myself short. I deserve more than this. I want more than what he's offering. "That may be true, Colton, but that admission, it's not enough for me." It breaks my heart to say these words to him.

"Rylee, just try it," he urges. "Try it my way."

"Oh save it, Colton!" I bite at him, throwing my hands up in the air. "I'm not one of your little floozies who's going to do whatever you say just because you say to. I'm sure you have those lining up waiting to be your plaything. Catch one of them and toss her back when you're tired of her. Not me, Ace. I don't work that way." My anger has resurfaced, despite my exhaustion and aching heart.

Colton just stares at me. We stand within a foot of each other, eyes locked, and yet I feel so far away from him. It's hard to believe it's been less than an hour since we were intimate.

"Rylee," he pleas.

"What, Colton?" I snap, immediately wincing from my tone.

"That first night …" he begins softly and then stops turning from me and walking toward the kitchen.

"What about it, Colton?" I follow him partway, leaning against the back of his couch. "I should have seen it then. You sleeping with me and then humiliating me by jumping out of bed like I'd burned you."

"You did, Rylee."

"What? What in the hell are you talking about?"

"That first night," he continues, ignoring my comment. "After the second time," he says, blowing out a loud breath. He continues to look at his bare feet, his hips resting against the counter, hands shoved in his pockets and discomfort rolling off him in waves. "I kissed you and asked you if you were all right." I nod my head acknowledging him, remembering the raw honesty in that simple moment between us. "I swear to God, Rylee … I felt like you saw me. *Really saw me.*" He raises his eyes to meet mine and they're swimming with emotion. "And you were sitting there, your dark hair falling all around you with that white sheet pooled around your waist..." he shakes his head before continuing "...your lips were swollen, your eyes were so wide and trusting … and I realized in that second that it meant more to me." His voice is hoarse with emotion. "That you meant more to me, Rylee, than anything I can remember. *Ever.*"

I stare at him, so many things running through my head, but more than anything, his words resonate in every dark part of me that craves to be wanted, needed, and desired. At least I know why he reacted how he did. Why he showed up this morning. Hope starts to soar in me. Maybe I can do this. Maybe with time, I can prove to him that there can be more. I wring my hands to try and stifle my sudden enthusiasm.

"You scared the shit out of me, Rylee. *You burned me.*" He runs his hand through his hair, his eyes darkening, "And then I realized, as I do right now, that in the end I'm going to break you apart."

"What?" I snap my head up to meet his eyes, my hopes crashing down around me. *Did I just hear him correctly?*

"I can't do that to you, Rylee." I see his fists clench as he fights his emotions. "I tried to warn you, but I'm so frickin' drawn to you. I just can't stay away."

I feel schizophrenic trying to keep up with his moods. "You tell me you can't do this, that you'll destroy me, but then you tell me you can't stay away even though you are the one warning me. You push me away then show up at my doorstep and give me tonight." I walk toward him in the kitchen until I stand in front of him. "Which way is up, Colton?"

Without a word, he grabs me and pulls me against his chest, wraps his arms tightly around me, and buries his nose in my hair. I press my hands against his back and absorb his warmth, surprised by his unexpected show of emotion. His need for me is palpable. It oozes off of him and wraps its way into my soul. It takes everything I have to not tell him yes. Tell him I'll do anything just to have a piece of him. That is how much he means to me. But my thoughts are louder than my heart. I wish that I could just quiet my head and sink into the reassuring feeling of his arms. Block out everything else.

"I'm going to hurt you, Rylee. And you already mean too much to me to do that to you." I stiffen at his words. But despite them, he holds me tighter. I try to push away from him but his arms will not release me. I relent eventually and lay my face against his chest, inhale the smell of us mingled together, feel the coarseness of the hair on his chest, and hear the strong, steady beat of his heart. "It's a first for me to care enough about someone to stop. But knowing it ahead of time isn't going to stop me from doing it. And I just can't do that to you, Rylee." His chest heaves a long breath. "And that's why I can't do this anymore with you. Why we can't ..."

"But why, Colton? Why can't you? Why can't we?" I'm panicked now. Now that I want him, he's telling me no. Or maybe that's exactly why. I'm grasping at straws now.

"Look, let's not get this confused here. I'm not and never have been the boy you bring home to mom, Ry. I'm the one you throw in her face to piss her off and show her you are asserting your independence. Let's not make me out to be better than I am."

I'm still not buying it. Why does he think so horribly of himself? He can repeat this crappy answer ad nauseam and I still won't believe it. "Who did this to you?"

We're quiet for a few moments as he mulls over my questions. Eventually he sighs. "I told you, Rylee, I've got a 747 of baggage."

I push against his chest. I need to see his eyes. Need to look into them. When I do, I can see he's hurting too. But he's also shutting down. Putting me at arm's distance emotionally so that it prevents further hurt in him. *But what about me?* I want to scream at him. What about my hurt? Why does this have to be so complicated? Why can't I just let it be and enjoy the ride? Hope that he'll see the real me and fall in love? Because I know that if he doesn't face whatever trauma has made him this way, he'll never get over it. He'll never be able to have a normal relationship. He's right. His 747 of baggage is going to ruin whatever chance we may have. "I'm not buying it, Colton."

With my words, he removes his hands from my arms, now physically distancing himself from me. "I can't give you any more, Rylee." He looks down and then looks back up, the mask effectively in place. "This is who I am."

Tears pool in my eyes, my voice a whisper. "*And this is who I am, Colton.*" When I speak those words I know. I have already started to fall for him. Warts and all. Somehow, someway, despite the short amount of time I've spent with him, he has penetrated that protective wall around my heart, and I've started the slow descent toward love. And that's why I know I can't do this. I can't walk knowingly into heartbreak. I've been devastated once. I don't think I can survive that again. And I know without a doubt that loving Colton and not getting love in return would devastate me.

"I guess we're at an impasse." His voice is gruff and he stuffs his hands in his pockets. The weight of his hands causes his jeans to hang lower on his hips. I have to physically stop myself from looking at the sexy inverted triangle of muscles that peeks over his waistband. I don't need a reminder of what is no longer mine.

"Then I guess it's time for you to take me home." I avert my eyes, unable to meet his as I choke the words out.

"Rylee ..." he says.

"I deserve more than this, Colton," I whisper, raising my eyes to meet his, "and so do you."

I can see his hands grip the kitchen counter as he digests my words, his knuckles white, and his face twisted in anguish. "Please, Rylee. Stay the night."

I hear the desperation in his voice, know that he really means it, but I know he is asking for the wrong reasons. He is asking to ease the hurt he knows he is causing me, not because he wants to make this more than the arrangement he desires.

"We both know that's not how this story goes." A tear slides down my cheek. "I'm sorry I can't be what you want me to be. Please take me home, Colton."

The ride home is silent. Adele's velvety voice sings softly on the radio about never finding someone like you, and deep down I feel the same way. It would be hard to compare anyone to Colton. I glance at him occasionally, watching the shadows and lights of the night play over the angles of his face. I know I am doing the right thing, self-preservation at its best, but my heart still aches at the thought of walking away from this mesmerizing man.

We arrive at my house with fewer than ten words spoken between us. Oddly, I'm still comfortable with Colton's presence despite my inner-turmoil.

He opens my door and escorts me out with a sad half-smile on his lips. He places his hand on my lower back as we walk up the walkway. At the front door, lit by a lone porch light, I turn to him. We both say each other's names at the same time and then smile softly at each other. The smiles never reach our eyes though. They reflect a weary sadness.

"You first," I tell him.

He sighs and just stares at me. I want so much for him to be able to express to me the emotions I can see swimming in his eyes, but I know that he'll never get the chance to tell me. He reaches out and brushes his knuckles over my cheek with the back of his hand. I close my eyes at the sensation. When he stops, I open them back up, tears pooling in them, to meet his. "I'm sorry," he whispers.

I know that his apology is for so many things. For what can never be. For what should be. For hurting me. For not being the person I need him to be. For not being able to confront whatever is in his past.

"I know." I reach up and run my fingers over his unshaven jaw and up through his wavy hair before returning back to his face. It's almost as if I am committing his lines and his features to memory. Something I can hold on to. For despite still having to work with him, I know that this will be the last time I'll allow myself to touch him. Touching him will be too dangerous for my weakened heart.

I step up on my tiptoes and brush my lips gently against his. Within moments, Colton has his arms around me and is lifting me up to his level. Our eyes lock on each other. He leans into me to resume our kiss. I feel something different in it. I realize that we are saying an unspoken goodbye. All of the hurt and unspoken possibilities are thrown into the unyielding softness of our exchange. The desperation and carnal need of earlier has been replaced with a poignant resignation. We slowly end the kiss, Colton gently lowers me, my body sliding down the familiar length of his. Once my feet are on the ground, he rests his forehead against mine. Our eyes remain closed as we take in this last moment with each other.

I move my hand between our bodies and place it over his heart, our foreheads still touching. "I wish you'd explain to me why you don't do relationships, Colton." My voice is barely a whisper, the threat of tears evident. "Maybe I could understand you—this—better then."

"I know," he breathes in response. He shifts and places his trademark kiss on the tip of my nose.

This action is my undoing. Tears silently coarse down my cheeks as Colton whispers, "Goodbye," before turning without looking back at me and hurrying down the pathway.

I can't bear to watch him leave. I fumble clumsily with the lock before shoving the door open and slamming it shut. I lean against the door and slide down it to sit on the floor, my silent tears turning into uncontrollable sobs.

This is how Haddie finds me moments later after being woken by my less-than-graceful entrance.

Chapter Eighteen

The week has sucked. My applicants for the new staff position at The House have been horrible. Unqualified. Underwhelming. Unexciting.

It might not help that my mind is not all here. I'm tired because sleep comes in short bouts interrupted by confusing nightmares of Colton and Max. My subconscious is obviously having a field day with my emotions.

I'm cranky because I'm eating everything in sight, and yet I have no desire to go run and work off all of the excess calories that I'm stuffing in my mouth to abate my misery.

I'm irritable because Haddie is watching me like a hawk, calling me every hour to check up on me, and turning off Matchbox Twenty anytime she catches me listening to it.

I'm petulant because Teddy just forwarded me an email from Tawny listing all of the events that CD Enterprises is requesting my presence at to promote our new partnership. And that means that I will have to stand side by side with Colton, the sole cause of my miserable state. Because despite the four days that have passed, nothing has helped to ease the ache radiating through my heart and soul from my last moments with Colton. I want to tell myself to get a grip, that we only knew each other a short time, but nothing works.

I still want him. I still feel him.

I'm pathetic.

The only personal contact I've had with him came via email the day after he dropped me off. He sent me a text saying:

***Whataya Want From Me* by Adam Lambert.**

I listened to the song, confused by the lyrics. He's telling me that we're not going to happen and yet he sends me a song asking me not to give up while he works his shit out. A part of me is pleased that he's still communicating, while another part of me is sad that he just won't let me lick my wounds by myself. I wasn't even going to respond until I heard the song playing on Shane's radio. I texted back:

***Numb* by Usher**

I was trying to tell him that until he confronts his same old modus operandi, nothing's ever going to change, and he's going to remain numb. He never replied, and I didn't expect him to.

I sigh loudly, alone at the kitchen counter at The House. Zander is at a counseling session with Jackson, and the rest of the boys are at school for another two hours. I'm on my last stack of resumes . One applicant is coming for an interview, but besides her, I've come across no one else even close to qualified.

The muffled sound of my cell phone ringing breaks me out of my trance. I scramble frantically to pick it up, my heart racing, hoping that it might be Colton even though we have not talked since Sunday night. My mind tells me it's not going to be him while my heart still hopes that it is.

My screen says *private caller* and I answer it with a breathless "Hello."

"Rylee?"

My heart swells at the rasp of his voice. Shock has me hesitating to respond. Pride has me wanting to make sure that the hitch in my voice is absent when I finally speak. "Ace?"

"*Hi, Rylee.*" The warmth mixed with relief in his voice has me shaking with an undercurrent of emotions.

"*Hi, Colton.*" I reply, my tone matching his.

He chuckles softly at my response before silence fills the phone line. He clears his throat. "I was just calling to let you know a car will pick you up at The House on Sunday at nine-thirty." His voice, so full of warmth moments before, is now disembodied and official sounding.

"Oh. Okay." I sag in my chair, overcome by disappointment that he's just calling to reiterate the email one of his staff members sent two days ago. I can hear him breathing on the line and can hear voices in the distance.

"You still have a total of ten, right? Seven boys and three counselors?"

"Yes." My tone is clipped, business-like. My only form of protection against him. "They are extremely excited about it."

"Cool."

Silence hangs in the air. I need to think of something to say so he doesn't hang up. Despite the tension between us, knowing he is on the other end of the line is better than him not being there at all. I know my line of thinking screams "desperate," but I don't care. My brain scrambles to form a sentence, and right when I say his name, Colton says mine. We laugh.

"Sorry, you go first, Colton." I try to rid my voice of the nerves that creep their way into my tone.

"How are you, Rylee?"

Miserable. Missing you. I infuse happiness into my next words, glad he's not in front of me to read through my lie. "Good. Fine. Just busy. You know."

"Oh. I'm sorry. I'll let you go."

No! Not yet! My mind grasps to think of something to keep him on the phone. "Are-are you ... ready for Sunday?"

"We're getting there." I think I hear a tinge of relief in his voice but chock it up to my imagination. "The car seems to be working great. We've made some adjustments to the lift/drag ratio, which seems to be working better." I can hear the enthusiasm in his voice. "We'll dial it in more on Sunday. And Beckett, my crew chief, thinks we need to adjust the camber, and you asked me why I don't do relationships."

What? Whoa! Direction change. I don't know what to say so I just murmur, "Hmm-hmmm," afraid that if I speak, it might reveal to him just how much I want to know, and at the same time, afraid to find out.

I can hear him sigh on the other end of the phone, and I imagine him running his hands through his hair. His voice is hushed when he finally speaks. "Let's just say my early childhood ... those years were ... more fucked up than not." I can sense his apprehension.

"Before you were adopted?" I know the answer, but it's the only thing I can think to say without him thinking I feel pity for him. And silence would be even worse.

"Yes, before I was adopted. As a result ... I ... how do I ...?" He struggles to find the right words. I hear another exhaled breath before he continues. "I sabotage anything that resembles a relationship. If things are going too well ... depending on which shrink you talk to, I purposely, unknowingly, or subconsciously ruin it. Screw it up. Hurt the other person." It all comes out in a quick jumble of words. "Just ask my poor parents." A self-deprecating laugh slips out. "Growing up, I fucked them over more times than I care to count."

"Oh ... I ... Colton—"

"I'm hardwired this way, Rylee. I'll purposely do something to hurt you to prove that I can. To prove that you won't stick around regardless of the consequences. To prove that I can control the situation. To avoid getting hurt."

So many things run through my mind. Most of them are about the unspoken words he's saying. That his history makes him test the limits of the person he's with to prove he's not worthy of their love. To prove they'll leave him too. My heart aches for him and for whatever unknown thing that happened to him as a child. On the other hand, he has opened up to me some, partially answering the question I asked against his lips on my front porch.

"I told you, a 747 of baggage sweetheart."

"It doesn't matter, Colton."

"Yes it does, Rylee." He laughs nervously. "I won't commit to anyone. It's just easier on everyone in the long run."

"Ace, you're not the first guy I've known with commitment issues," I joke, trying to add some levity to our conversation. But deep down I know that his inability to commit stems from something way deeper than just typical male reluctance.

I hear his nervous laugh again. "Rylee?"

"Yes?"

"I respect you and your need for the commitment and the emotion that comes with a relationship." He pauses, silence stretching between us as he finds his next words. "I really do. I'm just not built that way ... so don't feel bad. This would've never worked."

My hope, which has been rising despite my trying to control it, crashes back down. "I don't understand. I just—"

"What?" Colton says distracted, talking to a voice I hear in the background. "Saved by the bell! I'm needed on the track right now. More fine tuning." I can hear the relief in his voice.

"Oh. Okay." Disappointment fills me. I want to finish this conversation.

"No hard feelings then? I'll see you at the track on Sunday?"

I momentarily close my eyes, fortifying my voice with false nonchalance. "Sure. No hard feelings. See you on Sunday."

"See ya, Ryles."

The phone clicks and the dial tone fills my ear. I sit there not hearing it. Does he realize that he used his defense mechanism right now? Hurt me to keep me away? Put me in my place so that he can have all the control.

I'm unsettled. I want to finish our conversation. Tell him that it doesn't have to be this way. I want to comfort him. Ease the panic that laces his voice. Tell him that he makes me feel again after being numb for so very long. Confess that I want to be with him despite knowing deep down I will be destroyed in the end.

I pick up my phone, pondering what I'm going to say. In the end, all I text is:

Be safe on the track Ace!

He responds quickly.

Always. You know I've got great hands.

I smile sadly. My heart wanting so much that my head knows I'll never get.

Chapter Nineteen

The limo bus pulls through the gates of Auto Club Speedway in Fontana. The boys are buzzing with excitement, eyes wide as saucers taking in the sheer size of the complex. They have put on their shirts and all access lanyards that Colton's staff has left aboard the bus for them. Their wide smiles and their constant *oohs and aahs* fill the air and fill my heart with joy. Zander bounces unexpectedly on the seat, vibrating with an obvious energy that takes me by surprise. I look at Jackson and Dane, my fellow counselors, and note that they see it too.

For the first time in almost a week, I feel like I can smile, and ironically, it's Colton that has made me feel this way. I'm thankful to him for the little touches he has added for the boys: a personalized letter, the shirts, the lanyards, and glossy magazines with his car on the cover. Things that make them feel special. Important.

Our bus is directed down a tunnel under the stands before driving onto the infield. I didn't think it possible, but the boys' hooting and hollering becomes even louder. We come to a stop and the doors open. Within moments, a man hops on the bus, bounding with enthusiasm. He directs us off of the bus and has us follow him to a meeting room where he tells us we will meet up with Colton.

I feel small walking through this large arena. To the south of us, a large grandstand juts up to towering heights while the banked oval of the track encompasses the entire field around us. I can hear engines revving and see people scurrying to and fro in a garage on my right. With each step we take, my anxiety about seeing Colton again increases. How is he going to react after his telephone confession to me? Will it be business as usual or will there still be that magnetic pull between us? Despite my anxiety, I'm also excited to see Colton in action. To watch him in his element.

We arrive at a brick building and our facilitator, who we've learned on our walk is named Davis, leads us into a room with a red door. We heed his advice to gather around, the boys chattering excitedly. They call out random questions to Davis who patiently answers them.

When they settle down a bit, Davis explains the reason for testing. "When we're testing, a lot of time goes into tweaking the car. Little adjustments here and there that makes the car go faster or handle better. These changes are essential to the overall performance of the car when the season starts in late March. Along with these tweaks, Colton meets with his crew chief, Beckett Daniels, and reviews what they are working on. That is where Colton currently is now, discussing—"

"Not anymore." Chills dance up my spine as I hear the rumble of Colton's voice. Whoops go up as the boys greet him. I look down at Zander and the wide, genuine grin on his face causes my heart to lodge in my throat.

"Hey, guys!" he throws back at them. "So glad you're here! Are you guys ready for a fun day?"

The cheers go up again as I inhale deeply, preparing myself to turn around and face him. When I do, my heart squeezes tightly. Colton is on his haunches, eye level with the little guys of our group, and ruffling the hair on their heads playfully. He laughs sincerely at something Scooter says and then stands slowly, lifting his eyes, locking them with mine.

All thoughts leave my head as I drink him in. He's wearing a red fire safety suit, the top portion unzipped and tied around his waist to reveal a snug-fitting white t-shirt with a faded logo across the chest and a small hole in the left shoulder. His hair is a spiked mess and his jaw sports the shadow of a day's missed shave. My thoughts immediately focus on how much I'd love to run my tongue over his lips and fist my hands in his hair.

I bite my bottom lip, the quick pain a reminder that this is not going to happen—we're not going to happen—and to help me resist any urges that I might have of thinking otherwise. Colton's eyes stay locked on mine as the boys I love surround him. A slow, lazy grin spreads on his face.

All thoughts of resistance vanish. Shit! I'm in so over my head.

"Hello, Rylee." So much is behind those two words. All of the hurt and confusion and over-analyzing from the past couple of days disintegrates. In case I didn't know it before, it's obvious now that his proximity clouds both my judgment and my common sense.

"Hi." My nervous response is all I can manage as we continue to hold each other's gazes, as if we are the only two people in the room. I fidget with my hands, trying to ignore the desire blooming in my core. Kyle tugs on his hand, and after a beat, he drags his gaze away from me to focus back on the boys.

I slowly exhale the breath I didn't know I was holding. Dane scoots near me and leans in. "Damn, Rylee! What the hell's going on here?" I give him a bemused look, as if I don't know what he's talking about. "If I didn't know any better, that stare said he wanted to eat you for dessert." I laugh at him, nudging him playfully, trying to avoid having to answer. And to hide the blush crawling into my cheeks, remembering Colton's version of cotton candy dessert. "The man obviously wants you, girl!"

"Oh, whatever! You read the tabloids, Dane. He's a total player. I'm sure he gives that look to every woman." I'm grateful for the distraction when Zander sidles up next to me, and I place my hand on his shoulder. Colton notices and looks up from the other boys to meet Zander's eyes. He moves from the crowd of boys and walks over to kneel in front of us.

"Hiya, Zander. I'm so glad you could come today." Colton remains still, watching and waiting for an indication from Zander about how he should proceed.

I suck in a breath as I hear a hoarse sound from Zander's mouth. A croaked, "Hi," comes out and the cautious smile on Colton's face spreads to a megawatt grin. A tear trickles down my cheek, and I quickly dash it away, looking over to Dane and Jackson to see relief and pride on their faces as well.

Zander spoke his first word!

Colton clears his throat, and I think the moment may have gotten to him too. "So I'm going to need special help from you later, if that's okay?" When Zander nods, Colton slowly reaches out, showing Zander the intention of his actions, and when he doesn't flinch, Colton gently tousles his hair.

Colton glances up to me as he stands, and the tears swimming in my eyes are for both Zander's reaction and because of the man before me. Over everything that can't be with him. He gives me a resigned, knowing smile before turning his focus back on the other six boys. "So guys, are you ready to head down to the pits, check out the car, and get ready to test it all out?" Colton staggers back playfully at the roar of the boys' consent. "I take that as a yes!" He laughs.

Out of the corner of my eye, I notice a statuesque blonde enter the room with a clipboard in one hand, a worn baseball cap in the other, and an official-looking pass around her neck. She leans against the doorjamb watching Colton and must feel my stare on her because she turns, slowly eying me up and down. Her eyes finally meet mine, a small smirk on her lips and a less than friendly look in her eyes. And then it dawns on me who she is. She's Tawny Taylor: sometimes escort, CD Enterprises employee, and who knows what else to Colton. I bristle at the realization; her lengthy legs, sample size figure, long blonde hair, and stunning face making me feel beyond insecure. Why would Colton chase someone like me when he could have someone like her?

Colton looks over at her as she says his name in her throaty voice, interrupting his answer to Shane's question. "Just a minute, boys." He excuses himself and walks over to where she stands.

She holds out the battered baseball cap, and he runs a hand through his hair before placing it on his head. I hear their quiet voices and make out a few words in between the yells of my boys. Colton holds his hands on his hips, broad shoulders filling out the faded T-shirt, as he nods his head at Tawny. Her smile is wide, knowing, and when she reaches a hand out to place it on Colton's upper arm, I hate her immediately. My ears perk as I hear my name. *What?* Tawny glances over at me quickly before returning to Colton. It seems as if they are wrapping things up, so I busy myself by paying attention to the posters hanging on the walls. I hear Colton say, "Thanks," before returning to his audience. Tawny turns for the door and notices me studying her. She flashes me an insincere, catty smile as she walks out the door. Her smile says it all. Colton's her territory, and I'm just an intruder.

Well, game on, sweetheart!

With Tawny gone and at least one adversary known, I turn my attention back to Colton, who is telling the boys what to expect from testing. He patiently and simply answers their questions. Zander stands closely to Colton, engaged in watching the conversation, his eyes never leaving his face. When he finishes, Davis glances at his watch and pipes up, "Okay, guys, I'm going to lead you down to the pits. You guys can sit in the seats right above so you can see everything. We're also going to get you outfitted with headsets so that you can hear us talking back and forth with Colton." He grabs his clipboard and turns toward the door, "So if you'll follow me, we'll get you all set!"

The boys fidget animatedly as they fall into line behind Davis. I grab my bag and start to follow, anxiety rising at the possibility of being alone with Colton. I usually have strong will power but when it comes to Colton, it's nonexistent. I take my first step when I hear his voice behind me. "Can I have a sec, Ry?"

I ignore the raised eyebrows that Dane gives me before turning and following the boys out the door. Not trusting my voice, I figure that my lack of forward movement is enough of an answer for Colton.

"It's good to see you." His voice is gruff.

I take a deep breath and close my eyes momentarily, trying to clear the emotion from my face and remove my heart from my sleeve. I slowly turn around, a falsely calm smile on my lips as I remind myself of his words from the other day. The full force of the devastating effect he has on me hits me when I meet his eyes.

This would've never worked. "You too, Ace."

He's sitting on the edge of a table, one foot resting on the seat of the chair in front of him, his hands twirling his sunglasses. My heart twists at the sight of him, knowing I can have some of him but not the whole I need. I walk toward him, our chemistry irrefutable and his pull on me magnetic. I smile shyly at him, trying to keep my emotions under wraps. I stop in front of him, my fingers itching to touch. His eyes watch my hand as I reach out and wipe off an imaginary piece of lint from his shirt. "You look so official!" I laugh anxiously, saying the only thing that comes to my mind.

He cocks his head and raises an eyebrow at me. "What? You think I'm faking it and this is all for show?" he says dryly, rising from the table. When he unfolds himself and stands to his full height, his body is mere inches from mine. His scent envelops me and I take a step back to prevent myself from reaching out to touch him again. Any measure to try and preserve my dignity.

"No. That's not what I meant." I shake my head flustered, stepping back again to create some space. "Being here just makes it all so real—the track, seeing you in your suit, the grandstands ... the enormity of it all." I shrug. "Thank you so much, Colton." With these words I look down at my hands where I instinctively go to worry the ring that's no longer on my finger. Instead, I lace my fingers together and try to hide the emotion swarming in my eyes.

"For what?"

"You went over and above. The stuff in the bus for the kids. Having them here today. Everything." I look back up at him, tears of happiness swimming in my eyes, and say softly, "Zander's first word."

"A breakthrough is so important to healing invisible wounds." I know he understands these words more than most. He reaches out and wipes the lone tear that spills over. That simple act of compassion leaves me shaken. His eyes meet mine, and I can see the feelings he has for me. I just wish he could see them himself. He slips his sunglasses on his face, shielding my ability to read more, and holds his hand out to me. "Come walk me to the pits?"

When I just stand there staring at him, confused, he answers for me by grabbing my hand. We walk in silence, both occupied by our thoughts. So many questions I want to ask remain unspoken, for this is not the right time or place for them. I place a hand on my stomach to settle the nerves fluttering there.

"Why do you seem so nervous when I'm the one that's going to be hurling myself around the track at two hundred miles an hour?"

I stop and look at him and am unable to see through his dark lenses, wondering if he really doesn't get that spending time with him, being with him when I can't have him, does this to me. Has me walking on eggshells and thinking of what ifs. I decide to take the easy way out. "I'm nervous for you. Aren't you ever afraid that you are going to crash?"

"Oh, I've crashed plenty of times, Ryles." He lifts his sunglasses so that our eyes meet. "Sometimes you need to crash a couple of times to learn your mistakes, and then when the smoke clears, sometimes you're better off in the end. Lesson learned in case there is a next time." He shrugs, squeezing my hand and smiling shyly. "Besides, sometimes the dents just add more character in the long run. Looking pretty can only last so long." Our eyes hold each other's, and I know he is talking about more than racing. My eyes beseech his, silently asking the questions I'm afraid to voice, but he slips his glasses back on, pretending he didn't see them. He tugs on my hand again to start walking.

I try to think of something to say to add some levity to our walk. "Aren't you supposed to have a pre-race face on or something indicating you're *in the zone?*"

"Something like that." He laughs at me. "But it's not a race today. Besides, I usually get that way once I walk onto pit row. It pisses my sister off to no end."

"Why's that?"

"Because I can just tune everything and everyone out instantly," he says wryly, a small smile on his beautiful lips.

"Typical male." I laugh shaking my head. "Thanks for the warning, Ace."

"And she says I look mean. I try and tell her it's just part of my job but she doesn't buy it." We walk for a bit more in silence, a smile on my lips. I can hear an engine revving to my left and hear the clatter of a wrench on concrete somewhere to my right. "I wasn't sure if you were going to come today." His words surprise me. I think I do a pretty good job of hiding it on my face. "I thought you might send another counselor in your place instead."

"No," I murmur as we stop at the corner of a building, and I look up at him. Doesn't he realize that even when he pushes me away I am irrefutably drawn to him? That I couldn't stay away even if I wanted to? "I wanted to see you in your element. Watch the boys experience it."

He watches me for a moment, nodding at someone who walks past before returning his eyes to mine. "I'm glad you're here."

"Me too," I mouth back to him, fighting the urge to avert my eyes from the intensity of his.

"This is as far as I go," he tells me, leaning back against the wall, propping one foot back behind him.

"Oh." He runs his thumb over my knuckles on the hand he is holding.

A slow mischievous smile spreads across his lips. "Don't I get a good luck kiss, Rylee?" He tugs on my hand and has me falling against him. He splays his free hand against my back, holding me up against him.

His warnings, his mixed signals, the hurt he's caused all vanish when my eyes flutter up to see his sensual lips inches from mine. Every muscle beneath my waist clenches in desire. I close my eyes momentarily, wetting my lips with my tongue, before opening them back up to meet the clear green of Colton's. *Why the hell not?* It's not like the term levelheaded has been in my vocabulary the past few weeks when it comes to him anyway. Sensibility slips through my fingers like sand when I am near him.

"It's the least I can do," I murmur as he removes his baseball cap.

All sense of reason and modesty at our surroundings vanish the minute his lips capture mine. I pour all of the pent up hurt and emotion and need from the past few days into our kiss, and I know that I can taste the same from him. The pressure of his hand on my back urges me on, tempts me to run my hands up his chest, skim fingers on his neckline, and tangle in his hair curling at the back of his neck. Our hearts pound against each other as we each take what we need, regardless of the impasse we find ourselves at.

Our surroundings slowly seep into my consciousness as I hear someone shout out, "Get a room, Donavan!"

I feel Colton's smile against my lips as he breaks the kiss and turns his head to the right and yells laughing, "Fuck off, Tyler! You're just jealous!"

I hear a loud chuckle as Colton turns his head back to me, and I run my hands down to frame his face. "Good luck, Ace!"

We stare at each other a beat before he leans back down and brushes a tender kiss on my lips. A silent goodbye and now I am more confused then ever. "Remind me to bring you to my next race?"

"What? Why?"

"Because if that's how you kiss me good luck when I'm just testing, I can't wait to see what it's like when I'm really racing!" He raises his eyebrows, a playful smile turning the corners of his mouth, and he squeezes his hands around my waist. I laugh out loud.

"Colton?"

I turn to look into the startled eyes of a stunning woman a few feet to our left. She has a classic beauty that reminds me a lot of Haddie. She has tendrils of blonde hair that cascade around her shoulders, her caramel colored eyes regard me pensively, and her full, painted lips purse as she takes me in. I feel a punch in the stomach. Despite being pressed against Colton, in the split second I have to size her up, I can see true adoration and love in her eyes toward him. Something about her is different though, and the feelings I see in her eyes are much more intense than Tawny's or Raquel's.

Will the endless barrage of women in love with Colton ever end?

"Impeccable timing as usual," Colton says through gritted teeth without even looking at her. I look back at him, slightly confused as he kisses the tip of my nose and pulls back. "Rylee, meet my annoying little sister, Quinlan."

"Oh!" This makes sense now! I extricate myself from Colton's arms, the interruption not allowing me to even think about our intimate exchange. I hold out my hand in greeting, my cheeks blushing at the thought of the first impression she must have of me. "Hi. I'm Rylee Thomas."

Quinlan looks me up and down and then to my outstretched hand before eyeing Colton, an incredulous expression on her face. She shakes her head at him, a warning look in her eye as she completely disregards my hand. I let it fall as Colton sighs a warning to her. "Quin?" She just looks at him like a mother does when scorning her child. He glares back at her. "Q, quit being rude. I'll be right there. I'm a little busy right now."

She snorts rudely, surveying me again before turning on her heel and stalking off the way she came.

"Sorry," he mutters, "she can be an annoying little punk sometimes, regardless of how old she is." And with those words, for some reason, I think I get it. She thinks I'm one of Colton's little disposable playthings. And she acted how I probably would act if it were my brother. Disgusted. Fed up.

"It's okay." I step back from him. "You need to get going."

"That I do." He nods, running his fingers through his hair.

"Be safe, Colton. I'll see you at the finish line."

"Always," he says before flashing a quick, roguish smile at me and then turning to walk toward the pits. I watch his sexy swagger as he tugs his baseball hat on his head and adjusts it. He turns back to look at me, the bill of his hat shadowing his eyes and a wayward grin on his lips, *dangerous* written all over him. If nothing else, he is the definition of sexy. I sigh, shaking my head as I instinctively smile at him. He turns back around, and I watch him until I can't see him any more.

How do I even begin to process the last fifteen minutes?

Chapter Twenty

"Okay, boys, I think that last wing adjustment dialed it in. Great job! I'm going full throttle for the last twenty starting next time I hit the line," Colton's disembodied voice comes over the headset as we watch him on the stretch of track behind us.

"Don't push too hard, Colt. We'll need to make a couple more adjustments for next time out. I don't want you burning up the motor before we can mess with it."

"Relax, Becks." Colton laughs. "I'm not gonna break your baby." I can hear the engine rev up on the backstretch as Colton heads out of turn two. "Davis? You on?"

"What do you need, Wood?" Davis' voice fills my ears. *Wood?* What's that all about?

On the open mic, I can hear the car downshift as he heads into turn three. "Get Zander in the flag stand." I can hear the vibration of the car in Colton's voice as he increases his speed. "Let him wave. Then the rest of the boys."

"Ten-four."

The boys are all listening on their headsets and they turn to look at me with eyes big and grins wide. Davis climbs up the stairs to the little box where we sit above pit row and motions for the boys to follow him. Dane descends and then Jax looks back at me, eyebrows raised in question. "Go ahead, Jax," I motion for him to go as I remain seated. "I'll stay here."

I watch the boys make their way to pit row, heads turned to the right as Colton comes flying out of turn four toward the start-finish line. The rumble of the engine fills my ears and vibrates through my body, reverberating in my chest as he whips past us. Once gone, Davis leads them across the track and they disappear as they head to the flag stand. Moments later, Davis climbs into the little white boxed in platform with Zander at his side, and they wait for Colton to come back around the track again. I can hear the pitch of the motor heighten as Colton hits the accelerator down the backstretch. Before I know it, he is completing the two-mile circuit and tearing down the front straight away before me. Zander's hands are on the flag, and Davis cautiously helps his little arms wave it as Colton approaches and quickly zips past. I capture his smile with my camera before he heads back down the stairs for Aiden to have his turn.

It has been an incredible day. The boys have gotten a once-in-a-lifetime experience, thanks to Colton and his team. I've been interviewed by reporters from the Los Angeles Times and the Orange County Register about the fundraising collaboration of CD Enterprises on behalf of Corporate Cares. A photographer took pictures of us while we were watching the test laps. The boys have been filled with sugary treats as well as great food that Colton's team brought in for us. We've been treated better than I ever could've imagined, especially considering this was not a race or official engagement.

I snap a shot of Shane as he waves the flag when Colton passes by, pleased that I perfectly captured the look of joy in his face. When I look up from the digital image on my camera, Tawny is standing in front of me, a cool, calculating look in her frosty blue eyes. I give her a cautious but courteous smile.

When she continues to stand there and stare at me, I decide to make the first move. Her attempt at intimidation is ineffective. I just pray that for once in my life I can have that quick wit I always think about after the fact because I think I'm going to need it. "Can I help you?"

She crosses her arms across her ample bosom and leans a hip against the railing, her eyes never leaving mine. "You know you're not his typical type, right?"

Oh, so that's how this is going to be. I watch Colton come down the straightaway and wait for the deafening sound to pass us before pulling my headphones off. I lean back in my seat and allow the knowing smirk I feel to ghost my lips—the ones that Colton's lips had been on earlier. "And your point is what? That you are?" I cringe inwardly at my last comment, because I know that she actually does fit the Colton pre-approved mold. *So much for being witty.*

She laughs snidely. "*Oh, doll,* your innocent little self has no clue what you're getting yourself into, do you?"

Condescending bitch! "And what? If I had all of the experience that you do, I would?" My voice drips with sarcasm. "Let's get something straight, what's between Colton and me is none of your business. And I'm more than capable of taking care of myself, Tawny. Thanks for your misguided concern, though."

She stares at me through the slits of her eyelids, her face twisting in amusement. "Oh, Rylee, *everything Colton does is my business.* I make sure of it."

I stare at her momentarily, stunned by her impudence and wondering if there is any truth behind her words. I try to hide the bewilderment in my voice with cynicism. "I wasn't aware he needed a keeper. He seems quite capable of making decisions for himself." I cross my arms over my chest, mirroring her.

"You don't know anything, do you?" She laughs cattily, her patronizing tone grating on my nerves. "Every man needs a woman whispering in his ear, telling him what's best for him." She smirks. "And, *Rylee, doll,* I'm that person to Colton. Have been..." she arches an eyebrow "...and will continue to be."

I plug my ears as Colton comes back around again, thankful for the brief moment to let her comments sink in. "I'm pretty sure Colton doesn't let anyone tell him what to do, Tawny. Nice try, though."

If she laughs that annoying know-it-all laugh one more time, I'm going to strangle her. "You just keep thinking that, doll." She taps an acrylic nail to her perfectly white teeth. "And before you know it, you'll think you've reeled him in. And despite his little spiel about not wanting a girlfriend, you'll think he actually wants more with you. That you can change him and his ways. You'll think that you've tamed that rebellion and topped him and his domineering ways." She turns to watch him fly down the backstretch of the track before turning back to me and taking a step closer. "And just when that happens, you'll be over quicker than that lap he just clocked. You don't have what it takes to keep him. He gets bored quickly." Her eyebrows rise as she studies me. "Oh, my God!" She gasps, putting a hand over her mouth to hide her smarmy smile. "You've already fucked him, haven't you?"

I just stare at her, trying to hide the truth, silence my only answer. I don't want to let her know that she's getting to me. That her little bitchy comments are starting to get under my skin and feed the insecurities that I have in regards to why Colton likes me.

"Well, it won't be long now, then."

"'Til what?" I ask, already assuming what she's going to say.

I can see her move her tongue around the inside of her mouth as she thinks of how to best phrase her next piece of venom. "I've seen enough of his *hussies* come and go to say that I'll give you two months tops, doll. You'll be out of his bed and his life before the first race of the season." She squints her eyes, glaring at me, waiting for the reaction I won't give her. She takes a step closer. "Just know that it'll be me he turns to then. It'll be me telling him he's too good for someone like you. I told you. *I'm. The. Voice. In. His. Ear,*" she whispers the last words to me.

"And let me guess, it'll be you he finds happily ever after with, right?" I retort, my voice sugary sweet despite the ire bubbling beneath my surface.

"Eventually, once he's done biding his time with bimbos like you." She chuckles, eying me up and down. "You're smart. I'll give you that. But I've known him longer than anyone, and I've put in the time. His parents love me. I'm the only one he needs. He may not realize it yet, but he does love me—"

"Looks like you need to find something better to do with your time, doll," I say, rising from my seat and taking a step closer, fed up with her egocentric diatribe. "Waiting around to be second best must be really frustrating."

"A little testy are we? Don't shoot the messenger," she says, holding up her hands, "I just thought I'd save you the inevitable heartbreak."

I manage a single laugh. "Yeah, I can see the sincerity oozing out of your pores." I roll my eyes. "Your compassion is just overwhelming."

She purses her lips. "Us girls have to look out for one another."

Now I really laugh. What a bitch! "Yeah, I'm sure you have my back!" *With a knife pointing into it.* "I appreciate the heads up, but I'm a big girl, Tawny. I can take care of myself just fine."

She throws her head back and laughs loudly before eying me up and down again, a look of disdain on her face. "Oh, he is going to eat you alive and then spit you out, and I am so going to enjoy watching it!"

I see Colton complete his last lap and swing the car into the pits to the right of us. The boys will come looking for me any moment to go down and see the car, and frankly, I've had enough of Tawny's little "let me put you in your place" speech. I've tried to take the high road. I've tried to not be the catty bitch she's being. But enough's enough.

I take one step closer to her, my voice a spiteful whisper. "You better get used to watching, Tawny, because that's all you'll be doing. When he cries out a name, it'll be mine, sweetheart." The corners of my mouth turn up, my voice implacable. "Not yours."

"That's what they've all thought!" She snorts derisively.

How I'd love to throttle her right now. Wipe that sarcastic smirk off her face and show her she has no clue what she's talking about. But I can't. In the end, she may be right. *And that kills me.* Reminds me I need to keep my guard up. I give her the same, slow appraisal that she's given me, and I shake my head in disinterest. "This conversation has been stimulating, Tawny, but I'm going to go spend time with people that are worth my breath."

I rush down the stairs quickly, wanting to make sure that I get the last word in. At the bottom of the stairs, I walk toward where I can hear the engine of Colton's car. As I turn the corner, I see my boys following Davis down to the garage area of the speedway. I hurry to catch up, trying to let the anger and irritation from Tawny's words dissipate.

I shrug it off and tell myself that she's just a catty bitch trying to hold on to something that's not hers. A drop-dead-gorgeous catty bitch, but a catty bitch nonetheless. I think the combination of her being his type and my fear that there is some truth to her words, keeps the anger running through my system.

I catch up to the group as we approach the garage where Colton's crew has set up. The purr of the engine stops, and I see Colton hand the now-detached steering wheel to a crewmember before slowly pushing himself up from his seat. He lifts one leg over the side and then the other to stand on the ground. He takes a moment to settle on his legs before removing his helmet and the white fireproof balaclava from his face. He accepts the Gatorade that someone hands him and takes a long pull on it before running a hand back and forth through his sweat-soaked hair. Colton gives the man who approaches him a huge grin, and it takes me a moment to place him. He is the rakish gentleman who was at the Merit Rum party with him.

I stand back with the boys away from the flurry of activity in the garage. Several people are talking to Colton, who is motioning with his hands to demonstrate what he is saying. Other crewmembers are tending to the car, using instruments to measure things. Colton is completely in his element. It's not hard to sense his enthusiasm and respect for his sport.

His smile is wide and authentic, and I feel a pang in my heart when I see it. If he is this passionate about the sport that he obviously loves, I can't help but wonder what he'll be like when he finally accepts love from someone. My heart twists at the thought that it won't be me. I push the thought from my head, but it stays at the edge of my mind as I watch him.

The flurry dies down as several of the people who Colton is speaking to back off and attend to the engine in the back of the car. Now Colton is just speaking to the man from the club, and I observe an easy camaraderie between the two.

Davis motions for the boys to enter the garage, and they quietly follow in line, trying to stay out of the way. I remain rooted, choosing to watch from afar. Colton notices them and looks up from his conversation, giving the boys a wide smile. He waits until they approach before speaking. "So what did you think, guys?"

All of them shout out words at once ranging from "awesome" to "cool" to "unbelievable." He unzips his fire suit and pulls his arms out of the sleeves, letting them fall and hang below his waist. His shirt, darkened with sweat, clings to the defined muscles of his chest. The sight of him, sexy as hell, pulls at every part of me.

"I'm so glad you guys liked it! Now, this here," he says, putting his arm around the man from the club, "is one of the most important people out here. More important than me," he kids. "None of this..." he gestures to the garage around them "...would run so smoothly if it weren't for him. This is Beckett Daniels, my crew chief."

The boys say hello to him and he smiles back at them. Ricky throws out a question and Beckett smiles broadly, motioning the boys over to the car to look at something. Colton stays where he is and watches the boys follow. He rolls his shoulders and takes another long drink before looking up and around the garage. I feel that sudden crackle of electricity when his eyes meet mine, and that slow lazy grin turns up the corners of his mouth, his dimple deepening. He looks like sex: hot, sweaty, disheveled, and mouth-wateringly irresistible. He looks back at Beckett to make sure that things are okay before sauntering over to me.

"Well, hello there." I can't help the smile that forms on my lips when I speak to him.

"Still think I'm faking it?"

"No." I laugh as he stops in front of me.

"Well, as long as you're not, then I'm doing my job correctly," he quips, reaching out a hand to tug on a curl.

I shake my head at him with a soft smile before taking a deep breath. *Faking it is definitely not a necessity when it comes to Colton in the bedroom.* We stare at each other, the activity of the garage buzzing around us, as we become entranced by one another.

"You looked good out there, Ace," I finally manage to say, breaking our silence.

He takes another drink of his Gatorade. "You know nothing about racing, do you?" He laughs as I shake my head, laughing with him. "Didn't think so, but thanks for the compliment."

"But I have watched it with my brother before, and the boys obviously were Googling all about it to make sure they knew as much as possible." I shrug, glancing over his shoulder to check on the kids. "So, Wood, huh?"

He smiles shyly at me. "It's not what you're thinking. It's an old nickname." I raise my eyebrows at him, amused. "When I first started racing, someone called me Hollywood. The name stuck. Has been shortened to Wood over time. Anyone who calls me that has been around a long time." He looks back at Beckett for a beat. "Is someone I trust."

"Don't let the press get a hold of that or they'll have a field day with it."

"Believe me, I know." He laughs.

We both turn our heads as Shane's laughter fills the garage. Beckett has his arm around his shoulder and is laughing with him while Davis is lifting Ricky into the seat of the car to sit for a picture. "Thank you so much, Colton. For making them feel special for a day." He turns from watching the boys to look back at me. "For everything. I can't begin to tell you how much it means to the boys."

A dark look flashes across his face. "It's not a big deal." He shrugs it off, picking at the label on the Gatorade bottle. "I understand that need more than most." He shifts his attention back to the boys who are each getting their chance to sit in the car and get their picture taken. We watch them for a few moments, Colton taking his hat off of his head and running his hands through his hair. I watch him out of the corner of my eye as he looks at his watch and then turns his attention back to the boys.

Tawny's words ring in my ears. Two months, tops. What if she's right? Even if whatever we have lasts three or four months, I know it won't be enough. I don't think any amount of time will be enough to love someone like Colton. He is one of those guys who consumes every part of you. Makes you whole when you never thought you were incomplete. Gives you strength and makes you weak all at the same time. I know I am capable of loving him like that—like he deserves—but I know I will never get the chance. Tawny may be a catty bitch, but she knows him way better than I do. Between her words, Colton's own admissions, my research, and my intuition, I know that I will end up being destroyed if I allow myself to fall in love with Colton. And I can't allow that to happen. The rise might be more than fun, but the devastation after the fall will break me.

Colton breaks through my thoughts. "We have a meeting in ten minutes," he says, turning to look at me. "Can you stay and then I'll drive you home when it's over?"

I twist the ring I'd put back on this morning—a source of comfort to me. I desperately want to say yes. "It's probably not a good idea, Colton," I shake my head, avoiding his gaze.

"For who?" he says, turning and taking a step closer to me. His scent envelops me—the outdoorsy, clean scent of his cologne mixed with the scent of a man who has put in a hard day's work.

I eye him warily, trying to keep him at an emotional distance. "For both of us, Colton. You said so yourself the other night." He takes a step closer to me and I can feel my pulse surge.

"But maybe I think something different today ..."

I sigh deeply, telling myself that nothing's changed since Saturday night. He is who he is, and he's not going to change. That a few days away from each other has just made him horny, and he wants some relief. That's all this is. I push his last comment out of my head and try to carry on like he never said it. "Besides, I have to get the boys home. They're my responsibility."

He takes another step toward me, and I put my hands up on his chest to prevent him from getting any closer. I don't think I'd be able to bear the feeling of his body pressed against mine. My hands pressing against the firm muscles of his chest makes it hard enough for me to resist him as it is.

Colton takes a hand and lifts my chin up. "What's wrong, Ry?" His eyes search mine, trying to understand my hesitancy. How can he understand why his idea of a relationship is unacceptable to me? How do I explain that him pushing me away one minute and then kissing me senseless the next is making me question what I might concede in order to have him in my life?

"You," I whisper.

"Me?" he mouths.

"You confuse me at every turn, Colton." I shake my head softly and despite telling myself that touching him will only make walking away that much harder, I lift my finger and trace the hem of the neckline on his damp shirt. "One minute you tell me you can't stay away and the next you tell me you have to keep me at arm's length because you're going to hurt me. On Saturday you told me whatever is between us will never work unless I agree to your terms and then today you kiss me breathless." I step back from him and look over at the boys getting a tour of the garage, to avoid meeting his gaze. "I can't give you what you want and you can't give me what I need. That's all I know. All I understand, Colton."

He steps toward me again and tugs on my ponytail, forcing my head to lift and my eyes to meet his. And despite the chaos around us—the boys laughter, the clang of metal on metal, the sound of an air compressor in the distance—when his eyes hold mine, it all disappears. It's just he and I. A guy way too irresistible for his own good and a girl in way over her head.

"As much as I keep telling myself that this needs to be—should be—over, Rylee, for both our sakes ... I still want you." He cups the side of my face with his free hand and traces the pad of his thumb over my bottom lip. "Desperately," he whispers. His words resonate in my heart. "I think about how soft your skin is. The feeling of your body against mine. Of it under mine. How you tighten around me when I'm buried in you ..." His words, mixed with the intensity in his eyes, leave me breathless. Has my body vibrating with a deep-seated need for him that I'm not sure will ever be sated. "Christ, Rylee, it ... you ... are consuming me." He leans in and brushes a soft, brief kiss on my lips. The innocence and vulnerability behind it beguiles me. "And I intend to have you again."

I breathe in a sharp, audible gasp. I step back from him, holding his gaze for a second longer, before looking around the garage to check on the boys. I notice more people have joined us since we started talking. I notice a perplexed look pass between Beckett and Quinlan. I see Davis rounding the boys up, and I know our time here is ending.

"I'm sure you'll feel that way until you find someone else who fits your requirements," I quip, fearing my words speak the truth. I turn back to Colton, still trying to recover from the impact of his confession and yet needing to show him that I have some self-control when it comes to him. "Why waste your time on me when you can have any other girl willing to give you exactly what you want?"

"But. I. Want. You. Rylee. No. One. Else." He smirks.

The man is relentless, but I still think he's after the challenge when it comes to me. I shake my head. "You have a habit of telling me what you want, Ace, without asking me what I want."

Colton takes the baseball hat in his hands and tugs it down over my head, a Cheshire cat grin spreading across his face and a sinful gleam in his eyes. "Oh, sweetheart..." he emits a low rumbling chuckle as he takes two steps back from me "...I know exactly what you want." He holds his hand up to motion to Beckett that he's coming when his name is called. His grin widens into one of the wickedest and most carnal smiles I have ever seen. My core coils and I tense to stifle my desire. "*And I have just the right tools to give it to you.*" And with those parting words, he turns on his heel and walks over to Beckett, his laughter reverberating in the garage. Beckett eyes him up and down, a bemused look on his face as Colton says goodbye to the boys.

When Colton finishes, he turns back toward me and smirks. "All consuming experience!"

He laughs at my confused expression. "*What?*"

"*What it stands for.*" He grins and I finally get it. He's still guessing what Ace means.

"Nope," I say, fighting the smile that tugs at the corners of my mouth.

He takes a step backwards, biting his bottom lip in concentration. I can see the minute he thinks of another one as his eyes light up, the corners around them crinkling. "The amazing Colton experience," he shouts over to me, garnering an eye roll from Beckett.

"Oh geez!" I laugh at his lack of humility and mimic Beckett with an eye roll of my own. "Nope," I yell back, suppressing a laugh.

Colton takes another step backwards, his face filled with humor, and shakes his head at me. "Later, Ryles."

"Later, Ace," I mutter, begrudgingly accepting the fact that in so many ways Colton is right. That no matter how intelligent I am or how rational I try to be, his pull on me is just too strong.

I tug his hat down on my head, adjusting my now-wrecked ponytail, and watch him throw a playful arm around Beckett's shoulder as they walk down the pathway. I shake my head, overwhelmed by the day's events, and head over to collect my excited but very tired boys for the long ride home.

Chapter Twenty-One

"Check it out!" Dane throws a newspaper proof onto my desk as he walks by my office at Corporate Cares. "Your cleavage is going to be in the newspaper and we're going to get some good press."

I whip my head up to look at him, confused, before glancing down at the paper. On the lower half of the cover of the sports section is a side-by-side picture of our outing at the track and the accompanying article. The picture on the left is a picture of Colton's car with all of the boys kneeling in front of it with Colton in the middle. The picture to the right is a close up of Zander, Ricky, and myself. I am in between the two, and unfortunately, the way my arms are positioned, my cleavage is on display in the V of my snug T-shirt. "Lovely! Oh my God, that's embarrassing!"

"C'mon, Ry, you look hot. And the girls look great!"

I throw my pencil at him, laughing. "When does this go to print? Can we ask him to change the picture?"

"Yeah, right! You know they picked it so that the guys that open up the sports page will read the article and not flip past it." I roll my eyes, feeling the flush of embarrassment creep into my cheeks. "Just think of it as taking one for the team—"

"What?"

"It's a really good article that's going to give us good press." He laughs out loud. "Hell, if I was into playing for your team, I'd keep the picture for late night fun!"

"Oh, shut up!" I shout at him, unable to keep my laughter from bubbling up.

"C'mon, Ry—read it. You're gonna like what it says."

"Really?" I raise an eyebrow as I skim through it, pleased with what I see.

"Seriously. It is," he tells me, taking a seat in front of my desk. "A lot of good info about The House and about corporate and the new facilities."

"When's it running?"

"This Sunday, and the *OC Register* most likely will run then too, but I haven't seen their proof yet."

"Hmmm, not bad." I set it down on the side of my desk where I can read it more thoroughly later.

"How was your interview?" he asks, referring to the one good candidate I had for the open counselor position. I interviewed her earlier in the day and was quite impressed.

"She was actually really good. Almost too good to be true really, but her references check out, and I think I'm going to make her an offer. I think the boys will really take to her. I'll need you to help me train her but—" The ringing of my cell phone interrupts me. I glance down to see who is calling. "It's Teddy," I tell him.

Dane rises from the chair and mouths he'll come back later as I answer. "Hey, Teddy!"

"Rylee! Heard we got a good article from the *LA Times*. Great job!"

"You're breaking up on me, Teddy." The phone line crackles.

"I need to talk to you—" The call drops and the line goes dead.

I wait a second for my phone to ring again and when it doesn't, I go back to looking at the budgetary numbers I was working on before Dane interrupted. After a few minutes, my cell rings again.

"Hello?"

"Rylee Thomas, please," a monotone male voice says over the phone.

"This is she."

"Hi, Ms. Thomas, this is Abel Baldwin."

Oh, crap! What boy is it this time? "Good afternoon, Principal Baldwin. What can I do for you today?"

"Well, it seems to me that Aiden can't seem to keep his hands to himself lately. He was in yet another fight last period, Ms. Thomas." Disdain fills his voice at having to deal with this again.

This is Aiden's third fight in as many months that has been caught by school authorities. I have a feeling that there have actually been a couple more that have gone unnoticed as well. Oh, Aiden. "What happened?"

"Not quite sure. He won't really talk with me about it." *And I really don't think you care, either.*

"What about the other kid?" A question that I ask every time and always get a less than satisfactory answer to.

"They said it was a simple misunderstanding."

"They?" There's more than one? "I hope that they are in your office as well, Mr. Baldwin."

He clears his throat. "Not exactly. They are in class and—"

"What?" I shout at him, perplexed by his obvious bias.

"And I think it's better if you come and pick up Aiden—"

"He's suspended?" I ask through gritted teeth.

"No, he's not." I can hear the irritation in his voice at having me question him. "If you'd let me finish Ms. Thomas—"

"He's not suspended, but you want me to come get him while the other boys get to stay in class?" My rising frustration is more than evident in my voice. "Surely you can understand why I'm upset at what seems to be favoritism here."

He stays quiet for a moment as I gather up my things as best as possible with one hand so I can go pick him up. "Ms. Thomas, your accusation is unfounded and serves no purpose here. Now I would appreciate if you could come collect Aiden so we can let the two parties simmer down. This in no way indicates that Aiden is at fault in this matter. In addition, Aiden has blood on his clothing and seeing as it's against school policy for him to walk around with it there, I think it's in the school's best interest to send him home for the afternoon."

I sigh loudly, biting my tongue from telling this less-than-stellar principal exactly what I think of him. "I'll be right there."

Aiden is silent all the way home from school. My shift at The House doesn't start for another three hours, but I think that Aiden and I need to have a little alone time to talk about what happened. I haven't pushed him to tell me, but I need to know. Is he being bullied? Is he looking for attention that he's not getting? Is he releasing frustration from his past? I need to know so that I can figure out how to help.

Before we walk into the house, I motion for him to sit down on the front porch step next to me. He rolls his eyes but obeys. He stares at me as I take in the swollen lip with dried blood at the corner, the dark red mark on his right cheek and the start of bruising on the left eye. His cheeks flush deeply under my scrutiny.

"I know you don't want to talk about it, buddy, but you have to tell me what happened." I reach out and grab his hand while he lowers his head and watches an ant crawl slowly on the step beneath us. We sit in silence, and I allow it for a bit but finally squeeze his hand, letting him know he needs to talk.

"They were just being jerks," he grumbles.

"Who started it, Aiden?" When he doesn't respond, I prompt again. "Aiden? Who threw the first punch?"

"I did." His voice is so soft, so sad with shame that it breaks my heart. I see a fat tear slide down his swollen cheek, and I know that something is off.

"Talk to me, Aiden. Who was it and what did they do to make you want to hit them?"

He reaches up to dash away the fallen tear with the back of his hand and leaves a smear of dirt in its path. "They called me a liar," he mumbles, his bottom lip quivering. "Ashton Smitty and Grant Montgomery."

Little punks! The know-it-all, privileged, popular kids from his grade whose parents never seem to be around. I wrap my arm around his shoulder and pull him to my side, kissing the top of his head. "What did they say you were lying about?"

His voice is barely audible. "They told me I lied about going to the track on Sunday. That I didn't really meet Colton or know him ..."

My heart squeezes. He was so excited to go to school and tell all his friends about his experience. So excited to be cool for once and have something that the other kids didn't. I sigh loudly, squeezing him again. I want to tell him that the little punks deserved it and that he did the right thing, but that's obviously not the most responsible way to react. "Oh, Aiden ... I'm sorry, buddy. Sorry they didn't believe you. Sorry they pushed you ... but Aiden, fighting somebody with your fists is not the way to solve things. It only ends up making it worse."

He reluctantly nods his head. "I know, but—"

"Aiden," I scold sternly, "there are no buts here ... you can't use your fists to fix problems."

"I know, but I tried to tell Ms. McAdams when they started pushing and shoving and she wouldn't listen."

I can see another tear threaten to fall from his thick lashes. "Well then, I'm going to make an appointment to speak with her and Baldwin about this." His head whips up and his eyes open widely in fear. "I'm not going to make it worse, Aiden. I'm just going to ask them to keep their eyes open a little more. To make sure that they do not let this happen again. And I'll make sure that the other kids don't know."

He nods his head, releasing a noncommittal grunt. "Am I in trouble?" He looks up at me with fear in eyes.

I wrap both my arms around him and squeeze his little body that's known so much hurt and abandonment. I hold him to me, trying to reassure him and let him know that it's okay. That getting in trouble doesn't mean a severe beating and food withheld for days. "Yeah, bud, you are … but I think that icky feeling you have might just be the worst of it." I feel his shoulders sag in relief as a plan forms in my head.

"I knew you couldn't stay away from me for long." Colton's voice fills the other end of the telephone line, arrogance redefined. His sexy voice alone makes my pulse race, but I have to put how I feel aside as I put my plan to help restore Aiden's self-confidence at school into motion.

"I'm not calling for me, Ace."

"Ooooh, I love it when you're all business and straight to the point. It's such a turn on, Ryles."

"Whatever!" I say, but I can't help the slow smile that creeps over my face.

"No, seriously, what's up, sweetheart?"

Why do I love when he calls me that? Why does it make me feel like I'm special to him?

"It's Aiden," I tell him filling in the details as he listens attentively, despite the voices I hear in the background. "Is it possible that I can get some kind of signed picture of you or something he can bring to school tomorrow to prove that he's met you and actually was there on Sunday?"

Colton laughs loudly, and I'm confused by his reaction. "That's only going to get his teeth knocked in, Rylee. That's something only a geek would do … those brats would eat him alive."

"Oh … um … I had no idea."

"You wouldn't." Colton chuckles, slightly offending me.

"What's that supposed to mean?"

"And please don't go have a conference with the teacher or principal," he groans. "Inevitably someone will see you and then it will only make things harder for Aiden."

"I wasn't—"

"Oh yes, you were," he kids, and I'm shocked he has me pegged so well. "I just know you were one of those preppy kids who had their homework done before it was due, helped the teacher in class, and was part of the 'in' crowd. No offense, Rylee, but you have no idea what it is to be a misfit on the verge of puberty who gets the crap beat out of him *just because.*"

I'm flustered that he has such a good read on me, but more than that, his words about understanding the misfit crowd gives me more insight to him as a child. When I don't respond, he laughs again. "You were like that, weren't you?"

"Maybe," I answer slowly, heat flushing my cheeks.

"It's nothing to be embarrassed about, Rylee … it's just different for kids like Aiden."

And like you were. "What do you suggest I do then, since I obviously don't understand?" I try to hide the hurt in my voice.

"Are you on shift there tomorrow?"

"Yeah … what does that have to do with anything?" When he remains silent, I prompt him. "Colton?"

"Give me a second to think," he snips at me and I blanch at his tone. I hear someone call his name in the background. Of course it's a female. "What time do you leave for school in the morning?"

"At eight. Why?"

"I'm tied up right now," he says innocently, but my mind drifts to braided velvet ropes and cold counters. I jolt my mind from my thoughts, chastising myself. "Okay. I'll have something for him at The House before you leave."

"What are you—"

"Relax, control freak." He sighs, "I have something in mind. I just have to move some things around to make it happen."

"Oh, but—" I protest, wanting to know what he's bringing.

"Rylee," he interrupts, "this is the part where you let someone else handle the details. All you have to say is 'Thank you, Colton. I owe you one,' and hang up."

I pause momentarily, knowing he is right but wanting to know anyway. "Thank you, Colton," I comply.

"And?" he prompts.

I remain silent for a few moments. I can almost hear his smirk. "And I owe you one."

"And you can bet I'll collect on it." His seductive laugh fills the phone until I hear the dial tone on the other end.

Chapter Twenty-One

Colton—Raced

I rev the Aston. Her purr reverberates against the concrete walls in front of me and echoes through the early morning over the collective chatter that fills the air. If the boys only knew how many times as a kid I dealt with this shit. Fucking know-it-all punks who picked on me because I was that *"pity-case"* the Westins took in—what most assumed was an attempt to keep their holier than thou public persona up.

Yeah right. If those fuckers only knew the hell my parents had saved me from. A bully's fists and words were nothing compared to what I'd already lived through.

Sticks and stones. Sticks and stones.

Even if I didn't look in the rearview mirror at the boys and their grins in the backseat, I'd know they were smiling from the unmistakable energy zinging in the car. They'll get their due. I'll make sure of it.

I rev the car again, and I can see Ry tense beside me as she prevents herself from telling me I'm breaking the rules. Rule follower and rule breaker. Opposites must really fucking attract. Huh? If she only knew how opposite we really were.

God I would love to tear into this parking lot and lay some rubber. Give the boys a real entrance that would leave the rest of the students talking for months. It takes all of my restraint not to. Instead, I slide the Aston in between the curb and the waiting line of suburbanite moms in their SUVs or minivans and their judgmental attitudes.

Time to make an entrance, boys. Time to turn the tables, give them some positive attention for once, and put those fucking bullies to shame.

I park askew up onto the dip in the sidewalk, angling the car on purpose so that the boys can make their grand entrance. I rev the motor a few more times for good measure before opening my door and climbing out of the car. I take a quick look and notice a few of the moms in their sweatpants look my way. They stop, angling sunglasses down to see if I'm who they really think I am.

Damn straight, ladies. In the fucking flesh.

I stretch my arms above my head, taking my time and groaning aloud for good measure as I watch mouths fall lax and hands fly immediately to smooth down their unruly morning ponytails. I walk around the front of the car and stifle a laugh as I notice the shuffling through purses and sudden appearance of lipstick tubes. Fucking pretentious women.

Like I'd go for you when I have *her* in my front seat. Are you fucking kidding me? Plastic, botox, and ditz or real, intelligent, and sexy as fuck? A few weeks ago the decision may have been different, but now—since Rylee—there isn't one to be made.

Call me crazy.

Or pussy whipped.

I open the door for Rylee. My eyes instinctively scrape over her body and recall perfectly the feel of those curves beneath mine. She smirks at me—humor and curiosity mixed in her eyes—as she wonders how the reckless, quick to throw a punch Colton Donavan is going to handle these grade school punks.

I can't help the smile on my face as I squat down and flip the seat forward. The looks on Scooter, Aiden, and Ricky's faces are fucking priceless. I help them from the car and place my arms on their shoulders, the whisper of my name zipping through the crowd at my back.

That's right. *They're with me, folks.* No fucking with them any more.

I lean over to Aiden, the look of shock and fear and pride on his face makes me want to grab him and hug him. Tell him that no matter who you are or where you come from, there's always someone who'll stand up for you. "Do you see the bullies, buddy?"

His bruised little face looks around the crowd, and I know the minute he sees the punks. His body stiffens and fear or shame flickers momentarily through his eyes. For that look on his face alone, the fuckers should be suspended. I look to where he's staring and know instantly who my targets are. Seriously? I'm transported back twenty years in time and the fuckers could be interchangeable with those that tormented my years of school.

"Well, champ, it's time to go prove a point."

I urge the boys forward with my hands as I stand in the middle of the three of them, purposely moving as a solid unit. Mess with one of us, you get all of us. I can sense Ry's apprehension as to how I'm going to handle this, but she really needs to give me more fucking credit.

I plaster an easy going grin to my face as we approach the boys. Gonna kill them with fucking kindness. "Hey, guys!" I say in greeting as the boys' eyes widen like saucers and the shit-eating grins fade from their lips. "Hey, Aid, are these the boys that didn't believe you were my buddy?"

"Yeah," he croaks and looks up at me. And if I already didn't love this fucking kid, the look on his face makes me love him even more now. Eyes startled. Freckles scrunching. Lips turning up at the corners in a disbelieving smile. Yeah, *buddy*, you're more than worth sticking up for. It's time to start believing it.

"Oh man!" I say turning back to *dumb and dumber*. "You should've seen Aiden on Sunday. I let him bring six of his friends, including Ricky and Scooter here..." I squeeze their shoulders to let them know they're just as worthy "...with him to the track to test out the car, and boy were they the biggest help to me! We had so much fun!"

I can feel all three boys stand a little taller and I know that a bit of confidence has been restored in their damaged souls. They've still got a long way to go, but it's a start.

"Too bad you guys aren't friends of his or maybe you could have gone too!" It takes everything I have to not tell *dumber* to close his mouth because he's going to catch a fly if he keeps looking at me like that. Then again, it serves him right for picking on the weak. No, not weak—after everything these kids have been through, definitely not weak. *More like damaged*. Yeah damaged but hopefully repairable.

Unlike me.

The school bell buzzes and it's only now I realize the crowd around us. I've been too busy restoring the boys' dignity to notice. And honestly, fuck if I care. I note the bystanders' eyes flicker over my shoulder, and I have a feeling the dipshit authority is near. I don't even have to check because I know the look he'll have on his face already. It's embedded in my memory from too many trips myself. I guess pissing off principals is one thing I'll never stop doing whether I'm thirteen or thirty.

It's time to make sure the crowd understands where I stand in regards to the boys. I ratchet my smile up a notch and wink at the bullies. "Bye, boys! Make sure you say 'hi' to my man Aiden here when you see him in class!"

They just continue to stare at me as The Suit uses his hands to physically guide them toward the front doors of the school. He then turns back to Aiden, Ricky, and Scooter. "Boys, you too," he says in a monotone that makes me think of the teacher in Ferris Bueller.

I glance over at Rylee for the first time during this whole display, and I can see her fighting back a smirk. She just subtly nods her head at me when I ask her with my eyes if this is the prick taking sides. It takes everything I have to keep my temper reined in this time because the boys are still attached to my sides. Fucking judgmental asshole.

My smile is so fake it kills me. "One moment please, sir. I just need to say bye to my boys." I go to face the boys but I can't. I have to say something right here, right now. For the little boy in me always doubted and deemed at fault, for the hundreds of others like me, and for the boys beside me living it in the present.

I hang my head for a moment to make sure that my composure is nothing less than respectful. And that in itself is a fucking feat. "Next time, sir, it'd be best to remember that Aiden is telling the truth. It's the bullies that need to be sent home, not good kids like Aiden here. He may not be perfect, but just because he doesn't come from a traditional home, doesn't mean that he's at fault." I stare at him, holding those flustered eyes of his as he listens—not just hears but listens—to the words I've said. When I see them register, I do the only disrespectful thing that I can and turn my back on him, dismissing him without further comment.

My smile changes from tight to genuine when I look at the three pairs of eyes looking up at me. It's one thing to stick up for them with bullies that are the same age, it's another thing when it's done to an adult. I understand that more than anyone.

"I don't think they'll be bugging you anymore, Aiden." I reach out and when I see his eyes accept my intention, ruffle his hair. "In fact, I don't think anyone will be bugging you guys anymore. If so, you let me know, okay?" All three boys nod like bobble-head dolls, their minds and egos trying to comprehend what's just happened.

"Time to get to class," Ry tells them as she steps up beside me to watch them walk toward the doors, heads held high and pride in their posture. They reach the door, looking the principal in the eye and that alone fills me with a sense of right. Ricky and Scooter disappear through the door, but Aiden stops.

I immediately worry that he fears entering the school—years of belittling not fixable with one appearance by a guy like me—but when he looks up, his eyes meet mine and I see awe, clear as day. "Thanks, Colton." I can't help the feeling that twists within me. Two simple words but the way he says them implies so much more.

Rylee glances over at me as we walk back to the car. Pride is brimming in her eyes, and I swear to God something shifts and twists inside of me. A fucking foreign feeling. But fuck if I don't want her to look at me like that again.

I get the boys understanding why I did what I did. But Rylee? She's got to be assuming things that I'd rather remain hidden. She's got to wonder what exactly it is that burns so deep within me that I still fear it every minute of every day. Even twenty-two years later.

Too bad she wasn't around to save me way back then.

The question is, *can she save me now?*

"Why did you agree to come here if you don't like coffee?" That in itself says volumes to me.

She denied me at the track even though her body said otherwise. I got a ration of shit from the guys for her being there too. They're not used to a woman walking away when I ask her to stay. They thought it was the funniest fucking thing on the face of the earth, Rylee denying me.

And her reason for having to get the boys was a bullshit excuse. That much I know.

So she must be scared. Fuck, I'd be scared too after the shit I've pulled with her. Back and forth like a goddamn tennis match because my head's so fucked-up that I want her but know I can't give her what she needs.

The fucking problem is my wants are changing and I'm not sure just yet how to deal with that. Because I don't want them to change. So I let her in more than anyone I ever have and then lash out because I can't deal with the shit her being around churns up. The vulnerability of my past being exposed, my demons reawakened.

And yet she still called me when she needed help. Fuck if that call didn't surprise me, but blowing off the Penzoil rep was worth it to be standing beside her right now.

Trying to figure out what the hell I'm doing because fuck if I know.

I study her profile, a soft smirk on her face as she contemplates my question while staring at the muffins in the glass case in front of us. She's pretending to decide what to order, but I can tell she's figuring out how to answer me. With honesty because despite the smiles on our faces there is still an underlying tension of unanswered questions between us, or with humor to try and add some levity.

Pick, Ryles. Set the tone for the rest of this conversation because I'm sure as fuck uncertain where to go from here.

"I may not like the coffee part, but Starbucks has some damn good food that is oh-so bad for you."

You have no idea how true that statement is, sweetheart. I shake my head, my smile more genuine now but her comment weaving into my thoughts. Telling me that she gets this. Gets that anything between us will be a beautiful disaster.

We move up in line, and I can hear the comments starting behind me and at the tables around us. My name is a hushed murmur and usually I'm cool with the attention, but right now I need it to be her and me. I need to figure out why I keep coming back to something that we both know is going to happen again, but this time I fear will either break me or devastate her.

And that's a heavy fucking burden for a man to bear. I'd like to say I'll walk away right now and save her the pain but know sure as shit—because I'm standing here—that I can't. I'd like to think I'd sacrifice myself, take the hit my own demons will hand me, but fuck, I know how brutal that would be.

I'm not sure if I'm willing to face them in order to let this thing with her play out. And I know that makes me a man weaker than most but hell if I want to relive the horror that's robbed my soul more than once in a lifetime.

But then again why in the hell am I even wasting time thinking shit like this that I'm never going to allow. Love's not a possibility for me. Relationships have strings and expectations. Those are hard limits I won't cross, can't cross.

And yet here I am, curious what it is about her that I just can't let go.

"What wo-would you l-like?" The barista stammers when she recognizes me as we step up and thank fuck for that because she pulls me from all of the crap I am overthinking.

Fucking Rylee is rubbing off on me with her reading too much into shit. I can think of other things I'd like to rub off on when it comes to her.

The image that flashes in my head is so very welcome and makes me chuckle and shake my head. I think the cashier catches the suggestive tone of my laugh and infers the direction of my thoughts because she blushes. She busies herself with the cashier buttons as she takes our order and I can't resist, as we walk away I make sure to say thanks and wink before flashing a huge grin.

We're lucky to find a table in the corner since the place is packed, and I enjoy the view of Ry's ass when I pull her chair out before I sit down myself. We sit and stare at each other for a few moments, smirks on our faces and questions in our eyes.

"You know that after what you did today, you've most likely reached idol status with the boys now."

I roll my eyes at her. A hero, I'm far fucking from that. If she knew what I was thinking in line, she'd see I'm more a coward than anything. Idols don't hide in corners when monsters enter the room to steal things from them that can never be replaced. They fight back, they overcome, they escape and save the fucking day—not cower and cry and plead when pain is headed their way.

They don't need to call to superheroes because they become one themselves.

I can't answer her because I know the truth, so I avert my gaze and focus way too intensely on the muffin in my hand. I take a bite, pushing the ghosts back in their closet and finally look up to see her eyes fixed on where I just licked a crumb from my lip.

My thoughts vanish instantly as my dick stands up and takes notice of her physical reaction. She lifts her eyes to mine and we stare at each other for a moment, the buzz of the coffee shop allowing a comfortable silence between us despite the unspoken desire in both of our eyes.

"Ace." The barista calls my name and unknowingly breaks our connection. I stand to get my coffee and smile at Rylee, letting her know this visual conversation is far from over. And hopefully my vision will get the sight of her naked and beneath me sooner rather than later.

The thought occupies my mind as I doctor my coffee and the need to have her again only intensifies as I sit back down in front of her. I take a sip, the drink scalding my tongue. "Now I can think clearly."

And sitting here with her in front of me and the boys' status redeemed at school causes all kinds of clarity. Like how I sure as fuck want to let her in a bit, see where this takes us.

I'm not sure how to do it or where to go from here.

I've got a whole cup of coffee to figure it out, though, and time's a wasting.

Chapter Twenty-Two

Damn it! I knew I shouldn't have said anything to Aiden. I shouldn't have told him that I had something to fix what had happened yesterday. I shouldn't have depended on someone like Colton to come through when I am so used to relying on myself. He hasn't even answered my texts or calls this morning.

I glance at the clock and another minute has ticked by. It's seven fifty-two and I need to get the boys into action in order to get them to school on time. Mike's already left to take Shane and Connor to high school. Bailey has already come and left to take Zander to his therapist's appointment and Kyle to the eye doctor before dropping him back off at school. I'm left with the remaining three elementary school kids, and I know that getting them in the car should have started ten minutes ago.

I glance at the clock again and it's seven fifty-three now. *Shit!* "Rylee, are you going to tell me what it is yet?" Aiden begs again with hope in his eyes.

"Not yet, Aiden. It's a surprise." Now I have to scramble to think of something to do to make up for an empty promise.

I could strangle Colton right now. What did I expect from a careless playboy? I guess if there isn't a promise of getting laid at the end of the deal then he's not going to follow through. I pound a fist on the table, the silverware on it rattling, knowing I'm overreacting after how much he did for the boys. But at the same time, he's letting down one of my boys and he's letting me down too.

I start stuffing lunches into the backpacks that Aiden is handing me, concentration etched on his face as he tries to figure out what I can possibly have to help him. "C'mon, guys. It's time to go!" I shout. Aiden, my little helper, leaves the kitchen to go see what they are up to.

When after a few minutes I don't hear the usual scurry of feet, I sigh in frustration and head out toward the hallway. "Ricky, Scooter … C'mon, guys, its time to go!" I turn the corner to the hallway and do a double take when I see Colton standing in the foyer with the door open behind him. The sun is at his back, casting his body and dark features in a halo. Three little boys stand in front of him, their backs to me, but I can see all of their heads angled up to look at him. He steps further into the room smiling briefly at me, before turning his attention to Aiden.

"So, Aiden," Colton says, and I can see his subtle appraisal of the bruises on Aiden's sweet little face, "are you ready for school today?"

"What?" he asks bemused before looking back at me, a mix of anticipation and realization on his face. I look back at Colton, wondering what he's brought to help the situation.

Colton cocks his head to the side, realizing that no one gets what he's doing here. "I'm taking you guys to school," he says as silence fills the house before the boys start whooping and jumping around like loons. Their excitement is contagious and I feel my smile widen to match Colton's. He steps forward and kneels down in front of Aiden. "Hey, buddy, what do you say we go show those bullies that they're wrong and they can take a hike?" Aiden's eyes widen, moisture pooling at the corners, as he nods excitedly. "Go get your backpacks then," Colton instructs them as he stands back up.

My eyes follow him, and it is in this moment—with his dark features haloed by the bright light of the sun, when he's come to stand up for children that no one else cares to stand up for anymore—that I know I've fallen for Colton. That he has penetrated my heart's protective exterior and made me love him. I lift my hand and press the heel of it against my breastbone, trying to rub at the sudden ache there. Trying to will his self-professed, ending-filled devastation and hurt away. Trying to tell myself that I cannot let this come to fruition.

Colton looks questioningly at me. "Rylee?"

I shake my head. "Sorry." I shake my head again and smile at him as the three boys come barreling back down the hallway toward the front door.

"I guess they're ready." He laughs as he ushers the boys out of the house.

Colton purposefully revs the engine of the Aston Martin as I direct him into the school parking lot. I'm sitting in the front and the three boys are squeezed tightly together in the backseat, grins on their faces and bodies bristling with excitement. I glance over at Colton and he has a half-smile on his lips as if he is remembering a grade-school memory of his own. I'm about to tell him he can take the shortcut to the drop-off section in front of the school but I bite my tongue. I realize that he is taking a long, slow cruise through the parking lot, gunning the sexy purr of the motor every chance he gets, so that he draws the attention of everyone around us.

We finally make it to the drop-off line where Colton swerves around the long line of cars and carefully cruises down a narrow passage between the line and the sidewalk, despite the dirty looks shot at him. I know he'd love to floor the gas pedal and make a grand entrance, but he refrains. He pulls up right in front of the school's entrance, angling the car so that the passenger door faces the large crowd of students out front. He revs the engine a couple more times, its sound purring in the peacefully quiet morning air, before sliding out of the driver's seat.

He unfolds his long limbs gracefully and stands a moment by the opened car door. I can see him raising his arms over his head, stretching with a loud groan, making sure that all available eyes are on us. I glance around and notice the moms near us staring openly. I laugh as I watch them try to fix their bed-ridden hair.

Colton shuts the door and struts slowly around the front of the car toward my side. He opens the door for me and I exit, catching the amusement in his eyes and the gratified smirk on his lips. He squats down and flips the seat forward so the boys can exit one at a time.

The looks on their faces are priceless as they take in the crowd. Out of the corner of my eye, I see Principal Baldwin approach from the far side and his stern face startles at seeing a car parked improperly in his strictly rule enforced parking zone. I can hear whispers of Colton's name and my smile widens. Colton shuts the door and places himself with Aiden on one side and Ricky and Scooter on the other. He leans over and I hear him say to Aiden, "Do you see the bullies, buddy?" Aiden looks around the sea of faces, and I see him stiffen when he sees the boys. I follow his line of sight, as does Colton, to see the stunned expressions of Ashton and Grant. "Well, champ, it's time to go prove a point."

We move as a unit toward the two boys, their eyes widening with each step. I'm curious what Colton plans on doing once we reach them. I glance over to see his face relaxed in a huge, approachable grin as we come to a stop in front of Ashton and Grant. In the periphery of my vision, I notice Principal Baldwin scurrying over to us to stop any confrontation before it starts.

"Hey, guys!" Colton says enthusiastically, and I get the feeling he is going the kill-them-with-kindness route. Both boys just stand there gawking at Colton. He turns to Aiden. "Hey, Aid, are these the boys that didn't believe you're my buddy?"

I wish I had a camera to take a picture of the reverence on Aiden's face as he looks up toward Colton. His eyes are alive with disbelief, and I can see the pride brimming in them. "Yeah …" Aiden's voice comes out in a croak. The crowd around us has grown.

"Oh, man," Colton says to Aston and Grant, "you should've seen Aiden on Sunday. I let him bring six of his friends, including Ricky and Scooter here, with him to the track to test out the car..." he shakes his head "...and boy, were they the biggest help to me! We had so much fun!"

I see Ricky and Scooter bristle with pride now as well, and I wonder if Colton has any idea what he is doing, not only to their self-esteem but also to their status here at school. "Too bad you guys aren't friends of his," Colton said, shaking his head, "or maybe you could've gone too!"

The school bell buzzes. Principal Baldwin reaches us, slightly out of breath, and tries to disperse the crowd by ushering everyone to the doors. He looks down at the boys who are still staring at Colton before giving them a stern look and clearing his throat, making them snap out of it. Colton flashes his megawatt, no-holds-barred smile and winks at them. "Bye, boys! Make sure you say 'hi' to my man Aiden here when you see him in class!" They just nod their heads at Principal Baldwin, forcing themselves to take their eyes off of Colton, or they'll walk into a wall.

With their children safely inside, the mothers remain outside for no apparent reason—trying to look busy by retying their shoes or foraging in their oversize purses for something that they will never see because their eyes are locked on Colton.

"Boys, you too," Principal Baldwin tells my three.

Colton looks over at me questioningly and I nod subtly, letting him know this is the dipshit I told him about who favors everyone who fights Aiden. Colton flashes the same megawatt smile at him and says, "One moment please, sir. I just need to say bye to my boys." I didn't think it was possible for the grins to get wider on the boys' faces, but they do. Colton turns to talk to the boys and then turns back, in second thought, to address Principal Baldwin again. "Next time, sir, it'd be best to remember that Aiden is telling the truth. It's the bullies that need to be sent home, not good kids like Aiden here. He may not be perfect, but just because he doesn't come from a traditional home, doesn't mean that he's at fault." He holds his gaze and then turns his back on the wide-eyed principal, effectively dismissing him. The flustered look on Principal Baldwin's face is priceless.

Colton kneels down, bringing Ricky, Aiden, and Scooter around in front of him. He raises his eyebrows and grins at them. "I don't think they'll be bugging you anymore, Aiden." He reaches out and ruffles his hair. "In fact, I don't think anyone will be bugging any of you any more. If so, you let me know, okay?"

All three nod eagerly as Colton rises. "Time to get to class," I tell them, gratitude evident in my voice. They usually grumble at these words, but today they all obey and seem actually eager to enter the building.

Colton and I stand side by side as the boys walk through the door that Principal Baldwin is holding open for them. Nosy bystanders scurry by, pretending they are not watching. Aiden stops in the doorway and turns around, awe still on his face and says, "Thanks, Colton," before disappearing inside the building.

When we turn back to the car, I catch a look of accomplishment and pride on Colton's face. I have a feeling mine looks the same way.

"Why did you agree to come here if you don't like coffee?"

Against my better judgment, I've agreed to go get some coffee with Colton after leaving the school. I'm still floored by Colton's actions, and feel I at least owe him my time in return for what he's just done. I can still see the look on Aiden's face in my head. I don't think I will ever forget it.

"I may not like the coffee part, but Starbucks has some damn good food that is oh-so-bad for you." I laugh as he shakes his head at me. *Kind of like you, Colton.*

We place our order amid glances from the other patrons who recognize Colton. He's sans baseball hat and not incognito. We shuffle over to a corner that luckily has an empty table with two deep, comfortable-looking chairs on either side of it. We sit down and Colton pulls our muffins out of the bag and sets mine before me.

"You know that after what you did today, you've most likely reached idol status with the boys now."

He rolls his eyes at me and picks a piece of his muffin off and places it in his mouth. I watch it clear his lips and see his tongue dart out to lick a crumb. A flash of desire sears through me. I see the corner of his mouth twist up, and I force myself to look up to his eyes, which have noticed where my attention is focused. We stare at each other, unspoken words igniting the heat between us.

The barista at the counter calls out, "Ace," and Colton smirks at me before rising from the table to get the drinks. I watch him walk, his long, lean legs covered in denim with a forest green Henley shirt covering his broad shoulders and narrow waist, the long sleeves pushed halfway up his strong forearms. I watch the barista blush as she hands him our drinks and continues to stare as he turns to prepare his coffee.

I stare at him, confusion running through my head. We are so comfortable together. So drawn together. And yet we can't give each other what the other needs. Maybe I'm being selfish, but I know I won't be satisfied with just bits and pieces of him. Scraps he'll throw my way when he deigns to. But that notion confuses me even more since I've yet to see him act that way with me thus far. He tells me one thing about how his arrangements operate, but then acts another way with me.

Is he worth it? Colton sinks down into the chair across from me, a soft smile on his lips as he meets my eyes. *Yes. He definitely is.* But what do I want to do about that? He sighs after swallowing his first sip. "Now I can think clearly." *At least someone can, because it sure isn't me.*

"It seems to me like you were doing okay before your coffee," I kid as I swallow a bite of muffin. He smirks. "I have to tell you again, Colton, thank you so much for showing up and doing that. It was … you were … what you did for Aiden was above and beyond, and I really appreciate it."

"It wasn't anything, Rylee." He can see that I'm about to argue with him. "But you're welcome."

I nod my head and smile shyly at him, glad he has accepted my gratitude. "The looks on those brats' faces were priceless when you walked up!"

He laughs out loud. "No, I think the principal's face was even better," he counters, shaking his head at the memory. "Maybe next time he'll think twice before taking sides."

"Hopefully," I murmur, taking a tentative sip of my hot chocolate and trying not to burn my tongue. *You burned me.* Colton's words pick this moment to flash through my head. I push them to the back of my mind as I take a sip of my drink. The damn man clutters my mind, overwhelms my senses, and clouds my heart in one fell swoop.

We sit in an easy silence, watching store patrons and sipping our drinks. I put my hot chocolate down and absently fold the corners of my napkin, deciding if I should say the next comment that pops in my head or let it go. Typical me has to get it out. "Colton?" His eyebrows quirk up at the gravity of my tone. "You're so good with the boys, I mean way better than most people, and yet you tell me you'll never have any. I don't understand why."

"Having a child and being good with one are two completely different things." The muscle in his jaw tics as his eyes watch something outside in the parking lot.

"Colton, what you did today," I tell him, reaching out to put my hand on top of his. My touch draws his eyes back to mine. "You showed a little boy that he was worth something. That he was worthy enough to stand up for." Emotion fills my voice. My eyes try and tell him that I understand. That he did what should have been done for him as a child. Even though I don't know his circumstances, I know enough in my line of work to see that no one stood up for him or made him feel like he mattered, until he met his Andy Westin.

"Don't you do that every day, Rylee? Stand up for them?"

I mull over his words as I finish chewing my bite. "I suppose so, but not with your dramatic flair." I smile. "I guess I'm more behind the scenes. Not nearly as public and self-confidence boosting as you are."

"What can I say?" He picks at the cardboard guard on his coffee cup. "I know what it's like to be in Aiden's shoes. To be the odd kid out who doesn't fit in due to circumstances beyond your control. To be bullied and made fun of *just because*." He squeezes my hand. "You get the picture."

Sympathy engulfs me as I think of a raven-haired little boy with haunted green eyes. Of the pain he experienced and the memories that will forever be etched in his mind. Of the things he missed out on like comforting lips expressing unconditional love, warm arms to cuddle him tight, and fingers to tickle him into fits of deep belly giggles.

"Don't look at me like that, Rylee," he warns, pulling his hand away from mine and leaning back in his chair. "I don't want your pity or sympathy."

"I'm just trying to understand you better, Colton." My words the only apology that I'll give him.

"Delving into my dark and dirty past isn't going to help you understand me any better. That shit..." he waves a hand through the air "...it's not something I want to haunt you with."

"Colton—"

"I told you before, Rylee..." his stern voice silencing me "...I'm not one of your kids. My shit can't be fixed. I've been broken for way too long for that miracle to happen." The look in his eyes—a mix of anger, shame, and exasperation—tells me that this conversation is now over.

An uncomfortable silence hangs between us and I can't help but wonder what happened to him as a child. What is he so afraid to confront? Why does he think that he's so broken?

His voice pulls me from my thoughts, turning the focus of our conversation from him to me. "What about you, Rylee? You treat these kids like they're your own. What's going to happen when one day you meet Mr. Right and have kids of your own? How are you going to balance that?"

Even after two years, the pang that hits me still knocks me to my knees. I swallow purposely, trying to wash the acrid taste in my mouth. I pick at the corner of my napkin, watching my fingers rip tiny pieces off as I answer him. "I can't ... after the accident I was told that getting pregnant, that the chance of having a child is..." I shake my head sadly "...a very slim possibility. Like basically being on the pill for life. Most likely never going to happen." *Again*. I lift my eyes to his, rocking my head subtly from side to side. "So it's not something I put much thought into."

I hear him draw in a breath and can feel the pity roll off him. There is nothing worse than someone giving you *that look*. The pity look.

"I'm sorry," he whispers.

"It is what it is." I shrug, not wanting to dwell on what can never be. "I've come to terms with it for the most part," I lie, and in true Colton Donavan fashion I change the subject to something other than me. "So, Ace..." I wriggle my eyebrows "...you looked kind of hot in your race suit!"

He laughs, "Nice change of topic!"

"I learned from you," I reply, sucking a crumb off of my thumb. When I look up, Colton is watching me draw my finger from my mouth. Intensity and desire mingle in the depths of his eyes as he studies me. The sexual tension between us mounts. Our draw to each other is undeniable.

"Hot, huh?" he says.

I tilt my head and purse my lips as I study him back. "I wanted ..." My voice is quiet, unsure, when I speak. The small smile playing at the corners of Colton's lips gives me the surge of confidence I need to continue. Knowing that he desires me and wants more of whatever this is, emboldens me. It empowers me to finish my thought. "I wanted you to take me right there on the hood of your car." I can feel my cheeks flush as I look up at him through my eyelashes.

He takes in a sharp breath, his lips parting, eyes clouding with desire. "Why, Ms. Thomas..." he darts his tongue out to lick at his bottom lip "...we might just have to rectify that situation."

"Rectify?" Desire blooms in my belly at the thought.

He leans in across the table, his face inches from mine. "It's always been a fantasy of mine."

I think he's going to lean in and kiss me. My chin trembles in anticipation, synapses misfiring as I try to tell my brain to be the voice of reason here. To pull me back from the brink of Colton insanity. And then the alarm on my cell phone goes off. It startles us both and we jump back. "Oh crap! I have a meeting I have to get to," I tell him as I start gathering our trash and stuffing it inside my empty muffin bag.

Colton reaches out and grabs my hand, stopping my flurry of movement. He waits until my eyes meet his to speak. "This conversation isn't over, Rylee. You keep sending me so many damned mixed messages that—"

"What?" I screech, dumbfounded, trying to pull my hand back from his, but his grip holds my hand still. "What are you talking about? You're the one sending mixed messages. Whispering sweet nothings one minute and then pushing me away the next!" Are we experiencing the same thing here? How am I being confusing?

"I swear to God," he murmurs softly to himself, releasing my hand as he leans back in his chair shaking his head, amusement on his face. I can barely make out his next words when he speaks. "We haven't really even started this yet, and you're already topping me from the bottom." I can sense his exasperation as he runs a hand through his hair.

I look at him, unsure what exactly he means, but not really having the time to ask him to explain. I stand up and Colton grabs my hand again, pulling me up against him so I am forced to tilt my head up to see his face. He closes his eyes momentarily, as if he is resigning himself to something, before opening them again to lock onto mine. "I want you, Rylee. Any way I can have you."

His words create a vacuum of air, and I feel like I can't breathe. We're standing in a packed Starbucks with orders being called and people talking on cell phones and espresso machines steaming milk, but I hear none of it. It is just Colton and me and his deafening words.

I swallow loudly, trying to process them. Unable to speak, time passes until I find my voice. "Any–any way you can have me?" I stutter breathlessly, eyes wide with optimism. "Does that mean that you're willing to ... to try more than an *arrangement*? Try to compromise with me?"

I feel his body tense from my words and when I see the look in his eyes, I realize I misunderstand what he's saying. My chest deflates and my hopes sputter when he speaks, unable to look me in the eyes. "That's not what I meant, Rylee. All I know is how I operate. By my rules. They allow me that deep-seated desire for control that I so desperately need to be able to function. I have to have it on my terms." I feel his body shift before bringing his eyes to mine. I glimpse an unexpected vulnerability in them. "Rylee, this is all I can give you. *For now* ... Will you at least *try* my way? *For me?*"

For now? Try for me? What the fuck is that supposed to mean? That there is the possibility of a future? I try to stop my mind from reading into that comment. Colton's proximity and the words he just dropped like bombs on my rationality leave me stuttering as I try to respond coherently. "I thought you told me this wouldn't work. That we have two different sets of needs. That you ... I think your words were, that you're going to *break me apart*?" My words may sound strong and decided, but I'm anything but that.

He grimaces when I throw his words back at him and hangs his head, his voice soft. "Yeah, I know. I can't prevent the inevitable. But I still want you to try."

Blinded by my feelings for him, I ignore his admission of inevitable hurt because my head is still wrapping itself around that word: try. He's asked me to try. Am I willing to do that? For him? For a chance at us? To hope for the opportunity to show him that it's okay to want more. That he deserves more. My train of thought derails when Tawny's words flitter through my mind. *You'll think you can change him and his ways. And just when that happens, you'll be over quicker than that last lap he just took.* I shake my head, trying to rid her words from my head.

"Don't answer yet, Rylee." Colton's voice is a plea, mistaking the shake of my head as a denial to his request. "Have dinner with me first before you tell me no." I step back from him, needing the distance despite knowing I'm already going to tell him yes. "I have to have at least one more night with you. I need to." His eyes search mine for an answer. "I'll pick you up at three o'clock tomorrow."

I stare at him. "I can drive, Colton," I say, exasperated that once again he's made the decision for me. If I'm willing to try for him, shouldn't he try for me as well?

"Nope." He smiles, holding the door open for me as we leave. "I'm driving. That way you can't run away."

Chapter Twenty-Three

"*We don't have to fix each other. Come over. We don't have to say forever. Come over.*" I hum along with the Kenny Chesney song that is playing softly on the speakers of the Range Rover as we drive north along on the Pacific Coast Highway. I smile at the coincidence that Colton texted me this song earlier, and now it is playing on the radio as a member of his security staff, Sammy, drives me to wherever he is.

I reach beside me at my bag, rifling through the change of clothes and miscellaneous toiletries I packed. I pull out my compact mirror to check my reflection. My hair is piled on the top of my head in a stylish yet effortless disarray of curls with several wisps hanging loosely around my face and onto my nape. I set down my compact and bring my hands back to check the tie on my neck where the straps of my blue maxi dress meet, leaving my back bare until just below my shoulder blades. I say a silent thank you to Haddie for her suggestion to wear the dress. *Cute, casual, and just enough cleavage to keep him sneaking a peek* she told me over our second glass of wine.

As we drive north, the lush hills on my right give way to the ocean on our left. I place a hand over my stomach to try and settle the butterflies. I shouldn't be nervous to see Colton, but I am. I feel that tonight is going to be a turning point for whatever "we" are. I lean my head back and look out the window at the endless sea and hope that I can handle the repercussions of whatever that turning point may be. I close my eyes momentarily and wonder how an intelligent woman like me can knowingly walk into foreseeable devastation.

Taylor Swift's *Red* is playing when we start driving through Malibu. I listen to the words, relating to them. "Loving him is like driving a new Maserati down a dead end street." I shake my head, feeling like that dead end is going to come so much quicker than I want it to.

Sammy turns left onto Broadbeach Road, and I am pulled from my thoughts. Expensive houses line my left, bordering the coveted Malibu shoreline. Houses range from modern to Cape Cod to old world, with perfectly manicured landscaping and gated walls.

Within moments, we turn up to a driveway where large wooden gates are swinging open for us. We pull through the gates onto a cobblestone and grass driveway and come to a stop. Sammy escorts me from the car, and I look up at the two-story structure in front of me. It has an impenetrable-looking ledge stone façade, the top portion shaped like a stretched letter 'U' where an open-air deck sits between two sections of the house. There are no windows on the walls that face me, and I assume that the opposing walls are solely glass to showcase the Pacific. At ground level below the deck is a massive arched wooden door, and my eyes are drawn to it as it slowly opens.

Colton stands in the doorway, stopping me in my tracks when a slow, lazy smile lifts one corner of his mouth. The sight of him is like a sucker punch to my abdomen. I struggle to breathe as I drink him in. He is all kinds of sexy, wearing a pair of worn blue jeans, a faded black T-shirt, and bare feet. I'm not sure why the sight of his bare feet peeking out from beneath his pant legs is so attractive to me, but it's worth another glance. I regain my wits despite the humming of nerves and start moving toward him again as his eyes languorously appraise my body. I reach the doorway and stop in front of him, my smile matching his.

"I told you I'd hurt you and yet here you are," he murmurs captivated, astonishment flickering through his green eyes. Before I have a chance to process his words, he reaches out and takes my hand, pulling me against him. My hands land on his chest feeling every bit of muscle beneath the incredibly soft cotton of his shirt.

"Hi," he breathes, a shy smile on his lips and eyes steadfast on mine.

"Hi," is all I can manage before he leans in and brushes a slow, tantalizing kiss on my lips that speaks of the possibilities this evening holds. When he pulls away, every nerve in my body is humming.

"Beautiful as always, Rylee," he praises, taking my hand and ushering me in the door. "Welcome to my home."

The significance of his statement is not lost on me. This is his home. Not a place he brings his *sometimes girl*. I can't help wondering if he has invited me here to prove a point. To demonstrate that he is trying.

All thoughts leave my head as we enter the great room of the house. I am met with an unhindered view of a beautiful terrace and the ocean. Glass pocket doors have been slid aside, leaving the house open to the subtle breeze blowing in off of the water. My gasp is audible as I step past him without invitation and out onto the deck to admire the sight for several moments.

"It's beautiful. I—" I murmur, turning my head back to him. He is leaning against the back of a chocolate leather couch, his hands shoved casually in his pockets, and the look in his eyes as he connects with mine is so intense that I suddenly feel shy. I feel as if he can see everything deep within me: my hopes, my fears, and the fact that I've fallen in love with him. Uncomfortable that my every thought feels like it is on display, I try to break up the intense atmosphere. "Thank you for having me here, Colton."

He pushes off of the couch and saunters toward me, every part of my body aching for his touch. "I'm glad you're here. Would you like a tour or a drink out on the patio?"

"Patio," I tell him immediately, wanting to soak up the sun and the beautiful view with him. I wander out onto the sprawling deck complete with an infinity edge pool, built-in barbeque island, and the most comfortable looking patio furniture I have ever seen.

"Take a seat," he tells me. "I'm going to get us a couple of drinks. Is wine okay?"

"Sounds great." I ignore his request to sit and walk to the edge of the railing to take in the unobstructed view of the beach that stretches to the left and right of us. My thoughts turn to what it would be like to wake up every day to this spectacular view. *Beside Colton watching this spectacular view, to be exact.*

"I could sit here all day." I'm startled by his voice behind me.

"It's very soothing." He sidles up next to me and places a glass of wine on the railing beside me. "Thank you. I imagine it could be very distracting when you have other things to do."

Colton places a soft kiss on my bare shoulder and keeps his lips there as he murmurs, "Nothing could be more distracting than you standing here right now with the wind in your hair and your dress billowing around you, revealing those sexy legs of yours."

His words are like an electric pulse to my system, stoking my ever-present burn for him. Despite the warmth of him behind me, I have goose bumps on my arms. "Are you trying to sweet talk me, Ace, so that you can get laid tonight?"

"If it's working, then yes I am."

How will I ever be able to say no to him?

"I told you," I say, feigning disinterest, "I'm not really into race car drivers."

"Ah … yes." He laughs, moving to the side of me, resting his hip on the rail but keeping a hand on my lower back. "I forgot, only baseball players do it for you." He takes a long sip from his bottle of beer, watching me. "I'm sure you could be persuaded, though."

I raise an eyebrow and tilt my head, trying to hide my smile. "Might take an awful lot of persuading …"

He moves quickly so my back is to the railing now and his arms box me in on either side. His warm, hard body presses up against mine and a mischievous grin plays at the curves of his mouth. "You know I can be awfully convincing, Rylee."

In a flash, his lips are on my mouth and his tongue is pushing through my parted lips to meld with mine, attacking my mouth with purpose. I wrap my arms through his, hooking them up so I can press my hands against his shoulders. He deepens the kiss, demanding more, taking more, and igniting little licks of desire deep in my belly. One of his hands palms my butt and presses me against him while the other leaves whisper-soft touches on my bare back. I moan softly from the multitude of sensations his touch alone creates.

I hear a thumping sound and I screech suddenly, breaking away from our kiss as I feel something insistently trying to force itself between his hips and mine. I laugh loudly as I look down at the oversized ball of black, white, and tan fur. A beautiful and rather large dog wriggles against us, tail beating against the railing, wet nose pushing and prodding.

I take the dog's head in my hands. "Baxter!" Colton groans at him. "I apologize. He's a little out of control."

I coo to the gentle giant, and when I begin scratching behind his ears, he plops his bottom down on the ground complacently, tail thumping, and groans in pleasure.

"Holy shit! How'd you do that?"

"What?" I ask him over my shoulder as I squat down, continuing to rub the dog.

"He's never that calm with anybody except for me."

"I'm a dog person." I shrug casually, as if that explains everything, and move my hands to rub the dog's chest so that his back leg kicks out in pleasure.

"Obviously," Colton says, bending over to kiss the dog on the head and scratch the fur on his neck.

The sight makes me smile. "You're supposed to help me *get* the girls, big guy, not come in between us when we're kissing."

I laugh as Baxter groans on cue. "He's beautiful, Colton."

"Yeah, he's a keeper," he tells me as he takes my hand and pulls me up. "I haven't taken him for his walk yet today so he's mad at me."

"Then let's go take him," I offer up, a walk on the beach sounds like a perfect idea. Colton cocks his head and furrows his brow at me. Did I say something wrong? "What?"

"You just surprise me sometimes," he says, shaking his head at me.

"Good surprise or bad surprise?" I ask him over the rim of my glass of wine.

"Good," he says softly, reaching out and touching a loose curl on my neck. "You're just so different than what I'm used to."

Oh! Yes. I forgot to bleach my hair blonde before I came over. I fidget nervously under his gaze.

"Shall we?" he asks, nodding toward the steps that lead off the patio and on to the beach. I smile at him as he places a hand on the small of my back and ushers me down the stairway, pulling me quickly aside as Baxter bounds down the steps in excitement.

Barefoot, we walk side by side along the path where the wet sand meets the dry sand. Colton throws a ball for Baxter while we chat.

"You know, my sister was surprised to see you at the track the other day."

"Really? I couldn't tell. She seemed so warm and inviting when I met her."

Colton smiles ruefully. "I apologize. She's usually not like that."

"Hmm-hmm," I murmur, my expression telling him I find it hard to believe. "It's okay though because I thought she was another of the BBB."

"BBB?"

"Your Bevy of Blonde Beauties club."

"Oh, come on." He laughs. "I'm not that bad!"

"C'mon, Ace, have you Googled yourself lately?" He goes quiet and for the first time I think I see embarrassment wash through his cheeks.

"No, I don't Google myself," he says finally, "but it's kind of hot knowing that you're looking at me when you're not with me." I turn my head from him and look at the houses on our right, hiding my blush from him.

We walk a bit further, each lost in our own thoughts until I stop to absently dig up a shell with my big toe that is lying partially in the sand. Colton breaks the silence. "I lied to you the other day."

My foot stops digging at his words, curious where he is going with this. I look over at him. "Go on," I prompt.

"Well you asked me if I ever fear crashing." *Oh. Okay. Nothing bad.* "And I thought about it the other night when I was lying in bed. I mean we all fear crashing, but we try to push it out of our minds or it will affect our driving. I guess it's a knee-jerk reaction to say that I don't."

"Have you ever had a bad crash?" I envision him in a mangled car, and I don't like the feelings it evokes.

"Once or twice where it's shaken me up," he admits as he stops and stares out at Baxter biting at the tiny waves in the water. "So yeah, it scares the shit out of me. All it takes is that one time, but the minute I start driving like I have that fear … the minute I start letting up because of it … is the day that I need to quit."

"That makes sense," I say, although I can't fathom hurling myself around a track that fast. Can't comprehend experiencing that horrible disoriented and dizzying tumbling feeling more than once in my lifetime.

"Besides, I've feared much worse things in my life." He shrugs, still looking out toward the shoreline. "At least on the track, it's me that puts myself in danger … no one else. My whole team has got my back."

And you're not used to that. Not used to depending on others or needing anything from any body.

I hear a distant voice off to the right of us shout in a feeble voice. "Hi, dear!"

Colton looks over and a huge grin fills his face as he sees a figure standing in the second story window of the clapboard house we are passing. "Hi, Bette!" he responds, waving to her as we pass by before grabbing my hand. "That's Bette Steiner. Her husband was some software tycoon. He died last year so she calls me sometimes if she needs help with anything." He stoops down to scratch a wiggling Baxter before picking up the ball and throwing it toward the water again.

So the rebellious bad boy takes care of his elderly neighbors. Isn't he full of unexpected surprises?

We walk for a little while longer in comfortable silence, our fingers intertwined, hands swinging playfully. The houses are beautiful and the mixture of sun on my face, sand on my feet, and Colton beside me warms my heart. We follow a bend in the beach where the bluffs start to rise so that the houses are raised a bit rather than sitting right on the sand, and Colton pulls me toward a little alcove. A rather large rock with a flat top sits at the base of a small hill layered in various types of greenery that looks out at the ocean.

"I'll let you in on a little secret," he tells me as he helps me up onto the rock, before hopping up so that he can sit beside me.

"Oh?"

"This spot, right here, is my little slice of heaven. My place to go and sit when I need a break from everything."

I lean my head on his shoulder, watching Baxter crash into the waves, pleased that he's shared something with me. "Your happy place," I murmur, looking up at him. God, he looks gorgeous with his wind-blown hair and yet still a little aloof with his eyes hidden behind his sunglasses. He smiles at me and places a soft kiss on my forehead.

He is silent for a moment before speaking. "When I was little, I always had this image in my head, my *happy place* to use your term, where I'd go to when ..."

With his silence, I can feel his body tense up at some memory. I reach out and put a hand on his knee, drawing lazy lines with my fingernails. I know I shouldn't, but "the fixer" in me prevails. "When what, Colton?" I can feel him shake his head back and forth. "Do you want to talk about it?"

"Babe, it's old news," he says, shrugging his shoulders, effectively pushing me away before hopping abruptly off the rock. "I'm not the only kid who's had a rough go of things." Emotion clouds his voice as he walks a couple of feet away from me. I start to speak when he talks over me. "Don't bother, Rylee." He chuckles a self-deprecating laugh. "I've been picked apart and put back together by the best of them. A waste of my parents' money if you ask me, seeing as none of them fixed or erased anything." His next words are barely audible above the sound of the surf, and I'm not sure if he means for me to hear them anyway, but they bring a chill to my skin when he speaks. "I'm damaged goods."

I want to reach out to him. To tell him that a person who is damaged goods doesn't help elderly women with chores and make neglected boys feel special by standing up for them. I want to tell him that he is worthy of love and a real relationship. To tell him that what happened as a child—whatever horrible, unimaginable thing it was— does not define who he is today or where he is going. But I say nothing. Instead, I trace the lines of his body with my eyes, wanting to reach out, but unsure how he'd take it.

I am so focused on Colton, that I don't see Baxter bound up in my periphery until he decides to shake his wet fur all over me. I screech out loud at the bite of the cold water hitting my skin. Colton whirls around to see what happened and lifts his head up to the sky laughing at me. A deep, sincere laughter that lights up his face and eases the tension in his shoulders.

"Baxter!" I shout as Colton walks back to me, removing his sunglasses and hooking them onto his T-shirt's neckline. I look up to him, a false pout on my lips. "I'm all wet now."

Colton presses his thighs between mine so he stands in front of me while I stay seated. The rock's height brings us to almost eye level with each other. A slow, salacious grin spreads across his lips and he raises an eyebrow at me.

"All wet, huh?" he asks as he places his hands on my hips and pulls me into him, his hips between the apex of my thighs. "I like it when you're all wet, Ryles."

I swallow loudly, the clouded look in his eyes hinting at passion and desire and so much more. He leans forward, bringing his hands up to my shoulders, his thumbs rubbing back and forth at the hollow dip where my collarbones meet, before brushing a kiss on my lips. I bring my hands up to skim my fingernails up his chest and then around to the back of his neck and play in his hair before tugging his head forward, deepening the kiss. The low groan in the back of his throat excites me and ignites me, sending licks of white-hot pleasure to every nerve. Despite the barrage of sensation his lips evoke on mine, he keeps the kiss slow and soft. Soft sips, slow licks of tongue, slight changes in angle, and soft murmurs of sweet nothings that seep into my soul and wind around my heart. Colton backs away with a shaky sigh after placing a kiss on the tip of my nose.

Oh my, the man sure knows how to kiss a woman senseless. If I was standing right now, I think I'd need someone to help me because he's made my knees weak.

He tilts my head up so that my eyes are forced to look at him. I feel shy under the intensity of his gaze. He just smiles softly at me and shakes his head as if he can't believe something. Baxter nudges at him, jealous of the lack of attention, and Colton laughs, reaching his hand down to pet his head. "Okay, Bax, I don't mean to neglect you!" He takes the ball out of Baxter's mouth and turns around to chuck it down the beach.

I hop down off the rock and watch Baxter take off, kicking up sand as he goes. "He's fast!" I exclaim as I feel Colton's hands slide around my waist, pulling me back into him.

He wraps his arms around me, my back to his front, and he rests his chin on my shoulder. My body relaxes and yet perks up with awareness at the feel and warmth of his body pressed against mine. I close my eyes momentarily, drinking in the uncensored affection that Colton rarely displays.

"Hmmm, you always smell so good." He nuzzles my neck, and I can feel the vibration of his words against the sensitive skin beneath my ear where his lips press. "It's scary how easily I can get lost in you."

I still at his words. As much as I want and need to hear these words, my mind chooses this time for insecurity and disbelief to rear its ugly head. Images flash through my head. Page upon page of Google images with Colton and his BBB. He is so smooth. So practiced. How many women has he uttered these words to?

"What is it, Rylee?" *What? How does he know?* "I just felt your entire body tense up. What's going on in that beautiful and intriguing head of yours?"

I shake my head, feeling silly for my thoughts and yet afraid of the answers. When I try to pull away from him, his arms tighten around me. "It's nothing, Colton." I sigh.

"Tell me."

I take a deep breath and steel myself to ask the two simple words swimming around in my head. "Why me?"

"Why you what?" he asks, confusion in his voice as he releases his hold on me.

Despite being let go, I take a step away and keep my back to Colton, lacking the courage to ask him to his face. "Why me, Colton? Why am I here?" I can hear him take a deep breath behind me. "Why not one of the score of women before me? There are so many others that are so much prettier, sexier, skinnier ... why am I here and not one of them?"

"For someone so sure of yourself, your question astonishes me." His voice is closer than I had expected. We stand in silence and when I do not turn around to face him, he puts his hands on my arms and does it for me.

"Look at me," he commands, squeezing my biceps until I comply. He shakes his head at me, disbelief and, I think, a little bit of surprise etched in his features. "First of all, Rylee, you are an extremely beautiful, tremendously sensual woman. And that ass of yours," he pauses, the guttural sound in the back of his throat is one of pure appreciation, "is something men fantasize about." He snorts. "I could sit and admire you all day."

His eyes lock on mine and I can see the honesty in his eyes. A part of me wants to believe him. Wants to accept that I am enough for him. He moves his hands from my arms to the sides of my ribcage and then slowly runs them down to my hips and back up.

"As for these, I have to admit, sweetheart, that I've dated mostly waifs in my years, but damn, Rylee, your curves are so incredibly sexy. They turn me on like you wouldn't believe. I get hard just watching you walk in front of me." He leans into me, his arousal pushing against me, and kisses me softly on my parted lips. He rests his forehead against mine, his fingers playing idly with the tie at my neck. "As to why they are no longer here?" he murmurs, the words fanning over my face before pulling back so that his green eyes burn into mine. "It's simple. Our time was over."

I pull back from him, trying to wrap my head around that last part. "They just up and left?" I try to hide the desperation in my voice, as I suddenly need to know what I'm in for. "I mean, why was it over?"

He looks at me momentarily before answering. "Some found others that could give them more, some caused too much drama for my liking, and some wanted the white picket fence and two point five kids," he answers indifferently.

"And—and I assume that you ended things with them then?" He nods cautiously, the cogs in his head turning as he tries to figure out why I want to know. "Did you love any of them?"

"Jesus, Rylee!" he barks, running his hand through his hair, "What the fuck is this, fifty questions?" He walks a couple of feet away from me, exasperation emanating off him, but I've asked this much, I might as well find out what I really want to know.

I sit down in the sand, aware that Baxter is a ways down the beach, and hug my knees to my chest, twisting my ring around and around on my finger. "No, I need to know what I'm getting myself into." Colton's eyes snap up to mine, an indiscernible look on his face. "What I'm already into." I sigh more to myself than him, but I know he hears because I see the muscle in his jaw tic at the words. "You told me that you sabotage anything good. I need to know if you loved any of them."

He steps next to me and runs a hand through his hair. I have to crane my head up to meet his eyes.

"I'm not capable of love, Rylee," he deadpans, his voice a haunted whisper, before staring out to sea and shoving his hands in his pockets. "I learned a long time ago that the more you want someone, the more you covet them, and need and love them … it doesn't matter. In the end they're going to leave you anyway." He picks up a shell and tosses it. "Besides, someone can tell you they love you, but words can lie and actions can fake something that's not."

A shudder runs through me. What a sad, horrible way to go through life. To always want, but to never have, because you think it will be taken away without notice. To be so hurt that you think it's the words and actions that hurt rather than the person behind them. My heart is wrenched for the poor little boy who lived a life without unconditional love. It aches for the man before me. A man so full of passion and life and possibility but denying himself the one piece that can help make him whole.

Oblivious to my line of thinking and my overwhelming pity for the lonely boy within him, Colton continues. "Did I think I might have loved any of them? I'm not sure, Rylee. I know how they wanted me to feel. How they wanted me to demonstrate and reciprocate, but I told you, I'm just not capable of it." He shrugs his shoulders as if this is just a simple fact of life. He turns and looks at me, a ghost of a smile on his lips. "What about you, Rylee?" he asks playfully. "Have you ever been in love?"

I look at him for a beat and then back out to the waves, searching for the memories that are there but slowly fading. A wistful smile plays on my lips as they come back to me. "Yes. I have."

"Baxter, come!" Colton yells before holding his hand out to help pull me up from my seat in the sand. "Let's head back," he says as he keeps my hand in his, and it's not lost on me that he has not responded. We walk in silence for a while, and I can sense he wants to ask more but is unsure how.

He sighs. "I have no right to even feel this way," he says, running his hand through his hair, "seeing as how my past is so …" He drifts off without finishing when he meets my eyes. "Why does it bug me? Why does the thought of you with someone else drive me absolutely crazy?"

A part of me likes the fact that it bugs him. "You surely can't think that I've been waiting around my whole life to be your plaything, Ace." I laugh, shrugging away the unease I feel about the next question I know he is going to ask. I rarely talk about what happened. I never speak of the after effects. Of the indescribable loss that can never be forgotten. Of the horrid, callous words his family said to me. Their accusations that still haunt me to this day.

Despite the passage of time, I still feel that sharp pang of grief when talking about it. Time has dulled it some in the two years since the accident, but the images burned into my mind will never fade. The guilt still weighs so heavily on me at times that I can't breathe or function. In the past it has prevented me from living again. Taking risks and putting myself out there. From taking a chance like the one I am taking with Colton. I try to hide the shiver that runs through me at the memories and prepare myself for how much I to want to reveal.

Colton looks at me, a ghost of a smile on his sculpted lips. "Spill it, sweetheart. What happened?"

I take a deep breath. "There's not much to tell," I begin, staring at the sand in front of us as we walked casually. "We were high school sweethearts, followed each other to college, got engaged, were planning our wedding ..." I feel him stiffen beside me at my last words, his fingers tensing in mine. "And he died a little over two years ago. End of story." I glance over to find him looking at me. I'm glad the tears that usually fill my eyes don't come. How embarrassing to be in love with one man and crying about another.

He stops, tugging on my hand until I falter. Sympathy fills his eyes as they search mine. "I'm sorry," he says gently, pulling me into his chest and wrapping his arms around me. I bury my face in his neck, finding comfort in the steady beat of his pulse beneath my lips. I wrap my arms around him, inhaling his delicious scent—so new yet so comforting. He brushes a soft kiss to my temple, and his tenderness is so unexpected that tears burn in the back of my throat.

"Thank you," I whisper, leaning back to look at him and smiling softly.

"You want to tell me about it?" he prompts as he runs a hand down my arm and grabs my hand, bringing it up to his mouth and placing a kiss on it.

Do I want to talk about it? Not really, but he deserves to know. Most of it anyway. He pulls me to his side and puts an arm around me as we start to walk again. "There's not much to tell, really. Max and I had pre-calc together. He was a senior and I was a junior. Typical high school romance. Football games, prom, each other's firsts." I shrug. "I followed him to UCLA, stayed with him throughout, and then we got engaged my last year of college." I watch Baxter bite at the waves again, and it offers a welcome diversion from what I'm going to say next.

"One weekend, Max decided to surprise me with a road trip. He said it was just what the doctor ordered before …" I falter, wondering how I should continue. Colton squeezes my hand in encouragement.

"Before life got more hectic; new jobs, marriage … everything. We had no set destination, so we just drove. No one knew that we were going anywhere, so there was no one to expect us back home. We headed north and ended up by Mammoth, passing the town, but veering off a two-lane road not too far from June Lake. Thankfully it had been a dry winter, so there wasn't much snow on the ground. Just a few patches here and there. It was early afternoon and I was starving, so we decided to explore and find the perfect spot for a picnic. Stupid us." I shake my head. "We had cell phones with us, but without any service, we turned them off to not waste the batteries." I stop now, needing a minute to remember those last carefree moments before life changed forever. I release Colton's hand and wrap my arms around myself to stifle the shivers that race through me.

Colton senses my anguish and wraps his arms around me, his body ghosting mine. "You guys were young, Rylee. You did nothing wrong. Don't put whatever happened on yourself," he says as if he already knows that the guilt eats at me like a disease on a daily basis.

I take in his words, grateful that he's said them but still not believing them. "We came around a corner on this winding road we were driving on. There was an elk in the road and Max swerved the car to avoid him." I can hear Colton suck in an audible breath, knowing where this is going. "We veered into the oncoming lane and the tires grabbed the edge of the road because Max had overcorrected too much. I don't know. It all happened so fast." I shudder again and Colton holds me, his arms squeezing tighter around me as if their strength can ward off the inevitable. "I remember seeing the first trees as we went over the edge and started down the ravine. I remember Max swearing and it struck me as odd because he rarely swore." My stomach lodges in my throat as I remember the weightless feeling as the car lifted from the ground and the centrifugal force that tossed me around like a rag doll as the car tumbled down. I reach up and wipe the single tear that has slid out of the corner of my eye. I shake my head. "I'm sure you don't want to hear all of this, Colton. I don't want to put a damper on our evening."

I can feel him shake his head as it's resting on my shoulder. His arms are wrapped across the top part of my chest, from shoulder to shoulder, and I bring my hands up to hook onto them. "No, please continue, Rylee. I appreciate you sharing with me. Letting me get to know and understand you better."

Maybe if I open up to him, he'll feel comfortable enough to explain his past to me as well. I think about this for a couple of seconds and realize that as much as I can hope this might happen, the reality is that I feel relieved to be talking about it for the first time in a long time.

I draw in a shaky breath before I continue. "The next thing I remember is coming to. It was getting dark. The sun was already past the crest of the mountain so we were in the shadows of the deep ravine we were in. The smells—oh, my God—they were something I will never forget and will always associate with that day. The mixture of fuel and blood and destruction. We were at the bottom of a ravine. The car was sitting on an angle and I was on the high side while Max was on the low. The car was mangled. We had rolled so many times that the car had crushed into itself, making the interior almost half the size it should have been.

"I could hear Max. The sounds he made trying to breathe—trying to stay alive—were horrifying." I shudder at those sounds that I can still hear in my dreams. "But the best part about those sounds were that he was still alive. And at some point in those first moments of waking up, he reached over and held my hand, trying to take away my fear from regaining consciousness in the hell we were embroiled in."

"Do you need a minute?" he asks sweetly before pressing a kiss to my bare shoulder.

I shake my head. "No, I'd rather just finish."

"Okay. Take your time," he murmurs as we start to walk again.

"I panicked. I had to get help. It was only when I went to release my seatbelt that I felt the pain. My right arm wouldn't work. It was visibly broken in several places. I let go of Max's hand with my left hand and tried to undo the belt, but it was jammed—some freak thing the manufacturer studied after the fact. It was the result of metal jamming in the mechanism from the crash. I remember looking down and feeling like it was a dream, when I realized I was covered in blood. My head and arm and midsection and pelvis were screaming with pain so intense I think I would rather die than ever feel that again. It hurt to breathe. To move my head. I can recall Max mumbling my name, and I reached over groping for his hand. I told him that I was going to get us help and that he needed to hold on. That I loved him. I grabbed a shard of glass. Tried to use it to cut through my seatbelt but only ended up slicing my hand some and stabbing myself in the abdomen. It was brutal. I kept blacking out from the pain. Each time I would come to, the blinding panic would hit me again."

We reach the steps up to his house, and I watch Baxter bound up with endless energy. Colton sits on the bottom step and pulls me down to sit beside him. I use my toes to make mindless imprints in the sand. "The night was freezing and dark and terrifying. By the time the sun started to lighten the sky, Max's breaths were shallow and thready. He didn't have much time. All I could do was hold his hand, pray for him, talk to him, and tell him it was okay to go. Tell him that I loved him. He died several hours later."

I run the back of my hand over my cheek to wipe away the tears that have fallen and try to erase the memory in my mind of the last time I saw Max. "I was beside myself. I was losing my strength from all my blood loss, and I knew I was getting weaker and worse off by the hour. That was when the panic set in. I was trapped, and the longer I stayed in the car, the more I felt like it was closing in on me.

"When night fell near the end of the second day, the claustrophobia was smothering me, and I completely lost it. I couldn't deal anymore with the pain and the feeling of defeat so I thrashed around in fear, in anger, and in defiance that I didn't want to die yet. All of my movement somehow dislodged my cell phone that had gotten stuck up under the dash amidst the tumbling down the hill. It fell to the floor beneath me."

I take a deep breath remembering how it took every ounce of determination and strength that I'd had left to get that phone. My lifeline. "It took what felt like hours to reach it and when I turned it on there wasn't any service. I was devastated. I started yelling at everything and nothing until something clicked in the back of my mind about a story I had heard on the news. About how they'd found some missing hiker by following the pings on their cell phone despite a lack of service.

"I knew that when I didn't show up for work in the morning, someone would call Haddie and that would get the wheels in motion. She's a worrier and knew I was preparing for a big meeting I had that morning that I would've never missed. I figured that maybe they'd be able to track my cell phone to our location. It was a long shot, but it was the only hope I had." I touch the ring on my finger with my thumb. "I clung to it and willed every thought I had that it would work."

"I don't even know what to say," Colton says before clearing his throat. I'm sure that he never expected this to be my story. Nonetheless, I am impressed by his compassion.

"There's nothing you can say." I shrug, reaching over to place a hand gently on his cheek. A silent thank you for letting me talk and for listening without interjecting. Without telling me what I should have done as most people do. "It almost took another day and a half for them to find me. I was hallucinating by then. Freezing cold and trying to escape the confines of the car in my own head. I thought the rescuer was an angel. He looked in the window and the sun was behind him, lighting him up like he had a halo. Later he told me I screamed at him." I laugh softly at the memory. "Called him an SOB and that he couldn't have me yet. That I wasn't ready to die."

Colton pulls me onto his lap so that my body is cradled between his knees and softly kisses the tracks left by my tears. "Why does it not surprise me that you'd tell off an angel?" He laughs, his lips pressed to my temple. "You're very good at telling people off," he teases.

I lean into him, accepting and being grateful for his comfort. I close my eyes and let the heat of the sun's rays and the warmth of Colton against me melt away the chill deep in my soul. "I told you, Ace. *Baggage*."

"No," he says, his chin resting on the top of my head, "that's just a fucked up situation in circumstances way out of your control."

I wish everybody saw it that way. I shrug the errant thought away. "Too many sad thoughts for such a beautiful evening." I sigh, leaning back and looking at Colton.

He smiles wistfully at me. "Thank you for telling me. I'm sure it's not the easiest thing to talk about."

"What do you want to do now?"

Colton grins wickedly at me and grabs my waist, lifting me off of him as he stands up. He doesn't release me and continues to lift me up, ignoring my growing shrieks as I realize his intentions, and places me over his shoulder.

"I'm too heavy! Put me down!" I squeal as he starts to trot up the stairs. I smack him on the butt, but he continues.

"Quit wiggling." He laughs as he reciprocates the spank. By the time we reach the top, my sides hurt from laughing so hard and Baxter is barking loudly at us. Colton continues to carry me despite reaching the patio, and I swat at him again.

"Put me down!"

"It's taking everything I have to not toss you in the pool right now," he warns.

"No!" I screech, kicking wildly as he swings me so that I can see how close we are to the edge.

He hovers there momentarily as I cry out, but then steps away and I sag in relief. He stops and pulls my legs down, and my body slowly slides down the length of him. When our faces are even, he tightens his arms around me so I am standing on air, acutely aware of my chest pressed against his. "Now, there's that smile I like," he murmurs, his breath brushing over my face.

"Very funny, Ace!" I chastise. "You—" My next words are smothered as he captures his mouth with mine. Soft, tender, and seeking, I yield to him. Needing the virile man against me to make me forget my story earlier and to remind me why it's okay to move on. We sink into the kiss as he lets me slowly slide the rest of the way down his body, my hands holding his face. The calluses of his hands rasp across the bare skin of my back as he slides them down to hold my hips.

I mewl in protest as he pulls back from me. Emotions flicker through his eyes that are impossible to read. "You hungry?" he asks.

Yes, for you. I bite my bottom lip between my teeth and nod to keep the words from slipping out. "Sure," I say, stepping back from him to turn and find a table set up to the left of us, complete with food. "What? How?"

Colton smiles. "I have my ways." He laughs as he leads me over and pulls a chair out for me. "Thank you, Grace," he says toward the open doors into the house, and I hear a faint reply from inside.

"Your secret weapon?"

"Always!" He pours us wine. "Grace is the best. She takes care of me."

Lucky woman. "It smells delicious," I say, taking a sip of my wine as Colton dishes out what appears to be chicken with artichokes and angel hair pasta.

"It's one of my favorites," he muses, taking a bite. He watches me as I taste it, and I can see him visibly relax when I hum with approval.

Dinner is light and relaxed. The food is excellent, and I despise Colton telling me that Grace does not divulge her recipes. I tell him I'll talk her out of it somehow, someway.

We talk about our jobs, and Colton asks how Zander is doing. I tell him that he hasn't spoken any more words yet, but that he seems to be responding more. I tell him that hero status has been definitely bestowed on him by the boys, and that they can't stop reliving how he pulled up to the school. I explain what needs to be done next to get permits for some of the new facilities when Corporate Cares gets the green light.

He tells me that he's been busy with the media side of the upcoming season along with everyday operations at CD Enterprises. In the past week, he's filmed a commercial for Merit Rum, did a photo shoot for a new marketing campaign, and attended an IRL function.

We sink into a relaxed rhythm, mutually sharing with each other, and it feels normal in what is otherwise a surreal setting for me. When we finish dinner, he offers a quick tour of the rest of the house, which I have secretly been wishing for. Colton tops off our glasses and grabs my hand. He shows me a state-of-the-art kitchen with warm-hued granite accompanied by top-of-the-line stainless steel appliances.

"Do you cook, Ace?" I ask, running my fingers over the enormous island as my thoughts flash back to a different kitchen island. When he doesn't answer, I look up to meet his eyes and I flush, knowing that he is remembering the same thing.

He shakes his head and smirks. "I can throw a little something together when I need to."

"Good to know," I murmur as he leads me to the next room, a sunken family room that the kitchen overlooks. Deep, chocolate leather couches that look like you could sink into oblivion in are shaped in a semicircle facing a media unit. He takes me into an office oozing of masculinity in rich leather and dark wood. A broad desk takes up a large portion of the space, the walls are lined with bookshelves, and a lone acoustic guitar propped up against the far wall.

"You play?" I ask, nodding my head toward the guitar.

"For myself." His answer mixed with the unexpected softness in his voice has me turning to look at him. He shrugs. "It's what I do to help me think ... to work though stuff in my head." As he talks, I step back further into the office and run my fingers across bookshelves, looking at the scattered pictures of his family. "I don't play for others."

I nod my head, understanding the need to have something to help when your head is troubled. I continue perusing the bookshelves and one photo causes me to do a double take. A younger Colton looks exhausted, yet jubilant, in his race suit standing in front of his car, arms raised in victory, smile wide with accomplishment, and confetti raining down. The only thing detracting from the picture is a woman wrapped around his torso. She stares up at him, love, adoration, and reverence plastered on her face. I'd know her anywhere.

"What's this picture of?" I ask casually as I turn to where he's relaxed against the doorjamb, watching me.

"What's that?" he asks, tilting his head and walking toward me. I lean back and point toward the photograph.

A smile graces his lips and his eyes light up. "That was my first win in the Indy Lights circuit." He shakes his head in remembrance. "God, that was a year."

"Tell me about it." He arches an eyebrow at me as if wondering whether I really want to hear about it. "I want to know," I prompt.

"It was my second year and I thought I was going to lose my ride if I didn't pull a win. I had come close so many times and something always prevented it." He reaches out and takes the picture off of the shelf. "Looking back, I know now that I made a lot of rookie mistakes. But back then I was just frustrated and scared I was going to lose the one thing I really loved—too much ego, too little listening. Some things never change, huh?" He glances up and I smile at him. "Anyway, everything seemed to be going bad this race. We couldn't get the car adjusted right because the weather was erratic. But with five laps left I made a run at the lead. I passed the leader in a stupid risk that I never should have taken, but it paid off and we won."

"First of many victories, right?" I ask as I take the picture from his hand and study it again.

"Right." He smirks. "And hopefully more this season."

"Who's this?" I ask, pointing to Tawny, getting to my real question.

"You didn't meet Tawny at the track the other day?"

"Oh." I play stupid. "Is that who you were speaking with before you tested?"

"Yeah. I apologize. I thought you'd been introduced."

"Uh-uh." I place the frame back on the shelf and follow him as he steps out of the office. "Did she work for you way back then?"

"No." He chuckles, showing me into a den filled with racing memorabilia, a huge flat screen television, and a pool table. "She's a family friend and we kinda grew up together. We, uh, actually dated a while in college, and it was a long-running joke between our families that we would end up married someday."

Whoa! Did I just hear that right? Only a guy would think nothing of making that comment to the woman he is currently doing whatever we are doing together with. Their families think they'll end up married some day? Fuck! I swallow loudly as he takes me into a guest suite. "Why'd you guys break up?"

"Good question." He sighs, giving me an odd look, and I wonder if I am being too pushy. "I don't know. She was just too familiar. I thought of her like a little sister. It just didn't work for me." He shrugs. "When that picture was taken we were still dating. In the end, we remained good friends. She's one of the few people I can really trust and depend on. When she graduated from college with a degree in marketing and I started CDE, she helped me out. She was good at what she did, so when the company became a reality, I hired her."

Well, he might want a platonic relationship but she sure wants more than that. I turn from looking out at the ocean and look at him. He holds his hand out to me, "C'mon, let me show you upstairs."

We ascend the wider-than-normal freestanding staircase, and I find myself impressed with the lived-in feeling of his stone fortress. I tell him I assumed it was going to be cold and uninviting but it's the exact opposite. He tells me he opted for the stone exterior to limit the maintenance required from being exposed to the harsh beach conditions.

When we reach the top of the stairs, we come to an open room that is the patio I saw from the front of the house. "I think I found heaven," I murmur as I take in the indoor/outdoor space. Lights wrap around an overhead trellis covered in a growing vine, twinkling in the darkening sky. Four chaise lounges I could get lost in are arranged around the space.

Colton laughs at me as he tugs my arm. "We can enjoy that space later," he says, wiggling his eyebrows.

"Man with a one-track mind," I tease, but my words soon falter when he brings me into his bedroom. "Wow." I breathe.

"Now this is my favorite place in the house," he says, and I can see why. An oversized bed is facing the ocean. The room is covered in soft browns and blues and greens. A love seat sits on an angled wall and a coffee table is in front of it, where magazines and books are thrown. A large dog bed sits in another corner beneath a fireplace with chewed toys and a rumpled, blue blanket. The focal point of the bedroom is a wall of windows, and I can feel the breeze blowing in off the ocean.

I watch the distant lights of boats making their way home. I can see the silhouettes of surfers waiting to catch one last set before paddling in. "Your place really is magnificent."

Colton takes me by surprise when I feel his arms slide around my waist and pull me into him, his front to my back, and nuzzles his nose into my neck. "Thank you," he murmurs as he lays a trail of feather-light kisses down to my shoulder and back up.

My body shudders and a soft sigh escapes from my lips. His hand splays over my stomach and presses me against him, my curves mold to his firm lines. His mouth is at my ear again, kissing that sensitive spot just underneath.

"Can I tell you how much I enjoy having you here?" he whispers, licks of his breath tickling my ear.

I sigh into him, leaning my head back to rest on his shoulder. "Thank you for tonight, Colton."

He chuckles. "I sure hope you're not implying it's over yet, because I'm just getting started." His hands run up and down the side of my torso, fingertips skimming the edges of my breasts. Tiny hints at what's to come. I arch against him, my body humming with desire, my heart reveling in his tenderness.

I tilt my head up and he captures my mouth with his. His tongue delves past my lips and licks at mine. Teasing. Entwining. Tasting. Worshipping. I turn into him, needing more to feed my insatiable craving. He backs me up against the wall of glass. His forearms press against it, framing my head while his body pushes into mine.

A strangled sigh escapes him as I nip at his lower lip and run a tongue down the line of his unshaven jaw. I reach his ear and tug on his ear lobe with my teeth.

"No." I breathe into his ear. "The night is most definitely not over, Ace." I make my way down the line of his throat and back up to lay a kiss at the pulse in his throat. "It's just beginning."

"Rylee," he moans, a sound of pure appreciation.

I feel empowered by his unbidden reaction. I want to show him how he makes me feel. Tell him with actions since I am unable to with words. I dip my tongue in the indent of his collarbone, his coarse hair tickling my lips, his scent enveloping me, and then trail a row of soft kisses back up to his other ear. "I want to taste you, Colton."

I hear him suck in a breath, and suddenly his hands are on the sides of my cheeks, cupping them. He pulls my face back from his, his thumbs rubbing over my swollen lips. His eyes search mine, for what I don't know, but the depth of emotion that I see is all I need. We stare at each other for what feels like an eternity, trapped in our hazy state of desire.

Our silent interlude lasts until he groans, "God, yes, Rylee," before crushing his mouth to mine.

His kiss is a bombardment of what I see in his eyes: greed, passion, blazing need, and an unexpected urgency. I have no chance to offer anything for Colton just takes, and I submit willingly to his unspoken commands. I hand myself over to him, mind, body, heart, and soul.

I ease back from the kiss, a salacious look in my eyes that stops Colton from pulling me back to him. Our chests heave with anticipation. I bite my lower lip as my mouth spreads into a wicked grin. My thoughts turn to how I want to run my tongue down his body and feel him shudder in response to my touch.

I reach out, surprised by my reaction. Max's passive, shy girl who thought having sex with the lights on was adventurous is no more. Colton makes me need things I never knew I wanted. He makes me feel sexy. Desirable. Wanted.

I bunch the hem of Colton's shirt up until my hands graze his abdomen. I run a fingernail across his stomach just above the waistline of his jeans, and I smirk as his lips part and eyes darken with need from just my touch.

I start to pull his shirt up and off of him. "Let me," he rasps as he reaches up and grabs the back of the neck of his shirt and pulls it off in one fell swoop, as only a man who has no worries of messing up hair or make-up can.

"Just how I like you," I murmur, taking in his sculpted shoulders and lean torso all the way down to the trail of hair in the middle of the sexy V of muscle that disappears beneath his waistband.

"My body is yours to take advantage of." He breathes with a sexy smirk, hinting at the dirty things he wants me to do to him. He holds his hands out to his sides, offering himself up to me.

I reach out and cup his neck, bringing his face to mine. I press my lips to his and dart my tongue in his mouth, pulling back every time he tries to control the kiss. "I. Want. You," I whisper.

I skim my fingers down the plains of his torso, nails scratching softly so his body twitches in reaction. My mouth follows the same path but at a much more leisurely pace. Colton lets his head fall back and groans when I stop to lick the flat disks of his nipples. His hands trail down my arms, up and over my shoulders, and fiddle with the ties at the back of my neck.

"Uh, uh, uh," I chastise. I look up at him from beneath my eyelashes as I lace openmouthed kisses down the skin-gloved muscles of his abdomen. "My turn, Colton."

I step back from him, never breaking eye contact, raise my hands to the back of my neck, and slowly untie my dress. "It's a little hot in here, don't you think, Ace?" I toy with him as I take in a fortifying breath and let the material slowly slide down the curves of my body. I see the fire leap into Colton's eyes as he takes in what's underneath. I've worn my Agent Provocateur strapless bra and panty set in a rich, dark purple lace that hides little but highlights my figure perfectly.

"Sweet Jesus, woman! The sight of you is enough to drive a sane man crazy," he drawls as his eyes drag their way back up and down my body.

He rubs his thumb over his other fingers as if they are itching to touch me. I step toward him again, my body hyperaware of everything around us and between us. I reach out and lay my palms on his chest, his body quivering in anticipation.

I pull them down and undo the top two buttons of his jeans, relieving some of the tension. My hands slide around the inside of his jeans and boxer briefs and grasp the solid muscles of his very fine ass. I skim my fingers back up and over his lower back while I trace my tongue down the trickle of hair below his belly button. I look up at him as I sink to my knees and very slowly undo the last three buttons of his jeans.

He stares at me beneath eyelids heavy with desire, his lips parted, and need palpable. I lower his jeans and boxer briefs, his iron length springing free. I run my fingers down the dark smattering of hair and grip the base of his shaft. I lean forward and Colton sucks in an audible breath as I circle my tongue lightly around the bell-shaped tip and then flutter it slowly down to the root and back up. My hand moves slowly up and down the veined length while my other hand comes up to cup his balls beneath, gently grazing them with my fingernails.

I look up at Colton and I'm swallowed up by the look in his eyes as he watches me. His jaw flexes in expectancy as my fingers tease him, and when I take him very slowly into my mouth, he winces in pleasure before throwing his head back and hissing "Fuccckkk, Ryleeee!"

I tease him gently at first, only taking the tip of him into the warmth of my mouth, rubbing my tongue with pressure on the sensitive underside just beneath the rim of his crest. I twist my hand around his shaft, stimulating him with friction and wet heat.

When I've tormented him enough and can feel the tension in his thighs from anticipation, I sheath my teeth with my lips and take him all the way in until I can feel him hit the back of my throat. The guttural groan that comes from Colton's lips fills the room as the musky taste of his arousal and evidence of his desire for me churns an exquisite ache that invades the depths of my very core.

I bob my head down his length again, my throat convulsing when I reach maximum depth, and slowly press my tongue on the underside as I pull it back out. I feel Colton's fingers tangle into my hair as the blissful need for release starts building within him. The harsh exhale of words and beseeching calls of my name urge me to move faster. Quicker. I take him deeper and stroke him harder. He suddenly swells and I can taste him.

"Rylee," he grates out between clenched teeth, "I'm gonna come, baby. I want to be buried in you when I do."

With his length still hard in my mouth, I look up at him to see his face pulled tight with pleasure. A man on the razor thin edge of losing control. He convulses as I hollow my cheeks and pull tightly on him one last time.

My mind doesn't have enough time to register Colton hauling me to my feet and crushing his mouth to mine with near violent desire. Spirals of sensation whirl through me as he urges my back up against the windowed wall. The anticipation of what's to come causes the ache in my groin to intensify.

Raw need ricochets through my body and straight to my core when his calloused fingers find their way beneath my dampened panties. He parts me gently and finds my clit waiting and throbbing for his attention. I grow dizzy wanting more as his fingers work their magic, stimulating my nerve endings. His mouth plunders mine, filling me with his addictive taste.

"I want you in me, Colton," I pant out when I break from our kiss. He lifts me and pulls my legs around his hips. The delicate strap of fabric holding the two triangles of my lace panties together snaps as Colton rips them from me.

I'm no longer in control. The notion sends an unexpected thrill through me but the thought is short lived as Colton spans his hands across my sides and lifts me up, pressing me against the wall for leverage. He lowers me down while his hips thrust up, burying into me. I cry out, overcome by the feeling of fullness as he stills so I can adjust to him.

"Christ, Rylee," he gasps brokenly, his face buried in my throat. The gentle draw of his mouth on my skin causes me to dig my fingers into his solid shoulders and slowly flex my hips into him. "Oh, sweetheart," he pants as he rocks his hips out and then strokes back into my quivering softness.

His body slides against mine, his hands trapped between the glass and my hips, pressing me into him and pushing himself as deeply as possible. I draw a shuttered breath through parted lips as my body softens and heats up. "Colton," I mewl as I'm pushed toward the precipice. Filling me until I can hold no more. Connecting us in every way possible. Blood pounds in my ears and sensation rockets through my body as we find each other's rhythm.

"Hold on, Ry. Not yet!" he commands as he quickens his tempo and brings me closer to the brink. Our lungs pant in short, sharp breaths, hands grip sweat-slickened flesh, and mouths claim any part of the other we can taste.

I can feel my body quickening at the same time Colton stiffens inside me. "Colton," I warn, my body tensing around him.

"Yes, baby, yes," he shouts at the same time I'm unable to deny myself another single second. My thighs turn to steel as I crash over the edge, lost in the explosion. The intense contraction grabs hold of Colton and drags him over with me. A litany of pleasure-induced words falls from his lips, his face buried in the curve of my shoulder as his body shudders with his release. We stay like this, connected as one and locked around each other momentarily, until we slowly slide down the wall to the floor. We sit entwined, my face is nuzzled against his throat, and his arms encircle me.

And in this moment, I am completely and utterly his. Swallowed by him. Lost to him and the moment so much so that I am frightened by the power of my feelings.

We sit like this, tangled around each other in a spellbound state without speaking. The lazy tracing of fingers on cooling skin and the reverberation of our hearts against each other is the only communication we need. Our labored breaths finally even out as the sky falls dark, leaving us bathed in moonlight.

I'm afraid to speak. Afraid to ruin the moment.

"You okay, Ace?" I ask finally, my foot slowly falling asleep and needing to move. Colton grunts, and I laugh at him, pleased that I reduced him to incoherence. I try to pull away from him and lean my back against the glass behind me, but he shifts with me so his face is now in the crook of my neck. He moans a sigh of satisfied contentment that spears straight into my heart.

My eye catches my torn underwear on the floor and I snicker. "What is it with you and tearing my panties off, huh? I would have gladly stepped out of them for you." I scratch my nails languorously over his back.

"Takes too long." He snorts, his unshaven jaw tickling my skin.

"Those were one of my favorite pairs. Now I don't have any to match this bra," I pout.

Colton pulls away from me, a smirk on his lips and humor in his eyes. "Tell me where they're from and I'll buy you a hundred sets so long as you stand before me like you did tonight." Colton leans forward placing a slow kiss on my lips. "Better yet," he says, pulling back and tracing a finger along the line where my breast meets the lace of my bra. "Since that is such a mighty fine bra, maybe you should just wear that and nothing else under your clothes. Talk about sexy," he grunts. "No one would even have to know."

"You'd know," I counter, arching an eyebrow.

"Yes, I would." He grins wickedly, "And I'd walk around hard all fucking day thinking about it."

I laugh. A deep, soul-baring laugh because I am so overcome with emotions that I'm bubbling over.

"Shall we get off the floor?" he asks as he shifts and unfolds himself from me. He rises, reaching out for my hand, and helping me up to my feet. "The bathroom's through there..." he points to the wide opening to the left of the bed "...if you want to get cleaned up."

"Thanks," I murmur, suddenly self conscious about my nudity. I gather my dress, pressing it to my front and look for what's left of my panties. "What—?" I ask when I can't find them. I look up to see Colton watching me as he pulls his jeans up over his naked hips, the remnants of my underwear haphazardly stuffed in his front pocket. He stops when my eyes remain on his.

Leaving his fly unbuttoned, he walks to me and reaches out to tug my dress out of my hand. I try to pull it away but I realize his intentions a moment too late. "For God's sake, Rylee, there's no need to be shy. After you just stood before me like that?" He shakes his head at me. "You're hot as hell and having confidence about it is even sexier, sweetheart." He senses my unease and leans in to brush a kiss on my lips. "It's not like I haven't seen you naked before." He smirks and holds my dress out.

I stare at him, naked except for my bra, trying not to fidget. His compliment eases my insecurities a tad. I am plain old me and Colton frickin' Donavan is in front of me. Telling me I am sexy. That he loves my curves. I feel like I need to pinch myself. Instead, I push back my lack of self-confidence and tell myself

I can do this. A slow smile quirks at one corner of my mouth as I glance at my dress in his hand before I very deliberately walk past him.

I can feel his smile when I turn the corner into the oversized bathroom, filled with granite and tumbled stone. I release the breath I was holding, proud of myself for having the courage to do that. I glance up at my reflection in the mirror and am pleasantly surprised to see that my bag is sitting on the countertop. Grace must have brought it up.

"Feel free to grab one of my shirts off of the stacks in my closet," Colton calls to me from the bedroom.

"Um–Okay. Thanks."

"I'm going to run and get us a drink. Let Baxter out. I'll be right back. Take your time."

"Uh-huh," I reply as I wander around the ridiculously large space. I walk into an open doorway to find a closet that would make Haddie the Clotheshorse cry. I peruse his vast selection of T-shirts and settle on a heather gray one. I press my nose into the fabric and can smell the detergent that makes up part of Colton's scent that I love so much.

I clean up, freshen up my make-up, pull on a pair of boyshort panties I brought—because yes, I knew this was a forgone conclusion—and slip Colton's shirt over my head.

Chapter Twenty-Four

With Colton still gone, I wander down the hallway and out the open door onto the second story terrace. I walk to the railing that overlooks the lower patio and the ocean beyond and lean against it, enjoying the nighttime breeze and the moonlight on the dancing waves.

I am so overwhelmed by what's happened recently that I can't even begin to process it. One minute I am lonely, afraid, and feeling too guilty to live again and a few weeks later I am here with a man who's complicated and wonderful and so incredibly alive. I've gone from empty and aching and raw, to happy and sated and feeling like I am having an out-of-body experience.

"Just when I thought you couldn't get any sexier, I find you wearing one of my favorite shirts." His words startle me, and I turn to find him beside me, holding out a glass of wine.

"Thank you," I murmur, taking a sip and reaching a hand out to rub Baxter's head, as he tries to squeeze between us again.

Colton edges a hip up on the railing and turns to face me as I look out at the water. "I like seeing you here," he admits, his voice soft with reflection as he tilts his head and watches me. "I like seeing you in my surroundings, in my shirt, with my dog … more than I ever could've imagined." I transfer my gaze from the water to meet his, trying to read the emotions swimming beneath the surface. "That's a first for me, Rylee." He confesses in a soft whisper, and I can barely make out the words above the noise of the waves. But his admission speaks volumes to me. Holy shit! Does this mean that he means there is a possibility of more? That whatever we are is more than just one of his stupid arrangements? I can sense his unease so I try to lighten the mood.

"What? You don't drag all of your wenches to this hideous lair of yours?"

He reaches out, a quiet smile on his lips, and cups my neck, his thumb brushing over my cheekbone. "Just the one," he replies. I smile back at him, adoring the tender side of Colton as much as I love the stubborn, feisty one. He lifts his beer bottle to his lips and takes a long pull on it. "I brought up some dessert," he offers.

"Really? I thought that's what we just had." He smiles and a carefree laugh escapes his lips.

"C'mon." He tugs on my arm and pulls me down to sink into one of the chaise lounges. Colton walks over to a console hidden in the wall, and within seconds, I hear Ne-Yo's soft voice. Baxter groans in satisfaction as he plops his large body down in the open doorway.

"So," he says as he scoots a table next to me, "I have two options for you. Mint chocolate chip ice cream or chocolate kisses."

"You remembered!" I gasp.

"Well when it comes to you and sweets, I have a hard time forgetting." He smirks as he puts a hand on my back, urging me to sit up, and then slides himself behind me.

A smile he can't see spreads on my face as I think of Colton and his imaginative ways of eating a certain confection. I lean back into his bare chest, fitting myself to him, and reach out at the tray to grab a Hershey's kiss. I unwrap it and pop it in my mouth, laying my head back onto his shoulder and groan at its heavenly taste.

"If that's all it takes to hear you make that sound, I'm buying you a truckload of them," he breathes in my ear as he moves behind me, adjusting himself.

"Want one?" I tease as I bring it to his lips and then take it away and put it in my mouth, moaning intentionally this time. He laughs and I give him a Hershey's kiss for real this time. "A girl could get used to this," I murmur, liking the warmth of him against me.

We sit for a while and talk about families, travels, experiences, and work. I avoid the topic that I really want to delve into, knowing that his past is off limits. He is funny and witty and attentive, and I can feel myself falling deeper for him, entangling myself further in his tantalizing web.

"Awesome, charismatic, and exciting," Colton says, breaking the silence between us.

I can't help but laugh out loud. "Nope," I say again, leaning back further into the warmth and comfort of his chest.

"You're never going to tell me are you?" he asks lifting a hand to brush hair off the side of my neck, exposing my bare skin so that his mouth can place a kiss there.

"Nope," I repeat, fighting the shiver that runs through me as he nuzzles his nose down to my ear.

"How about addictive cock experience?" he murmurs, his breath tickling my skin.

The laugh that bubbles in my throat falls to a sigh as he nips at my earlobe and sucks gently on the hollow spot just beneath it. "Hmmmm, that could work," I manage as he wraps his arms around my chest, and I begin to run my fingers up and down the parts of his arms that I can reach. I angle my head further to the side, giving him more access to my sensitive skin as my nails cross a jagged line on his right forearm.

"That's a nasty scar," I murmur. "What super-masculine thing were you doing to acquire that?" I cringe at the thought of how much it must have hurt.

He's quiet for a beat, kissing my temple and pressing his face to the side of mine so I can feel him swallow. "Nothing of significance," he says then falls quiet again. "Do you surf, Rylee?" he asks, changing the subject.

"Nope. Do you, Ace?" I take a sip of wine as he murmurs in assent.

"Ever tried?" he asks, the rasp of his voice in my ear.

"Uh-uh."

"I should teach you sometime," he says.

"Probably not the best thing to do for someone like me who's scared of sharks."

"You're kidding, right?" When I don't respond, he continues, "Oh come on, it'd be fun. There aren't any sharks out there that'll bug you."

"Tell that to the people who've been chomped on," I challenge, and despite the fact that he's behind me, I cover my face in embarrassment when I say, "When I was little I was so scared of them that I never swam in our pool because I used to think they'd come out of the drain and eat me."

Colton laughs. "Oh, Rylee, didn't anyone ever tell you that there are much more dangerous things on dry land?"

Yes. You.

As I try to think of a witty retort, my ear catches the song playing over the speakers and I murmur, "Great song."

Colton stills as he listens to the music, and I can feel his head nod against the side of mine. "Pink, right?"

"Hmm-hmm. *Glitter in the Air*," I respond, distracted as I listen to the words of one of Haddie's and my all-time favorite songs. Colton runs his hands up my arms and starts to knead my shoulders. His hands are powerful and add just the right amount of pressure. "That feels like heaven," I breathe as my already relaxed body turns to gel beneath his skillful fingertips.

"Good," he whispers. "Just relax."

I close my eyes and hand myself over to him, humming softly to the song. Colton runs his fingers down the line of my spine and rubs my lower back, my head lolling to the side at the sublime feeling.

"Here comes the best part," I say. I sing along as the words wash over me, moving me as they always do. "*There you are, sitting in the garden, clutching my coffee, calling me sugar. You called me sugar.*"

"I don't get it," Colton says, "Why is that the best part?"

"Because it's the moment she realizes that he loves her," I say, a soft smile on my face.

"Why, Rylee, you're a hopeless romantic, aren't you?" he teases.

"Oh, shut up." I shift to swat him, but Colton grabs my wrist before I can, and pulls me into him. His lips slant over mine and make a languid sweeping pass before licking mine. He tastes of chocolate and beer and everything that is uniquely Colton. He cradles my head with one hand while the other runs aimlessly over my bare thighs. Fingertips graze softly, without urgency, or attention to any one spot. I could sit in this moment forever, his actions unraveling me.

Colton brushes a kiss on the tip of my nose before resting his forehead to mine, his hand still cupping the back of my head, fingers still knotted in my hair, his breath fluttering over my lips. "Rylee?"

"Hmm-hmm, Ace?"

He flexes the hand in my hair. "Stay the night with me." He says quietly.

I still, holding my breath. *Oh. My.* I can feel the emotion behind his request and can sense a change from the last time he said it to me. He's not saying it out of obligation but because this is what he wants..

"I've never said that before and truly meant it, Rylee." His voice is a hushed plea that tugs at my heart. He wraps his arms around me, cradling me in his lap, and pulls me with him as he leans back in the chaise, fingers playing in my hair. I remain silent, trying to clear the emotion from my voice before I speak.

"Hmmm, I don't think I could move even if I tried," I murmur.

"You'll stay?" The eagerness in his voice surprises me.

"Yes."

"In that case," he muses, "I might have to take advantage of you again."

"Again?" I laugh. His response is to grab my hips, lift me up, and place me astride him. He situates me on him so that our bodies fit together perfectly, each movement from him traveling through my thin panties and hitting me in just the right spot.

He sits up and kisses me forcefully, his tongue plunging between my parted lips, his hands pressing my body to him possessively. I grow dizzy wanting more of everything from him.

"I. Want. You. So. Much. Rylee." He pants between kisses down my neck. I bring my hands to his face, fingers touching coarse whiskers, and draw his head up to meet my eyes. "You're addictive."

"I know," I whisper, telling him with my eyes that I feel addicted to him too. The muscle in his jaw tenses momentarily before he crushes his mouth to mine, the connection between us a necessity like air.

"Ride me," he pants. Such a simple command, but the way he says it—as if the sun won't rise in the morning if I don't—has me pulling back. I stare into his eyes, so hypnotizing, so intense and so full of desire I wouldn't deny him even if I could.

So I begin to move, surrendering myself to him. Again.

Chapter Twenty-Five

The cool air that wisps over my skin is a stark contrast to the radiating heat pressing against me. My sleep-induced haze slowly clears from my mind as my eyes flutter open, startled by the natural light filtering in through the open windows.

I start to shift in the sinfully comfortable bed, wanting to stretch my muscles that oddly feel sore, until I realize why. Sex, sex, and more sex. A smug smile crosses my lips.

Colton is wrapped around me like a vine. He is on his side, one leg bent and slung over mine, and his hand splays possessively over my bare chest with his palm cupping my breast. I turn to find his head half on my pillow, half on his.

I study his face: the angles, the fan of thick, dark lashes against his golden skin, the curve of his nose. I reach over and brush an errant lock of hair off his forehead, careful not to disturb him. In sleep, Colton's dark and dangerous aura is softened by his disheveled hair, the absence of the intensity he carries around like a badge of protection, and the lack of tension in his jaw. I enjoy catching this rare glimpse of him—vulnerable and relaxed.

Staring at him, my mind drifts back to last night. I recall his complete and unyielding attentiveness to me and my every need. I think of the new experiences he introduced me to, and the pleasure he's induced in me. My thoughts stray to leather restraints, vibrating eggs, and ice cubes inserted to melt as we became one, evoking that walk down the fine line of pleasure edged by pain. I think of how he showed me slow and soft before pushing me to the brink of oblivion with hard and fast. How, by the light of the moon, in this expanse of a bed, he hovered over me, eyes intense, voice beseeching, and asked me to submit to him. Asked that I trust him to know what my body can handle and which threshold to push it to. And in that moment, I was so captivated with him, I handed myself over to him without question, or second thought. I agreed, knowing he already dominated my mind, heart, and body.

Afterward, as I drifted off to sleep, his warm body pressed against my back and his mouth pressed softly in my hair, I questioned my judgment. Before drifting off to sleep, I wondered what the hell I was getting myself into by accepting his seemingly innocent request, for what is simple under a blanket of moonlight never seems to be when the next morning dawns.

Colton shifts beside me, rolling over so his back is toward me, and pulls the covers with him and off me. I shiver from the chill but am happy that I can now stretch out my overused muscles. I wince as I flex my feet and extend my legs. I definitely wasn't treated like glass last night, but my body quite liked it too.

I'm starting to get cold. I look over at the artfully sculpted lines of Colton's back and I turn into him, tucking my body around him so I can enjoy the feeling of my bare skin against his. My chin rests on his shoulder and my breasts press up against his back as I curl my arms around him. I absently run my fingers across his chest, as I slowly sink back into sleep.

I'm in the first stages of sleep when Colton suddenly emits the most gut-wrenching, feral cry I've ever heard. I would've remained frozen in shock but he bucks his body violently back against me, connecting his elbow against my shoulder. "No!" falls from his mouth in a strangled shout. He jumps from the bed and turns around, legs spread, knees bowed, arms bent, and hands fisted in front of his face. His face is the picture of terror: eyes wild and haunted, flickering, teeth clenched, and tendons straining in his neck. His chest heaves shallow breaths, body tense and vibrating with acute awareness as sweat beads on his forehead.

I instinctively grab my shoulder where it is smarting with pain. The shock of what just happened is sinking in, my adrenaline is pumping, causing my body to shake. If I hadn't witnessed this reaction from a nightmare before, from my kids, I would have been more startled than I am right now. If Colton didn't have such a look of complete fear in his eyes, I would have laughed at him standing nude, looking like he's ready to throw down. But I know this isn't a joke. I understand that Colton has had a dream dredging up the past that silently chases him and continues to traumatize him on a daily basis.

I roll my shoulder, pain still shooting through it. "Colton," I say evenly, not wanting to startle him.

I see his eyes slowly come into focus and the tension in his stance slowly abate. He turns his head and looks at me, a plethora of emotions in his eyes: embarrassment, shame, relief, fear, and apprehension. "Oh, fuck!" He shudders a breath, bringing his hands up to rub the fear from his face. The only sounds in the room are his heaving breaths, hand chafing over his stubble, and the ocean outside.

"Fuuuccckkk!" he repeats again, his eyes narrowing on my hand rubbing my shoulder. I can see him clench and unclench his fists as he realizes he's hurt me. I remain still as his eyes lower and his shoulders slouch. "Rylee—I—" he turns abruptly and grabs the back of his neck with his hand, pulling down. "Give me a fucking minute," he mutters as he quickly strides into the bathroom.

I gather the sheets up to my chest and watch him leave, wanting to reach out to him and tell him things he doesn't believe or want to hear. I sit in indecision when I hear the unmistakable sound of Colton vomiting. A knife twists deep down in my gut, and I squeeze my eyes shut, wanting desperately to comfort him.

The toilet flushes followed by a muttered curse, and then I hear the faucet turn on and the brushing of teeth. I rise from the bed, sliding Colton's shirt on when I hear him sigh again. I enter the bathroom, needing to make sure he is okay. We stand frozen, as he focuses on the water running from the faucet. His angst is palpable and hangs in the air between us. Colton scrubs the towel over his face and turns toward me.

When he drops the towel from his face, the eyes that stare back at me are not his. The ones I've come to love. They are dead. Cold. Devoid of emotion. The muscle in his jaw pulses and the cords in his neck strain as he works his throat.

"Colton…" His glazed green eyes glare intently on mine causing my words to falter on my lips.

"Don't, Rylee," he warns. "You need to leave." His command is flat. As lifeless as his eyes.

My heart lurches into my chest. What happened to him? What memory has reduced this vibrant, passionate man to nothing? "Colton," I plead.

"Go, Rylee. I don't want you here."

My bottom lip trembles at his words, for he can't possibly mean them after the evening we've just shared. I saw the emotion in his eyes last night. Felt from his actions how he feels about me. But now … all I can do is stare at him, the man before me is unrecognizable.

I'm not quite sure what to do. I take a step forward and I hear his teeth grind. I've worked with traumatized children but I am way out of my element here. I look down at my clasped hands and whisper brokenly, "I just want to help."

"Get out!" he roars, causing my head to snap up in time to see his dead eyes spark to life with unfiltered anger. "Get the fuck out, Rylee! I don't want you here! Don't need you here!"

I stand there frozen, his unprovoked anger immobilizing me. "You don't mean that," I stutter.

"Like hell I don't!" he yells, the sound echoing off of the stone tiles and reverberating. Our eyes hold in silence as I process his words. Colton takes a threatening step toward me and I just stare at him, shaking my head. He throws the towel with a curse, the clatter of bottles it knocks over ricocheting around the pin-drop quiet bathroom. His eyes angle back toward mine as he clenches and unclenches his jaw. When he speaks, his voice is chillingly cruel. "I've fucked you, Rylee, and now I'm done with you! *I told you that's all I was good for, sweetheart …*"

His brow creases momentarily as the tears that burn the back of my throat well in my eyes and spill over. His callous words turn my stomach and wring my heart. My head tells my legs to move—to leave—but my body doesn't listen. When I just stand there, dumbfounded and shell-shocked, he grabs my bag from the bathroom counter and shoves it forcefully against my chest, propelling me through the door. "Out!" he grates through gritted teeth. His bare chest heaving. His pulse pounding in his temple. His fists clenched. "I'm bored with you already. Can't you see that? You've served your purpose. A quick amusement to bide my time. Now I'm done. Get out!"

Blinded by tears, I fumble with my bag and run blindly down the stairs. I can feel the weight of his stare on my back as I descend. I race through the house, my heart lodged in my throat and my head an absolute mess. My chest hurts so bad that pain radiates in it as I drag in each labored breath. Thoughts elude me. Hurt engulfs me. Regret fills me, for I thought what we had meant so much more.

I burst through the front door into the bright early morning sun, but all I feel is darkness. I stagger, drop my purse, and fall to my knees. I sit like that, staring at a beautiful morning, but seeing none of it.

Letting the tears wash over me.

Allowing the humiliation to consume me.

Feeling my heart break in two.

The End

Fueled

To J.P.—

Thanks for your patience while I take on this challenge that's always been a dream of mine. Oh and hey, it's not just a hobby anymore...

Prologue

COLTON

Fucking dreams. Jumbled pieces of time that tumble through my subconscious. Rylee's here. Filling them. Consuming them. And fuck if I know why the constant sight of her in a place that's usually clouded with such horrible memories fills me with a sense of calm—of what I think might be hope—allowing me to realize that I might actually have a reason to heal. A reason to overcome the fucked up things that lurk here. That the black abyss in my heart just might have the capacity to love. Her presence here in a place so dark lets me think the wounds that claimed my soul and have always been raw and festering just might be finally scabbing over.

I'm dreaming—*I know I'm dreaming*—so how come she's everywhere, even in my sleep? She's robbing me of thoughts every minute of every goddamn day, and now she's woven her way into my fucking subconscious.

She pushes me.

Unmans me.

Consumes me.

Scares the ever-loving shit out of me.

She feels like the start of a race, stopping my heart and speeding it up simultaneously. She makes me think thoughts I shouldn't. Digs deep into the black within me and makes me think in *whens,* not *ifs.*

Fuck me!

I must really be dreaming if I'm thinking fucking shit like this. *When did I become such a pussy?* Becks will hand my ass to me if he hears me talking shit like this. It can't be anything more than just needing to be buried in her again. Have her warm body beneath me to sink into. Soft curves. Firm tits. Tight pussy. *That's all it is.* I'll be fixed then. My head will return to where it needs to be. *Well, both heads actually.* And once satisfied, I'll be able to focus on something else besides useless shit like feelings and a heart beating that I know is incapable of giving or accepting love.

It has to be the newness of her that has me feeling like a needy little bitch—so much that I'm dreaming about *her specifically,* not just the faceless, perfect body that usually frequents my dreams. There's just something so fucking hot about her that I'm losing my mind. Shit, I actually look forward to the time spent before fucking her as much as I do the time I am fucking her.

Well, almost.

Unlike the numerous chicks that throw themselves at me with their overtly sexual ways: tits hanging out, eyes offering me to take them any way I want to, legs spreading at the drop of a dime—and believe me, most of the time I'm fucking game to their willingness. With Rylee though, it's just been different from the start, from the moment she fell out of that fucking closet and into my life.

Images flicker through my dreams. That first jolt as she looked up at me with those fucking magnificent eyes of hers. That first taste of her that seared my mind, crept down my spine, grabbed hold of my balls, and told me to not let her leave— that I had to have her at any cost. The image of her ass swaying as she walked away without a backward glance, reeling me in with something I'd never considered sexy before. Defiance.

Pictures continue to circle. Rylee kneeling down to Zander, trying to coax his damaged soul out of hiding; her sitting on my lap in my favorite t-shirt and panties, straddled over me last night on the patio; showing up at her office, confusion mixed with anger warring across her incredible features from my non-refutable offer; Rylee standing before me in lacy lingerie, offering herself to me, selflessly giving everything to me.

Wake the fuck up, Donavan. *You're dreaming.* Wake up and take what you want. She's right next to you. Warm. Inviting. Tempting.

Frustration fills me, wanting her so desperately and not being able to shake this damn dream to take her sexy as sin body as I see fit. Maybe that's what it is about her. That she doesn't realize how sexy she actually is. Unlike the countless others before who spent hours staring at and critiquing themselves and their best sides, Rylee has no fucking clue.

Images of her last night consume me. Looking up at me with violet eyes, her bee-stung bottom lip tugged between her teeth, and her body instinctively responding to me, submitting to me. Her signature scent of vanilla mixed with shampoo. Her addictive taste—sinfully sweet. She's irresistible and innocent and a vixen all mixed into one tempting, curvaceous package.

The thought alone makes my dick hard. I just need another fix of her. Can't get enough. *At least until the newness wears off and I move on like usual.* There's no way I'm gonna be pussy-whipped by any one woman. Why get attached to someone that will only leave in the end? To someone who will run the other way when they really know about the truths inside of me, the poison that clings to my soul. Casual is just what I need. The only thing I want.

The only thing I'll allow.

I feel her hands slither around my abdomen, and I sink into the feeling. *Fuck I need this right now. Need her right now.* The knowledge that the tight, wet, heat I crave is just within my grasp stirs my dick awake. Sinking into the softness of her body and forgetting all of this shit in my head is just mere moments away. My morning hard-on stiffens further so that it's almost painful, begging for her touch.

My body tenses as I realize the arms encircling me aren't soft or smooth or smelling of vanilla like Rylee's always are. Shivers of revulsion streak down my spine and turn my stomach. Bile rises and chokes my throat. Stale cigarettes and cheap alcohol permeate the air as it seeps from his pores with his heightened excitement. His paunchy gut presses against my back as his meaty, unforgiving fingers spread across my lower abdomen. I squeeze my eyes shut, the throb of my pounding heartbeat drowning out all sound including my feeble whimpers of protest.

Spiderman. Batman. Superman. Ironman.

I'm so hungry, so weak from the lack of food while Mommy has been away on her last *trip* that I tell myself to not resist. Mommy said that if I'm a good boy and do what I'm told, we'll both be rewarded—that doing this for her makes her love me; she'll get her fix of "Mommy feel goods" from him, and I'll get to have that half eaten apple and plastic wrapped pair of crackers she luckily found somewhere and brought back here. My stomach cramps and mouth waters at the notion of having something in it for the first time in days.

Spiderman. Batman. Superman. Ironman.

I just have to be good. I just have to be good.

I repeat the mantra to myself as his bearded jaw scrapes against my neck from behind. I try to stifle the heaving sensation from my stomach, and despite there being nothing to throw up, my body shudders violently, trying to anyway. The heat of his body against my back—always against my back—makes tears spring in my eyes that I fight to prevent. He groans into my ear—my fear exciting him—as the tears leak through my squeezed eyelids. They trail across my face to fall on my mom's musty mattress sitting on the floor. I tell myself not to resist as his thickening thing presses against my bottom. I remember all too well what happens when I do that. Resist or not, either option is painful, is a nightmare that results in the same ending— fists before pain or just accepting the pain without the struggle.

I wonder if there's pain when you die.

Spiderman. Batman. Superman. Ironman.

"I love you, Colty. Do this for Mommy and I'll love you again, okay? A good little boy does anything for his mommy. *Anything.* Love means you do things like this. If you really love me and know that I love you, you'll do this so that Mommy can feel better again. I love you. I know you're hungry. So am I. I told him you wouldn't fight this time *because you love me.*"

Her pleading voice rings in my ears. I know that no matter how hard I scream, she'll never open the door to help, despite sitting on the other side of it. I know she can hear my cries—the pain, the terror, the loss of innocence—but the haze of her withdrawal is so strong she doesn't care. She needs the drugs he'll give her when he's done with me. His payment. That's all she cares about.

Spiderman. Batman. Superman. Ironman. Spiderman. Batman. Superman. Ironman. I repeat the names of the superheroes, my silent escape from this hell. From the fear that races through my veins, coats my skin with sweat, and fills the air with its unmistakable scent. I repeat the names again. Praying any of these four superheroes will show up and rescue me. To fight evil.

"Tell me," he grunts. "Say it or it'll hurt more until you do."

I bite my lip and welcome the metallic taste of my blood as I try to prevent myself from crying out in fear and terror. From giving him what he wants, my screams for the help that I know will never come. He grips me hard. It hurts so bad. I give in and say what he wants to hear.

"I love you. I love you. I love you..." I repeat over and over, endlessly as his breath picks up from the excitement my words bring him. My fingernails dig into my clenched fists as his hands grope and grab their way down my torso. His rough fingers find the waistband of my threadbare underwear—one of the only pair I have—and I hear them rip under his excited and jerky movements. I suck in my breath, my body shaking violently, knowing what happens next. One hand cups my crotch, squeezing me too hard and hurting me, while I feel his other hand spreading me apart from behind.

Spiderman. Batman. Superman. Ironman.

I can't help it. I'm starving but…it just hurts too much. I buck against him. "No," gurgles past my chapped lips as I fight hard to escape what happens next. I thrash violently, connecting with some part of him as I spring from the bed and escape momentarily. Fear consumes me, engulfs me as he rises off the stained mattress and comes at me, a determined grimace on his face and desire in his eyes.

I think I hear my name being called and confusion flickers through my overwhelmed brain. *What is she doing here?* She has to go. He'll hurt her too. *Oh fuck! Not Rylee too.* My frantic thoughts scream for her to run. To get the hell out, but I can't get the words out. Fear has locked them in my throat.

"Colton."

The horror in my head slowly melds and seeps into the soft morning light of my bedroom. I'm not sure if I can believe my eyes. *What is real?* I'm thirty-two but I feel like I'm eight. The chilled morning air mingles with the sheen of sweat covering my naked body, but the cold I feel is so deep down in my soul I know that no amount of heat will warm me up. My whole body is taut with the impending assault that it takes a moment for me to believe that he's not really here.

I shift my gaze, my pulse thundering through my veins, and lock eyes with Rylee. She is sitting up in my beast of a bed, pale blue sheets pooled around her bare waist and her lips swollen from sleep. I stare at her, hoping this is real but not sure if I believe it. *"Oh fuck,"* I exhale on a shaky breath, unclenching my hands and bringing them up to rub them over my face to try and wipe away the nightmare. The coarseness of my stubble on my hand is welcome. It tells me I really am here. That I'm an adult and he's nowhere near.

That he can't hurt me again.

"Fuuuccckkk!" I grit out again, trying to get a hold on the chaos in my head. I drop my hands down to my side. When Rylee moves, my vision comes back into focus. She very slowly reaches her hand up to rub the opposing shoulder, her face grimacing with pain, but her eyes are chock full of concern as they remain focused on me.

Did I hurt her? Fuckin' Christ! *I hurt her.*

This can't be real. My nerves are shot. My mind is racing. If this is real, and that's really Rylee, then why do I still smell him? How come I can still feel the scrape of his beard against my neck? How come I can still hear his grunts of pleasure? Feel the pain?

"Rylee, I—"

I swear his taste is still in my mouth? *Oh God.*

My stomach revolts at the thought and the memory it conjures up. "Give me a fucking minute." I can't get to the bathroom fast enough. I need to rid the taste in my mouth.

I barely make it to the toilet, stumbling and falling to my knees as I empty the nonexistent contents of my stomach into the bowl. My body shakes violently as I do what I can to expunge every trace of him from my body even if those traces are only in my mind. I slide down to lean back against the tiled wainscot wall, the cool of the marble welcome against my heated skin. My hand trembles as I wipe my mouth with the back of it. I lean my head back, closing my eyes, and try to shove the memories back into hiding to no avail.

Spiderman. Batman. Superman. Ironman.

What the hell happened? I haven't had that dream in over fifteen years. Why now? Why did—*oh fuck! Oh fuck! Rylee.* Rylee saw that. Rylee was witness to the nightmare that I've never confessed to. The nightmare full of things that absolutely no one knows about. Did I say anything? Did she hear something? No, no, no! She can't find out.

She can't be here.

Shame washes through me and lodges in my throat, forcing me to breathe deep to prevent from getting sick again. If she knows the things I did—the things he made me do, the things I did without a struggle—then she'll know what kind of person I am. She'll know how horrible and dirty and unworthy I am. Why loving somebody, accepting love from somebody is not possible for me. *Ever.*

The deep-seated fear that lives just under the surface inside of me—over someone finding out the truth—bubbles up, sputters over the edge.

Oh fuck, not again. My stomach riots violently, and when I'm finished dry heaving, I flush the toilet and force myself up. I stumble to the sink and with shaking hands squeeze a heaping glob of toothpaste on my toothbrush and scrub my mouth aggressively. I close my eyes, willing the feelings away while trying to remember the feel of Rylee's hands— instead of any of the numerous women I've used unabashedly over the years to try and smother the horror in my mind—to take the memory away.

To use pleasure to bury the pain.

"Fuck!" It doesn't work so I scrub my teeth until I can taste the coppery hint of blood from my gums. I drop my toothbrush with a clatter on the counter and cup some of the water in my hands to splash onto my face. I focus on Rylee's feet through the mirror's reflection as she enters the bathroom. I take a deep breath. I can't let her see me like this. She's too smart—has too much experience with this kind of shit—and I'm not ready for the skeletons in my closet to be exposed and gone through with a fine-tooth comb.

I don't think I'll ever be.

I scrub my face with the towel, unsure of what to do. When I drop it, I look up to her. *God, she is so incredibly fucking beautiful.* She takes my breath away. Bare legs sticking out beneath my rumpled t-shirt, smudged eyeliner, hair tangled from sleep, and a crease in her cheek from the pillow do nothing to lessen her attraction. For some reason, it almost heightens it. Makes her seem so innocent, so untouchable. I don't deserve her. She is so much more than someone like me is worthy of. She's just too close right now, closer than I've ever let anyone get. And it terrifies me. I've never let someone this far in because that means secrets are shared and pasts are discovered.

And because it means you need. I've only ever needed myself—needing others only results in pain. In abandonment. In unspeakable horrors. And yet, *I need Rylee right now.* Every cell in my body wants to walk over, pull her against me, and cling to her right now. Use the warmth of her soft skin and the sound of her quiet sighs to alleviate the pressure expanding in my chest. To lose myself in her so I can find myself again—even if just for a minute. And for that reason alone, she needs to leave. As much as I want to, I can't…I just can't do this to her. To me. To my carefully constructed life and way of coping.

Alone is better. Alone, I know what to expect. I can map out situations and mitigate problems ahead of time. Fuck! How am I going to do this? How am I going to push away the one woman I've ever really thought of letting in?

Better to lose her now than when she bolts after finding out the truth.

I take a fortifying breath in preparation and meet her eyes. So many emotions swarm in her violet irises, and yet it's the pity that sets me off, that allows me to grab on to it and use it as my piss-poor excuse for what I'm about to do. I've seen that look so many times over my life and nothing irritates me more. I'm not a charity case. I don't need anyone's damn pity.

Especially not hers.

She says my name in that telephone sex rasp of a voice she has, and I almost cave. "Don't, Rylee. You need to leave."

"Colton?" Her eyes search mine, asking so many questions and yet none pass through her lips.

"Go, Rylee. I don't want you here." She blanches at my statement. My eyes trace down her face, and I watch her bottom lip tremble. I bite the inside of my lip as my stomach churns and feels like I'm going to be sick again.

"I just want to help…"

I wince inwardly at the break in her voice, hating myself for the pain I know I'm about to cause her. She's just so goddamn stubborn that I know she's not going to leave this without a fight. She takes a step toward me, and I grind my teeth in reaction. If she touches me—if I feel her fingertips on my skin—I'll cave.

"Get out!" I roar, her eyes snap up to meet mine, disbelief flashing in them, but I also sense her resolve to comfort me. "Get the fuck out, Rylee! I don't want you here! Don't need you here!"

Her eyes widen as she clenches her jaw to prevent her lip from quivering. "You don't mean that."

The quiet temerity in her voice hits my ears and tears into parts deep inside of me that I never knew existed. It's killing me to watch how I'm hurting her, how she's willing to stand there and listen to what I'm hurling at her just so that she can make sure I'm okay. She's proving now more than ever that she is in fact the saint, and I am most definitely the sinner.

Sweet fucking Christ!

I'm gonna have to destroy her with bullshit lies just to get her out of here. To protect myself from apologizing and keeping her here—from opening myself up to everything I've always protected myself against.

"Like hell I do!" I yell at her, throwing the towel in my hand across the bathroom in frustration and knocking over some stupid bottle-like vases. Her chin lifts up in obstinance as she stares at me. *Just go, Rylee! Make this easier on both of us!* Instead, she just holds my gaze. I take a step toward her, trying to look as threatening as possible to get her to leave.

"I've fucked you, Rylee, and now I'm done with you! I told you that's all I was good for, sweetheart..."

The first tear slides down her cheek, and I force myself to breathe evenly, to pretend that I'm unaffected, but the wounded look in those amethyst eyes is killing me. She needs to go—*now*! I pick up her bag off of the counter and shove it at her chest. I cringe when her body jerks backwards from the force I've used. Putting my hands on her like this makes my stomach churn even more.

"Out!" I growl, fisting my hands to prevent myself from reaching out and touching her. "I'm bored with you already. Can't you see that? A quick amusement to bide my time. Now I'm done. Get! Out!"

She looks at me one last time, her watery eyes still silently searching mine with a quiet strength before a sob tears from her throat. She turns and stumbles from my room as I brace myself against the doorjamb and just stand there, my heart pounding in my chest, my head throbbing, and my fingers hurting from gripping the doorjamb to prevent myself from going after her. When I hear the front door slam shut, I exhale a long, shaky breath.

What the fuck did I just do?

Images from my dream resurface, and that's the only reminder I need. Everything hits me at once as I stagger into the shower and turn the water on hotter than I can stand. I take the bar of soap and scrub my body violently, trying to erase the lingering feeling of his hands on me, trying to wash away the pain within from both remembering him and from pushing Rylee away. When the bar of soap is gone, I turn and empty a bottle of some kind of wash over me, and start again, my hands frantic in their quest. My skin is raw and still not clean enough.

The first sob catches me by complete surprise as it tears from my throat. *Fuck!* I don't cry. *Good little boys don't cry if they love their mommies.* My shoulders shake as I try to hold it in, but everything—all of the emotion, all of the memories, seeing all of the pain in Rylee's eyes—from the past few hours is just too much. The floodgates open and I just can't hold it back anymore.

Chapter One

As the sobs that rack my body slowly abate, the stinging on my kneecaps brings me back to the present. I realize that I'm kneeling on the coarse cobblestone in Colton's front entrance with nothing on but his T-shirt. No shoes. No pants. No car.

And a cell phone still inside on the bathroom counter.

I shake my head as hurt and humiliation give way to anger. I'm over the initial shock from his words, and now I want to give him my two cents. It's not okay to treat or talk to me this way. With a sudden rush of adrenaline, I push myself up from the ground and shove the front door back open. It slams back against the wall with a thud.

He may be done with me, but I haven't had my say yet. Too many things jumble around in my head that I might never get the chance to say again. And regret is one emotion I don't need added to my list of things to rue over.

I take the stairs two at a time, never more aware of how little I'm wearing as the cool morning air sneaks beneath the shirt and hits my bare flesh; Flesh that is slightly swollen and sore from Colton's more than thorough attention and adept skill the numerous times we'd had sex last night. The discomfort adds a quiet sadness to my raging inferno of anger. Baxter greets me with the thump of a tail as I enter the bedroom and hear the spraying water of the shower. My veins flow with fire now as his comments replay in my head, each one compounding upon the next. Each one transitioning from hurt to humiliation to anger. On a mission, I toss my bag carelessly on the counter alongside where my cell phone sits.

I stride angrily into the walk-in shower, ready to spew my venom back at him. To tell him I don't care who he is on the social scale, and that self-proclaimed assholes like him don't deserve good girls like me. I turn past the alcove in the shower and stop dead in my tracks, the words dying on my lips.

Colton is standing in the shower with his hands braced against the wall. Water streams down his shoulders, sagging and defeated in their carriage. His head hangs forward, lifeless and beaten. His eyes are squeezed shut. The distinct and always strong line of his posture that I've come to recognize is missing. The strong, confident man I know is nowhere to be found. Completely absent.

The first thought that flickers through my mind is it serves the asshole right. He should be upset and remorseful over how he treated me and for the abhorrent things he said. No amount of groveling is going to take back the hurt he's caused with his words or from pushing me away. I fist my hands at my side, warring within over how to proceed because now that I'm here, I'm at a loss. It takes a moment, but I've decided to leave undetected—call a cab—walk away without a word. But just as I take a step backwards in retreat, a strangled sob wrenches from Colton's mouth and shudders through his body. It's a guttural moan that's so feral in nature it seems as if it's taking every ounce of his strength to hold himself together.

I freeze at the sound. I'm watching this strong, virile man come undone, and I realize the anguish ripping through him is over something much bigger than our exchange. And it is in this moment, being witness to his agony, I realize there are so many different ways a person can ache. So many definitions I never realized held within such a simple word.

My heart aches from the pain and humiliation Colton inflicted with his words. From opening itself up after all this time to have it torn again with such cruelty.

My head aches with the knowledge that there is so much more going on here—things I should have noticed with my extensive training—but I was so blindsided by him, his presence, his words, and his actions that I didn't pay close enough attention.

I missed seeing the forest through the trees.

My soul aches at seeing Colton fighting blindly against the demons that chase him through the day and into his dreams to torture him at night.

My body aches to go to him and provide some type of comfort to try and ease the pain these demons cause. To run my hands over him and soothe away the memories that he feels he'll never be able to escape, that he'll never be able to heal from.

My pride aches from wanting to stand my ground, be stubborn, and stay true to myself. To never walk willingly back to someone who treated me the way he did.

I stand on the precipice of indecision, unsure which ache within to listen to when Colton strangles out another heart wrenching sob. His body shakes with its violence. His face squeezed so tight, his pain is palpable.

My debate on what to do next is minimal because I can't hide from the fact that whether he wants to accept it or not, he needs someone right now. He needs me. All of the cruel words he spat at me evaporate at the sight of my broken man. They fade elsewhere to be addressed at another time. My years of training have taught me to be patient but to also know when to step forward. And this time, I won't miss the signs.

I have never been able to walk away from someone in need, especially a little boy. And right here, right now, looking at Colton so bereft and helpless, that's all I see: a shattered little boy that's just broken my heart—is currently breaking my heart—and as much I know staying here will result in my own emotional suicide, I can't find it in me to walk away. To save myself at the expense of another.

I know if I were watching someone else make this decision, I'd tell them that they're stupid for walking back in the house. I would question their judgment and say they deserve what they get. But it's so easy to judge from the outside looking in, never knowing the decision you'd make until you're in that person's shoes.

But this time, this time I am in those shoes. And the decision is so natural, so ingrained in me to take a step forward when most others would step away that there isn't one to be made.

I move on instinct and cautiously enter the shower, *willingly walking into emotional suicide*. He stands beneath one of two huge rain showerheads while numerous jets in the stoned walls squirt water down the length of his body. A built-in bench spans the length of one wall; various bottles of product are shoved in a corner. In any other circumstance, my jaw would have dropped at the grandiose shower and thoughts of standing in there for hours would have flickered through my mind.

Not now.

The image of Colton—so magnificent in body yet isolated in emotion—as he stands there with water running in rivulets down the artfully sculpted lines of his body overwhelms me with sadness. The anguish that radiates off of him in waves is so tangible I can feel the oppressive weight of it as I walk up to him. I lean against the wall next to where he presses his hands. The scalding water that ricochets off of him tickles my skin. Indecision reappears as I reach out to touch him but pull back, not wanting to startle him in his already fragile state.

After some time, Colton lifts his head and opens his eyes. He gasps audibly at the sight of me standing before him. Shock, humiliation, and regret flash fleetingly through his eyes before he lowers them for a beat. When he raises them back to me, the uncensored pain that I see in their depths renders me speechless.

We stand there like this— motionless, wordless, and staring into the uncharted depths of each other for some time. A silent exchange that fixes nothing and yet explains so much.

"I'm so sorry," he says finally in a broken whisper before lowering his eyes and pushing himself off of the wall. He staggers back and collapses onto the built-in bench, and I can't hold myself back any more. I take the few steps to cross the shower stall and use my body to push his knees apart so I can step between his legs. Before I can even reach for him, he takes me by surprise, gripping his fingers into the flesh at my hips and yanking me to him. He finds his way beneath my now wet shirt and runs his hands up my torso, pushing it up as he goes until I cross my arms in front of me and strip it off. I toss it carelessly behind me and it lands with a loud slap against the tile. The minute I'm naked, he wraps his arms around me, and crushes my body to his. With him seated and me standing, his cheek presses against my abdomen, and his arms are like a vise gripping me tight.

I place my hands on his head and just hold him there, feeling his body tremble from the emotion that engulfs him. I feel helpless, unsure of what to say or do with someone so emotionally closed off. A child I can deal with, but a grown man has boundaries. And if I overstep my boundaries with Colton, I'm just not sure how he'd react.

I gently run my fingers through his wet hair, trying to soothe him as best as I can. My fingertips try to express the words he doesn't want to hear from me, the motion just as comforting to me as I'm sure it is to him. In this space of time, my thoughts process and begin to whirl. In the absence of his mind-numbing words, I'm able to read behind the venom of Colton's outburst. The pushing away. The verbal lashing out. Anything to get me to leave so I wouldn't witness him falling apart, trying to reaffirm to himself that he needs no one and nobody.

This is what I do for a living, and I missed all of the signs, love and hurt overriding my training. I squeeze my eyes shut and mentally chastise myself, although I know I couldn't have handled it any differently. He wouldn't have let me. He's a man used to being alone, dealing with his own demons, shutting out the outside world, and always expecting the other shoe to drop.

Always expecting someone to leave him.

Time stretches. The only sound is the splatter of the shower water against the stone floor. Eventually Colton turns his face so his forehead rests on my belly. It's a surprisingly intimate action that squeezes at my heart. He rolls his head back and forth softly against me and then takes me by surprise as he kisses the long line of scars across my abdomen. "I'm sorry I hurt you," he murmurs just above the sound of the water. "I'm just so sorry for everything."

And I know that his apology is for so much more than the verbal barbs and the cruelty in how he pushed me away. It's for things far beyond my comprehension. The angst in his voice is heartbreaking, and yet my heart flutters and swells at his words.

I lean over and press my lips to the top of his head, holding them there as a mother would a child—as I would to one of my boys. "I'm so sorry you were hurt too."

Colton emits a strangled cry and reaches up, pulling my face to his. Between one breath and the next, his lips are on mine in a soul-devouring kiss. Lips collide and tongues clash. Need crescendos. Desperation consumes. I sink down so my knees rest on either side of his on the bench as his lips bruise mine, branding me as his.

His trembling hands come up to cradle my face. "Please. I need you, Rylee," he pleads breathlessly, his voice choking on the words. "I just need to feel you against me." He changes the angle of the kiss, his hands moving my head, controlling me. "I need to be in you."

I can taste his need and can feel his desperation in his frenzied touch. I grab the sides of his face and pull back so when he lifts his eyes to search mine, he can see the honesty in them when I speak my next words. "*Then take me, Colton.*"

I can feel the muscle pulse in his jaw beneath my palms as he stares at me. His tentativeness unnerves me. My arrogant, self-confident man never hesitates when it comes to the physicality between us. Thoughts about what could make him react this way fill me with dread, but I push them from my head. I can process this all later.

Colton needs me right now.

I reach down with one hand and grab his rigid cock, positioning it at my entrance. A short, sharp breath is his only response. When he makes no indication of movement, his eyes squeeze shut and his forehead creases with whatever is still haunting the edges of his memory. I run my hand up and over his impressive length. Doing the only thing I can think to help him forget, I lower myself down onto him. I cry out, surprised when he thrusts up suddenly, our bodies connecting and becoming one. His eyes flash open and lock onto mine, allowing me to watch them darken and glaze with lust until he can't resist from feeling any more. He throws his head back and closes his eyes at the sublime sensation as he fights his control—fights to push out the bad and focus solely on me and what I'm giving him. Comfort. Assurance. Physicality. Salvation. I watch the struggle as it flickers across his face, silently egging him on.

"Don't think, baby. Just feel me," I murmur against his ear as I slowly move and create the sensation needed to try and help him forget.

He exhales shakily before biting his bottom lip and bringing his hands down to roughly grip my hips. Colton rocks into me again, burying himself deeper than I ever thought possible. I whimper, so overwhelmed from feeling him tense so deep inside me.

The only reaction I can give him is to part my lips and say, "Take more from me. Take everything you need."

He cries out, restraint obliterated, and holds me still while he pistons his hips into me in a relentless, punishing rhythm. Our bodies, slick with water, slide easily against each other. The friction against my breasts heightens my ache for release. He flicks a tongue over a nipple, sliding it across my chilled skin before capturing the other one in his mouth.

I moan out in pleasure, accepting every forceful stroke from him. Allowing him to take so that he can find the release he needs to forget whatever haunts him. The volatility in his movements increases as he drives himself higher and higher, giving himself no other option but to forget. His grunts and the sound of our wet skin slapping against each other echoes off the shower walls.

"Come for me," I grate out as I slam back down on him. "Let go."

He quickens his tempo, his neck and face taut with purpose. "Oh fuck!" he yells out, crushing me against him with his powerful arms and burying his face in my neck as he finds his release. He rocks our joined bodies back and forth gently as he empties himself into me. The desperation in his strangling grip tells me I've given him only an iota of what he needs.

He sighs my name over and over, lacing absent kisses between them, his emotion transparent. His utter reverence coming on the heels of his earlier insults steals my breath and completely immobilizes me.

We sit like this for a couple of minutes so that he can take a moment to compose himself. It can't be easy for a stoic and always in control man like him to have a witness to such an emotional episode. He runs his fingers over the chilled skin of my back, the hot water running a few feet behind me sounding like Heaven.

When he finally speaks, it's of nothing we've just experienced. He keeps his head buried in my neck, refusing to meet my eyes. "You're cold."

"I'm fine."

Colton shifts and somehow manages to stand with my legs wrapped around him. "Stay right here," he tells me, placing me in the stream of warm water before leaving the shower. I look after him confused, wondering if his display of emotion was too much for him and now he needs some distance. I'm not sure.

He returns quickly, water still running in rivulets off of his skin. He takes me completely by surprise when he swoops me up in his arms, turns off the water with an elbow, and carries me out. I shriek as the cold air from the bathroom hits me. "Hold on," he murmurs against the top of my head at the same time I realize his intent.

Within moments he has stepped into the bathtub that is filling with water, and sets me on my feet. He sinks down in the overabundance of bubbles and tugs on my hand for me to follow. I lower myself, the blissful heat surrounding me as I settle between Colton's legs.

"Ah, this feels like Heaven."

I lean back into him, silence consuming us, and I know he's thinking about his dream and the aftermath. He traces absent lines up and down my arms, his fingertips trying to tame the goose bumps that still remain.

"Do you want to talk about it?" I ask, his body tensing against my back with my question.

"Just a nightmare," he finally says.

"Mmm-hmm." Like I believe it was a run of the mill monster chasing you down a dark alley type of dream.

I feel him open his mouth and close it against the side of my head before he speaks. "Just chasing my demons away." I reach my hands up and lace them with his, wrapping our joined hands across my torso. Silence stretches between us for a few moments.

"Shit." He exhales in a whoosh. "That hasn't happened in years."

I think he's going to say more, but he falls silent. I debate what to say next and choose my words very carefully. I know if I say it the wrong way, we might end up right back where we started. "It's okay to need somebody, Colton."

He emits a self-deprecating laugh and falls quiet as my remark weighs heavy between us. I wish I could see his face so I can judge whether or not to say my next words. "*It's okay to need me*. Everybody has moments. Nightmares can be brutal. I understand that better than most. No one's going to fault you for needing a minute to collect yourself. It's nothing to be ashamed of. I mean…I'm not going to run to the first tabloid I see and sell your secrets—*secrets I don't even know*."

His thumb absently rubs the back of my hand. "You wouldn't be here if I thought you'd do that."

I struggle with what to say next. He's hurting, I know, but he hurt me too. And I have to get some things off of my chest. "Look, you want to shut me out, that's fine…tell me you need a minute—that you need…" I falter, searching for something he'll relate to "*…to take a pit stop*. You don't have to hurt me and push me away in order to have some space."

He mutters a curse into the back of my hair, his heated breath warming my scalp. "You just wouldn't go." He exhales in exasperation. I'm about to respond when he continues, "And I needed you to go. I was terrified you'd see right through me and into me, Rylee, in the way that only you've been able to…and if you did, if you saw the things I've done…you'd never come back." His last comment is barely a whisper, so soft I have to strain to hear him. The words unzipping his hardened exterior and exposing the vulnerability beneath. The fear. The shame. The unfounded guilt.

So you tried to make sure my leaving was on your terms. Not mine. You had to have control. Had to hurt me so I wouldn't hurt you.

I know his confession is difficult. The man who needs no one—the man who pushes people away before they get too close—was afraid to lose me. My mind spins with thoughts. My heart squeezes with emotions. My lips struggle to find the right words to say. "Colton—"

"But you came back." The utter shock in his voice undoes me. The significance behind his admission hangs in the air. He tested me, tried to drive me away, and I'm still here.

"Hey, I've gone up against a teenager with a knife before…you're nothing," I tease, trying to lighten the mood. I expect a laugh but Colton just pulls me back and holds me tighter, as if he needs the reassurance of my bare skin against his.

He starts to say something and then clears his throat and stops, burying his face back into the curve of my neck. "You're the first person that's ever known about those dreams."

His bombshell of a confession rocks my mind. In all his therapy dealing with whatever it is that has happened to him, he's never talked to anyone about this? He's that hurt, that ashamed, that traumatized, that *whatever*, that for almost thirty years he has kept this festering inside of himself without any help? *My God*. My heart twists for the little boy growing up and for the man that sits behind me—so disturbed by whatever happened that he's kept it bottled up inside.

"What about your parents? Your therapists?"

Colton is silent, his body taut and unmoving, and I don't want to push the issue. I lean my head back on his shoulder and angle my face so it nuzzles into the side of his neck. I kiss the underside of his jaw softly and then rest my head down, closing my eyes, absorbing this quiet vulnerability from him.

"I thought..." He clears his throat as he tries to find his voice. He swallows harshly and I can feel his throat work beneath my lips. "I thought that if they knew about them—really knew the reasons behind why I had them—they wouldn't..." He stops for a moment, and I can feel the unease rolling off of him, as if the words are physically hard for him to utter. I press another kiss on his neck in silent reassurance. "They wouldn't want me anymore." He exhales slowly and I know the admission has cost him dearly.

"Oh, Colton." The words fall from my mouth before I can stop them, knowing full well the last thing he wants is my sympathy.

"Don't..." he pleads, "*Don't pity me*— "

"I'm not," I tell him, although my heart can't help but feel that way. "I'm just thinking how hard it must have been to be a little boy and feeling all alone without ever being able to talk about it...that's all." I fall silent, thinking that I've said and pushed hard enough on a topic he obviously doesn't want to address. But I can't help the next words that tumble from my lips. "You know you can talk to me." I murmur against his skin. His hands tense in mine. "I won't judge you or try to fix you, but sometimes just getting it out, getting rid of the hate or shame or *whatever* is eating you makes it a tad bit more bearable." I want to say so much more but forcibly tuck it away for another day, another time when he's a little less raw, a little less exposed. "I apologize," I whisper. "I shouldn't have—"

"No, I'm sorry," he says with an agitated sigh, leaning forward and kissing the shoulder he tagged with his elbow. "For so very much. For my words and my actions. For not dealing with my own shit." The regret in his voice is so resonating. "First I hurt you and then I was rough with you in the shower."

I can't help the smile that forms on my lips. "Not going to say that I minded."

He laughs softly and it's such a good sound to hear after the angst that filled it moments ago. "About your shoulder or about the shower?"

"Um, shower," I say, noting his attempt to digress from my comment and thinking that a change in topic is just what is needed to add a little levity to our extremely somber and intense morning.

"You surprise me at every turn."

"How so?"

"Did Max ever treat you this way?"

What? Where is he going with this? His comment takes me by surprise. When, I turn and face him, he just tightens his arms around my torso and pulls me closer. "What does that have to do with anything?"

"Did he?" he insists, the master of deflection.

"No," I admit contemplatively. Sensing I've relaxed some, he unlaces his fingers from mine and moves them back up to draw aimless lines on my arms. I look down at my hand and watch as I poke absently at the bubbles. "You were right."

"'Bout what?"

"The first time we met. You told me that my boyfriend must treat me like glass," I whisper, feeling like I'm betraying Max's memory. "You were right. He was a gentleman in every way. Even during sex."

"There's nothing wrong with that," Colton concedes, bringing his hands up to massage the base of my neck. I don't speak, shocked at myself for feeling how I do. "What is it? Your shoulders just tensed up."

I exhale a shuddered sigh, embarrassed at my train of thought. "I thought that was how it was supposed to be...that was what I wanted sex to be. He was my only experience. And now..."

"Now what?" he prompts with a hint of amusement in his voice.

"Nothing." Heat rushes into my cheeks.

"Rylee, talk to me for Christ's sake. I just fucked you in my shower like an animal. Used you basically for my own reprieve, and yet you can't tell me what you're thinking?"

"That's exactly it." I aimlessly draw circles down his thighs that cradle my sides, the admission tackling all of my modesty and throwing it to the ground. "*I liked it.* I never realized it could be different. That it could be so raw and…" *Oh my God I'm drowning here.* I don't think I even spoke to Max about sex like this, and we were together for over six years. I've known Colton less than a month, and we're discussing how I think it's a turn on to be manhandled. *Sweet fucking Jesus* as Colton would say.

"Carnal," he finishes for me, and I can hear a tinge of pride in his tone. He kisses the side of my head, and I shrug, embarrassed at my lack of experience and unfiltered admission. Sensing my discomfort, Colton squeezes me tighter. "There's no need to be embarrassed. Lots of people like it lots of different ways, sweetheart. There's a lot more out there to experience than just the missionary position with whispered sweet nothings." He breathes into my ear, and I wonder how even he can turn me on with that statement.

My mind flickers back to Colton demanding that I tell him that I want to be fucked our first time together. Of him pushing me to the brink by taking me hard and fast. Of him whispering the explicit things he wants to do to me when we have sex—lifting me up, pressing me against a wall, and grinding us toward release. Of how the knowledge of any and all of these things can cause me to ache with a need so intense that it unnerves me.

My cheeks flush at the thoughts, and I am grateful he can't see my face because he'd know exactly where my mind has wandered. I exhale a shaky sigh, trying to stifle my mortification at the direction of conversation and my own self-revelations.

"That's one of the things I like about you. You're so uninhibited."

What? I feel like looking around the room to see whom else he is talking to. "*Me?*" I croak.

"Mmm-hmm," he murmurs. "*You're amazing.*" His voice feathers over my cheek, the movement of his lips grazing my ear.

His words leave me motionless. He's echoed my thoughts of him despite the chaos and hurt from earlier. Maybe this combustible chemistry between us is because I possibly mean more than some of his others? He's sending me all of the signals to validate this claim, and yet hearing it would mean so much more.

He lathers his hands up with a bar of soap and then proceeds to run them over my arms and down the front of my chest. I suck in a breath as his fingertips slide lazily over the peaks of my breasts and his mouth licks its way up the curve of my shoulder. "I don't think I could ever get my fill of you." Proving my point exactly. *Words that say it but don't really say it.* "You're always so reserved, but when I'm in you…" he shakes his head, a low hum deep in his throat "...you lose all sense of everything, become mine, submit completely to me."

His words are a seduction on their own, never mind his thickening cock pressed up against the cleft of my backside. "How does that make me uninhibited?" I ask, angling my head back so I can rub against the coarse stubble on his jaw.

Colton's laugh is a low rumble that reverberates through my back. "Let's see…we'll put it in baseball analogies for you since you seem to be so keen on them. Almost third base in a public hallway. Twice." He chuckles. "Second base on a blanket at a beach." With each word I can feel my cheeks redden. "Homerun, pressed against the window of my bedroom," he pauses "...that overlooks a public beach."

"What?" I gasp. *Oh. Fucking. Hell.* What is it about him that makes me lose my head? My ass was pressed against a glass wall while we had sex, and anyone could have enjoyed the show. I think dying from humiliation is a viable option right now. I have no other choice but to shift the blame. "It's all your fault," I tell him as I push away and splash water at him.

A cocky grin lights up his face. It's a welcome sight from the haunted look from earlier. The dark and brooding bad boy has returned and is sitting across from me, knees and torso peeking out from above an overabundance of bubbles with a playful look on his face. Is it no wonder I've fallen for this man who's such a juxtaposition of characteristics and actions?

And fallen damned hard without a safety line to hold on to. *Fuck, I'm so seriously screwed.*

"How's that?" He splashes water back at me and catches my wrist in a quick grab when I try to retaliate. He pulls me toward him playfully, and I resist in turn. He gives up and I flop back, sloshing water out of the tub at all angles. We both erupt in a fit of laughter, bubbles floating through the air at my sudden movements. "I've been with plenty of women, sweetheart, and most aren't as sexually candid as you've been, so you can't blame me."

I'm glad that we're laughing when Colton makes his off the cuff remark because I can see him tense even though a smile remains on his face. I make a quick decision to remain playful despite the pang his remarks cause. I really don't want to think about the *plenty of women* he's been with, but I guess I can't ignore them either. Maybe I can use this slip of his to my advantage, get more information on my fate as well as make a little point of my own.

"Oh really?" I arch a brow and scoot closer, a smile playing on my lips. "Plenty of women, huh? Glad I can surprise an experienced man such as yourself." I toy with him as I run my finger along the line of his throat and down between his pecs. His Adam's apple bobs as he swallows at my touch. "Tell me," I whisper suggestively as my hand dips beneath the water and rakes toward his already erect cock. "These plenty? How long do you usually keep them around for?"

He sucks in his breath as my fingers graze over the tip of his shaft. "This isn't the right time to—aar-rgh!" He whimpers as my hand cups his balls and massages them gently.

"It's never the right time, but a girl's gotta know these things." I lower my mouth to suck on one of his flat nipples, tugging it gently with my teeth. He groans deeply, his mouth parting when I look up at him from beneath my lashes. "How long, Ace?"

"Rylee..." he pleads before I take his other nipple between my teeth at the same time I press the pleasure point just beneath his balls. "Four or five months," he pants out in response. I laugh seductively, hiding the jolt that tickles up my spine at knowing the clock is ticking on my time with him. I lick my tongue up the line of his neck and tug on his earlobe. "Ah..." He sighs when I trace it around the rim.

"Good to know..."

He remains silent, his shallow breath the only sound. "You play dirty."

"Someone once told me that sometimes you have to play dirty to get what you want." I breathe into his ear, repeating his words back to him. My nipples, chilled from the air, skim over the taut skin on his chest.

He chuckles low and deep, and his eyes alight with humor because he knows he's not the only one affected. I slide my other hand down his chest beneath the water, and I watch him watch my hand disappear. He looks back up at me and raises his eyebrows, curious as to where I'm going with this. When he just continues to stare at me, I grip the base of his shaft with one of my hands and twist it up and back on his length while the pad of my thumb on my other hand pays special attention to the crest. "Oh God that feels good, baby," he moans. The look he sends me smolders so intensely with need and lust it's enough to ignite my insides.

I stroke him a couple more times, enjoying this game I'm playing. Enjoying the fact that I can create such a visceral reaction from this man. I stop all motion and Colton's eyes that have closed partway in pleasure fly open to meet mine. I smirk slowly at him.

"Just one more thing..." I can see the confusion on his face, his jaw grinding as he silently begs for the pleasure to return.

Now that I've gotten his attention, I continue again, altering my grip and angle of stroke. Colton hisses out at the difference in sensation, his head falling back against the edge of the tub. I stop again and cup his balls in my hand.

"Look, I know you were upset, but if you ever treat me like you did this morning again..." I enunciate each word, the teasing humor in my tone gone as I gently squeeze my hand around him "...disrespect me, degrade, or push me away by humiliating me, understand now that I will not be coming back like I did today—regardless of your reasons, how I feel about you, or what's between us."

Colton meets my implacable stare and doesn't flinch at my threat. His mouth slides into a ghost of a smile. "Well it seems you have me by the balls both *literally and figuratively*, don't you now?" he taunts, mischief dancing in his eyes.

I squeeze him softly, fighting the smirk that wants to play at the corners of my mouth. "Is that understood? Non-negotiable."

"Crystal clear, sweetheart," he says to me, his eyes conveying the sincerity within his response. Satisfied he understands what I am telling him, I shift in the water and release my hold on his balls. Keeping my eyes locked on his, I slide my hands up to his rigid length and repeat the motion that rendered him agreeable moments before. Colton groans a long, drawn out, "Non-negotiable." And I don't respond to his answer because I am so turned on watching his reaction. "*Christ, woman*," he grates out, grabbing my hips and pulling me toward him. "You like to play hardball, don't you?"

I accept his nudging and position myself over the top of his shaft. I lean forward, tunneling my fingers in his hair and place my cheek against his. As I lower myself at an achingly slow pace despite his hands urging me faster, I whisper in his ear, his own words back to him. "*Welcome to the big leagues, Ace.*"

Chapter Two

"Are you sure you can handle it?"

"Yes," he drolly calls out from the kitchen.

"Because if you can't, I can whip something up real quick."

"The image you just brought to my mind of you with a whip, high heels, and nothing else on is exactly what is going to prevent me from getting breakfast done." His laugh carries outside onto the deck where I sit.

"Okay, I'll just sit here quietly, enjoy the sun, and leave you with those images while I wait for my food."

I can hear the carefree note as he laughs again, and it lightens my heart. He seems to have tucked away the earlier nightmare and ensuing incident, but deep down, I know it's lingering just beneath the surface, always waiting patiently to remind him again of whatever atrocities he endured as a child. Nightmares. Shame. The overriding need for physicality with women. Memories so horrid he vomits with the reappearance of them. I can only hope the causes that flicker through my mind from my past work with other little boys with similar post-traumatic stress symptoms does not hold true for Colton.

I force myself to sigh away the sadness and soak up the welcome warmth of the early morning sunlight, to enjoy the fact that we've turned this morning around from the disaster that it began with. I can only hope that maybe, in time, Colton will trust me enough to open up and feel comfortable talking to me. Then again, who am I to think that I'll be the special one and make a difference in a man who's emotionally isolated himself from everyone for so long?

The speakers on the terrace come to life around me, and Baxter lifts his head momentarily before plopping it back down. Stretched out on the chaise lounge, I watch the early bird exercisers on the beach. I guess it's not that early now after our diversion in the bathtub. I swear I don't know what came over me and prompted me to act that way. That is so not me, but it sure was fun making Colton putty in my hands. And when all was said and done, with the bathwater growing cold, he made sure that my whole body ended up just as boneless as his.

And then there's the down side to our whole bathtub time. His admission that his average shelf life with a woman is four or five months. *Shit.* Tawny might be right. He's going to get bored with me and my lack of bedroom prowess. I shrug away the notion time is running out for me. The thought causes my breath to catch and panic to fill my every nerve. I can't lose him. I can't lose how I feel when I'm with him. He means too much to me already, and that's with me trying to be reserved in my emotions.

Jared Leto sings about being closer to the edge. I close my eyes thinking how I already have both feet over and beyond that edge that Colton has explicitly explained he does not want to teeter on. But how can I not plummet off it when he makes me feel so incredibly good. I try to rationalize that it's just the incredible—and it's mind-blowingly incredible—sex that's making me feel these insane feelings after only knowing each other for three weeks. And I know that sex does not equate love.

I need to remind myself of this. Over and over and over to prevent the fall.

But his words, his actions, tell me that I'm just more than an arrangement to him. They all flicker through my head—different things over the past three weeks—and I just can't see him not thinking that there are definite possibilities here. If not, then he has me fooled.

Matt Nathanson's voice fills the air around me, and I hum along to *Come on Get Higher*, my thoughts scattered and disjointed, but oddly content.

"Voila!"

I open my eyes to see Colton lower a plate onto the table beside me, and when I see its contents, I laugh loudly. "It's perfect, sir, and I so appreciate the depths of your fine culinary skills." I reach over and take a bite of my toasted bagel and cream cheese and moan dramatically in appreciation. "Delicious!"

He bows theatrically, obviously pleased with himself, and plops down beside me. "Thank you. Thank you." He laughs, grabbing a half off of the plate and taking a large bite of it. He leans back on an elbow, washboard abs bare and board shorts riding low on his hips. The sight of him is enough of a meal in itself.

We eat, playfully teasing each other, and I silently wonder what's next. As much as I don't want to, I think I need to get home and put some distance between the two of us before the night we've spent together and the feelings it solidified accidentally come stumbling out of my mouth.

"I told you to leave them," Colton says from behind me as I wash the dish in my hand. "Grace will get them or I'll clean them up later."

"It's no biggie."

"Yes it is," he whispers into my neck, sending an electric pulse straight to my sex as he slides his arms around my waist and pulls me backwards against him.

God, how I could get used to this. I'm grateful he can't see the look on my face that I'm sure is one of complete satisfaction. Adoration. Contentment.

"Thank you, Rylee." His voice is so quiet I almost miss the words over the noise of the water.

"It's one dish and a knife, Colton. Really."

"No, Rylee. Thank. You." His words are swamped with sentiment—a man drowning in unfamiliar emotions.

I set the plate down and turn off the water so I can hear him. So I can allow him the moment to express whatever it is he needs to say. I may not be very experienced when it comes to men, but I know enough that in the rare instances that they want to talk about feelings or emotions, it's time to be quiet and listen.

"For what?" I ask casually.

"For this morning. For letting me work through my shit the way I needed to. For letting me use you for lack of a better term." He moves my ponytail off of the back of my neck and places a soft kiss there. "For letting me have mine and for you not complaining when you didn't get yours."

His words, the thoughtfulness behind them, has me biting my lip to prevent me from making that verbal pitfall I was worried about earlier. I take a second to think of my next words so I don't take that stumble. "Well, you more than made up giving me *mine* in the bathtub."

"Oh really?" He nuzzles that sensitive spot just beneath my ear that drives me crazy. "That's good to know, but I still think I might need to further remedy the unsettled situation from earlier."

"Really?"

"Mmm-hmm."

"You are insatiable, Colton." I laugh, turning in his arms to have my lips captured in a tantalizing kiss that funnels sparks all the way to the tips of my toes. His hands map themselves down my torso and over my backside, pressing me into him.

"Now let's talk about that image I can't get out of my head of you with a whip and wearing only bright red stilettos." The wicked smile on his lips has the heat flowing from my toes back up.

"Ahem!" The clearing of a throat has me jumping back from Colton like I've been singed by fire.

I snap my head up, warmth burning through my cheeks when I hear Colton shout out, "Hey, old man!" and then embrace whoever it is in a huge bear hug. They have turned, hugging so fiercely that I can only see Colton's face, his pleasure evident.

I catch murmured words in gruff tones as they hold on to each other, hands slapping each other's backs, and when I think I know who it is, my blush deepens at the knowledge that he overheard what Colton had said to me. My hunch is confirmed when the two break apart and the visitor places a hand on the side of Colton's face and stares at him intently, concern etched on his face over something he sees in his son's eyes.

"You okay, son?"

Colton holds his father's stare for a moment, the muscle in his jaw pulsing as he reins in the emotions playing over his face. After a beat he nods his head subtly, a soft smile turning up the corners of his mouth. "Yeah…I'm okay, Dad," he acquiesces before glancing over to me and then back to his dad.

They draw each other into another quick man-hug of loud back slapping before they part, and the clear, gray eyes of Andy Westin dart over to me and then back to Colton, love and I think surprise bordering on shock reflected in them.

"Dad, I want you to meet Rylee." Colton clears his throat. "Rylee Thomas."

The woman you will forever think of in correlation with red stilettos and a whip. *Lovely*. Can I die now?

Andy mirrors my step forward and reaches out a hand to me. I try to act calm, to pretend like I'm not in front of a Hollywood legend who has just caught me in a compromising situation, and when I see the warmth mixed with disbelief in his eyes, I relax some. "Pleased to meet you, Rylee."

I smile softly, meeting his eyes as I shake his hand. "Likewise, Mr. Westin."

He's not big in stature like I expected, but something about him makes him seem larger than life. It's his smile that captivates me. A smile that could make the hardest of people soften.

"Pshaw, don't be silly," he scolds, releasing my hand and brushing his salt and pepper hair off his forehead, "call me Andy." I smile at him in acceptance as he shifts his gaze back to Colton, a bemused look in his eyes and a pleased smile on his face. "I didn't mean to interrupt anything—"

"You didn't," I blurt out. Colton turns to me, an eyebrow arched at my staunch denial, and I'm grateful when he lets it go without correcting me.

"Nonsense, Rylee. My apologies." Andy glances over at Colton again and gives him an indiscernible look. "I've been on location for work in Indonesia for the past two months. I got back late last night and wanted to see my boy here." He pats Colton on the back heartily, and his obvious love for his son makes me like him that much more. And even sweeter than Andy's adoration of his son is Colton's reciprocation. Colton's face lights up with complete reverence as he watches his father. "Anyway, I'm sorry I barged in. Colton never has..." he clears his throat "...Colton is usually out on the deck alone, recovering from whatever the chaos the night before has brought upon him." He laughs.

"You two obviously haven't seen each other in a while, so don't let me get in your way. I'm going to go grab my purse and I'll be on my way." I smile politely and then frown when I realize that I don't have my car to drive.

Colton smirks at me, realizing my oversight. "Dad, I've got to drive Rylee home. Do you want to hang here or I can stop by the house later?"

"Take your time. I've got some stuff to do. Stop by later if you get the chance, son." Andy turns toward me, an inviting smile warm on his lips. "It was very nice meeting you, Rylee. I hope to see you again."

The drive home from Malibu is beautiful as is expected, but the cloud cover starts to move in and smother the coastline the closer we get to Santa Monica. We talk about this and that, nothing serious, but at the same time I sense that Colton is distancing himself a bit from me. It's nothing he says per se, but it's more what's not said.

He's not rude, just quiet, but it's noticeable. Those little touches are absent. The knowing looks and soft smiles gone. The playful banter silenced.

I assume that he's taking the drive to think about his dream, so I leave him to his thoughts and stare out the window watching the coastline fly by. The radio's on low and the song, *Just Give Me a Reason* by Pink plays softly in the background as we exit the highway and head toward my house. I sing softly, the words making me think about this morning, and as I hit the chorus, I notice Colton glance over at me in my periphery. I know when he hears the lyrics because he shakes his head and the slightest of smiles graces his lips; his silent acknowledgement of my knack for finding the perfect song to express my feelings.

We remain in a contemplative silence for a bit longer until Colton finally speaks. "So um, I've got a crazy busy schedule the next two weeks." He glances over at me momentarily, and I nod at him before he looks back at the stoplight in front of us. "I've got a commercial to shoot for the Merit endorsement, an interview with Playboy, um…Late Night with Kimmel, and a whole lot of other shit," he says as the light turns green. "And that doesn't include all of the dog-and-pony shows coming up for the sponsorship with you guys."

I take no offense to the comment because I'm not too thrilled with the dog-and pony- show junket either. "Well that's good, right? Publicity is always good."

"Yeah." I can tell he's irritated at the thought as he slips his sunglasses on. "Tawn's doing a great job garnering press this year. It's good and all...and I'm grateful that there's the attention, but the more shit there is, the less time I have on the track. And that's where I need to concentrate my time with the season right around the fucking corner."

"Understandably," I tell him, unsure what else to say as we pull onto my street, unable to help the smug smile that tugs at the corners of my mouth. It's been a profound twenty-four hours with Colton. He's let me into his personal world some, and that counts for something. Our sexual chemistry remains off the charts, and I think it actually intensified after our night together. I told him about Max, and he listened with compassion and without passing judgment.

Then we had this morning. An hour filled with poisonous words and overwhelming emotions.

And not once did he mention his idiotic arrangement to me. How he'll only accept less when I'll only accept more; we find ourselves at a proverbial impasse despite his actions expressing the exact opposite.

Maybe my smile reflects my optimism over the possibilities between us. That Colton's unspoken words speak just as much to me as his spoken ones do.

I sigh as we pull into the driveway, and Colton opens the door for me. He offers me a tight smile before placing his hand on the small of my back and directing us up my front walkway. I struggle to figure out what his silence is saying, to not read into it too much.

"Thank you for a great night," I tell him as I turn to face him on the front porch, a shy smile on my lips, "and..." I let the word drift off as I figure out how to address today.

"A fucked up morning?" he finishes for me, regret heavy in his voice and shame swimming in his eyes.

"Yes, that too," I admit softly as Colton turns his attention to the absent fiddling with the ring of keys in his hand. "But we got through it..."

His gaze fixates on his keys, his eyes never lifting to meet mine when he speaks. "Look, I'm sorry." He sighs, shoving a hand through his hair. "I just don't know how to—"

"Colton, it's okay," I tell him, lifting my hand to squeeze his bicep—some form of touch to let him know I've said my piece about this morning and my lack of tolerance of it happening again.

"No, it's not okay." He finally lifts his head up, and I can see the conflicting emotions in his eyes, can feel the indecision of his thoughts. "You don't deserve to have to deal with this...with all my shit," he murmurs quietly, almost as if he's trying to convince himself of his own words. And I realize that his internal struggle has to do with so much more than just this morning.

His eyes swim with regret, and he reaches out to tuck a loose lock of hair behind my ear as I search his face to try and understand his unspoken words. "Colton, what are you—"

"Look at what I did to you this morning. The things I said. How I hurt you and pushed you away? That's me. That's what I do. I don't know how to—*shit!*" he grits out before turning and looking out toward the street where a teenager is making his way down the sidewalk. I focus on the thunk-thunk of his wheels as they hit the lines in the sidewalk panels while I process what Colton is saying. He turns back around and the lines etched in his striking features cause me to close my eyes momentarily and take a deep breath to prepare for what's coming next. For what I see written on his resigned expression.

"I care for you, Ry. I care about you." He shakes his head, the muscle in his jaw pulsing as he clenches his jaw, trying to find the right words. "I just don't know how to be..." He stumbles through words trying to get out what he wants to say. "You at least deserve someone that's going to try to be that for you."

"Try to be *what* for me, Colton?" I ask taking a step closer as he takes a step back, unwilling to allow him to break our connection. My bewilderment in regards to his confusing statements does nothing to squash the unease that creeps into the pit of my stomach and crawls up to squeeze at my heart. I part my lips and breathe in deeply.

His discomfort is apparent and I want nothing more than to reach out and wrap my arms around him. Reassure him with the physical connection he seems to need more than anything. He looks down again and blows out a breath in frustration while I suck one in.

"You at least deserve someone that's going to try to be what you need. Give you what you want...and I don't think I'm capable of that." He shakes his head, eyes fixed on his damn keys. The raw honesty in his words causes my heart to lodge in my throat. "Thank you for being you...for coming back this morning."

He finally says something I can latch on to, a diving board I have to jump from. "That's exactly right!" I tell him. Using one of his moves, I reach out and lift his chin up so he's forced to meet my eyes, so he's forced to see that I'm not scared of the way he is. That I can be strong enough for the both of us while he works through the shit in his head. "I came back. For you. For me. For who we are when we're together. For the possibilities of what we can be if you'll just let me in..."

I run my hand over the side of his cheek and cradle it there. He closes his eyes at my touch. "It's just too much, too fast, Rylee." He breathes and opens his eyes to meet mine. The fear there is heartbreaking. "For so long I've...your selflessness is so consuming that it..." he struggles, reaching up to take my hand framing his face in his own. "I can't give you what you need because I don't know how to live—to feel—to breathe—if I'm not broken. And being with you? You deserve someone that's whole. I just can't..."

The words to the song from the car flash into my mind, and they are out before I can stop myself. "No, Colton. No." I tell him, making sure his eyes are on mine. "*You're not broken, Colton. You're just bent.*"

Despite my saying it with serious intent, Colton belts out a self-deprecating laugh at the apropos corniness of me using a song lyric to try and express myself. He shakes his head at me. "Really, Ry? A song lyric?" he asks, and I just shrug at him, willing to try anything to break him out of this rut he keeps returning to. I watch as his smile fades and the concern returns to his eyes. "I just need time to process this...you... it's just too..."

I can feel his pain and rather than just stand there and watch it manifest in his eyes, I opt to give him what he needs to confirm our connection. I step up to him and brush my lips against his. Once. Twice. And then I slip my tongue between his lips and connect with his. He won't hear the words, so I need to show him with this. With fingertips whispering over his jaw and up through his hair. With my body pressed tight against him. With my tongue dancing with his in a lazy, decadent kiss.

He slowly lets go of the tension in his body as he accepts and gives in to the feeling between us. The desire. The need. The truth. His hands slide up to cup the sides of my face, thumbs brushing tenderly over my cheeks. Rough to soft, just like the two of us. He places a last, lingering kiss on my lips and then rests his forehead onto mine. We sit there for a moment, eyes closed, breath feathering over one another, and souls searching.

I feel settled. Content. Connected.

"*Pit stop*," he whispers against my lips.

The words come out of nowhere, and I jolt at their sound. *Come again?* I try to pull back to look at him, but he keeps a firm grip on my head and holds me against him, forehead to forehead. I'm not sure how to respond. My heart's unable to follow the path he's just chosen while my head is already five steps ahead of him.

"A pit stop?" I say slowly as my thoughts race one hundred miles per hour.

He eases his hold on my head, and I lean back so I can look at him, but he refuses to meet my eyes. "It's either a pit stop or I tell you that Sammy will drop by a set of keys for the house in the Palisades and we meet there from here on out," he slowly lifts his eyes to meet mine "…to keep the lines from getting fuzzy."

I hear him speak the words but don't think I actually listen to them. I can't comprehend them. Did he just actually tell me that after last night—after this morning—he's going to pull this shit on me? Push me back in to the *arrangement* category of his life.

So this is how it's going to go? *Fucking hell, Donavan.* I take a step back, needing the distance from his touch, and we stand in silence staring at each other. I look at the man that broke down in front of me earlier and is trying to distance himself from me now, trying to regain his isolated state of self-preservation. His request stings but I refuse to believe him, refuse to believe that he feels nothing for me. Maybe this all spooked him—someone too close when he's used to being all alone. Maybe he's using his fallback and trying to hurt me, put me in my place, so I can't hurt him in the long run. I so desperately want to believe that's what this is about, but it's so hard to not let that niggling doubt twist its way into my psyche.

I hope he can see the disbelief in my eyes. The shock on my face. The temerity in my posture. I start to process the hurt that's surfacing—the feeling of rejection lingering on the fringe—when it hits me.

He's trying.

He may be telling me he needs a break, but he's also telling me I have an option. I either give him the space he needs to process whatever's going on in his head or I can choose the arrangement route. He's telling me he wants me here as a part of his life—for now anyway—but he's just overwhelmed by everything.

He's trying. Instead of pushing me away and purposely hurting me to do so, he's asking me—using a term I told him to use if he needs some space—so I can understand what he's requesting.

I push down the hurt and the dejection that bubbles up because regardless of my acknowledgement, his proverbial slap still stings. I take a deep breath, hoping the pit stop he's asking for is the result of a flat tire and not because the race is almost over.

"Okay." I let the word roll over my tongue. "*A pit stop it is then*," I offer up to him, resisting the urge to wrap my arms around him and use the physicality of it to reassure myself.

He reaches out and brushes a thumb over my bottom lip, his eyes a depth of unspoken emotions. "Thank you," he whispers to me, and for just a second, I see it flash in his eyes. *Relief.* And I wonder if it's because he's relieved I chose pit stop over an arrangement or because he gets to walk away right now without being pushed any further.

"Mmm-hmm," is all I can manage as tears clog in my throat.

Colton leans forward and I close my eyes momentarily as he brushes a reverent kiss on my nose. "Thank you for last night. For this morning. *For this.*" I just nod my head, not trusting myself to speak as he runs his hand down the length of my arm and squeezes my hand. He pulls back a fraction, his eyes locking on mine. "I'll call you, okay?"

I just nod my head again at him. He'll call me? When? In a couple of days? A couple of weeks? Never? He leans forward and grazes my cheek with a kiss. "Bye, Ry."

"Bye," I say, barely a whisper of sound. He squeezes my hand one more time before turning his back and walking down the walkway. Pride over the small step he took today tinged with a flash of fear fills me as I watch him climb in the Range Rover, pull out of the driveway, and until he turns the corner from my sight.

I shake my head and sigh. Taylor Swift's definitely right. Loving Colton is like driving a Maserati down a dead end street. And with what he just said to me, I feel like I just slammed into it head first.

Chapter Three

Haddie and I have been like ships passing in the night the past couple of days, but she is awfully curious as to my cryptic notes about my night with Colton. I'm still confused as hell at what happened between leaving Colton's house and arriving at my doorstep. The two differing vibes have left me confused and moody and desperate to see him again, see if what I thought was between us was real or if I'd imagined it. At the same time, I'm angry and hurt and my heart aches at what I want so badly to be but am afraid never will. I have over-thought and over-analyzed every second of our drive home, and the only conclusion is that our connection unnerves him. That my willingness to return when all others would have run scares him. And even with that knowledge, the past few days have been unsettling. I've shed a few tears from my doubts and Matchbox Twenty has been on repeat on my iPod. It has also helped that I have a job where I have to work twenty-four hour shifts to occupy my time.

I take a sip of my Diet Coke, singing along to *Stupid Boy*, and finish adding ingredients to the salad when I hear the front door slam. I can't fight the smile that spreads on my lips when I realize just how much I've missed Haddie these past few days. She has been so busy working on projects for a new client that PRX is trying to land she's basically been sleeping at the office.

"My goodness, I've missed you, silly girl!" she announces as she comes into the kitchen and wraps her arms around me in a soul-warming hug.

"I know." I hand her a glass of wine. "Dinner's almost ready. Go get changed and get your butt back here so we can catch up."

"And you better not hold back on me," she warns with one of her looks before leaving the kitchen.

Our dinner has been eaten, and I think we are on our second or third bottle of wine. The fact that I've lost track tells me it's been enough for me to relax and tell Haddie everything. Her no-holds-barred responses to my replay of events have left me gasping for breath from laughing so hard.

As *Should I Stay* plays softly on the speakers around us, Haddie leans back against the chair behind her and stretches her legs out on the floor. Her perfectly manicured toes are a bright pink. "So, have you talked to him since then?"

"No. He's texted me a couple of times, but I've only given him one word responses." I shrug, not having any more clarity after relaying everything to her. "I think he might have a clue I'm hurt about something but he hasn't asked."

Haddie snorts loudly. "C'mon, Ry, he's a guy! Which means first of all he has no clue and, secondly, he's not going to ask even if he does think you're pissed."

"True," I concede, giggling. The aura of sadness that's been around me for the past few days continues to dissipate with my laughter.

"But that's no excuse for him being a dick," she says loudly, raising her glass up.

"I wouldn't exactly call him a dick," I argue, silently chastising myself for defending the one person that is responsible for my current confused and miserable state. Haddie just arches an eyebrow at me, a smarmy smirk on her face. "I mean, I am the one who told him to take a pit stop if he needed to deal with things instead of push me away. I just don't understand how he's kissing me one minute and then the next minute asking for one."

"Let me think about it a minute," she says, a look of amused concentration on her face. "My head's a little fuzzy from all this wine."

I giggle at her and the determined look on her face as she tries to work through everything. "Okay, okay, I got it," she shouts victoriously. "I think that...hmmm...I think that you freaked him the fuck out, Rylee!"

I throw my head back laughing hysterically at her. A drunk Haddie means a fouled mouth Haddie. "That's very astute, Had!"

"Wait, wait, wait!" She throws her hands up and luckily her wine doesn't slosh over the side. "I mean from what you've told me, you opened up to him, you talked about stuff, he fucked you seven ways from Sunday—"

I have to stop myself from spitting my wine out of my mouth at her last words. "Jesus, Haddie!"

"*Well, it's true!*" She shouts at me like I'm a dumbass, holding my gaze until I nod my head in compliance. "Anyway, back to what I was saying...you guys were flirty and fun and serious and had a great time. He found himself liking you in his surroundings. He saw himself being okay with you in his element. And then in walks his Dad. Having someone else see you there…with him…made it real for him. All of it combined probably freaked Mr. I-Only-Do-Casual out, Rylee!"

I eye her over the rim of my glass, adjusting my knees that are pulled up to my chest. Her words ring true to me, but it doesn't dissipate the hurt I feel. The ache that only reassurances from him can soothe. I need to do a better job of guarding my heart and pulling back more. I need to not give so freely to him when he isn't in return.

"God," I groan, laying my head on the back of the couch. "I've never been this wishy-washy in my life over something like I am over him. I'm driving myself crazy sitting here whining like one of those chicks I swore I'd never be. The ones we make fun of." I sigh. "*Shoot me now!*"

Haddie giggles at me. "You are kind of all over the place when it comes to him. Shit, the two of you are giving me fucking whiplash."

I continue to stare at the ceiling, expressing my agreement of Haddie's unsolicited opinion by giving a non-committal grunt before I lift my head back up and look at her. "You're probably right about the freaking out part," I muse, taking a sip to drain the rest of my glass, "but in all fairness, he told me from the start that he couldn't give me more."

"*Screw fairness!*" she shouts, raising her middle finger emphatically.

I laugh out loud at her. "I know, but it's my own damn fault for falling in lov—"

"I knew it!" She jumps up, pointing at me. I close my eyes and shake my head, cursing myself for slipping. "Shit, I need some more wine after that revelation!" She starts to walk past me and then steps back to look me in the eye. "Listen, Ry, have you cried over this? Over him?"

Uh-oh! She has her "I'm going to get to the bottom of this" look on her face. I just stare at her and my silence is enough of an answer. "Listen. I know he looks like a damn Adonis and probably fucks like a stallion, but, sweetie, if he's what you want, then it's time to make him sweat a little."

I snort at her. "That may be easy for you. You've played these games before, but I have absolutely no fucking clue what to do."

"You turn the tables on him. You've shown him what life's like when you're around…now that he's into you, you need to show him what it's like when you're not. Let him know that he's not your every breath or thought—even if it fucking kills you." She sits on the arm of the chair and stares at me. "Look, Ry, *every guy wants to be him and every girl wants to fuck him*. He's used to being wanted. Used to people pursuing him. You need to act like you did in the beginning—before you went and fell in love with the bastard—and let him chase you." I just stare at her, shaking my head at her frankness. She tilts her head and twists her lips up as she thinks. "I know he made you cry, but is he worth it, Rylee? I mean really worth it?"

I stare at her, tears pooling in my eyes, and I nod my head. "Yeah, he is, Haddie. He…he has this side to him that is the exact opposite of the brooding, bad boy player the media portrays him as. He's sincere and sweet. I mean it's more than just the sex." I shrug, a smile tugging at the corners of my mouth when she arches her eyebrow at me. "And yes, *it's really that good—*"

"I knew it!" she shouts and points her finger at me. "You've been holding out on me!"

"Shut up!" I shout back, giggling along with her. She stands, wobbling a bit before grabbing my empty glass.

"C'mon, spill the deets for dried up old me. How's his Aussie kiss? How many times did he make you come when you went to his house?"

I blush a deep crimson, loving and hating her at the same time. "*Aussie kiss?* What in the hell are you talking about?"

She lets out a naughty laugh and has an impish gleam in her eyes. "How's his mouth *down under?*" she laughs, deliberately looking down at my crotch and then back up at me with a raised eyebrow. I just stare at her with my mouth agape and a giggle I can't help bubbling out. "Let me live vicariously through you. *Pretty please?*"

I squeeze my eyes shut in embarrassment, unable to look at her. "Well I'd say he speaks Australian like a damn native."

"I knew it!" she yells, wiggling her ass in a little victory dance around the family room. "And…" she prompts.

"And what?" I play stupid.

"His stamina, baby. I need to know if he deserves the Adonis label in more than just the looks department. How many times?"

I twist my lips as I mentally run through the various times and places Colton and I had sex. "Hmmm…I don't know, eight times maybe? Or nine? I lost count."

Haddie stops mid-dance and her mouth falls open before spreading into a wicked grin. "And you were able to walk? You little vixen. Good for you!" She turns and teeters before heading toward the kitchen to grab another bottle of wine. "Fuck, I'd put up with a whole lot of shit from a guy if he can perform like that. I guess I was right about the stallion part," she teases from the kitchen, making a horse neighing sound that has me doubled over in laughter.

My phone rings and for the first time in several days. I don't jump up to get it. I've had enough to drink and have had enough false alarms that I know it's not Colton. Besides, according to Haddie I need to make him sweat a little.

Easier said than done. My resolve lasts two rings before I start to get up, stumbling in my inebriated state. I tell myself that I'm not answering it. No way. Haddie will kill me. *But…*even if I'm not going to answer it, I still want to see who it is.

"Well if it isn't the man of the hour," I hear Haddie say as she beats me to it and reads the screen of my phone. I stare at her with confusion as she flips on the stereo and picks up my phone to answer it.

This is not going to be pretty. Haddie drunk and being protective of me is not a good combination. "Give me the phone, Had," I say but know it's no use. *Oh fuck!*

"Rylee's phone, can I help you?" She shouts as if she's in a club, her voice rising with each word. She grins at me and raises her eyebrows while he must be speaking on the other end. "Who? Who? Oh, hey, Colby! Oh, I'm sorry. I thought you were Colby. Who? Oh, hiya, Colton, this is Haddie. Rylee's roommate? Mmm-hmm. Well look, she's a little drunk right now and a lot busy, so she can't talk to you, but I'd like to." She laughs loudly at something he says. "So here's the deal. I don't know you very well, but from what I do, you seem like a decent guy. A little too much in the press from your shenanigans if you ask me as you make jobs like mine a little harder, but hey, no press is bad press, right? But I digress..." She laughs, making a non-committal sound at Colton's response. "Wine for starters, but now we've moved on to shots," she answers him. "Tequila. Anyway, I just wanted to tell you that you really need to get your shit together when it comes to Rylee."

I think my mouth just fell to the floor. I wish I could see the look on Colton's face right now. Or maybe I don't want to.

"Yes, I was talking to you, Colton. I. Said. You. Need. To. Get. Your. Shit. Together." She emphasizes each word. "Rylee's a game changer, babe. You better not let her slip through your fingers or someone else is going to snatch her right out from under your nose. And from the looks of the sharks circling tonight, you better kick that fine ass of yours into high gear."

I'm so glad that I've had a lot to drink because if not, I would be dying of mortification right now. But the alcohol does nothing to diminish my pride in Haddie. The woman is fearless. Regardless of how I feel, I still glare at her and hold out my hand asking for my phone. She turns her back to me and continues making agreeable sounds to Colton.

"Like I said, she's quite busy right now, choosing which guy will buy her next drink, but I'll let her know you called. Uh-huh, yes. I know, but I just thought you ought to know. Game. Changer." She enunciates and laughs. "Oh and, Colton? If you make her fall, you better make damned certain you catch her. Hurting her is not an option. Understood? Because if you do hurt her, you'll have to answer to me, and I can be a raving bitch!" She laughs deviously. "Good night, Colton. I hope to see you around once you figure your shit out. Cheers!" Haddie looks over at me, a smug smile on her face as she switches off the stereo.

"Haddie Marie, I could kill you right now!"

"You think that now." She snickers, the neck of the wine bottle clinking against the rim of our glasses as she refills them. "But just you wait and see. You'll be kissing my boots when this pans out."

We finish our wine quotient for the night and are sitting on the couch, mellow, relaxed, and a little drunk, talking about the other events of the week. The local eleven o'clock news is wrapping up on low in the background when a spot for what's next on Jimmy Kimmel Live runs. I'm listening to Haddie when we both hear Colton's name mentioned as a guest. Our heads snap up and we stare at each other in surprise. With the events of the past couple of days, I'd completely forgotten his mentioning it to me.

"Well this will be interesting." She raises her eyebrows at me as she shifts her focus to the television.

We watch the opening monologue, and although the jokes are funny, I don't laugh. Maybe it's the somberness from too much wine or the apprehension of what's to come, but Jimmy's just not making me laugh. I know that Jimmy will mention the array of women on Colton's arm, and I'm not in the right frame of mind to hear it tonight.

"So our next guest is, how do I describe him? A master of many talents? *A man in the driver's seat?* Let's just say he's one of Indy's brightest talents—being listed as the driver to bring the circuit back into the spotlight—and one of Hollywood's hottest bachelors. Please give a warm welcome to the one and only Colton Donavan." The crowd in the studio erupts into a frenzy of female screeches with a few mixed in *I love yous.*

I suck in a breath as Colton walks out on stage in a pair of black jeans and a dark green button up shirt. Every part of my body leans forward in my seat as I drink him in. Study him. Miss him. The camera is at a distant angle, but I know firsthand the effect that his shirt will have on his eyes. How it will darken the circle of emerald around the exterior of the iris, leaving the center almost a translucent light green. He waves to the crowd as he walks, his megawatt smile in place.

Haddie makes a soft noise in the back of her throat. "Damn. That face is a definite work of art. You need to make sure you frame it between your legs every chance you get."

I choke on my drink as I look over at her and catch the wink she gives me. I burst out laughing. "Where in the hell do you come up with this stuff?"

"I have my sources." She shrugs with a naughty smirk on her lips.

I just laugh at her and shake my head as I turn my focus back to the interview. As Colton rounds the desk, one of Jimmy's papers flies off of it, and Colton bends over to pick it up. The slew of women in the audience go ballistic at the sight of Colton's ass in tight jeans, and Haddie laughs out loud. Colton turns around, shaking his head at the audience and their reaction.

"Well that's a way to make an entrance!" Jimmy exclaims.

"Was that planned?" Colton asks as he plays to the audience.

"No. There was such a large whoosh of air from the exhales of your female fans in here that they blew that paper off the desk."

The audience laughs and a woman screams, "Marry me, Colton!" I want someone to tell her to stick a sock in it.

"Thank you." Colton chuckles. "But none of that will be happening for a while."

"And the audience keels over in sorrow." Jimmy laughs. "So, how's it going man? Good to see you again. What's it been? A year?"

"Something like that," Colton says, leaning back in his chair and crossing his ankle over his opposing knee. The camera pans in for a close up of his face, and I breathe deeply. I don't think I'll ever get used to how striking he is.

"How do you not just stare at him all day when you're with him?" Haddie asks. I smile but don't respond. I'm too busy watching. "My God he's fine." She groans in appreciation.

"And how's your family?"

"They're doing good. My dad just got back a couple of days ago from being on location in Indonesia so I got to catch up with him, which as you know is always a good time."

"Yes, he's quite the character." Colton laughs at the comment and Jimmy continues. "For those of you who don't know, Colton's dad is Hollywood legend, Andy Westin."

"Let's not give him a big head by using the word *legend*," Colton says as Jimmy holds up a picture of his dad with his arm around him at some event. "There he is," he smiles with sincerity.

"So what have you been up to lately?"

"Just getting ready for the upcoming season to start. First race is at the end of March in St. Petersburg, so we're getting ramped up for that right now."

"How's the car running?"

"It's looking good so far. The guys are working hard to get it dialed in."

"That's great. Now tell me about your new sponsors this year."

Colton rattles off names of several of his advertisers. "And we picked up a new one this year in Merit Rum."

"Smooth rum," Jimmy says.

"Yeah, I can't complain about getting paid to drink good alcohol," Colton smiles, rubbing his thumb and forefingers over his shadowed jaw.

"I think we have a snippet of your new commercial for them."

I whip my head up to look at Haddie. "Have you seen it yet?"

"No." She looks as surprised as I do. "I've been so busy on this new client I haven't even caught up to speed with our other accounts."

"We just shot this the other day," Colton says.

The screen fills with Colton zipping his Indy car across a track, the Merit Rum logo splashed across his car's nose. His sexy rasp of a voice overlaying the scene. "When I race, I drive to win." The scene switches to him playing football on the beach with a bunch of other guys. Bikini clad women are on the sidelines cheering them on with drinks in their hands. He's shirtless with a pair of low-slung board shorts on. His chiseled torso is misted in sweat, sand sticking in some patches here and there, and an arrogant grin is on his face. He stretches out, dives for a pass, and catches it as he crashes into the sand. His voice says, "When I play, I always play hard." The commercial switches to a scene in a nightclub. Lights blaze and the crowd dances. Shots flash across the television. Colton laughing. Colton holding a drink and taking a sip while relaxing in a booth surrounded by gorgeous women. A shot of whom you assume is Colton dancing among a couple of women because all the screen shows is hands on hips, fingers gripping in hair, and mouths meeting in a kiss. The camera switches to a picture of Colton, his arm wrapped around the waist of a beautiful woman, the camera filming at their backs as they leave the club. He turns and looks over his shoulder, a smirk on his face saying "you know what happens next." The camera cuts to an empty Merit Rum bottle on the table at the club. "And when I party?" Colton's voice says, "I only drink the best. Merit Rum. *Like no other.*"

"Wow." Haddie breathes. "The ad turned out great."

I know she's looking at it from strictly a public relations perspective, and she's right. It's a great ad. Sex appeal, product placement, and an environment that makes you feel like you are there. Makes you want to be like him.

And his lips are on another woman's. I cringe at the thought.

"Great spot," Jimmy says as the audience's applause dies down. "I bet you had fun making that one." Colton just smirks at him, a sliver of a laugh escaping his lips that says it all. "The camera loves you, man. How come you've never hit up your old man for a job? I bet the ladies wouldn't mind seeing you on a jumbo screen somewhere."

The audience shouts out in agreement. Colton just curls the corner of one lip and shakes his head. "Never say never." He laughs and my stomach clenches thinking of millions of women getting to see him in action in some love scene. Theaters would sell out just for that.

"So tell me, Colton, what other things do you have going on?"

"Well we have a little something else in the works right now that legal doesn't want me to officially announce yet because it's still being wrapped up," the crowd "*awws,*" and Colton holds his finger up in a just wait moment. "But, since when have I ever done what I'm supposed to?" Colton's smirk is lopsided and mischievous as the audience laughs. I suck in my breath, shocked and pleased that Colton is going to give public notability to my company. "All I'll tell you is my company is working with a corporation who cares," he says, putting quotation marks on both title words of my company, "and we are uniting to raise money to benefit orphaned kids by providing better living situations for them…to give them more of a stable family environment on a permanent basis."

"A cause near and dear to your heart."

"Absolutely." Colton nods, leaving it at that.

"How fantastic. Can't wait until its official so we can learn more about it. But, I know you are not supposed to tell me." Jimmy rolls his eyes to the audience. "How are you going to be raising the money?"

Colton goes through the whole explanation, answering Jimmy's questions, and I just watch mesmerized, trying to decipher the Colton I know against the one that is on television before me. I see the same person and the same personality, but little nuances are different. I can see him holding back some. Playing up to the audience, and he definitely does it well.

"Well we're running out of time," Jimmy says and the audience grumbles, "but I think the audience might run me out of the studio if I don't ask the question that they want to know the most."

Colton looks around the audience, my favorite boyish smile spreading across his face. "What's that?" he prompts.

"Well, every time we see you in print or on television, you always seem to have a buxom beauty on your arm." Jimmy holds up the several magazine pages of Colton with various glamazons. "What's your status now? Are you dating? Is there a special lady in your life right now? Or perhaps *several special ladies?*"

Colton throws his head back laughing, and I wait with bated breath for his answer. "C'mon, Jimmy, you know how it is—"

"No, actually I don't." The audience laughs. "And please don't tell me you're dating Matt Damon," he deadpans.

This time I laugh at the startled look on Colton's face over Jimmy's long running joke over Matt Damon. "Definitely not Matt Damon." He laughs and then shrugs. "You know me. I'm always dating," Colton says, leaning back in his chair, hands gesturing casually to the crowd. "There are so many beautiful women out there, it'd be a waste to not enjoy them." Colton flashes his panty-dropping smile to the audience. "I mean look at all the beautiful women in the audience out there tonight."

"So in other words," Jimmy says, "you're avoiding the question."

"I wouldn't want to give away all my secrets," Colton smirks, winking at the audience.

"Sorry, ladies. That's all the time we have so I can't delve any further." The audience gives a collective groan. "Well, it's been great seeing you again, Colton. I can't wait to see you tear up the track this year."

"Hopefully you can make it out to a race."

"You can count on it. Best of luck to you."

Colton stands and shakes Jimmy's hand, saying something to him off mic that has him laughing. "Ladies and gentlemen, Colton Donavan." Colton waves at the audience and the show cuts to a commercial.

Haddie sits up and flips off the television. "Well," she muses, "That was entertaining."

Chapter Three and a Half

Colton—Raced

Why does it fucking matter?

I pace the confines of the greenroom, restless and on edge.

Why should I care if she's watching or not?

"Ten minutes, Colton."

I whirl around at Kimmel's production assistant peeking her face through the doorway, agitation giving way to aggravation. I just grunt a response, too wrapped up in my own goddamn head to say anything else.

Fuck! I wish I could yell it out! Get the pent up bullshit off of my chest. But I don't. Can't. It's my own damn fault. My own fucked-up head ruling my life.

I've got to get it together and soon before I walk out on stage and make a fool of myself because my head is wrapped around something else. Someone else. Just like I wish my body was.

Fucking Rylee.

I shouldn't.

I should.

I shouldn't.

Aw, fuck it!

My fingers are dialing before I even give myself a chance to stop.

What the fuck am I doing? I want this but I don't. Need her but don't want to need her. Whiplash is an understatement to describe the fucking tug-of-war raging inside of me right now.

Man the fuck up, Donavan. Grab your balls back and put them firmly in place. Wanting to fuck her is okay. You're calling because that's all you want to do. Nothing else. You don't need her. You don't need anyone.

I keep repeating the words to myself, the lie so ludicrous no way in hell I'd even convince Baxter of it. *Fuck*. I'm about done with the pussification of my thoughts, finger hovering over the end call button when music blasts on the other line. I freeze.

"Rylee's phone can I help you?"

I can barely hear her voice above the music and I'm immediately irked. And then I'm pissed at myself for even caring when I shouldn't be because she doesn't even really matter in the first place. Nice try, Donavan. Keep telling yourself that and you just might believe it.

"I'm looking for Ry. It's Colton."

"*Who?*" she shouts and I wince from the sound coming through the phone.

"Colton." My patience is about to run out. Why the fuck is Ry not answering her phone? And where exactly the hell are they?

"Who? Oh hey, Colby!"

What? I stop pacing and grit my teeth. What the fuck is going on here? "*Who's Colby?*"

"Oh, I'm sorry. I thought you were Colby."

"Not hardly," I say, jaw clenched, anger bristling. Whoever the fuck Colby is, he's going to wish he wasn't Colby if I find him trying to talk to Ry again.

But this is just for sex. Yeah, that's it.

"*Who?*"

And now I feel like I'm being fucked with. Does Ry not talk about me? Does whoever this person that's close enough she trusts to answer her phone not know who I am? Impossible.

You called pit stop, fucker. *No rings, no strings*. She can do what-the-fuck-ever she wants. So why do I want to punch the mirror in front of me?

I force a swallow down my throat, hating that I care if she's talking about me and hating that I don't care even more. Fucking Christ. I've been voodooed. Fucking sucked in by her magic and I never even knew it.

Uneasiness and disbelief crawls up my spine. I shake it off. No fucking way. There's no way I've been taken by her goddamn pussy. Time to prove it.

"Colton Donavan," I say, authority in my voice. Time to quit playing fucking games here.

"Oh, hiya, Colton, this is Haddie. Rylee's roommate."

Thank Christ, we're finally getting somewhere. "Hi, Haddie. I need to talk to Rylee." Need to? Why the fuck did I say I need to? I don't need anything from her.

"Mmm-hmm. Well look, she's a little drunk right now and a lot busy, so she can't talk to you, but I'd like to."

Drunk? *Rylee?* In a club on a weeknight? I'm so not liking the images in my head right now. Images like the fucking commercial I'm about to debut. Bodies grinding. Hands groping. Sexy clothes.

I can't help the groan that falls from my mouth and fuck if Haddie doesn't hear it because she laughs at me. Fucking laughs. I grind my molars and hope no one is grinding on Ry right now.

"So here's the deal. I don't know you very well, but from what I do, you seem like a decent guy. A little too much in the press from your shenanigans if you ask me as you make jobs like mine a little harder, but hey, no press is bad press, right? But I digress …"

"Thanks for the PR consult. Don't think I asked." I roll my shoulders as I look at the signatures of past guests on the walls and shake my head in frustration. Be nice. She's the only way you're going to find out what the fuck is going on. "Are you guys having something to drink with dinner?" I seriously just asked that? *Fish much, Donavan?* And then that laugh of hers again as if the joke's on me.

Fuckin' A.

"Wine for starters, but now we've moved on to shots. Tequila. Anyway, I just wanted to tell you that you really need to get your shit together when it comes to Rylee."

Wait a minute. *Tequila?* Images flash in my head of the last time I saw Ry doing a shot of that shit. It was after she left me at the Merit Rum party. Stood at the bar, downed the shot like a goddamn pro, and then ran from me. My dick pulses at the memory of what came next though: possession, claiming, some of the best fucking sex of my life.

"Yes, I was talking to you, Colton." She misunderstands my silence. Must think I'm not listening but instead am thinking of what it was like to see Rylee naked for the first time. Soft skin. Perfect fucking tits. Sinking into her. Hearing that sigh? Goddamn perfection.

So why the fuck is she in some club and not here with me? Because I called a damn pit stop. Motherfucker. I shake my head, the barrage of questions I want to ask fill my head but never have the chance to come out.

"I. Said. You. Need. To. Get. Your. Shit. Together," Haddie repeats, annoyance and don't-fuck-with-my-friend in her tone. But hell yeah, I want to fuck her friend. I start to speak, shout at her so she can hear me above that goddamn music, but she cuts me off.

"Rylee's a game changer, babe. You better not let her slip through your fingers or someone else is going to snatch her right out from under your nose. And from the looks of the sharks circling tonight, you better kick that fine ass of yours into high gear."

Sweet Christ! This is a one way conversation and yet I've just been knocked speechless. *Sharks circling.* Those fucking innocent eyes of hers and body that screams of sin put on display for others to watch. To touch. To want.

Fuck. Me.

"Where are you guys?" I'm about ready to blow off Kimmel, repercussions be damned. "Where?" I demand again.

"Like I said, she's quite busy right now choosing which guy will buy her next drink, but I'll let her know you called."

"Goddammit, Haddie! Where the fuck are you?" I bite the words out, ready to leave. To go get her. Claim her. Anything just so I can feel her again. Can have the peace she brings me again.

Because this is just fucking. That's all it is.

I shake my head and talk to Haddie as if I'm fucking trying to persuade myself. "You know what? I don't care where you guys are. She's a big girl. Can do her own thing." Jesus Christ, if you're gonna lie, at least make it sound convincing.

"Uh-huh, yes. I know, but I just thought you ought to know. Game. Changer," she says, like I'm a fucking two-year-old. As if I don't already know it. As if I didn't already cause this fucking situation because I called a pit stop to convince myself otherwise.

"Oh and, Colton? If you make her fall, you better make damned certain you catch her. Hurting her is not an option. Understood? Because if you do hurt her, you'll have to answer to me, and I can be a raving bitch!" Her taunting laugh fills the line. "Good night, Colton. I hope to see you around once you figure your shit out. Cheers!"

I go to speak, to participate in the conversation that's just fucked with my head more than it already is, and I hear a goddamn dial tone. What the fuck? Did I actually just get an ultimatum? As if I don't know I have shit to figure out.

I stare at myself in the mirror as I toss my phone on the counter and shake my head at my reflection.

Fucking hell.

Game changer? Like I didn't already know that.

Goddamn women.

I roll my shoulders and audibly exhale.

Holy shit ... I've been voodooed.

What the fuck am I going to do about it now?

Chapter Four

"That sounds great, Avery. All of the paperwork has been approved by HR, so I'd love to welcome you to the team. We'll see you next Monday." I hang up the phone and grab a pen, crossing that item off of my list. New girl hired, check.

Now, if I can just get the rest of my list completed. I glance at my week's schedule in my day planner, ignoring the inevitable date that looms tomorrow, and figure I can power through my "to dos" as I have no more shifts at The House this week.

That is if I can get motivated.

I have no one to blame for my lethargic pace this morning except for myself. Well and Haddie since she instigated the fourth, or was it fifth, bottle of wine. At least my headache has abated some so I can think without the hangover pounding in the background.

I grab the pile I've been avoiding, budgetary crap that takes too much time and in the end just gets overruled by the bosses upstairs, but I need to get through it. I sigh in fortification when I hear a tap at my door. I swear the next few moments take place in slow motion but I know they didn't.

When I look up, I cry out loudly and jump up in shock as I meet eyes that mirror mine. I round my desk and run full force into the arms of my brother. Tanner wraps them around me, spins around once, squeezing me so tight I can't breathe. All of the fear over his safety, anguish over not hearing from him, and loneliness from not having him near, vanish and manifest themselves in the tears that run down my cheeks in happiness.

He sets me back down on my feet and eases his hold on me, but I cling to him tightly and bury my face in his chest needing this connection with him. When I can't stop crying, he just holds on and kisses the top of my head. "If I knew I was going to get this kind of welcome, I'd come home more often," he says before grabbing my shoulders and pulling me back, his eyes searching mine. "What is it, Bubs?"

I smile at hearing the name he's called me our whole lives. I think I'm in shock. "Let me look at you," I manage, stepping back and running my hands over his arms. He looks a little older and a lot tired. Fine lines fan at the corners of his weary eyes, and the creases edging his mouth have deepened some in the six months since I have seen him last. His copper hair is a little longer than usual, curling up at the collar. But he is alive and whole and in front of me. The wrinkles make him more attractive somehow, adding a little ruggedness to his dynamic features. "Still ugly I see?"

"And you're even more beautiful," he recites, an exchange we've said at least a thousand times over the years. He holds out my arms to look at me and shakes his head as if he can't believe I am standing in front of him. "*God is it good to see you!*"

I grab a hold of him again and laughter bubbles up. "Do Mom and Dad know you're in the states?" I pull on his hand, bringing him into my office, not wanting to let go of him just yet.

"I flew in to San Diego and stayed with them last night. I'm leaving for Afghanistan this afternoon on a sudden assignment—"

"What?" I just get him back and now he's going to leave me again. "What do you mean you're leaving again?"

"Can you leave? Go to lunch with me and we can talk?"

"Of course."

Tanner's only request for his meal is that it be somewhere he can see and smell the ocean. I drive up the coast, deciding to take him to the beachside restaurant Colton took me to on what I consider our first date. It's perfect for him.

On the drive Tanner explains to me that he had taken a last minute week off to come home and visit us from his post in Egypt covering the unrest there. Once home, a fellow colleague had fallen ill and so now his trip was cut short so that he could head back to the Middle East to cover for him.

"So you flew all the way out here for two days just to see us?" I take a sip of my Diet Coke and stare at him. We're seated on the same patio where Colton and I ate just a couple of tables to the right. Rachel wasn't working but the hostess that is, heeded our request and set us out of the way from the steady flow of the lunch crowd.

Tanner just looks at me and smiles broadly, and I realize how much I've missed him and the calming effect he can have on me. He tilts his bottle of beer up to his lips and leans back, looking out at the waves beyond. "God, it's good to be home." He smiles. "Even if it's just for a day."

"I can't even imagine," I tell him, afraid to take my eyes off of him for just a second since my time with him is so fleeting.

Over food, we talk about the things going on in our lives. He tells me all about his living conditions and the things going on in Egypt that aren't making their way into the mainstream media. I learn he is casually dating another journalist but that it's nothing serious despite the softening of his features when he speaks of her.

I love listening to him. His passion and love for his job is so apparent that even though it takes him thousands of miles from me, I can't imagine him doing anything else.

I tell him about work and Haddie and everything in between. Except for Colton. Tanner can be a bit overprotective, and I figure why even mention something that I'm not sure even is a something. I think I'm doing a damn good job of it until he tilts his head and stares at me.

"What?"

His eyes narrow as he studies me. "Who is he, Bubs?"

I look at him perplexed, like I don't understand, but I know his investigative instincts have kicked in, and he won't back down until he gets the answer he wants. Hence why he's so good at his job. "Who's who?"

"Who's the guy that's got you tied up in knots?" He takes a draw on his beer. A smirk on his lips, his eyes never leave mine. Cocky son of a bitch. I just sit there and stare at him wondering how he knows. "Spill it!"

"Why would you even think that?"

"Because I know you *that well*." When I just fold my arms over my chest, he laughs at me. "Let's see, you are purposefully avoiding the topic rather than talking about it. You're twisting that ring around your damn finger like a worry stone. You keep biting the inside lip of yours like you do when you're trying to figure something out, and you keep looking at that table over there like you expect someone to be sitting there. Either that or you're remembering something that you and he did there." He arches an eyebrow at me. "Besides, you have a fire in your eyes that's been missing since…before," he muses, reaching out, grabbing my hand and squeezing it. "It's good to see." I smile at him, so happy that he's here. "So?"

"There is someone," I say slowly, "but it's confusing and I'm not sure what it is yet." I twist my ring around my finger and don't realize I'm doing it until Tanner raises an eyebrow at me. I stop immediately and give him the gist of things without giving him Colton's name. "He's a great guy, but I just think he's not looking for anything more than dating without commitment." I shrug, looking out at the scenery before looking back at him, a hint of tears in my eyes.

"Shit, Ry, any guy that makes you cry isn't worth it."

I bite my bottom lip and look down at the napkin I'm shredding mindlessly. "Maybe if he makes me cry it's because he *is* worth it," I say softly. I hear him sigh and I look back up at him. "It's a first step at least," I whisper with a trembling voice.

The compassion in his eyes almost undoes me, breaking the hold I have on the tears burning in the back of my throat. "Oh, Bubs, come here," he says, turning my chair and pulling it toward him. His pulls me into his arms where I just hold onto him, the one person I can always count on.

I close my eyes, my chin resting over his shoulder. "I know why you're here, Tan. Thanks for coming to make sure that I'm okay."

He squeezes me one more time before holding my arms and pushing me back to look at me with concerned eyes. "I just wanted to make sure with everything going on this week…I worry about you. I had to be here in case you needed me," he says softly. "So that if she calls, I can deal with her."

A surge of love rushes through me for my brother who has just flown halfway around the world for a day to make sure that I'm okay. It's hard to fathom the brother I grew up with, who I fought like cats and dogs with, has turned into such a thoughtful, caring man now. That he wants to deal with the fallout of the inevitable phone call I will receive from Max's mother tomorrow.

I reach up with both hands and hold my brother's cheeks and smile at him. "How'd I ever get so lucky to have you for a big brother?" Tears glisten in my eyes as I kiss him softly on his cheek. "You're the best, you know that?"

He smiles, uncomfortable with my affection for him. I stand up. "I'll be right back. I've gotta go to the bathroom." I start to leave the table and then without thought turn back around and grab him in a quick hug, wrapping my arms around his shoulders from behind as I stand behind him while he's sitting.

"Whoa, what's that for?" He laughs.

"Just because I'm going to miss you when you leave." I release him just as quickly as I hugged him and walk into the restaurant. The kitchen door shuts quickly as I walk past it toward the bathroom at the far side of the dining area.

When I emerge from the bathroom, I am preoccupied watching an adorable curly haired toddler trying to use a fork. One hand instinctively moves to rest on my lower abdomen and presses there. The pang hits me harder than usual watching her, and I can only assume it's because of what tomorrow's date signifies. The anniversary that took everything from me. Robbed me of the one thing I want more than anything in the world.

The one thing I would give up everything—everything—I have, if I could only have the chance again.

I'm so wrapped up in memories that I don't notice the commotion toward the patio until I hear, "*What the hell are you doing?*" It's my brother's voice, and it takes me a couple of seconds to maneuver around the tables to try and get in the line of sight of our table.

"The lady's with me, asshole. Keep your hands to yourself."

My heart stops.

I'd know that rasp of a voice anywhere. I rush quickly to the doorway, my pulse pounding and incredulity in my expression. I emerge out onto the patio to see Colton's hand fisted in the front of my brother's shirt, his jaw clenched, eyes full of fire. Tanner, who is still seated, is looking up at him, a smarmy look on his face. His shoulders are rigid, hands clenched quietly at his sides. The testosterone is definitely flowing.

"Colton!" I shout out.

He glances over at me and locks onto my eyes, a mixture of anger, jealousy, and aggression vibrating off of him. Tanner glances over at me, an eyebrow arching in question, his tongue tucked in his cheek.

"Colton, let go!" I demand as I stride toward him. "It's not what you think." I pull on his arm, and he shrugs out of my grasp, but he finally releases his hold on my brother. My heartbeat slowly decelerates. Tanner rises from his seat and squares his shoulders to Colton, an indiscernible look on his face. "Ace, meet my *brother*, Tanner."

Colton's head whips over to look at me, annoyance and hostility giving way to recognition. I can see a myriad of emotions flickering through his eyes: relief, discomfort, irritation.

I look at my brother, still unable to read him. "Tanner, this is my..." I falter, unsure what to label him. "Meet Colton Donavan." I watch Tanner as his synapses start firing, realizing who is standing in front of him. Who I'm dating.

The tension in Colton's shoulders relaxes some and a disbelieving smile tickles the corners of his mouth. Unapologetically, he reaches his hand out to shake Tanner's hand. Tanner looks at Colton and his outstretched hand and then over at me. "So, Bubs, this is the asshole?" he asks, his eyes silently imploring if this is who is the current cause of my tears.

I look at him, a timid smile gracing my lips. "Yes," I murmur answering both spoken and unspoken questions and glance over at Colton.

"Well shit," Tanner says, grasping Colton's hand and shaking it vigorously. "Have a seat man." He exhales. "I need a fucking beer after that." I stare at both of them, mystified at how men operate. Ready to go to blows one minute, in complete understanding the next.

"I'd love to, but I'm late for my afternoon meeting." He emits a sliver of a laugh. "Nice to meet you though. Maybe another time?" Colton turns his gaze on me. "Walk me out?"

I look at Tanner and he nods at me as if to tell me to go. I exhale, not realizing I'm holding my breath, suddenly nervous to be alone with Colton. Nervous to play the disinterested and aloof card. "I'll be right back," I tell Tanner, feeling like a little kid asking for his consent.

"Tanner." Colton nods at my brother in goodbye before placing his hand on the small of my back and steering me through the kitchen and out the side door of the restaurant.

The brief time it takes to walk toward a staff exit, I think of how we ended things the last time we spoke. Of the two options he gave me, *pit stop* or *arrangement*. That I gave him his pit stop, but I still feel unsettled. That because I've been swimming in lack of reassurance, regardless of the term, I still feel like one in a long line of bedtime companions.

I shake the thought away, forcing myself to step outside of my overemotional, over-analytical head and acknowledge that with most, success comes in baby steps. And even though Colton hasn't expressed wanting anything more than an arrangement with me, he took a baby step in calling 'pit stop'. *No more wishy-washy*, I tell myself as I recall Haddie's advice on how to interact with him. Aloof, unattainable, but desirable.

As Colton pushes open an exit door and ushers me outside, I'm preparing myself for the question of why I've not called him back. He's called me twice and I've physically forced myself to not react and pick up the phone.

Colton shuts the door and turns around to face me. *Screw being unattainable*. It takes all of my dignity to not push him up against the wall and kiss him senseless. The man makes me absolutely irrational and completely wanton.

He crosses his arms over his chest and stares at me, his head angled to the side. "So your brother's in town?"

I give an unladylike snort. "I think we already established that," I answer dryly, fighting the urge to gap the distance between us. "Got a short fuse, do we?"

I can't read the look that passes through his eyes because it flashes quickly. "When it comes to you, yes. I saw his arms around you." He shrugs—the only explanation I receive. "Is he here for long?"

I stare at him for a moment, confused by his nonchalance in regards to a fight he almost had with my brother over nothing. Finally, I glance down at my watch and rest my hips back against the retaining wall behind me, figuring I'll let it go for now. "Yeah, just for today. He's due at the airport in an hour and a half." I pick a piece of lint off of my tunic sweater as a means to keep my eyes and hands occupied before smoothing it down over my leggings.

Colton leans a shoulder against the wall in front of me, and when I look up I see his eyes run the length of my legs. They travel up the rest of my body, stalling when they come to my lips and then moving back up to my eyes. "Been busy?" he asks.

"Mmm-hmm," I answer vaguely. "And you?"

"Yeah, but this is the calm before the storm with the season just around the corner." He stares at me, his green eyes penetrating into mine. "Did you have a good night out?" he probes.

I give him a deer in the headlights look but recover quickly when I realize he's referring to Haddie's little performance on the phone the other night. "From what I remember of it, yes." I flash a sassy smirk at him, hoping my acting is convincing enough to fool him. "You know how it is when you go out…too many guys thinking they're way too cool, too much alcohol, and too little clothes—it all becomes a blur."

I see anger flicker through his eyes at my too many guys comment, and I like the fact that he's bugged by the idea. I like that he's thought about it enough to ask. And after his little altercation with Tanner, it's more than obvious that Colton has a little jealous streak running rampant through him.

It's kind of hot that such a streak is flaring over me.

He angles his head and studies me for a beat. For once, I don't avert my eyes under his severe scrutiny. I hold his gaze with boredom written in my expression. "Why do you seem so distant? Unapproachable?" He grunts, surprising me with his comment.

"Unapproachable? Me? I didn't realize I was being that way." I feign innocence when all I want to do is reach out and touch him.

"Well, you are." He sighs, exasperation glancing across the features of his face.

"Oh, well I guess I'm just trying to abide by your parameters, Ace. *Be exactly what you want me to be*." I smile sweetly at him.

"Which is what?" He huffs, confusion on his face.

"Emotionally detached, sexually available, and drama free." I can see the muscle in his jaw pulse as he takes a step near me, irritation flashing in his eyes at the defiance in my tone. "What are you doing here?"

He stares at me long and hard with such intensity that I nearly cave and tell him how bad I want him. Screw the mind games. "Luckily I escaped without the paps following me. Kelly let me up on the roof away from the crowd for some peace and quiet to eat my lunch." I arch a brow at him. "The owner," he says, breathing out an exasperated sigh at either the unease between us or for feeling like he needs to explain. *Maybe a bit of both*. I look down and focus on the chip in my manicure, desperately wanting to approach him. Kiss him. Hug him. "It's a good place to sit and mull things over."

"And what exactly are you mulling over?"

"The shit that I'm supposed to be getting together," he responds wryly. My eyes flash up to see a mixture of amusement and sincerity in his.

We stare at each other for a moment, my pulse accelerating from his proximity. I try to read the look on his face. *Is he serious?* Is he really trying to get his head straight or is he just mocking Haddie? I can't tell. "I-I sh-should get back inside. I don't have much more time until Tanner has to leave again." I push myself up and stand.

Colton takes a step closer to me, and our bodies brush against each other's briefly, his touch sending sparks of need spiraling through my system. I bite my bottom lip to stop myself from leaning in against him. "Can I see you later?" he asks, trailing a finger down the side of my face.

Does that mean the pit stop's over? Or he just needs to get laid? Either way, I need some clarity here. I fight the urge to lean my cheek into the feel of his fingertip on my cheek.

Stay strong, stay strong, stay strong, I repeat to myself. I struggle with how to answer. What to say?

"I'll send Sammy by the house at six to pick you up," he answers for me in my warring silence.

Wow, I guess he thinks that I'm a sure thing. And then the notion hits me that maybe all along he's wanted his arrangement with me, went further than he'd anticipated, and used the pit stop comment to try and put me back in my place. To put distance back between us.

Haddie's advice runs through my mind mixed with the notion that he thinks I'm going to just step back into this without a further explanation strengthens my resolve. "Sorry." I shake my head and avert my eyes so he can't see through my lie. "I have plans tonight."

I feel his body tense at my words. "What?" His tone is forced but quiet. It's obvious rejection is foreign to him.

"I have plans with Haddie," I volunteer, afraid he might think that I'm out with another guy. And if he thinks that I'm out with another guy then it'd be okay for him to be out with another girl. My stomach twists at the thought, and I realize I'm not very good at playing these types of games because all I want to do is tell him that yes I want to see him tonight. That I'd change any plans I have to be able to see him. And then I'd press him up against the wall and take with frustration everything that I want without a second thought of spooking him or crossing imaginary boundaries.

Colton lets out a dissatisfied grunt. "We're just having dinner at home," I tell him, "but it's a big deal because we haven't seen each other." Stop rambling, Rylee, or he'll know you're lying. "I can't go back on my promise to her."

Colton places a finger under my chin and lifts my head up to meet his green irises, studying me. "Well you're not trying very hard then," he admonishes despite humor alight in his eyes.

Confusion flits through me, unsure of what he's talking about. "Trying hard at what?" I shake my head not understanding.

He smirks arrogantly at me. "At being what I want you to be." The breath I exhale is audible as his eyes remain locked on mine. "Because if you were really trying," he explains, finishing the game I'd started, "you'd be where I want you. Wet, warm, and beneath me tonight."

I hold his stare while I try to think of what to say next. My body quivers at his words. It takes a few seconds for my brain to recover from his comment, and when it does, I take a step back from him. Distance is essential when dealing with him.

"Yeah, I guess you're right." I exhale, watching the surprise on his face from my admission. "Why would I want to be someone's beck and call girl? *Predictable is boring, Ace.* And from what I hear, you seem to get bored real quick."

When he just stands there and stares at me, a bewildered look on his face, I skirt around him. He reaches out and grabs on to my arm, turning me to face him. "Where are you going?" he demands.

"To see my brother," I tell him, looking over at his hand and then back at him. "Let me know when you get your shit together." I shrug from his grip and yank the door open to the kitchen without looking back. All I hear before the door shuts is Colton laughing and swearing at the same time.

Chapter Five

Colton

Fucking temperamental women!

My lungs burn. My muscles ache. My feet pound into the treadmill belt as if I'm trying to punish it. It doesn't matter. No matter how hard I push, my head is still screwed up. Rylee's still mucking up my thoughts. Constantly.

What the hell is wrong with me? I asked for the goddamn *pit stop*. Took my shot at putting it back on more familiar footing. So why am I the one that feels like she's left me behind?

Fucking women. Complicated. Temperamental. Necessary. *Fuck me.*

The music pounds in my earbuds. The driving beat of Good Charlotte pushes me harder, but the pressure in my chest doesn't dissipate. I count my footsteps when I run. Only to ninety-nine and then I start over again. I swear to God I've restarted the count a hundred damn times so far and nothing has helped.

I've never played games with women before, and I have no intention of starting now. I say when. I say whom. I give the terms.

I take what I want. When I want it.

And any and all of my previous bedside companions abide by my parameters without so much as a fucking flinch. No questions asked except for "Baby, how do you want me tonight? Knees or back? Cuffs or restraints? Mouth or pussy?"

All except for Rylee.

Fucking frustrating. First, I almost go to blows with her brother today, and then she walks away refusing to see me tonight. I know she wants me. It's written all over her ridiculously hot body. It's reflected in those magnificent eyes that draw you in and swallow you whole. And hell if I don't want her every minute of every hour. *But what the fuck?* She walked away, left me there, and didn't even hesitate at saying no about tonight.

No? *Are you fucking kidding me?* When is the last time I heard that? *Oh yeah. Right.* From Rylee. *Shit.* Now all I can think about is her. Seeing her. Hearing her. Burying myself in her until she sighs that little sound right before she's about to come. It's so goddamn sexy it's ridiculous.

I am not pussy-whipped. No way. No how. Not even close.

So why not call somebody else for a quick, uncomplicated fuck then? Why does the thought not even sound appealing? *You're losing it, Donavan.* I must've dipped my wick in the pool of crazies one too many times, and now it's fucking up my head.

I shove a finger at the screen and bump up the incline, forcing myself into ignoring my own damn thoughts. The song switches to Desperate Measures but the sarcasm in the lyrics I usually love does nothing for me.

Goddamnit! Nothing works. Music. Incline. Speed. *Shit!* I keep seeing her in the bathtub, fingers firm on my balls, eyes heated with intensity, lips telling me how exactly she deserves to be treated. What she won't put up with from me again.

That's a first. Someone setting parameters for me. Has hell frozen over and no one told me? She had my balls in a fucking vise, and all I could think of was how much I wanted her. In my bed. In my office. At the track. In my life.

And not just on her back.

She must have a voodoo pussy or something. Reeling me up and snagging me in her hooks without realizing it. I'm just fucking horny. That's gotta be why my head's all messed up. A week's a long time for me to go without sex. *Shit!* I can't remember the last time I've had a dry spell like this.

So why'd you pit stop her then the other day, dumbass? She'd have been beneath you tonight if you hadn't. Why'd you open your mouth?

I groan in frustration at my stupidity. At my need for release that this stupid-ass treadmill is definitely not helping with.

I can't stop rehashing the other morning. *Fuck!* It's official. Rehashing shit? *I'm without a doubt a goddamn chick now.* I must have lost my balls somewhere in the past week.

Only chicks rehash shit, but I keep thinking about standing with her on her porch…how I was just trying to do the right thing—protect her by pushing her away from the train wreck in my head. Trying to allow her the chance to find someone else that can give her what she needs—what she deserves—but I couldn't get the words out no matter how hard I tried. And then she stepped up and kissed me. Kissed me with such honesty and reassurance that I couldn't breathe. All I could do was feel. The moment was too real. Too raw. Too close.

Yep. I have a pussy. No doubt about it now.

But fuck if that simple taste of her didn't make me realize I've been starving for so very long.

And then I knew I had to put some distance between us and the foreign feeling of need that flashed through me. The need to covet. To protect. To care for. I had to push back from the one thing I know for fucking sure I don't want.

Love. Love and the things required of you with it.

Crying *pit stop* was like crying fucking wolf. Trying to tell myself I needed space to bring us back to the only set-up I'll accept. Back on arrangement status. I may have used her term to soften the blow, but my only thought was if I get us back to set parameters, then I'll be able to get the control back I felt slipping away. Regain the need to rely solely on myself.

I push a finger to the screen and wait for the treadmill to stop. I stand there, chest heaving, sweat dripping, and feeling no better for the hour of punishment I just put in. I glance out through the wall of glass at the shop down below, watching the guys finish with some engine adjustments we'd decided on yesterday before scrubbing the towel over my face and through my soaked hair.

My body feels like I'm floating a little when I hit the floor after being on the treadmill for so long. I head through the door on my left and into the bathroom that connects the gym to my office. I take a quick shower, glance in the mirror deciding to forgo the shave, and throw some shit in my hair.

Does she know how fucked up I am? Does she have any idea what a bastard I am? How I usually take when I need to and then discard? I need to tell her. Somehow. Someway. I need to warn her of the poison inside of me.

I'm pulling my shirt over my head when it hits me what I need to get out of my funk. I walk out into my office and head straight to my desk to grab my cell to make some calls and get the ball rolling. But first I need to send her a text. Need to give her a warning the only way she'll hear it.

I pull up her name on my phone and type: Push – Matchbox Twenty. Then I hit send, my mind running the lyrics over and over in my head: *"I wanna take you for granted. Well I will."*

"What crawled up your ass?"

Despite its familiarity, I jolt at the sound of the voice. I whirl around to see Becks sitting in one of the chairs in front of my desk with his feet propped up on another.

"You scared the shit out of me," I bark out, running a hand through my hair. "Fuckin' A, Becks!"

"From the looks of it, you need to fuck a B brother. It's got an extra hole and you sure as hell look like you can use the added release," he drawls out, amusement in his eyes as they narrow and study me trying to figure out what's going on.

A sliver of a laugh escapes my lips as my heart begins to decelerate. I sink down in my chair and prop my feet up on my desk, mirroring him. We just stare at each other, years of companionship allowing there to be comfort in the silence as I weigh what to say and he measures how much to ask.

He finally decides to break the silence. "It's a lot easier and cheaper to get it off your chest, Wood, than to break the damn treadmill, you know." I just give him a measured nod before glancing down at the garage again, one of my obsessive habits. "You gonna go all rogue on me with the silent treatment now?" When I look back at Becks, his eyes are now staring at the guys below, ignoring the sneer I'm giving him. "Or are you going to explain why you sat through that entire meeting after lunch with your head up your ass, giving little to no input and just being a dick in general. Only to end it without a decision so you could go break the treadmill?" He slowly moves his gaze back to mine with eyebrows arched in question and an appraising look in his eyes.

Leave it to Becks. The only person that can put me in my place. The only person I'll allow to call me on it. The only person that knows me well enough to know I'm pissed and to ask in our *guy speak* what the fuck's wrong.

"It's nothing," I shrug.

He chokes out a long laugh and shakes his head at me. "Yeah. It's nothing alright," he says, unfolding himself from his chair, his eyes never leaving mine. "Since you're so talkative, I think I'll be on my way then."

Fuck this. Before Becks reaches the door, I'm shoving my wallet into my back pocket, grabbing my cell, and striding toward the door. "Let's go," I mutter as I walk past him, knowing that he'll be right behind me. And I'm right because I hear his quiet laugh behind me. The one that says *yep, I was right.*

I give the universal 'another round' motion to the waitress with the nametag stating Connie. If she's just going to stand there and stare, she might as well do something to earn the free show. *Shit.* My buzz is humming now and I'm just starting to relax. I'm not drunk enough to push away my shitty mood, but I'm making progress.

Connie swivels her hips as she comes over to the table with our drinks in her hands. She leans over the table to set them down, making sure that I get the eyeful of tits she's putting on display. She's unquestionably hot in all of the right ways and in all of the right places. I'd definitely hit it—another time, another place, maybe—but I stifle back the smartass comment on my tongue about how all of a sudden from the drink request to the drink arrival her shirt just got lower and her skirt just got shorter. "Is there anything else I can get you two gentlemen?" she asks with a suggestive tone to her voice and her tongue licking over her lips.

"We're good here," Beckett deadpans, shaking his head and breaking her attempt at flirting. He's used to this shit and is a fucking saint for dealing with it all these years in his subtle, calculating way.

A text pings on my phone, and I reach for the fresh bottle as I look at it. "Smitty's on board," I tell him. I should be happy that Smitty's coming to Vegas with us. We've shared plenty of wild outings in the past. He'll definitely help get rid of my fucked up mood.

If I'm so happy, then why am I disappointed that it isn't Rylee's name on my phone's incoming text?

"Cool. Almost the whole gang then," Becks says, leaning back in his seat and taking a long pull on his beer. I can feel his eyes on me, waiting patiently for me to talk.

I lean forward and place my head in my hands for a moment, trying to shake my head out of where it keeps returning. *Fucking Rylee.*

"You want to tell me what we're doing here, Colton, at almost six o'clock on a Friday night? Who the hell put that stick up your ass?"

I just shake my head as I peel the label on my bottle and keep my eyes down. "Fucking Rylee," I mumble, knowing I've just opened the proverbial can of worms by admitting it to him.

"That so, huh?" he muses. I lift my head up slowly and meet his eyes, surprised by the lack of smartass comments that are his typical style. He peers at me over his beer bottle as he takes another sip, and I just nod my head. "What the hell'd you do to her?"

"Thanks for the vote of confidence, Becks." I laugh. "Who says I did anything?"

He just gives me a look that says *look who we're talking about here.* "*Well…*"

"Nothing. Abso-fucking-lutley nothing," I bark out, tossing back my shot to help bury the fact that I'm lying to my best friend. "She's just frustrating."

"Like that's a fucking news flash. We're talking about a woman here, aren't we?"

"I know. She's just gotten under my skin and now she's playing the hard to get card. That's all." I sigh, leaning back in my chair so I can meet Beckett's stare.

"She told you no?" Becks coughs out in shock. "Like no, no? Are you shitting me?"

"Nope." I catch Connie's eye again for another round.

"Well shit, Wood. We *are* leaving for the city of sin in a couple of hours. I'm sure there's a hot piece of ass there that you could tap for the night to forget about her. Or for that matter, several hot pieces." He shrugs and a slight, antagonizing smirk curls up the corner of his mouth. "Since all you're doing is just fucking Rylee…because that is all you're doing, right? Fucking her? There's no commitment there to ruin. No voodoo pussy hex."

I know he's trying to push my buttons. Get a reaction one way or another as to where I stand when it comes to Ry. But for some reason I don't take the bait. It's gotta be the alcohol running through my veins. Instead, I shrug at him in agreement about finding someone else for the night, but for some reason I have no desire to. None. And why the hell does that kind of comment—*that I'm just fucking her*—piss me off. This is Beckett I'm talking to. My best friend and brother for all intents and purposes—the man I discuss everything with, and I mean *everything*—so why does his off the cuff remark bug me?

It's like she still has my balls in her grip.

God Damn.

"She's got a hot friend."

Becks looks at me as if I've grown two heads."Come again? I'm not following you."

"Well, we can swing by Rylee's place on the way to the airport and the two of them can come with us." The words are out of my mouth before my brain can process the thought.

Beckett chokes on his swallow of beer and starts coughing. The look on his face is one of complete shock. Apparently I did grow an extra head.

I ignore him and turn my concentration back to my beer's label. Where the hell did that come from? Taking Rylee to Vegas with me? The one place I can most likely forget about her for a while? *The ultimate place to use pleasure to bury the pain.* Taking a girl to Vegas with you is like taking a wife to your mistress' house. That's why I've never done it. Never even thought about it. Avoided it at all costs. Companions, dates, whatever they're called, always stay home. They never even know I go. No exceptions. So why in the hell did I just suggest it? And more importantly, why the hell do I want her to go more than anything?

I must be outside of my fucking mind. *Voodoo pussy.*

Motherfucker.

"Holy shit..." Beckett says on a long drawn out drawl. "I never thought I'd see the day that Colton Fuckin' Donavan would say that." He whistles out a sigh, and then I swear I can hear something click in that head of his. "You're *barebacking,* aren't you?"

I can't help my eyes from snapping up to his with the comment. Our universal guy speak for sticking with one woman. For thinking of more than just sex without strings. For fucking without a condom because you have complete trust in the other person.

For being pussy-whipped.

Neither of us have ever barebacked. Ever. Kind of a silent solidarity we have between us. Neither of us that is, until now.

"Motherfucker!" Becks jumps up in his seat. "You are, aren't you, you cocksucker!"

"Shut the fuck up, Beckett." I growl as I toss back the rest of my beer and raise my empty shot glass up to Connie who hasn't stopped waiting attentively five feet away. Becks just sits and looks at me in silence until the newest round of shots are placed in front of us. I sit and stare back at him a while longer and let my comment settle between us, get comfortable rolling the idea around in my head...and then it hits me.

Hell yes, I want Ry to go with us. *Now what the fuck does that mean?* I throw back the shot, hissing at its burn before scrubbing my hand over my face as numbness spreads into my lips. Beckett keeps looking at me like I'm some kind of circus show freak. I can tell he's biting his cheek to keep from grinning at me, from saying the shit that's flying through his eyes at a lightning pace.

He holds his hand up to his ear and leans over the table. "I'm sorry. I don't think I heard you correctly. What was your answer?"

I can't help the grin that pulls up one corner of my mouth. This is being tame for Beckett, so I'm grateful that he's keeping himself in check against my obvious discomfort.

"No shit!" he says, shifting in his chair to stare at me for a little while longer with disbelief on his face. He looks down at his watch. "Well, if we're going to take off on time, loverboy, we best be going."

"That's all you're going to say?" I ask incredulously.

"I haven't even started yet, Wood! I need time to process...it's not every day Hell falls below zero."

Fine by me. If I can get away with only that being said right now, I'll take it. I nod my head at him and start typing away on my phone. "I'm texting Sammy to come get us." I tell him. The background music in the bar is playing, and I laugh at the fucking song playing. Of course it's Pink. Rylee and her fucking Pink. I send my text to Sammy and then hover over her name on my phone. Before I know it, I've entered a quick one to Rylee as well.

I'm in this far, might as well go balls deep.

Chapter 5/6

Colton—Raced

"Is there a reason Sammy is driving in the opposite direction of the airport?"

I need another beer. Need something to help numb the nonsense in my head telling me I really want this. Want her.

Fucking Rylee.

"I'm not *that* drunk. I do know the difference between east and west," Becks says as he tips his own bottle back again. "You can't pull one over on me."

"She's got a hot friend," I repeat, hoping the idea will shut him the fuck up and let me enjoy my buzz.

"Her ass better be fucking blazing and her tits better be perfection if you're actually dragging women—*walking vaginas*—to Vegas with us … land of free-balling, free-wheeling, *The Hangover* fucked-upness. Seriously, dude? You've lost your fucking marbles. Or handed over your balls." He shrugs with a chuckle. "They're about the same size."

"Fuck off, Daniels." I grunt at him as I lay my head back, the black interior of the limo all starting to fuse together as it spins like a fucking car doing donuts on the track.

Or the Tilt-A-Whirl at the carnival with Rylee.

How I wouldn't like to take her for a spin right now.

"Fucker? Are you listening to me?" Becks's voice breaks through my thoughts. The ones Rylee commandeers even when she's not even around.

"Yeah, what?" I angle my head over so that I can see him. "I was just thinking about … *stuff*."

"Dude, get the voodoo pussy out of your head for a second."

"Becks, there's nothing more I'd like right now than to have my head in her wet, willing voodoo."

"You are a disappointment to all men! Not only did you break the no barebacking pact, but you are fucking grinning about it."

"I need another beer if I have to listen to your whiny ass. Shit, we're going to the City of Sin and I'm putting a hottie on your arm … so quit your bitching, pact broken or not."

"I *know* you're riding without a saddle now because it's obviously fucking with your head," he says, holding up his hands to stop the retort he knows from years of friendship is on my tongue. The one about how much I want one of my two heads fucked with.

"Really chaps your hide, doesn't it," I say, fighting the laugh I want to release because fuck, even if I'm well on my way to getting drunk, I still know that was pretty damn witty.

"Fucking hilarious," he says sarcastically, shaking his head. "*Sooooo* … how are you going to handle Vegas with a chick on your arm?"

I'm instantly irritated at the comment. And now I'm wondering why. What is it about what Becks says that angers me?

"Don't look at me like that!" he says, and I can tell he's getting into Becks-knows-all mode. *Fuck!* I so don't need this right now. "Vegas is usually a flesh feast, so tell me how that's going to go over with Wonder-Rylee there? Did you think of that, cowboy?"

I close my eyes and emit a sliver of a laugh. "The only all-you-can-eat-buffet I'll be fucking dining at will be Ry's Thighs." I quirk my eyebrows up at him, challenge given. Got a comeback to that one now, fucker? "Besides, I wouldn't doubt she'd throw down if someone got in her way. She fights for what's hers."

And the words are out there before I can fucking take them back. Goddamn alcohol in my brain.

"*What's hers?* Did you just officially acknowledge—admit—what-the-fuck-ever that you're taken?" Becks spits out his beer. "Stop the car, Sammy!" he yells.

The limo swerves quickly to the side of the road and stops with a jerk. I know Sammy thinks Becks is gonna hurl. Did he really drink that fucking much? *Lightweight.*

Becks opens the door beside him and climbs out. "Hey, Wood?"

I'm confused by the amusement in his voice when he's supposed to be getting sick. "Yeah?" I ask as I angle my head out to look at him, beer in hand, lights from passing cars flashing over his face.

"Feel that?" he says, lifting his face up to the sky. "That's the fucking arctic chill right there!"

"What the fuck are you talking about?" He's starting to ruin my buzz here so I'm getting pissed.

"Dude, you're barebacking, we're taking chicks to Vegas with us, and that has to mean Hell is most definitely freezing over. What in the fuck is this world coming to?"

I just shake my head at him. "Get in the car, Beckett. If I'm gonna be around a pussy, it sure as fuck needs to be one I can get enjoyable use out of ... and you, my friend, are being one but hell if I'd enjoy you."

He slides in the car next to me and just stares at me, a smirk on his mouth and amusement in his eyes.

Me and my fucking mouth.

"Okay, Sam, we're good to go!" Becks says with a chuckle, and the car starts to take off.

I open the top of another beer. I think I'm going to need this to deal with him tonight. *I'm not fucking hers.* Becks is just out if his damn mind if he thinks I'm a kept man.

I'll tire of her. I always do. Shit, one woman isn't going to be able to change my MO. There's not enough game in the world that can change this player.

We drive for a bit, both of us staring out the window to the world beyond until he finally breaks the silence. "*Really?*" he asks with a shake of his head, meeting my eyes. And I know what he's asking. Are you sure? Is she really worth it? Is Rylee really going to Vegas with us?

Is she the real-deal voodoo?

I purse my lips for a second and nod my head. "Damn straight, she is."

Chapter Six

"You really said that to him?" Haddie asks incredulously, the look on her face over-exaggerated and hilariously funny.

"I swear!" I told her, holding up my hand in testament. I look down at my phone where a text just pinged. It's from Colton, and all it says is: *Get this Party Started – Pink.*

Haddie doesn't notice the odd look on my face when I read it because she is concentrating on filing her nails. What the hell? First the text about Matchbox Twenty today, which threw me for a loop, and now this? He's a little all over the place and a lot confusing.

"Shit! I'd have loved to see his face when you shut that door."

"I know." I laugh. "It felt kind of good to leave him stunned for once rather than the other way around."

"See, I told you!" she says, pushing on my knee.

"Besides the testosterone fest with Colton, did you and Tanner have a nice visit?"

"Yeah." I smile softly. "It was so good to see him. I don't realize how much I miss him until—" a knock on the door interrupts me. I look over at Haddie, my eyes asking her who could be knocking on our door at seven o'clock on a Friday night.

"No clue." She shrugs, getting up to answer it since I have a slew of work papers strewn across my lap and on the couch beside me.

Moments later I hear laughter and voices and Haddie exclaiming, "Well look what the cat dragged in!"

Curious, I start to clear my papers when Haddie enters the family room, a broad smile on her face. "Someone's here to see you," she says, a knowing look in her eyes.

Before I can ask her who it is, Colton comes barreling into the room in a less than graceful stride with a laughing Beckett right behind him. Something's amiss with Colton, and I'm not sure what it is until he sees me. A goofy grin spreads across his face and it looks out of place against the intensity of his features. Luckily, I'm shuffling up my papers because he unceremoniously plops down right beside me.

"Rylee!" he exclaims enthusiastically as if he hasn't seen me in weeks. He reaches out, calloused fingers rasping against my bare skin, grabs me, and pulls me onto his lap. All I can do is laugh because I realize that Mr. Cool and Always in Control is a tad bit drunk. No, make that well on his way to being drunk. And before I can even respond to his sudden appearance, Colton's mouth closes over mine.

I resist at first, but once his tongue delves into my mouth and I taste him, I'm a goner. I groan in acceptance and lick my tongue against his. It's only been a few days but God, I missed this. Missed him. I forget that other people are in the room when Colton tangles his hand in my hair and takes possession of me, holding me so all I can do is react. All I can do is absorb the feeling of him against me. He tastes of beer and mints and everything I want. Everything I crave. Everything I need. I bow my back so my chest presses to his, my nipples tingling as they brush against the firm warmth of his chest. Colton swallows the moan he's coaxed from me when his arousal pushes up through my thin pajama pants and rubs against me.

"Should we clear the room?" I hear Haddie say before she clears her throat loudly, shocking me back to reality.

I pull my head back slightly from Colton's, but his hand remains fisted in my hair holding my curls hostage. He rests his forehead to mine as we both draw in ragged breaths of need.

After a beat, he throws his head back on the couch and laughs loudly, his whole body shaking from its force, before choking out, "Shit, I needed that!"

I start to scramble off his lap, suddenly aware that I'm wearing a very thin camisole tank with some very aroused nipples sans bra, and Beckett—whom I've only met once—is sitting across from me, studying us with a quiet yet amused intensity. Before I can even cross my arms over my chest, Colton's hands grip me from behind, wrapping his arms around me and pulling me back against him.

"Hey!" I shout.

"I got it!" he shouts playfully in response. "And Colton's inebriated."

What? I shift in his lap, trying to turn and look at him. "Huh?"

He chuckles and it's such a carefree boyish laugh—so at odds with the intensity he exudes—that my heart swells at the sound. "Ace," he states confidently. "And Colton's inebriated."

He busts out laughing again, and I can't help but laugh along with him. "Nope." And before I can say anything else, Beckett jumps in.

"You're drunker than I thought. Inebriated starts with an 'I', you douchebag. Spell much?"

Colton flips him the bird, his boyish laugh returning again. "Whatever, Becks. You know you love me!" he says pulling me back against him. "Now, back to business," Colton announces loudly. "You're coming with us."

Haddie raises her eyebrows, amusement on her face at my flustered expression. "Colton, let me go!" I sputter loudly in between laughs, trying to wriggle out of his iron tight grip on me. He simply holds me tighter, resting his chin on my shoulder.

"Nope! Not until you agree that you're going with us. You and Haddie are going on a little road trip with Becks and me." I start to wiggle again, and I feel Colton's free hand slip up to cup my breast through my shirt, his thumb brushing over my nipple. I suck in a breath at his touch and embarrassment floods my cheeks.

"Uh-uh-uh," he teases, his breath feathering over my cheek. "Every time you fight me, baby, I'm gonna cop a feel." He nips at the skin between my shoulder and my neck, his arousal thickening beneath my lap. "So please, Rylee," he begs, "please, fight me."

I roll my eyes despite the shock wave of need that's reverberating through me at the sound of his bedroom voice, and I can't help the laughter that bubbles out, Haddie and Beckett joining in. Drunken Colton equals a very playful Colton. I like this side of him.

"Typical male," I tease. "Always misguided and thinking with the head in your pants."

He pulls me tighter against him, one arm around my shoulders while the other is around my waist. "Well then, don't be afraid to blow my mind," he murmurs, a low, seductive growl in my ear that has me laughing from the corniness of the line all the while tensing at the suggestion of it.

"So get your asses up, pretty ladies, and get ready!" he suddenly orders, breaking our connection, pushing me to my feet, and swatting my backside.

"What are you talking about?" I ask at the same time Haddie pipes up asking, "Where are we going?"

Beckett laughs out loud at Haddie's all-in reaction before bringing a bottle of beer to his lips. "Hey!" Colton shouts. "Don't be drinking my beer you bastard or I'll take you down."

"Chill out, Wood." He chuckles. "You left yours on the table by the front door."

"Shit!" he grumbles. "I'm a man in need of a beer and of women to get their asses moving. Time's a wasting!"

"What in the hell are you talking about?" I turn to him, arms across my chest.

A slow, roguish grin spreads across his lips as he stares at me. "Vegas, baby!"

Mysterious text solved.

"What?" Haddie and I shout, but both with different meanings. There is no possible way I am going to Las Vegas right now. What in the hell?

Colton holds up his phone, biting his lip as he tries to concentrate on its screen, and I realize he's trying to tell the time with his alcohol-warped mind. "We'll be back in the morning, but wheels up in one hour, Rylee, so you better get that fine ass of yours moving!"

What? We're flying? What am I even thinking? I'm not going anywhere. "Colton, you can't possibly be serious!"

He pushes himself up from the couch, and looks a little wobbly before getting control. He looks down at me, an errant lock of hair falling over his forehead with his shirt untucked on the right side. "Do I need to pick you up over my shoulder and haul you to your bedroom to show you just how serious I am, sweetheart?"

I look over at Beckett for some kind of help. He just shrugs his shoulders, silently laughing at our banter. "I'd just give in, Rylee," he drawls, winking at me. "He doesn't give up when he's in this mood. I suggest you go get changed."

I open my mouth to speak but nothing comes out. I look over at Haddie who has excitement dancing in her eyes. "C'mon, Ry," she prompts. "It couldn't hurt to escape with everything that's going on tomorrow." She shrugs. "Have some fun and forget a little." I nod at her and her smile widens. She whoops loudly. "We're going to Vegas, baby!"

Beckett stands from the chair asking for the bathroom. Haddie offers to show him on the way to her room to get ready. I turn to face Colton but am caught off guard as he swoops me up and over his shoulder, swatting my butt as he carries me rather unsteadily toward the hallway.

"Colton, stop!" I shriek, smacking his ass in turn.

His only response is a laugh. "Which room is yours?" I squeal as he tickles my feet. "Tell me, woman, or I'll be forced to torture you some more!"

Oh, I definitely like drunk and playful Colton!

"Last door on the right," I screech as he tickles me some more before throwing me unceremoniously onto my bed. I'm out of breath from laughing, and before I can even speak, Colton's body is flanking mine. The feeling of his weight on me, pressing intimately against me, creates a crack in my resolve. So much for being aloof. That card was thrown out the window the minute he wobbled into the family room with that playful and captivating grin on his face.

His mouth slants over mine and his tongue plunges into my mouth. I slide my hands up and under the hem of his shirt and run them up the planes of his back. The kiss is full of greed, angst, and passion, and I know I'm losing myself in it. To him. His hands roam, touching every inch of my bare skin he can find as if he needs this connection to tell him everything is alright between us. That our union is reassuring him, confirming that whatever's between us is still there.

I freeze when I hear a knock on the doorjamb. "C'mon, loverboy." Beckett chuckles uncomfortably. "Rein it in. You can do that later. Right now we've got a plane to catch."

Colton rolls off of me, groaning as he adjusts his arousal in his jeans. "You're such a buzz kill, Becks!"

"That's why you love me, brother!" He laughs as he retreats down the hall, giving me some privacy to get ready.

Colton props his hands behind his head and crosses his feet at the ankles as I scoot off of the bed. "God, you look sexy right now," Colton murmurs, his eyes focused on my nipples pressing against the thin cotton of my tank.

"She'll look sexier in about twenty minutes, Donavan, if you get the hell out of here and let her do her thing," Haddie says unabashedly as she breezes in my room holding a handful of barely-there dresses on hangers for me to try on.

"Well shit," Colton says, pushing himself up off of the mattress, "I guess I've been told. Beckett?" he bellows down the hall, "Time for another beer."

I twirl a lock of Colton's hair absently with my fingers as I stare down at his head resting in my lap. He's just fallen asleep and I shake my head watching the peaceful calm on his face. I'm still in shock at the direction the evening has taken. I smile, recalling the look on Colton's face when Haddie and I walked into the living room in our sexy Vegas outfits. The bottle of beer that was angling towards his lips stopped in midair when he saw me. His eyes ran the length of my body in a lazy perusal, a diminutive smile ghosting his lips before they met mine. What his eyes told me in that one look was everything that I'd needed to hear from him but hadn't heard over the past couple of days.

Desire. Need. Want.

And then unbeknownst to me, when Colton had mentioned flying, little did I know that there was a chartered jet waiting for us when we arrived via limo at the Santa Monica Municipal Airport. Haddie and I just looked at each other and shook our heads at the lavishness of it all. And when we boarded, in addition to Sammy sitting quietly at the rear of the plane, there was a flight attendant willing to fill any drink or meal order we desired. While Haddie, Becks, and I took advantage of the offer for a drink, Colton declined everything and crawled up on the couch beside me, laid his head in my lap, and declared he needed a quick nap to be ready for the night to come.

I shake my head thinking of it all, a wisp of a smile on my face when I look up to see Haddie and Beckett in a hushed conversation across from me. Haddie's heels are off and her feet are curled underneath her. Beckett's long legs are stretched out in front of him, and his fingers absently draw lines on the condensation of his bottle. He's quite handsome in a non-typical way. I stare at him, realizing that he has definite sex appeal, more than looks. His sandy blonde hair is cropped close to his head and spiked up with gel. His crystal clear blue eyes are fringed by thick lashes. They are quiet eyes that take in and observe in a reserved fashion. He has broad shoulders and a lean build like Colton.

I stare at him, the best friend of my lover, and there is so much I want to ask him about Colton. So many things I think he can shed light on but know he would never betray his buddy by telling me.

Whether by chance or because he feels the weight of my stare, Beckett looks up and meets my eyes, his sentence to Haddie faltering on his lips. He angles his head to the side and twists his lips up as if he's trying to decide if he should say something or not.

"You know why we're here right now...why Wood got drunk tonight, don't you?" His southern accent drawls out as he looks down and shakes his head at the sight of his friend before looking back up at me.

"No," I say.

Beckett leans forward resting his elbows on his knees and looks me straight in the eye. "Because you told him no, Rylee." He shakes his head, a smile growing on his face. "And nobody, except me, ever tells him no."

"That's absurd," I tell him, looking over at Haddie, who's arched her eyebrow at the turn in conversation, a pleased smirk on her lips. I realize that Beckett is telling me I am the first female to tell Colton no. To not ask how high when he says jump. I glance down at Colton and back up to Beckett. "Surely one of his *many others* have told him no before."

He thinks in silence for a moment before answering. "Not that I know of," Beckett says, tipping the bottle to his lips, "and if they have, I've never seen Colton care like this." He leans back and stretches out again, and I try to read the unspoken words in his eyes. "He came back from lunch one surly S. O. B., Rylee. I actually felt bad for the people on the other end of our meeting today." He smiles at the thought. "And then the next thing I know, he was pounding out his frustration on the treadmill. Pulling me to the bar with him to sulk and started making phone calls. Hatching a plan. Telling people we'll be in Vegas by ten, to get their asses there, and to meet him at the usual place."

The usual place? "You guys do this often?"

"Every couple of months." He shrugs like it's not a big deal. "But here's the thing, Rylee, no matter who he's with, I've never—never—seen him bring the woman he's seeing, or whatever the hell he's doing with them, along with us." He tips the bottle of the beer at me. "Now that's something to think about."

Beckett eyes hold mine until he knows I understand. There's something different between Colton and me that he hasn't seen before. I nod my head at him.

He leans forward again. "I've known Colton for a long time, Rylee. He can be cocky as hell and a stubborn ass at times, but he's a good guy. A really good guy." I can sense the sincerity in his voice and the brotherly love he has for Colton. He looks down at his slumbering friend and back at me. "He may not always go about things the right way, or even know how to go about them at all, but he usually has the best intentions behind his actions." When I don't say anything he just nods and continues. "I'm telling you this because you matter to him. More than he's willing to admit or can acknowledge right now, but it's important for you to know. Because if he matters to you like I think he does...really matters...not just for the recognition of being with him, but because of who he is, then you need to hear it. *Shit*," he swears, running a hand over his jaw and leaning back shaking his head. "I must be drunk if I just told you that. *Fuck*." He sighs. "He'd throttle me right now if he knew I was telling you any of this."

"Thank you," I tell him, my voice barely a whisper as I try to digest everything he's just told me—everything I wanted to ask him but was afraid to. My head is reeling with his confession. I try to keep a rein on the hope and possibilities that bubble up inside of me. I matter enough that his best friend notices the difference in him. I just need to remember that unless Colton acknowledges it, these feelings still mean nothing.

Haddie looks over at me and smiles softly, knowing how much I needed to hear this. That these words justify the depths of emotion I already feel for Colton.

He thanks the flight attendant as she hands him another beer. "I've said this much, I might as well finish," he mutters to himself with a sheepish smile spreading on his lips. Colton shifts and turns into me, his face nuzzling my abdomen, and all I want to do is bend down and kiss him. "Trying to control Colton is like trying to grab the wind. Don't even bother..." he shakes his head "...he's gonna fuck up, Rylee. He's going to make a lot of mistakes and say all of the wrong things because he doesn't know how to do anything other than what he's been doing."

Beckett takes a pull on his beer and sighs. "He'll never admit it Rylee. And unless you are one of the few that are close enough to him to see it, you'd never guess that he's a man drowning in his past. To accept that there might be more than just the usual arrangement per se with you—and by you being here, there obviously is—he might just pull you down so that you're drowning with him." He shifts some in his seat, eyes never breaking from mine. "When that happens, Rylee, more than anything he's going to need you to be his lifeline. He's going to be so consumed and obsessed with preventing his past from meeting his future that he's going to need everything from you to keep him afloat."

He holds my eyes for a minute longer and then eases back into his seat, a slight smile playing the corners of his mouth. "I love him to death, Rylee, but some days I hate him too." He shrugs without apology, "That's just Colton."

I look back up at Beckett and smile softly, a silent agreement to his assessment. "I'm beginning to understand that," I mutter.

The flight attendant comes over to fill our drinks one last time and to inform us that we will be beginning our descent into Las Vegas shortly. I look down at Colton and a feeling of warmth spreads throughout me as I realize how much I've come to care for and love—yes love—him. I shake my head and Haddie catches my eye, her happiness for me brimming in hers.

Chapter Seven

It's been several years since I've been to Las Vegas, and I can't believe how much the city of sin has changed in that time. New hotels have sprouted up while old ones have been torn down. Aging ones have been renovated and made over to match the caliber of the new ones.

I'm dying to get a moment alone with Haddie. We haven't really had one since this whole adventure started, and I need her advice on how I should act in light of Beckett's revelations. We had a quick moment alone in the airplane while we were freshening up, but not nearly long enough to have a real discussion about the night's events.

Lights and sounds surround us, assaulting our senses as we exit the limo. Sammy nods discretely to Colton and takes the lead as we walk up a set of stairs into an entrance at the Venetian. Within moments we are walking into TAO. Colton's hand is on the small of my back, and I notice conveniently that Beckett's hand is doing the same on Haddie's. I wonder if he's just being a gentleman or if there's something else possibly going on. *Interesting.*

I realize that people are starting to stare at us as Colton's name is hurriedly murmured around the Friday night crowd who've gathered in hopes of seeing a celebrity. Camera phones flash and I look up at Colton to see his reaction. He's all smiles with the crowd, but when he looks over at me, his eyes warm up with what's missing from his public one. His nap has sobered him up some, but I can still sense that playful Colton is just within reach.

We skirt around the long line of people waiting for the chance to enter. As we near the hostess podium, a woman steps out from behind it and motions for us to follow her. Wow, life must be nice when you're Colton Donavan. *No lines and women at your fingertips.*

Colton leads me by the hand as we walk past the giant Buddha on the way to our private table. Heads turn and flashes explode against the darkened atmosphere of the room as we pass through. I hear Colton's name murmured a couple more times within the crowd before he stops and turns to face me.

I look at him, a puzzled expression on my face as he steps toward me and unexpectedly captures my mouth with his. At first I freeze—I mean we are in the middle of a very swanky and completely packed restaurant—but as Colton deepens the kiss, as his fingertips cup my face and hold my head still, I succumb to him. His taste is just too devouring and his pull on me too magnetic to resist.

The sounds of the restaurant's patrons fade away. Colton kisses me like a man drawing his last breath and I am his air. It's passionate and possessive and provocative. *And holy fuck his addictive taste drags me under and takes hold.* My mind starts to come back to reality when the whistles and hollers of onlookers begin to register in my brain.

The crowd around us gets louder as they urge on our public display. Colton keeps his hands cupping my face but tears his lips from mine. His eyes register unfiltered lust, but the grin he flashes me is arrogant and mischievous. The only thought in my head is *wow*, but he's left me so breathless that forming that simple word isn't even a possibility. I give him a questioning look.

He just cocks his head to the side, a gleam lighting up his emerald eyes. "If they're gonna stare, Ryles, we might as well put on a good show!" He wags his eyebrows at me and brushes a chaste kiss on my lips before grabbing my hand and following the hostess standing off to the left of us. The dumbfounded look on her face reflects exactly how I feel.

Playful Colton has reappeared.

Cheers follow us out of the main room into our private dining area, and it is only then that I can read the stunned thoughts dancing across Haddie's expression. I shrug at her and she just grins back at me, eyes wide and dimples deep.

We reach our table and Colton pulls me into his arms before I have a chance to sit in the chair he's pulled out for me. "I haven't told you yet how absolutely stunning you look tonight." He breathes into my ear. "And now every guy in this restaurant knows you're mine," he says in case the claim he'd just staked wasn't clear enough. He presses his lips at the spot just below my ear. "You look sexy as hell in that dress, but I must confess that all I can think about is getting you out of it." He chuckles—a seductive sound that wraps its way inside my body and causes the fingers of desire to tickle in my lower belly. "Thank you for coming tonight, Ryles."

Dinner is delicious and seems uneventful compared to the whirlwind of the past couple of hours.

The conversation among the four of us flows easily, and I can see why Colton likes Beckett. He's funny and witty and really grounded, having no trouble putting Colton in his place when he needs to be. They banter back and forth like little old women, but their affection for one another is obvious.

Sammy sits at a table near us with eyes wary at all times. He's prevented our meal from being interrupted a couple of times from eager ladies wanting pictures with Colton, if not something more.

I catch myself staring at him randomly during dinner. His charisma and enthusiasm are infectious, and I love watching how his face lights up when telling a story or relaying an event. He's polite and attentive to everyone during the meal, making sure that all of our needs are met. He steals little kisses here and there coupled with the squeeze of my hand or the trace of a fingertip on my bare shoulder. I wonder if he has any clue the fire he is stoking within me with his casual affection.

I sip the last of my Tom Collins and realize I have a slight buzz going when Colton's phone alerts an incoming text. He looks down and laughs at the message. "Gotta hot date, Ace?" I tease him with a smirk on my face. He looks up from his phone to meet my eyes at the same time Haddie snorts at my nickname. He just raises an eyebrow and flashes that mischievous grin I adore. In the midst of staring at me, I see the moment his brain registers why Haddie's laughing.

"You," he says across the table pointing at Haddie.

"Me?" she says coyly as she takes a sip through her straw.

"You know what A.C.E. stands for," he says with excitement, and I can see the cogs turn in his head as he figures out how to play this.

"Now why would you think that?" Haddie flutters her eyelashes with feigned innocence.

"Spill it, Montgomery," Colton demands playfully. Haddie's eyes dart over to me and her smile widens, but she says nothing. "What can I bribe you with?"

"Well," Haddie replies in her best bedroom voice. "There's definitely a lot of things you could do to me to make me talk." She breathes out, licking her bottom lip and pausing. "You know Ry and I like to play a little on our own together," she says suggestively, eyeing him up and down. The look on Colton's face is utter shock and, being the guy that he is, unfiltered lust. It's taking everything I have to not burst out laughing. "If you want me to talk, you could always join us," she suggests, "and play a little…"

He works a swallow down his throat, his eyes darting back and forth between us before a lascivious smirk turns up that skillful mouth of his. "Very convincing, Haddie…And as much as my dick's enjoying the thought, I'm not taking the bait, sweetheart," he replies while Beckett barks out a laugh.

"Damn, Haddie." Becks shakes his head. "You had me going for a minute there!"

We all laugh as Haddie throws her napkin at him and turns to me with a smile on her face. "He'll never get it."

"Attractive, charming, and exquisite," Colton guesses and then blows on his knuckles and rubs them against his chest.

"Nope." I smirk at him as I play with the straw in my drink.

"More like all consuming ego," Beckett mocks.

"Nope," I repeat, my standard response.

"Saved by the bell!" Colton says as the waiter places dessert plates filled with chocolate confections in front of us.

We enjoy our dessert, the playful banter continuing, but no matter where my eyes wander, they always come back to Colton. He looks up as I'm admiring his devilishly handsome face and smiles softly at me.

"You ready?"

I return his smile and nod.

"Haddie? Becks? You game?" They both agree and gather their things. I start to stand up and find myself tugged backwards so I land on Colton's lap. I catch a glimpse of his wicked grin before his lips close over mine. His tongue slips between my lips and teases mine with tantalizing slow licks and sweeps into my mouth. He tastes of mint and rum, and all I can think of is how these little kisses here and there are not enough to last me all evening. They are a cruel tease when I've already had the real thing and know it's mind-blowingly better. His hand slides slowly up the outside of my thigh, fingertips gliding underneath the hem of my dress, kneading my soft skin with his roughened fingers.

Teasing me.

Before I can even process a coherent thought, he pulls back and kisses me on the tip of my nose. I release a frustrated sigh, needing so much more to soothe the ache he's seated in me.

He chuckles softly at my response. "Let's go," he says, nodding his head toward the door.

We've spent the last hour and a half occupying the casino floor with a flamboyant flair. Much to Sammy's dismay, Colton decided that he wanted to play some Craps. After some initial losing, Colton ended up at a table surrounded by a crowd as he rolled again and again to their cheers of encouragement and the benefit of his wallet.

His adrenaline is still amped up, and I can feel it vibrating off of him as our car pulls along a back entrance of the Palms Casino a little after midnight. We've all had a lot to drink and I'm more than ready to release some energy on the dance floor.

"Now the fun really begins, ladies!" he exclaims before tipping back the rest of his drink and grabbing my hand.

We exit the car and are whisked via a side door through the hotel and into a back entrance to the nightclub, Rain. The energetic beat of the song *Animal* fills the club and reverberates through my body. An employee leads us up a stairway and moves a velvet rope with a sign that notes *reserved* so we can pass into the VIP area.

Such an odd feeling to be treated as the only patrons in a club filled with hundreds of other people just feet away.

We're led onto the mezzanine level, and when we enter, a roar of cheers startles me. Colton doesn't seem surprised, and I realize that the thirty plus people in front of me are who Colton's been coordinating all night long. He is suddenly pulled into the crowd of people, collecting pats on the back from the guys and overly long hugs from the women.

I step back, allowing him to have the attention of his friends and look at our surroundings. I count six rooms on this level that overlook the dance floor and it seems as if Colton has rented them all out for the night. I step toward the railing and watch the mass of people below gyrate and move with the pulse of the music.

"You doing okay?"

I look over at Haddie, relieved to have her here, and smile. "Yes. It's just all a bit more than I'm used to."

"I guess he's a little over the top, huh?"

"Just a tad." I laugh. "So, Beckett?" I ask, arching my eyebrows.

"He is hella cute..." she shrugs "...but you know how that goes." She laughs in her typical carefree Haddie way. If she wants, she'll have him eating out of her hand by the night's end. *That's just Haddie.* "You wanna dance?"

I look for Colton to tell him that we're going down to the floor, but he's in the middle of a wildly animated conversation. He'll figure it out. Within moments we've made our way downstairs, and have worked ourselves into the crowd moving on the floor. It feels so good to let go and move with the beat, to get lost for a moment and forget the anniversary that started the minute the clock passed midnight.

After a couple of songs, I look up toward the balcony above us to see Colton standing at the railing. He searches the crowd and it takes a few moments before he finds me. I have a déjà vu moment when our eyes lock—a different club this time but the same intense heat between us. His face falls into shadow momentarily, and I can't help but remember wondering on our first date if he was an angel fighting through the darkness or a devil breaking into the light. Right now, looking up and completely consumed by him, he is most definitely my struggling angel. And yet I know the devil in him is always just beneath the surface.

I continue moving despite our irrefutable connection—the one that stops my breath and kick starts my heart every time he looks at me. I smile and motion for him to come down. He just shakes his head in a measured acceptance of whatever it is that he's thinking and smiles before disappearing from sight.

The song changes and I hear the opening notes to Usher's *Scream*. I throw my arms up and swivel my hips to the beat, letting the music wash over me. I sing my favorite line. "*Got no drink in my hand but I'm wasted, getting drunk on the thought of you naked.*" I snap my eyes open on the last word when I feel hands slide around my waist from behind and pull me backwards. Haddie's smile tells me that it's Colton, and I relax against him as I see Beckett and a few more of his friends from upstairs join us.

The soft curves of my body fit against the hard edges of his, and I close my eyes as we start to move together. Every movement against each other has my skin prickling and my insides igniting. Each nerve in my body is attuned to the feel of him against me. His strong hands map the lines of my torso: urging, grabbing, enticing. His hips move with mine, the ridge of his erection tempting me with each movement. We mimic each other in unfulfilled need, in mounting desire.

He turns me around to face him, the demand of his hands forcing me to do what he wants arouses me further. It evokes images of his skillful fingers running the length of my sex before parting me and slipping into me. I groan at the thought and somehow he hears me despite the music because the sexy smirk on his face and darkening eyes tell me he feels the same. I know he wants more than just this frustrating but sensual as hell petting with our clothes on.

Chapter Eight

We dance a few more songs. Each brush against him adds to the mounting need within me. A seductive game, that's tantalizing, sensuous, and felt by both of us despite the lack of words. The opening notes of Ginuine's *Pony* filters through the speakers, and the suggestive tone of the song is too much for Colton to handle. He grabs my hand and pulls me with obvious purpose through the crowd on the dance floor. Impatience, need, and determination radiates off of him and vibrates into me as he stops at the foot of the stairs. Every part of my body is on high alert when he puts his hand on my back to urge me up the steps. I'm on the first riser when he spins me around and captures my mouth in a blistering kiss filled with urgency.

He attacks my mouth with a definite purpose, thoroughly obliterating all hopes of self-discipline when it comes to him. But before I can give in to the temptation at my fingertips and react wholeheartedly, he ends the kiss just as abruptly as he began it, leaving me wanting for more and on the cusp of begging.

Colton starts up the stairs, my hand in his as I follow. When we reach the top where Sammy stands, Colton leans over and says something in his ear that the music drowns out. Sammy nods his head and turns on his heel, Colton and I right behind him.

We reach the sixth and last VIP room on the balcony, and I follow Colton's lead, stopping and looking out over the club below. I glance over my shoulder to see Sammy ushering his friends out of the last room before I look back to Colton. His eyes are focused on the crowd below, his jaw clenched, and I wonder if I've done something wrong to piss him off.

I'm a little taken aback. What in the hell did I do? He's going to choose right now to be pissed? I guess I should be used to his confusing, back and forth moods, but I'm not. We remain silent waiting for whatever Sammy is doing, and I resign myself that there is most likely a fight on the horizon for us. Can't we just have one night without it?

Sammy leans into Colton's ear and tells him something, and then we are on the move again. Colton leads me by my hand into the sixth and now vacant VIP area. The minute we clear the wall and are away from anyone's view, Colton's body crashes into mine instantaneously, forcibly pinning me against the wall.

I only have time for one coherent thought before the taste of Colton pulls me under. He's not pissed at me. *Not hardly. He's consumed with desire.*

All of the heat and urgency in the kiss on the stairs is intensified and then some. Our teeth clash and bodies mesh as his tongue pushes through my lips and licks into my mouth. His hands are everywhere on my body at once, each touch flaring my need and shooting desire like a mainline to my core.

I need him in me, filling me, moving inside of me, right now like I need my next breath.

His tongue continues its tormenting assault on my mouth, his hands seeking my bare flesh as the words of the song fuel the desire raging between us. He reaches down and pulls my leg up to his hip, his hands sliding up and under my hem. Desperate fingers dig into my willing flesh. His hand is so close yet so far away from where I need it to be that all I can do is groan out in a mixture of frustration and need. He nips my bottom lip, followed by the soothing lick of his tongue, prompting me to tighten my grip on his hair. I tug on it, my silent way of saying I need him too. Want him just as desperately.

Right here. Right now.

He drags himself away from me, his chest rising and falling with his labored breaths and his eyes bore into mine despite the fog of lust in them. "I don't like all of those guys dancing around you," he says, his strained voice is playful despite the violent desire I see raging in his eyes.

"It got your attention, didn't it?" I tease in a pant of breath, surprised by his jealousy.

"Sweetheart, if you want my attention..." he smirks, his hands cupping my ass and yanking me into him, the ridge of his erection pressing deliciously into my softness "...all you have to do is ask."

"And pull you away from your adulating *throng* of friends?" I tease, arching my eyebrows at him, my sarcasm apparent.

"So you'd rather go dance amidst a *throng* of random men?"

I suck in my breath as he moves his hands up the sides of my torso and stops beside my breasts. My body is so pent up, so on the edge of need that it responds instantly when it gets the touch it craves. His thumbs connect with my nipples and they pebble instantly as he rubs up and down. I lean my head back, closing my eyes, and allow myself to be swallowed in the sensation the stroke of his thumbs create.

My head clouds, trying to think of a witty comeback to this bantering foreplay between us. "It got you out there, didn't it?" I bait, running my tongue over my bottom lip. "Just think of it as a means to an end, Ace."

Colton brushes his thumbs up and down once more, making sure he has my attention. "Oh, baby," he murmurs, "the only end that's going to be sticking into your means, is mine." He leans in to nip at my bottom lip before pulling back to meet my gaze, one hand squeezing over my breast possessively. "*Mine*."

The intensity in his eyes prevents me from laughing. I lean into him, my hand reaching out to run over the ridge of his arousal and cup him through his pants. And I'm not sure where my brazen confidence comes from, but I bring my mouth up to his ear and whisper just above the noise. "Prove it."

Colton emits a strangled groan, and in a flash he grips my head and holds me still while his mouth crashes against mine before breaking apart way too soon.

"Come," he says, pulling me with him as he walks backwards to one of the chairs toward the back of the room. He sits down and pulls me onto him. "Straddle me," he commands, and the need in me is so overwhelming I obey without a second thought. I hike my dress up my thighs and place my knees on either side of him, lowering my center over his lap.

He looks at me, a wicked grin on his face that makes me want to earn the look he's giving me. Eyes locked on mine, he places his hands on my bare knees and runs his hands up my thighs. When he reaches my hem, he just keeps pushing my dress up. My lips part at their wanton progression, and in a quick moment of modesty, I twist my head over my shoulder to look at the doorway to make sure no one is watching.

"Don't worry," Colton whispers, unfettered need straining his voice, "Sammy's guarding the door. He's not letting anyone back here."

I'm relieved and yet uncomfortable with the thought that Sammy knows or can assume what we're doing in here. My worry falls to the wayside because Colton's hands squeeze my thighs, and I instinctively spread them wider as need thunders through my body.

"I've wanted to fuck this sweet pussy of yours all night," his voice growls in my ear. "Ever since I saw your nipples tight and pressed against your tank top. Since I watched you dancing, teasing me with this sexy body of yours." His thumbs brush over my dampened panties and I shiver, his touch like a lightning strike to my sex. "I want to feel you on the inside. I want to feel your cum coat me when I fuck you. Want to hear that sound you make when you lose it. And. I. Just. Can't. Wait. Any. Longer," he grits out between taunting kisses.

And then he finally gives me what I crave. His mouth captures mine, parting my lips and claiming my every reaction. At the same time one thumb pulls my panties to the side and the other connects with my clit. A blast of indescribable pleasure jolts through me with his touch, his lips smothering the moan he coaxes from me.

I dig my fingers into the muscled flesh of his shoulders, not caring if my nails mark him. His tongue delves into my mouth, a languorous exploration that is thorough and seductive while his fingers part my cleft and tease skillfully so that every part of me tightens in a frenzy of need. His hand slips down to where my legs are spread, and he wets his fingers with my obvious arousal before sliding them back up to coat me. On his caress back down, he doesn't stop but rather tucks two fingers into me.

I gasp out a broken breath at the sublime sensation, desperate for this and the anticipation of what is to come. His fingers start to move inside me and I flex my hips as best as I can, opening myself up to him so he can have complete access. I close my eyes, my head falling back as the ecstasy of his touch threatens to overwhelm me.

"Fucking Christ," he groans against the soft skin of my throat. "Baby, you are so fucking wet for me. So ready. Makes me so fucking hard for you. Come for me. Come so I can sink myself into you when you're still riding your orgasm."

His blatant words seduce me, pushing me higher toward the edge. The sensations his fingers incite make me forget we're in a public nightclub, but at the same time, I know. I know because the exhilaration of being where we can be caught so easily, heightens my arousal, makes me notice every brush and sweep of his body against mine. Every graze of flesh against flesh.

His lips tease the curve of my neck as his other hand gives me the friction I need on my clit to push me over the razor thin edge of sanity. The intense rush of heat hits me, pulling me under its rolling waves as I splinter into what feels like a million pieces. I drop my head on Colton's shoulder, my heartbeat racing and body pulsing with the orgasmic pleasure that washes through me. I suck in short, sharp breaths as he withdraws his fingers and fumbles with his zipper between my legs.

Before I have time to recover, Colton is guiding my hips up and positioning himself at my entrance. I'm so lost in the moment, in the pleasure, in Colton, that the outside world ceases to exist.

Right now it's me and Colton and the carnal need igniting an inferno between us. When we're like this—connected as one and absorbed in each other—I forget everything else. His taste, his scent, his domination of my senses, are my only focus.

I sink slowly onto him, feeling every thick inch of him as I lower my hips until fully seated. Colton's rough growl of a response and his fingers digging into my hips are the only reaction I need. I lean forward and cover his mouth with mine as I rock slowly onto him, his body tensing as mine tightens around him in acceptance. I continue my movement, sliding up and down his tortured length. My hands fan over the taut muscles of his back, and my tongue coaxes and demands for him to take everything from me because I want nothing less than all of him.

His hands push and pull me on each of his thrusts. I am so focused on giving him everything that he needs, everything that he wants, I don't even realize my body drowning in the liquid heat that fills me. Colton's face tightens and nostrils flare, a sure sign of his ratcheting pleasure and impending climax. His length thickens inside of me, expanding me so when he pushes into me the next time, I detonate in an explosion of sensation. He surges inside of me a couple more times and then his hands grip my hips forcibly, holding me still as his orgasm rushes through him. He throws his head back, his mouth falling open as his shattered moan fills our immediate space before being drowned out by the cacophony of noise in the club.

I watch his face, the reactions to his release flickering across his features when it hits me what I've just done. *Holy shit!* What in the hell am I thinking, and who took the real me and transplanted this wanton woman in my place? I start to shift off of Colton when he stops me from breaking our connection. Instead, he reaches up and gathers me against him, holding me for a sweet, unexpected moment before kissing the top of my head and then the tip of my nose.

We clean up and fix our disheveled appearances without speaking. I start fidgeting and fussing when Colton grabs my hand and squeezes it until I look up at him. A slow grin curls the corners of his mouth as he pulls me into him before pressing a chaste kiss on my mouth. He shakes his head at me. "You're constantly full of surprises, Ryles."

And you're the biggest surprise of them all.

I sip my drink as I sit back with Haddie in the VIP lounge, my body swaying subtly to the beat of the music below. I need a quick break from being on my feet, my shoes starting to take their toll. I see Sammy guarding the stairs and avert my eyes immediately, embarrassed about any conclusions he's drawn as to the less than innocent nature of Colton and my time alone.

I hear a high-pitched shriek as Sammy tries to avert someone from coming up the stairs. Colton, who's immersed in a conversation, turns his head toward the commotion. He steps back to see who it is and a wide grin spreads across his face before he motions for Sammy to let whomever it is up. My curiosity is definitely piqued when I see one of the guys he's talking to nudge him in an atta-boy manner.

Both Haddie and I turn our heads just in time to take in the longest pair of legs I've ever seen in what I think is the shortest skirt ever made strut toward Colton. The rest of the woman is just as spectacular as she tosses her head, throwing her long mane of blonde hair over her shoulder so that it falls just above her perfectly showcased backside.

She grabs Colton in a longer than necessary hug, her lips kissing the corner of his mouth as she leans back, a huge smile on her perfect face. It's when I see her that I suck in a breath, realizing who she is. Recognition dawns on Haddie at the same time, and we both look at each other in surprise. She is Cassandra Miller, the current darling of Hollywood as well as Playboy's latest celebrity centerfold. And despite completing their greeting, her hands are still resting on Colton's bicep, and her perfectly enhanced body is rubbing up against his with his hand resting politely on the small of her back.

I'm surprised by the twinge in my gut at the sight of them together. I've never been a jealous person, but then again, I've never been with someone as all-consuming as Colton Donavan.

I don't like her hands on him. *At all.*

Mine. He tells me that all the time. It's one of those possessive statements that I oddly find to be so damn arousing. And right now, I'd like to do nothing more than waltz up between the two of them and stake my claim on Colton as he did earlier to me in TAO.

But I don't move. I just sit and watch them interact, talk, her giggle stupidly and bat her eyelashes at a ridiculously fast pace while she keeps her hand on him. Why don't I move?

And then it hits me. They're stunning together. Absolutely stunning and this is who most would expect him to be with: the blonde bombshell, fantasy for many a men with the devastatingly handsome playboy, the desire of women everywhere. The picture perfect couple by Hollywood standards. He may have come here with me, and will be leaving with me, but like every woman, I have my own insecurities about my looks and my sex appeal.

And right now, looking from the blonde beauty then back to myself, those insecurities have just been put on display for everyone to see. For everyone to scrutinize. Even if I'm the only one who seems to be doing it.

I bring my fingers to my lips in thought and a cat ate the canary grin starts to spread across my face.

Fuck insecurity.

Fuck perfect, long-legged blondes.

Fuck playing it safe.

I close my eyes momentarily, remembering the feel of Colton's stubble scraping against the skin of my neck; his fingers bruising my hips as he helped me move over him; the look on his face as he came; the slight desperation with which he held me to him afterward in the room right next to where we're sitting now.

I remember Beckett's warning; trying to control Colton is like trying to grab the wind. He's gotten the playboy title for a reason. The short time we've been together isn't going to change that. Women are always going to be attracted to him, want him.

Cassandra obviously does. She's a dead giveaway with her constant touching and monopolizing demand on his attention. With how she leans in to speak to him, her hand pressed to his chest, leaving it there as he puts his mouth to her ear in response.

I'm not going to be irrational and deny the fact that I'm a tad bit jealous—alcohol most likely fueling my insecurity. Or maybe I'm just hormonal…I don't know. I'm a woman; insecurity is just par for the course in the grand scheme of things.

I snort out a laugh. Haddie looks over at me like I've lost it. "You're okay with…" She lifts her chin in the direction of Colton and Cassandra.

I look at them a moment longer before I nod my head. "It's not like I have to worry about him seeing her naked." I laugh, referring to her Playboy centerfold spread. "A huge portion of the male population has already done that and probably jacked off to her."

Haddie laughs out loud and shakes her head at me. I think she's a little surprised by my lack of a reaction. "*True*. At least you don't have staples in the middle of your body."

"Exactly." I smirk. "I have Colton *in me* instead." I love the look of shock on her face as I suck down the rest of my drink. "I need a shot and I wanna dance. You coming?" I walk out of the alcove without looking to see if she's following or not.

After downing our signature double shots of tequila, Haddie and I descend the stairs and enter into the rhythmic chaos of the dance floor. Songs come and go as we dance, and after a couple, I stop looking up at the balcony above to see if Colton's watching me. I know he isn't. That tingling of my skin telling me his presence is near is absent.

I'm thirsty and in need of a respite, so I motion to Haddie that I'm going to the bar to get another drink. Something to help dampen the dull edge of insecurity that is still holding my thoughts hostage.

I finagle my way up to the bar squeezing myself through the crowd, and prepare myself for a wait when I notice the numerous people in line. The guy beside me tries to start a conversation with me in his slurred voice, but I just smile politely and angle my body away from his. I focus my attention on watching the bartenders slowly inch their way back down the bar one order at a time.

The man beside me tries again, grabbing onto my upper arm and pulling me toward him, insisting he'll buy me a drink. I shrug my arm out of his grasp with an irritated but polite refusal. I think he's gotten the hint, but I'm proven wrong when he places his hand on my hip and forcefully tugs me against his side.

"C'mon, gorgeous." He breathes into my ear, the stale alcohol on his breath repulsing me. My discomfort grows, the hair on the back of my neck starting to rise. "Baby, I can show you a good time."

I push against his chest, trying to separate myself from him, but he just tightens his grip on my hip. I turn to search the crowd for help from Haddie when the guy's arm is suddenly yanked off of me.

"Get your fucking hands off of her!" I hear the growl a beat before Colton's fist connects with his jaw. His head snaps back and the guy stumbles and trips over someone's leg, landing on the ground. Despite my distaste for violence, a shiver of relief courses through me at the sight of Colton.

Before I can even react any further than shouting, "Colton, no!" one of the guy's buddies takes a swing at him. His fist glances off of Colton's cheek. I try to rush toward him, but my feet are cemented to the ground. Adrenaline, alcohol, and fear course through me. With lightning speed, Colton cocks his arm back to take another swing, murder in his eyes and an expressionless face. Before he can retaliate, Sammy's arms close around him and pull him back. Colton's rage is obvious. A vein pulses in his temple, his face is grimaced in restraint, and his eyes burn a threatening warning.

"Time to go, Colt!" Beckett shouts at him, a resigned look on his stoic face. "It's not worth the lawsuit they'll try to slap you with..." And then I see Haddie and several other guys from the crew in my periphery. The guys grab a still fuming but more collected Colton by the arms and take him from Sammy. Once Sammy knows that Colton's taken care of, he turns to the men, dwarfing them with his sheer size, a look of amused contempt on his face as if he's telling them, "Take a shot, I dare you." They look at him and then back at each other before scattering quickly as security makes its way toward us.

I stand there shaking until Sammy puts his arm around me and escorts me out of the club.

Chapter Nine

When Sammy pushes open the door for me, the cold air of the night hits me like a refreshing blast after the stuffy, smoke filled club. He leads me to the outskirts of the parking garage where the lone limo sits apart from the rest of the cars in the lot. As we get closer, I see Colton's back, his hands spread wide on the retaining wall bordering the edge of the garage, his weight leaning on them, and his head hanging down between his shoulders. I can sense the fury radiating off of him in waves as we draw near.

Beckett, who's leaning against the open door of the car, meets my eyes as we approach, uncertainty evident in his before nodding his head at me and sliding into the car next to Haddie. Sammy stops, but I continue forward toward Colton.

The click of my heels on the concrete alerts Colton that I'm near, but he remains facing away from me. I trace the lines of his body's silhouette against the expansive glitz of the Vegas strip, his imposing figure painting a striking contrast to the sparkle of lights beyond. I stop a few feet from him and watch his shoulders rise and fall in rapid succession as his tension slowly abates.

When he finally turns to face me, his shoulders squared, his eyes dancing with fire, and his jaw rigid with tension, I realize I'm wrong in thinking his anger is gone.

"What the fuck did you think you were doing?" His voice is ice cold.

His words hit me like whiplash, taking me aback with unbelievable force. I thought he was angry at the guy he punched, not with me. Where the hell does he get off being pissed at me? If he was paying attention to his date, he'd know the answer. "What do you think I was doing, Colton? That I was—"

"I asked you a question, Rylee," he grits out.

"And I was trying to fucking answer it before you so rudely cut me off," I spit at him, having no problem going toe-to-toe with him tonight. Maybe my intake of alcohol has taken a bit of the edge off, so I'm not intimidated by his intensity. His eyes pierce through the darkness and into mine. *Then again, maybe not.* "I was buying a drink, Colton. *A drink.* That's it!" I throw my hands up as I shout at him, my voice echoing off of the concrete walls.

He looks at me, the muscle in his jaw pulsing as he regards me. "Buying a drink, Rylee? Or flirting around to get someone to buy a drink for you?" he accuses, taking a step closer to me. Despite the lack of light, I can see the fire burning in his eyes and the rage fueling the tension in his neck. Where is all of this coming from?

What. The. Fuck? How dare he accuse me of paying attention to other guys when he was up there preoccupied with Ms. Bunny of the Month? I was being cool, not getting pissed off about how touchy-feely Cassandra was with him, trying to forgo the juvenile emotions I wanted to feel over it. *But fuck it.* If he's going to get mad about a guy offering to buy me a drink and touching me even though I said no, then I'm sure as hell going to be pissed about her blatantly displayed attraction to him. Attraction that he certainly didn't reject.

I'm done with this conversation. Alcohol and anger only result in words you can't take back in the morning. And we've both had way too much to be rational. "Whatever. We're done here," I huff as I turn on my heel, intent on heading back to the limo.

"Answer me," he commands as he grabs my upper arm, stopping me in my tracks. I see Beckett step back out of the limo, a wary look on his face as he stares down Colton over my shoulder. The silent warning is obvious, but the message behind it is unclear.

"What's it to you?"

"I'm waiting," he says, keeping his hand on my arm but stepping around to block my path toward the car.

"I was buying *myself* a drink. *That's it.* Big fucking deal!" I jerk my arm out of his grasp, fatigue from the night's events suddenly hitting me like a bat to the back of the head.

Colton's eyes bore into mine as if he's looking for my betrayal or confession of wrongdoing. "There was plenty of alcohol up top. Was that not good enough for you?" he taunts. "You had to go trolling for a guy to buy you one?"

His words slap at me, knock the wind from my sails. What the fuck is his problem? I can't believe that he'd even think that first of all, but second—and shockingly so—I'm surprised by the quiver in his voice that hints at a touch of insecurity.

Like I could want something more after having him.

I take a step toward him, my voice low but implacable. "I don't need a man *or* bottle service to make me happy, Colton."

He arches an eyebrow at me. "Uh-huh." He snorts derisively, clearly choosing to not believe me. *He's obviously dated some choice women.*

I sigh, frustrated already with our conversation. "You've spent enough money on tonight. On me. On everything." I huff. "You may be used to all of your *women* needing that to be satisfied. Not me."

"Of course not." He snorts sarcastically.

"I'm a big girl." I continue ignoring his flippant comment. "I can buy my own damn drinks and pay my own way, especially if when you pay it means that you have some kind of ownership over me."

His eyes widen at my words. "You're being ridiculous."

Does he not realize he does this? That he gives so charitably in exchange for people to like and love him? "Look, you're a very generous guy. More so than most people I know, but why?" I place my hand on his arm and squeeze. "Unlike most people in there, I don't expect you to pay my way."

"No girlfr—no one I'm with pays when they're with me."

"That's very chivalrous of you." I run my hand up his arm and lay it on his cheek, my voice softening, relieved that we have seemed to skirt around having this argument. "But I don't need any of that pomp and circumstance to want to be with you." He just stares at me, emerald irises trying to comprehend the honesty in my words. "You have so much more to give to someone than material excess."

I think my words have hit their mark because Colton falls silent, a war of emotions flowing through his eyes before they break from mine and look out at the city of sin. The muscle in his jaw tics as he pushes down whatever demons he's fighting internally. I notice his posture stiffen as he shakes my hand off his face, and I can sense his discomfort with the direction our conversation has taken. "You let a guy put his hands on you," he says in a dangerously quiet voice.

At first I'm hurt by his accusation, but when I look in his eyes, *I see it.* I see the truth behind Beckett's revelations about his feelings for me. I see that he's scared by it and unsure of how to handle it. I see that he's looking for a reason to pick a fight as a way to deny his feelings.

He wants a fight? I'll give him a fight because just below my surface is the fear that maybe I'm just what he needs and he might never acknowledge it. That he is exactly what I need and someone like Cassandra just might take that chance away from me. My mind flashes back to the thought of her hands on him. "And your point is what?" I counter with more confidence than I feel. "I'm not going to apologize because someone else finds me attractive." I shrug. "*You sure as hell weren't paying any attention to me.*"

He ignores my comment as only he can, shrugging it off as if I'm at fault here. "I've told you before, Ry, *I don't share.*"

I cross my arms over my chest. "*Well neither do I.*"

"What's that supposed to mean?" The bewildered look on his face tells me he really has no clue as to what I'm talking about. Typical, clueless male.

"Oh c'mon, Colton. Most of those women in there want you, and you were more than willing to be touchy-feely with them." I throw up my hands in frustration when he looks at me as if I've gone crazy, so I figure I'll give a specific example. "You seem to have no problem having your hands on Cassandra and hers on you," I accuse, flipping my hair like her and placing my hand on his chest, batting my eyelashes.

"Cassie?" he stutters incredulously. "Oh please."

"Really? It was obvious to every person up there that she wants you. Roll your eyes all you want and pretend you didn't notice, but you know you loved every minute of it—Center of attention, Colton. Life of the party, Colton. *Playboy, Colton,*" I accuse, turning my back to him, rolling my shoulders and shaking my head. I briefly lock eyes with Beckett who's still standing against the limo, arms crossed over his chest and stoic face devoid of judgment. I turn back to face Colton. "Why is that okay for you? Isn't turnabout fair play? At least I told the guy you punched to get his hands off of me. I didn't see you asking Cassie to stop…"

Colton takes a step toward me, lights from beyond playing against the shadows on his face. The devil has once again surfaced and is indeed trying to pull me into his darkness. "I believe it was you I was *fucking* up there tonight. Not any of them." His voice implacable and holding just a hint of edge as he watches for a reaction. I cringe knowing that Beckett just heard that.

"Yeah, you're right. You were with me, but I find it funny minutes later you were with her!" I shout back at him. "You punched a guy for touching me tonight and yet you stood there and let her rub up against you without so much as a thought to pushing her off you. Well I don't share either. The irony, huh?"

Colton's jaw flexes before he raises his eyebrows, a ghost of a smile gracing his lips. "I didn't take you for the jealous type."

"And I didn't take you for my type at all," I counter, my voice icy with contempt.

"Watch it," he warns.

"Or what?" I goad, taking a fortifying breath. "Like I said, I can take care of myself. The guy offered to buy me a drink. I was in the process of telling him no thank you in so many words when you stormed up to save the day." I'm not sure why I feel the need to lie about this. Maybe I'm trying to prove to Colton that I can in fact take care of myself. That I don't need the macho bullshit. I'm not sure, but I've thrown it out there, I might as well follow through with it. He doesn't have to know that I was getting a little unnerved at the situation. "The guy didn't deserve to be hit."

Colton's head snaps up as if I've just punched him. "Now you're defending him?" He brings his hands up to his neck and pulls down on it in frustration. "You're fucking unbelievable!" he shouts out into the empty garage.

"And you're drunk, irrational, and out of control!" I yell back.

"No one touches what's mine without consequences," he grates out.

"You have to have me first, Colton," I say with a shake of my head, "and you've made it quite clear that all you want from me is a quick fuck when it's convenient for you!" My voice is firm but betrays me when it wavers on my last words.

"You know that's not true." His voice is quiet with an undertone of desperation.

"I do? How's that?" I throw my hands up in exasperation. "Every time I get too close or things go beyond your stupid rules, you make sure to put me in my place."

"Jesus. Fucking. Christ. Rylee." He exhales through gritted teeth, running his fingers through his hair and turning from me to walk a few steps away.

"A *pit stop* isn't going to save you this time," I state calmly, wanting him to know that he can't cop out now to avoid the rest of this discussion. I *need* answers and deserve to know where I stand.

He hisses out a loud exhale of breath, his hands clenching and unclenching at his sides. We stand there in silence for a few moments as I look at his back, and he looks at the city beyond. After a moment he turns around and holds his arms out, his eyes full of a nameless emotion I can't decipher. "This is me, Rylee!" he shouts. "All of me in my fucked up glory! I'm not Max—*perfect in every way*, never making a god-damned mistake. I can't live up to the incomparable standard he's set, to the pedestal you've placed him on!"

I suck in a breath, his words hitting their target. How dare he throw Max and what we had in my face. Thoughts don't process. Words don't form. Tears well in my eyes as I think about Max and who he was and Colton and what he is to me. Confusion swamps me. Drags me under. Drowns me.

"How dare you!" I growl at him, hurt surrendering to anger before succumbing to grief.

Colton's not finished though. He takes a step toward me, pointing his finger at his chest. "But I'm alive, Rylee, and *he's not*!" His words rip into me. A tear slides down my cheek, and I turn my back to him, hiding from his words, thinking if I can't see the plea and hurt in his eyes, I won't have to accept the truth in his statement. "I'm the one here in front of you—*flesh and blood and needing*—so either you accept that it's you that I want. No one else," he rants, his voice echoing off of the concrete surrounding us and coming back to me twice as if to reinforce his words. "You need to accept me for who I am, faults and all..." his voice breaks "...or you need to get the fuck out of my life…because right now—*right now*—this is all that I can give you! All I can offer."

I can hear the pain in his voice, can feel the agony in his words, and it tears at me until a sob escapes my mouth. I bring my hand up to cover it while I clutch my other hand around my abdomen.

"That's enough, Colton!" Beckett's voice pierces through the early morning hour when he sees my anguish. "It's enough!"

In my periphery, I see Colton whirl toward him, fists clenched, emotion overwhelming him. Beckett doesn't flinch from Colton's imposing stare but rather takes another step toward him, taunting him with his eyes. "Try me, Wood," he challenges, his voice hard as steel. "You come at me and I'll knock you on that drunk, pretty-boy ass of yours in a heartbeat."

My eyes meet Beckett's for a fleeting second, the ice in his eyes surprising me before I turn to look at Colton. The features on his face are tight, and his dark hair has fallen over his forehead. The angst in his eyes is so incredibly raw. I study him as he glares at Beckett. His eyes flicker over to mine and whatever ex-pression blankets my face holds his stare. I can see his pain and fear and uncertainty in them, and I realize that as much as his words sting—as much as they hurt me to hear—there is so much truth to them.

Max is dead and never coming back. Colton is here and very much alive, and he wants me in his life in some form or another despite his inability to acknowledge or accept it. I see the plea in his eyes for me to choose him, to accept him. Not my ghost of memories. Just him. All of him. *Even the parts that are broken.*

And the choice is so easy, I don't even have to make one.

I step forward toward the eyes that flit frantically back and forth like a lost little boy. I glance over at Beckett and give him an unsure smile. "It's okay, Becks. He's right," I whisper, turning back to Colton. "You're right. I can't keep expecting you to be like Max or compare you to what I had with him." I take another timid step toward him.

"And I don't want you to think that you have to be like Cassandra," he says, taking me by surprise that his inference about my insecurity is spot-on. I reach out my hand to him, an olive branch to our argument, and he takes it, pulling me into him. I land against the firmness of his body as he gathers me to his chest, his strong arms wrapped around me a reassurance after the cruel and callous insults we've just hurled at each other. I press my face into his neck, the beat of his pulse beneath my lips. He runs a hand up my back, tunneling it into my curls and just holds my head there. He kisses the top of my hair as I breathe in his scent.

"You. *This*," he murmurs in a ragged exhale, "it scares the shit out of me." And my heart stops and breath catches as he falls silent, his pounding heartbeat the soundtrack to my thoughts. "I don't know *how* to…I don't know *what* to do…"

And if I hadn't already known, the raw emotion in his voice would have pushed me over the edge. My heart starts again, tumbles inside of me, and falls gloriously. I only hope he'll catch it. I fist my hand into the back of his shirt, his confession rocking me with hope and possibility. Offering us a chance. I close my eyes, taking a minute to score my memory with this moment. "*Me too, Colton*," I murmur into the skin of his neck. "*I'm scared too*."

"You deserve so much more than I'm capable of giving you. I don't know how or what to do to give you what you need. I just…"

I grip my fist tighter into his shirt, the fear so transparent in his tone it wrenches my heart and tugs at my soul. "That's okay, baby," I tell him, pressing another kiss against his neck. "We don't have to know all the answers right now."

"This is just…" He chokes on his words, his arms tightening around me as the sounds of Vegas swirl in the air around us. In this city of rampant sin and immorality, I have found such beauty and hope in the man holding me tight. "…so much…I don't know how…"

"We don't have to rush this. We can just take our time and see where this leads us." Desperation laces through my words.

"I don't want to give you false hope if I can't…" He shakes his head softly with an exhale to finish his statement.

I lean back and look up at the face of the man that I know has captured my heart. The heart I thought would never heal or love again. "Just try, Colton," I plead. "Please just tell me you'll try…"

Emotions war over Colton's features, his resistance to need. So much unspoken swims in his eyes. He leans down and brushes a soft, reverent sigh of a kiss on my lips before burying his face in the crook of my neck and just holds on.

I hold him there in the depths of a concrete garage. Giving as much as I am taking from the man consuming every part of me.

And it's not lost on me that he never answered my question.

The horizon is just starting to lighten to the east as we drag ourselves off of the plane and climb into the awaiting limo in Santa Monica. We are all exhausted from the whirlwind night.

I glance over at Colton's profile as we wait for Sammy to finish whatever he's doing. His head is leaning back against the headrest and his eyes are closed. My eyes track over the silhouette of his nose to his chin, down his neck and over his Adam's apple. My heart swells at the sight of him and what he's come to mean to me in such a short amount of time. He's helping me overcome some of my fears, and I can only hope in time he will trust me enough to let me in on his.

Beckett was right about Colton. He evokes such extreme emotions. He's easy to love and hate at the same time. Tonight was a breakthrough of sorts—for him to admit that I scare him—but I know in no way shape or form does that mean he's in love with me. Or that he's not going to hurt me in the end.

His lack of an answer tells me that his words and his heart are still in conflict. And that he's not sure if he can get them on the same page. He wants to. I can see it in his eyes, his posture, and the tenderness in his kiss.

But I also see the fear, sense the trepidation and inability to trust that I won't abandon him. That to love is not to give up control.

It seems like every time he gets too close, he wants to push me further away. Holding me at arms length keeps his fears at bay for a bit. Helps him push them down. Well, what if I just don't cower at the comments? Worry about his silent distance? What if instead of letting it get to me, I just shrug it off and keep going like nothing's been said? What will he do then?

Colton shifts his head over and looks at me with a softness in his eyes that makes me want to curl into him. How could I ever walk away from this face? Nothing short of him cheating on me would make me give up on him. He looks sleepy and content and still a bit buzzed.

Haddie hums the song that is playing softly on the speakers in the car. I strain to hear and meet her eyes when I recognize it as *Glitter in the Air*. Of all the songs to be on, of course it has to be this one.

"Fuckin' Pink," Colton snorts out in a sexy, sleepy voice that widens my smile.

Haddie laughs sluggishly in the seat across from us. "I could sleep for hours," she says resting her head on Beckett's shoulder.

"Mmm-hmm," Colton murmurs, shifting so he lies across the seat and places his head in my lap, "and I'm going to start now." He chuckles.

"You need all the beauty sleep you can get."

"Fuck you, Becks." Colton yawns. His voice is slurred from the mixture of both alcohol and exhaustion. "Should we finish what we started earlier?" He laughs softly as he tries to open his eyes. He is so exhausted they only open a fraction.

Beckett bellows out a laugh that resonates in the quiet of the car. "It'd be no contest. Us southern boys know how to throw a punch."

"You've got nothing on some of the fists that have been thrown my way." Colton nuzzles the back of his head into my abdomen.

"Really? Being bitch-slapped by a girl pissed off at finding out she's a one-nighter doesn't count," Beckett replies, meeting my eyes and shaking his head to tell me that he's making it up just to goad Colton. I have a feeling he might be lying.

"Mmm-hmm," Colton murmurs and then falls silent. We all assume that he's asleep, his breathing evening out, when he speaks again in an almost juvenile, dreamlike quality. "Try having your mom taking a bat to you…" he breathes "…or snapping your bone right through your fucking arm." He grunts. My eyes whip up to Beckett's, the same look of surprise I feel reflected in his. "Now that? That beats the one fucking punch I'd let you land before I knock you on your ass." He emits a sliver of a laugh. "It most definitely beats your fist any day, you cocksucker," he repeats before a soft snore slips from him.

My mind immediately flashes to the jagged scar on his arm—the one that I'd noticed last week. Now I know why he had changed the subject when I'd asked about it. I think of a little boy cowering in fear, green eyes welled with tears as his mother unleashes on him. The ache in my heart that moments before was because of my feelings for Colton has now shifted and intensified over something I can't even begin to understand or fathom.

The look on Beckett's face tells me that this is news to him. That even though he's known Colton for all these years, he hasn't had an inkling as to the horror his friend had endured as a young child.

"Like I said," Beckett whispers, "*Lifeline.*" My eyes snap up to his and he just nods with a quiet intensity. "*I think you're his lifeline.*" We exchange a silent acknowledgment and acceptance before looking back down at the man we love snoring softly in my lap.

Chapter Ten

The house is quiet and still despite the bright sun shining through the kitchen windows. It's close to noon but everyone is still asleep except for me. I'd awoken, hot and claustrophobic, with a dead to the world Colton haphazardly draped across my body. As delicious as his body felt against mine, and as much as I willed myself to go back to sleep, I couldn't. So despite Colton lying on the pillow beside me, I slowly extricated myself from him and the bed without waking him in search of Advil for my aching head.

I sit at the table, the soft snoring of Beckett asleep on the couch drifting into the kitchen. I swallow a big gulp of water hoping it will chase away the alcohol-induced fuzziness that clouds my head. I yawn again and rest my forehead on my arms that are folded on the table. *God, I'm tired.*

The distant and distinct ringing of my cell phone seeps into my dreams. I'm trying to help him. The little boy with dark hair and haunted eyes being pulled away from me by some unseen force. My hand is gripping his but my fingers are slipping ever so slowly as my muscles tire. He's pleading with me for help. The ringing of the telephone starts, startling me so I jerk and he slips away from me, crying out in fear. I scream at the loss and jolt myself awake, disoriented from my position at the kitchen table.

My heart is pounding and my breathing labored as I try to steady myself. *Just a dream,* I tell myself. Just a meaningless dream. I drop my head into my hands and push their heels into my eyes, trying to rub away the image of the little boy I couldn't save.

I hear the rumbling timbre of Colton's morning voice from my bedroom. I stand and start to walk to him when the inflection of his voice rises. "You've got a lot of nerve, lady!" resonates down the hallway.

It takes a moment for my mind to register what's going on...what day it is...the sound of my cell phone interrupting my dream. I shove the chair back and run down the hall to my bedroom. "Give me the phone, Colton!" I shout, my heart racing and my throat clogging with panic as I enter my doorway.

My eyes zero in on my cell phone at his ear. *On the bewildered look on his face.* My heart lodges in my throat, knowing the words filled with hatred that are assaulting his ears. I pray that she doesn't tell him. "Please, Colton," I plead, my hand outstretched for him to give me my phone. His eyes look up to meet mine, searching for an explanation as to what he's hearing. He shakes his head abruptly at me when I keep my hand held out.

He sighs loudly, closing his eyes before speaking. "Ma'am? Ma'am," he says more forcefully, "you've had your say, now it's time I get mine." Her voice through the speaker quiets down at his stern tone. Colton runs a hand through his hair, his V of muscle that sinks below the sheets flexes as he tenses up. "While I am truly sorry for the loss of your son, I think your accusations are sickening. Rylee did nothing wrong besides survive a horrible accident. Because she lived and Max died doesn't mean that she murdered him. No, you let me finish," he says sternly. "I understand that you're grieving and always will be, but that doesn't make Rylee guilty of killing him. It was a horrific, accident with circumstances beyond anyone's control."

I hear a litany of words in response that I can't decipher through the earpiece, my body still tense as I guess what she's revealing to him.

"And you don't think she feels guilty enough that she lived? You're not the only one who lost him that day. Do you really think a day goes by that she doesn't think about Max or the accident? That she doesn't wish it were her instead of him that died that day?"

Tears well in my eyes, Colton's words hitting too close to the truth, and I can't fight them. They slip down my cheeks and images flash through my head that will forever be burned there. Max struggling to live. Max struggling to die. My thousands of promises to God those days if we could just make it out alive.

All of us.

Something flickers through Colton's eyes at her words, and the tears come harder. There is silence between the two of them for several moments as Colton digests what she has divulged. They flash over to mine, and I'm unable to comprehend the enigmatic look they hold before darting back to look out the window outside.

"I truly am sorry for your loss, but this will be the last time you call Rylee and accuse her of anything. Do you understand?" he says with authority. "She picks up the phone because she feels guilty. She lets you bash her and accuse her and demean her because she loved your son and doesn't want you to hurt any more than you already do. *But no more*. You're hurting her, and I won't allow it. Understood?"

Colton blows out a large breath and tosses the phone onto the end of the bed where he stares at it for several moments without speaking. My heart pounds, the sound reverberating through my ears as I stare at him, emotions racing through me, tearing me apart as I wait.

Finally after what feels like hours, he shakes his head and looks down at his hands in his lap. "You are the most selfless woman I know, Rylee. Carrying around your own guilt. Allowing her to take her grief out on you. Giving everything of yourself to the boys…" My body trembles in anticipation of what he'll say next, of why he's looking at his hands and can't meet my eyes. So many emotions overwhelm me, thunder through me as I wait for him to collect his thoughts.

He looks over at me slowly, his eyes filled with a mixture of confusion and compassion. "Why didn't you tell me?" he asks gently, his eyes searching mine for an explanation.

I shrug, averting my eyes from his, trying to hold back the damn that threatens to break. I fail miserably, the dam splintering and the tears turn to sobs as he reaches out a hand and pulls me toward him. I sink onto my bed as he wraps his arms around me and gathers me to him. He smoothes a hand over my hair repeatedly, trying to soothe away my pain with reassuring words while I cry. He releases me momentarily, propping pillows behind him before lying back and pulling me with him so my head rests on his bare chest, my hand covering his heart.

The constant rhythm of Colton's heartbeat calms me. I realize that being here with Colton takes some of the sting out of today's date. It doesn't hurt any less, but it's getting easier. I realize that for the first time, I can think of Max and see him in good times, not just the final images I have of him broken, bloody, and dying. I can smile about the teenager I fell in puppy love with and the man I promised to spend my life with. I can remember the anxiety in his face the day he proposed and the surprise, love, and excitement in his eyes when I told him I was pregnant. God, I was so scared to tell him—hell I was scared myself—but when he hugged me and told me he was ecstatic and that everything would be alright, I allowed myself to feel the hope and wonderment I'd been holding back.

Colton places a soft kiss on the top of my head. "Do you want to talk about it?"

I almost laugh at his words. They sound so hypocritical coming from someone who never talks about his past. A few tears escape, falling onto his chest, and I quickly wipe them away. "I'm sorry," I apologize. I can't look at him. "I'm sure after last night, the last thing you want to deal with is a blubbering idiot."

He lifts his arm and runs his hand through his hair, sighing out loud. "I'm not good at this kind of thing, Rylee. Shit, I don't know what to do or say here…"

I can sense his discomfort at a woman falling apart in his arms. He hates drama. I know. I stroke my hand down his chest. "You don't have to do anything. You being here, sticking up for me with Claire..." I breathe out "...that's enough."

"How come you didn't tell me?" I can hear a trace of hurt in his voice, and it surprises me.

And I know he is referring to the baby. *My baby*. The part of me that forever died that day. The place that will forever be empty inside of me.

"It's not like you're exactly forthcoming about your baggage," I offer, the words hanging between us in silence. "You're so adamant about no children, I didn't think it was important for you to know. I didn't think you'd care."

I can feel him draw in a breath. "*Christ, Rylee.*" His voice strains, his hand fisting against my back. "Do you think that little of me? Just because kids are a deal breaker for me doesn't mean that I'm not sympathetic to your situation. To your loss."

I turn my head to prop my chin on my hand. I keep my eyes averted from his though by following my finger as it traces the lines of his tattoo that spans a portion of his rib cage. "I was…" I stop, trying to map out my memories. "I was shocked the day I found out I was pregnant. I mean I'd just graduated college. I was very black and white back then. I had a plan. First college, then marriage, and then a family," I smile softly.

"But you know what they say about best laid plans." I sigh shakily. "I was so scared of what Max's reaction was going to be. And when I told him, he looked at me in awe. I can still see him in my mind. He admitted he was scared but told me that it didn't matter because it was going to be okay. And I wondered how he could be so sure when everything was going to change so drastically."

I'm silent for a moment, my memories flashing through my mind like a slide show. I turn and shift my head to look at Colton as a tear slips silently from the corner of my eye. "She," I say on a shaky breath, "the baby was a girl." He nods his head at me and reaches out to wipe away the tear. "I was still scared and panicked at the thought of having a baby, but then I felt her kick." I stop, my chest tightening as I remember the feeling that I'll never experience again. "And I immediately fell in love with her. All of my reluctance faded." I clear my throat as Colton sits patiently, eyes locked on mine. "I was seven and half months along when we had the accident. I knew that first night she didn't make it, but I refused to acknowledge it. I was bleeding profusely and the cramping was…it was out of this world painful. I willed her to move. To kick me just once."

A shudder runs through me, those silent bargains I had made to God that night flickering through my head. "On some level, I knew the hope that she might still be alive is what kept me fighting to live."

"I'm so sorry, Rylee," he whispers.

"It took so long to be rescued that I got an infection from the bacteria. From what doctors saw, the damage was extensive enough that it essentially ruined my ability to get pregnant." I clear my throat before continuing. "Max's mom, Claire, blames me for everything."

"That's asinine," he interjects.

I shrug at his comment, agreeing but still letting guilt make me think differently. "She thought that if we hadn't been having premarital sex, this would have never happened."

Colton snorts at the comment. "You were together, what six years?"

I smile softly at him. "Almost seven."

"And she expected you to be abstinent that long?"

"To each their own beliefs." I shrug. "We went on the little trip because it was our last chance to get away. I was stressed about everything and the doctor was getting worried about my blood pressure. Max wanted to try and calm me down. To spend some time together before chaos ensued. So she blames me for killing him and her granddaughter."

"You know that's not true, Rylee."

"I know, but it doesn't take the guilt away. On the anniversary of the death and his birthday she calls me to vent her anger and sadness." I close my eyes momentarily, fighting away the horrible images that creep into my dreams. "It's her therapy I guess…and even though it tears me apart, listening to her is the least I can do." He pulls me farther up his chest and comforts me by wrapping his powerful arms around me and resting his chin on my head. "Oddly enough, meeting you, spending time with you, has allowed me to realize that I'm slowly coming to terms with what happened. Time has allowed me to remember Max and how he was before the crash, not just after. I think the hardest part is the baby." I exhale brokenly. "I will always cherish the feeling of a life growing inside of me, especially since I'll most likely never get that chance again." I nuzzle into the warmth of his neck and sigh. "She would have been two years old."

I catch the sob before it slips out, but Colton feels it. He squeezes me tighter, his even breathing and ability to listen is just what I need. I feel like a burden has been lifted off of me. All of my skeletons have been exposed. Now he knows. Everything. I cling to him because for some reason, his presence here completes the transformation for me.

I don't want to be alone anymore and am so sick of being numb. I want to feel again—in the extremes that Colton makes me feel.

I'm ready to live again. Really live. And in this moment I know that it is only Colton that I can imagine sharing these new memories with. I close my eyes and snuggle into him, the sleep I couldn't find earlier slowly claiming me now. I am just starting to drift off when his voice stirs my eyes open. "When I was six years old," he says so softly that if it weren't for the vibration in his chest, I wouldn't know to listen for his words. He stops for a moment and clears his throat. "When I was six, my—the woman who gave birth to me—beat me so badly that I ended up unconscious and in the hospital." He exhales loudly while I withhold my breath.

Holy shit! He's talking and hearing the pain in his voice I know that his wounds are still raw and wide open. Infected. How can you heal from your mother beating the crap out of you? How can you accept love from anyone when the one person that is supposed to protect you from everything is the one who harmed you the most? I'm at a loss for words, so I wrap my arms around him and squeeze before placing a soft kiss on his sternum. "Did the hospital call the police? Social services?" I ask timidly, unsure of how much he is willing to share with me.

I can feel him nod his head in assent. "My mom was the one who called 9-1-1. She told them my dad had done it. That she was the one who walked in and stopped it." He pauses, and I let him take a minute to compose himself and clear the emotion swimming in his voice. "I've never met my dad so...I was too scared of what she'd do to me to say otherwise…too young to know that life could be any better than what I had. She pulled me from school after that. Moved around a lot so social services couldn't check up on us…" His words drift off and there are so many thoughts running through my head, so many things I want to tell him to console him. That it wasn't his fault. That love doesn't have to be that way. That he is a true survivor for coming out of it and thriving. But I know my words will do nothing to take away the years of abuse that he must have endured or lessen its psychological after effects. Besides, I'm sure he's heard it all from psychiatrists time and time again.

I look up at him and the haunted look in his eyes tells me what he's just admitted is the least of his childhood nightmares. Do I tell him what he confessed last night in the limo? I struggle with the decision and choose not to. Sharing his past has to be on his terms. I open my mouth to speak, but he cuts me off before I can begin. "Rylee, please don't feel sorry for me."

"I'm...I'm not," I stutter, knowing that's the last thing he wants, but he can see right through my lie. How can I not feel sorry for the little boy he once was?

"That life was a long time ago for me. That little boy—he is a different person than I am now."

Bullshit. He is who he is because of what happened to him. Does he not see that?

I press a soft kiss on the center of his chest. "Do you know what happened to your mom?" I say in a hesitant voice, almost afraid to ask but also wanting to know as much as I can since he is talking.

He's quiet for a moment. He lifts his hand from my back and runs it over his stubbled jaw before exhaling loudly. "After my dad found me on the steps of his trailer…he brought me to the hospital. Stayed with me," he retells, utter reverence in his voice. "Little did I know he was this big time director. Not that I would have even known what that meant though. Later…much later, I learned that he'd wasted a whole day of studio time sitting with me in the hospital. At the time, all I remember thinking was he had the gentlest voice and his eyes. They didn't look mean even though I flinched when he touched me..." He trails off, lost in memories, and I let him for a moment.

"…and he ordered me every kind of food imaginable and had it delivered to the hospital room. I'll never forget the look on his face as he watched me eat things I'd never had. Things every boy at that age should have had many times over by then. I remember pretending to be asleep when the police told him they found my mom and were bringing her in for questioning…that the x-rays and exams had shown years of…" He pauses, trying to find the right word as I hold my breath wondering which one of the horrific options he'll use. "*Neglect.* And it is the only time in my life I've ever heard my dad use his stature to get what he wanted. I heard him ask the police officers if they knew who he was. To clear it with whomever they needed to, but that I was going to be under his custody from then on. That he'd get a team of lawyers if need be, but that's how it was going to be." He shakes his head with a soft laugh.

"That's…" I'm at a loss for words. I don't want to cheapen the memory by saying the wrong words, so I just leave it at that.

"Yeah." He breathes. "I saw my mom once more, but it was across the courtroom. I know she went to jail, but I don't know anything more than that. Never wanted to know. Why do you ask?"

"I just wondered how you left it. I thought maybe if you found out what happened to her…fill in any blanks you want to, that it might help. The nightmares might go away and—"

"I think that's enough *sharing* for today," he says, cutting me off and shifting our bodies abruptly so that I'm on my back and he's lying half on me, his legs scissored with mine.

"Oh really?" I smile when I see the tension ease from his face and pain fade from his eyes. "Is the only way to get you to talk, a trade? Tit for tat so to speak?"

"Well..." he smirks pressing me into the mattress with his hips "...you have seen my tats." He arches his eyebrows suggestively. "It's only fair..."

Colton's sudden change of subject is not lost on me. His inherent turn toward making things physical between us when I delve a little too deep. Normally I'd hesitate at using intimacy to ease the ache of sadness within, but this morning I just want him to help me forget for just a little bit the tears left in my soul from that day two years ago.

I wriggle beneath him, my body humming with need for his, loving the playful side that has re-emerged to lighten the dark of our morning. "And I thought you said we were *done with sharing* for today." The sound of his laugh is welcome as it rumbles through his chest into mine. I lift my head up and capture his bottom lip and pull on it. The low growl of desire in the back of his throat stokes my craving for him.

His hand brushes against my ribcage and palms my one breast not covered by his chest. He grazes a thumb over my already pert nipple, his touch a ripple of sensation slowly swelling through me. He leans down and presses a soft kiss to my lips. "Now about that tit," he murmurs, a smile curling the corners of his mouth. He squeezes my nipple between his thumb and forefinger and my gasp is absorbed by his mouth on mine.

"Will I ever get enough of you?" he asks against my lips. And I wonder the same thing. Will I ever tire of him? *Of this?* Of his taste or his touch or the rumble in his throat expressing how I make him feel when I touch him? Will he always bring me to such an aroused fever pitch? Surely my desire has to be sated at some point. From his touch alone, my thoughts are lost with only one remaining. Flickering through my mind.

Never.

Chapter Eleven

Avery smiles at me as I go over some of the schedules and our standard rules and procedures. "I know it's a lot to take in, but once you get familiar with it, you won't have to think twice about it."

She nods her head at me and looks over at Zander. He's sitting on the couch, tattered stuffed doggy clutched to his chest, watching television. "What's his story?" she asks quietly.

I look over my shoulder at Zander and smile. While still not talking much besides sporadic words here and there since the racetrack, he seems to be doing better. He is interacting a bit more with the boys, and I can see traces of emotion on his face whereas before it was blank. The therapist says he's starting to participate, starting to interact with her.

It's a start. Progress takes time.

Protective of my kids like a mother hen, I rarely share their backgrounds until a new employee has been with me for a while. "That's Zander. He doesn't talk much, but we're working on it. He was in a rough situation that he's dealing with internally. He'll get there though."

She gives me a quizzical look, but I ignore her interest and begin reviewing the next set of procedures. The doorbell rings and the unexpected interruption startles me. Jax is at baseball practice with Shane and Connor, so I rise to get the door.

When I look through the peephole, I'm caught off guard at the sight of Colton's sister. I open the door cautiously, curiosity getting the better of me. "What a surprise! Hello, Quinlan." I try to smile brightly at her all the while my heart beats rapidly at her presence. I marvel at how such a sweet looking, beautiful woman can instill such anxiety in me.

"Rylee." She nods, her perfect lips not quite forming a smile. "I came to get a tour of the place before I make a donation to the new project. I want to know exactly what my money is going to be used for."

Well, hello to you too! I smile tightly, inviting her in. She could at least grace me with a little warmth—anything to melt her icy façade. *What the hell have I done to her to deserve this deliberate chill?*

"I'd be glad to give you a tour," I force, wishing I could pawn her off on another counselor to show her around, but my manners and professionalism win out. Besides, something tells me this little visit is about more than checking out the facility for a donation. I plaster a fake smile on my face. "Please follow me."

I inform Avery that she's in charge of watching the boys and then proceed to show Quinlan the entire facility and explain its benefits. I'm probably rambling but she hasn't asked any questions. Rather she has just stared at me the whole time with a quiet yet critical appraisal. And after about twenty minutes, I realize the inspection isn't being done on The House or what we have to offer my boys. It's solely on me.

I've had enough.

I glance to make sure that all of the boys are still outside playing with Avery before turning to face her. "Why is it you're really here, Quinlan?" My tone matches the fuck you, no nonsense that I feel.

"To see if the facility is worthy of my donation," she responds too sweetly to be true. She holds my gaze but I see something flicker in the ice queen's eyes.

"I appreciate it as the facility and the kids are worthy of it," I tell her, "but let's be honest, why are you here? To see if the facility is worthy of your donation or if I'm worthy of your brother?" Quinlan's eyes flash as I hit a direct bull's-eye. Being protective of your brother is one thing. *I understand that.* Being a complete bitch is a whole different story. "Which one is it?"

She cocks her head and looks at me. "I'm just trying to figure out your angle."

"My angle?"

"Yes, your angle." Her voice is implacable and her eyes are right up there with Colton's on the intensity scale. "You're not the typical bimbo that Colton goes for...so I'm trying to figure out what exactly it is you want out of this. From him." She twists her lips as she stares at me. I'm sure the shocked look on my face is something to stare at.

"I beg your pardon," I sputter, more than offended.

"Are you a race groupie? Are you looking to land a part in my dad's newest film? An aspiring model looking to sleep your way up the ranks? I can't wait to hear what yours will be."

"*What?*" I just stare at her for a moment, shock ricocheting through me until it churns to anger. "How dare you—"

"Oh, I get it now." She smirks, sarcasm dripping from her words, and all I want to do is throttle her. "You need his money to finish this little project of yours," she says, motioning to the space around her. "You're using him to get your notoriety that way."

"That's uncalled for." I take a step forward, pushed to the point that I don't care that she's Colton's sister. I'd like to say something a lot worse, but I'm at work and I never know when impressionable ears are listening. But I can only be pushed so far before I throw my manners out the window, and she just shoved. "You know what, Quin? I've tried to be nice, tried to overlook your shitty attitude and your condescending sneer, but *I'm done*. Colton pursued me—not the other way around." She arches an eyebrow at me as if she doesn't believe me. "Yeah..." I laugh "...I find it hard to believe too, but he did. I don't want a damn thing from your brother except for him to open up to the possibility that he deserves more than what he's allowed himself thus far in his life." I step back, shaking my head at her. "I don't need to explain myself to you or justify your asinine accusations. Thanks for your false pretense of a donation, but I don't want your money. *Not in return for your judgment on me*. I think it's time you leave." I point toward the hallway, my body vibrating with anger.

She smiles broadly at me, her face dropping its guard and filling with warmth for the first time since I've met her. "Not yet. We're not done here."

What? Great, can't wait for the rest of this stimulating conversation.

"I knew you were for real." She smirks, pulling in a deep breath. "I just needed to make sure that I was right."

Whiplash.

Did I miss something here? I'm so confused right now that my mouth opens as I look at her like she's bat-shit-crazy. The schizophrenic changing of subjects like Colton does must run in the family.

When I just stand there staring at her with disdain she continues. "I've never seen Colton like that at the track before. He brings his bimbos, they flit around like arm candy, but he disregards them. He never lets someone distract him when he's in the car. *You distracted him*. I've never seen him so..." she searches for a word "...smitten with someone before." She crosses her arms across her chest and leans against the wall. "And my dad tells me you were at the Broadbeach house? *Then to top it off Becks tells me you went to Vegas with them?"*

What is it with the women in Colton's life keeping tabs on me and passing judgment?

Smitten? Colton may have said that I scare him, but in no way did he infer love or even hint at that. Definitely not smitten. I'm something different than his typical in-your-face, I-want-something-from-you-in-return type of girl. *I burn him. I scare him.* But for some reason despite all of that, I don't make him want to try for something more than what he's used to. I'm not enough to make him change his ways. He's not going to confront his demons when he's not even willing to talk about them. And that's the only way I think he'll be able to give into the emotion I see brimming in his eyes and feel in the worshiping actions of his touch.

I shake myself from my thoughts and focus on Quinlan. She stares at me. Really stares at me causing me to squirm under her silent scrutiny. "And your point is what, Quinlan?"

"Listen, as much as Colt tries to play Mr. Aloof and think that I don't—shit my whole family..." she exhales "...doesn't know about his little *arrangements*..." she rolls her eyes in disgust as she says the word, "It's no secret to us. *His stupid rules and sexist ways run amok*. And as much as I disagree with him and his antics, I know it's the only way he thinks he can have a relationship...*his necessary* way of dealing with his past." Her eyes hold mine and I realize she is apologizing for her brother. For what he thinks he can't give me. Over the fact that he's afraid to even try.

"Was it that horrible?" I whisper, already knowing the answer.

Finally a softness plies her steeped countenance as a true sadness fills her eyes. She nods her head subtly. "He rarely speaks of it, and I'm certain there are parts that he's never spoken about, Rylee. Experiences that I can't even begin to fathom." She looks down at her pink painted nails and twists her fingers into each other. "Having parents who don't want you is hard enough to come to grips with when you're adopted. Colton...Colton had so much more than that to overcome." She shakes her head and I can see that she is struggling with how much to tell me. She looks up at me, eyes clear yet conflicted. "An eight year old boy so hungry—locked in his room while his mom did God knows what for days—that he somehow escaped and went in search for food, luckily collapsing on my dad's doorstep."

I suck in a breath, my heart quickening, my soul wrenching, and my faith in humanity crumbling.

"That's just a small snippet of his hell, but it's his story to tell you, Rylee. Not mine. I'm only sharing so you have an iota of what he's been through. Of the patience and persistence you're going to need."

I nod in understanding, unsure of what to say next to a woman who moments before was berating me and who is now giving me advice. "So..."

"So I had to make sure you were for real." She offers me an apologetic smile of resignation. "And once I did, I wanted to get a good look at the first woman that might be the one to make him whole again."

Her words stagger me. "You've taken me by surprise here," I admit, unsure of what else to say.

"I know that I may be coming off a little strong, presumptuous even in being here...but I love Colton more than anything in the world." She smiles softly at his name. "And I'm just looking out for him. I want nothing less than the best for him."

This I can understand.

She pushes off the wall and straightens herself in front of me. "Look, if you look past the gorgeously rough exterior...there's a scared little boy inside that's afraid of love. That for some reason he associates love with horrific expectations one minute and then thinks he's not worthy of it the next. I think he's afraid to love someone because he knows that they'll leave. He'll most likely hurt you to prove that you will..." she shakes her head "...and for that hell alone, I apologize because from what I can tell, you deserve better than that."

Her words hit me in their full force. I understand the little boy inside because I have a backyard full of them right now with issues of their own. I just wish they had the unconditional love that Colton seems to have in Beckett and Quinlan. Someone who stands up for them and looks out for them because they want nothing but the best for them. This love—this protective feeling—I understand.

Quinlan reaches out and places her hand on my arm and squeezes to make her point. "I love my brother dearly, Rylee. Some would say that I worshiped the ground he walked on growing up." She reaches in her pocket and pulls something out, averting her eyes from mine. "I'm sorry for my intrusion. I really shouldn't be here...interfering." She seems embarrassed all of a sudden as she steps toward the door. She reaches out her hand and places a check in mine. Her eyes look up to meet mine, and for the first time I see acceptance in them. "Thank you for your time, Rylee." She takes a step past me and then hesitates and looks back at me. "If you get the chance, take care of my brother."

I nod in acknowledgement and all I can manage is a stilted, "Bye," as my head is in a whirlwind of chaos over her unexpected revelations.

Chapter Twelve

The scream wakes me in the dead night. It's a strangled, feral plea that goes on and on, over and over before I can even get out of the bedroom door. I race through the house toward the sound of unfettered terror, Dane and Avery right behind me, our footsteps pounding with urgency.

"Moooooommmmm!" Zander screams. I bolt through the door of his room as the soul shattering sound ricochets against the bedroom walls. He thrashes violently in his bed. "Nooooo! Noooo!"

I hear Shane's panicked voice in the hallway, trying to help Dane settle down the little guys who have woken up and are now frightened. The thought flits through my mind on how sad it is that night terrors are such a regular visitor in this house that Shane's no longer phased by them. But I focus solely on Zander now, knowing that Dane will take care of Shane and the rest of the boys. I hear Dane tell Avery to help me if I need it. *Welcome to your first night at The House, Avery.*

I cautiously sit on Zander's bed. His body twists and writhes beneath the sheet, his face wet from tears, his bedding damp with sweat, and fearful whimpers escape from deep in his throat. The unmistakable smell of his terrifying fear suffocates the small room.

"Zander, baby," I croon, careful to not raise my voice and add to the violence already haunting his nightmare. "I'm right here. I'm right here." His crying doesn't stop. I reach out to try and shake him awake and am taken aback when he thrashes ferociously, his fist connecting with my cheekbone. The pain registers just beneath my eye, but I shake it off, needing to rouse Zander to prevent him from hurting himself.

"Daddy, no!" he whimpers with such heartbreak that tears spring to my eyes. And despite it being a dream that cannot be used legally, Zander just confirmed the suspicion that his father killed his mother. Right before his eyes.

I struggle to wrap my arms around him. Despite his small size, the strength he has from the adrenaline induced terror is heightened. I manage to wrestle my arms around him and pull him into my chest, murmuring to him all the while. Letting him know I'm here and that I'm not going to hurt him. "Zander, it's okay. C'mon, Zand, wake up," I whisper over and over to him until he wakes with a start. He struggles to sit up and get out of my grip, searching the bedroom with hollow eyes to orient himself to his surroundings.

"Momma?" he croaks in such desperation that my heart shatters in a million pieces.

"It's okay, I'm right here, buddy," I soothe, rubbing my hand up and down his back softly.

He looks at me, eyes red and raw from crying and falls into my arms. He clings to me with such despair that I know I'd do anything to erase his memory of that night if given the chance. "I want my mommy," he cries, repeating it over and over. It's the first sentence I have ever heard him say and yet there is nothing to be excited about. There is nothing to encourage or celebrate.

We stay huddled together, arms wrapped tight for the longest time until his even breathing convinces me that he's fallen back asleep. I slowly shift him to lie down on the bed, but when I attempt to withdraw my arms from around him, he clings even tighter.

It's not until the sun's rays peek through the closed mini-blinds that we both fall into a deep sleep.

Chapter Thirteen

Colton

The shudder of the motor vibrates through my body as I flick the paddle coming into turn four. *Fuck.* Something doesn't feel right. Something's off. I ease up more than necessary as I cross over and into the apron coming out of the turn.

"What's going on?" Becks' disembodied voice fills my ears.

"Fuck, I don't know," I grate out as I bring the car back up to speed to try and decipher what she's telling me. Every shudder. Every sound. Each jolt of my body. My attention straining to try and pinpoint what feels off—something to substantiate why she doesn't seem to be handling how she should. I can't figure out what I'm missing, what I might be overlooking that could cost us a race.

Or put me headfirst into the wall.

My head pounds with stress and concentration. I pass the start/finish line, the grandstands to my right one big stretch of mixed colors. *The blur I live my life in.*

"Is—"

"How much preload in the differential?" I demand as I hit another paddle heading into turn one. The rear of the car starts to slide as I press the gas coming out of it, accelerating the car up to top speed. My body automatically shifts to compensate for the pressure imposed on it by the force and angle of the track's bank. "Possibly the clutch plate? The ass end is sliding all over the place," I tell him as I fight to get the car back under control on the chute before heading into turn two.

"That's not poss—"

"You driving the fucking car now, Becks?" I bark into the mic, my hands gripping the wheel in frustration. Beckett obviously reads my mood, because he goes radio silent. My mind flickers to the nightmares that plagued my sleep last night. Of not being able to talk to Rylee this morning when I called. Of needing to hear her voice to help clear the remnants from my mind.

Goddamnit, Donavan, get your head on the track. Irritation—at myself, at Beckett, at the damn car—has me pushing the pedal down harder than I should down the back straightaway. My fucked up attempt at using adrenaline to drown out my head.

I know Becks is probably beside himself right now, thinking I'm gonna burn her up. Trash all the time and precision we've dialed into the engine. I'm nearing turn three and a part of me wishes there was no turn. Just a straight stretch of road where I could keep going, drop the hammer, race the wind, and outrun the shit in my head—the fear squeezing at my heart.

Chase the possibilities just beyond the reach of my fingertips.

But there isn't one. Just another fucking turn. Hamster on a goddamn wheel.

I come into the turn too hot, my head too screwed up to be on the track. I have to consciously remember to try and not over-correct as the ass end gets too loose on me and slides to the right, drifting too high. A shiver of fear dances at the base of my spine for that split second when I'm not sure if I'll be able to pull the car out in time to avoid kissing the barrier.

Beckett swears on the radio as I narrowly escape, and I shout out one of my own. The only way to voice the high of fear that just jolted through my system. Adrenaline, my momentary drug of choice, reigns until the realization of my stupidity will take over in the moments to come. It always takes a few seconds to hit.

Fuck me. *I'm done.* I shouldn't be in the car right now. It's stupid of me to be here when my head's not right. I ease into turn four, decelerating when I hit pit row and stop where my crew stands behind the firewall. I silence the engine and blow out a loud breath. They all just stand there, no one stepping over, as I unbuckle my helmet and detach the steering wheel. I pull up on my helmet and it's yanked from my hands.

"You trying to kill yourself out there?" Beckett shouts at me as I remove my balaclava and ear buds. Now I know why the crew stayed behind the wall. They're used to the volatility and brutal honesty between Becks and me. They know when to stay clear. "Then do it on your own goddamn time. Not under my watch!" He's pissed and has every right to be, but fuck all if I'm telling him that.

I just stare at him, a slight smirk turning up the corners of my mouth at my oldest friend. My attempt at provoking him so that he doesn't notice the trembling of my hands. A surefire way for him to know I scared the shit out of myself as well and add fuel to his own fire. What the hell was I thinking getting in the car with a jacked up frame of mind? He just glares at me, jaw clenched and shoulders square before shaking his head, turning his back to me, and walking away.

The minute Becks turns the corner, my crew clears the wall and begins doing their various jobs as I climb out. I'm glad they steer clear of me, all obviously accustomed to my moodiness by now when testing goes to shit.

I scrub my hand over my face and through my sweat-soaked hair. I head the same way as Becks, knowing he's had enough time to calm down so that we can talk. Maybe. *Fuck.* I don't know. When things are off between the two of us, the rest of the team feels it. I can't have that coming into a new season.

I follow him to the RV and climb up the steps. He's sitting in the recliner across from the door, leaning forward, elbows on his knees. He just looks at me and shakes his head, causing a twinge of guilt to hit me for taking years off of his life with my careless stunt.

"What the hell was that?" he asks in an all too quiet voice—the voice of a disappointed parent to their child.

I unzip my suit to the waist and let the sleeves hang, before peeling off my shirt and falling back onto the couch. I close my eyes, swiveling so that my head rests on one armrest and my feet on the opposing one. I am so tired. I need sleep that's not filled with all the fucked up dreams that've been coming repeatedly since that morning with Rylee. I'm a damn mess. Can't think straight. Obviously can't drive worth a shit. "I don't know, Becks," I sigh out. "My head wasn't in the right place. I shouldn't have—"

"You're goddamn right you shouldn't have," he yells at me. "That was a stupid fucking stunt, and if you ever pull one like that again—get in the car when you're head's not straight—you can find yourself another goddamn crew chief." The squeak of the chair tells me he's just unfolded himself and stood. The motor home rocks with his movement and the door slams shut as he leaves.

I keep my eyes closed, sinking into the lumpy ass couch, just wanting to forget, wanting to talk to Rylee but knowing that she's probably sleeping herself after the events of her night.

I don't know why I got so panicked this morning when I couldn't reach her. My mind immediately veered to thoughts of her in an accident. Trapped in a mangled fucking car somewhere. Alone and scared. My chest tightened at the thought until I got a hold of Haddie who gave me the number to The House's landline. I felt better—and worse—after speaking to Jackson about the chaos of Zander's nightmare.

Poor fucking kid. Nightmares can be so damn brutal. Cause such a setback and fuck with your memories even more. Make them darker. Make you relive them in the worst possible way. Remember things you shouldn't. *Otherwise wouldn't.* Don't ever want to. But at least he had Rylee to comfort him, stay with him, and keep the demons at bay with her soft voice and reassuring touch.

Exactly what I needed from her last night. What I still need from her today.

I sigh at the thought of her, wanting her in the worst way...*in the best way.* I laugh out loud at myself in the vacant RV. I can't figure out what I want more, a dreamless sleep or to hear Rylee's voice.

Shit, my head must really be fucked up if all I want from Rylee is to hear her voice. I shake my head and scrub my hands over my face, feeling pussified from the thought. What I wouldn't give to go back to a couple of months ago when sleep came easy.

When my dick and balls were firmly attached and in charge of my thoughts. When the choice between sleep, sex, or wanting to hear a specific woman's voice was a no brainer; a few hours of uncomplicated sex led to the sleepless oblivion. Two down with one shot. *And the woman's voice?* Who cared if she talked or what she did with her mouth as long as she opened wide and swallowed without a gag reflex.

Rylee flashes through my mind. Her dark hair on the white pillow as I hover over her. The look on her face—lips jolting apart, eyes widening, cheeks flushing with color—as I sink inside of her. How she tightens like a vise around me as she comes. Fucking voodoo pussy.

My dick stirs at the thought—wanting, no needing her—but my exhaustion overwhelms, and swallows me whole into its oblivion.

Spiderman, Batman, Superman, Ironman.

Spiderman, Batman, Superman, Ironman.

I jolt from the nightmare with a start, disoriented from the unknown passage of time. My heart thunders in my ears. My stomach churns. My head forgets specifics instantly, but the nightmare's clutches of fear still hold me against my will, dragging me backwards through poisoned memories.

"Fucking Christ!" I yell out to the empty RV as I force myself to calm down and breathe. To try and forget the fear that'll never go away. Never. Fear gives way to anger as I pick up the closest thing to me, one of the crew's hackey-sacs and chuck it across the aisle as hard as I can. The thud it makes does nothing to abate the feelings clawing through me, embedding themselves in every fiber of my being, but it's all I can do. My only source of release.

I'm helpless and hostage to the poison within me. Sweat trickles down my cheek. I'm drenched with it. The smell of fear clings to me and my stomach twists in protest again. *Shit!*

I shove up from the couch and strip out of my fire suit as if the fabric is on fire. I need a shower. I need to clean the grime from the track and the stain of his imaginary touch from my unwilling flesh.

The water scalds. The soap does nothing to wash away the memories. I press my forehead against the acrylic stall, letting the water burn lines as it slides down my back. I will my brain to shut off and rest for five goddamn fucking minutes so I can have my own temporary radio silence.

Rylee's words keep looping through my head, badgering me, questioning me, making me wonder if it's a solution to the constant poison that I'm afraid is going to consume me. I pound a fist against the wall, the sound resonating through my fucked up thoughts. I drag myself from the shower, drape a towel around my waist, and grab my cell. I need to do this before I lose the courage. Before I puss out and think of the ramifications. The answers I'm afraid to find. The truth I fear will crumble me. I punch the number in my phone and swallow the bile threatening to rise, preparing myself with each passing ring of the phone.

"Colton? I thought you were testing today?"

Warmth spears through me at the sound of his voice, at the concern flooding into it. And then fear. How is he going to handle the questions I need to ask? The ones that Rylee thinks might help me, might ease the weight on my soul and torment in my mind.

I labor to ask the man who gave me possibilities about the woman who robbed me of everything. My youth. My innocence. My trust. My ability to love. My self.

Of the concept of unconditional love.

"Son? Is everything okay?" Concern creeps into his voice as a result of my silence. "Colton?"

"Dad…" I choke out, my throat feeling like it's drowning in sand.

"You're scaring me, Colt…"

I shake my head to get a grip. "Sorry, Dad…I'm fine. I'm good." I can hear him exhale audibly on the other end of the line, but he remains silent, allowing me a moment to gather my thoughts. He knows something is amiss.

I feel like I'm thirteen and I've fucked up again. That adolescent fear fills me—the anxiety that if I push too hard or screw up one more time, they'll send me back. They won't want me anymore. The funny thing is I thought I'd conquered this fear a long time ago, but as the question weighs heavy on my tongue, it all comes back. The fear. The insecurity. The need to feel wanted.

Dread strangles my words.

"I...uh...just had a question. Don't know how to ask it really…"

Silence fills the line and I know my Dad is trying to figure out what the hell has gotten into me. Why I'm acting like the little boy I used to be.

"Just ask, son." It's all he says, but his tone—that soothing, acceptance at all costs tone—tells me that he knows something has brought me back to that place in time. And even though all I feel is fear and uncertainty, all I hear is patience, love, and understanding.

I suck in a breath of air and exhale it shakily. "Do you know what happened to *her*? Where she is? What became of her?" My fingers tremble as I bring a hand to run through my hair. I don't want him to worry or think that I want to find her and…*I don't know what with her*. Reconcile? *Fuck no*. Never.

But it scares the hell out of me that the idea of her—just the thought of her—can get me this worked up. Can fuck with my head more than the dreams. "Never mind, I—"

"Colton…It's okay." Reassurance fills his voice.

"I just don't want you to think—"

"I don't think anything," he soothes in a way only a father can to a son. "Take a breath, Colt. It's okay. I've waited a long time for you to ask—"

"You're not mad?" The one fear I have bubbles out of my mouth.

"No. Never." He sighs, resigned to the fact that a small part of me will always worry regardless of the passage of time.

I feel like a hundred pound weight has been lifted from my chest. Freed me from the fear of asking. "Really?"

"It's natural to wonder," he assures. "Normal to want to learn about your past and—"

"I know all I need to know of my past..." The words come out in a whisper before I can stop them. Silence hangs through the line. "I just...fucking Rylee..." I mutter in exasperation.

"You're having dreams again, aren't you?"

I struggle to answer. I want to tell him because I feel obligated to be honest after everything he's done for me, and at the same time feel the need to lie so that he doesn't worry about the memories that debilitated me as a child. So he doesn't remember how detrimental they were. So he doesn't find out *everything* that had happened. "I saw it in your eyes when I got back from Indonesia. Are you okay? Do you need—"

"I'm fine, Dad. It's just that Rylee had asked if I knew what had happened to *her*. That maybe if I knew I might get some closure. Be able to shut some old doors..."

He's silent on the connection for a moment. "I kept tabs on her for a while. I wanted to make sure when she got out of jail that she didn't come back to find you or make trouble for you when you were just starting to do so well. I stopped about ten years ago," he admits, "but I'll call the PI that I used, he'll know her habits better than anyone—and we'll see what he can find. If that's what you want..."

"Yeah. Thanks. I just..."

"No need to explain, Colton. You do what you need to fill in that piece you've always felt is missing. Your Mom and I knew this day was coming, and we want you to do whatever you have to do to find peace. We're okay with it."

I pinch the bridge of my nose and close my eyes, fighting the burn that threatens within. "Thanks, Dad." There's nothing else I can say to the man who gave me life after being dead for the first eight years of my existence.

"Sure, son. I'll call you when I have any news. Love you."

"Thanks, Dad. Me too."

I'm just about to hang up when he speaks again. "Colton?"

"Yeah?"

"I'm proud of you." His voice wavers with emotion, which in turn makes me swallow the lump in my throat.

"Thanks."

I hang up the phone, toss it on the table, and lean my head back against the wall. The loud breath I exhale into the silence does nothing to ease the overwhelming emotions swimming through me. I sit there for a bit, knowing I need to apologize to Beckett and wanting Rylee in the worst way. Needing something to clear my head.

The idea hits me like lightning, and I'm up, dressed, and climbing out of the RV in less than five minutes. I see the guys working in the garage off to my right, but I can't talk to anyone right now. Don't want to. I walk into the open bay where the favorite of all my babies is parked—*Sex*.

I don't even take a second glance to appreciate the F12's clean lines and flawless fire engine red perfection, but I sure as hell will enjoy her speed in about one minute. I climb behind the wheel and when the engine rumbles to life, I feel a piece of myself return. Spark back.

I zip past the garage, noting Beckett's refusal to meet my eyes—*stubborn bastard*—and exit the track. I crank up the volume as *The Distance* comes through the speakers. Great fucking song. The minute I hit the 10 and see it's unbelievably empty for this time of day, I drop the hammer and fly. Fly faster than is safe but the feeling—luxury cocooning me, perfection in my hands, and an engine that talks to me—clears my head, and eases the self-inflicted tension pulling from all directions.

Sex never disappoints me when I need her the most.

By the time I approach traffic, my head is a little clearer and my mind is made up. I pick up my phone and make the call.

Chapter Fourteen

As I look across the kitchen at Zander and his tutor working on his spelling words, I hear the front door slam open. The excited chatter of the boys fills the hallway. They are usually animated when they get home, but today the noise is off the charts. So much so that Zander looks up from his paper and raises his eyebrows at me.

Ricky comes barreling around the corner, so excited he stutters—as he normally does when overly excited—for a second. "Ry-Rylee and Za-Zander…Hurry up and get your stuff!"

"No running in the house, Ricky," I warn. "What are you talking about?"

The other boys come flying into the great room before he has a chance to respond. I look over at the boys to scold them for running in the house when my voice falters.

Standing at the entry to the room is Colton. Reckless. Sexy. Devastating. The three words hit me at once at the sight of him.

I know it's silly. It's only been four days since I've seen or talked to him, but now that he's in plain sight, I'm staggered at how much I've missed him. How much I've wanted to see him. Be near him. Hear his voice again. Have a connection with him again. *So much for needing space to clear my head.*

I drink him in, my eyes dragging their way up his body. When I meet his eyes, a slow, lopsided grin curls up one corner of his mouth making that dimple I find irresistible deepen. I swear my heart skips a beat at the smoldering look in his eyes. I swallow loudly trying to gain the equilibrium that he's just knocked out from underneath me.

We stare at each other, the boys' raucous noise fading to white as we speak without talking. Kyle grabs my hand and tugs on it, breaking the trance between us.

"Colton's taking us to the go-kart track!" he exclaims, excitement dancing in his eyes.

"He is, is he?" I ask, raising my eyebrows and looking over at Colton.

"Yep, he is," Colton says as he takes a step toward me, his lopsided grin now at its full megawatt capacity. "Go put your stuff away guys and get in the van. Jackson's waiting." My eyes widen at his comment, and I wonder how he coordinated this.

Colton turns and meets Zander's hopeful eyes. "Hey, Zander, I thought you guys could use a break from all of this school stuff. I know it's really important, but sometimes a guy needs a break, don't cha' think?" Zander's eyes grow as big as saucers and his mouth spreads in a huge grin. It's a small miracle how the grace of a smile can ease the severity of the nightmare's effects on his precious face. "Let's go get your shoes and we can meet everyone in the van. You game?" he asks.

Zander jumps up and races toward his bedroom, and I bite back the inherent scold of no running. I apologize to the tutor and send her on her way with eyes dazed from the sight of Colton. Poor thing.

When she exits the room, I can hear the boys making their way to the front door with gusto. It is only then that Colton approaches me and backs me up against the kitchen counter. He presses his hips into me at the same time his mouth captures mine in a mind-altering, head-dizzying, soul-emptying kiss. *God, I missed the taste of him.* The kiss is too brief to fulfill my four days of missing him. When our lips part, he wraps his arms around me in a tight hug that I could lose myself in—one teeming with a quiet desperation. He holds me to him, his face nuzzled in the side of my neck, and I can feel him breathe me in drawing strength from our connection.

"Hey," I murmur softly as his hands press into my back. "You okay?"

"Yeah." He breathes. "Now I am."

His murmured confession rocks me. Hits those parts deep within in me, unjaded and still full of hope and possibility.

He finally releases me when he hears sounds in the hallway. I gaze up at his face and look beyond the handsome features that still make my breath catch in my throat. I notice darkened smudges under his tired, wary eyes. He's not sleeping. More nightmares? I don't know and I don't want to ask. He'll tell me if he wants to. When he's able to.

I stare at him for a beat and try to figure out what's different about him. It's only when he angles his head to question my silent appraisal that it hits me. He's clean-shaven. I reach up and run my hand across his jaw, his face leaning into my touch. And it's something about that little gesture mixed with his earlier confession that causes my heart to swell.

"What's this?" I ask, averting my eyes to prevent him from seeing my emotional transparency. "So smooth and clean-shaven."

"It doesn't bode too well doing a razor commercial with a five o'clock shadow," he smirks, running his palms up and down the sides of my torso. Licks of desire flicker low in my belly at his touch.

I laugh out loud. "Understandably. I like it though," I tell him, running my fingers over it again when he frowns. "It's okay, Ace, you still ooze bad boy without the stubble. Besides, I'll get to sleep with someone different than this scruffy-jawed man I've been wasting my time on."

He flashes a wicked smile. "Wasting your time, huh?" He takes a step toward me, lust clearly edging the humor out of his eyes.

Every part of my body tightens at the predatory way his body moves toward mine. My God. *Take me*, I want to tell him. *Take every part of me that you already haven't stolen, taken, or claimed.*

"Oh, most definitely. He's a rebel..." I scrunch my nose up, playing along "*...and I definitely don't do the bad boy type.*"

"No?" He wets his lips with a quick dart of his tongue. "What type exactly, *do you do?*" A devilish grin snakes up the corner of his lips as he reaches out to touch my face, and in an instant it disappears. His eyes narrow upon noticing the bruise from Zander on my cheek. My cover-up has obviously worn off. "Who did this to you?" he demands, his hands cupping my neck, angling my head to the side so he can see the severity of the bruise. "Is this from Zander last night?"

I startle at his words. "Yeah, it goes with the territory." I shrug. "How'd you know about it?"

"Poor fucking kid." He shakes his head. "I called you this morning. You were still asleep after being up with Zander all night. I hadn't heard from you and got worried." He pauses and those words—his admission that he cares for me coming on the heels of him telling me in so many words that he needs me—ignites my soul and makes my lips curl automatically. "So I called the house and Jackson answered. He told me what happened." He angles my chin up to look at my cheek again. "Are you sure you're okay?"

"Yeah." I shake my head, his concern endearing.

"So, I figured the kids might need a break to shake off last night." He leans in and brushes his lips against mine again. "And I really wanted to see you," he murmurs breathlessly, his words shooting straight into my heart and embedding themselves into my every fiber.

How can he say he doesn't subscribe to romance when he says things so casually when they're least expected?

"I have a work function tonight, so I don't have much time, but I wanted to go have some fun and release some stress." He subtly shakes his head, and I can see a hint of sadness creep back into his eyes. "Besides, it's been a rough day and I needed to get away. Do something to relax."

"Everything okay?"

"Nothing for you to worry about." He forces a tight smile, leans in, and kisses the tip of my nose. "Besides, I thought the boys might enjoy it too."

"I'm sure they will," I tell him. "I've gotta go get my purse." I start to head toward the staff's room when I hear Zander call my name from the opposite side of the house. I pause, a wide smile spreading across my face over hearing him call my name like all the other kids in the house do. It makes my heart happy. "What's wrong, Zand?" I ask.

"Shoe." It's only one word. But it's a word. And he's actually communicating so that makes it even better. I smile broadly and Colton follows suit in understanding.

"Go get your purse," he tells me. "I'll go help him."

"You sure?" I ask, but he's already turning the corner to the hall.

I gather my stuff, lock up the back door, and get ready to leave. When I near the hall, I hear the murmur of voices. I take a few steps and then stop when I realize that Colton and Zander are talking about last night.

I know I shouldn't eavesdrop—that I should walk away and leave them some privacy—but my curiosity is piqued. And when I hear Colton say, "You know, I used to have really bad dreams too, Zander," I know that I won't be going anywhere.

I can't see them but I have a feeling that Zander acknowledges Colton somehow because he continues. "When I was little, I had some really bad things happen to me too. And I used to get scared. So scared." I can hear Colton sigh and some shuffling. "And when I'd get that scared, do you know what I'd say to try and make me not so scared? I'd repeat in my head, '*Spiderman. Batman. Superman. Ironman.*' I'd say it over and over. And you know what? If I squeezed my eyes really, really tight—just like this—it would help."

I stand in the hallway. My heart melting as I listen to a man who is so damaged he's sworn off ever having children but is so unbelievable with them. Especially the broken ones. The ones that need him the most. The ones he understands better than anyone. I feel a phantom pang in my abdomen, and I push away the thoughts of what can never be. For me. And with him.

Then the best sound pulls me from my self-pity. It's meek but it's a laugh that warms my insides. I wish I could see what Colton's doing to make him laugh. What barrier he's breaking down to get that sound from Zander. "You know what? I'll let you in on another secret…even now—even though I'm an adult—when I have a bad dream or am really scared, I still say that. I promise I do..." Colton laughs and I take a step forward toward the open doorway. And what I see steals my breath. Colton is sitting on the bed and Zander is sitting sideways on his lap, looking reverently up at him. A soft smile on his lips. Colton glances up for a split second when he notices me, the gentle smile on his face widening, and then turns back to focus on Zander. "And it still helps. Now, are you ready to drive a go-kart and beat me?"

Zander looks over to me and smiles widely. "Okay, then go get in the van!" I tell him. He looks back toward Colton and nods his head once before hopping off and running toward the front door.

Colton stays seated for a moment, and we just stare at each other. A silent exchange that tells him I heard everything and that he's glad I did. That exchange—watching him with Zander—has the protective wall around my heart fracturing into a million pieces and love seeping from the cracks. I shake my head to clear it of all of the things I want to say to him in this moment and hold my hand out to him instead.

He rises slowly and gives a half smile. "C'mon." He takes my hand and tugs it. "Do you think you can beat me in a race?"

"I know I can beat the pants off of you," I reply suggestively.

He chuckles at my comment. "As much as I like your line of thinking, Ry, we're gonna be surrounded by a crowd of people."

I release his hand and wrap my arm around his torso, wanting the feel of his body against mine. It's me who needs to feel close to him now. He laughs at my sudden assault of him. "I thought being dirty in a crowd turned you on," I whisper against his ear.

"Sweet Jesus, woman." He groans. "You know what to say to get me hard."

I place an open mouth kiss at the spot just beneath his jaw. "I know. Too bad we're going to be surrounded by seven little boys who hang on your every word or I'd let you scratch this itch I seem to have."

"God, you're such a cock tease," he laughs as we walk out of the front door of the house. He releases me so I can lock the front door, a look of desire clouding his eyes as he watches me.

"You think so?" I murmur coyly, batting my eyelashes at him as he nods. "Maybe I'll have to show you just how good of a cock tease I am," I quip as I sashay down the walkway in front of him, swinging my hips back and forth. I know that sex is off of the agenda for the evening because he has to leave right after karting with the kids, and Saturday night will be the next time I get to see him.

I turn back to face him, taking a step backwards as I watch him. "Too bad you shaved," I say, fighting the smirk I want to give him. "I kinda liked the roughness of it between my thighs." I raise my eyebrows as he sucks in a breath.

This could be fun. A buildup of anticipation. I can spend the week taunting him and ramp up the expectation so that by Saturday night we can't keep our hands off of each other. *As if we need help with that anyway.*

"C'mon, Rylee! You have to beat him. You're our last hope!" Shane yells across the railing at me as I stand beside my kart waiting for my rematch.

The past two hours have been a blast. From the racing to the boys' laughter to the constant banter between Colton and me, I couldn't have thought of a better way for the boys to let off steam and reconnect after the chaos of Zander's nightmare last night.

After an hour of free-for-all racing, the boys begged to race one on one against Colton. He willingly obliged and in turn set up my current situation. Colton beat all of the boys, everyone that went up against him, except for me. I accused him of letting me win, which had him instantly calling for a rematch. The second race went in his favor. Now we're in the tiebreaker.

"Best out of three, Thomas. Whoever wins next gets bragging rights," he calls over to me, amusement in his eyes and challenge in his smile. *God, I love him.* Especially when he has this look about him: confident, carefree, and downright sexy.

"You're all talk, Donavan. Your win was a total fluke." The arrogant smile he flashes goads me further. "Big, bad professional racer like you has to maintain your dignity, you know. Can't have rookies like me showing you up! Especially a woman."

"Oh baby, you know me, I'll let a woman do whatever she wants to me." He smirks and raises an eyebrow suggestively.

I laugh out loud as I walk the ten feet between us. I look back over my shoulder at the boys who are egging me on and wink at them to show I'm on their side. As I approach, Colton turns to face me, his hand holding his helmet against his hip as if it's the most natural stance in the world for him, and the fingers of his other hand rubbing together as if he is itching to reach out and touch me.

Good, it's working. My subtle brushes against him. My little suggestive comments whispered to him here and there. My slow perusal of his body so he notices. Despite having to do them all under the detecting eyes of our audience, I'm glad to know that none of them have gone unnoticed. I can see it in his eyes and the pulsing muscle in his jaw as I approach him.

"You worried you're going to lose, Ace?" I smirk. My back is toward our audience so I bend over and tie my shoe, purposefully putting my cleavage on display. When I look up, Colton's pupils have darkened and his tongue darts out to wet his lips.

"I know what you're doing, Rylee," he murmurs softly from beneath his smirk, "and as much as your little antics have had me wanting to push you up against that wall over there and take you hard and fast more than once since we've been here—regardless of who's watching—it's not going to work." He flashes his megawatt smile at me. "I'm still gonna beat that fine ass of yours to the finish line."

"Well as much as I could use a good spanking..." I breathe out, looking up at him from beneath my lashes and catch his sharp intake of air at my words "...I was just coming over here to see if you needed any help getting your motor revved up." I smile innocently at him, although my body language says anything but.

I watch his throat constrict as he swallows, his lips twisting as he tries to prevent himself from smiling. "Oh, my motor's running just fine, sweetheart," he teases as his eyes travel the length of my body again. "Revved and raring to go. Do you need any help getting yours tuned and ready to race?"

I bite my bottom lip as I stare at him and angle my head to the side. "Well I seem to be running a little tight in the ass end. Nothing a quick lube job wouldn't fix," I toss over my shoulder as I walk back to my car, wishing I could see the reaction on his face.

The boys keep up their shouting and heckling as we put our helmets on and get strapped in our carts. I glance over at Colton and nod my head as I rev my gas pedal. And then we are off, racing side by side through the twists and turns of the track. My competitive nature surfaces as Colton noses past me. I can't hear the boys cheering me on over the sound of the motors, but I catch passing glimpses of their arms waving frantically in my periphery. We come to the next turn and I edge the nose of my cart in first, taking the corner at full speed and powering past him. We race down the straightaway toward the finish line, edging back and forth. When we finally cross it, I'm pretty sure that I won by the hysterics from the boys and Jackson on the sidelines.

I screech my kart to a stop and jump out, unable to suppress the wide grin on my face. I pull off my helmet at the same time Colton does and when I turn to him, I swear his grin is as wide as mine. I do a silly, little victory dance around him to amuse the boys who are doing their own celebrating. He just shakes his head, laughing at me with a genuine, carefree smile on his face.

"Ha!" I smirk at him. "How do you like them apples?" I taunt as I follow him to the little office at the edge of the track and out of the spectators' view. The minute we're out of the boys' line of sight, Colton spins me around and has me pinned against the wall. His long, lean body presses against every curve of mine as if we fit together like yin and yang.

"Do you have any fucking clue how turned on I am, Rylee?" He growls at me. "How much I want to take what you've been flaunting in front of me all afternoon?"

It takes every ounce of my concentration to appear unaffected by him. Every ounce. I arch my eyebrows at him in nonchalance. "Well I have a feeling that your dick pressing into me is an indication."

"God, I want to fuck that smirk off your face right now."

His words alone incite my core muscles to clench at the mere thought. I never realized that the act of seducing can provoke equal parts of desire in both parties.

My nipples harden at the feeling of his firm chest pressed against them. His breath feathers over my face and his eyes remain locked on mine. He tilts his head forward and meets my lips, his tongue licking between them, and tangling with mine. There is a quiet passion to his kiss, and I groan as he releases me, leaving me wanting more.

"I couldn't agree more, Ryles, but I gotta get going...and I have a feeling your fan club is going to come barging through that door any moment." He takes my helmet from my hand and places it on the table at the same time the door opens up and the boys come barreling through. Colton looks over at me and arches his eyebrows as if to say *I told you so.*

I bite back a careless giggle when I see all of the boys carrying bundles of cotton candy. My thoughts revert to my more than memorable experience with the confection and Colton. He groans, his own little acknowledgement, causing my lips to twitch with a devious little smirk.

"One second, guys!" I yell above their raucous noise as I take a pinch from Ricky's funnel. I step back toward Colton and deliberately run my tongue over my lips before placing the fluff of sweetness on my tongue. I close my eyes and play up savoring its taste. When I open them back up, Colton's eyes have darkened and his jaw is set with frustration and desire—just the response I was looking for.

I lean close to his ear, purposefully withholding any touch of my body against his, my voice a seductive whisper for his ears only. "Hey, Ace?" He looks over and arches a brow at me. "*I'm not wearing any panties.*" I smirk. He audibly sucks in a breath in acknowledgement before I sway my hips a little more than normal as I walk away from him.

What he doesn't know, won't hurt him, I think as I picture the pair of white cotton underwear I'm wearing beneath my Levis.

Chapter Fifteen

Colton glances over at me as he listens to his publicist give him the order of events for the evening. We're gliding through Los Angeles in a limo headed toward a charity gala. This is the first of several events in the coming weeks where Colton and I will make the rounds, formally promoting our companies' joint venture, and hopefully enlist some participants for the car's lap sponsorship program.

I stare at him unabashedly as I hum to *Hero/Heroine* floating gently through the background from the speakers. I take in everything about him that has become so familiar, so addictive, so *everything* to me in such a short period of time. He's so striking in the formal tuxedo—the clothing that he's already confessed to detesting several times—and I can't stop thinking what a lucky girl I am. His face is clean-shaven again, and yet even without the usual shadow of hair, he still *exudes* the aura of careless bad boy.

It's just something that oozes off of him regardless of what he's wearing. He's almost sexier with his look tonight because I know that beneath his sophisticated exterior lies a reckless rebel at heart.

Colton glances over me again, feeling the scrutiny of my stare, and a salacious smirk spreads on his lips. His eyes meet mine and I know he is aching just as bad as I am to feel our bare skin connect. The remainder of our week since the go-kart track has been filled with provocatively taunting emails and texts explaining in depth what we want to do to one another once this evening is over. *My God, with words alone the man can make a woman need, crave, desire—and most likely beg if it takes too long—like I've never known possible.* But I'm pretty confident that the unfulfilled ache goes both ways though, from the hissing of his breath when I answered the front door in my sexy, red dress.

"Okay, so we'll be there in about five minutes. I'll jump out before your call time and get into place while the car circles around the block," Chase says, looking at both of us above her black-rimmed glasses. I hold a hand to my stomach at the thought of being photographed on the red carpet in front of all of those people. *Yikes*! I thought this was a little function. I didn't realize it was a full-blown Hollywood filled gala with questioning press. The publicity will be good for the charity, but can't I just sneak in the back door and avoid the spotlight?

Obviously that will never be the option if I'm with Colton.

He reaches over and squeezes my hand. "Don't be nervous." He winks at me. "I've got you covered."

"That's what I'm afraid of." I smirk at him, our eyes doing the talking for us. I swear I can see the electricity crackle in the air as sexual tension fills the limo. Chase busies herself by keeping her head down, her cheeks staining red at our silent yet obvious exchange.

"Well, here's my stop," she mumbles, gathering her papers as Colton rubs the back of my hand with his thumb.

"Thanks, Chase. We'll see you in a few minutes," he tells her, never taking his eyes off of mine.

The minute the limo door shuts, Colton shifts and has me pressed against the backseat. His hand tangles in my loose curls, and I arch my chest off the back of the seat, aching to feel the heat of his body against mine, but he stops inches from my face. My lips part and my breath quickens as I look into his eyes. The quiet intensity held within that flash of green undoes me.

Strips me.

Fuels me.

"Do you have any idea how many times this week I've wanted to do this to you?" He ever so slowly lowers his lips to mine, just a whisper of a touch that has me groaning with a teeming desperation.

"Colton," I plead as his lips withdraw a fraction, leaving my body focused solely on the slow slide of his hand up my ribcage to just below the underside of my breast before it makes the slow descent back down. My breath exhales in a shuddered sigh that has his lips turning up and eyes crinkling at the corners.

"Is there something you want?" he whispers against my lips as he pulls my hair gently back so my neck is exposed. His tongue glides a slow trail down the column, clearly drawing out the anticipation that we've built over the past couple of days, but I'm so addled with need, I just want him inside of me. Now. To fill the void aching for him.

"Yes. I. Need. You. In. Me. Colton. Now," my splintered voice pants as his tongue licks at my proffered cleavage.

His laugh is low and throaty, the tenor of it filling my ears, stoking my fire of need until his tongue leaves my skin. I open my eyes, looking at him from beneath eyelids weighted with desire to find his gaze trained on my face. "You didn't think I'd let you off—or rather *let you get off*—that easy did you?" He smirks and I can see the mirth dancing in his eyes. *Oh shit!* My body already taut with need tenses further. "You've given me blue balls all week, and I think turnabout's fair play." He smirks. "*To use your term.*"

As much as I want to take pride in the fact he's confessed that I've successfully driven him crazy, the knowledge that my itch is not going to be scratched any time soon causes me to groan in frustration. Colton's smile only widens at the sound, and the mischief in his eyes has my own narrowing at him in turn.

"You've been killing me softly all week, Rylee, with your little suggestions…little teases…and so it's time to show you exactly how it feels."

Oh fucking hell! *Seriously?* What does he have in mind here? "I *do know how it feels*," I try to emphasize but only succeed in sounding breathy. Desperate. "Your responses have done the same to me."

He kisses my neck softly, working his way to my pleasure point just below my ear lobe. His whisper of a touch makes me slick with arousal. "No. I don't think so, Rylee," he murmurs, his lips moving to my ear. "Do you know how hard it is to concentrate on a meeting, trying to hide my hard-on because I can't get your texts out of my head? What an idiot I look like when I draw a blank at a question about wing adjustments to the car because all I can think about is savoring the sweet taste of your pussy again?" He brings a hand up and lays his palm on the base of my neck, holding my head still, so that I have no option but to meet the challenge in his eyes. "*Did it feel the same for you, Rylee?*"

I bite my bottom lip and shake my head no, our eyes, violet to green, in a silent exchange. "Say it."

"No." I take in a shaky breath, completely under his spell. Captivated. Mesmerized.

"Then tonight I'll show you," he tells me, sinking to his knees on the floor of the limo as he moves between my legs and captures my mouth again. His tongue licks in and slowly moves with mine as his hand slides up the outside of my thigh, pushing my dress up as he goes. "Sweet Jesus." He exhales as his fingers skim over the garter belts I wore specifically with seducing him in mind. For some reason though, I seem to think the tables have turned now.

I'm the one being seduced.

"Now I'm going to think about undressing you all night until you're standing in your heels and these and nothing else," he says, pulling on a garter strap so it snaps back against my thigh. The slight sting mainlines a jolt straight to my already quivering sex.

"I think you're a little overdressed." He smirks, the devilish look back on his face. I look at him with trepidation, all my focus on the carnal look in his eyes, until I feel his fingers dancing over the dampened silk of my panties. The slight fabric barrier mutes his touch, and I instinctively lift my hips up, begging for more.

"Colton," I gasp.

"And I'm a little underdressed," he murmurs, a teasing quality to his voice. I have a quick second to wonder what the hell he means by his comment, but then the limo's cool air bathes my heated flesh as he pulls my panties to the side and the question falls from my mind. I keep my eyes on him, body humming with uncontrollable need as he ever-so-slowly trails one finger up and then down my slowly swelling folds. And I am gone—my thoughts lost to the dance of fingertips, the searing heat of desire, and the unyielding ache of need.

He leans in and teases me with a soft, tantalizing kiss—fucking my mouth with reverence—that pulls all the way from my toes and back up. He's assaulting all my senses, hindering all coherent thoughts, manipulating my body with a focused purpose.

I cry out and into his waiting lips as he tucks three fingers into me, circling them around so that they rub all of my sensitive walls. I throw my head back without shame and emit a strangled moan, his fingers invading the depths of my sex and manipulating me in the way I so desperately need. I angle my hips up, straining to be closer, his fingers to delve deeper, needing this release brought on by him. The connection.

My body climbs. Tightens with the anticipation of my mounting orgasm. I'm so close to free falling into ecstasy that I can't hold back the moan that falls from my lips.

And then suddenly I'm empty.

"What?" I cry, flashing my eyes open to see Colton's green ones filled with humor and a heavy dose of lust before me.

"Not 'til later, Ry." A lascivious smirk finds its way on to that gorgeous mouth of his. "When I can take my deliriously slow, sweet time with you. Take you to places you don't even know exist yet," he says, reiterating his promise from the first night we met, except right now I have no witty comeback for him. I just want him. Now. Any way possible.

Because this time I know he can fulfill that promise. *And then some.*

When I start to protest, he brings a finger up to my bottom lip, and coats it with my own arousal before capturing my mouth with his. His tongue licks his way into mine, the hum in the back of his throat is sexy as hell. He frames my cheeks in his hands and then pulls back a fraction, laving my bottom lip again upon retreat. He looks into my eyes—that hum rumbling through his throat again. "My two favorite tastes in the whole world."

I groan in frustration. Is he fucking kidding me? He can't talk to me like that and not think I'm going to jump him and take what I want.

"Shhhh," he whispers. "I told you it's your turn to be tortured with need." I close my eyes momentarily, resigning myself to having this deep, fastidious craving remain unfulfilled for the time being. "And I intend to show you just how exquisite that torture can be *all night long*, sweetheart."

The dark promise of his words has my entire body thrumming with an unrequited desire and my pussy pulsing in anticipation. I have a feeling that this is going to be a very long, very frustrating evening.

"Starting now," he murmurs, flashing me a wicked grin while he slowly moves himself down my body, and lowers his mouth to take a slow, sweet taste of me. I groan wildly at the soft swipe of his tongue that immediately renders me defenseless and leaves me his for the taking.

He slides his tongue back and forth momentarily, his fingers whispering across and spreading my swollen flesh.

"Colton," I say in a drawn out whimper as an earthquake of sensation rocks me when he plunges his tongue inside of me. I can barely breathe. Can't even focus. My fingers grip into the flesh of my thighs—urging, pushing, building toward the earth shattering release just within reach.

"That's it, Ry." He blows on my seam, my head falling back against the seat, eyes closed and body willing. "I want you just like this all night."

I hear, rather than feel the snap of fabric as Colton falls back on his heels. And I'm so pent up with my denied release that I don't even find it amusing that he's claimed yet another pair of my panties. The low, guttural groan he emits has me flashing my eyes up just in time to see him wipe my moisture from his mouth with the remnants of my red silk panties. I just stare at him, lips parted, eyes wide, breath panting, and heart racing.

And frustrated.

"Is there something you want?" He smirks.

My head is clouded with need. Screw the game he's playing. All I want is him. Right now. Urgently. "Yes. Please, Colton. Please." I basically beg and don't care one bit that I did.

Our silent stare is broken when his phone chirps a text. He looks at it and then up to me with amusement dancing in his eyes. "Perfect timing. It's our turn in line."

I just shake my head at him as my body remains in its suspended state of negligence. He smirks, smoothes my gown back down over my legs, sans panties, and sits back in the seat next to me.

And in this moment I can see it in his eyes. The razor thin edge his control is teetering on. How his body is driven with such an incredible need and fueled by such an intense, overwhelming desire. How much this little seduction of his is killing him as much as it is me.

"A single word," he says, slowly leaning forward so one of his hands can cup the side of my face. He brushes the pad of his thumb back and forth over my bottom lip. "*Anticipation.*"

The simple word sends a tingle of awareness through my body. He grazes his lips tenderly against mine before pulling back a fraction. I lean in wanting to deepen the kiss and drown in the taste that I've been craving, but he withdraws, denying me with a seductive chuckle and a mischievous yet naughty gleam in his eye.

And for some reason, my mind picks this moment to remember the comment he'd made moments ago. "*Underdressed?*" I ask, my eyes narrowing in thought, trying to figure out what exactly he means.

He holds up my panties and works his tongue inside his mouth as he figures what words to taunt me with. "You see, now these have been exactly where I've wanted to be nestled all fucking week long. And since I haven't been allowed to be there, neither will these." He leans in to place the most tender of kisses on my lips before resting his forehead against mine. "Tonight, Rylee," he murmurs against my lips, "I want you thinking about me all night long. More specifically everything I plan on doing to you later when I have you alone." He breathes out, his voice a seductive whisper that has the desire within me igniting into a raging inferno. "Where my tongue is going to lick. Where my fingers are going to grip. Where my mouth is going to taste. Where my cock is going to stroke. How my body is going to worship every incredible inch of yours."

My hands reach out to squeeze his biceps as my mouth goes dry and my sex gets wet from the provocation of his words. He has to know I'm affected—has to know that I'm desperate for his touch already—but he continues.

"I want to know that while you are talking to all of these potential donors, looking so poised, elegant, and fucking breathtaking, that beneath this dress you are wet and dripping with need for me." I draw in a ragged breath, his words almost too much to hear in my current state. "That you ache so much it hurts. That your pussy pulses at the thought of how later tonight my cock is going to be buried in it. *For hours.*" His voice is pained as he says the last words, and I have some degree of satisfaction that he is suffering as deliciously as I am. I can't help the hum of desire in the back of my throat, as I feel his mouth curl in a smile at my response.

"Every time I look at you I want to know that I'm killing you slowly on the inside while you look so perfectly proper on the outside." He angles his head forward and gives me the kiss that he's been withholding from me. I'm breathless by the time he releases me. "And knowing that will leave me wanting just as much as you will be."

He pulls back from me and shifts in the seat beside me. I've said nothing this entire time, and yet I feel exhausted and totally overcome from our conversation. "Underdressed," he says, a mischievous grin tugging at the corners of his mouth as he holds up my panties and starts folding them. "You are no longer overdressed with these taken out of the picture…" He tucks the scrap of red silk into his pocket square opening and winks at me. "and now I'm perfect."

I stare at him wondering what depths of desire he is going to bring me to tonight. A blush spreads over my cheeks and he smirks, knowing that I'm more than along for the ride. I shake my head softly at him. "You can really be naughty, you know that?"

Something flashes through his eyes which I akin to fear, but I know that's not possible. What does he possibly have to fear from me? "You have no idea, Rylee." His jaw clenches as he looks at me, the mood is suddenly serious and I'm confused as to why. We sit staring at each other in silence for a moment before he turns to look out at the passing scenery. His voice is eerily soft and contemplative when he finally speaks. "If you were smart…if I could let you…I'd tell you to walk away."

I stare at the back of his head, confusion bewildering me. What does he think is so horrible within him that he's not worthy of me? The fact that after all of this time he still feels that he's tainted by his childhood kills me. If only he would let me try and help him. I reach out and lay my hand on his back. "Colton, why would you say that?"

He looks back at me, his face guarded. "I like your naivety way too much to give you the sordid details."

Naivety? Does he not know the horrors I have seen working at The House? Either that or it's another excuse to run from his past. "Whatever it is Colton, it doesn't affect how I feel about you. I need you to know that—"

"Colton?" I startle as the intercom from the front of the car buzzes to us in the back.

"Drop it, Ry," he warns quietly. "Yeah, Sammy?"

"ETA two minutes."

He lowers the privacy partition dividing us. Sammy turns his head toward Colton. "Sammy, please get Sex here. I feel like driving tonight."

Sex? Driving? What the fuck is he talking about?

"Sure thing," Sammy says, a crooked smile lighting up his face before the partition slides back up.

"*Sex?*" I look at him like he's crazy, glad for the change of topic to add some levity to the sudden heaviness of our conversation.

"Yeah. My F12. *My baby*. That's her name." He shrugs as if it's the most perfectly normal thing in the world, but he lost me at F12, baby, and sex.

"Ummm, can you explain that in a language for those of us with dual X chromosomes?" I laugh bewildered.

He gives me a boyish grin that would melt my panties if I had any on. "F12 is my favorite of all of my collection. She's a Berlinetta Ferrari. The first time Beckett drove her he told me that the feeling was equivalent to the best sex he's ever had. It was a joke at first, but the name stuck. So…" he shrugs his shoulders, and I just shake my head at him "...Sex."

"*Collection?*"

"Women have shoes. Men have cars." It's the only explanation he gives. I'm about to ask more when he announces, "We're here." He shifts in his seat so that he's closer to the door and butterflies take flight in my stomach. "Show time."

Before I can mentally prepare myself any further, the door to the limo opens. Even though Colton's body standing in the doorway partially blocks the flash of cameras, I am temporarily blinded by their intensity.

Colton calls out a casual laid-back greeting to the paparazzi as he buttons up his jacket before turning to help me. I take a deep breath as I take his hand and scoot out of the limo. I exit the car and look up at him, a reassuring smile on his face. Gone is the brooding guy in the car from moments before. *Hello Hollywood playboy.*

"You okay?" he mouths to me and I nod my head subtly, overwhelmed by the onslaught of people yelling at us along with the repeated camera flashes. He pulls me toward him, his mouth resting against my ear. "Remember to smile and follow my lead," he murmurs. "You look stunning tonight." He pulls back, squeezing my hand and graces me with one of his panty wetting smiles before turning to walk the carpet.

And the only thought that breaks through the buzz surrounding us is that from this point forward, I am no longer anonymous to the press.

Chapter Sixteen

My eyes still have bright white spots in my field of vision, but I survived the red carpet. I feel so disoriented and oddly taken advantage of by the press' invasive questions and incessant picture taking. I have no idea how Colton can be so relaxed in such a situation. *Maybe years of practice.* He was calm and polite, and avoided answering the questions thrown at him—were we an item, how long had we been together, what was my name?—and deflected them with the flash of his smile, giving them the perfect picture for their cover page instead.

Colton squeezes my hand in sympathy. "Sometimes I forget how nerve wracking that can be to someone who's never done it before." He gives me a quick, chaste kiss on the lips before directing me toward the ballroom. "Forgive me. I should have prepped you for it before hand."

"Don't worry about it," I tell him, relaxing at the warmth of his hand on my back. "I'm fine."

The red carpet is one thing, but I don't think anything could have prepared me for what I'd feel entering a room with Colton. It seems as if every head in the room turns when we walk through the doorway, all of their attention focused on the man beside me. The man is just simply magnetic in every sense of the word: looks, attitude, charisma, and personality. I falter at the sudden attention. Colton feels my hesitancy and pulls me closer against his side, a not so subtle demonstration of ownership and possession to the assessing stares. The unexpected action both surprises me and warms my heart. He leans his mouth to my ear. "Breathe baby," he murmurs, "you're doing just fine. And I can't wait to fuck you later." My eyes flash up to his and the smirk he gives me tames the nerves.

The next hour or so goes by in a flash. Colton and I mingle throughout the crowd, and I'm in awe of the number of people that he knows or is acquainted with. He is so unpretentious that I find myself forgetting the circumstances in which he grew up—where celebrities are family friends and tuxedos are everyday wear.

He's really quite charming, always knowing the right comment to make or when to add a little levity to the conversation with a light joke. He subtly works the sponsorship program into each conversation and patiently answers questions about it in a laid-back fashion that has people committing to the cause without feeling propositioned or badgered.

And he wears my panties as a pocket square—a constant reminder to me of our little interlude in the limo and the seductive promises he made.

I glance around the room and notice several women talking together and stealing glances our way. At first I assume that they're looking at Colton because let's face it, it's hard not to gawk at him. And then when I take a second look, I realize that their gazes are not in admiration of Colton but rather in judgment of his date—me. They eye me cattily, sneers on their faces before turning back to each other to carry on. *Criticizing me, no doubt.* I try to not let it bother me or to let my insecurity get the best of me, but I know what they're thinking. I see Tawny's observations echoed in their looks.

I am so immersed in my thoughts that I didn't realize Colton has maneuvered me behind a tall bistro cocktail table. He turns his back to the room behind us and kisses me to renew my torturous need for him. He pulls his face back to watch me as his hand, blocked to the crowd beyond by his dinner jacket, cups the V between my legs. "Fast and hard? Or nice and slow, Rylee? Which way should I fuck you first?" he murmurs quietly, the timbre of his voice carrying to my ears. My breath catches in my throat as one finger presses between my folds through the fabric of my dress—not enough pressure to set me off, but just enough to cause a ripple of sensation to travel throughout my body.

"Colton?"

A voice interrupts us from over Colton's shoulder. I jolt in awareness from what he was just doing, while a smooth smile slides across his mouth as he turns to address the acquaintance. He greets the gentleman and introduces me even though he knows I most likely need a moment to regain my wits. I'm sure the flush of my cheeks can tell him that much, but when I glance over at him, he's immersed in his conversation about some event they'd attended together in the past. His eyes flick over to me, a lopsided, ghost of a smirk on his face and his eyes suggesting so much more.

I watch Colton, only partially listening to what he's saying, until the couple is called elsewhere, all the while my body humming with desire. To have him so close to me—at my fingertips really—and not be able to touch him? To slide my hands up that sculpted chest beneath that dress shirt? Run my tongue down the V at his hips and taste him? Absolute torture. He leans into me, obviously guessing where my thoughts have drifted off to, and his face brushes against my hair. "God, you're sexy when you're aroused," he whispers to me before pressing a kiss to my temple.

"This is so unfair," I chastise him, pressing a hand against his chest, a foolish grin on my lips. My smile falters momentarily as I catch a nasty look from a passing female out of the corner of my eye. *What's your problem?* I want to ask her. *What have I done to you?*

"Do you want another drink?" he asks, breaking through my mental dress down of unknown bimbo number one. I figure I should number them because I have a feeling there might be more than a few here tonight. I nod my head to his request, knowing the night's just begun and I need a little liquid courage if I'm going to remain at Colton's sexual mercy. "I'll be right back," he tells me before squeezing my hand and heading off to the bar.

I watch him and see several A-list actors stop him on his way to shake his hand or pat his back in greeting. A statuesque blonde sidles up to his side trying to get his attention. I observe Colton, curious as to how he'll interact with her and noting their level of familiarity—the way she touches him, the lean in her body language towards him, the way he looks at her, but at the same time seems annoyed by her presence—makes me wonder if he's slept with her before. I can't tear my eyes away from watching them because deep down I already know the answer.

I know that he's had his fill of women, and I accept that, but at the same time, my acknowledgement does not mean that I'm okay with it. That I want to be privy to it with my own eyes. I watch him dismiss the blonde and continue across the room. By the time he actually makes it to the bar, he is surrounded by a group of people, all vying for his attention, ranging from young to old, men to women.

"He's not going to keep you around you know," an accented voice beside me says quietly.

"Excuse me?" I turn to look at the stunning beauty beside me with the requisite straight, blonde hair.

Hello, bimbo number two.

She smirks at me, her head shaking side to side in disapproval as she sizes me up. "Just what I said," she deadpans. "He doesn't keep us around for long."

Us? As if I want to be any part of anything with her, let alone the newest member of the Colton Donavan Cast Off Club. *Great! Another of his women scorned.* "Thanks for the heads up," I tell her, not hiding my disdain for her presence, "I'll make sure to keep that in mind. *Now if you'll excuse me.*"

When I start to walk away she grabs me by my upper arm. Anger fires in my veins. Every polite bone in my body riots to not whirl around and show her that underneath this glamorous dress is a scrapper willing to fight for what's mine. And right now, Colton is *mine*. My hand itches to reach out and slap her hand off of me. *Or to just slap her in general.*

"Just so you know, when he's done with you and tosses you aside, I'll be there to take your place." With these words, I successfully shrug out of her grip and turn to face her. When I just stare at her with icy contempt, shocked into silence from her audacity, she continues. "Didn't you know Colton likes to dabble with his exes when he's in between women?"

"So what? You just sit around and wait? Seems pathetic to me," I say, shaking my head at her and trying to hide the fact that her words unnerve me.

"He's that good," she rebukes.

As if I didn't know already.

And with her words, I realize that is why all of these exes are so possessive of him, even if in memory. He's the total package in more ways than one. *Less the ability to commit of course.* Suddenly, the sneer on her face is replaced by a dazzling smile. I notice her body language changing and shifting, and I know that Colton is behind me even before my body hums with the awareness of his proximity.

I turn and give him a smile, my countenance one of gratitude for saving me from this woman's talons. "Teagan." He nods to her, a reserved smile on his face and indifference in his voice. "You look lovely as always."

"Colton," she gushes breathlessly, her demeanor completed changed. "So good to see you again." She steps forward to kiss his cheek, and he absently brushes her off by placing his hand on my waist and pulling me tighter into his side. I can tell she is hurt by his lack of attention, so she tries again without success.

"If you'll excuse us, Teagan, we have a room to work," he says politely, dismissing her by steering me away.

He nods to another acquaintance and continues once we are out of earshot. "She's a nasty piece of work," he says before taking a swallow of his drink. "I'm sorry I didn't rescue you sooner."

"It's okay, she was busy informing me that when you discard me, she'll be your in-between-girl until you find someone new. That you always dabble with your exes while searching for your next conquest." I roll my eyes and try to make my tone lighthearted as if her words didn't bug me, but I know later they'll hit me full force when I'm least expecting it.

Because I'm more than sure she was speaking the truth.

Colton throws his head back and laughs loudly. "When Hell freezes over!" he exclaims, brushing off her remarks. "Remind me to tell you about her later. She's a piece of work."

"Good to know. I'll make sure I steer clear of her."

We mingle a bit more, talking up our joint venture in a room filled with deep pockets. We are separated here and there, different conversations tugging us in opposing directions. In those instances when we are apart, I can't help but look over at Colton, my soft smile is the only answer I can give to his wicked smirk.

I find myself alone for a moment and decide to head to the bar to refill my drink. I'm waiting in the rather long line when I hear the three women a couple of patrons behind me. At first I don't think they realize that I can hear them. The rude comments about my choice in dress. About how I am so not Colton's type because I'm not exactly *sample size*. How I'd benefit from a nose job and some lipo. How I wouldn't know how to handle Colton in bed even if he gave me a road map. And it goes on and on until I know for sure that they're saying it loud on purpose, in the hopes of getting to me.

No matter how much I know that they're just jealous and trying to get under my skin, they've most definitely burrowed deep and are succeeding. They've gotten to me despite the knowledge in my head that I'm the one Colton's with tonight. I decide the drink refill I want—that I currently feel like I most definitely could benefit from—isn't worth the mental angst that these bitches are inflicting.

I opt out of line and take a deep breath in fortification, planning to ignore them as I walk by. But I can't do it. I can't let them know they've succeeded. Instead I stop just as I pass them and turn back. I don't care how I feel on the inside. I'm not letting bimbos numbers three, four, and five know that they've gotten to me. I look up to meet their judgmental eyes, take in their condescending sneers, and shrug off their disapproving glares.

"Hey, ladies." I smirk, leaning in closer. "Just so you know, the only road map I need is the little moan that Colton makes as I lick my way down his delicious happy trail that points straight to his obscenely large dick. Thanks for your concern though." I flash a catty smile of my own before walking away without looking back.

My hands are shaking as I walk, veering towards the hallway near the restrooms for a moment to collect myself. Why did I let them get to me? If I'm with Colton, isn't that the only answer I need? *But am I really with Colton?* I see it in his eyes, hear it in his unspoken words, and feel it in his skillful touch. In Vegas he told me that he chose me, but when I asked him to try and give me more than his stupid arrangement, he never answered me, never gave me any of the security a simple, "Yes, I'll try," would have given me.

Maybe it's noticing all of, what I assume to be, his cast-offs here tonight—seeing them still want what they can no longer have and parading around in front of me. Couldn't he have at least warned me?

And then the thought snakes into my psyche. Is that going to be me in a couple of months? One of the many women scorned by the notorious Colton Donavan. I'd like to think not, but after seeing them here tonight, why do I think that I even have a shot at taming the uncontrollable man? Why would he change for me when the myriad before didn't even tempt him to?

I can think that I'm different all day long, but my thoughts mean nothing when his words could mean everything.

I sigh, my nerves calming and unsettled simultaneously as I look down into my empty glass. I let out a little shriek as hands slide around my waist from behind. "There you are," Colton's voice murmurs into my ear, his lips grazing the curve of my shoulder up to my neck. "I couldn't find you."

"*Well hello there, Ace*," I say back to him, the whisper of his lips momentarily quieting my doubts.

"*Ace*, huh?" He chuckles and I try to turn into him, but he keeps his body ghosted to mine with his arms around my torso. He starts walking forward, my legs instinctively moving from the momentum of his. With each step, I can feel him hardening against my lower back. The ache that never really left roars back to life.

Colton's resonating chuckle against my ear snaps me out of thoughts of what I want him—no need him—to do to me right now. It's just too much for me to have our bodies connected from thigh to shoulder. Begging is within the realm of possibilities right now.

"A closet experience?" he asks, and it takes me a moment to get that he's offering up another lame attempt for the meaning behind Ace.

"Nope," I laugh at him, "Where'd that one—"

"God, it couldn't be any more fucking perfect if I'd planned it."

And I see it the minute the words are out of his mouth. He's walked us down toward the isolated end of the janitor's alcove, and ironically we are standing in front of a door marked *Storage*.

I start to laugh but before it can even escape, he has me turned around and pinned against the wall, his body pressing into me, his steel into my softness. Colton props his hands on either side of my head and leans his face into mine, stopping a whisper from my lips. Our chests press together as our desperation to taste one another consumes our air, hijacks our ability to breathe, and steals the process of reason.

Despite our close proximity, our eyes remain open, the connection between us unwavering. *Electric. Combustible.* "Do you have any idea how desperate I am to fuck you right now?" he murmurs, the movement of his lips brushing ever so slightly against mine.

I drown in the liquid heat his words evoke, begging him to pull me under and take me there, but all I can do is exhale an unsteady breath. He leans in and tastes me. My hands itch to fist in his jacket and rip open his shirt, buttons be damned.

Colton pulls back when he hears the click of heels but pulls open the closet door and presses me inside. The minute the door shuts to the darkened closet, Colton has my arms pinned above my head. The only illumination in the closet is the light seeping through the crack of the doorjamb. My mind never once registers my internal demons—the claustrophobia from the accident that usually smothers me at the first inkling of being confined. My only thought is Colton. Fear ceases to exist. I shudder, anticipating the moment his body will crash into mine, push me against the door, and take from me what we've both been so desperately needing.

Release. Connection. Intensity.

But it doesn't happen. The only connection between us is his hands holding my wrists hostage above my head. The closet is too dark to decipher the outline of his body, but I can feel his breath feathering over my face. We stand here like this for a moment, so close that the hairs on my arms stand up, every nerve in my body itching to feel the touch he's yet to give, suspended in this hazy state of need.

"Anticipation can enhance," he whispers, and right now, it is most definitely the definition of Ace. *No doubt.* But I don't have any time to comprehend let alone respond because his lips finally meet mine. And this time, they do more than just taste. They devour. Take without asking. Brand the claim being staked.

The world on the other side of the door ceases to exist. The doubts rioting in my head fall silent. Everything is lost to the sensation of his mouth worshiping mine.

Our tongues dance. Our reverent sighs meld. Our bodies succumb, but never touch. Besides Colton's hands on my wrist and lips on my mouth, he doesn't allow any other part of our bodies to connect.

And I so desperately need to touch him, feel the tightened buds of my nipples rubbing against his chest, feel his fingers trailing up my thighs and touching my most intimate of places.

But he refuses me that silent request, completely in control of the satiation of my detonating desire.

He pulls back on a groan from both of us. "Christ woman," he swears. "You're making it incredibly difficult to pull away from you."

"Then don't." I pant as lust coils so intensely, having him so close yet so far from me in more ways than one.

He growls in a frustrated response and just as quick as we entered the ironic storage closet, we are out of it. I momentarily close my eyes at the sudden wash of light. When I open my eyes again, Colton stands a few feet in front of me, the tension set in his shoulders a result of what I assume is the slippery hold he has on his restraint.

He looks back over his shoulder at me, his jaw set and his eyes warring with something within. "Colton?" I ask, trying to figure out his state of mind.

He just shakes his head at me. "I'm gonna hit the head. Meet you out there?"

I just look at him, a stuttered, "Okay," falling from my lips.

He starts to walk away but stops and turns back and steps toward me. Without preamble, he grabs the back of my neck and pulls me into him for a chaste kiss on the lips before walking away. I hear him call over his shoulder. "I need a minute."

And I need a lifetime.

I'm immersed in a conversation about the merits of my organization and what the new facilities will have to offer when I'm interrupted.

"Rylee!" a voice booms behind me, and when I turn around, I find myself swallowed up in a big bear hug by the arms of Andy Westin. I return the hug, his affection contagious, and then he leans back and holds my arms out to take me in. He whistles. "Wow! You're looking absolutely stunning this evening," he compliments, and I can see exactly who Colton learned how to charm from.

"Mr. Westin, so glad to see you again," I tell him, and I am surprised that I really am. In a room full of pretension, he brings vibrancy and sincerity.

He waves a hand in the air. "I told you, please call me Andy."

"Alright, Andy then. Does Colton know you're here? Can I get you a drink?"

"Nonsense. I'll get myself a drink in a moment," he says, patting my arm while searching the crowd. "We haven't seen him yet. We've been busy seeing old friends and hearing about this great cause."

"Kids Now definitely is," I muse.

He grins widely. "Speaking of good causes, I hear you and my boy are working on a little something together for your own organization."

"Yes we are!" I exclaim, a thrill shooting through me at the sudden realization that this is really happening. I am actually here promoting the new facility and its culmination. "With Colton's help—"

"There you are," a sultry voice interrupts me. I turn to see its owner and find that I am face to face with Dorothea Donavan-Westin. She is absolutely stunning, and there is a gracefulness about her—in her movement, in her smile, in how she holds herself—that makes you want to just watch and admire.

"Dottie, sweetheart! I didn't know where you went off to," Andy says as he kisses her cheek.

Dorothea looks over to me, her sapphire blue eyes alight with humor. "He's always losing me." She laughs.

"Dottie dear, this is Rylee..."

"Thomas," I finish for Andy.

"Thomas. Yes," he says, winking at me, thankful for my assistance. "Please meet my wife, Dorothea..." he turns to her "...she's the one that Colton is working with on—"

"Yes I know, dear..." she pats his arm affectionately "...I am on the board after all." She turns to face me and extends a perfectly manicured hand. "So glad to finally meet you in person, Rylee. I've heard such great things about your work through the committee."

I reach out to shake her hand, surprised by my nerves. Where Andy is warm and inviting, Dorothea is reserved and regal. A person who makes you want to have their approval without so much as saying a word. Commanding. "Thank you. So lovely to meet you as well," I smile warmly at her. "Your husband and I were just talking about that. Your son's generous donation has made the facility become a tangible reality for us. Once his team figures the total lap match sponsorship, we just might be able to start pulling permits."

Pride fills Dorothea's face at the mention of her son, and I can see the unconditional love in her eyes. "Well I guess it was a good thing I fell ill and forced him to attend in my place then." She laughs. "Despite the incessant grumbling I had to listen to about being forced to wear a tux."

I can't help but smile at her words; I heard the same grumbling earlier. "We are overwhelmed by his generosity. Words cannot express how much it is appreciated. And then to go above and beyond and try to get sponsorships to complete the funding..." I place my hand over my heart. "It just leaves us—me—speechless. Overwhelmed, really."

"That's our boy!" Andy exclaims, reaching for a flute of champagne from a passing waitress and handing it to Dorothea.

"You should be so proud of him. He's a good man." The words are out of my mouth before I even realize it, and I find myself slightly embarrassed. My unexpected admission to his parents is insight into my feelings for their beloved son.

Dorothea angles her head to the side and regards me over her champagne flute as she takes a sip. "So tell me, Rylee, are you here with Colton tonight on a professional or a personal level?"

I must look like a deer in the headlights at her words and I look from Dorothea to Andy and back again. What am I supposed to say? That I'm in love with your son, but he still thinks of me as a woman he fucks because he refuses to accept that he might have feelings for me? I hardly think that's an appropriate thing to say to one's parents regardless of its truth or not. My mouth opens to say something when Andy intervenes.

"Don't badger the girl, Dottie!" he says playfully, winking at me as I silently thank him.

"Well..." she shrugs in apology, although I doubt she's remorseful "...a mother likes to know these things. In fact, I think—"

"What a pleasant surprise!" I hear the smooth rasp of Colton's voice, and relief floods me that I won't have to answer her question.

"Colton!" Dorothea exclaims as she turns to face her son. I'm surprised when he grabs his mom in a huge bear hug, rocking her back and forth before kissing her on the cheek, his face lighting up with love for her. She accepts his affection openly and places both hands on his cheeks and looks into his eyes. "Let me look at you! It feels like forever since I've seen you!"

He smiles at her, his adoration apparent. "It's only been a couple of weeks." He smirks at her as he pats his dad on the back in greeting. "Hey, Dad!"

"Hey, bud," Andy says, putting an arm around Colton's shoulders and squeezing momentarily. "What's this?" he asks, bringing a hand up to playfully rub Colton's cheek. "You actually shaved for tonight? Your mother was surprised when she saw the picture from the event the other night of you and—"

"You looked so handsome, Colton. All clean-shaven..." She cuts her husband off with a warning glance before smiling adoringly at her son. "You know how much I like when you shave that scruff off of your face. You look much better without it!"

Colton looks over at me, a crooked smirk on his face, his eyes telling me that he remembers my comment about just how much I enjoy the scruff against my inner thighs. "I see you've met Rylee?" he says as he slides an arm around my waist and pulls me against him, leaning over to brush his lips to my temple. I instinctively lean into him, not missing the look of surprise that's exchanged between his parents. Over what I'm unsure, but Andy's look to Dorothea appears to say *see what I mean.*

"Yes, we were just speaking about her company's new project," his mother replies, studying him closely, a bemused look on her face.

"Rylee's done a great job," he says, the pride brimming in his eyes surprises me. "If you saw the boys—the ones that are currently under her charge—what great kids they are, you'd understand why becoming involved was a no-brainer. Why this project needs to be completed." His enthusiasm is heartfelt and that is endearing to me. "But you already know that, don't you, Mom?"

We speak for a few moments before Andy excuses himself to go get a drink, and I do the same heading for the restroom. I take a few steps away when Colton places his hand on my lower back and stops me with the murmur of my name. His body presses up behind me, connecting us together like puzzle pieces.

"Don't even think about getting yourself off in that bathroom." He growls quietly into my ear causing spirals of need to electrify my every nerve. "I know you're desperate to feel me buried inside you as much as I am. I know the ache is so intense it burns. But, baby, I'm the only one allowed to take you there." He runs his hand up the side of my ribcage. "Not your fingers. Not a toy. Not any other fucker in this room." He exhales and I'm envious of his ability to breathe at this moment. "Just me. And I'm nowhere near done with you yet." He presses a kiss to the back of my head. "Mine. Understood?"

I swallow, trying to find my voice. His words were just so seriously hot that I swear I can feel the moisture pooling between my thighs. I nod my head and only when I am several feet away from him—when I can actually think without him clouding my coherency—am I able to draw a breath.

The bathroom is empty when I enter, and I head to the furthest stall against the wall. I just need a moment to myself. I'm finishing my business when I hear the door creak open and two pairs of heels clicking on the concrete floor, and their laughter echoing off of the tiled walls.

"So who's he here with tonight? He seems pretty serious about her seeing as his eyes aren't wandering astray as usual."

The other woman laughs a throaty reply and something about the familiarity of it causes me to pause with my hand on the door to the stall. "*Oh her?* She's absolutely nothing to worry about."

I hear the smack of lips as if someone is blotting their freshly applied lipstick. "Well by the looks of Page 6, you seem to be right."

"You saw that?" throaty-voiced girl says.

"Yes! You and Colton looked so great together. Like the perfect fucking couple." I bristle at the words when I recognize that throaty-voiced girl, the one saying that I am nothing to worry about, is Tawny.

"Thanks, doll! I think so too. It was such a great evening, and as usual Colton was his ever-attentive self."

Whoa! What in the hell is she talking about? Evening? As usual? My conversation with Colton's parents comes back to my mind. Andy telling Colton that his mother saw a picture of him and someone else before Dorothea cut him off. The picture was with Tawny? I swallow the bile that rises in my throat, trying to calm my thoughts from getting too far out of whack and reading into the comments. I try to push away the pounding rush of my pulse filling my ears, desperate to eavesdrop some more. I feel nauseous, so I back up and sit back down, fully clothed, on the toilet seat.

"I can't believe you ever let him get away in the first place!"

"I know." She sighs. "But he's a man that's definitely hard to sway once he makes his mind up. I've made sure that he knows without question that he can no longer use the excuse that I'm like a sibling to him though." She giggles suggestively. "And I've made sure to be there every step of the way so that in the end he'll turn to me."

"Shut-up! No you didn't..."

"Someone's gotta whip that boy into shape." My stomach revolts at her words.

"Well, I don't think it'll take him much longer now by the looks of that picture," her friend says, and I can mentally see the smirk she has spreading across her lips.

"Yeah, I know." Tawny replies. "She can't give him what he needs. She's so damn naïve. The two of them are like Little Red Riding Hood and the Big Bad Wolf. He's going to eat her alive, spit her out, and then move on to the next."

"*He does have quite the sexual appetite.* Big Bad Wolf...hmm, that fits. Definitely some of the best sex I've ever had." *Wait a minute! Colton's been with the friend too? Deep breath, Rylee. How fucking many of his exes are there here tonight? Deep breath.*

I hear the zipper of a purse close. "He'll tire of her soon enough when she can't fulfill him. I mean look at her...she doesn't have a seductive bone in that body. She's too boring...too plain...*too blah* to keep his rapt attention. And if she's like that on the outside, I can't imagine how utterly lackluster she is between the sheets. You know how he is, predictability is one thing he doesn't tolerate." She laughs. "Besides, I dropped a few hints to him the other night to let him know I was still game. And more than willing to be anyone or do anything he wanted."

Her friend hums in agreement. "Who wouldn't be when it comes to him? *The man's a tireless fucking God in the sack.*"

"I know that better than anyone." Tawny chuckles, the sound crawling up my spine. "Besides, I can be patient. Time is most definitely on my side."

"You ready?" I hear a second purse zip and the clicking of heels again until the door closes shut, bathing me in silence.

What the hell? I fumble in my purse for my phone. I click on Google and type in "Page 6, Colton Donavan." I click on the first link that pops up and brace myself when the image fills the screen. It is a picture of Colton walking out of the Chateau Marmont. His hand is placed on Tawny's lower back, who is decked out in a stunningly sexy, red dress. She is turned, looking up at him, her hand on his lapel, adoration filling her eyes, and a suggestive smile on her face. Colton is looking down at her, his face crinkled in laughter as if they've just shared a private joke. When I can finally tear my eyes away from the obvious chemistry between them, I glance at the date of the photo.

The date is this past Wednesday. The same day that Colton took the kids and me to the go-kart track. I groan out loud in the empty restroom at the realization that I got him all riled up in sexual frustration, and then I sent him off to a function with Tawny. *Fucking great!* I glance at the photo again, hoping maybe it is a stock photo the paper used to fill space, but then I take a closer look and notice that Colton is clean-shaven. He's never clean-shaven. Wednesday was the first time since I've known him that he's been like that. I feel a sharp pain in my gut as I stare at the picture again. Colton had told me that he had a work function to go to. At the Chateau Marmont with Tawny? What the hell type of function were they at, and why were they leaving together looking so damn cozy?

I take a deep breath, my thoughts rioting violently around in my head as Tawny's verbal digs enter my conscience again and take hold.

I start to feel suffocated in the confines of the bathroom stall. I fumble with the lock on the stall and hurry past the vanities. I glance at myself in the mirror quickly and am shocked that my appearance is so calm and collected when my insides twist over this newfound information.

I force myself to calm down and not jump to conclusions. Tawny is a family friend and a business associate. Of course they have to go to functions together. The picture was probably snapped at just the right moment to capture a scene people could talk about. One they could make assumptions about. There are probably twenty other pictures in that scene that are boring and non-gossip worthy. Besides, the fact that Tawny still has a thing for Colton shouldn't surprise me; she let me know as much at the track.

When I exit the bathroom, I'm still trying to talk myself down from the ledge of insecurity. I can't find Colton, so I head toward the bar, needing another drink to soothe my frayed nerves. I tell myself that I know Colton's had his share of women, but he told me in Vegas that I'm who he wants. It'd be so much easier to accept if he'd just admit to me that we were something more—that we were exclusive—anything to tell me verbally that emotions are a part of the picture. That I'm not just his physical plaything.

Get that out of your head, Rylee! I have to accept that he shows me with actions, not words. That's all he's willing to give me, and I have to accept this or walk away. I sigh in frustration. I thought I was mentally okay with this. Really I did, but then you add the mix of bimbos tonight and my insecurities have resurfaced. And having them thrown in my face repeatedly by Tawny and then tonight by Teagan—as well as bimbos three through five—makes it that much more difficult. Colton's the total package. I should be flattered that other women want to be with him.

Keep telling yourself that, Ry, and maybe someday you'll believe it.

I order a drink from the bar and when I turn to walk away, I spot Colton talking to some gentlemen across the room. I smile, the sight of him dissipating all of my doubts. As I start to walk toward him, his conversation ends and before he turns to walk away, a woman walks up to him and embraces him in a hug that lasts a little too long for my liking. And of course she is a blonde, breathtaking beauty that rivals him in the stunning looks department. When she turns so I can see her, it's none other than bimbo number five from the bar line earlier.

The flames of irritation flicker to life inside of me.

Here we go again. I stop in my path and watch their interaction. Whereas Colton's exchange with Teagan was pleasant but detached, his conversation with bimbo number five is anything but distant. When I see him smile sincerely at her and leave his hand pressed to her lower back instead of moving it, I bite back the jealousy that streaks.

He's done nothing wrong or improper, but the familiarity between them is obvious. I force myself to look away, and it is then that my eyes meet Tawny's from across the room. Her blue eyes hold mine, contempt and condescension thrown at me in the simple glare. She crosses her arms across her torso as she flicks her eyes over to Colton and then back to mine. A derisive smirk lifts one corner of her mouth as she shakes her head. She makes a show of looking down to her watch and tapping on the face of it before looking back up at me. *The clock's ticking, Rylee. Your time is almost up.*

I turn back toward Colton, careful not to give her any reaction in my facial expression despite my surmounting anger. There's not enough alcohol in this room right now for me to hold a conversation with her. I could use a good Haddie-pep-talk right now. *Where the hell is she when I need her?*

I start to make my way toward Colton when the blonde he's with lifts her eyes from his to meet mine. She gives me the same quick but appraising look she had earlier, but his time it's followed by the flash of an insolent smile. Yet another female that wants me out of the picture so that she can make her move. Then again, it doesn't seem like anyone's waiting. They don't seem to have any problem making their moves right in front of me.

I need a break from all of this frickin' drama and the inferno of irrationality that's smothering all of my oxygen. I decide to head outside to get some fresh air and regain my sense of self that these blonde leaches seem to be sucking from me bit by bit.

Colton's gaze follows bimbo number five's and meets mine. A smile lights up his face as I approach, but it falls slightly when he sees the look on my face. "You okay?"

"Mmm-hmm," I murmur, purposely avoiding looking at his companion. "I just need to get some air," I say and continue right past him without stopping to answer the questioning look on his face.

I hurry out of the ballroom, making it to the exit unscathed. I push open the doors and draw in the fresh, night air. It's cold but more than welcomed. I need it after the stifling atmosphere inside. I walk hastily toward the gardens I'd noticed on the way in, hoping that they're empty at this time of night.

Needing solitude.

Chapter Seventeen

"Rylee!" Colton calls my name but I keep walking, needing some momentary distance from him. *"Rylee!"* he repeats, and I can hear the heavy fall of his footsteps on the sidewalk behind me. They echo off of the concrete walls, confirming how I feel—that no matter how far I go, Colton will always be there. In thought. In memory. In everything. He's ruined me for anyone else. I have no other option but to stop when I come to the end of a path.

"Stop running!" He pants from behind me as he catches up. *"Tell me what's wrong."*

Colton's technically done nothing wrong tonight, but all of my angst and insecurity brought on by the various women from the night boils inside of me. Even the most confident, self-secure woman would be affected by his many admirers tonight. I know I should be confident in the notion that Colton came here with me—will be leaving with me—but then again, isn't that what Raquel thought the night of the Merit Rum launch?

I need words from him. I need to hear it. And he hasn't given me that yet. Actions can be misconstrued. Words cannot...and let's face it, I'm female. Aren't we programmed to read into things?

When he reaches out to touch my arm, it all comes to a head. I whirl around. "How many, Ace?" I shout at him, my breath turning white against the cool night air.

"What?" His face is a mixture of confusion and surprise. "How many what?"

"How many of your exes are here tonight?"

"Rylee—"

"Don't Rylee me," I yell at him, stepping back so I can have the space I so desperately need to keep my head clear. "If you're going to bring me here tonight and parade your bevy of blonde beauties in front of me—all the women that you've fucked—the least you can do is give me a heads up." When he starts to interrupt me, I meet his eyes and the look in mine causes the words on his lips to falter. "It's bad enough that you have Tawny—your permanent go-to-girl—who still wants you and is around constantly. Working for you. Pushing her perfectly manufactured tits in your face. Making sure you know that she'll be there for you when you tire of the current flavor of the month." The look of utter shock on his face is priceless. He looks as if I've told him the sky is yellow. Has he never noticed this? Her willingness? A part of me sags in respite knowing that he doesn't see Tawny this way, but *what about all of the others from tonight?* "And then you bring me here tonight and parade more in front of me? The least you could have done was forewarn me…prepare me for the onslaught of nasty looks and catty barbs. So how many, Ace?" I demand, *"or do I even want to know?"*

Colton looks at me and shakes his head, the corners of his mouth turning up sheepishly. "C'mon, Ry, it's not that bad. Tawny's just an old friend—she works for me for fuck's sake—and the others…we just run in the same circles. We're bound to see each other sometimes." He takes a step toward me, a lascivious smirk spreading across his gorgeous face. "You're just frustrated because you're on edge..." he moves closer, his voice suggestively smooth "...and you have needs. You're sexually frustrated."

I stare at him, my mouth falling open. *Did he really just say that?* That's his fucking response to my reasons for being so upset? To why I'm going off the deep end? *I need to come and it will make everything better?* After that all of his whores will go back and bury themselves in the holes they've been hiding in?

"C'mere, let me take care of that for you." He reaches out, unbeknownst to him how angry I am at his callous comment and tries to pull me toward him. And as much as I want him to take care of the ache burning deep inside of me, as much as intimacy with him would assuage my doubts for how he feels about me, my anger and dignity override my needs. I shrug my arms from his grasp and take a step back.

Colton's face blankets with shock, his mouth parting slightly as he stares at me. *"You're telling me no?"* he asks incredulously.

I snort out in disgust. "A new concept for you no doubt, *but yes."* I sigh. *"I'm telling you no."*

He stares at me for a moment, his eyes narrowing and then his face softens into acknowledgment. "You have more restraint than me. I see what you're trying to do here," he murmurs, shaking his head, and for some reason I get the sense that he thinks I'm toying with him. That I'm telling him no, just to play hard to get.

"Sex isn't going to fix things, Colton." I huff at him, rubbing my hands up and down my arms to ward off the chill.

"It might just a little bit," he jokes, trying to get a smile out of me. While I continue to glare at him, shaking my head and sighing deeply, he mutters a curse and walks away from me a few steps. He brings a hand to his neck and pulls down while angling his head up to the night sky and exhaling loudly. "Shit!" he mutters before falling silent for a beat. "I can't change my past, Rylee. I am who I am and I can't change that. You knew that going into this when you started all your goddamn talk about not being able to accept the *only thing* I can give you."

"What? So now we're back to that? An *arrangement?* I'm not one of your whores, Colton. *Never have been. Never will be.*" My voice cuts through the silence of the night around us.

He steps back toward me, lowering his head and looking at the ground in front of him, his jaw clenching as he finds his next words. When he finally speaks, his voice is unbending. "I told you I'd fuck this up."

His words—his excuse—followed on the heels of everything tonight, enrage me. "Don't be such a martyr!" I shout at him. "Grow the fuck up and quit using your so-called goddamn defense mechanism as an excuse, Colton!" The words are out before I can stop them, anger overriding common sense. He snaps his head up, his eyes blazing with anger as they meet mine. He takes a step back from me, the physical distance just emphasizing the emotional detachment I can sense happening. I know I'm probably overreacting. But that knowledge does nothing to stop the freight train of emotions running through me. "*Fuck. This,*" I mutter. "If you've had your way with me and don't want me anymore…if you want one of your cookie cutter blondes inside…then man-up and just tell me!"

He says nothing to me, just sits there, jaw clenched, shoulders tense, and eyes staring at me, a mixture of reactions crossing his shadowed face. I'm not sure what I expect him to say, but *I'd hoped that he'd at least say something.* I thought that maybe he'd put up a fight to keep me with him, to prove to me that I'm worth it.

I guess if I'm going to make ultimatums than I'd better be prepared to stand by them. Fear snakes down my spine when he doesn't utter a sound. I stare at him, willing him to speak. To prove my words wrong. To prove them right. *Anything.*

But he says nothing. Just a shell of a man staring at me with eyes emotionless, lips silent, and patience wearing thin.

Anger fills me. Hurt consumes me. Regret weighs heavy. I knew this was going to happen. He predicted it, and I ignored it. I thought I was *enough* to change the outcome. "You know what, Colton? Screw you!" I yell, the only words I can verbalize to portray how I feel. Not very intelligent sounding, but it's all I have. "Just tell me one thing before you walk away and move on to the next willing candidate…*besides the obvious,* what does screwing all of these women do for you, Ace?" I step closer to him, wanting to see the reaction in his eyes, needing to see some type of response from him. "What need does it fulfill that you refuse to acknowledge? Don't you want more? Deserve more out of that connection than just a warm body and a fleeting orgasm?" When he doesn't respond but rather has irritation flash across his face, I continue. "Fine, don't answer that question…but answer this one: *Don't you think that I deserve more?*"

I see pain in his emerald eyes and a flicker of something darker, deeper, and I know that I've churned something within him. Hurt him. *But I'm hurt too.* He remains silent, and that pisses me off even more.

"What? You're too chicken shit to answer that?" I goad. "*Well I'm not!* I know I deserve more, Colton! I deserve so much more than you're willing to even try for. You're missing out on the best part of being with someone. All of the little things that make a relationship special." I throw my hands up to emphasize my point, all the while he stares at me, stone faced and jaw clenched. I pace back and forth in front of him trying to contain my pent up frustration. "Your four to five month time limit doesn't give you any of that, Ace. It doesn't give you the comfort of knowing someone cares for you so much that they are there for you even when you're being irrational. *Or an asshole.*" I sneer at him, my blood pumping and thoughts coming so fast I can't spit them out of my mouth fast enough. "You rob yourself of knowing what it's like to surrender yourself—mind, body, and soul to someone. To be completely naked—exposed and selfless—when you're *fully clothed*. You don't understand how special any of that is," I rant, realizing how sadly deprived he is with his choices. "Well I do. And that's what I want. Why has this always been about what you want? *What about me?* Don't I deserve to feel how I feel and not hold back because of some implied rules?"

He just stares at me, his body tense, his voice silent, and I can feel him slipping away. A tear slides silently down my cheek, my breath panting out in white puffs after my verbal diatribe. I don't feel any better because nothing's been solved. The wall he's hid behind for so long—that he's been slowly peeking over—is suddenly reinforced with steel.

I look at him, *the man I love*, and my chest tightens and heart twists in pain. This is what I was afraid of. What my head and heart fought over and against. And yet here I am, scared and scarred, but still fighting for him, because Teagan is right. *He's just that good.* His words run through my head.

You burned me, Rylee.

You. This. It scares the shit out of me, Rylee.

I can't seem to get enough of you.

I step forward, wanting to touch him. Craving any kind of connection with him, needing to remind him of that spark between us when we touch and to try and prevent him from slipping through my fingers. *Like trying to grab the wind.* I reach my trembling hands out, his eyes following their movement, and lay them on his chest. I feel him stiffen in response, a proverbial slap at my attempt to connect with him that pushes me over the edge.

My eyes flash up to his, and I see that he knows how much he just hurt me with that small flinch—the nonverbal rejection that just spoke volumes. He instinctively brings his arms up to wrap them around me, to try and placate me, and I can't let that happen. I can't let him pull me into the one place I want to be more than anywhere else right now because nothing between us has changed. And I know if I'm wrapped in his arms, I will succumb to everything all over again so I won't lose what I fear the most—*him*. But I deserve the whole him that he's unable—*no, unwilling*—to give me.

I push against his chest, but his hands tighten their grip on my shoulders. He tries to pull me into him, but I struggle against him. When he doesn't react…I lose it. "Fight damn it! Fight, Colton!" I yell at him, desperation seeping as my voice wavers and tears threaten. "For you. For us. For me," I plead. "You don't get to pull away from me. You don't get to walk away without a second thought." I'm still trying to resist his hold, but the dam breaks and the tears overflow. "I matter, Colton. I deserve the same *more* that you do. *What we have is not inconsequential!*"

Overcome with emotion, I succumb to my tears, my fears, the emptiness looming. I stop resisting him and he gathers me in his arms and pulls me to him, his hands running up and down over my back and arms and neck. The feeling is bittersweet because I know it's fleeting. I know that the words I so desperately want and need to hear—that this is something…that we are something…anything to him—are never coming.

I consciously etch this moment to my memory.

His warmth.

The rasp of his calloused fingers across my bare skin.

The clenching of his jaw against my temple.

The timbre of his hushed murmurs.

His scent.

I close my eyes to absorb it because I know I've scared him. I know I'm asking for too much when there are so many others willing to settle for so much less.

"Rylee…" My name is a whispered hush over my now tearless sobs.

I fall silent, my hitching breath the only sound in the night. I lean back, his hands on my shoulders guiding me so he can see my face. I steel myself before looking up to meet his eyes. I can see fear and confusion and uncertainty in them, and I'm waiting for him to verbalize what's on the tip of his tongue. His internal struggle plays out on his usually stoic face before he reins it in. My chest aches as I try to draw in a breath and prepare myself because what I see makes me panic. Has me resigning all of my fate because I know he's preparing himself to walk away.

To say goodbye.

To break me apart.

"I deserve more, Colton." I breathe out, shaking my head as a single tear trails down my cheek. His eyes follow it before looking back at me, and for a moment they soften with concern, his throat working a swallow as he nods his head in agreement. I reach a hand out and place it on his jaw, his eyes cautiously tracking my movements. I feel his jaw muscles tighten beneath my palm. "I know this is the whole reason you have your rules and stipulations, but I can't abide by them anymore. *I can't be that girl for you anymore.*"

I lower my head at my last comment, avoiding his eyes because I can't bear to see the reaction. Wanting and not getting one or wanting and being rejected—either one will shred my heart more than it already is. I sigh deeply, eyes focused intently on his impromptu pocket square and my mind marveling how simple things seemed just a couple of hours ago when he was underdressed and I was overdressed.

He tenses his fingers on my biceps, and I force myself to look back up at him—glad I did because the look in his eyes takes my breath away. My gorgeous bad boy looks like a child—panic stricken and petrified. I struggle to find words to speak because standing there with that look in his eyes; he looks just like one of my damaged boys. It takes a moment, but I'm finally able to find my voice.

"I'm sorry, Colton." I shake my head. "You did nothing wrong tonight but be the man that you are…

but seeing your exes here tonight still wanting more..." I sigh "...I don't want to be them in three months. *On the outside looking in*. I can't stand by and blindly obey the parameters you dictate anymore. I want to have a say." He shakes his head back and forth, automatically rejecting the idea, and I don't even think he realizes he's doing it. The grip of his hands tightens on my arms, but he says nothing to refute what I'm saying.

"I'm not asking for love from you, Colton." My voice is barely a whisper when I speak, but my conscience is screaming that I am. That I want him to love me the way I love him. His eyes widen at my confession. His sharp intake of air audible. "I'm not even asking for a long-term commitment from you. I just want to be able to explore whatever this is between us without worrying about overstepping imaginary boundaries that I don't even know exist." I stare at him, willing him to hear my words. Really hear what I'm saying, not just what he wants to hear. "I'm asking to be your lover, Colton, not your happily ever after or your structured arrangement. All I want is a chance..." My voice trails off, asking for the impossible. "For you to tell me you'll try..."

"You were never an arra—"

"Let's call a spade a spade." I arch my eyebrows at him, trying to summon the fire that coursed through my veins moments before that has since been replaced with desolation. "You have an uncanny way of putting me in my place any time I overstep one of your asinine boundaries."

We stare at each other, unspoken words on our lips, and he is the first to look away and break our connection. He shrugs out of his dinner jacket, and wraps it around my shoulders, ever the consummate gentleman even in the midst of turmoil, but where his fingers would normally linger on my skin, he recoils instantly.

"I never meant to hurt you, Rylee." His voice cracks with a quiet vulnerability I've never heard before. I'd never expect from him. He lowers his head, shaking it subtly, and mutters *fuck* under his breath. Déjà vu hits me from the night in the hotel room, and all the air punches from my lungs. "I don't want to hurt you any further."

This is it.

He's going to end it right here, right now. Doing what I can't for the life of me do myself. I press the heel of my hand to my chest, trying to press away the ache that sears through me. He runs his hands through his hair, and I tremble in anticipation, waiting for him to continue but hoping he doesn't. He lifts his head and reluctantly meets my eyes. He is stripped bare—haunted, desolate—the emotion so transparent in his eyes it's hard to hold his gaze.

And in this moment, it hits me. I realize that I've been chastising him for not fighting for me, but has anyone ever really fought for him besides his parents? Not for his material possessions or his notoriety, but for the little boy he was and for the man he is now? For the years of abuse and neglect I'm sure he endured. Has anyone ever told him they love him not despite it but rather because of it? And that all of those experiences combined have in fact made him a better person. A better man. That they accept all of him regardless—every maddening, confusing, heartwarming, piece of him.

I bet no one has.

And as much as I'm hurting and want to lash out at him in return, a part of me wants to leave him with something no one else has ever given him. Something to remember me by.

"For you, Colton..." My voice may be soft when I speak, a resignation to our fate, but my honesty comes through loud and clear. "...I'd take the chance." I can visibly see his body stiffen at my admission. His lips part slightly and the tension leaves his jaw, as if he is shocked that I'd be willing to take the chance on him. *That I believe he's worth the risk.*

He takes a step toward me and reaches a hand out tentatively to frame my jaw. He stares into my eyes with an unfettered intensity, his lips opening several times to say something but closing without a sound. I inhale a sharp breath at the resonance of his touch as he rubs the pad of his thumb over my bottom lip—the roughness of his calloused fingers against the softness of my lips. A horrible sadness takes hold when I realize rough and soft is in a way a lot like us.

"For you, Rylee," he whispers, his voice breaking. His usually steady hands tremble ever so slightly against my cheeks, and I swear I can see fear flicker through his eyes before he blinks away the moisture that pools in them. "*I will try.*"

He will try? My mind has to switch gears so quickly that I'm left disoriented. Talk about going from an unbelievable low to an unexpected high. "*You'll try?*" my broken voice asks, not believing my ears.

Just a trace of the crooked, roguish smile that I find irresistible curves up one side of his mouth, but I can hear the trepidation in his tone. "*Yes,*" he repeats. His eyes burn into mine until my eyes flutter closed as he leans in and gives me the gentlest, most reverent kiss I've ever received. He then kisses the tip of my nose before resting his forehead against mine. His breath whispers against my lips, and his heart pounds a frantic tattoo against my chest all the while my insides are leaping for joy, bubbling over with hope.

Holy shit! Colton is going to try. He is going to fight for us. For me. For him. There is so much unspoken beneath his declaration. So much promise, fear, vulnerability, and willingness to overcome whatever plagues his dreams at night and incessantly haunts his memories—just to try and be with me.

He dips his head down and kisses me again. A slow, soft brush of lips and dance of tongues that is so packed with unspoken words it causes tears to well in my eyes. He finishes by kissing my nose again and then pulling me into him in a crushing embrace. I sigh, welcoming his warmth, his strength, and enjoying how the long, lean line of his body fits perfectly against my curves. I drink in his scent and the sound of his heart beating beneath my ear. He leans his face down, his cheek rubbing against my temple, as he emits a sigh that sounds similar to a muttered oath. And I swear it sounds like he mutters something about a *voodoo pussy*, but when I snap my head up to look at him, he just shakes his head and smirks.

"What am I going to do with you, Rylee?" He holds me tighter, chills dancing up my spine. "What am I going to do?" He sighs again and I suppress a smothered chuckle as I wriggle against him. The mixture of his body on mine, the relief in knowing he is going to try, and the anticipated buildup of the evening has me more than desperate for just a platonic hug in a garden.

How can such a simple statement leave me breathless with anticipation and desperate for his touch—emotionally and physically? He trails a finger down the line of my neck before dipping it down into the bodice and then descending the long torturous path downward, parting the draped slit of my dress to my hypersensitive sex. His deft fingers find me weeping and wanting, and when he touches me I swear I'm ready to splinter into a million pieces of pleasure. I gasp a strangled moan from its effect.

I lean into him, my forehead pressing against his chest, my hands gripping his biceps. I'm not sure if my responsiveness is from Colton's willingness to try or the onslaught of sensation, but my body climbs the precipice quicker than normal. I am so close. So close to the brink that my nails dig into his arms.

Colton slides his fingers back and forth one more time before emitting a feral growl. "Not yet…I want to be buried in you when you come, Rylee," he murmurs against the crown of my head. "I'm desperate to be."

I suck in an audible breath, my muscles so taut and nerves so aware of the feeling of his body against mine that I can't contain myself. I launch myself at him like an addict needing a fix. One hand grips the back of his neck, automatically fisting his hair, and pulls his face lower so I can meet his mouth. My other hand reaches down to rub the hard length of his growing erection against his slacks. His guttural moan tells me he's bound with as much need as I am.

I kiss him with a hungry desperation, passion unfurling between us, as I pour everything I've been holding back into our melding of mouths. He snakes his hands between his jacket that I'm wearing and my dress, his hands mapping the lines of my backside and hips, inciting a need so strong that it rocks me senseless and leaves me breathless.

"Colton," I moan as he laces open mouth kisses down the line of my throat, sending earthquakes of sensation rocketing through me.

"Car. Parking garage. Now," he says between kisses with a teeming desperation, restraint non-existent.

I agree with a non-coherent moan, but my body doesn't want to let up or let go. His hand fists my hair and pulls it down so my face is forced up. The dark desire that clouds his eyes has my thighs clenching together, begging for relief. "Ry? If we don't walk right now, you're going to find yourself bent over that bench right there in plain view of all of these hotel rooms." His husky warning has me swallowing loudly. He leans down and kisses me chastely, his tongue tracing the line of my bottom lip. "You've annihilated my control, sweetheart. Elevator. Now," he commands.

He pulls me to his side, his hand clamped on my hip as we walk quickly. With his free hand, Colton pulls his iPhone out of his pocket. "Sammy? Where's Sex?" He listens for a moment. "Perfect. That works." He laughs loudly, the timbre of it echoing off of the concrete walls we walk past. "Like you read my mind. You're fucking awesome Sammy...Yeah. I'll let you know." He slips his phone back in his pocket as we reach a path, and I'm mystified as to the conversation he just had. Colton looks left and then right, weighing his options with a forced urgency before veering right.

Within moments we are in an elevator at the outskirts of a concrete parking garage. The drab grey doors shut, Colton's presence dominating the small space, and before the elevator starts to move upwards, Colton has me pinned against the wall with his hips and his mouth feasting on mine with a raw carnality. I don't even have time to catch my breath before the car pings. He drags his mouth from mine, leaving me shaken by his consuming desire.

Chapter Eighteen

When we exit the elevator, a giggle escapes my lips. Who in the hell is this girl that I turn into when I'm with Colton? This brazen, wanton woman so sure of her sexuality? I definitely wasn't her an hour ago. I swear it's the *Colton effect*.

I jolt in surprise when we turn the corner and Sammy is standing there. "Hi, Sammy," I say shyly, for once again he's seeing me in my Colton-induced path to indecency. He nods at me, his face remaining stoic as he hands a set of keys out to Colton.

"Thanks. All clear?" Colton asks.

"All clear," Sammy nods before stepping onto the elevator car.

"Come," Colton commands as he pulls my hand so I land against him forcefully before his lips meet mine again in a greedy kiss. I push him back momentarily despite his protests and glance around at our surroundings to make sure we don't have an unsuspecting audience. My eyes focus immediately on a sexy-as-sin, sleek, red sports car in the far corner. I'm not really into cars, but all I know is that if *that's* her name? It most definitely fits her.

When I pull my eyes away from the Ferrari, I'm surprised to find the monochromatic garage completely vacant. "How'd…?" He just smirks at me with that *it's good to be me* kind of smirk and I shake my head. "*Sammy?*"

"Mmm-hmm." His hand roams up my waist and cups my breast through my dress. I exhale a soft moan at the muted sensation, wanting his body, naked and moving, on mine. In mine.

"Oh, Colton…" I sigh, turning into putty in his hands as his finger dips beneath the fabric. "That man needs a raise," I murmur as we pseudo-walk, pseudo-grope each other across the desolate garage. He laughs loudly at my comment, the sound mixed with the click of my heels echoing off of the walls. I push away the niggling feeling in my head that I wonder just what else Sammy has seen under Colton's employment. That was the past. His past.

And now, he's my future. All that matters now is that Colton's willing to try.

We reach the car, relief that we can get out of here flooding through me. Right now I'm being selfish. I'm not thinking about the gala below or my charity or anything. All I can focus on is the feelings coursing through me. The ones I need met as I steer our bodies toward the passenger side.

But Colton stands still—*doesn't budge*—just keeps my hand in his, our arms outstretched from the connection. I look over at him, his eyes trailing over the front of his car and then looking back to me. The lascivious smirk that turns up the corners of his mouth rocks my world off its balance. "Uh-uh," he says, confusing me.

What? Now he doesn't want to…*oh… Oh! Oh fuck!*

He recognizes the minute I understand his intention. "You. Here." He points to the sleek, red hood. I blush and hesitate, remembering my off the cuff comment in Starbucks that now feels likes years ago about how I wanted to *take him on the hood of his car*.

"Now!" He growls.

Me and my big mouth. I glance around and swallow before my eyes come back to meet his. *Always back to his.* "Here?"

"Here." He smirks as a thrill chases through me. "*I'm gonna corrupt you yet.*"

"But…"

"Don't question it, Rylee. If you obey all the rules, baby, you miss all of the fun." *Only Colton could quote Hepburn at a time like this and make it sound seductively sexy.*

His eyes dance with the thrill of what we are about to do. There is no way in hell that I'm going to pass up the chance to be with him. After everything tonight—the limo, the buildup of anticipation, the fact that he'll try—wild horses couldn't drag me away.

I don't even have a moment to be concerned with our location because he grabs me and brands his lips to mine. I can taste his desire. His hunger. His impatience. His willingness. Their mixture is a heady combination that sends chills up my spine and causes goose bumps to cover my skin as he leads me backwards. Our lips part only for him to whisper the naughty promises of what he wants to do to me.

How hard he's going to fuck me. How loud he wants me to scream. How many times he plans on making me come. How insanely beautiful I am. How he craves the taste of me.

The backs of my knees hit the front bumper of the car, and he slips his jacket off of my shoulders. He takes the jacket and lays it inside out on the hood behind me as I fumble with the zipper on his pants, my dexterity ruined by the liquid heat that fills me.

"Hurry," he demands, his voice laced with anguished need.

I laugh, hysterics tingeing the sound from my desperation. His hands still as he pulls back from our close proximity and looks into my eyes. *A moment of calm amidst our storm of need.* He reaches up and runs his fingers down my cheek, a smile of disbelief on his face and a look in his eyes—one that says he can't believe I'm real. *That this is real.* He shakes his head and his mouth curls up to one side, his dimple winking. And with his eyes locked on mine, he runs his hand back to my hair and fists it, angling my head to the side, exposing the curve of my neck.

And then need and desire take over as he lowers his mouth to that expanse of bare skin. The feelings, the sensations, the emotions pull me under, consume me.

My eyes close. My body softens and heats up simultaneously. I feel Colton's dick pulse and they spring to life, my hands finally working so I can pull his pants down far enough to release his engorged length. He hisses out an incoherent litany in appreciation as my fingers encircle him and dance over his heated flesh.

"Rylee. Please. Now." He pants between open mouth kisses. My hands continue their pleasurable torture as I feel Colton's fingers bunch the length of my dress up until his hands are beneath it, cupping my bare ass.

I feel the warmth of Colton's fingertips as they part my legs, and I tense, knowing that his touch is all I'll need to push me over the edge. His hands smooth across my skin, and his deft fingers find their destination, making me cry out as they tease and torment.

My nails dig into his shoulders as my legs start shaking from the mounting pressure within me. "Colton." I breathe as pleasure rakes over me, a low keening in the back of my throat the only other sound I make as he pushes me higher and higher. His mouth catches mine again as I throw my head back, the heat from his skillful fingertips ripping through me and searing every imaginable nerve in my body. My fire ignites as he slips two fingers in to invade the depths of my sex with one hand while the other grips my hip possessively. Fervent fingers digging into willing flesh. I'm so worked up—so on the cusp—that it doesn't take long until I crash over the edge into a rapturous free fall.

All of the anticipation, flirting, highs, and lows from the night intensify the mix of sensations that splinter through me. Colton brings a hand up to cup my neck, his thumb resting just under my chin as my eyes flutter open. The simple brush of his touch there is like adding gasoline to a roaring fire. My body tenses again as another ripple of pleasure pulses through me, all the while his gaze on mine.

Colton's eyes flicker and flame with lust as he watches me regain some semblance of equilibrium from the earth he just helped to move beneath my feet. Before I can even comprehend what's happening, his control snaps, and he pushes me back on to his jacket on the cool, polished metal of his hood. He grabs my hips, pushing my dress up so I am clothed from the waist up and bare from the waist down, except for garters and stockings. He lifts my hips up to meet the height of his so that just my shoulders and neck are resting on the cool silk of his jacket.

His eyes roam over my bared flesh. "Sweet Christ, woman," his voice husky with desire murmurs as I close my eyes to revel in the need he's about to fill because even though I've come, my body is aching so desperately to have him in me, filling me, and stretching me to sublime satisfaction. "Open your eyes, Rylee," he commands as he places his steely head at my entrance. I gasp at the feeling, needing more. Always needing more and never being able to get enough of him. "I want to watch you while I take you. I want to see those eyes of yours turn hazy with desire."

My eyes flash open to lock on his. My mouth goes dry from the absolute lust reflected in them. In this moment, the calm before the storm, I am irrevocably his.

I cry out in unison with his guttural groan as he enters me in one slick thrust, holding himself deep as he grinds his hips against my pelvis. The heels of my shoes dig into his backside as I tense at his invasion, my slick channel clenching onto him with every swivel of his hips. "Oh, Rylee." He grunts, his head thrown back, lips parted, and face pulled tight with pleasure.

He starts moving now. Really moving. Fitting himself to me—in me—so that each drive devastates my senses. All I can do is absorb the impossible sensations he draws out of me with each thrust, ride out the blistering onslaught with him.

The jacket beneath me serves as a slide of sorts. With each drive I glide back and up the hood, only to be pulled back onto him to start the delicious descent and thrust back up all over again. The motion causes a myriad of overwhelming sensations that only serves to coax my orgasm to come faster. Harder. Quicker.

My muscles clench around him as I lift my head to watch our union. To see my arousal coating him as he withdraws from my pussy before plunging back in. And the sight of what I do to him, of what he does to me, is unbelievably hot. "Colton," I moan in a stilted breath as one of his fingertips grazes over my clit. My body shudders from his touch.

"You. Are. Mine. Rylee," he growls between thrusts. "Tell. Me. Tell me you're mine, Rylee," he demands.

"Colton." I gasp as my body is pulled under the pleasure swamping me. His fingers dig into my hips as his muscles tense up and I'm able to resurface momentarily. "Yes. Yours. Colton." I pant between thrusts. "I'm. Yours!" I shout as I drown in the liquid heat of ecstasy the same time he climaxes with a hard groan, my name spilling from his lips.

Several moments have passed but our chests are still heaving for air. Our bodies are still pulsing with the adrenaline from our union. I open my eyes first. Colton is still gripping my hips, his cock still within me, but completely clothed otherwise. He stands before me, so tall, so imposing. It's no wonder he dominates both my thoughts and my heart. My everything.

My whole world.

His eyes flutter open slowly, looking down at me through heavy lids, a Cheshire cat grin lazily spreading across his lips. He exhales a sated sigh, and we both wince as he withdraws before slowly lowering my legs. He grabs my arms to help me up before the jacket beneath me slides me off of the too low hood of the car. My dress makes an odd sound against the immaculate paint as he pulls me up, and I gasp aloud. In my desperate need to have Colton, the thought never crossed my mind that I might scratch—or even worse, dent—the car. A car that probably costs more than I make in several years.

"What is it, Rylee?" he asks, looking over his shoulder thinking someone has just been voyeur to our escapade, and then looking back at me after seeing no one.

"Your car…*Sex*." I cringe but at the same time feel ridiculous calling the car that name. "I hope I didn't scratch it."

Colton angles his head and looks at me as if I'm crazy before he throws his head back, a full bodied laugh flowing from his mouth. He tucks himself back inside his slacks and zips them up. "Relax, baby, it's just a car."

"But—but it's worth a small fortune and—"

"And it can be fixed or replaced if damaged." He leans in and catches my mouth in a dizzying kiss and then pulls back with a smirk. "Then again, if it's damaged, I may just have to keep it just like it is as a reminder. ." He lifts his eyebrows at me as he straightens his vest before reaching up to straighten his bow tie.

"A souvenir of sorts," I muse, smoothing my dress down over my hips.

He cocks his head and looks at the car over my shoulder before looking back at me. "That's one helluva souvenir, sweetheart." He whistles between his teeth, a lascivious smirk on his handsome face. "And now *her* name has a whole new meaning to me."

"Yes, it does." I smile shyly in return as he pulls me into him and tightens his arms around me. He looks at me, that naughty smirk I can't resist lighting up his features and those intense eyes filled with so much emotion. He leans down and brushes a soft kiss on my lips—the kind that is nothing more than lips on lips—that is so soft, so packed full of meaning, it causes my whole body to ache in the sweetest way.

Colton pulls back and places his jacket back over my shoulders before holding his hand out to me. "Come. We should get back or people will be wondering what we've been doing." I snort loudly in the most unladylike way. As if the flush in my cheeks and glimmer in my eye won't be a dead giveaway. He squeezes my hand as we walk toward the elevator, my head still reeling from the intensity and thrill of what just happened. Colton pulls me closer into his side, a laugh falling from his mouth.

"*What?*"

"A car experience," he says looking at me and raising his eyebrows.

It most definitely was. "Nope. Not even close," I tease him back at his creative yet hopeless attempt.

By some stroke of luck, we slip back into the function a moment after dinner service is announced. Colton guides me to our assigned table just as the other patrons are sitting down. He pulls out my chair for me and removes his jacket from my shoulders, placing it on the back of the chair. I catch the libidinous smirk on his face as he shakes his head at me before leaning in and whispering, "Homerun." I can't contain the laugh that bubbles up at the thought.

During dinner I watch Colton interact with the other guests at the table, championing his various causes at the same time answering questions about his upcoming race. The older women at the table are charmed by him, and the men are envious of his good looks and bucket list lifestyle.

He's such a mix of contradictions. Emotionally closed off and isolated, but at the same time so open and giving in regards to the causes he cares about. He's arrogant and overly confident, and yet has a quiet understated vulnerability that I'm getting sneak peeks of when he doesn't close himself off. He can hobnob with the extremely wealthy in this room and also understand a traumatized seven year old boy and his needs. He's brash and aggressive, yet compassionate and considerate. And my God can the man infuriate me one moment and then make me weak in the knees the next.

I smile at the checkered flag cuff links and know that only Colton could get away with making such a novelty item appear sophisticated and classy. But more than anything, I find myself staring at his hands and wondering what it is about them that I find so incredibly sexy. I watch his fingertips absently toy with the stem of his wine glass before sliding it up and over the condensation forming. My mind wanders to those fingers and their skillful mastery on other things.

When I look up Colton is watching me, an amused look in his eyes, and I know he knows my thoughts are anything but innocent. He raises the glass to his lips and takes a sip, his eyes remaining on mine.

He leans over, his lips a breath from my ear. "Every time I take a drink, I can smell you on my fingers. It's making me count the minutes until I can take my slow, sweet time with you, Rylee," he whispers. The resonance in his voice permeating every nerve in my body. "*I want to explore every delicious inch of you.*" He presses a kiss to my cheek. "*And then I'm going to fuck you senseless.*" He growls.

My core clenches and coils at the thoughts his words evoke. "*Check, please.*" I murmur, and Colton throws his head back in laughter, drawing the attention of those at our table.

We sit through the rest of the dinner and the host's enlivened speech about the cause of the evening. Colton sighs with relief when the applause ends and people start to rise from the tables. "Thank God!" he mutters under his breath bringing a smile to my face. At least I'm not the only one anxious for the nightcap to our garage rendezvous. "You ready, Ry?"

"Ready and willing," I admit, enjoying the interruption to his movement from my words.

"Willing's good," he whispers. "Wet's even better."

"I've been that way all night, Ace," I murmur in response, smiling to myself when I hear his sharp intake of air as he follows me through the maze of tables.

"Colton! Hey, Donavan!" a voice to the right yells out.

Colton curses under his breath as I turn to face him. "I'll make this quick," he says before placing a chaste kiss on my lips. He turns and walks across the room meeting the gentleman. "Vincent!" I hear Colton say in greeting as the two shake hands and slap each other on the backs like two men who are more than casual acquaintances.

I watch the exchange from afar, a soft smile on my face as I marvel at Colton and this evening's unexpected turn of events.

"That smile on your face won't last you know," a voice says beside me.

I bristle at the sound of it. *Here comes the rain to fuck with my parade.* "What a pleasant surprise," I say, my tone saccharine laced with sarcasm. I keep my eyes straight ahead, focused on Colton. "Are you having a good time, Tawny?"

She ignores my question and goes straight for the jugular. "You know he's already getting bored with you, right? Already looking for his next willing piece of ass?" She laughs low and snidely, and in my periphery I can see her turn to face me, looking for a reaction I refuse to give her. "And you know as well as I do that there are plenty of women vying for that coveted spot."

I'm riding high from Colton's revelation tonight. I feel brazen and am sick of Tawny's crap. "Oh, believe me, I know." I smirk. "But don't worry, I'm not as naïve as you think I am when it comes to Colton's needs. Little Red Riding Hood, I'm not." I hear Tawny suck in an audible breath as she realizes that I overheard her conversation. Colton glances up from his discussion and his eyes meet mine, a quizzical look crossing his face as he sees who's standing beside me. I smile sweetly back at him as if everything is under control.

It will be momentarily anyway.

"Your time's up, Rylee," she antagonizes.

I take a sip of the champagne in my hand and carefully choose my next words, my voice low and spiteful. "Well, I think it's time you get a new watch then, Tawny, because it seems to me like you're stuck in the past. You really need to get current with the here and now...because when you do, you'll see that you no longer have a say or hold on Colton's personal life."

I watch her chest rise and fall as the anger fires within her. I feel like telling her that if what she feels is anger, then I've got a fucking inferno of fury in comparison. *And I'm just getting started.* "It must suck for you, Tawny, when all you have to look forward to in life is being Colton's sloppy seconds. Thinking you're only good enough to go back to once he's tried everybody else that he thinks might possibly be better. Talk about a hit to that overinflated ego of yours."

"*You bitch!*" she sputters. "You can't fulfill his needs. You're—"

I turn quickly toward her, the look on my face stopping her words. "*Oh, doll,* I just did. Was it you he was fucking on the hood of Sex in the parking garage before dinner? I didn't think so," I patronize with a smirk, but my eyes tell her he's mine and to back the fuck off.

The look on her face is priceless: eyes wide, lips parted as she digests what I've just said. "*Colton would never. .*" she huffs getting herself worked up ". .the Ferrari is his baby. He'd never risk scratching it."

"Well I guess you don't know him as well as you thought you did." I give her the same catty smirk she's graced me with several times. "Either that or you just didn't mean more to him than his car." I twist my lips and look at her while her ego tries to process what I've just said. "We're done here then," I say with a laugh as I walk away from her toward Colton.

God, that felt good! Serves her right.

When I reach Colton, he extends a hand to me and wraps it around my waist, pulling me into his side as he finishes his conversation with Vincent. They say their goodbyes and as he walks away, Colton leans down and kisses me gently. "What was all that about?" he asks warily.

I angle my head to the side as I look at him and run my fingers along the line of his jaw. "Nothing... it was *inconsequential,*" I tell him, scrunching up my nose at the word.

Chapter Nineteen

"Are you sure you're not too cold?"

"Uh-uh," I murmur as Colton rubs his hands up and down my arms, the ocean breeze a biting chill against my bare skin, but I don't want to ruin the moment. This evening—post garden argument—has been one that I'll never forget.

Something has changed in Colton with the evening's progression. It's not something I can put my finger on exactly but rather several things that are subtly different. The little looks he's given me. The casual touches here and there for no specific reason other than to let me know he's at my side. That shy smile of his that I noticed he's reserved for only me tonight. Or maybe it's always been there, and I'm looking at things through different lenses now that I know Colton is going to try for the possibility of an us. He's willing to try to break a pattern that he swears is ingrained in him. For me.

The pitch-black night is lit solely by the sliver of moon hanging in the midnight sky. I close my eyes, hum softly to *Kiss Me Slowly* floating from the speakers, and lift my face as the salty breeze drifts up onto the terrace where we stand. Colton rests his chin on my shoulder as he wraps his arms around my waist from behind. I melt into his warmth, never wanting him to let me go. We stand there, lost in our separate thoughts, soaking in the dark night's atmosphere, and completely aware of the underlying current of desire between us.

Baxter barks at the gate to go down to the beach, and Colton reluctantly releases me to take him out. "Do you want a drink?" I ask, my body chilled the minute his warmth leaves mine.

"Beer, please?"

I wander into the kitchen and get our drinks. When I walk back out, Colton is standing, hands propped on the railing, looking out toward the empty night, completely lost in thought. His broad shoulders are silhouetted against the dark sky—the white of his untucked dress shirt a stark visual contrast—and once again I'm reminded of my angel fighting to break through the darkness.

I place my wine glass down on a patio table and walk up behind him, the crash of the waves drowning out the sound of my footsteps on the deck. I slip my hands through his arms and torso, my front to his back, and wrap my arms around him. A second after my body touches his, Colton spins around violently, a harsh yelp echoing in the night air, his beer flying from my hands, and shattering on the deck. As a consequence of his actions, I am shoved to the side, my hip smarting against the railing. When I clear the hair out of my face and look up, Colton is facing me. His hands are fisted tight at his sides, his teeth are gritted in rage, his eyes are wild with anger—or is it fear—and his chest is heaving in shallow, rapid breaths.

His eyes lock with mine, and I freeze mid-movement with my hip angled out, hand pressing on it where it hurts. A myriad of emotions flash through his eyes as he stares at me, finally breaking through the glaze of fear that masks his face. I've seen this look before. The utter and consuming fear of someone traumatized when they have a flashback. I purposely keep my eyes on Colton's, my silence the only way I know how to let him breach through the fog that's holding him.

My mind filters back to the last morning I spent in this house and what happened when I curled up behind him. And now I know, deep down, that whatever happened to him, whatever lives within the blackness in his soul, has to do with this. That the action—the feeling of being hugged, taken, held from behind—triggers a flashback and brings him momentarily back to the horror.

Colton breathes in deeply—a ragged, soul cleansing drag of air— before breaking eye contact with me. He looks down at the deck momentarily before shouting a drawn out, "*Goddamnit!*" at the top of his lungs.

I startle at his voice as it echoes into the abyss of night around us. That one word is filled with so much frustration and angst all I want to do is gather him in my arms and comfort him, but instead of turning to me, he faces the railing, bracing himself against it once again. The shoulders I admired moments before are now filled with a burden I can't even begin to fathom.

"Colton?" He doesn't respond but rather keeps his face straight ahead. "Colton? I'm sorry. I didn't mean to..."

"Just don't do it again, okay?" he snaps. I try not to be upset by the vehemence in his tone, but I see him hurting and all I want to do is help.

"Colton what happen—"

"Look..." he whirls to face me "...we all didn't have perfect-fucking-suburban-white-picket-fence childhoods like you, Rylee. Is it really that important for you to know I'd go days without food or attention? *That my mom would force—*" He stops himself, his fists clenching and his eyes getting a far off look in them before refocusing on me. "That she'd make me do whatever was needed to ensure her next fucking fix?" His voice is void of all emotion except anger.

I suck in my breath, my heart breaking for him and the memories that plague him. I want to reach out to him. Hold him. Make love to him. Let him lose himself in me. *Anything to make his mind forget for just a moment.*

"Shit, I'm sorry." He sighs with remorse, scrubbing his hands over his face and looking up to the sky. "I find myself apologizing a lot around you." He looks back down and meets my eyes, shoving his hands in his pockets. "I'm sorry, Ry. I didn't mean—"

"It's okay to feel that way." I take a step toward him and raise my hand and place it on his cheek. He leans his face into my hand, turning it briefly to press a kiss to the center of my palm before closing his eyes to absorb whatever emotions he's processing. His acceptance of comfort from me warms my soul. Gives me hope that in time he might talk to me. His unfettered vulnerability tugs at my heart and opens my soul. Draws me in. When he opens his eyes, I look into them, searching their depths. "What happened, Colton?"

"I told you before. Don't try and fix me..."

"I'm just trying to understand." I rub my hand over his cheek one more time before I run it down and rest it over his heart.

"I know." He exhales. "But it's something I don't like to talk about. Shit…it's something no one should have to talk about." He shakes his head. "I told you, my first eight years were a fucking nightmare. I don't want to fill your head with the details. It was—*fuck*!" He pounds his hand on the railing beside us, startling both Baxter and myself. "I'm not used to having to explain myself to anyone." He clenches his jaw, making that muscle pulse. We stand in silence for a while before he looks down at me with a sad smile. "*I swear to God it's you!*"

"Me?" I stutter flabbergasted. What did I have to do with what just happened?

"Mmm-hmm," he murmurs, staring at me intently. "I've never let my guard down. Never opened myself up to…" He shakes his head, his confusion and clarity written on his face. "I've been able to block things out for so long. Ignore emotions. Ignore everything, but you? You tear down walls I didn't even know I was building. *You make me feel, Rylee.*"

I feel as if all of the air has been sucked from my lungs. His words render me thoughtless and yet inundated with thoughts at the same time. Possibilities flicker and flame. Hope sets in. My own walls crumble. My heart swells at his acknowledgement.

He purses his beautifully sculpted lips as he brings a hand up and sets it on my shoulder, his thumb aimlessly rubbing back and forth over my bare collar bone. "Feeling like this when I'm so used to living life in a blur…it's drudging up old shit…old ghosts that I thought I'd buried long ago."

He reaches his other hand out and places it on my waist, pulling me into him. I nuzzle my face into the underside of his neck, inhaling the uniquely Colton scent that I can't seem to get enough of. He wraps his strong arms around me, clinging to me as if he needs the feel of me to help wash away some of his memories.

"I've lived for so long trying to close myself off from people. From this kind of emotion…Rylee? Do you have any idea what you're doing to me?"

His words nurture the love blooming in my heart, but I know he's uncomfortable with his unexpected admission, and I don't want him to suddenly freak out when he realizes it. *Call for a pit stop*. I feel the need to do something—add some levity—to chase away his demons if just for the night. I lean into him and brush a slow, intoxicating kiss on his lips until I can feel his erection thickening against my midsection and wiggle against it. "*I think I can feel that easy enough*," I murmur against his neck.

His laughter vibrates through his chest against mine. "So beautiful." He brings a hand up to my chin and tilts it back as he leans down and teases my lips with his. My name is a reverent sigh on his lips. His tongue caresses mine over and over, teasing me with a dance intent on complete seduction and utter surrender. I never thought it was possible to make love to someone by kissing alone, but Colton is proving me wrong.

He flutters his tongue gently against mine, the softness of his firm lips coaxing me to need more from him—to need things I never thought possible or could even exist again. His tenderness is so unexpected, so overwhelming, tears sting the back of my eyes as I lose myself in him. Lose myself to him.

"You are so breathtakingly beautiful, Ry. Not what I deserve, but just what I need." He breathes into my mouth, his hands cupping my neck. "Please let me show you..."

As if he even has to ask.

I step up on my toes and thread my fingers through the hair at the nape of his neck. I look up at him, his eyes framed with thick lashes and chock-full of all of the unspoken words his actions are trying to express. I tip my head up and bring my lips to his as a response.

I laugh as he leans down and places his arm behind my knees, picking me up and carrying me over the broken glass of his beer that's scattered all over the decking. He continues inside and carries me up the stairs into his bedroom. He flicks a switch with his elbow as we enter the room and a fire roars to life in the fireplace in the corner of the room.

He stops at the edge of the bed and places me on my feet.

"Is this the part where you take your *deliciously, slow, sweet time with me?*" I whisper, using his words from earlier.

I see his eyes spark at my words. He leans down and delves his tongue between my parted lips. "Baby, I want to enjoy every single inch of this ridiculously sexy body of yours." I feel his hands on the zipper at my back and then my skin becomes chilled from the room's air as he slowly parts my dress. He hints at the things he wants to do to me. His rasp of a voice caresses over me, matching the feel of the fingertip he trails down the path he's unzipping. I feel the tug on the fabric, and it slides down and pools around my high heels.

"Christ, woman, you test a man's restraint," he swears at me, his pupils dilating as he absorbs the entire visual of my lingerie that he's seen only in bits and pieces tonight.

I smooth my hands over the black lace piped with a fire engine red bra portion of my basque and continue down the fabric until I reach the garters attached to it. "You like?" I ask coyly, a smirk on my lips.

"*Oh, baby.*" He sucks in a breath of air closing the distance between us, his eyes devouring the sight in front of him. He wraps his arm around me and yanks me against him so we are face to face, our lips a whisper from each other's. "I more than like. *I want.*" He growls as he moves us backwards and pushes me down onto the bed.

I lean my weight on my elbows and look up at him standing before me as he unbuttons the rest of his shirt. My mouth waters and desire coils as I get an inch by inch glimpse of the magnificence beneath. The hunger in his eyes is a promise of what he wants to do to me, and it leaves me revving with need. He shrugs off his shirt, the hard-edged muscles of his chest and abdomen leave my fingers itching to touch them. He crawls onto the bed, his knees nudging my legs apart as he sits between them. His fingertips trace heated lines up and down my inner thighs. My muscles tense at the feeling and tremble in anticipation.

"Colton," I plead as his touch ignites the ache deep inside me. The need is so intense my hands snake down my abdomen and my fingers dig into the flesh at my hips in restraint. I'm bound up so tight that I need release.

"Oh yes." He groans. "Touch yourself, sweetheart, and let me watch. Show me how much you need me."

His words are all I need to throw my modesty out the window. My fingers dance down my mound, and I part myself, sighing in relief as my fingers begin to add the friction I need over my most sensitive part. Colton groans in lust as he watches, and the sound urges me on. I draw my bottom lip between my teeth as the sensation starts to pull me under.

"Rylee." He rasps out a tortured breath. "My turn."

My eyes flicker up to meet his, lids weighted with desire as I drag my fingertips over my clit one last time before pulling them away. His lips part in reaction to the moan that escapes between my lips and then curve in a wicked smile that has me arching my back, begging for more of his touch. His eyes hold mine as he leans down. I feel the gentle draw of his warm mouth on my aching hot spot and once again he drowns me. His passion swallows me whole.

Chapter Twenty

We lay on our sides facing each other, our heads propped on pillows, our bodies naked, and our current desire temporarily sated. Craig David plays softly through the speakers in the ceiling. I drink in Colton, our eyes speaking volumes despite our lips remaining silent. So many things I want to say to him after what we've just exchanged. It wasn't just sex between us. Not that it ever has been for me, but tonight especially, the connection was different. Colton has always been a more than generous lover, but how he was tonight—his slow, worshipping touch—has left me in a state of blissful daze. I find myself becoming so lost in him, so blanketed by everything that he is, that in a sense, *I have found myself again.*

I am whole again.

"Thank you." His words break our silence.

"Thank me? I think I'm the one who's just come multiple times."

The crooked, cocky grin fills me with such happiness. "True," he concedes with a nod of his head. "But thank you for not pushing earlier."

"You're welcome," I tell him, feeling like the smile on my face is a permanent fixture.

We fall silent again for a bit before he murmurs, "I could look at you for hours." I blush under the intensity of his stare, which is funny considering I should be blushing rather in regards to all of the various things he just did to please me. But in this moment I realize that I am blushing because I am completely naked to him—stripped, bared, open—and not in just in the literal sense. He is looking at me, seeing into my eyes and through the guard I have lowered to reveal the transparency of my feelings for him.

I shake myself from my thoughts. "I think I should be the one saying that," I tell him, the dancing flames from the fire bathing a soft light across his dark features.

He snorts at me and rolls his eyes. Such a childish reaction from such an intense man that it softens him, makes my heart stumble that much more. "Do you have any idea how much crap I got as a kid for being so *pretty*," he says with disdain. "How many fights I got in to prove that I wasn't?"

I reach out and run my fingertips over the lines of his face and then down the crooked line of his nose. "Is that how you got this?" I ask.

"Mmm-hmm." He chuckles softly. "I was a senior in high school and had the hots for the football captain's girl. Stephanie Turner was her name. He wasn't too thrilled when the school rebel snuck out of a party with his girl." He smiles sheepishly. "I was...I had quite a rep back then."

"Only back then?" I tease.

"Smartass," he says, giving me that bashful smile. "Yes, only then." When I roll my eyes at him, he continues. "Anyway, I was quite the hot head. Got in fights constantly for no reason except to prove no one had a say in what I could do or how they could control me. I had a lot of anger in my teenage years. Because of that, the next day he got his buddies to hold me down while he beat the shit out of me. Broke my nose and fucked me up pretty bad." He shrugs. "Looking back, I deserved it. You don't touch another man's woman."

I stare at him, finding his last comment oddly sexy. "What did your parents say?"

"Oh they were pissed," he exclaims before continuing on to explain how they reacted. We talked like this for the next hour. He explained what it was like growing up with his parents, filling in little stories here and there that had me laughing at both his rebellions and his shortcomings.

We fall back into a comfortable silence after a while. He reaches out and pulls the covers up my back after noticing I've become chilled and tucks an errant curl behind my ear. "I'm proud of you," he says softly, my drowsy eyelids opening fully in question. "You walked into that storage closet tonight and didn't freak out."

I look at him, awareness seeping into me that he's right. That I didn't think twice about it. With him beside me, I was able to forget my fear. "Well I didn't actually walk into it…I believe I was *coerced*. It's the *Colton effect*," I tease. "You had my thoughts focused elsewhere."

"I could do that again right now if you'd like?" he suggests.

"I'm sure you could, Ace, but..." I stop and stare at him, Tawny's bathroom conversation seeping into my thoughts. Curiosity melds with insecurity and it gets the better of me. "Colton?"

"Hmm?" he murmurs, his eyes drifting closed as his fingers draw aimless circles on the top of my hand.

"Do I give you what you need?"

"Mmm-hmm" The nonchalance of his response tells me that either he doesn't understand my question or is lost to the clutches of sleep.

Her words echo in my head. "Do I satisfy you sexually?" I can't help the break in my voice when I ask.

Colton's body tenses at my words, his fingertips become motionless on my skin, and his eyes open with deliberate slowness and confusion. He stares at me as if he is looking straight into my soul, and the intensity of it is so strong that I eventually avert my eyes to watch my fingers pluck at the sheet. "Why would you ask me such a ridiculous question?"

I shrug as embarrassment colors my cheeks. "I'm just not very experienced and you—you most definitely are so I was just wondering..." My voice fades off, unsure how to ask what is in the forefront of my mind.

Colton shifts in the bed and sits up, tugging on my arm so that I have no choice but to follow suit. He reaches out and tips my chin up so that I'm forced to look into his eyes. "You're just wondering what?" he asks softly, concern etched in his features.

"How long until you're bored with me? I mean, I'm—"

"Hey, where is all of this coming from?" Colton implores as he brushes his thumb gently over my cheek.

How is it I can let this man have his way with me sexually, but right now, confronting him about my lack of experience makes me feel more naked than ever? Insecurity clogs my throat when I try to explain. "It's just been a rough night," I say. "I'm sorry. Forget I said anything."

"Uh-uh, you're not getting off that easy, Rylee." He shifts in the bed and despite my protests, pulls me so that I'm seated between his thighs—face to face—my legs astride his hips. I have no choice but to look at him now. "What's going on? What else did I miss tonight that you're not telling me?" His eyes search into mine looking for answers.

"It's silly really," I admit, trying to downplay my feelings of inadequacy. "I was in the bathroom stall and overheard some ladies talking about what a God you are in the sack." I roll my eyes for good measure not wanting his ego to get any bigger than it already is. "...And how it's obvious that I'm more than inexperienced." I look down and focus on his thumbs rubbing absently back and forth on my thighs. "How you're going to take what you want, chew me up, and spit me out. They said you don't do predictability and—"

"Stop." His voice is stern, and I can't help but look up to meet his bemused eyes. "Look, I don't know how to explain it." His voice softens and he shakes his head. "I can't really. All I know is that with you, things were just different from the start. *You broke the mold, Rylee.*"

His words elate the feelings of hope inside of me, and yet I still feel the roots of inadequacy weighing down my soul. We sit here both trying to gain our bearings on the ever-shifting ground beneath our feet. "I know," I interject, "I just—"

"You don't get it do you?" he asks. "You may not have the experience but..." He fades off trying to find the right words. "...you're the purest person I've ever met, Rylee. That part of you—that innocence in you—*it's so goddamn sexy*. So fucking incredible."

He rests his forehead against mine, pulling my body further into his. He sighs and laughs softly, his breath feathering across my lips. "You know, a couple of months ago, I might have answered you differently. But since you fell out of the damn storage closet, nothing has been the fucking same." He pauses momentarily, his fingertip trailing down the bare line of my spine. "No one's mattered before. Ever. But you? Fuck, somehow you changed that. *You matter*," he says with such clarity that his words delve into places deep inside of me I thought could never be healed. Places and pieces now slowly stitching themselves back together.

I still as Colton's warm arms wrap around the chilled skin of my back. He pulls my hair to the side and presses his lips to the curve of my neck. The scrape of this returning stubble sends shivers down my spine. "What is it with you and jumping to conclusions tonight?" he murmurs, keeping his lips pressed against my skin. The vibrations of his lips ricocheting across hypersensitive nerves.

I shrug without explanation, suddenly embarrassed at confessing my moment of blatant insecurity to him when he so obviously showed me tonight that I'm the one he wants. Silence settles around us for a bit as we breathe each other in. "If there's something you're not getting from me—that you need—you'd tell me right?" He leans back to look at me, his hands resting on my shoulders, thumbs brushing absently over the dip of my collarbone, question in his eyes. I continue, "When Tawny said—"

Colton's eyes snaps alert. "*Tawny?*"

"She was in the bathroom," I confess and see irritation flicker across his face.

"Fuckin' Tawny," he mutters dragging a hand through his hair. "Look at me, Rylee," he commands. I raise my eyes up to meet the raw intensity in his. "Tawny's just jealous that she doesn't have a tenth of the sex appeal that you have. And the best part about it—about you—is that you don't even realize it. Do you remember that night at the Palisades?" he asks and all I can do is nod, mesmerized by his words and the soft smile ghosting his lips. "That's what I was struggling with. Why I was such an ass. How could I bring you there and treat you like everybody else when you were like no one I'd ever been with before? And then I walked over to you, and you were standing there trying to figure out what my problem was, looking so goddamn beautiful and unintentionally beguiling. And even though I'd been a dick, you stepped toward me *and gave everything of yourself* to me without a single explanation." He reaches up and traces a line down my forehead and nose and then stops on my lips. "It's such a fucking turn on, Rylee. *Like no one else I've ever been with*. No one."

I draw in a ragged breath, afraid to believe what he's really telling me. *That I give him what he needs. That things between him and I are different for him.* A first of sorts for him. I swallow loudly before clenching my jaw. If I speak right now, three words he doesn't want to hear are going to come tumbling out of my mouth. It's been an emotional night, and I'm more than overwhelmed. All I can manage is a simple nod.

"I've never had to work so hard to get something I never thought I wanted," he confesses and the words feather through me and embed themselves in my swelling heart and transparent soul.

How is it possible to feel love this intense when I thought the ability for me had died with Max?

I lean in and express the words my tangled tongue cannot, by pressing my lips to his. "Thank you," I whisper to him for the many things I don't even think he could understand even if I told him.

He pulls back and I can't miss the smirk on his devilishly sexy mouth. He raises and eyebrow at me, amusement in his eyes. "*A God in the sack, huh?*"

I can't help the laughter that bubbles up and spills out, not surprised he didn't forget. "Did I say that?" I tease as I run my fingertips down the ridges of his abdomen. I can feel his thickening arousal pulse beneath me from my touch. "Must have been a slip of the tongue."

"Oh really?" He asks with a playful grin on his lips, and a look in his eyes that tells me his sated needs are no longer fulfilled. "Tongues are funny things don't you think?" He leans in and traces my lower lip with his tongue. "They can lick like this," he whispers. "And they can kiss like this," he says branding his mouth to mine, his tongue parting my lips and dominating my mouth. He shifts us backwards on the mattress so that his weight presses deliciously on top of me.

He breaks the kiss and the lust in his eyes has desire unfurling in my belly. "And they can lick like this," he whispers before grazing his way down my neck to tease the tightened bud of my nipple. "They can tease and pleasure like this." His tongue caresses one then another before trailing down my abdomen at an achingly slow pace. My muscles flex in anticipation as he stops at the top of my sex.

He looks up at me and I catch a flash of a grin. "And they most definitely..." He blows against my seam, the heat of his breath feathering over my sensitive flesh. "...love to taste like this."

His tongue laves over me and my sharp intake of air followed by a soft moan is all I can manage. My words are lost and mind is clouded from the soft slide and adept skill of his tongue.

As he consumes me. Pleasures me. Undoes me.

Chapter Twenty-One

Colton

God, she's fucking gorgeous. I can't help but reach out and pull a curl off of her cheek. The feeling—that fucking foreign feeling that's not so foreign any more—courses through me, grabs me by the balls and then hands them back to me on a platter.

Makes fear shiver at the base of my spine in a constant state of reverberation.

My fingers linger on her shoulder, touching her to make sure she's real. There's no possible way that she can be. She scares the hell out of me. That not so foreign feeling scares the hell out of me. But I can't force myself to walk away. From that very first encounter I haven't been able to. Shit, at first it was definitely the challenge. That smart mouth, those violet eyes, and the sway of that ass—what red-blooded male would have?

Christ. Tell me I can't have something, I'm sure as shit going to go after it until I get it. *Game on*. I'm in it until the motherfucking checkered flag.

But then, that first time I showed up at The House—that look in her eyes that told me to get the hell out and to not mess with *her Zander* or she'd take me down herself—everything changed. *Shifted*. Became real. The challenge ceased to exist. All I saw in that moment was myself as a kid. Myself now. Knew that she loved the broken in us. Was okay with the darkness because she was so full of fucking light. Knew she'd understand so much more than I'd ever be able to say.

That selfless soul of hers and come-fuck-me body just pulled at me, twisted through parts inside of me that I thought had died and would never regenerate. *Made me feel* when I've been so content to live in the blur around me. I mean who really does the shit she does? Takes fucked up kids—*lots of fucked up kids*—and treats them as her own. Defends them. Loves them. Fights for them. Is willing to make a deal with the devil such as myself for their benefit.

That day in the conference room when I trapped her into my little deal, I could see the trepidation and the knowledge that I'd hurt her in those bedroom eyes, and as much as she knew it, she agreed for the sake of the boys, regardless of the damage it'd cause to her personally. And of course I'm a selfish bastard for wondering the whole time how sweet her pussy would taste. I mean if her kiss was that goddamn addictive, then I couldn't even imagine how the rest of her body would drug me. She's sacrificing herself for her boys, and there I was thinking of my end game.

And that in itself screwed me up, forced me to keep my guard up. I knew she was going to let me have her, but had no fucking clue that first time together—when she looked at me with such a definitive clarity afterward—that she'd be able to look right into my goddamn soul. It freaked me the fuck out, stirred things within me I never wanted churned up again. Things I had accepted living a lifetime without. No one knows the things I did—the things I allowed to be done to me. The poison living inside. How I loved and hated and did unimaginable things for reasons I didn't understand at the time and still don't understand now.

And I fear every minute of every damn day that she'll figure it out, learn about the truths inside of me and then leave me so much worse off than she found me. She's unlocked things in me I'd never intended to allow to see the light of day again. She pushes the concept of vulnerability to a whole new level.

But I can't push her away. I can't stop wanting to for her sake. But every time I try—every time I crack and she sees a glimpse of my demons—I'm scared shitless. God, I try to make her leave—even if it's only in my fucked up head—but I'm never successful. And I'm just not sure if it's because she's stubborn or because it's a half-assed attempt on my part just so I can tell myself I actually tried.

I know what's best for her is not me. Shit, last night…last night was…*fuck*. I handed myself to her. Told her I'd try when every part of me screamed in protest from the fear of being ripped to shreds by allowing myself to feel. I've always used pleasure to bury the pain. Not emotions. Not commitment. Pleasure. How else can I prove to myself that I'm not that kid I was forced to be? It's the only way I know. The only way I can cope. *To hell with* the therapists who had no clue what happened to me. My parents wasted so much money on people telling me how to overcome the issues they thought I had. That I could use hypnosis to regress and overcome. *Fuck that*. Give me a tight, wet, willing pussy to bury myself in momentarily and that's all the proof I need.

Pleasure to bury the pain. So what do I do now? How do I cope with the one person that I fear can give me both? And she does, yet I still hurt her last night. I have a feeling I always will in some way or another. At some point she's just going to stop forgiving or coming back. Then what, Donavan? What the hell are you going to do then? If I'm broken now, I'll be fucking shattered then.

I stare at her sleeping, so innocent *and mine* and fuck all why I can't stay away from her. I'm scared shitless and she did this to me. She fucking grabbed hold, forced me to listen to the silent words she spoke, and *really hear them*. Now what the hell am I supposed to do?

My God the way she looked at me last night with eyes filled with naivety and jaw set with obstinance, asking me if she was enough for me. First of all—fucking Tawny—and then secondly, enough? I'm the one that's not enough. Not hardly. I'm drowning in her, and I'm not even sure I want to come up for air. Enough? I shake my head at the irony. She stays despite, if not because of the darkness deep in my soul. A saint I'm not worthy of, shouldn't taint.

She makes a soft noise in her throat and rolls onto her back. The sheet slips down off of her chest exposing her perfect tits. Fuck me. My dick starts stirring to life at the sight. It's been what, like three hours since the last time I was buried in her, and I'm already ready to have her again. Addictive voodoo pussy. I swear to God.

She whimpers again and rocks her head back and forth on the pillow. I hear Baxter's tail thump at the sound and the possibility that someone might be up already. My eyes trail over her lips and back to her tits. I groan at the sight of her pink nipples pebbling from the morning chill. I really should cover her back up, but fuck me, the view's pretty fucking fantastic, and I don't want to ruin it just yet.

Her shriek scares the shit out of me. It's a piercing keening that causes my chest to tighten. She cries out again and it's a tortured sound followed by her throwing her arms up to block her face. I sit up and try to gather her against me, but she bucks back.

"Rylee. Wake up!" I say, shaking her shoulders a couple of times. She finally wakes with a start and struggles out of my grip to bolt up in the bed. The sound of her gasping for breath makes me want to fold her into my arms and take the fear and pain that's rolling off of her in waves away from her. I do the only thing I can think of and run my hand up and down the bare skin of her back—the only comfort I can offer. "You okay?"

She just nods her head and looks over at me. And in that one glance I'm paralyzed. *Fucking paralyzed.* As a guy you're supposed to have that instinct to protect and care for. You always hear about how that's your job. It's ingrained. What-the-fuck-ever. Besides the few times when Q had some bullies at school mess with her, I've never remotely felt that way. Never.

Until right now. Rylee looks at me and those violet eyes are pooling with tears and filled with such absolute pain and fear. I do the only thing I want to even though I know it's not enough for her, it'll assuage my needs. I reach out pulling her toward me and onto my lap before leaning back against the headboard. When I wrap my arms around her, she lays her cheek over my chest. Over my heart. And despite the calm that the feel of her bare skin on mine brings me, I can't help but keep feeling the single connection of her face over my heart.

The one place I never expected to feel again just quickened at such a simple, natural gesture. I swear that her pulse and breathing are evening out and mine are accelerating. I run my fingers through her curls, needing to do something to combat the panic I feel setting in.

First I feel like I need to protect her, take care of her, covet her. And then the simple notion of her getting comfort from my heartbeat freaks me the fuck out. Can you say pussy, Donavan? More like pussy whipped. *What. The. Fuck?* This shit is not supposed to happen to me. Telling her I'll try is one thing. But this goddamn feeling taking hold of me like a vise grip in my chest? No fucking thanks.

I hear my mom's voice. It seeps into my head and my hand stills in Rylee's hair. I swear I stop breathing. "Colty. I know how much you love me. How much you need me. That you understand that love means doing whatever the other person tells you to. So I'm telling you that because you love me, you'll go lay down on my bed for me and wait like the good little boy that you are. You want food right? It's been days. You've got to be hungry. If you're a good little boy—if you love me—you won't fight this time. Won't be the *naughty* boy you were last time. If you're bruised up, the police might take us away from each other. And then you won't get anything to eat. And then I won't love you anymore."

Rylee's hand tracing absent circles on my tattoos jolts me back to the here and now. The irony in that—her touching the tattoos that represent so much—is enough in itself. I force myself to breathe calmly, try and clear the revulsion in my stomach. Quiet the tremor in my hand so she doesn't notice. Shit. Now I know the feeling earlier really was a fluke. How can I want to protect and take care of Rylee when I can't even do that for myself? *Breathe, Donavan. Fucking breathe.*

"I wonder if we're drawn to each other because we're both fucked up emotionally somehow," she murmurs aloud, breaking the silence. I can't help the breath that hitches in my chest. I swallow slowly, digesting her words—realizing they're just a coincidence—but how true they ring for me.

"Well gee thanks," I say, forcing a chuckle, hoping to calm both of us with some humor. "Us and everyone else in Hollywood."

"Uh-huh," she says, snuggling deeper into me. The feeling is so soothing I wish I could pull her inside of me to ease the pain there as well.

"I told you, a seven forty seven baby." I leave it at that. I can't force any more words out without her catching on that something's amiss with me.

She moves her hand from my tattoo to tickle through the slight smattering of hair on my chest. "I could lie here forever," she sighs out in that throaty morning voice of hers. I pray for my dick to stir at the sound. Need it to. Need to prove to myself that the unexpected reminder of my mother and my past can't affect me anymore. That they aren't who I am.

My thoughts flicker to what I'd normally do. Go call up my current flavor and use her. Fuck her into oblivion without a second thought of her needs. Use the fleeting pleasure to bury the endless goddamn motherfucking pain.

But I can't do that. I can't just walk away from the one person that I want and fear and desire and have grown to need. Balls in a fucking vise.

And before I even think, the words are out of my mouth. "Then stay here with me this weekend." I think I'm as shocked as Ry is at my comment. She stills at the same time I do. The first time my lips have *ever* uttered those fucking words. Words I never wanted to say before, but know without a doubt I mean right now.

"On one condition," she says.

One condition? I just handed her my balls on a platter in exchange for the whip to her pussy and she's going to add a condition? Fucking women.

"Tell me what a voodoo pussy is."

For the first time this morning I feel like laughing. And I do. I can't contain it. She just looks up at me, with those eyes that do wild things to me, like I'm crazy. "Shit, I needed that," I tell her, leaning down and pressing a kiss to the top of her head.

"Well?" she asks in that no-nonsense tone she has that usually turns me on. And I breathe a slight sigh as I start to harden at the thought of her wet heat I plan on taking advantage of in mere moments.

"Voodoo pussy?" I choke on the words.

"Yeah. You said it last night in the garden."

"I did?" I ask, unable to hide the amusement in my tone, and she just nods her head subtly with her eyebrows arched waiting for an answer. Oh yeah. Definitely hard and raring to go now. Thank Christ. "Well…it's that pussy that just takes hold of your dick and doesn't let go. It's so good—feels, tastes, everything good—that it's magical." I feel so stupid explaining it. I don't think I ever have. I just say it and Becks knows exactly what I mean.

Rylee laughs out loud and the sound is so beautiful. *Beautiful?* Fuck. I am pussy whipped. "So you're telling me that I have a magical pussy?" she asks as her finger trails a circle around my nipple before looking up at me and licking her lips. I can't manage a word at the moment because all of the blood needed to supply a coherent thought in my brain has just traveled south, so I just nod my head. "Well maybe I should show you—"

The cell phone on the dresser rings—it's a different ring than her normal one—and something about it has her scrambling off of the bed in a flash. She's breathless when she answers. And fucking breathtaking. She stands at the wall of windows looking out to the beach down below, her phone to her ear, and the sun bathing her naked body in its light.

The concern in her voice pulls me from my perverse thoughts of all of the ways I can take her. Position her. Corrupt her.

"Calm down, Scooter," she soothes. "It's okay, buddy. I'm okay. I'm right here. Shhh-shhh-shhh. Nothing's happened to me. I'm actually sitting on the beach right now, looking out at the water. I promise, buddy. I'm not going anywhere." The concern in her voice has me shifting in the bed. She notices my movement and looks over and smiles apologetically at me. As if I'd be mad that she left me to talk to one of the boys. Never. "You okay now? Yes. I know. Don't be sorry. You know that if I'm not there, you can always call me. Always. Mmm-hmm. I'll see you on Monday, okay? Call me if you need me before then." Rylee walks back toward the dresser as she wraps up her call. "Hey, Scoot? I Spiderman you. Bye."

I Spiderman you? Rylee hangs up her phone and tosses it on the dresser before walking back to the bed. My eyes roam over the line of her curves, thinking how lucky I am to have her naked and walking toward me with an extremely durable bed beneath me.

"Sorry," she says. "Scooter had a really bad dream and was afraid that I'd been hurt. That I was going to be taken away like his mom was. He just needed to make sure that I was okay. Sorry," she says again, and I swear that my goddamn heart twists in my chest at her apologies for being selfless. Is she for fucking real?

"Don't be," I tell her as she climbs into the bed beside me and sits on her knees. I tell myself to ask now before I become distracted at the sight of her sitting there looking so damn obedient. "*I Spiderman you?*"

She laughs with this adorable look on her face. "Yeah." She shrugs. "Some of the boys have trouble with affection when they come to us. Either they feel like they're betraying their parents, regardless of how fucked up their situation, by having feelings for their counselors, or feelings in general had a negative connotation from whatever situation they came from… It all started with Shane really, but it kind of caught on and now most of the boys do it. We take the one thing that they love more than anything and use that as the emotion instead. Scooter loves Spiderman so that's what he uses."

I look at her with bemusement, a little unnerved that she has these kids pegged so well—me, so well—if I allowed her to look close enough. She's just unknowingly fucked with my mind so much that my eyes haven't roamed south of her face to take in her gloriously naked body below as they normally would.

She mistakes the look I give her to be that I don't understand so she tries to clarify. She shifts off of her knees and situates herself closer to me. "Okay, for instance pretend you are one of my boys—tell me one thing that you love more than anything."

"That's easy." I smirk at her. "*Sex with you.*"

The smile spreads on her lips and her cheeks flush. So sexy. "Well, that's an answer I've never gotten from one of my boys before," she jokes, laughing at me. "No seriously, Colton, g— ive me the one thing."

I shrug, saying my first and only love. "I love to race."

"Perfect," she says. "If you were one of my boys and you wanted to tell me you loved me, or vice versa, you'd say 'I race you, Rylee.'"

My heart stutters again at hearing her say those words, and I think she realizes what she's said the minute the words are out of her mouth. She stills and her eyes dart to me and then down to her hands twisting in her lap. "I mean..." she backpedals and I'm glad this conversation is making her as nervous as I am right now "...if you were one of the boys that is."

"Of course." I swallow, desperately needing a distraction. I reach out to trace a finger down the midline of her chest—from her neck, down between the center of her breasts, and stopping at her bellybutton.

I race you, Rylee fleets through my mind. Just to hear what it sounds like for no other reason than to see how one of the boys would feel saying it. The tightening of my chest forces me to focus on the one thing that always allows me to forget. There will be no *racing* between Rylee and I. *None*. I look up from where my finger rests on her stomach to meet her eyes. "Now, I think you were just about to show me just how magical that pussy of yours was before we were interrupted."

Chapter Twenty-Two

The ringing of my cell phone startles me awake, and in the muted light of the dawn, I fumble for it on my nightstand. "Hello?" I mumble groggily, afraid that even though it's not the designated ring, something is possibly wrong with one of the boys at The House.

"Good morning, sleepy." Colton's velvety smooth rasp fills my ears. I can hear his smile through the line, and it sends shivers straight down my spine to the tips of my toes. I'm definitely awake now.

"Morning," I murmur, sinking back into the comfort of my warm bed.

"Do you have any idea how much I wish I was tangled up with you in that bed of yours? And that I was waking up with you and having lazy morning sex rather than just calling your cell?"

His subtle yet seductive words serve their purpose as I shift in my bed to still the ache he's just unfurled in me. "I was just thinking that same thing." I sigh softly, my mind wandering to how much I already miss him. How much my body automatically responds to the sound of his voice. I look down at my cotton camisole and panties and smirk. "Considering I'm very cold and very naked and I know you'd know exactly what to do to warm me up." A little lie never hurt anyone when one was trying to keep the fires burning, right?

I hear him suck in a hiss of a breath. "Sweet Jesus, woman, you know how to make a man want," he says quietly as I hear other voices in the background and realize that he's not alone.

It's only been four days since our blissful weekend together, but it feels like forever since I've been able to touch him. He drove me home on Monday morning on his way to the airport, and since then I've had to survive on texts and phone calls that leave me bereft and acting like a love-struck teenager.

"I'll be right back," he tells someone off the speaker, and I hear the chatter fade into the background. "I'm not sure that the people having breakfast here in the hotel want to watch me rub one out because my girlfriend's so fucking hot," he chuckles that seductive bedroom laugh of his through the line and I let it wash over me.

And then I still when the one word he said breaks through my sleep hazed brain. *Girlfriend*. I want to ask him to say it again so I can hear the word that is so simple but just literally took my breath away. But it's the fact that he's said it so casually, as if that's how he thinks of me, that I don't want to draw attention to it.

I sink further into the comfort of my bed with a huge smile plastered on my lips. "How's Nashville?"

"It's Nashville," he replies drolly. "Not bad, just not home. I'm sorry to wake you up with the time difference, but I'm going to be crazy busy all day, and I wanted to make sure that I got to talk to you. To hear your voice."

His words soften my smile, knowing that he's thinking about me even though he's doing work and prepping with his top sponsor. "Your voice is definitely a better wakeup call than my alarm clock..." I falter, holding back before I say screw it and just say what's on my mind. "I miss you," I tell him, hoping he hears what I really mean behind the words. That I miss more than just the sex. *That I miss him as a whole.*

He's silent on the other end of the line for a moment, and I think maybe I've expressed too much verbalized affection for Mr. Stoic. "I miss you too, baby. More than I thought possible." His last statement is said very quietly as if he can't believe it either. I smile broadly and snuggle deeper in my covers as his words warm me. "So what are your plans for the day?"

"Hmmm...sleeping some more and then a run, laundry, cleaning house...Maybe dinner with Haddie." I shrug although I know he can't see it. "What's your schedule like?"

"Brand meetings with the Firestone team, sponsorship junkets, a trip to Children's hospital—best part of the day if you ask me—and then some formal dinner thing tonight. I'll have to check with Tawny on the exact order." He sighs as I roll my shoulders involuntarily at her name. "The days just all run together sometimes on these trips. It's all important but it's also rather boring."

"I bet it is." I laugh. "Next time you're nodding off in one, just picture what my mouth did to you last Sunday," I murmur to him in my breathiest voice. Images flash through my mind and I can't fight the smile that comes with the memory.

A strangled moan comes from the other end of the line. "Jesus, Ry, are you purposely trying to make me walk around with a permanent hard-on today?" When my only response is a contented sigh, he continues, the edge in his voice expressing his unsatisfied desire. "When I get back, I'm locking you in my bedroom for an entire weekend—tying you up if I have to—and you'll be my sex slave. Your body will be mine to use as I please." He chuckles. "Oh and don't worry Ryles, your mouth will be used and then some."

Hello, Mr. Dominant! "Why are you limiting us to just your bedroom? I believe you have numerous surfaces in that large house of yours that are usable."

The groan he emits causes need to coil inside of me. "Oh, don't worry about where. Just worry about how you're going to walk afterward." His laugh is strained and sounds like how I feel.

"Promise?" I whisper, my body heating up at the thought of it.

"Oh, sweetheart, I'd stake my life on that promise." I hear his name called in the background. "You ready, Becks?" he says away from the speaker before sighing loudly. "I gotta go but I'll call you later if it's not too late, okay?"

"Okay," I reply softly. "It doesn't matter the time. I like hearing your voice."

"Hey, Ry?"

"Yeah?"

"Think of me," he says, and I can hear something in his voice: insecurity, vulnerability, or is it the need to feel wanted? No, not wanted. He has that all of the time. Maybe it's the need to feel needed. I can't decipher it, but that little request has my heart constricting in my chest.

"Always." I sigh, a smile on my lips as the line goes dead.

I sit with the phone to my ear for quite some time, so many thoughts running through my head about Colton and the sweet and affectionate side of him. The side that I'm getting glimpses of more and more. I can't help the broad smile on my face as I hang up my phone and sink back into my bed. I will myself to go back to sleep, but thoughts of him and endless possibilities prevent it.

The next time I glance at the clock, I'm startled an hour has passed while I've been lost in my thoughts, thinking about our time together. About how in such a short time he has brought me from such maddening lows to the incredible high like I am feeling now.

I finally start to drift off to sleep when my phone rings again. "*Seriously?*" I groan until I see who the caller is.

"Hey, Momma!"

"Hi, sweetie," she says, and just hearing her voice makes me want to see her again. I feel like it's been forever since I've been able to hug her. "So when were you going to tell me about the new man in your life?" she asks, tone insistent.

Nothing like getting straight to the point. "Well don't beat around the bush or anything." I laugh at her.

"How do you think I felt when I was flipping through last week's People magazine and lo and behold, I thought I saw a picture of you. So I flipped back and sure enough there you were, *my daughter*, looking absolutely breathtaking, on the arm of that tall, dark, and sinfully handsome Colton Donavan." I start to talk but she just keeps on going. "And then I read the caption and it said that 'Colton Donavan and his reported new flame heat up the night at the Kids Now charity function.' Do you know what a shock it was to see you there? And then to think that you're *dating someone* and I don't even know about it."

I can hear the shock in her voice. And the hurt over not telling her about my first date since Max. That she had to find out from a magazine. I glance over to my dresser where the copy of People sits. "Oh, Mom, don't be silly." I sigh, knowing I've hurt her by not confiding in her.

"Don't be silly?" She scoffs. "The man has donated a boatload of money to bring your project to fruition to get your attention and you're telling me I'm being silly?"

"Mom," I warn, "that's not why he donated the money." She harrumphs on the other end of the line at my answer. "No, really. His company picks one organization a year to focus on, and this year it happened to be mine. And I wasn't not telling you…things have just been crazy."

"Well, I think it's rather telling that you told me about his company donating the money for the project, but neglected to say that you'd actually met him…so?" she asks skeptically.

"I met him at the charity function," I answer without giving more away.

"And what happened at that function?"

"Have you been talking to Haddie?" I ask. There is no way she knows what to ask without having talked to Haddie.

"Quit avoiding the question. What happened at the function?"

"Nothing. We talked for a few minutes and then I was pulled away because of a problem with the date auction." Dear old mom doesn't need to know about the brief interlude backstage before that.

"And what was the problem?"

"Mother!"

"Well, if you'd just answer me straight the first time, we wouldn't have to play this cat and mouse game you're playing now would we?"

What is it with mothers? Are they clairvoyant? "*Okay, mom.* A date contestant got sick. I took her place. Colton bid on a date with me and won. Are you happy now?"

"Interesting," she says, drawing out every syllable, and I swear I can hear the smirk on her face in the single word. "So you tell me that I'm being silly when one of the sexiest men alive is pursuing my daughter, donating to her charity to get her attention I assume, and taking her to high profile events to show her off? Really? And how is that being silly, Rylee?"

"Mom—"

"How serious is it?" she deadpans, and I shouldn't be shocked at her frankness, but even after all of these years, I still am.

"Mom, Colton doesn't do serious," I try to deflect.

"Don't try to play it off, Rylee," she scolds. "I know you well enough to know that any man you give your time to is obviously worth it. And you wouldn't waste your time on someone that is in it for a quick lay." I cringe at her words. If only she knew about Colton's arrangements, I'm sure she wouldn't be so sure of my judgment then. "So tell me, honey, just how serious is it?"

I sigh loudly, knowing that my mother is tenacious when she wants an answer. "Honestly, from my viewpoint, it could be something. From his...well, Colton isn't used to doing the more than a couple of months type of thing. We're just feeling it out as we go," I answer softly and as honestly as possible.

"Hmmm," she murmurs before falling silent. "Does he treat you well? Because you know that they always treat you the best in the beginning of the relationship, and if it's not good in the beginning then it's not going to get any better."

"*Yes, Mother,*" I say like a child.

"I'm serious, Rylee Jade," she says, her voice implacable. She must be serious if she's using my middle name. "Does he or doesn't he?"

"Yes, Mom. He treats me very well."

I hear her warm laughter on the other end of the line, and I can tell she's relieved. "Just remember what I always say; don't lose yourself trying to hold onto someone who doesn't care about losing you." I finish mouthing the words she's saying. Words she's told me since I started crushing on boys as a teenager.

"I know."

"Oh, honey, I am so happy for you! After everything that you've been through…you deserve nothing but happiness, my sweet child."

I smile at her unconditional love and concern for me, appreciating what a great mother I have. "Thanks, Mom. We're just taking things a day at a time right now and seeing where it leads us."

"There's my girl. Always with a level head on her shoulders."

I sigh, a soft smile on my face. "So how are things going? How have you been? How's Dad?"

"All's good here. Dad's fine. Busy as ever, but you know how he is." She laughs and I can imagine her running her tongue over her top lip as is her habit. "How are the boys?"

I smile at my mom's question. She treats them like they're family too, always sending them treats or cookies or little things to make them feel special. "They're good. I think Shane has his first pseudo-girlfriend, and Zander is slowly making progress." I go through the boys and talk about each one with her, answering her questions, and I can sense another care package coming for them.

We talk for a bit more before she has to go. "I miss you, Mom." My voice cracks with my words because she might be tough and overbearing, but she only wants the best for me. I love her more than anything.

"I miss you too, Ry. It's been too long since I've seen you."

"I know. I love you."

"Love you too. Bye."

I hit call end and snuggle back into my warm bed that for some reason no one will let me sleep in this morning. I glance over at the dresser at the People and grab it. I flip it open to the marked page and there I am.

I stare at the picture of Colton and me at the Kids Now function on the red carpet. He is standing, his shoulders squared to the camera, with his hand in one pocket of his slacks and his other hand wrapped around my waist. His pocket square front and center. His face is looking toward the camera, but his chin and eyes are angled toward me with a huge smile on his face.

My eyes gravitate to the part of the picture that I love the most, the way his hand grips my hip, a possessive hold announcing to the world that I am his.

I reread the caption again and sigh. I'm so glad the press hasn't gotten a hold of my name yet. I'm not ready to be thrust in to the media circus but I know it's inevitable if I'm with Colton.

"In for a penny, in for a pound," I mutter to myself.

I hold the picture in my hand, staring at it until I talk myself into taking my run. I shift out of my bed when my phone dings a text. I laugh out loud at technology's rule over my life this morning and nonetheless pick up my phone to see Colton's name. I can't help the smile on my lips.

Thinking nasty thoughts of you in the middle of my meeting. Won't be standing for a while now. Bruno Mars – Locked Out of Heaven.

I laugh out loud, knowing the song and feeling flattered at the same time at the song's lyrics. I text him back.

So glad I could help with your boredom, Ace…it's the least I can do. Think more thoughts! TLC – Red Light Special.

I smirk as I toss my phone onto my nightstand, knowing that he's going to have a lot harder time concentrating in his meeting now.

Chapter Twenty-Two

Colton—Raced

"You know what I think?"

"Huh?" I look over to where Becks is sitting on the chair across from me, but I move too fast and the room spins for a minute before I can focus again.

"I think," he says, laughing and tilting God knows what number beer we're on at me, "I think we need to have a moment of silence."

"*Who died?*" I'm drunker than I thought. What did I miss? I lift my bottle to my lips and try to figure out what he's talking about.

"Your single, non-pussy-whipped self."

"Bullshit!" I spout through his damn laughter that's a little too loud right now for my drunk ears.

"*Bullshit?*" he says as he scoots to the edge of his chair, and I want to tell him not to stand, that he'll fall on his ass. Then again, he's fucking with me and I could use a good laugh at his expense so I refrain. "Were you just not looking at your phone like you wanted to call her and get off?"

I lay my head back and laugh because hell if he's not right. It's been five fucking days since I've had her, since she stayed the weekend at my place. Hours occupied with sex that rocked my world and downtime where she challenged me, pushed me, laughed with me. A first for me on so many levels, but the most important one was that I wasn't freaked the fuck out about it.

And that never happens.

"It's called Skype," I tease, closing my eyes momentarily. No amount of alcohol can fuck with the perfect image in my head of answering my iPad to find Rylee sitting on her bed, lace and garters and come-fuck-me-gear on the other end of the picture connection. Manicured fingernails parting pink flesh to show me just what I'm missing. Dirty talk I'd never expect to fall from her lips but perfectly fitting in that telephone-sex rasp of hers.

"*Exactly*. When have you ever had Skype-sex? You usually snap your fingers in whatever town you're in and you can pick from the hundred that come running and drop to their knees." I hear the pop of a bottle top and then another and open my eyes to see him holding a fresh one out to me.

I think for a second as I accept it and fuck if he's not right.

"See? *I told you*. When you brought her to Vegas with us I thought she was just a passing fad. Thought you were testing the waters because you weren't used to having a challenge and it got a rise out of you. *Literally*," he deadpans, drawing a shake of my head. "But, Wood, after the past few weeks, you bailing from work early to go to go-kart tracks and shit … It's more than obvious that we need to say our parting words and have a moment of silence for your dearly departed dick."

"Becks—"

"Shh!" he responds, trying to hold his pointer finger to his lips but his depth perception is so off I laugh when he tries several times to get it there despite his dead serious face. "A moment of silence is needed to kiss your unvoodooed ass goodbye."

"You're such an asshole," I tell him but know I'm lucky to have him as my partner in crime.

"Shh!" he says again, and I give up. I take a deep breath and roll my eyes but humor him and remain silent. I swear he's passed out but he's still sitting at the edge of the chair and hasn't fallen over.

Yet.

But his eyes are still closed when a huge-ass grin turns his mouth up and he claps his hands together and rubs them. "Shit, that was easier than I thought."

"What was?" My buzz is humming now and I'm finally relaxed after a fuck-all day with the Firestone guys and negotiations over shit they're going to cave on in the end anyway.

"Getting you to admit you're a kept man now."

"Fucking Christ, dude!" I spit my beer out. "Kept? You're calling me kept?" That's like the equivalent of telling Jenna Jameson she's a virgin.

"It's pretty fucking obvious when there's a huge neon sign above your head flashing no vacancy for your stabbin' cabin that you're a kept man. Have a woman now."

"A woman now? I'm sure Ry would love to hear you refer to her as that."

He eyes me over his bottle. "So she's not your woman, then? Because usually when you hang up the phone you don't think twice, back to business. Now you hang up with a little smirk on your face and you're lost in la-la land for a bit."

"La-la land?" I laugh.

"What would you call it, then? Girlfriend-ville?" He eyes me. Dares me to deny his reference since I'm the self-proclaimed *don't do the girlfriend thing* kind of guy.

I begin to argue but then stop. *Fucking Becks*. He knows me like the back of my hand and yet this is uncharted fucking territory for me. A woman that I want to color outside the lines with. No, scratch that. A woman that fucks with me on so many levels that I'm so busy being challenged and seduced by her words, her body, and her defiance that I don't even realize the parameters I'm used to controlling don't really matter anymore ... because she does.

Fuckin' A, he's right, but hell if I'll tell him that.

"We'll go with *woman*," I concede, but the word *girlfriend* rolls around in my head, sticking here and there as I get used to the idea of it.

"Holy shit!" Becks says, pounding on his chest acting like he's choking and I just stare at him unamused despite the smile on my lips. He stops laughing and tosses a bottle cap at me as he leans back in his chair. "Well, admission is half the battle. Keeping her is the other half."

"Keeping her?" Dude's got my head spinning. I mean, fuck, I just told her I'd try, asked her to spend the weekend at Broadbeach with me when no one ever has, and he's talking about how to keep her? I didn't realize she was going somewhere.

"Baby steps, Becks. Don't give me a heart attack here. I hear keeping her but I think rings and strings and weddings and shit."

And he only thinks my reaction makes the whole situation funnier by how he curls up and can't stop laughing. "The look on your face is priceless," he finally gets out, "but I'm not talking about marriage."

Thank fuck for that. We can put away the defibrillators now. I look over at him, eyes telling him to get to the fucking point so I can enjoy my beer again without any more cardiac arrests.

"I'm talking about romance. Shit girls like, man."

"You don't need romance when you have my skills," I tell him, already waiting for the smart-ass comment to come from his mouth.

"Okay, *one-pump chump*."

"Fuck off!" I sneer and flip my middle finger up, but he's laughing so hard he doesn't even see it.

"Shit. I've got to take a piss," he says and rises on unsteady feet to head to the bathroom of my suite.

I lift my feet up and prop them on the table in front of me, hands clasped behind my head. Through the open balcony doors I can hear Bruno Mars's newest song playing in the bar across the street, but in the muted silence I start thinking about the word girlfriend. Wondering if that's a definition we really need when we have our own language between us. Then Beckett's words start running over again in my head until he comes back out zipping up his fly.

He walks over to the open doors and I feel a slight pang of guilt that he wanted to go hang out at the bar and I just didn't want to deal with the crowd tonight. I'm usually interested in the eye candy and playing the game.

But I just don't feel like it this trip.

I shake my head. What in the fuck is Rylee doing to me? All her talk about Scooter saying *I Spiderman you* and that look on her face as she sat naked on her knees beside me undoes me bit by bit when I'm already a mess of unraveled memories.

I lean forward and grab another beer from the bucket of ice in front of me and stare at the label for a few minutes. "So uh, romance, huh?"

I see his body register my words, but he keeps his face toward the street because he can tell I'm so far out of my fucking element here, the periodic table wouldn't even be able to help me.

Romance? I don't do it. Flowers die, food gets eaten. It's not real. I've watched people flip the switch on and off enough in my life between my dad's movie sets to women wanting something with me that I'm not fucking stupid enough to see the farce.

So why the fuck am I wondering what Becks thinks I'm screwing up here?

"What are you not saying to me? You think I'm not giving her the flowery shit a girl wants so she's gonna bail?" The thought doesn't settle well in my stomach. In fact it makes me shove up out of my chair and walk back and forth.

Well more like stumble.

"I didn't say shit, dude." Becks keeps looking out the window. He knows he's questioned me and I don't take too easy to that.

And fuck if he doesn't have me questioning myself now. I told her I'd try to give her more. That has to be enough in the end here. I'm already pushing myself past my comfort zone and now I have to think about this kind of shit?

I'm annoyed with Becks for butting his nose in and irritated at myself for not even thinking about it. But I shouldn't have to, should I?

I roll my shoulders and plop back down on the couch. Did he really have to ruin my stellar buzz by bringing this up? Then again, the room's still moving a bit so maybe he didn't.

"What do you think I should do? Send her poems and shit? C'mon, dude, that's not me."

He snorts out a laugh. "Yeah. I'm sure a classy 'roses are red' poem is just what a lady like her wants."

I sit there in silence, ignoring the dig, thoughts running through my semi-cloudy mind and plaster a grin to my face when the words connect. "Roses are red, tires are black, you're the only pussy I wanna ride bareback."

Becks spits out the beer in his mouth in a huge spray out the balcony doors. He wipes his mouth as his laughter falls to match mine. He turns to face me and raises an eyebrow. "That was pretty fucking good. If you're that witty when you're drunk, I think we should work under the influence more often." He walks toward me and I can already see his mind turning, trying to match my poem. "I've got one. Roses are red, violets are fine, you be the six, and I'll be the nine."

"Now that's a good image to have," I say, my mind immediately back on her in that fucking outfit from Skype.

"Down, boy. Poetry, not pornography," he says, tapping the neck of his bottle against mine before sitting back in his chair. "Not with me anyway."

"No worries there. You're cute and all but not my type." I lean back and fall into thought before I start laughing. Look at us. Two guys in our thirties making up fucking nursery rhymes. This is some funny shit.

Becks chuckles to himself, his eyes closed, and I wait for him to speak. "Roses are red, violets are blue, get in my bed and be ready to screw."

"How fucked-up are we?" I laugh.

"Hey, this is poetry in its truest form." He lifts his beer to me, his eyes still closed as the alcohol mixed with the clock hitting past midnight begins to get to him. "In fact, you should send her one of them tomorrow. That's something a good *boyfriend* would do."

"You and your boyfriend bullshit," I tell him, taking my hat off and tossing it on the table. "I'm so good, dude, labels like that don't apply to me."

"Oh Jesus." He throws his hands up, his beer splashing up the top of his longneck that has him sputtering to wipe it off his shirt. "Forgive me, Oh-King-of-All-Things in his own mind."

"Damn straight," I say, loving to get his feathers ruffled.

"Let me ask you something," Becks says as he props his feet on the table. "Do you fuck her regularly?"

I nearly spit my beer out but don't because I may be feeling more than good, but no one talks about Ry this way. I make sure my eyes tell him exactly that.

"Oh, excuse me, choirboy Colton. Let me rephrase. Are you having *regular relations* with her?" he asks in a prim and proper voice.

I can't help but laugh. *Fucker*. He just stares at me, eyebrows raised, waiting for me to answer. "Every chance I get."

He nods his head and works his tongue in his mouth while he thinks. "What's she doing tonight?"

What's up with the questions? "She was at The House until nine and then heading to dinner with Haddie. Why?"

"So you know her schedule then?"

"And your point is ...?" He's starting to irritate me with this cryptic bullshit.

"When's her birthday?" He ignores my question by asking another, a regular fucking Socrates.

"September fifteenth." Becks chuckles and I blow out an exhale at the condescending sound of it.

"Impressive." He nods his head in approval. "Now I know you'll know her bra size, but what about her shoe size?"

"What the fuck dude? What are you getting at?"

"Patience, young grasshopper. Bra and shoe size?"

"I'll *young grasshopper* your ass if you don't get to the fucking point."

He leans forward and lifts a beer from the bucket toward me in offering. I nod my head and take it. Fuck it. I might as well answer him than deal with his crap. Besides, I've gotta admit I'm curious where he's going with this. "Thirty Six D and size nine and half."

"Nice," Becks says, drawing it out in a sound of approval. "What are her parents' names?"

"Daniels," I grit out, patience lost amidst his amusing twenty questions.

"Last one, I promise." He puts his hands up in surrender.

"Mr. and Mrs. Thomas." *Take that*. I can be a smart ass just like you.

"Just answer." He sighs in exasperation.

"If I answer, are you going to get to your point?" He nods his head, his grin spreading even wider as I tell him their names.

"Huh."

"Huh?" After all the build up, that's all he's going to give me? I lean forward and rest my elbows on my knees waiting for an answer.

He angles his head and looks me in the eyes for a beat. And despite the spinning in my head, curiosity is killing the cat. And of course cat leads me to thinking of pussy and pussy to Rylee. *Fuck*. I'm definitely drunk.

"Boyfriend," he says, breaking through my thoughts, know-it-all grin spreading from ear to ear.

"*Fuck off*." It's the only comeback I have because he just baited the hook and I thought he was going to tell me something unexpected. What an ass. I throw the pillow beside me at him and flop back on the cushions.

He catches it and laughs loudly. "Those are things boyfriends know. Not fuck buddies, not random assholes—although, you qualify for the asshole part too—but boyfriends."

"Isn't it time you head back to your room? Isn't your hand and some lotion waiting for you there?"

"Best offer I've had all night," he says, pushing himself up off the couch, and I laugh when it takes him a moment to steady his feet. "I think I'll try to enjoy it before I pass the fuck out ..."

"You go do that," I tell him, slipping my shoes off and turning my feet so I can lift them onto the couch and lie down. "Tell Rosy and Palmela to do you right," I tease, making the jerking-off motion with my free hand.

"No worries, they never disappoint," he says and so many comebacks flicker in my mind but are just beyond my drunken haze so I nod my head instead. "You just lie there and enjoy thinking about the sex you have regularly now with the woman you claim isn't your girlfriend but who really is." He opens the door. "Catch ya in the morning, *boyfriend*."

Asshole is the word that comes to mind but all I say is, "Hmm ..." as the door clicks shut and my eyelids begin to feel heavy. I start to doze, my mind on Rylee, wondering if the boys were good during her shift today. If she made it home okay afterwards. Shit! I'm thinking about stuff I normally don't give a flying fuck about ... stuff a *boyfriend* would think about.

There's that fucking word again.

Thoughts come and go but they're all focused on the one person I never expected to be thinking about. The damn voodoo she's grabbed me by the balls with and is now somehow twisting around my hardened heart.

... *If you were one of my boys and you wanted to tell me you loved me, or vice versa, you'd say 'I race you, Rylee'*...

The words flicker through my buzzed mind. I try to shake them, try to forget that look in her eyes when she made the statement. Try to focus on the incredible sex we had afterward.

But as I fall asleep on the couch in some overpriced hotel suite in Nashville, my mind should be focused on tomorrow's negotiations and the upcoming season. I should be dreaming of great sex with a hot blonde.

But I'm not.

I'm thinking of roses and violets, of *my girlfriend*, and learning that maybe Spiderman and racing off the track just might have a thing or two in common.

Chapter Twenty-Three

"Stella?" I call out from the door of my office. "Stella? What happened to my schedule for today?"

I lower my very tired and aching head into my hands and rest it there while I try to figure out how to juggle everything this week: budget projections, schedules, project meetings, along with the usual daily grind. And now I can only hope that the sudden four hour meeting blocked on my schedule for after lunch is just a computer glitch. Why didn't Stella enter any details? I swear it wasn't there thirty minutes ago. Maybe I'd looked at the wrong day.

"Fuck," I mutter under my breath as I rub my temples to assuage the beginning of a headache. I hope it's not one of Teddy's endless brainstorming sessions. Our optimism had been tested earlier in the week when new budget projections showed us falling short of funding due to changes in California insurance laws. And since we've tapped every fundraising well dry, we're crossing our fingers and hoping that Colton's team pulls through with the needed sponsorships to keep everything on track. I look down at my schedule again, reining in my impatience at Stella's lack of response, and remind myself of Haddie's accusation when I'd snapped at her earlier this morning.

"Ooooh, someone's having Colton withdrawals," she chided as she added creamer to her coffee.

"Shut up," I muttered, shoving my bagel in the toaster with more force than necessary.

"I guess it's the toaster's fault you're pissy then." I shot her a glare of death, but her only response was a smarmy smile. "Look, I get it. You're so used to getting fucked into next week that when you're stuck in this week you're beyond sexually frustrated. You've gotten used to having incredible sex regularly, and now he's been gone now for what? Nine days?"

"Eight," I snapped.

"Yeah." She laughed. "But it's not like you're counting right? And now Momma needs to *get some* to make her happy." I stifled my smile then even though my back was to her. "Christ, Rylee, it's nowhere near the real thing, but Skype the man and get yourself off if it's going to stop you from being such a bitch!"

"Who says I haven't," I responded coyly, extremely happy that she didn't see the blush creep over my cheeks as I remembered Colton's and my chat last night. *Oh the marvels of technology.*

"Well hot damn!" She slapped the kitchen table. "At least someone's getting some in this house this week." She laughed. I caved and finally turned around, my laughter joining hers. She brought the cup to her lips again and looked at me while she blew the steaming coffee cooler. "I'm happy for you, Rylee. Really happy. The man looks at you as if you're the only woman in the world." When I snorted at her telling her she's completely wrong, she just continued. "Colton's put that spark back in your eye. Made you confident and sure of yourself again. He's made you feel sexy too…don't give me that look," she told me when I narrowed my eyes at her. "I've seen the lingerie hanging to dry in your bathroom, sister, so don't even try to deny it. I love it! So when does the handsome stud get back anyway?"

"Two more days," I sighed.

"Thank God! Then you can stop being such a raving bitch!" she teased with a smile. "You've got it bad girl!"

"I know. I know." I shot her a quick smile as I stuffed my lunch into my bag, knowing the following forty-eight hours were going to drag big time. "I gotta go before I'm late. Love ya – bye."

"Love ya – bye."

I take a deep breath as I shake myself from my reverie. Haddie's right, *I've got it bad.* I turn in my chair and buzz Stella again.

"Yes?"

"There you are…hey what's up with this meeting taking up my whole afternoon?" I try to keep the irritation out of my voice, but it's hard. I've been working non-stop since Sunday and just want the afternoon to catch up.

"Um, I'm not sure."

What? Who took my overly efficient assistant and hid her? "*What do you mean you're not sure?*"

"Well…" I sense her discomfort even through her disembodied voice on the intercom. "I mean—"

"What's it for?"

"Well someone from CDE called over and asked that I clear your schedule for a very important meeting about the sponsorship program. Teddy was right here when they called and okayed it. Said he'd tell you… and I'm guessing by the sound in your voice that he didn't?"

My heart flutters at the mention of Colton's company and then deflates knowing that he's not going to be there. And then my mind starts turning and my heart accelerates because I have a feeling that this means I'm going to have to be one-on-one with Tawny and her team. Just the person I want to spend four hours confined in a room with.

"No, he didn't. Are you fucking kidding me?" I say before I can catch myself.

"Nope." She chuckles sympathetically, knowing I've been burning the candle at both ends. "I'm sorry. I know your day was packed, but I was able to move everything around. I left you a voicemail…I guess you didn't get to that either, huh?"

"Haven't even had a chance to listen to them since I first checked them this morning."

"Well at least you might get to see that hot hunk of a man hmmm?"

I laugh overtly at her comment, knowing the rumors are swirling around the office about what Colton and I are or aren't doing. I've yet to justify any of them except to say that we attended the gala together to promote the sponsorship despite what the caption in People said. I'm not sure if anyone believes me or not—and honestly I am way too busy to care—but I'm sure the water cooler has been a busy place as of late.

"Nah. When we spoke last week he mentioned that he'd be out of town for the week for some kind of promo junket," I lie.

"Too bad," she murmurs. "Looking at him during a four hour meeting would definitely put some pep in anybody's step." Her hearty laugh comes through the line, and I can hear it echo in stereo outside my office door.

"You're incorrigible, Stella. What time do I have to be there?"

"They're sending a car for you. It'll be here in just under thirty minutes."

Sending a car? Tawny probably wants to make sure I have no way to escape her evil plans for me. I snort a laugh at my thoughts and bring a hand up to cover my mouth to stifle it. "Okay, Stell…I don't like it but I guess I have no choice, huh?"

"Nope," she agrees before I disconnect the line.

"Fucking great!" I mutter aloud before reaching for a tootsie roll in the bowl on my desk. I think I'm going to need the whole lot of them to help me cope with the rest of my afternoon.

"We're almost there," Sammy says from the driver's seat. "About ten more minutes."

"Okay. Thanks, Sammy," I murmur as I take in the beautiful interior of the G-class SUV. This must be yet another one of his collection of cars. I fight the smirk that wants to come. I don't think it matters how many he has; Sex is definitely my favorite.

Sammy glances at me in the rearview mirror, and I smile at him. I was shocked when he was the one who came to pick me up. I told him so, expressing that I was surprised Colton had left him behind on his trip. I thought that they were inseparable. Sammy had just given me a non-committal shrug without saying a word. And now my overactive imagination starts to roam on the ride over, and I begin to worry about Colton. What if he needs help to keep some crazy, irrational fan away from him and Sammy's not there to help protect him? I shake my head, telling myself I'm crazy. Colton admitted to me he was quick to throw down in his youth. I'm pretty sure he could hold his own if he needed to.

My phone beeps a text and I pull it out of my purse, a smile spreading on my face when I see it's from Colton.

Beckett scolded me for not giving you romantic gestures. RME. He says I need to give you the flowers and poetry variety. Here's the closest I get and the best we could come up with. Roses are red. Violets are blue. Sitting in Nashville. Thinking of you.

I laugh out loud at the image of Beckett and Colton sitting in Nashville and having a discussion about me. I can very clearly see Colton rolling his eyes at Beckett's big brotherly recommendation of romantic gestures, all the while making up a nursery school rhyme to send to me instead. I quickly pull up the web on my phone and search for different versions of the preschool poem. After a few different links, I find the perfect one.

How sweet! And you said you didn't do romance. Be still my beating heart. Those must be some really boring meetings. Now, I have one for you. Roses are red. Violets are blue. I'm using my hand, while thinking of you. Xx.

I smirk as I hit send, pleased with my witty response and wishing I could see his face as he reads it. We drive a couple more minutes when my phone chimes again.

FYI – Dick's hard like a teenage boy. My turn—typing with one hand now: Roses are red. Lemons are sour. If you open your legs, I'll be there in an hour.

I bite back the laugh that bubbles up in my throat, squeezing my knees together to stifle the ache our little text tête-à-tête has stirred up. I look up and meet Sammy's eyes in the mirror, my cheeks blushing as if he knows what I'm reading, the dirty thoughts I'm thinking. I quickly avert my eyes and reply.

Quite the poet, Ace. Too bad you're not here. The flight's at least four hours. I don't know if I can wait that long. Might just have to take care of myself. xx Gotta go. I need my hands for other things now.

I hit send as we pull into the parking lot of a large, nondescript, gray three-story building with a mirrored glass exterior. The building spans the better part of the block, and the only marker denoting its occupants are the letters "CD Enterprises" in electric blue at the top row of windows.

"Here we are," Sammy murmurs, and my anxiety ratchets up at the thought of having to sit across from Tawny. I close my eyes momentarily and inhale a long breath while Sammy moves around to my side of the car to open my door. I need to keep my cool with Tawny because the last thing I need is to be known as Colton's bitch of a girlfriend. Thank God I had my little texting distraction to ease the dread.

Within moments he's taken me in a side entrance and leads me up the stairs to a waiting conference room. "Someone will be right with you," he says as he walks out.

"Thank you, Sammy."

"My pleasure, Ms. Thomas."

I turn and appraise the conference room I've been ushered into. There is a long, typical looking conference table in the midst of the room with walls painted a warm coffee color, but the focal point of the room is the wall opposite the doorway. It's a wall of tinted glass, and as I step closer to it, I realize that the opening looks down upon a massive garage of sorts. Around several race cars there is a flurry of activity with men moving here and there. Snap-on tool boxes in cobalt blue line one wall of the garage with a chair rail of sorts, made of stainless steel diamond plate across the midsection, with various posters and banners above it on the wall. I step closer, fascinated and feeling the energy from all of the activity below.

"Roses are red. Violets are blue." The voice at my back startles me, but I whip around knowing that rasp anywhere. "It better be only *my* hands on you."

"Colton!" His name comes out in a breathless rush of air and despite every nerve in my body tingling at his proximity, my feet remain cemented to the floor. I swear my heart rate doubles at the sight of him, and although my intention is to remain cool and mask the excitement wreaking havoc on my system, I can't help the wide grin that spreads over my lips.

"Surprise!" he exclaims, holding his arms out to the side. He steps into the room and shuts the door behind him.

It's seeing him in the flesh that makes me realize how much I've missed him. How in such a short amount of time I've gotten used to him being a part of my day-to-day life. We both take a few steps toward each other, drinking the other in. The hungry look in his eyes steals my breath and hints at things that make my center ache with liquid heat.

My eyes move to that sensuous mouth of his. It's quirked up at one corner, as if his thoughts aren't exactly pure and innocent. And I hope they aren't because then they'd be matching mine.

My body vibrates with his nearness, confirming that time has done nothing to dampen the instant pull he has on me. I surpassed stepping cautiously off of the edge of falling in love with him a long time ago and am now currently plunging headfirst.

Our eyes lock as we slowly close the distance between us, and I know it's not possible, but in that instant I swear that I see a flash of my future in his eyes. The revelation unnerves me and releases the butterflies I have flitting around in my stomach.

We stop within a foot of each other, and I angle my head up so that my eyes can remain on his. "Hiya, Ace." I smile at him, my pulse still jumping erratically.

"Hi," he mouths, that shy smile tipping up the corners of his lips. We stare at each other for a beat, and before I can process the thought, Colton's hands are fisted in my hair, yanking me forward, his lips claiming mine. He tastes of mint and urgency and everything Colton, and even though I'm drowning in him, I still can't seem to get enough. His tongue licks in my mouth and teases by pulling back and then darting back in again.

His mouth captures my moan as he lowers his hand on my back and skirts under my sweater to draw his calloused fingers against my bare skin before pressing me into the hard length of his body. And just when the kiss starts to soften and become tender, Colton's mouth dominates mine again, our hands becoming a series of touches and movements as if we can't feel enough of each other.

He breaks from our kiss, his forehead resting on mine and his breath panting against my lips. "I couldn't let you resort to your hand, Rylee," he murmurs, and I can feel his lips form a smile as they press against mine, smothering the carefree laugh his words incite. "You're mine now. I'm the only one allowed to give you pleasure."

Before I can think of a witty retort, Colton's mouth is on mine again, his tongue delving between my lips, his body pushing me backwards so my hips hit the edge of the conference table. He presses me to sit down, nudging my legs apart with his knee, and steps in between them. I am now at a height disadvantage to him, and he leans over and cups my cheeks in his hands, his tongue soothing over where he just nipped my bottom lip. I keen with need as he continues his tantalizing assault on my mouth and all sense of coherence is lost.

In an unexpected move, he pulls his face back, his hands still framing my cheeks in possession, and stares at me. His eyes swim with emotion as his jaw clenches from unspoken words. We stare at each other and pant from the need that is driving every action and subsequent reaction. Feelings I want to confess die on my lips as the pad of his thumb reaches over to graze them tenderly. Something has shifted between us, and I can't put my finger on it, but the look in his eyes tells me all I need to know: He wants me as much as I want him. Any doubts of mine that he wants another vanish with this singular look.

"I missed you, Rylee," he says softly before wrapping his arms around me and folding me into him. He places his cheek on the top of my head, his arms squeezing tighter. Hearing him say it, admitting that I am a part of his everyday life too, warms me on the inside.

"I missed you too," I murmur as I melt into the comfort of his arms, "more than I want to admit." A small sound rumbles in his chest, and I know that my words have affected him. We sit like this for a few moments, reveling in the warmth and comfort from each other that we've missed over the past week and a half; we're absorbing what we've finally acknowledged, verbalized, and are both accepting in our own ways. I plant a soft kiss over his heart without thinking. "I really like my surprise. You sure know how to spoil a girl. Thank you."

"You're welcome," he tells me, kissing the top of my head again. "I wasn't sure how your office would react if I were to waltz in and take you over the edge of your desk."

"What?" I laugh out loud as my body heats at the thought. I lean back so I can look up at his eyes. "That was your plan, huh?"

"Desperate times call for desperate measures."

"I believe you once told me that you were far from desperate," I tease, throwing his words back at him.

He chuckles softly before pursing his lips. "That was before I spent an endless amount of time, in God knows how many boring meetings, thinking about what exactly I'd like to be doing with you." A lascivious grin spreads across his lips. "And to you."

"That's a lot of dirty thoughts."

"Oh, Rylee, you have no idea."

I swallow loudly, the lust that leaps in his eyes and darkens his irises giving me a hint. "So, you planned on acting out these impure thoughts in my office? On my desk?" I arch my brow in mock disapproval, but the smirk on my face betrays me.

"Yep. I told you," he says, playing along, "I take what's mine when I want it..."

"With an audience of my co-workers?"

"Ah-huh." He grins like a mischievous schoolboy. "I'd planned on coming straight from the airport this morning but I didn't think Teddy would approve of it."

I run my tongue across my top lip as I look up at him, placing my hands behind me on the table so I can lean back on them—my shoulders arching and my breasts pushing forward. I take notice of Colton's eyes and their languorous appraisal of my new posture—his eyes heating and tongue darting out to wet his lip. "Since when do you care what people think?"

"Oh, sweetheart, believe me, I don't..." he smirks "...but we still have to preserve your reputation."

"I think that was ruined the minute I started going out with you."

"Probably." He shrugs in nonchalance. "I still think that your boss might object to his star employee being fucked on her desk."

"But your boss?" I ask playfully. "He's okay with his employees doing something like that? Here?"

A slow, suggestive smile curls one corner of his mouth, his dimple deepening. "Oh I think so," he says, leaning down and laying his hands beside my knees on the table.

"You think so? Why's that?" I ask, narrowing my eyes at him as I continue to play along.

"Oh, he has quite a vested interest in this situation here," Colton murmurs as he leans closer into me.

"Oh really?" I breathe as I involuntarily arch my back so my breasts brush against his chest. I bite my bottom lip as we stare at each other.

Colton's breath whispers over my face. "*Sometimes it's fucking great to be the boss,*" he says before lowering his lips to mine again, but this time it's an achingly slow kiss that tantalizes and torments me to the point of no return.

I want him, and I want him now. My God the man makes me crave with an intensity I never thought was imaginable. His fingers begin a slow, languid slide up my arms, my body coiling at the thought of where his talented fingers will trail to next.

I lean my head back as his mouth skims down my jaw and expose my neck for him. I reach his hip with one hand and pull him harder against me as his mouth tempts and dips below the neckline of my sweater.

"Colton." I exhale as need swelters through my core and fire spreads in my veins.

A loud beep fills the room suddenly and Colton sags against me as I hear, "Excuse me, Colton?" coming from the phone on the credenza.

"Fuck," he mutters quietly against my neck. "Yes?"

"Beckett's looking all over for you. Something about an issue with Eddie…" she trails off as if she's afraid of his response.

"Christ!" he swears aloud, his body tensing in response to her comment.

"My thoughts exactly."

"Where?"

"They're on the garage floor."

"I'll be right there. Thanks, Brooke."

The phone clicks off as Colton straightens his frame to its full height. I push myself off of the conference table as he walks over to the glass-viewing wall to look at the garage below. When he turns back toward me he has transformed from the playful lover to the consummate businessman.

"I apologize, Ry. I have to go take care of something down below. Come with me?" he asks, holding his hand out, and I'm slightly taken back. Mr. I-Don't-Do-Commitment wants to hold my hand at his work? Isn't that a little too much of a 'public display' for someone with his history?

"I can stay here if you'd like," I offer meekly, not wanting to leave his side.

He just looks at me oddly before reaching out and grabbing my hand and pulling me with him. "I'm not letting go of you, Ryles, until I get my fill of you," he warns in a promise that causes flames of desire to lick at my center, "and that may just take a long fucking time."

Chapter Twenty-Four

Beckett nods to me, the ghost of a smile curling his lips as Colton leads me from the garage floor. We make our way to a side door that Colton ushers me through, and I find us in a stairwell of sorts. "Up." Colton points as he places a hand on my back.

I ascend in front of him, his hand remaining on the swell of my backside the entire first flight. "Did I tell you how damn sexy you look today?" His voice rasps from behind me.

I look over my shoulder and smile at him. "Thank you," I reply, recognizing the salacious look in his eyes. "But I have a feeling that your view is a little jaded from a lack of sex."

The hum of appreciation in the back of his throat makes me smile. "Oh, baby, there's definitely nothing wrong with my view," he says with a chuckle. I start to go up the second flight again, but this time Colton's hands seem to be touching me in various places with every step. A soft caress up the back of my thigh. A slight brush down my bare arm. A quick tap on my backside.

I know exactly what he's doing, but it's not like he needs to stoke the embers because I'm already a wild fire of need. Knowing that he wants me like this, needing and aching for more of his touch, makes me feel wanton and willing to play the game too. I sway my hips a little more than usual as I walk across the second landing. My hand purposely snagging my hem to reveal just a trace of what's beneath it.

Colton's lightning quick as he grabs me from behind, both of his arms wrapping around me in a vise like grip. "You little minx." He growls in my ear as I feel the play of his muscles against my back. "Are you really going to tease me like that when I've been without being inside of you—tasting you for way too long? Especially when you know how desperate I am to have you."

Thank God he's as needy as I am because I'm not going to be able to hold out much longer. He nips my earlobe when I try to shrug away, the need almost debilitating. "Desperation doesn't suit you. It's not like you're going to do something about it with a building full of your employees nearby?" I taunt playfully.

Colton spins me around, his body presses against mine, and his hands clasp at my lower back. The smirk on his face matches the wicked gleam in his eye. "*Oh, Ryles, didn't you know that dares like that are what rebels like me live for?*" He leans in, his lips a breath from my ear as my heart pounds against my rib cage. "I will have you, Rylee, when I want, where I want, and how I want. *It's best you remember that.*"

The dominance in his voice excites me. The threat-filled promise arouses me. The feel of his body against mine vibrating with need and his hands possessing my skin cause moisture to pool at the apex of my thighs. I tilt my head up and my lips part—needing his mouth on mine desperately. From what I read in Colton's eyes, he feels the same way. The days apart have fueled our desire into a raging inferno. All I want to do is take anything and everything he can give me. The temptation of paradise at my fingertips.

I lean in to him succumbing to my craving, but before I can have a single taste, he spins me around and emits a deviously pained chuckle. "One more flight," Colton says smacking my backside before placing both hands on my waist and urging me forward. I sigh out in sexual frustration and from the ache strangling parts deep within me. I'm on my second step when I feel the cool air of the stairwell on my ass as he lifts up the back of my skirt to discover what's beneath.

I smile to myself, knowing exactly what he'll find. It was one of those mornings where I didn't feel particularly attractive, and I was grumpy because I was missing him, so I decided to make myself feel better by wearing something sexy and girly underneath. For some reason wearing lingerie always makes me walk with a little added bounce to my step when I need it. Little did I know how well that decision would pay off, but I do now when I hear Colton suck in a hiss of breath at what he finds.

"Sweet Jesus," he mutters on a pained draw of air.

I move one of my legs to prop it up on the next riser and stop as I feel his finger trace the top line of my stockings and then up the strap of my garter. I look coyly back over my shoulder at him, "Is there a problem, Ace?"

He just smirks at me and shakes his head subtly, his eyes steadfast on what I can assume is the mixture of lace and satin beneath. "Woman, you really don't play fair do you?" he exhales in a groan before tearing his eyes away to look up at mine.

"Whatever do you mean?" I bat my eyelashes at him and purposely bite my lower lip. I love watching his mouth part and his tongue dart out to lick his lower lip as his eyes darken and cloud—his stare unwavering on mine—green eyes to violet. I love knowing that I can bring him to such a state of desire without even touching him. And it's all because of him that I can do this. He makes me feel confident and sexy and desirable when all I've ever felt before is run of the mill and unable to own my sexuality.

Colton's eyes remain on mine but his fingers feather over my flesh to the edge of my panties. My muscles quiver at the proximity of his touch—so close yet so far from where I want his fingers to claim. *Where I need them to.* "Two can play this game," he murmurs as he steps closer. "I seem to recall you saying predictability doesn't suit me. Why don't I show you how absolutely right you are... *right now?*"

I bite down harder on my lip to stifle a moan as his deft fingers pull my panties aside and he slips a finger into my molten core. I brace my hand on the stair rail beside me as he pulls out, sliding up and down the folds of my sex before tucking three fingers in me. "Oh, baby, I love how wet and ready you are for me." He growls as I gasp out. "Do you have any idea what that does to me? How much knowing you want me turns me inside out?"

"Colton, please," I plead. Right now I am not beneath begging for him to fill me. To take me to that unprecedented edge that only he can help me climb at a lightning pace.

"Tell me what you want, Rylee." He chuckles as he withdraws his fingers, and I groan at the sudden feeling of emptiness.

I throw my head back. My eyes close as my body convulses with such need that its evidence glistens on Colton's hand. "You. Colton." I pant. "I. Want. You."

He runs his finger over my bottom lip before leaning in and replacing his fingertip with his tongue, darting it between my lips before pulling away. I can't help the whimper that falls from my mouth. "Tell me, baby."

"Only you, Colton."

In a flash he has me spun around, my back pressed up against the wall of the stairwell. His chest heaves and his jaw clenches as he looks at me with such intensity that I am lost to him. The outside world ceases to exist in this moment as I stand here exposed and unbidden. I am stripped physically and emotionally. I have never been more his.

Colton lifts my skirt back up, and forces my legs further apart. He smiles lasciviously as he sinks slowly to his knees, his eyes never leaving mine.

My rational thoughts should kick in now. My head should be treading atop of the waterfall of lust I'm drowning in and tell me that I'm in the stairwell at his work, but it does no such thing. Instead, my traitorous body shudders in anticipation, and when Colton notes it, his eyes spark and smile taunts as he leans into me. Within seconds a single laugh slips between my trembling lips as he rips my panties off of me effortlessly and stuffs them in his pocket. My mind and body are so focused on him, on what I need from him, that I don't give the fact that he's ruined yet another pair of underwear a second thought.

His fingers part my folds, his eyes never leaving mine, and he closes his mouth over my nub of nerve endings. My hands fly to fist in his hair, and I fight with everything I have to not close my eyes and give into the ecstasy of his clever tongue. I want to watch him while he drives me up and over, but the sensation is so strong that it overtakes me and I arch—my neck, my head, my back—pushing my hips out so I can rock against him.

He pulls my leg up and drapes it over his shoulder before adding his fingers to the mix. They press, push, and circle inside of me. My muscles clench so tight that when my climax claims me, I feel like my body shatters in a million pieces of ecstasy. Colton runs his tongue up and back over my sex before licking inside of me, drawing out every last tremor of my orgasm.

I sag against the wall behind me, needing its support because my legs have just been rendered boneless. I close my eyes and try to calm myself, but he has just obliterated my senses with such devastation that *I've now lost a part of myself to him forever.*

"My God, woman, a man could get drunk on the taste of you." He groans as he places a soft kiss on my abdomen before rising from his knees. I open my eyes to his smug, satisfied smirk and eyes lidded heavy with desire. He leans in and kisses me forcefully, the taste of myself on his lips unexpectedly arousing.

I moan into his mouth, my hands snaking down his body to cup his erection through his pants, still wanting more, still needing more. He breaks from the kiss with a tortured groan and pulls away from me. "Colton," I murmur, "let me take care of you."

"Not here," he tells me, smoothing my skirt down and smirking as he stuffs what's left of my panties further down into his pocket. "I want to hear you scream out my name when I take you. I want to hear it when you fall apart from the things I'm going to do to you, Rylee. I want to claim you. Make you mine. Ruin you for any other man that dares to think of touching you." He grimaces from the conviction of his words.

"You already have, Colton," I breathe out without thinking, reaching out to place my fingertips to his lips. "I'm yours..." My words trail off as he stares at me, his jaw working overtime as he absorbs the words I've said.

A ghost of a smile mixed with an uncertain disbelief plays on his lips before shaking it away and pushing it aside. "I—we can't continue here with what I want to do, but this," he says, motioning to me and the wall, "will tide me over." He flashes a quick grin at me before grabbing my hand and climbing the last flight of stairs.

I follow him, knowing my heart and body are far from recovered from that little episode. Haddie's words flash through my head, and I can't help but disagree with her. When it comes to Colton, I don't just have it bad. I've drowned, been consumed, and am utterly and undeniably his.

Colton pushes open the door at the top of the stairwell, and I'm surprised to find us in the interior of a very masculine and sparsely decorated office. Assumptions aside, I know it's his because it's so similar to his office in Malibu. I step in behind him when I hear a gasp.

"Oh, Colt, you scared me half to death!" the feminine voice exclaims, and instantly my back bristles at her familiarity with him. Does the woman have to be everywhere? *Fuucckk!*

"Can I help you with something, Tawn?" Colton asks, and I swear that I hear an edge to the curiosity in his question.

Tawny straightens up from where she is leaned over his desk and straightens the papers she is fumbling with. Of course she looks flawless in her cleavage defying shirt, skin-tight pants, and freshly made-up face. The woman is absolutely, fucking perfectly stunning. Her lips form a startled O shape as she looks at Colton before her eyes dart over to me and then back to him. The catty, territorial girl inside of me wants her to notice the flush on my cheeks and that just fucked smirk on my face so it's reaffirmed that she's nothing more than a blip on Colton's radar.

"Sorry. You scared me." She exhales. "I was just looking for the Penzoil contract. I wasn't sure if you'd had a chance to sign it. That's all." She smiles too sweetly.

I've got a place she can shove that fake smile.

Colton looks at her for a moment as if he's trying to decipher something, but shakes his head absently. "Tawny, you've met Rylee, right?"

Tawny's eyes flit back and forth between us noting our joined hands before re-plastering the smile that has slightly fallen from her lips. "Something like that," she says as she steps out from behind his desk and walks—no, saunters—toward us. There really is no other way to describe it. Her eyes remain steadfast on Colton's. She is definitely one of those women who are acutely aware of every move of her body and its effect on the opposite sex.

If I disliked her before, I truly detest her now.

Colton gives me a warning look as he feels my hand tense at her approach. "So good to see you again," I lie, and I wonder if he has any idea of the future WWE Smackdown he's just initiated. I have to stifle the giggle I feel bubbling up at the image of Tawny and me flying off of the ropes of a wrestling ring with bad costumes and even worse moves as we fight over the trophy of Colton.

"Yes, how unexpected to see you here." She smiles, and I'm observant enough to note Colton's eyebrows raise in amusement at the obvious tension between the two of us.

He turns to me, his eyes reissuing the warning to be on my best behavior as if he knows my WWE thoughts. "As you know, Tawny here is the head of my marketing team and is actually the one who came up with the lap match sponsorship idea."

Yes, please remind me again so I don't reach across and slap her because it's so damn tempting.

"Yes," I exclaim indifferently, knowing I should thank her properly but not wanting to. I pause for a moment, but my manners finally prevail. "And Corporate Cares is appreciative of all of the hard work you've put behind this," I say with sincerity.

"You're welcome," she says, her eyes never leaving Colton's although she is addressing me. Does he not see her infatuation with him? It's so obvious it's ludicrous. "We've already landed some sponsors, but we have a few more irons left in the fire for some big name corporations. We're wrapping that up right now and most likely will get that magic number to solidify the funding for the project."

"Incredible," I say, trying to express my enthusiasm while hiding my complete disdain for her as she oozes—yes oozes, for that's what she does—her charm all over Colton.

I observe her watching Colton, and it irks me that I suddenly feel like an outsider. She turns slowly to me, a snarky smirk on her face, and I have to remind myself it was me that Colton was just doing inappropriate but hot as hell things to in the stairwell. Not her. *And with that mental reminder, I'm more than ready to play this game.*

"If you think you can contribute in any way…Rylee, right?" she asks apologetically as I just tilt my head to the side and bite my tongue at her catty barb because she damn well knows my name. "Please feel free to let me know."

"Thank you—but I'm sure that any help I could provide…would be…" I look up in thought as I search for the perfect word "...*inconsequential*." My eyes shift from her to Colton as I speak. A smile plays at the corners of my lips, and I arch an eyebrow in question. "Don't you think, Ace?"

"Inconsequential," Colton mouths, a smirk on his lips as he shakes his head at my word choice. He holds my stare and I can see that even with this stunning woman beside me he desires me.

Me.

The air between us fills with an electricity as our gazes hold. I can sense Tawny's discomfort as she shuffles from foot to foot in the charged silence. "Thank you, Tawny," Colton says dismissing her without breaking our connection, "Rylee and I have somewhere we need to be," he concludes, standing and reaching out for my hand.

And hopefully that someplace he needs to be is in me.

Chapter Twenty-Five

"You know, Rylee, you sure are changing how I look at certain things in the world," Colton comments as we pull into my driveway.

"Why's that?" I murmur distractedly, my mind still trying to process the events of the day—that Colton is here—with me.

"I'll never wipe down the hood of my car or trudge up a stairwell again without thinking of you," he says, flashing his megawatt grin at me. "You'll forever be the one who made me look at mundane things in a new light."

I laugh out loud as he leans over to give me a chaste kiss before getting out of the car. I watch him come around the hood to open my door, and I'm suddenly shaken by his comment. A part of me smiles at the knowledge that he will never be able to forget me while another part saddens at the notion that this won't last forever. Even if we could, I don't think he'd ever accept it. The problem is that I'm the one who keeps getting pulled under, deeper and deeper. I'm the one trying to stay afloat. I'm the one who needs a pit stop.

Colton swings the door open and the comment on his lips dies when he sees the look on my face. I've tried to mask my sudden sadness, but obviously I haven't been too successful. "What is it?" he asks, stepping into the doorway of the car between the V of my legs.

"Nothing." I shrug, shaking it off. "I'm just being silly," I tell him as his hands slide up my thighs and under my skirt to where my naked sex is.

I sigh at the feathered touch of his fingertips over my skin as I look up at him. The smirk on his face draws me from my mood, and I smile back at him. "You know, we need to do something about this habit you have of ripping my panties off."

"No we don't," he murmurs as he leans down and slants his mouth over mine.

"Don't distract me." I giggle as his hands slide farther up my thighs and his thumbs brush at my strip of curls, my body arching into him in reaction. "I'm being very serious."

"Uh-huh…I prefer you distracted," he says against my lips. "And I also like you when you're very serious." He imitates my tone, causing me to giggle again.

"You're starting to put a dent in my drawers," I respond breathlessly as his thumbs graze lower this time.

"I know and I hope to be again very soon." He chuckles against the side of my neck, the vibration soothing.

"You're a hopeless case." I sigh as I run my hands up his chest and loop them around his neck before claiming his lips with mine.

"That I am, Rylee..." he sighs when we part lips "...that I am."

We enter the quiet of my house. Haddie will be working late at an event tonight so the house is all ours, and I intend to take full advantage of that. "You hungry?" I ask him as I lay my stuff down on the kitchen counter.

"In more ways than one," he smirks at me and I just shake my head at him.

"Well how about I fix us something and take care of your first hunger, get you nice and fortified, and then I'll make sure I offer up some dessert for your second hunger," I tell him over my shoulder as I bend over and peer in the refrigerator.

"Whether it's offered up or not, sweetheart, *I'll be taking it*," he says, and I can hear the smile in his voice. I forget a moment too late about my bare nether region as I'm bending over because Colton runs a finger across my naked backside before landing a playful slap on it making me jump and jarring my constant ache for him into a smoldering burn.

We eat the simple meal I've concocted in a comfortable exchange. He tells me about his endless meetings in Nashville and what he'd hoped to accomplish during them. I tell him about the progress on the project at the office as well as little tidbits about the boys' week. I find it endearing that he actually listens when I talk about the boys and that he asks questions letting me know that he has a genuine interest in them. It's important to me that he understands what a big part of my life they are.

"So why'd your trip get cut short?" I ask him while we finish up our meal.

He wipes his mouth with a napkin. "We started reviewing meetings we'd already had. It started to get redundant..." he shrugs "...and I hate redundancy."

That's not what Teagan says, flickers through my head thinking how she told me that Colton likes to dabble with past flings while in between current ones. I chastise myself for trying to sabotage a perfectly good time.

"Besides," he says, looking up from his plate to me, "*I missed you.*"

And now I feel like crap for my little mental barb. "*You missed me?*" I ask incredulously.

"Yes, I missed you," he says, smiling shyly, his foot nudging mine beneath the table to emphasize his words.

How is it four simple words from his mouth could mean so much to me? The emotionally unavailable bad boy I tried so hard to keep at arms' length, I now never want to let go.

"I could tell by the beautiful poetry you wrote me," I tease.

He flashes me a heart-warming grin that makes me want to pinch myself to know this is real and that smile is meant for me. "Those were clean compared to some of the nasty ones we wrote." He raises his eyebrows and his eyes alight with humor.

"Oh really?"

"Yep. I think I'd rather show you though."

"Is that so?" I smirk as I bite into my last strawberry.

"Yep, and we brainstormed the meaning of Ace as well."

"Oh, I can't wait to hear these…" I raise my eyebrows at him and laugh.

"Always creating ecstasy."

"Nope." I laugh. "You do know that you've made such a big deal about this that you're going to be so disappointed at the real answer right?"

He just smirks at me as I get up and start clearing the dishes, rejecting his offer of assistance. We chat about the sponsorship some until the ringing of his phone interrupts us.

"One sec," he says as he answers the phone. He holds a short conversation about something work related and then says, "Thanks, Tawny. Have a good night."

I automatically roll my eyes at the name and he catches me. "You really dislike her, don't you?" he asks, a bemused look on his face.

I sigh deeply, wondering if I want to tackle this right here and right now. She is an ex-girlfriend, friend of the family that his parents obviously love, and an important member of his CDE team. Do I really want to fight a losing battle here? If I'm going to be with Colton, I have to face the fact that she is going to be a part of his life, whether I like it or not. I twist my lips as I contemplate the right words to use. "Let's just say that she and I have had a couple of exchanges that lead me to believe she's not as innocent as she seems…and I'll leave it at that," I tell him.

He stares at me for a long time and a lopsided smile forms on his lips. "You're jealous of her, aren't you?" he asks as if he's just had an Oprah ah-hah moment.

I return the same measuring stare at him before averting my eyes and rising to wipe off the counter that I've already cleaned. "Jealous no…but c'mon, Colton." I laugh with disbelief. "Look at her and look at me. It's pretty easy to see why I'd feel that way."

"What are you talking about?" Colton asks as I hear the chair scoot out from underneath him.

"Seriously? She's a walking wet dream. Perfect in every way whereas I'm just…I'm just me." I shrug in acceptance.

Colton rests his hips on the counter beside me as I fiddle with the dishtowel, and I can feel the weight of his stare on me. "You're something else, you know that?" he says, exasperation in his voice.

"Why's that?" I ask, suddenly feeling embarrassed about revealing my insecurities when it comes to Tawny. Why did I even say anything? Me and my big mouth.

Colton pulls on my hand, but I don't budge. Someone as attractive as Colton has no clue what it's like to be insecure. "C'mon," he says, pulling my hand again without taking no for an answer. "I want to show you something."

I follow him reluctantly down the hallway to my bedroom, curious as to what he's being so adamant about. We enter my bedroom and Colton leads me to my en suite bathroom. He ushers me in so that my back is to his front. His eyes blaze into mine as his hands run up the sides of my torso and back down. On their second pass, his fingers veer over and start undoing the buttons on my sweater. Although I feel and see what he's doing in the mirror, my eyes instinctually look down.

"Uh-uh, Rylee," he murmurs, his voice a seductive whisper against my neck. "Don't take your eyes off of mine." My eyes flicker back up to his, and we stare at each other like this for a few moments, neither of us speaking. Colton's fingers finish undoing my sweater, and he steps back as he pulls it off of my shoulders. His fingers rasp across the bare skin of my lower back, and then I feel the zipper on my skirt being lowered. Colton's hands run over my waist and then slide inside the loosened waistline of my skirt. He pushes my skirt down until it clears my hips and falls to the floor.

I chance a glance down to where his hands remain in the front of my pelvis, their olive color a stark contrast to my pale skin. The look of ownership they have over my body—big strong hands lying over silk and lace and flesh—cause my breath to hitch between my parted lips.

"Eyes right here, Rylee," Colton commands as he steps up against me once more, placing his head to the right of mine. I keep my eyes fastened to his as they give a leisurely appraisal of my body and the bra, garter, and stockings I have on, sans the panties he took care of earlier. When his eyes finish their sweep, and they connect with mine again in our mirrored reflection, I see so many things swimming in their depths.

"Rylee, you are breathtaking. Can't you see that?" he questions, his hands running up my rib cage and stopping at by bra. "You are so much more than any one man could handle in a lifetime." He sweeps a finger inside the cup of one side of my bra and pushes it down so that my breast rests above the collapsed cup, my nipple already pebbled and aching for more. He moves to the other side and repeats the same process, but this time I can't help the soft moan that escapes my lips at his touch. I lay my head back on his shoulder and close my eyes at the sensation.

"Open, Rylee," he orders, and I snap them back open to his. "I want you to see what I see. I want you to see how sexy and desirable and fucking hot you are," he whispers against the bare skin of my shoulder. "I want you to see what you do to me. How you—in this body that is beautiful inside and out—cause me to come undone. *Can unravel me.*" His hands travel down to my hips before one slowly travels back up, rubbing back up between my breasts and then holding onto the side of my neck while the other travels lower to slide softly over the mound of my sex. "Can reduce me to nothing and build me up all at the same time." His words seduce me. The eroticism of the moment entices me. He completely mesmerizes me.

It takes everything I have to not close my eyes, tilt my head back, and give into the thunderstorm of sensation that he is evoking with his touch, but I am unable to due to his firm grip on my neck. His sweet seduction of words leaves me wet and wanting while the intimate connection between our gazes fills me emotionally.

"I want you to watch me while I take you, Rylee. I want you to watch each of us as we crash over that edge. I want you to see why this is enough for me. *Why I choose you.*"

His words course through me, opening locks on places deep within that I've been trying to keep guarded. My soul ignites. My heart swells. My body anticipates. I inhale in a shuddered breath, his foreplay of words successful in their pursuit of arousal. His eyes smolder with a mixture of need and desire.

"Hands on the counter, Rylee," Colton orders as he pushes me forward on the back with one hand while the other hand grips onto my hip. I can feel him hard and ready against my backside through his pants and push back into him. "Head up!" he commands, and I comply as his hand snakes south and slowly parts me.

"Colton." I gasp, fighting the natural inclination to close my eyes at the overwhelming sensations rocking through my body when he eases a finger in me and then out to spread my moisture around. I keep my eyes on his and smirk when I notice that he's having trouble with his own composure as well. The rigid tension in his jaw and fire leaping in his eyes incites me. His fingers slide up and tease my bundle of nerves while I feel him fumbling at my backside with his button and zipper. "Now," I plead, my insides unfurling into an oblivion of need. "Quickly."

I can see the wicked grin that blankets Colton's face in the crinkles around his eyes as he positions his rigid head at my opening. "Do you want something, Rylee?" he asks as he just barely pulses into me.

"Colton." I gasp, lowering my head in the painfully exquisite agony of needing more.

"Eyes!" He growls against my shoulder as he denies us both the pleasure we so desperately want. "Say it, Rylee."

"Colt—"

"Say it!" he orders, his face the picture of a man on the verge of losing control.

"Please, Colton..." I gasp "...please." And he plunges inside of me completely in one slick thrust. The unexpected movement steals my breath and catapults me with an explosion of white-hot heat.

"Oh God, Rylee." He groans wildly, his eyes turning to slits, his eyelids weighted with desire. He wraps his arms around me, his fingertips pressing into my flesh, and his cheek pressed against the back of my neck as my body adjusts to his invasion.

He places a row of open mouth kisses on the line of my shoulder and up to my ear before he straightens up and starts to move. Really move. Giving me exactly what I need because right now I don't care about slow and steady. I want hard and fast, and he doesn't disappoint when he sets a punishing rhythm that drags out inexplicable sensations from my depths with every thrust out and drive back in.

I lose myself in his steady tempo, our eyes still locked on each other. The look on Colton's face takes my breath away as his eyes darken and face pulls tight with pleasure. He reaches a hand forward to my breast and rolls my nipple between his fingers. An incoherent moan slips from my lips, the fire inside me almost too much to bear. With his one hand still gripped on my hip, he moves his other from my breast to my shoulder and pulls us against each other, my back to his front, slowing his relentless pace to grind his hips in a circle inside of me.

"Look at yourself, Rylee," he murmurs in my ear between movements. "Look how goddamn sexy you are right now. Why would I want anyone else?"

I break from his reflective gaze and look at my own reflection. Skin red from his hands. Nipples pert and pink from pleasure. The folds of my sex swollen with desire. My lips are parted. My cheeks are flushed. My eyes are wide and expressive. *And alive.* My body reacts instinctively to Colton's movements—driven by such unexpected need, fueled by such a relentless desire, and crashing into unimaginable possibilities. I look at this mysterious woman in the mirror, and a slow, sensuous smile ghosts my lips as I look back to Colton. Our eyes lock again and I acknowledge for once that I see what he sees. That I accept it.

Colton pushes my back forward so that my hands can brace on the sink as he slowly eases in and out of me several times. One of his hands maps my hip and over the front to tease my clit, and my body squeezes at the sensation, my velvet walls milking his cock.

"Fuuucckk!" He groans, throwing his head back, forgetting his own rule about eye contact momentarily. He is absolutely stunning at this moment. Magnificent like an Adonis. Head back, lips parted in pleasure, neck strained with impending release, and my name a pant on his lips. He starts moving again, picking up the pace, dragging me to the edge of ecstasy with each relentless drive. He tilts his head back up and locks his eyes on mine.

The wave pushes me higher and higher, the intensity building, my legs weakening as pleasure tightens everywhere. And just before I crash into oblivion, I can see in his face that he's past the point of no return as well.

We crash over the cusp together: eyes clouded, lips parted, souls united, hearts spellbound, and bodies drowning in spirals of sensation.

My knees buckle beneath me as my muscles reverberate with my climax. Colton's rough hands hold me in place as he empties himself into me. His hands remain tight on my hips for a moment longer, as if the single action is enough to keep us from both sliding to the floor. Eventually I straighten up and lean back against him, angling my head back onto his shoulder where I finally close my eyes, allowing myself a moment to absorb what I've just experienced.

I am overwhelmed and emotionally shaken. I know I loved Max with everything I had, but it pales in comparison to what Colton and I just shared. Together we are so intense, so volatile, so powerful, so intimate that I don't think I've ever felt closer to another human being as I do with Colton right now. My body trembles with the acceptance of it as he withdraws slowly from me and turns me to face him.

I try to bury my head in his shoulder, to avoid eye contact with him because I feel completely stripped bare, naked, and vulnerable—more so than any other time in my life. Colton puts a finger to my chin and lifts my face up to his. His eyes search mine in silence, and for a moment I think I see how I feel reflected in his, but I don't know if that's possible. How was it a few weeks ago this man before me was a complete stranger and now when I look at him, I see my whole world?

I know Colton senses something different in me, but he doesn't ask, just accepts, and for that I'm grateful. He leans down and brushes a tender kiss on my lips that brings tears to my eyes before wrapping his arms around me. I revel in the feeling of his silent strength, and before I can even think properly, my mouth is opening. "Colton?"

"Hmmm?" he murmurs against the top of my head.

I love you. It takes everything to stifle the words on my lips. I want to scream it out loud. "I...I...that was *wow*," I recover, silently saying the other three words I want to say.

"Wow is right." He chuckles against my temple.

Chapter Twenty-Six

I awake to Colton's warm body pressed up against the back of mine. His hand cups my bare breast, and his finger draws lazy circles around its shape, over and over until my nipple tightens from his touch. I smile softly to myself and sink back into him, absorbing the moment and the emotions I'm feeling.

"Good morning." His voice rumbles against the back of my neck, and he places a soft kiss there as his hand slowly traces lower down the curve of my body.

"Hmm," is all I can muster as the feeling of him hard and ready against me already has me willing and wanting.

"That good, huh?" He laughs.

"Mmm-hmm," I respond again because there is nowhere else I'd rather be right now than waking up in this man's arms.

"What time does your shift start today?" he asks as his erection grows harder and presses into the cleft of my backside.

"Eleven." I'm on a twenty-four hour shift at The House today. I'd much rather stay in bed with him all day instead. "Why? Did you have something in mind?" I ask coyly as I wiggle my hips back against him.

"Most definitely," he whispers as he nudges his knee between my thighs from behind so I'm opened up for his hand that is slowly tickling my tender folds. "What time do you have to be at work...aahh—" I'm distracted as his fingers find their target.

"Later." He laughs against my skin. "Much later."

"Then we better make the most of the time we have." I sigh as he shifts us so I sit astride him.

"Your pleasure is my number one priority, sweetheart," he says, flashing his megawatt grin.

He reaches up and cups the back of my neck, pulling me down to him. I moan as his mouth finds mine and I become lost in the haze of lust.

"You sure you don't mind me using your razor?" Colton asks me, his eyes meeting my reflection in the mirror.

"Nope." I shake my head as I watch him from the doorway to my bedroom. A towel is fastened around his waist sitting just below that sexy V, drops of water still cling to his broad shoulders and muscular back, and his hair is in wet disarray. My mouth isn't the only thing that moistens when I look at him. The sight of him, so gorgeous and fresh from the shower, makes me want to drag him back to my bed and dirty him up all over again.

I'm not sure if it's because he's in my bathroom making himself at home with my things after a long night and early morning of incredible sex, but I know I've never thought him sexier.

I bite my lip as I walk behind him thinking how normal this feels. How domestic and comforting it is. I put my arms through my bra straps as I move, feeling Colton's eyes on me as I clasp it and adjust myself. I look up at him in the mirror and notice that he has paused, the pink handle of my razor halfway up to his face, a soft smile on his lips.

"What?" I ask, suddenly shy under the intensity of those gorgeous green eyes.

"You own more bras than any woman I've ever known," he says as his eyes home in on the one that I've just put on. It's light pink, edged in black, and does a perfect job creating just the right amount of cleavage.

His eyes flash up to meet mine, and I purse my lips at him. "I can take that several ways," I tease him. "I can be quite offended that you're comparing me to all of the other women you've been with, or I can be pleased that you appreciate my vast array of lingerie."

"I'd tell you to go with the latter." He smirks. "Only a dead man would be able to ignore your penchant for sexy underthings."

I smile brazenly at him as I hold up a matching thong that is made of lace and very little of it at that. "You mean like this?"

His tongue darts out to lick his bottom lip. "Yeah, like that," he murmurs, his eyes tracking my movements as I step into the panties. I make sure to give him a little floor show as I bend over to pull it up over my wiggling hips. "*Sweet Christ, woman, you're killing me!*"

I laugh out loud at him as I grab my T-shirt and tug it over my head. "Can't fault a girl for having a soft spot for sexy underthings as you put it."

"No ma'am." He smirks at me as he moves the razor up and clears a clean path of shaving cream under his chin—such a masculine act and so sexy to witness. I lean against the door and watch him with thoughts of tomorrows and the future running through my mind.

I thought I knew what love felt like, but standing here, breathing him in, I realize I had no clue. Loving Max was sweet, gentle, naive, and what I thought a relationship should be. Like what a child sees when they look at their parents through rose-colored glasses. Comfortable. Innocent. Loving. I loved Max with all my heart—always will in some capacity—but looking back at it in comparison to what I feel for Colton, I know that I would have been selling myself short. Settling.

Loving Colton is so different. *It's just so much more.* When I look at him, my chest physically constricts from the emotions that pour through me. They're intense and raw. Overwhelming and instinctual. The chemistry between us is combustive and passionate and volatile. He consumes my every thought. He is a part of everything I feel. His every action is my reaction.

Colton is my air in each breath. My endless tomorrow. My happily ever after.

I watch the line form between his eyebrows as he concentrates, angling his face this way and that. He's just about finished, little smudges of shaving cream left on his face here and there when he notices me.

As he wipes his face on a towel, I walk up slowly behind him and to the left, his eyes on mine the whole time. I reach out and run a hand softly up and down the line of his spine, stopping at the nape of his neck so I can run my fingers through his damp hair. He leans his head back at the sensation and closes his eyes momentarily. I want so badly to nuzzle up against his broad back and powerful shoulders and feel my body pressed against his. I hate that the horror from his past robs me—and him—of the chance to snuggle up against him in bed or being able to walk up to him and wrap my arms around him, nuzzling into him from behind—another simple way to connect with him.

I lean up on my toes and press a soft kiss to his bare shoulder while my fingernails trail up and down the line of his spine. I can feel his muscles bunch and move as my touch tickles his skin, and my lips form a smile against the firmness of his shoulder.

"You're tickling me," he says with a laugh as he squirms beneath my touch.

"Mmm-hmm," I murmur, my cheek now pressed against his shoulder so I can meet his eyes in the mirror, and watch his face tense as I tease my fingernails up the side of his torso. I can't help the smile that forms on my lips as his face scrunches up to try and prepare for the graze of my fingers over his ribcage—a little boy's expression on the face of a grown man. I find my purchase and make sure to be extra thorough in my tickling.

"Stop it, you evil wench." He struggles trying to remain stoic, but when my fingers continue their relentless torture, he wriggles his body away from me.

"I'm not letting you get away." I laugh with him as I wrap my arms around him and try to prevent him from escaping.

He's laughing, the razor thrown and forgotten into the sink, his towel dangerously close to falling from his hips, and my arms wrapped around him from behind. Unintentionally, I've maneuvered him into the one position I'd just been thinking about. I know he realizes it the moment that I do because I feel his body tense momentarily and his laughter fades off before he tries to cover it up. Colton's eyes glance up to the reflection of the mirror to meet mine. The look I've seen in any one of my boys' flickers through them, and it breaks me apart inside, but as quick as it flashes there, it's gone.

Regardless of the length of time, I know how much that small concession is a huge step between the two of us.

Before I know it, Colton's twisted out of my grip and is assaulting my rib cage with the tips of his fingers.

"No!" I cry, trying to escape him but unable to. The only way I can think to get him to stop is to wrap my arms around his torso and press my chest to his as hard as I can. I'm breathless and know that I'm no match for his strength.

"Are you trying to distract me?" he teases as his fingers ease up and slide up the back of my shirt to the bare flesh beneath. The protest on my lips fades as I sigh into him and welcome the warmth of his touch and the arms that he tightens around me. I find comfort here, a peace I never thought I'd know again.

We stand here like this for some time—the length I don't know. It's long enough, though, that his heartbeat beneath my ear has slowed significantly. At some point I press my lips into his neck and simply absorb everything about him.

I'm so overwhelmed with everything. I know that he's just shared something monumental with me—bestowed a depth of trust to me—and maybe subconsciously I want to give him a piece of me in return. I speak before my head can filter what my heart says. And by the time I do, it's too late to take it back.

"*I love you, Colton*." My voice is even and unfaltering when the words come out. There is no mistaking what I've said. Colton's body stiffens as the words suffocate and die in the air around us. We stand there in silence, still physically entwined for several more moments before Colton unlaces his fingers from mine and deliberately removes my hands off of him. I stand still as he steps to the edge of the counter to grab his shirt and shove it over his head, an exhaled "*Fuck!*" coming from between his lips.

I follow him in the mirror and the panic in his eyes, on his face, reflected in his movements are hard to watch, but I'm silently pleading with him to look into my eyes. To see that nothing has changed. *But he doesn't*. Instead, he briskly walks past me into my bedroom without looking at me.

I watch him drag on yesterday's jeans before sitting on the bed and shoving his feet in his boots. "I've got to get to work," he says as if I hadn't spoken.

The tears that threaten fill my eyes and blur my vision as he rises from the bed. I can't let him go without saying something. My heart is hammering in my ears, the sting of his rejection twisting my insides as he grabs his keys off the dresser and shoves them into his pocket.

"Colton," I whisper as he starts to walk past me to the doorway. He stops at the sound of my voice. His eyes remain focused on his watch as he fastens it on his wrist, his damp hair falling onto his forehead. We stand there in silence—me looking at him, him looking at his watch—the chasm between us growing wider by the second. The silence so loud it's deafening. "Please say something," I plead softly.

"Look, I—" He stops, sighing heavily and dropping his hands down but not meeting my eyes. "I told you, Rylee, *that's* just not a possibility." His rasp is barely audible. "I'm not capable of, not deserving..." he clears his throat "...I've got nothing but black inside of me. The ability to love—to accept love—is nothing but poison."

And with that Colton walks out of my bedroom and what I fear most possibly out of my life.

Chapter Twenty-Seven

Colton

I can't breathe. *Fuck.* My chest hurts. My eyes blur. My body shakes. The panic attack hits me full force as I grip the steering wheel, knuckles turning white and heart pounding like a motherfucking freight train in my ears. I try to close my eyes—try to calm myself—but all I see is her face inside the house in front of me. All I hear are those poisonous words falling from her mouth.

My chest constricts again as I force myself to pull out of her driveway and make myself concentrate on the road. To not think. To not let the darkness inside take over or allow the memories to seep through.

I do the only thing that I can do—I drive—but it's not fast enough. Only on the track is it ever fast enough to push myself into that blur around me—get lost in it—so that none of this can catch me.

I pull into the dive bar: blacked out windows, no sign above the door with it's name, and a myriad of overflowing ashtrays on the window ledges. I don't even know where the fuck I am. I park my ride next to some piece of shit clunker and don't even think twice about it. All I can think about is how to numb myself, how to erase what Rylee just said.

The bar is dark inside when I open the door. Nobody turns to look at me. They all keep their heads down, crying into their own fucking beers. Good. I don't want to talk. Don't want to listen. Don't want to hear Passenger on the speakers above singing about letting her go. I just want to drown everything out. The bartender looks up, his sallow eyes sizing up my expensive clothes and registering the desperation on my face.

"What'll you have?"

"Patron. Six shots. Keep 'em coming." I don't even recognize my voice. Don't even feel my feet move toward the bathroom in the far corner. I walk in and up to the grungy sink and splash some water on my face. Nothing. I feel absolutely nothing. I look up at the cracked mirror and don't even recognize the man in front of me. All I see is darkness and a little boy I no longer want to remember anymore, don't want to be anymore.

Humpty fuckin' Dumpty.

Before I can stop myself, the mirror is shattering. A hundred tiny fucking pieces splinter and fall. I don't register the pain. I don't feel the blood trickling out and dripping from my hand. All I hear is the tinkling as it hits the tiles all around me. Little sounds of music that momentarily drown out the emptying of my soul. Beautiful on the surface but so very broken as a whole. Irreparable.

All the king's horses and all the king's men, couldn't put Humpty back together again.

The bartender eyes my wrapped hand as I walk up to the bar. I see my shots lined up by some fellow patrons, and I walk to the other vacant end of the bar and sit down. My stomach churns at the thought of sitting between the two men there. The barkeep picks up and delivers my shots to me and just stares as I place two one hundred dollar bills on the bar top. "One hundred for the mirror," I say, lifting my chin toward the bathroom, "and one hundred to keep them coming, no questions asked." I raise my eyebrows at him, and he just nods in agreement.

The bills slip off the counter into his pocket before my second shot is being tossed back. I welcome the sting. The imaginary slap to my face for how I just left Rylee. For what I'm going to do to Rylee. The third one's gone and my head still hurts. Pressure's still in my chest.

You know that you're only ever allowed to love me, Colty. Only me. And I'm the only one who'll ever really love you. I know the things you let them do to you. The things you enjoy them doing to you. I can hear you in there with them. I hear you chanting 'I love you' over and over the whole time. I know you're convinced you let them because you love me, but you really do it because you like how it feels. You're a naughty, naughty boy, Colton. So very bad that no one will ever be able to love you. Will never want to. Never. And if they did and found out all of the naughty things you've done? They'd know the truth—that you're horrible and disgusting and poisoned inside. That any love you have inside of you for anyone but me is like a toxin that will kill them. So you can't tell anyone because if you do, they'll know how repulsive you are. They'll know the Devil lives inside of you. I know. I'll always know and I'll still love you. I'm the only one that is ever allowed to love you. I love you, Colty.

I try to push the memories from my mind. Push them back into the abyss that they're always hiding in. Rylee can't love me. No one can love me. My head fucks with me as I glance down the bar. The man sitting with his back to me causes sickness to grapple though me. Greasy dark hair. A paunchy gut. I know if he turns around what he'll look like. What he'll smell like. What he'll taste like.

I toss back the seventh shot, trying to force the bile down. Trying to numb the fucking pain—pain that won't go the fuck away even though I know in my right head that it's not him. Can't be. It's just my mind fucking with me because the alcohol hasn't numbed enough yet.

I push my forehead in my hands. It's Rylee's voice clear as day that I hear in my head—but it's his face that I see when I hear those three words.

Not Rylee's.

Just his.

And my Mom's. Her lips and that ragged smile giving me her constant affirmation of the freakish horror inside of me.

The blackness has already poisoned me. There's no way in hell I'm going to let it kill Rylee too. Number ten goes down and my lips are starting to not work.

A catastrophic exit. The perfect fucking meaning to Ace. I start laughing. It hurts so fucking much that I can't stop. I'm barely holding it together. And I'm afraid that if I do stop, I'm going to fracture just like the goddamn mirror.

Humpty fuckin' Dumpty.

Chapter Twenty-Eight

"This is the way you want it to be. Guess you don't want me," I sing solemnly with my old standby, Matchbox Twenty, as I drive home after my shift the next day. I still haven't heard from Colton, but then again I hadn't expected to.

I pull into my driveway, the past twenty-four hours a blur. I should have called in sick to work as it wasn't fair to the boys to have a guardian around who's so wrapped up in their own head they weren't really present.

I've relived the moment so many times that I can't think about it anymore. I didn't expect Colton to confess his undying love for me in return, but I also didn't think he'd act as if the words were never spoken. I'm hurt and feeling the sting of rejection and am uncertain where to go from here. I took an important moment between us and fucked it up. *What to do now?* I'm not sure.

I trudge in the house, drop my bag rather unceremoniously on the floor by the front door, and collapse on the couch. And that is where Haddie finds me hours later when she walks through the door.

"What'd he do to you, Rylee?" Her demand rouses me from sleep. Her hands are on her hips as she stands over me, and her eyes search mine for an answer.

"Oh, Haddie, I screwed up royally," I sigh as I let the tears that I'd been holding back flow. She sits down on the coffee table in front of me, hand on my knee in support, and I relay everything to her.

When I finish she just shakes her head and looks at me with eyes full of compassion and empathy. "Well, sweetie, if anything's screwy, it's definitely not you!" she says. "All I can say is that you need to give him a little time. You probably scared the shit out of Mr. Free-Wheelin'-Bachelor to death. Love. Commitment. All that shit..." she waves her hand through the air "...is a big step for someone like him."

"I know." I hiccup through my tears. "I just didn't expect him to be so cold…so nonchalant about it. I think that's what hurts the most."

"Oh, Ry." She leans in and hugs me tightly. "I'll call in sick to the event tonight so you're not alone."

"No don't," I tell her. "I'm fine. I'll probably just eat a gallon of ice cream and go to sleep anyway. Go..." I shoo her away with my hands "...I'll be fine. I promise."

She just stares at me for a moment, debating whether I'm lying or not. "Okay," she says, taking a deep breath, "but just remember something…you're awesome, Rylee. If he doesn't see that...if he doesn't see everything you have to offer in and out of the sack...then fuck him and the horse he rode in on."

I give her a slight smile. Leave it to Haddie to put it eloquently.

The next morning passes without hearing from him. I decide to text him.

Hi, Ace. Call me when you have a chance. We need to talk. XO.

My phone remains silent for most of the day despite how many times I've looked at it and checked to see if I have good service. As the day drags on, my unease settles in, and I start to realize that I've probably done irrevocable damage.

Finally at three o'clock I receive a response. My hopes soar at the prospect of having contact with him.

Busy all day in meetings. Catch you later.

And then my hopes take a nosedive.

On the third day post the I-love-you disastrous confession, I get up the nerve to call his office on my way in to the office. "CD Enterprises, can I help you?"

"Colton Donavan please," I answer, my knuckles white from gripping the steering wheel.

"May I ask who's calling please?"

"Rylee Thomas." My voice cracks.

"Hi, Ms. Thomas, let me check. Just a moment please."

"Thanks," I whisper, anxiety eating at me as I hope he answers and then at what to say if he does.

"Ms. Thomas?"

"Yes?"

"I'm sorry. Colton's not in today. He's out sick. Can I take a message? Can Tawny help you with anything?"

My heart moves up into my throat at the words. If he is in fact sick, she wouldn't have had to check. She would've known.

"No. Thank you."

"My pleasure."

The past few days have started to take their toll on me. I look a mess, so much so that even make-up isn't helping. On day four I feel like I would give anything to take my words back. To take us back to the moments before where we were connected in the moment of his unyielding trust in me. *But I can't.*

Instead, I sit at my desk and stare aimlessly at the pile of work on my desk without any desire to do anything. I look up at the knock on my open door to see Teddy. "You okay, kiddo? You don't look so good."

I force a smile. "Yeah. I think I'm coming down with something," I lie. Anything to avoid the questioning look and the I-told-you-so tone. "I'll be fine."

"Okay, well don't stay too late. I think you're the last one. I'll tell Tim down in the lobby you're still up here so that he can walk you to your car."

"Thanks, Teddy." I smile. "Good night."

"Good night."

My smile fades as he turns his back from me. I watch Teddy walk to the elevators and into the open car while I muster up the courage to call him again. I don't want to come off desperate, but I am. I need to talk to him. To show him that even though I said the words, things are still the same between us. I pick up my cell phone but know he probably won't pick up if he sees my number. I opt for the office line.

On the third ring the phone picks up "Donavan."

My heart pounds in my chest at the sound of his voice. Keep it light, Rylee. "Ace?" I say breathlessly.

"Rylee?" His voice seems so far away as he says my name. So distant. So detached and bordering on annoyed.

"Hi," I say timidly. "I'm glad I got ahold of you."

"Yeah, sorry I haven't called you back," he apologizes, but he sounds off. He's talking to me in the same irritated tone that he spoke to Teagan with.

I swallow the lump in my throat, needing any type of connection with him. "Don't worry about it. I'm just glad you picked up."

"Yeah, I've just been real busy with work."

"Feeling better then?" I ask, then cringe when there's silence on the line— the pause that tells me he has to think of something quick to say to cover the lie.

"Yeah…just getting some last minute details done to try and push a patent through on one of our new safety devices."

My insides twist at his disembodied tone because I can feel it. I can feel him removing himself from all we shared together. From all the emotions I thought he felt but couldn't put words to. I try to hide the desperation in my voice as the first tear trails down my cheek. "So how's it going?"

"Eh, so-so…look, babe..." he laughs "...I've gotta run."

"Colton!" I plead. His name falls from my mouth before I can stop it.

"Yeah?"

"Look, I'm sorry," I say softly. "I didn't mean..." My words falter as I choke on getting the lie out.

The line is silent for a moment, and that's the only reason I know he's heard me. "Well that's a slap in the face," he says sarcastically, but I can hear the annoyance in his voice. "Which one is it, babe? *You either love me or you don't, right?* It's almost worse when you say it and then take it back. Don't you agree?"

I think it's the obvious derision in his voice that breaks me this time. I catch the sob before it comes out loudly. I hear him laugh with someone on the other end of the line. "Colton…" is all I can manage to say, the hurt swallowing me whole and pulling me under.

"I'll call ya," he says, the phone clicking off before I have a chance to say what I fear could possibly be my final goodbye. I keep the phone to my ear, my mind running through all of the other ways that conversation could have gone differently. Why did he have to be so cruel? He forewarned me. I guess I'm at fault all around in this case. First for not listening and then for opening my big mouth.

I cross my arms and lay my head down on my desk, groaning when I realize I've laid my head on top of the schedule his office has sent over to me. Of the events that I've been contracted to attend. With him. What the fuck did I do to myself? How could I have been so damn stupid agreeing to go along with this? *Because it's him,* the small voice in my head reiterates. *And because it's for the boys.* I pick up the schedule, crumple it up, and throw it across the room hoping for a thump at least, but the soft sound of it hitting the wall does nothing to assuage the pain in my chest.

Within moments, sobs rack my body. Fuck me. Fuck him. *Fuck love.* I knew this was going to happen. *Bastard.*

I wake Saturday morning still feeling like shit but with a renewed purpose. I get up and force myself to go for a run, telling myself it will make me feel better. It will give me a fresh outlook on things. I take the run and pound my feet into the pavement at a relentless pace to relieve some of my heartache. I arrive home, out of breath, body tired, and still feeling the ache deep in my soul. I guess I lied to myself there.

I take a shower and tell myself no more tears today and definitely no more ice cream.

I am scooping the last of the mint chocolate chip out of the carton when my cell phone rings. I glance at the unknown number, curiosity getting the best of me. "Hello?"

"Rylee?" I try to place the feminine voice on the other end of the line but can't.

"Yes? Who is— "

"*What the hell happened?*" the voice demands of me in a clipped and obviously annoyed tone.

"What? Who— "

"It's Quinlan." A small breath squeaks past my lips in shock. "I just left Colton's house. What the hell happened?"

"Wh-what do you mean?" I stammer because I can answer that question in so many different ways.

"God!" She sighs in frustration and impatience on the other end of the line. "Will you two get your shit together and pull your heads out of your asses? *Fucking Christ.* Maybe then you'd realize you two have got something real. Something that's undeniable. It would take an idiot not to see that spark between you guys." I remain silent on the other end of the line. The tears I told myself I couldn't cry, leak out of the corners of my eyes. "Rylee? You there?"

"I told him I loved him," I tell her softly, wanting to confide in her for some reason. Maybe needing some kind of validation about his response from someone that's closest to him so I don't keep replaying it over in my head endlessly.

"*Oh shit.*" She breathes in shock.

"Yeah..." I laugh anxiously "...that about sums it up in a nutshell."

"How'd he take it?" she asks cautiously. I tell her his reaction and how he's been since then. "Sounds like what I'd expect from him." She sighs. "He's such an ass!"

I remain silent at her comment, dashing away my tears with the back of my hand. "How is he?" I ask, my voice breaking.

"Moody. Grouchy. Surly as hell." She laughs. "And from the number of his friends Jim and Jack, empty and lining his kitchen counter, I'd say he's trying to drink himself into oblivion to either help forget his demons or so he can push down the fear he has in regards to his feelings for you." I exhale the breath I'm holding, a part of me reveling in the fact that he's hurting too. That he's affected by what's happened between us. "And because he's missing you terribly."

My heart wrenches at her final words. I feel like I've been in a world without light for the past couple of days, so it's welcome to know that he's drowning in darkness too. And then the part of me that acknowledges that notion doesn't want him to hurt, feels sorry for causing all of this pain with those stupid words, and just wants to make everything right again.

My voice is thick with tears and wavers when I speak again. "I really fucked up by saying it, Quinlan."

"No you didn't!" she scolds. "Ugh!" She groans. "*God, I love him and hate him so much sometimes!* He's never opened himself up to this possibility before, Rylee...he's never been in this predicament. I can only guess how he'll react."

"Please," I plead. "I'm at a loss for what to do. I just don't want to screw up and push him away further."

She is silent for a few moments as she contemplates things. "Give him a little time, Rylee," she murmurs, "but not too much time or he might do something stupid on purpose, and risk fucking up the one good girl he's ever truly cared about."

"Not Tawny..." The words are out before I can stop them. I cringe, knowing I've just openly insulted a family friend.

"Don't get me started on her." Quinlan sneers in contempt, causing a small part of me deep down to smile at the knowledge that it's not just me who detests her. I laugh through my tears. "Hang in there, Rylee," she says, sincerity flooding her voice. "Colton is a wonderful yet complicated man...worthy of your love, even if he is unable to accept that concept yet." The lump in my throat prevents me from responding, so I just murmur an agreement. "He needs a lot of patience, a strong sense of loyalty, unrelenting trust, and a person to tell him when he steps out of line. All of that is going to take time for him to realize and accept...in the end though, he's worth the wait. I just hope he knows it."

"I know," I whisper.

"Good luck, Rylee."

"Thank you, Quinlan. For everything."

I hear her chuckle as she clicks off the phone.

Chapter Twenty-Nine

Quinlan's advice still rings in my ears as I lie in bed the next morning. The pain in my chest and ache in my soul is still there, but my resolve has returned. I once told Colton to fight for us. For me. Now it's my turn. I told him he is worth the risk. That I'd take the chance. Now I need to prove it.

If Quinlan seems to think I matter to him, then I can't give up now. I have to try.

I drive up the coastline, Lisa Loeb playing on the speakers, and my mind a whirl of thoughts— what I'm going to say and how I'm going to say it— as the clouds above slowly burn off and give way to the morning sun. I take it as a positive sign that somehow when I see Colton face-to-face, he'll see it's just him and me, how it was before, and that the words mean nothing. That they change nothing. That he feels the same way and that I act the same way. And that we are us. That the darkness I feel will dissipate because I'll be back in his light once again.

I steer down Broadbeach Road and pull up to his gate, my heart pounding a frantic tattoo and my hands shaking. I ring the buzzer, but no one answers. I try again, and then again, thinking maybe he is asleep. That he can't hear the buzzer because he is upstairs.

"Hello?" a feminine voice asks through the speaker. My heart drops into my stomach.

"It's Rylee. I...I need to see Colton." My voice is a tangle of nerves and unshed tears.

"Hi, dear. It's Grace. Colton's not here, sweetie. He hasn't been here since yesterday afternoon. Is everything okay? Would you like to come in?"

The rush of blood into my head is all I hear. My breath hitches as I rest my head against the steering wheel. "Thanks, Grace, but no thank you. Just tell…just tell him I stopped by."

"Rylee?" The uncertainty in her voice has me leaning out the window of the car.

"Yes?"

"It's not my place to say it..." she clears her throat "...but be patient. Colton's a good man."

"I know." My voice is barely audible, my stomach lodged in my throat. If only he would realize it.

My drive back down the coastline is not as filled with hope as my drive up it was. I tell myself that he probably went out with Beckett and was too drunk to drive home. That he went out with the crew and grabbed a hotel in downtown L.A. after partying a little too hard. That he decided it was time for another trip to Las Vegas and is on the plane home right now.

The endless scenarios run through my head but do nothing to alleviate the ripples of fear that ricochet within me. I don't want to think of the one other place that he could be. The townhome in the Palisades. The place he goes to be with his arrangements. My heart races and thoughts fly recklessly at the notion. I try to justify that he crashed there. That he's alone. But both Teagan's and Tawny's comments flicker through my mind, feeding the endless stream of doubt and unease churning within me.

My mind fills with the many warnings he's given me. *"I sabotage anything that resembles a relationship. I'm hardwired this way, Rylee. I'll purposely do something to hurt you to prove that I can. To prove that you won't stick around regardless of the consequences. To prove that I can control the situation."*

I don't remember steering the car in that direction, but before I know it, I'm turning down his street from memory. Tears spill over and down my cheeks as I grip the steering wheel tightly. The need to know outweighing the agony of acknowledging what my mind fears. What my heart worries. What my conscience already knows.

I pull up to the curb, a small sigh escaping my lips in momentary relief when I see that none of Colton's cars are there. But then I see his garage door and wonder if it's inside. I have to know. I have to.

I push my hair out of my face and suck in a deep breath before I slide out of my car. I walk on weak knees up the pathway and into the cobblestone courtyard. My heart pounds so loudly that its thundering is all hear, all I can focus on besides telling my feet to place one foot in front of the other.

Chapter Thirty

Colton

My fucking head. I groan as I roll over in the bed. Stop pounding on the goddamn drums. Please. Somebody. Anybody. *Fuck me.*

I shove the pillow over my head, but the throbbing continues in my temples. My stomach rolls and twists, and I have to concentrate on not getting sick because my head really doesn't want me to get up just yet.

Fucking Christ! What the hell happened last night? Bits and pieces come back to me. Becks coming to get me to shake me out of the voodoo pussy funk. A funk I'm not really sure I want to be shaken from. Drinking. Rylee—wanting Rylee. Needing Rylee. Missing Rylee. Tawny meeting us at the bar for some signatures. A lot of fucking alcohol. Way too much fucking alcohol according to my head right now.

Pleasure to bury the pain.

I struggle to fight through the fuzz in my head to remember the rest. Snapshots of clarity amidst the haze. Coming back here. Palisades house closer than Malibu. Drinking more. Tawny not comfortable in her business suit. Getting her a shirt of mine. Standing in the kitchen looking at the fucking Tupperware container of cotton candy on the counter. Memories of the carnival making the ache burn.

"*Oh shit.*" I groan as the next recollection flickers through loud and clear.

Sitting on the couch. Becks, the fucker looking no worse for the wear even though he's gone drink for drink with me, sitting in the chair across from me. His feet propped up and his head angled back. Tawny next to me on the couch. Reaching over her to the end table to grab my beer. Her reaching up. Hands around my neck. Mouth on my lips. Too much alcohol and a chest still burning with need. Hurting so bad because I need Rylee. Only Rylee.

Pleasure to bury the pain.

Kissing her back. Getting lost in her momentarily. Trying to get rid of the constant damn ache. To forget how to feel. All wrong. So wrong. Pushing her off. She's not Rylee.

Looking up and meeting the disapproving eyes of Becks.

Fuuccckkk! I shove myself up from the bed and immediately cringe at the freight train that hits my head. I make it to the bathroom and brace myself on the sink for a moment, struggling to function. Images of last night keep flashing. Fuckin' Tawny. I look up to the mirror and cringe. "You look like shit, Donavan," I mutter to myself. Bloodshot eyes. Stubble verging on beard. Tired. And empty.

Rylee. Violet eyes begging me. Soft smile. Big heart. Fucking perfect.

I love you, Colton.

God, I miss her. Need her. Want her.

I brush my teeth. Trying to rid the taste of alcohol and misery from my mouth. I start shoving off my shirt and underwear—needing to get the feel of Tawny's hands off of me. Her perfume off of me. Needing a shower desperately. I'm just about to flick the water on when I hear a knock at the front door. "*Who the fuck?*" I grumble before looking over at the clock. Still early.

I look disjointedly for something to wear, trying to shake the fuzz from my head. I can't find my pants from last night. Where the hell did I put them? Frustrated, I yank open my dresser, grab the first pair of jeans I find, and hastily shove my legs in them. I hurry down the stairs starting to button them up as I try to figure who the fuck is at my door. I glance over to see Becks passed out on the couch. Serves the asshole right. I look up to see Tawny and her mile long legs opening the door. The sight of her—T-shirt, legs, and nothing else—does nothing to me, for me—when it used to do everything.

"Who is it, Tawn?" My voice sounds foreign as I speak. Gravelly. Unemotional because the only thing I want is Tawny gone. I want her out of my house so I don't need a reminder of what I could have done. What I almost fucked up. Because it matters now. *She* matters now.

And when I step into the blinding morning light through the doorway, I swear to God my heart stumbles in my chest. There she stands. My angel. The one helping me break through my darkness by letting me hold on to her light.

Chapter Thirty-One

My knock sounds hollow on the front door. I lay my hand on it, contemplating knocking again, just to make sure. My shoulders start to sag in relief that he's not holed up inside with someone when the door pushes inwards beneath my fingers.

All the blood drains to my feet as the door swings open and Tawny stands before me. Her hair is tousled from sleep. Make-up is smudged under her bedroom eyes. Her long, tan legs connect to bare feet that stick out from under a T-shirt that I know is Colton's, right down to the small hole in the left hand shoulder. The morning chill showcasing her braless breasts.

I'm sure that the look of shock on my face mirrors the one on hers, if only momentarily, for she quickly recovers, a slow, knowing, siren's smile spreading across her face. Her eyes dance with triumph, and she licks her tongue over her top lip as I hear footsteps from inside.

"Who is it, Tawn?"

She just widens her grin as she uses her hand to push the door open further. Colton strides toward the door with nothing on but a pair of jeans; jeans his fingers are fumbling to button the fly on. His face sports more than its usual day's worth of growth, and his hair is unwashed and messy from slumber. His eyes are bloodshot causing him to flinch at the morning sunlight as it comes in through the doorway. He looks rough and reckless and as if the alcohol from the night before has taken its toll. He looks how I feel, shitty, but no matter how much I hate him in this moment, the sight of him still causes my breath to hitch in my throat.

It all happens so quickly, but I feel as if time stops and moves in slow motion. Stands still. Colton's eyes snapping to mine when he realizes who is at his door. When he understands that I know. His green eyes hold mine. Imploring, questioning, apologizing, all at once for the hurt and crushing devastation that is reflected in mine. He steps forward into the doorway and a strangled cry escapes my lips to stop him.

I struggle to breathe. I try to drag in a breath, but my body is not listening. It does not comprehend my brain's innate commands to draw in air because it is so overwhelmed. So crushed. The world spins beneath me and around me, but I can't move. I stare at Colton, the words in my head forming but never making it past my lips. Tears burn in my throat and sting my eyes, but I fight them back. I will not give Tawny the satisfaction of seeing me cry as she smirks at me from over his shoulder.

Time starts again. I draw in a breath and thoughts start to form. Anger starts to fire in my veins. Emptiness starts to register in my soul. Pain radiates in my heart. I shake my head in disgust at him. At her. In resigned shock. "Fuck this," I say quietly but implacably as I turn to walk away.

"Rylee," Colton calls out in despair, his voice gravelly from sleep as I hear the door slam behind me. "Rylee!" he shouts at me as I all but run down the path, needing to escape from him. From her. From this. "Rylee it's not what you— "

"Not what I think?" I yell over my shoulder at him in disbelief. "Because when your ex answers your door this early in the morning with your shirt on, what else am I supposed to think?" His footsteps are heavy behind me. "Don't touch me!" I yell as he grabs my arm and spins me around to face him. I yank it from his grip, my chest heaving, my teeth clenched. "Don't fucking touch me!"

Albeit temporarily, anger has replaced the hurt now. It is coursing through me like a wild inferno, emanating off of me in waves. I clench my fists and squeeze my eyes shut. I will not cry. I will not give him the satisfaction of seeing how deeply he has torn me apart. I will not show him that giving my heart away for the second time might be the biggest regret of my life.

When I look up, his eyes meet mine, and we stare at each other. My love for him still there. So deep. So raw.

So forsaken.

His eyes swim with emotion as he clenches and unclenches his jaw trying to find the right words. "Rylee," he pleads, "let me explain. Please." His voice breaks on the last word, and I close my eyes to block out the part of me that still wants to fix him, comfort him. And then the anger hits me again. At me for still caring for him. At him for breaking my heart. At her for...just being.

He runs a hand through his hair and then scrubs it over the stubble on his face. The sound of its rough scratch—the one that I usually find so sexy—does nothing but drive the proverbial knife deeper into my heart. He takes a step forward, and I mirror him taking a step back. "I swear, Rylee. It's not what you think..."

I snort incredulously, knowing the consummate playboy will say anything—do anything— to talk his way out of this. The image of Tawny snuggled in nothing but his shirt flashes in my mind. I try to quiet the other ones that form. Of her hands on him. Of him tangled with her. I close my eyes and swallow purposefully, trying to wipe the images away. "It's not what I think? If it looks like a duck and walks like a duck..." I imply with a shrug "...well then you know what they say."

"Nothing hap— "

"*Quack!*" I shout at him. I know I'm being childish, but I don't care. I'm pissed and hurting. He shakes his head at me, and I can see the desperation in his eyes. Tawny's smug smirk fills my head, her previous taunts echo in my mind, and they fuel my fire.

Colton's eyes search mine as he steps toward me again, and I retreat. I see the sting of rejection glance across his face. I need my distance to think clearly. I shake my head at him, disappointment swimming in my eyes and pain drowning my heart. "Of all people, Colton...why choose her? Why turn to her? Especially after what we shared the other night...after what you showed me." The memory of the intimacy between us as we looked in the mirror at each other is almost too unbearable to envision, but it floods into my mind. Him behind me. His hands on my body. His eyes drinking me in. His lips telling me to look at myself, to realize why he chooses me. That I'm enough for him. A sob I can't hold back escapes and is wrenching and comes from so deep within me that I wrap my arms around my torso to try and stifle its effects.

Colton reaches out to touch me but pauses when I glare at him, his face etched with pain, and his eyes frantic with uncertainty. He doesn't know how to assuage the pain he's caused. "Rylee, please," he begs. "I can make this right again..."

His fingertips are so close to my arm that it takes everything I have to not lean into his touch. Visually shunned from touching me, he shoves his hands in his pockets to ward off the early morning chill. Or perhaps mine.

I know I'm hurt and I'm confused and I hate him right now, but I still love him. I can't deny that. I can fight it, but I can't deny it. I love him even though he won't let me. I love him even through the hurt he's inflicted. The floodgates I've been trying to hold back burst and tears spill over and down my cheeks. I stare at him through blurred vision until I'm able to find my voice again despite the despair. "You said you'd try..." It's all I can manage to say, and even then my voice breaks with each word.

His eyes plead with mine and in them I can see the shame. For what, I can only imagine. He sighs, his shoulders sagging and his body defeated. "I am trying. I..." His words falter off as he removes his hands from his pocket and something falls out of one. The scrap of paper flickers to the ground in slow motion, the sun catching its reflective silver packaging. It takes my mind a moment to process what has landed at my feet—and not because I don't understand, but rather because I am hoping against hope that I'm wrong. I stare at the emblazoned Trojan emblem on the torn package, synapses slow to fire.

"No, no, no—" Colton repeats in shock.

"You're trying?" I shout at him, my voice rising as anger blazes. "*When I meant try, Ace, I didn't mean try to stick your dick in the next available candidate the first time you got scared!*" I'm yelling now, not caring who hears. I can sense Colton's rising panic—his uncertainty of how to have to actually deal with the fallout of his actions for once—and the notion that he's never had to before...that no one else has ever called him on it, made him accountable, feeds my anger even further.

"That's not what I— I swear that's not from last night."

"Quack!" I shout at him, wanting to grab him and hold him and never let him go and at the same time wanting to hit him and push him and show him how much he's hurt me. I'm on a fucking roller coaster, and I just want to jump off. Stop the ride. Why am I still here? Why am I even fighting for something he so obviously doesn't want? Doesn't deserve from me?

He runs his hands through his hair in exasperation, face pale, eyes panicked. "Rylee. Please. Let's just take a pit stop."

"*A fucking pit stop?*" I shout at him, my voice escalating, pissed that he's patronizing me right now. A pit stop? More like an engine rebuild. "Did you not believe in us enough?" I ask, trying to understand through the hurt. "You told me the other night that Tawny had a tenth of the sex appeal I had? Guess you chose to go slumming, huh?" I know I'm being overdramatic but my chest hurts with each breath that I take, and frankly I'm beyond caring at this point. I'm hurt—devastated—and I want him to hurt like I do. "Did you not believe enough in me that you had to run to someone else? Fuck someone else?" His silence is the only answer that I need to know the truth.

When I finally have the courage to look up and meet his eyes, I think he sees the resignation in mine, which in turn causes panic to flicker through his. He holds my gaze, emerald to amethyst, a volume of emotions passing between us— regret the biggest of all. He reaches out to wipe a tear from my cheek, and I flinch at his touch. I know that if he touches me now, I will dissolve into an incoherent mess. My chin trembles as I turn to go.

"I told you I'd hurt you," he whispers behind me.

I stop in all two steps of my walk away from him. So much for distance, but his words infuriate me. I know if I walk away without saying this, it'll be something I will forever regret. I whirl back around to face him. "Yeah! You did! But just because you warned me doesn't mean that it's okay!" I shout at him, sarcasm dripping with anger. "Suck it up, Donavan! We both have baggage. We both have issues we have to overcome. Everyone does!" I seethe. "Turning to someone else...*fucking someone else,* is unacceptable to me. Something I won't tolerate."

Colton sucks in his breath as my words hit him like punches. I can see the torment on his face and a part of me is relieved to know that he is hurting–maybe not as much as I am–but at least I know what I thought we were wasn't all a lie. "You can't possibly love me, Rylee," he says quietly resigned, his eyes on mine.

"Well you sure tried to make sure of that, didn't you?" I say with a wavering voice. "Did you sleep with her, Colton?" My eyes beseech his, finally asking the question I'm not sure I want answered. "Was fucking her worth losing me?"

"Does it matter?" he snips back, emotions warring over his face as he goes on the defensive. "You're going to think what you want to think anyway, Rylee."

"Don't turn this on me, Colton!" I scream at him. "I'm not the one who fucked this up!"

He stares at me for a few moments before he responds, his eyes accusing, and when he does, his voice is an icy barb. "Didn't you though?"

His words are a stinging slap to my face. Callous Colton has resurfaced. Tears re-emerge and run down my cheeks. I can't stand here anymore and deal with my pain.

Something behind him catches my eye, and I glance over to see that Tawny has opened the door. She is leaning against its frame, watching our exchange with amused curiosity. The sight of her there gives me the strength I need to walk away.

"No, Colton," I answer him sternly, "this is entirely on you." I close my eyes and breathe deep, trying to control the tears that won't stop. My breath hitches and my chin trembles at what I should have done the first night we met. "Goodbye." I whisper, my voice thick with emotion and my eyes full of unshed tears.

My heart full of unaccepted love.

"You're leaving me?" His question is a heart-wrenching plea that snakes in my soul and takes hold. I shake my head sadly as I look at the little boy lost inside the bad boy in front of me. Vulnerability encased in rebellion. Does he have any idea how irresistible he is right now? What a wonderful, empathetic, caring, passionate man he is? How he has so much to give someone, to contribute to a relationship, if he just conquers his demons and lets someone in?

How can I even be thinking of that right now? How can I be worrying about how my leaving will hurt him when the heartbreaking evidence is at my feet and within my sight?

His eyes dart frantically as panic sets in. The pain is too much to bear. Hurting him. Him hurting me. Walking away from the man I love when I never thought it was possible to feel this strongly again. Walking away from the man who's set the bar that all others will be compared against. My chest squeezes as I try to control my emotions. I need to go. I need to walk to the car.

Instead, I step closer to him, the drug to my addiction. His eyes widen as I reach up and run my fingers gently over his strong jaw and perfect lips. He closes his eyes at the feel of my touch and when he opens them I see devastation welling there. The sight of him coming silently undone squeezes something in my chest. I step up on my tiptoes and kiss him oh-so-softly on the lips, needing one last taste of him. One last feel of him. One last memory.

One last fracture in my shattered heart.

A sob escapes my mouth as I step back. I know this will be our last kiss. "Goodbye, Colton," I repeat as I take in everything about him one last time and commit it to memory. *My Ace.*

I turn on my heel and stumble down the pathway, blinded by my tears. I hear my name on his lips and push it from my head, ignoring his plea to come back, that we can fix this, as I force my feet to move to my car. Because even if we fix it this time, with Colton, there will always be a next.

"But, Rylee, *I need you...*" The broken desperation in his voice stops me. Undoes me. Breaks the parts of me that aren't yet broken. Tears into my depths and scorches me. Because for everything that

Colton isn't, there is so much that he is. And I know he needs me as much as I need him. I can hear it in his voice. Can feel it in my soul. But need isn't enough for me anymore.

I stare at the ground in front of me and shake my head. Not able to turn to face him because I won't be able walk away from what I see in those eyes of his. I know myself too well, but I can't forgive this. I squeeze my eyes shut and when I speak, I don't recognize my own voice. It's cold. Absent of all emotion. Guarded. "Then maybe you should have thought of that before *you needed her*."

I tell my body to leave as Colton sucks in a breath behind me. I yank the door open and throw myself into my car just in time to succumb to all of my tears and the endless hurt. And it hits me. How alone I've been over the past two years. How until I had to walk away from Colton, I didn't realize that he's the only one that's been able to fill that void for me. Has been the only one that has made me whole again.

I don't know how long I sit there, emotions exploding, world imploding, and heart breaking. When I can compose myself enough to drive without crashing, I start the car. As I pull from the curb, Colton is still standing there in my rearview mirror with a wounded look on his face and regret dancing in his eyes.

I force myself to drive away. From him. From my future. From the possibilities I thought were a reality. From everything I never wanted but now don't know how I'm ever going to live without.

Chapter Thirty-Two

My feet pound the pavement to the driving beat of the music. The angry lyrics help relieve some of the angst, but not all of it. I make the final turn on the street to reach my house and just wish I could keep running right on past it— past the reminders of him that blanket my house and overload my phone on a daily basis.

But I can't. Today is a huge day. The corporate big wigs are visiting, and I have to present the final details of the project as well as give the requisite dog- and- pony- show Teddy wants for them.

I've thrown myself into preparing for this meeting. I've pushed aside—or tried to as best as possible—the sight of Tawny's face as it flickers smugly through my mind. I've tried to use work to drown out Colton's voice pleading with me, telling me he needs me. I've tried to forget the sun glittering off of the foil packet. Tears well in my eyes but I push them back. Not today. I can't do this today.

I jog the last couple of steps up the front porch and busy myself with my iPod so I'm able to overlook the newest bouquet of dahlias sitting on the doorstep. As I open the door, I pluck the card from the arrangement without really looking at the flowers and toss it in the dish on the foyer table already overflowing with its numerous unopened and identical counterparts.

I sigh, walking into the kitchen and scrunching my nose at the overbearing smell of too many unwelcome flowers that are scattered randomly throughout the house. I pull out my earbuds and lean into the refrigerator to grab a water.

"Phone?"

Haddie's contemptuous voice startles me. "Jesus, Had! You scared the shit out of me!"

She eyes me with pursed lips for a moment as I chug down my water, her usually cheerful countenance has been replaced with annoyance. "What? What did I do now?"

"Sorry if I worried about you." Her sarcasm matches the smarmy look on her face. "You were gone a lot longer than usual. It's irresponsible to go running without your phone."

"I needed to clear my head." My response does nothing to lessen her visible irritation. "He calls and texts me constantly. I just needed to escape from my phone…" I gesture to the ludicrous amount of flower arrangements "…from our house that smells like a damn funeral parlor."

"It is a little ridiculous," she agrees, scrunching up her nose, her features softening as she looks at me.

"Asinine is what it is," I murmur under my breath as I sit at the kitchen table to untie my shoes. Between the one to two bouquets delivered daily, with cards that go unopened, to the numerous text messages that I delete without reading, Colton just won't get the hint that I'm done with him. Completely. Over him.

And regardless of how strong I try to sound when I say those words, I'm quietly falling apart at the seams. Some days are better than others, but those others—*they are debilitating*. I knew Colton would be hard to get over, but I just didn't know how hard. And then to add to the fact that he just won't let me go. I haven't spoken to him, seen him, read his texts or cards, or listened to the voicemails that are sapping up the memory of my phone, but he remains relentless in his attempts. His persistence tells me that his guilt really must be eating at him.

My head has accepted the finality of it; my heart hasn't. And if I give in and read the cards or acknowledge the songs he refers to in his texts depicting how he feels, then I'm not sure how resolute my head will remain with its decision. Hearing his voice, reading his words, seeing his face—any of them will crumble the house of cards I'm trying to reconstruct around my broken heart.

"Ry?"

"Yeah?"

"Are you okay?"

I look up at my dearest friend, trying to hold it together so she can't see right through my false pretense, and bite my bottom lip to quell the tears that threaten once again. I shake my head and push it back. "Yeah. Fine. I just need to get to work."

I start to stand up and shuffle past her, wanting desperately to avoid the Haddie Montgomery pep talk. I'm not quick enough. Her hand reaches out and holds my arm firm. "Ry, maybe he didn't…" she stalls when my eyes meet hers.

"I don't want to talk about it Haddie." I shake her hand loose and walk toward my bedroom. "I'm going to be late."

"All set?"

I glance over at Teddy as I finish my final run through of my Power Point presentation on the conference room screen and make sure that my smile reflects confidence. In case Teddy's heard the rumors, I can't let him know that anything is amiss between Colton and I. If I do, then I know he'll fret about losing the funding. "Definitely. I'm just waiting for Cindy to finish running off copies of the agenda to place on the top of the binders."

He steps into the room as I refasten a diagram to an easel. "I'm sure you noticed that I adjusted and added a couple of items on the agenda. It doesn't affect your portion but— "

"It's your meeting, Teddy. I'm sure whatever you added is fine. You really don't have to run any changes by me."

"I know, I know," he says, looking at the slide up on the projector screen, "but it's your baby being presented to the bigwigs today."

I smile genuinely at him. "And I'll get them up to speed. I have my updates, budget projections, estimated schedules, and everything else relating to the project updated and ready to present."

"It's you, Ry. I'm not worried. You've never failed me." He returns the smile and pats me on the back before looking at his watch. "They should be here any minute. Do you need anything from me before I go down to meet them?"

"Not that I can think of."

Cindy passes Teddy on his way out of the conference room. "Do you want to see the agendas first or should I just lay them out on top of the binders?"

I glance up at the clock, realizing that time is slipping away from me. "You can just lay them on the binders. That'd really help. Thanks."

I clean up my mess, get my presentation back to the beginning slide, and just escape the conference room to stash the unneeded items back in my office when I hear Teddy's resonating voice down the hallway. Time to put my game face on. "And here she is," he booms loudly, his voice reverberating off of the office hallways.

I stop, hands full of items, and smile warmly at the stuffed suits. "Gentlemen." I nod my head in greeting. "So glad to have you here. We can't wait to get you up to speed on the project and get your input." I look down at my overloaded hands and continue, "I just need to go put this stuff away real quick, and I will be right back."

I dash into my office, throw the items on top of my desk, and take a quick minute to check my appearance before making my way back to the conference room. I enter right as Teddy starts addressing the group before him. Trying not to interrupt his welcoming comments, I sit in the first seat available at the front of the massive, rectangular table without looking around at the room's occupants behind me.

Teddy rambles on about expectations and how we will be exceeding them as I square up the papers in front of me. The agenda being the top paper, my eyes travel over it dismissively since I know it like the back of my hand. And then I do a double take when I notice one of Teddy's changes. Right beneath my time slot, the words, "CD Enterprises" mars the page.

My heart stops and pulse races simultaneously. My breath pauses and I begin to feel light headed. *No! Not now.* I can't do this right now. This meeting means too much. He can't be here. Panic starts to overwhelm me. The rush of blood fills my ears, drowning out Teddy's words. I slowly lay down the paper and place my hands in my lap, hoping that no one notices their trembling. I lower my head and close my eyes tightly as I try to steady my breathing. How stupid was I to assume that he wouldn't be here? After all, his donation and sponsorship program are the reason our hands are hovering over the *go* button. I've been so wrapped up in avoiding him and being conveniently sick for some of the other functions that I was supposed to attend, I completely shut out the possibility from my subconscious.

Maybe Colton didn't come. Then of course that means Tawny would most likely be sitting here. I'm not sure which one would be worse. When I can't stand it anymore, I take a fortifying breath, and raise my eyes to scan the occupants of the room.

And I immediately lock onto the pale green irises of Colton whose attention is focused solely on me. The house of cards surrounding my heart flutters to the ground and all of the air punches out of my lungs at the sight of him. No matter how hard I tell myself to break eye contact, it's like a car accident. I just can't help but stare.

Only because I have intimate knowledge of his face, do I notice the subtle differences in his appearance. His hair is longer, the scruff is back around his jaw, slight shadows bruise beneath his eyes, and he seems slightly unkempt for a man who's always so well put together. I drag my gaze over his magnificently stoic face and am drawn back to his eyes. It is on this second pass that I realize the usual mischievous spark that lights them from within is absent. They look lost, sad even, as they silently plead with me. I see his jaw tic as the intensity in his eyes strengthens. I tear my eyes away from him, not wanting to read the unspoken words he is conveying.

After what he did, he doesn't deserve a second glance from me. I close mine for a beat to try and blink away the tears that threaten, telling myself that I have to keep it together. I have to keep my composure. And regardless of what I tell myself, images of Tawny barely covered by Colton's T-shirt flash through my head. I have to bite back the sickening pang in my stomach and fight the urge to leave the room. My shock at seeing him here slowly churns itself into anger. This is my office and my meeting, and I can't let him affect me. Or I at least have to give the pretense of it anyway.

I clench my jaw and shake away my misery as Teddy's voice slowly seeps through the buzzing in my brain. He's introducing me and I rise on wobbly legs to make my way to the front of the conference room, all too aware of the weight of Colton's eyes locked on me.

I stand at the front of the room, thankful that I've rehearsed my presentation numerous times. My voice breaks as I begin, but I slowly find my confidence as I continue. I make sure to meet the eyes of the suits as well as avoid one set of eyes in particular. I channel my hurt and anger at him and his actions—and him just being here in general—to fuel my enthusiasm for the project. I speak of CD Enterprises and their monumental contributions, but never once look in his direction. I finish my presentation smoothly and succinctly and smile at the group before me. I answer the few questions that are posed and then gladly take my seat as the same time that Colton rises from the table and makes his way to the front of the room.

I fiddle with the papers in front of me as Colton addresses everyone. I curse myself for my last minute entrance into the meeting and my proximity to the front of the room. He is so close to me that his clean, woodsy smell lingers in the air and wraps itself into my head, evoking memories of our time together. All of my senses are on high alert, and I'd give anything to be able to leave the room right now.

It's torture to have the person inches from you that makes you love inexplicably, desire desperately, despise viciously, and hurt unfathomably, all in the same breath.

I doodle aimlessly on my papers trying to distract myself as the rasp of his voice pulls at me. My eyes desperately want to look at him—to search out a reason or explanation for his actions, but I know that nothing will erase the images in my head from that day.

"In partnership with Corporate Cares, CD Enterprises has gone down every avenue possible to ensure the largest sum of donations. We've knocked on all doors, called in all outstanding favors, and answered all incoming phone calls. *Everyone gets equal attention.* No one is overlooked as we've found in projects past, that usually when you least expect it, someone will come along—someone that you might have originally written off—and they will be the one that ends up turning the tide. Sometimes the one that you assumed would be *inconsequential,* turns out to be the one that *makes all the difference.*"

My eyes reflexively flash up to Colton's on the word that holds so much significance between us. Despite the audience, Colton's eyes are transfixed on mine as if he's waiting for any reaction from me to tell him that I've heard his private innuendo. That I still care. And of course I played right into it. *Damn it!* The emerald of his eyes bore into mine and the muscles play in his jaw as our stare lasts longer than is professional, the message within his words registering in my psyche.

A diminutive smile curls up the corner of his mouth as he breaks his gaze from mine to continue. And that little smile, that little show of arrogance that proves he now knows he still affects me, both pisses me off and overwhelms me. Or is he trying to tell me that I'm the one who matters to him? I'm so confused. I don't know what to think anymore.

The one thing I am sure of is that I refuse to be *that girl.* The girl that we all look at and think is stupid because she continually goes back to the guy that is always doing wrong by her— screwing around behind her back, leading her on, telling her one thing while doing the other. I have a backbone, and as much as I want Colton—as much as I do love Colton—I value the things I have to offer someone too much to let him or any guy trample me and my self-esteem. I just have to keep telling myself this as his voice seduces my ears, trying to draw me back in and strengthening his hold over me like nothing I've ever experienced.

"And such a phone call came in yesterday to my office. And by no means are we done with our fundraising efforts, but with that unexpected phone call, I am pleased to announce that in addition to the funds already pledged by CD Enterprises, another two million dollars has been confirmed in donations for the completion of your project."

A collective gasp echoes through the room with Colton's declaration. Voices buzz with excitement and the knowledge that our project is now fully funded, that all of our hard work will come to fruition.

I hang my head down amidst the commotion and squeeze my eyes shut as the roller coaster soars me up and then yanks me back down. I can't even begin to process the gamut of emotions coursing through me. On one hand, all of my efforts on behalf of my boys will pay off in a monumental way. More kids will benefit from the program and have the chance to become positive contributors to society. On the other hand, Colton is the one handing me this victory. *Talk about irony*. I'm being handed everything I've dreamed of on a professional level by the one person that I want more than anything in the whole world, but can't have on a personal level.

As much as I fight the emotions, they are just too much to bear. I'm overwhelmed. The flip-flopping between hurt and anger and misery has exhausted me. A tear slips down my cheek, and I hastily dash it away with the back of my hand as my shoulders tremble from the threat of so many more. The pain of having Colton just within reach and yet so far away from me is just too much. Everything is too fresh. Too raw.

I've lost myself so much to my emotions that I've forgotten my surroundings. When I come back to myself, the room is silent. I keep my head down, trying to pull myself together when I hear Teddy's hushed voice. "It's meant everything to her. She's put her heart and soul into this...you can't fault her for being overwhelmed."

I hear murmurs of agreement, and I'm relieved that my coworkers have mistaken my visible emotion as elation in respects to the good news on the project rather than as a result of my personal heartache. I force a thready smile onto my lips and look up at the room of people despite the tears pooling in my eyes. I meet Teddy's gaze, warmth and pride reflected on his face, and I smile sheepishly at him, playing into the charade. *Anything to escape from Colton*. "If you'll excuse me, I just need a moment," I murmur.

"Of course." He smiles softly as does the rest of the room, assuming correctly that I need to go pull myself together but for all of the wrong reasons.

I rise and calmly walk to the door, leaving a wide berth to where Colton stands, and exit the room. I can hear Teddy's voice congratulating everyone and declaring the meeting over seeing as there is no need to brainstorm how to secure the remainder of the funding anymore. My pace quickens as the distance increases from the conference room. I hold up my hand to Stella, effectively dismissing her, as she calls out my name. I make it to my office and shut the door in the nick of time before the first sob tears from my throat.

I let them roll through me as I lean against the wall opposing the door. I've tried to be so strong and hold them in for so many days, but I can't anymore. I'm disappointed in myself for still caring about him. Upset that I still want him to think about me. Pissed that he can affect me in so many ways. That he still makes my heart swell for him while my head acknowledges that he turned to Tawny when things between us went beyond the mandated Colton dating stipulations.

I ignore the gentle knock on the door, not wanting anyone to see me in such a wrecked state. The person persists and I try to rub away the tears from my cheeks knowing it's useless. There is no way I can hide my crying jag. I snap my head up as the door opens and Colton slides inside, shutting it behind him and leaning against it.

I'm staggered by his presence in my office. He dominates the small space. It's one thing to try and get over him when he's not tangible, but when he is right in front of me—when I can touch him with my fingertips—it's that much more unbearable. Our eyes lock onto each other's and my mind whirls with so many things I want to say and so many things I fear to ask. The silence is so loud between us it's deafening. Colton's eyes are saying so much to me, asking so much of me, but I'm unable to respond.

He pushes off the door and takes a step toward me. "Rylee..." My name is a plea on his lips.

"No!" I tell him, my quiet yet useless defense against him. "No," I say again with more resolve as he takes another step. "*Don't do this here, Colton. Please.*"

"Ry..." He reaches out to touch me, and I bat his hand away.

"No." My lip trembles as he stands inside my personal space. I look down at the ground. Anywhere but his eyes. "Not here, Colton. You don't get to come into my work—*my office*—and take the one place that has been keeping me sane after what you did to me and taint it." My voice breaks on my last words as a tear escapes and makes a path down my cheek. "Please..." I push against his chest to try and gain some distance, but I'm not quick enough because he grabs my wrists and holds them. The jolt of electricity still remaining between us has me gritting my teeth and fighting back more tears.

"Enough!" He grates out. "I'm not a patient man, Rylee. Never have been and never will be. I've given you your space, dealt with you ignoring me, but I have half a mind to tie you down to your chair and force you to listen to me. Keep it up and I will."

"Let go!" I yank my wrists from him, needing to break the connection.

"I didn't sleep with her, Rylee!" He grates out.

"I don't want to hear the sordid details, Colton." I have to stop him. I can't listen to the lies. "Two words, condom wrapper." I'm proud of myself for the quiet steel in my voice. Proud that I can process a thought when my insides are shredding.

"Nothing happened!" he snaps harshly at me as he paces the small confines of my office. "Absolutely nothing!"

"I'm not one of your typical airheads, Colton. I know what I saw and I saw—"

"Jesus fucking Christ woman, it was just a goddamn fucking kiss!" His implacable voice fills the room.

And empties my heart.

I force myself to swallow. To unhear what he's said. "What?" I ask, disbelief dripping from my question as he grabs the back of his neck and pulls down on it, a grimace of regret on his face. "First you swear that nothing happened. Now you're telling me that it was just a kiss. What next? You're going to tell me you forgot that your dick accidentally slipped into her? The story keeps changing, but I'm supposed to believe that this time you're telling the truth?" I laugh, hysteria mixed with the hurt bubbling up. "Last I checked, you didn't need a condom to kiss someone."

"It's all just a misunderstanding. You're totally blowing this out of proportion and I—"

A knock on the door jolts us from our bubble. It takes me a moment to find my voice and sound composed. "Yes?"

"Teddy needs you in five," Stella says timidly through the door.

"Okay. I'll be right there." I close my eyes momentarily, resigning my soul to this continuous anger and hurt.

Colton clears his throat; his face clearly conflicted between forcing me to hash this out and allowing me to retain my dignity here at work. Reluctantly he nods his head in defeat. "I'll go, Rylee. I'll leave, but I'm not letting you run away from this—from us—until I get to have my say. This is by no means over. Understood?"

I just look at him, missing him so desperately but unable to wrap my head around telling him I love him and then him running into another woman's arms. Unable to accept the ever-changing story about what happened between him and Tawny. I nod my head once, panic fluttering through my body when I realize that as much as I need distance, a part of me is relieved to know that I will get to see him again. It's a silly thought seeing as the sight of him churns my stomach and causes my heart to hurt, but you can't undo the addictive haze of love.

Tears well in my eyes as I brace myself when he leans in and places a lingering kiss on the top of my head. Chills dance up my spine despite my initial reaction to pull away from him in self-preservation.

He holds my head to his lips for a moment so that I can't squirm away. "I had to see you, Rylee. I moved Heaven and earth to get that sponsorship so that I could call Teddy and tell him to let me present today." My breath hitches at his words. I can feel his throat work a swallow as I drown in him despite the pain he's inflicting. "It's killing me that you won't talk to me—that you won't believe me—and I'm not sure what to do with how that makes me feel." He pauses but keeps his cheek against my head, and I know opening up like this is difficult for him. "*I can still feel you, Rylee.* Your skin. The way you taste. Your lips when you smile against mine. Smell the vanilla you wear. Hear your laugh...you're everywhere. You're all I can think about."

With those parting words, Colton turns and leaves my office, shutting the door behind him without looking back. I nearly cave. I nearly give into the urge to call his name and go back on the promises I made to myself long ago about what I deserve in a relationship. The memory of Tawny in his doorway draws me back to myself. Allows me to keep the slippery hold on my resolve.

I exhale slowly, trying to locate my composure because his words have undone me. They were the words I needed to hear weeks ago. The words I needed to hear in response to telling him I loved him. But now I'm just not sure if they're too late. My stumbling heart says they're not, but my sensible head says yes as it tries to protect my vulnerable feelings.

After a few minutes, I stop trembling and freshen up my make-up in time to participate in a smaller conference with the bigwigs from corporate. During the meeting, my cell phone vibrates signaling an incoming text, and I grab it quickly as to not interrupt the conversation. In my fleeting glance, I see the short text from Colton.

Sad by Maroon 5 - x C

I know the song. A man talking about the two paths of a relationship. A man admitting that he chose the wrong one to take. That he never said the words she needed to hear. That he realizes it now that she's gone.

I take a small victory in knowing he's affected by the turn of events, but it doesn't feel good. Nothing about this situation feels good.

I hate that I want him to hurt as much as I do. I hate myself for wanting him even when he hurt me. And more than anything, I hate that he made me feel again because right now I just wish I could go back to being numb.

I pull myself from my thoughts and wonder for the hundredth time if Colton really misses me or if he's once again trying to repair that fragile ego of his from being rejected.

Regardless, he's a big boy and big boys have to take responsibility for their screwed up actions. He says nothing happened but it's hard to believe when I saw them wearing the same pieces of a matching outfit.

Consequences. I'm sure that's a word he's never had to own up to before. I don't plan on responding, but I do just for measure.

I Knew You Were Trouble – Taylor Swift.

Chapter Thirty-Three

"So you're still not going to talk to him?"

"Nope." I put the Xbox game back on the shelf, trying to remember if Shane has it already.

"Nope? That's all you're going to give me?"

"Yup." I furrow my brow in indecision as I look around the various possible presents at Target.

"Are you going to say more than one word for an answer?"

"Hmm." I stall for a moment. "What do you get a sixteen year old boy for his birthday?"

"Beats me. I realize avoidance is really your thing right now, but you're an idiot if you think that you're going to be able to steer clear of him at the race."

"I've done a pretty good job so far and after yesterday, I've got enough of a reason to keep avoiding him," I shrug, not really wanting to have this conversation with Haddie. I just want to get Shane's birthday present, and then go home and shower before my shift and Shane's birthday party.

I hear Haddie's loud sigh of frustration but ignore it. "Ry, you've got to talk to him. You're miserable. You said yourself he said nothing happened."

I snort in jest. "'He' being the operative word Haddie." I say, turning to her, a chill in my voice as a result of her constant meddling in regards to how I'm handling the relationship that I no longer have with Colton. "Put yourself in my shoes. Let's say that you went to talk to the guy you're seeing and some long-legged bimbo, the one who has made it crystal clear to you in previous conversations that she wants your man, opens his door. In the morning. The only thing she is wearing is his T-shirt. *Definitely no bra*. And your boyfriend comes to answer the door, buttoning up his jeans, happy trail showing *and then some* to let you know that he was naked just prior to that moment. You realize that Long-Legged-Bimbo is most likely wearing the T-shirt that is missing from your boyfriend's bare chest. You ask said boyfriend what the hell is going on, and you can see his mind trying to figure out how to explain what you've just seen." I shove another game back on the shelf. "As he's denying nothing happened, a condom wrapper falls from his pocket. He still claims nothing happened. I believe the actual words he used were absolutely nothing happened, but push him a little—get him flustered—and oops, out slips that it was just a kiss. Only a kiss. I guarantee if I push him a little harder, more truths will spill out. *Nothing happened my ass!*"

"There could be a perfectly good reason…" she throws in there but stops when I glare at her.

"That's what I thought."

"I just hate seeing you like this." She angles her head at me and twists her lips. "Look, I understand where you're coming from, Ry, I do. I really do, but I wouldn't be a good friend if I just sat back and watched you make a mistake. I think you're so upset—and rightfully so—at what happened that you're not seeing the forest through the trees right now. You need to talk to him and hear him out. I mean the guy is still chasing after you relentlessly."

I raise my eyebrows in agitation, my feathers automatically ruffled. "Guilt will do that to you," I mutter as I move on looking at other possible gift options.

"It will," she agrees, "but so will being falsely accused of something." I peer up from the case of iPods and accessories, meeting her eyes. She reaches out and places a hand on my upper arm. "I've seen the way he looks at you. I'm watching his non-stop attempts to get your attention. Shit, he's been to our house three times in the last week trying to get you to listen to him. I'm not going to lie to him anymore for you and tell him you're not home. I know you're scared to let him back in again, but I think that fear might be healthy. The man's got it bad for you. Just like you do him. Please, keep that in mind."

I stare at her for a moment and then turn back to the case, needing a minute to digest what the one person that knows me better than anyone else has just said. "I'll think about it," is all I can manage. "Am I missing something here? Why are you pushing this so hard when you are the queen of moving on to the next guy when there is the smallest transgression let alone the guy screwing someone else? I just don't get it."

"Because he makes you happy. He challenges you. Pushes you outside your comfort zone. Makes you feel again—both good and bad—but at least you're feeling. How can I not when in the short time you've been together, you've come back to life again?" She throws a box of cereal in the cart I'm pushing. "I know I'm supposed to side whole-heartedly with you because you're my best friend, but I'm holding out hope."

I try and let her words sink in. "You didn't see what I saw, Haddie. And let's face it, words mean nothing. One minute he says nothing happened and then the next that it was just a kiss, but you know what? Something did happen, and I'm not just talking about between him and Tawny. I told him I loved him—and the something that happened was him running away and turning to another woman." My voice cracks on my last words, my resolve weakening. "I understand that he might have issues because of his past—I get that. Running away for a while to figure your head out is one thing, but running to another woman? That's unacceptable."

"I've never known you to be so hard on someone. To not give him the benefit of the doubt. From what you said, he seems to be as miserable as you are."

"We're done here," I tell her, and I mean more than just the shopping. I don't want to listen to her sympathize with Colton any more. I roll my eyes on a sigh as Haddie steps in front of the cart to block me.

"A man like Colton isn't going to wait around forever," she warns. "You need to figure out what you want or else you're going to run the risk of losing him. Sometimes when you love someone, you have to do and say things you never thought you ever would—like forgiving. It sucks donkeys, but that's just the way it is." She steps to the side of the cart, her eyes steadfast on mine. "There's a fine line between being stubborn and being stupid, Rylee,"

"Hmpf," is all I manage to say in response, pushing the cart past her, but her words hit their target. I blow out a long breath as I fight back the tears threatening and the images that flood my memory. I struggle to figure out where exactly that line is. At what point do I actually open myself up and listen to Colton's explanations with the possibility of believing him? And at what part of that process do I become stupid for either forgiving or not forgiving him. Am I willing to let the man I love walk away on principle alone?

It's a no win situation, and I'm so sick of thinking about it and dwelling over it. Seeing as how I will be spending time with him and his team in St. Petersburg starting Thursday, I think I'll have more than ample time to dwell some more on it then. Right now, I just want to buy Shane his birthday present and go enjoy his party without the complication of Colton's presence.

Fuck! I groan internally. I'm being a coward and I know it. I'm just so afraid to forgive and get hurt again. To get sucked up in the tornado that is Colton and be hurled back into emotional suicide. I laid myself out bare and he chewed me up and spit me out just like Tawny said he would. But what if Haddie's right? What if I'm fucking this up? What if he didn't do it?

And it's in the middle of my self-deprecation that I look up and my eyes catch the latest issue of People. And there he is—the current cause of my misery and schizophrenic emotional state—gracing the cover of the magazine. A candid shot of him and Cassandra Miller together at a party.

The pang hits me in a flash and I do my best to recover quickly. Unfortunately I've been getting good at it over the past few days.

"As miserable as I am?" I question Haddie, sarcasm rich in my voice. I try to tear my eyes away but they won't budge. They scrape over every detail of the picture. "Yeah he looks like he's really suffering."

Haddie sighs in exasperation. "Ry, it was a charity auction. One that you were supposed to attend as his date if I recall, and I read online that he showed up alone."

I swallow the lump in my throat. It's bad enough to think of him with Tawny, but now I have to push the image of Cassie out of my head too. "Arriving alone and leaving alone are two completely different things," I respond wryly, forcing my eyes from the cover.

"Ry—"

"Just drop it, Haddie," I say, knowing I'm being irrational but so beyond caring any more.

Haddie and I chat about everything but Colton as we leave the store, our earlier conversation tucked away for me to ponder later and a new set of noise canceling head phones and an iTunes gift card for Shane under my arm. Haddie and I are a few feet from my car when I hear, "Excuse me, Miss?"

I glance at Haddie before turning to the voice at my back, suddenly grateful that Haddie asked to accompany me on my errand. There is nothing more unnerving to a female than a random man approaching you in a parking lot when you're alone. "Can I help you?" I ask the gentleman as he nears me. He's of average height with a baseball cap covering his longish brown hair and eyes masked behind a pair of blacked out sunglasses. He looks completely normal, but he still makes me uncomfortable. Something about him seems familiar, but I know I've never met him before.

"Are you...no, you couldn't be?" he says in a uniquely sounding grate of a voice while shaking his head.

"Excuse me?"

"You look like that young lady that was featured in the paper with those orphaned kids and that racing guy. Was that you?"

His comment surprises me. I look at him for a moment thinking how to best respond and trying to figure out why he'd remember that particular article. Odd but possible. "Uh…yeah."

He just tilts his head and despite not being able to see his eyes behind his dark lenses, I get the distinct feeling that he is running his eyes over the length of my body and it unnerves me. Just as I'm about to say screw this and get in the car, he speaks again. "What a great program you have there. Just thought I'd let you know."

"Thanks," I say absently as I climb in my car, dismissing him and breathing a sigh of relief when he walks away without another word.

Haddie looks over at me, concern etched in her eyes. "Creepy," she mutters, and I can't help but agree.

Chapter Thirty-Four

"*Not yet!*" I chastise Shane as he begs again to open one of his presents.

"Oh c'mon, Ry," he flashes his lady killer grin at me. "Can't I at least open one?"

"Nope! No presents are being opened until after cake. You have to make a wish first!" I smirk as I finish the last portion of dinner clean-up. "Besides, you already opened the presents from your friends last night when you all went to the movies."

"Can't fault a guy for trying," he says as he sits on a barstool.

"What'd you guys see?"

His eyes light up like a normal sixteen-year-old boy at the mention of his coed movie night out, and it warms my heart. This kid is a heartbreaker, and I remind myself to speak to Jackson about having a little man-to-man with him about being responsible. "That new zombie movie. It was way cool!"

"Mmm-hmm…did Sophie go with you guys?" His cheeks redden at her name, and I know that Jackson definitely needs to have that chat soon.

Shane fills me in on the details about his evening while the rest of the boys are outside with Dane, Bailey, Jackson, and Austin—the other counselors here to help celebrate. They are decorating the patio area for the birthday party, as is our practiced tradition here at The House.

"Okay, we're ready for the birthday boy!" Austin announces as he enters the kitchen. Shane rolls his eyes at the babyish idea of a birthday party, but I know deep down he secretly enjoys the fuss.

We head out to the patio where streamers and balloons hang haphazardly yet affectionately. It's obvious that the younger boys helped with decorating. A cake sits on one table and another has a small gathering of birthday presents on it. Shane smiles brightly at the sight and at the chorus of cheers that erupt when he walks through the doorway.

We visit for a bit and play childish party games because for these kids nothing is silly. They've missed out on numerous ridiculous traditions in their lifetimes, and we want to try and provide such things for them here. After pin the tail on the donkey, we decide it's time for cake.

"Oops, I forgot the party plates," Bailey whispers to me as she places seventeen candles on the cake.

"I'll get them!" Scooter pipes up.

"No! I've got them," I say quickly as Bailey looks at me oddly. "All the stuff for the Easter baskets are in the same cabinet," I whisper to her, not wanting Scooter to accidentally see the Easter Bunny's secret stash. She just smiles and calls him back to help her.

It takes me a while to get the plates out of the cabinet in the garage because I move and re-stash the Easter garb onto a higher shelf and place some stuff in front of it for better hiding. Austin is walking down the hall to find me when I come back in the door from the garage to the house.

"Everything okay?" he asks, his English accent turning the corners of my mouth up a tad. He really is the epitome of handsome with his blond hair and golden skin and very serious girlfriend whom I've come to call a friend.

"Yeah." I smile. As we walk through the great room and out toward the back door, he slings an arm over my shoulder and pulls me close into his side to whisper what he got Shane for his birthday as we walk onto the patio. I laugh out loud as he tells me about his gag gift and then his real gift, when I refocus my attention on the party. And although it is completely innocent, Austin's mouth is nuzzled into my ear divulging his birthday present secrets when I raise my head and surprisingly meet Colton's eyes across the yard.

I feel like the world falls out beneath my feet, my heart staggering in my chest and breath catching in my throat. His comments mingled with Haddie's mix and meld in my head, and every part of my body and soul wants every part of his right now. I want the complications gone, the images in my head of him and Tawny to vanish, and to just be back to where we were with him shaving in my bathroom with the pink handle of my razor in his hand.

And as much as I want to see him again regardless of the pain his presence causes, I can't find it in me to forgive what he did. Wouldn't it just happen again?

His eyes hold mine for a beat, shooting daggers at Austin and his arm draped on my shoulder, before turning back to his conversation with of all people, intern Bailey. Yes, that Bailey. The girl I believe he'd messed around with prior to helping me out of the storage closet that first night we met. And even though

Colton keeps glancing over at me, Bailey is clueless, all of her blatant flirting focused solely on him. My stomach revolts when I see her place a hand on his bicep and smile suggestively up at him.

"Someone didn't get the memo," Dane whispers in my ear as Austin goes to help Ricky with something.

"What?"

"Bailey didn't seem to get the memo that Colton's no longer on the market."

"She can have him." I snort, rolling my eyes as I see him dart another glance over at me. Dane looks at me oddly, and I realize that I've let our little no-longer-seeing-each other predicament slip. I've purposely kept what has happened quiet, not wanting anyone at the company to get wind that Colton and I are at odds so it wouldn't get back to Teddy. It's really been easy since I never spoke about it anyway; rather I just let the rumors run without confirming or denying them.

"Uh-oh." Dane smirks, always one for juicy gossip. "Sounds like trouble in paradise."

"Paradise is most definitely not the word I'd use to describe it," I murmur, unable to take my eyes off of Colton. "Try a sinking ship without life preservers and a whole shitload of issues."

"Everybody's got issues, honey. Too bad he doesn't swing my way because I could definitely take care of any mommy issues he may have by making sure he tends to *my big daddy issue* if you catch my drift." He wags his eyebrows playfully.

"Eew gross!" I slap his shoulder but burst out laughing. I can't help it. It's the first good laugh I've had in weeks, and it feels good to just let go.

"I have a feeling there are going to be fireworks in St. Petersburg, and it's nowhere near the fourth of July." Dane snickers.

I have a serious case of the giggles, my catharsis over my pent up emotions happening at the oddest time, and several of the boys look at me as if I've lost my marbles. "Okay...c'mon you guys," I say, struggling to contain my laughter, "it's time to cut the cake."

Everyone gathers around the table, Shane sitting in front of the cake as we light the candles and sing to him. His face full of excitement when he closes his eyes to make his wish, and I wonder what it is he is hoping for. The cake is cut and everyone is enjoying a piece, so I slip inside to bring the ice cream back to the freezer and clean off the knife. I shut the freezer door and jump out of my skin when I see Colton standing there in the kitchen.

"*Who's the Brit?*"

"Jesus! You scared me!"

I keep my hand on the refrigerator handle, unsure what to do as we just stare at each other. Several times over the past few weeks, I've wished that I could rewind time and take back those three little words that I'd said, but I realize right now in this moment—as he stands before me so achingly beautiful inside and out—that I don't think I would. I did love him. I still love him. And he needed someone to tell him so that at some point in the future he can look back and accept the fact that he is worthy of such a love. I just don't know if I'm willing to stick around and accept the pain that I'm positive he'll inflict on the person willing to assert such a notion.

"Sorry." He smirks halfheartedly, but the smile never reaches his eyes. Rather, I sense irritation and impatience from him. "*Who is he?*" he demands again, and there is no masking his annoyance now. "Is he with you because you sure looked cozy? You moved on awfully quick, Rylee."

Every part of me that sagged in relief at seeing him here tonight is now bristling with irritation. Who the hell does he think he is coming here and accusing me of having a date? If he thought this was the right way to start our conversation, he's sadly mistaken.

"Seriously, Colton?" I roll my eyes using Shane's word, not wanting to deal or spend the time to assuage Colton's fragile ego. When he just stands there and stares at me, I relent for the sake of not making a scene despite the jealous, alpha-male tantrum he's throwing. "He's a counselor here." I huff out.

He angles his head and stares at me, muscle ticking in his jaw, eyes piercing. "*Have you fucked him?*"

"That's none of your goddamn business." I sneer at him, anger rising as I try to brush past him.

He reaches out and grabs my bicep, holding me in place so my shoulder hits the middle of his chest. I can feel the rapid beat of his heart against my arm and hear his uneven breathing as I stare straight ahead. "Everything about you is my business, Rylee." A disgusted snort is my only response. "Did you?"

"Hypocrite. Unlike you, Ace, I don't make a habit of *fucking* the people that work for me." I tilt my chin up and look into his eyes to let him see the anger, hurt, and defiance brimming in mine. The grimace he emotes on his otherwise stoic countenance lets me know I've made my point. We just stand like this for a moment, staring at each other. "Why are you here, Colton?" I eventually ask with resignation.

"Shane invited me to his birthday party." He shrugs, taking his hand from my arm and shoving both hands deep into the pockets of his jeans. "I couldn't let him down just because you refuse to see me."

What can I say to that? How can I be mad at him for being here, when he's here for one of the boys?

"And because..." He runs a hand through his hair and steps back while he struggles to figure out what to say next. He blows out an audible breath and is about to speak again when Shane comes barreling into the house.

"We're going to...open presents now," he finishes after looking back and forth from Colton and me, his brow furrowing with uncertainty as he tries to figure out the dynamic between the two of us.

I inhale deeply; glad to be saved because I don't think I'd made my mind up on what to do just yet. My heart tells me I want to listen to him, understand what happened, and figure out where to go from here. But my head, my head tells me, "*Quack.*"

"Presents!" I repeat as I walk out of the kitchen and brush past Colton without acknowledging his comment.

Shane's excitement is more than contagious to the rest of us bystanders as he opens his gifts. His eyes are full of excitement, and his smile reflects a teenager who feels loved. I stand on the fringe of the crowd, watching the action and reflecting a bit on what a good job we're doing here with these boys. It's odd how sometimes it just hits you, and right now is one of those moments. I lean against the beam of the patio cover as Shane lifts his last present up and shakes it as the little ones yell out what they think it might be.

It's a flat rectangular box that I hadn't seen on the table before, and I take a step closer to see what it is, my curiosity getting the better of me. Shane rips the paper off and when he opens the box, a card slides out. He turns the card over in his hand, and when he sees nothing on the envelope, he shrugs and tears it open. I watch his eyes widen and his lips fall open as he reads the words inside. His head snaps up and he searches the partygoers to meet Colton's eyes. *"Seriously?"* he asks, incredulity in his voice.

I'm curious as to what's written in the card and my sight focuses on Colton's as a shy smile spreads across his lips, and he shakes his head, "Seriously, Shane."

"You're shittin' me?"

"Shane!" Dane snaps out at him in warning, and Shane's cheeks turn red as he blushes at the reprimand.

Colton laughs out loud. "No, I'm not. Keep your grades up and I will. *I promise.*"

Still mystified as to what the two of them are talking about, I ease out of the shadows and walk up to Shane. He holds the card out for me to see. The card is a typical birthday card, but it's the penmanship inside that makes my heart flop.

Happy Birthday, Shane! What I remember the most about turning 16 is wanting desperately to learn how to drive...so this card entitles you to driving lessons—from me. (I get to pick the car though...and the Aston is off limits). Have a good one bud. –Colton

I look down at Shane who still seems like he can't believe that a famous race car driver has offered up to be his behind-the-wheel instructor. And I see in his eyes the self-worth that Colton has given him in this one offering and bite back the tears that burn my throat. He doesn't offer him something of material value that he can buy easily, but rather gives Shane something much more valuable—*time*. Someone to look up to. Someone to spend time with. Colton understands these boys so well and what they need at what times, and yet he can't comprehend what I need and how I feel about what I walked in to.

Shane gets up and walks over to Colton and shakes his hand to thank him before passing the card to everyone to show them what it says. I look away from observing Shane to see Colton silently watching me. I just shake my head softly at him trying to convey my appreciation for his well thought out gift. He holds my gaze as he slowly walks over to me. I bite my bottom lip in hesitation. My body is filled with a civil war of emotions, and I just don't know what to do anymore.

Colton places his hand on my lower back, the contact sending my nerves dancing even more than they already are. His signature scent envelops me, and I reflexively part my lips, craving the taste of him that I've missed so much.

He leans in to me and asks for the second time tonight, "Can we speak for a moment?" His rasp fills my ears and the warmth of his breath feathers over my cheek.

I step back from him, needing distance to keep a clear head. "Um...I don't think it's a good idea... The House isn't the best place to..." I fumble with the words.

"Don't care. This won't take long," is his only response as he steers me to the fringe of activity on the patio. The short reprieve gives my mind time to think. To rationalize. To decide. "I'm talking, you're listening. Understood?"

I turn to face him and look up at the lines of his magnificent face partially hidden by the shadows of the night. My angel struggling between the dark and the light. I take a fortifying breath before I open my mouth to speak, options and indecision swirling around with mixed emotions. "Colton…" I begin before he can speak and when I see the annoyance flash across his face, I decide to change tactics. Try to protect my heart from further devastation even though it's crying in protest over what I'm about to do. "There's nothing to explain." I shrug; swallowing down the lump clogging my throat so the lies can prevail. "You made it clear from the beginning what was between us. I mistook our physical chemistry for love." Colton's eyes narrow and his mouth falls lax at my words. "*Typical female mistake.* Great sex doesn't mean love. Sorry about that. I know how much you hate drama, but I realize that you're right. *This would've never worked.*" I grit my teeth, knowing this is for the best as I watch the confusion flicker across his face. "It's not like we were exclusive. What you did with Tawny is your business. I may not like it, but that's the breaks right?"

If I write him off, it might make having to work together less awkward for the both of us despite knowing deep down that having to be beside him when my heart still desires him—*hell, when every cell in my body wants him in one way or another*—will be brutal.

Trying to prevent the memory of the wounded look in those crystalline green eyes, I start to turn away from him, moving so he can't see the welling tears or my trembling chin. He reaches out and holds his favored spot on my bicep. "Get back here, Rylee…"

I squeeze my eyes shut at the forlorn sound of my name from his lips and try to infuse nonchalance in my voice when I actually find it. "Thanks for the good time. It was real while it lasted." I shrug my arm out of his grasp, and only when I open my eyes to walk away do I see Shane watching the interaction, concern in his eyes at the expression on my face.

Colton mutters a curse beneath his breath as I walk away under the pretense of going to help clean up. Rather than going in to the kitchen to wash dishes, I walk right past it and go into the counselors' room. I sit on the edge of one of the twin beds there and hold my head in my hands.

What did I just do? I try to catch my breath, my conscience and my heart not agreeing with what my head decided was the best course of action. I fall back on the bed and rub my eyes with my hands, a litany of curses falling quietly from my lips as I chastise myself. A soft knock is at the door and before I can sit myself up, Shane pokes his head into the open doorway.

"Rylee?"

"Hey, bud." I sit up and the smile I think I'm going to have to force comes naturally at the look of concern on his face. "What's up?" I ask as I pat the spot on the bed next to me. I can tell something is bugging him.

He shuffles over and sits down next to me, eyes angled down as he laces and unlaces his own fingers. "I'm sorry." He breathes.

"For what?" I'm usually pretty good at following the moods of the boys, but I'm thrown here.

"I just…you've been sad…and he makes you happy…usually…so I invited him so that you'd be happy again. And now you're sad…and it's because of him. And I…" He clenches his fists and grits his teeth.

Shane's discomfort is obvious as it hits me what he's saying. My heart breaks as I realize that he's invited Colton here to try and cheer me up without knowing he's the reason I've been so somber the past few days. And then I feel guilty because I obviously did let my relationship with Colton affect my work. I reach out and squeeze his hand.

"You didn't do anything wrong, Shane." I wait until he raises his eyes to mine—eyes of the man he's becoming but still reflecting the unsettled little boy deep inside. "What makes you think I've been sad?"

He just shakes his head, tears starting to collect at the corners of his eyes. "You just have been…" He stops, and I wait for him to finish the thought I can see working its way to his mouth. "My mom was always so sad…always so upset because it was just us two…I never did anything to help…and then…" *One day you found her dead with the empty bottles of pills beside her bed.* "I'm sorry, I was just trying to make things better…I didn't realize he's the one who made it worse."

"Oh, sweet boy," I tell him, pulling him into my arms as a lone tear slides down his cheek. My heart swells with the love I have for this boy, so much older than his years for unfathomable reasons but with such a tender heart, trying to make me feel better. "That is one of the nicest things that anyone has ever done for me." I lean back and frame his face in my hands. "You, Shane—you and the rest of the boys in our family—are what makes me happy on a daily basis."

"Kay… Well, I don't have to accept his present if it upsets you," he offers without a hesitation.

"Don't be silly." I pat his leg, the gesture touching me. "Colton and I are fine," I lie for good measure. "He's just being a guy." I get a slight smile out of him with that line despite his eyes still reflecting uncertainty. "Besides, think how cool it'll be to tell all of your friends that a real race car driver taught you how to drive!"

His grin widens, "I know! It's so cool!" And once again we are back on even footing. He stands and starts toward the door, my little boy who is growing up so fast.

"Hey, Shane?"

"Yeah?" He stops at the door and turns around.

"Happy birthday, buddy. *I football you* more than you'll ever know."

A sheepish smile spreads across his face, his hair flopping down over his forehead when he just shakes his head and looks at me. "I'm sixteen now. We can stop with the whole football thing." He pushes his hair out of his eyes as they meet mine. "I love you too," he says before shrugging as only a sixteen year old can and walking away. I stare after him with a smile plastered on my face, a heart overflowing with love, and tears of joy pooling in my eyes.

Chapter Thirty-Five

The beautiful Florida sunshine feels magnificent on my skin and elevates my spirits. Arriving a day earlier than needed in St. Petersburg, I have taken full advantage of the ever-present warm weather and lavish pool of the Vinoy Resort and Golf Club. The home base of CD Enterprises and Corporate Cares for the next few days. There's nothing like relaxation and the touch of sun on my skin to rejuvenate me before my official duties and the whirlwind that will ensue tomorrow.

It's not that I mind the crazy schedule—in fact, I look forward to meeting and thanking the people that have helped make the project a reality—it's that I will have to stand side by side with Colton to show the unity between our two companies. There are photo ops and sponsorship appreciation events among other things before the actual race on Sunday.

I cringe at the thought of my schedule—my close proximity to Colton—seeing as how I was able to avoid him the rest of the night at Shane's party and therefore didn't follow through on my promise to talk with him. I'm sure my due will come tomorrow when I see him, but for now, my head swims of sun and relaxation.

Rihanna's *Stay* plays in my earbuds, the lyrics hitting a little too close to home. Wanting to forgo getting sunburn on the first day here, I gather my belongings and head back toward the room.

I step into the empty elevator, and just as the door starts to close, "Hold the elevator!" echoes off of the marbled walls of the lobby. A hand sticks in the small space between the moving door and the wall, and it immediately retreats back open. I suck in a breath when a very sweaty, extremely delectable Colton jogs his way into the elevator. His momentum dies when his eyes meet mine.

A pair of sweat soaked gym shorts ride low on his hips while the top portion of his torso remains bare. His tan is darker, no doubt from his work out in the bright sun, and sweat glistens off every inch of his bared skin. My eyes wander helplessly over the well-defined ridges of his abdomen, the intricate markings of his tattoos, and to where rivulets of sweat drip down into the deep V that travels below his waistband. I swallow reactively at the memory of my hands mapping those lines and the feel of them bunching beneath my fingertips as he buries himself in me. I drag my eyes away and up to those magnificent pools of green that stare at me with a somber intensity.

Of all of the elevators in the entire frickin' resort, he has to pick this one?

A cautious smile turns up the corners of his mouth as he steps farther into the elevator toward me. He knows I'm affected. "Glad to see you got in okay."

"Yeah…" I clear my throat, finding it difficult to make my thoughts form into words when the temptation is so painstakingly clear in front of me. "Yes, I did. Thank you."

"Good," he says, eyes locked on mine.

The doors start to close again, and when a gentleman starts to walk in, Colton breaks our visual connection and steps in front of him, spreading his arms across the entrance. "Sorry, this elevator's taken." His voice that denotes that there is no arguing the matter.

I start to protest as the doors close and Colton whirls around to me, his predatory glare matching the posture of his body. "Don't even start, Rylee…" He growls, silencing me as he takes a step toward me. His chest is heaving and I'm not sure if it's a result of the exertion from his run or because of our close proximity. His dominance of this small space is all consuming. "This ends right now."

He takes another step closer, his jaw clenched, his eyes unforgiving as they leave mine and roam over my bikini-clad torso. My swimsuit seemed to provide more than adequate coverage when I bought it, but standing here in an elevator with Colton's eyes scraping over every single curve of my body, it feels indecently suggestive. And I know it's because even though he's not touching me—even though I'm hurt and want nothing to do with him—my body remembers all too well the havoc he can wreak on my system with the simple graze of his fingertips or caress of his tongue.

I tell myself to snap out of it. To remember what he did to me, but it's so damn hard when his heady after-workout scent is dominating the small space. The ache resurfaces deep within my body at the sight of him, creating desires I know only he can satisfy. The man's pull on me is relentless, even when he doesn't even realize it. "Now's not a good time, Colton."

He chuckles a sliver of a laugh, but his face doesn't depict a single trace of humor. He takes a final step toward me, my retreat leaving my back pressed against the wall. He leans forward and presses his hands on either side of me, boxing me in. "Well, you better make it one, Rylee, because I really don't care. This ends right here, right now. Non-negotiable."

My breath hitches, betraying my false façade as his body brushes against mine. The heat of his skin radiates off of him and into me. His lips are mere inches from mine. All I'd have to do is lean forward to feel them. To taste him again. And then I realize that this is exactly what he wants. He wants to remind me physically so I forgive and forget about what happened emotionally.

Wrong tactic to use with me.

I want him—God yes I want him—but not on these terms. Not with lies still hanging between us. Not with the hurt from his deception poisoning my heart.

We breathe each other in, our eyes unwavering, and I'm proud of myself for holding my own. "I think you've forgotten how good we are together," he grates out in frustration when he realizes that I'm able to resist him.

I angle my head and look at him. "It's easy to forget when Tawny opens the front door of your whorehouse with nothing but your T-shirt on, Ace." I sneer, timing it perfectly so my last word coincides with the elevator's ding to our destined floor. I take the sound as my cue and duck quickly beneath his hands, bolting into the hallway to the sounds of a cursing Colton. I should know better by now how fast he is, but my mind is jumbled with everything else.

I can hear his footsteps behind me as I fumble with the keycard into my room. I think I may be in the clear, but the minute I have the door open, his hand slams against the door forcing it open with a bang. I don't even have a moment to yelp before he spins me around and crashes my back against the wall with the full force of his body.

"Then let me remind you," he growls, and in my surprised state, I barely register his words, but they seep into my fuzzy conscience the moment before his lips claim mine. It's amazing that regardless of how long it's been—how hurt I am—when we connect, I feel like I'm home. A home currently set ablaze, but a home nonetheless. His mouth fervently possesses mine, and his hands map over every inch of my exposed flesh. Kneading. Stimulating. Possessing. I get lost in his taste; his touch; the low groan emanating in the back of his throat; the hard length of his body pressing into mine as one hand wraps around the waterfall of curls down my back and holds me captive to his mind-altering onslaught.

It takes a moment for my mind to work through the chaos and the bang of arousal he's just created between my thighs. I struggle out of the desire-induced haze that renders my body boneless. *Shit! Shit! Shit!*

"*No!*" It's a broken, strangled cry but a cry nonetheless. I push forcibly on his chest, tearing his mouth from mine. "I can't. I just can't! This doesn't fix anything!"

I stand there staring at him with our chests heaving and pulses racing—a sure sign that our chemistry still remains—and his more than addictive taste still on my lips. His hands are wrapped around my wrists, holding my hands against his damp and alluring chest. "Rylee..."

"No!" I try again to push against his chest, but my strength is no match for his. "You don't get to just take what you want, when you want it."

"My God, woman, you are driving me insane!" he mutters into the air.

"Why? Because you got caught?"

"You have to do something wrong to get caught!" he shouts, releasing my wrists and pushing away from me, his face a mix of exasperation, frustration, and unsatisfied desire. "*Nothing! Fucking! Happened!*" His voice bellows around the empty room and echoes in the emptiness of my hurting heart.

"*Tigers can't change their stripes, Ace.*"

"You and your fuckin' tigers and ducks," he mutters before turning his back and walking farther into my room and away from me.

"Don't forget jackasses!" I shout.

"Goddamn frustrating, pig-headed woman!" he says to himself before turning back around.

The man is infuriating, thinking he can just waltz in here and kiss me senseless so that I forget everything else. "C'mon, since when does the infamous ladies' man, Colton Donavan, resist a half-naked woman?" I sneer, taking a step toward him, infusing sarcasm in my next comment. "And to think you were even generous enough to offer her the shirt off your back." I snort. "With a track record like yours, I'm sure you offered what was in your pants as well. Oh, I'm sorry—we know you did because you made sure it was jacketed up. Nothing happened? Just a kiss? *And I'm supposed to believe that?*"

"Yes!" he shouts loud enough to make me wince. "Just like I was supposed to believe your excuse at Shane's party. It was bullshit and you know it."

"Don't you dare turn this on me!" I yell at him.

"You really believe that we were just sex?" He grates out, jaw clenched, voice challenging.

"Oh, were we something more?" Sarcasm drips from my words.

"Yes goddamnit!" He pounds his fist against the wall, "and you know it!"

I take a step toward him, anger overriding any intimidation I normally would have felt. "Well by you acknowledging it, it just makes what you did even worse?"

"What did I do, Rylee? Tell me exactly what I did!" He shouts at me, stepping well within the realm of personal space.

"Now you want to rub it in? You want to shove my face in it by making me say it out loud? Fuck you, Colton," I shout at him, anger starting to snake through my body and permeate through the hurt.

"No. I want to hear you say it. I want you to look in my eyes and see my reaction for yourself. What did I do?" he commands, giving my shoulders a slight shake. "Say it!"

And I refuse to. I refuse to watch the little smirk that I know will play at the corners of his mouth if I obey him so instead I say the only thing that comes to mind. "*Quack!*"

"Now you're just acting like a child!" Exasperated, he releases me and shoves his hand through his hair before taking a few steps from me to control his temper.

"A child?" I sputter, shock radiating through me. Talk about the pot calling the kettle black. "A fucking child? Look who's talking!"

"You," he says with a sneer and an arch of an eyebrow, "the child throwing the goddamn tantrum. The one so wrapped up in your own head, that you don't realize your little fit is for all of the wrong fucking reasons."

I stare at him for a moment, our eyes locked on one another's and I realize that we're tearing each other apart and for what? We obviously can't get past this. Me accusing. Him denying. "This is such a waste of time," I say quietly, a single tear slipping down my cheek and resignation in my voice.

He takes another step toward me, and I just shake my head at him, unable to let go the tumultuous emotions inside of me. How can I love this beautiful man before me and despise him at the same time? How can I crave and desire him, all the while wanting to throttle him? I sag against the wall as I try to process everything that I was afraid of happening transpire.

"Why was she there, Colton?" I stare unflinchingly into his eyes, asking but not really wanting to know the answer. His eyes look down for a moment, and his hesitancy makes me miserable. I gather every ounce of hurt I have in my voice, and when I speak, it drips with it. "I told you that cheating was a deal breaker for me."

"Nothing happened." He throws his hands up as the image of Tawny's legs, hard nipples pressed against his T-shirt, and her smug smile flickers through my head. "*What is it going to take to make you believe me?*" The sound in his voice takes me by surprise. As if he really can't believe my doubt in him. Haddie's comments flicker through my mind, but I push them away. She wasn't there. *She didn't see what I saw.* She didn't see Tawny tousled from sleep with that victorious siren's smile across her swollen lips. The condom wrapper fluttering to the ground like a nail sealing the coffin lid shut. "Rylee, Tawny came to the house. We were drunk. Things got out of control. It all happened so fast that—"

"Stop!" I shout, holding up my hand, not wanting to hear the gory details that I know for sure will break my heart even further. "All I know, Colton, is that you pushed me to open up—to feel again after everything that happened with Max—and I did exactly what you said. I trusted you, despite my head telling me not to. I allowed myself to feel again. *I gave everything of myself to you.* Was willing to give so much more…and the minute you got spooked, you ran into the arms of another woman. *That's not okay with me.*"

He leans back against the wall opposite me, and we just stare at each other, sadness smothering the air between us. I can see him struggle with something but push it back. "I don't know what else to say, Rylee…"

"Saying nothing and running away are two completely different things." He pushes himself off of the wall and takes a step toward me. I shake my head at him. The fact that not once has he acknowledged that I told him I loved him slingshots into my head. He's here trying to make things right, but he can't acknowledge the words I spoke to him. *This is so fucked up.* "I could've lived with you saying nothing. I could've accepted you running away. But you ran into the arms of another woman. I can't bring myself to trust that it wouldn't happen again. You made your choice when you slept with Tawny."

His shoulders sag and his eyes flash with fire at my words before settling with defeat. "*I need you.*" The unhindered honesty behind his words strikes me and twists my heart.

"There's a fine line between wanting me and needing me, Colton. I needed you too." *And I still do.* "But you obviously needed her more. I just hope she was worth it." I choke on the words and shake my head. Anything to try and erase the sound of his voice saying he needs me. Anything to prevent the doubt from creeping in.

Hurt propels my thoughts. Devastation controls my actions. "I think it's best you go." I whisper, forcing the words past my lips.

He just looks at me, pools of green silently pleading with me. "You've made your choice then…." His voice is broken. Silent. Resigned.

I can't bring myself to agree with him. My body is a riot of conflicting answers, and saying it out loud will just add permanence to something half of me wants over and done with while the other half would kill to have a second chance at. There is nothing left for me to say. But I say it anyway.

"Yes, I have. But only because you did it for me."

"Rylee..."

"And mine's no longer you."

I break from his gaze and stare at the floor. *Anything to get him to leave.* He stands staring at me for a time, but I refuse to raise my head and look at him.

"This is fucking bullshit, Rylee, and you know it," he says evenly to me before turning to walk out. *"I guess you don't love the broken in me after all."*

The sob catches in my throat at his words and it takes everything I have to stay on my feet. And even standing proves to be too much because the minute I hear the door close, I slide down the wall until I hit the floor.

The tears come. Hard, jagged sobs that shudder through my body and steal little pieces of my soul with each one. His parting words echo over and over in my head until I know for sure that I'm the one that's broken, not him.

Doubts creep through. Sorrow sets in. Devastation reigns.

Chapter Thirty-Six

I slip back into my hotel room for a quick respite before the next event occurs. I tell myself that I just need to take a breather, but I know for a fact that I'm just being a coward and avoiding Colton as I've done for the better part of the day. He's been nothing but cordial in front of others but aloof when no one is watching. Hurt is evident in his eyes, but then it's prevalent in mine as well.

In one of the rare instances that we were alone, I tried to talk to Colton about his parting words to me. I wanted to tell him that I do love the broken in him—that I still want the parts of him that he's hiding away and afraid to let out—but when I opened my mouth to speak, he just dismissed me away with a glacial glare. His patience has obviously run out. It's what I wanted, so why do I feel like I'm dying inside.

What am I doing? *Am I making a huge mistake?* I press the heels of my hands to my eyes and sigh. Having him move on should make me happy. Should make me relieved that I don't have to put up with the "let me explain" routine. Then why am I so utterly miserable? Why do I have to swallow the huge lump in my throat every time I think of him or look at him?

I'm screwing this up. Maybe I need to listen to him. Give him the chance to explain. Maybe if I know the whole story it will help me push through this pain and move on once I hear all of the sordid details of his night with Tawny. And I think these details are exactly what I fear…but what if there are no sordid details? What if everything Haddie has been pushing into my ears is legitimate?

What if I'm in the wrong?

Crap. I am screwing this up. I can't even think straight—thoughts fragmenting in a million directions—but I know I'm fucking this up.

My cell phone chirps a text notification, and it drags me from my schizophrenic thoughts. It's a text from Dane about Zander. I dial him immediately. "What's wrong?" I ask in response to his greeting.

"He had a pretty rough night, Ry." He blows out a loud sigh. "Actually talked about that night. It was his dad, Ry. And he swears that he saw his dad in his window last night. Freaked out. Literally. But Avery was in the room with him, and she said that there was no one there."

"*Oh God!*" is all I can say, imagining the fear tearing through his little body.

"Yeah… Avery did a great job with him though. In fact, he hasn't left her side all day."

"Is he still talking?" My mind immediately thinks of all of the progress he's made in the past month. Of how in therapy he's started drawing pictures depicting what happened that horrific night and started piecing it together for both his counselors and the authorities. A set back like this could wipe all of that away and then some.

"Not as much but it's still fresh in his mind. I'm just keeping Avery with him. The two of them have really bonded."

"Do I need to come home? I can…" Guilt spirals through me. I should be there with Zander right now. Comforting him. Helping him through this. Holding him.

"Don't be silly, Ry. We've got it covered. I just know how you like to know everything about the kids when it happens."

"You're sure?"

"Positive," he reiterates. "How's it going resisting the Adonis? Is the ship still sinking or are you diving into his bits of paradise?"

I can't help the smile that forms on my lips. "You've been talking to Haddie, haven't you?" His silence is the only answer that I need. Resigned and needing someone to bounce things off of, I reluctantly respond. "It's…confusing." I sigh.

"Men always are, babe."

I laugh. "I don't know, Dane. I know what I saw. I'm not stupid. But between Haddie telling me I'm being stubborn and Colton's non-stop denial, I wonder if I'm making a mistake. I just don't get how one plus one doesn't equal two."

He just makes a non-committal sound on the other end of the line while he thinks. "Shit, Ry, not everything is black and white if you know what I mean. What does it hurt to hear him out?"

I breathe out audibly, fear snaking through me that I really might be wrong. That I might already be too late. "My pride."

"Sugar, maybe you should be holding on a little tighter to that Adonis instead of your pride. That'll just cause you to end up alone with lots of cats."

A silence settles between us, his words striking a little closer to home than I care to admit. "Yeah…I know."

"Then get off your ass and do something about it! A gorgeous man like that isn't going to wait around forever regardless of how delicious you are. Shit, I just might try to turn him."

I laugh again; always appreciative of Dane and his unsolicited advice that no doubt puts me in my place. Crap! I thank him quickly and hang up, my mind made up. I scramble quickly, slipping my practical outfit over my head, and grab the sexiest dress I have in my suitcase.

In the time I've had to sit and think about everything, I've reapplied my make-up and given myself a pep talk to regain some of my confidence. I'm not sure what I'm going to say to Colton, but I have to say something. I have to fix the damage of this cluster-fuck that we're continually finding ourselves in.

It's time for me to put on my big girl panties.

I figure if I can speak to him quickly, then I can make some plans to see him afterward and talk things through. I double-check my reflection in the mirrors of the elevator. My quick change has done wonders for both my appearance and my attitude. I head toward the ballroom where the event of the evening is taking place. An event that I had not been scheduled to attend, but I don't care. I have to do this now.

I can't wait any longer. I can't waste another minute clutching to my pride.

And besides, I really hate cats.

The evening's event is a charitable cocktail party where people pay the requisite donation and get the rights to say they had drinks with the elusive Colton Donavan. As much as I'm thrilled that the funds will be going toward a local St. Petersburg organization for orphaned children, I have a hunch that the attendees of this evening's event will be more concerned with trying to grab Colton's attention—or rather what's in his pants—than the kids their money will be helping.

I take a deep breath as I walk. My mind's made up. I need to talk to Colton. Tonight. I need to either bury this or take a chance, trust him, and listen to what he has to say. Believe him when he tells me that he didn't sleep with Tawny—that he'd never cheat on me. I silently rehearse the words I want to say. Nerves jingle in my stomach. I smooth my hands over my dress, turning the corner to the foyer leading to the ballroom and stop dead in my tracks when I come face to face with the one person I have dreaded seeing this entire trip. The one person I am most certain that Colton has purposely kept my eyes from even catching a glimpse of.

"*Well isn't this an unexpected surprise*," her unmistakable voice chides, causing the hairs on the back of my neck to stand up. It takes everything I have from launching myself at her. From slapping that smug, smarmy smirk off of her face and showing her how I really feel about her.

And I'm just about to lay into her when the gentleman passing by catches my eye and nods at me, a murmured, "Rylee," on his lips—a corporate sponsor.

I nod back at him, forcing a slight smile in greeting, knowing that as much as I'd like to attack Tawny right here and show her what I think of her, I can't commit the professional suicide that would result from it. And I know that Tawny knows it because she works her tongue in her cheek as her smirk widens.

"What?" she says, looking me up and down. "You're finally ready to forgive Colton for his indiscretions?" She quirks her eyebrows, so much more than contempt dancing in her eyes. And it's not lost on me that the word 'indiscretions' is plural. I stare at Tawny, so many things I'd like to spew at her running through my mind. I physically have to clench my fists to prevent them from reaching out and slapping her. Anger is so thick in my throat that words don't come. Feelings—emotions—hatred overwhelms, but words don't come.

"Did you think he'd change just for you, doll? Maybe you should ask him *what* or should I say *who* he's been up to these past couple of weeks." A sliver of a laugh escapes her botox enhanced lips as she takes a step closer. "Neither Raquel nor Cassie nor…" she raises her eyebrows with the insinuation of herself "…had any complaints in your absence."

Her words shock me at first and then catapult me into fury. "Go to Hell, Tawny," I grit out as I take a step closer to her, infringing well inside the bounds of her personal space. My hands shake. My blood rushes. She has singlehandedly replaced my hope of reconciling with Colton with unfiltered ire and absolute despair. What should I expect? She's the one who took it from me in the first place.

I'm done. So fucking done. Just when I had worked myself up to believe that I was the one in the wrong—place the blame for all of this heartache on myself—here comes the truth, slapping me in the face. My hope splinters and falls to the ground around me.

"You know what?" I sneer, wanting to shove her up against the wall behind us and wrap my hand around her throat. "I don't care who gets him anymore, but sure as hell, *I'll make certain it's not you!*"

She laughs coyly, my words not affecting her. "Well big shock, sweetie, you've already fucked that up since Colton's mine for the rest of the night." She smirks, winking at me before turning and walking off. I stand there watching her back as she retreats, and I can't even begin to process my whirlwind of thoughts.

He's been with other women? This whole time he's been trying to win me back, he's been screwing his exes? Teagan's words from the gala come back to me. *What an ass I am.* I actually believed him that he wanted me back. *That he was willing to change for me.*

The Big Bad Wolf definitely has tricked Little Red Riding Hood.

The all too familiar feelings of hurt turned into rage course through me. Before, where I would have run and hidden, right now—right now—I want to unleash my fury on Colton. Unload on him and tell him exactly what I think. And although it's not the right time or place, my feet obviously don't give a flying fuck because before I know it I'm pushing through the entrance into the ballroom.

A woman on a mission.

When I enter, the venue is already full of patrons, seeing as this is one of the hot tickets for this evening. I scan the crowded room to try and catch a glimpse of Colton. It's not hard—my body always seems to know just where he is regardless of location—but the congregation of people at the far corner, bordering on a small mob, confirms the hum that buzzes through my body.

A buzz at this point and time I wish would electrocute itself and die out because I'm done. *I'm so fucking done.*

I stalk across the room, my heart thumping in my chest, noting that cleavage, legs, and form fitting seem to be the dress code of the evening. I hear Colton's laughter erupt from the mob causing me to roll my shoulders and my stomach to churn.

As I approach the gathering of people, I swear the group parts with my approach and opens up to highlight the spectacle before me. Colton stands amidst a crowd of women who willingly seem to adhere to the dress code of *easy*. He is completely relaxed and obviously the unyielding center of attention in this circle. Both of his arms are casually draped over the two women at his sides with one hand holding an empty snifter.

Something about his smile seems off. His eyes aloof. Something missing from his expression. Maybe this is just Colton in full, public persona mode. Or maybe, by the looks of the empty snifters on the table behind him, he's drunk.

I stand from a distance watching the display of estrogen edged with desperation, my rage building, and just when I'm about to walk up and interrupt the little gathering, Colton looks up and his eyes lock onto mine. Some unnamed emotion flickers through them, but it's gone before I can really comprehend it. I take a step forward as a diminutive smile ever so slightly turns up one of the corners of his mouth. And very slowly, very deliberately, Colton leans down to the blonde on his right—his eyes still on mine—and proceeds to kiss her. And I'm not talking a peck on the lips. I'm talking a full-blown kiss.

Green eyes all the while held steadfast on mine.

I think my mouth drops open. I think a feeble squeak even escapes from between my lips. I know that all of the blood rushes from my head and into my veins. "Fucking bastard!" The words fly from my mouth, but they are so low, so grated, that I'm unsure if anyone even hears them.

I turn my back on him and rush from the room. The image burned in my mind of what I just saw. The bimbo's face flickers and changes to Tawny. To Raquel. To the faceless, nameless others that Tawny threw in my face. I blow past a server, not caring that I almost topple his tray in my wake, and push through the closest exit I can find.

The tears that scorch the back of my throat threaten, but the anger firing through me burns them out. I have so much pent up rage—so much hurt—that I don't know what to do. I walk toward one end of the empty room I've found myself in to find no exit.

A bubble of hysteria slips out as the song on the fucking speakers assaults my ears as I try to calm myself and look for a way out other than back through the ballroom. *Slow Dancing in a Burning Room.* Like that song couldn't be any more perfect at this fucking moment.

I press my hands against a table in the hall and try to catch my breath. The replay of his mouth on that skank, so blatantly in my face, makes my stomach turn. What the hell am I doing here? Trying to reconcile? *Who is this woman that I've become?* And I was willing to compromise my own morals for him? I hear the door open behind me. I try to straighten up and dash away the tears from my eyes.

"Rylee..."

I glance back at Colton, so completely done with him. How many times am I going to walk headfirst into heartbreak without learning from my own stupidity? "Go away, Colton! Leave me alone!"

"Rylee, I didn't mean it."

This time I turn around. Colton stands a few feet from me, hands shoved deep in his pockets, shoulders hunched, eyes utterly apologetic. But I'm not falling for it this time. I cross my arms across my chest, a useless protection over my heart. "*Fuck you*! For someone so hung up on me, you sure do move fast, *Ace*! You definitely earned the nickname now!"

His eyes search mine, questioning my comment, but he doesn't ask it once he notices my fists clenching and unclenching in anger.

"It's not what you think, Rylee."

"I'm so sick of hearing you say that! *Not what I think?*" I say, raising my voice. "I just watched you shove your tongue down some bimbo's throat and it's not what I think?" How stupid does he think I am? I start to laugh. Really laugh. Almost in hysterics, the push and pull of emotions from the day almost too much to bear. "Oh wait. You didn't mean to with that skank, but you did with *all of the others of your BBB that you fucked* while trying to win me back? Pretending it was me you wanted? Just tell me one thing, Ace...did you get a good laugh at my expense?"

Colton grabs my upper arm, his fingers digging in to my skin. His grip is so tight that when I try to recoil from his touch, I can't. "What. The. Fuck. Are. You. Talking. About?" he says quietly. "Who—"

"Raquel. Tawny. *Who else, Ace?* Cassie? Did they give you what you needed? Sit on their knees patiently and kiss your feet *like a good girl should?* Take what you give and shut the fuck up otherwise? Did you order the flowers for me in between screwing them?"

Colton's fingers grip harder to the point that I think I'll have bruises tomorrow. His eyes pierce into mine. "Do you mind explaining to me—"

"I don't have to explain anything to you!" I yank my arm from his grasp. "To think I was coming down here to try and fix things between us. To apologize for being stubborn. To tell you I believed you." I shake my head in defeat, and I start to walk away but turn back. Hurt consuming every fiber of my being. "Tell me something...you said they weren't whores, but you pay Tawny a salary right?" I arch my brow and I know by the look on his face that my implication is understood.

"She works for me," he says, releasing one of my arms and shoving his hand through his hair. "I pay her because she does her job. I can't fire her because you don't li—"

"Yes. *You can.*" I scream at him. "And it's not that I don't like her. *I fucking hate her! You fucked her, Colton. Fucked! Her!* I think your choice is pretty fucking obvious. Don't you?"

"*Rylee...*"

"You know what, Colton? You make me sick. I should've trusted my gut instinct when it came to you the first time around. You really are nothing but a whore."

When I stop and wipe the tears from my eyes that I didn't even realize were flowing, Colton still remains standing there, his face stoic and his eyes hard as steel. When he speaks, his voice is low and unforgiving. "Well if I'm going to be accused of it—lose the one girl I choose because of her misperception and absolute obstinance—*then I might as well do it.*"

I stop mid-motion at his words. So sarcastic. So accusatory. I meet his eyes and my breath catches in my throat before closing them and taking a deep breath as his comment sinks in. My world spirals in black, looping with confusion that just became quite clear. It's the first time that he hasn't denied sleeping with her. He didn't confess—I didn't hear the words come from his mouth—but he didn't deny it either. Pain staggers through my chest as I focus on trying to breathe—on trying to think—but he just keeps talking. My fractured heart shatters and splinters into a million pieces.

"This is how I'm used to dealing with pain, Rylee. I'm not proud of it, but I use women to cover up the hurt. I lose myself in them to block everything out." He hangs his head for a second as my mind tries to grasp the shock waves his words create.

He's just told me two things, and I'm not sure which one my scattered mind can focus on. His admission causes his comment from several weeks ago to float into my head. The comment he made in my house the morning after our first time sleeping together. How his 747 of baggage makes him crave the sensory overload of physicality—the stimulating indulgence of skin on skin. *But why?*

And at what point is a convenient explanation just a bullshit excuse for a playboy caught in his own lies? An opportune way for the man who always gets what he wants, to well, get what he wants. I can love the broken in him, but I can't accept the lies any more.

"You told me the other day that we're over. I'll be the first to admit it's fucked up, but I'm coping the only way I know how," he says.

I search his face, looking so far within him that it scares me. I can see the pain in his eyes. Can hear the hesitation and utter shame in his confession. *Is this what I want?* A man who every time we have an argument or every time he gets spooked about our relationship turns to someone else? Runs off to another woman to help lessen the pain? I told him I loved him. I didn't tell him I want to marry him and be the mother of his unwanted children for God's sake.

"So you're telling me that I'm so important to you that if you bag some unmemorable chick, you'll forget me?" I shake my head at him. "That if we're together, every time the going gets tough you'll run off with Tawny or another willing candidate? *Gee, you're really building the foundation of a great relationship here.*" He tries to interrupt me, but I just hold up my hand to stop him. "Colton..." I sigh. "Coming to talk to you tonight was obviously a mistake. The more you talk, the more I'm really starting to realize I don't know you at all."

"You know me better than anyone!" he shouts, taking a step closer as I take one back. "I've never had to explain anything to anyone...I'm not doing a good job at it."

"You can say that again," I snip back at him.

"Let's get out of here and talk."

"Colton?" a seductive female voice calls to him from over my shoulder. Everything in my body tenses at the sound. Colton's face blanches.

"Out!" He grates between gritted teeth at her.

I unclench my jaw and take in a deep breath. "Talking's overrated. Besides, it's obvious you found someone to help you bury the hurt." I nod my head toward the door behind me. "And you know what? I think it's time I try it too." I shrug. "See if finding a guy for the night fixes everything like you seem to think it does."

"No!" The pained look of desperation on his face upsets me, but I'm so far past caring right now. So far past feeling. So numb.

"Why not? What's good for the goose and all that," I say, adding another animal to the imaginary menagerie I'm building as he just stares at me. One last look. "Enjoy your cocktail party, Ace."

Chapter Thirty-Seven

I wander aimlessly around the resort for what feels like an eternity. I watch the sun sink into the horizon, snuffing out the light of the day like the emotions darkened in my heart. Sadness overwhelms me but it's nothing new since I've been there the past few weeks anyway. I think it's worse because I allowed myself to believe that when I went to Colton, he'd accept why I was upset and that would be it. I never thought he'd play the idiotic game he did to purposely try and hurt me further.

I replay his admission to me over and over in my mind. His acknowledgement that he uses women to bury his hurt. On one hand I understand him a bit better now, but on the other it tells me that I really know nothing of his past—of the things that make him who he is.

But he's so in denial—or maybe so used to getting away with things—that he doesn't even realize the excuses he's giving for his actions are inexcusable.

As I take a seat on a bench in one of the many gardens of the hotel, my phone rings. I look down, debating on answering it, but know that this might be the one person that might help me get my head on straight.

"Hey, Had," I say, trying to muster up as much normalcy as possible.

"What happened?" Her insistent tone rings through the phone line loud and clear. I guess I failed at fooling her.

The tears come. They don't stop. When they eventually subside, I relay the events of the evening. Haddie speaks. "That's the biggest bunch of bullshit I've ever heard."

What? "Come again?"

"Well first of all, Tawny. She's just a jealous bitch trying to get to you and she succeeded!"

"Whatever..." I blow my nose, completely dismissing Haddie's remark.

"Seriously, Ry...that's like *Bitch 101*. If you can't have the guy, make the girl the guy wants doubt him so that you can have him." She sighs loudly. "I'm not proud to say it, but I've done the exact same thing before."

"Seriously?" My mind starts to comprehend what she's saying.

"Rylee...for a smart girl sometimes you're really dumb."

"Way to add insult to injury, Had."

"Sorry, but it's true. You're so wrapped up in your own head right now that you're not seeing it from the outside. If Colton wanted to fuck around, then why would he pursue you relentlessly? The guy's got it bad for you, Ry. Tawny's just one of those devious bitches that's going to get her due sometime. I hope Karma kicks that bitch's ass sooner than later."

I start to hear what Haddie is saying. When the hell did dating become so complicated? *When the someone you're dating is so incredibly worth the fight.*

"I hear what you're saying, Haddie, but what about tonight then? The kiss. The...he cheated on me." I breathe the last part out.

"*Did he though?*" she says, and it lingers on the line between us.

"Fucking Christ, Haddie! You're not helping me here." I squeeze my eyes shut and pinch the bridge of my nose.

"I'm not in your shoes, Ry. I can't tell you what to do—what to feel—all I can tell you is to use your gut instinct." She sighs. "Women are vicious bitches and men are confusing bastards—you just have to figure out which of the two you trust the most."

"Fuck!" I groan, feeling less resolved than when our conversation began.

"Love ya, Ry."

"Love ya, Had."

I hang the phone up and walk some more along the edge of the golf course thinking about Haddie's comments and lack of advice. I wander around the grounds of the resort, attempting to stop my mind from thinking, but I'm unsuccessful. I walk past one of the hotel cocktail lounges and uncharacteristically find myself turning into it and taking a seat at the bar. The lounge is not overtly busy, but it's not quiet by any means either. Both the bar and the various tables are peppered with patrons, some alone and others coupled here and there.

It's not until I take a seat that I realize how much the arches of my feet ache from my heels and my aimless wandering. I look up at the clock on the wall and am astounded to see that over two hours have passed.

I lean into the back of the chair and shake my head at the day's chain of events that have hit me like a head-on collision. I order a drink and take a long sip on the straw as my attention turns to the television in the corner to the right of me. Of course the channel is on something or other pertaining to the race tomorrow—the whole city has been transformed for the road track—so I can understand why the television is tuned to it. Unfortunately for me, the panel of men on the program discuss one Colton Donavan and review his highlights from last year. Images of the number thirteen car at various venues flash on the screen. I swear I can't escape the man no matter where I go.

Without thinking, I lean forward as I hear the announcers mention Colton's name. "Well, Leigh, Donavan seems to be lighting up the track this week," one announcer says. "He's been like a man on a mission the way he's barely letting up in the turns in his practice runs."

"He's obviously worked on his skills in the off season because it's definitely showing. I'm just wondering if he's running a little too hard. Going in with a game plan that's a little too aggressive for the race tomorrow," the other announcer observes. "Maybe taking too many risks. He's definitely driving like a man scorned for sure though." The other announcer laughs, and I just roll my eyes at the comment.

"If he runs laps tomorrow like he did today, he's set to break a course record."

The screen flashes to the media headshot of Colton and then flashes back to the highlights. Ludacris' *The Rest of My Life* plays as the background music during the spotlight of Colton's testing runs, and I shake my head for I couldn't think of a more fitting song.

I sigh heavily and take another draw on my straw, averting my eyes that are drawn to the sight of his face on television.

"Rough day?"

I turn to face the masculine voice that has spoken to my left. I'm in no mood for company really, but when I see the set of chocolate brown eyes filled with compassion framed by a rather handsome face, I know that I can't be rude. "Something like that," I murmur with a slight smile before turning back to my drink, just wanting to be left alone. My nervous hands start to shred tiny pieces of my napkin apart. "Another please?" I motion to the bartender as she walks past.

"Let me get it," the man beside me says.

I look over at him again. "That's really not necessary."

"Please, I insist," he tells the bartender, sliding his card across the counter to start a tab, which makes me a bit uncomfortable seeing as I don't plan on being here long enough to have a tab.

I stare at him again. My eyes take in his clean-cut appearance and attire but are drawn back to his eyes. All I see is kindness. "Thanks." I shrug.

"Parker," he says, holding his hand out.

"Rylee," I reply, shaking his hand.

"You here for work or pleasure?"

I laugh softly. "Work. You?"

"A little of both actually. Looking forward to the race tomorrow."

"Hmpf," is all I manage as I focus back on shredding my napkin. I realize I'm being rude, but I'm really not in the mood to make polite conversation with someone that possibly wants more than just a drink and quick chat at the bar. "I'm sorry," I apologize, "I'm not much company right now."

"It's okay," he says wistfully. "Whoever he is…he's a lucky man."

I look over at him. "That obvious, huh?"

"Been there, done that before." He chuckles as he takes a long sip of his beer. "All I'll say is the man must be an idiot if he's willing to let you walk away without a fight."

"Thanks," I resign, a flash of a smile lighting up my face for the first time since I've met him.

"Wow! There's a smile," he teases, "and a beautiful one at that!"

My cheeks flush as I avert my eyes and take a drink of liquid courage. We talk idly about nothing in particular for a while as the lounge slowly fills up and the night progresses. At one point Parker scoots his stool closer to mine as we're having trouble hearing each other over the increased noise. He's easy to talk to, and I know that if we were in another place and another time, I'd enjoy his casual attempts at flirting with me, but my heart's just not in it so his harmless attempts remain unreciprocated.

I've had a couple of drinks, and a slow hum is buzzing through my system—not enough to stifle the hurt from the day but just enough to allow me to forget for sporadic moments of time. My attention is drawn to loud laughter outside the open entrance to the lounge, and when I look up, I stifle a gasp as my eyes meet Colton's. We stare for a beat, and then I see his eyes narrow in on Parker and the angle of his body leaning in to hear me over the noise.

I hear Beckett and Sammy shouting in the background over the noise, and I pull myself away from Parker when I hear Colton growl. I search through the shifting crowd and see Beckett in front of Colton, hands pressed against his chest as Sammy stands behind him, restraining him by the shoulders. Colton is not looking at them at all. His eyes are boring holes into mine as he works his jaw back and forth on gritted teeth, muscles straining in his neck.

I look back at Parker, who has heard the distraction in the hallway but can't see anything with his line of sight. He looks to me and shakes his head. "Let me guess," he says with a resigned laugh. "He's come back to fight for you?"

"Something like that," I murmur.

I hear more shouting as I look back toward the door and the rest of the patrons have taken note of the chaos ensuing. The noise level has hushed some as all of the onlookers stare and I hear Beckett shout, "No! You've got other priorities, Wood!" before I see Colton break free from his grip and stalk through the crowd that parts for him without hesitation.

Parker has since taken note of the scuffle in the hallway, and when he sees who is bearing down on us, I hear him suck in a breath. "That's the guy?" he says incredulously, with a mixture of fear and astonishment filtering through his voice simultaneously. "Colton fuckin' Donavan? *Christ, I'm dead*!" He groans.

I stand up from the stool and step in front of him. "Don't worry. I can handle him," I tell him confidently, but when I catch a glimpse of the unadulterated rage reflected in Colton's eyes, I question if I can.

And I'm sure it's the numerous cocktails under my belt and buzzing through my system, but the thought sends an unexpected thrill through me regardless of the events of the past couple of days. Something on his face besides his anger pulls at parts deep within me. It's that look in his eye. The one that says he's had enough. That says he's going to waltz into this room, pick me up, throw me over his shoulder, and take me somewhere to have his way with me. In those few seconds before he reaches me—as I watch the muscles bunch beneath the fitted fabric of his shirt—every part of me below the waist coils with desire. I am so not into the cave man thing, but damn if the man doesn't make a woman want like no other.

And then when he stops in front of me, those cold, calculating, emerald green eyes visually pin me motionless, and my mind regains control of my traitorous body, pushing my libido to the wayside. "What the fuck are you trying to pull, Rylee?" he growls, low but it resonates above the chatter of the bar.

I hear Parker shift restlessly behind me. Without looking, I reach my hand back and pat his knee to tell him I've got this. "What business is it of yours?" I respond flippantly, the alcohol allowing me to reflect the courage that I really don't feel.

I'm ready for his hand as it reaches to grab my arm, so I yank it out of his reach before he can grasp it. We stare at each other, both seething for the same reasons. I see Beckett approach us with trepidation in his eyes and Sammy not far behind him.

"I don't like games, Rylee. I won't tell you that again."

"You don't like games?" I laugh with disgust. "But it's okay for you to play them?"

He leans in, his face inches from me, his alcohol laced breath feathering over my face and mingling with mine. "Why don't you tell your little boy toy he can run along now before things get even more interesting?"

Knowing that we have both been drinking and should stop this little charade before we can't turn back should make me walk away—but rational exited the building a long time ago, leaving crazy and scorned to reign. I shove against his chest as hard as I can to get him out of my face, but he just grips my hands and pulls me with the momentum that I've caused. "*You. Arrogant. Conceited. Egomaniac*!" I shout brokenly at him, unconsciously giving him the meaning behind his nickname, but I know he doesn't catch it. I fall against him and the action draws even more stares from the crowd around us. Our chests rise and fall with our angry, harsh breaths as we both clench our jaws in frustration.

"What the fuck are you trying to prove?" he grits out.

"I'm just testing your theory," I lie.

"My theory?"

"Yeah." I scoff. "If losing yourself in someone helps get rid of the pain."

"How's that working for you?" He smirks.

"Not sure." I shrug nonchalantly at him before I reach back and tug on Parker's hand. I know I shouldn't involve him any further. It's extremely selfish of me to use him in this, but Colton makes me bat-shit crazy sometimes. "I'll let you know in the morning." I raise my eyebrows at him as I take a step past him.

"Don't you walk away from me, Rylee!"

"You lost the right to tell me what to do the minute you slept with *her*." I sneer at him. "Besides, you said you like my ass…enjoy the view as I walk away because that's the last you'll be seeing of it."

Within moments, so many things happen that I feel like time stands still. Colton lunges at Parker, pulling him so our hands disconnect. In that split second I hate myself for involving Parker in our bedlam, and when I look at him I try to convey that thought with my eyes alone, I see Colton's arm cock back to throw a punch. Before it surges forward, Sammy has his arms around Colton, preventing him. I start yelling at Colton, throwing everything but the kitchen sink into my accusations. I feel an arm close around my shoulder, and I buck it off but to no avail. I turn my head to see it's attached to Beckett. He shoots me a warning glance as he forcefully leads me out of the bar.

Chapter Thirty-Eight

By the time we reach the elevator, the burst of adrenaline has subsided, burning off the remaining alcohol in my system. My entire body starts to shake. The emotion of what just transpired overwhelms me. Makes me realize the crazy-ass woman I just became in a public place that I in no way recognize. Of how I involved an innocent guy who didn't deserve the wrath of Colton bearing down on him for no reason. I feel like I've just stepped out of a scene from Bravo's Real Housewives, and I was the star attraction.

My knees give way as everything—having Colton, not having Colton, wanting Colton—becomes too much.

"No you don't," Beckett says as he tightens his grip around my waist before I slide to the floor. I take his lead as he nudges me out of the elevator and toward my room. My insides are numb with hurt and bewilderment. I glance up at him as he just shakes his head at me and murmurs so quietly that I think he's talking to himself. "Jesus Christ, woman, are you purposely trying to push every single one of Colton's buttons? Because if so, you are damn well succeeding!"

He holds his hand out when we reach my room, and I fumble in my purse for my keycard and hand it to him. He unlocks it and pushes open the door for me, pressing a hand to my lower back to usher me in.

I walk immediately over to my suitcase start yanking dresses off of hangers and shoving them and anything else I can find into the suitcase, hysterical tears spitting out every chance they can.

"Uh-uh. No way! Don't you dare, Rylee!" Beckett shouts from behind me as he sees what I'm doing. I just ignore him, throwing, shoving, stuffing. Beckett's protests continue, and I yelp out as I feel his arms circle around me from behind me, holding my arms down, trying to tame my hysterics.

He just holds me awkwardly, hushing me like a tantruming child who needs soothing. He embraces me as I break down and succumb to the tears and the heartbreak of the day. And to what will never be.

"I thought you guys were trying to figure this out. *Could figure this out*. You're both miserable fucks apart."

"And we're miserable when we're together as well," I whisper. Tears he can't see fill my eyes again, and I just shake my head at him. "He needs to concentrate, Becks. I'm…this…is a distraction he doesn't need right now."

"That's a fucking brilliant statement if I've ever heard one…*but what does that mean, Rylee?*"

I wipe a fallen tear off my cheek with the back of my hand. "I don't know…I feel like I don't know anything anymore…I just need some space from him to be able to think and figure it out."

"So what? You're going to pack up and leave without him knowing? Sneak out?" He breathes out as he paces the room in front of me. "Because that's just so much better, right?"

"Beckett…I can't…" I mumble, "I just can't…" I grab the handle of my suitcase and start to pick it up.

Beckett yanks it out of my hand, stepping around me to grab both of my shoulders and gives them a hard shake. "Don't you dare, Rylee. Don't you fucking dare!" he shouts at me, anger now firing in his veins. "You want to leave him?"

"Becks…"

"Don't you *Becks* me. On any other day I'd tell you that you're just as big of a fucking coward as he is…that both of you are so goddamned stubborn you'd rather cut off your noses to spite your faces. You didn't work your shit out? I get it. I really do. It happens." He sighs loudly, releasing me and walking a few feet from me before turning around and getting back in my face. "But by you walking out, Rylee, you're fucking with my team—my driver—this race—*my best friend*. So suck it up and pretend for me. At least pretend until the race starts. That's all I ask. You owe me that much, Rylee." When he speaks again, he's eerily calm and full of spite. "Because if you can't do this for me, so help me God, Rylee, if something happens to him…it's on you!"

I swallow loudly, my lips falling lax as I look at Beckett, a one-man army on a mission. "Look, Ry, I know it's easier for you to do it this way…to leave this way…but if you love him—if you ever loved him? You'll do this for me. If you leave, it's too dangerous…I can't have Colton flying close to two hundred miles an hour tomorrow with his head focused in la-la land thinking about you instead of being focused on the goddamn track." He grabs my suitcase and sets it back down.

All I can do is look at him through blurred eyes and with a hurting heart. He's so right on every level, and yet I don't know if I can find it within me to pretend. To act like I'm unaffected when the sight of Colton causes my breath to hitch and heart to twist. When we continually tear each other apart and purposely hurt one another. I cry out a strangled sound, hating the woman that I've become in the last few days. Hating Colton. Just wishing that I could be numb again even though it felt so damn good to feel again. But if I can't have him—have my beautifully damaged man—then I'd rather be numb than live in this endless abyss of pain.

Beckett sees the hysteria surfacing—sees the moment that I realize how much I actually love Colton and the devastation I foresee on the horizon—and mutters, "Motherfucker!" in exasperation at being the one left to tend to my irrationality before calmly walking me over to the bed and pushing my shoulders down. "Sit!" he orders.

He squats down in front of me, the motion much like a parent does to a child, and it makes me realize what a good guy Beckett really is. He reaches out and puts his hands on my knees, looking me squarely in the eye.

"He fucked things up, right?" All I can do is nod my head, my throat clogged with emotion. "You love him still, correct?"

I tense at the question. The answer comes so willingly into my mind that I know even though I love him—that loving him will most likely bring me a truckload of continual hurt—it's just not enough. "Beckett…I can't keep doing this to myself." I lower my head, shaking it as my breath hitches again.

"Remember when I told you that Colton was going to push you away to prove a point?" I nod my head, listening to him but really just wanting to be by myself, wanting to take my suitcase with items sticking out of it at all angles and make a mad dash to the airport—back to structure and predictability and a life without Colton.

And that thought alone robs me of every emotion possible.

Beckett squeezes my knees to get me to focus back on him. "*Right now is that time, Rylee*. You need to push away everything in your head. Clear all of the assumptions out and think with your heart. Just your heart, okay?"

"I can't do it anymore, Becks—"

"Just listen to me, Ry. If you really love him, then keep knocking on that fucking steel gate he has around his heart. If he's really worth it to you, you'll keep at it." He shakes his head at me. "The damn thing's got to give sometime, and you're the only one I think is capable of doing it." When I just stare at him with my mouth lax, he just shakes his head at me. "I told you, you're his lifeline."

I just stare at him, unable to speak, trying to digest his words. Am I his lifeline? Can I possibly be his lifeline? I feel more like a weight dragging us toward the bottom of the ocean than a lifeline. And why does Beckett keep telling me to clear all assumptions?

"That can't be. Love doesn't fix—"

I'm startled from my thoughts from a knock on the door. I start to stand but Beckett just pushes back down on my shoulder and goes to answer it. When he opens it, I see Sammy shove Colton through the door before Beckett slams it shut.

Despite everything Beckett said, just the sight of Colton ignites my temper. I'm off the bed in a flash the minute he stalks into my room. "Uh-uh! No way! Get that egotistical asshole out of here!" I shout at Beckett.

"Fuckin' A, Becks! What the fuck is this?" he yells, confusion in his voice. He glances down at the haphazard packed suitcase and grunts. "Thank Christ! *Don't let the door hit you in the ass, sweetheart*!"

I step toward him, fueled with fury and ready to detonate.

"This is over here and now!" Beckett's voice booms at us like a parent scolding his children. We both stop mid-motion as Beckett turns toward us, exasperation on his face and obstinance in his stance. "I don't care if I have to lock you in this fucking room together, but you two are going to figure you're shit out or you're not leaving. Is that understood?"

Colton and I both start yelling at him at the same time, and Beckett's voice thunders over ours. "Is that understood?"

"No way, Becks! I'm not staying in this room another second with this asshole!"

"Asshole?" Colton whirls on me, his body mere inches from mine.

"Yeah! Asshole!" I sneer.

"You want to talk about assholes? Try that stunt you pulled with bar boy back there. I believe you claimed the title right then, sweetheart."

"*Bar boy?* Wow, because having a harmless drink is so much worse than you with your gaggle of whores earlier, right?" I shove at his chest, the physicality of the action giving me a small iota of the release that I need.

Colton steps back from me and walks to the far side of the room and back, blowing out a puff of air from his lungs. My room feels small with Colton eating up the space, and I just want him gone.

He looks over to Beckett and shoves his hands through his inky hair. "She's driving me fucking crazy!" Colton yells at Beckett.

"You'd know all about the *fucking part* seeing as you fucking Tawny is what started this whole thing in the first place," I scream back at him.

Since Colton is standing beside Beckett, it's hard not to notice the completely dumbfounded look on his face. "What?" Beckett stutters.

"What? He didn't tell you?" I grind out looking at Beckett, my fists clenched as images flash through my head. "I told the asshole that I loved him. He bailed as fast as he could. When I showed up at the Palisades house a couple days later, Tawny opened the door. In his T-shirt. Only his T-shirt." I focus completely on Beckett because I can't bring myself to look at Colton right now. "Colton didn't have much more on than that either. Told me nothing happened. But that's a little hard to believe with his notorious reputation. Oh and the condom wrapper in his pocket."

I finish my little rant, for some reason wanting to show Beckett what an ass his friend is, as if he didn't know it already. Trying to explain to him why I have a case of the crazies right now. But when I stop, the look I expect to see is not there. In its place is utter confusion, and when he turns to look at Colton, it morphs into incredulity. "Are you fucking kidding me here?"

Now I'm confused. "*What?*"

Colton growls. "Leave it, Becks."

"What the fuck, man?"

"I'm warning you, Beckett. Stay out of this!" Colton steps chest to chest with Beckett.

"When you start jeopardizing my team and the race tomorrow, then it becomes my business…" he shakes his head at him. "Tell her!" he bellows.

"Tell me what?" I shout at the both of them and their damn man code.

"Beckett, she's like talking to a goddamn brick wall. What good will it do?"

Colton's words hit my ears but don't really seep in. I'm so focused on Beckett's reaction that I don't hear them.

"She's right. You're an ass!" Beckett snickers with disbelief. "You won't tell her? Fine! Then I will!"

In a heartbeat Colton has Beckett pressed against the wall, his hands pressing against his chest, his clenched jaw inches from his. I suck in a breath at the sound of Beckett's back hitting the wall, but I notice that he has no reaction otherwise to Colton's temper. "I said leave it, Becks!"

They stare at each other for a few moments, testosterone oozing between them in two entirely different ways: Colton's with force and Beckett's with a simple look. Finally Beckett raises his hands and shoves back against Colton's chest. "Then fucking fix this, Colton! Fix! It!" he shouts, pointing at him before yanking the hotel room door open and slamming it behind him.

Colton expels a litany of curses as he paces back and forth the length of the room with his hands clenched and his temper flaring.

"What was that all about?" Colton ignores my comment and continues to wear a path in the carpet in front of me, refusing to meet my eyes. "Damn it, Colton!" I stand in his path. "What don't you want me to know?"

The eerie calm in my voice stops him momentarily, his head down, jaw clenched. When he lifts his head to look into my eyes, I can't get a read on what underlies the anger I see boiling over on the surface. "You really want to know?" he shouts at me. "You really want to know?"

I step up to him, confronting him, standing on my toes to try and stretch my height to be eye level with him. "Tell me." Fear snakes up my spine at what I might hear. "Are you that goddamn chicken shit you can't fess up and just admit it? I need to hear it come out of your mouth so that I can get the fuck over you and get on with my life!"

He angles his head down and looks unflinchingly into my eyes, green to violet. My chest hurts so bad breathing feels impossible as time stretches.

His voice is quiet steel when he speaks. "*I fucked Tawny.*" His words float out into the space between us but stab sharply into my heart.

"You coward!" I scream, pushing against him. "You goddamn fucking coward!"

"Coward?" he bellows. "Coward? What about you? You're so fucking stubborn that you've had the truth staring you in the face for three fucking weeks. You're up there so high and mighty on your goddamn horse you think you know everything! Well you don't, Rylee! *You don't know shit!*"

His words that mean to hurt and push me away just fuel my temper even more, egging me on. "I don't know shit? Really, Ace? *Really?*" I step closer to him. "Well how's this? I know a bastard when I see one," I seethe.

We stare at each other, both so willing to hurt the other that we neglect to see that we're both tearing the other apart for the same reason. "*Been called worse by better, sweetheart.*" He smirks, taking another step toward me, the smarmy look on his face setting me off.

Before I can think, my hand flashes out in front of me to connect with his cheek. But Colton's quicker. His hand jerks up and grabs my wrist mid-flight, our chests bumping against each other from our momentum. My wrist is locked in his hand and when I start to struggle away from him, he takes his other hand and grabs hold of my free arm that's flailing. I'm frustrated and struggling against him, and I hate him so much right now that my chest hurts. His face is inches from mine, and I can hear his exertion in the breath that pants against my face.

"If you were done with me...had your fill of me? You could have just told me!"

He looks at me, face strained as he holds my arms from pummeling him. "I'll never have my fill of you." And then before I can even process what he's doing, Colton's mouth crashes against mine. It takes me a moment to react, and I'm so angry—so furious with him—that I buck against his hold and tear my mouth from his.

From the taste I crave but the man I hate.

"You want rough, Rylee?" he asks, my head not comprehending his words but my body reacting instantly. "I'll give you rough!"

And from one beat to the next, Colton's mouth crushes down on mine and takes every sensation in my body hostage for his sole manipulation. His hands still grip mine as I struggle to refuse his kiss, trying to push him off and away from me. Regardless of how much I thrash my head, his lips remain on mine, tiny grunts of satisfaction coming from deep within his throat.

I try desperately to deny the desire that starts to seep through the anger-induced haze in my brain. I try to reject the ache deepening at the apex of my thighs from the taste of his tongue melding with mine. I attempt to fight the pebbling of my nipples at the firmness of his chest as he brushes against mine.

Rage turns into desire. Hurt expels into yearning. Absence fuels our fervor. His touch blocks out all rationality. A soft moan catches in my throat as his mouth continues to tempt and torment every spot of my lips and within.

At some point Colton realizes that I'm struggling against him not to get away but rather to touch him. He releases my wrists and my hands go immediately to his chest where they fist into his shirt, aggressively pulling him into me. His hands, now free, are on the move, mapping the lines of my curves over and over again as our mouths convey the unbridled desire we still have for one another.

Every action and reaction reflects urgency. Necessity. Hunger. Longing. Desperation as if we're afraid that at any minute we're going to be pulled away from one another to never experience this again.

Colton brings a hand to cup the rounded curve of my butt as he jerks me into him while the other holds my neck still. I don't even realize that the moan in the room is from me when the hard length of his arousal rubs against the V of my thighs as he pushes us backwards to the dresser behind me. He lifts me up and settles my backside on the top of it, pushing my dress up my thighs as he steps between my legs, all the while continuing his mind-numbing dexterity to my lips and tongue.

I lock my legs around his hips, pulling him farther into me. I know this is wrong. I know that after what he just told me, I shouldn't be here doing this with him. *But I am so sick of thinking.* So sick of wanting him when I know we don't belong together. Our two completely different worlds just don't mesh. But I am so tired of missing him. So tired of wanting to hear his voice when I pick up the phone. So tired of needing him.

So tired of loving him without being loved in return.

I need this connection with him. I need the silence in my head that the all-encompassing feeling of him against my skin brings to me. There is a peace in the physicality of it all that I never realized before. A peace that I know Colton has used over and over in his life to numb his pain.

And right now, I need to numb mine.

I know it's temporary, but I turn myself over to him. To the feel and taste and sound and smell of him. My troubling, all-consuming addiction. I willingly let myself get lost in him to forget for just a moment the pain I know I'll feel when we're no longer one.

I grip the waist of his shirt and pull it up over his head; our lips break for the first time since we've reconnected with each other. Immediately after the material is gone, we crash back together again. He tugs the straps of my dress off of my shoulders as his mouth laces open mouth kisses down the line of my neck and to the lacy edge of my bra. I cry out in shock and need as he yanks down one of my bra cups and closes his mouth over my nipple. I throw my head back at the sensation while one of my hands fists in the hair at the back of his neck. The burn in my core turns into a raging inferno directing my free hand to fumble with his belt and undo his pants.

I successfully unzip them, shoving my hands between the cotton of his briefs and his heated skin. I grab his rock hard erection in my hands, and he groans at the feeling of my skin on his flesh. His hands are instantly on my thighs, shoving my dress up higher and yanking my dampened thong to the side. He slides a finger along my seam, and I buck my hips at the feeling of his fingertips on me again. I press my hips into his hands, greedy and unashamed to lose myself in the pleasure. I cry out as he slips a finger into my core and then spreads my wetness around.

Before I can open my eyes and notice the absence of his fingers, he enters me in one fervent thrust. We both cry out as he stills and seats himself as far as possible within my wet heat. My walls clench around him as I adjust to the over-fullness of him within me. The muscles in Colton's shoulders strain beneath my hands as he tries to hold onto his control. I feel it slipping—know that he's a man about to snap—so I take the reins and start to move against him, moving my hips to tell him to go. Urging him to lose his control. To be rough with me. I don't need foreplay right now. All I need is him. I've craved this for the past couple of weeks, and he feels so damn good right now I don't need anything else to push me over the edge.

Colton grips his fingers, bruising the flesh at my hips, and holds me still on the edge of the dresser as he pistons his hips into mine. Over and over. Drive after delicious drive.

"God, Rylee!" He moves relentlessly within the confines of my thighs. He brings his mouth down and devours mine again, his tongue mimicking the actions below. And from one kiss to the next he pulls me into him, cupping my ass so we remain connected as he lifts me up and turns me around so we fall onto the bed behind us.

His mouth claims mine as he finds his rhythm again. I can feel the pressure building—can feel the conflicted bliss just within my reach—and grab the back of Colton's neck and hold his mouth to mine as I drink him in. "You. Feel. Incredible," he murmurs against my lips.

I can't speak. Don't trust myself to. Don't know who I am right now. So instead I just I arch my back into him so I can change the angle of my hips allowing him to hit that nerve-laden spot deep within, over and over.

Colton knows my body so well already—knows what I need to bring me to climax—that he takes the hint of the subtle repositioning. He rears back onto his knees, grabs my legs, pushes them back, and places my feet flat against his chest. The angle allows him to surge even deeper, and I can't hold back the moan of utter rapture as he bottoms out inside of me before pulling back out slowly and driving back in.

I look up at him, a sheen of sweat on his face and shoulders with my pink painted toenails bright against his tanned torso, and I meet his eyes. I hold his stare as long as I can until it's too much for me to bear; it's the first time since we've met that there is nothing guarding the emotion flickering through his eyes. It's too much for me to comprehend—too much for me to think about when all I want to do is lose myself in this moment and block out everything else. To lose all train of thought.

I throw my head back, my eyes closed and hands gripping the sheets beneath me as the sensations threaten to overtake me. Colton must sense my impending release from my rapid breathing and the tightening of my thighs.

"Hold on, Ry." He pants. "Hold on, baby." He plunges into me, picking up his pace until I can no longer hold it back.

"Oh God!" I cry out as my body fractures into a million pieces of mindless pleasure. Release surging though me and consuming my every breath, thought, and reaction. The continual pulsing of my orgasm milks Colton to his climax. He cries out my name brokenly and throws his head back, welcoming his own release and jerking harshly within me. When he comes back to himself, I am still catching my breath and my thoughts with my eyes closed and my head angled back. I feel him remove my feet from his chest, and without breaking our connection, flanks his body over mine, resting his weight on his elbows propped on either side of me. He brings his hands to the side of my face and cups it, running his thumbs gently over the skin on my cheeks.

I can feel his breath feathering over my lips—know that his eyes are staring at me—but I can't bring myself to open mine yet. I need to get a hold on my emotions before I open my eyes because no matter how wonderful that just was, it doesn't fix anything. It doesn't take away the fact that he ran away when I told him I loved him. It doesn't erase that he slept with Tawny to bury the very idea that someone might actually want more than just an arrangement with him. All it solidifies is that we can have incredible, mind-numbing sex.

And numb—right now—is how I feel.

I can feel the weight of Colton's stare, but I can't bring myself to open my eyes because I know the tears will fall. He sighs softly and I know he's trying to understand me and what's going on in my mind. He leans his head down and rests his forehead on mine, his thumbs still caressing the line of my jaw softly. "God, I missed you, Rylee," he murmurs softly against my lips.

It's harder to hear those words from his lips than it is to accept that we just had sex. The vulnerability in the way he says them with his rasp of a voice tugs at my heart and twists in my soul. I think maybe the idea that he's had sex with numerous people but most likely never murmured those words to anyone before is what gets to me.

"Talk to me, Ry." He breathes into me. "Baby, please talk to me," he pleads.

It's now that a tear slips out of the corner of my eye and slides down my cheek. I just keep my eyes shut and shake my head subtly, emotions warring violently inside of me. Our connection is enough to fix things for him. Not for me. *How can I ever trust him?* How can I ever trust me? This girl who sleeps with someone after they cheat on her—that's not me. How can I live and love him knowing I have to constantly walk on eggshells because I fear that if I say anything to spook him, I'll drive him into the arms of someone else?

For him, this is a reconciliation. For me, it's a last memory. My final goodbye.

I hate myself terribly. Hate that I used him to try and soothe the pain that I know is going to own my heart and soul in the weeks and months to come. I hate that just as he seems to be needing me, I can't bring myself to need him anymore. I can't lose the *me* that I've just found—that ironically he's just helped me find. Look what he's doing to me. To the person I'm becoming. I'm a fucking neurotic lunatic around him. And yes—*God yes, I love him*—but love's definitely not worth it if it's one sided and this is the return I get.

He pulls back and kisses the tip of my nose, my chin trembling as I hold my realization in. "Tell me what's going on in your head, Ry?" he urges as he laces tender kisses along the track of my lone tear and then up to both of my closed eyes before back to my lips. Such tenderness from a man that swears he can't feel has me fighting the opening of the floodgates. And even though he hasn't withdrawn from me, I sense that he feels like he's losing our connection for as his lips brush mine again, he presses his tongue to part between them. He licks slowly into my mouth, his tongue dancing tenderly with mine, expressing his desire for me with a subtle, gentle desperation.

I respond to him and his unspoken request, needing this connection to hold on to everything I feel for him even though I know it's just not enough anymore. Unreciprocated love never is. Eventually Colton ends the kiss and sighs when he pulls back and I keep my eyes closed.

"Give me one sec," he says to me. I wince as he slips out of me, *one now becoming two*, and I feel the bed dip as he pushes himself up off of it. I hear the water running in the bathroom. I hear his footsteps come across the bedroom and am startled as he takes a warm washcloth and cleans me ever so gently before padding back into the bathroom. "Baby, I desperately need a shower. Give me a minute and then we need to talk, okay? *We have to talk.*" He brushes another kiss to my forehead, and I feel the bed dip again as he rises from it. I hear the shower start and hear the stall click closed.

I lie there in silence, my head humming with so many thoughts it's starting to hurt. Do I love this man so magnificent, yet so damaged? Without a doubt…but where I used to think love conquers all, I'm not sure of that any more. He may care for me in his own way, but is that enough for me? Is always wondering when the other shoe is going to drop what I want in my relationship?

I've spent the past two years numb to emotion—fearing what it would be like to feel again—and now that I found Colton, and he's made me do just that, I don't think I can go back to how I was before. Merely existing, not living. Can I really be with Colton and hold back everything inside of me bursting to finally get out? I don't think I want to revisit that life of void. I don't think I can. I'm just not sure if he'll ever be able to accept my love. I squeeze my eyes shut and try to tell myself that we can overcome all of this. That I can be strong enough and patient enough and forgiving enough to wait him out while he tackles his demons and accepts the love that I've offered. But what if he never does?

Look at the two of us tonight. We purposely hurt each other. We purposely used other people to get back at the other. Tried to tear each other apart. That's not healthy. You don't do that to someone you love or care about. My mom's words flicker through my mind. About how someone always treats you the best in the beginning of a relationship, and if it's not good in the beginning, then it's not going to get any better. If the past twenty-four hours is any indication, then we definitely aren't going to make it.

We are passionate, fiery, unyielding, and intense when we're together. In the bedroom, that leads to immeasurable chemistry; in the relationship arena, that leads to disaster. And as heavenly as it would be to contain Colton to the bedroom so he could have his way with me over and over, that's just not realistic.

The tears come now and I don't have to hide them anymore. They rack my body and tear through my throat. I cry and cry until I have no more tears for the man just within my grasp yet so incredibly far away. I close my eyes momentarily and steel myself for what I'm about to do. In the long run, it's for the best.

And I move without thinking. Use the numbness to guide me before I can't bring myself to do this. Colton's right. He's broken. *And now I'm broken.* Two halves don't always make a whole.

I fucked him—yes, it was most definitely fucking because there was nothing soft or gentle or meaningful about it—especially after he admitted to me that he fucked someone else. *Tawny of all people.* That's not acceptable to me. Ever. But when I'm near him—when he dominates the air I breathe—I compromise on things I never would otherwise. And that's not a way to exist. Compromising everything of yourself when the other person compromises nothing.

I catch the sob in my throat as I have trouble pulling my clothes on. My hands are trembling so badly I can barely slip my clothes to their proper position. I steal a glance in the mirror and it stops me in my tracks. Pure and utter heartbreak is reflected looking back at me. I force my eyes to look away and grab my suitcase as I hear Colton drop something in the shower.

I wipe the tears that start to fall in their familiar tracks down my cheeks. "Bye, Ace. I love you," I whisper the words to him that I can't say to his face. That he'll never accept. "I think I've always loved you. And I know I always will." I open the door as quietly as possible and slip out of the hotel room, luggage in hand. It takes me a moment to physically release the door handle because I know once I lose the connection, it's over. And as sure as I am about this decision, I'm still shattering into a million pieces.

I take a deep breath and let go, grab my luggage, and start to make my way toward the bank of elevators, tears flowing freely.

Chapter Thirty-Eight

Colton—Raced

"I told you, Becks, I'm sick of her shit. I'm not buying the *I'm innocent* act she pulled in the team meeting." I glance over to him as we walk down the hallway, enough alcohol humming through my veins for me to speak my mind.

Then again, I don't need alcohol to do that.

"What the fuck did Tawny do now?"

"I don't know, man, but she's being squirrely and fuck if I can figure out what she's up to."

Sammy snorts behind me and I turn to look at him, figure what the hell he means by it, but he just looks right past me like it's not his place to say anything. Ha. Like he's held back before.

Becks catches my eye with his raised brows as we turn a corner because I'm heading in the opposite direction of our wing of rooms for the team. "You can deal with it when we get back home. I need your head focused on the race."

"No shit, Sherlock." I shake my head, eyes scanning over all of the places I've seen Rylee since she's arrived. I need to see her, need to set the shit right that I did earlier. My dumb-ass move to kiss bar-girl just to make Rylee jealous, show her that I can have anybody I want.

Even though it's her I want.

So I hurt her on purpose as a payback for her twisting the knife a little more every time I see her. Sitting at appearances, promoting the fundraiser—everything beside me—but the minute the attention is off of us, she disengages. Goddamn frustrating woman.

So why are you looking for her, then? Why do you still care, Donavan? She doesn't believe a fucking word you say, said she's done, so how are you going to prove otherwise?

Fuck if I know but I'm so sick of this ache in my chest that I'm trying to ignore regardless of how much it continues to burn.

"So you ever going to tell me what the fuck happened between you and Rylee? Why you're moping around like I kicked your dog?" Becks asks for the hundredth time, even though he knows Baxter would bite his ass if he kicked him.

I don't want to talk about this. Never do. I just want it all back how it was. Ry and me in a good place. Then why the fuck did you kiss that chick? Pull your head out and fight for what you want.

I glance over and Becks is giving me the look like he's waiting for an answer. My head's so fucked-up right now I forgot to respond.

"Nothing. Something." I exhale. "She thinks I cheated on her."

Becks starts laughing and pats me on the back. "Dude, does she not see how goddamn pussy whipped you are? I saw you shove Tawny off you like a hot fucking coal that night she kissed you." He laughs at the memory that caused the *morning after* that still haunts me. When Tawny opened the fucking door when Rylee knocked. "If you're not having your fallback girl, you sure as hell aren't locking lips—or anything else for that matter—with anyone else."

I sigh, that ache returning with a vengeance.

"It'll sort itself out as long as you don't go and do something stupid, Wood."

"I won't," I lie, then cringe at the memory of Rylee's eyes filled with hurt as I *locked lips* with that bimbo earlier. Fuckin' A.

"Because she sure as hell wouldn't do something stupid like …" Becks's words trail off as we pass the bar before he takes an abrupt turn down the hall in the opposite direction. I start to follow when I see him glance at Sammy. I stop and turn around, the unspoken words causing the heart I've thought dead for so long to roar to life.

I see her instantly, body turned, knees touching, and face close to some fucking douchebag sitting beside her in the bar. I freeze for a moment when I see her leaning forward. *The kiss I see is all in my fucked-up mind* but I don't fucking care because I see it anyway, feel it hit me like a goddamn sucker punch. Just like she must have felt when I did it to her earlier.

The hurt barrels through me. Grabs hold and doesn't let go.

And I don't allow myself to get hurt. *Ever.* I lived a lifetime of fucking pain caused by the one that was supposed to care about me the most. I know better now. Know that the minute someone gets too close, I push them away. The minute I feel like I'm going to be hurt, I lash out without regret.

... and I let Rylee in close enough to hurt me ...

She senses me, looks up, and our eyes lock. I see defiance, finality, and fuck if I'm going to let that bastard sitting beside her reinforce it being there. She told me she was going to find a guy for the night to see if it helps with her pain. Apparently she was serious.

But this isn't like her—acting like me, throwing the confession I gave her about how I cope back in my face—so it kills me to see her do this to spite me. *To hurt me on purpose.*

Bar-boy leans in closer, his mouth near her ear, and she breaks her eyes from mine. And now that ache turns into motherfucking pain.

Defense mechanism locked and loaded. She's not going to believe me? Going to pull shit like this? I need to get back to *every man for his fucking self* ... well, after I take care of this I'll get right on that.

I'm ready to lash out and thank God the fucker sitting beside her is the perfect size for a punching bag because my fists are clenched and vision is red.

No one touches what's mine.

Even when she tells me she's not.

No one.

Things happen so fast. A shout sounds and I don't even realize it's mine until Becks is pushing my chest from the front and Sammy holds my shoulders from behind. It doesn't fucking matter who's on me because right now I want blood. I need an excuse to release my anger, at her for not believing me, at me for the stunt I pulled, and because I want to touch her so fucking badly it's not even funny.

And he's touching her instead.

"Let me go," I say through gritted teeth, trying to shrug them the fuck off of me. And I don't care how hard they hold me back because nothing is stopping me. I break free, Becks says something about priorities to which I think I only have one right now and that's getting this fucking guy away from her.

The crowd is smart and moves apart as I stalk toward her, mind focused, heart armoring up. She says something to the guy and stands as I near. Her eyes meet mine and they make me so fucking angry and so goddamn whipped that I push it away and focus on him.

If I was smart I'd haul her over my shoulder, take her upstairs and show her just exactly how I haven't cheated. But fuck smart and fuck being reasonable because she's being neither of those right now either.

Two wrongs don't make a right but hell if it doesn't feel good in the process.

I stop in front of her, lips so fucking close I can taste them, and she lifts that chin of hers up in a non-verbal *fuck you*. That defiance I find so goddamn sexy is in full effect but right now I'm also scared shitless because the hurt I see mixed with it is my doing ... and my undoing.

What the fuck am I doing?

My head is such a clusterfuck of emotions and thoughts. The biggest one is hurt her first. Deliver the first blow. And I know it's not right, know it's the worst kind of way to be, but my chest hurts so goddamn bad I can't think straight.

"What the fuck are you trying to pull, Rylee?" I ask. I know the answer, *payback's a bitch*, but I don't care because bar-boy shifts behind her and his eyes lock and then glance away from mine.

Good. At least he knows who's calling the shots here. Too bad Rylee doesn't.

And then she reaches back and pats his knee. I have flashbacks of the Merit launch party and Surfer Joe, the déjà vu almost comical.

Almost.

Because then she was just an addictive challenge I had to conquer and now ... now she's part of my fucking world. I'm a man with something to lose and that's not a good place to be.

"What business is it of yours?" she sneers as my eyes keep flickering back and forth to her hand on his knee.

And I can't help it, need to take it off of him, so I reach out to grab her arm and she yanks it away from me. I know why she did it, but the look she gives me mixed with the action flashes me back to my other hurt. When I fought away from any touch at all because of what would come next. The calling to my superheroes.

I'm staggered.

And fucking furious.

At her for fighting me and at me for making her feel *that* way. It takes a moment to pull me from the thought, to separate the two events that just melded when one has nothing to do with the other and fucked up my head even further.

I look in her eyes—see the hurt, the defiance, the sadness—and use what I see there to gain my bearings again.

"I don't like games, Rylee. I won't tell you that again."

"You don't like games?" she says, her tone laced with disgust. "But it's okay for you to play them?"

Fuck yes I played them, but that's not the point. The point is right here, right now. At the Merit party she gave me the choice: go or stay. Now it's my turn to ask.

"Why don't you tell your little boy toy he can run along now before things get even more interesting."

Watcha gonna do, Ryles?

Pick me.

Go with me.

Fix this shitstorm I started and get us back.

She shoves against me as hard as she can. "*You. Arrogant. Conceited. Egomaniac!*" spewing from her lips as she falls into me.

And every part of me stands at attention at the feel of her against me, wanting and needing but knowing I can't have, because she sure as fuck didn't give me the answer I wanted.

"What the fuck are you trying to prove?" I ask, wanting her to say she wants me, wants to fix this, believe I didn't cheat on her.

But she doesn't. Not even fucking close.

"I'm just testing your theory," she says with a smirk.

"My theory?" What the fuck is she talking about?

"Yeah, if losing yourself in someone helps get rid of the pain."

Ah fuck. In a single second I rein in everything that tumbles inside of me at the thought of her being with someone else, *everything but my anger*. I sure as shit hold onto that.

"How's that working for you?" It's all I can think to say because her rejection stings something fierce.

"Not sure." She shrugs with a smirk. "I'll let you know in the morning."

And I'm so focused on that look on her face when she pushes away from me that I don't even notice the fucker's hand in hers.

When I see it, anger turns to motherfucking fury. "Don't you walk away from me, Rylee!"

"You lost the right to tell me what to do the minute you slept with *her*." She says, her voice breaking through the haze of my colliding emotions. "Besides, you said you like my ass ... enjoy the view as I walk away because that's the last you'll be seeing of it."

I snap. No excuses, no regrets. My fist is clenched, fury ready to unleash on bar-boy.

But none of it fucking matters because I feel the steel grip of Sammy on my arm before I get my chance. And then the melee ensues.

Rylee is screaming at me, insults and names. Sticks and stones, baby. Sticks and stones.

You got to me.

You beat me at my own game.

At least it's Becks leading her away from me and not the fucking bar-boy. I'll take any kind of victory I can get at this point.

The crowd's buzzing seeps through my rage, drowns out her voice as it fades. And then Sammy's arm is around my shoulders leading me out of the bar and down a hallway.

"Calm the fuck down, Wood."

My pulse pounds in my ears, my head all is over the place, and my chest hurts even worse. "Just let me the fuck go, Sam," I grit out. My only thought is: Fuck the race tomorrow, I need to visit with Jack and Jim for a bit.

"Nope," he says, ushering me into an elevator in this damn maze of a resort. All I want to do is walk, run, pound out this anger then get fucking plastered so I can't feel the emptiness inside of me right now.

We're done.

She just made it clear as day and I don't want us to be done.

But it really doesn't fucking matter what I want or don't want because she doesn't fucking believe me. And why the fuck should she, Donavan, when you go kissing bimbos to spite her?

I groan and run a hand through my hair, fucking beside myself as Sammy pushes me out of the elevator car and down the hall.

"She's irrational and fuck she was going to sleep with that asshole and ... motherfucker!" I shout into the hallway, not caring who the hell is asleep or if anyone is listening. I'm feeling everything all at once when I'm so fucking used to feeling nothing that I can't concentrate.

Anger vibrates through me.

My teeth grind. My hands fist. My blood pounding.

Fucking Rylee.

Sammy points to the door to his right and when I stop he puts both hands on my shoulders. "Get your fucking hands off of me, Sammy!"

He just laughs at me in that snarky way he has, and I've just added him to the list of people I want to punch. Right after that fucking bar-boy he prevented me from plowing. I try to jerk my shoulders from his hands as he steers me down the hall, but I should know better by now. He's stronger than a fucking ox.

I'm so angry at him.

So pissed at her.

So disgusted with myself for the shit I pulled earlier without trying to make things right.

Rage blinds me and since every fucking room in this resort looks the same, I don't even realize what room Sammy shoves me into. By the time I look up, it's too fucking late.

"Uh-uh! No way! Get that egotistical asshole out of here!"

My head snaps up the minute I hear her voice. Sugar and spice laced together. Rage and lust and pure need collide momentarily until my mind flashes back to the image of Rylee with that fucker in the bar. The emotion hits me like a freight train.

I hate her.

I want her.

I hate that I want her so much that this is fucking killing me.

And she comes into view but without the dim light of the bar, I really see her. Hurt staining her face and defiance in her eyes, and I do the only thing I know how to do … push away the good and prepare for the pain. "Fuckin' A, Becks! What the fuck is this?" I yell, furious that I was coerced into a confrontation that I don't want. That I do want. *I don't know what the fuck I want because she doesn't want me anymore.*

I notice her packed suitcase and my heart fucking constricts in my chest. She's leaving me? The part of me that hoped this was all just a show dies a fast fucking death. And I thought her always saying she'd stay meant she would. That she understood I'd push and hurt to prove otherwise. I guess she doesn't understand me as much as I thought she did.

I say the only thing I can to hide the hurt lancing through me, to lash out. To hide the unexpected let down that drops through my soul knowing she doesn't want to be here and watch me chase the green flag tomorrow.

I confessed that I use pleasure to bury the pain … but fuck, right now, I'm about to use anger to hide the foreshadowed devastation.

"Thank Christ! *Don't let the door hit you in the ass, sweetheart!*"

She steps toward me and I can see the fire in her eyes, the fury in her lips, and that goddamn defiance in her posture. That defiance that makes me ache to take her like no other fucking woman I've ever met before, ever had before.

"This is over here and now!" Beckett's voice booms at us in a tone I've heard very few times during our friendship. Instinct has me turning to look at him because last time I heard him like this he threw a punch at me. I don't need this shit right now. Not Becks pissed and sure as hell not him interfering. "I don't care if I have to lock you in this fucking room together, but you two are going to figure your shit out or you're not leaving. Is that understood?"

I start to argue with him the same time that Rylee's voice rises, but he cuts us both off. "Is that understood?"

The anger in his voice stuns me momentarily, and fuck me, Rylee gets the first word in. "No way, Becks! I'm not staying in this room another second with this asshole!"

"Asshole?" It rolls of my tongue as if it's a question, but she's right. Fucking right in every sense of the word but I'm so beyond angry right now. First her and now Becks turning against me? The hairpin trigger had been pulled tight in the bar, and I'm primed and ready to fight.

I whip around to face Rylee, only to find her body fucking inches from mine. How can I hate and hurt right now but my body vibrates from her nearness? Fuck me, she's my kryptonite.

Where are the fucking superheroes now?

And I'm so grateful when she speaks because it pulls me from my thoughts—thoughts that are so fucking scattered I can't figure out which one to focus on. The woman makes me have more personalities than the splintered images of my reflection in that shattered mirror. For some reason though, I don't think all the king's horses and all the king's men will be able to put this Humpty Dumpty back together again.

She snorts in disgust. The sound forces me to focus on the here and now rather than the memories of what she feels like against me. Beneath me. Part of me.

"Yeah! Asshole!" She sneers at me with such derision that I can feel it pulse in waves off her.

Good. The wall's back up. Right where I need it to be. Fucking Christ! If she thinks that's going to hurt me, she's gonna have to try a whole fucking lot harder. It's hard to hurt a man that died inside years ago.

But I swear to God she brought me back to life.

Get your head straight, Donavan. Hurt her before she hurts you. You told her the truth. You chased. You tried. She wouldn't listen. Still isn't going to listen.

Which means she's not going to hear me. She's going to believe whatever the fuck she wants to. And in turn she's going to leave me.

Broken.

Shattered.

Irreparable.

Break her before she'll break me.

"You want to talk about assholes? Try that stunt you pulled with bar-boy back there. I believe you claimed the title right then, sweetheart."

"*Bar-boy?* Wow, because having a harmless drink is so much worse than you with your gaggle of whores earlier, right?"

She shoves at my chest like she did downstairs and I accept her anger. I welcome the physicality that comes with the force of the push. I welcome the sting in my heart from that goddamn look in her eyes that says she hates me, loves me, is hurt by me.

I need a fucking minute, a pit stop second. I need to stop that burn in my gut and get my fucking head back in the game. I pace back and forth, blowing out a breath to shove the emotion aside and bury it down deep with the rest of my secrets.

I notice the smirk on Becks's face out of the corner of my eye—the one telling me I'm in so fucking deep and the cement's starting to harden around my feet … and around my heart—and I can't help the words that fly out of my mouth. "She's driving me fucking crazy!"

I'm talking to Beckett, friend to friend, searching for some kind of help here to quiet the confliction within and of course Rylee latches on to the one word I leave hanging out there for her like a checkered flag in the wind.

"You'd know all about the *fucking part* seeing as you fucking Tawny is what started this whole thing in the first place," she screams at me.

I don't even have time to register the jolt of Beckett's body beside me before he stutters out, "*What?*"

Oh fuck.

"What? He didn't tell you?" She sneers at him.

Shut the fuck up, Rylee. Becks is in big brother mode and this is my fucking business.

Motherfucker.

"I told the asshole that I loved him. He bailed as fast as he could. When I showed up at the Palisades house a couple days later, Tawny opened the door. In his T-shirt. Only his T-shirt." She takes a deep breath, focused completely on Beckett and ignoring me. "Colton didn't have much more on either. Told me nothing happened. But that's a little hard to believe with his notorious reputation. Oh and the condom wrapper in his pocket."

I cringe, her words hitting every part of me that wants to hide. Becks turns to look at me and I can see it hitting him, lie by fucking lie. That I let this argument fester to become this because I'm so fucking stubborn that I didn't tell her the truth. I see the disbelief in his eyes and how infuriated he is in the clench of his jaw. "Are you fucking kidding me here?"

"*What?*" I can hear the confusion in her voice, but I can't look at her because I'm too focused on the look on his face.

"Leave it, Becks."

"What the fuck, man?" Here comes the bulldog. Fuckin' A. He's not going to leave this alone, is he?

"I'm warning you, Beckett. Stay out of this!" I'm so pissed at myself—at everything that's happened tonight—the anger inside ignites and I turn the inferno toward him. My fists clench. My blood boils.

He takes the bait, focusing on me rather than Rylee, and adds kerosene to my fire. "When you start jeopardizing my team and the race tomorrow, then it becomes my business …" He shakes his head. "Tell her!"

"Tell me what?" Rylee shouts out in the silence of the room. The only other sound is the testosterone reverberating between Becks and me.

He gives me the look—that look that tells me he is so disappointed in me, mixed with *what the fuck are you trying to pull.* I give him the only answer I can because right now I don't even know what I'm fucking doing. "Beckett, she's like talking to a goddamn brick wall. What good will it do?"

"She's right. You're an ass!" he says, and I can see the challenge in his eyes even before he spits out his next words. "You won't tell her? Fine! Then I will!"

I'm done, trigger pulled, buttons pushed successfully.

My hands grip his shirt and I'm pressing him against the wall without a second thought, jaw clenched, fists itching. "I said leave it, Becks!"

What the fuck am I doing? About to go to blows with my best friend over a fucking chick? She must be the real deal. Fucking voodoo pussy, my ass. More like schizophrenic pussy. She has me all over the goddamn place.

I can see the amusement in his eyes. The look that says, *she's got you by the balls, Wood, and I think you like it, want it, but are scared shitless.*

No fucking way.

My emotions are ruled by anger and I'm so confused my game's off and no one knows that better than him. He could have our positions reversed in a millisecond. So why hasn't he pushed back? Taken the bait? Hurt me so I'm given the due I deserve?

Instead he just lifts an eyebrow telling me to show him differently, then—show him that Rylee isn't my final rodeo—before pushing me away.

"Then fucking fix this, Colton! Fix! It!" He shouts the dare at me before yanking the hotel room door open and slamming it shut.

Unsure what to say. Not sure how to escape these confines—from feeling and not wanting to feel and everything in between—I cuss out a storm as I pace the room again, trying to ignore the fact that Ry is watching my every movement—dissecting it and trying to draw conclusions I don't want her to form. If she's not going to believe me when I told her nothing happened, then she'll never trust me anyway.

How could she really believe I'd want something more when I have her? Perfection. Necessity. The Holy motherfucking Grail.

Does she know how much it kills me that she thinks I'd do that to her? Rips my fucking gut to shreds. I've given more of myself to her than anybody else I've ever met and she doesn't trust me? My poison has tainted her now and I can't let it continue to any further. I want to punch something—need to desperately—to get rid of this overload of shit coursing through my body.

"What was that all about?" Her voice cuts through the haze, but I'm so angry I push it away, keep walking trying to calm the fuck down before I say something I'll regret. "Damn it, Colton! What don't you want me to know?"

She blocks my path and as much as I want to physically pick her up and move her out of the way so I can wear a hole in the fucking carpet until I can think rationally, I can't. I want to touch her so bad. Take her. Hold her. Accept her.

But I can't.

... no one will ever be able to love you ...

She doesn't trust me.

... you're horrible and disgusting and poisoned inside ...

She's going to leave me.

... you're like a toxin that will kill them ...

Shatter me.

... I'm the only one that is ever allowed to love you ...

Break me.

... you're worthless, Colty ...

I can do worse and she can do better.

Let her go.

Push her away.

Save her.

"You really want to know?" I shout at her, hoping she flees and runs at the question but knowing not in a million years that she will. "You really want to know?"

She stands on her tiptoes, those glints of violet boring into mine, daring me to confirm what she already thinks is true in her heart. "Tell me." Her voice is a quiet calm when she says it. "Are you that Goddamn chicken shit you can't fess up and just admit it? I need to hear it come out of your mouth so I can get the fuck over you and get on with my life!"

I don't know how I swallow. I don't know how I speak, but the words are out of my mouth before I know it. Walls re-erected and solitary confinement a Siren's song calling to me. "*I fucked Tawny.*"

Poison spread.

Ship crashing against the treacherous ocean rocks.

Silence settles around us but I can hear the locking of the cell.

Feel the quicksand smothering my lungs.

The death of my resurrected soul.

"You coward!" she screams, hysteria bubbling up. "You goddamn fucking coward!"

"Coward?" I shout. Does she have any fucking clue I'm trying to save her? Trying to push her away before I can fuck this up even further? Fuck her over any further? Trying to stem the sudden feeling of need? "Coward?" I ask, trying to cover up every emotion that wants to pour out of my mouth and make this even worse. I'll take the pain, but fuck me if I don't want her to know that I tried to tell her. That I tried and she ignored.

Get your head on straight, Donavan. You either want her or you don't. Decide. Figure it out because this cerebral war is fucking killing you.

Turn it back on her.

"What about you? You're so fucking stubborn that you've had the truth staring you in the face for three fucking weeks. You're up there so high and mighty on your goddamn horse you think you know everything! Well you don't, Rylee! *You don't know shit!*"

"I don't know shit? Really, Ace? *Really?*" The quiet calm in her voice scares me. Does her lack of fight mean she's over me? Fuck, no. "Well how's this? I know a bastard when I see one."

Self preservation wins.

"Been called worse by better, sweetheart." I'm not sure if the words are meant as a challenge or a coup de grace. Will she fight for me or flee while she can?

I know my answer in the flash of her hand aiming for my face. Her wrists collide into my hands without a thought, our bodies crashing together with the motion, our lips inches apart. And I'm fucking frozen. Paralyzed in that space of time where I immediately take back everything I said, everything I did, and just crave the simplicity of her addictive taste.

Just want it to be her and me back in front of that mirror. Just want to be man enough and not fucked-up enough that when she says those words to me, I don't cringe. I don't feel the blackness swallow me whole and smother the air in my lungs, but rather look in her eyes and smile.

Accept.

Reciprocate.

Love.

Her voice breaks through my haze of regret. "If you were done with me … had your fill of me … you could have just told me!" Hurt fills her eyes and trembles across her lips.

And now that I've done it—now that I've pushed her away and hurt her with my callous comments—all I want is her back in my arms, my life, at my side. Because done with her? Does she really think that?

As if a single taste of her will ever be enough.

"I'll never have my fill of you." I say the words but see the disbelief still warring in her eyes so I give into the ache. Show her the only way that I know how. Search for the balm to soothe my aching soul and the bleach to purify my blackened heart.

My mouth slants over hers. Takes and tastes and demands. I accept her struggle, accept the fact that she hates me because I hate myself too, but I can feel the need vibrate between us. Can sense that this hunger will never be satisfied. That I'll never want it to.

She keeps struggling, keeps wanting to hurt me. And I want to tell her to do just that. Hurt me like I deserve. Hurt and love are equivalent to me. The only way I know that love is supposed to be.

But I see it in her eyes. The pain I've caused. And yet I still feel the love from her. Still feel like she wants this. Wants me. And even despite all of this … all of the hurt and confusion and spiteful words we spit at each other, I want her desperately. Have to have her desperately.

And I plan to take. I have to get us back to where we were. Where we need to be. To the only place my soul has felt at peace over the past twenty-odd years.

Back to Rylee.

"You want rough, Rylee?" And despite the contempt in her eyes, I do the only thing I know how to reclaim her. "I'll give you rough!"

My lips connect with hers and I do the only thing I can: I take what I want so desperately. What's mine.

To save myself.

Chapter Thirty-Nine

The descent of the elevator feels like it takes forever as my tired eyes and heavy heart force my feet to stand, urge my lungs to breathe. Try to figure a reason to move. I knew that getting over Colton would be hard—absolutely devastating—but I never in a million years imagined that the first step would be the hardest.

The doors ping and open. I know I need to hurry. Need to disappear because Colton will try and track me down and drag this out.

Then again, maybe he won't. Maybe he got his quick fuck and he'll let me go. It's not like he's easy to figure out, and to be honest, I'm so tired of trying. Thinking one thing and him doing another. If I've learned one thing being with Colton, it's that *I know nothing.*

I rub my face, trying to blot the tears from my cheeks but know that nothing is going to lessen my damaged appearance. And frankly, I don't have enough left in me to care what people think.

I know I've been here for a couple of days, but my mind is in such a haze that it takes me a second to figure out which way I need to go to find the main entrance in order to catch a cab. I have to walk out through a garden and then into the main lobby. I see it and start shuffling toward it, all of my luggage overflowing and awkward. I'm in a state of numbness, telling myself that I'm doing the right thing—that I've made the right decision—but the look in Colton's face as he buried himself in me—raw, open, unguarded—haunts me. We can't give each other what we need, and when we do we only end up hurting each other. One foot in front of the other, Thomas. That's what I keep telling myself. As long as I keep moving—keep my mind from wandering—I can keep the questioning panic that is just beneath the surface from bubbling up.

I make it about twenty feet into the garden, empty at this time of the night, and I'm struggling desperately to keep moving.

"I didn't fuck her."

The deep timbre of his voice causes the words to slice through the still night air. My feet stop. My head says go, but my feet stop. His words shock me, and yet I'm so numb from everything—from needing to feel and then not wanting to feel then to emotional overload—that I don't react. *He didn't sleep with Tawny?* Then why did he say that he did? Why did he cause all of this heartache if nothing happened? In the back of my mind I hear Haddie telling me that I'm so stubborn I didn't allow him to speak—didn't allow him to explain—but I'm so busy trying to remind myself to breathe that I can't focus on that. My heart thunders in my chest, and I find myself completely at a loss for what to do. I know his words should relieve me, but they still don't fix *us*. Everything that seemed so clear—conflicted yet clear—no longer is. I need to walk away, but I need to stay.

I want and I hate and more than anything, *I feel.*

"I didn't sleep with Tawny, Rylee. Not her or any of the others you accused me of," he repeats. His words hit me harder this time. Hit me with a feeling of hope tinged with sadness. We did this to each other—tore each other apart verbally and played stupid games to hurt one another—*and for no reason?* A tear escapes and slides down my face. "When I heard the knock at the door, I grabbed an old pair of jeans. Haven't worn them in months."

"Turn around, Ry," he says, and I can't bring myself to do so. I close my eyes and take a deep breath, emotions running rampant and confusion in a constant state of metamorphosis. "We can do this the easy way or the hard way," he says, his implacable voice closer than before, "...but have no doubt, *it will be my way.* You are not running this time, Rylee. Turn around."

My heart stops and my mind races as I slowly turn to face him. And when I do, I can't help the breath that catches in my throat. We're standing in this garden full of exotic plants with exploding colors but by far the most exquisite thing in my line of sight is the man standing before me.

Colton stands in a pair of blue jeans and nothing else. Bare feet, bare chest heaving with exertion, and hair dripping with water that runs in rivulets down his chest. He looks as if he literally stepped out of the shower, noticed I was gone, and chased me. He takes a step toward me, his throat working a nervous swallow, and his face a mask of conviction. He is utterly magnificent—breathtakingly so—but it's his eyes that capture me and don't let go. Those beautiful pools of green just hold mine—imploring, apologizing, pleading—and I'm frozen in the moment.

"I just need time to think, Colton," I offer as a justification of my actions.

"What is there to think about?" He blows out a loud breath, a harsh curse following right after. "I thought we were..."

I stare at the paint on my toenails; flashbacks flit through my mind of them on his chest not too long ago. "I just need to think about us...this...everything."

He steps closer to me. "Look at me," he commands softly, and I owe him this much regardless of how much I fear seeing the look in his eyes. When I raise my eyes to meet his, searching mine in the full moonlight, I see worry, disbelief, fear, and so much more in the depths of his eyes and as much as I want to look away—to hide from the damage that I'm about to cause—I can't. He deserves better than that from me. His voice is so soft when he speaks that I barely hear him. "Why?" It's a single word, but there is so much emotion packed behind it that it takes a minute for me to find the words to respond.

And it's the same question I need to ask him.

"If this is real, Colton...we're supposed to complement each other—make each other better people—not tear each other apart. Look at what we did to each other tonight." I try to explain. "People who care for each other don't try to purposely hurt one another...that's not a good sign." I shake my head, hoping he understands what I'm saying.

His throat works as he thinks of what to say. "I know we've made a mess of this, Ry, but we can figure this out," he pleads. "*We can get us right.*"

I close my eyes momentarily, tears spilling over as I remember where we are and what tomorrow signifies. "Colton...you need to focus right now...on the race...we can talk later...discuss this later...right now you need to get your head on the track where it belongs."

He shakes his head emphatically at me. "You're more important, Rylee."

"No, I'm not," I murmur as I avert my eyes again, silent tears endlessly sliding down my cheeks now.

I feel his finger on my chin, guiding my eyes to look back at his. "If you leave, it's not just to think. You're not coming back, are you?" He stares at me, waiting for a response and my lack of one is his answer. "Did us—you and me—earlier not mean anything to you? I thought that..." his voice drifts off as I can see it dawning on him "...you were getting closure. That's why you were so upset," he says, talking more to himself than me. "You were saying goodbye weren't you?"

I don't respond but rather just keep my eyes fixed on his so maybe through his pain he can see how hard this is on me too. It would be so much easier if he raged and threw something instead of these soft pleading words and eyes filled with disbelief and hurt.

"I just need some time to think, Colton," I finally manage, repeating myself.

"Time to distance yourself to make it easier on you is what you really mean, right?"

I bite the inside of my cheek as I carefully chose my next words. "I—I just need some time away from you, Colton, and the disaster that we've made of the past couple of days. You're so overpowering—so everywhere—that when I'm near you I become so lost in you that it's like I can't breathe or think or do anything on my own. I just need a little time to process this..." I look around before turning back to him. "*Time to try and figure out why we're so broken...*"

"No, Ry, no," he insists, the rasp in his voice breaking as he brings his hands up to frame the sides of my face at the same time he bends his knees to bring us inches apart, eye to eye, thumbs caressing over the line of my jaw. "We're not broken, baby...we're just bent. *And bent's okay.* Bent means that we're just figuring things out."

I feel like my heart is going to explode in my chest as he recites my words—the lyrics of the song I once said to him—back to me. It hurts so much. The look in his eyes. The raw simplicity in his explanation. The pleading conviction in his voice. The subtle irony that the one person who doesn't ever "do the relationship thing" is giving the advice here on how to fix one.

Ours.

I just shake my head at him, my mouth opening to speak but closing again to just taste the salt of my tears when I can't find the words to answer him. He's still bent down, eye level with me. "There's so much that I need to explain to you. So much I need to say...so much I should have already said to you." He breathes out in a desperate plea. Colton puts both hands up on to the back of his neck, elbows bent, and paces back and forth a few steps. My eyes follow him and on his fourth pass, he grabs me without preemption and crushes his mouth to mine, bruising my lips in a kiss teeming with desperation. And before I can regain my footing beneath me, he tears his lips from mine, hands on my shoulders, eyes boring into mine. "I'll let you go, Rylee. I'll let you walk away and out of my life if that's what you want—*even if it fucking kills me*—but I need you to hear me out first. Please, come back to the room so I can tell you things that you need to hear."

I take a deep breath as I stare at his eyes, inches from mine and pleading with me for some scrap of hope. The rejection is on my tongue, but for the life of me I can't get it past my lips. I drag my eyes from his and swallow, nodding my head in consent.

The room is dark except for the light of the moon. In the space between us on the bed, I can make out Colton's shadow. He's on his side, head propped on his angled elbow, staring at me. We sit like this in silence for a while—him staring at me, me staring at the ceiling—as we both try and process what each other is thinking. Colton reaches out hesitantly and takes my hand in his, a soft sigh escaping his lips.

All I can think to do is swallow and keep my eyes fixed on blades of the ceiling fan above as they rotate endlessly.

"Why?" My voice croaks as I speak for the first time since we've come back to the room, asking the same question he's asked me. "Why did you tell me that you slept with Tawny?"

"I…I don't know." He sighs in frustration as he shoves a hand through his hair. "Maybe because since that's what you thought of me—expected of me without even letting me explain—then maybe I wanted you to hurt as much as I did when you accused me of it. You were so sure that I slept with her. So sure that I'd use her to replace you that you wouldn't listen to me. You shut me out. *You ran away*, and I never got a chance to explain that whole fucked up morning to you. You wouldn't let me…so a part of me felt like I might as well give you the affirmation you needed to think of me like the bastard-asshole that I really am."

I remain silent, trying to process his rationale, understanding and not-understanding all at the same time. "I'm listening now," I whisper, knowing full well that I need to hear the truth. Need it all laid out on the table so I can figure out where to go from here.

"I truly didn't know how alone I was, Rylee," he starts on a shaky breath and for the first time, I can sense how nervous he is. "How isolated and alone I've made myself over the years, until you weren't there. Until I couldn't pick up the phone and call you or talk to you or see you…"

"But you could, Colton," I reply, confusion in my voice. "You ran from me…not the other way around. I was the one sitting and waiting for you to call. How could you think otherwise?"

"I know," he says softly. "I know…but what you said to me—*those three words*—they turn me into someone I won't ever let myself be again. It triggers things—memories, demons, *so fucking much*—and no matter how much time has passed, I just…" he fades off, unable to verbalize what the words *I love you* do to him.

"What? Why?" What in the hell is he talking about? I want to scream at him, but I know that I have to have patience. Look where my obstinance has gotten us thus far. Verbalization is not his strong point. I have to just sit back and be quiet.

"Ry, the explanation—when, as a kid, those words are used as a manipulation…as a means to hurt you…" He struggles and I so desperately want to reach out and hug him. Hold him and help him through it, so maybe I can understand him better—comprehend the poison he says sears his soul—but I refrain. He looks at me and tries to smile but fails miserably, and I hate that this conversation has robbed him of that brilliant smile of his. "…it's too much to go in to right now and probably more than I'll ever be able to explain." He exhales on a long, shaky breath. "This, talking right now, is more than I ever have…so I'm trying here, okay?" His eyes plead with me through the shadow of darkness, and I just nod at him to continue. "You said those words to me…and I was immediately a little boy, dying—wishing I was dead—hurting inside all over again. And when I hurt like that, I usually turn to women. *Pleasure to bury the pain…*" My free hand grips the sheet beside me for the little boy that was in so much pain he'd rather die and for the man I love beside me that's still so haunted by it and for what I fear is going to spill from his lips next. His confession. "*Usually*," he whispers, "but this time, after you, there was no appeal in it. When the thought crossed my mind, it was your face I saw. Your laugh I missed. It was your taste I craved. *No one else's*." He shifts onto his back, keeping his fingers still laced with mine as my heart squeezes at his words. "Instead, I drank. *A lot*." He chuckles softly. "The day before…everything happened…Q came by my place and read me the riot act. She told me to clean myself up. Told me to find some friends other than Jim and Jack to hang out with. Becks showed up an hour later. I know she called him. He didn't ask what was wrong—he's good like that—but knew I needed some company.

"He took me out surfing for a couple of hours. Told me I needed to clear my head from whatever was fucking it up. He had to assume it had something to do with you, but he never pried. After we surfed for a while, I told him we needed to go out, hit a couple of bars, something to make me numb." He rubs his thumb softly back and forth over our clasped hands, and I turn onto my side so now it's me watching him staring at the ceiling. "We did and in the process, Tawny called and had some documents she needed me to sign since I hadn't been in the office for several days. I told her where we were and she showed up. I signed the documents and the next thing I knew, a couple of hours had passed and all three of us were shitfaced. Lit like you wouldn't believe. We were closer to the Palisades house, so I had Sammy drive us there and figured we'd pick up their cars in the morning.

"We walked through the front door, and I realized that I hadn't been there since that night with you. Grace had been there of course—the shirt I'd thrown on the couch before we..." He fades off remembering. "It was folded neatly on the back of the couch for me to see the minute I entered the house. My first reminder. When I walked into the kitchen, she'd taken the cotton candy and it was sitting in a container on the counter. I couldn't escape you—even drunk, I couldn't escape you. So I drank some more. Tawny and Beckett followed suit. Tawny was uncomfortable in the clothes she had so I grabbed a shirt for her so she could be more comfortable. We were all sitting in the family room. Drinking more. I was trying anything to numb how much I needed you. I don't remember the exact sequence of events, but at some point I reached for my beer and Tawny kissed me..."

Those words hang in the darkened room like a weight on my chest. I grit my teeth at the thought even though I'm appreciative of his honesty. I'm starting to think that maybe I don't need to hear all of the story. That in this case truth might not be the best policy. "Did you kiss her back?" The question is out of my mouth before I can stop it. I feel his fingers tighten momentarily around mine, and I know my answer. I worry my bottom lip between my teeth as I dread hearing the confirmation come from his lips.

He sighs again and I can hear him swallow loudly in the quiet of the room. "Yes..." he clears his throat "...at first." Then he falls silent for a few moments. "Yes, I kissed Tawny back, Rylee. I was hurting so much and drinking wasn't helping to numb it anymore...so when she kissed me, I tried my old fallback method." I audibly suck in my breath and try to pull my hand from his but his grip remains firm. He doesn't allow me to pull away from him. "But for the first time ever, I couldn't." He turns on his side again so that although the darkness of the room doesn't allow us to completely see each other, I know that he is staring into my eyes. He reaches his free hand up to run the backside of his fingers over my cheek. "She wasn't you," he says softly. "*You ruined casual for me, Rylee.*"

I sniffle at the tears burning the back of my throat, and I'm unsure of whether they're a result of the fact that he did try to start something with her or if they're because of his reasons why he couldn't. "I told you I loved you, Colton, and *you ran away*. Basically into the arms of another woman," I accuse. "A woman who has harassed and threatened me no less in regards to you."

"I know..."

"What's to say you won't do that again, Colton? What's to say that the next time you get spooked you won't do the same damn thing?" Silence falls around and between us, wiggling its way into the doubts in my head. "I can't..." I whisper as if talking normally is too much for the words I'm about to utter. "I don't think that I can do this, Colton. I don't think I can let myself believe again..."

Colton shifts suddenly in the bed and sits up, grabbing both of my hands in his as I fall onto my back. "Please, Rylee...don't decide yet...just hear the rest of it out, okay?" I can hear the desperation in his voice, and it undoes me for I know exactly how it feels when that tone is in your voice.

That was the same one I had right after I told him I loved him.

We sit there and his hands hold mine—our only connection despite feeling as if he is the only air that my body can breathe. I feel the tension radiate off of him as he tries to put the thoughts swarming in his head into words.

"How do I explain this?" he asks the room as he blows out a loud breath before beginning. "When you race, you're going so fast that everything outside of your car—the sidelines, the crowd, the sky—everything becomes a big, stretched out blur. Nothing specific can be identified. It's me in the car, alone, and everything outside of my little bubble is part of the blur." He stops momentarily, squeezing my hands to stop the nerves trembling through his as he regroups to try and explain better. "Kind of like when you're a kid and you spin in circles...everything in your line of sight becomes one big continuous image all blurred together. Does that make sense?"

I'm unable to find my voice to answer him. His anxiety seeping into me. "Yes," I manage.

"I've lived my life for so long in that state of blur, Rylee. Nothing is clear. I never stop long enough to pay attention to the details because if I do then everything—my past, my mistakes, my emotions, my demons—will catch up to me. Will cripple me. It is always easier to live in that blur than to actually stop, because if I stop, then I might actually have to feel something. I might have to open up to the things I've always protected myself against. Things ingrained in me from the shit that happened to me as a kid. Shit that I don't ever want to remember but that I constantly do." He releases one of my hands and scrubs it over his face. The chafe of the stubble against his hand is a welcome sound to me, a comforting one.

"My past is always there, just on the edge of my memory. Always threatening to overwhelm me. To drag me back and pull me under." I can hear the emotion thickening in his voice, and on impulse, reach out and grab his hand again. I squeeze it—a silent sign of support for the hell inside of his head. "Living inside of that blur is like living in a bubble. It allows me to control the speed I'm going…to slow down if I need a breather, but to never really stop. I've always been in the driver's seat…always in control. Always able to speed up, push the limits, when things get too close…

"And then I met you…" The astonishment in his voice is raw and honest and tugs so deep within me that it causes me to sit up, so I'm now cross-legged with my knees pressing against his. His hands find mine again and squeeze them tightly. "The night I met you it was like a firecracker shot out of that blur of color and exploded above me. So bright and so beautiful…and so hostile..." he chuckles "...that I couldn't look away even if I tried. It was like life slammed the brakes on me and I'd never touched the pedal. I was immediately drawn to you, to your attitude, to your refusal of me, to your wit…to your incredible body." I can feel him shrug unapologetically at the last comment, and I can't help the smile that curls up my lips or the hope that begins to bloom in my soul. "…to everything about you. That first night you were a spark of solid color to me in a world that's always been one big mixed blur of it."

Words escape me as I try and process what he's telling me. Just when I've made up my mind one way, he says something so poignant and achingly beautiful that I can't help but feel my heart swell with love for him. Colton accepts my silence and reaches out to cradle my head in his hands before he continues. The tenderness in his touch brings tears to my eyes. "That first night you created a spark, Rylee, and every day since then, you've allowed me the strength to slow down long enough to see into the blur I've always feared. Even when I don't want to do it, your quiet strength—knowing that you are there—pushes me to be a better person. A better man. Since you've come into my life, things finally have definition, specific colors assigned to them…I don't know…" I can hear his struggle, and I turn my face into the palm of his hand and kiss it there softly as he sighs. "I don't know how else to explain it, but I know that I can't go back to how I existed before. *I need you in my life, Rylee.* I need you to help me continue to see the color. To slow things down. To allow me to feel. I need you to be my spark …"

He leans in and brushes his lips so softly, so tenderly against mine. "Please be my spark, Ry…" he pleads as the words cause his lips to brush against mine.

I lean in and press my lips against his, instigating the kiss to go deeper by slipping my tongue into his mouth because the words and thoughts in my head and heart are so jumbled that I'm afraid to speak. Afraid that in this moment of his revelation—that if I pour out what's spilling over in my heart—I will overwhelm him. So instead, I pour it all into my kiss. He gathers me to him, cradling me in his lap while he worships my mouth in the way that only he knows how. The reverence in which he breathes my name between kisses causes a tear to slide down my cheek.

"I might not be able to tell you the things you need to hear with the traditional words you need to hear them in, but I swear to God, Rylee, *I will try*. And if I can't, then I'll show you. I'll show you with everything I have—anything it takes—where your place is in my life," he murmurs to me, shattering every last form of protection I have guarding my heart.

He just stole it completely.

And I just more than willingly handed it over.

He wraps his arms around me and buries his face in my neck, holding me tightly for a long while, his vulnerability palpable. My mind thinks in sensations and emotions and shuts all sensibility out so that I can just enjoy this unguarded side of Colton that is such a rarity. I breathe in the scent of us mixed together. I feel the beat of his heart against my chest. The warmth of his breath against my neck. The strength of his arms as they hold me tight. The scrape of his scruff against my bare skin. The comfort his presence brings to me by just being near. So many things to absorb—to pack away for another day—so I can remember them when I need them the most.

Because I know that being with Colton—staying with Colton—loving Colton—guarantees that I will need these memories at the most random of times to help me get by in the trying ones I know will inevitably come.

"I'm drowning here. Your silence is killing me. Can you say something? Throw me a lifeline please?" he says and the comment has me immediately thinking of Beckett's words on the way to Vegas and earlier to me.

"C'mon," I whisper to him as I run my hands up and down his back. He pulls me tighter and nuzzles deeper into the underside of my neck. "You have a long day tomorrow. It's late. You need to get some sleep."

His head startles back and in our close proximity I can see the crystalline green of his eyes—their clarity, their utter shock, their acceptance—of my unspoken words. "You're not leaving?" he asks so brokenly. "You're staying?"

I catch the sob that almost escapes my throat with his words. That I think he's worth it. His hands run over my face and down the curve of my shoulder and back up. Touching to make sure that I really am before him—flesh and blood and accepting of him. Accepting the journey that he wants to try and take with me.

"Yes, Colton. I'm not going anywhere," I'm finally able to say once the burn in my throat dissipates.

He holds my head with both hands and leans in to press a sigh of a kiss against my lips before wrapping his arms around me and pulling me tightly into him. "I don't want to let you go just yet," he murmurs against my temple. "I don't think I ever will."

"You don't have to," I tell him softly as I lay down on the bed and pull him down with me. He shifts so that we are both on our sides, bodies pressed together, arms wrapped around each other, and my face nuzzled in his neck now.

We've been quiet for some time, the silence around us not so lonely anymore, when Colton sighs out a soft sound of contentment and then murmurs, "*A chance encounter.*" He plants a kiss on the top of my head and clears his throat. "I don't know what it meant before me, but to me, now, it means a chance encounter. One that's changed my life."

I snuggle in closer to him, planting a soft kiss at my favorite spot beneath his jaw, my heart overflowing with love and my soul brimming with happiness.

After some time of just absorbing each other and our new found balance, his breathing slows and evens out. I lie there for some time, just breathing him in, feeling his warmth, and my heart lodges in my throat when I realize that my decision was never really mine to make. It was made the minute I fell out of that damn storage closet and into his life.

I turn onto my side so I can watch him. My chest physically hurts as I stare at the beautiful man he is inside and out. He looks so peaceful in sleep. Like he can finally rest from the demons that chase him so frequently while he's awake. So much like the dark angel I think of him as that's breaking through the inescapable darkness to grasp and hold on to the light. His spark of light.

Chapter Forty

COLTON

For the first time in a month, the riot in my head is quiet as I sleep. Nightmares are non-existent. The events of last night flicker through my head as the morning hour pulls me from slumber.

That and the feel of Rylee's weight settling over me.

I groan involuntarily as she sinks down, sitting astride me. The heat of her pussy has me straining to be released from the sheets she's now pinned against my body. Talk about sweet goddamn torture.

Fuck me if this isn't the best wake-up call ever.

Fingertips feather up my abdomen, circle around my nipples, and then trail back down to my hip-bone. "Good morning," she whispers in that rasp of hers before pressing a soft kiss against my lips. Her fingers continuing to tease my skin. To taunt me with the drug to my addiction.

I grunt a response and squint open my eyes to find one of the most terrific sights I have ever seen. Tits—Rylee's tits to be exact—full and pert with pink nipples hardened in arousal dominating my line of sight. I take a moment to admire God's greatest creation ever before I drag my eyes away and scrape them over the rest of her sun-kissed skin to meet her eyes.

Those eyes.

The ones that have held me captive and owned parts of me I never even knew existed since that first moment they looked up at me amidst a mass of fallen curls.

"Good morning," she says again, her sleepy eyes hold mine and a sluggish smile tugs up the corners of her mouth.

I feel like my heart beats for the first time. She's real and she's here. Relief floods me. Today may be the first race of the season, but waking up with her, here with me after all the shit from the past couple of weeks? I've already fucking won.

I cock an eyebrow up at her as her fingers tickle further south, my cock pulsing up in response to her touch. "It is good indeed," I grumble needing my mind to catch up with my body that's already revved and raring to go. "Any time I can wake up with a sight like this, is indeed a good fucking morning." I can't help the smile that curls up my lips. God, she's gorgeous.

And mine.

Seriously? What the fuck did I do to deserve her? Hell has most definitely frozen over.

"Well," she says drawing the word out into a purr. "We seem to have a dilemma here?"

"A dilemma?"

"Yes, I seemed to be underdressed and you Mr. Donavan, you seem to be very overdressed."

I quirk an eyebrow up at her, all systems fully awake now, and more than ready to go. "I think you look fucking perfect." I shift some and prop the pillow further under my head so that I most definitely do not miss a single thing from the vision in front of me. "But you think I'm overdressed, huh?"

"Most definitely," she says, "and I think it's time to fix the situation." She shifts her weight, and I can feel her fingers scrape over my hips as she pulls the sheet down. Fuck if she's not teasing me. My cock springs free from the confines of the sheet and it aches for her to touch it. To be buried in that sweet heat of hers. I watch her look at my cock and when she licks her tongue over her bottom lip it takes everything I have to not pin her to the bed and take what that mouth is tempting.

"Oh, there is most definitely a situation." She smirks and her eyes look up to meet mine, lust and mischief dancing beneath her lashes.

"And how do you suggest we fix it?" I ask enjoying the role of temptress she's playing despite my balls desperately begging for release.

She reaches out and wraps her hand around my cock. *Damn that feels good.* I lay my head back and drown in the sensation of her fingers on my tortured flesh. She strokes me with slow, even strokes that feel so fucking good it takes everything I have to not put my hand on top of hers and urge her to go faster. To pump harder.

When it comes to Rylee, begging is not beneath me.

"Well, it is race day, and I can't exactly let my man go to the track without fixing this little problem we have here."

I flash my eyes open and take in the arch of her eyebrow and taunt on her lips. "Oh baby, *there's nothing little about it.*"

She moves forward, her hand still on my cock but tits back front and center in my view as she leans in close to my face. "There isn't?" She angles her head watching my mouth fall lax as she works her dexterous fingers back up my dick. All I can do is bite my lip in response and shake my head as she pays special attention around its crest. Talking right now is not an option. "I guess I'll have to find out for myself then. Don't you think?"

I stare at her. Take all of her in as she kneels over me—cheeks flush, eyes dancing, and mouth tempting—and I can't believe after how bad I screwed up, that she's still here. Still fighting for us. My fucking saint.

A reply is on my lips—and hell if I remember what it is because it flies from my mind the minute she sinks down onto my cock.

Wet fucking heat. Pleasure swamps me the instant I feel the velvet grip of her tight pussy wrapped around me. From the bottom of my spine all the way to the top of my sac tightens in a tingling surge of eye-roll into the back of your head type of ecstasy.

"Sweet Jesus!" I groan out as she seats herself root to tip and stills so that she can adjust to my invasion.

"No, not Jesus," she murmurs as she leans in and slips her tongue between my lips adding torment to her tantalization. "But I can still take you to Heaven," she whispers against my lips.

And then she starts to move. Up and down. Her slick, wet heat spasming over my cock with her every rise and fall. Skin on skin. Soft to hard. Hers and mine. So damn good.

Fucking Rylee.

My fucking voodoo pussy.

Shit. *I stand corrected.* Now this—Rylee's voodoo pussy—is God's greatest creation.

Ever.

And hell if Rylee wasn't right.

She does feel like fucking Heaven.

I shove my legs into last night's jeans, knowing I need to get my ass in gear. I'm excited for the day ahead of me—for the organized chaos and the rev of the motor at my command—but I'm just not ready to share Rylee yet. Not ready to burst this bubble around us and step into the blur.

I look over at her as she shoves her arms through her T-shirt and I shake my head. What a fucking shame to cover those perfect tits up. But I have to admit, I kind of like the idea of a T-shirt with my name emblazoned on it pressed against them. Staking a claim.

A sharp knock sounds on the door and before either of us can respond the door is shoved open. "You guys decent?"

Beckett walks in, fire suit on but the sleeves are tied around his waist.

"And if we weren't?" I ask a little miffed. What if Ry wasn't dressed yet? Or even worse, laid out beneath me naked and moaning. So not fucking cool. It's not like Becks and I haven't been drunk and screwing women in the same room before—but shit—this is Rylee we're talking about here. My spark.

"How the hell did you get in here?" I ask and he knows I'm pissed at the intrusion. And of course being fucking Becks, he smirks a little knowing smile to let me know he's just testing the waters. That he's pushing my buttons to see where she and I stand.

Beckett looks back and forth between Rylee and myself before tossing the key card on the bed. "From last night," he says in explanation to his room access. "You guys good now?" He looks over at Rylee, eyes holding hers for a beat, and I can see him searching her face to make sure that she is in fact okay. That we worked our shit out. Fucking Becks. He may be a cocksucker but he's the best goddamn wing man a guy could ever have.

"Yeah, we're good now," she answers him and the soft little smile she gives him has me shaking my head. Could she be any more perfect?

"Good," he states glancing over at me with a cat ate the canary grin, eyes telling me *it's about fucking time.* "Don't let it happen again."

I just shake my head at him as I rise from the bed and start buttoning up my jeans. I glance over to Rylee and notice her eyes watching my fingers trail over the ridged lines of my bare abdomen. The look in her eyes has me wanting to lock Beckett out and drag Rylee to the floor—or shove her up against the wall—I'm not picky and frankly beggars can't be choosers—until I get my fill of her.

Then again, that might take a long-ass time. I don't think I'll ever get my fill of her.

"No time for that lover-boy." Becks snorts when he sees the look Ry and I exchange. I have half a mind to tell him to get the fuck out so that I can get one more taste to last me through the race. Especially when I look over and see her cheeks flushed at being caught thinking naughty thoughts.

"You've got fifteen minutes before we leave. Make the most of your time." He winks at Rylee and I know she's dying of embarrassment right now.

Oh, I fucking plan on it.

The air vibrates with anticipation around me as we walk through the pits. The guys are checking and making sure that everything is in order and ready for the green flag, but let's face it, they're just busying their hands to keep from looking nervous. And I love that my crew gets nervous about a race. Lets me know they care about it as much as I do.

I should be nervous, but I'm not. I look over at Rylee beside me and squeeze her fingers that are laced with mine. She's the reason that I'm not. Fucking Rylee—the balm to soothe all problems: nerves, nightmares, broken souls, and healing hearts.

My new superstition number one—her beside me.

She smiles at me, eyes hidden behind her sunglasses, and the sexiest fucking smile on those lips.

Out of habit I walk over to the car where it's parked in front of my pit row designation and rap my knuckles on the hood four times. Superstition number two down. Rylee looks over at me and quirks an eyebrow. I just shrug in response.

Superstitions are stupid fucking things but hey, whatever works.

"Why the number thirteen?"

She's referring to the number on my car. My unlucky, lucky number. "It's my lucky number." I tell her as I wave at Smitty passing by.

"How unconventional." She smirks at me, pushing her sunglasses up into her hair and tilting her head to the side, her eyes steadfast on mine.

"Would you expect anything less of me?"

"Nope. Predictability doesn't suit you." She shakes her head and drags her bottom lip through her teeth. Hell if that's not sexy. "Why thirteen?"

"I've defied enough odds in my lifetime so far." I lean back against the car behind me. "I don't think a number's going to change my luck now." *And it's the date of the day my Dad found me.* The thought unexpectedly flashes through my head, but I don't say it—just think it—not wanting to put a damper on the moment.

I tug on her hand and pull her against me, needing to feel her. The soothing balm to my aching soul. She lands solidly against me, and I swear more than our bodies jolt.

My fucking heart does too. It jolts, trips, falls, tumbles, freefalls—no that's not it—it *crashes* into that foreign fucking feeling pulsing through me.

I lean down, needing a taste of her. I slant my lips over hers and revel in her sweetness. The move of her tongue. The taste of her lips. The scent of her perfume. The quiet moan she sighs into me.

The claiming of my heart.

My God. The woman is my fucking kryptonite. How did this happen? How did I let her own me? More importantly and fucking shocking, *I want her to own me.*

Every damn piece of me.

Game over baby.

She's my motherfucking checkered flag.

Chapter Forty-One

"Don't I get my good luck kiss?" Colton looks over and smirks at me as he pulls his lucky shirt over his head and throws it on the couch behind him. *My God.* The man knows how to knock the wind out of me. He stands before me, that arrogant as sin grin spreading his mouth wide and his eyes reflecting all of the dirty things he'd love to do to me right now.

And the thoughts are not unreciprocated.

"Good luck kiss? Or good luck..." I let my words trail off, raising my eyebrows at him, my eyes licking their way over the bronzed skin and defined lines of his naked torso and stopping at those completely devastating lips. I let my gaze rest on his amused sparks of green as he watches me appreciatively take in the sight of him.

He quirks his eyebrow up as he unties the loose sleeves of his fire suit around his waist. "Good luck what?" he teases as he takes a step toward me and leans over, bracing his hands on either side of the arms of my chair.

I look up at him and feel a million miles away from where the two of us were twenty-four hours ago. I feel like it was a really bad dream but am oddly glad it isn't. There is something between us now, an ease or contentment I guess, that has shown us we can muddle through. That we can fight and love and despise, but in the end, *we can find us again.* That we can use each other's pleasure to bury the pain.

"Not sure...I've never done this race thing before..." I smirk as I give into the temptation—take what really is mine now—and tease my fingertips up his chest and tickle them along his jaw until they find their way into his hair.

He dips his head down and captures my mouth with a languorous exploration of his tongue against mine. The slide of my fingertips over his skin. The hum of approval deep within his throat. My soft sigh he breathes in and deepens the kiss. He shows me how he feels about me with an underlying urgency and complete veneration.

The pounding on the motor home door has me jerking back from Colton and him swearing one of his favorites as he looks over at it. I look up at him and allow the emotions to flow through me, welcome them in their still dreamlike state. My achingly handsome rogue standing before me, *really is mine.*

"Showtime?" I ask on a sigh.

"Checkered flag time, baby." He smirks and presses one last, chaste kiss against my lips. I catch him by surprise as I cup the back of his neck and slip my tongue between his lips and just take. Take everything I've needed and wanted and been too afraid to ask for over the past few months. And although I catch him by surprise, he gives unflinchingly without questioning. I end the kiss and pull back a fraction to look into his eyes—telling him without words how much he just gave me. A smile ghosts his lips, that lone dimple I love deepening, and he just shakes his head at me, trying to figure out what that was all about.

"Checkered flag time, baby." I smile at him as I rise from the chair. He reaches behind him and tugs on a new T-shirt—an endorsement T-shirt—to wear beneath his fire suit now that the requisite lucky T-shirt has been worn for the superstitious allotted amount of time. I glance over at the clock and am struck by the nerves that start fluttering when I realize that there's only a short time left before the cranking of the engines while he seems so calm and collected.

"Don't worry," Colton says bringing me back to the here and now, not realizing that I had pressed a hand to the butterflies in my stomach. "They'll hit me the minute we walk out of the RV." He points to my stomach and then nods his head toward the door before shoving a hat on his head. *His lucky hat.* And I smile softly when I realize it's the same hat that he wore on our date to the carnival.

Mr.-I'm-So-Sure-Of-Myself wore his lucky hat on our first official date. As if my heart could swell any more.

"You ready?" he asks as he walks a few steps and then turns and holds his hand out to me.

"Hey, Ace?" Colton stops with the door ajar and looks back at me with curiosity. Time for me to show him just what's waiting at the finish line. I'd found the skimpy pair of black and white checkered panties that have *Revved and Raring* embroidered across the butt at a little novelty store back at home. With the state of things between Colton and me, I'm not sure why I'd even brought them on the trip, but obviously with last night's turn of events, I'm glad that I did. His eyes widen as I unzip my shorts and wiggle my hips, pushing them down so that he can see a hint of the lace and checkering on the fabric. "This is the only checkered flag you need, baby."

His smile widens and the open door is forgotten as he strides two steps back toward me and yanks my body against his. He stops a moment and stares at me, mouths a whisper apart and emotion brimming in our eyes before he crashes his lips to mine in a kiss of pure hunger and carnality. He breaks away just as suddenly as he starts it and looks at me with a smirk. "You can bet your ass that's one checkered flag I'm definitely claiming."

Chapter Forty-Two

COLTON

I can feel it.

That complete certainty that hits you like a fucking freight train on very few days in your life. I have it today. I feel it today. It's in the air circling around me as my head flickers here and there through what I need to do today when I hit the track and the rubber connects. Stay clear of Mason—the fucker's got it out for me—like I knew he had his sights on that barfly last year. It's not like he was waving a flag or anything staking his fucking claim. Bad blood is never good on the track. Never. Stay high and tight through turns two and three. Binders light. Pedal heavy. Bring it in low on one. I keep repeating my responsibilities in my head, over and over. My way of making sure that I don't have to think down the chute. Just react.

Today I'm taking the checkered flag, and not just those dick hardening panties that fucking Rylee has on. *Sweet Christ, am I claiming that flag.* But I can feel it. Everything feels right with the world, and shit, maybe I'm being a pussy but that *right* feeling started when I woke up with Rylee wrapped in my arms, head nuzzled under my neck, lips pressed to my skin, and heart beating against mine.

Right where she's supposed to be.

I take a bite of another of my pre-race superstitions—a Snicker's bar—and look up to search her out. She's sitting quietly out of the way toward a corner, and her eyes lock with mine immediately. Her lips form that shy smile that turns me motherfucking inside out, and instead of the fear that usually snakes through my system, I feel settled. At ease. Can you say fucking pussy to the whip? But you know what? I'm okay with it because I'm pretty sure she'll be gentle with me. Won't crack it too hard. Well, unless I want her to.

"Wood?" I turn and look at Beckett.

Now Becks on the other hand is still going to hand my ass back to me in a hand basket once the stress of this race is over and he realizes it's minutes before a race and I'm thinking about my fucking voodoo pussy. *My fucking Rylee.*

I flash a quick smile at Ry before I turn to Becks. "Yup?" I say as I stand and begin the routine of zipping up my suit.

Getting ready to race.

Getting ready to do the one thing I have always loved.

Getting ready to take that motherfucking checkered flag.

Chapter Forty-Three

There is so much to take in. So many sights and sounds to assault and overwhelm. Hand over my heart, I stand beside Colton as the national anthem is sung on the stage at our backs. Flags wave. The breeze blows. The crowd sings. And my nerves go into overdrive for the man beside me who has transformed into an intense, introspective man as he focuses on the task at hand.

He reaches out a free hand and places it at the small of my back as the camera crew makes its way down the line of drivers standing on pit row with their crew and significant others at their sides. The fact that he's trying to comfort me in a moment strictly about him warms my insides. I'd tried telling him that I could sit in the pit box during the anthem—that it wasn't a big deal to me—but he refused. "I've got you now, sweetheart, I'm not letting you out of my sight," he'd said. Argument won. Hands down.

Fireworks boom as the song comes to an end, and all of a sudden pit row is a flurry of activity. Crews going to work to try and make all of their hard preparation come to fruition for their driver. Men descend around Colton before I can wish him one last good luck. Ear buds are stuffed in and taped down. Velcro is fastened. Shoes are double checked to make sure nothing will interfere with the pedal. Gloves are pulled on and situated. Last minute directions are given. I allow myself to be led from the craziness and am helped over the wall by Davis.

"Rylee!" In all of the complete, organized chaos, his voice rings out. Stops me. Starts me. Completes me.

I turn around and face him in all of his suited up glory. His white balaclava is in one hand and helmet in the other. So achingly handsome. So damn sexy. And all mine.

I look at him confused since we already had our moment of privacy in the motor home. Did I do something wrong? "Yeah?"

His smile lights up. A solid figure standing still while everyone else moves in one big blur around him. His eyes hold mine, intense and clear. "*I race you, Ryles,*" he says in a voice that's implacable and unwavering amidst the swirling chaos.

My heart stops. Time stands still and it feels like we're the only two people in the world. Just a damaged boy and a selfless girl. Our eyes lock and in that exchange, words that I can't shout out in the chaos between us are said. That after the little he explained last night, I know how horribly difficult it is for him to utter those words. That I understand he's telling me he's still a broken child inside, but like my boys he's giving me his heart and trusting that I will hold it with gentle, compassionate, and understanding hands.

"I race you too, Colton." I mouth to him. Despite the noise, I know he hears what I've said for a shy smile graces his lips, and he shakes his head like he's trying to understand all of this too. Beckett calls his name and he gives me one last glance before his face transforms into work mode. And I can't help but just stand there and watch him. Love swells, overwhelms, and heals my heart that I once thought was irreparable. Fills me with happiness over the man that I can't tear my eyes away from him.

My storm before the calm.

My angel breaking through the darkness.

My ace.

My chest reverberates as the cars fly down the backstretch. Fifty laps in and I'm still a nervous wreck, my eyes flicking between the track and the television monitor in front of me when the cars are at my back and out of my sight. My knee jiggles, my fingernails have been picked clean of nail polish, and the inside of my lip has been chewed raw. And yet Colton's voice comes through confident and focused at the task at hand every time he speaks on the headset I'm wearing.

Each time he talks to Beckett or his spotter I feel a trickle of ease. And then they hit a turn, cars side by side—masses of metal flying at ungodly speeds—and that trickle of ease turns into a pound of anxiety. I check the monitor again and smile when I see "13 Donavan" under the number two spot fighting his way back to the lead after a pit stop prompted by a caution.

"Dirty air ahead," the spotter says as Colton comes out of turn three and heads toward traffic a lap down.

"Ten-four."

"Last lap fastest yet," Beckett pipes into the conversation as he studies a computer screen several seats down from me that's reading all of the gauges in number thirteen. "Doing great, Wood. Just keep her steady in that groove you've got. The high line has a lot of pebbling already so stay clear."

"Got it." His voice strains from the force of the car as he accelerates out of turn number one.

There is a collective gasp from the crowd as a car comes into contact with the wall. I turn to look, my heart jumping in my throat, but I can't see it from our position. I immediately look to the monitor where Beckett is already focused.

"Up one, Colton. Up!" The spotter yells in my ears.

It all happens so fast but I feel like time stops. Stands still. Rewinds. The monitor shows a cloud of smoke as the car that hits the wall first slings back down the track at a diagonal. The speeds are too fast so the remaining cars are unable to adjust their line in that quick amount of time. Colton had once told me you always race to where the accident first hits because it always moves afterwards due to the momentum.

There's so much smoke. So much smoke, how is Colton going to know where to go?

"I'm blind," the spotter yells, panicked as the mass of cars and the ensuing smoke is so large that he can't direct Colton. Can't tell him the safe line to drive with his car flying close to two hundred miles per hour.

I watch his car fly into the smoke. My heart in my throat. My prayers thrown up to God. My breath held. My soul hoping.

Chapter Forty-Four

Colton

Motherfucker.

The smoke engulfs me. The blur around me now gray with flashes of sparking metal as cars collide around me. I'm fucking blind.

Don't have time to fear.

Don't have time to think.

Can only feel.

Only react.

Daylight flashes on the other end of the tunnel of gray. I aim for it. Not letting up. Never let up. Race to where the crash was.

Go, go, go. C'mon, one-three. C'mon, baby. Go, go, go.

The flash of red comes out of nowhere and slings in front of me. No time to react. None.

I'm weightless.

Lifted.

Weightless.

Spiraling.

Spinning.

White knuckles on the wheel.

Daylight again.

Too fast.

Too fast.

"Fuck!"

Chapter Forty-Five

I see Colton's car rise above the smoke. It's up on the nose. Spiraling through the air. I hear Beckett yell, "Wood!" It's only one word, but the broken way he says it has lead dropping through my soul.

I can't react.

Can't function.

Just sit in my seat and stare.

My mind fracturing to images of Max and Colton.

Broken.

Interchangeable.

Chapter Forty-Six

Colton

Spiderman. Batman. Superman. Ironman.

The End

Crashed

To Mom and Dad ~

Thank you for teaching me that life isn't about how you survive the storm,
but rather how you dance in the rain.

And I'm finally dancing…

Prologue

Thwack. Thwack. Thwack.

The resonating pain in my head pulses to the sound assaulting my ears.

Thwack. Thwack. Thwack.

There is so much sound—loud, buzzing white noise—and yet it's eerily fucking quiet. Quiet except for that damn thwacking sound.

What the hell is that?

Why the fuck is it so damn hot—so hot I can see the heat coming in waves off of the asphalt—but all I feel is cold?

Motherfucker!

Something to the right of me catches my eye—mangled metal, blown tires, skins shredded to pieces—and all I can do is stare. Becks is going to throttle me for fucking up the car. Shred me to pieces just like my car strewn all over the track. What the fuck happened?

A trickle of unease dances at the base of my spine.

My heartbeat accelerates.

Confusion flickers at the far away edges of my subconscious. I close my eyes to try and push back the pounding that's suddenly playing percussion to my thoughts. Thoughts I can't quite grasp. They sift through my mind like sand through my fingers.

Thwack. Thwack. Thwack.

I open my eyes to try and find that goddamn sound that's adding pressure to the pain …

… pleasure to bury the pain …

Those words whisper through my mind, and I shake my head to try to comprehend what's going on when I see *him:* dark hair in need of a trim; tiny little hands holding a plastic helicopter; a Spiderman Band-Aid wrapped around his index finger that's spinning the pretend rotors.

Spiderman. Batman. Superman. Ironman.

"*Thwack. Thwack. Thwack,*" he says in the softest of voices.

So why does it sound so loud then? Big eyes look up at me through thick lashes, innocence personified in that simple grace of green. His finger falters on the rotor as his eyes meet mine, cocking his head to study me intently.

"Hi there," I say, the deafening silence reverberating through the space between us.

Something's off.

Completely not fucking right.

Apprehension resurfaces.

Hints of the unknown whirl around my mind.

Confusion smothers.

His green eyes consume me.

Anxiety dissipates when a slow smile curls up the corner of his little mouth smudged with dirt, a lone dimple winking at its side.

"I'm not supposed to talk to strangers," he says, straightening his back some, trying to act like the big kid he wants to be.

"That's a good rule. Did your mom teach you that?"

Why does he seem so familiar?

He shrugs nonchalantly. His gaze runs over every inch of me and then comes back to meet mine. They flicker to something over my shoulder, but for some fucking reason I can't seem to drag my eyes from him to look. It's not just that he's the cutest fucking kid I've ever seen … No, it's like he has this pull on me that I can't seem to break.

A little line creases his forehead as he looks down and picks at another superhero Band-Aid barely covering the large scrape on his knee.

Spiderman. Batman. Superman. Ironman.

Shut the fuck up! I want to yell at the demons in my head. They have no right to be here … no reason to swarm around this sweet looking little boy, and yet they keep swirling like a merry-go-round. *Like my car should be around the track right now.* So why am I taking a step toward this polarizing little boy instead of preparing for the ration of shit Becks is going to spew at me, and by the looks of my car, that I obviously deserve?

And yet I still can't resist.

I take another step toward him, slow and deliberate in my motions, like I am with the boys at The House.

The boys.

Rylee.

I need to see her.

Don't want to be alone anymore.

I need to feel her.

Don't want to be broken anymore.

Why am I swimming in a sea of confusion? And yet I take another step through the fog toward this unexpected ray of light.

Be my spark.

"That's a pretty bad owie you got there …"

He snorts. It's so fucking adorable to see this little kid with such a serious face, nose scattered with freckles scrunched up, looking at me like I'm missing something.

"Thanks, Captain Obvious!"

And a smart-ass mouth on him too. *My type of kid.* I stifle a chuckle as he glances back over my shoulder again for the third time. I start to turn to see what he's looking at when his voice stops me. "Are you okay?"

Huh? "What do you mean?"

"Are you okay?" he asks again. "You seem kind of broken."

"What are you talking about?" I take another step toward him. My fleeting thoughts mixed with the somberness of his tone and the concern etched on his face is starting to unnerve me.

"Well, you look broken to me," he whispers as his Band-Aid wrapped finger flips the propeller again—*thwack, thwack, thwack*—before motioning up and down my body.

Anxiety creeps up my spine until I look down at my race suit to find it intact, my hands patting up and down to calm the feeling. "No." The words rush out. "I'm okay, buddy. See? Nothing's wrong," I say, sighing a quick breath of relief. The little fucker scared me for a second.

"No, silly," he says with a roll of his eyes and a huff of breath before pointing over my shoulder. "Look. You're broken."

I turn, the calm simplicity of his tone puzzling me, and look behind me.

My heart stops.

Thwack.

My breath strangles in my chest.

Thwack.

My body freezes.

Thwack.

I blink my eyes over and over, trying to push away the images before me. The sights permeate through a viscous haze.

Spiderman. Batman. Superman. Ironman.

Fuck. No. No. No. No.

"See," his angelic voice says beside me. "I told you."

No. No. No. No.

The air finally punches from my lungs. I force a swallow down my throat that feels like sandpaper.

I know I see it—the chaos right before my eyes—but how is it possible? How am I here and *there?*

Thwack. Thwack. Thwack.

I try to move. To fucking run! To get their attention to tell them I'm right here—that I'm okay—but my feet won't listen to the ricocheting panic in my brain.

No. I'm not there. Just here. I know I'm okay—know I'm alive—because I can feel my breath catch in my chest when I take a step forward to get a closer look. Fingertips of dread tickle over my scalp because what I see … that can't be … it's just not fucking possible.

Spiderman. Batman. Superman. Ironman.

The gentle whir of the saw pulls me from my ready-to-rage state as the medical crew cuts the driver's helmet down the center. The minute they split it apart, my head feels like it explodes. I drop to my knees, the pain so excruciating all I can do is raise my hands up to hold it. I have to look up. Have to see who was in my car. Whose motherfucking ass is mine, but I can't. It hurts too goddamn much.

... I wonder if there's pain when you die ...

I jolt at the feel of his hand on my shoulder ... but the minute it rests there, the pain ceases to exist.

What the ...? I know I have to look. I have to see for myself who is in the car even though I ultimately know the truth. Disjointed memories fracture and flicker through my mind just like pieces of the splintered mirror in that fucking dive bar.

Humpty fucking Dumpty.

Fear snakes up my spine, takes hold, and reverberates through me. I just can't do it. I can't look up. *Don't be such a pussy, Donavan.* Instead, I look to my right into *his* eyes, the unexpected calm in this storm. "Is that ...? Am I ...?" I ask the little boy as my breath clogs my throat, apprehension over the answer holds my voice hostage.

He just looks at me—eyes clear, face serious, lips pursed, freckles dancing—before he squeezes my shoulder. "What do you think?"

I want to shake a fucking answer out of him but know I won't. Can't. With him here at my side amidst this whirling chaos, I've never felt more at peace and yet at the same time more scared.

I force my eyes from his serene face to look back at the scene in front of me. I feel like I'm in a kaleidoscope of jagged images as I take in the face—my fucking face—on the gurney.

My heart crashes. Sputters. Stops. Dies.

Spiderman.

Grey skin. Eyes swollen, bruised, and closed. Lips lax and pale.

Batman.

Devastation surrenders, desperation consumes, life sputters, and yet my soul clings.

Superman.

"No!" I yell at the top of my lungs until my voice falls hoarse. No one turns. No one hears me. Every fucking person is unresponsive—my body and the medics.

Ironman.

The body on the gurney—*my body*—jolts as someone climbs on the stretcher and starts compressions on my chest. Someone fastens the neck brace. Lifts my eyelids and checks my pupils.

Thwack.

Wary faces. Defeated eyes. Routine movements.

Thwack.

"No!" I shout again, panic reigning within every ounce of me. "No! I'm right here! Right here! I'm okay."

Thwack.

Tears fall. Disbelief stutters. Possibilities vanish. Hope implodes.

My life blurs.

My eyes focus on my hand hanging limp and lifeless off of the gurney—a single drip of blood slowly making its way down to the tip of my finger before another compression on my chest joggles it to drip on the ground beneath. I focus on that ribbon of blood, unable to look back at my face. I can't take it anymore.

Can't stand watching the life drain from me. Can't stand the fear that creeps into my heart, the unknown that trickles into my subconscious, and the cold that starts to seep into my soul.

"Help me!" I turn to the little boy so familiar but so unknown. "Please," I beg, an imploring whisper, with every ounce of life I have in me. "I'm not ready to ..." I can't finish the sentence. If I do then I'm accepting what is happening on the gurney before me—what his place beside me signifies.

"No?" he asks. A single word, but the most important one of my fucking life. I stare at him, consumed by what is in the depths of his eyes—understanding, acceptance, acknowledgment—and as much as I don't want to leave the feeling I have with him, the question he's asking me—to choose life or death—is the easiest decision I've ever had to make.

And yet, the decision to live—to go back and prove like fucking hell that I deserve to be given this choice—means that I'll have to leave his angelic little face and the serenity his presence brings to my otherwise troubled soul.

"Will I ever see you again?" I'm not sure where the question comes from, but it falls out before I can stop it. I hold my breath waiting for his answer, wanting both a yes and a no.

He tilts his head to the side and smirks. "If it's in the cards."

Whose fucking cards? I want to yell at him. God's? The Devil's? Mine? Whose fucking cards? But all I can say is, "*The cards?*"

"Yup," he responds with a little shake of his head as he looks down at his helicopter and back up to me.

Thwack. Thwack. Thwack.

The sound becomes louder now, drowning out all noise around me, and yet I can still hear the draw of his breath. Still hear the pounding of my heart in my eardrums. Can still feel the soft sigh of peace that wraps around my body like a whisper as he places his hand on my shoulder.

All of a sudden I see the helicopter—Life Flight—on the infield, the incessant sound of the rotors—thwack, thwack, thwack—as it waits for me. The gurney shunts forward as they start to move quickly toward it.

"Aren't you going?" he asks me.

I work a swallow in my throat as I look back at him and give him a subtle, resigned nod of my head. "Yeah ..." It's almost a whisper, fear of the unknown heavy in my tone.

Spiderman. Batman. Superman. Ironman.

"Hey," he says, and my eyes come back into focus on his perfect fucking face. He points back to the activity behind me. "It looks like your superheroes came this time after all."

I whirl around, heart lodged in my throat and confusion meddling with my logic. I don't see it at first, the pilot's back is to me, helping load *my* stretcher in the medevac, but when he turns around to jump in the pilot's seat and take the joystick, it's clear as day.

My heart stops.

And starts.

A hesitant exhale of relief flickers through my soul.

The pilot's helmet is painted.

Red.

With black lines.

The call sign of Spiderman emblazoned on the front of it.

The little boy in me cheers. The grown man in me sags with relief.

I turn back to say goodbye to the little boy, but he's nowhere to be found. How in the hell did he know about the superheroes? I look all around for him—needing the answer—but he's gone.

I'm all alone.

All alone except for the comfort of those I've waited a lifetime to arrive.

My decision's been made.

The superheroes finally came.

Chapter One

Numbness slowly seeps through my body. I can't move, can't think, can't bear to pull my eyes from the mangled car on the track. If I look anywhere else, then this will all be real. The helicopter flying overhead will really be carrying the broken body of the man I love.

The man I need.

The man I can't lose.

I close my eyes and just listen, but I can't hear anything. The only thing in my ears is the thumping of my pulse. The only thing besides the blackness that my eyes see—that my heart feels—is the splintered images in my mind. Max melting into Colton and then Colton fading back to Max. Memories that cause the hope I'm grasping like a lifeline to flicker and flame before dying out, like the darkness smothering the light in my soul.

I race you, Ryles. His voice so strong and unwavering fills my head and then dissipates, glittering through my mind like ticker tape.

I double over, willing the strangling tears to come or a spark to fire within me, but nothing happens, just lead dropping through my soul and weighing me down.

I force myself to breathe while I try to fool my mind into believing the past twenty-two minutes never happened. That the car never cartwheeled and pirouetted through the smoke-filled air. That the metal of the car wasn't cut apart by somber-faced medics to extricate Colton's lifeless body.

We never made love. The single thought flits through my head. We never had the chance *to race* after he finally told me the words I'd needed to hear—and that he'd finally accepted, admitted to, and felt for himself.

I just want to rewind time and go back to the suite when we were wrapped in each other's arms. When we were connected—overdressed and underdressed—but the horrific sights of the mangled car won't allow it. They have scarred my memory so horribly for a second time that it's not possible for my hope to escape unscathed.

"Ry, I'm not doing too good here." They're Max's words seeping into my mind, but it's Colton's voice. It's Colton warning me of what's to come. What I've already lived through once in my life.

Oh God. Please no. Please no.

My heart wrings.

My resolve falters.

Images filter in slow motion.

"Rylee, I need you to concentrate. Look at me!" Max's words again. I start to sag, my body giving out like my hope, but arms close around me and give me a shake.

"Look at me!" No, not Max. Not Colton. *It's Becks.* I find it within myself to focus and meet his eyes—pools of blue fringed with the sudden appearance of lines at their corners. I see fear in them. "We need to go to the hospital now, okay?" His voice is gentle yet stern. He seems to think that if he talks to me like a child I won't shatter into the million pieces my soul is already broken into.

I can't swallow the sand in my throat to speak, so he gives me another shake. I've been robbed of every emotion but fear. I nod my head but don't make any other movement. It's utterly silent. There are tens of thousands of people in the grandstands around us, and yet no one is talking. Their eyes are focused on the clean-up crew and what's left of the numerous cars on the track.

I strain to hear a sound. To sense a sign of life. Nothing but absolute silence.

I feel Becks' arm go around me, supporting me as he directs us out of the tower on pit row, down the steps and toward the open door of a waiting van. He pushes gently on my backside to urge me in like I'm a child.

Beckett scoots in next to me on the seat and pushes my purse and my cell phone into my hands as he fastens his own belt and then says, "Go."

The van revs forward, jostling me as it clears the infield. I look out as we start to descend down the tunnel, and all I see are Indy cars scattered over the track completely motionless. Colorful headstones in a quiet graveyard of asphalt.

"Crash, crash, burn ..." The lyrics of the song float from the speakers and into the lethal silence of the van. My blank mind slowly processes them.

"Turn it off!" I shout with panicked composure as my hands fist and teeth grit, as the words embed themselves into the reality I'm unsuccessfully trying to block out.

Hysteria surfaces.

"Zander," I whisper. "Zander has a dentist appointment on Tuesday. Ricky needs new cleats. Aiden has tutoring starting on Thursday and Jax didn't put it on the calendar." I look up to find Beckett's eyes trained on mine. In my periphery I notice some of the other crew seated behind us but don't know how they got there.

It bubbles up.

"Beckett, I need my phone. Dane is going to forget and Zander really needs to go to the dentist, and Scooter ne—"

"Rylee," he says in an even tone, but I just shake my head.

"No!" I yell. "No! I need my phone." I start to undo my seat belt, so flustered I don't even realize it's in my hand. I try to scamper over him to reach the sliding door of the moving van. Beckett struggles to wrap his arms around me to prevent me from opening it.

It boils over.

"Let go of me!" I fight against him. I writhe and buck but he successfully manages to restrain me.

"Rylee," he says again, and the broken tone in his voice matches the feeling in my heart taking the fight out of me.

I collapse into the seat but Beckett keeps me pulled against him, our breathing labored. He grabs my hand and squeezes tightly, the only show of desperation in his stoic countenance, but I don't even have the wherewithal to squeeze it back.

The world outside blurs, but mine has stopped. It's lying on a gurney somewhere.

"I love him, Beckett," I finally whisper.

I'm driven by fear...

"I know," he says, exhaling a shaky breath and kisses the crown of my head. "I do too."

... Fueled with desperation ...

"I can't lose him." The words are barely audible, as if saying them will make it happen.

... Crashing into the unknown.

"Neither can I."

The whoosh of the electric doors to the emergency room is paralyzing. I freeze at the noise.

Haunting memories flicker from the sound, and the angelic white of the hallways bring me anything but calming peace. It's odd to me that the slideshow of fluorescent lights on the ceiling are what flash through my mind—my only possible focus as my gurney was rushed down the hallway—medical jargon sparred between doctors rapidly, incoherent thoughts jumbling, and the whole time my heart pleading for Max, for my baby, for hope.

"Ry?" Beckett's voice pulls me from the panic strangling my throat, from the memories suffocating my progress. "Can you walk in?"

The gentleness in his tone washes over me, a balm to my open wound. All I want to do is cry at the comfort in his voice. The tears clog my throat and burn my eyes and yet they never well. Never fall.

I take a fortifying breath and will my feet to move. Beckett places an arm around my waist and helps me with the first step.

The doctor's face flashes through my mind. Stoic. Unemotional. Head shaking back and forth. Apology in his eyes. Defeat in his posture. Remembering how I wanted to close my eyes and slip away forever too. The words "I'm sorry" falling from his lips.

No. No. No. I can't hear those words again. I can't listen to someone telling me I've lost Colton, especially when we've just found each other.

I keep my head down. I count the laminate tiles on the floor as Becks leads me toward the waiting room. I think he's talking to me. Or to a nurse? I'm not sure because I can't focus on anything but pushing the memories out. Pushing out the despair so maybe just a sliver of hope can weasel its way into its vacated spot.

I sit in a chair beside Beckett and numbly look down at the constantly vibrating phone in my hand. There are endless texts and calls from Haddie, ones I can't even think to answer even though I know she's worried sick. It's just too much effort right now, too much everything.

I hear the squeak of shoes on linoleum as others file in behind us, but I focus on the children's book on the table in front of me. *The Amazing Spiderman*. My mind wanders, obsesses, focuses. Was Colton scared? Did he know what was happening? Did he call out the chant he told Zander about?

The thought alone breaks me and yet the tears don't come.

I see surgical booties in my periphery. Hear Beckett being addressed.

"The specialist needs to know exactly how impact was made so we best know the circumstances. We've tried to catch a replay but ABC stopped airing it." No, no, no. Words scream and echo through my head and yet silence smothers me. "I was told you'd be the person who'd most likely know."

Beckett shifts beside me. His voice is so thick with emotion when he begins to speak that I dig my fingers into my thighs. He clears his throat. "He hit the catch fence inverted … I think. I'm trying to picture it. Hold on." He drops his head into his hands, rubs his fingers over his temple, and sighs as he tries to gather his thoughts. "Yes. The car was upside down. The spoiler hit the top of the catch fence with the nose closest to the ground. Midsection against the concrete barrier. The car disintegrated around his capsule."

The collective gasp of the thousands of people in response still rings in my ears.

"Is there anything you can tell us?" Beckett asks the nurse.

The unmistakable noise of metal giving under force.

"Not right now. It's still the early stages and we're trying to assess everything—"

"Is he going to be …"

"We'll give you an update as soon as we can."

The smell of burned rubber on oiled asphalt.

Shoes squeak again. Voices murmur. Beckett sighs and scrubs his hands over his face before trembling fingers reach over and pull the hand gripping my leg free and clasps it in his.

The lone tire rolling across the grass and bouncing against the infield barrier.

Please just give me a sign, I beg silently. Something. Anything. A tiny little thing to tell me to hang on to the hope that's slipping through my fingers.

Ringing cell phones echo off of the waiting room's sterile walls. Over and over. Like the beeps on the life supporting machines that filter out into the waiting room. Each time one silences, a little part of me does too.

I hear the hitch of Becks' breath a moment before he emits a strangled sob that hits me like a hurricane, shredding the paper bag I have preserving my resolve and faith. As hard as he tries to push away the onslaught of tears that threaten him, he's unsuccessful. The grief escapes and runs down his cheeks in silence, and it kills me that the man who has been the strength for me is now crumbling. I squeeze my eyes shut and will myself to stay strong for Beckett, but all I keep hearing are his words to me last night.

I shake my head back and forth in a panicked disbelief. "I'm so sorry," I whisper. "I'm so, so sorry. This is all my fault."

Beckett hangs his head momentarily before wiping his eyes with the palms of his hands. And the gesture—pushing away tears like a little kid does when ashamed—wrings my heart even more.

I can't help the panic that flutters as I realize that I'm the reason Colton's here. I pushed him away and didn't believe him—made him tired the night before a race—and all because I was stubborn and scared. "I did this to him." The words kill me. Rip my soul apart.

Beckett lifts his red-rimmed eyes from his hands. "What are you talking about?" He leans in close, his conflicted blue eyes searching mine.

"Everything …" My breath hitches and I pause. "I messed with his head the last couple of days, and you told me that if I did, it was on me—"

"Ryl—"

"And I fought him and left him and we stayed up so late and I put him in that car tired and—"

"Rylee!" he finally manages in a harsh tone. I just keep shaking my head at him, eyes burning, emotions overloading. "This is not your fault."

I jolt as he puts his arms around me and pulls me into him. I fist my hands into the front of his fire suit, the coarseness of its fabric rough against my cheek.

"It was a crash. He drove into it blind. That's racing. It's not your fault." His voice breaks and falls on deaf ears. His arms are around me, trapping me, and claustrophobia threatens. Suffocation claws.

I stand abruptly, needing to move, to release the unease scavenging my soul. I pace to the far end of the waiting room and back. On my second pass the little boy in the corner chair scoots off his seat to pick up a crayon. The lights on his shoes flash red and grab my attention. I narrow my eyes to look closer, to take in the inverted triangle with the S in the center.

Superman.

The name feathers through my subconscious, but my attention is drawn to the television as someone changes the channel. I hear Colton's name and I suck in a breath, afraid to look but wanting to see what they're showing.

It seems like the whole room stands and moves collectively. A mass of red fire suits, faces conflicted with emotion, focus on the screen. The announcer says there was a crash that halted action for more than an hour. The screen flashes to the image of the cloud of smoke and cars careening off of each other. The angle is different than ours was on the track and we are able to see more, but as Colton's car comes into the turn, the broadcast cuts the footage. All of the shoulders around the television sag as the crew realizes that what they were anxiously anticipating will not be shown. The segment ends with the announcer saying that he is currently being treated at Bayfront.

I see Colton's lifeless body on the gurney, Max's beside me in his seat. The similarities of the situation knock the wind out of me, pain without end. Memories colliding.

I turn to see the Westins walk into the waiting room. Colton's regal and commanding mother looks pale and distraught. I swallow the lump in my throat, unable to tear my eyes from the sight of them. Andy supports her gently, guiding her to sit down as Quinlan grips her other hand.

Beckett's at their side in a flash with his arms wrapped around Dorothea and then Quinlan in quick but meaningful embraces. Andy reaches out and grabs Beckett in a longer hug, teeming with heart-wrenching desperation. I overhear a choked sob and almost break from the sound of it.

Watching the whole scene unfold causes memories to flicker through my mind of Max's funeral. A miniature pink casket laid atop a full-sized black casket, both blanketed with red roses, remind me of the words I can't hear again: *ashes to ashes, dust to dust.* Makes me remember the hollow, empty hugs that do nothing to comfort. The ones that leave you feeling over-sensitized, raw when you've already been scraped to the core.

I start to pace again amidst the hushed murmurs of "how long until there is an update?" Faces usually so strong and energetic are etched with lines of concern. And when my feet stop I'm looking into the eyes of Andy and Dorothea.

We just stare at each other, faces mirrors of each others' disbelief and anguish, until Dorothea reaches a trembling hand out for mine. "I don't know what … I'm so sorry …" I shake my head back and forth as words escape me.

"We know, sweetheart," she says as she pulls me into her arms and clings to me, both of us holding each other up. "We know."

"He's strong," is all Andy says as his hand rubs up and down my back to try and comfort me. But this—hugging his parents, all of us comforting each other, the tear-stained cheeks and muffled sobs—makes it all too real. My hope that this is all a really bad dream is now shattered.

I stagger back and try to focus on something, anything, to make me feel like I'm not losing it.

But I keep seeing Colton's face. The look of absolute certainty as he stood amid all of the chaos of his crew—the same crew that sits around me, heads in hands, lips pulled tight, eyes closed in prayer—and admitted his feelings for me. I have to stop to try and catch my breath, the pain radiating through my chest, in my heart, just won't stop.

The television pulls at me again. Something whispers through my mind and I turn to look. A trailer for the new Batman movie. Hope reawakens as my mind reaches into its depths—into the past hour.

The Spiderman book on the table. The Superman shoes. The Batman movie. I try to rationalize that this is all just a coincidence—that seeing three of the four superheroes is a random occurrence. I try to tell myself that I need the fourth to believe it. That I need Ironman to complete the circle—to be the sign that Colton will pull through.

That he will come back to me.

I start searching, eyes flitting around the waiting room as hope looms and readies itself to blossom, if I can just find the final sign. My hands tremble; my optimism lies beneath the surface cautious to raise its weary head.

There is sound toward the hallway and the noise—the voice—causes every emotion that pulses through me to ignite.

And I'm immediately ready to detonate.

Blonde hair and long legs breeze through the door and I don't care that her face looks as devastated and worried as I feel. All of my heartache, all of my angst rears up and is like a rubber band snapping.

Or lightning striking.

I'm across the room within seconds, heads snapping at the growl I let loose in my fury-filled wake. "Get out!" I scream, so many emotions coursing through me that all I feel is a mass of overwhelming confusion. Tawny's head whips up and her startled eyes meet mine, her enhanced lips set in a perfect O shape. "You conniving bit—"

The air is knocked out of me as Beckett's strong arms grab me from behind and yank me back into his chest. "Let me go!" I struggle against him as he grips me tighter. "Let me go!"

"Save it, Ry!" He grunts as he restrains me, his reserved yet firm drawl hitting my ears. "You need to save all of that fire and energy because Colton's going to need it from you. Every goddamn ounce of it." His words hit me, punch through the holes in me, and sap my adrenaline. I stop struggling, his grip around me still iron clad, and the heat of his breath panting against my cheek. "She's not worth it, okay?"

I can't find my words—don't think I'm capable of coherency at this point—so I just nod my head in agreement, forcing myself to focus on a spot on the floor in front of me, rather than on the long legs off to the right.

"You sure?" he reaffirms before slowly letting go and stepping in front of me, forcing me to look into his eyes, to test if I'll be true to my word.

My body starts trembling, held captive to the mixture of anger, grief, and the unknown coursing through me.

My breath hitches as my lungs hurt with each breath. It's the only hint of the turmoil I feel inside when I meet the kindness edged with concern in Beckett's eyes. And I feel so horrible that he's here trying to take care of me when he loves Colton and is reeling from the unknown just as much as I am, so I force myself to nod. He mimics my action before turning around, his body blocking my line of sight to Tawny.

"Becks ..." She sighs his name and her voice alone chafes over my exposed nerves.

"Not a fucking word, Tawny!" Beckett's voice is low and guarded, audible only to the three of us despite the numerous pairs of eyes watching the confrontation. I see Andy rise to his feet from the other side of the room as he tries to figure out what's going on. "I'm letting you stay for one reason and one reason only ... Wood is going to need everyone he has in his corner—behind him if he ..." he says, choking on the words, "when he pulls out of this ... and that includes you, although right now after the stunt you pulled between him and Ry, *friend* is a very loose term when it comes to you."

Becks' words take me by surprise. I hear the noncommittal sound she makes before a momentary silence hits ... and then I hear her start to cry. Quiet, sorrowful whimpers that break through the hold on me that Beckett's voice couldn't.

And I snap. My reassurance to Becks that I'd save my strength vanishes right along with my restraint.

"No!" I scream, trying to push Beckett out of the way and take a swing. "You don't get to cry for him! You don't get to cry for the man you tried to manipulate!" Arms close around me from behind, preventing me from landing my punch, but I don't care, reality's lost to me. "Get out!" I shout, my voice wavering as I'm dragged away from her stunned face. "No!" I struggle against the restraining arms. "Let me go!"

"Shh-shh-shh!" It's Andy's voice, Andy's arms that are holding me tight, trying to soothe and control me at the same time. And the only thing I can focus on—can grasp onto as my heart races and body shakes with anger—is that I need a *pit stop*. I need to find Colton. I need to touch him, to see him, to quiet the turmoil in my soul.

But I can't.

He's somewhere close, my rebellious rogue unable to let go of the damaged little boy within. The man who has just started healing is now broken, and it kills me that I won't be able to fix him. That my murmured words of encouragement and patient nature won't be able to repair the immobile and unresponsive body that was loaded onto that stretcher and rushed to somewhere within these walls—so close yet so very far away from me. That he has to rely on strangers to mend and heal him now. Strangers that have no idea of the invisible scar tissue that still lingers beneath the surface.

More hands reach out to touch and soothe me, Dorothea's and Quinlan's, but they're not the ones I want. They're not Colton's.

And then a terrifying thought hits me. Every time Colton is near, I can feel that tingle—the buzz that tells me he's just within reach—but I can't feel anything. I know he's physically close, but his spark is nonexistent.

Be my spark, Ry. I can hear his voice say it, can feel the memory of his breath feather over my skin ... but I can't *feel* him.

"*I can't!*" I shout. "I can't be your spark if I can't feel yours, so don't you dare burn out on me." I don't care that I'm in a room full of people, being turned around and encircled into Dorothea's arms, because the only one who I want to hear me, can't. And knowing that causes desperation to consume every part of me not already frozen with fear. I fist my hands into the back of Dorothea's jacket, clinging to her while I plead with her son. "Don't you dare die on me, Colton! I need you dammit!" I shout into the now sterile silence of the waiting room. "I need you so much that I'm dying right here, right now without you!" My voice cracks just like my heart, and as much as Dorothea's arms, Quinlan's hushed murmurs, and Andy's quiet resolve helps, I just can't handle it all.

I push away and stare at them before I stumble blindly down the hall. I know I'm losing it. I'm so numb, so hollow, that I don't even have the energy to argue with Beckett and refire the hatred I feel for Tawny. If I'm to blame for Colton being here, then she sure as fuck needs to share some of that blame too.

I turn the corner to head toward the bathroom and have to push myself to move. I press my hands against the wall for support or else I'll collapse. I remind myself to breathe, tell myself to put one foot in front of the other, but it's nearly impossible when the only thought my mind can focus on is that the man I love is fighting for his life, and I can't do a goddamn thing about it. I'm hopeless and powerless.

I'm dying inside.

My guiding hands hit a doorjamb, and I stagger between its frame and into the nearest stall, welcoming the cocooning silence of the empty bathroom. I unbutton my shorts, and when I shimmy them over my hips, my eyes catch sight of the checkered pattern on my panties. My body wants to quit, wants to slide to the floor and sink into oblivion, but I don't. Instead, my hands grip onto the belt loops of the shorts still hanging off of my hips. I can't catch my breath fast enough. I start to hyperventilate and get dizzy, so I brace my hands against the wall but nothing helps as the panic attack hits me full force.

You can bet your ass that's one checkered flag I'm definitely claiming.

I welcome the memorized sound of his voice. I let his rumble permeate through me like the glue I need to hold my broken self together. My breath drags in ragged rasps between my lips as I try to hold onto the memory—that incredible grin and the boyish mischief in his eyes—before he kissed me one last time. I bring my fingers to my lips wanting to make a connection with him, fear of the unknown weighing heavy in my heart.

"Rylee?" The voice jolts me to the here and now and I just want her to go away. I want her to leave me intact with my memory of the warmth of his skin, taste of his kiss, possession in his touch. "Rylee?"

There's a knock on the stall door. "Mmm-hmm?" is all I can manage because my breathing is still forced and irregular.

"It's Quin." Her voice is soft and uneven, and it kills me to hear the break in it. "Ry, please come out ..."

I reach forward and unlock the door, and she pushes it open looking at me oddly, her tear stained face and smudged mascara only emphasizing the devastation looming in her eyes. She purses her lips and starts laughing, in a way that's borderline hysterical so when it echoes off of the tile walls around us all I hear is despair and fear. She points to my half-shoved down shorts and checkered panties and keeps laughing, the tears staining her cheeks an odd contrast to the sound coming from her mouth.

I start laughing with her. It's the only thing I can do. Tears won't come, fear won't abate, and hope is wavering as the first laugh falls from my lips. It feels so wrong. Everything is just so wrong and within an instant, Quinlan—the woman who hated me at first sight—reaches out and wraps her arms around me while her laughter turns into sobs. Gut wrenching hiccups of unfettered fear. Her tiny frame shakes as her anguish intensifies.

"I'm so scared, Rylee." It's the only thing she can manage to get out between hitches of breath, but it's all she needs to say because it's exactly how I feel. The defeat in her posture, the fortitude of her grief, the strength in her grip reflects the fear that I'm not able to express, so I cling to her with everything I have—needing that connection more than anything.

I hug her and soothe her as best as I can, trying to lose myself in the role of patient counselor I know so well. It's so much easier to assuage someone else's despair than to face my own. She tries to pull away, but I just can't let go. I don't have the wherewithal to walk out the doors and wait for the doctor to report news I'm terrified to hear.

I fasten my shorts and look up to meet my own reflection in the mirror. I can see the haunting memories flickering in my eyes. My mind flashes to a shattered rearview mirror, sun reflecting on its blood-specked, jagged edges as Max gurgles his last breath. And then my mind grasps onto a happier memory with another mirror. One used in the heat of passion to demonstrate why I'm enough for Colton. *Why he chooses me.*

"C'mon," she whispers, breaking my trance as she releases me but moves her hand down to wrap around my waist. "I don't want to miss an update."

Chapter Two

Time has stretched. Each minute feels like an hour. And each of the three hours that have passed feels like an eternity. Each swoosh of the doors has us all startling and then sinking back down. Empty Styrofoam cups spill over the wastebasket. Fire suits have been unzipped and tied around waists as the waiting room grows stuffy. Cell phones ring incessantly with people searching for updates. But there's still no news.

Beckett sits with Andy. Dorothea has Quinlan on one side of her and Tawny on the other. The waiting room is full of hushed murmurs and the television plays background to my thoughts. I sit by myself and except for the constant texts from Haddie, I welcome the solitude so I don't have to comfort or be comforted—the schizophrenia in my mind only getting louder with each passing second.

My stomach churns. I'm hungry but the thought of food makes me nauseous. My head pounds but I welcome the pain, welcome the drum of it to count to as I try to speed up time. Or slow it down—whichever is to the benefit of Colton.

The electronic beep of the door. The squeak of shoes. I don't even open my eyes this time.

"I have an update on Mr. Donavan." The voice jolts me. Feet shuffle as the guys stand and an understated anxiety hums through the room in anticipation of what is going to be said.

Fear grips me. I can't stand. Can't move. I'm so petrified of the words that are going to pass through his lips that I force a swallow down my throat but remain paralyzed with trepidation

I squeeze my hands, gripping them into the bare flesh of my thighs, trying to use the pain to bury the memories. Willing the past to not repeat itself—to not trade one wrecked car with a man that I love for another.

He clears his throat and I suck in a breath—praying, hoping, needing some kind of scrap to hold on to. "Let me just say that scans are still ongoing at this point but from what we can tentatively see, it's obvious that Mr. Donavan has suffered a sudden deceleration injury with an internal organ disruption from the force in which he hit the catch fence. The injury occurs because the body is forcibly stopped but the organs inside the body remain in motion due to the inertia. From what we can tell …"

"English, please," I whisper. My mind tries to comprehend the medical jargon, knowing that if I wasn't swimming in this fog of uncertainty, I'd be able to process it. He stops at my comment and even though I can't lift my eyes to meet his, I say it louder this time. "English, please, doctor." Fear overwhelms me. I cautiously lift my eyes to meet his, the crew turning to look at me while I stare at the doctor. "We're all very worried here and while you may understand what you're saying, the terminology is scaring the shit out of us..." my voice fades and he nods kindly, "...our minds are too overwhelmed to process this all right now … it's been a long wait for us while you've been with him … so can you please just tell us in simple terms?"

He smiles gently at me but his eyes are grave. "When Colton hit the wall, the car stopped—his body stopped—but his brain kept going, slamming into the skull surrounding it. Fortunately he was wearing a HANS device which helped to protect the connection between his spine and his neck, but the injury he sustained is serious nonetheless."

My heart races and my breath labors as a million different possible outcomes flicker through my mind.

"*Will he …?*" Andy moves into my view facing the doctor and asks the question he can't complete. Silence descends upon the room and the nervous shifting of feet stops as we all wait for the answer with baited breath.

"Mr. Westin, I presume?" the doctor asks as he holds out his hand to a nodding Andy. "I'm Dr. Irons. I'm not going to lie to you … your son's heart arrested—stopped twice during transport."

I feel as if the bottom of my soul has dropped out with those words. *Don't leave me. Please don't leave me.* I plead silently, willing the words to hit him somewhere within the confines of this hospital.

Andy reaches out and squeezes Dorothea's hand.

"We were able to get his heart regulated after a bit which is a good sign as we were afraid that possibly his aorta had torn from the force of the impact. At this point in time we know that he has a subdural hematoma." The doctor looks up and meets my eyes before continuing. "This means that the blood vessels ruptured and the area between his brain and the skull is filling with blood. The situation is twofold because Colton's brain is swelling from the trauma of hitting his skull. At the same time, the pooling blood is putting pressure on his brain because there is nowhere for it to escape to relieve said pressure." Dr. Irons scans the eyes of the crew surrounding him. "At this time he's more stable than not, so we are prepping him for surgery. It's imperative that we go in and relieve the pressure on his brain to try and stop the swelling."

I watch Dorothea reach over and cling to Andy for support, the obvious unconditional love for her son pulls on my every emotion.

"How long is the surgery? Is he conscious? Were there any other injuries?" Beckett speaks for the first time, rapidly firing off the questions we are all thinking.

Dr. Irons swallows and steeples his fingers in front of him while meeting Beckett's eyes. "As for other injuries, just minor ones in comparison to the head injury. He is not conscious nor has he regained consciousness at this time. He was in the typical comatose state we see with these injuries—mumbling incoherently, struggling against us—in very sporadic bouts. As for everything else, we'll know more when we get into surgery and see how bad the bleed on the brain is."

Beckett exhales the breath he's been holding, and I can see his shoulders slump with its release, although I'm unsure if it's in relief or resignation. None of the doctor's words have made the dread weighing down the pit of my soul lessen any. Quinlan steps forward and grabs Becks' hand as she glances over at her parents before asking the one thing we all fear. "If the swelling doesn't stop with the surgery..." her voice wavers, Beckett pressing a brotherly kiss onto the top of her head in encouragement "...what ... does that mean? What I'm trying to say is you're talking brain injury here so what is the prognosis?" Her breath hitches with a swallowed sob. "What are Colton's chances?"

The doctor sighs aloud and looks at Quinlan. "At this time, before we go into surgery and see if there is any damage, I'm not comfortable giving one." The strangled gasp that comes from Andy breaks the silence. Dr. Irons steps forward and places a hand on his shoulder until Andy looks up and meets his eyes. "We are doing absolutely everything we can. We are very practiced in this sort of thing and are giving your son every benefit of that training. Please understand that I'm not giving a percentage because it's a lost cause, but rather because I need to see more to know what we're up against. Once I know, then we can establish a game plan and go from there." Andy nods subtly at him, rubbing a hand over his eyes, and Dr. Irons looks up and scans the faces of everyone in the room. "He is strong and healthy and that's always a good thing to have on our side. It's more than obvious Colton is loved by many people ... please know I carry that knowledge into the operating room with me." With that he gives a tight smile then turns and leaves the room.

Upon his departure, no one moves. We are all still in shock.

All still letting the severity of his words slither into the holes poked through our resolve. People slowly start moving and shifting as thoughts meld and emotions attempt to settle.

But I'm unable to.

He's alive. Not dead like Max. Alive.

The dull ache of relief I feel is nothing compared to the sharp stab of the unknown. And it's not enough to assuage the fear seated deep in the depths of my soul. I start to feel the leeching claws of claustrophobia burn over my skin. I blow out a long breath trying to abate the sweat beading on my upper lip and sliding down the line of my spine. My breath slips from my lungs without replenishing my body.

Images flicker again. Max to Colton. Colton to Max. Blood tricking slowly from his ear. At the corners of his mouth. Flecking in specks across the shattered car. My name strangling on his lips. His pleas scarring my mind. Etching them like a brand marked to haunt me forever.

The sprinkling of unease turns into a downpour of panic. I need fresh air. I need a break from the oppression that is smothering this goddamn waiting room. I need color and vibrancy—something full of vigor and life like Colton—something other than the monochromatic colors and overwhelming memories.

I push myself up and all but run out of the waiting room ignoring Beckett's call after me. I stagger blindly toward the exit because this time the whoosh of the doors calls to me, offers a respite from the hysteria siphoning my hope.

You make me feel, Rylee ...

I stumble through the doors, the memory feathering through my soul but hitting me like a sucker punch to the abdomen. I gasp loudly, pain radiating through my every synapse. I draw in a ragged breath, needing something, anything to help recoup the faith I need to face the reality that Colton might not make it through the surgery. The night. The morning.

I shake my head to rid the poison eating my thoughts when I turn the corner of the building and am thrown into a maelstrom. I swear there are over a hundred cameras that flash all at once. The roar of questions thunders so loudly that I'm blasted by a tidal wave of noise. I'm surrounded immediately, my back pressed against the wall as microphones and cameras are shoved in my face documenting my slowly depleting grip on reality.

"Is it true they're issuing Colton his last rites?"

Words trap in my throat.

"What is the status between you and Mr. Donavan?"

Anger intensifies but I'm overwhelmed by the deluge.

"Is it true that Colton's on his death bed and his parents are at his side?"

My lips open and close, my fists clench, eyes burn, soul tears, and my faith in humanity crumbles. I know I look like a deer in the headlights, but I'm trapped. I know that if I thought I felt the claws of claustrophobia inside, I feel the cinch of my windpipe as the hands of the media squeeze the air from me. My breath comes in short sharp bouts. The blue sky spins above as my mind warps it into a lazy eddy, blackness starts to seep through as my conscious fades.

Just as I am about to sink into the welcoming oblivion, strong arms wrap around me and prevent my crash to the ground. My weight slams into Sammy's like a freight train, and memories spear through my mind of the last time I fell into the arms of a man. Bittersweet images flicker of lost auction paddles and jammed closet doors. Vibrant green eyes and an arrogant, self-assured grin.

Rogue. Rebel. Reckless.

Sammy's voice breaks through my clouded mind as he chastises the press. "Back off!" he grunts as he supports my dead weight, arm around my waist. "We'll give an update when we have one." Flashes reignite the sky.

Again, the whoosh of doors, but this time I don't cringe. The beast on the inside is much more palpable than the one outside. My breath begins to even some and my heart decelerates. I am pushed down into a chair, and when I look up Sammy's eyes meet mine, searching for something.

"What in the hell do you think you were doing? They could've eaten you alive," he swears. It is such a flagrant show of emotion from the otherwise stoic bodyguard that I realize my mistake in going outside. I'm still finding my footing in Colton's very public world; and then I feel horrible because while I've been in the waiting room surrounded by everyone, I realize Sammy's been out here by himself making sure that we're left alone and undisturbed.

"I'm sorry, Sammy," I breathe an apology. "I just needed some air and … I'm sorry."

Concern lingers in his eyes. "Are you okay? Have you eaten anything? You almost fainted there. I think that you need to eat some—"

"I'm fine. Thank you," I say as I stand slowly. I think I surprise him when I reach out and squeeze his hand. "How are *you* doing?"

He shrugs nonchalantly, although the gesture is anything but. "As long as he is okay, then I'll be fine."

He nods at me as he turns to reclaim his post at the hospital doors before I can say anything else. My eyes track his movements for a moment, the callous comments from the press reverberating through my mind, while I build up the courage to walk back to the waiting room.

I close my eyes for a moment. I will myself to feel anything other than the numbness that consumes my soul. I try to pull from my depths of despair the sound of his laugh, the taste of his kiss, even his stubborn nature and staunch resolve—anything to cinch together the seams of my heart that Colton's love stitched backed together.

Not inconsequential, Rylee. You could never be inconsequential.

The memory whispers through my mind and is like flint re-sparking to life tiny flickers of hope. I take a deep breath and will my feet to move forward down the long corridor to where everyone else waits impatiently. I am just passing the nurses station when I hear Colton's name mentioned by two nurses whose backs are facing me. I slow my stride, trying to catch any bit of information I can. I try to force my mind from fretting that we're being lied to about the gravity of the situation, when I hear the words that punch the air from my lungs.

Makes my heart stop.

Causes a shiver to ricochet through my body.

"Who's in OR One with Mr. Donavan?"

"Dr. Irons is lead on the case."

"Well hell, if there's anyone I'd want operating on me in this circumstance, it sure as hell would be *Ironman*."

Spiderman.

I gasp, the nurses turn to take notice of me. The taller of the two steps forward and angles her head at me. "Can I help you miss?"

Batman.

"What did you just call Dr. Irons?"

Superman.

She looks at me, a slight crease in her brow. "You mean our nickname for Dr. Irons?"

Ironman.

All I can do is nod my head because my throat chokes with hope. "Oh, he's known around here as Ironman, sweetie. Do you need something?"

Spiderman. Batman. Superman. Ironman.

I just shake my head again then take the three steps toward the waiting room, but sag against a wall and slide down to the floor, as I become overwhelmed with hope, overpowered by the presence of Colton's beloved superheroes.

A childhood obsession now turned into an adult's grasp on hope.

I rest my face on my bent knees as I cling to the notion that this coincidence is more than just that—a coincidence. I rock my head back and forth, their names falling from my lips in a hushed chant that I know for the first time ever has been uttered with absolute reverence.

"Colton used to say that in his sleep as a little boy." Andy's voice startles me as he slides down the wall next to me, a heavy exhale falling from his lips. I shift some so I can look over at him. He looks years older in the hours since the race started this morning. His eyes hold a quiet grief and his mouth tries to lift in a soft smile but fails miserably. The man I've only known to be full of life has been sapped of his exuberance. "I haven't heard that in forever. Actually forgot about it until I just heard you say it." He chuckles softly, reaches out and pats my knee as he stretches his legs out in front of him.

"Andy ..." His name is a murmur on my lips as I watch him struggle with emotion. I desperately want to tell him about the signs—the random occurrence of his son's dearly loved superheroes—but worry he'll think I'm losing my grip on reality just as I fear Beckett thinks I am.

As I worry I might be.

"I'm surprised he told you about them. It used to be this secret code he'd chant as a little boy when he had a nightmare or was scared. He would never elaborate ... would never explain why those four superheroes were so comforting to him." He looks over at me, the soft smile falling. "Dottie and I could only ever imagine what he was hoping those superheroes would save him from ..."

The words drift between us and settle in questions we both want to ask but neither say aloud. What does Andy know that I don't and vice versa? He dabs the back of his hand at his eyes and exhales a shaky sigh.

"He's strong, Andy ... he's going to be ... he has to be okay," I finally say when I trust the resolve in my voice.

He just nods his head. We see a set of doctors running past us and my heart lodges in my throat, worried it's because of Colton. He scrubs a hand over his face and I watch the love fill his eyes. "The first time I ever saw him, he broke my heart and stole it all with one, single look." I nod my head at him to continue because more than anything I understand that statement, for his son did the same thing to mine.

He captured it, stole it, broke it, healed it, and forever owns it.

"I was on set working in my trailer on a scene rewrite. It had been a long night. Quin was sick and had been up all night." He shakes his head and meets my eyes for a moment before looking back down to focus them on the band of his watch that he's fiddling with. "I was late for a call time. I opened the door and almost tripped over him." He takes a moment to will the tears I see welling in his eyes to dissipate. "I think I swore aloud and I saw his little figure jolt back in unmistakable fear. I know he scared the shit out of me, and I could only imagine why a child would have that type of a reaction. He refused to look at me no matter how gentle I made my voice."

I reach over and take his hand in mine, squeezing to let him know that I know Colton's demons without him ever revealing them. I may not know the specifics, but I have seen enough to get the gist.

"I sat on the ground next to him and just waited for him to understand that I wasn't going to hurt him. I sang the only song I could think of." He laughs. "*Puff the Magic Dragon*. On the second time through, he lifted his head up and finally looked at me. *Sweet Christ* he stole my breath. He had the hugest green eyes in this pale little face and they looked up at me with such fear ... such foreboding ... that it took everything I had not to wrap my arms around and comfort him."

"I can't imagine," I murmur, going to withdraw my hand but stopping when Andy squeezes it.

"He wouldn't speak to me at first. I tried everything to get him to tell me his name or what he was doing, but it didn't matter. Nothing mattered—my missed call time, the wasted money, nothing—because I was mesmerized by the fragile little boy whose eyes told me they'd seen and experienced way too much in his short life. Quinlan was two at the time. Colton was so small in stature compared to her that I guessed he was about five. I was shocked later that night when the police told me he was eight years old."

I force the swallow that's stuck in my throat down as I listen to the first moments in Colton's life when he was given unconditional love. The first time he was given a life of possibilities rather than one of fear.

"I eventually asked him if he was hungry and those eyes of his got as big as saucers. I didn't have much in the trailer that a kid would like, but I did have a Snickers bar and I'll admit it," he says with a laugh, "I really wanted him to like me ... so I figured what kid couldn't be bribed with candy?"

I smile with him, the connection not lost on me that Colton eats a Snickers before every race. That he ate a Snickers bar today. My chest tightens at the thought. Was that really only hours ago? It feels like days.

"You know Dottie and I had talked about the possibility of more kids ... but had decided Quinlan was enough for us. Well, I should say that she would have had more and I was content with just one. Shit, we led busy lives with a lot of travel and we were fortunate enough with one healthy little girl, so how could we ask for more? My career was booming and Dottie took parts when she wanted to. But after that first few hours with Colton, there wasn't even a hesitation. How could I walk away from those eyes and the smile I knew was hiding somewhere beneath the fear and shame?" A tear slips over and down his cheek, the concern for his son, then and now, rolling off of him in waves. He looks up at me with gray eyes filled with a depth of emotions. "He's the strongest person—man—that I've ever met, Rylee." He chokes on a sob. "I just need him to be that right now ... I can't lose my boy."

His words tear at places so deep inside of me, for I understand the anguish of a parent scared they're losing their child. The deep seated fear you don't want to acknowledge but that squeezes at every part of your heart. Sympathy swamps me for this man that gave Colton everything, and yet the numbness inside me incarcerates my tears. "None of us can, Andy. He's the center of our world," I whisper in a broken voice.

Andy angles his head to the side and looks over and studies me for a moment. "I fear every time he gets in that car. *Every goddamn time* ... but it's the only place I see him free of the burden of his past ... see him outrun the demons that haunt him." He squeezes my hand until I look back up to see the sincerity in his eyes. "The only time, that is, until recently. Until I see him talk about, worry about, interact with ... you."

My breath catches, tears well for the first time but don't fall. After having Max's mom, Claire, hate me for so long, the unspoken approval from Colton's father is monumental. I hiccup a breath, trying to contain the tornado of emotions whirling through me.

"*I love him.*" It's all I can manage to say. Then it's all I can think about. I love him, and I might not ever get to really show him now that he's admitted to feeling the same way about me. And now I stand on the precipice of circumstances so out of my control that I fear I might not ever get the chance to.

Andy's voice pulls me from my rising panic attack. "Colton told me you encouraged him to find out about his birth mother."

I look down and draw absent circles on my knee with my fingertip, wary that this conversation can go one of two ways: Andy can be grateful that I'm trying to help his son heal or he can be upset and think I'm trying to drive a wedge between them.

"Thank you for that." He exhales softly. "I think he's always been missing a piece and maybe knowing about her will help fill that for him. Just the fact he's talking about it, asking about it, is a huge step..." he reaches out and places an arm around my shoulder and pulls me toward him so my head rests on his shoulder "...so thank you for helping him find himself in more ways than one."

I nod my head in acknowledgment, his confession causing words to escape me. We sit together like this for some time, accepting and pulling comfort from each other when all we feel is emptiness inside.

Chapter Three

It's a perfect day. Blue sky overhead, sun warming my cheeks, and not a thought on my mind. The waves crash into the sand with a soothing crescendo, roll after roll. I come here often, the place we had our first official date, because I feel close to him here. A memory, something to hold onto when I can never hold onto him again.

I wrap my arms around my knees and breathe it all in, accepting that sadness will always be a constant ache in my heart and wishing he were here beside me. But at the same time, I know I haven't felt this at peace since he's been gone. I might be turning a corner in my grief—at least that's what the therapist thinks—since it's been days without the blind panic and strangling screams that consume my thoughts and skew my grip on reality. I think that maybe after all of this time, I might be able to move forward—not on—but forward.

The lone car in the parking lot to my right catches my eye. I'm not sure why. Maybe it's because the car is parked near where Colton parked the Aston Martin on our first spontaneous outing—the most expensive beach date ever—but I look, my heart hoping what my mind knows is not possible. That it's him parking the car to come join me.

I turn to look just in time to see a figure walk up to the passenger side and lean over to talk to the driver through the open window. Something about the person causes me to rise from the sand. I shield my eyes from the sun's glare and study his profile, suddenly feeling that something is off.

Without thinking, I start walking toward the car, my unease increasing with each step. The stranger straightens up and turns to face me for a second, the sun lighting his dark features and my feet falter, breath lost.

My dark angel standing in the light.

"Colton?" My voice is barely a whisper as my brain attempts to comprehend how it's possible that he's here. Here with me when I saw them load his unresponsive body on the stretcher, kissed his cold lips one last time before they laid his casket to rest. My heart thunders in my chest, its beat accelerating with each passing second as the hope laced with panic starts to escalate.

And although my voice is so soft, he tilts his head to the side at the sound of his name, his eyes filled with a quiet sadness, lock onto mine. He starts to raise a hand but is distracted momentarily when the passenger door is shoved open. He looks into the car and then back to me, resignation etching the magnificent lines of his face. He hesitantly raises his hand again but this time finishes the wave to me.

I bring my fingertips to my lips as the grief rolling off of him finally reaches across the distance and collides into me, knocks the breath clear out of my lungs. I feel his absolute despair instantly. It rips through my soul like lightning splitting the sky.

And in that instant I know.

"Colton!" I say his name again, but this time my desperate scream pierces through the quiet serenity of the beach. Seagulls fly at the sound but Colton slides into the passenger seat without a second glance and shuts the door.

The car slowly heads toward the parking lot's exit, and I break out into a full sprint. My lungs burn and legs ache but I'm not fast enough. I'm not going to get there in time and can't seem to make any progress no matter how fast I run. The car turns to the right, out of the lot onto the empty road, and is angled to head past me on its way south. The blue metallic paint shimmers from the sun's rays and what I see stops me dead in my tracks.

It feels like forever since I have seen him like this. All-American, wholesome with blue eyes and that easy smile I love all too much. But his eyes never break from their focus on the road ahead.

Max never even gives me so much as a second look.

Colton, on the other hand, stares straight at me. The combination of fear, panic, and resignation etched on his face. In the tears coursing down his cheeks, the apologies his eyes express, in his fists pounding frantically against the windows, in his words I can see him mouth but can't hear him plead. All of it twists my soul and wrings it dry.

"No!" I yell, every fiber of my being focused on how to help him escape, how to save him.

And then I see movement in the backseat and am knocked clear to my knees. The gravel biting into them is nothing compared to the pain searing into the black depths of my core. And although I'm hurting more than I ever thought imaginable, a part of me is in awe—lost in that unconditional love you never think is possible until you experience it for yourself.

Ringlets frame her cherubic face, bouncing with the car's movement. She smiles softly at Max, completely oblivious to the violent protests from Colton in the seat in front of her. She twists in her car seat and looks toward me, violet eyes a mirror reflection looking back at me. And then ever so subtly, her rosebud lips quirk up at one corner as childhood curiosity gets the best of her and she stares at me. Tiny fingertips rise above the windowsill and wiggle at me.

I have to remind myself to breathe. Have to force the thought into my head because she's just singlehandedly ripped me apart and pieced me back together. And yet the sight of her has left me raw and abraded with tomorrows that will never be.

That I can never get back.

That were never mine to keep.

And from my place on the ground, my soul clinging for something to hang onto before being swallowed into the darkened depths of despair, I yell at the top of my lungs the name of the only person that can still be saved.

"Colton! Stop! Colton! Fight damn it!" My voice falls hoarse with the last words, sobs overtaking and despair overwhelming me. I hang my head in my hands and allow myself to be dragged under and drowned, welcoming the devastating darkness for the second time in my life. "No!" I scream.

Invisible hands grab me and try to pull me away from him, but I struggle with every ounce I can muster against them so I can save Colton.

Save the man I love.

"Rylee!" The voice urges me to turn away from Colton. No way in hell am I walking away again.

Never.

"Rylee!" The insistence intensifies as my shoulders are shoved back and forth. I try to flail my arms but I'm being held tight.

I awake with a start, Beckett's aqua blue eyes staring intensely into mine. "It's just a dream, Rylee. Just a dream."

My heart is racing and I gulp in air but my body doesn't seem to accept it. I can't grab my next breath fast enough. I bring a trembling hand up and rub it over my face to gain my bearings. It was so real. So impossible, yet so real ... unless ... unless Colton is ...

"Becks." His name is barely a whisper on my lips as the remnants of my dream gain momentum and I start to understand why Colton would be with Max and my daughter.

"What is it, Ry? You're white as a ghost."

The words strangle in my throat. I can't tell him what my mind is processing. I stutter trying to get the words out when we are interrupted.

"The family of Colton Donavan?"

Everyone in the waiting room stands and moves to congregate near the entrance of the waiting room, where a short woman in scrubs stands untying her surgical mask. I stand too, fear driving me to push my way to the forefront with Becks clearing the path ahead of me. When we stop next to Colton's parents, he reaches his hand over and grips mine. It's the only indication that he's as scared as I am.

Her eyes take in the lot of us and she shakes her head with a forced smile. "No, I need to speak to his immediate family," she says. I can hear the fatigue in her voice and of course my mind starts racing faster.

Andy steps forward and clears his throat. "Yes, we're all here."

"I see that, but I'd like to update his immediate family in private as per hospital protocol, sir." Her tone is austere yet soothing, and all I want to do is shake her until she says "screw the rules" and gives me an update.

Andy shifts his eyes from her to glance over at all of us before he continues. "My wife, daughter, and I may be Colton's immediate family, but everyone else here? They're the reason he's alive right now ... so in my eyes, they are family and deserve to hear the update at the same time we do, hospital protocol be damned."

A look of slight shock flickers across her features and in this moment I can see why all those years ago the police officers in the hospital didn't question Andy when he told them Colton was going home with him for the night.

She nods slowly at him, lips pursed. "My name is Dr. Biggeti and I teamed up in the operating room with Dr. Irons on your son's case." In my periphery I see most of the guys nod their heads, bodies leaning forward to make sure they hear everything. Dorothea steps up next to her husband, Quinlan on the opposite side, and grabs his hand like Becks is clutching mine. "Colton made it through surgery and is currently being moved to the ICU."

A collective gasp fills the room. My heart thunders at an accelerated pace and my head dizzies with the news. He's still alive. Still fighting. I'm scared and he's scarred but we're both still fighting.

Dr. Biggeti puts her hands up to quiet the murmuring among us. "Now there are still a lot of unknowns at this point. The bleeding and swelling were quite extensive and we had to remove a small section of Colton's skull to relieve the pressure on his brain. At this time, the swelling seems to be under control but I need to reiterate the words *at this time*. Anything can happen in these cases and the next twenty-four hours are extremely crucial in telling us which way Colton's body will decide to go." I feel Beckett sway next to me and I detangle our hands and wrap my arms around his waist, and take comfort in the fact we are all here, feeling the same way. That this time I'm not alone in watching the man I love struggle to survive. "And as much as I have hope that the outcome will be positive, I also need to prepare you for the fact that there may be possible peripheral damage that is unknown until he wakes up."

"Thank you." It's Dorothea who speaks as she steps forward and grabs a surprised Dr. Biggeti in a quick embrace before stepping back and dabbing the tears beneath her eyes. "When will we be able to see him?"

The doctor nods her head in compassion at Colton's parents. "Like I said, right now they are getting him situated and checking his vitals in the ICU. After a bit, you'll be able to see him." She looks over toward Andy. "And this time, I must follow hospital policy that only immediate family be allowed to visit with him."

He nods his head.

"Your son is very strong and is putting up one hell of a fight. It's obvious he has a strong will to live … and every little bit helps."

"Thank you so very much." Andy exhales before grabbing Dorothea and Quinlan in a tight embrace. His hands fist at their backs and expresses just an iota of the angst mixed with relief vibrating beneath his surface.

As the doctor walks away her words hit me, and I close my eyes to focus on the positive. To focus on the fact that Colton is fighting like hell to come back to us. To come back to me.

All of us—crew and family—have been moved to a different waiting room since we were taking up all of the space in the emergency area. This one's on a different floor, closer to the ICU and to Colton. The room's a serene light blue, but I'm nowhere near calm. Colton is near. The thought alone has me hyperventilating. I'm not immediate family so I'm not going to get to see him.

And that alone makes every breath an effort.

Leaves every emotion raw, nerves bared as if my skin has been peeled back and exposed to a fire hose.

Each thought focused on how much I need to see him for my own slipping sanity.

I stand and face a wall of windows overlooking a courtyard below. The parking lot beyond is swarming with media trucks and camera crews all trying to get something more on the story than the station next to them. I watch them absently, the mass becoming one big blur. *You were a spark of solid color to me in a world that's always been one big mixed blur of it …*

I'm so lost in my thoughts that I jolt when someone places their hand on my shoulder. I turn my head and meet the grief-stricken eyes of Colton's mother. We stare at each other for a moment; no words are spoken but so much is exchanged.

She's just come from seeing Colton. I want to ask her how he is, what he looks like, if he's as bad as the images I have in my mind. I open my mouth to speak but close it because I can't find the words to express myself.

Dorothea's eyes well and her bottom lip trembles with unshed tears. "I just …" she starts to say and then drifts off, bringing her hand to her mouth and shaking her head. After a moment, she begins again. "I can't stand seeing him like that."

My throat feels like it's closing as I try to swallow. I reach my hand up to my shoulder and squeeze hers, the only solace I can even remotely offer. "He has to be okay …" The same words I've uttered over and over today that fix nothing, but I say them nonetheless.

"Yes," she says with a determined nod as she takes in the circus of the parking lot. "I haven't had nearly enough time with him. I missed the first eight years of his life, so I'm owed extra ones for not getting the chance to save him sooner. God can't be that cruel to rob him of what he deserves." She looks over toward me on her last words, and the quiet strength of this mother fighting for her son is unmistakable. "I won't allow it." And the commanding woman that had slipped momentarily is back in control.

"Mom …" The sob is hiccupped as Quinlan re-enters the waiting room. We both turn to face her as she walks toward us, all eyes in the room on her. I watch Dorothea's face shifts gears as she goes from fierce protector to maternal soother. She pulls Quinlan into her arms and kisses the top of her head, squeezing her own eyes shut tight as she whispers words of encouragement that she fears are lies.

I feel like a voyeur—wanting my own mother more than anything right now—when Dorothea looks up at me over the crown of Quinlan's head. Her voice is a hushed murmur but it stops my breath. "It's your turn now."

"But I'm not …" I don't know why I'm so shocked that she's giving me this opportunity. The rule follower in me bristles, but my traumatized soul stands at attention.

"Yes, you are," she says, a tight smile on her lips and sincerity flooding her eyes. "You're helping make him whole—the one thing I've never been able to do as a mother and that kills me, but at the same time the fact that he's found it in you …" She can't finish the sentence and tears well in her eyes, so she reaches out and squeezes my hand. "Go."

I squeeze it back and nod at her before I turn to go to the man I can't live without, fear mixed with anticipation streaks through me like fireworks on a pitch black night.

Chapter Four

I stand outside of the intensive care unit and prepare myself. Fear and hope collide until one big ball of anxiety has my hands trembling as I turn the corner to stand at his doorway.

It takes me a moment to gain the courage to raise my eyes and take in the broken body of the man I love. The images in my head are worse—bloody, bruised, total carnage—but even those couldn't have prepared me for the sight of Colton. His body is whole and unbloodied, but he lies there so motionless and pale. His head is wrapped in white gauze and his eyelids are partially closed, the whites of his eyes showing somewhat from the swelling of his brain. He has tubes coming out of him every which way, and the monitors beep around him constantly. But it's not the sight of all of the medical equipment that breaks me—no—it's that the life and fire of the man I love is nonexistent.

I shuffle toward the bed, my eyes mapping every inch of him as if I've never seen him before, never felt him before. Never felt the thunder of his heart beating against my own chest. I reach out to touch him—needing to desperately—and when I hold his hand in mine, it's cold and unresponsive. Even the calluses I love—the ones that rasp deliciously over my bare skin—are not there.

The tears come. They fall in endless streams as I blindly sink down into the chair beside the bed. I grip Colton's hand with two of mine, my mouth pressed to our joined hands, my tears wetting his skin. I cry even harder when I realize the all too familiar Colton scent that feeds my addiction has been replaced by the antiseptic hospital smell. I didn't realize how much I needed that scent to be there. How much I needed that small, lingering piece of the man I love to remain when everything else has changed so drastically.

Incoherent words cross my lips and muffle against our entwined hands. "Please wake up, Colton. Please," I sob. "You can't leave me now. We have so much time we need to make up for, so many things that we still need to do. I need to cook you horrible dinners and you need to teach me how to surf. We need to watch the boys play little league and I need to be in the grandstands when you win a race." The thought of him getting back in a car makes my heart lodge in my throat, but I can't stop thinking of all the things we still have left to experience together. "We need to eat ice cream for breakfast and eat pancakes for dinner. We need to make love to each other on a lazy Sunday afternoon, and when you walk in the door, I'll push you up against it because we just can't get enough of each other. I haven't had my fill of you yet ..." My voice fades as I close my eyes and rest my forehead against our hands, Colton's name a repeated prayer on my lips.

"You know, I've never been as angry with him as I was last night." Beckett's voice jars me from my scattered focus.

I look up through blurred eyes to see him leaning against the doorjamb, arms crossed over his chest, and his eyes focused on his best friend. I know he's not expecting a response from me—and frankly, I'm hoarse from crying so I give him the only answer I can manage, an incoherent murmur before turning back to look at Colton.

"I've been pissed at him plenty of times, but last night took the cake." Becks breathes a long, frustrated sigh, and then I hear his feet shuffle across the floor. He sits down in the chair opposite me and hesitantly reaches out to squeeze Colton's free hand. He looks over toward his friend's impassive face before holding my gaze across the lifeless body of the man we love. "When I knew Colton was willing to let you walk away without telling you the truth or putting up a fight..." he shakes his head in disbelief as tears swim in his eyes "...I don't think I've ever been so pissed off or wanted to throw a punch at someone as much as I did when he told me to leave your room."

"Well, we were both being stubborn asses," I concede, wishing that we could be back in that hotel room—repeat the day—so that we just could stop fighting and I could wrap my arms around him a little tighter, a little longer. I wish I could rewind time so I could warn Colton of what was going to happen at the track. But I know it wouldn't matter. My reckless rebel thinks he's invincible and would have climbed into the car anyway.

I look back up at his face and he's anything but invincible now. The sob rises in my throat, and I try to hold it back but fail miserably.

"He's so used to thinking he's not worth any of the good fortune that's come his way. He's never given me specifics, but I know he thinks he doesn't deserve any better than what he was from, wherever he came from. He thinks he's not enough for you and—"

"He's everything," I gasp, the truth in my words resonating clear within my soul.

A ghost of a smile turns up the corners of Beckett's mouth despite the sadness in his eyes. "I know, Rylee." He pauses. "You're his lifeline."

I lift my eyes from Colton to meet his. "I don't know how that's going to help him now. I left him last night after you walked out of the room," I confess, staring again at our two hands intertwined, guilt consuming me. "After what he said to me, I kept thinking, *I can't be with him anymore under these circumstances.* I thought I could stick around—help him heal everything that's broken—but I couldn't stand around and be cheated on, so I left."

"You did the right thing. He needed a taste of his own medicine. He was being an ass and was using his fear to fuel his insecurity … but he went after you, Ry. That in itself tells me he knows how much he needs you."

"I know." My voice is almost a whisper and is drowned out by the incessant beep of the machines. "I'd gladly walk away from him again and never look back if it would prevent us from being here right now."

I say the words without any conviction because I know deep down that wherever Colton is, I would never be able to stay away from him.

We sit for a bit, each battling our own thoughts when Becks stands abruptly, his chair scraping across the floor and shattering the antiseptic silence in the room. "This is fucking bullshit. I can't sit and look at him like this." His voice is thick with emotion as he starts to walk out.

"He's going to pull through, Becks. He has to." My voice breaks on the last few words, betraying my confidence.

He stops and sniffles before turning around to look at me. "That fucker is stubborn in everything he does—everything—he better not disappoint me now." He shifts his attention to Colton and strides to the side of the bed, the grief turning into anger with each passing second. "It's always got to be about you, doesn't it, Wood? *Self-centered bastard.* When you wake the fuck up—and you will wake the fuck up because I'm not letting you go out like this—I'm going to kick your ass for making us worry."

He reaches his hand out and, in contradictory fashion to his gruff words, lays a hand on Colton's shoulder for a brief moment before turning and walking out of the room.

I'm left alone with the man I love, the weight of the unknown pressing down upon us but hope finally starting to bleed through the edges of the pain.

Chapter Five

Colton

I can feel the car—the engine's rumbling in my chest that tells me I'm alive—before I even see it slingshot out of the backside of the turn. I focus on my hands. They're shaking, fucking trembling. I can't hold onto the wheel, to my thoughts, to anything at all. The wheel shudders beneath my goddamn fingers. Fingers that can't quite grip to control the chaos unraveling around me.

The confidence I own in a place that's always been my salvation is gone. Dust in the motherfucking wind.

What the hell is going on?

The sound of metal giving—fucking shredding—mixed with the squeal of rubber sliding across asphalt echoes all around me. Jameson's car slams into mine. And with the impact—the jolt of my body, the theft of my thoughts—my memories crash and collide like our cars do.

The thought of Rylee sucker punches me first.

The bright ray of light against my goddamn darkness. The sun shining through this crash-crazed haze of smoke. The one and only exception to my fucking rule. How can I hear her sobs through my headset and yet see her doubled over in shock from a distance? Something's messed up here. Like bat-shit crazy messed up.

But what? How?

And even though there's all this smoke, I can still see her face clear as day. Violet eyes giving me something I don't deserve—motherfucking trust. Begging me to let her in, to let her help heal the parts of me forever damaged from a past I'll never outrun—never escape—even when slamming head first into the damn wall.

I see my car rise above the smoke—above the goddamn fray of broken trust and useless hope—and I lose my breath and my chest feels like it's exploding, detonating like the shrapnel of memories embedding themselves so deep in my mind I can't quite place where they land. Even though I'm watching it, I can still feel it—the force of the spin, the strain on my muscles, the need to hold tight to the wheel. My future and past coming down all around me like a goddamn tornado as I roll out of control struggling to fight the fear and the pain I know is coming next.

That I can't ever escape.

Debris scatters … on the track and in my head.

Collateral damage for another poor fucking soul to deal with. I've had more than my share of it. I choke on the bile that threatens—the soul siphoning fear that stabs into my psyche—because even mid-flight, when I should be free from everything, *she's* still there. *He's still there*. Always a constant reminder.

Colty, when you don't listen, you get hurt. Now go be a good boy and wait for him. When you're naughty, naughty things happen, baby boy.

The crunch of metal, his masculine grunt.

The smell of destruction, his alcoholic stench.

My body banging into the protective cage around me, his meaty fingers trying to take me, own me, claim me.

Tell me you love me. Say it!

I love you. I love you. I love you. I love you.

I welcome the impact of the car because it knocks those words off my tongue. I can see it, feel it, hear it all at the same time as if I'm everywhere and nowhere all at once. In the car and outside of it. The resonating, unmistakable crunch of metal as I become weightless, momentarily free from the pain. Knowing that once I've spoken those *three words* only hurt can come.

The fucking poison will eat at me piece by piece until I'm the nothing I already know I am.

The goddamn fear will paralyze me—fucking consume me—dynamite exploding in a vacuum chamber.

My body slams forward but my shoulder harnesses strangle me motionless, like Rylee urging me to move forward. Like the memory of *him* holding me back—unforgiving arms trapping me as I fight against the blackness he fills me with. Against the words he forces me to say, forever fucking up their goddamn meaning.

The impact hits me full force—car against barrier, heart against chest, hope against demons—but all I see is Rylee stepping over the wall. All I can see is *him* coming at me while she's walking away.

"*Rylee?*" I call out to her. Help me. Save me. Redeem me. She doesn't turn, doesn't respond. All my hope is fucking lost.

... I'm broken ...

I watch the car—feel its movement encompassing me—slowly come to a stop, the damage unknown as the darkness consumes me.

... and so very bent ...

My final exhale of resistance—from him, for her—as the fight leaves me.

Spiderman. Batman. Superman. Ironman.

"We're losing him. He's crashing!

... I wonder if there's pain when you die ...

"Colton, come back. Fight goddammit!"

Chapter Six

Minutes turn into hours.

Hours turn into days.

Time slips away when we've lost too much of it as it is.

I refuse to leave Colton's bedside. Too many people have left him in his life, and I refuse to do it when it matters the most. So I ramble to him incessantly. I speak about nothing and everything, but it doesn't help. He never reacts, never moves … and it kills me.

Visitors drift in and out of his room in sporadic bouts: his parents, Quinlan, and Becks. Updates are given in the waiting room where some of the crew and Tawny still gather daily. And I have no doubt that Becks is making sure Tawny keeps her distance from me and my more than fragile emotional state.

On the fifth day I can't take it anymore. I need to feel him against me. I need that physical connection with him. I carefully move all the wires to the side and cautiously crawl on the bed beside him, placing my head on his chest and my hand over his heart. The tears come now with the feel of his body against mine. I find comfort in the sound of his heartbeat, strong and steady beneath my ear, instead of the electronic beep of the monitor I've grown to rely on as a gauge of his momentary status.

I snuggle into him, wishing for the feel of his arm curling around me, and the rumble of his voice through his chest. Little bits of comfort that don't come.

We lie there for awhile and I'm fading off into the clutches of sleep when I startle awake. I swear it's Colton's voice that is pulling at me. Swear I hear the chant of superheroes, a tumultuous sigh on his lips. My heart races in my chest as I reacquaint myself with the foreign surroundings of his room. The only thing familiar is Colton next to me, and even that's a small comfort to the riot in my psyche because he's not the same either. His fingers twitch and he moans again, and even though it's not the words that awoke me, deep down I know he's calling to *them*. Asking for the help to pull him from this nightmare.

I don't know how to soothe him. I wish I could crawl inside of him and make him better, but I can't. So I do the only thing I can think of, I start singing softly, his dad's comments ringing in my ears. I thought I'd forgotten the words to the song I'd heard long ago, but they come to me easily after I struggle through the first few.

So in this cold and sterile environment, I attempt to use lyrics to bring warmth to Colton by singing the song of his childhood: *Puff the Magic Dragon*.

I don't even realize I've fallen asleep until I jolt awake when I hear the squeak of shoes on the floor and look up to meet the kind eyes of the charge nurse. I can see the reprimand about to roll off the tip of her tongue but the pleading look in my eyes stops her.

"Sweetie, you really shouldn't be up there with him. You risk the chance of pulling a lead out." Her voice is soft and she shakes her head when I meet her eyes. "But if you want to while I'm on shift, I promise not to tell." She gives me a wink, and I smile gratefully at her.

"Thank you. I just needed to …" My voice trails off because how do I put into words that I needed to connect with him somehow.

She reaches over and pats my arm in understanding. "I know, dear. And who's to say it won't help pull him from his current state? Just be careful, okay?" I nod in understanding before she leaves the room.

I'm left alone again in the darkness with the eerie glow from the machines illuminating the room. Still snuggled into his side, I angle my head up and press my lips to that favorite place of mine on the underside of his jaw. His scruff is almost a beard now, and I welcome the tickle of it against my nose and lips. I draw him in and just linger in the feel of him. The first tear slips out quietly and before I know it, the past few days come crashing down around me. I am lying holding on to the man I love—still afraid that I might lose him—overcome with every form of imaginable emotion.

And so I whisper the only thing I can to express the fear holding my soul hostage.

Spiderman. Batman. Superman. Ironman.

My tears subside over time, and I slowly succumb to the clutches of sleep again.

I awake disoriented, eyes blinking rapidly at the sunlight filtering in through the windows. Murmured voices fill my ears but the one that surprises me the most is vibrating beneath my ear.

Awareness jolts me when I realize the rumble is Colton's voice. In a split second my heart thunders, breath catches, and hope soars. My head dizzies as I sit up and look at the man I love, all others in the room forgotten.

"Hi." It's the only word I can manage as my eyes collide with his. Chills dance over my flesh and my hands tremble at the sight of him awake and alert and aware.

His eyes flicker over my shoulder before coming back to rest on mine. "Hi," he rasps as my elation soars. He angles his head slightly to observe me, and even though confusion flickers over his face, I don't care because he's alive and whole.

And he's come back to me.

I just sit there and stare at him for a moment, pulse racing and the shock of him awake robbing my words. "*Iron-Ironman* ..." I stutter, thinking that I need to go get the doctor. I don't want to move. I want to kiss him, hug him, never let him go again. He just looks at me as if he's lost and understandably because he's just woken up to a frantic mess and the only thing I say is the name of a superhero.

I start to shove off the bed but he reaches out and grabs my wrist. "What are you doing here?" His eyes search mine asking so many questions that I'm not sure that I can answer.

"I—I—you were in an accident," I stutter, trying to explain. Hoping the trepidation snaking up my spine and digging its claws into my neck are just from the overload of emotions over the past few days. "You crashed during the race. Your head ... you've been out for a week ..." My voice fades as I see his eyes narrow and his head angle to the side. I can see him trying to work through the memories in his head, so I give him the time to do that.

His eyes glance back over my shoulder again, and it's now that I remember there were voices in the room—more than one person—but something about the look on his face makes me afraid to look away. "Colton ..."

"You left me." His voice is broken and heart wrenching, filled with disbelief.

"No ..." I shake my head, grabbing onto his hand as fear starts to creep into my voice. "No. I came back. We figured it out. Woke up together." I can hear the panic escalating in my tone, can feel the pounding of my heart, the crashing descent of the hope I'd just gotten back. "*We raced together.*"

He shakes his head gently back and forth with a stuttering disbelief. "No, you didn't." He looks back over my shoulder as he pulls his hand from mine and holds out his now free hand to the person behind me. "You left. I chased you but couldn't find you. She found me in the elevator." The smile I'd been silently needing, wanting to reaffirm our connection, is given ... but not to me.

The air punches from my lungs, the blood drains from my face, and a coldness seeps into every fiber of my soul as the smile I love—the one he only reserves for me—is given to the person at my back.

"Colton couldn't remember everything, *doll*." The voice assaults my ears and breaks my heart. "So I filled him in on all of the missing pieces," Tawny says as she comes into view, scrunching up her nose with a condescending smirk. "How you left and we reconnected." She works her tongue in her mouth as the victorious smile grows wider, eyes gleaming, message sent loud and clear.

I won.

You lose.

The bottom drops out of my world, blackness fading over my vision, and nothingness left to contend with.

Chapter Seven

I awake with a start. My lungs are greedy for air and my mind reaches to cling to anything real through its groggy haze. The scream on my lips dies when I realize I'm in Colton's room, alone, with him beside me. My head is still on his chest and my arm still hooked around his waist.

I blow out a shaky breath as my adrenaline surges. It was a dream. *Holy shit, it was just a dream.* I tell myself over and over, trying to reassure myself with the constant beep of the monitors and the medicinal smell—things I have grown to hate but welcome right now as a way to convince myself that nothing has changed. Colton's still asleep and I'm still hoping for miracles.

Just ones that don't involve Tawny.

I sink back down into Colton, my nightmare a fringe on the edge of my consciousness that leaves me beyond unsettled and my body trembling with anxiety. I'm so lost in thought—in fear over both nightmares—that as the adrenaline fades, my eyes grow heavy. I'm so lost to the welcoming peace of sleep that when a hand smooths down my hair and stills on my back, I sink into the soothing feeling of it in my hazy, dreamlike state. I nestle closer, accepting the warmth offered and the serenity that comes with it.

And then it hits me. I snap my head up to meet Colton's. The sob that chokes in my throat is nothing compared to the tumble in my heart and awakening in my soul.

When our eyes meet I'm frozen, so many thoughts flitting through my mind, the most prevalent one is that he came back to me. Colton is awake and alive and back with me. Our eyes remain locked and I can see the confusion flicker through his at a lightning pace and the unknown warring within.

"Hi there," I offer on a shaky smile, and I'm not sure why a part of me is nervous. Colton licks his lips and closes his eyes momentarily which causes me to panic that he's been pulled back under. To my relief he reopens them with a squint and parts his mouth to speak, but nothing comes out.

"Shh-Shh," I tell him, reaching out and resting my finger on his lips. "There was an accident." His brow furrows as he tries to lift his hand but can't, as if it's a dead weight. He tries to angle his eyes up to figure out the thick bandages surrounding his head. "You had surgery." His eyes widen with trepidation and I mentally chastise myself for fumbling over my words and not being clearer. The monitor beside me beeps at an accelerated pace, the noise dominating the room. "You're okay now. You came back to me." I can see him struggle to comprehend, and I wait for something to spark in his eyes but there is nothing. "I'm going to get the nurse."

I reach out to pull myself off the bed and Colton's hand that's lying on the mattress clasps around my wrist. He shakes his head and winces with the movement. I immediately reach out to him and cradle his face with one hand, his skin paling and beads of sweat appearing on the bridge of his nose.

"Don't move, okay?" My voice breaks when I say it, as my eyes travel the lines of his face searching to see if he's hurt anything. *As if I would know if he had.*

He nods just barely and whispers in an almost absent voice, "Hurts."

"I know it does," I tell him as I reach across the bed and push the call button for the nurse as the hope deep within me settles into possibility. "Let me get a nurse to help with the pain, okay?"

"Ry ..." His voice breaks again as the fear in it splinters in my heart. I do the only thing I know might reassure him. I lean forward and brush my lips to his cheek and just hold them there momentarily while I control the rush of emotions that hit me like a tsunami. Tears drip down my cheeks and onto his as the silent sobs surge through me. I hear a soft sigh and when I pull back, his eyes are closed and his mind lost to the blackness behind them once again.

"Is everything okay?" The nurse pulls me from my moment.

I look over at her, Colton's face still cradled in my hand and my tears staining his lips. "He woke up ..." I can't say anything else because relief robs my words. "He woke up."

Colton comes in and out of consciousness a couple more times over the next few days. Small moments of lucidity among a haze of confusion. Each time he tries to talk without success, and each time we try to soothe—what we assume from his racing heartbeat—are his fears, in the few minutes we have with him.

I refuse to leave, so fearful that I'll miss any of these precious moments. Stolen minutes where I can pretend nothing has happened instead of the endless span of worry.

Dorothea has finally convinced me to take a few moments and head to the cafeteria. As much as I don't want to, I know I'm hogging her son and she probably wants a minute alone with him.

I pick at my food, my appetite nonexistent, and my jeans baggier than when I first arrived in Florida a week ago. Nothing sounds good—not even chocolate, my go to food for stress.

My cell rings and I scramble to get it, hoping it's Dorothea telling me Colton's awake again, but it isn't. My excitement abates. "Hey, Had."

"Hi, sweetie. Any change?"

"No." I just sigh, wishing I had more to say. She's used to this by now and allows the silence between us.

"If he doesn't wake anytime soon, I'm ignoring you and flying my ass out there to be with you." Here comes Haddie and her no-nonsense attitude. There's no need for her to be here really. She'd just sit around and wait like the rest of us, and what good is that going to do?

"Just your ass?" I let the smile grace my lips even though it feels so foreign in this dismal place.

"Well, it is a fine one if I may say so myself … like bounce quarters off of it and shit." She laughs. "And thank God! There's a bit of the girl I love shining through. You hanging in there?"

"It's all I can do," I sigh.

"So how is he? Has he come to again?"

"Yeah, last night."

"So that's what, five times in two days according to Becks? That's a good sign, right? From nothing to something?"

"I guess … I don't know. He just seems so scared when he wakes up—his heart rate on the monitors sky rockets and he can't catch his breath—and it's so quick that we don't have time to explain that it's okay, that he's going to be okay."

"But he sees you all there, Ry. The fact you're all there has to tell him he has nothing to fear." I just give a non-committal murmur in response, hoping her words are true. Hoping that the sight of all of us soothes him rather than scares him into thinking he's on his deathbed. "What does Dr. Irons say?"

I breathe in deeply, afraid if I say it my fears might come true. "He says Colton seems stable. That the more often he wakes up the better … but until he starts talking in full sentences, he won't know if any part of his brain is affected by everything."

"Okay," she says, drawing the word out so that it's almost a question. Asking me what I fear without asking. "What are you not telling me, Ry?"

I push the food around on my plate some, scattered thoughts focusing for bouts of time. I work a swallow in my throat before drawing in a shaky breath. "He says sometimes motor skills might be temporarily affected …"

"And …" Silence hangs as she waits for me to continue. "Put your fork down and talk to me. Tell me what you're really worried about. No bullshit. You're not a lesbian so stop beating around the damn bush."

Her attempt to make me laugh results in a soft chuckle turned audible exhale of breath. "He said that he might not remember much. Sometimes in cases like these, the patient may have temporary to permanent memory loss."

"And you're afraid he might not remember what happened, good and bad, right?" I don't respond, feeling stupid and validated in my fears at the same time. She takes my lack of a reply as my answer. "Well, he obviously remembers you because he didn't freak out when you were lying in bed with him the first time, right? He grabbed your hand, stroked your hair? That has to tell you he knows who you are."

"Yeah … I've just found him though, Haddie, and the thought of losing him—even if it's in the figurative sense—scares the shit out of me."

"Quit thinking about something that hasn't happened yet. I understand why you're worried but, Ry, you've made it through some pretty random shit so far—Tawny the twatwaffle's antics included—so you need to back away from that ledge you're sitting on and wait to see what happens. You'll cross that bridge and all when it comes, okay?"

I'm about to respond when my phone beeps with an incoming text. I pull my phone from my ear and my heart rockets when I see Quinlan's text. *He's awake.*

"It's Colton. I gotta go."

Chapter Eight

Colton

Pain pounds like a jackhammer against my temple. My eyes burn like I'm waking up after downing a fifth of Jack. Bile rises and my stomach churns.

Churns as if I'm back in that room—dank mattress, crab weeds of trepidation blooming in me as I wait for *him* to arrive, for my mom to hand me over, *trade me* … but that's not fucking possible. Q's here, Beckett. Mom and Dad.

What the fuck is going on?

I squeeze my eyes shut and try to shake away the confusion, but all I get is more of the goddamn pain.

Pain.

Ache.

Pleasure.

Need.

Rylee.

Flashes of memories I can't quite grasp or understand blindside me before disappearing into the darkness holding them hostage.

But where is she?

I fight to gain more memories, pull them in and grasp them like a lifeline.

Did she finally figure out the fucking poison within me? Realize this pleasure isn't worth the pain I'll cause in the end?

"Mr. Donavan? I'm Dr. Irons. Can you hear me?"

Who the hell are you? Ice blue eyes stare at me.

"It may be tough to speak. We're getting you some water to help. Can you squeeze my hand if you understand me?"

Why do I need to squeeze his hand? And why is my hand not moving? How the hell am I going to drive in the race today if I can't grip the wheel?

My heart hammers like the pedal I should be dropping on the track right now.

But I'm here.

And last night I was there, with Ry. Woke up with her … and now she's gone.

… checkered flag time, baby …

It all zooms into focus at once. And then complete darkness. Checkered holes of black—polka dots of void—throughout the slideshow in my head. I can't connect the dots. I can't make sense of anything except that I'm confused as fuck.

All eyes in the room stare at me like I'm the side show at the goddamn circus. *And for his next act folks, he'll move his fingers.*

I try my left hand and it responds. Thank Christ for that.

My mind flashes back. Crunching metal, flashing sparks, engulfing smoke. Crashing, tumbling, free-falling, jolting.

… It looks like your superheroes came this time after all …

My mind tries to figure out what that means but comes up empty.

Rylee's gone.

She doesn't love the broken in me after all.

I try to shake the bullshit lies from my head but groan as the pain hits me.

Max.

Me.

She left.

Can't do this again.

I can't believe I was selfish enough to even ask her to.

"Colton." The doc is talking again. "You were in a bad accident. You're lucky to be alive."

A bad accident? The flickering images in my head start to make more sense but gaps of time are still missing. I try to speak but my mouth's so dry all that comes out is a croak.

"You injured your head." He smiles at me but I'm wary.

Never look a gift horse in the mouth.

He may have given me life again, but the fucking reason for living isn't here. She's smart enough to leave because I just can't give her what she needs: stability, a life without racing, the promise of forever.

"The nurse is bringing you some water to wet your throat." He notes something on his tablet. "I know this might be scary for you, son, but you're going to be okay. The tough part's over. Now we need to get you on the road to recovery."

The road to recovery? Thanks, Captain Obvious—more like the speedway to Hell.

Faces fill my immediate space. Mom kissing my cheek, tears coursing down her face. Dad hiding his emotion but the look in his eyes tells me he's a goddamn wreck. Quin beside herself. Becks muttering something about being a selfish bastard.

This must be pretty fucking serious.

And yet I still feel numb. Empty. Incomplete.

Rylee.

After a few moments they slowly back away at my Mom's insistence to give me space, to let me breathe.

And the air I've just gotten back is robbed again.

I turn to look at the vague blur I notice in my periphery, and there she stands.

Curls piled on top of her head, face without makeup, hollow, tear-stained cheeks, eyes welled with tears, perfect lips in a startled O standing in the doorway. She looks like she's been through Hell, but she's the most beautiful thing I've ever seen.

Call me a pussy, but I swear to God she's the only air my body can breathe. Fuck if she's not everything I need and nothing that I deserve.

Her hands are fiddling with her cell phone, my lucky shirt hanging off her shoulders, and I can see the trepidation in her eyes as they flit around everywhere but at me.

Breathe, Donavan. Fucking breathe. She didn't leave. She's still here. The neutralizer to the acid that eats my soul.

Her eyes finally find and lock onto mine. All I see is my future, my salvation, my singular chance at redemption. But her eyes? Fuck, they flicker with such conflicting emotions: relief, optimism, anxiety, fear, and so many more unknown.

And it's the unknown I focus on.

The unspoken words telling me all of this is tearing her apart. That it's not fair for me to put her through this again. But racing is my life. Something I need as much as I need the air that I breathe—ironic considering she's my fucking air—but it's the only way I can survive and outrun the demons that chase me. The black ooze that seeps in every crack of my soul making sure it can never be eradicated. I can't be selfish and ask her to stand by me when all I want is to be the most self-centered bastard on the face of the earth.

Urge her to go but beg her to stay.

But how can I let her go when she owns every single part of me?

I'll gladly suffocate so that she can breathe freely. Without worry. Without the constant fucking fear.

Be selfless for the first time ever when all I've been my entire life is self-serving.

I should have told her—got over the fear that consumes my soul—but I couldn't ... and now she doesn't know.

... I Spiderman you ...

Words scream through my head but choke in my throat. The words I don't know if I'll ever be healed enough to say.

She robbed me of that all those years ago.

And now I'll pay for it.

By letting my one fucking chance go.

Then I hear the sob wrench from her throat. Hear the disbelief and torment in that singular sound as her shoulders shake and her posture sags.

And I know what I want and what is best for her are two completely different things.

Chapter Nine

Out of nowhere the sob tears from my throat at the sight of him, lucid and groggily alert. My damaged man that is the most beautiful sight I've ever seen.

My heart tumbles even further if that's even possible. And we just stare as the noise and excitement in the room abates, everyone taking a step back and silently watching our exchange.

Yet my feet are frozen in place as I try and read the emotions racing rapid-fire through Colton's eyes. He seems apologetic and maybe unsettled, but there's also an underlying emotion I can't place that has trepidation eating at the corners of my mind.

A nurse whisks past me, brushing my shoulder and breaking Colton's hold on me. She brings the straw from a cup of water to his mouth and he sips eagerly until it's gone.

"Well, you're a thirsty one, aren't you?" she teases before adding, "I'll go get you some more but let's make sure this stays down before we waterlog you, okay?"

I try to quiet my hiccupping draws of breath but can't seem to calm my anxiety. I feel Quinlan's arm go around my shoulder as she sniffles herself, but I don't even acknowledge her. I can't bear for my eyes to focus on anything but the tear–blurred vision in front of me.

The nurse reaches over and takes a chart from Dr. Irons and leaves. I haven't moved yet. I can't seem to. I just stare at Colton as Dr. Irons examines him: tracking his eyes, testing his reflexes, feeling the strength in his grip as he squeezes. I notice he asks Colton to repeat the grip test for his right hand a couple of times, and I can see panic flicker over Colton's features. I can't drag my eyes away. I trace over every inch of him, so very afraid I'll miss something—anything—about these first few moments.

"Well, all seems quite well," Dr. Irons says eventually after he examines him some more. "How are you feeling, Colton?"

I watch his throat work a swallow and his eyes close with a wince before opening them again. I take a step forward, wanting to help take the pain away. He glances around at everyone in the room while he finds his voice. "My head. Hurts," he rasps. "Hand?" He looks down to his right hand and then back up, confusion apparent in his eyes. "Happened? How long?"

Dr. Irons sits down on the edge of the bed next to him and begins to explain about the crash, the operation, and the amount of time he has been in a coma. "As for your hand, that could be a result of some residual swelling still in your brain. We'll just have to watch it and see how it progresses over time." Colton nods at him, concentration etched on his face. "Can you tell me the last thing that you remember?"

I suck in a breath as Colton blows one out. He swallows again and licks his lips. "I remember … knocking four times." His voice comes out, his vocal chords scraping over gravel.

"What else?" Andy asks.

Colton looks over at his dad and subtly nods his head at him before squeezing his eyes shut in concentration. "It's like snippets in my head. Certain things are clear," he rasps before swallowing and then opens his eyes to look at Dr. Irons. "Others … they're vague. Like I can feel them there but can't remember them."

"That's normal. Sometimes—"

"Fireworks on pit row," he cuts the doctor off. "Waking up *overdressed*." Colton's eyes lift and find mine with the words that let me know he remembers me, remembers my memorable pre-race wake-up call. A slight smile curls up one corner of his mouth looking so out of place against the pallid tone of his usually bronze skin.

And if he didn't own my heart already—if he hadn't tattooed every single inch of it with his unmistakable stamp—he just did.

I can't help the laugh that bubbles up and spills over. I can't stop my feet from moving and stepping up to the edge of the bed as his words fade and his eyes track my movement. My grin widens, my tears fall faster, and my heart swells as I feel relief for the first time in days. I reach out and squeeze his hand resting on the mattress beside him.

"Hi." It sounds stupid, but it's the first and only word I can manage, my throat clogged with emotion.

"Hi," he whispers, that lopsided grin I love ghosting his mouth.

We just stare at each other for a beat, eyes saying so much and yet lips speaking nothing. I lace my fingers with his and I see the alarm trigger in his eyes again when he tries to respond but his hand doesn't.

"It's okay," I soothe, unable to resist. I reach my other hand out and cup the side of his face, welcoming the feeling of the muscle in his jaw ticking beneath my palm. "You've gotta give it some time to heal."

Emotions dance at a lightning pace in the green of his eyes as he tries to comprehend everything. And in this moment the ache in my chest transforms from the fear of the unknown to sympathy over watching the man I love struggle with the knowledge that his usually virile, responsive body is anything but.

"Rylee's right," Dr. Irons says, breaking the connection between us. "You need to give it some time. What else do you remember, Colton? You woke up underdressed and knocked four times," he prompts, his face masking the mystification he must feel over not understanding the meaning behind these statements. "Then what?"

"No," Colton says, wincing when he shakes his head instinctively. "First knocking and then waking up."

My eyes snap up to Beckett's because of all people he'll understand that this is not the order in which the events happened. Dr. Irons notes the startled look on my face and shakes his head for me to remain quiet.

"Not a problem. What else do you remember about the day regardless of the order?" Colton gives him a strange look and the doctor continues. "Sometimes when your brain has been traumatized like yours has, memories have a way of shifting and changing. For some, the sequence of events may be off but they'll still be there. For others there are some memories that are completely clear and others that are lost. I have some patients who remember the day of their trauma perfectly fine but have a void of time during other times or events that have happened. Every patient is unique."

"For how long do these voids usually last?" Andy speaks up from the side of the bed.

"Well, sometimes for a little while and sometimes forever ... but the good thing is that Colton seems to have memories of the day of the crash. So it would seem that a small chunk of time has been lost for him. As days pass, he may realize he doesn't remember other things ... because really, until he is reminded of something, he doesn't even know he's missing it." Dr. Irons looks around the room at all of us and shrugs. "At this time it wouldn't seem far off to reason that you'll regain all of it, Colton, but I advise caution because the brain is a tricky thing sometimes. In fact—"

"The national anthem," Colton says, relief flooding his voice at reclaiming one more memory from the darkness within. I smile at him in encouragement as he clears his throat. "I ... I can't ..." Frustration emanates off of him in waves as he tries to remember. "What happened?" He blows out a breath and looks around at everyone in the room before scrubbing his left hand over his face. "You were all there. What else happened?"

"Don't force it, sweetie." It's Dorothea speaking. "Right, Dr. Irons?"

We all look over at Dr. Irons, who nods his head in agreement, but when we look back at Colton, he's fallen asleep.

We all breathe in a collective gasp. All fearing he's slipped back into a coma. All our minds racing into overdrive. Dr. Irons puts the brakes on our panic when he says, "This is normal. He's going to be exhausted the first couple of times he wakes up."

Shoulders relax, sighs are exhaled, and relief is restored, but our concern never completely abates.

"We know he seems to be—that his brain seems to be—functioning well so far," Quinlan says as she steps up to the bed. "What can we expect now?"

Dr. Irons watches Colton for a beat before he continues, meeting all of our eyes. "Well, each person is different but I can tell you that the longer it takes Colton to remember, the more frustrated he may become. Sometimes in patients their disposition changes—sometimes they have a temper or are more mellow—and sometimes it doesn't at all. At this point it's still a waiting game to see how all of this has affected him long term."

"Should those of us that were there fill in the blanks for him of what he can't remember?" Becks asks.

"Of course you can," he says, "but I can't guarantee how he'll respond to it."

I resume my seat bedside as Dorothea comes over to kiss me goodbye on the cheek before leaning over to press her lips to Colton's forehead. "We're just heading to the hotel to get some rest. We'll be back in the morning. Don't you dare give up." She steps back and stares at him for a beat more before smiling softly at me and leaving to join Andy and Quinlan in the hall.

I sigh out loud as Beckett gathers the remaining trash from our late night dinner we'd had while impatiently waiting for Colton to wake. I glance over from my book that I'm really not paying attention to and watch Becks' methodical movements. I can see the toll the past week has taken on him in the bruises beneath his eyes and the scruff on his usually clean-shaven face. He seems lost.

"How you doing?" I ask the question softly, but I know he can hear me because his body stops momentarily before he puts the last bit in the trash can and shoves it down.

He turns and leans his hip against a counter behind him and just shrugs as our eyes meet. "You know," he drawls out in his slow, resonating tone that I've come to love. "In the sixteen years we've known each other, this is the longest we've ever gone without talking." He shrugs again and stares out the window for a moment at the media trucks in the parking lot. "He may be a demanding smart-ass, but I miss him. Call me a pussy, but I kinda like the guy."

I can't help the smile that spreads on my lips. "Me too," I murmur. "Me too."

Becks walks over to me and presses a kiss to the top of my head. "I'm going to head back to the hotel. I've gotta take a shower, check in with my brother, and then I'll be back, okay?"

A growing adoration for Becks blooms within—the ever true best friend. "Why don't you stay there tonight and get a good night's sleep? In a real bed instead of the crappy chairs in the waiting room."

He chuckles derisively and shakes his head at me. "Pot calling the kettle black, huh?"

"I know, but I just can't ... and besides, I've been sleeping in these crappy chairs in here." I pat the seat of the one I'm sitting on. "At least this has more padding than those out there." I angle my head and watch him mull it over. "I promise to call if he wakes up."

He exhales loudly and gives me a reluctant look. "Okay ... but you'll call?"

"Of course."

I watch Becks leave and welcome the unique silence of the hospital room. I sit and watch Colton, feeling truly blessed indeed that he's here and whole in front of me—that he didn't forget me—when it could be so much worse. I send a silent prayer up as time passes, knowing I have to start following through with the various barters I made to the great beyond to get Colton to come back to me.

I field a couple of texts from Haddie, check in on the boys and see how Ricky's math test went today, before texting Becks good night and telling him Colton's still out.

The early morning hours approach and I can't resist anymore. I slip off my shoes, pull the clip out of my hair, and position myself in the only place in the world I want to be.

At Colton's side.

Chapter Ten

The morning light burns through my closed eyelids as I try to rouse myself from the deepest sleep I've had in over six days. Instead I just burrow in deeper to the warmth beside me. I feel fingers brush across my cheek and I'm instantly alert, my body jolting with awareness.

"Morning." His voice is a whispered murmur against the top of my head. My heart floods with an array of emotions but what I feel more than anything is complete.

Whole again.

I start to move so I can look into his eyes. "No doctors yet. I just need this. Need you. No one else, okay?" he asks.

Seriously? *Is the sky blue?* If I could, I'd whisk him out of this sterile prison and keep him all to myself for a while. Forever or more if he'd let me. But rather than letting the flippant comment roll off my tongue, I just make a satisfied moan and tighten my arms around him. I close my eyes and just absorb everything about this moment. I so desperately wish we were somewhere else, anywhere else, so I could lie with him skin to skin, connect with him in that indescribable way. Feel like I am doing something to help heal his broken memory and damaged soul.

We lie there in silence, my hand over his heart and the fingers of his left hand lazily drawing lines up and down my forearm. There are so many questions I want to ask. So many things that run through my head, but the only one that I manage to say is, "How are you feeling?"

The momentary pause in his movement is so subtle I almost don't catch it, but I do. And it's enough to tell me that something's wrong besides the obvious.

"This is nice." It's all he says and that further solidifies my hunch. I give him a bit of time to gather his thoughts and work out what he wants to say because after the past few weeks, I've learned so many things, least of which is my inability to listen when it matters the most.

And right now it matters.

So I sit in silence as my mind wars with the possibilities.

"I've been awake for a few hours," he starts. "Listening to you breathe. Trying to make my right hand fucking work. Trying to wrap my head around what happened. What I can't remember. It's there. I can sense it but I can't make it come to the forefront ..." he trails off.

"What do you remember?" I ask.

I desperately want to turn, to look into his eyes and read the fear and frustration that is most likely marring them, but I don't. I give him the space to admit that he's not one hundred percent. To balance that inherent male need to be as strong as possible, to show no weakness.

"That's just it," he sighs. "I remember bits and pieces. Nothing flows though, except you were there in most of them. Can you tell me what happened? How the day went so I can try to fill in what's missing?"

"Mmm-hmm." I nod my head gently, smiling at the memory of how our morning started.

"I remember waking up to the best sight ever—you naked, on top of me." He sighs in appreciation that causes parts within me that have been ignored over the past week to stir to life. I don't even fight the smile that spreads across my lips when I feel his growing arousal beneath the sheet next to me. Glad I'm not the only one affected by the memory.

"Becks came in without knocking and I was pissed at him for that. He left and I do believe your jeans were on the floor and your back was up against the wall in a matter of seconds after the door was shut." We fall silent for a moment, that undeniable charge crackling between us. "Sweet Christ what I wouldn't give to be doing that right now."

I start laughing and this time when I shift myself to sit up and look at him, he allows me. I turn to face him and can't help the chills that blanket my skin when I lock eyes with his. "Now I don't think Dr. Irons would approve of that," I tease, silently sighing with relief that we feel like we are right back where we left off before the accident. Playful, needing, and each other's complement. I can't stop my hand from reaching out and lingering on his cheek. I hate the thought of not being in contact with him.

"Well," he says, "I'll make sure that's the first thing I ask Dr. Irons when I see him."

"The first thing?" I ask and swallow around my heart that's just somersaulted into my throat when he turns his face and presses a kiss into the palm of my hand. The simple action knotting the bow on the ribbon already tied around my heart.

"A man has to have his priorities." He smirks. "If one head's fucked up, at least the other one can be used to its *maximum potential*." He starts to laugh and winces, bringing his left hand up to hold his head.

Alarm shoots through me and I immediately reach out to push the call button, but his hand reaches out and stops me. And it takes a second for me to register that it's his right hand he's just used. I think Colton realizes it at the same time.

He works a swallow down his throat, his eyes shifting to watch his hand as he releases my arm. I follow his gaze to see his fingers tremor violently as he unsuccessfully tries to make a fist. I notice a sheen of sweat appear on his forehead below the bandage as he wills his fingers to tighten. When I can't bear to watch him struggle any more, I reach out and grab his hand in mine and start massaging it, willing it to move myself.

"It's a start," I reassure him. "Baby steps, okay?" All I want to do is wrap him in my arms and take away all of his pain and frustration, but he seems so fragile that I fear touching him, despite how much it would lessen the lingering unease that tiptoes in my head. My usual optimism has been put through the ringer these past few weeks, and I just can't seem to shake the feeling that this isn't the worst of it. That something else is lurking on the horizon waiting to knock us down again.

"What else do you remember?" I prompt, wanting to get his mind off of his hand.

He gives me his recollections of the day, little pieces are missing here and there. The details aren't too major but I do notice that the closer he gets to the start of the race, the bigger the voids are. And each piece of the puzzle seems to get harder and harder to recall, as if he has to grab each memory and physically pull it from its vault.

Giving him a moment to rest, I return from the in-suite bathroom to put away the mouthwash he'd requested. I find Colton looking out the window, shaking his head at the media circus below. "I remember being in the trailer. The knock on the door." His eyes angle over to me, salacious thoughts dancing within his glints of green as I return to my seat on the bed beside him. "A *certain* checkered flag I never got to claim." He purses his lips and just stares at me.

And resistance is futile.

It always is when it comes to my willpower and Colton.

I lean in, doing what I've wanted to do desperately. Giving into the need to feel that connection with him—to feed my one and only addiction—and brush my lips against his. I know it's ridiculous that I'm nervous about hurting him. That somehow the lascivious thoughts behind our innocent brush of our lips are going to cause pain to his healing head.

But the minute our lips touch—the minute the soft sigh escapes his mouth and weaves its way into my soul—I find it hard to think clearly. I withdraw a fraction, needing to make sure he's okay when all I want to do is devour the apple tempting me.

But I don't have to because Colton hands it to me on a silver platter when he brings his left hand to the nape of my neck and draws my mouth back down to his again. Lips part, tongues meld, and recognition renews as we sink into each other in a reverent kiss. We're in no hurry to do anything other than enjoy our irrefutable connection. The annoying beep of the monitors is overtaken by the soft sighs and satisfied murmurs signaling the affection between us.

I am so lost in him, to him—when I feared I might never taste him again—all I can think about now is how will I ever get enough of him?

I feel the tightening of his lips as he grimaces in pain and guilt immediately lances through me. I'm pushing him too hard, too fast to soothe my own selfish need for reassurance. I try to pull away but his hand holds my head firm as he rests his forehead against mine, noses touching, breaths feathering over each other's lips.

"Just give me a sec," he murmurs against my lips. I just nod my head slightly against his because I'll give him a lifetime if he asks.

"These headaches come on so quick it feels like a sledgehammer hits me," he says after a moment.

Concern douses the flames of lust instantly. "Let me get the doctor."

"No," he says, pounding his left hand against the bed making the rails shake. "This place brings me back to being eight." And the argument that was about to roll off the tip of my tongue dies. "Everyone looking at me with worried eyes and no one giving me answers ... except this time I'm the one who can't give answers."

He laughs softly and I can feel his body stiffen again with the pain. "Colton ..."

"Uh-uh. Not yet," he says again, stubbornly, as he rubs his thumb back and forth across the bare nape of my neck trying to soothe me when it should be the other way around. "I remember my interview with ESPN. Eating my Snickers bar." He gets a rather odd look on his face and averts his eyes momentarily. "Kissing you on pit row and then nothing for a bit," he says, trying to distract me from wanting to get the doctor.

"The drivers' meeting." I fill in. "Becks was with you then."

"Why would I remember eating a candy bar but not the meeting?"

And I draw the connection in my own mind with the missing information that Andy had filled in. Because the traditional good luck Snickers bar is tied to his past—the first chance encounter he had with hope in his life. "I don't know. I'm sure it will all come back to you. I don't think—"

"You were next to me during the anthem. The song ended ..." His voice fades as he tries to recall the next events, while mine catches in my throat. "I watched Davis help you over the wall, wanting to make sure you were safe while Becks started last minute checks ... and I remember feeling the weirdest sense of being *at peace* as I sat at the start/finish line but I'm not sure why ... and then nothing until waking up."

And the lingering tiptoe of unease that I'd felt earlier turns into a full-on stampede.

My heart plummets. My breath hitches. *He doesn't remember*. He doesn't remember telling me the phrase that's glued the broken pieces of me together. It takes every ounce of strength I have to not let the unexpected slap to my soul show in the stiffening of my body.

I didn't realize how much I needed to hear him say those words again—especially after thinking I'd lost him. How knowing he remembered that defining moment between us would mend together the last fissures in my healing heart.

"Do you?" His voice breaks through my scattered thoughts as he kisses the tip of my nose before guiding my head back so he can look into my eyes.

I try to mask the emotions that I'm sure are swimming there. "Do I what?" I ask, forcing a swallow down my throat over the lie that clogs it.

He angles his head as he looks at me and I wonder if he knows I'm holding something back. "Do you know why I felt so *happy* at the start of the race?"

I lick my lips and mentally remind myself to not worry my bottom lip between my teeth or else he'll know I'm lying. "Uh-uh," I manage as my heart deflates. I just can't tell him. I can't force him to feel words he doesn't remember or make him feel obligated to repeat words that make him recall the horrors of his childhood.

... What you said to me—those three words—they turn me into someone I won't ever let myself be again. It triggers things—memories, demons, so fucking much ...

His words scrape through my mind and score a mark that only he will ever be able to heal. And I know as much as I want to, as much as it hurts me to suppress my need to hear it, I can't tell him.

I force a diminutive smile on my lips and meet his eyes. "I'm sure you were just excited about the start of the season and thinking that if your practice runs were any indication, you were going to be claiming the checkered flag." The lie rolls off of my tongue, and for a minute I worry he's not going to believe it. After a beat one corner of his mouth lifts up and I know he hasn't noticed.

"I'm sure there was more than one checkered flag I was focused on claiming."

I shake my head at him, the smile on my lips beginning to tremble.

Colton's face transforms instantly from amusement to concern at the unexpected change in my demeanor. "What is it?" he asks, bringing his hand up to cradle the side of my face. I can't speak just yet because I'm too busy preventing the dam from breaking. "I'm okay, Ry. I'm going to be okay," he whispers reassurances to me as he pulls me into him and wraps his arms around me.

And the dam breaks.

Because kissing Colton is one thing, but being encircled in the all-encompassing warmth of his arms makes me feel that I'm in the safest place in the entire world. And when all is said and done, the physical side to our relationship is earth shattering and a necessity no doubt, but at the same time this feeling—muscular arms wrapped around me, his heated breath murmuring reassurances into the crown of my head, his heart beating strong and steady against mine—is by far the one that will carry me through the tough times. The times like right now. When I want him so much—in so many ways—that I never realized were possible. That never even flickered on my radar before.

I'm crying for so many reasons that they start to mix and mingle and slowly fade with each tear that makes the all too familiar tracks down my cheeks. I'm crying because Colton doesn't remember. Because he's alive and whole and his arms are wrapped tight around me. I'm crying because I never got the chance to experience this with Max and he deserved it. I'm crying because I hate the hospital, what it represents, and how it affects and changes the lives of everyone inside for the good and for the bad.

And when the tears stop—when my catharsis is actually over and all of the emotions I've kept pent up over the past week abate—I realize what matters most is this, right here, right now.

We can get through this. *We can find us again.* A part of me worries deep down that he'll never remember that moment so poignant in my mind, but at the same time we have so many more moments ahead of us, so many ready for us to make together, that I can't feel sorry for myself any longer.

My breath hitches again and all I can do is hold on a little tighter to him, hold on a little longer. "I was so worried," is all I can say. "So scared."

"Spiderman. Batman. Superman. Ironman," he whispers in what seems almost a reflex.

"I know." I nod and pull back from him so I can look him in the eyes as I wipe away the tears from my cheeks. "I called to them to help you."

"I'm sorry that you ever had to." He says the words with such honesty that all I can do is stare into his eyes and see the truth within them. That his apology knows how truly scared I was.

I lean in and press my lips gently to his one more time, unable to resist. Wanting him to feel the sense of relief finally settling in my soul. Wanting to prove to him that I can be the strong one while he heals. That it's okay for him to let me.

"Well lookie here. Sleeping Beauty finally woke his ugly ass up."

We break from our kiss at the sound of Beckett's voice, heat flooding my cheeks. "I was just going to call you."

"Really? Is that what you were doing?" he teases as he approaches the bed. "Kiss a lot of frogs? Because it looks to me like the comatose prince here has you under his spell."

I can't hold back the laugh that bubbles up. "You're right. I'm not sorry at all." I reach out and squeeze the hand he offers me. "But I was going to call you next."

"No worries. I know you would have." He turns and looks at Colton, his smile the brightest I've seen since race day. "Aren't you a sight for sore eyes. Welcome to the land of the living, man." And I know he sounds tough, but I catch the break in his voice and the water beading at the corners of his eyes when he focuses on Colton. He reaches out and cuffs his shoulder. "Shit. That freakish-looking shaved patch on your head might just knock you back down to the realm of good looking people. How's it feel leaving the land of I'm-a-fucking-God?"

"Fuck off. This coming from the land of I'm-a-fucking-comedian?"

Beckett barks out a laugh with a shake of his head. "At least in my land we don't have to modify door casings to allow overinflated egos to walk through."

"This is the kind of welcome back to the world I get? I feel the love, dude. I think I prefer the drugs they're giving me to hold me under rather than wake up and listen to this shit." Colton squeezes my hand and his eyes dart over to mine before returning back to Beckett.

"Really? Because I may not have just awoken from a coma, but I assure you that the fuzzy feeling those drugs give you is nothing compared to being awake and the feeling of a warm, wet—"

"Whoa!" I hold my hands up and scoot off the bed, not wanting to hear where the rest of this conversation is going. The faint smell of last night's dinner in the trash gives me all the excuse I need to give them a moment alone. "That's enough for me, boys. I'm going to head down, stretch my legs, and take this trash out."

"Oh, Ry! C'mon ..." Becks says, holding his hands out to the side of him. "I was going to say bath. A warm, wet bath." He laughs loudly and then I hear Colton's laugh and I feel like the world that had been shifted off its axis has just been righted somewhat.

"Yeah," I chide as I pull the liner from the trash can. "I know I always use the adjectives warm and wet when referring to a bath." I shake my head and catch Colton's gaze for a beat. "Be back in a couple of minutes."

Chapter Eleven

My heart feels so much lighter as I walk down the corridor back toward Colton's room. I've texted his parents and Quinlan about him being awake again, and I'm sure they'll be here momentarily. I head to the end of the hall, where the staff of the hospital has so graciously placed Colton's room. His room is more private than most of the others so he can stay out of the sight of other hospital visitors. And there's less chance of the media getting a coveted picture of him.

I'm just about to enter his room when I realize he might want some water. I turn around, not paying attention, and almost run head on into the one person I have no desire to see.

Ever.

At all.

Tawny.

We both startle when we see each other. And of course I'm looking ragged from intermittent sleep and days' old clothes, while she is looking perfectly polished and camera ready. And I have to give her credit, she's kept her distance since Becks gave her the dressing down in the waiting room. But when she offers me up a consolatory smile, I don't care that it's not meant in her usual catty way, because all of the emotions I've pent up over the past few days erupt.

"What are you doing here?" I spit out between gritted teeth. If you could make revulsion a sound, my voice would definitely be laced with it right now. My fingernails dig into my palms, my hands fist, and every muscle in my body is vibrating with indignation.

It takes a minute for the shock to fade from her face, but when it does, I recognize the mask of superiority slip in its place.

"Colton's awake." She shrugs, a smirk ghosting over her pink painted lips. "He wants to speak with me privately," she says as she juts her chin out in case I didn't already know her disdain for me.

"Anything that's Colton's business, is my business."

"Keep dreaming, doll."

"Wipe the smug look off your face, Tawny."

"Are we feeling a little guilty for fucking with Colton's head the night before a race. Everyone knows you were playing your little games with him. That you made him tired. That you—"

The air whooshes out of her when my hands grip her arms and shove her up against the wall, fury sheathed in calm. "Let me make something perfectly clear to you, Tawny. I'm only going to say it once, but it's best you listen, understood?"

I watch her swallow, and her breath comes out in a shaky shudder as she nods. Her eyes flicker around the hallway but there is no one around to come to her rescue.

I lean in closer, fire in my veins and ice in my voice. "You are the reason that Colton is here. Not me. You. There's a special place in hell for women like you—women who fuck with other women's men—and if you keep your shit up, rest assured one of those spots is going to have your name written all over it." I squeeze her arms a little harder, a silent warning that I'm just getting warmed up.

"Here's how this is going to play out, just in case you haven't gotten that new watch and are still living in the past. Colton's no longer on the market. He's mine and I'm his. Is that clear?" I don't care that she doesn't respond because I'm on a roll and nothing's going to stop me. I see her eyes widen and I continue. "Second, if you ever try to insinuate or imply to anyone that there is anything more between you and Colton than a business relationship with family ties, you're going to have to deal with me … and I guarantee that it's not going to be pretty. You haven't seen anything yet, *doll*. I protect what's mine without a second thought to collateral damage." She tries to shrug her shoulders out of my grip, and that just causes me to lean in closer and squeeze a little tighter. "You will treat me with respect and keep your gaggle of whoring friends away as well."

Despite my hands holding her hostage, she regains some of her composure and responds. "Or what?"

I continue on as if she never speaks. "You will keep your relationship with Colton completely professional and will keep your tits and other *assets* out of his face. Is that clear enough or do I need to spell it out for you?"

I loosen my grip, message delivered, although I feel no better for it because Colton is still in the bed on the other side of the wall. Tawny eyes me up and down. "Oh I think you've made it crystal clear … too bad you don't get that Colton needs me in his life."

In a heartbeat I slam her back up against the wall, this time my forearm pushes against her chest and my face is within inches of hers. "Your expiration date was years ago, *sweetie*. I am all he needs. And if you attempt to show him otherwise, that very prestigious job of yours might just go bye-bye ... so I'd definitely think twice before opening your mouth again." I start to walk away but turn back and glare at her, her eyes reflecting the anger in mine. "Oh, and, Tawny? Colton will not know about this conversation. That way you can keep your job and he can keep the notion that his childhood friend and college sweetheart really is the nice person he believes her to be, and not the underhanded bitch you really are."

"He'd never believe you. I'm still here, aren't I?" She says the words to my back, and I turn slowly trying to gain some semblance of control over the inferno of rage boiling just beneath the surface.

"Yeah, *for now*," I say with a raise of an eyebrow and a disbelieving shake of my head, "but the clock's ticking, *doll*." Tawny starts to speak but I cut her off. "Try me, Tawny. Try me, because there's nothing I'd rather do than prove to you how serious I am right now."

"Is there a problem here?" The voice jolts me out of my rage induced haze as I look over to the nurse from earlier, who's now leaving Colton's room.

I look from her and then back at Tawny for a second. "No problem," I say, saccharine lacing my tone. "I was just taking out the *trash*." I shoot Tawny one more warning look before I take the ten steps to Colton's room and enter it with a smile plastered on my face.

I breathe out in relief that Dr. Irons is busy examining Colton when I enter the room, because I need a minute to settle my thundering pulse and calm my fingers trembling from anger. Colton glances up and smiles softly at me before focusing back on the doctor and answering his questions.

I exhale the shaky breath I was holding and see Beckett angle his head as he looks at me, bemusement in his eyes as he tries to figure out why my cheeks are so flushed. I just shake my head at him, and at that moment, Dr. Irons decides to remove the bandage from Colton's head.

I have to withhold the gasp that instinctively wants to escape from my lips at the sight. There is a shaved patch of hair with a two inch diameter circle of staples on the upper portion of the right side of his skull. It's still swollen and the silver staples juxtaposed against the pink incision with the dark red of the dried blood make a ghastly contrast.

Colton must see the look on my face because he looks over at Beckett while Dr. Irons examines the incision and says, "How bad?"

Beckett just chews the inside of his cheek and twists his lips as he looks at it and then back at Colton. "It's pretty nasty, dude."

"Yeah?"

"Yeah," Beckett says and nods his head.

"Whatever." Colton shrugs with nonchalance. "It's just hair. It'll grow back."

"Think of the serious sympathy points you could get with Rylee though if you play it up."

Colton glances over at me and smirks. "I don't need any sympathy points with her." I'm about to speak when his gaze shifts over my shoulder. "Tawny."

My back bristles instantly but I try to smooth it down as best as I can. I've said my piece. I've given her enough rope to hang herself; let's just see if she chooses to swing or stand.

"Hey," she says softly. "It's good to see you awake."

I step to the side of the bed next to Colton—staking my claim in case I hadn't made it crystal clear earlier—and reach out to squeeze his right hand, noting its strength has still not returned.

"It's good to be awake," Colton replies as he winces at Dr. Irons' intrusive fingertips against his scalp and hisses in a breath of air. "Give me a minute, okay?"

"Sure."

We all stand there quietly watching Colton until the exam is over and the doctor steps back. "So what other questions do you have, Colton, because I'm sure you have some besides what we spoke about earlier?"

Colton looks over to me and I'm sure he sees the dare in my eyes because mirth begins to dance in his. He works his tongue in his cheek as his grin widens with a lift of his eyebrows.

"Not yet, young man." Dr. Irons laughs out in amusement as he guesses the question and pats him on the knee. I'm sure embarrassment stains my cheeks but I don't even care. "What I wouldn't give to be in my early thirties again," he sighs.

Colton laughs and looks over at me, eyes locking, sexual tension crackling, and the underlying ache starting to smolder. "At any time and in any place, sweetheart," he repeats the words back to me he'd said the night we met.

Everyone else in the room ceases to exist. My insides coil with craving from his words and the salacious look in his eyes. The muscle in his jaw tics as he stares at me for a beat before looking back at Dr. Irons. He shrugs in mock apology as a mischievous grin lifts one corner of his mouth.

"Sorry, Doc, but you gave me a rule and that just tempts me to break it that much more."

Dr. Irons shakes his head at Colton. "So noted, son, but the ramifications of …" he continues on in warning about needing to watch the pressure of blood flowing through the major arteries in his brain while they heal, and thus certain strenuous activities can cause that pressure to be stronger than is safe at this stage of healing. "Anything else?"

"Yes," Colton says, and I don't miss the look that passes between him and Beckett. He pulls his eyes back to the doctor's and says, "When will I be cleared to race again?"

Of all the questions I had expected him to ask, it wasn't that. And of course I'm stupid for hoping that on the off chance Colton might not want to race again, but hearing him actually say it causes panic to course through me. As much as I try to hide the mini-anxiety attack his words have evoked, my body instinctively tenses, my hands jerking tight around his hand while my breath audibly catches in my throat.

Colton averts his eyes from Dr. Irons momentarily to look into mine. Obviously Dr. Irons senses my discomfort because he waits a beat before answering. And during that time, Colton's eyes convey so much to me but at the same time are guarding his deepest thoughts. The moment I start to catch more, he looks away and back to the doctor.

This immediately puts me on edge, and I can't quite place why. And that scares the shit out of me. The unknown in a relationship is brutal, but with Colton? It's a downright mindfuck.

My pulse is racing from Colton's question alone, and now I have to worry about the cryptic warning in his eyes? What the fuck is going on? Maybe like Dr. Irons said earlier, his emotions and disposition have been affected by the accident. I try to tell myself this is the reason—to play it off as such—but deep down I hear warning bells and when it comes to our relationship, that's never a good sign.

Dr. Irons snaps me from my turbulent thoughts with the clearing of his throat. And I fear how he is going to answer Colton's question. "Well …" He sighs and looks down at his iPad before looking back up to meet Colton's gaze. "Since I'm getting the sense that whatever I tell you *not* to do, will just encourage you to do it even faster—"

"You're a quick learner," Colton teases.

Dr. Irons just sighs again, trying to fight the smile tugging on the corners of his mouth. "Normally I'd tell you that getting back in the car is a bad idea. That your brain has been jarred around enough and even when your skull is fully healed, it will still have a weak spot where the bone has reconnected and that could be dangerous … but I know no matter what I say you're going to be back on the track, aren't you?"

I have no option but to sit down now because despite how calm I appear on the outside, my insides have just been shredded by Dr. Irons' correct assumption.

Colton blows out a long breath and looks out the window for a bit, and for just a moment I notice the chink in his armor. It's fleeting, but it's there nonetheless. He may never admit it, but he's scared to get in the car again. Scared to recall the moments during the crash that he can't remember right now. Afraid he might get hurt again. And he's so consumed by his thoughts that he doesn't notice that he's withdrawn his hand from mine.

"You're right," he finally says, and chills immediately blanket my body. "I will. I have no other choice … but I'll follow your advice and wait until I'm medically cleared. I'll have my doctors in California connect with you to make sure nothing is missed."

Dr. Irons swallows and nods his head. "Okay, well I'm going to bank on the fact that you're a sensible guy … well, as sensible as one can be that drives two hundred miles an hour for a living." Colton smiles at the comment. "I'll be back to check on you later."

Dr. Irons leaves and for a moment there is an awkward silence between the four of us. I imagine it's because all of us are secretly wondering what it's going to be like if—no *when*—he hops back in the race car, but no one says anything.

Dread weighs heavy on me, and I have no clue how I'm going to be able to handle it. How I'm going to be able to watch him climb inside a car nearly identical to the one he almost died in.

Colton breaks the startled silence. "Becks?"

"Yeah." Becks steps forward and stares at his friend.

"Make sure to tell Eddie that he needs to get my records from Dr. Irons so we can study my injury. See how we can make it complement the HANS even better."

I know Colton is talking about the top secret safety device he was wearing during the accident. The one that CD Enterprises is getting ready to submit for patent protection, so I'm not sure why Beckett's face falls. I watch his eyes dart over to Tawny momentarily, a flash of worry flickering through them, before looking back at Colton.

"What, Becks? What aren't you telling me?" Obviously Colton notices the reaction too.

Becks clears his throat and takes a deep breath. "You fired Eddie a couple of months ago, Colton."

"What? C'mon, Becks. Quit fucking with me and just get the records for him, okay?"

"I'm not fucking with you. A second set of schematics disappeared. With his gambling debts and other issues, too many factors pointed to him, so you fired him," Beckett says as Colton's eyes flicker around the room, his head toggling back and forth as if he's trying to comprehend what he's being told.

"Seriously?" When Becks just nods, Colton looks over at Tawny and she nods too. "Fuckin' A," he grits out as he rolls his shoulders and stares out the window for a moment before looking back at Beckett. "*Stealing?* I don't remember that at all." His voice is dead quiet and full of disbelief.

I reach out and squeeze his hand, causing him to look over and meet my eyes. "Hey, it's okay. It'll come back. It's only temporary," I say, trying to reassure him as best as I can.

"But ... if I don't remember something like that, what else don't I remember that I don't even know about?" His eyes swim with confusion and he grimaces momentarily causing my heart to speed up with worry.

"Don't worry about it, dude. Think of all the crap you can claim amnesia on that normally you'd get shit for."

Thank God for Becks and his easygoing personality because even though I can still see Colton struggling as he tries to grasp everything, I can also feel some of the tension relax from his hand that I'm holding. I meet Becks' eyes, a silent thank you passing between us.

Tawny clears her throat softly and all of a sudden it's like we all snap from our private thoughts with the sound. Colton breathes in deeply and says, "Tawny, I need you to issue a press release right away."

"What would you like it to say?" Ms. Ever-efficient asks while walking to the bedside opposite me, as Colton gathers his thoughts. And with just the slightest glance my way, she refocuses on him and softens her voice. "Colton?"

"Yeah?" he answers, raising his eyes to meet the question in her voice.

She reaches out and squeezes his bicep, her eyes roaming over his wound before withdrawing her hand when he doesn't respond. "I'm so glad that you're okay."

I can hear the sincerity in her voice—know she means it—but it still doesn't make me like her any more.

"Coulda been a lot worse from what I'm told, so I'll get there." Colton takes a sip of water while his brow furrows in concentration. "Tell them I'm awake and have been for a day or so. I'm on the road to recovery and will be heading back to California within the week, once I'm cleared, and returning to the track in no time. Thank them for their support and prayers, and instead of any flowers or gifts, I'd rather they make a donation to Corporate Cares. The boys need it more than I do."

Tawny looks up from her phone where she's typing all of this and asks, "What about your memory loss?"

"None of their business," Colton says, glancing up at Becks again, a silent understanding passing between them. "That's all." Tawny lifts her focus from her phone and looks at Colton as if she doesn't understand. "You can go now," he says to her, and I have to hide the look of shock on my face at the unexpected dismissal.

Tawny's head snaps up as she shoves her phone in her purse. "Well, um, okay," she says, color staining her cheeks as she heads for the door.

"Hey, Tawn?" Colton's words stop her and the acid in his tone surprises the hell out of me.

"Yes?" she asks as she turns around to face the two of us side by side.

"After you issue the press release, you can get your stuff and head back home."

She angles her head and stares at Colton for a moment, confusion flickering over her face. "It's okay. It's better if I stay here and deal with the media—"

"No," Colton says. "I don't think you understand what I'm saying." Tawny's tongue darts out and wets her bottom lip as nerves start to eat at her. She takes a step toward the bed as he begins to explain. "We've known each other, what? Most of our lives? Long enough for you to know that I don't like being fucked with." Colton leans forward as her eyes widen and I hold my breath in disbelief at the ice in his voice. "You fucked with me, T. And more importantly you fucked with Rylee. *Now that?* That I most definitely remember. Game over. Pack your shit. You're fired."

I hear Beckett suck in a breath. At the same time Tawny sputters out, "Wh-what? Colton, you—"

"Save it." Colton holds up a hand to stop her and shakes his head in disappointment. "Save your ridiculous excuses and go before you make things any worse for yourself."

She just stares at him, blinking away the tears before glancing over at Beckett, spinning on her heels, and rushing out of the room.

I watch her leave, trying to fathom what it would be like to be in her shoes. To lose both your job and the man you've believed is yours.

And as I hear Colton breathe out a huge sigh beside me, I actually feel sorry for her.

Well ... *not really.*

Chapter Twelve

A muffled sound pulls me from sleep. And I'm so tired—so wanting to sink into the blinding oblivion because I've had so little sleep over the past two weeks—that I keep my eyes closed and write it off as the purr of the jet's engine. But because I'm now awake, when I hear it a second time, I know I'm wrong.

I open my eyes, startled at what I see. The sight of my reckless bad boy—eyes squeezed tight, teeth biting his bottom lip, and face painted with the grief that courses down his cheeks—coming completely undone in disciplined silence. I'm momentarily frozen with uncertainty.

I'm uncertain because I've felt a disconnect between us in the past few days. On the one hand I felt like he was trying to push me away—keep me at arms' length—by keeping all discussions superficial. By saying his head hurts, that he needed to sleep, the minute I brought up any serious subject.

And then there were the odd moments when he thought I wasn't paying attention to him when I'd notice him looking at me from the reflection in the room's window with a look of pained reverence, one of longing laced with sadness. And that singular look always caused chills to dance over my flesh.

He hiccups out a sob and opens his eyes slowly, the pain so evident in them, my grown man scarred by the tears of a scared little boy. He looks away momentarily and I can see him trying to collect himself but only ends up squeezing his eyes shut and crying even harder.

"Colton?" I shift from my reclined position, starting to reach out, but then pulling back in uncertainty because the absolute desolation reflected in his eyes. My hesitation is answered by Colton looking at my hand and shaking his head as if one touch from me will crumble him.

And yet I can't resist. I never can when it comes to Colton.

I can't let him suffer in silence from whatever is eating his soul and shadowing his face. I have to connect with him, comfort him the only way that has seemed to work over the past few weeks.

I unbuckle my seat belt and cross the distance between us, my eyes asking if it's okay to make the connection with him. I don't let him answer—don't give him another chance to push me away—but rather settle across his lap. I wrap my arms around him as best I can, nestle my head in the crook of his neck, and just hold on in reassuring silence.

Hold on as his chest shudders and breath hitches.

As his tears fall, either cleansing his soul or foreshadowing impending devastation.

Chapter Twelve

Colton—Raced

The turbulence jars me awake. Scares the fuck out of me really, seeing as I was having that damn dream again about the crash—the dream where I can't remember shit except for the dizzying, sickening feeling in the pit of my stomach and the out of control feeling in my head. Add to that the jolt of the plane, and my mile-high wake up is a hell of a lot more stressful that the one I'd really like to have with Ry.

God, how badly do I want to take that for a ride. I'm fucking hard as a rock as I've been for the past three days when I wake up but one, doctor's fucking orders. Two, we're constantly surrounded by other people, and three, after overhearing her conversation with Haddie the other night when she thought I was asleep, how can I touch her when all I'm going to do is end up hurting her.

I don't want to do that to her. Don't want her to live life always waiting for the worst to happen. I don't mind the car, don't mind what a crash could possibly do to me because the shit I lived through was much more painful than hitting a concrete barrier.

Impact can kill your body.

What my mom did to me killed my soul.

I shake the shit from my head and lift it up from the chair Ry insisted I adjust to recline. I look around to see Nurse Ratchet, the hospital approved medic sent to monitor my flight home, sit up at attention when she notices that I'm awake.

Leave me the fuck alone.

I've had enough prodding fingers and concerned eyes looking at me to last a fucking lifetime. Oh and then there were the fucking ludicrous sponge baths. Grown men sure as fuck are not supposed to have someone wash their nuts unless it's to be followed by a blowjob in the shower. On a bed with a sponge? *Fucking ridiculous.*

Good riddance to the hospital and its torturous type of solitary confinement.

Nurse Ratchet starts to unbuckle her seatbelt, and I just shake my head to tell her that I'm fine. I lie back down, angling my head to the right so I can stare at the sight across the aisle from me. Rylee's sound asleep, curled up on her side so she's facing me, no doubt so that she can watch and make sure that I'm okay.

The fucking self-sacrificing saint.

And I know she's exhausted. She misses the boys desperately despite being on the phone with them every chance she gets. Add to that the nightmares she's been having every night that wake me, allowing me to be the silent witness to the fucking agony I'm inflicting upon her. She shouts out Max's name. My name. Begs for us to live. Begs to take our place so she can die instead. Begs for me not to race again. Screams for a car to stop and let me out. And I know this because I lie awake holding her while she trembles in her sleep. Holding her—holding on to her as I breathe in everything I can—so that I can live with the ghost of her when I finally bring myself to do what I need to do.

Be selfless for the first time in my life.

And the time has come.

Way too soon—forever would be too fucking soon—but it has come.

And the thought has every single fucking part of me protesting over the gut-wrenching hurt that's to come. That I'll be inflicting on myself. Pain I'm sure that will be a thousand times worse than these ear-splitting headaches that come and go on a fucking whim, because this kind will be from tearing myself apart, not from trying to put myself back together.

Humpty fuckin' Dumpty.

She sighs softly, shifting in her sleep, and a curl falls over her cheek. I give into the need—the one that is so inherent now that I'm fucking scared to death of how I'll be able to lessen it in the coming days—reach out and move it off of her face. I curse my fucking fingers as they tremble from the after effects of what we still hope is just swelling. They stop shaking and so I let them linger, enjoying the feel of her skin against my fingertips.

What the fuck is going on with me? How is it I fought my whole life to not need, *to not feel* ... and now that I do, I'll gladly take the pain so she doesn't have to?

But the thought I can't shake keeps tumbling through my obviously screwed-up head. If she's my fucking pleasure, how in the hell am I going to bury the pain when I push her away? From pushing her away? I shake my head, unsure, and welcome the stab of pain from the action because it's got nothing on what's going to happen to my heart.

But there's no other option. Especially after overhearing her on the phone with Haddie last night when she thought I was asleep. Hysterical hiccupping sobs. Denials of how she's ever going to watch me get in a car again. Hearing the brutal reality of what she went through killed me, fucking ripped me to shreds as I lie with my back to her, remorse hardening my heart, tears burning my eyes, and guilt submerging my soul. Learning that her abrupt trips out of my hospital room are so she can throw up because she's so sick with worry over it. How she's eating Tums like candy to lessen the constant acid eating through her stomach from my need to return to the track. How she'll support me, urge me, help me get back in the car, but will have to sneak out before the pace car is off the lead lap. How she won't be able to hear the sounds and see the sights without replaying the images that are etched in her mind. Won't be able to look me in the eyes and wish me luck without thinking she's sending me to my death.

A shiver of recourse revolts through my body.

And then there's the other hint that I'm getting from her—that I can see in her eyes when she shifts them away—that tells me she knows something I don't. She has one of my memories and is holding it hostage. But which fucking one?

The hints swirl of what I've lost in the black abyss of my mind. Ghosts of memories converge, overlapping and all shouting for attention at once. They scream at me like fans asking for autographs—all begging for attention—faceless, nameless people all wanting something—yelling at the tops of their lungs—and yet all I hear is white noise.

All I see is a blur of mixed color.

Why is it I can still remember the shit that stains my soul but I can't seem to remember the bleach I've found that washes it away? And I have a feeling that whatever Rylee is guarding is that important. That monumental. She wouldn't be keeping it from me unless she was trying to protect me. Or her.

But from what?

In my dreams I hear her saying she can't do this anymore. Is that it? Is she going to end this? Is she going to walk away and never look back? Break me into a million fucking pieces?

What the fuck, Donavan? You're going to do it to her. Walk away to save her from yourself. And you think it's going to be any easier just because you're doing it? Think that the acid-laced knife that's going to barb through your heart is going to hurt any less because it's by your own hand?

Fucking crash.

Goddamn prescriptions that I swear are messing up my head.

Fucking voodoo pussy.

My fucking Rylee.

I watch her. Can't move my eyes away from those thick lashes on cream-colored skin. Over her all-consuming lips and down over the swell of her tits. She's arms' length away but I still know how she smells. How she tastes and sounds and feels. It will forever be embedded in my mind.

Irremovable.

Irreplaceable.

Yeah, my dick stirs to life—it's Rylee, isn't it? But so much more stirs and swells and hopes that I don't even fight the tears welling in my eyes. For the second time in more years than I can count, I let the tears fall. Silent tracks of impending devastation staining my face.

Who knew that doing what was right for someone else could feel so incredibly wrong? Could break the strongest man by weakening his heart?

Will reduce me to nothing?

I know she can give me what I need—quiet the demons in my head that torment my soul and parasitic heart—like the adrenaline of losing myself in the blur at the track, but I can't do that to her. I can't in good conscience hold on to her so tightly in order to lose my demons when it's causing hers to invade her sleep. I can't take the pleasure when it's causing her all of the pain.

Before, I could. I would have. But this is Rylee here. The selfless soul who means too fucking much to me. So, no I can't.

Not now.

Not ever to Rylee.

It feels so good to let it all out—the confusion, the loss of hope, the dying of my redemption—yet hurts so badly as the tears fight their way out and scorch my face. Singe my soul. Crumble possibilities.

I squeeze my eyes shut and try to shut out the memories that I do have. The ones flickering like a strobe light through the haze of my time with Rylee. The tears turn to silent sobs and eventually even those dissipate into hitching breaths.

When I open my eyes, violet pools of concern are staring at me with a mix of confusion and sympathy. "Colton?"

Fuck. I don't want her to see me like this. Remember me like this. Some pussified man bawling his eyes out for reasons she can't fathom.

I can hear the worry in her voice but all her face shows is compassion, understanding, acceptance. And that makes what I have to say so much harder. The words are there on the tip of my tongue and I fool myself into believing that I'm about to say them.

Acid on my taste buds.

Bile in my throat.

The fracturing of my heart.

She reaches out and cups her hand to the side of my face, her thumb wiping away the stains—just like her heart has brushed away vile memories—and a soft smile ghosts her mouth.

I race you, Rylee.

The words feather through my mind and another tear slips over.

And I've never felt more exposed in my life.

Guard down.

Heart open.

Soul needing.

Accepting.

Wanting.

I'm so fucking lost right now. Lost even though I've been found. Even though she's found me.

And I get it now. Get why she can't watch me get in the car again. Get why she'd be so selfless—encourage, push, help—even when it's killing her. Breaking inside while pretending on the outside that she's whole.

But I'm nowhere near okay.

Not going to be for a long time.

If ever again.

I open my mouth but I can't bring myself to do it. I can't bring myself to tell her this isn't what she deserves. That I'm not what she deserves. That I could do so much worse—have done so much worse—and she can do so much better. That I understand she can't go through this again. I'm not sure how to. I try to force the words off my tongue but they die, self-preservation at its finest. Silence is my only option. The only way to quell the guilt that eats at me every time she looks in my eyes and gives me the same soft smile she's giving me now.

She has to be wondering why I'm crying. Why I'm being such a chick, but she doesn't ask. Instead, she sits up slowly and looks around the private jet before rising and closing the distance between us. She gives me a look as if she's asking if it's okay and before I can even answer, she's settling in my lap, nuzzling her head under my chin, wrapping her arms around me as best she can.

The soothing balm to my aching soul.

She doesn't say a word, but just holds on, easing whatever she thinks is wrong with me by her mere presence. And of course now the tears well again like a fucking broken faucet and I hate it. Hate myself right now.

And I am so wrong.

I thought I could live with the pain—manage—but holy shit I feel as if my body is broken—fucking shattered into a million pieces, and I haven't even told her yet. Haven't even taken a step away but holy mother of God, I'm already knocked to my knees.

Already struggling to breathe when the air is cocooning me.

It's time to hit the concrete barrier head on without a seat belt, without my lifeline.

How in the fuck am I going to do this?

Chapter Thirteen

"I don't need a goddamn wheelchair!"

It's the fourth time he's said it, and it's the only thing he's said to me since waking up on the airplane. I bite my lip and watch him struggle as he glares at the nurse when she pushes the chair once again to the back of his knees without saying a word to her difficult patient. I can see him starting to tire from the exertion of getting out of the car, and walking the five feet or so toward the front door, before stopping and resting a hand on the retaining wall. The strain is so obvious that I'm not surprised when he eventually gives in and sits down.

I'm glad I texted everyone ahead of time and told them to stay inside the house and not greet us in the driveway. After watching the effort it took for him to get off the plane and into the car, I figured he might be embarrassed if he had an audience.

The paparazzi are still yelling on the other side of the closed gates, clamoring to get a picture or quote from Colton, but Sammy and his new additions to the staff are doing their job keeping this moment private, which I'm so very grateful for.

"Just give me a fucking minute," he growls when she starts to push him, and I can see that a headache has hit him again when he puts his head in his hands, fingers bending the bill of his baseball hat, and just sits there.

I take a deep breath from my silent place on the sideline, trying to figure out what is going on with him. And after his silent breakdown on the jet, I know it's more than just the headaches. More than the crash. Something has shifted and I can't quite put my finger on the cause of his warring personalities.

And the fact that I can't pinpoint *the why* has my nerves dancing on edge.

Colton presses his hands to the side of his hat, and I can see the tension in his shoulders as he tries to brace for the pain radiating from his head. I walk toward him, unable to resist trying to help somehow although I know there's nothing I can really do, and just place my hands on his shoulders to let him know I'm there.

That he's not alone.

"I don't need a fucking nurse watching over me. I'm fine. Really," Colton says from his partially reclined position on the chaise lounge. Everyone left shortly after our arrival, everyone but Becks and me, realizing what a surly mood Colton was in. Colton's parked himself on the upstairs patio for the last thirty minutes because, after being trapped in the hospital for so long, he just wants to sit in the sun in peace. A peace he's not getting since he's been arguing with everyone about how he's perfectly fine and just wants to be left alone.

Becks folds his arms across his chest. "We know you're hardheaded and all, but you took quite a hit. We're not going to leave you—"

"Leave me the fuck alone, Daniels." Colton barks, annoyance evident in his tone as Becks steps toward him. "If I wanted your two cents, I would've asked."

"Well crack open the piggy bank because I'm going to give you a whole fucking dollar's worth," he says as he leans in closer to Colton. "Your head hurts? You want to be a prick because you've been locked up in a goddamn hospital? You want sympathy that you're not getting? Well too fucking bad. You almost died, Colton—*died*—so shut the fuck up and quit being an asshole to the people that care about you the most." Becks shakes his head at him in exasperation while Colton just pulls his hat down lower over his forehead and sulks.

When Becks speaks next, his voice is the quiet, calculating calm he used with me when we were in the hotel room the night before the accident.

"You don't want sponge baths from Nurse Ratchet downstairs? I get that too. But you have a choice to make because it's either her, me, or Rylee washing your balls every night 'til you're cleared by the docs. I know who I'd choose and it sure as fuck isn't me or the large, gruff, German woman in the kitchen. I love ya, dude, but my friendship draws the line when it comes to touching your junk." Becks leans back, his arms still crossed and his eyebrows raised. He shrugs his shoulders to reiterate the question.

When Colton doesn't speak, but rather remains ornery and stares Becks down from beneath the brim of his cap, I step up—tired, cranky, and wanting time alone with Colton—to try and right our world again.

"I'm staying, Colton. No questions asked. I'm not leaving you here by yourself." I just hold up my hands when he starts to argue. *Stubborn asshole.* "If you want to keep acting like one of the boys when they throw a tantrum, then I'll start treating you like one."

For the first time since we've been out on the patio, Colton raises his eyes to meet mine. "I think it's time everyone leaves." His voice is low and full of spite.

I walk closer, wanting him to know that he can push all he wants but I'm not backing down. I throw his own words back in his face. Words I'm not even sure he remembers. "We can do this the easy way or the hard way, Ace, but rest assured it's going to be *my way*."

I make sure Becks locked the front door on his way out before grabbing the plate of cheese and crackers to head back upstairs. I find Colton in the same location on the chaise lounge but he's taken his hat off, head leaned back, eyes closed. I stop in the doorway and watch him. I take in the shaved patch that's starting to grow back over his nasty scar. I note the furrow in his forehead that tells me he's anything but at peace.

I enter the patio quietly, the song *Hard to Love* is playing softly on the radio, and I'm grateful that it masks my footsteps so I don't wake him as I set his pain meds and plate of food down on the table next to him.

"You can go now too."

His gruff voice startles me. His unexpected words throw me. My temper simmers. I look over at him and can't do anything other than shake my head in sputtering disbelief because his eyes are still closed. Everything over the past couple of days hits me like a kaleidoscope of memories. The distance and avoidance. This is about more than being irritated from being confined during his recovery. "Is there something you need to get off your chest?"

A lone seagull squawks overhead as I wait for the answer, trying to prepare for whatever he's going to say to me. He's gone from crying without explanation to telling me to leave—not a good sign at all.

"I don't need your goddamn pity. Don't you have a house full of little boys that need you to help fulfill that inherent trait of yours to hover and smother?"

He could've called me every horrible name in the book and it wouldn't sting as much as those words he just slapped me with. I'm dumbfounded, mouth opening and closing as I stare at him, face angled to the sun, eyes still closed. "Excuse me?" It's no match for what he's just said, but it's all I've got.

"You heard me." He lifts his chin up almost in dismissal but still keeps his eyes closed. "You know where the door is, sweetheart."

Maybe my lack of sleep has dimmed my usual reaction, but those words just flicked the switch to one hundred percent. I feel like we've time warped back to weeks ago and I immediately have my protective guard back up. The fact that he won't look at me is like kerosene to my flame. "What the fuck's going on, Donavan? If you're going to blow me off, the least you can do is give me the courtesy of looking at me."

He squints open an eye as if it's irritating him to have to pay attention to me and I've had it. He's managed to hurt me in the whole five minutes we've had alone together, and the fact that my emotional stability is being held together by frayed strings doesn't help either. He watches me and a ghost of a smirk appears, as if he's enjoying my reaction, enjoying toying with me.

Unspoken words flicker through my mind and whisper to me, call on me to look closer. But what am I missing here?

"Rylee, it's just probably best if we call it like we see it."

"Probably best?" My voice escalates and I realize that maybe we're both a whole lot exhausted and overwhelmed with everything that's occurred, but I'm still not getting what the hell is going on. Panic starts burgeoning inside me because you can only hold on so tight to someone who doesn't want to be held on to. "What the hell, Colton? What's going on?"

I push off the chair and walk to the ledge and look out over the water for a moment, needing a minute to shove down the frustration so patience can resurface, but I'm just plain worn out from the whiplash of emotions. "You don't get to push me away, Colton. You don't get to need me one minute and then shove me away as hard as you can the next." I try to keep the hurt out of my voice but it's virtually impossible.

"I can do whatever the hell I want!" he shouts at me.

I whirl back around, jaw clenched, the taste of rejection fresh in my mouth. "Not when you're with me you can't!" My voice echoes across the concrete of the patio as we stare at each other, the silence slowly smothering possibilities.

"Then maybe I shouldn't be with you." The quiet steel to his words knocks the wind out of me. Pain radiates in my chest as I draw in air. What the hell? Did I read this all wrong? What am I missing?

I want to tear into him. I want to unleash on him the fury I feel reverberating through me.

Colton deflects his eyes momentarily and in that moment, everything finally clicks. All of the puzzle pieces that seemed amiss over the past week finally fit together.

And it's all so transparent now, I feel like an idiot that I didn't put it together sooner.

It's time to call his bluff.

But what if I call it and I'm wrong? My heart lurches into my throat at the thought, but what other option do I have? I smooth my hands down the thighs of my jeans, hating that I'm nervous.

"Fine," I resign as I take a few steps toward him. "You know what? You're right. I don't need this shit from you or anyone else." I shake my head and stare at him as he grabs his hat, places it on his head, lowering the bill so I can just barely see his eyes that are now open and watching me with guarded intensity. "*Non-negotiable, remember?*" I throw my threat back at him from our bathtub agreement weeks ago, and with those words I see a sliver of emotion flicker through his otherwise stoic eyes.

He just shrugs his shoulder nonchalantly, but I'm onto his game now. I may not know what it is, but something's wrong and frankly this *been here, done that* bullshit is getting old. "Didn't you learn fucking anything? Did they remove the common sense part of your brain when they cut it open?"

His eyes snap up to mine now and I know I've gotten his attention. *Good*. He doesn't speak but I at least know his eyes are on me, his attention is focused. "I don't need your condescending bullshit, Rylee." He yanks the bill of his hat down over his eyes and lays his head back, dismissing me once again. "You know where the door is."

I'm across the patio and have flipped his hat off of his head within seconds, my face lowered within inches of his. His eyes flash open, and I can see the wash of emotions within them from my unexpected actions. He works a swallow in his throat as I hold my stare, refusing to back down.

"Don't push me away or I'm going to push back ten times as hard," I tell him, beseeching him to look deep within and be honest with himself. To be honest about us. "You've hurt me on purpose before. I know you fight dirty, Colton ... so what is it that you're trying to protect me from?" I lower myself in the chaise lounge, our thighs brushing against each other's, trying to make the connection so he can feel it, so he can't deny it.

He looks out toward the ocean for a few moments and then looks back at me, clearly conflicted. "Everything. Nothing." He shrugs, averting his eyes again. "From me." The break in his voice unwinds the ball of tension knotted around my heart.

"What ... what are you talking about?" I slide my hand into his and squeeze it, wondering what's going on inside his head. "Protect me? You ordering me around and telling me to get the hell out is not you protecting me, Colton. It's you hurting me. We've been through this and—"

"Just drop it, Ry."

"I'm not dropping shit," I tell him, my pitch escalating to get my point across. "You don't get to—"

"Drop it!" he orders, jaw clenched, tension in his neck.

"No!"

"You said you couldn't do this anymore." His voice calls out to me across the calming sounds of the ocean below despite the turbulent waves crashing into my heart. The even keel of his tone warns me that he's hurting, but it's the words he says that have me searching my memory for what he's talking about.

"What—?" I start to say but I stop when he holds his hand up, eyes squeezing shut as the cluster headache hits him momentarily. And of course I feel guilty for pushing him on this, but he's crazy if he thinks I'm going anywhere. I want to reach out and soothe him, try to take the pain away but know that nothing I can do will help, so I sit and rub my thumb absently over the back of his tensing hand.

"When I was out ... I heard you tell Becks that you couldn't do this anymore ... that you'd gladly walk out ..." his voice drifts off as his eyes bore into mine, jaw muscle pulsing. The obstinate set to his jaw asking the question his words don't.

"That's what this is all about?" I ask dumbfounded and struck with realization all at once. "A snippet of a conversation I had with Becks when I said I would have gladly walked away from you—done something, anything differently—if it would've prevented you from being comatose in a hospital bed?" I can see how his mind has altered bits and pieces of my conversation with Beckett, but he's never asked me about it. Never communicated. And that fact, more than the misunderstanding, upsets me.

"You said you'd gladly walk out." His repeats, his voice resolute as if he doesn't believe I'm telling him the truth. "Your pity's not needed nor welcome."

"You've been pulling away because you think I'm only here out of pity? That you got hurt and now I don't want you anymore?" And now I'm pissed. "Glad you thought so highly of me. Such an asshole," I mutter more to myself than to him. "Feel free to make assumptions, because in case you haven't noticed, they've done wonders for our relationship so far, right?" I can't help the sarcasm dripping from my voice, but after everything we've been through together—everything we always seem to come back to when all is said and done—I'm hurt that he even remotely thinks I'm going to want him any less because he's not one hundred percent.

"Rylee." He blows out a loud breath and reaches for my hand but I pull it back.

"Don't *Rylee* me." I can't help the tears that swim in my eyes. "I almost lost you—"

"You're goddamn fucking right you did, and that's why I have to let you go!" he shouts before swearing out a muttered curse. He laces his fingers at the back of his neck and then pulls his elbows down, trying to staunch some of his anger. My eyes flash up to meet his, my breath choking on confusion. "I heard you on the phone with Haddie the other night when you thought I was asleep. Heard you tell her that you're not sure you'll be able to watch me get back in the car again. I can't be made to choose between you and racing," he says, anguish so palpable it rolls off him in waves and crashes into the desperation emanating off of me. "I need both of you, Rylee." The desolation of his voice strikes chords deep within me, his fear transparent. "Both of you."

And now I get it. It's not that he thinks I don't want him because he's hurt, it's that I won't want him in the future because I'll fear for every minute of every second that he's in that car, as well as the minutes leading up to it.

I had no idea he'd heard my conversation. A conversation with Haddie that was so candid, I cringe recalling some of the things I said, without the sugarcoating I'd use with most others.

I lift my hand to his face and bring it back to look at mine. "Talk to me, Colton. After everything we've been through, you can't shut me out or push me away. You've got to talk to me or we can never move forward."

I can see the transparent emotions in his eyes, and I hate watching him struggle with them. I hate knowing something has eaten at him over the past week when he should have been worried about recovering. Not about us. I hate that he's even questioned anything that has to do with us.

He breathes out a shaky breath and closes his eyes momentarily. "I'm trying to do what's best for you." His voice is so soft the sound of the waves almost drowns it out.

"What's best for me?" I ask in the same tone, confused but needing to understand this man so complicated and yet so childlike in many ways.

He opens his eyes and the pain is there, so raw and vulnerable they make my insides twist. "If we're not together … then I can't hurt you every time I get in the car."

He swallows and I give him a moment to find the words I can see he's searching for … and to regain my ability to breathe. He's been pushing me away because he cares, because he's putting me first and my heart swells at the thought.

He reaches up and takes the hand I have resting on his cheek, laces his fingers with it, and rests it in his lap. His eyes stay focused on our connection.

"I told you that you make me a better man … and I'm trying so fucking hard to be that for you, but I'm failing miserably. A better man would let you go so that you don't have to relive what happened to Max and my crash every time I get in the car. He'd do what's best for you."

It takes a moment to find my voice because what Colton just said to me—those words—are equivalent to telling me he races me. They represent such an evolvement in him as a man, I can't stop the tear that slides down my cheek.

I give in to necessity. I lean in and press my lips to his. To taste and take just a small reassurance that he's here and alive. That the man I thought and hoped he was underneath all of the scars and hurt, really is there, really is this beautifully damaged man whose lips are pressed against mine.

I withdraw a fraction and look into his eyes. "What's best for me? Don't you know what's best for me is you, Colton? Every single part of you. The stubborn, the wild and reckless, the fun loving, the serious, and even the broken parts of you," I tell him, pressing my lips to his between every word. "All of those parts of you I will never be able to find in someone else … those are what I need. What I want. You, baby. Only you."

This is what love is, I want to scream at him. Shake him until he understands that this is real love. Not the unfettered pain and abuse of his past. Not his mom's twisted version of it. This is love. Me and him, making it work. One being strong when the other is weak. Thinking of the other first when they know their partner is going to feel pain.

But I can't say it.

I can't scare him into remembering what he felt for me or said to me. And as much as it cripples me that I can't say *I race you* to him, I can show him by standing by his side, by holding his hand, by being strong when he needs me the most. By being silent when all I want to do is tell him.

He just stares at me, teeth scraping over his bottom lip, and complete reverence in his eyes. He sniffs back the emotion and clears his throat as he nods his head, a silent acceptance of the pleading in my words. "What you told Haddie is true though. It's going to kill you every time I get in the car ..."

"I'm not going to lie. It is going to kill me, but I'll figure out how to handle it when we get to that point," I tell him, although I already feel the fear that stains the fringes of my psyche at the thought. "*We'll* figure it out," I correct myself and the most adorable smile curls one corner of his mouth, melting my heart.

He just nods his head, his eyes conveying the words I want to hear, and for now, it's enough for me. Because when you have everything right before you, you'll accept anything just to keep it there.

"I'm not any good at this," he says, and I can see the concern fill his eyes, etch across his features.

"No one is," I tell him, squeezing our linked fingers. "Relationships aren't easy. They're hard and can be brutal at times ... but those are the times you learn the most about yourself. And when they're right," I pause, making sure his eyes are steadfast on mine, "they can be like coming home ... finding the rest of your soul ..." I avert my eyes, suddenly embarrassed by my introspective comments and my hopeless romantic tendencies.

He squeezes my hand but I keep my face toward the sun, hoping the color staining my cheeks isn't noticeable. My mind races with the possibilities for us if he can just find it within himself to let me have a permanent place there. The silence is okay now because the empty space between us is floating with potential instead of misunderstanding. And on this patio, bathed by sunlight, we're lost in thought because we're accepting the fact that there are tomorrows for us to experience together, and that's a good place to be.

As my mind wanders I see the plate of food and pain meds on the table next to us. "Hey, you need to take your pills," I say, finally turning toward him and meeting his eyes.

He reaches out and cups the side of my face, brushing the pad of his thumb over my bottom lip. I draw in a shaky, affected breath as he angles his head and watches me. "You're the only medicine I need, Rylee."

I can't help the smile spreading across my lips or the sarcastic comment that slides off my tongue. "I guess the doctors didn't mess with your ability to deliver smooth one-liners did they?"

"Nope," he says with a devilish smirk that has me leaning into him the same time he does, so that we meet in the center.

Our lips brush ever so gently, once then twice, before he parts his lips and slides his tongue between mine. Our tongues dance, our hands caress, and our hearts swell as we settle into the tenderness of the kiss. He brings his other hand up to cup my face, and I can feel it trembling as he tries to keep it there. I lift my hand up to hold onto the outside of his and help him hold it against my cheek. Desire coils deep in my belly and as much as I know I can't sate my body's yearning, per doctor's orders, it doesn't mean I don't want to desperately.

When we connect through intimacy, it's more than just the mind blowing orgasm at the hands of the oh-so-skillful Colton, but rather something I can't exactly put words to. It's almost as if, when we connect, there is a contentment that weaves its way deep down in my soul and completes me. Binds us. And I miss that feeling.

A sexy as hell groan comes from the back of his throat that doesn't help stem the ache I have burning for him. I reach my free hand out and run it up the plane of his chest, loving the vibration humming beneath my fingers as a result of my touch. Chills prickle my skin and it's not from the ocean breeze but rather the tidal wave of sensations my body misses desperately.

"Fuck, I'm dying to be in you, Ry," he whispers against my lips as every nerve in my body stands at attention and begs to be taken, branded, and remade his all over again. And I am so close to saying *fuck the doctor's orders* that my hand is sliding down his torso to slip beneath his waistband, when I feel his body tense and his breath hiss out.

I'm immediately swamped with guilt over my lack of willpower to take the temptation so readily at my fingertips and I switch to high alert. "A bad one?"

The grimace on Colton's face remains, eyes squeezed shut, as he just nods his head softly and shifts backward in the chair until he's reclined. I reach for the medicine and put them in his hands.

I guess I'm not the only medicine he needs after all.

Chapter Fourteen

I wander the halls of the Malibu house—worry over Colton, homesickness for the boys, and missing Haddie all robbing me of sleep. This has been the longest I've been away from any of them, and as much as I love Colton, I'm needing that connection with *my life*.

I need their energy that always lifts my soul and feeds my spirit. I've missed Zander's deposition, Ricky's first home run, Aiden being called into the principal's office for stopping a fight rather than starting one … I feel like a bad mother neglecting her children.

Not finding solace, I climb the stairs for the umpteenth time to check on him. To make sure he's still knocked out from the cocktail of medications Dr. Irons prescribed on the phone earlier when Colton's headache would not let up.

I'm still worried. I think I subconsciously fear falling asleep because I might miss something he needs.

Then I think of Colton's revelations earlier before the headache hit, and I can't help the smile that softens my face. The knowledge that he was trying to push me away to protect me may have been misguided, but perfect nonetheless.

There is most definitely hope for us yet.

I walk toward the bed, Halestorm playing softly on the stereo overhead, and can't help the breath I hold as I sit down on the bed beside him. He's lying on his stomach, his arms buried beneath the pillow and his face angled to the side of the bed facing me. The light blue sheets have fallen down below his waist, and my eyes trace the sculpted lines of his back, my fingers itching to touch the heated warmth of his skin. My eyes roam over the scar on his head and note that the patch of hair is starting to grow in with stubble. In no time at all no one will even know the trauma beneath his hair.

But I'll know. And I'll remember. And I'll fear.

I shake my head and squeeze my eyes shut, needing to get control of my rampant stampede of emotions. I notice his discarded shirt on the bed beside him and can't help picking it up and burying my nose in it, drinking in his smell, needing the mapped connection in my mind to lessen the worry that's now a constant. It's not enough though, so I crawl into bed beside him. I lean forward, careful not to disturb him, and press my lips to the spot just between his shoulder blades.

I inhale his scent, feel the warmth of his heated flesh beneath my lips, and thank God that I get this moment again with him. A second chance. I sit like this for a moment, silent *thank yous* running through my mind when Colton whimpers.

"*Please no*," he says, the juvenile tone in the masculine timbre is haunting, unnerving, devastating. "*Please, Mommy, I'll be good. Just don't let him hurt me*."

He thrashes his head in protest, body tensing, arms bracing as the sounds he's making become more adamant, more upsetting. I try to wake him, take his shoulders and shake him.

"*Please, Mommy. Pleeeaaassseeee*," he whimpers in a pleading voice wavering with terror. My heart lodges in my throat and tears spring to my eyes at that eerie combination of little boy within the grown man.

"Wake up, Colton!" I shove his shoulder back and forth again as he becomes more animated, but the strength of the prescriptions that Dr. Irons had me give him are too strong to pull him from the nightmare. "C'mon, wake up," I say again as his body starts rocking, the all too familiar chant falling from his lips.

I hiccup a sob as he shifts again, voice silenced and rolls onto his back. He shifts a couple more times and I'm relieved that his nightmare seems to have left him. He still seems uneasy though, so I crawl up beside him and lay my head on his chest, leg hooked over his, and rest my hand on his frantically beating heart. And I do the one thing I can in hopes of soothing him, I sing.

I sing of little boys and imaginary dragons. Of believing in something unbelievable. Of forgetting and moving on.

"My dad used to sing that to me when I had nightmares."

His rasp of a voice scares the crap out of me. I didn't even know he had woken up. He places an arm around me and pulls me in closer to him. "I know," I whisper into the moonlit room, "and you were."

Silence hangs between us as he blows out a soft breath. I can tell his dreams are still on his mind, so I grant him the silence to work through them. He presses a kiss onto the top of my head and keeps his mouth there.

When he speaks, I can feel the heat from his breath as he murmurs into my hair. "I was scared. I remember the vague sense of being scared those last few seconds in the car as I was flipping through the air." And it's the first time he's admitted to me anything to confirm my fears in regards to the crash.

I run my hand over his chest. "I was too."

"I know," he says as his hand finds its way beneath the waistband of my panties and cups my bare ass, pulling me up his body so my eyes can meet his. "I'm sorry you had to go through that again." I can see the apology in his eyes, in the lines etched in his forehead, and I'm unable to speak, tears clogging in my throat at his acknowledgment of my feelings so I show him the next best way I know how. I lean in and brush my lips against his.

His lips part as I slip my tongue between them, a soft groan rumbling in the back of his throat, spurring me on to taste the one and only fix to my addiction. My hands run over his stubbled jaw to the back of his neck, and I take in the intoxicating mixture I've grown to crave. His taste, his feel, his virility.

His hands cradle my face, fingers tangled in my curls as he draws my face back momentarily so we're inches apart, our breath whispering against each other's and eyes divulging emotions we've previously kept guarded under lock and key.

I can feel the pulse of his clenched jaw beneath my palms as he struggles with words. "Ry, I ..." he says and my breath catches. My soul hopes with bated breath. And I mentally finish the sentence for him, fill in the two words that complete it, complete us. Express the words that I see in his eyes and feel in the reverence of his touch. He works a swallow down his throat and finishes, "Thank you for staying."

"There's nowhere else I'd rather be." I can see the words I breathe out sink in and register as he pulls me toward him, guiding my body to shift and settle in a straddle over his lap while his mouth crashes to mine. *And it does crash.* A frenzy of passion explodes as my need collides with his desperation. Hands roam, tongues delve, and emotions intensify as we refamiliarize ourselves with the lines and curves of one another.

Colton runs his left hand down my back and grips the flesh on my hip as I rock over the ridge of his boxer-brief clad erection. Sensation swells within, creating an ache so powerful, so intense it borders on painful. My body craves the all-consuming pleasure I know only he can evoke.

I swallow his groan as I am engulfed in the emotion—the connection between us—in this moment. I feel Colton's right hand slide down to my other hip as he brings his hands to the sides of my tank top trying to pull it up and off. But when I feel his right hand fail to grasp the material, I quickly take control, not wanting it to affect this moment. I cross my arms over my front, grab the hem, and lift it over my head.

I sit astride him, bare except for a scant pair of panties, as his eyes scrape over the lines of my body, raw male appreciation apparent in his gaze. Unfettered lust. Undeniable hunger. He reaches back out to touch, to dance fingertips up my ribcage enabling him to guide my face back to his so that he can take, taste, tempt.

I moan at the feeling of my breasts pillowing against his firm chest, hardened nipples hypersensitive to the touch. Colton urges my hips back and forth again, and the sensation rocks me, nerves ready to detonate. I angle my body back, lost in the feeling when his mouth finds my breast, warm heat against chilled flesh.

I want him. Need him. Desire him like I never thought possible.

Our breaths pant and hearts race as we act on the instinct that has pulled us together since day one. And it's in this moment that I feel his hand flex and hear the warning of Dr. Irons flash through my head. I want to ignore him, tell it to go the fuck away so I can take my man again, pleasure him, own him as he owns me in every sense of the word. But I can't risk it.

I bring my hands down to my hips and lace my fingers with his. I break from our kiss and rest my forehead against Colton's. "We can't. It's not safe." The strain is apparent in my voice, expressing how hard it is for me to stop from taking exactly what we both want. Colton doesn't utter a sound. He just presses his hands into my hips as our labored breathing fills the silence in the bedroom. "It's too much exertion."

"Baby, if I'm not exerting myself then I'm sure as fuck not doing it right." He chuckles against my neck, stubble tickling my skin that's already begging for more of his touch.

I force myself to sit up so I'm farther away from the temptation of his mouth, but neglect to realize that my new positioning causes more pressure on the weeping apex between my thighs as my weight settles down on his erection. I have to stifle the moan that wants to fall from my mouth at the feeling. Colton smirks, knowing exactly what just happened, and I try to feign that I'm not affected but it's no use as he rolls his hips again.

"*Colton*," I moan, drawing out his name.

"You know you don't want me to stop," he says with a smirk and as he starts to speak again, I reach out and put a finger to his lips to quiet him.

"*This woman* is just trying to keep you safe."

"Oh, but you forget that the patient is always right and *this patient* thinks that *this woman*," he says as he draws my finger into his mouth and sucks on it causing desire to coil within, "needs to be thoroughly fucked by this man."

My legs tighten around him and I dig my hands into the top of my thighs as my body remembers just how thorough a fucking by Colton Donavan can be. And despite my resolve, my body screams take me, brand me, claim me. Own every part of me, right here, right now.

"Safety," I reassert, trying to regain some type of control over my body and the situation. Trying to think of his safety rather than the constant ache burning like a wildfire within me.

"Ryles, when have you ever known me to play it safe?" He smirks that devilishly handsome grin he knows I can't resist. "Please … let me exert myself," he pleads, but I know that beneath the playful tone is a man scavenging what's left of his restraint. "I'm dying to take the driver's seat and set the pace."

I can't help my laugh because his words cause a certain comment to come back to me. "When we first met, Haddie wondered if you fucked like you drive."

He snorts out a laugh, a mischievous grin gracing his lips and leaving that dimple I love. "And how's that?"

"A little reckless, pushing all the limits, and in it until the very last lap …" I let my voice trail off as I tease a fingernail over the midline of his chest, his muscles flexing as he anticipates my touch.

He angles his head to the side and his arrogant smile grows wider. "Well, was she right or do I need to take you for another spin around the track to refresh your memory?"

I love seeing the Colton I know, the Colton I missed, so vibrant that I decide to have a little fun—play him at his own game. He wants sex that I'm not going to give him, but that doesn't mean I can't put on a good show to tide him over. Give him a little something to ease the burn.

Or intensify the ache.

I run my fingers back down his chest and then to my parted knees and up and over my thighs. His eyes follow their wanton progression as they sit on top of the triangular swatch of fabric covering my sex. "Not sure I remember, Ace. It's been a while since I've seen you in action."

He sucks in a hiss of breath and the reaction drives me, spurs me to go one step further. I rub my hands over my naked stomach and up to cup my breasts already weighted with desire. I purposefully drag my teeth over my bottom lip, breathing out a soft moan as I pinch my nipples between my thumbs and forefingers, the sensation ricocheting through my every nerve. Colton's eyes darken, his lips part, and I feel his cock throb under my core at the sight of me pleasuring myself.

His reaction empowers me, allows me to have the courage and confidence to carry this out. A few months ago I would have never done this—touch myself so brazenly under the scrutiny of his stare—but he's done this for me, shown me that my curves are sexy; the body I used to readily criticize is something he desires, something that turns him on. *Is more than enough for him.*

And because of that knowledge, I can give him this gift with steady hands and complete confidence.

I let another moan fall from my mouth, and as much as I can see the desire swell in his green eyes, I can tell the minute he's on to me. The slow, lopsided spread of a smile turning up one corner of his deliciously handsome mouth. He just shakes his head subtly, mirth dancing over his expression as he shows me he's more than willing to play this game.

"Baby, if you're trying to get me to stop, then you shouldn't throw around comments like that."

He rolls his hips beneath me, his rock hard length pressing exactly where I ache for it to fill—where I'm silently begging for it to stroke—and feeds my pleasurable pain. I try to stifle the reaction on my lips, try to play coy, but it's no use when he does it again. My mouth falls lax, a satisfied purr comes from deep within my throat, and my hands fall without thought to press against the outside of my damp panties. Needing something to stifle the urge to take what I so desperately need, so desperately want.

Him.

When his hips settle, my fingers dig into the flesh of my thighs to prevent me from taking what I want—fingers ripping down boxer-briefs, taking his steeled length in my hands, guiding him into me, stretching me to sublime satisfaction—I gain enough composure to raise my eyes back up and lock onto his. To feign that I have a tight hold on the control that's begging to be snapped.

He reaches a hand up and draws a line down the middle of my chest at an excruciatingly slow pace.

His smirk spreading to both corners when my nipples pebble from his touch, proving that despite my strong façade, I'm affected by him in every possible way.

"Well, if you think I fuck like I drive, you should see me drop the hammer and *race* you to the finish line."

I can't help the breath that catches in my throat. It has to be coincidence that he uses the term *race*—it is his profession after all—but every single part of me hopes momentarily that I'm wrong. That he's using the term to tell me he remembers. But as quick as the thought soars with hope, it burns out, shutters the breath in my lungs. So I do the only thing I can to help make me forget and help him remember.

It's time to give him the show I've been tempting him with.

As his eyes flicker back and forth between my eyes and my fingers, I spread my legs further apart wanting to make sure he can see everything I'm doing. My fingers slip just beneath the waistband of my panties and then stop, my own body aching for my touch as much as I can see he is by the look in his eyes and his own fingers rubbing together, itching to touch me himself. But he's still in control. Still so calm.

Time to test that restraint.

"I thought racing wasn't a team sport," I say from beneath my lashes. "You know, more of an every man for himself kind of thing." I make sure he's watching, make sure he sees my fingers slide a little farther south. And I know he does because his Adam's apple bobs as he works a swallow down his throat.

"Every man, yes," he finally says, his voice strained. "Racing can be a dangerous sport too, you know?"

"Oh really?" I respond.

I take it upon myself to give into the sweet torture of parting myself and rubbing the evidence of my arousal around so I can apply the much needed friction to my clit. And as good as it feels—the pressure, the friction, his hardened dick rubbing against me—nothing turns me on more than the look on Colton's face. Undeniable arousal and complete concentration as he watches movements he can't see but can only guess at through the silky red fabric.

I want more from him. I want that stoic restraint snapped, and so I give into the feeling, into the eroticism of the moment—of him watching me while I pleasure myself—and I do the one thing I know will help push him over the edge, pull that hair-string trigger I know he has so tightly wound. I lift my head back, close my eyes, and let "Oh, God!" slip from my lips.

"Sweet Jesus!" he swears, restraint snapped right along with the strings of fabric holding my panties together.

I keep my head back knowing he's watching me move my fingers—absorb the pleasure—because there is something unexpectedly liberating about him stripping my clothes so he can see. I am unbound, unashamed, and utterly his for the taking, both physically and mentally.

I feel my pulse quicken. Warmth spreads through me like a tidal wave of sensation that I willingly want to be drowned in. Colton groans out in front of me and I come back into the present, lift my head up, and open my eyes to find his trained on the delta between my thighs. I hiss a moan as I bring my hand out for him to see the evidence of my arousal glistening on my fingers. I struggle to control the burning fire spreading through me, igniting places I didn't even know exist and try to find my voice.

"Well, Ace, danger can be overrated. It seems I know how to handle a *slick track* perfectly well," I purr, unable to fight the smirk that plays as his fingers dig deeper into the flesh at my hips. I keep my eyes locked and taunting on his as I bring my fingers up to my lips and suck slowly before withdrawing them.

The muscle in his jaw tics. His dick pulses beneath me in reaction. His breath rasps out. "Slippery and wet, huh? Danger has never been more fucking tempting," he drawls before his tongue darts out and wets his lips as he tracks my hands sliding back down my torso, over my breasts, down my stomach, and back down to between my thighs. This time though, I spread my knees wider as I use one hand to part my cleft so he can see my other hand slide down between the swollen, pink flesh. I can see the struggle flicker across the magnificent lines of his face, watch the desire swamp him, and the knowing smile that curls up his lips somehow fits him with absolute perfection.

My handsome, arrogant rogue.

A little cocky.

A lot imperfect.

And completely mine.

"You know," he rasps, trailing a fingertip up one thigh, purposely missing my core clenching in anticipation before continuing down the other leg. "Sometimes in a race, in order to reach the finish line, rookies like you have to tag team to get the result you want."

I don't fight the smile that comes or hide the shudder of breath as his fingers leave my skin. I lean forward placing my hands on his chest and look straight into his eyes. "Sorry, but this engine seems to be doing just fine running solo," I say, scraping my fingernails in lines down his chest as I sit back up. His muscles convulse beneath my fingers proving that even though the arrogant curl to his lips remains, his body still wants and needs what I have to offer. I slip my fingers between my thighs again and deliver the line I'm hoping will push him over the edge. "I know exactly what it's going to take to get me to the finish line."

"Oh, so you like to race dirty, huh? Break all the rules?" he taunts, tossing the ball right back into my court.

"Oh, I most definitely can race dirty," I tease with a raise of my eyebrows before I reach a hand out, his eyes narrowing as I bring a finger, coated with my moisture, to his lips. His hand flashes up immediately and grabs my wrist, guiding my fingers into his mouth, the low hum in the back of his throat reverberating over me, through me, into me. And my own restraint is tested as his tongue swirls over them, my hips grinding down and rocking over him in automatic response. *Holy shit that feels like Heaven.* My nerves reach the fever pitch of ache as I rock back again, his hard to my soft, and all I can think about is the need coursing through me. The moisture pooling between my legs. The thought of his fingers on me, in me, driving me.

Fuck, I need him now. Desperately. So I do the only thing I can without downright begging. I deliver the last coherent dare I have left because all of my thoughts are jumbling in my head with this onslaught of sensation. I lean forward, the feather of my lips up his whiskered jaw line, and inhale his scent before I whisper, "Being a seasoned pro such as yourself, you just might have to show this rookie exactly why they say rubbing's racing."

I rotate my hips over the top of him and I can feel his teeth grind in willpower. I repeat the motion one more time, a satisfied exhale slipping between my lips as my body begs for more. "Big bad professional race car driver like you afraid to show a newbie how to drive stick, huh?"

I forgot how fast Colton can move, bad hand and all. Within a heartbeat he's pushed me so I'm sitting back up again. My feet have been pulled forward so they're flat on the bed on either side of his rib cage, and he pushes my knees as far out as they can go.

Bingo.

Fuse lit.

That razor thin edge of control snapped.

Thank God!

He must be mistaking the look on my face—the one of relief edged with desperation—as confusion because he says, "I'm shifting gears, sweetheart, because I'm the only one allowed to drive this car." I can hear the hum deep in his throat as he slides his hands up my thighs, stopping to sweep his thumbs up and down my tight strip of curls. A teasing touch that sends tiny tremors ricocheting through me, hinting at what's to come, the level of pleasure he can bring me to.

His fingers still and he drags his eyes up my body to meet mine, a smug grin ghosting his mouth. He holds my stare—almost as if daring me to look away—as he moves one hand to part my swollen flesh while the other tucks his fingers inside of me. My head falls back as I cry out at the feeling, fingers moving, manipulating, circling to stroke over the responsive bundle of nerves. He slides his fingers in and out, my walls clenching around him, gripping onto him in pure, carnal need. Greed.

I watch his face. See his tongue slip between his lips, the desire cloud his eyes, watch the muscles ripple in his arms as he works me into a fever pitch. Causes me to climb quickly because I'm so pent up—so addled with need—that the sight of him, the feel of him, the memory of him, pushes me over the edge.

My fingernails score down his forearms as my body tenses, pussy convulses, and the broken cry of his name fills the room around us. I fall forward, collapsing on top of Colton's chest as the heat spearing through me in waves liquefies my insides. Makes coherency a distant possibility. I want the feel of my skin on his. Need to feel the firmness of him against me and the security of his arms wrapped around me as I swim through the sensation he just flooded me with.

I pant out in short, sharp breaths as my body settles, his fingertips tracing lines up and down my spine. I can feel his soft chuckle against my chest. "Hey, rookie?"

I force myself to look up at him—to pull myself from my post-orgasmic coma. "Hmm?" is all I can manage as I meet the amusement in his eyes.

"I'm the only one that's allowed to drive you to the motherfucking checkered flag."

I can't help the laugh that comes out and bubbles over. He can claim my checkered flag any day.

Chapter Fourteen

Colton—Raced

Dragons live forever, but not so little boys …

The lyrics filter into my head, my own dragons—and not the playful, puffy kinds—are front and fucking center, but that's not the problem. The problem is I'm not a little boy and yet I'm still living with this shit.

I slowly ease awake and can't believe how nice it feels with her arms wrapped around me instead of that soul-jarring, mind-fucked moment when you wake up alone with only your demons lurking in the dark corners to keep you company.

I close my eyes for a second, accepting that she's still here after everything I've put her through.

"My dad used to sing that to me when I had nightmares."

Her body jolts at the sound of my voice as I put my arm around her and pull her closer, skin to skin. My own personal balm to coat the inked reminders on my torso that reflect the stains on my soul.

"I know," she whispers, "and you were."

I press a kiss to the top of her head and leave my mouth there, breathing her in. Trying to wash the dream from my mind. Needing to.

I think of how I'd much rather dream about the crash than *him*. How almost dying, going headfirst into a wall, is ten times easier to cope with than the smell of the musty mattress, the feel of his hands on me, the taste of anticipatory fear.

I need to talk, to scavenge some of the thoughts from within and release them so I can start to breathe again. I pick the one she knows the most about, the one that won't make her look at me and think I'm weak for succumbing to its clutches.

"I was scared. I remember the vague sense of being scared those last few seconds in the car as I was flipping through the air." I don't know why that's so hard to admit to her.

She runs her hand over my chest. "I was too."

"I know," I say evenly but hate myself for putting her in that position. Loathe that she fears anything because of me. I reach down, my hand sliding beneath the band of her panties to cup the curve of her ass and pull her up so she can look into my eyes. I hate rehashing shit, but I owe her this ten times over and then some. "I'm sorry you had to go through that again."

Her eyes glisten with tears and now I hate that I've made her cry bringing it up, but when she leans forward and brushes her lips against mine, all thoughts are lost but one.

Take.

And hell if it's the emotion of the day, needing to erase my dreams, or simply being so fucking relieved to be alive, but I do just that.

I squeeze her ass in my hands so her tits rub up against me, and every part of my body begs, craves, and is starved for more of her. I need to hear that sigh she makes, need her taste on my tongue, and I don't hesitate. I slip my tongue between her lips and don't even realize the groan is coming from me.

Thank fuck I survived the crash because I need this little slice of Heaven right now, and I sure as shit know this was going to be one of the first things I'd miss if I'd died and landed in Hell.

I bring my free hand to her face and slide my other one from her ass up her back and put them in my favorite place tangled in her curls so she has no other option but to open up to me. And when I pull her head back, I see just that in her eyes: vulnerability, need, and desire all balled into one dick hardening look.

Hell, I was hard before that, but shit, there's no turning back now.

"Ry, I …" My mind fires, fleeting flashes of stolen thoughts but none stick against the wall. Things I want to say flicker and fade just as quick as they come, but the feeling within me remains burning bright. I clear my throat, trying to buy time for them to come out but nothing does so I say the only thing I can. "Thank you for staying."

Fuck this. That's not what I want to say. Man the fuck up, Donavan. You told her if you can't say it, you'll show her any way you can. So fucking show her.

"There's nowhere else I'd rather be," she says, snapping me from my conflicting thoughts. I meet her eyes, a man on a mission now. Wanting to take and needing to prove.

My hand pisses me the fuck off because I want to lift her up and onto me so I can keep my head still and not trigger another goddamn headache and ruin this, but it's not working. And fuck do I need it to work more than ever right now. But Ry anticipates what I want, so she straddles my hips and looks down at me.

I take her all in, lips parted, nipples hard beneath her tank, and the fucking heat of her pussy on my very desperate cock. Desire ignites between us and within moments our lips are on one another's, hands touching, bodies aching for so much more than this.

My good hand grips onto her hip, urging her to rock like that again over my dick and when she does, fuckin' A. All thoughts flee because my mind and body are in total agreement on what they want: *her*. Any way I can get her because it's been so fucking long since I've buried myself in her addictive pussy.

My right hand moves to her other hip because I need my woman naked right now. Need to see her tits, rub my thumbs over her nipples for my own fucking pleasure and hers. I'm so lost in the taste of her kiss that when I go to grip her tank top, I forget about my hand—that it can't pull the fabric up and over her head.

Without missing a beat, Rylee comes to the rescue—like always—and has the shirt off. And fuck I've seen her tits before but don't think I've ever wanted her more than right now.

Screw what the doctor says, what my head is going to feel like, because this man is not waiting. No fucking way when she is sitting like this atop me. Vixen, siren, mine. The last one mattering the most.

Her mouth meets mine again, her tits against my chest. My hand on her hip guides her to slide over my boxer-brief clad cock, making me ache in the worst way, in the best way. And when she moans and sits back up, I fight every primal instinct in me to flip her over and fuck her into oblivion. She is the epitome of sex right now and all I want to do is taste, take, and sate my desire.

I lean up, the slight twinge of pain in my head drowned out by the desire owning my body, and take the tip of her tit into my mouth. Her cool flesh against my warm tongue only adds to the riotous frenzy within me.

I flick my tongue over her nipple and claim her mouth again while my right hand lamely palms her breast. I know the minute she feels my hand's fucked-up grip because she brings her hands to mine, laces her fingers with them, and moves them to her hips.

I groan as she drags her lips from my mouth and leans her forehead against mine, dreading and knowing what she's going to say.

"We can't. It's not safe."

We can. Fuck safety. Fuck any reason you're going to deny me because I'm not ashamed to admit I'm a desperate man willing to break every rule to have you.

"It's too much exertion," she explains.

"Baby, if I'm not exerting myself, then I'm sure as fuck not doing it right." I can't help but chuckle against that spot on her neck. I feel goose bumps across her skin as I rub my stubble against it to let the flash of pain in my head abate.

Her nipples press into my chest and I know she sits up to fight her own urge to take and fuck if that doesn't make her even sexier. But even better is she positions herself perfectly so that my dick presses against the damp spot on her panties. Her lips part and eyes close momentarily as I purposely adjust my hips, pushing my cock against our double cloth barrier into the dent of her pussy. I get a low groan but I want more from her. I want to hear her tell me to take her.

"*Colton*," she moans and fuck, saying my name like that is like my own personal verbal Viagra. There's no way I'm turning back now because then both heads will be throbbing in pain.

"You know you don't want me to stop," I say, hoping she's willing to break a few rules, but she reaches out and places her finger on my lips to quiet me

"*This woman* is just trying to keep you safe." Her voice has that husky rasp to it that tells me she's fighting this just as hard as I am. And damn her restraint is a challenge I can't wait to test.

Game on, baby.

"Oh, but you forget that the patient is always right and *this patient* thinks that *this woman*," I say as I open my mouth and suck on her finger, swirl my tongue around it, eyes locked on hers, "needs to be thoroughly fucked by this man."

She squeezes my hips with her knees, and I can feel her control slipping, my dick pulsing against her. Almost there, baby.

"Safety," she reiterates with unwavering resolve and fuck, I thought she was closer to caving than this. Time to bring out the big guns. Well the big guns beside the one she's sitting astride rubbing herself against right now.

"Ryles, when have you ever known me to play it safe? Please … let me exert myself," I plead, flashing her that no-holds-barred grin of mine. The one that she's told me makes her wet because it means I'm about to take her. But fuck if my voice isn't strained from the painful ache in my balls. I roll my hips again, and this time she grinds down at the same time so she's testing more than just my control, she's testing my sanity too. I lick my lips and look at her, eyes taunting, dick teasing. "I'm dying to take the driver's seat and set the pace."

Her laugh fills the room and I just look at her, confused to why the hazy look in her eyes has been replaced with humor. What the fuck, Ry? This is not a laughing fucking matter.

"When we first met, Haddie wondered if you fucked like you drive."

Talk about shifting gears when the only one I want to be shifting is into her … but her comment finally makes its way through my pussy-possessed mind and I can't help but laugh at Haddie's question. Hmm. Wonder how she answered.

"And how's that?"

"A little reckless, pushing all the limits, and in it until the very last lap …" she says, her fingernail scraping down my chest causing my balls to tighten and priming every muscle in my body to pounce.

But I hold myself back, know she's playing some kind of game here. I can see it in her eyes, and I'm torn between letting it play out and giving in to fucking her senseless.

I angle my head to the side and stare at her. I love when feisty Rylee comes out to play, so fuck yes I'll accept the painful ache drawing this out will cause me.

I'll play the game all right, follow her lead, but she better be ready to let me win this round when all is said and done. A man has only so much restraint after all.

"Well, was she right or do I need to take you for another spin around the track to refresh your memory?"

You gonna say no, sweetheart? I love the look on her face, love that I caught her off guard. Tell me, show me, what's flickering through those eyes of yours.

Our eyes lock for a moment as I try to read what she's thinking but fuck if I can hold them there when her fingers slide over my happy trail and then up over the scant excuse she's wearing for panties.

And then they sit there. Taunting me. They move slightly over the waistband like she's as desperate to touch herself as I am.

"Not sure I remember, Ace. It's been a while since I've seen you in action."

This is the game she's playing? Drive me crazy? Fuckin' A, measure me for the straight jacket because I'm sure we could put it to some kind of kinky use.

I don't think she has any clue how much she owns me right now.

Fucking owns every single part of me and doesn't have a damn clue. Sitting astride me, fingers atop the little piece of Heaven that I'd die to claim right now, and the sarcastic dare falling from her mouth. My mind wanders to what exactly those fingers would look like nestled between those folds of flesh, and I have to stifle the groan at how fucking hot the vision is. And I think that's exactly what she's trying to do—tease me with what she won't give me. With what I can't claim yet.

She wants to play, huh? Oh, I am so fucking game right now. Ready to knock it out of the goddamn park.

"Baby, if you're trying to get me to stop, then you shouldn't throw around comments like that." I shift in the bed and *accidentally* roll my hips again, feeding into the pleasurable pain as my aching cock rubs against her tempting pussy yet again. And this time I know I've hit her right where it counts because she throws her head back and the soft sigh that falls from her mouth is a dead giveaway no matter how unaffected she's trying to play it.

I can't take my eyes off of her. The sight of her tits, weighted globes of perfection, right in front of my face. I force my eyes to move upwards and meet the challenge in hers. "If you think I fuck like I drive, you should see me drop the hammer and *race* you to the finish line."

I see her breath catch and her body stutter in its motion momentarily before she quickly recovers and regains her composure. My mind starts to try and figure what I just missed but my thoughts are pulled out from underneath me when she spreads her legs apart further, the wetness on her panties spreading wider. My fingers rub together, itching to touch.

"I thought racing wasn't a team sport," she says coyly. "You know, more of an *every man for himself* kind of thing." Her eyes hold mine as her fingers slip beneath the band of her red silken panties and still, my eyes darting between the two waiting for her to move them. Begging her to move them. The visual consuming my thoughts.

I force myself to look away, to work a swallow in my throat that's suddenly become dry. "Every man, yes," I finally am able to get out. "It can be very dangerous too, you know?"

"Oh really?" she asks, eyes locked on mine, the moan of pleasure that falls from her lips has my breath laboring as I look down to watch the movement of her fingers beneath the fabric in front of me.

"*Sweet Jesus!*" I can't handle the unknown, needing to see for myself the show on display. And thank fuck my right hand decides to work when I need it most because the fragile fabric of her panties is snapped and dropped in an instant without a second thought.

And Rylee doesn't even skip a beat.

Oh fucking my. The white French tips of her nails are a mind-dizzying contrast to the darkened pink flesh they dance across. Perfection. Addiction. Absolution. I glance up knowing she's going to have that taunting smile on her lips and for the second time in as many seconds I'm knocked breathless.

Fucking kryptonite.

Rylee's head is thrown back, curls tumbling all over the place, lips parted, tits pushed out, and the sexiest moan coming from her lips as she doesn't just revel in the moment but becomes the fucking moment. *Fuck me*. The woman who used to tighten the sheet around her months ago in modesty now sits astride me in all of her glory, owning her body and sexuality with such a confidence that I've never thought her to be more sexy, more sensual, more everything than right now.

She lifts her head forward, her hand sliding out from between her legs, moisture glistening off of her fingers for me to see. "Well, Ace, danger can be overrated. It seems I know how to handle a *slick track* perfectly well." She smirks that smug smile I want to fuck off her face right now just before she slips her arousal coated fingers into her mouth and sucks on them, eyes taunting me all the while.

Is she trying to kill me right now? Fucking voodoo pussy is back with a vengeance and fuck if I'm not ready to be the first and only victim. The woman has me strung tighter than a hair string trigger—volatile and ready to blow. My balls tighten, my body tenses wanting her so desperately, but my stubborn streak tells me I have to hold out, take the reins when the time is right. My body screams that time was ten fucking minutes ago, while my head loves when Ry gets feisty and defiant. When she makes me work for it like no one else ever has.

"Slippery and wet, huh? Danger has never been more fucking tempting," I tell her, my eyes watching as she pulls her fingers from between her very fuckable lips and follows the descent back down south. She adds torment to her tantalization by parting her seam with one hand so I can more than handily see her other fingers add the friction her sighs say is more than pleasurable.

Fuck me this is brutal to watch and not partake in when all I want to do is urge her hips closer to my face and have her sweet taste on my tongue again. For that alone, it's time for me to mess with her a little more and knock her out of the pleasure inducing coma that's darkening the violet in her eyes.

"You know, sometimes in a race, in order to reach the finish line, rookies like you have to tag team to get the result you want."

Her head snaps up, lips parting, and eyes flashing with shock momentarily until she regains her composure. Perfect. Threw you there didn't I, sweetheart?

"Sorry, but this engine seems to be doing just fine running solo." She smirks at me, so arrogant that she thinks she dodged the proverbial bullet. Too bad I'm holding the only gun allowed to shoot that shell. And fuck me, she's sliding her hands back down to my place between her thighs, her moan of pleasure when she finds purchase—my own personal Heaven and Hell.

And then she stops and looks at me, lust in her eyes and evidence of her arousal on her hands. "I know exactly what it's going to take to get me to the finish line."

"Oh, so you like to race dirty, huh? Break all the rules?" I ask, fingers trailing up her thighs, leaving visible goose bumps in their wake, her body angling toward me the higher I go. Fuckin' A straight. She can play the aloof card all she wants but she can't deny that her body readily submits to me when I want it to. And fuck, how I want it to right now.

"Oh, I most definitely can handle dirty," she taunts as she trails a finger up my chest and rubs some of her moisture across my lips. My tongue darts out, unable to resist the temptation to taste what I'm craving and fuck me if it doesn't make me want to flip her over, cuff her hands over her head, and fuck the defiance out of her until she's screaming my name and owning my heart more than she already does.

She grinds her hips down, that smarmy smile still teasing the corners of her mouth as she rocks back and forth over me. She leans forward, her breath a taunting whisper against my ear. "Being a seasoned pro such as yourself, you just might have to show this rookie exactly why they say rubbing's racing."

She's playing the temptress card and passing with flying fucking colors. I don't even have time to recover from the notion that her pussy's wetness is starting to soak through my boxer-briefs when she rocks her hips again. I try to remain unaffected, play her game, but I have to grit my teeth to prevent my eyes from closing at the rocket of sensation that just shot through me.

When I look from her hand back up to her eyes, she raises her eyebrows in the final coup de grace. "Big bad professional race car driver like you afraid to show a newbie how to drive stick, huh?"

And I can't take it anymore. Fuse lit and control shot. Within a beat, I've pushed her back up to sitting, pulled her feet flat on the bed beside my ribs and knees spread wide, because if I'm watching the feature presentation, I better have a goddamn front row seat.

"I'm shifting gears, sweetheart, because I'm the only one allowed to drive this car." My hands slide up again until they reach the juncture of her thighs. My thumbs brush over her tight strip of curls before I readjust and tuck my fingers into her. She cries out, her tight walls flexing around me and milking against my fingers as they stroke the nerves within. And between her wetness on my fingers and the memories of her gripping my dick has me pre-coming like a fucking adolescent school boy but fuck me, I'll take it. I'll take anything I can from her because Rylee? *She's fucking everything.*

She doesn't take long to climb because she's so addled with pent up need—and the fact that it's only for me is not lost in the frenzied moment. Her fingernails score my skin, body tenses, and pussy convulses as the broken cry of my name fills the room around us.

My name moaning from her lips. God-fucking-damn is that not the sexiest sound I've ever heard.

I give her a moment to gain her breath, the senses I've just finger-fucked out of her, and when I think she's coherent enough, I let her know that even though she's just come, I'm the one who just won the race.

"Hey, rookie?"

She lifts her head forward and looks at me from beneath weighted eyelids heavy with satisfaction. "Hmm?" is all she can manage and I fucking love that drowsy just-been-fucked-right look on her face. The one that only I can put there.

"I'm the only one that's allowed to drive you to the motherfucking checkered flag."

She just throws her head back and laughs, cheeks flushed, tits jiggling.

Fucking gorgeous.

Like I said, she's everything.

The Holy motherfucking Grail.

Chapter Fifteen

"Oh, buddy, I'm so proud of you!" I fight back the wave of guilt that rolls over me. I missed helping Connor study for a test in his most dreaded subject—math. "I knew you could do it!"

"I just used that little trick you told me about and it worked!" The pride in his voice brings tears of joy to my eyes, and at the same time, grief over not being there.

"I told you it would! Now go get ready for baseball. I'm sure Jax is waiting for you already!" He laughs telling me I'm right. "I promise I'll see you a little later in the week, okay?"

"'Kay. I Lego you."

"I Lego you too, bud!"

I hang up and look out toward the patio as laughter filters in above the crash of the waves—years worth of friendship breaking though Colton's bad mood. I'm so thankful to Beckett for stopping by. I hear them belt out another laugh, and as much as I wish I was the one putting the smile on Colton's otherwise scowling face of late, I'm just grateful that it's there.

Beggars can't be choosers.

I watch them clink the necks of their beer bottles over something and I sigh out loud, wanting the tension between Colton and me to go away. I'm sure it's because we're both sexually frustrated. To need and want and desire when temptation is right beneath your fingers, but to not be able to take and devour, is brutal in every sense of the word.

And yes, his more than skillful fingers brought me a small ounce of the release I needed the night before last, but it's not the same. The connection was made but not cemented, because when Colton is in me, literally stretching me to every depth imaginable, I am also completely filled figuratively in every sense of the word. He completes me, owns me, has ruined me for anyone else ever again.

I feel closer to him right now—spending so much time with him—and yet further away. And I hate it.

I shake myself from my pity party and think how much worse things could be right now. I slip my shoes off and head out onto the deck for fresh air. I walk between Colton and Beckett's lounge chairs and sit in one of my own, facing them.

Behind my sunglasses I take in the sight before me, and I know there isn't another woman in the world that wouldn't want to be in my shoes right now. Both men are relaxed, clad in board shorts, ball caps, and sunglasses. I let my eyes roam lazily with more than ample appreciation for the defined lines of their bare torsos and fight the smile that wants to pull at the corners of my mouth.

"Well if it isn't Florence Nightingale," Beckett drawls in that slow, even cadence of his as he brings the bottle to his lips.

"Well I think if I was Ms. Nightingale, I'd be telling my patient, Mr. Donavan here, that he probably shouldn't be drinking alcohol with all of those pain meds running through his blood."

"More like Nurse Ratchet." Colton snorts, looking at me from beneath the shadow of his bill, green eyes running over the length of my legs stretched out on the chaise in front of me. A quick dart of his tongue over his lips tells me he wants to do a whole lot more than just look.

"Nurse Ratchet, huh?" I ask as I slide my foot up and down the calf of one of my legs trying to not feel insulted.

"Yep," he says, pursing his lips as his eyes watch me over the top of his beer bottle. "If she gave me what I really wanted, I'd be able to recover that much quicker." He raises his eyebrows at me, the suggestion in his eyes devouring me.

"Well shit," Beckett swears, "if I'm not trying to get the two of you back together, I'm fucking trying to keep you apart."

"*Fucking*," Colton drawls in Beckett fashion, "now there's a word."

Becks just snorts a laugh and rolls his eyes. "Definitely a good word indeed."

Colton breaks our eye contact for the first time and angles his head over to look at his oldest and best friend. "Rest assured, bro, when the doc clears me, nothing—and I mean nothing—is going to be coming between Rylee and me for a long *fucking* time, except for maybe a change of sheets."

My cheeks burn red at his frankness but my body clenches at the promise of his words. And I don't care that Beckett just heard because I'm focused on the words *long, fucking time*.

"So noted," Becks says as he takes another tug on his beer.

"I gotta take a piss," Colton says, shoving himself up from the chaise. As I've learned to do over the past days, I force myself to remain seated as Colton struggles momentarily with his lack of balance and the sudden dizziness that I know assaults him. After a few moments he seems steady and goes to place his beer bottle on the table next to him. About a foot from the table, Colton's right hand's grip gives way and the bottle clatters to the deck below.

Becks' eyes flash to mine momentarily, concern passing through them before he laughs and pretends not to notice. "Party foul!" he laughs. "I think Nurse Ratchet just might be on to something in regards to mixing all those drugs with that alcohol."

"Fuck off," he tosses over his shoulder as he turns toward the house. "Just for that I'm grabbing another!" I watch Colton walk into the kitchen, and when he thinks no one is looking, he looks down at his hand and tries to make a fist out of it before shaking his head.

"How's he doing?"

I turn to face Becks. "The headaches are coming less and less but he's frustrated. He keeps finding little things here and there he can't remember. And he's feeling confined." I shrug. "And you know how he gets when he feels confined."

Beckett blows out a loud breath with a shake of his head. "He needs to get back out on the track as soon as possible."

I stare at him, mouth lax. "*What?*" slips from between my lips, feeling a stab of betrayal at his words. This is his best friend. Doesn't he want to keep him safe? Keep him alive?

"Well, you say he's feeling confined ... the track is the one place he's always been free of everything," Becks says, holding my stunned stare. "Besides, if he doesn't get behind the wheel soon, he's going to let that fear he has eat at him, embed itself in his head, and fucking paralyze him so when he does actually think he can get back in the car, he'll be a danger to himself."

I'm an intelligent person and maybe if I weren't still surprised by Beckett's first comment, I would really hear what he's saying—see the whole picture—but I don't. "What are you talking about? Since he's been home all he's been grumbling about is getting back on the track."

He just chuckles and even though it's not condescending, I feel like my back is up against the wall here and grit my teeth at the sound. "Fuck yeah, he's scared, Ry. Scared out of his fucking gourd. If it's not his hand that he uses as an excuse, it will be something else ... and he needs to get over it. If he doesn't, the fear is just going to eat him alive."

My mind jogs back to the past week. Things Colton has said about racing. Actions that contradict the words he's saying, and I begin to realize that Beckett is right.

"But what about *my* fear?" I can't help the desperation that laces through my voice.

"You think I'm not scared? That it's going to be easy for me too?" The bite in Becks' voice has me turning to look at him. "You think I'm not going to relive those seconds over and over in my mind every time I buckle him in the car? Every time he flies down the chute? Fuck, Ry, I almost lost him too. Don't think this is going to be easy for me because it's not. It's going to be *fucking brutal* but it's what is best for Colton." He shoves up from his seat and walks over to the railing, hands spread out supporting himself as he leans into them. "Until you came along it was the only thing he cared about. The only thing that kept him fucking sane." He blows out a biting breath. "It's the only thing he knows." He turns back around to face me, eyes hidden behind aviators. "So yes, he needs to get his ass on the track and I'll be his biggest fucking cheerleader, but don't let that fool you into thinking my heart's not going to be racing every goddamn minute he's out there."

My eyes follow him as he paces to one end of the patio to let his agitation abate and then back toward me before grabbing his bottle and turning the end up, downing the remainder of his beer.

"Racing's about eighty percent mental and twenty percent skill, Rylee. We've got to get his head back in the game, thinking he's ready, then he'll be ready."

I see the logic behind his reasoning, but it doesn't mean I'm not scared to death.

I lift my face up to catch the last rays of sun before they dissipate and sink into the horizon. I hum along to *Collide* playing softly on the outdoor speakers as my mind wanders to Beckett and our conversation, to how I'm going to feel watching Colton get behind the wheel again and if he'll fear it as much as I do.

"Hey, what are you doing out here all by yourself?" Colton's rasp pulls at me on every level, and I open my eyes to find him looking down at me from my comfortable spot on the chaise. Warmth spreads through me when I see the pillow crease in the side of his cheek, and I can't help but wonder what he was like as a little boy.

"Did you have a good nap?" I scoot over as he sits down beside me, but I purposefully don't move too far so I can snuggle up closer to him.

He wraps his arms around me and pulls me in. "Yeah, I was out." He laughs pressing a kiss to the top of my head. "But no more headache so all is good.

"I can't imagine why you'd have any type of pain with the amount of beer you two put away."

"Smart ass."

"I'd rather be a smart ass than a dumb ass."

"Aren't we feisty tonight?" he says as he tickles my rib cage. "You know what feisty does to me, baby, and I sure as fuck could use it right now."

I squirm out of his grasp. "Nice try, but we most likely only have a couple more days and then I'll be any kind of feisty you want me to be," I say with a raise of my eyebrows as his fingers ease up and smooth down my back.

"Don't promise shit like that to a man as desperate as I am, if you're not going to deliver, sweetheart."

"Oh, no worries, Ace," I say, snuggling back into him, "I'll deliver truckloads of feisty as long as I know you'll be okay."

Colton doesn't say anything, rather he makes a non-committal sound in response. We settle into a comfortable silence for a while, and I welcome it because this is the first time in the past few days where there isn't that inexplicable tension vibrating between us. As the sun sinks and the ocean waves sigh into the oncoming night, my mind begins to wander back to my conversation with Becks. And being me, I have to ask, have to know Colton's thoughts about racing again.

"Can I ask you a question?"

"Mmm-hmm," he murmurs into the crown of my head.

I hesitate at first, not wanting to bring up any thoughts if they're not there already, but ask anyway. "Are you scared to get back on the track? To race again?" The words rush out and I wonder if he can hear the underlying trepidation in my tone.

His hand pauses momentarily on its trek up my spine before it continues, and I know I've touched on something he's not completely comfortable talking about or admitting to. He sighs out into the silence I've given him. "It's hard for me to explain," he says before shifting so that we're side by side, our eyes meeting. He shakes his head subtly and continues. "It's like I fear it and I need it all at the same time. That's the only way I can put it."

I can sense his unease so I do what I do best, I try to soothe him. "You've figured it out with me."

Confusion flickers in his eyes. "What do you mean?"

I had no intention of taking the conversation here, making him feel uncomfortable in talking about the "us" that was there before the crash. The "us" he *raced* and doesn't remember. I reach out and rest my hand on the side of his stubbled jaw and make sure I have his attention before I speak. "You feared and yet needed me ..." My voice fades.

He draws in a breath as emotions flicker through his eyes. His lips purse momentarily. The silence mixed with the intensity in his eyes unnerves me. I can hear the hitch of his breath, the sound of the ocean, the pound of my heart in my ears, and yet silence from him. He looks away and I prepare myself, for what I'm not sure. But when he looks back at me, a slow, shy smile curls up one corner of his mouth, and he nods his head in acceptance. "You're right, I do need you."

Parts way down deep sag in relief that he's finally acknowledging our connection. Accepting it. And I don't care that he isn't telling me he races me, because this, the fact that he needs me, is more than I could ever have hoped for.

He brings a hand up gently to cup the side of my face and brushes his thumb over my bottom lip. He leans in and whispers his lips over mine tenderly before kissing the top of my nose. When he pulls back I see the wicked grin on his face. "Now it's my turn."

"Your turn?" I ask as his fingers play over the buttons of my top.

"Yep. It's question and answer time, Ryles, and it's your turn in the hot seat."

"I'd like a turn in your hot seat," I say back to him, earning the lightning fast grin that pulls on every hormone in my body like a magnet.

"Watch it, sweetheart, because I'm a walking case of blue balls that wants nothing more then to be buried in that finish line between your thighs." As he speaks, he leans forward, close enough to kiss but doesn't grant me one. Talk about sweet torture. When he speaks next, his breath feathers over my lips. "It's best not to test my restraint."

Every part of my body angles into him—wanting, needing, daring him—but he proves he still has control when he chuckles out a pained laugh. "My turn. Why haven't you seen the boys yet?"

Of all of the questions he could have asked me, I had not expected this one. I must look a little shell-shocked because he's right. I do desperately want to see the boys, but I don't know how to see them without bringing the circus with me. The circus that their already fragile lives don't need and can't handle.

"You need me more right now," I tell him, not wanting to give him the exact reason, so that he doesn't have something besides recovering to worry about.

"That's bullshit, Ry. I'm a big boy. I can be left alone for the night. Nothing is going to happen to me."

But what if it does? What if you need me and no one is here and something horrible happens? "Yeah … I just," I trail off, needing to say it and at the same time not wanting to offend him. "I don't want your world to collide with theirs. They don't need cameras in their faces telling everyone they're orphans—that no one wanted them—or any of the fallout I'm sure would come with it."

"Ry, look at me," he says as he lifts my chin up to meet his eyes. "You and me? I don't ever want it—me, the craziness around my life, the press, whatever—to come between you and the boys. They are what's important, and I understand that more than most."

Between telling me he needs me and then this declaration, I swear I could have just won the lottery and it wouldn't matter because those two things just made me the richest person in the world. *He really gets me.* Gets that my boys make me who I am and that in order to be with me, he needs to love them. Beckett says I'm Colton's lifeline, but I think he just proved it goes both ways.

I swallow back the lump of tears in my throat as he continues staring at me, to make sure I hear what he's saying. I murmur in agreement, my voice robbed of emotion. "I'll figure something out," he says, leaning in to brush a kiss to my lips. "I'll make sure you get to see the boys soon without interference, okay?"

I nod my head and then curl myself into him as my mind whirls with numerous questions when one jumps out at me. "My turn," I say, wanting and fearing the answer to the question.

"Mmm-hmm."

"That first night," I pause, undecided about how to ask the question. I decide to dive in head first and hope I'm in the deep end. "What were you doing with Bailey in the alcove before you found me?"

Colton barks a laugh followed by a curse, and I think he's a little surprised by my question. "You really want to know?"

Do I? Now I'm not so sure. I nod my head and close my eyes in preparation for the explanation to come.

"I walked backstage to take a call from Becks." He laughs. "Shit, the minute I hung up she was on me like a pit viper. She had my jacket stripped, the front of her dress unzipped, and her mouth on mine faster than …" He fades off as I try not to react to the words, but I know he feels my body tense because he presses a kiss into the top of my head in reassurance. "Believe me, Rylee, it was not what it sounds like."

"Really? Since when does the infamous ladies' man, Colton Donavan, turn down a willing woman?" I can't hide the sarcasm in my voice. Even though I asked the question, it still hurts to hear the answer. "Besides, I thought you like women taking control."

He laughs again. "There's no need to be jealous, sweetheart … even though it's kind of hot that you are." I poke him with my finger, content that he's trying to soften the blow of the truth, and instead of pulling away, he just holds on to me tighter. "And I've only ever let one woman take control because she's the only one that's ever mattered."

I scrunch up my nose as my heart sighs at the comment, but my head questions whether he is just trying to exercise self-preservation. Cynicism wins. "Hmpf." I puff out. "I do believe I heard *sweet Jesus* come out of your mouth and not *get off me*."

I feel Colton's body shudder as he laughs in that full bodied way I love. "Think of it more like being eaten alive by a piranha with dull teeth." I can't help the laugh that bubbles up from his comment, and I just shake my head. "No seriously," he says. "The minute I was able to come up for air, that was the first thing that came out of my mouth because the woman kisses like a fucking bulldog." I can't stop laughing now, my jealousy easing toward relief. "And the funniest part was at that moment my mom called to see how things were going and unknowingly rescued me from her claws."

"You mean from her voodoo pussy?"

"Fuck no," he chuckles. "You, baby—you're my voodoo pussy. Bailey? She's more like a piranha pussy."

We laugh a bit more as his analogies get funnier and funnier and then he says, "Okay, so..." he trails a finger down the bare skin of my arm leaving tiny sparks of electricity in its wake "...*Ace?*"

I was waiting for the question, and I just pull back from him and shake my head. "You're going to waste your next question on that? You're going to be so disappointed." I twist my lips and look at him. "Don't you want to know something else?"

"Quit stalling, Thomas!" His fingers dig into my ribs, and I squirm trying to evade them.

"Stop," I tell him as I keep wriggling. "Okay, okay!" I put my hands up and he stops right before I shove his shoulders. "Tyrant!" He tickles me one more time for good measure and then grunts as I try to explain. "Haddie tends to have a ridiculous penchant for rebellious bad boys." I stop mid-sentence as he raises his eyebrows at me.

"Talk about the pot calling the kettle black, huh?" I can see him trying to keep the smile off of his face.

"I told you that night at the carnival that I *don't do* bad boys."

"Oh, baby, you most definitely did me."

I don't even fight the laugh that comes out because the cocky, mischievous grin is back on his face, lighting up his eyes, and solidifying the theft of my heart. "I sure did, but you were most definitely the exception to the rule," I tell him with a smirk.

"As you were mine," he says, and I think back to how easy it seems for him to say these things now when a month ago I never thought it would be a possibility. He leans forward and brushes his lips against mine, his tongue delving between them to taste and tantalize. I groan, unsatisfied, when he pulls away. "Now give me answers, woman. Ace?" he says with the raise of his eyebrows.

"Okay, okay," I relent, although I'm still very distracted by how close Colton's lips are to mine and how much I crave just one more taste even though my lips are still warm from his. "Like I said, Haddie goes for tattooed men destined to break her heart. Some are good for her, most are not. Max and I used to always laugh at the revolving door of rebels that surrounded her. In college she dated this guy named Stone." I just nod when Colton shakes his head, making sure he heard me correctly.

"Yes, Stone was in fact his name. Anyway, the guy was a jerk but Haddie was madly in lust with him. One night he stood her up for his boys, and as we sat with a bottle of tequila and a bag of Hershey kisses, I told her he was a "real ace in the hole" she'd picked this time. One thing led to another shot, and then another shot." I laugh at the memory from all those years ago. "And the more we drank, we decided to make ace stand for something ... we thought we were hilarious with our guesses and once we decided on the perfect one for Stone, we couldn't stop giggling. Later that night after he'd been out on the town with his buddies, he showed up at the door and when Haddie answered it, she said "Hey, Ace!" and the nickname stuck. He thought she was telling him he was an ace in the sack when she was really telling him he was an *arrogant, conceited egomaniac*." Colton's eyes meet mine when I finally give him what he wants to know. "And from there on out, every time she dated a guy who was like Stone, we called him Ace."

He just stares at me for a second before nodding his head subtly. "Hmpf," is all he says after a beat, his expression stoic and unexpressive. I worry my bottom lip between my teeth as I wait, and then a slow, lazy grin curls up one corner of his mouth. "It's still *a chance encounter* to me, but I guess I earned that title the first night we met."

I snort. "Umm, yeah, you can say that again."

"Don't kick an injured man when he's down." He pouts in mock sadness, and I lean in and brush my lips against his.

"You poor thing," I croon.

"Yep, and just because you feel sorry for me, you're going to let me ask another question. What other memory am I forgetting that you're not telling me?"

I swear my heart skips and lodges in my throat. I try to not falter. Try not to show the break in my figurative stride, which would most definitely let him know that I know something he doesn't. "Nice try, Ace," I tease, swallowing hard and figuring distraction is key at this point.

I lower my lips and kiss little pecks down his neck and chest and then instantly know my next question. I probably shouldn't ask it—know it's a no-go area and I really intend to ask about the knock four times on the hood of the car thing—but the question is out of my mouth before I can stop it. "What do your tattoos mean?" I feel his chest hitch momentarily as I look up and meet his eyes. "I mean, I know what the symbols represent ... but what is their meaning to you?"

He stares at me, tumult in his eyes and uncertainty in his grimace. "Ry ... " My name is an exhale on his lips as he tries to find the words to express the warring emotions dancing at a rapid pace through his irises.

"Why'd you get them?" I ask, thinking maybe I'll switch gears, anything to get rid of the fear flickering in them.

"I figured I was scarred permanently on the inside—live with it every day, a constant reminder that never goes away—I might as well scar myself on the outside too." He shifts his eyes away from mine with a deep breath and looks out toward the ocean. "Show everyone that sometimes what you think is a perfect package is filled with nothing but damaged goods, scarred and irreparable." His voice breaks on the last word and with it so does a little piece of my heart. His words are like acid eating at my soul.

I can't stand the sadness that overtakes him so I take the reins. I want him to see that whatever the tattoos represent, it doesn't matter. Show him that only he could take what he deems an invisible disfigurement and make it visibly, beautiful art. Explain to him that the scars inside and out are meaningless because it's the man that wears them—*owns them*—who is important. Is the man I've fallen in love with.

And I'm not sure how to show him this, so I move on instinct, touching his arm so he raises it up. I very slowly lean forward and press my lips to the uppermost one, the Celtic symbol representing *adversity*. I feel his chest vibrate beneath my lips as he tries to control the rush of emotion swamping him when I move ever so slowly down to the next one: *acceptance*.

The notion that anyone should ever have to scar themselves permanently to accept horrors I can't even fathom hits me hard. I leave my lips pressed against the artistic reminder and close my eyes so he doesn't see the tears pooling in them. So he doesn't mistake them for pity. But then I realize I want him to see them. I want him to know that his pain is my pain. His shame is my shame. His adversity is my adversity. His struggle is my struggle.

That he no longer has to battle it alone, body and soul stained in silent shame.

As I lift my lips from the symbol of *acceptance* and move it down to *healing*, I look up at him through my tear blurred eyes. His eyes lock on to mine and I try to pour everything in myself into our visual conversation.

I accept you, I tell him.

All of you.

The broken parts.

The bent parts.

The ones filled with shame.

The cracks where hope seeps through.

The little boy cowering in fear and the grown man still suffocating in his shadow.

The demons that haunt.

Your will to survive.

And your spirit that fights.

Every single part of you is what I love.

What I accept.

What I want to help heal.

I swear neither of us breathe in this silent exchange, but I can feel walls crumbling down around the heart that beats just beneath my lips. Gates that once protected are now forced apart from the rays of hope, love, and the trust breaking through. Walls collapsing to let someone else in for the first time.

The absolute impact of the moment causes the tears to fall over and trail down my cheek. The salt on my lips, his scent in my nose, and the thunder of his heart breaks me apart and puts me back together in a magnitude of ways.

He squeezes his eyes shut, fighting the tears, and before he opens them, he's reaching down and pulling me up so we're at eye level. I can see the muscles in his jaw tic and see the fight over how to verbalize it in his eyes. We sit like this a moment as I allow him the space he needs.

"I ..." he starts out and then his voices fades, lowering his eyes for a beat before raising them back up to mine. "I'm not ready to talk about it yet. It's just too much and as much as it's clear in my head—in my soul and my nightmares—saying it out loud when I never have, is just ..."

My heart splinters for the man I love. Fucking shatters into the tiniest shards possible from the memories that just put that lost, apologetic, shameful look in his beautiful eyes. I reach out and cup his jaw in my hands trying to smooth away the pain etched in the magnificent lines of the face.

"Shh, it's okay, Colton. You don't need to explain anything." I lean in and press a kiss to the tip of his nose as he does to me and then rest my forehead against his. "Just know I'm here for you if you ever want to."

He exhales out a shaky sigh and pulls me tighter against him, trying to make me feel secure and safe when I should be doing that for him. "I know," he murmurs into the darkening night. "I know."

And it's not lost on me that he let me kiss all of his tattoos—express love for all of the symbols of his life—except for the one denoting vengeance.

Chapter Sixteen

Colton

"Motherfucker!"

Where the hell am I? I jerk awake and sit up. My heart's racing, head's pounding, and I'm out of breath. Sweat beads on my skin as I try to wrap my head around the jumbled images floating, then crashing through my dreams. Memories that vanish like goddamn ghosts the minute I wake up and leave nothing but an acrid taste in my mouth.

Yeah, the two of us—nightmares and me—we're tight. Thick as motherfucking thieves.

I glance at the clock. It's only seven-thirty in the morning, and I need a drink already—screw that—*a whole damn fifth* to deal with these dreams that are going to be the death of me. Talk about motherfucking irony. Memories of a crash I can't remember are going to kill me trying to remember them.

Can you say fucked up with a capital F?

I laugh out loud only to be answered by the thumping of Baxter's tail against his cushion on the floor beside me. I pat the bed for him to jump up on it, and after a bit of petting, I wrestle him to lie down, laughing at his wildly licking tongue.

I lie back on my pillow and close my eyes trying to remember what I was dreaming about, what empty spaces in my mind I can try and fill. Absolutely fucking nothing.

Sweet Jesus! Throw me a goddamn bone here.

Baxter groans beside me. I open my eyes and look over at him, expecting puppy dog eyes begging for attention. Nope. Not in the slightest. I can't help but laugh.

Fucking Baxter. Man's best friend and shit and also comedic relief when needed most.

"Seriously, dude? If I could lick myself like that, I wouldn't need a woman." My words don't even make him hesitate as he finishes cleaning himself. After a beat Baxter stops and looks at me, head angled, handy tongue hanging out the side of his mouth. "Don't give me that smug look, you bastard. You might think you're top dog now with all that flexibility and shit, but, dude, you'd hold out too for Ry's pussy. Fucking grade A voodoo, Bax." I reach out and scratch the top of his head and laugh again with a shake of my head.

Am I that damn desperate that I'm talking to my dog about sex? And the doc says my head's not screwed up? Shit, I think he's taken one too many right turns on an oval track.

Baxter stands and jumps off the bed. "I get it, use me and then leave me," I say to him, and Rylee's words to me the first night we met resurface. *Fuck 'em and chuck 'em.* Fucking Rylee. Pure class, gorgeous with a defiant mouth and feisty attitude. How the hell did we get from there to here?

I swear to God life is a fucking series of moments. Some unexpected. Most not. And very few inconsequential. Hell if I would have ever expected a stolen kiss to lead to this. Rylee and me.

Motherfucking checkered flags and shit.

Blowing out a breath as the headache starts, I roll over on the bed to grab my pain meds from the nightstand. It feels like my head explodes with a bright burst of white—a flash of memories from the drivers' meeting hits me like a fucking sledgehammer—and then disappears before I can hold on to more than a tenth of what flickered.

"Goddamnit!" I shove up and out of the bed, the dizziness not as bad as yesterday. As the day before yesterday. I feel restless as I try to force myself to remember, to make my jacked up head recall all that I'd just glimpsed. I pace, my mind drawing nothing but blanks. I'm frustrated, feeling confined, unsettled.

More fucked up than not.

I don't feel like me anymore. And I need that right now more than anything. To be me. To be in control. To be on top of my game.

To still be Colton *fucking* Donavan.

"Aaarrrrggghh!" I shout because *fucking* is most definitely what I need right now. What will help me find the fucking me I need to be again. I may be pacing in front of my bedroom window, but my dick is hard as a rock and my balls are so fucking blue I'm gonna turn into goddamn Papa Smurf if the doc doesn't clear me soon.

Pleasure to bury the pain, *my ass*. When you can't have the pleasure, what the hell do you do with the pain?

And fuck me if it's not the worst—sweetest—torture sleeping next to the only woman I've ever ached for. I can't take another damn day of this. Even though it aches like a bitch, just the thought of her has me reaching down to palm my dick, make sure it didn't shrivel up and fall off from lack of damn use.

Yep, still there.

And then my hand trembles. Shakes so that my fingers can't even hold my own dick anymore.

Motherfuck, cocksuck! I'm shaking with frustration right now. At me, at Jameson for crashing into me, at the damn world in general! This confinement is suffocating me. Making me lose my shit! I'm going fucking crazy!

I pick up the pillow next to me on the couch and chuck it at the wall of glass in front of me before flopping down into a chair. "Shit!" Squeezing my eyes shut, I suddenly feel like images zoom and collide at a rapid pace slamming against the front of my mind. The bright flash of white returns with a vengeance, crippling and freezing me at the same fucking time.

Go, go, go. C'mon, one-three. C'mon, baby. Go, go, go.

Too fast.

Fuck!

Spiderman. Batman. Superman. Ironman.

I jolt my eyes open as memories lost to me rush back in high definition color.

My stomach tumbles to my feet as the forgotten feelings hit me. Fear strangles me as I try to piece the crash together from the Swiss-cheese sized holes still in my memory.

The anxiety attack hits me at full force and I can't shake it. Dizziness. Vertigo. Nausea. Fear. All four mix like a Long Island Iced Tea I'd kill to gulp down right now as my body trembles with the tiny bits of knowledge my memory has chosen to return.

I feel like I'm on a roller coaster, mid free fall as I struggle to draw in a damn breath.

Suck it up, Donavan. Quit being such a pussy! Fuck me because all I want right now is Rylee. And I can't have her. So I rock myself back and forth like a goddamn puss to prevent myself from calling her on her first full day back with the boys.

But hell if I don't need her, especially because I get it now ... get her now. Understand the claustrophobia that cripples her, because right now I can't even function. All I can fucking do is lie flat on the floor with the edges of my vision blurring, the room spinning, and my head pounding.

And in a moment of lucidity amidst the strangling panic, my mind acknowledges that if I didn't feel like myself before, then I most definitely hate this pussified version of myself—falling to pieces, lying on the floor like a little bitch because of a few memories.

I close my eyes as my mind swims in a goddamned fog.

... If it's in the cards ...

More memories graze my mind, but I can't reach them or see them long enough to hold on to the fuckers.

... Your superheroes finally came ...

I push the memories back, push them down into the blackness. I'm so useless right now. As much as I need to remember, I'm not sure if I can handle them. I've always been a balls-to-the-wall kind of guy, but right now I need motherfucking baby steps. Crawl before you walk and all that shit.

I close my eyes to try and make the room stop the fucking Tilt-A-Whirl it's become.

Thwack!

And another flash of a memory hits me. Five minutes ago I couldn't remember shit and now I can't forget. Screw being broken or bent, I'm a motherfucking scrap yard of parts right now.

Breathe, Donavan. Fucking breathe.

Thwack!

I'm alive. Whole. Present.

Thwack!

I take in a couple of deep breaths, sweat staining the carpet as it pours off of me. I struggle to sit up, to piece together the parts of me scattered all over the damn place to no avail, because it's gonna take a whole hell of a lot more than a torch to weld me back the fuck together.

And it hits me like a motherfucking freight train what I need to do right now. I'm on the move. If I were more coherent, I'd laugh at my naked ass crawling across the floor to reach the television's remote, at how low I've stooped.

But I don't give a flying fuck because I'm so goddamn desperate.

To find myself again.

To control the one fear I can control.

To confront the memories and take their power away.

To not be a fucking victim.

Ever.

Again.

I reach the remote with more effort than it usually takes me to run my typical five miles, and I've only crawled ten feet. I'm weak right now in so many ways I can't even count them. I'm out of breath and the jackhammer is back to work in my head. I finally reach my bed and I push myself on my ass so I can prop my back against the footboard.

Because it's time I face one of the two fears that dominate my dreams.

I aim the remote at the television, push the button, and it sparks to life. It takes me a minute to focus, my eyes have trouble making my double vision merge. My fingers are like Jell-O, and it takes me a few tries to hit the right buttons, to find the recording on the DVR.

It takes every ounce of everything I have to watch my car slingshot into the smoke.

To not look away as Jameson's car slams into mine. Lighting the short fuse on a fireworks display.

To remember to fucking breathe as it—the car, me—flies through the smoke-filled air.

To not cringe at the sickening sound and sight of me hitting the catch fence.

To watch the car shred to pieces.

Disintegrate around me.

Barrel roll like throwing a fucking Hot Wheels down the stairs.

And the only time I allow myself to look away is when I throw up.

Chapter Seventeen

Expectation vibrates and contentment flows through me as I drive the sun drenched highway back to Colton's house, back to what I've been calling home for the past week. A silent tiptoe within a monumental step of our relationship.

It's just out of necessity. Not because he wants me to stay with him for an unspecified period of time. Right?

My heart is lighter after spending my first twenty-four hour shift in over three weeks with the boys. I can't help but smile, recalling Colton's self-sacrifice to get me out of the house and to the boys without a paparazzi entourage. As I was behind the wheel of the Range Rover and its heavily tinted windows, Colton opened the gate on his driveway and walked right out into the media frenzy, drawing all of the attention on himself. And as the vultures descended, I drove out the other side and left without anybody tailing me.

Anticipation is not inconsequential. The phrase dances through my mind, a parade of possibilities rain from the four words Colton texted me earlier. And when I tried to call him to ask what he meant, the phone went to voicemail and another text was sent in response. **No questions. I'm in control now. See you after work.**

And the simple notion that after being with him basically non-stop for three weeks and now I'm not allowed to talk to him—that in itself has created serious anticipation. But the question stands, what exactly am I supposed to be anticipating? As much as my body has already decided, vibrating at what it knows to be the answer, my mind is trying to prepare me for something else. I'm afraid that if I think he's really been cleared by the doctor, and he hasn't, I'll be so frenzied with need and overwhelmed with desire that I'll take what I want—am desperate to have—even though it's not safe for him.

I can't help but smile in satisfaction as I think of what tonight just might bring, on the heels of a great shift with the *other* men in my life. I felt like a rock star walking into The House from the warm and loving reception I received from the boys. I missed them so much and it was such a comforting sound to hear Ricky and Kyle bickering over who is the best baseball player, to hear the sweet sound of Zander's voice in its sporadic but steady bouts, to listen to Shane rattle on about Sophia and Colton getting better so he can teach him how to drive. There were hugs and affirmations that Colton really is okay and all of the headlines in the papers saying otherwise were not true.

I turn up the radio when *What I Needed* comes on and start singing aloud, the lyrics bolstering my good mood, if that's even possible. I look over my shoulder and change lanes, noticing the dark blue sedan for the third time. Maybe I didn't escape the paparazzi after all. Or maybe it's one of Sammy's guys just making sure I get home okay. Regardless, I have a slightly unnerving feeling.

I start to get paranoid and reach for my phone to call Colton and ask him if he had Sammy put a security detail on me. I reach across to the passenger seat and my hand hits all of the homemade gifts the boys made for Colton. It's then I realize that when I loaded my stuff into the back of the car, I set my phone down, and forgot to pick it back up.

I glance in my mirror again and try to shake the feeling away that eats at me, that makes me worry when I see the car still a few lengths back, and force myself to concentrate on the road. I tell myself it's just a desperate photographer. Not a big deal. This is Colton's territory, something he's completely used to but not me. I blow out an audible breath as I make my way through the beachside community and onto Broadbeach Road.

I shouldn't be surprised that the paparazzi still obstruct the street outside of Colton's gates. I shouldn't cringe at having to navigate the street as they descend upon me when they notice I'm driving his car. I shouldn't check my rearview mirror again as I push the button for the gates to open and see the sedan park itself against the curb. I should notice that the person in the car never gets out—never claims his camera to take the shot he's been following me for—but driving with camera flashes exploding around me, it's hard to concentrate on anything else.

I breathe out a shaky breath as the gates shut behind me and park the Rover. I exit the car, my hands a little jittery and my head wondering how anyone gets used to the absolute chaos from the frenzied media as I hear them still calling my name from over the wall. I look up to where Sammy stands just inside the gate and accept the nod he gives me. I start to ask if he's added a man on me but I suddenly remember Colton's text.

Anticipation is not inconsequential.

Everything in my body clenches and coils, my nerves are already frenzied and aching for the man inside the house in front of me. I open the back of the car and grab my purse, figuring I'll leave everything else and get it later. I move quickly to the front door, have the key in the lock, and the door open in seconds. When I close the door the cacophony outside is silenced, and I lean back against the wood, my shoulders sagging at the literal and figurative notion that I've just shut out the world and am now in my little slice of Heaven.

I'm now with Colton.

"Tough day?"

I almost jump out of my skin. Colton steps out of the shadowed alcove, and it takes everything I have to remember to breathe as he leans against the wall behind him. My eyes greedily scrape over every defined edge—every inch of pure maleness—of his body, covered only in a pair of red board shorts hanging low on his hips. My gaze roams up his chest and over inked reminders to take in the lopsided ghost of a smile, but it's when our eyes lock that I catch the spark right before the dynamite detonates.

And from one breath to the next, predicated by a carnal groan, he is on me—body crashing into mine, pressing me against the door, mouth doing so much more than kissing. He's taking, claiming, branding me with unfettered need and reckless abandon. I immediately reach up and fist the hair at the back of his neck while one of his hands does the same to me, the other is on my hip, his desperate fingers digging into my willing flesh. My breasts pillow and pebble against the firmness of his chest, the warmth of his skin adding heat to the blaze building inside of me.

An inferno of need rises inside me that I don't think will ever be sated.

We move in a series of fervent reactions, his hand holds my curls hostage so my mouth is at the mercy of his dexterous lips. So his tongue may delve and tantalize and taste like a man savoring his last meal, like a man saying fuck off to his restraint and accepting gluttony as a welcome sin.

My hands graze down the blades of his shoulders as he gasps—so grateful to have the chance to feel again—before he hikes my leg up and over his hip. I moan, the change in position allowing his rock hard erection to be perfectly placed against my aching core. I throw my head back against the door as the muted friction swamps me, and Colton takes advantage of my newly exposed neck. His mouth is on the tender flesh in the beat of a heart, his tongue sliding against nerves, bringing them to life and then simultaneously singeing them with desire.

My fingers grab onto flexing biceps as his hands make quick work of the button on my jeans. I wiggle my hips when his hands slide between the fabric and my anticipatory flesh. I step out of them as his fingers roam, feathering over my swollen folds to tempt but not take. His other hand palms my backside, a barrier between me and the door, and presses me further into him.

Need swells to unfathomable heights as the parasitic strains of desperation consume every part of my body.

"Colton," I groan, wanting—no needing—him to complete our connection. My hands grope his torso and tear apart the Velcro on his board shorts. I hear the hiss of his breath as my hands find and encircle his tortured length. His whole body tenses at the feel of my skin on his.

"Ry …" He pants my name as I slide my hand up and down him. His hands find their way beneath my top, stripping it off me and making fast work of my bra clasp. "Rylee," he says between gritted teeth. He's so overwhelmed with the sensations ricocheting through him that he stops kissing me, stops moving his hands over my flesh, and braces them against the door on either side of my head. He presses his forehead against mine as he vibrates with the need coursing through him, his breath coming out in short, sharp breaths against my lips.

He says something so quietly I can't hear it underneath the heavy breathing filling the otherwise silent room. I move my hands again, enjoying the feeling of him trembling against me. "Stop," he says quietly against my lips, and this time I hear him. I instantly stop and move back to look at him, fearing that his head is hurting. And I am immediately unnerved by the sight of his eyes squeezed shut.

He draws in a pained breath and opens his eyes slowly to meet mine, as his fingers gently knead my ass. "I'm fucking desperate to bury myself—feel, lose, find myself—in you, Ry …" he says, the strain in his neck visible and his desperation audible. "You deserve soft and slow, baby, but all I'm going to be able to give you is hard and fast because it's been so fucking long since I've had you."

My God the man is so damn sexy, his admission such a turn on, that I don't think he realizes I don't care about soft and slow. My body is strung so tight—emotions, nerves, willpower—that a single touch from him will undoubtedly break me, shatter me into a million fucking pieces of pleasure that oddly will make me whole again.

I angle my head up to him, lean in, and brush my lips to his. I hear his pained intake of breath, feel the tension in his lips as I pull gently on his bottom one from between my teeth. When I pull back, I meet his lust-laden eyes.

"I want you," I whisper to him, one hand wrapped around his iron length and the other fisted tight in the hair at his nape, so he can feel the intensity of my desire. "Any way I can have you. Hard, fast, soft, slow, standing, sitting—it doesn't matter so long as you're the one buried in me."

He stares at me for a beat, disbelief warring with the need raging in his eyes. I can see him try to rein it in, can feel him tremble with need, and know the instant his resolve crumbles. His mouth meets mine—bruising lips and melding tongues—as he takes, tastes, and tempts as only he can. Strong hands map the lines of my torso, thumbs brushing the underside of my breasts already heavy with need, before descending back down the curve of my hips.

If I thought the seeds of desire planted before had bloomed, I have never been more wrong because right now—*right now*—I'm a garden of need.

He grows even harder in my hand as I rub my thumb over the moisture at his crest and am rewarded with a groan from deep in his throat. My other hand scratches up the skin of his back as my lips brand his with just as much fervor. In an instant, Colton has his hands on my hips, lifting me up and pressing my back against the door. My legs try to wrap around his waist but he holds me up, suspended so the one connection I want the most isn't made, so the steeled length of him against my thighs is a torturous tease to my begging apex.

He sucks in a breath as I reach between my legs and grip him, wanting to control the man who is uncontrollable. Needing him in the worst way. The best way. In any way.

His eyes flicker with some undecipherable emotion, but I'm so pent up, so preoccupied with what's going to happen in the next few moments I don't even give a second thought to what it is.

I release him momentarily and reach between my legs to wet my fingers with the pool of moisture within before encircling his crest and coating it, preparing him physically and showing him figuratively what he does to me, and what exactly I want from him. And my little demonstration weakens all of his restraint.

His fingers dig into my hips and lift me up a little higher as I line him up before he pulls me back down and onto him. We both cry out as our connection is made. As my wet heat stretches past its limits to accommodate his invasion.

And it feels like it's been so long since he's filled me, my body has forgotten the pleasurable burn his presence can evoke. "My God," I breathe as my body takes him in. "I'm so tight," I tell him, chalking it up to the fact that it's been over three weeks since we've been intimate.

"No, baby," Colton says, mirth dancing in his eyes as he stills his hips so I can adjust. "I'm just that big."

The laughter fills my mind but never makes it to my lips before I see a flash of his cocky grin and then his mouth is on mine again. But this time as his kiss claims mine, his hips begin to move, hands begin to guide, and his cock begins to stroke over every attuned inch within my nerve-laden walls. He is in complete control of our movements, our motions, our escalation of sensations.

I lift my head up from its leaning position against the door and take in the sight of him. His own eyes are closed, lips slightly parted, hair mussed from my hands, and shoulder muscles rippling as he moves us in rhythmic motion.

My broken man is now in pure dominant mode, and every nerve in my body screams to be taken. To be made his. To be the one he proves his virility to.

"Fuuuccckkk you feel good," he tells me as he pushes me up and then plunges back into me as my muscles clench and nerves are paid the attention they most definitely have been craving.

"Colton," I pant, my fingers digging into the tops of his shoulders as he drives me higher and higher. Sensation spirals—little shock waves of pleasure preparing me for him to shake the earth beneath my feet—and warmth starts to spread like a wildfire through my core. He drives back in again as my thighs tighten around him, my fingernails score lines, and my mouth seeks his with a frenzied need.

It only takes a few more seconds before the pleasure ratchets into an explosion of white in the abyss of darkness that has consumed me. And I am instantly lost to a world beyond our connection. It's just him and me—sensation overwhelming and breath robbed— as I drown in the liquid heat and lose myself to the feeling, his name a repeated pant from my lips.

Within moments, Colton's cry breaks through my pleasure induced coma at the same time his hips convulse wildly beneath mine, finding his own release. He rocks back and forth in me a few times trying to draw out the moment, his breath ragged and chest gleaming with our combined sweat.

His body sags against mine as he buries his face into the crook of my neck. My arms wrap around him from my position atop his pelvis and pressed against the door. I absorb the moment—the rapid rise and fall of his chest, the warmth of his breath against my neck, the unmistakable scent of sex—and understand without a doubt that I'd move Heaven and earth for this man without a second thought.

Colton adjusts his grip on my hips, and I slowly lower my feet to the ground; although my head is still figuratively in the clouds. He slips out of me and yet our connection is not lost because he gathers me in his arms, skin to skin, as if he doesn't want to let me go just yet.

And I'm okay with that because I don't think I'll ever be able to let him go either.

"Fuck, I needed that," he sighs with a slight chuckle and all I can give him is a noncommittal answer because frankly I'm still riding my own high.

We fall silent for a few moments, lost in the moment, enjoying the comforting feel of just being together.

"I can't believe you didn't tell me," he says, breaking the silence and shakes his head back and forth before pulling back so he can look at the questioning look on my face.

"Tell you?" I'm confused.

A ghost of a smirk graces his mouth as he brings one hand up to cup the side of my face, his thumb brushing ever so softly over my lips still swollen from his kisses. "What I said to you before I got in the car ..."

My inhaling breath dies and my heart skips a beat, lodging itself in my throat from the words on his lips and the emotion in his eyes. I want to ask him to say it, to tell me the words himself, because hell yes I know what he said, but I want to hear that he remembers those words and still feels the meaning behind them.

I try to control the hitch in my breath and wavering in my voice but I have to ask. "What do you mean?" I'm a horrible liar and I know he can see right through my feigned confusion.

He chuckles a quiet laugh and leans in to brush a tender kiss against my lips and then the tip of my nose before leaning back so he can look into my eyes. He darts his tongue out to wet his lips and says, "*I race you, Ryles.*"

My heart melts and my soul sighs at hearing him repeat those words I've used like glue to bind the broken pieces the crash created. Even though the words bring me peace, I can hear nerves shake his voice, can sense the anxiety in the bottom lip he worries between his teeth. And now I'm starting to get nervous. Did he say the words and now doesn't feel the same way he did then? I know it's a ridiculous thought, considering what happened between us moments ago, but the one thing I've learned about Colton is that he is anything but predictable.

"Yeah," I sigh, meeting the temerity in his eyes. "Those words ... are you saying them now because you've reclaimed the memory or because you still mean them?" *There*. I've laid it out on the table, given him the option to say it's the former and not the latter—an *out* in case he no longer *races* me. In case the accident has changed how he feels and this—us, me and him—have reverted back to a *just casual* status.

Colton angles his head and studies me a moment, eyes beseeching but lips motionless. The silence stretches as I wait for the answer, as I wait to see if he'll rip me apart or be the soothing balm to my healing heart.

"Ry ... don't you know I never forget a single moment when I race ... *on or off* the track?" It takes a moment for the words to register, for the words and what they mean to sink in. That he remembers and that he still feels the same way. And the funny thing is now that I know—now that all of this worry can go away and we can move forward—I'm frozen in place.

We're naked, leaning against a door that a hundred or so reporters are on the other side of, the man I *race* has just told me that he races me back, and yet all I can do is stare at him as my soul realizes the hope filling it, is finding its permanent home.

Colton leans in so his mouth is a whisper from mine, hands framing my face as he looks into the depths of my soul. "I race you, Rylee," he says to me, mistaking my silence as not understanding his prior statement. Little does he realize I'm so head over heels in love with him, right here, right now—body naked and heart bared—that I'm robbed of the ability to speak. So instead I accept the brush of his lips over mine in a kiss that's soft and reverent before he rests his forehead against mine. "Don't you know?" he asks. "You're my motherfucking checkered flag."

I can feel his lips curve up in a smile as they brush against mine, and I let the laughter that bubbles up fall free. It feels so good to suddenly have that thorn removed from my side.

To know the man I love, loves me in return.

To know he's caught my free-falling heart.

Colton's hands start the descent back down the line of my spine—the tremor of his right hand so slight now I barely notice it—and then back up as I feel him start to harden again against my lower belly.

"I take it you've been cleared from the doc?" I ask, my sated body already thrumming with newfound desire.

"Yeah I did, but after my day," he says, kissing my forehead and pulling me back into the comfort of his arms, "it didn't fucking matter if I got the okay or not, I was taking what was mine."

"What was yours, huh?" I tease him despite the words warming my heart.

"Yep."

And then the words he said before register and have me pulling back to search for an answer. "What was wrong with your day?"

I see something cloud his eyes momentarily before he pushes it away. "Don't worry about me," he says, and I'm immediately concerned.

"What else happened, Colton? Was there something you remembered—something that—"

"No," he says, quieting me with a press of his lips against mine. "I only remembered what was important. Some voids are still there." Ever the master of deflection, he continues, "It seems I've been neglecting you as of late."

So whatever is bugging him, he doesn't want to talk about. Okay … well, then on the heels of the past twenty minutes, I will most definitely give him the unasked for space and not push. "*Neglecting me?*"

"Yes, not treating you properly," he says as he slaps my butt; the sting it leaves has nothing on the shock waves that ripple through the hypersensitive flesh between my thighs. "You've been taking care of me—of everyone else but yourself as usual—and I haven't properly taken care of you."

"I do believe you did just take care of me … *and quite properly,*" I tease, wiggling my naked body up against his and earning the hum that comes from deep within his throat. "If that's considered not taking care of me—neglecting me—Ace, *then please...*" I nip at the skin on the underside of his jaw "...neglect me some more."

"My God, woman, you test a man's restraint," he groans as his hands run down my spine and clasp together against my lower back. "But, that was just a minor sidetrack to—"

"*Minor* is not what I'd call it," I quip with a raise of my eyes and another wiggle of my hips that causes him to laugh out loud. "I'll take one of your sidetracks any day."

"Bet your ass you will," he teases with a quick squeeze of my hips, "but as I was saying, it's time I treated you to a proper night out rather than gross hospital food and keeping me occupied while I lie in bed." When I just quirk a suggestive eyebrow at the occupy in bed part, he just shakes his head at me and that grin I love lights up his face. He leans in and kisses me softly, murmuring his next words against my own lips. "There'll be plenty of time for you to occupy me in bed later because right now—tonight—I'm taking you to a movie premier."

His words catch me by complete surprise. "Wh-what?" I look at him with incredulity on my face and lips parted in shock. He just grins at me with a cat-that-ate-the-canary look because he's surprised me.

A little thrill of excitement shoots through me at the thought of experiencing something new with Colton—making new memories—but at the same time that means I'll have to share him with *them*. The *paparazzi* who sit outside the gate and will no doubt be at the event with their intrusive questions and in-your-face cameras. And it also means we have to step outside of this world, away from our cozy little realm where we can make sweet, lazy love whenever and wherever we want.

I know which one I prefer.

His sarcastic comment to Becks from days earlier chooses right now to hit my ears and take hold. The words are out of my mouth before I can filter them. "I thought once you got the okay, nothing was going to come between you and me but a change of sheets for a *long, fucking time.*" I repeat his own words back to him.

Colton's eyes instantly darken with lust and spark with mischief as his mouth twists, his mind figuring out which option he'd prefer. "Well," he says with a laugh, "I did in fact say that." He traces a finger lazily down my cheek, to my neckline, and then down between my breasts. I can't help the breath I suck in, the pebbling of my nipples, or the swelling of my heart. "And you know me, Ryles, always a man of my word … so how exactly am I going to keep you naked with the exception of a sheet and at the same time attend a premier I've already committed to? Hmm … decisions," he whispers as he leans down and traces the curve of my neck with the tip of his tongue. "What shall we do?"

I open my mouth to answer but all I can do is try and breathe when his teeth tug playfully on my earlobe. "I guess the world's about to learn how damn sexy you look wrapped in a sheet."

My eyes snap open to meet his as shock kicks my libido down a notch. Within a second Colton and his devilish grin have picked my naked self up and placed me over his shoulder.

"No!" I shriek as he starts toward the stairs. "Put me down!"

"The media's going to have a field day with this one," he taunts as I swat his ass, but he carries on. "Well one way to look at it, it's not going to take you long to pick out what to wear."

"You've lost your marbles!" I shout, my comment earning me another smack on my bare ass perched so seamlessly over his shoulder.

"My loss is your gain, sweetheart!" He chuckles as he climbs the last step up the stairs.

"Gain, *my ass!*" I mutter under my breath, and he belts out another laugh.

"Oh really," he says, angling his head to the side and placing a chaste kiss on my hip beside his face. "I didn't know you liked to play *that way*, but I'm sure we could explore that avenue when the time's right."

My mouth gapes open and I sputter a nervous laugh as Colton stops and slowly slides my body down every firm inch of his until my feet touch the floor. The impish gleam in his eye causes me to wonder if that's yet another something Colton might be into that's never crossed my mind before. I'm so lost in my momentary thoughts and the quiet calculation in his eyes that I miss the fact he's set me down on the private, second story terrace.

And when I realize it—when I notice my surroundings—I'm shocked once again ... but this surprise is one that melts my heart.

"Oh, Colton!" The words fall out of my mouth as I take in all of the preparations around me. A portable movie screen has been set up on the far end of the patio and the chaise lounges have been arranged in theater style seating, draped in several layers of none other than sheets. A smile spreads over my face and warmth permeates my soul as I take in the little touches, little things that let me know he cares: a bowl of Hershey's kisses, a bottle of wine, funnels of cotton candy, lighted candles sprinkled everywhere, and clouds of pillows to lie back on.

I can't help the tears that well in my eyes nor do I care when one slips over and slides silently down my cheek. The thoughtfulness that went into everything that sits beautifully in front of me leaves me at a loss for words. I turn back to face him and just shake my head at what I see ... because if what's behind me robs my words, the beauty inside and out of the man before me steals my heart. He stands there naked—unshaven, hair mussed and, not including the shaved patch, in desperate need of a haircut, and a look in his eyes that reinforces the words he said to me downstairs.

"Thank you," I tell him with a broken breath. "This is the sweetest thing ..." My voice drifts off as he takes a step toward me and brings his hands up to cup my cheeks and angle my head up so I can meet his eyes. "The best kind of night out. A movie with my Ace and sheets ... *nothing between us but sheets*."

He smiles that shy smile that undoes me and leans in for a whisper of a kiss before pulling back. "That's exactly right, Ry. Nothing between us but sheets. *Nothing between us ever again but a set of sheets*."

His words stagger me, move me, complete me, and all I can do is step forward and press my lips to his—feel his heart against me, the scrape of his unshaven jaw against my chin, see the love in his eyes—and say, "*Nothing but sheets*."

Chapter Eighteen

The heat of the morning sun warms my skin, chased by the cool blow of the ocean's breeze. The stereo we forgot to turn off last night plays Matt Nathanson's voice just barely audible above the noise of the surf. I snuggle in closer to Colton, so content with the unexpected turn our lives have taken when we more or less crashed into one another that I swear my heart hurts from the enormity of it all. With the second chances we've both been given—that we're both slowly accepting—that a year ago we could have never imagined.

I squint my eyes, thankful for the trellis above that blocks the sun from where we fell asleep last night on the bed of chaise lounges. I don't even bother to suppress the sigh of a more than satisfied woman as I reminisce making slow, sweet love to him under a blanket of stars and in a bed made of possibilities.

I recall rising over him, sinking down onto him, and watching the unguarded emotion flow through his eyes. How the soft and slow with Colton is just as mind blowing as the hard and fast. How a man used to showing no emotion—used to guarding his heart at all costs—is slowly opening up, moving each brick one at a time, allowing the key to turn in the lock.

I smile softly as I lift my head and look at all the reminders of last night. How sweet the gesture was from a man who swears he doesn't subscribe to the notion of romance, when everything around us screams just the opposite. What man calls in a favor from his dad to get a copy of his not-released-yet but soon-to-be-blockbuster movie so he can have an uninterrupted date night with his girlfriend? And even though I came to find out he had Quinlan's help, it was all his idea … the little touches here and there, because it's the little things that mean so much more to me than the extravagant ones.

I raise my head up from where it rests on his chest and watch him sleep, let my love for him warm the parts of me the breeze has cooled. "I can feel you watching me," he says groggily with a curl of his lip even though his eyes remain closed.

"Mmm-hmm." I can't help the smile on my face.

"Whose idea was it to sleep out here? It's too damn bright." He shifts, eyes still closed, but brings the arm that rests behind his head down to pull me closer to him.

"I believe the words were, 'Your voodoo pussy has worked its magic and stolen mine. I have no energy to move,'" I repeat, not hiding the smug look on my face or the pride in my voice.

"Nope, definitely not my words," he says before cracking open an eye and looking over to me, that salacious smirk I love displayed proudly. "I've got magic in spades, baby, it must have been some other guy your voodoo sucked the life from."

I fight back the urge to laugh because that gravelly morning voice and those sleepy eyes are the perfect combination of sexy, making it extremely hard to feign nonchalance. "Yeah, you're right. Remember, I don't do bad boys such as yourself." I shrug. "It was that clean-shaven guy I see on the side. The one who gives me what you can't," I taunt as I lift the sheet resting over our hips and peek under it, my eyes roaming greedily over his impressive morning hard-on. My muscles, slightly sore from last night, immediately clench in welcome anticipation of more to come. I close my eyes to hide the desire I'm sure clouds them and make a satisfied moan.

"See something you like? Something he can't give you?" I love the playful tone in his voice.

I make sure my voice is even when I speak because all of this bantering foreplay is making me crave what is beneath my fingertips.

"No worries." I force the words out as I look up from beneath my eyelashes to find his eyes dancing with humor. "*This woman* is more than satisfied. No need to experience your magic when that man can drive his stick down the homestretch like you wouldn't believe."

Within a heartbeat Colton has flipped me on my back and hovers over me, weight resting on one elbow, and his other hand cuffing my wrists above my head. His face is inches from mine, smirk locked in place, and eyebrows raised in challenge. "I believe my words the other day were a *long, fucking time*," he says, pressing his erection at my apex. "There's the *long*, sweetheart, now we just need to fulfill the *fucking time* part of it."

I start to belt out a laugh but it ends in a pleasurable moan as he sinks into my willing body. I'm not fully ready for his entrance, and although this would normally hurt, it doesn't. Instead it adds the perfect amount of friction to awaken every nerve possible, including any he might have missed last night.

"Sweet fucking Jesus, you feel like Heaven woman," he murmurs into my ear as his hips pull out and slide back forward, his one hand still pinning my hands above me. In an oddly intimate action, he lowers his face and rests it just beneath the curve of my neck so each time he withdraws and sinks back into me, the scrape of his stubble and the warmth of his breath teases my skin. And maybe it's because of his face being so closely positioned by my ear or just that we are so in tune with one another again, but there's something about the sounds he makes that are such a turn on. Grunts turn into moaning sighs, audible satisfaction.

I try to move my arms but his grip holds me still. "Colton," I pant as my body starts to quicken, warmth spreading, the desire coiling so tight I'm waiting for it to spring free. "Let me touch you."

"Hmm?" he murmurs, the vibration of his mouth against my neck rolling through me. He moves again, grinding his hips in a circular motion, cock hitting hidden nerves, before he pulls back out and angles up so he rubs against my clit adding a pleasurable friction that has me forgetting all thoughts about needing my hands to be released. He chuckles, knowing exactly what he's just done. "That feel good?"

"God yes!" I moan as he does it again, my thighs starting to tense and my skin becoming flushed as the tidal wave of sensation surges in preparation for its final assault on my body.

"I know I'm good, baby, but God might get a little jealous if you start comparing us."

The playful tone, the lazy lovemaking, because this is making love for us—he may call it racing, but this ... murmured words, utter acceptance, complete knowledge of the other's body, comfort—is most definitely him showing me how he loves me.

I can't help the carefree laugh that falls from my mouth any more than I can help the arch of my back and the angling of my hips on his next thrust in his slow, skillful rhythm. "Well ... be prepared to get jealous in turn," I taunt, causing him to lift his head from his position on my neck and scrape his whiskers purposefully across my bare nipple causing unfettered need to mainline straight to where he is manipulating so expertly between my thighs. He raises his eyebrows at me in amusement, trying to figure out what exactly I mean as his hips rotate again within me, and I'm lost.

To the moment.

To him.

To the orgasm singlehandedly ripping through my body and drowning me in its overwhelming sensations.

To the, "*Oh God, oh God, oh God!*" that falls from my lips as wave after wave surges through me.

And I succumb to the haze of my desire but I hear him chuckle when he realizes just why I thought he might be jealous. My body is still pulsing around him, still coming, when he leans down into my ear, his morning rasp adding a soft tickle to the violent sensations reverberating through me. "You may be calling his name now, sweetheart, but in a minute you're going to be thanking me," he says as he nips my shoulder with his teeth before my hands are released and the warmth of his body leaves mine.

I'm so lost in riding out my climax that the warmth of his mouth on my already sensitive flesh has me calling out his name, hands fisting in the hair on his head positioned between my legs, tongue sliding along the length of my seam. "Colton!" I cry as his tongue licks into me, drawing out the intensity of my orgasm, prolonging the free fall of ecstasy. "Colton!" I say again, starting to squirm my hips against his mouth as the pleasure becomes almost too much to bear.

He licks his tongue back up again and this time keeps going, drawing a line of open mouth kisses and licks up my belly, chest, and neck to my mouth so when his tongue pushes between my lips, I can taste my own arousal. His mouth on mine absorbs my gasped moan as he enters me once again and begins to chase his own orgasm.

When he pulls back from my mouth and sits back on his knees, holding my legs apart as he starts to move within me, he grants me that lightning flash grin I can never resist. "I told you, it would be my name you were calling in the end."

I start to say something but he grips my hips and rears back and thrusts into me. The start of a punishing rhythm that has my hands gripping the sheets and his name becomes a pant on my lips as he takes us to the edge together.

"What'd Becks want?" I ask Colton as I walk into his office and lean my backside on the desk to face him. If it weren't for my positioning, I would have missed the uncertainty flicker through his eyes before he grimaces.

"Is it a bad one?" I ask of the headache I can tell he's trying to hide.

"Nah, not too bad. They're getting fewer and farther between," he says falling silent as he unbends the paperclip in his hand with fierce concentration.

"Becks?" I prompt, sensing that something is wrong.

"He uh, asked if I wanted to reserve some time at the track since they book out far in advance. To make sure I had some time if I wanted it." He averts his eyes and focuses on the paperclip he's unfolding with his fingers. "He thinks I should get back in the car."

Fucking Beckett!

I want to scream at the top of my lungs but settle for chastising him silently. Okay. I've gotten my unfounded anger out at him for doing what I agree is right, but it still doesn't mean I like it … at all. I'd feel a whole hell of a lot better if I had a punching bag too because I'm still terrified by the thought of Colton suited up and behind the wheel, but the question is, is Colton?

"What are your thoughts on it? Are you ready?"

He sighs and leans back in his chair, lacing his fingers behind his head and looking up to the ceiling. "Nah," he says finally, drawing the word out, stalling for time for his explanation. "Yesterday I—" he stops mid-thought and shakes his head. "Doesn't matter … My hand's still too fucked up to grip the wheel," he says. And I know it's a bullshit lie since he had no problem holding me up so he could have his way with me against the front door yesterday, but I know saying it out loud would be akin to kicking a man when he's down; not only would I know he's scared, but I'd also be proving he's lying.

But his aborted explanation that he didn't complete, mixed with his comment yesterday about it being a rough day, collide together not so subtly in my mind. I move without asking and sit across his lap and nestle into him. He blows out a resigned breath before unlacing his fingers and closing his arms around me.

"What happened yesterday?" I ask after a moment. I can feel his body pause momentarily, and I kiss his bare chest beneath my lips as a silent sign of support.

"I watched the replay."

He doesn't need to say anything further. I know perfectly well what *replay* he's referring to because I still can't bring myself to watch it. "And how did you handle it?"

His body vibrates with an unsettled energy, and when he starts to shift beneath me, I can tell that he needs to release some of it. I move off his lap and when he rises and walks to the window, I sink back into the leather, still warm from his body.

Colton shoves a hand through his hair, tension evident in the bare muscles of his back as he looks out the window to the beach down below. He forces out a laugh. "Well, if you call a grown man crawling around on the fucking floor naked while he dry heaves from the goddamn panic attack after every single fucking feeling from the crash hits him like a sucker punch," he says, voice thick with sarcasm, "then shit, if that's considered handling it? Then fuck yeah … I'd say I aced that motherfucking test." He rolls his shoulders and walks out of the office without a backward glance. I exhale the breath I'm holding when I hear the door to the patio slide open and then shut behind him.

I let some time pass, lost in my thoughts, my heart hurting for Colton's obvious struggle between needing and fearing racing, and I stand up to go find him.

I walk out onto the patio and hear the splash of water before I see his long, lean figure slicing through the top of the water with graceful fluidity. He covers the distance of the pool quickly, reaches the end and does some kind of underwater flip and resurfaces before heading the other way.

I sit cross-legged on the edge of the pool and admire his natural athleticism—the rippling of muscles, his complete control over his body—and wonder if this absolute attraction I have for him has any limitations.

After a bit, he does his underwater turn at the edge farthest from me and instead of immediately starting his stroke again, he flips over on his back and floats, his momentum causing him to drift toward where I'm sitting. He looks so peaceful now, despite his chest expanding from his exertion, and I wish I could see this type of serenity in his features more often.

His torso rises from the water as he lowers his feet to the bottom and scrubs his hands over his face. When he removes them, he looks up, startled to see me sitting there watching him, and the most breathtaking smile spreads across his lips. He scrunches his nose up, reminding me of what he'd look like as a little boy, and any of my concern over his state of mind vanishes.

He walks over to where I sit, eyes locked on mine. "I'm sorry, Ryles." He shakes his head with a sigh. "It's hard for me to admit I'm scared to get back in the car."

His admission shocks the hell out of me. I reach out and run a thumb over his cheek, never more in love with him than right now. "That's okay. I'm scared too."

He reaches out to my hips and pulls me closer toward him so he can kiss me. A brush of his lips and the scent of chlorinated water on his skin is all I need to feel right with him again. He starts to say something and then stops. "What?" I ask softly.

He clears his throat, licks his lips, and averts his eyes to the beach beyond. "When I get back in the car ... will—will you be there?"

"Of course!" The words are out of my mouth and my arms are wrapped around his wet body instantly, a physical emphasis to my words. I feel his chest shudder and hear the hitch in his breath as he squeezes me tighter. I bring my fingers up and tease his hair with my nails as his face remains nuzzled under my neck.

I love you. The words are in my head, and I have to stop them from coming out of my mouth because the intensity of what I feel for him is indescribable. Unconditional love.

The distant sound of the doorbell ringing from inside the house has us pulling back from one another. I look at him confused. "It's probably one of the security guys," he says as I rise and he swims towards the steps.

"I'll get it," I tell him as I walk in the house, pulling my now wet shirt away from my body, glad I opted for the red tank top instead of the white one.

My hand is turning the knob, pulling on the slab of wood, when I hear Colton's voice from outside tell me to "*Wait!*" but it's too late. The door's swinging open and unbeknownst to me, one of my worst nightmares is standing opposite me.

All I can do is sag my shoulders at the sight. Long legs, blonde hair, and a condescending smirk is all I catch before she starts to walk past me and then stops, angling her head over her shoulder to look back at me. "You can run along now, little girl. Playtime is over because Colton doesn't need you anymore. He's in good hands now. Momma's here."

My jaw drops open, her audacity renders me speechless. Before I can find my words, she breezes into the house like she owns the place, leaving me in the wake of her overpowering perfume.

"Colton?" I shout out at him the same time he walks into the foyer, the towel he's using to dry his hair drops to the ground.

Several emotions flicker through his eyes, the most prevalent one being annoyance, but his face shows absolutely nothing.

And with Colton, when his face is that cold and devoid of emotion, it means a storm is brewing just beneath.

"What the fuck are you doing *here*, Tawny?" The ice in his voice stops me in my tracks but doesn't even faze her.

"Colt, baby," she says completely unaffected by the bite in his words. "We need to talk. I know it's been a while and—"

"I'm not in the mood for your melodramatic bullshit so cut the crap." Colton takes a step farther into the room. "You know you're not welcome here, Tawny. If I wanted you here before, I would've invited you myself."

I shrink back at the venom lacing his voice, but at the same time, I'm pissed. Pissed that she just waltzed in here—a home where I'm the only woman he's ever brought—like she deserves to be here.

"Testy, testy," she scolds playfully, unfazed by his complete disinterest. "I was so concerned about you and how you're doing and if you've gotten your memory back yet that—"

"I don't give a flying fuck about your concern! You have two seconds. Start talking or I'm throwing your ass out." Colton takes another step toward her and I can see his grinding jaw and his complete callous disregard for her.

"Just because you're pissed your recovery is going so slow—that you can't remember *important* things—doesn't mean you get to take it out on me." Tawny lets out a condescending laugh and turns slightly to look over at me with disbelief in her eyes as if she's saying "*Really? He's picked you over me?*" before she says, "I'm sure this is amusing to you being his nursemaid and all, doll, but you're no longer needed."

I'm off the wall in an instant, a ball of anger flying at her, but Colton beats me to the punch. Rage emanates off of him in palpable waves as he grips her bicep. "Time to go!" he growls out as he starts to direct her toward the door. "You don't come into my house and disrespect, Ry—"

"I'm pregnant."

The words that float out of her mouth die in the sudden silence of the room, and yet I can see them vibrating within Colton. His body stops, fingers flex on her arm, and teeth grind. It takes a beat for him to catch his stride again, pulling her toward the front door.

"Good for you. Congrats." He bites out, sarcasm dripping from his words. "Nice knowing ya." He starts to open the front door as she yanks her arm free.

"It's yours."

Colton's hand stills on the doorknob as my heart twists at the words coming from her lips. I'm watching this unfold—all of it right before my eyes—but I feel like a complete outsider, a hundred miles away. I watch his head sag down between his shoulders for a beat, notice his hands clench in fists at his sides, see the fury rage in his eyes as he turns ever so slowly around. His eyes dart over and hold mine for a beat, and what I see knocks the wind out of me. It's not the rage they glisten with—no—it's the disbelief laced apology he's offering up to me. The apology that tells me deep down he fears her words are true. Lead drops into my stomach as the mask he's let slip is reapplied, and he turns to direct his anger toward Tawny.

"You and I both know that's not possible, Tawny." He takes a step forward and I can see every ounce of restraint he has—how he's trying so hard to not pick her up and physically throw her out. His eyes dart from her face to her stomach and then back up again.

"What?" she gasps, shock laced with hurt in her voice. "You don't remember?" She holds a hand to her mouth, tears welling in her eyes. "Colton you and I … the night of Davis' birthday party … you don't remember that?"

My stomach wrenches because if I thought she might be acting—playing the part to get him back—she just stole the show with the hurt look on her face and desperation in her voice.

Oh my God. Oh my God. It's my only coherent thought because my entire body trembles with every imaginable emotion possible.

"No," Colton says, shaking his head back and forth, and the look on his face—the one that says if he keeps repeating no over and over this will all just be a nightmare—kills me. Tears into parts deep inside of me opening me up, preparing me for the onslaught of hurt to come.

"It's the only possibility," she says quietly, placing her hand over her midsection where I can see the slight bump now that her shirt is smoothed down. "I'm five months, baby."

I have to fight the bile that rises in my throat as my faith falters. I have to force myself to breathe. To focus. To realize that this isn't about me. That this is about Colton's worst nightmare coming true on the heels of a truly magical night between us. But it's hard not to.

All my mind can focus on is dates—days past—as her words sink their claws into me. *Five months, five months, five months,* I repeat over and over because time is so much easier to focus on than the world that's just been shifted beneath my feet. When my mind can formulate coherent thoughts again, I realize it's been a little shy of five months since we met. Fuck, *it's possible*.

I tell myself she's lying. That she's trying to dig her hooks into Colton—catch the prize she wants more than anything—by pulling the *I'm pregnant* card. The oldest one in the book. But the evidence is there in her swollen belly and the terrified look on Colton's face says it's a possibility—that he's reaching deep within the locked vault of memories and trying to find the one she's telling him about. Fear flickers across his face, embeds itself in those eyes of his that all of a sudden refuse to look at me.

And no matter how much I want to, I can't look away. It's like if I keep staring at him, he's going to look up at me and give me that smile he gave me moments ago in the pool and she'll just disappear.

But it never comes.

He stands in the middle of us, motionless, lost in thoughts I can only imagine. The playful man I love from last night is nonexistent. I can see the cogs in his head turning, notice the wince of pain that I'm sure is from another headache hitting him … but if he's completely frozen, then I'm fucking paralyzed.

Tawny's eyes flicker over and assess me with complete disregard, before looking back at Colton, a soft smile on her face. "You drove me home from Davis' house, asked to come in … we had sex, Colton. The first time we were drunk … desperate to be with each other again and didn't use a condom."

And if her dagger isn't already breaking skin and pushing into my heart, she has to add the notion that they were together multiple times to twist it a little deeper.

"Before … when we dated before..." he clears his throat "...you used to be religious about taking your pill." I don't recognize his voice, and I've been on the receiving end of Colton's wrath, but right now the absolute contempt in his tone sends shivers up my spine.

"I wasn't on the pill," she says softly with an unapologetic shrug as she takes a step toward him, the possible mother of his child. The gentle intimacy in her tone causes tears to spring in my eyes. She reaches out to touch Colton's arm and he yanks it out of her reach.

His reaction and the unfettered panic in his eyes causes the reality of this all to begin to seep through my denial, the possibility that this isn't a ploy to merely get him back.

I sag against the wall behind me, my ghosts and inadequacies as a woman threatening to rear their ugly head. I place a hand on my abdomen to stifle the pang I feel in my useless womb. The one that will forever remain empty. The one that can't give him the only thing *she can*. I feel the beginnings of a panic attack—breath laboring, heart racing, eyes unable to focus—as I wonder if the man who professes to never want kids just might change his mind when faced with the possibility of one. It happens all the time. And if it does, then where does that leave us? Leave me? The woman who can't give him that.

"No!" It falls from my lips in response to my silent thoughts.

Colton whips around to look at me quickly, distress etched in his features at my unexpected words. And then she snorts out in disregard and adds gasoline to Colton's fire.

"Get out!" He shouts so loudly I jump, and for a moment, because he's facing me, I fear that he's speaking to me. I force a swallow, his eyes flicking over me before he turns his back to me and points toward Tawny and then the door. "Get. The. Fuck. Out!"

"*Colty* ..."

"Don't you ever call me that!" he yells, grated steel in his voice as he raises his eyes to look toward where she's not moved an inch. "*No one gets to call me that*! Do you think you're special? Do you think you can just waltz in here and tell me you're five fucking months pregnant? That I'd care? Why are you telling me now, huh? Because it's too late for me to have a say in anything, so you think you've trapped me? Found your golden fucking ticket?" He begins to pace, lacing his fingers behind his head and blowing out a loud breath. "I'm not Willy fucking Wonka, sweetheart. Go find yourself another sugar daddy."

"You don't believe me?"

Colton whirls around in a flash, his gaze meeting mine and the void in his expressionless eyes startles me. Dead eyes look at me momentarily before he breaks our connection and strides back across the room to where Tawny still stands. "You're goddamn right I don't believe you. Quit the crap and get the fuck out with your bullshit lies." He's inches from her face, eyes glaring, and posture threatening.

"But I still love—"

"You don't get to love me!" he bellows, fist slamming down on the sideboard next to him, vases rattling and noise resonating in the otherwise quiet of the house. Tawny lets out a sob and Colton remains completely unaffected by her outburst of emotion. "You don't get to love me," he repeats again so quietly that I can hear his pain beneath it, feel the desperation roll off of him in waves.

He reaches up and rubs his hands over his face. He looks out the window for a moment toward the tranquility of the ocean as I watch the storm rage inside of him. I'm rocked in the turbulence of his emotions without a lifeline to hold on to. When he looks back at Tawny, I can see so many emotions behind his slipping mask that I'm unsure which one he is going to grab and hold onto.

"I want a paternity test."

Tawny gasps, her hand resting protectively over her belly, but when I look back up to her face, I watch the transformation happen. I see the damsel in distress morph into the vindictive vixen. "This baby is yours, Colton. I don't sleep around."

Colton snorts a laugh with a shake of his head. "Yeah, you're a regular patron fuckin' saint." He stalks to the front door and turns back to look at her. "Go tell it to some other gullible son of a bitch who cares. My lawyer will be in touch."

"You're gonna have to come at me with something a hell of a lot bigger than threatening me with your attorney to get out of this one," she says, straightening her spine. "Get your checkbook ready and your ego prepared for some serious damage, *sweetheart*!"

"Did you actually think you could just waltz in here, drop your bullshit bomb, and I'd take your word for it? Write you off with a hefty check or marry you and ride off into the motherfucking sunset?" His voice thunders. "It's. Not. Mine!"

Tawny shrugs her shoulders and a smarmy expression transforms her features. "The press is going to have a field day with how I spin this one ... a nice juicy scandal to sink their teeth into."

She starts to walk toward the front door and just when I think I might be able to take a breath, Colton's palm slams against the door, the sound assaulting the dead silence of the room. He turns and gets back within inches of her face, his voice trembling with rage. "Newsflash, *sweetheart*, you better hit me with something stronger than that threat if you think the press scares me. Two can play that game," he says opening the door. "Make sure you tell them all the juicy details because I sure as fuck won't hold back. It's amazing how quick a promising career can be dashed in this town when rumors hit the papers about what a demanding diva one can be. No one wants to work with a fucking bitch, and you definitely fit that bill. Now get the fuck out."

Tawny walks up to him, stares at him, although he refuses to meet her eyes, and then walks out the front door that shuts with a resounding slam behind her. Colton immediately grabs one of the vases on the sideboard he'd hit moments earlier and throws it against the wall. The shattering sound of glass followed by tinkling as it bounces off the tiled floor is such a contrast to the heaviness of the moment. Not getting the release he needed, he places his hand on the sideboard and braces his weight against it.

I step forward from the shadows of the foyer, still not sure what to do when he looks up and locks his eyes with mine. I try to get a read his emotions but I can't—his guard is back up and locked in place. The knowledge of how much work it's going to take to break that wall back down causes a little piece of me to die, to die and fall to rest beside the piece that broke off the day the doctor told me it'd be nothing short of a miracle for me to get pregnant again.

The emptiness of my womb hits me again as I walk toward him. He watches me, jaw ticking, body tense. "Colton ... I—"

"Rylee," he warns, "back the fuck off!"

"What if it's true? What if you guys really did and you don't remember?" It's the only coherent thought I can verbalize, my mind spinning with *what-ifs* and *never-going-to-bes*.

"*Why?*" He turns to face me, and I swallow nervously. "So you can play house?" He takes a step toward me and the look in his eyes has me cringing. "Because you want a baby so bad that you can taste it? Would do anything to have one? Take one that might or might not be mine so you can sink your hooks in me too? Get the best of both worlds, huh? A hefty sum and a baby—every woman's fucking dream." His words whip out and slap me, rip apart the part of me that knows I would do anything to have the chance to have a baby. "It's not true!" His voice thunders at me. "It's not true," he says again in too calm of a voice.

I'm stuck in place—wanting to run, wanting to stay, hurting for me, devastated for him—at a crossroads of uncertainty, and all I want to do is curl into a ball and shut the world out. Shut Colton out, and Tawny out, and the ache that will never go away, to feel a baby move within me. To create something out of love with someone I love. Bile threatens at the thought, and I cover my mouth as I gag audibly to prevent myself from puking.

"Yeah, the thought of me being a dad makes me want to puke too." He sneers at me, so much more than contempt lacing his voice. And that's not why I'm going to be sick, but I can't tell him that because I'm too busy trying not to be. "*Between the sheets.*" He belts out a patronizing laugh, looking up at the ceiling before looking back at me. "How fucking ironic is it when it's between the sheets with someone else that's causing this little dilemma, huh, Ryles? How's that phrase working for ya now?"

"Fuck you." I say it more to myself than to him, a quiet voice laced with hurt. I've had it. He can be upset. His horrible past can be dredging through his mind, but that doesn't give him the right to be a fucking asshole and take his shit out on me.

He turns to look at me, a picture of fury against the tranquility behind him. "Exactly." He spits out. "*Fuck me.*"

And with those parting words, Colton yanks open the door to the deck. I don't call out to him—don't care to—and watch him jog down the stairs to the beach with a whistle beckoning Baxter.

Chapter Nineteen

The longer I sit and wait for him to come back the more nervous I become.

And more pissed.

I'm nervous because besides his swim earlier, Colton hasn't exercised since being cleared … and he was only cleared yesterday. I know his anger will push him to run harder, faster, longer, and that only unnerves me because how much can the healing vessels in his brain withstand? It's been almost an hour since he left, how much is too much?

And I'm pissed that after everything he said to me, I even care.

I shake my head, the words he said to me rattling around as I look down the stretch of beach. I get his anger, the inherent need to lash out over his rather fragile hold on his preconceptions, but I thought we were past that. Thought that after everything we've been through in our short time together that I'd proven otherwise to him. Proven that I am not like *other women*. That I need him. That I will never manipulate him to get what I want like so many other women in his life have. That I will not abandon him. And I so desperately want to leave right now—escape the argument and further hurt I fear will happen upon his return—but I can't. More than ever I need to prove to him right now that I'm not going to run when he needs me the most, even if the thought of him having a child with someone else is killing me now.

I swallow the bile that wants to resurface again, and this time I can't hold it down. I run to the bathroom and upset the contents of my stomach. I take a moment to compose myself, talk myself down from the ledge I want to leap from because this is too much for me. So many things are happening in such a short amount of time that my mind wants to shut off.

But if it's true, what does that mean? To him as a person and us as a couple and to me as the woman who can't ever give him that? And especially given to him by *her*? My stomach revolts at the thought again, and all I can do is drop my forehead on the lid of the toilet, squeeze my eyes close, and shut out images of an adorable little boy with inky hair, emerald eyes, and a mischievous smile. A little boy I'll never be able to give him.

But she can. And if that's the case, how in the fuck am I going to be able to handle it? Love the man but not the baby that's his because I'm not the mother—simply because he's part Tawny—now what kind of horrible person would that make me? And I know that's not true, know I could never not love a child because of circumstances he has no control over, but at the same time, there would be that constant devastating reminder of what someone else can give him that I can't.

The ultimate gift.

Unconditional love and innocence.

I wipe away the tears I didn't even realize were falling when I hear the distant bark of Baxter and make my way out onto the deck. The harmless beast of a dog clears the top of the stairs coming up from the beach and plops down exhausted on the deck with a groan. I take a deep breath and prepare myself for Colton's arrival, unsure which version of him I will be facing.

Within moments he appears, hair dripping with sweat, cheeks red, and chest heaving from the exertion. I want to ask how he's feeling, where his head is, but I think better of it. I'll let him set the tone of this conversation.

He looks up and I see the shock flicker across his features when he sees me. He stands, hands propped on his hips, and just stares at me for a beat. "Why the fuck are you still here?"

So that's how this is going to be.

I thought I had calmed down, hoped that he had with his run, but obviously we're both still bound with a barbed wire ball of hurt. We're both still hell-bent on proving our points. The question is how is he going to handle what I have to say? Is he going to lash out again? Rip me apart for a second time? Or is he going to realize that despite Tawny's bombshell, our figurative race doesn't stop? That we can withstand the collateral damage?

"You don't get to run anymore, Colton." I hope my words—words he'd used with me before—will hit their target and sink in.

He stops mid-stride beside my chair but keeps his head angled down to avoid looking at me. "You don't fucking own me, Ry. You don't get to tell me what I can or can't do any more than Tawny can." His voice is a whisper but his words sucker punch me.

"Non-negotiable, *remember?*" I warn him with challenge I don't feel reflected in my eyes. He just stands there impatiently, muscles tense, and I feel compelled to continue. To either stop or start the fight brewing between us. "You're right." I shake my head. "I don't own you … nor do I want to. But when you're in a relationship, you don't get to hurt someone because you're hurting and then bail. There are consequences, there are—"

"I told you, Rylee …" He turns to face me now, his eyes still averted, but the tone of his voice—one of pure disgust—has me rising to my feet. "I do as I damn well please. It's best you *remember* that."

"Colton …" It's all I can manage, feeling like I've been knocked back a few steps by his sudden assertion, his sudden need to grab his life that he feels is spiraling out of control. But he doesn't get it. It's not just *his* life anymore. It's my life too! This is about the man I love and the possibilities I feel. This is killing me just as much as it is him, but he's too wrapped up in his own head to see differently. I force a swallow as I try to find the words to tell him this, to show him we're both hurting, not just him. But I'm too slow. He beats me to the punch.

"You tell me we're in a relationship, Rylee … Are you sure it's what you want because this is how my life goes," he shouts, his body moving restlessly with all of his negative energy. "The *charmed* life of Colton fuckin' Donavan. For every up there's a motherfucking free fall down. For every good there's a goddamn bad." He takes a step toward me, trying to antagonize me and push my buttons. I dig my nails in my palms to remind myself to let him get it off of his chest. To let him blame everyone in the world if need be, so he can calm down, realize this is not the end of his world, despite it feeling like it is for me. "Are you ready for that kind of *spin* on the track of my life?" He finishes, the sarcasm dripping from his words as he steps within a few feet of me. I can feel the anger vibrate off of him, can sense his desperation at which straw to grab and hold onto to get me to react. I force a swallow and shake my head.

"Okay," I say, drawing the word out, buying time as I try to think of what to say. "What is the good and the bad then?"

"The good?" he asks, his eyes widening as sweat drips down his torso. "The good is I'm alive, Rylee. I'm fucking alive!" He shouts, thumping his chest with his fist. I cringe as his voice rings in my ears. He mistakes my reaction and feeds off of it. "What? Did you think I was actually going to say *you?*" I tell myself not to cry, tell myself that's not the answer I was hoping for, but who am I kidding? Did I really think that in the midst of all of this he'd hold onto me as his strength? His reason? I can hope, but for a man so used to relying on himself, I shouldn't be surprised.

"You think you can waltz in here and play house, nurse me back to health, and all my troubles—all my fucking demons—are going to disappear? I guess Tawny just proved that theory wrong, huh?" He laughs a patronizing chuckle that eats tiny holes in what resolve I still have left. "The perfect fucking world you think exists, sure as fuck doesn't. You can't make lemonade with a lemon that's rotting from the inside out."

And I'm not sure which hurts more, the acid eating at my stomach, his anger hitting my ears, or the ache squeezing my heart. The aftershock left by Tawny turns into a full-blown earthquake of disbelief and pain as my thoughts spin out of control and slam headfirst into the wall just like Colton did. But this time the collateral damage is too much to handle as it all comes crashing down around me. My stomach heaves again as I try to grasp on to something, anything, to give me an iota of hope.

I need air.

I can't breathe.

I need to get away from all of this.

I take a few steps backwards, needing to escape, and stumble against the railing. I fight the need to throw up again, my hands squeezing the wood beneath my fingers as I try to steady myself.

"You don't get to run anymore, Rylee, *we're in a relationship*. Aren't those your rules?" His mocking voice is closer than I expect and something about the way he says them, the intimacy laced with sarcasm, sets me off.

I whirl around. "I'm not running, Colton! I'm hurting! Fucking falling apart because I don't know what to say or how to respond to you!" I scream. "I'm fucking pissed that I'm angry at you for being so goddamn callous because *you're right*! I would give anything to have a baby. *Anything*! But I can't and the thought that someone can give you the one fucking thing that I can't is tearing me apart."

I bring my hands up to my head and just hold them there for a moment as I try to stop crying, as I try to collect the thoughts I need to say. I lift my head and meet his eyes again. "But you know what? Even if I could, I would never use or manipulate you to get one. I am not fucking Tawny, and I am not the poor excuse of life your mother was." Tears stream down my face and I look at him, standing there stunned by my outburst through my blurred vision.

He starts to say something, and I raise a hand to stop him, needing to finish what I have to say. "No, Colton, I'm not running and I'm not leaving you, but I don't know what to do. *I have no fucking clue*! Do I stay here and let you rip me apart more? I'm dying inside, Colton. Can't you see that?" I wipe the tears from my eyes and shake my head, needing some kind of reaction from him. "Or do I just leave? Give us a couple of days to fix the shit that's fucked up in our own heads? So I don't resent you for getting a choice when I don't. So you realize I'm not like every other woman who's ever used you."

I take a step toward him, the man I love, and I wish I could do something—anything—to ease the turmoil inside of him, but know that I can't. I can sense he's at a breaking point just like I am, that being faced with the possibility of a child is more than even he—a man who has survived so much—can bear, but I'm at a loss how to help when I'm filled with turmoil too.

The muscle in his jaw pulses as I watch him struggle to remain in control over his emotions, his anger, his need for release and wish I could do something more for him because if my heart is breaking, then I can't imagine what his is doing. And the only thing I think I can do is give us some space ... let us calm down ... figure ourselves out so we can be good again.

Find us again.

I take another step toward him and he finally raises his eyes to meet mine so I can read what he's feeling. And maybe it's the fact that we really know each other now, have broken down each other's walls, because regardless of how hard he's trying to mask his emotions I can read every single one of them flickering through his eyes. Fear, anger, confusion, shame, concern, uncertainty. The truth is there—what I knew would be—he's pushing me, daring me to run to prove to him I am in fact what he perceives all other women to be. And at the same time, I see remorse swimming there, and a small part of me sighs at the sight, gives me something to hold on to.

He takes a step toward me so we stand close but don't touch. I can see the emotion flickering across his face, how his muscles tense as he tries to contain everything I see in his eyes. I fear if I touch him, we'll both break and right now one of us needs to be strong.

It has to be me.

"Look at me, Colton," I tell him, waiting for his eyes to find mine again. "It's me, the one who races you. The one who'll fight tooth and nail for you. The one who will do anything—anything—to make that hurt in your eyes and the pain in your soul disappear ... make Tawny's accusation go away ... *but I can't*. I can't be anything to you until you stop pushing me away." I step closer, wanting to reach out and touch him and erase the pain in his eyes. "*Because all I want to do is help*. I can handle you being an asshole. I can handle you taking your shit out on me ... but it's not going to fix things. It's not going to make Tawny or the baby or anything else go away." I choke on the tears that fill my throat. "I just don't know what to do."

"*Rylee* ..." It's the first time he's spoken and the desperation in the way he says my name with such anguish sends chills up my spine. "My head's pretty fucked up right now." I force a swallow down my throat and nod my head so he knows I hear him. He closes his eyes for a beat and sighs aloud. "Look I—I ... I need some time to get it straight ... so I don't push you farther away ... I just ..."

I bite my lower lip, not sure if I'm upset that he's telling me to go or relieved, and nod my head. He reaches out to touch me and I step back, afraid if he does, I won't be able to walk away. "Okay," I tell him, my voice barely audible as I take a step backwards. "I'll talk to you in a couple of days."

And I can't look at him again, both our pain right now is so palpable for different reasons, so I turn and head toward the house.

"Rylee," he says my name again—no one can say it like he does—and my body stops instantly. I know he feels like I do—uncertain, unresolved, wanting me to stay and wanting me to go—so I just keep my back to him and nod my head.

"*I know*." *I know* he's sorry—for hurting me, for loving me and that I'm being put through this, for Tawny, for the uncertainty, for my own insecurities when it comes to what I can't give him ... so many things I know he's sorry for ... and the biggest one is that he's sorry for letting me walk away right now because he can't find it in him to ask me to stay.

Chapter Twenty

"I'm so proud of you, buddy." I look into Zander's eyes and fight my own tears. I want him to see the depth of feelings I have for him and for what he just did. For giving the district attorney all they needed to press formal charges against a man that's disappeared like the wind. To sit at a table full of scary grown-ups and explain, in a voice you just found again, how your father murdered your mother—how he attacked her from behind, stabbed her repeatedly and then waited for her to die while you hid behind the couch because you were supposed to be in bed. Now that, is a courageous kid. I squeeze him tight in my arms, more for me than for him, and wish I could take away the memory from him.

"How'd you get so brave?" I ask him.

I don't expect an answer, but when he responds it stops me in my tracks.

"The superheroes helped me," he says with a shrug. I force a swallow down my throat burning with so much emotion I can't speak. I look into the eyes of a little boy that I love with all my heart, and I can't help but see pieces of the grown man who owns it too. My heart twists for both, and even though I am filled with such an incredible sense of pride, it's tinged with a bit of sadness because I know Colton would want to know what Zander did today. The imaginary barriers he vaulted over that most adults could never fathom.

But I can't tell him.

It's been four days since I left his house.

Four days without speaking.

Four days for him, for us to get our individual shit together.

And four days of absolute chaos for me in more ways than one: The House, my emotions, the media frenzy over a possible baby, missing Colton.

I tell Zander I'll put his beloved stuffed dog in his bedroom and tell him to go play tag with the rest of the boys. Go be a kid, play, laugh, and forget the images that haunt him—if that's even possible.

I go through the motions of getting dinner together, while the familiar and comforting sounds of the boys outside help me cope.

I miss Colton. We've been together every day for over a month and I'm used to his presence, his smile, the sound of his voice. I'm hurt he hasn't called but at the same time I don't expect him to. Other than texting to make sure I'd gotten home okay and the song *I Am Human,* I haven't heard from him. He has a lot to figure out, a lot to come to terms with. And *God yes,* I want to be there by his side, helping him figure it all out, but it's not my situation to figure out. Plain and simple.

I can't count how many times I've picked up the phone to call him—to hear his voice, to see how he's doing, to just say hi—but I can't. I know better than anyone that until Colton lets me back in to his barricaded heart, a call won't do any good.

I frost the cake I'd made earlier as a little reward for Zander's bravery today, when my phone rings. I look over at the screen and push ignore. It's an unknown number and most likely a journalist wanting to pay me handsomely for my side of Tawny's story. She's told the press that I am the mistress who broke up her, the pregnant victim, and the love of her life … Colton.

The only blessing is that the paparazzi have not discovered The House yet. But I know it's not long until they do, and I'm still trying to figure out *what do I do then?*

And for some reason, the story Tawny's painted makes me laugh. I don't believe the inside scoop on Page Six that says she and Colton have rekindled their love affair. I was in Colton's house. I know how much he despises her and everything she represents. That's not why I'm sad.

I just miss him. Everything about *him.*

The funny thing is, this time around, I'm not worried he's going to turn to another. We've passed that hurdle and quite frankly adding another woman to the mix would just complicate his life further. No, it's not him turning to another woman I worry about, it's him not turning to me.

Voices break through my thoughts as I cut the potatoes up for dinner. I catch Connor saying, "The douche bag's here again."

"We could always egg him." That one was Shane.

What in the heck are they talking about?

"Hey, guys?" I call out to them as I wipe my hands off and head out to the living room. "Who's here again?"

Shane tilts his head toward our front window. "That guy," he says, pointing. "He thinks he's so incognito parked over there."

"Like we can't see him," Connor interjects. "And don't know he's a *photographer*. Camera's a dead giveaway, dude."

I'm immediately pulling the curtains back, looking down the street. Before I even spot the car, I know what I'm going to see. The dark blue sedan is parked a couple of houses down partially hidden by another car. I had completely forgotten about it.

At least this lone paparazzo is greedy and keeping my whereabouts quiet so he can get all the monetary gain for himself. For that I can be grateful. But it also means that if he's figured it out, others will soon follow wanting to get the scoop from the home-wrecker I am purported to be.

Fuck! I knew The House's anonymity was too good to be true.

"C'mon guys. Time to—"

"That's so cool that you're gonna be famous!" Connor says as he starts walking down the hall.

I start to correct him when Shane does it for me, with a playful shove to his shoulder. "No she's not, dickweed! Colton's the one who's famous. Don't you know anything?"

"Hey! Clean it up!" I shout after them.

"Thanks for picking me up."

"Not a problem," Haddie says as she guns the motor when the light turns green. "It was kind of fun teasing the photographers, although I don't think any of them believed me when I said you were hiding away inside the house."

I groan. It's taken a while to get used to photographers milling about the house, but now I fear that the few I'm used to will turn into a whole yard full. "Dare I ask?"

Haddie looks over at me and just flashes her devil-may-care grin. "Nope, you may not because we're not thinking about it … or Colton … or me … absofuckinglutely nothing of any significance."

"We're not?" I look over at her and can't help but smile, can't help but be happy she was available to pick me up from work to try and keep the vultures at bay.

"Nope!" she says as the tires squeal on a turn. "We're gonna find a dark corner and drown our sorrows, and then we're going to find a wicked hot beat to dance to until we can't remember shit!"

I laugh with her, the idea sounding like Heaven. A moment to escape from the thoughts constantly running through my head and the heaviness in my heart. "What's going on with you? What sorrows are you drowning?" And for a minute I'm sad we've been so busy over the past few weeks that I don't know the answer to the question, when before I would never have had to ask.

She shrugs and is unusually quiet for a beat before she speaks. "Just some stuff with Lexy." I'm about to ask what she's talking about, because she and her sister are so close, but she beats me to the punch. "We're not talking about anything that needs to be talked about, remember?"

"Sounds good!" I tell her as music springs to life in the car and we both start singing along.

I set my glass down with a clink, realizing my lips are a little bit numb. No, make that a *lot* numb. I watch Haddie smirk at the man across the bar and then turn her focus back on me, her smirk spreading into a full out grin. "He looks kinda like Stone," she says with a shrug, and I'm glad my drink is empty or else I would have spit it out.

I don't know why it's so funny, because it really isn't, but my head starts playing connect the dots with memories. Stone makes me think of Ace and Ace makes me think of Colton and the thought of Colton just makes me *want* … him. Everything about him.

"Uh-uh-uh," Haddie says realizing what I'm thinking about. "Another round," she says to the bartender. "Don't think about him. You promised, Ry. No boys. No sadness. No penis perturbance allowed."

"You're right," I tell her with a laugh, hoping she believes me even though I know I'm not being very convincing. "No penis perturbance allowed." The waiter slides new glasses in front of us. "Thank you," I murmur as I concentrate on stirring the ice with my straw instead of thinking of Colton and wondering what he's doing, where his head is at. And I fail miserably. "I told him about Stone the other day."

I'm surprised Haddie can hear me. My voice is so soft, but I know she does because she slaps her hand on the bar. "I knew you couldn't do it!" she shouts, garnering the attention of the people around us. "I knew that no matter how much you've had to drink we'd end up there."

"I'm sorry," I tell her, twisting my lips. "I really am." I focus back on my drink, upset over letting my friend down.

"Hey," she says, rubbing a hand up my arm. "I can't imagine … I'm sorry … I was just trying to shake the dick dominance and embrace our inner slut for a bit." I arch an eyebrow at her smirk and just shake my head.

"Inner slut embraced," I say, resting my head on her shoulder but not really feeling like it.

"So have you talked to him?" She asks.

"I thought we weren't talking about dick dominating, penis perturbing men named Colton or *Stone*." I snicker.

"Well," she draws the word out. "Yours is damn hard not to talk about when he looks like that with his sexy swagger, come-fuck-me eyes, and all around holy hotness. Shit, the only reason to kick a man like him out of bed would be to fuck him on the floor."

I start laughing, really laughing until all of a sudden the laughter has tears welling in my eyes and causes my lower lip to tremble. I hiccup back the sob and I immediately curse the alcohol—it has to be the alcohol's fault—that I am suddenly sad and missing him like crazy.

Get a grip, Thomas! It's been one frickin' week. Man up. My internal pep talk fails because one day or ten days, it doesn't matter. I miss him like crazy. Whatever the opposite of pussy whipped is, I've got it bad.

"And she finally lets it out," Haddie says, putting her arm around my shoulders and pulling me into her side.

"Shut up!" I tell her but don't mean it.

I mean I'm sitting in a bar on a Friday night with my best friend and I should be having a great time, but all I can think about is Colton. Is he okay? Has he taken the paternity test yet? Is he going to call me? Why hasn't he called me? Is he thinking about me like I am him?

"So I'm gonna throw this out there because we both know that even though we're sitting here together, Colton is figuratively between us. And as much as the idea might excite him …"

I finally give her the laugh she's been working for. "Ugh! I hate this."

"Then why don't you call him?"

And therein lies the million dollar question.

"This whole thing with Tawny fucked him up. It's dredging up shit from his past and as much as I want to be there—to call him—I won't take the brunt of it. I called Becks to check on him, make sure he's okay." I shrug. "He said he did and that Colton's still kind of fucked up. I want to talk to him," I admit as she smooths a hand up my arm, "but I need to give him the space he asked for. He'll call me when he gets his shit together."

"Hmm, I wonder where I've heard that phrase before?" she teases and I just shrug.

"A very wise woman said it, I believe."

"Very wise indeed," she laughs, rolling her eyes and clinking her glass to mine. "And being as I am *that* woman, may I offer you another tidbit of advice?"

"A Haddie-ism?"

"Yes, a Haddie-ism. I like that term." She nods her head in approval as she takes another sip of her drink and smiles again at the guy across the bar. "I asked you once before if you thought Colton was worth it … and now that you have more time invested in it, do you still feel that way? Do you see the possibility of a future with him?"

"I love him, Had." The answer is off of my tongue in a split second. No hesitation, no doubt, complete conviction.

She stares at me a second and I can tell that beneath the surface she is gauging my reaction, trying to figure out the whole picture and a little surprised at my *all in* response. "Do you love him because he's the first guy since Max or because he's the one you choose? Not because you want to fix him, because we both know you like the damaged souls, but because you choose *the him* he is now and *the him* he'll be five years from now?"

I don't answer her, not because I don't know the answer, but because I can't form the words over the lump that's strangling them in my throat. And she can see my answer, knows the person I am enough to know how I feel.

"And if the baby is his?"

I find my voice. "Geez … you're really hitting with the hard questions tonight. I thought tonight was supposed to be thinking about absofuckinglutely nothing? I thought there was a Haddie-ism in here somewhere?" And it's not like I haven't asked myself these questions, but hearing her say them makes it all seem so real.

Because sometimes baggage can be a powerful thing and love just isn't enough to overcome it.

"I'm getting there," she says, pushing my drink toward me. "But this is important because my bestie is hurting so take a drink and answer the question."

I take a sip and can't fight my resigned smile. "It's not if the baby's his that's the problem … it's his reaction that scares me." And for the first time, I'm actually admitting aloud what I fear the most. "What if he is the father and he can't handle it? How can I love a man that can't love his own child regardless of who the mother is? Writing a check to buy her off and acting as if a child doesn't exist? What if that's the option he chooses? How could I spend the night in the bed of a man who writes his own child off and then go to work in a houseful of boys who had the very same thing happened to them? What kind of hypocrite would that make me?"

And there. *It's out there.* My biggest fear, I'm in love with a man that will walk away from his own child. That I'll have to walk away from the man I love because he can't face his own demons, can't accept the fact that he can be the man his child would need him to be. Compromising choices, preferences, and wants to be in a relationship are one thing, compromising who you are—the things ingrained in you, your beliefs, and your morals—are non-negotiable.

I sigh and just shake my head. "What happens then, Haddie? What if that's the choice he makes?"

"Well..." she reaches out and squeezes my hand "...there are no answers yet so it's a moot point right now. Secondly, you have to give him the benefit of the doubt … he was shocked, upset, pissed off the other day when she blindsided him … but he's a good person. Look how he is with the boys."

"I know, but you weren't there. You didn't see how he reacted when—"

"You know what I say?" she says, cutting me off and raising the two shots of tequila that have been sitting untouched on the bar in front of us. I look at her, trying to figure out why all of a sudden she wants to toast mid-heart to heart talk, but I raise my shot glass. "I say, never look down on a man unless he's between your legs."

I choke on the simple breath of air I'm drawing in. I should be used to her by now, I really should, but she continually surprises me and makes me love her that much more. When I stop laughing I look up at her. "One for luck …"

"And one for courage," she finishes as we toss the alcohol back.

I welcome the burn, welcome the here and now with my best friend, and when I wrap my head around what the hell she's just said, I look over at her out of the corner of my eye. "Unless he's between your legs, huh? Is that an old family adage? One passed down from generation to generation?"

"Yep," she says, twisting her lips, fighting the smile I know that's coming. "Never disturb a man when he's eating at the Y."

"Haddie," I laugh. "Seriously?"

"I can keep going all night long, sister!" She clinks her glass with mine again, my cheeks hurting from smiling so hard. "And here's another one. When your best friend is sad? It's your job to get her shit-faced and go dancing."

"Well," I say, sliding off of the barstool and taking a minute to let the room stop spinning, "I think that's a fucking perfect idea!"

Haddie squares up our tab and calls for a cab as we clumsily walk to the front door. And I talk myself out of making her take me to Colton's house because right now, I just really want Colton—in the best way, in the worst way—in all ways.

"C'mon, we're good to go. Three hours in a bar is way too long," she says as she puts her arm around me and helps me walk respectably to the exit.

And as we clear the bar's door, the darkened night sky explodes into an electrifying barrage of blinding camera flashes and shouts.

"How does it feel being known as the home wrecker?"

"Don't you have any remorse coming between Colton and Tawny?"

"Isn't it hypocritical that you tried to make Colton abandon his baby when that's what you do for a living?"

And they keep coming at me. One after another after another. I feel trapped as Haddie tries to guide me through the congestion of cameras and microphones and flashes and contempt.

I guess the press has found me.

Chapter Twenty-One

Colton

"You're fucking kidding me, right?" I fight the urge to smash something. That urge driving my every emotion, the one that makes me crave the sound of destruction. The sound of my fucking life imploding.

My mind pushes out the images flashing through it from the past couple of days.

Blood draws and DNA markers and goddamn paternity tests.

Tawny and her bullshit lies and crocodile tears the fucking vultures are eating up like fresh meat.

Visiting with Jack and Jim and getting so sick of looking at my life through the bottom of an empty glass, I just choose to drink straight from the goddamn bottle.

And then there is Rylee.

Motherfucking Rylee.

Little pieces of her everywhere. Sheets that still smell like her. A ponytail holder on the bathroom counter. The cans of her beloved Diet Coke lined perfectly in the refrigerator. Her Kindle on the nightstand. The strands of her hair on my shirt. Evidence that her perfection exists. Evidence that something so good—so pure—actually can want someone like me—tainted and fucked up with a capital F.

I want, need, hate that I want, hate that I need her so damn bad, but I can't do it. I can't pull her into this rainstorm of bullshit surrounding me, don't want her to deal with the fucked up me that even I hate until I can wrap my head around everything. Until I can control the emotions that are ruling my actions.

Until I get a negative on the DNA match.

My mom was fucking right. Fucking right and she only knew me for eight of my thirty two years … if that doesn't say something, I'm not sure what else does. I can't be loved. If someone loves me—if I let someone in too much—my own demons will start in on them too. Work their way through the cracks in me and find a way to ruin them.

"Colton, are you there?"

I pull myself from my thoughts—the same goddamn ones that have been running like a hamster on the wheel through the shit in my head over the past week. "Yeah," I reply to my publicist. "I'm here, Chase." I push the rags on the table in front of me away, but it doesn't matter if I throw them in the trash or set a match to the fuckers because the image of Rylee coming out of that bar is still burned in my brain. Shocked eyes, parted lips, and an all-around look of being overwhelmed from the maelstrom that hit her when she left.

And it fucking kills me! Rips me apart that my bullshit—being with me—caused that look on her face. The fear in her eyes. All I want to do is be the one with her, my arm around her, but I'm not. I can't because I don't have the words or actions to make it better. To make it go away. To protect her.

"This is fucking bullshit and you know it."

I hear my publicist sigh on the other end of the line. She knows I'm pissed, knows no matter what she says I'm not going to be happy unless she tells me to find the bastards that are harassing Ry, and let loose my need to destroy. "Colton, in light of Tawny's accusations, it's best that you do nothing. If you react, your public image—"

"I don't give two fucks about my public image!"

"Oh believe me, I know," she sighs. "But if you react the press eats it up and then the longer they hang around to see you screw up or lose it. That means the longer they hang around Rylee …"

Fuck all if she's not right. But shit, what I wouldn't give to walk outside the gates and give them my two cents worth. "One of these days, Chase," I tell her.

"I know, I know."

I toss my phone on the couch across from me and scrub my hands over my face, before sinking back in the couch and closing my eyes. What the hell am I going to do? And since when do I give a shit?

What the hell happened to me? I went from not giving a fuck about anything or anyone to missing Rylee and wanting to see the boys. Strings and shit. *Fuck me.*

A voice thanking my housekeeper, Grace, brings me back to the present from the unicorns and rainbow shit that doesn't belong in my thoughts. Crap that's associated with pussies and whipped assholes. Shit that has no place in my head mixed with the other poison living there.

I wait a second. I know he's there, watching me, trying to figure out my current state of mind, but doesn't say anything. I crack open an eye and see him leaning against the doorjamb, arms folded across his chest and concern filling his eyes.

"You just gonna stand there and watch me or are you going to come in and pass judgment on me face-to-face?"

He stares at me a beat more and I swear to God I hate this feeling. I hate knowing that along with every other fucking person on the long and distinguished list, I am letting him down too. "No judgment, son," he says as he makes his way into the room and sits on the couch across from me.

I can't bring my eyes to meet his and thank Christ for Grace or this place would be a disaster, and he'd really know how much this whole Tawny situation has screwed me up. I draw in a deep breath wishing I had a beer right now. Might as well get this party started, right? "Lay it on me, Dad, because I sure as shit know you're not here to just say hi."

He sits silent for a bit longer and I can't fucking stand it. I finally look at him. He meets my gaze, gray eyes contemplating what to say as he twists his lips in thought. "Well, I can honestly say I stopped by to see how you were doing in the midst of all of this," he says, waving his hand in the air with indifference, "but it's pretty obvious since you're in such a shitty mood." He leans back in the chair and props his feet up on the coffee table and just stares. *Shit, he's making himself comfortable.* "You gonna talk, son, or are we going to sit and stare at each other all night? Because I've got all the time in the world." He looks at his watch and then back up to me.

I don't want to talk about this shit. I don't want to talk about babies and gold digging women and little boys I miss and a woman I can't stop thinking about. "Fuck, I don't know."

"You're gonna have to give me more than that, Colton."

"Like what? That I fucked up? Is that what you want to hear?" I goad him to react. And it feels good to push someone for a change. Everyone else has been walking around me, treating me with kid gloves this past week afraid of my temper snapping, so it feels good even if I'm going to feel like shit later for doing it to my dad. "You want me to tell you I fucked Tawny and now I'm getting what I deserve because I dumped her like a hot coal and now she's coming after me saying she's pregnant? That I don't want a kid—*will not have a kid*—with her or anyone else? *Ever*. Because I refuse to let someone use a child as a pawn to get what they want from me. Because how the hell can someone like me be a father to a kid when I'm just as fucked up now as I was when you found me?"

I shove up off of the couch and start pacing the room. I'm annoyed with him that he hasn't taken the bait—hasn't pushed back and given me the fight I'm itching for—and is just sitting there with that look of complete acceptance and understanding. Pacification. I want him to tell me he hates me, that he's disappointed in me, that I deserve all that I'm getting right now because that is so much fucking easier for me to hold on to and believe than the opposite.

"And what does Rylee think of all of this?"

I stop and turn to look at him. *What?* I didn't expect that to come out of his mouth. "What do you mean?"

"I asked, what does Rylee think about all of this?" He leans forward, elbows on his knees, eyes questioning me beneath arched brows.

"Hell if I know." I grunt and my dad shakes his head. *God, I hate having to explain myself.* But it's my dad. My end game superhero, how can I not? "She was here when Tawny dropped the bomb. We got in a fight because I was taking everything out on her, being an inconsiderate ass. Bitching about a baby I don't want when she can't have one. I was in stellar form," I tell him with a roll of my eyes. "We agreed to a few days apart to get our heads straight again. Get my shit together."

"And you haven't talked to her since?"

"What is this, Dad? Twenty fucking questions? Does it look like I have my shit figured out yet?" I snort out a derisive laugh. One step forward and then fucking twenty steps backwards. "Is Tawny still pregnant? Have the test results come back yet? Yes, and a *big fucking no* ... So no, I haven't called her back yet. Chalk it up to just another thing for you to hold against me."

He just stares at me. "Is that what I'm doing? Holding your shit against you? Because it looks like you're doing a damn fine job of it yourself, son. So let me ask you the question you should be asking yourself: Why haven't you pulled your head out of your ass and called her?"

I blow out a loud breath. Fuckin' A. "I don't want to go there right now, Dad." *Just go away.* Let me down the next bottle of Jack while the clock ticks for the doctors to take their sweet ass time to decide if I've just fucked up the life of an unborn child. Because if the kid's mine, shit, he's already starting off with a tainted soul and that—that's something I can't have on my conscience."

"Well I do want to go there, so pull up a chair to your own pity party, Colton, because I'm not leaving until we finish talking. Understood?"

My mouth falls open, and I'm transported back to fifteen years ago and my one night in custody for drag racing. To that moment in time when he picked me up, raked me over the proverbial motherfucking coals, and told me how it was going to be from there on out. Damn. I've got chest hair and houses and shit now, but he can still make me feel like a teenager.

Anger flashes through me. I don't need a fucking shrink right now, I need a negative blood test. And Rylee wrapped around me with a soft sigh falling from her lips as I sink into her. The ultimate pleasure to bury all of this bullshit pain.

"So," he says, pulling me back to him instead of thoughts of her. "You're seriously going to let her go without a fight? Let her walk out of your life because of *Tawny?*"

"She's not walking away!" I shout at him, upset that he would even think she would. *Would she?*

He just quirks an eyebrow. "Exactly." My eyes snap up to meet his. "So quit treating her like she did. She's not your mother."

I want to scream at him that I sure as shit know she's not. To not even put her in the same sentence as my mother, but instead I play with the seam on the couch as I search for the answer I think he wants to hear. That I'm trying to convince myself is the truth. "She doesn't deserve this … the shit that comes with me. My past … now my possible fucking future."

He makes a hum in his throat, and I hate it because I can't figure out what it means. "Isn't that up to her to decide, Colton? I mean you're making decisions for her … shouldn't she get a say?"

Shut up, I want to tell him. Don't remind me what she deserves because I already know. I already fucking know! And I know because I *can't give it to her.* I thought I could … thought I might be able to and now with this, I know I can't. It's reinforced all of the things *she* said … all of the things I'll never be able to cleanse from my damned soul.

"You say she's not going to leave you when things get tough, son, but your actions are telling me something completely different. And yet you didn't see her fighting for you every damn day you lay in that hospital bed. Every damn day. Never leaving. So that leads me to believe this little dilemma you have here isn't about her at all."

Every part of me revolts against the words he says. The words that said by anyone else would have me ready to rage, but respect has me holding back from yelling at the man who's words are hitting a little too close to home.

"It's about you." The quiet resolve in his voice floats out in the room and slaps me in the face. Taunts me to take the bait, and I can't hold back anymore.

And I don't want to do *this* any more than I want to spend another night without Rylee in my bed. Looking too close causes dead ghosts to float to the goddamn surface, and I don't have any more room for ghosts because my closet's already full of fucking skeletons.

But the match is lit, gasoline thrown. Fire inside fucking ignited and all of the frustration and uncertainty and loneliness from the past week comes to a head, explodes inside of me. I wear a hole in the goddamn floor pacing as I try to fight it, try to rein it in, but it's no use.

"Look at me, Dad!" I shout at him while he perches on the couch. I hold my hands out to my side, and I hate myself for the break in my voice, hate myself for the unanticipated show of weakness. "Look what *she* did to me!" And I don't have to explain who *she* is because the contempt dripping from my voice explains enough.

I stand there arms out, blood pumping, temper raging, and he just sits there, calm as can fucking be and smirks—fucking smirks—at me. "*I am, son.* I look at you every day and think what an incredible person you are."

His words knock the wind out of my sails. I yell at him and he comes back at me with *that?* What kind of game is he playing? Fuck up Colton's head more than normal? Shit, I hear the words but don't let them sink in. They're not true. Can't be. Incredible and damaged don't go together.

Incredible can't be used to describe a person who tells the man molesting him that you love him, whether the words are forced or not.

"That's not fucking possible," I mutter into the silence of the room as vile memories revive my anger, isolate my soul. I can't even meet his eyes because he might see just how messed up I really am. "That's not possible," I repeat to myself, more emphatically this time. "You're my dad. You have to say that."

"No, I don't. And technically, I'm not your dad, so I don't have to say anything." Now that stops me dead in my tracks … brings me back to being a scared kid afraid to be sent back. He's never said anything like this to me before, and now I'm fucking freaked out about the direction this conversation has taken. He stands and walks toward me, eyes locked on mine. "You're wrong. I didn't have to stop and sit with you on the doorstep. I didn't have to take you to the hospital, adopt you, love you ..." he continues feeding into every childhood insecurity I've ever had. I force myself to swallow. Make myself keep my eyes locked on his because all of a sudden I'm scared shitless to hear what he has to say. The truths he's going to admit. "... but you know what, Colton? Even at eight years old, scared and starving, *I knew*—I knew right then the amazing person you were, that you were this incredible human being I couldn't resist. Don't you walk away from me!" His voice thunders and shocks the hell out of me. From calm and reassuring to angry in an instant.

I stop in my tracks, my need to escape this conversation that's causing so much shit to churn and revolt within me begging me to keep walking right on out the door to the beach below. But I don't. I can't. I've walked away from every fucking thing in my life, but I can't walk away from the one person who didn't walk away from me. My head hangs, my fists clench in anticipation of the words he's going to say.

"I've waited almost twenty years to have this conversation with you, Colton." His voice is calmer now, steadier, and it freaks me out more than when he rages. "I know you want to run away, walk out the fucking door and escape to your beloved beach, but you're not going to. I'm not letting you take the chickenshit way out."

"Chickenshit?" I bellow, turning around to face him with years of pent up rage. Years of wondering what he really thinks of me coming to a head. "You call what I went through the chickenshit way out?" And the smirk on his face is back, and even though I know he's just goading me, trying to provoke me so I take the bait and get it all out, I still take it. "How dare you stand there and act like even though you took me in, it was easy for me. That *life* was easy for me!" I shout, my body vibrating with the anger taking hold, the resentment imploding. "How can you tell me I'm this incredible person when for twenty four years you've told me a million goddamn times that you love me—*LOVE ME*—and not once have I *ever* said it back to you. Not fucking once! And you're telling me you're okay with that? How can I not think I'm fucked up when you've given me everything and I've given you absolutely nothing in return? I can't even give you three goddamn words!" When the last words leave my lips I come back to myself and realize I'm inches from my dad, my body shaking with the anger that's eaten me whole for a lifetime as tiny flecks of it are being chipped away from my hardened fucking heart.

I take a step back and in a flash, he's right back in my face. "Nothing? Nothing, Colton?" His voice shouts out into the room. "You gave me *everything*, son. Hope and pride and the goddamn unexpected. You taught me that fear is okay. That sometimes you have to let those you love chase the fucking wind on a whim because it's the only way they can free themselves from the nightmares within. It was you, Colton, who taught me what it was to be a man ... because it's easy to be a man when the world's handed to you on a silver platter, but when you're handed the shit sandwich you were dealt, and then you turn into the man you are before me? Now that, son, that's the definition of being a man."

No, no, no, I want to scream at him to try and drown out the sounds I can't believe. I try to cover my ears like a little kid because it's too much. All of it—the words, the fear, the fucking hope that I just might in fact be a little bent and not completely broken—is just too much. But he's not having any of it, and it takes every ounce of control I have to not take a swing at him as he pulls my hands from my ears.

"Uh-uh." He grunts with the effort it takes. "I'm not leaving until I've said what I came to say—what I've pussyfooted around saying to you for way too long—and now I realize how wrong I was as a parent not to force you to hear this sooner. So the more you fight me, the longer this is going to take so I suggest you let me finish, son, 'cause like I said before, I've got all the time in the world."

I just stare at him, lost in two warring bodies: a little boy desperately begging for approval and a grown man unable to believe it once he's been given it. "But it's not poss—"

"No buts, son. None," he says, turning me around so he's not touching me from behind knowing I can't handle that still all these years later, so he can look into my eyes ... so I can't hide from the absolute honesty in his. "Not a single day since I met you have I ever regretted my choice to choose you. Not when you rebelled or fought me or drag raced down the street or stole change off of the counter ..."

My body jolts from the comment—the little boy in me devastated I've been caught—even though he's not angry.

"... Did you think I didn't know about the jar of change and box of food you hid beneath your bed ... the stash you kept in case you thought we were going to not want you anymore and kick you out on the streets? You didn't notice all the change I suddenly left everywhere? I left it out on purpose because I didn't regret a single moment. Not when you pushed every limit and broke every rule possible, because the adrenaline of the defiance was so much easier to feel than the shit she let them do to you."

My breath stops at his words. My fucking world spins black and acid erupts like lava in my stomach. Reality spirals at the thought that my biggest fear has come true ... *he knows*. The horrors, my weakness, the vile things, the professed love, the stains on my spirit.

I can't bring my eyes to meet his, can't push the shame far enough down to speak. I feel his hand on my shoulder as I try to revert back to focusing on the numbing blur of my past and escape the memories tattooed in my mind—on my fucking body—but I can't. Rylee has made me feel—broken that goddamn barrier—and now I can't help but do anything but.

"And while we're clearing the air," he says, his voice taking on a much softer tone, his hand squeezing my shoulder. "*I know, Colton*. I'm your dad, I know."

The fucking floor drops out beneath me, and I try to pull my shoulder out of his grip but he doesn't let me, won't let me turn my back on him to hide the tears burning my eyes like ice picks. Tears that reinforce the fact that I'm a pussy who hasn't handled anything at all.

And as much as I want him to shut the hell up ... to leave me the fuck alone ... he continues "You don't need to say a word to me. You don't need to cross that imaginary line in your head that makes you fear an admission will make everyone leave you, will prove you to be less of a man, will make you the pawn she wanted you to be ..."

He pauses and it takes every ounce of everything inside of me to try and meet his eyes. And I do for a split second before the door to the patio, the sand beneath my feet, and the burn of oxygen in my lungs as my feet pound down the beach calls to me like heroin to an addict. Escape. Run. Flee. But I'm fucking frozen in place, secrets and lies swirling and colliding with the truth. The truth he knows but I still can't bring myself to utter after twenty-four years of absolute silence.

"So don't speak right now, just listen. I know she let *them* do things to you that are vile and repulsive and make me sick." My stomach pitches and rolls, my breath shuddering at hearing it aloud. "... Things no one should *ever* have to endure ... but you know what, Colton? *That doesn't make it your fault*. It doesn't mean you deserved it, that you let it happen."

I slide down the wall behind me until I am sitting on the floor like a little kid ... but his words, my dad's words ... have brought me back there.

Have scared me.

Changed me.

Messed with my head so memories start pushing through the wormholes in my fucked up heart and soul.

I need to be alone.

I need Jack or Jim.

I need Rylee.

I need to forget. Again.

"Dad?" My voice is shaky. The sound of a little bitch asking for permission and shit, right now, isn't that what I am? On the damn floor once again about to throw the fuck up, body shaking, head racing as my stomach revolts?

He's sitting on the floor beside me like he used to do when I was little, his hand on my knee, his patience calming me some. "Yeah, son?" His voice is so soft, so tentative, I can tell he's afraid he's pushed me too far. That he's broken me more when I've already been fucking shattered and held together with scotch tape for way too long.

"I need—I need to be alone now."

I hear him draw in a breath, feel his resigned acceptance, and his unending love. And I need him to go. Now. Before I lose it.

"Okay," he says softly, "but you're wrong. You may have never said the words aloud—may have never told me you loved me—but I've always known because you have. It's in your eyes, how your smile lights up when you see me, the fact that you'd share your beloved Snickers bars with me without asking." He chuckles at the memories. "How you would let me hold your hand and let me help you chant your superheroes as you lay in bed so you could fall asleep. So words, no, Colton ... but you told me every day in some way or another." He's silent for a moment as a part of me allows the fact to sink in that he knows. That all the worry I've had over all of these years that he didn't know how much I felt didn't matter. *He knew*.

"I know your worst fear is having a child ..."

The elation that lifted me is choked by fear with his words. This is all just too much—too much, too fast when for so long I've been able to hide from it. "Please don't," I plead, squeezing my eyes shut.

"Okay ... I've thrown a lot of shit at you, but it was time you heard it. And I'm sorry I probably messed with your head more than you needed me to, but, son, only you can fix that now—deal with it now that all of the cards are on the table. But I have to tell you, you're not your mother. DNA doesn't make you a monster like her … just as if you were to have a child, your demons won't be transferred to that new life."

My fists clench and teeth grind at the last words—words that feed off the worst of my fears—the urge to break something returning. To drown the pain that's back with a vengeance. I know he's pushed me to the breaking point. I can hear his quiet sigh through the screams of every ounce of my being.

He stands slowly and I tell myself to look at him. To show him that I've heard him, but I can't make myself do it. I feel his hand on the top of my head, like I'm a little boy again, and his uncertain voice whispers, "I love you, Colton."

The words fill my fucking head but I can't get them past the fear lodged in my throat. Past the memories of the chant I used to say that was followed by the brutality and unspeakable pain. As much as I want to tell him—feel the need to tell him—I still can't.

See, perfect example, I want to tell him, to demonstrate how fucked up I am. He just bared his self to me and I can't give him a goddamn response because *she* stole it from me. And he thinks I could be a parent? She made my heart black and my core rotten. There's no way in hell I could pass that on to someone else if there were the remote chance it could happen.

I hear the door shut and I just remain on the floor. The outside light fades. Jack calls to me, tempts me, allows me to drown myself in his comfort, no glass needed.

Confusion fucking swamps me. Drags me under.

I need to clear my fucking head.

I need to figure my shit out.

Only then can I call Ry. And God *I want to call her*. My finger hovering over the damn Call button. Hovering there for well over an hour.

Call.

Call End.

Call.

Call End.

Shit!

I squeeze my eyes shut, head fuzzy from however much I've drank. And I start to laugh at what I've been reduced to. Me and the floor are becoming best fucking friends. Fuckin' A.

It's not hard to go up when you're already at rock bottom. Time to ride the damn elevator. I start laughing. I know there's only one other way to clear my head—my only other fucking high besides Rylee—that will help keep the demons at bay for a bit. And as much as I need Rylee right now, I need to do this first to get my shit figured out. My right hand trembles as I go to push Call, and when I do, I'm scared out of my goddamn mind, but it's time.

Head straight.

Then Rylee.

Motherfucking baby steps.

"Hey, douche bag. I didn't realize you knew my phone number it's been so damn long since you've called me."

Such a fucking old lady. God, I love this guy.

"Get me in the fucking car, Becks."

His laughter stops in an instant, the silence assuring me he's heard me, heard the words I know he's been waiting to hear since I got the all clear.

"What's going on, Wood? *You sure?*"

What's with everyone questioning me tonight? "I said get me in the goddamn car!"

"Okay," he drawls out in his slow cadence. "Where's your head at?"

"Seriously? First you push me to get in the fucker and now you're questioning the fact that I want to? What are you, my goddamn wet nurse?"

He chuckles. "Well, I do like my nipples played with, but shit, Wood, I kinda think you touching them would give me a reverse boner."

I can't stop the laugh that comes. Fucking Beckett. Always a bucket of laughs. "Quit screwing with me. Can you get me on the track or not?"

"Can you get the slur out of your voice and put down Jack, because that's a dead giveaway your head is still screwed up … so I'll repeat my question again. Where's your head at?"

"All over the fucking place!" I shout at him, failing miserably to not sound drunk "Goddamn it, Becks! *That's why I need the track.* I need to clear the shit from it to help fix me."

There's silence on the line, and I bite my tongue because I know if I push he'll hang up on me. "The track's not going to fix that fucked up head of yours, but I think a certain wavy haired hottie could do that for you."

"Drop it, Becks." I bite the words out, not in the mood for another shrink session.

"Not on your life, fucker. Baby. No baby. You really gonna push the best thing you got going for you out the damn door?"

And session number two begins.

"Fuck you."

"No thanks. You're not my type."

His condescending tone pisses me off. "Stay the hell out of it!"

"Oh! So you are going to let her go? Isn't that a song or some shit? Well, since you're gonna let her go, I guess I'll give her a run then."

Motherfucker. Are my buttons that easy to push tonight? "If you're smart, you'll shut the hell up. I know you're pushing me ... trying to get me to call her."

"Wow! He does listen. Now that's a news fucking flash."

I'm done. "Quit fucking around, do your job, and get me on the goddamn track, Beckett."

"Be at the track at ten tomorrow morning."

"What?"

"It's about time. I've had it reserved for the past week waiting for your ass to get with it."

"Hmpf." He had me pegged.

"You won't show." He laughs.

"Fuck off."

"You wish."

Chapter Twenty-Two

I blow out a breath and roll my shoulders, welcoming the burn as I stretch my warm and thoroughly tired muscles. I desperately needed this run—the escape into our backyard and through the gate of the neighbor behind us so I could get away undetected from the persistent press.

I look up from my stretch and something across the street catches my eye. I'm immediately on guard when I see the dark blue sedan across the street with the man leaning against it, camera in hand with a telephoto lens blocking his face. Something about him strikes me as familiar, and I can't put my finger on it … but I know my little piece of freedom—by secret passage—has been compromised.

The thought pisses me off and although I've yet to engage with any press, my feet have a life of their own and start walking toward him. My mind running the verbal lashing I'm about to give him over and over in my head. He watches my approach, the shutter clicking at rapid fire pace, the camera still blocking his face. I'm just about to start my spiel when I'm about fifty feet away and my phone rings in my hand.

Even after many days of no contact, my pulse still races at the sound, hoping it's Colton but knowing it's not before I even look at it. But I'm taken back a bit when I look at the screen and see Beckett's name. I stop immediately and fumble with my phone, worried that something's happened.

"Becks?"

"Hey, Ry." That's all he says and falls silent. *Oh shit.* Dread drops like a lead weight through me.

"Beckett, what's wrong with Colton?" I can't stop the worry that weighs heavy in my voice. The silence stretches and my mind runs as I glance at the photographer momentarily before turning my back and hurrying home.

"I just wanted you to know that Colton's on his way to the track right now."

I'm standing outside in the open, but I suddenly find it hard to draw in a breath of air. "What?" I'm surprised he can even hear me, my voice is so soft. Images flash through my head like a slideshow: the crash, the mangled metal, a broken Colton unresponsive in the hospital bed.

"I know you two … the whole baby thing and he hasn't called you." He sighs. "I had to call you and let you know … thought you'd want to know." I can tell he's conflicted over breaking his best friend's trust and doing what he thinks Colton needs the most.

"Thanks." It's the only thing I can manage as my emotions spiral out of control.

"Not really sure you mean that, Ry, but I thought I should call."

Silence stretches between us and I know he's just as worried as I am. "Is he ready, Becks? Are you pushing him?" I can't hold back the contempt that laces my question.

He breathes out and chuckles at something. "Nobody pushes Colton, Ry, but Colton. You know that."

"I know, but why now? What's the urgency?"

"Because this is what he needs to do …" Beckett's voice fades as he finds his next words. I push open the gate and scramble over the little fence separating the neighbor's yard and mine. "First of all, he needs to prove he's just as good as before. Secondly, this is how Colton deals when there's too much going on in his head and he can't shut it all off, and thirdly …"

I don't hear what Beckett says next because I'm too busy remembering our night before the race, our conversation, and the words fall from my mouth as I'm thinking aloud. "The blur."

"*The what?*"

It's when Beckett speaks that I realize I have in fact said it out loud and his voice shocks me from my thoughts. "Nothing," I say. "What's the third reason?"

"Never mind."

"You've already said more than you should, why stop now?"

There is an uncomfortable silence and he starts and stops for a moment. "It's nothing really. I was just going to say that in the past he's turned to one of three things when he gets like this. I'm sorry—I shouldn't have—"

"It's okay. I get it—get him. In the past he turned to women or alcohol or the track when life got to be too much, right?" Becks remains silent and there's my answer. "Well, I guess I should be lucky there was an opening at the track, right?"

Beckett belts out a laugh, and I can tell he's relieved. "God, he doesn't deserve you, Rylee." His words bring a smile to my face despite the worry eating at my insides. "I just hope you both realize how much he needs you."

Tears prick my eyes. "Thank you for calling, Becks. I'm on my way."

I'm thankful that traffic is light as I speed to the track in Fontana, and that the security at the parking lot prevent the press from following me into the facility. I park the car on the infield and freeze as I hear the crank try to start the car. The engine roars to life, its sound echoing against the grandstands and vibrating in my chest.

I don't know how I'm going to do this. How I'm going to be able to watch Colton, belted in and flying around the track, when all I can see in my head is the smoke and feel the fear? But I promised him I would be there the day he climbed back behind the wheel. Little did I know I'd get a call to collect on that promise when everything was unsettled between us.

But I can't not be here. Because I keep my promises. And because I can't stand the thought of him being out there without knowing he's okay. Yes, we've not spoken and are confused and hurt, but that doesn't mean I can turn my feelings off.

The motor revving again pulls me from my thoughts. My trepidation and the need to be there for him, for me, for my sanity, pushes me to put one foot in front of another. Davis meets me at the outskirts of pit row and nods as I take the hand he offers in greeting, before leading me to where Colton's crew is working.

I stop when I see the car, the curve of Colton's helmet in the capsule behind the wheel, Beckett's body bent over him, tightening his belts as only Colton will let him do. I force my throat to swallow but realize there is nothing to ingest because my mouth is filled with cotton. I find myself going to worry the ring I no longer wear, out of nervous habit, and have to make do with clasping my hands.

Davis leads me up the flight of stairs to the observation tower above, much like the one I sat in while I watched Colton spiral out of control. Each step up reminds me of *that* day—the sound, the smell, the churning of my stomach, the absolute terror—each riser is another memory of the moments after the car hit the catch fence. My body wants to turn and flee, but my heart tells me I have to be here. I can't quit on him when he needs me the most.

The pitch of the engine changes and I don't have to turn and look at it to know he's driving slowly down pit row toward the banked asphalt of the track. I stand in the tower, a few members of the crew focused on gauges reading the car's electronics, but in the mere seconds I stand there, I can sense the nervous energy, can feel that they are as anxious about Colton being in the car as I am.

I hear footsteps on the stairs behind me and know it must be Becks. Before I even have a chance to say anything to him, the sound of the car's motor eases, and we both look toward it at the end of the vacant pit row. After a moment, the engine's rumble revs again and the car moves slowly onto the track.

Beckett looks over to me quickly and hands me a headset. The look in his eyes tells me that he's just as on edge and uneasy about this as I am, and a small part of me is relieved by this. He leans in close before I situate the headphones on my ears and says, "He doesn't know you're here."

I just nod at him, eyes telling him thank you, lips telling him, "I think that's for the best."

He motions toward a chair at the front of the tower, but I just shake my head resolutely. There is no way in hell I can sit down right now. Nervous energy assaults my senses, and I shift back and forth on my feet while my soul remains anchored solid from my fear.

The engine purrs gently into the back end of turn one, and I twist so my eyes can track Colton, although I want to scream for him to stop, to get out, to come back to me. The car starts to accelerate into turn two.

"That's it, Wood. Nice and easy," Becks says to him in a gentle coaxing voice. All I hear on the open mic is the cadence of the engine and Colton's harsh breathing, but no response from him. I bite my lip and glance over at Beckett, not liking the fact that he's not speaking. I can only imagine what is running through Colton's head.

"Goddammit, Becks!" It's the first time I've heard his voice in over a week and the sound in it—the fear woven through the anger—has me holding tight onto the ear pieces. "This car is shit! I thought you checked everything. It's—"

"Nothing's wrong with the car, Colton." The evenness of Becks' voice comes through loud and clear, and Beckett glances over to another crew member and subtly shakes his head no at something.

"*Bullshit!* It's shuddering like a bitch and is gonna come apart once I open her up." The vibration that's normally in his voice from the force of the motor isn't there, he's not even going fast enough out of turn two to affect him.

"It's a new car. I checked every inch of it."

"You don't know what the fuck you're talking about, Beckett! Goddammit!" he yells out into the car as it comes to a stop on the backstretch between turns two and three, frustration resonating over the radio.

"It's a different car. No one's on the track to hit you. Just take it nice and easy."

There is no response. Nothing but the distant hum of an idling motor that I'm sure will die soon and then they'll need to get a crank start out on the track to get it going again. More time for Colton to sit and think and remember and relive the crash that is incapacitating him.

And as time stretches, my concern for the man I love has my own anxiety escalating. Even though we're all here supporting him, I know he's over there feeling all alone, isolated in a metal casket on wheels. My heart lodges in my throat as the panic and helplessness I feel starts to strangle me.

Beckett paces back and forth, his hands shoving through his hair, uncertain how to coax his best friend off of the ledge when he's not listening already. I shift again—Colton's ragged breathing the only sound on the radio—and I can't take it anymore.

I walk up to Beckett. "Get everyone off the radios." He looks at me and tries to figure out what I'm doing. "Get them off," I say, desperation tingeing the urgency in my request.

"Radios off everyone," Beckett orders immediately as I move to the mic on the counter at the front of the box. I sit down in the seat and wait for the nod from Beckett once he realizes what I'm doing.

I fumble with the buttons on the mic and Davis leans over and pushes down on the one I need. "Colton?" My voice is shaky but I know he hears me because I hear the hitch in his breath when he does.

"Rylee?" It's my name—a single word—but the break in his voice and the vulnerability in the way he says it causes tears to well in my eyes. He sounds like one of my boys right now when they wake from a terrifying dream, and I wish I could run out onto the track so that I can hold and reassure him. But I can't, so I do the next closest thing.

"Talk to me. Tell me what's going through your head. No one's on the radio but you and me." Silence stretches for a bit as my palms become sweaty with nerves and I fret that I'm not going to be able to help him through this.

"Ry," he sighs in defeat, and I'm about to jump back on the mic when he continues. "I can't … I don't think I can …" His voice fades as I'm sure memories of the accident assault him, as they do me.

"You can do this," I say with more resolve than I feel. "This is California, Colton, not Florida. There's no traffic. No rookie drivers to make stupid mistakes. No smoke you can't see through. No wreck to drive into. It's just you and me, Colton. You and me." I pause a moment and when he doesn't respond, I say the one thing circling in my mind. "Nothing but sheets."

I hear the sliver of a laugh, and I'm relieved that I got through to him. Used a good memory to break through the crippling fear. But when he speaks I can still hear the trepidation in his tone. "I just …" He stops and sighs, vulnerability a hard thing for a man to accept, especially in the face of a crew who idolizes and respects him.

"You can do this, Colton. We can do this together, okay? I'm right here. I'm not going anywhere." I give him a few seconds to let my words sink in. "Are your hands on the wheel?"

"Mmm-hmm … but my right hand—"

"Is perfectly okay. I've seen you use it," I tell him, hoping to ease some of the tension. "Is your foot on the pedal?"

"Ry?" His voice wavers again.

"Pedal. Yes or no?" I know right now he needs me to take the reins and be the strong one, and for him, I'll do anything.

"Yes …"

"Okay, clear your head. It's just you and the track, Ace. You can do this. You need this. It's your freedom, remember?" I hear the engine rev once or twice, and I see relief mixed with pride in Beckett's eye before I focus back on Colton. "You know this like the back of your hand … push down on the gas. Flick the paddle and press down." The engine's pitch purrs a little higher and I continue. "Okay … see? You've got this. You don't have to go fast. It's a new car, it's going to feel different. Becks will be pissed if you burn up the engine anyway so take it slow."

I turn to watch the car with bated breath as Colton starts slowly into turn three. He's nowhere near even practice speeds, but he's going and that's all that matters. We're facing our fear of him getting back into the car again together. I just never figured it would be me coaxing him to drive that would lessen my own.

The motor guns again, the reverberation hitting my chest as he nears turn four and I hear him cuss. "You okay?" There is nothing but silence around me and the roar of the approaching engine. "Talk to me, Colton. I'm right here."

"My hands won't stop shaking." I don't respond because I'm holding my breath as he picks up the pace and enters into turn one. "Becks is gonna be pissed because my head's fucked up."

I glance over at Becks again and see the smile flash on his face, and I know he's listening in, making sure his best friend is okay. "It's okay … watching you out there? Mine is fucked up too … but you're ready, you can do this."

"Aren't we a fucking pair?" He snorts into the radio and I can sense a little of his anxiety and fear dissipating with each passing second. I see the guys around me relax some as they notice the smile widen on Beckett's face.

"We are indeed," I laugh before releasing an exhale in relief. God, I love you, I want to say, but refrain. The rumble increases down the backstretch and I can't fight the grin on my face at the sound of success. "Hey, Ace, can I bring the guys back on?"

"Yeah," he says followed quickly by, "Ry … I …"

My heart swells at the emotion in his voice. I can hear the apology, feel the absolute sincerity behind it. "I know, Colton. Me too."

I fight the tears of happiness that well up, and when I look up at Beckett he has a soft smile on his face. He shakes his head ever so subtly and mouths the word *lifeline* to me.

Chapter Twenty-Two

Colton—Raced

Fear is a brutal bitch to face.

It squeezes your lungs so you can't breathe, locks your jaw to bear the brunt of your stress, and cinches your heart so your blood rushes through your body.

The guys are at my back pretending to be busy. Ignoring the fact that I'm standing in front of my car, staring at the cause of my biggest fucking fear right now and my greatest goddamn salvation. I need it more than ever between the bullshit Tawny hit me with and not having the one person I want most but don't want to taint any further around.

Rylee.

She said she'd be here when I got in the car for the first time. I need her here, need to know she's here to come back to at the end of the run. The salve to my stained soul. But how in the fuck could I call her and ask her when I've pushed her so far away?

So here I stand, surrounded by my crew but battling the shit in my head all alone. And of course my mind veers to the vultures at the gates that shoved cameras in my face and spewed Tawny's bullshit lies about Rylee when I left the house earlier. Then it slides back to Rylee and how much I want her here right now.

Fuck this, Donavan. Quit being such a pussy and get in the goddamn car. You've faced shit ten times worse than this. You've got this. Man the fuck up and get in the car.

I take a deep breath and squeeze my eyes shut momentarily as I lift my helmet and push it down on my head. My silent acknowledgement to the guys that I'm ready to tackle this.

It takes me a minute to buckle my helmet; my hands tremble like a motherfucker. Becks steps forward to help and I glare at him to back the fuck off. If I can't fasten this then I don't deserve to get behind the wheel.

I slide my hand up the nose toward the cockpit. I knock softly out of habit to ease my superstitious mind.

Spiderman. Batman. Superman. Ironman.

Four knocks, one for each of the superheroes that the little boy in me still thinks will help protect him. They pulled me through the last crash, I know they're good for it.

I take a deep breath and try not to think as I lift one leg and then the other so I can drop into the driver's seat. I sit there, try to make myself numb so I can't feel the fear coursing through me and trickling down the line of my spine in rivulets of sweat.

Becks steps up and locks the steering wheel in place and thank fuck for that because now I have somewhere I can put my hands and grip so that they stop shaking. I feel his hand pat the top of my helmet like he usually does, but before he clicks my HANS device he pulls my helmet up so I'm forced to look at him.

I see the fear flicker in his eyes but I also see resolve. "All you, Wood. Take your time. Ease into her." He nods at me. "Just like riding a bike."

A bike my ass. But I nod at him because I have a feeling I could argue the point just to cause a distraction from actually having to do this. I focus on the wheel in front of me as he studies me, gauging whether I really am okay being here.

"I'm good," I lie. And he stands there for a minute more before the guys bring the crank out and we fire the engine.

The reverberation through my body and sound in my ears of the engine's rumble is like coming home and making me question myself all at once. Kind of like Rylee.

I hold onto that thought—to the idea of her being here when she's not—as I rev the motor a few times. It sounds the same and yet so very different from the memory still hit and miss in my mind from the wreck.

The crew gets over the wall and it's just Becks and me. He leans over and pulls on my harness, the same way he has for the past fourteen years. It's comforting in a sense because he doesn't act like anything is different, knows that this is what I need. Routine. The sense that everything is the same when it's a clusterfuck in my head.

He raps the hood twice as is his habit and walks away. I don't follow him because if I do, I know I'll see the falter in his step. And his hesitancy will reaffirm my fear that I'm not ready.

I give it some gas, let the car rumble all around me to clear my head, and psych myself to do this. And I sit here long enough that I know I look like a pussy who shouldn't be in the car so I put the car in gear and begin to ease out onto pit row. My heart is in my throat and my body vibrates from more than just the car. Nerves and anxiety collide with the need to be here, to do this, to be able to outrun my demons and find the freedom-laced solace I've always been able to find on the track.

I exit pit row and squeeze the wheel, frustrated that my fucking grandmother can drive faster than I am.

"That's it, Wood. Nice and easy," Becks says, and it takes everything I have to shut him out, to listen to the car like I always do and try and hear what she's telling me. But I can't drown out the bullshit in my head so I close my eyes momentarily and tell myself to just push the gas and go.

And I do. I push it, flick the paddle as I change gears, and enter the high line into turn two because I'm not going fast enough to have to worry about drifting into the wall.

But the more I accelerate, the less I hear. She's not talking to me. The noises aren't the same. "Goddammit, Becks! This car is shit! I thought you checked everything. It's—"

"Nothing's wrong with the car, Colton."

"*Bullshit!* It's shuddering like a bitch and is gonna come apart once I open her up," I grate out, pissed at that placating tone in his voice. I'm the one in the fucking car—the one that can possibly slam headfirst into the wall—not him.

"It's a new car. I checked every inch of it."

"You don't know what the fuck you're talking about, Beckett! Goddammit!" I pound my fist against the steering wheel, completely backing off the gas.

I know he says something about taking it nice and easy but I don't really hear it because the flashback hits me so hard I suffocate in the open air.

The car stops but dizziness spirals through me.

My body slams to a stop but my head hasn't.

A breath shocks into me as I realize what just happened. That I survived that tumbling pirouette into the catch fence. That I escaped the shredded fucking mass of metal on the track at my back.

Pain radiates around me like a motherfucking freight train. My head splinters into a million damn pieces, hands grabbing and groping and pushing and prodding. That familiar pang twists in my gut because I don't want anyone's hands on me, can't handle the feeling. I don't want to be reminded of the little boy I used to be and the fear that used to course through me when I was touched by others. *By him.*

Medical jargon flies at a rapid pace and it's so technical I can't catch the gist. Just tell me if I'm going to be fucking all right. Just tell me if I'm dead or alive, because I swear to God my life really did just flash before my eyes and what I thought was going to be ... what I thought I wanted out of life ... just got twisted and turned more than the aluminum of my car.

How could I have been so wrong? How could I have thought change would be the catalyst when it ended up being my fucking epiphany? Shows me to try and change the road fate's already set for me.

I writhe to get away from the hands that touch, twisting and turning to find her. To go back and tell her that I was so wrong. Everything I put her through. Each rejection and rebuff was my fault. Was a huge mistake.

How do I make it right again?

Pain grapples again and mixes with the fear that ripples under the surface. My head feels like it is going to explode. Lazy clouds of haze float in and out and eat the memories away. Take them with them as they leave and fade. Darkness overcomes the edges until I can't take it anymore. Voices shout and hands assess my injuries, but I fade.

My thoughts.

My past.

My life.

Bit by bit.

Piece by piece.

Until I am cloaked in the cover of darkness.

"Colton?" It's her voice that shocks me from my memory like a drowning man finally breaking the surface for air. I gasp in a breath just as hungrily.

I shake my head and look around. I'm all alone on the backstretch of the track, sweat soaking through my fire suit. Did I really hear Ry or was that part of my flashback?

"Rylee?" I call her name. I don't care that there are guys on the mics that probably think I'm losing it because she's not here ... because they're right. I am losing it.

"Talk to me. Tell me what's going through your head. No one's on the radio but you and me."

She's here. It's her. I don't even know what to do because I feel like I'm hit with a wave of emotions. Relief, fear, anxiety, need.

"Ry ... I can't ... I don't think I can ..." I'm such a fucking head case that I can't string my thoughts together to finish a thought.

"You can do this," she tells me like she actually believes it, because I sure as fuck don't. "This is California, Colton, not Florida. There's no traffic. No rookie drivers to make stupid mistakes. No smoke you can't see through. No wreck to drive into. It's just you and me, Colton. You and me, nothing but sheets."

Those words. I know they don't belong right here in this moment but fuck if they don't draw a sliver of a laugh from my mouth but that's all I can manage because they also make me think of everything I've put her through. How nothing but sheets between us has led to her having to deal with the fallout of Tawny and all of that bullshit.

And yet somehow she's here. She came for me. Does she have any fucking clue what that means to me especially when I'm the last one on earth that deserves her right now?

I pushed and now she's pulling.

"I just ..." Can't do this anymore. Push you away and hurt you. Push the gas and drive the car. Not have you near me.

I know my head's fucked up but I'm in overload mode again and then she speaks and lets light into my darkness.

"You can do this, Colton. We can do this together, okay? I'm right here. I'm not going anywhere."

I don't deserve you. Your faith in me. Your belief in me.

"Are your hands on the wheel?" The confidence in her voice staggers me when I feel anything but.

"Mmm-hmm ... but my right hand—"

"Is perfectly okay. I've seen you use it," she says and the thought flickers through my head of just how she saw it the last time we had sex.

"Is your foot on the pedal?" she asks.

"Ry?" I want to stay in these thoughts of her, don't want the fear to ride the wave back into my psyche.

"Pedal. Yes or no?"

"Yes ..." *But I'm not sure I can do this.*

"Okay, clear your head. It's just you and the track, Ace. You can do this. You need this. It's your freedom, remember?"

She knows the words to pull me back from the edge. I take a deep breath and hold on to the confidence that she has to try and override the fear crippling my thoughts with images and sensations of tumbling into the wall. The wall that looks exactly like the one to the right of me.

Surrounding me.

C'mon, Donavan. Engage the motor. Prevent it from dying. The engine revs and a part of me sighs at the progress.

"You know this like the back of your hand ... push down on the gas. Flick the paddle and press down."

I make myself focus on her voice, hold on to the thought that she came back to help fix the broken in me. And the car starts to move down the backstretch and into turn three.

"Okay ... see? You've got this. You don't have to go fast. It's a new car, it's going to feel different. Becks will be pissed if you burn up the engine anyway so take it slow."

I push a little harder, accelerator unsteady, but I'm starting to move around the track. I pass the point similar to where I went into the wall in St. Petersburg and I force my mind to tune out the unease and focus on listening to the car talk to me.

"You okay?" I can't answer her because I may be trying to engage mentally but my body is still owned by the fear. "Talk to me, Colton. I'm right here."

"My hands won't stop shaking," I tell her as I look at the gauges and realize I'm going faster. And with speed I need to concentrate on the feeling of the track beneath me, the pull of the wheel one way or another, the camber when I hit the corners. Routine items I can diagnose without thinking. Because I don't want to think. Then doubts come, fear creeps.

I shake the thought and sigh, knowing how much shit I'm going to get from Becks since I'm not focusing like I should on the task at hand. "Becks is gonna be pissed because my head's fucked-up."

She doesn't respond and I start to crawl back in my own mind for a moment when she clears her throat. She has my attention now. Is she crying?

"It's okay … watching you out there? Mine is fucked-up too … but you're ready. You can do this." Something about her willingness to be vulnerable to me when I know she's standing around all the guys hits places inside I'm glad I can't analyze right now.

"Aren't we a fucking pair?" I laugh, finding it rather humorous how screwed up we both are.

"We are indeed," she says, and the little laugh she emits tells me so much. I press the accelerator down some. I've never needed approval from anyone, but right now I need it from her. Need her to see that I'm trying, both on and off the track.

"Hey, Ace, can I bring the guys back on?"

"Yeah," I reply quickly. I hit turn four again and feel a little more confident, a lot more sure that I can do this. And I know how a large part of that is because she's here. Shit, even after I was an asshole to her, have put her through hell with the paparazzi chasing her, she's still here. "Ry … I …" My voice fades but my mind completes them.

I'm sorry.

I race you.

Thank you.

"I know, Colton. Me too." Her voice breaks when she says it, and I feel like I can breathe again, like my world was just somehow set right when it's been inside out the time without her.

Chapter Twenty-Three

The car enters the pits and rolls to a stop. Beckett's at its side in an instant while I fidget behind the wall, wanting to see Colton face to face to make sure he's okay. He removes the steering wheel and hands it to Becks before unbuckling his helmet. Becks helps him unfasten it from the HANS device, and when he pulls it from his head, removing the balaclava with it, the crew erupts into a roar of cheers.

Chills dance at the celebratory sounds as Becks helps him out of the car. I step over the wall with the rest of the crew, unable to stay at a distance any longer because now Colton stands there hot, sweaty, and oh my God sexy. Pride tinged with desire spears through me at the sight of him.

Attending to the car is forgotten as his crew pats him on the shoulders and welcomes him back. Beckett just looks at him with a shit-eating grin on his handsome face. "I'm proud of you, dude, but fuck, *your lap times sucked.*"

Colton laughs again, slinging an arm around his friend. "I can always count on you to knock me down a few pegs." He goes to say something else and then stops when he sees me.

I have a déjà vu moment, Colton standing amidst the whirling chaos of his crew, eyes locked on mine, sexy-as-sin grin wide on his lips. Time stops again as the world falls away and we stare at each other.

I know there are so many things we need to talk about—need to figure out from the last time we spoke—but at the same time I need this connection with him. Need the carnal physicality between the two of us that hits me like a shock wave as it crosses the distance between us and crashes into me before we can figure the rest out.

And I know he feels it too because within a beat Colton strides toward me with purpose. Within an instant of reaching me, my legs are wrapped around his waist and our mouths are on one another's with a frenzied need. My hands grip his shoulders. One of his grabs my backside while the other grips my neck, holding my mouth to his, so he can take everything I am offering, and then some.

"God, I fucking missed you," he growls into my mouth between kisses. And without preamble we are on the move. His powerful legs stride beneath me, and strong arms hold me secure while his lips bruise mine in unbidden possession.

Noise filters back. Hoots and hollers of the crew ring through the empty stadium as Colton makes no apologies for walking away without a second thought. Someone shouts "Get a room!" and I am so overwhelmed, so desperate to sate the desire unfurling within and shocking through my system that I answer before Colton can.

"Who needs a room?" I say before my lips crash back against his, hands fisting in his hair, hips grinding into his as his erection rubs against me with every step.

Laughter rings out followed by catcalls, but they're only background noise to the freight train of desire bearing down on us. "Hurry," I tell him in between desperate kisses.

"Fuck," he mutters as he tries to find an open door at my back without wanting to take his mouth from mine.

"Oh, you better plan on it," I reply as I pull back so he can find the handle. He belts out a laugh as my tongue glides to his neck, the taste of salt on my tongue, the vibration of his laughter beneath my lips.

We're on the move again, up a set of stairs in a darkened corridor, and I have no clue where we are. I hold on for the ride, laughter bubbling up, relief flowing through me as my body tenses with the anticipation of what's to come.

We're suddenly bathed in a muted light, and I turn my head and blink my eyes to take in our surroundings. We are in one of the luxury boxes on pit row: plush couches, a concessions bar on one side, a table spanning the length of the wall of tinted windows that looks down on the track, where his crew is tinkering with his car.

That's all I have time to take in because Colton's lips find mine again, his mouth a toxic concoction of need and lust. My legs fall from his hips, feet dropping to the ground, as we move toward the counter in a clumsy choreography of steps. We reach the lip of the counter, and I lean my hips back against it, as Colton's hands roam down my torso, before I feel bare hands beneath my shirt on my ribcage.

And I'm not sure if it's the heightened arousal from the adrenaline of the race track, or our reconciliation, but I feel like I can't get enough of him—his touch, his taste, the sound in the back of his throat, my name on his lips. I reach up and unfasten the Velcro against his throat so I can pull his zipper. And even this small action pains me because I have to pull away from his lips. But the minute I yank the zipper down, my mouth meets his again. Our hands unfasten, arms pull out of our sleeves, fingers shove down my shorts and underwear, clothes thrown haphazardly to the floor, our mouths never leaving one another's.

"Ry," he says between kisses, one hand gripping my hair tightly while the other tests my readiness for his entrance. Foreplay isn't an option right now. We're so pent up, so desperate to right the wrongs of our last conversation that without speaking, we both know we need this connection. Talking will come later. Cuddling and niceties later. Right now desire consumes, passion overwhelms, and love takes hold. "Fuck, I need you right now."

"Take me." Two simple words. They're out of my mouth without a second thought, but within a second of saying them, Colton has me flipped over, hands braced on the counter, his hands gripping my hips, his throbbing cock lined up at my entrance from behind. He rests the crest in between my folds and then slides it up and back causing my body to tense and a moan to fall from between my lips.

And there's something about this moment, about Colton on the precipice of taking me without asking, that has every part of me aching for release, begging for more of his touch. "Please. Now," I pant as my sex quivers with need, body so in tune to his every action that my body automatically responds, opens, invites.

I rear back and try to take him on my own, trying to demonstrate the need spearing and spiraling throughout my every nerve, robbing my rationality, and making my senses crave more. "*Behave!*" He chuckles out a laugh of pure male appreciation as one hand fists in my mane of hair as his other lands smartly on the left side of my ass. The sting shocks my head back but has nothing on the assault of sensation that occurs as he enters me in one slick, earth-shattering thrust. I can't help the hitched breath followed by a soft sigh that falls from my mouth as sensation ripples and my walls convulse around him.

He pulls on my hair, angling my head back, so when he leans forward his lips are at my ear. "That is the sexiest fucking sound in the world," he growls before his lips find my bare shoulder, stubbled beard tickling the usually forgotten erogenous zone of my back. His teeth nip my shoulder followed by the press of his lips as his hips grind into me, and I moan in pure rapture as the scrape of his beard moves down my spine.

And now it's my turn to enjoy the sounds he makes as we start to move in rhythm with each other. Goose bumps appear despite the heat spreading through my body. One hand grips the flesh on my hip, controlling each pleasure inducing drive in and subsequent withdrawal tantalizing every single nerve. My body quickens, overtaken by the animalistic nature of his hold on my hair and my body.

"Oh God!" I pant, needing, wanting, not being able to take any more all at the same time. My hands start to slide on the surface of the counter as they dampen with sweat.

"Fuuuuccckkk!" he grates out, his desire to control his tempo apparent in his voice. And call it a challenge, or me just channeling the inner vixen he's helped me find, but I want to break that control. I want to push him harder, faster—to take with reckless abandon—because my God, the guttural sound in his throat, the fullness as he seats himself to the hilt when he thrusts into me, the clockwise motion of his hips as he moves within me pushes me harder, faster, than I've ever known. Makes me want to bring him an ounce of the pleasure that his body gives me.

I reach a hand down between my legs, fingers sliding over the temptation to caress my own clit, and instead grab a hold of his balls as he grinds his hips into me again. Fingers caress, nails tease, and hands cradle as he pulls back tighter on my hair. I can hear the sounds he's making, know he's clenching his jaw, that he's riding that razor-thin edge of being controlled versus relinquishing to the carnal nature of the act. To take for himself without thought. And it eggs me on, tempts me to push him harder, force him over that edge that much quicker, because fuck if he's not driving me there in the process.

I get lost in the feeling, the sounds of his body smacking against mine, the feel of his hand possessing my hip, the fall of my name from his lips and without realizing it, I'm there, teetering on my own razor thin edge. I crash into the endless free fall of bliss as my climax overwhelms me, my body an inferno of warring sensations.

"Colton!" I cry, over and over as he slows his pace, sliding his tongue up the plain of my back to help draw out my orgasm.

I can feel my muscles pulse around him still within me, moving slowly, and then a feral cry fills the air as he can't hold back anymore. His hips thrust a few more times before his arms suddenly wrap around my torso and hold my weight as he pulls me to a standing position, his front still to my back.

In an unexpected move of tenderness in complete contrast to the thorough dominance of my body, he squeezes me back into him and buries his face into the curve of my neck. We stand like this for some time, absorbing each other, accepting the silent apologies.

Chapter Twenty-Four

The silence descends around us as we pull our clothes back on. Now that we've had our way with each other physically—now that our bodies are no longer connected—my mind worries about how we're going to connect verbally.

Because we can't leave things as is. And we can't ignore them. Hopefully the miserably lonely time apart has helped us so we can move forward.

But even if we can, where exactly do we go from here?

I steal a glance over at him as he zips up his fire suit and looks through the tinted window at the crew below, and I just can't get a read on him. I pull my shirt over my head and lick my lips as I try to figure out how to start this conversation.

"We need to talk," I say softly as if I'm afraid to disturb the blanket of silence smothering the room.

"I'm putting the Palisades house up for sale." He speaks the words quietly, never once looking my way, and I'm so focused on him and his lack of emotion, it takes a moment for his words to sink in.

Whoa! What? So that's how we're going to play this? Classic avoidance?

Even though he's not looking at me, I know he's aware of me so I try to visibly hide the shock from the words he's just hit me with, as well as the ones he hasn't said.

"Colton?" I say, his name like a question—one that asks so many different things. Are we going to address this? Are we going to ignore this? Why are you selling the house?

"I don't use it ..." he answers my unasked question, sliding a glance over at me, before he looks back at his guys down below. And the way he says it, almost apologetically, makes me feel like this is something he's doing to tell me he's sorry for everything that's happening—Tawny, a possible baby, the space he needs.

When I don't respond and just watch him patiently, he turns and faces me. Our eyes lock and we stare at each other for a moment, asking unanswered questions without words.

"I don't need it anymore," he explains as he watches me for a reaction.

And as much as there is unresolved drama between us, what he's just said tells me he's really in this for the long haul. That even with everything thrown at us over the past week that might turn his world upside down, he's selling the one place I'd vowed never to return to. That I mean enough to him that he's willing to get rid of a place signifying his old way of life full of stipulations and mitigations.

"Oh ..." It's all I can manage to say because I'm at a loss for words, so we just continue to stare at each other in this room that still smells like sex. I can see him thinking, trying to figure out what to say—how to go from here—so I begin. "What's on your mind, Colton?"

"Just thinking," he says, pursing his lips and running a hand through his hair, "about how I didn't realize how much I needed to hear your voice today out on the track until you came through the headset."

The gentle sigh of satisfaction comes from every part of me, warming me inside and out, as it weaves its way around the hold he has on my heart. And the old me would have rolled my eyes at his comment and said he's trying to get on my good side, but the old me didn't need and miss Colton as much as I do now, didn't know all he had to offer.

"All you had to do was call me," I say softly, reaching a hand out and placing it on top of his beside me. "I promised you I'd be here your first day back."

He emits a self-deprecating chuckle with a shake of his head. "And say what? I've been an asshole—haven't called at all—but I need you on the track with me today?" The sarcasm is thick in his voice.

I squeeze his hand. "It's a start," I tell him, my voice trailing off. "We agreed to figure our shit out, get our heads straight, but I would've been here in a heartbeat if you'd called me."

He sighs, angling his head out toward the track beyond. "I'm sorry for what I said to you ... the things I accused you of ... I was an ass." Emotion causes his voice to waver, which makes what he's saying that much more endearing.

I don't want to ruin the moment, but I have to let him know. "You hurt me. I know you were upset and lashing out at the person nearest to you ... but *you hurt me* when I was already torn apart. We struggle day to day with our pasts, and then something like this happens and ... I ..." I can't find the right words to say it, so I just don't finish my thought.

Colton steps toward me and reaches out to grab my hand, pulling me gently toward him so the only barrier between us is our clothes. "I know." He draws in a shaky breath before he continues. "I've never done this before, Ry. I'm trying to figure it out as I go and fuck, I know the excuses are getting old and pretty soon aren't going to be excusable, but … fuckin' A, I'm trying." He shrugs.

I nod at him, words escaping me because he's doing something he's never been good at: communicating. And they may seem like baby steps to him, but they gain us massive ground in our relationship.

He leans forward and brushes an unexpected kiss on my lips before murmuring, "C'mere." He leans his butt against the ledge behind him the same time he pulls me into him so we stand with my back to his front, his legs surrounding mine. I lean my head against his chest and feel stupidly content as he brings his arms around me and holds me tight. He rests his chin on my shoulder. "Thank you for today. No one's ever done something like that for me before."

His words kind of surprise me but after a minute I understand his line of thinking and need to correct it. "Becks, your family, they do it all the time. You just don't allow yourself to see or accept it."

"Yeah, but they're family, they have to." He pauses and even though I can't see the look in his eyes, I can sense his mind working as I wonder what exactly he classifies me as. "And you? You're my fucking checkered flag." I angle my head to the side just enough so I can see a diminutive smile spread on his lips as a full-fledged one lights up mine. "It's a little hard to get used to the idea when I've never done this before. I have to get used to you being there for me and needing you, and fuck if that doesn't knock me back a few pit stop steps sometimes because it scares the ever-loving shit out of me."

Holy shit! I'm stunned to silence once again by his attempt to explain the trepidation I'm sure is tickling the outer edges of his psyche. I put my hands over his arms that are locked around me and squeeze them in a silent acknowledgment of the growth he is trying to show.

"I'm not going to run, Colton," I say, my voice resolute. "I haven't yet, but you *really* hurt me. I know you're going through a lot of shit, but hell if you aren't a lot to take in. I'm going to need a pit stop sometimes too. I mean, between you, the limelight, the women still wanting you and hating me, the possibility of …" I can't finish the thought, can't force the word *baby* from my lips or rid the sudden acrid taste from my mouth.

"*Hello elephant in the fucking room.*" He lets out an audible sigh, and his jaw tenses on my shoulder.

I don't want to ruin the moment—the heart-to-heart we need to have more of—but since I unexpectedly brought it up, I'd rather address it and get it over with. "What's going on with … that?" I close my eyes and grit my teeth as I await the answer.

"I don't care what she says about what I supposedly did or didn't do that I can't fucking remember. I know it's not mine, Rylee."

The simplicity of his statement and the vigor with which he delivers it causes my hope to soar. And then to fall. If he got the results back, then why didn't he call me? "You got the test results back already?" I say cautiously, trying to hide my wariness.

"No." He shakes his head as the hope I have falls completely. "I took the test two days ago. Results will come any day now. But I know … I know it's not mine." And from the sound of his voice, I can't tell who he's trying to convince more: himself or me.

"How do you know, Colton, if you can't remember?" I say loudly, frustrated and needing this to just be over, needing more emotion from him than what I'm getting. I take a deep breath and try to calm myself. "I mean even if you and Tawny did..." I stop, unable to finish the thought "...she said you didn't use a condom." My voice is so quiet when I speak, hating that we even have to have this discussion. Hating that once again our moment of contentment is ruined by the outside world and the consequences of our pasts.

"You're the only person, Ry … the only woman I've ever not used a condom with. I don't care if you think I slept with her, but I know, Rylee … I know I would have used a condom." I can hear the pleading in his voice for me to believe him. For me to understand an iota of the fear he's feeling at the prospect of a child. When I don't respond he pushes back away from me and starts to pace back and forth on the deck. The calm of five minutes ago is now replaced with pure agitation, a caged animal needing to escape its confines.

"It's not mine!" he says, raising his voice. "There's no fucking way it can be mine!"

"But what if it is?" I reiterate with full knowledge of the fire I'm lighting.

"It's not," he shouts. "Fuck! All I know is that I don't know fucking anything! I hate the goddamn media following you and fucking harassing you. I hate the look on your face right now that says you're going to fucking lose it if it is my baby even though you tell me you won't. I hate fucking Tawny and everything she represents. The bullshit lies she's fucking spewing about you that Chase says I can't respond to because they'll only hound you more. I hate that once again I'm fucking hurting you … that I'm going to fuck this up because my past is what it is … " He closes his eyes and rolls his shoulders as he tries to rein in his anger.

This is the kind of fighting I can handle. Him venting, me listening, and then hopefully a little bit of the pain in his eyes and the weight on his shoulders will be eased, even if just for a bit.

"You've got enough on your plate. You don't need to worry about me." I tell him this and yet I love the fact that he's upset by the fallout affecting me.

"I don't?" he says with incredulity. "It's my fucking job to look out for you, and I can't even do that right now because everything's so fucked up!"

"Colton—"

"I swear to God, your life gets turned upside down by me and you're more worried about me and the boys than yourself." He walks toward me with a shake of his head. He points to me and I look at him with confusion. "You are most definitely the fucking saint I don't deserve."

"Every sinner needs a saint to balance them out," I say with a smirk.

He laughs softly and reaches out to cup my cheeks in his hands. And even though we've already had each other, my body vibrates instantly at his nearness, at wanting him, at needing him. His eyes lock on mine, hints of what he wants to do to me dancing behind the fringe of lashes.

"God, I fucking race you." The emphatic words on his lips are followed by a lopsided smirk and a shake of his head, as if he's still comprehending the depths of his emotions.

How many more times can my heart fall harder for this man? Because there it is again, the unpredictability of Colton that makes what he says just that much more poignant. Every part of my body shivers at his words.

It's useless to try and fight the moisture pooling in my eyes because those words mean so much more than just "racing" to me. They mean he's trying, he's apologizing for the times when he's going to fuck up. And for a man previously closed off from everyone, he's handing me the key to the lock, and giving me an all-access pass.

I reach my free hand out and cup the back of his neck, pulling him into me because a man this magnificent, inside and out, is just too irresistible. I kiss him tenderly, licking my tongue between his lips so it dances intimately with his. No urgency, just soft, gentle acceptance. It's only been minutes since our last kiss but it already feels like a lifetime. As the kiss ends, he rests his forehead against mine and I say, "I race you too."

I can feel his smile spread against my lips, and in this moment, I know he actually gets it. He actually accepts the fact that I love him and it's such a figurative ray of light from this dark angel of mine that I grasp onto it, silently vowing to always remember how I feel right here, right now.

We may not have everything figured out, may not know what the future's going to hold, but at least I know we're in this race together.

"C'mon," he says, pulling on my hand. "Let's get out of here."

We head toward the garage area where the guys are working on the car. As we enter, Beckett shakes his head and smirks at us. I avert my gaze quickly, so very aware that every guy in the garage knows exactly what we were just doing. The walk of shame is one thing, but when you have an audience that knows you're doing it, well … that's a lot more embarrassing.

Colton laughs beside me and squeezes my fingers laced with his. "What's so funny?" I mumble, still keeping my eyes trained on the ground.

"You're cute when you blush," he teases. "I prefer the pink parts elsewhere on you more though."

My mouth shocks open and before I can even recover, his mouth is on mine. The clang of tools surround us and yet all I hear is the beat of my heart. The kiss is merely a tease of what we did earlier, but when he pulls back after kissing the tip of my nose, a smirk curls up one corner of his mouth.

"What was that for?" Like I even care what the answer is. He can do that to me anytime, anywhere.

"You know me, sweetheart. If they're gonna stare, you might as well give them something good to stare at, right? Besides, if it wasn't clear enough earlier, I want everyone in here knowing you're mine."

My heart swells at his words before the sarcasm is off my tongue. "Staking a claim are we?"

"Baby, claim's already been made," he says, stopping to look at me with a smirk. "No doubt about that."

I roll my eyes and laugh at him as I keep walking. "C'mon, Ace," I say over my shoulder, "can't you keep up?"

I feel his hand smack my butt. "You sure as hell know I can keep anything up," he says, wrapping an arm around my shoulders and leaning down so his mouth is near my ear. "My dick, you pressed against the door, my stamina, and any other thing that can be considered up … but those are the most important ones, don't you think?" He chuckles as I shake my head and make a sound of amusement.

We sort out the fact that Sammy is going to take my car home for me and then Colton leads me to a covered parking area where Sex sits. I can't deny that the sight of the sexy-as-sin car brings back a rush of more than memorable memories that put a smirk on my face. From my locked gaze on the hood, I stare over to Colton where a lascivious grin meets mine. He raises his eyebrows, mischief dancing in his eyes, his tongue darting out to wet his bottom lip as he opens the door for me.

"Nice choice of car today," I tell him as I slide into the opulent interior.

"This reminds me of you, and I needed you here today," he says before shutting my door so I can't respond. And maybe it's best that I can't, because his simple statement means so very much to me.

Baby steps.

Within seconds we're on the freeway with the sounds of the Dave Matthews Band floating around us, the purr of the motor cocooning us, and the frenzied media following us. Colton looks in the rear view mirror before looking over at me from behind his sunglasses. "You buckled in?" he asks and all of a sudden my stomach twists in knots, fearing what's going to happen next.

I don't even have a chance to respond before the car surges forward, the motor revving, Colton laughing as the car flies faster than the press chasing us can go. I feel a surge of adrenaline and for a split second I can understand the pull of his addiction, but then I look up as he weaves in and out of traffic, and my heart lodges in my throat as the world beyond blurs.

Chapter Twenty-Five

I square up the documents on the kitchen counter. I'm satisfied with the transcription of Zander's deposition to bring formal charges against his father. I tuck them in the manila folder and realize I've lost track of time; the clock reads seven-forty and the boys have to be at the field by eight. Oh crap! I need to finish getting the stuff together for their games. I rise from the table and start filling sport bottles and putting them on the counter next to bags of sunflower seeds. I strain to hear the commotion in the bedrooms and can tell that Jackson has the boys on task and almost ready to leave.

"Hey, Ry?"

"Yeah?" I look up to see Jackson leaning his shoulder against the wall with concern in his eyes.

"Zander and Scoot are still asleep." He pauses for a minute and then continues. "Were you awake when Shane came in last night?"

I look at him, trying to figure out why he's asking. "Yes. I was reading in my room. Why?"

"Did you physically see him? Talk to him?"

Now alarm bells sound in my head, and I stop what I'm doing and turn to face him. "Uh-uh. I called out his name and he said goodnight and went to his room. You're scaring me, Jax, what's going on?"

"Well, it looks like Shane tied one on last night. He's passed out in his bed, his room reeks of beer, and by the looks of the bathroom he was reliving the night backwards into the toilet." He has a half-smirk on his face, and I know it's not appropriate but I have to stifle a laugh that Shane did something so normal for his age.

And then the responsible part of me takes over. I bite my lip and look at Jax. "We knew this would happen someday … shit, do you want me to deal with him or do you want to?"

"We'll be out in the van, Jax!" Ricky yells.

"Kay!" he responds before looking back to me. "I can stay here with Zand, Scoot, and Shane if you want to take baseball today?"

"No, that's cool," I tell him as he grabs the bottles. "We'll meet you at the field later to watch the games. I can handle Shane."

"You sure?"

"Positive."

Jax says goodbye and as he closes the door I don't feel so sure anymore. I sit down on one of the barstools and contemplate how exactly to handle a hungover sixteen year old. He's the oldest and the first of the lot to go through this, so I'm kind of lost. Of course I was too scared to drink in high school—always the consummate good girl—so I'm on foreign ground here.

My phone rings and I look down, a smile immediately lights up my face when I see it's Colton. "Good morning," I say as warmth fills my heart. The past few days have been good between us despite the underlying tension we've blatantly been ignoring over the impending paternity test results. Colton's been excited that he'll be returning to the office next week, wanting to be there to oversee the new adjustments to the safety device they're working on. I laughed and told him I thought it was funny that he'd returned to the track before the office, but he just said with a smirk that the track was a necessity and the office not so much.

"Hey … this bed is awfully lonely without you in it." His sleepy morning rasp pulls at me and his words seduce me when I have no business being seduced.

"Believe me, I'd much rather be there with you—"

"Then get here as quick as you can, baby, because time's wasting. I have a long list of things to do today," he says, humor edging the suggestive tone of his voice. And I love this about him—about us—that just his voice can help ease the stress of my morning.

"What is it you have to do today?"

"You on the couch, you on the counter, you against the wall, you just about any place imaginable …" His voice drifts off as the parts of my body still asleep suddenly snap awake.

I groan into the phone. "You have no idea how tempting that sounds because today's already turned to shit."

"Why? What happened?" he asks concerned.

"Shane had his first experience with alcohol and from what Jax says, it doesn't sound like it was a good one."

Colton belts out a laugh. "He got shit-faced? Attaboy, Shane!"

"Colton! I'm trying to raise respectable boys here!" And the minute the words are out of my mouth I realize what an old-fashioned prude I sound like, but it's true.

"Are you telling me I'm not respectable, Ryles?"

I smirk because I can picture the impish grin on his face right now. "Well, you do in fact do dirty things to me ..." I tease, my body tensing and the ache in my lower belly pulsing at the thought of our last little sexcapade on the stairs of the Malibu house the day before last.

His chuckle is seductive yet naughty. "Oh, baby, dirtying you up is what I do best, but I'm talking about everyone else. I got drunk with the best of them in high school, and I turned out all right."

"That's debatable," I tease. "So you're saying it's no big deal? To let him off the hook without any repercussions?"

"No, that's not what I'm saying. I just think it's a good sign that he's out being a typical sixteen-year-old kid. Not that it's good or bad, just typical. And as long as it's a one time deal—that he's not drinking to escape his past—then good for him."

In a sense I agree with Colton, but at the same time I know I need to address it with Shane, need to tell him it's not okay and it can't happen again, even though I know it will. "So how, man-that-used-to-be-a-reckless-teenager, should I handle this best?"

"I'm still reckless, Ry," he says with amusement in his voice. "That, my dear, will never change. Jax needs to deal with him because he's not going to listen to you."

"I beg to differ." I don't want the boys to not want to talk to me or listen to me because I'm one of the few female counselors in the house.

"Don't get your panties in a bunch, Thomas," he says with a laugh. "I'm not saying you can't handle it. I'm just saying that he's going to listen better if it comes from a man."

"Well, Jax, is at baseball so it has to be me."

"You're at the house alone?" I can hear the concern fill his voice immediately, and smile at his sudden need to watch out for me, protect me. It's quite cute.

"Colton." I sigh. "There are fifty photographers out front. I'm perfectly fine."

"Exactly. Fifty photographers that have no fucking business being there except to harass you and the boys. Fucking Christ!" He barks out to himself. "I'm so sick of my goddamn bullshit being on your doorstep."

"Really, it's not a—"

"I'll be there in thirty minutes," he says and the line clicks dead.

Okay. So he's coming to deal with the press, which will do no good, and I still have to figure out how to deal with Shane.

Fuck!

"You can play for another hour or so, Scooter, and then we have to head to the field, okay?"

"Yep!" he yells to me as he hustles down the hallway toward the family room where I'm sure Saturday morning cartoons will be in full swing momentarily.

I continue down the hall and stop when I pass Zander and Aiden's room. Zander's on the bed, blanket wrapped around his shoulders, precious stuffed dog grasped to his chest, and he is rocking back and forth with his eyes closed. I angle my head, take a step into the room, and watch him for a moment so I can figure out if he's dreaming or awake. When I step closer, I hear the quiet keening within his chest and then I move on instinct.

"Hey, Zander, you okay, buddy?" I ask gently, as I lower myself ever so slowly onto the mattress next to him.

He just continues rocking but lifts his head up to look at me, tears staining his face and utter heartbreak reflected in his eyes. Because no matter how much time passes, the memories will always be there burrowing their tentacles of destruction as deep as they can so he will never be able to forget. He might be able to move on at some point, but he will never forget.

"I want my mommy," he whimpers, and if my heart could shatter into a million pieces, it would for this little boy, who I love more than anything.

I ever so slowly pull him into my lap and wrap my arms around him, nestling his head under my neck so he doesn't see the tears I'm crying for him, his lost innocence, the part of him he'll forever ache for—his mother.

"I know, buddy," I tell him as I rock him. "I know. She'd be here if she could. She never would have left you if the angels hadn't needed her."

"But—but I need her too ..." He sniffs and there is nothing I can say to that. Nothing. So I press a kiss to his head and just hold him tighter, trying to let my love for him ease some of the heaviness in his heart, but know it will never be enough.

We sit there for a bit, him drawing comfort and solace from me as much as I am from him. He calms down some as minutes tick by, my hand smoothing over his hair and back as I try to figure out something to make him smile. "Hey, bud? Colton's on his way over."

I feel his body jerk to attention as red-rimmed eyes look up at me. "Really?"

And as if on cue, I hear commotion outside the front of the house. Even with the windows and blinds shut I can hear the purr of an engine, the clicks of the camera shutters, and the questions being called out.

"Yep, in fact I think he just got here."

Grateful for Colton's timing and the instant spark it puts in Zander's eyes, we rise and head toward the front of the house. I make sure the boys are in the family room so when I open the front door, they're out of the camera lens' way.

Colton pushes into the narrow opening of the doorway with a muttered curse as the door shuts behind him. He looks at me, lines of frustration etched in his face, and a brown grocery bag propped under his arm. He smiles. "Hey."

"Hiya, Ace," I say, stepping toward him to give him a kiss hello but his body stiffens. I immediately step away realizing one of the boys is behind me. Colton is always so aware of them and cautions kissing me in their presence, even a peck on the lips, because he knows how overprotective they are, and he never wants to upset that balance.

"Just kiss her and get it over with!" Scooter's exasperated voice behind me has Colton and me bursting out laughing as I turn to face him, a smile plastered on my lips.

I feel Colton's free hand on my lower back as he steps beside me and squats down in front of Scooter. "It's okay?" he asks the little boy whose eyes have just become the size of saucers. "I mean, it's not really polite to walk into another man's house and kiss his girl ... but since you're one of the men in the house, I guess I could kiss her if you tell me it's okay."

Scooter's mouth falls lax at Colton's comment and his spine stiffens with pride. "Really?" The excitement in his voice has me putting a hand over my heart. "Yeah ... it's okay. As long as you don't make her sad."

"Deal." Colton sticks his hand out, and they shake on it. My heart overflows with love, and I have to fight back the tears welling in my eyes for the second time today, but this time they're from the pride I feel for two of the men in my life.

"Well then," Colton says as he stands and looks at me, "the man of the house says I can kiss you."

My smile widens as Colton leans in and pecks my lips in a brotherly fashion. "Eeeewwww gross!" Scooter says, wiping his mouth off with the back of his hand and turning to run into the family room to tell Zander.

Colton looks over his shoulder to make sure Scooter is gone and when he turns back his lips find mine without a second thought. It's a brief kiss, but man does it pack a punch, more than reinforcing that he's the drug I can't live without. "Wow!" I say as he pulls back.

"He said I could do it." He just smirks and shrugs. "Where's our drunk skunk at?"

"Still asleep," I tell him as I look down at the brown bag under his arm. "What's that?"

Colton just grins. "A little something to make sure that he remembers this morning for a long time. Hair of the dog and all that."

"Colton," I warn as I notice the shape of the bag looks a little too similar to a six pack. "I can't give him beer! I'll get fired," I shout at him in a hushed tone.

He has the gall to just stand there and chuckle. "Exactly. That's why I am." And with that, Colton strides down the hallway to my right into Shane's room. Colton's words earlier that Shane won't listen to me has me walking down the hallway to see what he's going to do.

Colton pulls the blinds up, and bright light floods the room, before he looks over to his dresser, a huge smile spreading on his face. Within seconds, the pair of speakers that Shane's iPod is plugged into blare to life with a base thumping beat. Shane springs out of bed instantly, shouting and covering his ears and does a double take when he sees who is standing in front of his bed, arms crossed over his chest and eyebrows raised.

They stare at each other for a moment before Shane grabs the pillow and pulls it over his head to stop the sound and block the bright light. "Stop it!" he yells. Colton laughs and walks over to the iPod and flicks it off. "Thank you!" Shane's muffled voice says from beneath the pillow.

"Uh-uh," Colton says to him as he bounces on the bed beside him and pulls the pillows from his hands as Shane then uses his arms to cover his eyes. "By the smell of your room and the look on your face, I'd say you tied one on nice and hard last night. That right, bud?" He laughs, an amused borderline sinister laugh, when Shane doesn't respond. "Is your head pounding? The room spinning? Your eyes hurt? Does your stomach feel like you want to throw up but there's nothing there?"

"Shut up," Shane groans as he tries to pull the covers over his head, and Colton just yanks them back down.

"Nope. You wanna hang with the big boys—get plastered like they do—then it's time to wake up and take it like a man." From my vantage point in the hallway I watch Colton prop his back against the wall and get comfortable before he digs into the brown paper bag. I hear the crack of the beer can opening and Shane immediately sits up in bed, and looks at Colton like he's lost it.

"Are you fucking crazy?" Shane croaks in a panicked voice.

"Yep," Colton says as he looks over at Shane and grins. He takes a sip of the beer and then holds it out to Shane. "Sure as hell am. Drink up, son."

"No way!" Shane says as he backs away from the can like it's on fire. "You can't give me a beer!"

Colton raises his eyebrows. "I believe I just did. Now quit using that as an excuse. You were grown up enough to chug it down last night, right? So it's time to remind you just why you liked it so much." Colton shoves the beer back at him. "C'mon, take a drink. I dare you."

"What the—"

"Drink!" Colton pressures him. "What? You're cool enough to drink with your friends but not me?"

"It's going to make me puke!"

"Now you're catching on!" Colton says with a smirk as he reaches with his free hand back into the bag and grabs another beer. "I've got five more here for ya when you finish this one."

Shane's eyes grow huge and his face pales when Colton's words hit him. "No way! I'm going to throw up."

"*Good,*" Colton says as he gets in close to Shane's face. "Drink this," he says. "I want you to remember just how good it tastes coming back up the second time around. The next time your buddies push you to drink or you want to drink to look cool for the ladies ... I want you to remember how fucking cool you look bent over the toilet throwing this back up because I guarantee you from experience, it's not a pretty sight." Colton backs away from him and returns to his position against the wall, a smug smile on his face. He leans his head back but angles his eyes over to watch Shane. "You sure you don't want this beer? Don't want to remember what it tastes like?"

Shane shakes his head, a little shocked at the verbal lashing his idol just gave him, as am I.

When Colton speaks next, his voice is eerily calm. "Now that I've got your attention, a few ground rules, shall we?" He doesn't wait for Shane to respond. "How'd you get home last night, Shane?"

The question surprises me, just as it does Shane. "Davey brought me home."

"Did Davey drink last night too?" The quiet calm in Colton's voice has Shane averting his gaze, which makes my heart sink.

"He had a few." I can hear the shame in Shane's voice; he knows it was wrong.

"Eeeehhh! Wrong answer!" Colton says as he turns his head to look at him again. "You wanna be stupid and get drunk? That's one thing I can get. You want to step in a car and let someone else drive you who's drunk—because let's face it you were shit-faced so how do you know how many Davey had—that's something I won't tolerate! You have way too many people who love you in this house. *Care about you, Shane*—Ry, the boys, *me*—we don't want something to happen to you. So let me rephrase the question, okay? I'm not going to ask you if you're going to get drunk again because then you'll have to lie to me. Here's my question: Are you going to get in a car with another person who's been drinking?"

Shane swallows loudly and shakes his head no. When Colton just stares at him, he says aloud, "No."

"Good! Now we're getting somewhere ..." Colton says, pounding his hand against the wall loudly that has Shane jumping and grabbing his head, while Colton belts out a laugh. "You sure you don't want this beer?" He offers again to a frantic shake of Shane's head. "I love a smart kid so listen up, I don't care how the fuck you get home, call me if you have to, but don't do it again. Last thing ... *why?*"

Shane's eyes lift up to meet his. "What do you mean *why?*"

Colton stares at him long and hard and it drives me crazy that I'm not close enough to see the unspoken words pass between them. "To be cool? To impress a girl? To cover the pain from your mom? You don't have to tell me, Shane, but the answer is very important. It's something you need to answer for yourself." I see Shane's head lower and I suck in a breath with concern. Shane shifts and leans against the wall like Colton, legs crossed out in front of them, arms crossed over their chests, and heads angled up at the ceiling. The sight of them together like this is priceless, and I know this is one moment that will forever be etched in my memory.

Colton blows out a breath and when he starts speaking, his voice is so soft that I strain to hear him. "When I was little I had some bad shit happen to me. *Really bad shit.* And no matter what I did, or how good I was, or how hard I tried ... nothing mattered ... nothing stopped it. No one helped. So in my seven year old brain, it was my fault and even some days now, I still think that way. But the worst part was living with the pain and guilt from it." He sighs and turns his head from the ceiling and waits for Shane to do the same so they're looking at one another. "Shit, I started drinking when I was a helluva lot younger than you, Shane ... and I drank because it hurt so fucking much. And after some stupid stunts and some situations I was lucky enough to walk away from, my dad sat me down and asked me the same question I just asked you. Said the same things I said to you. But then he asked, 'Why drink to cover it up because hurting is feeling and feeling is living, and isn't it good to be alive?'" Colton shakes his head. "And you know what? Some days I thought it was bullshit, that I would never be able to spend a single day without thinking about it or hurting from it or feeling guilty about it ... and fuck, those days? I wanted to drink. At fifteen Shane, I wanted to drink to deal with it ... but my dad would sit me down and repeat those words to me. And you know what? He was right. It took time. Lots of time. And it never, ever goes away ... but I'm so glad I chose to feel over being numb. So glad I chose living over being dead."

I don't realize that I have tears sliding down my cheeks like Shane does until Colton reaches out and hooks an arm around his neck and pulls him close. He gives him a quick, but gruff man-hug that causes a sob to shake through Shane's body. Colton presses an uncharacteristic kiss to the top of his head and murmurs again, "Remember, hurting is feeling and feeling is living, and isn't it good to be alive?"

My heart is in my throat, my breath robbed, and any hope I ever had of walking away from this beautiful disaster of a man is completely stolen from me forever.

The damaged man helping the broken child.

He releases Shane from the hug and I can immediately sense they are both uncomfortable with their show of emotion. Colton shoves off of the bed and laughs when he offers Shane the beer again and he pushes it away. He gathers the bag with the rest of them and starts to walk toward the door but turns back. "Hey, Shane? You stink, dude. Take a shower and get dressed, we've got some baseball to go watch."

Colton walks out of the door and stops to stare at me, so many emotions swimming in his eyes as he sees the tears staining my cheeks. I say the only thing I can. "Thank you," I mouth. He nods as if he doesn't trust himself to speak and walks down the hall.

Chapter Twenty-Six

Colton

"You've got them now, Jax?" I ask as I watch Scooter buy some sugary crap from the snack bar with the cash I gave him. Shane refused. Fucker's still green in the face. He won't be eating anything for a while, unless he wants it to come back up.

Ah, sweet memories of being a teenager and getting lit like a goddamn Christmas tree. I can't help but feel sorry for him, but hell if it's not kind of funny watching this rite of passage.

Jax adjusts his baseball cap, sets his bat down and walks over to me. "Yeah, I got 'em." He reaches out to me and we shake hands. "Thanks for …" He lifts his chin over in Shane's direction.

"No prob." I laugh. "He had nothing on my first dance with the bottom of the bottle, but I talked to him."

"Thanks. Did Ry change her mind? Is she not coming?"

"No," I shake my head as I watch Ricky take a swing and rip the ball out of the infield during his batting practice. I whistle so he knows I saw him and he has the cutest damn grin on his face when he looks at me. I know more than anyone that acknowledgment in any form goes a long way. "She is. I guess Zander had a rough morning so she didn't want him paraded around in front of the press. So I brought the boys, hoping they'd follow me."

Fucking vultures. I look out toward the parking lot by the Range Rover and see them all standing there, cameras slung around their necks, long range lenses pointing at me; hoping to catch … fuck if I know what at a kids' little league game. But shit, they maintain their distance and don't bombard me when I'm with the kids, and I'm a little shocked. Since when do they have any goddamn manners? It's not like I'm going to be doing anything exciting behind the bleachers and creating any more unfounded illegitimate children. "Anyway..." I shrug "...it seems to have worked."

Jax laughs as he looks at the mob of them in the parking lot. "Ya think? Craziness, man, to live with that all the time. Do you ever get used to it?"

"Can a car drive without wheels?" Stupidest fucking question ever but it's Jax. Dude's cool. Looks out for Ry.

"True," he says with a nod.

I make a bit more small talk with him before I head out to give the parasitic shitbags by my car the close up pictures that'll land them some money. That will hopefully keep them at bay for another goddamn day.

They hit me with their cameras as I walk by, and it takes everything I have not to throw a punch because hell if it wouldn't feel good to just let loose and have at 'em. Fucking Chase. Her words stop me only because it will harm Ry if I pull the reckless bad boy gone crazy that they're pushing for with their bullshit questions about her being a home wrecker.

Motherfucking promises. Fuck them all to hell. This is why I never make them. Never did before Rylee anyway. Who'd have thought the day would come that I'd be pussy whipped and okay with it.

Add another layer of ice to Hell because it's become colder than the arctic circle with the shit she's changing in me.

I told her I was trying to be a better man. Well, fuck me. Little did I know we were going to get thrown into this shit storm that was gonna pull us every which way like a motherfucking tug-of-war.

I've been good so far. Haven't picked up my phone and ripped Tawny apart for this bullshit charade she's pulling, for throwing Rylee to the damn wolves to try and hurt me. But I know if I do it's just going to prove that she's gotten to me. And to her, that's winning half the battle.

"So when's the wedding, Colton?"

"Does Tawny know you're with Rylee today?"

"Have you picked out names for your son yet?

Another cameraman jostles me from the side, and I whirl on him, fists clenched, jaw grinding. "Back the fuck off, man!"

Rylee. Rylee. *My fucking Rylee*. I have to repeat it over and over to help me ignore their bullshit lies and prevent myself from losing my shit.

At least the guy backs off so I can open the door to the car. Thank God for expensive ass cars because the minute I slam the door shut the sound silences and the tinted windows make it hard for the cameras to get their shot of me about to go apeshit. As much as I need to sit here and calm the fuck down, there's no way I can with the circus surrounding me.

I rev the engine and hope they get the clue and back off so I don't run them over. One more rev of the engine and the slight movement backwards has them all running off to get in their cars so they can chase me.

Fucking Christ.

Have drama, please follow. If I put stupid-ass bumper stickers on my car, that's what it would say.

I check for kids and rev the engine once more before I quickly leave the lot. I get clear of the craziness when I lose most of the cars at a red light I fly through on the tail end of a yellow. I finally breathe a sigh of relief, can have a minute of peace humming along to *Best of You* on the radio, and then I look down at my phone.

And the air I just got back gets sucker punched right out of me. My foot falters on the gas like a fucking rookie driver from the text displayed on the screen.

Sealed envelope sitting on my desk. Results are back. Call me.

My entire body freezes—lungs, heart, throat, everything. I stare straight ahead, my knuckles turn white as I grip the steering wheel, trying to get a grip on the onslaught of emotions burying me alive.

I force myself to breathe, to blink, to think. The minute my head's commands to my body click, I swerve across the lane causing horns to blare. I pull into the closest driveway I see, a strip mall parking lot, and slam on the brakes.

I pick up my phone to call my lawyer but put it back down as I squeeze my eyes shut and try to get a handle on the nerves suddenly shooting through me. *This is it.* The answer on the other end of the line is going to be either my biggest fuck up or my greatest relief.

The certainty I felt before that this couldn't be true, doesn't feel so goddamn certain anymore. I blow out a breath, pound a fist on the console, grab a figurative hold of my balls, and pick up the phone.

Each ring destroys me. It's like waiting for the chair to be kicked out from beneath my feet with a noose looped harmlessly around my neck.

"Donavan."

It takes me a minute to respond. "Hey, CJ." My voice sounds so foreign, like a little kid waiting for his punishment to be decided.

"You ready?"

"Fucking Christ, tell me already, will you?" I bark.

He chuckles as I hear the paper tear. Easy for him to laugh right now when my heart's hammering, head is pounding, and foot is bouncing on the floorboard. And then I hear CJ exhale.

"You're good."

There's no way I heard him right. "*What?*"

"She lied. The baby's not yours."

I pump my fist out into the air and shout. I squeeze my head in both of my hands as the adrenaline hits me at full force, hands tremble and tears well. I can't even process a thought. I know CJ is talking but I can't hear him because my heart is pounding in my ears from the adrenaline hitting me like it does at the start of a race. I raise a hand to run it through my hair but stop midair to pound on the steering wheel before scrubbing at my face because I'm so overwhelmed … so inundated with fucking relief I can't keep a single thought straight, except for one.

It's not mine.

I didn't fuck up a poor soul's life by tainting it with my blood.

By being born to a manipulative bitch like Tawny.

"You okay, Wood?"

It takes me a minute to swallow and find my voice. "Yeah," I sigh. "Better than okay. Thanks."

"I'll have Chase issue a press release for—"

"I'll cover that," I tell him, wanting nothing more to than to feed the vultures a taste of crow and get their fucking obtrusive cameras out of our lives for a bit. Let Rylee adjust to my crazy-ass life while we find our footing.

There I go again. Thinking about finding our footing and the future and shit with her. My fucking kryptonite.

Motherfucker.

And it hits me.

Rylee.

I need to tell her.

"Thanks again, CJ, I gotta call—I gotta go."

I hang up and immediately start to dial Rylee but my hands are shaking so badly from the adrenaline racing through my blood, I stop for a second.

And then I realize I want to end this once and for all before I talk to Ry. I want to call her with the slate clean so I can tell her this is all behind us. Baby, Tawny, lies—everything is over and fucking done with.

I take a deep breath as I dial the number that used to be so familiar but now just makes my blood boil.

"Colton?" I like the fact she's surprised, that I've caught her off guard.

Time to play ball.

"Tawny." My voice is flat, unemotional. I don't say anything else. I want her to squirm. I want her to wonder if I know or not. She's ballsy enough to lie to my face, let's see if she's gonna keep up the charade or lay her cards on the table.

Because fuck if the paternity test isn't my ace in the hole.

"Hi," she says so softly that I can't really figure out if she's being timid or trying to sound seductive.

Either one has my stomach churning.

I chew my cheek, trying to figure out where I want to go with this conversation because as much as I want to make her suffer, I just want her gone. Sayonara, adios, the whole fucking goodbye. She clears her throat and I know the silence is killing her.

Good.

"Colton," she says my name again, and I have to bite my tongue, let her suffer. "Did you need something? I—I'm surprised to hear from you ..."

"Really? Surprised?" The sarcasm drips from my voice like fucking motor oil. "Now why would that be?"

She starts to stutter out words but none of them get past the first syllable. "Save it Tawn. Just tell me one thing. *Why?*"

When the hell did she get like this? When did she go from my college sweetheart to the conniving, manipulative bitch on the other end of the line? What the fuck did I miss?

"Why?" she asks, drawing the word out. We've been friends for so long, I can tell she's fishing. She's looking for a clue so she can take it and twist it and manipulate it into whatever I'm going to say that suits her best.

And I'm done. The innocent routine ended a long time ago when it comes to her and her goddamn lies. At least I recognize it now. After what she did to Ry? And now tried to do to me?

Batter up, sweetheart.

"Yeah, why?" I bite out. "Because you fucking lied through those perfect white teeth of yours? Used my accident to—"

"Colton I didn't try to—"

"Shut up, Tawny! I don't care about your goddamn pathetic excuses!" I shout at her because I'm on a roll and fuck if it doesn't feel good to let it out. Release all of the anger and the fear and the uncertainty that's ruled my life over the past few weeks. Left me a goddamn disoriented mess just like driving blindly into the smoke after a crash to hope I come out the other side of its oppressive fucking haze. "You didn't try to what?"

My anger's eating me raw. I need to move. Need to expel some of it so I shove open the door of the Rover and start pacing back and forth, shoving my free hand through my hair as my feet hit the ground beneath me.

"You didn't try to use my accident—*my fucked up head*—as a means to get what you wanted? Tell me I slept with you when I didn't? Trap me into being the daddy for your illegitimate kid? *How fucked up is that?* What kind of piece of shit does that, Tawn? Huh? Can you answer me why the woman I used to know—*was my friend* once upon a fucked up time—had to stoop so damn low that you used a kid to try and get me back?"

There's not enough asphalt in this parking lot right now to help me abate the fury in my veins, because the more I think about it—about what she was trying to do to me—the stronger my rage grows.

Goddamn right she's quiet, I tell myself, when she doesn't respond to a single thing I've said. All I hear are whimpering cries on the other end of the line.

"To think I used to care about you. Fucking unbelievable, T." I shake my head and swallow a huge gulp of air. "Is this how you treat the people you claim to love? Use a kid to manipulate? To deceive to get love?"

"You got back the results." It's not a question, just a soft statement that's eerily calm.

And she knows.

"Yeah, I got them back." The quiet steel in my voice should have her running for cover.

"You fucked with me once, Tawn. I dealt with it as gently as possible since our families are connected." I lean my back against the Rover and just keep shaking my head, my pulse racing, and breath panting out in shallow breaths. "But you obviously don't care about that because you just majorly screwed with me again. Tried to ruin me with the one thing you know would fuck me up more than anything else. So I suggest you listen closely because I'm only going to say this once. I'm done with you. Don't contact me. You sure as fuck better not contact Ry. And family functions?" I laugh and it sure as shit isn't because I'm feeling happy. "I suggest you have the stomach flu or some other reason not to attend. Got it? You were my friend and now you're just ... nothing."

"Please listen," she pleads and her voice—the voice that used to mean something—does absolutely nothing to me. At all. "Don't be so cold—"

"Cold?" I shout at her, my body vibrating with anger. "Cold? Cold? Get ready for the polar fucking ice cap because we're done. You're dead to me, Tawny. Nothing else left to say." And I hang up the phone despite the sob I hear coming through the other end. I turn and brace my hands on the side of my car as I process everything. As I try to comprehend how a childhood friend could do that to me.

And I realize it doesn't really fucking matter. The *whys*, the *what fors*. Any of it.

Because I have Ry now.

Holy shit. I'm so wrapped up in my head and what I just did, that I forgot the whole reason I did it.

Rylee.

I get in the car as I fumble with the phone in my hand, and it takes me a second to bring her up from my recent calls list. The phone rings but I'm impatient. "C'mon, Ry!" I pound the steering wheel with my fist as the ringing filters through the speakers of the car.

"Hey!" She laughs.

The sound. *My fucking God*, that carefree sound in her voice grabs a hold of my damn heart and just squeezes it so tight I feel like I can't breathe. It's like all of a sudden all of the bullshit is gone with Tawny and the crash, and even though I can't take a breath, I feel like I can breathe for the first time in a long ass time. Is this what it's supposed to feel like? Fucking clarity and shit?

I start to speak and I can't. What the hell? It's like I want to say everything to her at once and yet I can't think of how to start. I start laughing, like batshit crazy laughing, because I'm the middle of some shitty strip mall and it hits me now?

"You okay?" she asks in that sexy tone of hers.

"Yeah," I choke out through my laughter. "I just—"

The giggle comes through the speaker loud and clear and I just stop talking. It's Zander's and it's the first time I've ever heard it. The sound cuts me open like a filet knife. I swear to God I couldn't be any more of a chick right now with my emotions all over the fucking place.

"Go get your glove in the backyard and we'll get going, okay?" I hear him agree through the line. "Sorry, you were going to tell me what was so funny."

And I start to talk, begin to tell her about the test results when I hear a sound that is so horrifying it reaches into my chest and tears into my hardened heart. "What the fuck is that?" I can't say it quickly enough because despite the high-pitched scream that sounds like a wounded animal fighting for his life, I can still hear Rylee moving through the phone line.

My stomach churns at the sound and her goddamn silence. "Ry? Tell me what's going on. Ry?"

"No, no, no, no!" she says and there's something in her voice—fear, disbelief, and shock mixed with defiance—that has shivers dancing up my spine and has me immediately starting the car and throwing it into gear.

"Goddammit, Ry! Talk to me. What the fuck is wrong?" I yell into the phone, panic overtaking me, but all I hear is her heavy breathing. And then whimpering. "Rylee!"

"You can't have him!" she says in an eerily calm voice, which sounds far away and has me cutting off some poor schmuck in the lane next to me.

"Who's there, Ry? *Tell me, baby, please*," I plead, fear like I've only ever known in my youth tasting like bile in my mouth. Fear in my every fucking nerve. I struggle with deciding whether to hang up and call 9-1-1, but that would mean I'd have to hang up on her—not hear her, not know she's okay.

"You fucking bitch!" is all I hear before she cries out in pain and the phone goes dead.

"No!" I scream and smash my hand into the steering wheel. My eyes blur as I try to push the numbers on my phone, but my fingers are shaking so damn bad that I can't even manage 9-1-1 until after the third try.

"9-1-1. What's your emergency?" The disembodied voice answers.

"Please help them. They're screaming and ... they're screaming!" I plead with her.

"Who's screaming, sir?"

"Rylee and Zand..." I can't fucking think straight; ice floods my veins and my only thought is I need to get to them so I don't even realize I'm not making any goddamn sense. "Please, someone is there and—"

"Sir, what's your name? What's the address?"

"Co-Colton," I stutter out when I realize I don't even know the address. Just the street. "Switzerland Avenue."

Oh fuck. Oh fuck. *Hang on, baby. Hang on.* I'm coming. It's all I repeat in my head—over and over—as my body shakes.

"What's the address sir?"

"I don't fucking know!" I shout at the 9-1-1 operator. "The one with all the goddamn paparazzi out front. There's no one else in the house but her and a little boy. *Please*! Quickly."

And when I look up from ending the call, I have to slam on the brakes as I hit fucking road construction.

"Fuck!" I yell, laying in on my horn like it's my lifeline.

Rylee.

She's my only thought.

Rylee.

Please God, no.

Chapter Twenty-Six Bonus Scene

Colton

No.

Please no.

Rylee.

She's my only focus as my tires squeal around the last turn onto her street. I'm a goddamn mess and the sight of police cars scattered all over the block – doors open, lights on, sirens off – scares the shit out of me.

Then a sliver of relief.

If they were injured, ambulances would be here. And if they were still inside, then the police would be running around in a frenzy to try and help them. But they're not. No one is doing a goddamn thing except for all huddling together, a line of black uniforms, shoulder to shoulder.

See? They must be safe.

Something to my right catches my attention. I freeze. Never mind. The ambulance is here; its lights are flashing but its siren is silent.

Spiderman.

Why isn't the siren on?

Batman.

Why is everyone standing around?

Superman.

Where the fuck is Rylee and Zander?

Ironman.

Thoughts scream in my own head, but I can't process them. They're lost in the fear clenching every single fucking part of me. The damage must be done. He's already taken them.

Or worse.

Numbness hits and the tang of fear I've only ever tasted before back in that dank fucking room of my youth fills my mouth. Owns my soul. Takes over.

I drive as far as I can into the melee. With fumbling fingers I fling the door open, the Rover still running, and sprint as fast as I can down the sidewalk. I try to shout, to call for her so she knows I'm here, but all that comes out is a rasp of sound, her name broken.

Policemen shout at me. I can't hear a word they say because my only focus is on the front door, the caution tape I can now see being pulled tight across the street, and the intensity on the faces of the wall of uniforms.

Two cops rush me. I resist, try to shove them off me and push as far as I can toward the house.

"Rylee," I grunt out as they slam me against the cruiser behind me. Even with adrenaline owning my body, I have nowhere near enough strength to break free from a two officer tag team.

But that doesn't stop me from trying.

"*Where is she?*" I yell as I continue to struggle, fear and adrenaline dominating my body and mind. "*Rylee!*" I resist but when I see other officers put their hands on the butts of their holstered guns, I relent.

Calm the fuck down, Donavan. Good luck with that.

"Okay," I tell them as I shrug their hands off of me. "Please just tell me—I'm the one who called—I know who's in there!"

And now I have their attention.

Within moments I've explained everything I can think of, but they haven't said a single word to me. Nothing.

An officer tells me to stay put, another keeps his hand on my shoulder, afraid I'm going to fucking bolt. And he's right. I do want to. So I do the only thing I can, I put my head in my hands and try to keep from choking over the fear lodged in my throat.

And I repeat the chant that she's said for me in my time of need. Over and over. Fucking Christ. Where are the superheroes when I need them?

Or are they not coming because it's already too late?

The officer must sense my restlessness, must know that if I don't move some, I'm going to implode with the pressure in my chest and fear in my heart – the one Rylee brought back to life. So he releases my shoulder and I'm immediately on the move, feet eating up the same six concrete panels of sidewalk, over and over.

I look up when I hear footsteps. "Talk to me. *Please*," I beg. "Tell me she's okay. Zander's okay. He's fucking traumatized. *Please*." My voice breaks as tears prick the back of my eyes like pins. I welcome the pain, hold onto it because it's the only way I can cope right now with all of the unknowns.

"The woman and little boy—"

"Her name is Rylee!" I shout. "She's not a faceless, nameless victim. She's my Rylee." *My checkered flag*. Oh god! "And Zander. Rylee and Zander. Call them their names. Acknowledge that they're people with families goddammit!" I fist my hands, desperate to hurt something, break anything, to abate my restlessness. But it won't help. Nothing will. Except for getting to see them.

I lace my fingers on my neck and pull down, force myself to breathe. I need to calm the fuck down or they're going to kick me out of here. My chest aches and if I had any doubt before I know for sure now: That woman owns this heart of mine.

Rylee. Hang in there, baby. Be strong. For me. For Zander. Please.

The police office looks at me again and I'm such a fucking mess—so inside my own head—that I forgot he was coming to give me information.

"Rylee and Zander," he says using their names, "and the suspect are isolated in the backyard."

"Then go in there and get them the fuck out of there! C'mon! Do your goddamn jobs!" I shout with hands fisted and teeth gritted. My mind is so overwhelmed that the stupidity of my comment doesn't register until I notice the officer before me glance to the one beside me.

And then I know.

"Has he hurt her?"

Silence.

"A gun?"

Crickets.

"Has he hurt Zander?"

"No."

No to all of the questions or just the one about Zander? What are they not telling me?

My chest constricts. My world spirals like the tumbling of the car in the wreck. One second. That's all I allow myself to feel before I shut down. Fuck this. Fuck everyone.

I shove away from them, pace down the sidewalk, and try to wrap my head around all of this. Take a moment. Then I stride back to him, know it won't do a bit of goddamn good, but ask anyway. "You've gotta get me in the house. Right. Fucking. Now!" I demand as a dog starts barking somewhere.

"Sir, keep your voice down. The suspect doesn't know we're here and we're trying to keep it that way. We've got tactical in the kitchen to take a shot if need be. We don't want to escalate the situation."

And all I hear is that he doesn't know we're here. So that means Rylee doesn't know we're here. She doesn't know help is here. And that scares the shit out of me more than anything.

My selfless saint.

"If need be? He has a fucking gun right? What more do you need to know?"

"We're doing everything we can," he says in that placating tone I want to rip from his throat.

"No you're not!" I bark. "Do you have them safe? NO YOU DON'T!"

"Sir, if you can't settle down, we're going to have to escort you from the premises."

Panic rifles through me. I can't be taken farther away than I already am. I look over at the house and think of earlier today: my welcome kiss with Rylee, my chat with Shane. How could a perfect morning turn into this? How could I leave her to face this alone?

I squeeze my eyes shut and drop my head for a beat before looking back at the man in front of me. "Officer..." I glance at his name tag, try to make a connection with him so that he understands how important my next words are. "Officer Destin – Please. You have to let her know we're out here. Zander's one of her boys. She'll do anything—*anything*—to keep him safe." The thought terrifies me. *Fuck being calm*. I grab the front of the his shirt. "Do you understand what I'm saying? She'll sacrifice herself for one of her boys...so fucking do something *now*!"

Hands yank me backwards. Voices threaten me. I shrug them off and hold my hands up in an apology. "We're doing everything we can to—"

"Don't give me the bullshit line. Don't stand here. Do something!"

They nod their heads like they get it but they don't. Not even fucking close. They don't have a freight train of fear derailing inside of them because the people they care about are in a backyard with a murderer.

Time fucking stretches.

Seconds.

Minutes.

Forever.

It feels like years are being scraped off of my life by a dull knife with each and every passing second. Eventually I'm moved into a tactical van near the front of the house. They say it's to keep me better apprised of the situation. I know it's because they can see me about to explode from the unknown and that when I do, I'll take matters into my own hands and compromise their operation.

My mind races but I can't focus on a goddamn thing but Rylee and Zander and being stuck inside this tiny truck where I can't pace and can't talk. All I can do is sit here with guys in headsets and monitors with white snow, a constant on their screens.

"I'm not letting you take him."

And then I hear her voice.

My body jolts to attention. Adrenaline pumps through my veins from the goddamn defiance in her voice. *She's all right.*

I lean forward and focus on the grainy image that springs to life on the bank of monitors in from of me. I have to fight the sob of relief when I see her, hear her voice, when all I've felt for the past however fucking long it's been is fear.

And the wave of reprieve is short lived because when I'm finally able to tear my eyes from her, there's only one other thing I can focus on: the gun that is aimed directly at her.

Chapter Twenty-Seven

"Spiderman. Batman. Superman. Ironman. Spiderman. Batman …" Zander repeats it over and over as he sits balled up in a corner behind me in the backyard. It's the only thing I can hear over the buzzing in my head right now from the force of the punch. Zander's hands are over his ears and he rocks back and forth as he chants, withdrawing into himself. Into the world he wants to exist, where there are no bad men wielding guns or fathers holding knives cutting their wives apart.

The problem is that in Zander's world, they are one in the same.

I notice all of this in the split second after I'm punched in the face, my body flinging and twisting from the impact to see my sweet boy shrinking into himself. Time stands still then begins to move in slow motion. The pain in my cheek and eye does nothing to abate the fear in my heart as I look up to meet the eyes of the man that's been a constant presence in my life over the past few weeks. His hat and dark glasses have been knocked off and it hits me.

I know this man.

I've seen him before.

He's the man who gave me the creeps in the Target parking lot. He's the man from the dark blue sedan parked outside of The House and my house, following me. Without his hat and sunglasses I can see Zander in him. I know why he seemed so familiar in the parking lot that day. He has the same color eyes, the same features; his hair is longer and a bit darker, but the resemblance is unmistakable.

My eyes skim over the matte black metal of the pistol he has pointed at me and then to his eyes—dark pools of unemotional blackness—that are flickering back and forth from me to Zander and his incessant chanting of superheroes in the background.

"What did you do to him?" he shouts at me angling the gun over to Zander and then back to me. "Why's he doing that? Answer me!"

Stay calm, Rylee. Stay calm, Rylee.

"He—he's scared." *You did this to him,* I want to scream at him. *You did this, you useless piece of murdering sack of shit,* but all I do is repeat myself, trying to hide my fear and keep myself from stuttering. I try to focus on the pounding of my heart, counting the beats thumping in my ears to keep me calm. I can feel the rivulets of sweat trickle between my shoulder blades and breasts. I can smell the fear and my stomach revolts, knowing it's mine that I smell—mixed with his.

And I hold onto that thought.

That he's scared too.

Think, Ry. Think. I need to keep him calm but protect Zander, and I have no clue how to do that. The unfettered fear I feel is scattering my thoughts, robbing me of coherency. Of what in the hell I should do, because I know he's murdered before. Murdered the mother of his child, his wife no less.

What's going to stop him from murdering me?

He has nothing to lose.

And that more than anything scares the shit out of me.

I force a swallow, my eyes flicking all over the backyard. I see his camera and fake press pass on the ground by the gate. I see my cell phone in the edge of the grass, where it scattered when he hit me, and I immediately think of Colton.

I instantly grab on to the hope that he heard me, knows we're in trouble, will call for help—because if he didn't, I have no chance at protecting Zander against this madman. Of protecting myself.

My tears sting, and the swelling in my eye from where he ambushed me, hurts like a bitch. My hands are shaking and my breath hitches in fear, while the increased volume of Zander's chant is adding a heightened level of stress to the whole situation.

It's the only sound I can hear in the early morning silence—the chants of a little boy knowing he has no hope left. And with each passing moment, the whispered words get louder and louder as if he's trying to drown out the sound of his dad's voice.

"Wh—what do you want?" I finally ask over Zander's voice, sensing his grasp on reality is long gone. And I don't know how to rationalize with a crazy person.

He steps toward me, his eyes running down the length of my body, and even though my nerves are already on high alert, the look in his dead eyes when he scrapes them back up causes new ones to hum.

Warning bells go off and my stomach squeezes violently—so much so that I have to fight the nausea that threatens.

He reaches the gun out, and I freeze as he runs the tip of it up and down the side of my cheek. The cold of the steel, the hard reality of the metal on my flesh and what it represents, causes the blood in my veins to turn to ice.

"You're a pretty little thing aren't you, *Rylee*." The way he says my name, as if he's fucking it with his tongue, has me gagging. In an instant he has my cheeks squeezed tightly in his hands, his face inches from mine. Tears start streaming down my face. I want to be tough. I want to tell him to fuck off and die. I want to scream for Zander to run and get help. I want to plead with God, *with anyone*, for help. I want to tell Colton I love him. But I can't because none of that is possible right now. My knees are shaking, my teeth are trying to chatter inside of his grip. Everything I am—my future, my possibilities, my next breath—is at this man's whim.

He comes in closer so I can feel his breath feather over my lips as his fingers dig deeper into the sides of my cheeks, and I can't help the cry of fear that falls from my lips. "The question is, *Rylee* ... exactly how far would you go to protect one of *your boys?*"

"*Fuck you*." The garbled words are out of my mouth before I can stop them, anger removing the filter between my head and mouth. And before I can blink, his fist slams into my abdomen, and I'm propelled backwards. I land with a thud against the concrete patio, my shoulders and head hitting the wood fence behind me.

The terror consuming my body overshadows pain from the blow. I've landed near Zander so I scramble as quickly as I can over to his side and pull him into me, trying to protect him in any way I can. I know he's behind me, can feel the heavy presence of the gun I know is pointed at me, but I rock Zander.

"It's okay, Zand. He's not going to hurt you. I'm not going to let him hurt you," I tell him in a hushed voice, but Zander doesn't stop rocking, doesn't stop chanting, and I'm so petrified right now I start chanting for the superheroes with him as we sit in a backyard built on hope and what I fear will soon be marred with violence.

"I've come to take my son." If I thought his voice was cold before, his tone now matches the steel of his gun.

"No," I tell him, the waver in my voice betraying the confidence of what I want to say.

"Who the fuck do you think you're dealing with?" he growls, pointing the gun into my back, its hard nose digging deep between my shoulder blades. "It's time to step away from my son."

I squeeze my hands into fists to quit their shaking so Zander doesn't know how scared I am. I don't want his father to realize it either. I force a swallow as Zander's sobs start racking through his body, and if I didn't already know, I know now with such clarity—with a cold sweat breaking over my skin and fear in my heart—that I can't let his father take him. That I'll protect him with everything I have because no one else could before.

The muzzle in my back digs deeper, and I bite back a yelp of pain as tears freely flow down my cheeks. I begin to worry my bottom lip between my teeth, because in a moment I'm going to stand up. And when I turn around I have to show him I'm not scared of him. I have to put on the performance of a lifetime in order to save this little boy.

"Now!" he shouts at me, my body jumping as his voice cuts through the constant hum of Zander's chanting.

I lean my mouth down by Zander's ear and try to still him as he rocks, hoping that my words get to him—break through the world he's transported his mind to—in order to save himself from the fear and memories of his father.

"Zander, listen to me," I tell him. "I'm not going to let him take you. I promise. The superheroes are coming. They're coming okay? I'm gonna stand now but when I say Batman I want you to run as fast as you can into the house okay? *Batman*."

I just finish my words when I feel the gun leave my shoulder blades but feel his boot connect with my left side. I groan in pain as I absorb the impact, tensing my arms around Zander as we push harder into the fence we're cornered against.

"Get the fuck up, *Rylee*."

"Batman, okay?" I say again, gritting my teeth as I breathe through the pain and force myself to rise on wobbly legs. I take a deep breath and turn to face him.

"You're a tough cookie!" He sneers at me. "I *like* my women tough."

I swallow the bile rising in my throat and force evenness in my tone that I hope I can maintain. "I'm not letting you take him."

He laughs out loud, raises his face up to the sky, before looking back at me, and I wonder if I just missed my one chance to tell Zander to go. To run. My heart twists at the thought. "Now, I really don't think you're in the position to be telling me what exactly I *can and cannot* be doing. Right?"

My head races for things to say. Ways to calm down the nerves I can see are starting to overtake him with each passing second. But all the same, I need this time. The longer I have, the more likely help might be coming. "There's a yard full of press out front. How are you going to leave with him?"

He laughs again and I know the sound will haunt my dreams for the rest of my life. "That's where you're wrong. They all left with your hotshot boyfriend and followed him." He steps closer and raises the gun to my face. "It's just you, and me, and Z-man over there. So what do you have to say to that, huh?"

I swear all of the blood in my body drains to my feet because I have to struggle to remain focused on standing as the dizziness assaults me. After a moment, I manage to steady myself, to see through the blackness clouding my vision, and try to figure out what to do next.

The only thought I can come up with is to distract him somehow, lunge for the weapon, and scream at Zander to run.

But how?

When?

We stand for what seems like forever—a silent standoff where it's more than evident who holds all the power in this forced relationship. As time stretches I see his hands starting to shake, his facial muscles twitching, and the sweat beading, all while the sound of Zander's escalating chants continue to add more pressure to the unstable situation.

"Shut him the fuck up!" he screams at me as his eyes flicker all over the yard like a trapped animal unsure of its next move.

I startle when I hear a noise behind Zander's dad. My heart leaps in my chest as the next door neighbor's dog barks viciously through the fence. Zander's father twists at the sound, the gun moving with him. I act on instinct, not allowing myself to think of the consequences.

"BATMAN!" I scream at the same time I lunge at Zander's father. I collide into him, the harsh impact of my athletic frame against his knocks all thoughts from my head, except for one, I hope Zander heard me. That I got through to him and he's running to save himself because I just sealed my fate if I'm not successful.

The sound is deafening.

The crack of the gun going off.

The jerk of his body from its recoil.

My scream, a primal sound I hear but don't even recognize as my own. Then it stops. The wind is knocked out of me as we slam to the ground. I'm momentarily stunned—my body, my mind, my heart—as I land on top of him, before I try to struggle to get away. I have to get the gun, I have to make sure Zander is gone.

I push up off the vile man beneath me, still struggling. My only thought is *get the gun, get the gun, get the gun*, and my hands slip in the slickness beneath me. I shove backwards as panic and pain radiate through me. I land with a thud on my ass, the force jolting all the way up my spine and snapping my mind out of the shock it's in.

I lose focus on the man, as I look at the blood on my trembling hands. I take in the blood covering my T-shirt with Ricky's team's mascot printed on the front. My mind scrambles to think, frantically searches its recesses for what I'm supposed to be doing because the sight—so much blood—is making me dizzy.

I'm confused.

I'm scared.

Dizzy.

My world goes black.

Chapter Twenty-Eight

"Please, baby, please wake up."

Colton? My head is foggy as I hear his voice and smell him near. I try to figure out what exactly is going on. My eyelids feel so heavy, but I can't open them just yet.

"Sir, you need to let me examine—"

"I'm not going fucking anywhere!"

It's so warm and cozy here in the darkness—so safe—but why is Colton ... Then it all hits me like a tidal wave of overwhelming emotions. I start to fight to sit up. "Zander!" His name is barely a croak as I struggle against arms, hands, not sure what else is holding me down.

"Shh, shh, shh! It's okay, Ry. It's okay."

Colton.

My whole body sags momentarily. Colton is here. My eyes open, tears already welling in them, and the first sight I see is him. My ace. A shining light in all of this darkness. His eyes meet mine, the lines around his deep with concern and a forced smile on those devastating lips of his. "You're okay, baby."

I blink rapidly as everything else comes into focus, the flurry of activity around us in the backyard—policemen, medics. "Zander. Gun. Dad." My mind is reeling and I can't get the thoughts into words fast enough, my eyes flitting back and forth, focusing on a group of men hunched over something to the side of me.

I keep repeating the words until Colton leans down and presses a kiss to my mouth. I taste salt on his lips and my mind tries to grasp why he's been crying. When he pulls back, his smile is a little less shaky. "There's my girl," he says softly, his hands smoothing over my hair, my cheeks, my face. "You're okay, Ry. Zander's okay, Ry." He leans his forehead against mine.

"But there was blood—"

"Not yours," he says, his lips curving into a relieved smile against mine. "Not yours," he repeats. "You were ridiculously stupid and I'm so angry at you for it, but you went for the gun and the police took their shot. His blood, baby. It was his blood. He's dead."

I suck in a breath. Relief I didn't realize I hadn't released yet rushes out of my lungs. And the tears come now—hard, ragged, body shaking sobs that release everything. He helps me sit up and pulls my body into his so I'm sitting sideways across his lap, his arms hold me so tight, supporting me, ensuring my safety. He buries his nose in the side of my neck as we cling to one another.

"Zander's safe. He's inside. Jax is keeping the boys away so they don't know—don't see—what happened. He called Avery to come be with Zander. His therapist is on the way to come help him if he needs it," he tells me, knowing all of the worries I'd have and assuaging them with every word he speaks. "Are you—where do you hurt?"

"Sir, can we please—"

"Not yet!" Colton snaps at the voice at my back. "Not just yet," he says so softly I can barely hear him before he pulls me in tighter, breathing me in. I'm completely alert now, can see the activity around Zander's father's body. I think I understand the risk I took until I feel Colton's body shake beneath mine, shudder as he holds in the quiet sobs racking his body.

I'm lost. I don't know what to do for this strong man silently coming undone. I start to move so I can shift and turn into him, and he just squeezes me that much tighter. "*Please,*" he pleads in a gruff voice, "I don't want to fucking let go yet. Just a minute longer."

So I let him.

I let him hold me in this backyard, on a plot of grass where violence tried to rob Zander of hope for the last time.

Colton closes the car door for me and climbs into his side of the Range Rover before starting it. He pulls out of the police barricades and past the flashing lights of the awaiting media as we leave The House. Three very long hours have passed. Three hours of questions and retelling everything I could remember about the backyard exchange. About telling Zander to run on "Batman." The constant looks from Colton sitting in the corner as I refused medical assistance or a check-up at the hospital. His growing anger as I replayed Zander's father's comments and physical attacks. Signing statements and having photographs taken of the bruises on my body as evidence. I field phone calls from Haddie and my parents to reassure them that I'm okay, that I'll call them later to explain more.

Three hours of feeling helpless to comfort my boys, wanting to tell them I was okay. The therapist thought it was best they didn't see me with my bruised eye and swollen cheek, because it might dredge up their own histories. As much as it hurt not to see them—show them I'm okay—I kissed Zander and held onto him as long as I could while I repeated my praise over and over to him that this time he didn't hide behind a couch. This time he helped save someone. I know I'm not his mom, but to ease the guilt and assuage the feeling of helplessness in his traumatized psyche was huge.

We merge onto the freeway and besides Rob Thomas' voice ironically singing *Unwell* through the speakers, the car is silent. Colton doesn't say a word despite his hands gripping the steering wheel so tight his knuckles are white. I can sense his anger, can feel it vibrating in waves off of him, and the only reason I can think of that he's mad is because I've put myself in danger.

I lean my head back on the seat and close my eyes but have to open them immediately because all I see are *his* eyes, all I feel is the cold steel pressed against my cheek, all I hear is Zander chanting over and over.

I want to ease the tension between Colton and me, because right now I just really need him. I don't need him closed off in Colton-I'm-pissed-off-land. I need his arms wrapped around me, the warmth of his breath on my neck, the security I always feel when I'm with him.

"He did what you told him to do." My voice is so soft I'm not sure he hears me tell him the one thing I didn't tell the police officers. The one thing I felt would violate a part of the trust Colton had instilled in me. After a few minutes, I hear him blow out a sigh and see him glance over at me. So I continue. "When I went outside, Zander had curled up in a ball and all I could hear the whole time we were out there was him calling to your superheroes."

I yelp as Colton swerves abruptly across two lanes, car horns blaring, and slams the car into park on the side of the freeway. I don't even have a chance to catch my breath or for my seat belt to unlock before he is out of the car and stalking toward the shoulder of the road to my side of the car. I dart my eyes back and forth trying to figure out what in the hell is going on. Is something wrong with the car? I watch him as he passes my door and paces to the end of the Rover and back up past the front. He keeps walking for about ten feet, and with his back to me I hear him yell something at the top of his lungs in a feral rage I've never heard from him before.

If I'd thought about getting out of the car, I know for sure I'm not now. I can see the tension in his shoulders as they rise and fall with his labored breaths. His hands are fisted as if he's ready to fight, him against the world.

I watch him, can't take my eyes off of him, as I try to figure out what's going on inside his head. After some time, he turns back and walks to my car door and yanks it open. I turn instinctively toward him as I take in his grinding teeth, the strain in his neck, and then my eyes lock onto his. We stare at each other and I'm trying to read what his eyes are saying, but it's such a contradiction to his posture that I must be wrong. I see his jaw muscle pulse as his hand reaches out toward my cheek and then pulls back. I angle my head in question, my bottom lip trembling because I'm just on overload from everything today. I notice his eyes flicker down to my mouth, take in my vulnerability, and within an instant I'm crushed against his chest, one arm spanning my back, one hand holding the back of my head as he clutches me to him in a hug teeming with absolute desperation.

My tears fall onto his shirt as we cling to each other. "I've never felt so helpless in my entire life," he tells me, voice weighed down with emotion as he squeezes me tighter. "I'm so angry right now and I don't know how to handle it." I can hear the growl of his rage simmering just beneath the surface.

"It's over now, Colton. We're okay—"

"He had his goddamn hands on you!" he yells as he pushes away from me and walks a few feet before spinning around and shoving his hands through his hair. He just stares at me, his eyes pleading for forgiveness that isn't for him to ask because he didn't do anything wrong. "He put his hands on you and I wasn't there! I didn't protect you, and that's my fucking job, Rylee! To protect you! To take care of you! And I couldn't! Fucking couldn't!" He looks down at the gravel on the side of the road and the anguish in his voice kills me, rips me to shreds, because there was nothing he could have done, but I know telling him that is useless.

When he looks back up, I see the tears glisten in his eyes as he stares at me. "I fought the officer at the barricade. They put me in the back of a car to calm me down because I was going in the house with or without them. I heard you on the phone, Rylee, heard your voice and it just kept replaying over and over in my head and I couldn't get to you." He shakes his head as a single heartbreaking tear slides down his face. "I couldn't get to you." His voice breaks and I shift to get out of the car, and he just holds up his hand for me to stop, to let him finish.

"The gun went off," he says, and I can see him fight to hold back the emotions overtaking him, "and I thought ... I thought it was you. And those few moments waiting and then seeing Zander run out of the front of the house screaming and waiting to see you and you didn't come ... fucking Christ, Ry, I lost it. Fucking lost it." He takes a step closer to me, dashing away a tear with the back of his hand. I force a swallow over the emotion swelling in my throat.

"I made sure Zander was okay before I pushed into the house. I had to get to you, see you, touch you ... and I came into the family room and you were both on your backs on the grass. You both had blood all over your chests. And neither of you were moving." He steps between the V of my legs, making the physical connection I so desperately need, and cradles my cheek in his hand.

"I thought I'd lost you. I was so fucking petrified, Ry. And then I got to you and fell to my knees to hold you, to help you, to ... I don't know what the fuck I was going to do with you, but I had to touch you. *And you were okay.*" His voice breaks again as he leans in and rests his forehead against mine. "You were okay," he repeats before pressing his lips to mine and holding them there as his shoulders shake and tears fall down his cheeks until I taste the salt of them mixed between our lips.

"I'm right here, Colton. I'm okay," I reassure him as we press our foreheads together, our hands holding the back of each other's necks as the outside world whizzes past us at eighty miles per hour, but it's just him and me.

Feeling like we're the only two people in the world.

Accepting that the emotions we're feeling are only getting stronger with the passage of time.

Coping with the notion that we won't always be able to save the other.

Loving one another like we never thought possible.

We turn down Broadbeach Road, our hands linked between us, and drive into a media frenzy bigger than I have ever seen. Colton blows out a loud breath. Our emotions have been put through the ringer, and I fear how much more Colton can take before he snaps.

And I pray this unruly crowd isn't going to be the straw that breaks the camel's back because, frankly, I just can't take any more.

I bow my head and put my hand up to shield the swollen side of my face from the constant flashes and thumps on the car for us to look up. Within minutes Colton drives slowly forward and we edge into the opening gates as Sammy and the two other security guys on duty step forward to prevent the press from entering the property. We park and within moments Colton is opening my door, the sudden roar from the media over the gates hits me like a tidal wave.

He helps me out of the car, and I wince in pain as my body starts to stiffen from everything it has been put through. Colton notices my grimace and before I can object, he has me cradled in his arms and is walking us toward the front door. I lay my head under his neck, feel the vibration in his throat as he says, "Sammy," and nods his head in acknowledgment at him.

And then he stops dead in his tracks. I'm not sure what's he's heard or what sets him off, but he unexpectedly turns and is walking toward the gates at the front of the driveway. "Open the fucking gates, Sammy!" he barks as we near them, and I immediately shrink into Colton as confusion and uncertainty fills me.

I hear the clank of metal as the motors start moving, hear the reporters become even more frenzied at the sight of the gates opening, and then I hear them go absolutely ballistic when they see the two of us standing there. My heart is pounding and I have no idea what in the hell he is doing. We stand there for a moment, him holding me, me burying my face into his neck, the incessant questions ringing out one after another, and the camera flashes so bright I can see them through my closed eyelids.

Colton angles his face down and places his mouth close to my ear, and even though there is all this outside noise, I can hear him clear as day. "This is something I should have done when this first started. I'm sorry." He presses a chaste kiss to my cheek. "I'm gonna put you down now, okay?"

I try to figure out what he's referring to, but I just nod my head. *What is he doing?*

He lowers me to the ground. "You okay?" he asks as he looks in my eyes like we are the only two people standing here. When I nod he gets that little smirk on his face, and before I can read it his lips are on mine in a soul-devouring, heart thumping, thigh-clenching-together kiss that leaves no questions about who Colton's heart and emotions belong to. His lips claim me, tasting like a needy man starving. And I am so lost in him, to him—just as needy for him—that I don't hear the people around us, the clicks of the cameras, because regardless of the outside world, it always comes back to us.

He breaks the kiss with a gasp from me and gives me that smirk again. "If they're gonna stare, Ryles." And shrugs his shoulders unapologetically as I mentally finish the phrase he said to me in Vegas ... *we might as well put on a good show.*

"Did you all get a good picture?" he shouts to the crowd around us, and I look over at him confused. "Now this is what you can print with your goddamn picture. Rylee isn't the home wrecker folks. Tawny is. Just like Tawny is a fucking liar." He glances over at me as I stand there with my mouth agape over his comment. "Yep," he shouts. "Paternity test is negative. So your story? Isn't really a story anymore!"

It takes a minute for the meaning of his words to sink in and I just stare at him as he looks at me with the hugest grin on his face, and shakes his head as he pulls me under his arm and tucks me against him. "Wha—why—how?" I stutter as so many emotions flicker through me at a rapid pace, the most prominent one: relief.

"Chase is going to kill me for that one," he mutters to himself with a smirk on his face that I don't quite understand. Before I can ask, Colton turns us around and starts walking back through the gates as questions are yelled out about what happened today at The House. He ignores them and waits for the gates to shut before turning and looking at me. "That's what I was calling to tell you ... and then everything happened."

I just stare at him. I can see the burden that's been heavy in his eyes is gone—has probably been gone all day—but then again I've been a little preoccupied. I nod my head, unable to speak as he takes my hand and raises it to his lips.

And it hits me harder than ever before.

We can do this. All of the obstacles between us have been removed in one way or another. It's just this selfless girl and this healing boy and we can really make this work.

He looks at me as tears well in my eyes, and I step into his arms and don't let go, because I'm exactly where I want to be.

Exactly where I belong.

Home.

Chapter Twenty-Nine

"Are you sure you're okay?"

It's only the hundredth time he's asked me, but a part of me smiles silently at how well he's taking care of me. The day had just gotten longer and longer as I assured an adamant Haddie I was okay and that she didn't need to fly home from her job in San Francisco to physically see I was all right, and that I'd call her again in the morning. Next it was my parents and the same reassurances, and then the boys … checking in on Zander and wishing I was there to speak to him face to face as well as talk to the rest of the boys. Colton cut me off after that, telling the rest of the people who called—his parents, Quinlan, Beckett, Teddy—that I needed rest and I'd call them in the morning.

"I'm fine. I'm not feeling too well but I think it's because I'm exhausted. My stomach is upset. I should've eaten more food before I took the pain meds. And now they're making me super sleepy …"

He sits up in bed. "Do you want me to go get you something to eat?"

"No," I tell him, pulling his arm so he lies back down. I look over at him. "*Hold me?*"

He instantly shifts and gingerly places his arms around me, pulling me into him so our bodies fit against each other. "Okay?" he murmurs into the crown of my head.

"Mmm-hmm," I say, snuggling in as close as my sore body will allow because the pain is a little more bearable with his arms holding me tight.

We sit there for a bit, our breathing slowly evening out. I'm just on the cusp of sleep when he murmurs, "I race you, Ry. I really, really race you."

Every part of me sighs at those words, at the admission I know is hard for him. I press a kiss to my favorite place beneath his jawline. "I race you too, Colton."

More than you'll ever realize.

The cramps in my stomach wake me up.

I lie in the pitch black, moonless night as the little, continuous stabs of pain combined with the sweat coating my skin, and the dizziness in my head, tell me I need to get to the bathroom quickly before I throw up. I slide out of Colton's loosened grip on me, trying to be quick but also trying not to disturb him. He mumbles something softly, and I still momentarily before he rolls onto his back and quiets down.

My head's fuzzy as I stand, and I'm super groggy from the pain medication. Talk about feeling like I'm walking through water. I laugh because the floor even feels kind of wet and I know it's just my drug laden brain. I run my hand along the wall to help steady myself and guide me through the dark room so I don't accidentally bump something and wake up Colton.

My God, I'm going to be sick! I feel the huge rugs covering the bathroom floor beneath my feet and almost moan out in pain mixed with relief knowing the toilet is so close. I slip some as I hit the tile and curse Baxter and the damn water bowl he always drips from. I shut the bathroom door and flick on the light, the sudden brightness hurting my eyes so I squeeze them shut as the dizziness hits me at full force. I bend over, hand on the toilet rim, stomach tensing and ready to puke, but all I feel is the room spinning. My stomach revolts, the dry heave hitting me over and over. My stomach is tensing so forcefully I feel wetness run down my legs.

And I start laughing, feeling so pathetic that I'm puking so hard I've just peed myself, but my mind is so sluggish, so slow to piece my thoughts together that instead of figuring out what to do next, I sink down on my knees. I slide on the slick marbled floor coated with urine, but my stomach hurts so badly and my head's so dizzy I don't really care. All I can think of is how pathetic I must look right now. How there is no way in hell I'm going to call Colton for help.

And I'm so tired—so sleepy—and afraid I'm going to throw up again, I decide to lay my head atop my hands on the rim of the toilet and just rest my eyes for a minute.

My head starts to slide off of the toilet, and I don't know how much time has passed but the falling motion jerks me awake. I'm immediately assaulted with such a wave of heat through my body followed up by an absolute chill that I force myself to stop a minute and take a deep breath.

Something's not right.

I feel it immediately, even though my mind is trying to snap my thoughts together, line them up so that they're coherent. And I just can't. Nothing's making sense to me. My head is heavy and my arms feel like a million pounds. I try to call out to Colton for help, not caring anymore if I'll be embarrassed about sitting in a pool of piss. Something's just not right. I put my hand on the wainscot to help support myself so I can stand up and open the door so he'll hear me call his name, but my hand slips. And when I can open my eyes, when I can focus, my handprint is smeared in blood down the wall.

Hmm.

I kind of laugh as delirium takes over. As I look down to see that I'm not sitting in urine.

No.

But why is the floor covered in blood?

"Colton!" I call, but I'm so weak I know my voice isn't loud enough.

I'm floating and it's so warm and I'm so tired. I close my eyes and smile because I see Colton's face.

So handsome.

All mine.

I feel sleep start to pull on me—my mind, my body, my soul—and I let its lethargic fingers begin to win the tug-of-war.

And right before it takes me, I understand the why, *but not the how*.

Oh, Colton.

I'm sorry, Colton.

Darkness threatens to pull me under its clutches.

Please don't hate me.

I have nothing left to resist its smothering blackness.

I love you.

Spiderman. Batm—

Chapter Thirty

Colton

The sound of the gunshot startles me awake. I spring up in bed and have to catch my breath as I tell myself it's all over. Just a goddamn nightmare. The fucking bastard is dead and got what he deserved. Zander is fine. Rylee is fine.

But something's off. Still not right.

"Say something I'm giving up on you …" I jolt from the panic I feel from hearing the lyrics as they pass through the overhead speakers. *Shit*. I forgot to turn them off last night. Is that what scared the hell out of me? I scrub my hands over my face trying to snap me from my sleep-induced haze.

That had to have been it.

"… I'm sorry that I couldn't get to you …"

I reach for the control on the nightstand to shut the music off. And then I hear it again, the sound that I'm sure was what woke me up. "Bax?" I call out into the room as I realize Ry's side of the bed is empty. He whimpers again. "Fuckin' A, Bax! You really have to take a piss now?" I say to him as I place my feet on the floor and stand, waiting for a second to steady myself and thank God this is getting easier because I'm sick of feeling like an eighty-year-old man every time I stand.

I immediately look out toward the top of the stairs to see if any lights are on downstairs and the hairs on the back of my neck stand up when it's dark as fuck. Baxter whimpers again. "Relax, dude. I'm coming!" I take a few steps toward the bathroom and feel a bit of relief when I see the sliver of light around the closed door to the toilet room. *Jesus, Donavan, chill the fuck out, she's fine.* No need to go smothering her and shit just because I'm still freaked out.

Baxter whimpers again and I realize he's in the bathroom too. What the hell? The dog's licked his balls one too many times and is going crazy. "Leave her alone, Bax! She doesn't feel good. I'll take you out." I walk into the bathroom, knowing he's not going to come with me unless I grab his collar. I yell a hushed curse trying to get him to obey but he doesn't move. I'm beat and not in the mood to deal with his stubborn ass. I slip on the water on the floor and my temper ignites. "Quit drinking the goddamn water and you won't have to go to the bathroom in the middle of the fucking night!" I take another step and slip and I'm pissed. I've had it right now and am having trouble keeping my cool.

Baxter whimpers again at the bathroom door and when I reach it, I rap my knuckle against it. "You okay, Ry?" Silence. *What the fuck?* "Ry? You okay?"

It's a split second of time between my last word and the door flinging open but I swear to God it feels like a lifetime. So many thoughts—a fucking million of them fly through my mind, like at the start of a race—but the one I always block out, the one that I never let control me, owns every goddamn part of me now.

Fear.

My mind tries to process what I see, but I can't comprehend it because the only thing I can focus on is the blood. So much blood, and sitting in the middle of it, shoulders slumped against the wall, eyes closed and face so pale it almost matches the light marble behind it, is Rylee. My mind stutters trying to grasp the sight but not processing it all at once.

And then time snaps forward and starts moving way too fucking fast.

"No!" I don't even realize it's my voice screaming, don't even feel the blood coat my knees as I drop to them and grab her. "Rylee! Rylee!" I'm shouting her name, trying to jostle her the fuck awake, but her head just hangs to the side.

"Oh God! Oh God!" I repeat it over and over as I pull her into my arms, cradle her as I jolt her shoulders back and forth to try to wake her up. And then I freeze—I fucking freeze the one time in my life I need to move the most. I'm paralyzed as I reach my hand up and stop before it presses to the little curve beneath her chin, so afraid that when I press my two fingers down there isn't going to be a beat to meet them.

God, she's so beautiful. The thought flickers and fades like my courage.

Baxter's wet nose in my back snaps me to, and I suck in a breath I didn't even know I was holding. I get a little better grip on my reality—my fucking sanity—and it's not very strong but at least it's there. I press down and let out a shout in relief when I feel the weak pulse of her heart.

All I want to do is bury my face in her neck and hold her, tell her it's going to be okay, but I know the thirty seconds I've wasted sitting here have been more than too much.

I tell myself that I need to think, that I need to concentrate, but my thoughts are so fucking scattered I can't focus on just one.

Call 9-1-1.

Carry her downstairs.

So much goddamn blood.

I can't lose her.

"Stay with me, baby. Please, stay with me." I plead and beg but I don't know what else I can do. I'm lost, scared, fucking beside myself.

My mind whirls out of control with what I need to do and what's most important ... but the one thing I know more than anything else is I can't leave her. But I have to. I pull her out of the small room housing the toilet, my feet slipping on the blood all over the floor, and the sight of it smearing—dark marring the light floor—as I drag her to the rug causes new panic to arise.

I lay her gently down. "Phone. I'll be right back." I tell her before I run, slipping again to the nightstand where my phone is. It's ringing in my ear as I reach her and immediately bring my fingers to her neck as it rings again.

"9-1-1—"

"5462 Broadbeach Road. Hurry! Please—"

"Sir, I need to—"

"There's fucking blood everywhere and I'm not sure—"

"Sir, calm down, we—"

"Calm down?" I scream at the lady. "I need help! Please hurry!" I drop the phone. I need to get her downstairs. Need to get her closer to where the ambulance can get to her faster.

I pick her up, cradle her, and I can't help the sob that overtakes me as I run as fast as I can through my bedroom to the stairs and down them. Panic laced with confusion and mind-numbing fear runs through me. "Sammy!" I'm screaming. I'm a madman, and I don't fucking care because all I can see is her blood coating the bathroom. All I can think of is being a little kid and that damn doll Quin used to have—Raggedy Ann or some shit like that—how her head and arms and legs lolled to the side regardless of how she held her. How she'd cry when I'd tease her over and over that her doll was dead.

And all I keep thinking of is that fucking doll because that's what Rylee looks like right now. Her head hangs back over my bicep completely lifeless, and her arms and legs dangle.

"Oh God!" I sob as I hit the bottom of the stairs, the image of that doll stuck in my head. "Sammy!" I scream again, worried that I told him to go home last night like usual, rather than sleep in the guest room because the press were so out of control.

"Colton, what's wrong?" He runs around the corner and I see his eyes widen as he sees me carrying her. He freezes and for the odd moment I think how mad Rylee would be at me right now for letting him see her like this—in just a tank top and panties—and I hear her voice chastising me. And the sound of her voice in my head is my undoing. I drop to my knees with her.

"I need help, Sammy. Call 9-1-1 back. Call my dad. Help me! Help her?" I plead with him as I sink my face into her neck, rocking her, telling her to hold on, that it's going to be okay, that she's going to be okay.

I know Sammy's on the phone, can hear him talking, but my shocked brain can't process anything other than the fact that I need to fix her. That she can't leave me. *That she's broken.*

"Colton! Colton!" Sammy's voice pulls me from my hypnotic panic. I look up at him, the phone held up to one ear as I'm sure he's getting instructions from the 9-1-1 operator, and am not even sure if I speak or not. "Where's she bleeding from?"

"*What?*"

"Look at me!" he shouts, snapping me somewhat out of my fog. "Where is she bleeding from? We need to try and stop the bleeding."

Holy shit! What is wrong with me? I open my mouth to speak, to tell him, and I realize that I'm so panicked I have no fucking clue.

Sammy's eyes lock on mine as if to tell me I can do this, that she needs me, and he's able to break through my slow motion mental state. I immediately lay her down—as much as it kills me to because I feel like she's so cold that I need to keep her warm. I start running my hands over her body, and I start shaking I'm so mad at myself for not thinking of this, so scared at what I'm going to find.

I cry out in fear as I realize blood is still running down her legs, and I can't even begin to process why. "Her accident. Something from her accident," I tell Sammy as I lift her shirt up her abdomen to show him the scars that mar her skin as if that will explain it. And then I grab her and pull her onto me again—her cold body against my warm skin—as Sammy starts talking again to whomever's on the other end of the phone.

"Hang tight, sweetheart. Help's coming," I tell her as I rock her, knowing that there is no way I can stop the bleeding—hers or my heart's.

I hold her tight and I swear I feel her move. I scream out her name to try and help her come back to me. "Rylee! Rylee! Please, baby, please." But there's nothing. Fucking nothing. And when I sob in despair her body shudders again, and I realize it's me moving her. It's my body shaking and begging and pleading that's moving her.

"Oh God!" I cry out. "Not her. Please not her. You've taken everything good from me," I scream into an empty house to a God I don't really believe exists any more right now. "*You can't have her,*" I yell at him, holding onto the only thing I can because everything else I hold true is slipping through my fingers. I bury my face in her neck, the sobs ruining me as my warm breath heats up her skin cooling beneath my lips. "*You … can't … have … her.*"

"Colton!" A hand jolts my shoulder and I snap out of my trance, unsure of how much time has passed, but I see them now. The medics and the flashing lights swirling on my walls through the open front door. And I know they need to take her from me to help her, but I'm so fucking scared right now I don't want to let her go.

She needs me right now but I damn well know I need her more.

"Please, please don't take her from me," I croak as they lift her from my arms and I'm not sure who I'm talking to, the paramedics or God.

"How long, Sammy?" I shove up from the chair, nerves gnawing at me and my legs not able to eat up enough ground to make them go the fuck away.

"Only thirty minutes. You gotta give them time."

I know everyone in this waiting room is staring at me, watching the man with blood all over his clothes pace back and forth like a caged animal. I'm antsy. Restless. Fucking terrified. I need to know where she is, what's wrong with her. I sit back down, my knee jostling like a goddamn junkie needing a fix and realize that I am. I need my fix. I need my Ryles.

I thought I lost her today only to know I didn't, and then when I think she's safe— protected in my arms as we fall asleep—she's ripped the fuck away from me. I'm so goddamn confused. So fucking angry. So … I don't even know what I am anymore because I just want someone to come out from behind those automatic doors and tell me she's going to be okay. That all the blood looked a hundred times worse than it really was.

But no one is coming. No one is giving me answers.

I want to scream, want to punch something, want to sprint ten fucking miles—anything to get rid of this fucking ache in my chest and churning in my stomach. I feel like I'm going crazy. I want time to speed the fuck up or slow the fuck down, whichever is best for her, as long as I can see her soon, hold her soon.

I get out my phone, needing to feel a connection to her. Something. Anything. I start to type her a text, express to her in the way she understands best how I feel.

I finish, hit send, and hold on to the thought that she'll get this when she wakes up—because she has to wake up—and know exactly how I feel in this moment.

"Colton!"

It's the voice that's always been able to fix things for me and this time he can't. And because of that … when I hear his voice call out to me, I fucking lose it. I don't stand to greet him, don't even lift my head to look at him because I'm so overtaken by everything that I can't function. I drop my head in my hands and start sobbing like a damn baby.

I don't care that there are people here. I don't care that I'm a grown-ass man and that men don't cry. I don't care about anything but the fact that I can't fix her right now. *That my endgame superhero can't fix her right now.* My shoulders shake and my chest hurts and my eyes burn as I feel his arm slide around me and pull me into his chest as best he can and try and comfort me when I know it's not going to do a goddamn fucking thing for her. It's not going to erase the images of her lifeless Raggedy Ann body and pale lips that are staining my mind.

Humpty fuckin' Dumpty.

I'm so upset I can't even speak. And if I could, I don't even know if I could put words to my thoughts. And he knows me so damn well he doesn't even say a word. He just holds me against him as I expel everything I can't express otherwise.

We sit in silence for some time. Even when my tears are gone, he keeps his arms wrapped around my shoulders as I lean forward with my head hanging in my hands.

His only words are, "I've got you, son. I've got you." He repeats them over and over, the only thing he can say.

I squeeze my eyes shut, trying to rid my mind of everything but it's not working. All I can think of is that my demons have finally won. They've taken the purest thing I've ever had in my life and are stealing her fucking light.

Her spark.

What have I done?

I hear shoes squeak on the floor and stop in front of me, and I am so scared of what the person has to say that I just keep my head down and my eyes closed. I stay in my dark world, hoping I have the control to keep it from claiming her too.

"Are you the father?" I hear the soft, southern accent ask the question, and I feel my dad shift and assume he's nodding to her, ready to listen to the news for me, bear the brunt of the burden for his son.

"Are you the father?" The voice asks again, and I move my hands off of my face and look over at my dad, needing him to do this for me, needing him to be in charge right now so I can close my eyes and be the helpless little kid I feel like. When I look over, my dad is looking straight at me—meets my eyes and holds them—and for the first time in my life I can't read what the hell they're saying to me.

And they don't waver. They just look at me like when I was in little league and afraid to go up to the plate because Tommy-I always-hit-the-batter-Williams was on the mound, and I was scared to get beaned with the ball. He looks at me like he did way the fuck back then—gray eyes full of encouragement telling me that *I can do this*—I can face my fear.

My entire body breaks out in a cold sweat as I realize what that look is trying to tell me, what she's trying to ask me. I swallow loudly as the buzzing in my head assaults me, then leaves me shaken to the core, as I angle my head up to look at the patient brown eyes of the woman in front of me.

"Are you the father?" she asks again with a somber pull to her lips as if she's smiling to abate the words that she's about to tell me.

I just stare at her, unable to speak as every emotion I thought I'd just emptied out of myself while my dad held me comes flooding back into me with a fucking vengeance. I sit stunned, speechless, scared. My dad's hand squeezes my shoulder, urging me on.

"Rylee?" I ask her, because I have to be mistaken. She has to be mistaken.

"Are you the baby's father?" she asks softly as she sits down next to me and places her hand on my knee and squeezes. And all I can focus on right now is my hands, my fucking fingers, the cuticles still caked with dried blood. My hands start to tremble as my eyes can't move away from the sight of Rylee's blood still staining me.

My baby's blood staining me.

I raise my head, tear my eyes away from the symbol of life cracked and dead on my hands, and hope and fear for things I'm now not sure of all at the same fucking time.

"Yeah," I say barely above a whisper. I swallow over the gravel scraping my throat. "Yes." My dad squeezes my shoulder again as I look over at her brown eyes as mine beg for a yes and no at the same time.

She starts out slowly, like I'm a two year old. "Rylee is still being tended to," she says, and I want to shake her and ask what the fuck does *tended to* mean. My knee starts jogging up and down again as I wait for her to finish, jaw grinding, hands squeezing together. "She suffered from either a placental abruption or a complete previa and—"

"Stop!" I say, not understanding a word she's saying, and I just look at her like a goddamn deer in the headlights.

"The vessels attaching her to the baby severed somehow—they're trying to determine everything right now—but she lost a lot of blood. She's getting transfusions now to help with—"

"Is she awake?" My mind can't process what she just said. I hear baby, blood, transfusion. "I didn't hear you say she's going to be okay, because I need to hear you say she's going to be fucking okay!" I shout at her as everything in my life comes crashing down around me, like I'm back in the goddman race car, but this time I'm not sure what parts I'm going to be able to piece back together … and that more than anything scares the fuck out of me.

"Yes," she says softly, that soothing voice of hers makes me want to shake her like an Etch A Sketch until I get a little more assurance. Until I erase what's there and create the perfect fucking picture that I want. "We've given her some meds to help with the pain of the D & C, and once she gets some more blood transfused, she should be in a lot better state, physically."

I have no clue what she just said, but I cling onto the words I understand: she's going to be okay. I hang my head back into my hands and push my heels into my eyes so I don't cry, because any relief I feel isn't real until I can see her, touch her, feel her.

She squeezes my knee again and speaks. "I'm so sorry. The baby didn't make it."

I don't know what I expected her to say because my heart knew the truth even though my head hadn't quite grasped it yet. But her words stop the world spinning beneath my feet and I can't breathe, can't draw in any air. I shove myself to my feet and stagger a few feet one way and then turn to go the other way, completely overwhelmed by the buzzing in my ears.

"Colton!" I hear my dad, but I just shake my head and bend over as I try to catch my breath. I bring my hands to my head as if holding it is going to stop the turmoil bashing around inside of it. "*Colton.*"

I push my hands out in front of me gesturing for him to back off. "I need a pit stop!" I say to him as I see my hands again—the blood of something I created that was a part of Rylee and me—saint and sinner—on my hands.

Untouched innocence.

And I feel it happen, feel something shatter inside of me—the hold the demons have held over my soul for the last twenty-something-years—just like the mirror in that goddamn dive bar the night Rylee told me she loved me. Two moments in time where the one thing I never wanted to happen, happens and yet … I can't help but feel, can't help but wonder why hints of possibilities creep into my mind when I knew then and know now this just can't be. This is something I never, ever wanted. And yet everything I've ever known has changed somehow.

And I don't know what this means just yet.

Only how it feels: different, liberated, incomplete—fucking terrifying.

My stomach turns and my throat clogs with so many emotions, so many feelings that I can't even begin to process this new reality. All I can do to keep from losing my sanity is focus on the one thing I know that can be helped right now.

Rylee.

I can't catch my breath and my heart's pounding like a fucking freight train, but all I can think of is Rylee. All I want, all I need, is Rylee.

"Colton." It's my dad's hands on my shoulders again—the hands that have held me in my darkest hours—trying to help me break away from this smothering darkness trying to pull me back into its clutches. "Talk to me, son. What's going through your head?"

Are you fucking kidding me? I want to scream at him because I really don't know what else to do with the fear consuming me but lash out at the person closest to me. Fear that is so very different than ever before but still all the same. So I just shake my head as I look up at the brown-eyed lady trying to figure out what to do, what to feel, what to say.

"Does she know?" I don't even recognize my own voice. The break in it, the tone of it, the complete disbelief owning it.

"The doctor's spoken to her, yes," she says with a shake of her head, and I realize in that moment Rylee is dealing with this all by herself, taking this all in … *alone*. The baby she'd give anything for—was told she would never have—she actually had.

And lost.

Again.

How did she take it? What is this going to do to her?

What is this going to do to us?

Everything is spiraling out of control, and I just need it to be in control. Need the ground to stop fucking moving beneath me. Know the only thing that can right my world again is her. I need the feel of her skin beneath my fingers to assuage all of this chaos rioting through me.

Rylee.

"I need to see her."

"She's resting right now but you can go sit with her if you'd like," she says as she stands.

I just nod and suck in my breath as she starts to walk down the corridor. My dad's hand is still on my shoulder, and his silent show of support remains until we walk farther down the hallway to the door of her room.

"I'll be just outside, if you need me. I'll wait for Becks," my dad says, and I just nod because the lump in my throat is so huge that I can't breathe. I walk through the doorway and stop dead in my tracks.

Rylee.

It's the only word I can hold on to as my mind tries to process *everything*.

Rylee. She looks so small, so pale, so much like a little girl lost in a bed of white sheets. When I walk to her side I have to remind myself to breathe because all I want to do is touch her, but when I reach out I'm so scared that if I do, she's going to break. Fucking shatter. And I'll never get her back.

But I can't help it because if I thought I felt helpless sitting in the back of the police cruiser, then I feel completely useless now. Because I can't fix this. Can't charge in and save the damn day, but this ... I just don't know what to do next, what to say, where to go from here.

And it's fucking ripping me to shreds.

I stand and look at her, take all of her in—from her pale bee-stung lips, to the soft-as-sin skin that I know smells like vanilla, especially in the spot beneath her ear; and I know this feisty woman full of her smart-mouthed defiance and non-negotiables, *owns* me.

Fucking owns me.

Every goddamn part of me. In our short time together she's broken down walls I never even knew I'd spent a lifetime building. And now without these walls, I'm fucking helpless without her, because when you feel nothing for so long—when you choose to be numb—and then learn to feel again, you can't turn it off. You can't make it stop. All I know right now, looking at her absolute beauty inside and out, is that I need her more than anything. I need her to help me navigate through this foreign fucking territory before I drown in the knowledge that I did this to her.

I'm the reason she's going to have to make a choice, one I'm not even sure I want her to make any more.

I sink into the seat beside her bed and give in to my one and only weakness now, the need to touch her. I gently place her limp hand between both of mine, and even though she's asleep and doesn't know I'm touching her, I still feel it—still feel that spark when we connect.

I love you.

The words flicker through my mind, and I gasp as every part of me revolts at the words I think, but not the feelings I feel. I focus on the fucking disconnect, on shoving those words that only represent hurt out, because I can't have them taint this moment right now. I can't have thoughts of him mixed with thoughts of her.

I try to find my breath again as the tears well and my lips press against the palm of her hand. My heart pounds and my head knows she just might have scaled that final fucking steel wall, opened it up like Pandora's box so all the evil locked forever within, could take flight and exit my soul with just one thing left.

Fucking hope.

The question is, what the hell am I hoping for now?

Chapter Thirty-One

My head is foggy and I'm so very tired. I just want to sink back into this warmth. *Ah, that's so nice.*

And then it hits me. The blood, the dizziness, the pain, the rectangular tiles on the ceiling as the stretcher rushes down the hallway, once again foreshadowing the doctor's words I never expected to hear again. I open my eyes, hoping to be at home and hoping this is just a bad dream, but then I see the machines and feel the cold drip of the IV. I feel the pain in my abdomen and the stiff salt where tears have stained my cheeks.

The tears I'd sobbed when I heard the words confirming what I'd already known. And even though I'd felt the life slipping out of me, it was still heartbreaking when the doctor confirmed it. I screamed and raged, told her she was mistaken—wrong—because even though she was bringing my body back to life, her words were stopping my heart. And then hands held me down as I fought the reality, the pain, the devastation until the needle was pressed into my IV and darkness claimed me once again.

I keep my eyes closed, trying to feel past the emptiness echoing around inside of me, trying to push through the haze of disbelief, the unending grief I can't even comprehend. Trying to silence the imaginary cries I hear now but couldn't hear last night as my baby died.

A tear trickles down my cheek. I'm so lost to everything I feel, so I focus on every single feeling as it makes the slow descent because I feel just the same.

Alone. Fading. Running away without any certainty but the unknown.

"And she's back with us now," a voice to my right says, and I look over to a lady with kind eyes in a white coat—the same lady that broke the news to me earlier. "You've been out for a while now."

I manage a weak smile, my only apology for my reaction, because the one person I wanted to see, the one person I need more than anyone isn't here.

And I'm devastated.

Does he know about the life we'd created? Part him, part me. Could he not handle it so he left? The panic starts to strangle me right away. The tears start to well as I shake my head, unable to speak. How is it possible that God would be so cruel to do this to me twice in my life—lose my baby and the man I love?

I can't do this. I can't do this again.

The words keep running through my mind, the scalpel of grief cutting deeper, pressing harder, as I try to feel anything but the unending pain, the incomparable emptiness owning every part of me. I grasp for anything to hold on to except for the handfuls of razorblades I keep coming up with.

"I know, sweetie," she says, rubbing her hand over my arm. "I'm so very sorry." I try to control my emotions over the baby and Colton—two things I can't control—and two things I now know I've lost. My chest hurts as I draw in breaths that aren't coming fast enough. As I try to swallow over the emotion that's holding my air hostage. And then I think it'd be easier if I choke. Then I'd be able to slip away, creep back under that cloak of darkness, and be numb again. Have hope again. Be bent and not broken again.

"Rylee?" she says in that questioning way to see if I'm okay or if I'm going to freak out on her like I did when she told me about the miscarriage.

But I just shake my head at her because there's nothing I can say. I focus on my hands clasped in my lap and I try to get a hold of myself, try to get used to the loneliness again, the emptiness.

When I've finally calmed down some, she smiles. "I'm Dr. Andrews. I told you that before but understandably you probably don't remember. How are you feeling?"

I shrug, the discomfort in my empty womb is no match for the deep ache in my heart. "I'm sure you have questions, should we start or do you want to wait for Colton to come back first?"

He didn't leave me? I gasp in a huge breath of air as the lump in my throat loosens, lets air in, and her words help the slice of the proverbial scalpel hurt a little less. She just angles her head and looks at me with sadness, and I feel like she's telling me something without telling me. *But what? Colton's reaction to the news?* I'm so scared of facing him, of having to speak to him about this on the heels of knowing how he reacted with Tawny's bombshell, but at the same time a flicker of relief shudders through me that he's still here. "He's here?" I ask, my voice barely audible.

"He just left for the first time since you've been here," she explains, sensing my fears. "He's been beside himself and his father was finally able to get him to go stretch his legs for a minute."

The words fill me with such a sense of relief, shivers dancing over my arms as it hits me that he didn't leave me. *He didn't leave me.* Silly really to even think he would, but we've been overloaded with so many things lately and every person has a breaking point.

And mine passed a long time ago.

I finally find my voice and look back up to meet her eyes. "Now is fine." I have so many questions that need explanations. So many answers that I fear Colton is not going to want to hear. "I'm trying to process everything still." I swallow as I bite back the tears again. "What… ?"

"…happened?" she finishes for me when I don't continue.

"I was told I could never get pregnant, that the scarring was so …" I'm so shaken, mentally and physically, that I can't finish my thoughts. They hit my mind like rapid fire so I can't focus on one for more than a few minutes.

"First off, let me say that I spoke to your OB and reviewed your files and yes, the chance of you being able to carry a fetus, conceive even, was extremely slim." She shrugs, "But sometimes the human body is resilient … miracles can happen, nature prevails."

I smile softly, although I know it doesn't reach my eyes. How was I carrying a life—my baby, a piece of Colton—and I didn't know it? *Didn't feel it?*

"How did I not know? I mean how far along was I? Why did I miscarry? Was it my fault, something I did or was the baby—*my baby*—never going to make it full term anyway?" The questions come out one after another, running together, because I'm crying now, tears coursing down my face as I wear the vest of guilt over the miscarriage. She just lets me get all of my questions out as she stands there patiently, compassion filling her eyes. "Was this a one-time thing, or is there a possibility that this can happen again? I'm just so overwhelmed," I admit, my breath hitching. "And I don't know … I just don't know what to believe anymore. My head's swimming …"

"That's understandable, Rylee. You've been through a lot," she says, shifting her position, and when she does he's right there leaning against the doorjamb, hands shoved in his pockets, shirt stained with blood—my blood, the baby's … *our baby's blood*—and if I thought the floodgates had burst before, they completely disintegrate at the sight of him.

He's at my side in an instant, face etched with pain and eyes a war of unfathomable emotions. He reaches out to comfort me and hesitates when he sees my gaze flicker down and focus through my tear blurred vision on the stains of his shirt. Within a flash, he has his jacket off and his shirt over his head, throwing them into the chair before wrapping his arms around me, pulling me into him.

The ugly tears start now. Huge, ragged, hitching sobs that rack through my body as he holds onto me—completely at a loss for what to do to make it better—and lets me cry. His hands move up and down my back as he whispers hushed words that don't really break through my haze of disbelieved grief.

And there are so many things I feel all at once that I can't pick a single one out to hold onto. I'm confused, scared, devastated, hollow, shocked, safe, and I feel like so many things have been forever altered.

For me.

Between us.

Hopes, dreams, wants, that were ripped away from me and predetermined by a fate that I never got a say in. And the tears continue to fall as I realize what I've lost again. What hopes might just be a possibility I never expected to be able to get back.

And all the while Colton laces my tear stained face with kisses, over and over, trying to replace the pain with compassion, grief with love. He leans his head back and his eyes fuse with mine. We sit there for a moment, eyes saying so many things and lips saying nothing. But the worst part is, besides utter relief, I can't get a read on what his are telling me.

The only thing I know for sure is that he's just as lost and confused as I am, but deep down, I fear he feels this way for the exact opposite reason I do.

"Hey," he says softly as a soft smile tugs up the corner of his mouth. I can feel his hands tremble slightly. "You scared the shit out of me, Ryles."

"Sorry. Are you okay?" My voice sounds sleepy, sluggish.

Colton looks down and shakes his head with a stilted laugh. "You're the one in the hospital bed and you ask me if I'm okay?" When he looks up I see the tears welling in his eyes. "Rylee, I …" He stops and blows out a breath, his voice swamped with emotion.

And before he can say anything further there is a knock on the door jamb. It's Dr. Andrews asking if it's okay for her to return. Neither of us even realized she had left because we were so absorbed in one another.

"Are you ready for your answers?"

I nod at her, hesitant and yet needing to know. Colton releases me momentarily—the loss of his touch startling to me—as he puts his arms through his sweatshirt. He comes back to take my hand in his as she walks back over to the side of the bed and sighs. "Well, unfortunately nothing I can tell you is concrete because we only had the aftermath of everything to try and piece together. Now that you're a little more coherent than when we first met, do you mind telling me what you remember?"

My head feels like I'm swimming underwater but I go through everything I remember, up to sitting on the bathroom floor and then nothing until I was here. She nods and makes some notes on her iPad. "You're very lucky Colton found you when he did. You'd lost quite a lot of blood and by the time you reached us you were going into hypovolemic shock."

There are so many questions I want to ask her ... so many unknowns my mind is still processing. I glance over at Colton and hesitate to ask the question I want answered the most because of everything we went through with Tawny. So I opt for another one that's been nagging at my mind.

"How far along was I?" My voice is soft and Colton holds my hand tight. The idea that I'd ever even get to ask those words strikes me to the core. I was carrying a baby. *A baby*. My chin quivers as I try desperately not to cry again.

"We're guessing around twelve to fourteen weeks," she says, and I squeeze my eyes shut trying to comprehend what she's telling me. Colton's fingers tense around mine, and I hear him exhale a controlled but uneven breath. She waits a beat to let everything sink in before continuing. "From what we can tell, you either experienced a placental abruption or a complete previa where the vessels burst."

"And what does that mean?"

"By the time you were admitted, the bleeding was so extensive and so far advanced we can only guess as to the cause. We are assuming it was a previa because we rarely see an abruption this early on in a pregnancy unless there is some sort of violent trauma to the abdomen and ..."

She keeps talking but I don't hear another word, and neither does Colton, because he's off of my bed in an instant, legs pacing, body vibrating with negative energy, and anger etched in the lines of his face.

And it's so much easier for me to focus on him and the explosion of emotions on his face than my own. My overwhelmed brain thinks that by looking at him, I don't have to face how I feel. I don't have to wonder if I pushed Zander's dad a little too hard, a little too much, and I am the reason this all happened.

Dr. Andrews looks at him and then back at me, concern in her eyes, as I relay the events of the day. Each time I mention Zander's father hitting me, I can physically see Colton's agitation increase. I don't know what this is doing to Colton, not sure where exactly his head is or how much more he can take, and I'm afraid of so many things because I know how I feel.

"That very well could have been the cause—the trigger of everything—that led to the miscarriage," she says after a few seconds.

I squeeze my eyes shut momentarily and force a swallow down as Colton barks out a curse under his breath, his body still restless, his hands clenching into fists. And I study him, trying to read the emotions flickering through his eyes before he stops and looks at me. "I need a fucking minute," he says before turning and barreling out of the doorway.

Tears return and I know I'm an emotional mess, know that I'm not thinking clearly when the notion flickers through my mind that Colton's mad at me for being pregnant, not because the loss of our child. I immediately push the thought away—hate myself for even thinking it—but on the heels of the past few weeks and everything we've been through, I can't help it. And then that thought causes so many more to spiral out of control that I have to tell myself to get a grip. That Colton cares about me, wouldn't walk away from me because of something like this. I force myself to focus on answers and not the unknown.

And without another thought, the next question is off of my tongue and hanging in the air still vibrating with Colton's anger. "Is it possible for ... can I get pregnant again? Would I be able to carry to term?"

She looks at me, sympathy flashing over her stoic face, a sigh on her lips, and tears welling in her eyes. "Possible?" She repeats the word back to me and closes her eyes for a moment as she gently shakes her head back and forth. She reaches out and grabs my hands in hers and just stares at me for a moment. "This wasn't supposed to be possible, Rylee." Her voice breaks, my grief and disbelief obviously affecting her.

"I'd hope fate wouldn't be cruel enough to do this to you two times and not give you another chance." She quickly dashes away a tear that falls and sniffles. "Sometimes hope is the most powerful medicine of all."

I can feel him before I even open my eyes, know he is sitting beside me. The man who waits for no one is waiting patiently for me. My body sighs softly into the thought and then my heart wrings at the thought of a little boy lost forever to me—dark hair, green eyes, freckled nose, mischievous grin—and when I open my eyes, the same eyes in my imagination meet mine.

But his eyes look tired, battle weary, and concerned. He leans forward and takes the hand I'm reaching out.

"Hey," I croak as I shift from the discomfort in my abdomen.

"Hey," he says softly, scooting forward to the edge of his seat, and I notice his shirt has been replaced with a pair of hospital scrubs. "How are you feeling?" He presses a kiss to my hand as my tears well again. "No." He rises, sitting his hip on the edge of my bed. "Please don't cry, baby," he says as he pulls me against his chest and wraps his arms around me.

I shake my head, feelings running a rampant race of highs and lows through me. Devastated at the loss of a child—a chance that I might not ever get again despite the dash of possibility this whole situation presented—and at the same time guilty feeling relief because if I had been pregnant, where would that leave Colton and me?

"I'm okay," I tell him, pressing a kiss to the underside of his jaw, drawing strength from the steady pulse beating beneath my lips, before leaning back on my propped up pillows so I can look at him. I blow out a breath to get my hair out of my face, not wanting to use my hand and break our connection.

The look in his eyes is so intense, jaw muscle clenching, lips strained with emotion, that I look down at our joined hands to mentally prepare myself for the things I need to say to him but fear his responses. I take a deep breath and begin. "We need to talk about this." My voice is barely a whisper as I raise my eyes back up to meet his.

He shakes his head, a surefire sign of the argument that's about to fall from his lips. "No." He squeezes my hand. "The only thing that matters is that you're okay."

"Colton ..." I just say his name but I know he can hear my pleading in it.

"No, Ry!" He shoves up off the bed and paces the small space beside it, making me think of him on the side of the freeway yesterday, overwhelmed with guilt. Was it just yesterday? It feels like a lifetime has passed since then. "You don't get it, do you?" he shouts at me, making me cringe from the vehemence in his voice. "I found you," he says, his eyes angled to the ground, the break in his voice nearly destroying me. "There was blood everywhere." He looks up and meets my eyes. "Everywhere ... and you ...you were lying in the middle of it, covered in it." He walks to the edge of my bed and grabs both of my hands. "I thought I'd lost you. For the second time in one fucking day!"

In an instant, his hand is holding the back of my neck tightly and he's pressing his lips possessively against mine. I can taste the raw and palpable angst and need on his tongue before he pulls back and rests his forehead against mine, hand still tight on the back of my neck while his other one comes up and cups the side of my cheek.

"Give me a minute," he whispers, his breath feathering over my lips. "Let me have this okay? I just need this ... you ... right now. To hold you like this because I've been going out of my fucking mind waiting for you to wake up. Waiting for you to come the fuck back to me because, Ry, now that you're here, now that you're in my life ... become a part of me, I can't fucking breathe without knowing you're all right. That you're coming back to me."

"I'll always come back to you." The words are out of my mouth before I can think, because when the heart wants to speak it does so without premeditation. I hear him breathe in a shaky breath, feel his fingers flex on my neck, and know how hard the man who's never needed anybody is desperately trying to figure out what to do now that the one thing he's never wanted he suddenly can't do without.

We sit like this for a moment, and as he leans back to press a kiss on the tip of my nose, I hear the commotion before I see her barrel into the room. "Christ on a crutch, woman! Do you enjoy giving me heart attacks?" Haddie is through the door and at my side in an instant. "Get your hands off of her, Donavan, and let me at her," she says, and I can feel Colton's lips form into a smile as he presses them against my cheek. Within seconds I am engulfed in the whirlwind that is Haddie, held tight as we both start crying. "Let me look at you!" she says, leaning back, smiling through the tears. "You look like shit but are still beautiful as ever. You okay?" The sincerity in her voice makes the tears well again, and I have to bite my lip to prevent them from falling. I nod and Haddie looks up and over my bed, and meets Colton's eyes. They hold each other's gaze for a few moments, emotion swimming in both of their eyes. "Thank you," she tells him softly, and I close my eyes for a moment as the enormity of everything hits me.

"No tears, okay?" Her hand's squeezing mine and I nod my head before I open my eyes.

"Yeah." I blow out a breath and look over to meet Colton's eyes. There's something there I can't latch onto, but we've both been through so much in the past few days it's probably emotional overload.

We sit for some time. Each moment that passes, Colton becomes more withdrawn, and I can tell Haddie notices it too but she just keeps chatting away as if we aren't in a hospital room and I'm not mourning the loss of a baby. And it's okay that she is, because as usual, she knows just what I need.

She's in the middle of telling me that she's spoken to my parents and they're on their way up from San Diego when her phone receives a text. She looks at it and then looks over at Colton. "Becks is down in the parking lot and wants you to come show him where to go."

He gives her an odd look but nods, kissing me on the forehead and smiling softly at me. "I'll be right back, okay?"

I smile back at him and watch as he walks out the door before looking over at Haddie.

"You want to tell me what the fuck is going on here?" I laugh, expecting nothing less than her frankness. "I mean shit." She blows out a breath. "I told you to have reckless sex with him, clear the cobwebs and shit. You couldn't be any more Jerry Springer if you tried. Getting knocked up, wrestling a gun-wielding man, and miscarrying a baby you didn't even know you were carrying."

The tears come now—tears of laughter—because anyone else listening to this conversation would think Haddie is being callous, but I know deep down she is dealing with her sudden anxiety the only way she knows how—with sarcasm, and then some. And for me, it's my own personal therapy because it's what I've clung to the past two years on the really rough nights after Max's accident.

She's laughing with me too but her laughter is chased by tears as she looks at me and continues. "I mean who knew the man had sperm with super powers that could just swoop on in, rescue and repair a broken womb like a damn superhero?"

I choke out a cough, startled by what she's just said because I've never told her about Colton and his superheroes, never wanting to betray his trust. And she never notices, she just keeps going. "From now on, every time I see a Superman logo, I'm going to think it stands for Colton and his super sperm. Breaking through eggs and taking names."

I laugh with her, all the while silently smiling softly at her words and looking toward the doorway, wanting him—needing him—to come back in the worst way.

"How's he doing?" she asks after her laughter tinged tears slowly abate.

I shrug. "He's not really addressing the—the baby." I struggle even saying the word and squeeze my eyes shut to try and push the tears back. She squeezes my hand. "He won't say it but he blames himself. I know he thinks that if he hadn't left me at the house alone then Zander's dad wouldn't have been there. Wouldn't have hit me. I wouldn't have ..." And it's silly really that I can't say the words—miscarriage or lose the baby—because after all this time, you'd think my lips would be used to saying them. But each time I think it ... say it, I feel like it's the first time.

She nods her head and looks at me before looking down at our joined hands. I wait for her to speak, one of her Haddie-isms to fall from her mouth and make me laugh, but when she looks up, tears are welling in her eyes. "You scared the shit out of me, Ry. When he called me ... if you could have heard what he sounded like ... it left no doubt in my mind how he feels about you."

And of course my eyes tear up because she is, so she stands and shifts to sit on the bed next to me, pulling me into her arms and holding on tight—the same position we'd spent hours in after I lost Max and our baby. At least this time, the burden weighing down on my heart is a little lighter.

Chapter Thirty-Two

I feel like I'm in a parade as Colton pushes my wheelchair toward the hospital's exit. I don't need the wheelchair but my nurse says it's hospital policy. My mom is chatting quietly with Haddie and my dad is listening with a half smile on his face because even he isn't immune to Haddie's charm. Becks is pulling the Range Rover up front for Colton while Sammy stands at the entrance to the hospital, wary of any press who luckily have not caught wind of the story. Yet.

Colton is quiet as he pushes me, but then again he has been for the better part of the last two days. If it were anyone else I'd chalk his withdrawal up to the unexpected meeting with my parents. I mean, meeting your significant other's parents is a huge step in any relationship, let alone someone like Colton who has a nonexistent history with this kind of thing. Add to that meeting your girlfriend's parents after she miscarried a baby she never knew existed.

But not Colton—no—it's something different. And as much as I love my parents for rushing up here, Haddie and her nonstop humor, Becks with his unexpected wit, and every other person who has stopped by to wish me well, all I want is to be alone with Colton. When it's just the two of us he won't be able to hide from me and ignore whatever is on his mind. The silence is slowly smothering us, and I need us to be able to breathe. I need us to be able to yell and scream and cry and be angry—get it all out—without the eyes of our families watching to make sure we don't crack.

Because we need to crack. We need to break. Only then can we pick up each other's pieces and make each other whole again.

I glance behind me and steal a quick glance at Colton and his sedate expression. I can't help but wonder what if Zander's dad hadn't happened? What if I was still pregnant? Where would we be then?

Don't focus on that, I tell myself, even though it's all I can think of—me being pregnant. It feels like such a real possibility, tangible even, that it's constantly flickering through my mind. Colton stops the wheelchair as we exit the doors of the hospital and walks around the front of me. His eyes meet mine, a softness to the intensity that I've noticed there over the past few days. A smile creeps over his lips. Could I ever walk away from this man because I want a child and he doesn't? Would I be willing to leave the one man I know I can't live without for the one thing I once thought I'd do anything to have?

No. The answer is that simple. This man—damaged, beautiful, work-in-progress man—is just too much of everything I need to ever walk away from.

Colton leans in, pressing a soft kiss to my lips as guilt flickers through me for even thinking such thoughts. "You doing okay?"

I reach up and place my hand softly on the side of his cheek and smile with a subtle nod of my head. "Yeah, you?"

The grin lights up his face because he knows I'm referring to the looks we've both seen my dad giving him as he figures out if this man is good enough for his little girl. "Nothing I can't handle," he says with a wink and a shake of his head as he stands up, eyes still locked on mine, smile still warming my heart. "Do you doubt my abilities?"

"No, that's one thing I most definitely do not." I laugh and stop when he tilts his head to the side and stares at me. "What?"

"It's just good to see you smile," he says softly before his eyes cloud and he averts his attention to something over my shoulder. When he looks back his eyes are clear and his expression is gentler. "You ready to blow this joint?"

Colton holds one elbow and my mom the other, as I stand, both remaining there to make sure I'm stable, which is unnecessary. "I'm fine, really," I tell them.

My mom wraps her arms around me and holds me against her a little longer than normal. "If you want us to we can stay in town an extra day. Make sure you're nice and comfy before we head back home."

"She's not going home." I swear, everyone's heads whip over to look at Colton, including mine. Despite all eyes on him, his are only on me. "You're staying with me. No questions."

And with that decree, Colton walks around a smirking Beckett, a satisfied Haddie, and my stunned parents. He closes the back of the Rover and walks over to my parents. "You're more than welcome to come and stay at my place. I have plenty of room." He raises his eyebrows at them, welcoming any argument that might come.

"No. That's fine," my dad says, reaching out to take the hand Colton has extended. "I'm trusting that you'll take good care of her."

And it's as simple as that. The unspoken bond from father to the man his daughter loves passes between the two of them. Man to man. Protector to protector. Colton holds my father's hand firm and nods his head in acceptance of the trust just bestowed to him. Colton is now responsible—in *man-speak*—for me. They hold each other's eyes and hands a moment longer. Emotions lodge in my throat as I slide my eyes over to my mom who is watching the exchange, a tear in her eye as well.

We both watch them for a moment before my mom helps me get in the car. She straps the belt across my lap and then looks at me, holding my cheeks in both of her hands. "You told me once that you weren't sure what was between you and Colton." She moves an errant curl from my ponytail off of my face. "The man is head over heels in love with you, honey." She smiles softly and nods her head when I automatically start to speak and downplay it. "I'm your mom, it's obvious to me, Ry. Men never see it, accept it, want it, until they trip and fall face first into it. You're lucky to get the chance twice in your life, to have a man willing to trip on purpose, to take that bottomless step. Even when he messes this up—" She holds her hand up when I start to defend him and just rolls her eyes before continuing. "Let's face it, he's a man, he's going to mess this up ... have some patience because he loves you just as much as you love him. The words he can't speak are written all over that handsome face of his."

I just nod, my bottom lip worrying between my teeth to prevent the endless stream of tears from starting again. "I know." My voice is so quiet, happiness and sadness overwhelm me.

She reaches down and squeezes my hands where they're clasped in my lap. "If a baby's meant to be, Ry, it will happen. I know it doesn't make you feel better to hear me say it, but in the middle of the night when you're sad, you'll be able to hear my voice telling you. Remember, life isn't about how you survive the storm, but rather how you dance in the rain." She leans in and presses a kiss to my cheek. "I love you."

"I love you too, Mom," I reach out and wrap my arms around her, her words of wisdom dancing in my head. "Thank you."

Goodbyes are said quickly with everyone else since the car is in the loading zone. Beckett is last to say goodbye. He reaches into the car and gives me a quick hug while Colton talks to Sammy about something outside of the car. He starts to close the car door and then stops a moment and looks at me with a shake of his head. "That lifeline thing goes both ways, you know? Use it. Use him. He won't break if you do ... but you just might if you don't."

"Thanks, Becks. You're a really good friend to him."

"Asshole's more like it!" Colton says, sliding into the seat beside me. "He'd be an even better friend if he got his hand off of my girl and let me take her the fuck home."

"Speaking of our mild-mannered friend," Becks says with a laugh, squeezing my hand. "I love you too, Wood!"

"Ditto, dude!" Colton laughs as he pushes the button on the dash and the engine roars to life.

"Keep him in line," Becks says with a wink to me and a shake of his head before he shuts the door.

We pull out of the parking lot, both of us falling into a comfortable silence as we drive. I'm anxious to get home, sleep in my own bed with Colton's reassuring warmth against me. I close my eyes and lean my head back, my mind racing over every chaotic event that's happened in the last few weeks. I sigh into the silence and Colton switches the radio on before reaching over to hold my hand.

Sarah Bareillis' voice floats through the air, and I can't help but hum softly and smile at the poignancy of the lyrics. I know Colton hears the words too because he squeezes my hand, and when I open my eyes to look over at him, I'm startled by the sight in front of me.

"Colton, what...?"

"I know you're still sore, but I wanted to bring you somewhere that made you happy."

"You make me happy," I say, locking eyes with him to reinforce my words before looking out at the stretch of beach beyond us.

"I'm prepared this time around." He smiles shyly at me. "I have blankets, jackets, and some food if you'd like to go sit a while in the sun with me."

Tears well in my eyes again and I start laughing. "Yes. I'm sorry," I say in reference to the tears I'm wiping away. "I'm an emotional mess. Pregnancy hormones and ..." My voice fades, realizing I've touched on the taboo topic we've yet to discuss. The uncomfortable silence settles between us. Colton grips the steering wheel tight and blows out a loud breath before climbing out of the car without another word.

He opens the back door, and collects some things, and then helps me out of the Rover. "Easy," he says as I slide gingerly off of the seat.

"I'm okay."

We link hands and walk a ways down the beach in silence. There are people here today, unlike the last time we were here months ago—our first official date. The fact that he thought to bring me to a place I find solace in makes my heart happy.

"This okay?" he asks as he lets go of my hand and lays a blanket out onto the sand. He sets a brown paper bag down and then puts his hands on my hips as I start to sit down.

"I'm not going to break," I say softly to him even though I love the feeling of his hands on me—strength, comfort, and security—all three things given with their simple placement.

He sits down behind me, frames my legs with his, and pulls me back against his chest, leaving his arms wrapped tight around me. He lowers his mouth and chin to the curve of my neck and sighs. "I know you're not going to break, Ry, but you came damn close. I know you're strong and independent and used to doing things all by yourself, but please just let me take care of you right now, okay? I need … I need you to let me do this." He ends his words with a kiss pressed to my skin but never moves his mouth, he just keeps it there so I can feel the warmth of his breath and the chafe of his stubble.

"Okay," I murmur, a deep sigh on my lips and a twinge in my abdomen reminding me that we need to talk. I tilt my chin toward the sun and close my eyes, welcoming the warmth because I still feel the cold inside of me.

"Just say it," he tells me, exasperation lacing his voice. "I can feel you tensing up, pretending your mind isn't going a million miles a minute with whatever it is you want to ask me. You're not going to relax like you need to until you say it." He chuckles, his chest vibrating against my back, but I can sense he's not too thrilled.

I close my eyes a moment, not wanting to ruin the peace between us but at the same time needing to address the underlying tension. "We need to talk about … the baby …" I finally manage and am proud of myself that my voice didn't waver like it has over the past few days every time I try to bring this up. "You're not talking to me and I don't know what you're thinking … what you're feeling? And I need to know …"

"Why?" The single word snaps out, a knee jerk reaction I'm sure since I can't see his face, but can feel his body tense up. "Why does it matter?" he finally asks again with a little more control in his voice.

Because that's what you do when you're in a relationship, I want to tell him but exhale softly instead. "Colton, something major happened to us … to me at least—"

"To us," he corrects, and his comment throws me for a moment. It's the first time he's really acknowledged the baby we lost. Something we created together that linked us together indefinitely.

"… to us. But I don't know how you feel. I know my world has been rocked and I'm reeling with everything. I just … You're here and going through this with me, but at the same time I feel like you're closing yourself off, not talking to me." I sigh, knowing I'm rambling but not sure how to break through to him. I give it one last try. "You tell me you need me to let you take care of me. I understand that. Can you understand that I need you to talk to me? That you can't shut me out right now? The last thing I need to be right now is worried about where we stand."

I force myself to stop rambling because I can hear the desperation in my voice, and he still hasn't responded, so now we're surrounded by an awkward silence. Colton starts to pull away from me, and I immediately prepare myself for the emptiness of him distancing himself when I need him the most. Then I feel his nose nuzzle into the back of my hair and just breathe me in. I close my eyes as chills dance over my skin because I know he's not going to push me away, but rather is taking his Colton way of taking a minute to gather his thoughts.

"Rylee…" he sighs my name in that way that makes me hold my breath because there's so much emotion packed in it. He rests his forehead against the back of my head as his hands squeeze my arms. "I can't talk about *it*. I just can't." And the way he says *it* tells me that he's referring to the baby. "I can only deal with one thing at a fucking time, and right now I'm still trying to wrap my head around the fact that I almost lost you."

He rocks his forehead back and forth against my head. "I'm not used to feeling, Ry. I'm used to being numb … running the first time shit gets too real. And you, us, this …" He sighs "… it's as fucking real as real can get. I feel like I've been sucker punched by what happened when I was just getting used to the new fucking normal. I'm shaken up. I don't know which goddamn way is up, but I'm dealing with it the best way I know how right now. And that means dealing with getting the image of you looking like a lifeless Raggedy Ann doll out of my head."

His words reach into the depths of my soul and give me back the tiny pieces of hope I lost with the miscarriage and the fears that ate at me from his silence. So he doesn't want to—can't—deal with the baby, at least he's told me. And as much as I want and need to speak to him about it, reassure him that he's what I need and everything else can be figured out later, I keep quiet and let him deal with what happened to me.

I shift between his legs so I'm sitting sideways in his lap, my legs resting over the top of one of his. I need to see his face, need to show him I'm okay. I look into his eyes brimming with confusion and reach a hand up to rest on his cheek with a soft smile on my lips. "I'm okay, Colton. You saved me." I lean in and brush a tender kiss on his lips that I can't seem to ever get enough of. "Thank you for saving me."

"I think I should thank you." He subtly shakes his head. "You're the one who's saving me."

His words rob all thoughts from my head except for the words I can't tell him. *I love you.* I love you more than you'll ever know or I'll ever be able to express. Doesn't he realize the only way I could possibly save him was because he finally let me in? When is he going to accept that he is worth saving? Our eyes are locked onto one another's as unspoken words are exchanged. I'm surprised by the tears pooling in the corners of his eyes and the shuddered inhale of his breath.

"We're fine, Ry. I just need a minor pit stop to work through all the crap in my head I'm not used to, okay? I'm not asking for space or time apart, just a little patience as I try to figure it all out."

I nod my head, bottom lip between my teeth because I can't speak—physically can't speak—because he's just rendered me speechless. He gets my biggest fear and wants to assuage it before my mind can over-think and over-analyze everything, as I typically do.

We sit for a bit, the silence settling around us into an easy comfort. "You hungry?" he asks after a while. I just shrug, enjoying my head nuzzled under his chin and his arms wrapped around me. "The first time we came here, you threw me for a loop."

"Why?" My voice is sleepy and content. There is nowhere else I'd rather be right now.

I can feel his shoulders shrug against me. "I don't know. I was expecting you to get pissed that I brought you to a beach and fed you salami and cheese and wine out of Dixie cups." He chuckles. "Little did I know you were going to rock my fucking world."

Warmth floods through me. Images flicker through my mind of sitting here months ago with this achingly handsome man, wondering what in the hell he saw in me. And I get it now. He saw the pieces of me that could make a whole. Accepted the jagged edges that needed to be healed, because he too had the same thing. And here we sit again, in parts and pieces, needing to be put back together. But this time we have each other to lean on, to look to for help.

"God you were cocky as hell but I just couldn't resist you, *Ace*."

"Oh, baby, I've still got all of the arrogance and definitely a whole lot of cock."

I roll my eyes and giggle. "My God!" I can't stop laughing as he presses a kiss to the top of my head. "The man has arrogance in spades."

"Nope," he says. "Just in aces."

"Lame!" I say, enjoying the lighthearted banter between us and leaning back to look at his face. "Seriously? That's all you can give me? You can't come up with anything better than that?"

"Oh, Ry." He smirks at me, a salacious look in his eyes, as he leans in and presses a quick kiss to my lips. "No worries about the coming or the getting it up part because you'd be hard pressed to find any man that can give a fucking better than I can."

Before I can even respond, his lips are on mine, his hands winding around my back, and our hearts entwining in a way I never thought possible.

We've loved.

We've lost.

And now we're just finding our footing again. Us again. And it's never felt so good to lose myself in someone so I can find myself again.

"You sure you're okay?"

I feel his weight on the bed as he sits down next to me, his cologne momentarily masking the antiseptic smell the cleaning crew left behind. "Mmm-hmm. I'm just tired," I tell him as I roll on my side so I can look at him. "Thank you for this afternoon," I say, thinking about our time on the beach. Our conversation, our food from the deli reminiscent of our first date, and of the silence between us that isn't so lonely or pained any more. "Are you okay?" I ask the same question back to him.

He pets Baxter on the head and leans down to press a tender kiss to my lips, and it's not lost on me that he never answers the question. "I'm gonna go do some work for a bit," he says as he rises from the bed. "You sure you'll be okay?"

"I'm fine, Colton. I'm just going to go to sleep." I squeeze his hand as he turns to walk out of the bedroom. "Hey, do you know where my phone is so I can let Haddie know I'm all right?"

He walks over to the dresser and brings it to me, pressing another kiss to my forehead and then my nose before walking out of the room. I watch him leave knowing the sight of him will never get old. I will never take it for granted since it has taken so much work for us to get to this point.

I power on my phone, surprised it has any battery left since it's been here since the night everything happened. It turns on and I shake my head at the endless texts of well-wishes. I read a few about the ground breaking ceremony we have coming up to commemorate the new project beginning. And then my last text completely throws me.

Knocks the wind out of me, and steals my heart.

It's from Colton and I don't think words from him have ever been so honest or the depths of his despair so raw.

I'm lost here. You're somewhere in this damn hospital and I need to talk to you. Fucking touch you. Something to you because I'm scared as fuck … so I'm going to tell you the way I know you'll hear me. *Broken* by Lifehouse.

And the tears come now. They fall freely down my face and I don't try to stop them or hide them because no one is here to see them now. And because they are tears of joy.

He loves me.

Chapter Thirty-Three

COLTON

"You going to sit out here and drown your sorrows all night like a whiny little bitch or what?"

The voice coming from the pitch black night scares the shit out of me. "Jesus Christ, Becks!" I bark as I turn to see him walking down the side of the house. "What the fuck, dude? You ever heard of the front door?"

"Yeah, well, you ever heard of answering your cell phone? Besides, knocking's for friends and I'm fucking family so quit your bitching."

"I've been in the hospital more than enough over the past two months, a heart attack's not part of my fucking game plan." I take a long tug on the beer, my head finally becoming fuzzy enough that when I think of Rylee, the image of her cold, covered in fucking blood, and unresponsive isn't what comes to mind first.

"Well, what is part of the game plan then?" he asks as he opens the beer he's pulled out of the fridge, that smirk on his face telling me he has a point and *fuck me*, I don't need any more points or advice or fucking anything right now.

"Really, make yourself at home," I tell him. "Steal my beer."

"Nah, just borrowing it," he says as he plops down in the chair beside me and we sit in silence, trying to gauge the other's mood. "We didn't get a chance to talk much at the hospital."

"Yeah? Well, I had more important things on my mind than shooting the shit with you." And fuck if I'm not being an asshole. I needed him there too, but I'm not real comfortable with where he's going with this. I feel a Becks' dress down coming. *Shit!*

"She asleep?" he asks, lifting his chin up toward the second story.

"It's past midnight, what do you think?"

"Don't be such an asshole. Look, you've been handed a lot of shit to deal with and—"

"Butt the fuck out, Becks. Let me just drink my goddamn beer in peace." I toss my empty bottle toward the trash can and fucking miss. I must be drunker than I thought. Fuckin' A.

"No can do, brother." He sighs as I mutter *asshole* under my breath which garners a drawn out chuckle from him. "You've fucked this up one too many times so I'm here to help."

"Don't let the door hit you in the ass on the way out, *sweetheart*." I just want to be left alone. Me, my beer, my dog, and my fucking peace.

"Nice try but you're stuck with me. Kind of like herpes, only better."

What? "Dude, did you just actually compare yourself to fucking herpes?" I lean my head back and look at the stars in the sky before angling it over to stare at him and shake my head. "Because at least with herpes, my dick gets serviced first. With you, it's more like being bent without any lube."

He laughs that laugh of his that tugs a smile up at the corner of my mouth. The stubborn fucker is getting to me when all I want is to be left alone.

"Well at least it's nice to know you'll let me in somehow," he says, winking and staring at me until I can't take it. I let out the laugh I've been holding in.

"You're a sick fuck, you know that?" I say, uncapping another bottle of beer.

"You wouldn't want me any other way."

"Mmm-hmm," I say as I down half of the bottle letting the night's silence settle around us. As much as I want to be left alone—to deal with the jacked up shit in my head that's telling me a decision's going to have to come sooner than later—it's nice that Becks is here, even if he's a pain in my ass. I drum my thumbs to Seether playing through the speakers as he gives me a couple of minutes before he starts playing shrink to the fucking poisonous shit in my head.

"Remember that girl, Roxy Tomlin?" he asks finally, throwing me for a loop.

"*Hoover?*" I laugh, curious as to why he's bringing up the blow job queen from our past. The one who sucked Becks off just to get to me. And normally, I'd be shoving that shit out the door with a stunt like that, but after he'd bragged she gave the best head he'd ever had, I took advantage of the more than willing offer.

"Yeah, fucking Hoover. The suction that never stopped." He laughs with me, shaking his head at the memory. "Still pretty goddamn high on the ranking scale in my book."

"No fucking Rylee, but yeah." I shrug. "She was decent."

"Decent?" he barks out. "I swear to God, the woman had no gag reflex."

"Maybe that's 'cause you're not big enough to reach the back of her throat." I quirk my eyebrows as I finish another beer. He wants to come to my house and fuck with my head, I sure as shit am going to mess with his.

"Fuck off, Wood."

His bottle cap hits me in the chest as I sit back and smirk. "I've had much better offers, my friend, but thanks anyway." My head's spinning trying to figure out where the hell he's going with this line of thinking, but hell if I can figure it out.

"I ran into her the other day." His calm cadence makes me to turn my head and look at him.

"And ...?"

"Shocked the shit out of me is what she did."

"Why's that?" I pretend to be interested but he's losing me. I glance up at the bedroom window behind me where the light's still off, and even though I'm way beyond the road to drunk, I like knowing Ry's up there. I try to focus back on Becks but why the hell do I care about the easy piece we both had way back when with a head so screwed up it rivaled mine?

"I barely recognized her. Still gorgeous as sin. Filled out in all the right places now."

Yeah, yeah, get to your fucking point, Beckett.

"And she had three kids in tow."

"Look, dude, I know there's some kind of six degrees of Kevin Bacon happening here right now, but I'm not fucking following you so just spit out your goddamn point." Then it hits me. *Oh shit!* "They're not your kids are they, Becks?"

"Jesus Christ, Donavan, you're drunker than I thought." He chokes out a cough before raising his hand in the air and pointing to himself. "King of double bag before you stab, right here!"

"And who taught you that, douche bag?"

"Apparently not you since you obviously didn't practice what you fucking preach."

His unexpected words cause a twinge in my gut that I hate. The same damn twinge I get every time I think of Rylee lying there on the goddamn floor all by herself, for who knows how long, and every time I think of the small piece of me dying inside of her. I gulp down the beer, pushing the thoughts from my head and force myself to breathe.

"Where the hell are you going with this, Daniels, because I'm drunk, have no fucking patience, and kind of think you're trying to push my buttons to get me to react to whatever point you're taking your sweet ass time getting to. So just fucking get to it."

"Remember that one night we all got plastered at Jimmy's bonfire?"

"Beckett!" I growl at him because my tolerance ran out like five goddamn minutes ago.

"Chill out, shut the hell up, and listen." I snap my head over to look at him because I'm in no fucking mood. "We were wasted and she started talking about the shit that had happened to her—bad shit—you remember?" I give him a measured nod, still not following the fucking road map he's lost himself on, but recall the story of abuse in all forms. A conversation I took no part in. "And she said she never wanted kids, that life's too messed up and she didn't want them to go through the shit she did. And now she has three kids, is married, and seems genuinely happy."

"The fucking point?" I growl at him

"Quit being so goddamn stubborn, Donavan, and connect the fucking dots, will you?"

"I'm not a fucking constellation. Your dots aren't drawing a picture so help me the fuck out."

"You look like the Little Dipper to me." He smirks.

I pick up the pillow next to me and chuck it at him. "Fuck off! Big Dipper's more like it." I take a long tug on my beer. Shit, it's empty. They're disappearing faster than I can count them. Usually I'd just crash right here, but fuck Ry's up there. No way I'm sleeping without her next to me. I sigh, Becks' words running circles in my head, hinting at his point but never really landing on the damn bull's-eye. "Seriously, Becks, what are you trying to tell me here? Just spit it out."

"Things change, dude! Life changes. Priorities change. Pre-fucking-conceived notions change. You have to adjust and change with them or your ass gets left behind." He shoves up out of his chair and walks to the railing and looks out into the blackness beyond. When he turns back around, he is dead serious. "We've been best friends for what? Almost twenty years. I love ya, man. I never interfere with the shit you've got going on ... which woman's warming the sheets, but fuckin' A, Wood ..."

I'm not liking where this conversation is going. Deflection is my only thought. "I thought you told me I needed to fuck a B instead," I say, trying to add some humor to this serious conversation, and fuck all if I can follow how we went from Hoover Tomlin to Becks sticking his goddamn nose where it doesn't belong.

He laughs—has the balls to fucking mock me—before walking over to me and shaking his head at me. "You don't get it, do you? Fuck the A or the B, you have the *whole goddamn alphabet* upstairs and she's asleep in your bed right now, but the only letter that can fuck this up is U!" he shouts at me.

What the fuck? He's taking her side? I swear to God, Ry's worked her voodoo pussy magic on him and he's never even had it before. Talk about super powers and shit.

"Becks? How am I going to screw this up? She's here isn't she? I want her here, brought her here, so what the hell else do you want from me? And how does Hoover factor into this shit?"

"Jesus fucking Christ!" he swears as he paces in front of me and takes a long pull on his beer. "She's here for now! She's here until you start thinking too damn much about how, now that she might be able to have a baby, she just might not want you anymore because you've never wanted one. Until you start pushing her the fuck away and trying to hurt her so she makes the decision for you so you don't have to make it for yourself. But things change, Colton! Look at Roxy 'Hoover' Tomlin. She never wanted kids because of the shit that happened to her as a kid and now her kids? They're her whole goddamn world!"

"Fuck. You." The ice in my voice rivals the chill of the polar ice cap.

"No, fuck you, Colton! You sat in that goddamn hospital room when she needed you the most and sure as hell you were there ... but fluffing pillows doesn't fix the shit that's hurting inside of her. Or in you. I sat there and plain as day watched you start to pull away from her."

"I'm warning you, Becks!" I say, standing up, fists clenched, fury racing through my veins. His words hit a little too close to home. A little too close to a truth I always said I never wanted—would never tolerate—but now all of a sudden I can't get out of my mind. Ideas of a life I never even thought could exist for me. But how is that even fucking possible? The broken merry-go-round in my head keeps whirling, but all I can think about is shutting Becks up because he's right about me pulling away. About me not being there for her when she needed me most. So right my stomach is a motherfucking mess.

"Truth hurt, dude? You want to throw a punch at me? Take the truth you don't want to face out on me?"

I grit my teeth and throw my bottle into the can and watch it shatter into a million fucking pieces. And once again I'm back here—broken glass, broken mind, and fucked up all around. He pushes my shoulder from behind, egging me on, and I take the goddman bait so quick it's not even a thought. I whirl around, arm cocked back, fists clenched, and a fucking freight train of anger tears through me.

And Becks just stands there, eyes locked on mine, chin raised in that *fuck you* position daring me to take a shot. "What's your problem, hotshot? Not so tough now, are ya?"

My body hums, vibrates with every fucking ounce of emotion I've held in over the past week, but all I can do is stare at him, wanting so desperately to expel the guilt eating at every goddamn piece of me.

Guilt that all of this happened because of me—not stepping up to be a man, leaving her alone with Zander, not getting to The House quick enough, not getting to the bathroom quick enough. The guilt clings to so many fucking things inside of me—the poison and the hope— that the only thing I want to do is drink another beer, numb myself, and push it away.

"You wanna fight? How 'bout you save it? How about you fight for what fucking matters? Because she," he says, pointing up to the bedroom window and lowering his voice to a quiet steel, "she's worth the fight, dude. Worth every goddamn fear eating at you. Every piece of it, Colton—A to motherfucking Z." He steps into me and jabs a finger into my chest. "Time to deal with your past, because Rylee?" He points up to the room again and then back at me. "She's your goddamn future. It's fight or flight time, man. Let's just hope you're the man I've always thought you were."

My whole body tenses at his words, and I'm so pissed at myself that I don't immediately tell him he's full of bullshit. I'm so motherfucking angry that for a moment—just a flicker of a moment—fear consumes me so I think of flight.

Think of flight when she's done nothing but prove she's a fighter—a gorgeous, defiant, scrappy brawler when it comes to what's hers—while I fucking hesitated. My teeth are gritted so goddamn hard I swear my molars are going to break, and I turn my back to him and walk over to the railing and cuss out into the darkness that rivals the black I feel in my soul right now.

I don't deserve her. Sinner and saint. My caution to her motherfucking checkered flag. And as much as I know this—as much as my chest hurts with each breath because of this—she's the only thing I see. The only one I want. *My fucking Rylee.*

"Cat got your tongue, Colt?" he taunts from behind me. "Are you that stupid you're going to walk away because she got pregnant? Because of some shit that hap—"

And I'm done.

Temper snapped.

Gas added to my fucking fire.

"You have no fucking clue about what happened!" I yell at him, my voice breaking as I turn to face him. "Not a clue!"

Beckett's in my face in five strides. "You're right! I don't have a fucking clue!" He grabs my shoulders so I can't turn away from him, and as hard as I try I can't shrug them off of me. "But, Colton, *brother*, I've watched you struggle for years with whatever the fuck that bitch of a mother did to you as a kid, but *that's not you anymore*. You're not that kid. *Never again*. And, dude, Rylee accepts that. Accepts you. *Fucking loves you*. Figure out how to accept it and the rest will figure itself out." He reaches out and cuffs the side of my face with a hand before stepping back and shaking his head. "It's time to man the fuck up and realize you love her too, before it's too goddamn late and you lose the one person who's made you whole again. Figure out how to deal with your past so you don't lose your fucking future."

And with that the fucker nods his head and walks toward the house as if he didn't just mess with me. He stops as he opens the door and turns back to face me. "When we were younger I didn't get it, but what your dad used to tell you about hurting is feeling and some shit like that?" I just nod. "Yeah, I think you need to remember that now."

He turns back around and disappears into the house, leaving me all alone with nothing but an empty night and haunting memories.

Hurting is feeling and feeling is living, and isn't it good to be alive? My dad's mantra passes through my mind as I walk into my room and see Ry asleep.

Fuck me.

She still takes my breath away. Still makes me want and need and ache like no one ever has. And shit I still want to corrupt her—that part will never go away. I laugh at my fucked up mind, but I know deep down corruption doesn't matter anymore. Because she's what matters now.

Rylee. Motherfucking checkered flags and shit.

I walk toward the bed knowing I could sit and stare at her for hours. Dark curls fanned across my pillow, tank top covering those perfect fucking tits and riding up on her abdomen so the moonlight shows the scars of her past. The scars that robbed her of a future she thought was impossible, until three days ago.

I rub my hand down my side as I watch her, slide it over my inked scars that remind me of a future I never imagined was a possibility—until three days ago, and my fingers linger over the last one—uncolored and empty. The one thing left I have to figure out before I know for sure if I can do what my head and heart agree on.

Because baggage can be a powerful thing. It can contain you. Prevent you from moving on. Kill you. And sometimes feelings aren't enough to break its hold. To allow you to move on. But right as rain, standing here, watching her chest rise and fall, it's time my 747—baggage and all—takes fucking flight.

Because I chose fight.

My breath catches in my throat as I come to the realization that I want this. I fucking want her. In my life—day, night, now, later—and the thought staggers me. Breaks and mends me. Tames the un-fucking-tamable. Fuckin'A.

I shake my head and laugh softly. I guess I should say *A to fucking Z*. And I can't resist anymore. I sink down softly into the bed next to her and push away images of what happened the last night we lay there together.

I give into the necessity coursing through me like the adrenaline I crave. I reach out and pull her in tight against me. When I do, she rolls over in my arms so her face is nestled under my chin, her arms pressed between our chests, and the heat of her breath tickling my skin as she murmurs, "I love you, Colton."

It's so soft I almost don't hear it. So quiet and sluggish that I realize she's still asleep but it doesn't matter, my breath stops. My pulse races and my heart constricts. I open my mouth but then close it to swallow because I feel like I just ate a mouthful of cotton. I do the only thing I possibly can. I press a kiss to the top of her head.

I want to blame it on the alcohol. And I want to think that someday it might be possible to actually say those words without feeling like I'm opening old wounds just to re-infect them.

I want to have hope that normal might just be a possibility for me. That this woman curled up beside me really is my cure.

So I settle for the only words that will come, the ones I know she knows matters.

"I race you, Ry." I press a kiss to her shoulder. "Night, baby."

Chapter Thirty-Four

"The ceremony starts at four. You'll be there right?"

"Yes, Mother! We'll be there." Shane calls out to me as he heads out the front door with a huge grin on his face, a little swagger in his step, and car keys rattling around in his hand.

"I fear we're creating a monster." I laugh as I look over at Colton, who has one shoulder leaned against the wall and is staring at me with a quiet intensity. I notice the dark circles still under his eyes that have been there for the last few weeks, and it saddens me he's having nightmares again and isn't talking to me about them. Then again he isn't really talking to me at all about anything, other than work or the boys or the ribbon cutting ceremony later today to kick off the project. And it's weird. It's not as if anything is off between us, actually it's the opposite. He's more attentive and physical than ever before, but it feels like this is his way to make up for the fact we still haven't talked about the miscarriage.

He asked for space and I've given it to him, not talking about the loss or how I'm feeling, how I'm coping. I even went so far as to not tell him about my follow-up appointment yesterday.

I get that we're both dealing with this in our own ways. His way is to wall himself off, figure it out alone, when mine is to hold on a little tighter, need him a little more. The momentary distance between us I can handle—I know it's temporary—but at the same time, it's killing me to know he's hurting. To be hurting myself when I need him and can't ask for any more from him. Needing the connection that's always been a constant between us.

To give him the space he asked for, when all I want to do is fix.

Late at night when I wake from dreams filled with car crashes and floors filled with blood, I watch him sleep and my mind wanders to those deep, dark thoughts that I can hide from in broad daylight. I wonder if he's not addressing or dealing with the miscarriage because he's worried that maybe a baby is what I want now. That maybe we're doomed because he never will.

But if I can't talk to him, if he changes the subject any time I try to bring it up, I can't tell him otherwise.

And yes, while thoughts of a baby have crossed my mind, I can't hang my hat on the idea. I can't let myself think that I'll be granted that post-accident miraculous chance more than once in my lifetime. Hope like that can ruin you if it's all you're holding on to.

But what if I'm hanging on to the hope that he'll talk to me—come back to me—rather than slowly slip away through my fingers? Won't that hope ruin me too? Becks has told me to sit tight, that Colton's figuring out his shit as much as he can tell from their years of friendship, but to not let him pull too far away. How in the hell am I supposed to know exactly how far is too far?

I need him to need me as much as I need him while I go through the emotions of losing a piece of something that was uniquely ours ... and the fact that he doesn't, kills me. Yes, his arms are wrapped around me at night while we sleep, but his mind is elsewhere. Lost perhaps in his endless texts and hushed conversations as of late. The ones that unnerve me, despite knowing deep down, he's not cheating on me.

But he's hiding something, dealing with something, and it's without me when I need him to help me deal with this.

I try to tell myself it's the lack of our physical connection that's making me read into everything way too much. Over analyzing everything. While I lie in his arms every night, pulled tight against his chest exactly where I long to be, we've yet to make love since coming back from the hospital. We kiss and when I try to deepen it, move my hands down his body and entice him to want me like I crave him, he'll cuff my wrists and tell me to wait until I feel better, despite me telling him I'm not hurt and that I'm perfectly fine. That I want to feel him in me, connecting with me, taking me again.

The rejection stings something fierce because I know Colton—know the virile, physicality he needs when he's hurting—so why isn't he taking it, taking me, if he's in the pain I see rampant in his eyes?

I shake myself from my thoughts and focus on the emerald eyes locked onto mine. The man I love. The man I fear like hell is slipping away from me.

"A monster? No," he says with a shake of his head and a smile tilting up the left corner of his mouth so his dimple deepens. "A teenager on the loose? Most definitely."

I smile at him as he closes the distance between us, free to touch me since the rest of the boys are at baseball practice and will meet us at the ribbon cutting afterward. "You okay?" I ask him, probably for the umpteenth time in the past week.

"Yeah, I'm fine. You?"

"Mmm-hmm." And so goes our usual thrice daily conversation—at least. Our affirmation that everything is all right even though everything feels so very different. "Colton …" My voice fades as I lose the courage to ask him more.

He senses my hesitation and reaches out to cup the side of my face, his thumb rubbing gently over my cheek. I close my eyes and absorb the resonance of his touch because it's so much more than just skin to skin. It vibrates through me and delves into every fiber of my being, seeping into places unknown and forever stamping them with his presence, ruining me for anyone else ever again with invisible tattoos.

When I open my eyes, his are front and center in my line of sight. "Hey, quit worrying. Everything's going to be okay. We're okay." He swallows and lowers his eyes before bringing them back up to mine. "I'm just trying to figure out my shit so it doesn't affect us."

"But—" My question is cut off when his lips meet mine. It's a soft sigh of a kiss that he slowly deepens when he slips his tongue between my lips to dance in a slow entanglement with mine. I taste need laced with desire, but all my head can think about is why won't he act on it?

I move my hands up so my fingers can twist in the hair curling over his collar and tell my mind to shut up, tell it to quiet down so I can enjoy this moment, enjoy him. I feel the tears well as the tenderness behind his touch overwhelms me. As if I'm fragile and will break.

I'm not sure if he can feel the shudder of my breath as I try to rein in my emotions, but he places one more soft kiss to my lips and then to my nose, that almost breaks my floodgates, before pulling back to look at me. Hands frame the side of my face and eyes search mine. "Don't cry," he whispers before leaning in and pressing another kiss to my forehead. "Please don't cry," he murmurs.

"I just … " I sigh, words escaping me on how to express what I feel and need and want from him without pushing him too hard.

"I know, baby. I know. Me too." He presses a kiss to my lips that causes another tear to slide down my cheek. "Me too."

The crowd is clapping as I finish my speech and step down from the podium, my eyes sweeping over the audience. I see Shane sitting next to Jackson, clapping like the rest of the boys, but I don't see Colton.

I scramble to come up with a valid excuse for why the biggest sponsor of the project is going to be AWOL at the ribbon-cutting ceremony and press photo session, taking place in less than ten minutes.

Where in the hell is he? He would never purposefully miss something for the boys or the project he was so instrumental in making a reality. I look down at my phone as I head toward Shane to ask him where Colton is and there is nothing. No missed call, no text, no anything.

The clapping subsides as Teddy takes the podium again to wind the press conference down. "Shane!" I whisper loudly as I motion him over to me. "Shane!"

Jax nudges him so that he stands and walks toward me. I turn my back and start walking away from the crowd, assuming he's following me. We turn a corner so we're away from the press and I force myself to take a breath.

"Where's Colton?" I ask without trying to sound like I'm anxious.

"Well," he says, shuffling his feet before looking back up to meet my eyes. "When we were on our way here, he got a phone call from someone named Kelly and he made me pull over to the side of the road so he could get out and talk to her privately."

My heart skips and lodges in my throat despite telling myself that there has to be a perfectly logical explanation for this. Telling myself and convincing myself are two very different things though.

"Are you okay?" he asks me, blue eyes looking over my face and meeting my eyes.

I mentally chastise myself and have to remember that Shane is no longer a twelve year old but rather a teenager on the verge of manhood who notices things. "Yeah, I'm good, fine, just surprised he's not here. That's all."

"Well he got back in the car and told the lady he'd call her back in a couple of minutes because he had to get us here on time. We parked right before the speeches started and he told me to head on in and he'd be right there. He got out and watched me sit next to Jax and I saw him talking on the phone as he waved goodbye to me. Why? Is something wrong, Ry?"

"No. Not at all. I just missed his call," I lie to Shane, and most likely myself, to soften the blow. "I wanted to see if he told you when he'd be back because I'd hate for him to miss the ribbon cutting ceremony."

"Yeah, well I'm sure something pretty important came up for him to not be here. He knows how much it means to you and stuff," he says, twisting his lips, trying to comfort me in that awkward prepubescent way that makes my heart swell with pride.

"It must have been very important." I smile at him. "You guys mean the world to him." I put my arm around his shoulder and start walking back toward the crowd, hoping he misses what I'm not saying, that maybe I don't mean the world to him anymore.

We make it back in time for the ribbon cutting ceremony, and I can't stop my eyes from frantically searching the crowd for him. My mind repeats Shane's words over and over. *It must be something very important.* Something huge, but the question is what?

And then of course doubt creeps in and nibbles at my resolve. Did something come up with Tawny? With his family? But if it had, he would have called me, texted me, something, right?

By the time the ceremony is over and I've said goodbye to the boys, my nerves are frayed. I've gone from concerned, to pissed, to uneasy, to angry, and as I speed up Pacific Coast Highway toward Broadbeach Road—his voicemail answering every time I hit dial—I'm sick to my stomach with worry.

By the time I reach the gates and pull into an empty driveway, I'm a freaking mess. I unlock and fling open the front door, his name a shout of my lips. But before I even make it past the kitchen, I know he's not home. It's not just the frantically excited Baxter that tells me but also the eerie silence in the house.

I open the sliding glass door to let Baxter out as a new thought hits me. What if something happened to his head? What if he's injured somewhere and needs help and no one knows?

I run back to the kitchen counter and dial Haddie.

"Hey!"

"Has Colton called the house?"

"No, what's wrong?" Concern floods Haddie's voice but I don't have time to go into details.

"I'll explain later. Thanks." I hang up on her while she's still talking, telling myself I'll apologize later while the phone's already ringing for the next person.

"Rylee!"

"Becks, where's Colton?"

"No clue, why?"

I hear a female giggle in the background and I don't even give a second thought about interrupting whatever it is I'm interrupting. "He didn't show up at the ceremony. Shane said he got a call and that's the last anyone's seen of him."

I hear Becks tell the woman to be quiet. "He didn't show?" Apprehension laces his voice as I hear shuffling on the other end of the line.

"No. Who's Kelly?"

"Who?" he asks before the line goes silent for a moment. "I have no clue, Ry."

His silence makes me question his honesty and the scattered thoughts in my mind reach my mouth. "I don't give a fuck about man code and all that, Beckett, so if you know—I don't care if it's going to hurt me—you have to tell me because I'm worried fucking sick and ... and ..." I'm rambling frantically and I force myself to stop because I'm starting to get hysterical and I really have no reason to be, except for the intuition that tells me something isn't right.

"Calm down. Take a breath. Okay?" I squeeze my eyes shut and get a grip. "Last I talked to him he was taking Shane out driving and then heading to the ceremony. You know—"

"Why is he not answering his phone then?"

"Ry, he's got a lot of shit he's sorting through, maybe he just ..." He fades out, not sure what to say to me. I hear him blow out a loud breath as I walk over to shut the door Baxter's just come in through. The house phone on the counter starts ringing and the caller ID says Quinlan. Something's going on and the sight of her name tells me that I'm right to be worried.

"Q's calling. Gotta go," I tell him, switching the phone as I hear him tell me to call him back.

"Is he okay?" My words come out in a rush of air as I answer her call, anxiety causing acid to churn in my stomach.

"That's what I was calling to ask you." The concern in her voice rivals mine.

"What? How did you know something's wrong?" *I'm confused.* I thought she knew what was going on.

"I was in class all day and had my phone off. I just turned it back on and he left a message." I'm afraid to ask her what that message said. "He sounded upset. He rambled saying that he needed to talk to someone because his head was all fucked up. *That he knows*. But he didn't say what that meant."

Lead drops through my soul as I try to connect puzzle pieces that don't belong together.

"Did something happen, Ry? Is it because of the miscarriage? I've just … I've never heard him sound like that before."

Thoughts flicker and fade in my mind as I try to figure out what could have happened to Colton. And I'm already on the move and racing upstairs as my brain starts grasping at the possibilities of where he could be. "Q, I think I know where he is. I'll call you when I know for sure."

I toss the phone on the bed as I rush into the bathroom stripping my business suit off, leaving a trail of clothes as I go. Within minutes I've changed into my exercise clothes and am lacing up my shoes as fast as I can. I grab my phone and am down the stairs, out the doors leading to the deck, and racing down to the beach below.

I break out in a full sprint toward the place Colton took me on that first fateful night here, his happy place, where he goes to think. The more I think of it, the more confident I am that this is where he is. He's probably sitting on his rock watching the sun sinking into the sea and coming to terms with everything that's happened.

But why did he not take Baxter? Where is his car? I push the doubts away, convincing myself that he's just there contemplating things, but uncertainty starts to grow with every pounding step.

But I know when I round the bend I'm not going to find him here. And as I come to the clearing, I already have my phone dialed and ringing.

"Did you find him?" I can tell Becks is freaked, and I feel bad for making him feel that way, but I'm worried.

"No. I thought I did but …" I have to stop to catch my breath because my lungs are burning from my sprint down the beach.

"Ry, what's going on?"

"He called Quin and said he *knows* and his head is fucked up." I pant out. "So I ran to his place on the beach but he's not here. You know him better than anyone … where does he go when he needs to clear his head besides here?"

"You."

"What?"

"He goes to you." The honesty in his voice resonates through the phone line.

My legs stop moving at his words. They strike deep and make my heart twist with love and worry. Tears spring in my eyes as I realize how desperately I miss him in this moment—the him I'd only gotten back weeks ago to be taken away again by God's cruel twist of fate with the miscarriage. I swallow the lump in my throat and it takes me a minute to find my voice. "Before me, Becks …"

"The track."

"That's where he's gotta be." I start running back toward the house. "I'm headed there now."

"Do you want me to—"

"I have to do this, Becks. It's gotta be me." I've never spoken truer words because deep down I know he needs me. I don't know why, I just know he does.

"I'll text you how to get in the facility, okay?"

"Thanks."

Chapter Thirty-Five

It feels like it's taken me forever to reach the speedway because of the traffic on the freeway. I pull off the exit in Fontana, my heart lodged in my throat and my hope up in the air as I wonder what I'll be walking into when I find him.

Panic strikes when I pull through the gates of the complex because it's pitch black except for a few random parking lot lights. I drive around the side of the facility toward the infield tunnel, and I breathe out a huge sigh of relief when I see Colton's Range Rover.

So he's here, but now what am I going to do?

I pull up beside it, the darkness of the empty speedway seeming ominous. I put my car in park and shriek when I hear a knock on the passenger side window. My heart is hammering, but when I see Sammy's face in the window I tell myself to breathe and get out of the car.

The concern in his eyes has me even more worried. "Please just tell me he's okay, Sammy." I can see him struggling about speaking to me, and betraying his boss and his friend.

"He needs you." That's all he says—the only thing he needs to.

"Where is he?" I ask, although I'm already following him through a darkened entrance underneath the massive grandstands. We reach a gap between the bleachers and I realize I'm in the middle of the grandstands, looking out on an eerily empty race track. I meet Sammy's eyes through the darkness, and he signals over my left shoulder. I turn around instantly.

And I see him.

There is a single light on in a section of the grandstands and just in its fringes I see a lone shadow sitting in the darkness. My feet move without thinking and start climbing the stairs, one by one, to him. I can't see his face in the darkness, but I know his eyes are on me, can feel the weight of his stare. I reach the row of bleachers he's sitting on and I start walking toward him, anxious and calm all at the same time.

I try to think of what to say, but my thoughts are so jumbled with worry I can't focus. But once I'm able to see his shadowed face, everything vanishes but heart wrenching, unconditional love.

His posture says it all. He sits leaned over, elbows on his knees, shoulders sagging, and face stained with tears. And his eyes—the ones always so intense but dancing with mischief or mirth—are filled with absolute despair. They lock onto mine, begging, pleading, asking so much of me, but I'm not sure how to respond.

When I finally reach him, his grief crashes into me like a tidal wave. Before I can say a single thing, he strangles out a sob the same time he reaches out and pulls me into him. He buries his face into the curve of my neck and just hangs on like I'm his lifeline, the only thing keeping him from slipping under and drowning. I wrap my arms around him and cling to him trying to give him what he needs.

Because there is nothing more unsettling than watching a strong, confident man come completely undone.

My mind races as his muffled sobs fill the silence and the trembling of his body ricochets through mine. What happened to reduce my arrogant rogue to this distraught man? He continues to hold on as I shush him and rock subtly back and forth—anything I can to quiet the storm that's obviously raging inside of him.

"I'm here. I'm here." It's the only thing I can say to him as he releases all of the tumultuous emotion. And so I hold him in the dark, in a place where he made his dreams come true, hoping that just maybe he's coming to terms—stopping and facing head on—the demons he usually uses this track to outrun.

Time passes. The sounds of traffic on the highway beyond the empty parking lot lessen and the moon moves slowly across the sky. And yet Colton still holds on, still draws whatever he needs from me while I revel in the fact that he still needs me when I thought he didn't anymore. My mind jockeys back and forth from memories of a shower bench and him clinging to me then like he is now. Of what could figuratively knock this man of mine to his knees. So I just hold him now like I did then, my fingers playing in his hair for comfort until his tears slowly subside and the tension in his body abates.

I don't know what to say, what to think, so I just say the first thing that comes to my mind. "Are you okay? Do you want to talk about it?"

He loosens his grip and presses the palms of his hands into my back, pulling me tighter against him, if that's even possible, while drawing in a shaky breath. He's scaring me, not in a bad way but in the sense that something huge had to have happened to draw this kind of reaction out of him.

He leans back and squeezes his eyes shut before I have a chance to look into them, scrubbing his hands over his face before blowing out a loud breath. He hangs his head back down and shakes it, and I hate that I can't see his face right now.

"I did …" He blows out another breath and I reach out and place a hand on his knee. He just nods his head as if he's talking to himself and then his body tenses up again before he speaks. "I did what you said I should do."

What? I try to figure out what exactly I told him to do.

"I did what you said and now … now my head is just so fucked up over it. I'm a goddamn mess."

The raw grief breaking his voice has me sitting beside him and waiting for him to look up into my eyes. "What did you do?"

He reaches out and grabs my hand, lacing our fingers together and squeezing tightly. "*I found my mom.*"

The breath catches in my throat because when I made that comment, never in a million years, would I have thought he'd actually do it. And now I don't know what to say, because I'm the catalyst for all of this pain.

"Colton …" It's all I can say, all I can offer besides lifting our hands and pressing a kiss to the back of his.

"Kelly called me while I was … Oh fuck! I missed the ceremony. I stood you up." And I can tell by the absolute disbelief in his voice that he really, truly forgot.

"No, no, no," I shush him, trying to tell him that it doesn't matter. That only facing his fears is what matters. "It's okay." I squeeze our hands again.

"I'm so sorry, Ry … I just … I can't even fucking think straight right now." He breaks his eyes from mine and averts them in shame as he uses his other hand to wipe the tears from his cheeks. "You know..." he shakes his head as he looks out at the darkened track in front of us "...it's kind of funny that this is the place I come to forget everything and tonight it's the first place I thought to go in order to come to terms with it all."

I follow his eyes and look out at the track, taking in the enormity of it all—the track and his actions. We sit in silence as the importance behind his words hit me. He's trying to face things, to move on, to begin to heal. And I've never been more proud of him.

"I asked my dad a couple of months ago if he knew what had happened to *her*. He got me in touch with a PI—Kelly is his name—that he'd hired when I was younger who kept tabs on her for ten years to make sure she didn't come back for me." His voice is even, flat, such a contrast to the hiccupping despair from moments ago, and yet I can feel the extremity of the emotion vibrating just beneath the surface. "He called me today. He found her." He looks over at me, and the forlorn look in his eyes—a lost little boy trying to find his way—undoes me, breaks the hold on the emotion I'm trying to hold in so I can be strong for him.

Be the rock while he crumbles.

My first tear falls as I reach out and place my hand on his cheek, a simple touch that relays so very much about what I think, how I feel, what I know he needs from me. I lean in, his jaw clenching beneath my palm, his eyes fused with mine, and place a feather soft kiss to his lips. "I'm so proud of you." I whisper the words to him. I don't ask him about what he found or who she is. I focus on him, on the now, because I know his head is desperately trying to reconcile the past while trying to figure out the future. So I focus on the here, the now, and hope he understands that I'll be here for every single step of the way if he lets me.

We sit like this, the silence reinforcing the reassurance of my touch and the understanding behind my kiss. And for once, the silence is comforting, accepting of his tortured soul.

He works a swallow in his throat and blinks his eyes rapidly as if he too is trying to understand everything, and yet he has so many more pieces of the puzzle than I do, so I sit and wait patiently for him to continue. He breaks our eye contact and leans back, eyes drawn back to the track.

"My mom is dead," he says the words without any emotion, and even though they float out into the night, I can sense them suffocating him. I stare at him, take in his moonlit profile against the night sky, and I choose to say nothing, to let him lead this conversation.

Restless, he shoves up out of his seat and paces to the end of the aisle and then stops, his figure haloed by the single light beyond him. "She never changed. I guess I shouldn't have expected to find anything different," he says so quietly, but I can still hear every single inflection in his tone, every break in his voice. He turns to face me and walks a few feet toward me and stops.

"I'm … I'm—my head is such a fucking mess right now I just …" He scrubs his hands over his face and through his hair before emitting a self-deprecating laugh that sends shivers up my spine. "I don't even have any positive memories of her. None. Eight years of my fucking life and I don't remember a single thing that makes me smile."

I know he's struggling and I so desperately want to cross the distance between us and touch him, hold him, comfort him, but I know he needs to get this out. Needs to rid himself of his self-proclaimed poison eating his soul.

"My mom was a drugged out whore. Lived by the sword and died by the sword ..." The spite in his voice, the pain, is so powerful and raw I can't help the tears that well in my eyes or the shudder in my breath as I inhale. "Yep," he says, that laugh falling out of his mouth again. "A druggie. She wasn't discriminate though. She'd take anything to get that rush because it was what was important. Fucking more important than her little boy sitting scared as fuck in the corner." He rolls his shoulder and clears his throat as if he's trying to choke back the emotion. "So I just don't get it ..." His voice fades and I try to follow what he is saying but I can't.

"Don't get what, Colton?"

"I don't get why I fucking care that she's dead!" he shouts, his voice echoing through the empty stadium. "Why does it bug me? Why am I fucking upset over it? Why does it make me feel anything other than relief?" His voice cracks again, his words ricocheting off the concrete.

My stomach knots up over the fact that he's hurting because I can't do a goddamn thing about it. I can't fix or mend or resolve, so I reassure. "She was your mom, Colton. It's normal to be upset because deep down I'm sure in her own way she loved you—"

"Loved me?" he screams, startling me with the sudden change from confused grief to unfettered rage. "Loved me?" he yells again, walking toward me and pounding on his chest with his words before walking five feet and stopping. "Do you want to know what love was to her? Love was trading her six year old son for fucking drugs, Rylee!"

"Love was letting her drug dealing pimp rape her son, *fuck her little boy while he had to repeat out loud how much he loved it, loved him,* so she could get her next fucking fix! Treat him worse than a fucking dog so she could score enough drugs to ensure her next high! It was knowing the fucker is giving her the smallest fucking quantities possible because he can't wait to come back and do it all over again. Love was sitting on the other side of the closed bedroom door and hearing her little boy scream in the worst motherfucking pain as he's ripped apart physically and emotionally and not doing a goddamn thing to stop it because she's so fucking selfish."

He cringes at the words, his body strung so tight I fear his next words will snap the tension, relieve the boy but break the man within. I look at him, my own heart shattering, my own faith dissolved imagining the horror his small body endured, and I force myself to stem the physical revulsion his words evoke because I fear he'll think it's for him, not the monsters who abused him.

I can hear him struggling to catch his breath, can see him physically revolt against his own words with a forceful swallow. When he starts speaking again, his voice is more controlled but the eerily quiet tone chills my skin.

"Love was snapping her little boy's arm in half because he bit the man raping him so hard that now he won't give up her next fucking speedball. Love was telling her son he wants it, deserves it, that no one will ever love him if they know. Oh and to seal the deal, it was telling her son that the superheroes he calls to while being violated—ruined—*yeah those,* they're never fucking coming to save him. Never!" He's shouting into the night, tears coursing down both of our faces, and his shoulders are shuddering with the relief of being unburdened from the weight he's carried for over twenty-five years.

"So if that's love?" He laughs darkly again, "...then yeah, my first eight fucking years of my life, I was loved like you wouldn't fucking believe." He walks up to me, and even through the darkness I can feel the anger, the despair, the grief that's running rampant through his body. He looks down for a beat, and I watch the tears falling from his face darken the white concrete below. He shakes his head once more, and when he looks up, the resignation in his eyes, the shame that edges it, devastates me. "So when I ask why I'm confused about how I can feel anything other than hatred to know she's dead? That's why, Rylee," he says so quietly I strain to hear him.

I don't know what to say. Don't know what to do, because every single part of me has just shattered and crashed down around me. I've heard it all in my job, but to hear it from a grown man broken, lost, forlorn, burdened with the weight of shame over an entire lifetime, a man I would give my heart and soul to if I knew it would take away the pain and memories, leaves me at a complete loss.

And in the split second it takes me to think all of this, it hits Colton what he's just said. The adrenaline from his confession abates. His shoulders begin to shake and his legs give out as he crumbles to the bench behind him. In the heartbeat of time it takes me to get to him, he is sobbing into his hands. Heart wrenching, soul cleansing sobs that rack through his entire body as, "Oh my God!" falls from his lips over and over again.

I wrap my arms around him feeling completely helpless but not wanting to let go, never wanting to let go. "It's okay, Colton. It's okay," I repeat over and over in between his repeated words, my tears falling onto his shoulders as I hold tight letting him know that no matter how far he falls, I'll catch him.

I'll always catch him.

I try to hold back the sobs racking through my body but it's no use. There's nothing left for me to do but feel with him, grieve with him, mourn with him. And so we sit like this in the dark, me holding onto him, and him letting go in a place that's always brought him peace.

I just pray that this time the peace will find some permanence in his scarred soul.

Our tears subside but he just keeps his head in his hands, eyes squeezed tight, and so many emotions stripping him straight to the core. I want him to take the lead here, need him to let me know how to help him so I just sit quietly.

"I've never … I've never said those words out loud before," he says, voice hoarse from crying and eyes focused on his fidgeting fingers. "I've never told anyone," he whispers. "I guess I thought that if I said it, then … I don't know what I thought would happen."

"Colton," I say his name as I try to figure out what to say next. I need to see his eyes, need for him to see mine. "Colton, look at me please," I say as gently as possible, and he just shakes his head back and forth like a little kid afraid of getting in trouble.

I allow him time, allow him to hide in the silence and darkness of the night, my thoughts consumed with pain for this man I love so very dearly. I close my eyes, trying to process it all, when I hear him whisper the one line I'd never expect in this moment.

"*Spiderman. Batman. Superman. Ironman.*"

And it hits me like a ton of bricks. What he's trying to tell me with the simple, whispered statement. My heart falls and my head screams. "No, no, no, no!"

I drop to my knees in front of him, reaching out my hands to the side of his face and direct it up so that his eyes can meet mine. And I cringe when he flinches at my touch. He's petrified to take this first step toward healing. Scared of what I think of him now that I know his secrets. Worried about what kind of man I perceive him to be, because in his eyes, he allowed this to happen to him. He's ashamed I'll judge him based on the scars that still rule his mind, body, and soul.

And he couldn't be any further from the truth.

I sit and wait patiently, my fingers trembling on his cheeks for some time until green eyes flicker up and look at me with a pain I can't imagine reflected in them.

"There are so many things I want and need to say to you right now … so many things," I say, allowing my voice to tremble, my tears to fall, and goose bumps to blanket my entire body, "that I want to say to the little boy that you were and to the incredible man you are." He forces a swallow as his muscle in his jaw tics, trying to rein back the tears pooling in his eyes. I see fear mixed with disbelief in them.

And I also see hope. It's just beneath the surface waiting for the chance to feel safe, to feel protected, to feel loved for it to spring to life, but it's there.

I am in awe of the vulnerability he is entrusting me with, because I can't imagine how hard it is to open yourself up when all you've ever known is pain. I rub my thumb over his cheek and bottom lip as he stares at me, and I find the words I need to convey the truth he needs to hear.

"Colton Donavan, this is not your fault. If you hear one thing I tell you, please let it be this. You've carried this around with you for so long and I need you to hear me tell you that nothing you did as a child, or as a man, deserved what happened to you." His eyes widen and he turns his body some, opens up his protective posture, and I'm hoping it's a reflection of how he feels with me. That he's listening, understanding, *hearing*. Because there are so many things I've wanted to say to him for so long about things I'd assumed, and now I know. Now I can express them.

"You have nothing to be ashamed of, *then, now, or ever*. I am in awe of your strength." He starts to argue with me and I just put a finger to his lips to quiet him before I repeat what I was saying. "I am in awe of your strength to keep this bottled up for all this time and not self-destruct. You are not damaged or fucked up or hopeless, but rather resilient and brave and honorable." My voice breaks with the last word, and I can feel his chin quiver beneath my hand because my words are so hard to hear after thinking the opposite for so very long, but he keeps his eyes on mine. And that alone signals that he's opening himself up to the notion of healing.

"You came from a place of unfathomable pain and yet you … you're this incredible light who has helped to heal me, has helped to heal my boys." I shake my head trying to find the words to relay how I feel. So he understands there is so much light in him when all he's seen for so long is darkness.

"Ry," he sighs, and I can see him struggling with accepting the truth in my words.

"No, Colton. It's true, baby. I can't imagine how hard it was to ask your dad for the help to find your mother. I can't imagine how you felt taking that call today. I can't fathom how hard it was for you to just confess the secret that has weighed so heavy on your soul for so very long … but please know this, your secret is safe with me."

He sniffles back a sob, his eyes blinking rapidly, his expression pained, and I lean forward and press a soft kiss to his lips—a touch of physicality to reassure the both of us. I press a kiss to his nose and then rest my forehead against his, trying to take a moment to absorb all of this.

"Thank you for trusting enough to share with me," I whisper to him, my words feathering over his lips. And he doesn't respond, but I don't need him to. We sit like this, forehead to forehead, accepting and comforting each other and the boundaries that have been crossed.

I don't expect him to share any more, so when he starts to speak, I'm startled. "Growing up I didn't know how to deal with it all, how to cope." The absolute shame in his voice washes over me, my mind reeling from the loneliness he must have endured as a teenager. I rub my thumb back and forth over his cheek so that he knows I'm here, knows I'm listening. He sighs softly, his breath heating my lips as he finishes his confession.

"I tried quickly to prove that I wasn't damned to Hell even though he did those things to me. I ran through the gamut of girls in high school to prove to myself otherwise. It made me feel good—to be wanted and desired by females—because it took that fear away … but then it also became my way of coping … my mechanism. *Pleasure to bury the pain.*"

I whisper it the same time he does. The line he said to me in the Florida hotel room that stuck with me, ate at me, because I wanted to understand why he felt that way. And I get it now. I get the sleeping around. The fuck 'em and chuck 'em. All of them a way to prove to himself that he was not scarred by his past. A way to place a temporary Band-Aid over the open wounds that never healed.

I squeeze my eyes shut, my mind and heart aching for this man, when his voice interrupts the silence.

"I don't remember everything, but I remember that he used to come up to me from behind. That's why …" his voice so soft it trails off, answering a question I asked the night of the charity gala.

"Okay," I tell him so he knows I hear him, knows I understand why he was robbed of the ability to accept such an innocent touch.

"The superheroes," he continues, his stark honesty stealing my breath. "Even as a kid, I had to hold on to something to try and escape the pain, the shame, the fear, so I would call to them to try and cope. To have some kind of hope to hold on to."

I taste the salt on my lips. I assume it's from my own tears but I can't be sure because I can't tell where he ends and I begin. And we don't move, remaining forehead to forehead, and I wonder if it's easier for him to sit like this—eyes shut, hearts pounding, souls reaching—to get it all out. So he doesn't have to see the despair, pain, and compassion in my eyes. But even though his eyes are closed I can still feel the chains that have bound his soul for so long begin to break free. I can feel his walls starting to crumble. I can feel hope take flight out of this place in the dark. Just him and me in a place where he can now chase his dreams without his past closing in on him.

I angle my head down and press a kiss to his lips. I feel them tremble beneath mine, my self-assured man stripped bare and open. He finally eases his head back, our foreheads no longer touching, but now I can look into his eyes and I can see a clarity that's never been there before. And a small place within me sighs that he just might be able to find some peace now, just might be able to lay the demons to rest.

I smile solemnly at him as he draws in a ragged breath and reaches his hands out and urges me up from my knees and onto his lap, where he wraps his arms around me. I sit there cradled, comforted, and loved by a man capable of so much. I hope he's finally able to see it and accept it. A man who swears he doesn't know how to love and yet that's exactly what he's giving me right now—love—in the midst of being in the darkest of despairs. I press a kiss to the underside of his jaw, his stubble tickling my sensitive lips.

The dust of a broken past settles around us as hope rises from its remnants.

"Why tell me now?"

He draws in a quick breath and tightens his arms around me, pressing a kiss to the top of my head and chuckles softly. "Because you're the fucking alphabet."

What? My head shakes back and forth, and I lean back so I can look at him. And when I meet his eyes, when the smile that spreads on his face lights up the green in the dark around us, my heart tumbles to new depths of love for this man. "*The alphabet?*"

I'm sure it's the look on my face that has his grin widening, dimple winking, and his head shaking. "Yep, A to motherfucking Z." A spark of his personality that he'd lost shines through fleetingly, and it warms my heart to hear that touch of amused arrogance in his voice. He chuckles again and says "Fucking Becks" before leaning forward and pressing his lips to mine without answering my question.

He pulls back and looks at me, eyes intense. "Why now, Ry? Because of you. Because I've pushed and pulled and hurt you way too much … and despite all of that, you've fought for me—to keep me, to help me, to heal me, to *race* me—and for once in my life, I want someone to do that for me. And I want to be free to do that for someone else. I …" He sighs trying to find the words to match the emotion swimming in his eyes. Eyes still haunted on the fringes but so much less now than ever before, and that alone eases the ache in my soul. "I want the chance to prove I'm capable of it. That all of this …" he says with an irrelevant wave of his hand, "didn't rob me of that. That I can be who you need and give you what you want," his voice pleads.

I hear the sadness from his confessions still tingeing his voice, but I can also hear hope and possibility woven in there as well. And it's such a welcome sound that I purse my lips and press them against his.

I can still feel the emotion shuddering through him as he slips his tongue between my parted and willing lips to deepen the kiss. I can still sense him trying to grasp this new ground he's trying to find his footing on, but I know that he'll find it.

Because he's a fighter.

Always has been.

Always will be.

Chapter Thirty-Six

I glance over to him watching the light of the streetlights play over the angles of his face as I sing softly to Lifehouse's *Everything* on the radio. It's late, but time was of no importance as we sat together in the grandstands laying old wounds to rest and bringing new beginnings to the table. Sammy's driving my car to the house but as Colton and I exit the freeway in the Range Rover, I realize we're not going home just yet.

Home.

What a crazy notion. That I'm going home with Colton, because right now, after tonight, the word means so much more than just a brick and mortar building. It means comfort and healing and Colton. *My ace*. I sigh, my chest tightening with love.

I look over at him again and he must feel the weight of my stare because he glances over at me with eyes still slightly red from crying. They lock on mine momentarily as he smiles softly and then shakes his head subtly, as if he's still trying to process the events of the past few hours before looking back at the road. But I keep my eyes on him because I know deep down that's where they'll always land no matter where else they look.

I'm so deep in thought I don't even recognize our location when Colton pulls into a parking lot and puts the car in park. "There's something I've gotta do. Come with me?"

I look at him confused about what we're doing at eleven o'clock at night in some random parking lot in the outskirts of Hollywood. Obviously it's important because after tonight all I can think of is that he's probably exhausted and just wants to go home. "Of course."

We exit the car and I look around, a little leery leaving such a nice car in this rundown, poorly lit lot, but Colton is completely unfazed. He pulls me in close to his side and leads me toward a very formidable wooden door that looks like it came straight out of the medieval times. Colton opens it and I'm immediately confronted with bright lights, music playing softly, and a strangely unique buzzing sound.

I whip my head over to Colton, who's watching me with a bemused curiosity. He just chuckles and shakes his head at my slack jawed reaction and widening eyes.

I've never even stepped foot in one of these places before. Deep down a part of me knows why we're here, but it doesn't make sense.

Colton links his fingers with mine as we walk down a narrow hallway toward a room where there are bright lights. Colton crosses the threshold ahead of me and stops momentarily until the buzzing ceases.

"Well motherfucking cocksuck! The fucking wonder boy pays a visit," a rumbling voice yells out, and Colton laughs before being pulled farther into the room. "Well goddamn, you're a sight for sore eyes, Wood!"

I watch as arms, sleeved in a variety of colors and images, wrap around Colton and bring him in for a quick hug. I see a pair of hazel eyes catch sight of me over Colton's shoulder.

"Oh fucking shit! I'm so sorry about all of the fucking cussing," the voice belonging to the eyes says as he shoves Colton backwards and steps toward me. "Dude, if you bring a fucking lady in here you need to make sure to give me warning so I can be respectable and shit!"

Colton laughs as the man wipes his hand off on his jeans before reaching it out to shake mine. My eyes roam over the heavy set, tattoo riddled man with closely cropped hair and a long unruly beard, but what I find the most endearing is the blush staining his cheeks. It's actually quite adorable, but I doubt he'd be amused if I said that right now.

"So fucking sorry! Christ, I just did it again," he shakes his head with a wheeze of a laugh and I can't help but smile.

"No worries," I tell him, lifting a chin over toward Colton. "His mouth's just as bad. I'm Rylee."

"Okay, well I'll try to keep *the fucking* to a minimum," he says and then blushes again. "I mean—not with you of course—well unless you wanted to because then—"

"Don't even think about it, Sledge," Colton warns with a laugh as Sledge, I assume, shakes his head and just laughs that unique laugh of his again before ushering us into the tattoo parlor.

"So, dude, really?" Sledge asks Colton.

"Yeah." He looks over to me and smiles. "Really." And I'm completely lost.

"Whatever yanks your dick man," he says, shaking his head as he walks over to a counter and starts rifling through some papers. "Speaking about yanking dicks and shit …" He glances over at me and his face scrunches up in apology before continuing to look for something. "How's that fine ass sister of yours that I'd love to have yank mine, among other things."

I expect Colton to freak out, but he just throws his head back and bellows out a laugh. His reaction makes me realize these two go way back.

"She'd eat you alive and you know it, dude … you're such a pussy."

"Fuck you!" Sledge laughs as Colton starts pulling his shirt over his head. And even with so many new sights to take in here, I can't tear my eyes from his chiseled abdomen. I take in the four symbols—representations of his past—and wonder what he's going to do now.

"Yeah … quite the hard ass," Colton teases as he ushers me to a chair and presses a chaste kiss on my lips. He looks me in the eye for a moment, as if to say *trust me*, before sitting down in a chair himself. "The inked up man who listens to Barbara Streisand and keeps his five pussies in the back room." *What in the hell is he talking about?* "Didn't you know, if you're gonna pretend to be a badass you need to listen to death metal and have a man-eating pit bull instead of enough cats to rival an old spinster." Colton is laughing, carefree even, and I love that whoever this contradiction of a man is brings this out in Colton.

"I'm a delicate flower!" Sledge quips before yelling out, "A-ha!"

"Flower my ass!" Colton says, shaking his head and laughing as Sledge walks over to him with a piece of paper in his hand. "That it?" Colton asks, and I straighten my posture to try and see what's on it. He stares at it a moment, lips pursing, head subtly bobbing as he considers it. "You sure? It'll really work?" He flicks his eyes up at Sledge, his expression reinforcing the question.

"Like you have to fucking ask. Oops, there I go again with the fucking." He raises his eyebrows as he glances over to me in a silent apology. "Dude, if I'm gonna stain you, I'm gonna research it to make sure."

"Like Google research or bottom of a bottle research?" Colton asks.

"Get out of my fucking chair!" Sledge teases, throwing his arm toward the direction of the door before looking over at me. "You really put up with this shit on a daily basis?"

I nod my head and laugh as Colton leans forward and stares at me, and for a second I see sadness flicker there but it goes away just as quickly as it came. "Ryles?"

"Yeah?" I scoot to the edge of my seat, still curious what the paper has on it.

"Time to lay the demons to rest," he says, his eyes locked on mine, "and move on."

I force myself to look away from his eyes and down to the sketch of curved, interlinking lines. I know the symbol is a Celtic knot and it's similar but different to the others, but I don't know why it's significant.

I look up from the paper, my eyes beseeching Colton's for an explanation. "New beginnings," he says, his eyes telling me he's ready, "…rebirth."

I suck in a breath, my eyes burning with tears, the significance of the symbol is so poignant I can't find the words to speak so I just nod.

"Okay, I get you're all fucking lovey-dovey and shit, but I'm itching to cause you some fucking pain, Wood, so scoot your ass back," he says, pressing Colton's shoulders back and winking at me with a smirk. "Because you ain't gonna have a chance to be reborn, motherfucker, if you sit and stare at her so long that you fucking die in the meantime."

I laugh, my love for this man I just met is already profound. Colton complies but not without a comeback. "Dude, you're just jealous!"

"Fuck yeah, I am. I'm sure that she can..." he stalls, eyes darting back to me and then down to where he's busy setting up his supplies "...whip up a mean bowl of macaroni and cheese." He chortles out that laugh again.

"Damn straight," Colton says, slapping him on the shoulders. "Nice and creamy."

I choke on my breath the same time Sledge does, both of our faces staining red with embarrassment. I give Colton a disbelieving look and shake my head while mischief glimmers in his eyes. And the sight of it—troublemaker in full effect—makes me smile even brighter.

"Just for that I oughta give you a fucking pansy instead …" He shakes his head as the needle buzzes to life and Colton jolts at the sound. Sledge throws his head back and laughs a deep belly rumble. "Pansy ass motherfucker! Oops, there's a heart. Oops, there's a vagina. Oops, there's a daisy!" Sledge teases pretending to place the needle on Colton's body.

I am dying with laughter, so desperately needing this humor after the heaviness of our night.

"Oops, there's a boot up your ass, is more like it." Colton starts laughing but stops the minute Sledge angles the needle near his side. I've never seen anyone get a tattoo before and I'm quite curious. I stand and walk over to an empty chair next to Colton so I can watch.

I don't even look at first—can't as I see Colton's body tense and his breath hiss out as the needle touches him for the first time.

"God nothing changes," Sledge says, exasperation in his voice. "Once a puss, always a puss." The buzzing stops and he lifts his head to look up at Colton. "Seriously, dude? If I've gotta worry about you shivering like a fucking chihuahua, then we're gonna have some serious fucking issues and I'm not gonna claim this job as mine."

Colton just lifts a hand and flashes Sledge his middle finger before flicking his eyes over to me and then closing them as the needle starts again. This time the buzz remains steady, and after Colton relaxes some, I move around to the other side of Sledge to test if I can handle watching him draw Colton's blood. And when I get the courage to finally look down, I'm confused.

Sledge's needle is working over the symbol for vengeance. He's cut dark red lines that make me cringe at the thought of what that must feel like against Colton's rib cage. I look up to find Colton's eyes locked on mine as I try to figure out what's going on.

"Sledge figured out how to overlay the new knot on top of vengeance."

"Vengeance is gone," I whisper, and for some reason this concept is so moving to me that I just stand there, lips parted, head shaking, and eyes watching Sledge reconfigure a concept that would only destroy Colton further and give him one filled with hope instead.

"Time to lay the demons to rest."

I swallow over the lump in my throat at Colton's words and reach out to hold his hand as we watch the slow transformation of one of his inked scars. One that is now a symbol of hope and healing.

After some time and more ribbing between the two of them—along with me falling further in love with Sledge—Colton's tattoo has been transformed.

"I want to see it before you bandage it up," Colton says as Sledge slathers it with petroleum jelly. "Go pet your pussies and make sure you didn't sneak any hearts or rainbows in there somewhere since you kept blocking my view, you fucker." Colton stands from the chair and I notice the time it takes to steady himself from the after effects of his accident is a lot shorter now. He heads off to the back room where the mirror is.

And I don't know what it is—maybe the events of the night or maybe the hope weaving its way into our lives—but my decision's made before Colton even clears the door to the back. I have to act now before I lose the courage, before my rational head catches up with my irrational heart.

Before I chicken out.

"Hey, Sledge," I say as I sit down in the chair Colton's vacated, pulling the elastic band of my exercise pants down over my hip bone, and point there. "I think it's the perfect time to get my first tattoo. I want the same thing only a lot smaller."

He looks over at me, eyes dancing and startled. "Darlin', when I said fucking, I didn't think you'd offer, much less bring your pants down for it with Wood in the back fucking room." He winks at me and smiles before staring into my eyes. "You trying to get me killed?"

I laugh. "He'll go easy. I think he has a soft spot for you, Sledge."

"Yeah soft spot in his head more like it." He just licks his lips and looks down at my hip before back up to my eyes, concern and uncertainty in his. "You sure? It's kinda permanent," he questions with an amused raise of an eyebrow. I nod my head before I lose the courage to go through with it—to prove to Colton that I want to be there for him every step of the way on this journey.

Sledge laughs and rubs his hands together. "I always love being the first to touch virgin skin. Makes my fucking balls tighten up and shit ..." He blows out a breath. "Fucking shit, I'm sorry. Again." He shakes his head as he starts to trace the image on my hipbone after looking up at me to make sure it's where I want it.

"You positive?" he asks again, and I nod because I'm so frickin' nervous I can barely force a swallow down my throat.

I'm not a tattoo type of girl, I tell myself, so why am I doing this? And then I realize I'm not a bad boy kind of girl either. Look how wrong I was with that assumption.

I jolt when the needle buzzes on, my breath hitching and body vibrating with anxious anticipation. I bite my bottom lip and fist my hands as the first sting hits me. Holy shit! It hurts so much more than I expected. *Don't wimp out, don't wimp out*, I repeat over and over in my head to try and drown out the needle that's stinging my hip like a bitch. And my chant doesn't ease the pain so I close my eyes and exhale a breath, nodding at Sledge to continue because I'm okay when he stops and looks up to check on me.

I don't hear him or see him, but I know the minute that Colton re-enters the room because I can feel him. His energy, our connection, his pull on me has me opening my eyes and lock on his instantly.

The look on his face is priceless—shock, pride, disbelief—as he steps closer to see around Sledge's hands. I know when he sees it because I hear him suck in a startled gasp before his eyes flash up to mine.

"New beginnings." It's all I say as I watch the emotion dance in his sparks of green.

"You know that's permanent, right?" he murmurs, shaking his head at me, still floored by what I'm doing.

"Yeah," I say, reaching out to lace my fingers with his, "kinda like we are."

Chapter Thirty-Seven

I can't help but laugh and feel sentimental as Colton finishes explaining the whole alphabet comment he'd made earlier. The lighthearted sound from Colton makes me content, causes me to remember the dark days in the hospital when all I wanted was to hear that sound again, and the request is out of my mouth before I think twice. "Can we have ice cream for breakfast?"

Colton's hand stills on my thigh as he stutters out a laugh. "What?" I love the look on his face right now. Carefree, careless, and unburdened from the secrets that are no longer between us.

I just smile at him lying on his side next to me as I adjust the pillow behind me and lie back, sighing, his amused eyes still staring at me. Music plays overhead as I shrug at him, suddenly feeling silly for my comment. It's just that I feel like everything is coming full circle. Things I said I wanted to do, I needed to do, promises I made when he was lying in that hospital bed, I need to keep.

"Yes, ice cream for breakfast," I tell him, wincing as I move and my panties tug on the bandage over my new tattoo—the tattoo my mother is going to kill me over when she finds out about it. But the sudden startled look in his eyes pulls me from my thoughts and causes me to lean forward to look at him closer, curious as to what just put it there. He stares back at me momentarily, and then after blinking his eyes a few times as if he's trying to figure something out, he just shakes his head and smiles at me, melting my heart, and confirming that I have absolutely no regrets.

About being with him or the tattoo I just got to prove it.

Of the ups and the downs that our relationship has gone through, endured, persevered, and come out stronger for.

None of it, because it brought us here to this point—right here, right now.

Healing together and loving one another.

Taking the first steps toward our future.

He angles his head on his hand propped on his elbow beneath him and quirks his lips. "Well, what the woman wants, the woman gets."

"I like the sound of that," I say, wiggling my hips, "because I have a whole lot of wants, Mr. Donavan."

"Oh really? And what might those be?" He raises his eyebrows, a lascivious smile tugging at one corner of his mouth as he leans forward and presses a soft kiss to the edge of my bandage. He looks up at me, lust and so much more dancing in the depths of his eyes as he slowly crawls his way up my body until his lips are inches from mine.

And my God, do I want to lean in and taste those lips and feel my skin hum to life from his touch, but I opt for one more request before losing myself in him, to him. "For dinner, I want—"

"Pancakes." Colton finishes my sentence. "Ice cream for breakfast and pancakes for dinner. I remember hearing you say that." His voice is filled with awed reverence as my heart soars at the revelation that he heard me when he was unconscious in the hospital. I watch him try to process everything with a soft shake of his head. "You talked a lot," he murmurs, leaning closer to my lips but not touching, and I know he's smiling because I can see the lines bunch around his eyes.

"So we have our menu planned for tomorr—"

Colton leans forward and captures my mouth with his in a soft kiss. "It's time to stop talking, Ryles," he says as he leans back to look me in the eyes, humor and unguarded love reflected in them.

"Colton," I say, arching my back to try and brush my breasts against his bare chest because everything in my body at this moment is desperate for his touch, his taste, the connection between us. And when he stays still and doesn't move, I reach out and grab the back of his neck, trying to pull him into me, but he doesn't move.

He just remains motionless, staring at me with such intensity. And for the first time I understand what he meant when he told me I was the first one to ever really see him—to see into the depths of his soul—because right now there's nothing I can hide from him. Absolutely nothing. Our connection is that strong, that irrefutable.

It's been such an emotional evening, more so for him than for me, but my body is humming for a physical release. It's vibrating with need and all I want is him.

"Rylee ..." It's that one word plea of my name on his lips that gets me every time.

"Don't *Rylee* me," I implore as I watch concern edge the desire from his eyes. I move my hands to frame his cheeks and hold him still so he has no option but to hear me. "I'm *fine,* Colton."

"I'm so afraid I'm going to hurt you ..." His voice fades and the concern that floods it makes every part of me slip further under his tidal wave of love.

"No, baby, no. You're not going to hurt me." I lean forward and brush my lips to his and then lean back until I can see his eyes again. "You not wanting to be with me, that hurts me. Destroys me. I need you, Colton, every side of you—physical and emotional. After tonight, after we've stripped away everything that's been keeping us apart, I need to share this with you. Connect in every way possible because it's the only way I can truly show you how I feel about you. Show you what you do to me."

I can hear his shuddered exhale moments before the heat of it hits my lips. His hand flexes on my bicep and then softens as if he wants and then doesn't want at the same moment. He just stares at me, indecision written across his face. And then that muscle pulses in his jaw, his last tell of resistance, because the desire clouding his eyes tells me his decision has already been made.

When he leans in to kiss me, I don't think victory has ever tasted so sweet.

His lips brush softly against mine, once, twice, and then his tongue delves between my lips and licks against mine. He slides his hands behind my back and gathers me against him while our tongues dance a seductive ballet. His hands find their way beneath the hem of my shirt and then tease my bare skin as he draws my shirt up and over my head.

A soft sigh escapes my lips as we part so my shirt can clear my face and then our lips find each other's again. I release my tangled grip on the back of his hair and scrape my fingernails down the steeled muscles of his biceps, his body responding, tensing to my touch. The guttural moan he emits from the back of his throat turns me on, entices me, has me wanting and needing more.

Desire coils and need springs with each passing second, my thighs clenching together, my breath coming faster. "Colton," I murmur as his lips travel down my jawline to the pleasure point just beneath my ear that has me arching my back and moaning out loud on contact, heated warmth on willing flesh. His hands scrape over my rib cage and cup my breasts, already weighted with desire. Sensations spiral into and then through every part of me.

"Fuck, Ry, you test a man's control. I've been craving the taste of that sweet pussy of yours. That sound you make when I bury my cock in you. The feel of you coming around me."

He groans as I slide my hands between his shorts and grip his heated flesh. And as incendiary as his words are, as much as they stoke the fires already raging out of control, there's an added tenderness in his touch that's a stark contrast to their explicitness.

"I want every inch of you trembling, *fucking shaking,* begging for me to take you, Ry, because fuck if I won't be doing the same. I want to be your sigh, your moan, your cry out in pleasure and every fucking sound in between." He leans in and nips my lip, and I can feel him quiver, and know that he's just as affected as I am.

"*I want to feel you.* Your fingernails digging into my shoulders. Your thighs tense around mine as I drive you closer." He breathes out, the dominance of his tone fringed with a raw necessity has my entire body vibrating with need. "I want to see your toes curl as they push against my chest. Want to watch your mouth fall open and your eyes close when it becomes too much—the pleasure so fucking intense—because, baby, I want to know I make you feel that way. I want to know you feel just as fucking alive inside as you make me."

And I can't take it anymore, his words the most seductive foreplay for my body that's already craving his touch. I pull him toward me, hesitancy a distant memory. Our bodies and hearts crash together as we fall back on the bed beneath us as hands and mouths explore, taste, and tempt.

I force him on his back by scoring my nails down his chest, his muscles tensing and throat humming with a desperate groan. My mouth traces a languorous trail down the line of his neck, over the ridged muscles of his abdomen scrunching and flexing with each lick of my tongue or scrape of my fingers. I kiss my way down one side of his sexy as hell V and then back up the other side, cautious of his freshly tattooed rib cage as my fingertips find and encircle his steeled length through his shorts.

I look up and meet his eyes, clouded with desire and weighted with emotion, as I pull down his shorts. I kiss my way down the tiny line of hair and then move down and tease the crest of his dick with the wet, warmth of my lips. His cock pulses against my lips as he hisses out, "*Fuck!*" The drawn out way he says the word encourages me to take him further into my mouth, and press my tongue to the underside as I slide down and take him deeper.

His hands sitting idly on the bed clench into fists, and his hips twitch as I slide him back out until just his tip is in my mouth. I roll my tongue around it, paying special attention to the nerves on the underside, before sliding back down until he hits the back of my throat. In an instant, his hands are fisting my hair as pleasure overtakes him. "Sweet Christ," he pants out between labored breaths as I continue to work him with my mouth. "So fucking good."

Fingertips tease his sensitive skin beneath, tickling and pressing, as I hollow my cheeks out with each slide down and subsequent suck back out. I look up at him and can't help the satisfied smile that tries to form despite his place in my mouth. Colton's head is thrown back, lips pulled tight in pleasure, and the muscles are strained in his neck. The sight of him slowly coming undone would have me wet and wanting if I wasn't already.

I fist my hand around him and work it in circular motions while I bob my head up and down over the remainder of him. He groans, turning to steel in my mouth, and in an instant he is dragging me up the length of him, my nipples aching from the skin on skin contact.

His mouth is on mine the minute my lips are within reach, a greedy clash of lips, tongues, and teeth as he dominates the kiss, taking what he wants even though I'm giving it up more than willingly. He shifts our position in the blink of an eye so I am on my back, atop the pillows propped behind me. He scrapes his eyes down the length of my torso, a mischievous grin lighting up his face as he looks at my panties and then back up at me.

"I'm out of practice," he says with a shake of his head and a flash of his lone dimple. And then despite the carnal need raking through every one of my nerves, I can't help the laugh that falls from my lips as the fabric of my panties is ripped in half. "There," he says, lowering his mouth to my abdomen and pressing a kiss there. "Much better."

And it's not the kiss in itself, but the unexpectedness of his lips holding still momentarily, just below my navel, that sobers the moment for me. But at the same time, makes it that much sweeter. His eyes are closed and his lips are pressed atop the womb that held his child, and chills immediately race across my anticipatory flesh.

After a moment, his lips make their torturously slow ascent up my rib cage to my breast. I can feel his heated breath, the slide of his tongue, the suction of his mouth as he closes over my nipple, and I cry out involuntarily. The sensations his mouth evokes are like a lightning strike to my sex, my inhibitions singed and body lit afire.

"Colton," I pant as the ache in my core intensifies and fingernails score the skin on his shoulders as his mouth pleasures and hints at things to come. When my nipples are tightened and teased so thoroughly they're on the edge of pain, he moves back up my body. One of his hands fists in the back of my hair, holding my curls hostage, while the other slides down my body and slips between my legs.

I hold my breath in that space of time between feeling his fingers move my thighs apart and them actually touching me. Lungs robbed of air and body full of anticipation, Colton brands his mouth to mine in a soul-searing, gravity-defying kiss, and just when it leaves my head spinning and desire spiraling out of control, his fingers part me and stake their claim. His mouth captures the moan he coaxes from me as my nerves are expertly manipulated. Heat ignites and a rapturous moan emanates from the back of my throat as I am entirely consumed and completely undone by Colton.

His fingers coated in my arousal slide back out and up to add friction to my already throbbing clit. "Ah!" I can't help the garbled cry as his fingers connect, sensations overwhelm, and emotions swell. His fingers stroke and his mouth tempts the skin along my neck as my body climbs the wave at a rapid pace. My nipples tighten and thighs tense as desire ricochets through me and then comes back to hit me ten times harder.

And I am lost. Stepping into an oblivion that's assaulting all my senses, and overwhelming all thoughts. My hands grip his arms and my hips buck as my body detonates into a million splinters of pleasure. The only thing I hear besides my pulse thundering in my ears is a satisfied groan falling from his lips.

Within a second of riding out the last wave of my orgasm, Colton is shifting, pushing my thighs apart with his knees as he places the head of his cock against my still pulsing entrance.

And then it hits me—breaks through my hazy state of desire—and shocks me back to my senses. I push against his chest, shaking my head. "Colton … we need a condom …" I tell him, reality hitting me stronger than the climax tremors still rumbling through me.

Colton's body tenses and his head snaps up from where he's watching our connection. He angles his head and just stares at me, the only sounds in the room are my still shuddered breathing and the soft strains of *Stolen* on the speakers overhead. But the way he looks at me—as if I am his next draw of breath—halts any further protests from my lips.

"I don't want to use a condom, Rylee." His words startle me but more than that, it's the way he says them, resigned disbelief laced with irritation.

But why?

Disbelief because I ruined the mood to ask? Irritation because he has to now? "C'mon, Colton, don't be such a guy. I know it doesn't feel the same but we need to be smart and—"

Colton's sudden shift in the bed, pulling me up and into him so I straddle his lap, surprises me so much that I abandon my protest. His hands find the nape of my neck, thumbs framing the sides of my face, and his eyes bore into mine with a reverent intensity that I've never seen before. "No, Ry. I don't want to use a condom and it's not because of lack of feeling. Fuck, baby, I could have burlap wrapped around my dick and I'd still feel you."

I want to laugh as my mind tries to figure out just what Colton is telling me. "What do you—what are you trying to say?" And even though he hasn't answered me yet, my heartbeat quickens and my fingers start to tremble.

I watch him swallow, his Adam's apple bobbing, and his lips turn up in a ghost of a smile. He shakes his head slightly as that smile deepens. "I don't know how to explain it, Ry. *That night* was horrible. It was something that will forever be etched in my mind—you, me ... the baby ..." His voice fades as he shakes his head softly, looking down for a moment because I know he's still trying to come to terms with the fact that we lost a baby together. He exhales a shaky breath, and when he looks up the raw honesty in his eyes has me holding my own. "I was scared shitless," he says, leaning in and brushing the most tender of kisses against my lips before kissing my nose and then leaning back. "It still scares me every time I think about it and what could have happened. I—I'm just not sure how to even explain it." He blows out a loud breath, and I can see the need in his face to try and capture the right words to express how he feels.

"Take your time," I whisper, knowing I'd give him all the time in the world if he asked for it.

He rubs his thumbs back and forth on my cheek, goose bumps dancing over my skin at the poignancy of the moment. "A part of me ..." His voice breaks and I can see the muscle in his jaw tic as he attempts to control the emotion I see swimming in his eyes. "... a part of *us* died that day. But it was the part of me that I've been holding on to."

When he refers to the baby as *ours*, my breath catches in my chest and my hands reach out to hold onto his biceps.

"I sat in that waiting room, Ry, with your blood, our baby's blood, on my skin and I don't think ... I don't think I've ever felt so fucking alive." That soft smile is back on that magnificent mouth of his, but it's his eyes that captivate me. Those sparks of green that are pleading, asking, and searching to make sure I understand the words—spoken and unspoken—that he is telling me right now.

He looks down at his hands for a beat, emotion flickering over his face as he remembers how he felt before looking back to me. "The blood of a baby I'll never meet, but that was something we'd created together ..." The gravel of his voice breaks on his last words, but his eyes remain steady on mine, making sure I see everything in his—grief, disbelief, loss.

"All the emotions ... everything that was happening ... trying to process it all felt like taking a sip of water from a fucking fire hose." He exhales another breath, closing his eyes momentarily as he becomes overwhelmed with the memory and how to best explain it. "And I still don't know if I'll ever be able to process it, Ry. But the one thing I do know," he says, his fingertips tightening on my cheeks to reinforce the certainty of his words, "is that when I sat in that waiting room and the doctor told me ... about the baby ... feelings I never thought possible filled me," he says, eyes unflinching and complete reverence in his voice that causes my heart to swell with hope for things I never thought I could imagine.

His thumb wipes away a tear that runs down my cheek I didn't even know I'd shed and he continues on. "And sitting there in that damn hospital room, waiting for you to wake up ... I realized what you meant to me, what we had created together—the best parts of us combined. And then it hit me," he says with so much tenderness in his eyes that when I go to open my mouth to say something nothing comes out. He smiles softly at me, darting his tongue out to wet his bottom lip. "I realized that what *she* did to me *doesn't have* to happen again. That I can give someone the life I never had, Rylee. The life you showed me is a possibility."

I bite back the comments that rush into my head as Colton's words break down every last form of protection I've ever woven around my heart. My fingers tense on his biceps and my chin quivers from the emotions coursing through me.

"No, don't cry, Ry," he murmurs as he leans in and kisses the tracks of tears coursing down my cheeks. "You've cried enough already. I just want to make you happy because fuck, baby, it's you that's the difference. It's you that allowed me to see that my biggest fear—darkest goddamn poison—wasn't really a fear at all. It was an excuse for me to not open myself up by saying all I could do was bring pain and pass my demons on. But I know—*I know*—that I could never hurt a child—a baby that is my own flesh and blood. And I sure as fuck know you could never hurt one just to spite me."

Tears well in his eyes as he lowers them for a moment and shakes his head, the confession and cleansing of his soul finally taking its toll. But when he looks up at me, despite the tears swimming in his eyes I see such clarity, such reverence, that my breath is stolen. My heart that was robbed long ago is undeniably his. "It's like out of the horrible darkness I've had to live with my whole life came this incredible ray of light."

His voice breaks and a tear drops as we sit in this beast of a bed, bodies bare, pasts no longer hidden, hearts naked and completely vulnerable, and yet I have never felt more certain about any other person in my life.

He tilts my head back up to look at him. "So are you okay with this?"

I look at him not sure what he's asking, but hoping my assumptions are true.

Chapter Thirty-Eight

Colton

"God, I need to know you're okay with this, Ry?" I search her face for any indication that she's along for the ride, because right now, my fucking heart's pounding and my chest is constricting with each damn breath.

Those violet eyes of hers—the only ones that have ever been able to see straight into my soul and see everything I've hidden—blink back tears and try to process what I've been telling her I've never wanted, I now want with her.

Tomorrows.

Possibilities.

A fucking future.

The ultimate motherfucking checkered flag.

And deep in my heart I know with absolute certainty how I feel about this woman who crashed into my damn life, grabbed me by the balls—and apparently my heart—and never let go. I can't resist one brief taste to calm the apprehension coursing through me, to ease the upheaval of a soul I always thought was doomed to Hell. I lean in and press my mouth to hers using her soft lips as a silent reassurance she doesn't even know she's giving me.

I look at my hands trembling on her cheeks, and I know this tremor has nothing to do with the fucking accident and everything to do with the healing of wounds so old and scarred I never thought they could be mended. I lift my eyes to meet hers again because when I tell her, I need her to know that there may have been many before her, but she is the only fucking one who will ever hear this.

"I told you in Florida that I've always used adrenaline—the blur, women—to fill the void I've always felt. And now ..." I shake my head, not sure how I'm going to get the words racing laps around my fucking head to sound coherent. I take a deep breath because these words are the most important ones I've ever spoken. "Now, Ry, none of that matters. All I need is you. Just. You. And the boys. *And whatever it is we create together.*"

Chills dance on my skin and I'm so overwhelmed with everything—the moment, the feeling, the fucking vulnerability—that I have to force a swallow as I close my eyes momentarily. And when I open them, the compassion and love in hers—and the simple notion that I see her love, accept it— has my pulse racing from the euphoria it brings, and it breaks the final barrier of my past.

"*I love you, Rylee.*" I whisper the words. The weight in my chest fractures, splinters into a million fucking pieces freeing my soul like a 747 taking flight.

Chapter Thirty-Nine

He loves me.

The thought races around my mind, over and over as adrenaline surges through me.

He just told me he loves me.

Words escape me as a swell of love and pride for this man engulfs me, wraps me in its cocoon of possibilities, and quiets any remaining doubt I might have had. "Colton …" I'm so overcome with emotion I can't even find the words to tell him what I've waited so long to say.

"Shhh," he says, bringing a finger to my lips while a shy smile forms on his. "Let me finish. *I love you, Rylee.*" His voice is more certain now in his declaration, as he finds his footing in this newfound world. His smile widens and so does mine with his finger still pressed against my lips. "I think I always have … from that first damn night. You were that bright spot—that fucking spark—I couldn't hide from even when the darkness claimed me. My God, baby, we've been through so fucking much that I …" His voice fades as the moisture pooling in his eyes leaks, a single tear sliding down the side of his face.

I hiccup the sob I've been holding back because it's impossible to keep it at bay. I reach up and hold his cheeks, his stubble coarse and comforting beneath my palms, and press my lips to his as his arms wrap around me and pull me in tight against his body. I lean my forehead against his as my fingers fist in his hair so I can pull his head back to see his eyes. "I love you, Colton. I've wanted to say those words to you again for so long." I laugh, unable to contain the happiness bubbling inside of me. "I love you, you brave, amazing, complicated, stubborn, gorgeous man that I can't seem to ever get enough—"

His lips capture mine, our mouths joining in a kiss packed with so much emotion I can't contain my tears that fall or the repeated murmurs of the words I've had to withhold for so long finally being set free.

The calluses on his fingers rasp across my back as he presses me into him, his steeled skin against the softness of my breasts reigniting the licks of desire deep in my belly. Tongues delve, sighs expel, needs intensify as we slide into a slow but utterly body-tingling, mind-numbing kiss. Every nerve in my body itches for his fingers to graze and stake its claim anywhere and everywhere.

I rock my aching apex over the tip of his erection at the same time his tongue leaves me weak and defenseless, branding his indelible mark on me from his kiss alone. My fingers stroke absently over the hard edged muscles of his shoulders before I thread them in his hair, holding his head captive like he's already done to every single piece of me.

He pulls back, breaking our kiss, and I cry out in protest feeling like I'll never fully sate my desire for him. I take in his mussed hair and sparkling eyes before being drawn down to his lips curled up in a smile that completely knocks my world off balance. His fingertips trace feather-light lines down the column of my spine as I try to gauge what it is his eyes are telling me.

"Let me make love to you, Ry," he says, the huskiness of his voice laced with affection.

How many more times tonight is he going to leave me breathless? How many more times is he going to give me the broken pieces of him so I can hold them and heal with him to make him whole again?

I just stare at him, my lips forming a smile as I say, "I *always* have been." I shake my head as emotion stains my cheeks. It's silly really, to be embarrassed by my confession when everything else between us has been shared, but I love the spark in his eyes and parting of his lips as my words hit him. I run a hand up his arm and rest it over his heart. "I've always made love to you, you just never knew."

He breathes out a laugh, that grin deepening as he shifts and lays us down on the pillows behind me. His face is inches from mine, his body supported on his elbows, and his knees between my thighs.

"Well this time, we'll both know," he says, inhaling a shaky breath as his steeled length presses at my opening.

I close my eyes as my body trembles beneath his, needing and wanting the bombardment of the all-consuming sensation I know is coming. "Look at me, Ry." My eyes flutter open and look up to lose myself in the beauty of his face. "I want to watch you as I take you. I want to watch you as you let me love you." He leans his head down and teases my lips with the whisper of a kiss before finding my eyes again. "I love you."

As he says the three words he pushes his way into me, and I swear sparks ignite with our union because this time it's more than just the physical connection. It's the joining of our hearts, souls, and everything in between. I watch his eyes cloud with desire and darken with emotion as he seats himself fully into me.

"Sweet Jesus!" He groans as he begins to move, raking over every interior nerve possible. My body reacts instinctively, hips angling and back arching so I can draw every possible ounce of pleasure from this incredible man.

I feel bombarded by sensation. The slide of his skin across mine. The unhindered lust and unfettered love in his eyes. The soft groan of pleasure from the back of his throat. The rush of heat enveloping me as he grinds into me circling his hips before slowly pulling back out only to start all over again.

My body vibrates from this sensual high—a collision of everything with the most perfect timing that I couldn't escape even if I wanted to.

Pressure builds and pleasure catapults me to a dizzying high as Colton finds a slow but steady cadence that allows him to draw out and drag over every last nerve. His eyes still hold mine, but I can see the pleasure start to edge out the need to watch me as his eyes close momentarily, his jaw set tight in concentration, his eyelids heavy, and nostrils flared.

"Colton ..." I moan as a desirable devastation begins to rock through me, my muscles tense in preparation for the onslaught of sensation just within reach. With the call of his name, he shifts, drawing his hands down the length of my body as he sits back onto his knees. His hands sweep over the top of my sex, thumb grazing over my clit making me buck my hips up asking for more.

The lines of concentration on his face ease as his lips curl into a lascivious smirk. "You want more of that?"

All I can do is nod, my words lost to the onslaught of sensation. His fingers, careful of my newfound ink, grip the flesh at the sides of my hips, holding me firmly as his smile still plays over his face but his hips continue their painfully exquisite surge in and subsequent withdrawal. There is nothing I can do but focus, try to manage the all-consuming attack on my senses as he holds my gaze, driving me higher and higher. My thighs tense and my head falls back as the force of my impending climax heightens.

And then nothing.

Colton stops all movement stealing my orgasm with his sudden lack of motion. My head snaps up to look at him, frustrated, to meet green eyes dancing with mirth and full of restraint.

He leans forward, his heated length surging to unimaginable depths inside of me, dragging out an insuppressible moan I don't even attempt to stop. His hands push the backs of my thighs forward as his face fills my entire line of sight. I can feel the heat of his panting breath on my face and see his muscles tighten as he controls his need to pound into me with reckless abandon and drive us to the brink fast and hard, the way I know he likes.

"Fuck, baby, you feel like Heaven," he says as he leans forward and brushes his mouth to mine. He surprises me as he pushes his tongue between my lips and dominates the kiss in much the same fashion as he dominates my heart. I can sense his restraint slipping, can feel every sweet inch of him expand inside of me, can taste the desire mounting, need edging out all reason.

His mouth brands and claims me while his body slowly starts moving again—taking, taunting, pushing mine to accept his challenge. Liquid fire flickers to life again, molten lava singeing and refueling the inferno he's just forced me to abandon. I swallow his groan as he rocks deeper into me, throbbing sparks of pleasure igniting my nerve endings.

He nips my bottom lip and breaks the kiss as he starts to pick up his tempo, drives into me with a passionate desperation as he drops his forehead to my shoulder. My body begins to tremble from the intense pull at my core while he continues his punishing rhythm. The room is filled with my soft moans, his inarticulate grunts, and the slap of skin against skin as he edges me higher and higher.

The scrape of his teeth along my collarbone is my undoing. Mindless pleasure seizes me as my body tightens all around him and free falls into rapturous oblivion as I surrender myself to him.

I have forgotten everything—he has made me forget everything—except for his scent, his sounds, his taste, his touch. My body crashes into the wave of sensation, his name on my lips, our bodies united as one.

"So fucking hot to watch you come undone," he whispers as his stubble scrapes against my neck, his body stilling and then moving in and out of me ever so slowly to draw out the last remnants of my orgasm still firing through me. I pulse and tighten around his cock, my fingernails scoring his shoulders as I hold tight with each surge of pleasure.

"Fuck, Ry, that feels so fucking good!" He groans out as his hips start jerking, my own orgasm starting to milk his from him. And within a moment Colton is back on his knees, hands pushing my thighs up, and his hips are pounding into me as he chases his own climax.

"Come on, baby," I pant out as I try to meet him thrust for thrust, surrendering myself completely to his needs.

His guttural groan fills the room as he hits his peak, his shuddering and body tensing while he rides out his own high. After a beat, he rolls us over, our hips remaining connected in the most primal of ways so that I'm lying atop him, my cheek on his chest where I can hear his thundering heartbeat.

And we sit like this for a moment, fingers drawing lazy lines over each other's bare flesh, regaining our breaths, and calming our pounding hearts. The silence around us is so comfortable without the demons haunting the shadows. Yes, he'll always have a part of him haunted and damaged, but for the first time ever he has someone he can share them with. Someone to help ease the burden, to help heal.

I sigh at the thought and am completely content as he presses a kiss to the top of my head. "I love you," I whisper the words still overwhelmed with everything that has transpired this evening. His fingers continue tracing aimlessly over my spine. I close my eyes and enjoy the feeling of our bodies pressed against one another's and the simplicity of his touch. And then my OCD kicks in as I mentally trace what his fingers are spelling, and I shift my head so my chin rests on my hands covering his sternum.

"What?" he asks innocently, despite the smile tugging at the corner of his mouth and eyes reflecting the mischief I've come to love and expect from him. When all I do is raise my eyebrows, I feel the rumble of his chuckle through his chest and into mine.

"The alphabet, Ace?" I raise an eyebrow and try to bite back my own smile, but it's useless.

"Yep. I'm seeing the alphabet in a whole new light these days," he says, abandoning his letter tracing and trailing his finger down the top of my backside.

My laugh is overtaken by a sigh as his hand palms my ass. I can feel that ache he always has on low burn start to simmer anew. He starts to harden inside of me again and moisture starts to pool as desire is heightened by the complete connection of our bodies.

"And just what might your favorite letter be?"

He emits a full bodied laugh, his shaking body reverberating all the way down to his cock, now alert and fully buried within me. "Oh, baby, I'm kind of partial to your V. That's the only place that I want to B."

I can't even laugh at his corny line because he chooses this moment to thrust his hips upward, my body moving with it, his skin rubbing my nipples and coaxing a pleasurable groan from my throat. My eyes close and body softens as his movements draw heightened responses from the flesh already swollen from him.

"Good God!" I sigh as he pulls me out of my post-catatonic orgasmic state and drags me under his spell once again.

Chapter Forty

Colton

The sun feels just as good as the ice cold beer sliding down my throat and the sight of Rylee bending over in front of me. *Fuck* is my only thought as I adjust myself and think thoughts I shouldn't be thinking with the boys here.

Will this ever end? To want her near? The want to watch her sleep and wake up next to her? My need to be buried in her? It's been only three damn hours since we've left my bed and fuckin' A, I'd love to drag her upstairs right now and have her again.

"Down boy!"

And there's the voice that will make me go limp.

"'Sup, Becks."

"Apparently you, if you don't stop looking at her like you want to bend her over that lounge chair and fuck her into oblivion," he says, taking a long sip of his beer.

Well, that's always a thought.

I groan. "Thanks for the visual, dude, because that's really not helping right now," I reply with a roll of my eyes and shake of my head, before looking around to make sure the boys are far enough away they can't hear us talking about how I want to defile their sexy-as-fuck guardian. And my God is she a walking wet dream. I shift in my chair again as I watch her squat down and adjust the top of her suit before slathering sunscreen all over Zander.

I shake my head thinking about her concern earlier in picking which swimsuit to wear with the boys coming over for a pool party. Even in the red one piece that she deemed matronly, every curve of hers is on display like a goddamn road map tempting me to take it out for a test drive.

Dangerous curves ahead? Fuckin' A. *Bring. It. On.* I'm a man that lives for danger. The thrill I get from it. And hell if I'm not itching for the keys, right now.

Talk about revved and raring.

"By that sappy ass look on your face, I take it things are going good?" Becks asks as he sits down beside me and snaps me from my dirty thoughts.

"Pretty much." I pop the top off of another bottle with the opener and take a drink.

"Please don't tell me you're gonna get all domesticated and shit on me now."

"Domesticated? Fuck no." I laugh. "Although the woman is hot as hell in her heels pushing that grocery cart in front of me." I can visualize it now and damn if the thought's not making me ache to take her.

"*You*—Colton Donavan—stepped foot into a grocery store?" he sputters.

"Yep." I raise my eyebrows and smirk at the look of shock on his face.

"And it wasn't just to buy condoms?"

I can't help it now. I love fucking with him. It's just too goddamn easy. "Nah, no longer a requirement when you hold a frequent flier card to the barebacking club."

"Jesus Christ, dude, are you trying to get me to choke on my beer?" He wipes beer off his chin that he spit out.

"I got something else you can choke on," I murmur as my eyes are drawn back to Rylee bending over, my constant semi wanting to fly full staff. I'm so focused on her and my corrupt but oh-so-fucking awesome thoughts of what I can do to her later that I don't hear what Becks says. "Huh?" I ask.

"Dude, you are one whipped motherfucker, aren't you?"

I look over at him ready to defend my manhood when I realize it's right where I want it to be, held in Rylee's hands—the perfect mixture of sugar and spice. So I laugh out and just shake my head, bring the beer to my lips and shrug. "As long as it's her pussy doing the whipping, I'm fucking game all day long."

Becks chokes again but with laughter this time, and I pat him on the back as Ry looks over at us making sure he's okay. "My God! That must be the best voodoo pussy ever to tame Colton fuckin' Donavan."

"*Tame?* Never." I chuckle and shake my head, leaning back on the chair behind me to look over at him. "But some asshole—er friend—made me realize how much I like the fucking alphabet."

"That *friend* deserves a shitload of beer as a thank you then." He shrugs. "That, or a mighty fine piece of ass in return."

I snort out a laugh, grateful for his sarcasm to avoid talking about deep feelings and shit that I'm not really comfortable discussing. I'm just getting used to saying this kind of shit to Ry, I'm sure as shit not going to be getting touchy-feely with Becks.

"*She's got a hot friend*," I tell him with a raise of my eyebrow, earning me a snort in return as I repeat what I said the night I talked him into inviting Ry to Vegas with us.

"She sure does," he murmurs, but before I can respond, Aiden cannonballs into the pool and the splash hits us full on. We start laughing, comment forgotten, sunglasses now splashed with water.

"Hey," he says, and I look back over at him. "I have to give you shit because that's just the way we roll ... but I'm really happy for you, Wood. Now don't fuck it up."

I grin at him. *The fucker.* "Thanks for the vote of confidence, dude."

"Anytime, man. Anytime." We sit in silence for a moment, both watching the boys around us acting like they're supposed to be, kids. "So you ready?"

Becks' voice pulls me from my thoughts and back to what I should really be focusing on: the race next week. First time back in the car since the accident. Pedal to the floor and the next left turn. And just the thought makes my blood pressure spike.

But I got this.

"Fuck, I was born ready," I tell him, tapping the neck of my beer bottle to his. "Checkered flag's mine for the taking."

"Fuck yeah it is," he says as he looks down at his phone that's received a text, and my eyes drift back to Rylee and thoughts of a particular pair of checkered panties I never did get to claim. I sure as hell need to fix that.

I shake my head as I sink back into my chair and watch the boys jumping in the pool and chicken fight one another. I sit and wait for it, but it doesn't happen. That fucking pang of jealousy I used to get when I saw boys acting their age, acting how I never got to. Because even after I was adopted, the fear was still there, still raw as fuck.

Rylee catches my eye from across the deck and those sexy-as-sin lips spread wide. Fuck me running. My balls tighten and chest constricts at the notion that I put that smile on those lips. The woman is my fucking kryptonite.

Who else would I allow to invite seven boys to my house for a pool party to celebrate summer being here? What other woman could I share my demons with and instead of running like a banshee, she looks me in the eyes and tells me I'm brave? Who else would scar their skin to prove to me she's in it for the long haul?

Motherfucking checkered flags and alphabets and sheets. When did all of this become okay with me?

I shake my head, pretending I don't want it but fuck if I can't look away from her for one goddamn second before my eyes find her again.

I lift the fresh beer Becks hands me and start to take a sip and look over at him as he shakes his head laughing at me. "*What?*"

"You are so going to fucking marry her."

It's my turn to choke on my beer. I double over in a coughing fit as Becks pounds me a little too hard on the back. "He's fine!" I hear him say as I try to control the choking mixed with laughter burning its way up my throat. "He's fine," he says again, and I can hear the amusement in his voice.

"Fuck off, Becks!" I finally manage to get out. "Not gonna happen! *No rings, no strings*," I say our old motto with a laugh. And then I look up to find Ry. She's across the patio sitting on the edge of the pool, Diet Coke in hand, and is playing referee to the boys' game of Marco Polo. Ricky gets caught as a fish out of water, and Rylee throws her head back in laughter at something Scooter says to him.

And there's something about her right now—hair highlighted from the sun, a carefree sound to her laugh, and obviously in love with everyone around her. Something about her being with the boys, making life normal for them at a place that has never really been a home until now—until her—hits me harder than that fucking rookie Jameson did in Florida. Has me thinking about the forevers and shit that six months ago would have never once crossed my mind.

It's just gotta be Becks getting in my head. Mucking it up. The bastard needs to shut the hell up about shit that's not gonna happen.

Never.

So why the fuck am I wondering what Ry'd look like wearing white? Why am I wondering how *Rylee Donavan* sounds out loud?

Never. I try to shake the thoughts from my head, but they linger, spooking the shit out of me.

"*So not gonna happen.*" I laugh, not sure if I'm repeating the words to convince Becks or myself. I look back over at Ry for a second. Talk about jumping the gun when I haven't even found the bullets to load it yet. Fucking Beckett. "Taming's one thing, fucker. Ball and chaining?" I whistle out. "That's a whole 'nother ball game I have no interest in playing." I shake my head again at that shit-eating grin on his face as I rise from the chair. "Never."

"We'll see about that," he tells me with that smirk I want to wipe from his face.

"Dude, do you feel that?" I ask, raising my arms out from my side and lifting my face to the sun before looking back down at him.

"Huh?"

"That's called heat, Daniels. Hell can't freeze if it's still hot outside," I toss over my shoulder before walking to the edge of the pool. Conversation over. No more discussion of marriage and shit like that.

Is he trying to give me a heart attack?

Fuck.

"Cannonball!" I yell before jumping in, hoping to create more turmoil in the pool than what Becks is trying to create in my head.

Chapter Forty-One

Déjà vu hits me like a runaway train as I step from the RV ahead of Colton. The humid heat of Fort Worth hits me instantly, but the sweat trickling in a line down my back has nothing to do with the weather and everything to do with the anxiety coursing through every nerve.

Over Colton.

And over the car we're walking toward.

I know he's nervous, can feel it in the tightened grip of his fingers laced with mine, but his outward appearance reflects nothing but a man preparing to do his job. People around us chatter incessantly but Colton, Becks, and I walk off the infield as one unit, completely focused.

I attempt to push away the memories bombarding my mind, to appear calm even though every fiber of my being is vibrating with absolute trepidation.

"You okay?" His rasp washes over me, the concern in it tugs on my guilt since it should be me reassuring him.

I can't lie to him. He'll know if I am and it will only cause him to worry more. The last thing I want is him to be thinking of me. I want him focused and confident when he buckles into the car and takes the green flag all the way to the checkered one.

"I'm getting there," I breathe and squeeze his hand as we reach the pits and the mass of photographers waiting to record Colton's first race back after the accident. The click of shutters and shouting of questions drowns out the response he gives me. And as I tense up further, Colton seems to relax some, comfortable in this environment like it's his second skin.

And I realize that while all of this is uncomfortable and foreign to me, this is part of the blur that Colton used to permanently reside in. Surrounded by the shouts and the flashes of light, he's one hundred percent back in his element. The utter chaos is allowing him to forget the worry I know is plaguing his thoughts, and for that I'm so thankful.

I step to the side and watch him answer questions with a flash of his disarming smile that gets me every time. And as much as I see the cocky bad boy shining through with each answer, I also see a man in utter reverence of the sport he loves and the role he plays in it. A man gaining back bits and pieces of the confidence he left on the track in St. Petersburg with each response.

As much as I'm dreading the familiar call of "*gentlemen start your engines,*" a part deep down within me sags in relief that he's back. My reckless, rebellious rogue just found his footing and is stepping back in his place.

Silence descends around us—the constant noise fading to a white humming as the minutes tick away, bringing us closer and closer to the start of the race. I can feel Colton's restlessness rising, can see it in his constant movement, and wish I could ease it somehow, someway, but fear he'll sense mine and that will only make matters worse.

I see him toss his empty Snickers wrapper into the trash beside him as he goes over pit stop scheduling with Becks and some of the other crew members, his face intense but his body language fluid. I watch him step away and look at his car, his head angling to the side as he stares at it for a beat—a silent conversation between man and machine. He walks up to it slowly; the crew, still making last minute adjustments, steps back. He reaches a hand out and runs it up the nose to the driver's cockpit, almost a caress of sorts. Then he raps his knuckles on the side, his customary four times. The last time he holds his fist there, resting against the metal for a second before shaking his head.

And even with the chaos of all the last minute preparations happening around me, I can't tear my eyes away from him. I realize how wrong I was to hope he'd give this all up as I sat beside his hospital bed. How asking him to give up racing would be like asking him to breathe without air. To love without me being the one he's loving. Racing is in his blood—an absolute necessity—and that has never been more evident than right now.

I wonder how different this race will be for him without the constant pressure of the demons on his heels, of the need to drive faster, to push harder to outrun them. Will it be easier or harder without the threat he's had his whole life?

The PA hums to life shattering my thoughts and Colton's moment of reflection. When he looks over his shoulder, his eyes immediately lock with mine. A shy smile spreads over his lips, acknowledging that our connection is so deep that we don't need words. And that feeling is priceless.

People scramble around us but with his eyes on mine, he wraps his knuckles two more times on the hood before turning and walking toward me.

"Starting a new tradition?" I ask with a quirk of my brow, a smile a mile wide and a heart brimming with love. "Two more for extra luck or something?"

"Nah." He smirks, scrunching his nose up in the cutest way—such a contrast to the strong lines of his face—that my heart melts. "All the extra luck I need is right here," he says as he leans in and presses the tenderest of kisses to my lips and just holds his mouth against mine for a moment.

Emotions threaten—war really—inside of me as I try to tell myself his sudden affection isn't because the fates above are giving me one last memory with him because something bad is going to happen again. I try desperately to fight the burn of tears and enjoy the moment, but I know he knows, know he senses my unease, because he lifts his hands up to hold my face as he draws back and meets my eyes.

"It's gonna be okay, Ry. Nothing is going to happen to me." I force myself to hear the absolute certainty in his voice so I can relax some, be strong for him.

I nod my head subtly. "I know ..."

"Baby, Heaven doesn't want me yet, and fuck if Hell can handle me, so you're kinda stuck with me." He flashes me a lighting fast grin that screams everything I never thought was sexy—unpredictable, adventurous, arrogance—and now can't help the ache it creates.

"Stuck with you, huh?"

He leans in and brings his mouth to my ear. "Stuck *in you* is more what I'm thinking," he murmurs, his heated breath against my ear sending shivers down my spine. "So please, *please*, tell me you're wearing some type of checkered flag I can claim later because fuck if I don't want to throw you over my shoulder and take a test lap right now."

Every part of my body clenches from his words. And maybe it's my heightened adrenaline and excessive emotion being back in the moment so precious yet stolen so brutally from us months ago, but fuck if I don't want him to do just that.

"I love a man willing to beg," I tease, my fingers playing with the hair curling over the neck of his fire suit.

"You have no idea the things I'm willing to beg for when it comes to you, sweetheart." He disarms me with that roguish grin of his, his words causing my breath to catch in my throat. "Besides, my begging leads to you moaning and fuck if that's not the hottest sound ever."

I exhale a small groan of frustration, needing and wanting him desperately when I can't have him ... and I know that's exactly why the ache is so intense. I start to speak, but am cut off by the opening chords of the Star Spangled Banner. Colton holds tight to the sides of my face and looks at me a moment longer before pressing one more kiss to my lips, and then nose, before turning toward the flag, removing his lucky hat, and placing his hand over his heart.

As the song plays on, its last notes sounding, I take a deep breath to prepare myself for the next few moments—to be strong, to not show him my fear's still there, regardless of how certain he feels. And then chaos descends around us the minute the crowd cheers.

Colton gets suited up, taped down, zipped up, gloves on. Engines start to rev farther down the line, and the rumble vibrates through my chest. He's in the zone, listening to Becks and getting ready for the task at hand.

Superstition tells me to make this race different. To step back over the wall without Davis' help. To do anything to not let time repeat itself. And then his voice calls to me. Shattering all my resolve with the shards of nostalgia.

"*Rylee?*"

My eyes flash up immediately, the breath knocked clear from my chest with his words and the bittersweet memories they evoke, and lock onto his as he strides toward me, shrugging off a groan from Beckett about running out of time.

My mouth parts and my eyebrows furrow, "Yeah?"

He reaches out, the short barrier of a wall between us and yanks my body to his so our hearts pound against one another's. "Did you actually think I was going to let you walk away this time without telling you?"

The smile on my face must spread a mile wide because my cheeks hurt. Tears pool in my eyes and this time it's not from fear.

But from love.

Unconditional adoration for this man holding me tight.

"I love you, Ryles." He says the four words so softly in that rasp of his, and even with everything around us—revved engines, a packed grandstands, the crackle on the PA system—I can hear it clear as day.

His words wrap around my heart, weave through its fibers, and tie us together. I exhale a shaky breath and smile at him. "I love you too, Ace."

He smirks before pressing a toe-tingling kiss to my lips and says, "Checkered flag time, baby."

"Checkered flag time," I repeat.

"See you in victory lane," he says with a wink before turning and walking back toward a crew standing motionless, waiting for their driver.

I watch them help him slide his helmet on, mesmerized with both love and fear, and then allow Davis to lead me up the stairs to the pit box so I can watch from an elevated level. I place the headset on as I look down over the sill and watch them fasten Colton's HANS device, yank on his harnesses, and tighten the steering wheel down.

"Radio check, Wood." The disembodied voice of Colton's spotter fills my ears, startling me. "Check one, two. Check one, two."

There's silence for a moment and I look down as if I'd be able to actually see him through his helmet and the surrounding crew.

The spotter tries again. "Check one, two."

"Check, A, B, C." Colton's voice comes through loud and clear.

"Wood?" The spotter calls back, confusion in his voice. "You okay?"

"Never better," he laughs. "Just giving a shout out to the alphabet."

And the nerves eating at me dissipate immediately.

"*The alphabet?*"

"Yep. A to motherfucking Z."

Quinlan grips my hand as I look up at the ticker on the top of the screen counting down the laps left to go.

Ten.

Ten laps to go through the gamut of emotions—nervous, excited, frantic, hopeful, enamored—just like I have the past two hundred and thirty eight laps. I've stood, I've sat, I've paced, I've yelled, I've prayed, and have had to remind myself to breathe.

"He's gonna pull it off," Quinlan murmurs beside me as she squeezes my hand a little tighter and while I agree with her—that Colton is going to win his comeback race in a flurry of glory—I won't say it aloud, too afraid to jinx the outcome.

I look down below to where Becks is talking furtively with another crew member, their heads so close they're almost touching as they scribble on a piece of paper. And I don't know much about racing, but I know enough that they're worried their fuel calculations are so slim in margin that Colton may literally be running on fumes on the final lap.

I watch as the lap number gets lower, my pulse racing and heart hoping as it hits five. "You've got Mason coming up hard and fast on the high side," the spotter says, anxiety lacing his usually stoic voice.

"Ten-four," is all that Colton says in response, concentration resonating in his voice.

"He's going for it!" the spotter shouts.

I glance at the monitor in front of me to see a close up version of what I'm seeing on the track, and my body tenses in anticipation as they fly into turn three, masses of metal competing at ungodly speeds. I swear that everyone leans forward from their position in the booth to get a closer look. I fist my hands and rise up on my toes as if that will help me see more, quickly pushing my prayers out to Colton as Mason challenges him for the lead.

I hear the crowd the same time my eyes avert back to the monitor, just in time to see rear tires touching together, Mason overcorrecting and slamming into the wall on the right of him, while Colton's car swerves erratically on the bank of asphalt from the force of their connection.

Everyone in the box is on their feet instantly, the same sound, different track, wreaks havoc on our nerves. My hands are covering my mouth, and I'm leaning out of the open-windowed booth to see the track.

"Colton!" Becks shouts out as I gasp, a blaze of red car sliding out of control onto the apron. Colton would normally reply instantly, but there is absolute radio silence. And I think a little part of me dies in that instant. A tiny part forever lost to the notion that there will always be this trickle of unease and flashback of the riotous emotions from Colton's crash every time I see smoke or the wave of the yellow flag.

I see Beckett pull on the bill of his baseball cap as his eyes fixate on the track. Anxiety rules over my body right now, and yet I still feel those seeds of certainty Colton planted with his confidence earlier ready to root and break through. And I can't imagine what's going through his head—the mix of emotions and memories colliding—but he doesn't let up. The car doesn't slow down one bit.

And yet he still hasn't spoken.

"C'mon, son," Andy murmurs to no one in particular down the line from me, hands gripping the edge of the table he stands behind, knuckles turning white.

Only seconds pass but it feels like forever as I watch Colton's car aim erratically toward the grass of the infield, heading straight for the barrier, before miraculously straightening out.

And then the whole booth lets out a collective whoop when the telltale red and electric blue nose of the car flies back up the apron and onto the asphalt, under control. And still in the lead. Colton's voice comes through the speaker. "Fuckin' A straight!" he barks, the overflow of emotion breaking through both his voice and the radio, followed by a "Woohoo!" The adrenaline rush hitting him full force.

"Bring it home, baby!" Becks shouts at him as he paces below us and blows out a loud breath, taking off his headset and hat for a moment to regain his composure before putting them back on.

Four laps left.

I feel like I can breathe again, my fingers twisting together, my nerves dancing, and my hopes soaring to new heights. *C'mon, baby. You can do this,* I tell him silently, hoping he can feel my energy with the thousands in the stands pushing for him to claim this victory.

Three laps left. I can't stand it anymore. My body vibrates from more than the rumbling of the engines as the cars pass us one after another in an endless sequence. I shove back from the counter and shrug at Quinlan when she gives me a questioning look about where I'm going. I want to be as close to him as possible so I make my way to the stairs and start running down them.

"Two to go, baby!" Becks shouts into the mic as I make it to the bottom step and stay close to the wall below on the inside border of the pits. I can't see the track very well from here but I smile as I watch Becks look at the monitor and shake his head back and forth, body moving restlessly, energy palpable.

I look up at the standings and see that Colton is still in the lead before my eyes are drawn to the flag stand where the flagger is getting the white flag denoting last lap ready. And then it waves and my heart leaps into my throat. Becks pumps a fist in the air and reaches over to squeeze the shoulder of the crew member next to him.

Someone brushes against my shoulder and I look over to see Andy beside me, cautious smile ready to light up his face when the checkered flag takes flight. I look back up but my view of the flag stand is obstructed by the row of red fire suits standing atop the pit row wall, watching, waiting, anticipating.

And then I hear it.

The crushing roar of the crowd and the jubilant whoops of the crew as they jump off the wall hooting and hollering in victory. I'm so overcome with emotion I don't even remember who grabbed who, but all I know is that Andy and I are hugging each other out of pure excitement. He did it. He really did it.

The next few minutes pass in a blur as hugs and high fives are given all around, headsets are removed, and we all move quickly in a big mass toward victory lane. The motor revs as Colton pulls into his spot fresh off his victory lap.

And I don't know what the protocol is for non-crew members, but I'm right in the thick of it, fighting my way to see him. Wild horses couldn't keep me from him right now.

My view is blocked temporarily by camera crews and I'm so anxious—heart pounding, cheeks hurting from smiling so wide, heart overflowing with love—that I want to push them out of the way to get to him.

When they shift to get a better shot, I see him standing there, accepting congratulations from Becks, bottle of Gatorade to his lips, hand running through his sweat soaked hair sticking up in total disarray, and the most incredible expression on his face—exhaustion mixed with relief and pride.

And then as if he can feel my gaze on him, he locks his eyes on mine, the biggest, most heart-stopping grin blanketing his face. My heart stops and starts as I take him in. I swear the air zings with sparks from our connection. He doesn't even say a word to Beckett but leaves him behind and starts pushing through the crowd, the mass moving with him, his eyes never leaving mine, until he's standing before me.

I'm against him in an instant, his arms closing around me and lifting my feet off the ground as he throws his head back and emits the most carefree laugh I've ever heard before crushing his mouth to mine. And there is so much going on around us—utter chaos—but it's nothing compared to the way he's making me feel inside right now.

Everyone and everything fades away because I'm right where I belong—in his arms. I feel the heat of his body pressed against mine rather than the press jostling us to and fro to get the perfect shot. I inhale his smell, soap and deodorant intermingled with a hard day's work—and it has my pheromones snapping to attention, has them silently urging him to take me, dominate me, own me so I'm marked by that scent. I taste Gatorade on his lips and it's nowhere near enough to satiate the desire coursing through me, because with Colton, one taste will never be enough. I hear his laugh again as he breaks from our kiss and presses his forehead to mine for a moment, his chest rumbling from the euphoric sound.

"You did it!"

"No," he disagrees, pulling his head back to look in my eyes. "We did it, Ry. It was us together because I couldn't have won without you."

My heart tumbles in my chest and crashes into my stomach that's jolted up as if I'm free falling. *And in a sense I am.* Because my love for him is endless, bottomless, eternal.

I smile at him, tears blurring my vision as I press one more chaste kiss on his lips. "You're right," I murmur. "We did it."

He squeezes me tight one more time and lowers me to the ground with another heart-stopping grin as the world around us seeps back. I step away, allowing everyone else their five seconds with him, and yet all I can think of are his words, *we did do it.*

And I watch him—the man I love—and know his words have never been more true. We've really done it. We've faced our demons together.

His past, his fears, his shame.

My past, my fears, my grief.

He looks over in the midst of an interview question and winks at me with a smirk. Pride, love, and relief flow through me like a tidal wave.

Holy shit.

We really did do it.

Chapter Forty-One and a Half

Colton—Raced

She switched it. When the hell did she do that?

I pick up the picture from my bookshelf, the one that sits in exactly the same place the one of Tawny and me used to. Frame's the same, picture's not.

The new one is of Ry and me at my comeback race. I don't fight the smirk when I think that wasn't the only victory lane I claimed that night with her arms wrapped around my waist.

And something else around my cock.

Fuck, she's gorgeous. Her head is angled back, grin on her face, but her eyes are on me. And that look in them—that frozen moment of time—reflects clear as fucking day her feelings for me. Not a single doubt.

I'm one lucky son of a bitch.

Well shit. When I look at my image, there's no denying I feel the same way about her. The look on my ugly mug tells anyone who sees the picture that she's snagged me hook, line, and double-sinker.

Funny thing is I see a man completely voodooed and I'm not even spooked by it.

I'm still getting used to the thought of it, the taste of it. And hell if I'm quite liking the foreign feeling, especially because it means I get to slide between those sexy as fuck curves of hers and claim the finish line every chance I get.

I know the game has caught up with this player because as much as that thought's a turn on, I like the idea even more that when I wake up I can reach over to find her in my bed next to me, that sleepy smile on her lips and that rasp to her morning voice.

God, I sound like a fucking pussy. All sappy and shit.

The woman has topped me from the bottom when I never thought it was a possibility. But fuck me, being beneath her means I get a damn good view of those tits of hers while I'm looking up.

My balls tighten at the thought alone.

Yep. I'm a damn voodooed man. Who would've known it'd feel so good to be under a woman's spell.

I'm starting to feel cracks in the ground beneath me because Hell sure as fuck is starting to freeze over.

I set the picture down, glancing one more time at it with a shake of my head. Nice, Ry. A sly removal of Tawny and subtle claiming of me.

And fuck if I don't like that claim. Who would've thought? Huh. Stranger fucking things have happened over the past few months I shouldn't be so shocked by feeling so okay with this.

Those baby steps of mine have turned into full on leaps. I guess I should start practicing for the long jump if this shit keeps up.

I wander out of the office forgetting the article from *Race Weekly*, so completely lost in thought. And then I see the woman who holds them captive. She's out on the patio in deep discussion with my mom and Quinlan over something.

And it's fucking weird how perfectly she fits here, there, everywhere in my life.

Jesus, I sound like a fucking Dr. Seuss poem.

"How come you're not at the track?"

My dad's voice pulls me from my thoughts, and I immediately realize I forgot to grab the article for him, distracted by Ry's bait and switch. And then I wonder how long he's been standing there watching me watch Rylee.

"What? Why would I be at the track?" He's lost me. It's Sunday, a non-race day and no testing scheduled, so why the fuck would I be at the track?

He looks me in the eyes like he always has to judge how I'm doing from what he sees there since talking's not really my forte. And for the first time in forever, he gets this ghost of a smirk and just nods his head like he knows something I don't. He stares at me a moment longer and then hands me the bottle of beer in his hand before sitting down in one of two leather chairs facing the fine-ass view in front of us.

Of the ocean and the women.

"Sit down, son."

Famous fucking last words. I suddenly feel like I'm thirteen again and about to get read the riot act for something or other that I most likely deserve to get punished for. I take a pull on the beer, enjoying my last meal before the sentence is handed down.

I sigh and plop down next to him and repeat my question. "Why would I be at the track?"

"Because that's where you go when you need to think things through."

I look over at him like he's lost it because he sure as fuck is losing me. "Is there something you know that I don't? Like what exactly I'm supposed to be thinking through?"

"You know life is one big scavenger hunt," he says before falling silent. I stare at him as he looks out the window and try to follow the bread crumbs he seems to be dropping here. "Fate hands you a list of things to experience. Ones you never expected, ones that break you, ones that heal you. So many of them you swear you'll never even attempt or want to cross off your list. You get caught up in the day to day, moment to moment, and then one day you look at your list and realize you've unexpectedly completed some of the tasks. It's only then you realize that the brutal truths the scavenger hunt has made you face has not only made you a better person, but has also given you an unforeseen prize when all is finally said and done."

Has he been hitting the bottle today when I didn't know? He's gone from the track to a scavenger hunt. I get he's talking about my life in some context, but I need help connecting the dots here.

"Dad." I sigh the word, part question, part exasperation. Throw me a goddamn bone here.

Rylee laughs and the sound floats inside causing me to look back at her.

Always back to her.

"I'm not going to lie, your list has had some pretty fucked-up shit on it, son."

The way he says it, like he blames himself for the shit he couldn't prevent, stabs at the parts deep inside of me. Parts I'd always thought dead until recently. The kid in me starts to apologize and then I stop myself. Can't apologize if I don't know what the fuck I did wrong, so I just sip my beer and give a noncommittal sound, not wanting him to feel guilty for the demons that came before he could protect me.

"I just think it's time that you look at your list. Take stock of all of those things—expected and unexpected—and look at what extra things you've earned for crossing those items off."

Silence falls between us as his words and what I think they mean start to sink in. The weight that has been lifted from my shoulders. The poison exorcised from my soul. The new chance at life without the demons snipping at my heels.

All because of the defiant as fuck contradiction of a woman my eyes keep drifting back to.

"Sinner and saint," I murmur without thought. My dad either doesn't hear me because he just pulls the beer to his lips and takes another sip or chooses to let my comment slide. And as thoughts connect, puzzle pieces begin to fall in place. "Dad?"

"Hmm?" He doesn't look at me, just keeps his eyes forward when I slide a glance his way.

"What is it you think I'm thinking about?" My voice doesn't sound like mine when I ask it. It's cautious, quiet, and I don't care because all I want to know is his answer.

"How you're going to ask Rylee to marry you."

He delivers the statement so matter-of-factly that it takes a moment for me to register that I'm choking out, "Fucking Christ, Dad!"

Disbelieving laughter follows right behind my words. I scrub my hands over my face, more than aware of his scrutiny, and yet my mind races with his comment. Parts way down deep that I'm not sure I want to acknowledge flutter to life like nerves right before the green flag is waved on race day. Nerves that tell me my adrenaline need is about to get its next fix.

A fix.

A necessity.

Something you can't fucking live without.

Rylee.

Dots connected. Bread crumbs scattered and gone so I can't find my way back again.

The question is, do I want to?

Shit, I've got Becks chewing my ear about it and now my old man starting in. Fuck yes, the thought has crossed my mind. But shit I just realized I'm capable of loving someone, let's not shoot the gun without loading it first.

Ruin a good thing by fucking it up with something that's so bad for so many.

And things are good between us. Like fucking stellar. We've never talked marriage. Never even brought the word up. I told her I wanted to see what life hands us and she was cool with that. Didn't say first comes marriage and shit.

So why all a sudden is the idea mulling around in my head when it's a finish line I swore I was never going to officially cross.

Fuck me running. C'mon, Donavan. Speak the fuck up. Assert yourself. Say hell no instead of wondering what it would feel like to have her name be Rylee Donavan.

"Well, I don't hear you saying no, now do I?" He glances my way, raises his eyebrows, and then leans back to put his feet up on the coffee table.

Ah fuck, he's getting comfortable. I know what this means.

Can't we just back the hell up here? I prefer the guessing game. I can fill in another answer we can get stuck on. Anything but this because it's causing me to think of things I shouldn't be thinking.

I pinch the bridge of my nose and squeeze my eyes shut momentarily as I try to wish the conversation away. And when I do, all I see is that goddamn vision of Rylee in a white dress that Becks's comments at the pool party caused me to think of. And shit, that vision comes back with a vengeance. Veils and rings and shit I shouldn't be thinking of. Shit that's getting way too comfortable as a visitor in my thoughts lately.

I shake my head. Need to clear this nonsense. Rid it of the road this man is never going to race down. So why do I see the metaphorical finish line at the end of the track all of a sudden?

My heart pounds momentarily until I push away the thoughts his words are creating. What the fuck is going on here? Why does my dad have me thinking of scavenger hunts and marriage proposals? *Sweet Jesus.*

"You're not pulling any punches today, are you?"

"I don't believe I threw one," he says, completely unaffected.

Is he fucking kidding me? Must be nice to sit there so calm and collected when he's doling out sucker punches to make a damn point.

I slump down in the chair and rest my head against the back of it, eyes looking up at the pool's reflection on the ceiling. I focus on it as he allows me the silence I need to swish the thoughts around like mouthwash. A necessary evil that burns before it leaves you cleansed.

Marriage.

The word lingers. There's something about it that I can't quite put my finger on. First causing panic, then banging around like a ping pong ball before feeling like that fucking grain of sand in my swim trunks. The one you feel at first, irritating with every movement—your mind thinking of how you need to strip your suit off so you can wash it out—but then as minutes pass to hours, you don't feel it anymore.

It's still there, in that spot right between your nuts and your thigh, and you're kind of okay with it.

And it's all because of her.

Fucking Rylee. I shake my head, one thought more than all others front and center. With temerity and defiance, obstinance and patience, she chipped away at every hard edge of me until there was nothing left but the truths I feared. The bent and broken. The ones buried so goddamn deep I knew they'd push her away.

And yet when all was said and done, when the poison in my soul was lying on the table so she could see how fucking dark it was, she looked me in the eyes and told me I was brave, loved the broken in me. I gave her my darkest and her response was to give me her light. Her love.

I blow out another sigh and scrub my hand over my face, words forming and then dying before I can speak.

"C'mon, Dad, me? Marry someone?" I spit the words out—words that used to be a given fact—so why in the fuck do they feel like lies when they come from my mouth while I'm looking at her?

"I call bullshit. Nice try though."

And there's the knock-out punch.

I stare at him, waiting for him to look at me, wanting the fight to prove he's wrong. To prove that nothing's changed. I can be with Rylee but that's enough for me. No rings, no strings.

But that half-ass smirk is the only reaction he'll give me to the buttons of mine he's pushing with expertise. One by fucking one.

So why doesn't that pitching feeling in my stomach come when I think of it all of a sudden? I have so many fucking excuses why I'll never get married and yet even with the last push of my button, not a single one comes to mind.

The only thing that does cross my mind is the woman sitting feet away, well within perfect reach.

"Life only hands you so many chances, Son. You seem to have used quite a few this year already. I don't think you should take many more for granted." He turns his head now and locks eyes with mine. The man that's sat beside me most in my life, held my hand to help me conquer my biggest fears, called my superheroes with me, is telling me there's one left I have yet to face.

That there's one item left on my scavenger hunt that will give me an even bigger reward than I ever thought I deserved or was imaginable.

Something happens.

Fuck if I can explain it other than that dead calm right before the green flag waves. When your body is amped up on adrenaline, mind is blanking sound out, everything is happening at a lightning-fast speed, but you sit there like time is in slow motion. Calm. Resolute.

At peace.

I force a swallow down my throat, past my heart lodged there, because motherfucker ... this broken man who was once held together with Scotch tape is now rock solid, and it's all because of Rylee.

She may be my kryptonite but fuck if I'm the superhero worthy of her.

His words echo in my head. Pushing me. Questioning me. Making me want things I never expected to want or deserve. Ever. I look down at the label, my fingers playing idly with it as ideas form, possibilities arise.

"How did you know Mom was the one?" I don't give him a yes or no answer that my thoughts just might be veering in the direction his questions ask me about. I keep my head down, needing to get used to this idea myself.

Let the grain of sand irritating my nuts become a bit more familiar first.

I can feel his eyes on me, know he wants me to look up at him, but I can't. Fucking sand isn't all that comfortable just yet.

"How did I know?" He chuckles and the tone of his voice has a corner of my mouth pulling up into a smile. "Your mother walked into the cafeteria on the lot one day. She was an extra and I was an assistant director and she intimidated the hell out of me. She was gorgeous and commanded attention. And then she looked up and smiled at me and I knew. Just like that." He pauses for a beat until I raise my eyes to meet his.

"How did I know? Because I let her in, let her see the good, bad, and ugly about me. I gave your mother the power to destroy me when I fell in love with her, and she didn't. She was my prize at the end of my scavenger hunt. Without her I wouldn't have this," he says, motioning to my sister and then me. He glances out to my mom and smiles softly before looking back at me. "In racing terms, she was my checkered flag, Son."

... I gave her the power to destroy me ...

His words stagger me. Open me. Urge me. Seal a fate I never had control of until now.

He has no idea I call Rylee my checkered flag—no fucking clue—so I'm knocked back a pit stop second, pulse pounding, mind thinking of possibilities that were never mine to think.

I'm so focused on my thoughts and the bottle of beer in my hand, I jump when he cuffs me on the shoulder. "You'll figure it out, Colton. You'll make the right decision when or if you want to." He rises from the chair and stands there looking outside for a moment. "You're a good man. She'd be lucky to have you, just like your mom and I have been."

He starts to walk away, his unending confidence in me still staggering after all this time, after all the shit I've put him through.

Even at my darkest.

"Dad." I don't know why I stop him when the conversation itself has made me uncomfortable, but I do.

He stops but doesn't turn around, his back to me.

Words tumble. Thoughts scramble. But for some reason the ones that never stuck before are the only ones that do now.

"I love you." The words are out without thought, my hands shaking, the little boy in me hoping he hears them.

I immediately hear the hitch of his breath as his whole body freezes. He slowly hangs his head forward, his shoulders shuddering momentarily. He raises his head and nods a couple of times. "And that is my unexpected reward for my scavenger hunt." His voice is thick with emotion. "I love you too, Son." He says it so softly before waiting a beat and walking into the kitchen area.

I exhale the breath I was holding, thankful he didn't make a big deal and embarrass me when he heard the words it's taken me a lifetime to say. Grateful we're so close that he knows what I needed.

I shake my head. Shit, that was intense. All of it. Revelations and confessions I never expected to make all of a sudden fall like rain around me.

Fuckin' A.

I look up and Rylee's eyes lock with mine. The smile comes so naturally to her lips that my body—head and heart—react immediately to her.

And I know.

Just like that.

Something I've spent a lifetime fighting is all of a sudden knocked out by this defiant as fuck woman who owns the heart she showed me could beat again.

Fuck me. I just keep knocking 'em down one right after the other. Might as well tackle this bad boy while I'm on a roll.

My mind starts churning, ideas forming. The scavenger hunt of my life continues. I smile back at her as I stand and just stare.

My future.

My salvation.

The woman I want to marry.

Fuck. That grain of sand just became comfortable.

I guess the plus side is if marriage is sand, at least I know my dick is going to be covered in it.

Chapter Forty-One and 3/4 Bonus Scene

"You can stop driving me to work you know."

"I'm perfectly aware of that but I'm kind of partial to the view I get when you walk towards the house." Curves. Attitude. One helluva package that's now my whole world.

Rylee flashes that smile of hers—pure innocence—but I know the fucking truth behind it. Know the defiant vixen that owns me hook, line, and huge ass sinker. And fuck how I'd love to pull her back into the Range Rover and take her back to our bed—or any convenient location—and have my way with her again.

I can't get enough of her.

Sliding a glance at the back seat, I grin as my mind contemplates the possibilities.

"Dream on, Donavan." She laughs the words and rolls her eyes.

I can think of better ways to make her eyes roll back. That back seat's looking better and better by the second.

She starts to close the door and then stops before looking toward The House where I'm sure at least four pair of eyes are on us before turning those violet eyes back to me. Angling her head to the side, she studies me in silence and now I'm fucking worried that she knows.

But she can't. It's not possible.

Then again falling in love wasn't possible either and look at me now.

"What?" I ask as unaffected as possible despite my thumb beating against the steering wheel. Thank fuck I have sunglasses on or else she'd probably see my eyes widen in fear that's she's caught on.

"I'm okay, Colton. You don't need to worry about me anymore. Zander's dad is gone, I've recovered from . . . everything. Nothing's going to hurt me." The sincerity in her voice plays me like a fucking violin, pulling on the strings I thought that had been broken and irreparable.

Her words make me feel and that in itself is crazy as fuck.

"I know. I like driving you. I like coming in to see the boys when I can...and I love kissing you goodbye."

"Hm. I do especially like that last part." She steps onto the running board and leans into the cab toward me. Our lips meet, tongues touch, and fuck if she's not the sweetest addiction a man can have.

Only this man, though.

And I plan on making that notion a step further today.

We break apart, her taste still on my tongue. "Baby, there's no doubt about that. Have a great shift. Tell the boys I'll come in when I pick you up tomorrow and they better be ready for me to kick their butts on the Xbox, game of their choice."

"I've been warned of the impending overflow of testosterone," she groans.

"You like my overflow of testosterone." I lift my eyebrows, the sound of her laugh turning me one.

Fuck. I've got it bad. Her damn voodoo pussy calling to me on every level: eyes, dick, heart . . . soul.

"Have fun in San Clemente."

My heart stops at her statement. "What?" I cough the word out.

"I heard you on the phone with Becks. Something about going there today."

"Yeah. Yes. Going to lunch with one of the Penzoil reps."

Real smooth, Donavan. Sweet Jesus, why don't you just tell her what you're doing already by overreacting?

"Cool. Have fun." She shuts the door and then looks in the window.

"I love you."

The emotion in her eyes is like an arrow to my heart. Shit, I'm pathetic, thinking cupid and shit. But damn if the words—the ones that used to choke me, make me ill - don't come to my tongue like they can't wait to be said.

"I love you too." She gives me one last smile. The kind that makes my balls and heart constrict. The one that tells me she's mine.

Once the door shuts behind her, I pull away from the curb.

Lunch with the Penzoil reps, my ass.

I'm going to do something that's so not normal for me I'm at a loss.
I'm far from traditional. Way fucking far from it . . .
But this time it matters that I try to be.
This one time I'm going to do something right from the start.
I'm going to ask Rylee's dad for her hand in marriage.

Chapter Forty-Two

I sit back and watch Zander and his counselor work together, and my heart surges at seeing him so actively engaged. He's talking so much now and beginning to heal. I allow the pride I feel to swell and the tears to blur my vision because he's doing it.

He's actually doing it.

I walk from his room where they're having their session and out toward the kitchen, listening to the music in Shane's room and the chatter of the rest of the boys building a Lego city out on the backyard patio. Dane's emptying the last of the silverware from the dishwasher when I walk into the kitchen and plop down on a stool with an exhausted sigh.

"I agree!" he says, closing a drawer and sitting down beside me. "So," he says when I don't say anything. "How's it going with the panty melting Adonis?"

I roll my eyes. "You just wish he was a boxer-brief melting Adonis." I snort.

"Hell to the yeah I do, but I've given up hope that I can turn him to the better side. Only a blind man would miss the way he looks at you."

"Oh, Dane." I sigh, a smile spreading on my lips at just the thought of Colton and how great things have been over the past few weeks. At the comforting rhythm we've settled ourselves into without even speaking about it. Things just feel natural. Like they were meant to be. No more drama, no more lack of communication, and no more hiding secrets. "Things are great. Couldn't be more perfect."

And when I say it, I really believe it. I'm not waiting for the other shoe to drop like before. I'm not expecting anything anymore because if being with Colton has taught me anything, it's that our love isn't patient, nor is it kind, it's just uniquely ours.

"So living together hasn't been a horrible disaster?"

"No," I say with a softness as I think of how it's been quite the opposite. "It's been pretty incredible actually."

"C'mon, the man has to have something that's horrific about him," he teases.

"Nah, he's pretty damn *perfect*," I reply, loving the chance to say perfect again when it comes to Colton and me.

"I don't believe it," he says, smacking a fist to the counter. "He's got to pick his nose or snore horribly or fart like a rhino."

"Nope!" Laughter rocks through me and he tries incredibly hard to not crack a smile but his resolve is short lived.

"You have to be lying, Ry, because no man can be that fucking perfect." He shrugs. "Well, unless of course, it's me."

"Well, of course," I say, laughing and shaking my head. "Let's see ..." I smirk, thinking of something to satisfy him. "He did refuse to buy me a box of tampons on the way home from work the other day."

The look on his face is priceless, lips lax and eyes wide. "The prick!" he spits out in mock disgust before shaking his head. "Shit, he just went up twenty points in my book. Sweetie, you can't ask an alpha-Adonis like him to buy your girly shit. That's the equivalent of asking him to hand over his balls on a platter."

The water in my mouth almost comes out my nose I'm laughing so hard. "Dane!"

"Well it's true." He shrugs. "I'm glad to see they're still firmly attached."

"Yeah." I snort. "Just 'cause you want them."

"Well," he draws out, "we would make a cute couple, and fuck if I don't like balls firmly attached to the people I date."

And my next sip of water isn't as lucky as my last one. I spit it out as laughter forces a spray causing us to laugh even harder. It takes a few minutes for us to settle down because each time one of us looks at the other, we start laughing again.

I'm hung up at the office again. Haddie's picking you up for me. Call you on the way home. Crash My Party, Luke Bryan. - Xx C

My heart soars and soul warms at the song he's texted. My sentimental, alpha male full of continuous contradictions. I sigh to push away my disappointment because I missed him terribly today, but I'm ecstatic about spending a little time with Haddie. I haven't seen her much lately.

I pick up my phone and reply. **I miss you. Hurry home. All of Me, John Legend. -XXX**

I check the clock and realize time's gotten away from me, so I start getting my stuff together and saying my goodbyes to the boys.

When I exit the house she's sitting in her car outside. I open the passenger side door to her squeal of delight. "Well fuck me sideways it's so good to see you!"

"I know!" I tell her as she pulls me in for a quick hug across the console, before gunning the motor and taking off with a laugh.

I throw my head back in a laugh that matches hers and close my eyes for a minute, letting the wind of the open window rush over my face. The wind dissipates as she rolls the window up, and I turn to see her eyes glancing from the road ahead of her over to me.

"Thanks for picking me up. If I had known Colton was going to work late, I wouldn't have let him drop me off. Sorry."

"I know, you're such a pain in the ass!" she says as she flicks her blinker and makes a left turn. "So since Mr. Fine-as-fuck has dumped you for now, how about a few drinks to catch up on things? Like why even though all your things are in our house, you never are … despite you adamantly denying that you've "officially" moved in with him."

I laugh and shake my head. "I don't want to jinx things." I shrug. "You know how I am."

"Yep, I sure do. So that's why we're going to knock back a few so you relax, get loosey-goosey and talk to me."

As much as I want to catch up with her, I'm dead tired. "Why don't we go to his house and we can sit on the deck, look out at the water, and have some wine. Besides," I say, looking down at my T-shirt and jeans, "I'm not dressed for a bar."

"Exactly what I thought you'd say," she says, reaching behind my seat and grabbing something. She places a tote bag on my lap. When I look over at her, she just smirks. "Nice try, Ry, but we're going out for drinks." She nods her head at the bag. "A shirt, sexy shoes, and makeup."

"What?" I say, surprised but at the same time not surprised that she's going to get her way.

"Hussy-up baby! I'm a driving and time's a wasting." I laugh and shake my head at her. "You'll thank me before the night is through." We slow to a stop at a light and she picks up her phone and sends a quick text, before putting it down and looking over at me. "You're not getting out of this, Thomas. I miss my friend, I want a drink, end of story."

The light changes and she takes off as a smile spreads on my lips. God, I love her.

I don't really pay attention to where we're going because I'm looking in the visor mirror and fixing my makeup and primping my hair. Haddie's only input is "Leave it down," when I try to put it up in a clip. We chat about this and that, to catch each other up on the day to day. I'm zipping up my pouch of makeup when my phone rings.

I fumble with it clumsily when I see it's Colton. My immediate thought is that he's done with work and can meet up with us for a drink.

"Hi!" I say as I shove everything back into the bag at my feet on the floor.

"Hey, sweetheart."

And just the sound of his voice causes a wave of love to wash over me. "Are you done with work?"

"I lied," he says, and I'm immediately confused. "I'm not working because I'm busy planning the perfect date for you, so look up because that date starts right now."

I snap my head up and cannot contain the sob that catches in my throat as I take in the dirt field and the quiet carnival in front of me. The motionless Ferris wheel, the vacant Midway, the locked turnstiles

"Colton … what … why?" I attempt to ask as astonishment passes through me, his amused chuckle resonating through the line.

"We haven't been on a real date since our night at the carnival, so I thought this would be the most fitting way to start this one. I know you're not good with the unknown, but promise me you'll go with it. For me."

What? Holy hell! "Yes … of course," I stutter.

"See you soon," he says and the line goes dead.

I immediately look to Haddie who has the hugest grin on her face. "You!" I say to her, my voice breaking from so many overwhelming emotions. "You knew?"

"Do men have penises?" She laughs with mock abhorrence. "Of course I'm in on it!"

I just sit in the car with my mouth hanging open, as I look around and my mind tries to process this. Tries to process how the man that swears he isn't romantic is a hopeless romantic at heart. "How ... what?" I try to spit out the questions my head is forming, but they're not coming out.

"Colton thought you deserved a real date—a night out to thank you for hanging with him through everything so he asked for a little help." She shrugs. "I agreed with him, so here we are."

Tears well in my eyes as I breathe in deeply, still trying to comprehend that I'm sitting at the same carnival seven months later. While I sit stunned, Haddie reaches behind my seat and produces a box larger than a shoebox.

I laugh. "Do you have a whole store back there?"

"Nope. This is the last thing." She places the box in my hand and I cough out a nervous laugh, not because I'm actually nervous, but because of my dislike for the unknown and my need for control.

Colton knows me so well.

I sit there and stare at the rectangular gray box and can't help the soft smile that graces my lips as I recall something Colton told me a long time ago—*sometimes not being in control can be extremely liberating.*

"Jesus, woman, open the damn box already, will you? The suspense is killing me!" Haddie says beside me, her body vibrating with anticipation.

I let out a deep breath and crack open the top like something is going to jump out at me. And when I lift the top off, an envelope sits atop some black and white checkered tissue paper, my name written on it. I lift it up and slide the paper out of it.

Ryles-

I know you're probably wondering what in the hell is going on, so let me try and explain. You always put everyone else first—me, the boys, the stray dog on the corner—so I thought it was time to switch places and let you be the one front and center. So with the help of others, I've put together a bit of a scavenger hunt for you. In order to get to the prize, you have to follow and answer all of the clues.

Good luck.

Here's your first clue: The carnival is the place I knew you were so much more than I'd ever expected. I knew sitting atop the Ferris wheel with you that no matter how hard I was fighting it, I couldn't do casual with you and that you deserved so much more than that from me. So the first item is waiting for you at the first ride we went on.

Love,

Colton

I wipe away the tears that slide down my cheeks without messing the makeup I'd just put on, but it's damn near impossible. Haddie reaches over and squeezes my forearm to help steady my trembling hands. I look over at her trying to comprehend what it took for Colton to organize all of this, as well as put the words he has a hard time expressing verbally to paper.

"Get your ass out of the car and go find your man before I have a heart attack from the anticipation," she says as she pushes my shoulder toward my open car door.

I slide out of the car, my heart pounding and head trying to understand that he cares enough about me to do this. I walk up to the gated entry to find a single turnstile unlocked. I walk through it and into the eerily deserted carnival, my pace starting to quicken with each step as memories flood back to me. Stuffed dogs, stolen kisses, and cotton candy. Dares to a bad boy who had already captured my heart even though I didn't want to admit it just yet. Fears and firsts and a shy, lopsided grin on his magnificent face.

I reach the ride section and head for the Tilt-A-Whirl. I let out a gasp as Shane and Connor step out of the shadowed ticket booth with huge grins on their faces and a box in their hands.

My hand presses to my chest from utter shock and absolute adoration at Colton for including my boys in his scavenger hunt. For allowing them to help him do something nice for me. "You guys!" I exclaim as I jog over to where they stand and take in the mischievous looks in their eyes. "You kept this from me?" I step forward and hug both of them tightly as we all laugh.

"We were sworn to secrecy," Shane says, blushing.

"Colton said we wouldn't get in trouble for lying to you either," Connor adds, shaking his head.

"No." I laugh, completely overwhelmed by everything. "You'd never get in trouble for something like this."

Shane clears his throat and I look over to him. "We have your next clue."

"Oh, okay," I say with a laugh, my nerves returning.

"You have to answer this question right in order to get the next clue, okay?" I nod. "When you see this item, which Con is going to hold up, what one word answer comes to your mind?"

Connor holds up a yellow, rubber ducky and I erupt into a fit of giggles, fresh tears appear at the corners of my eyes. I shake my head trying to staunch my laughter but can't when I say, "Quack!"

And more recollections hit of shouting and hurt cutting through the morning chill on the front lawn of the Palisades house to a hotel room in Florida and my menagerie of animals I threw at Colton when trying to preserve my heart from misconceived truths. Of being so stubborn I didn't really listen, didn't hear what he was telling me.

But I'm listening now. He's not the only one who's learned during our time together.

Connor and Shane let out a little cheer and they hand me another envelope in which I hurriedly tear open. It says: ***The memories this next clue remind me of are burned in my mind just as much as the ink of my tattoos. And you were sexy as fuck. Damn! "In case you need a little sweetener after I dirty you up." Where exactly would you buy that?***

Everything below the waist tightens at the memory of Colton and cotton candy and I smile at the thought and then feel weird thinking those thoughts near the boys. "Are you guys going to be okay?" I ask them immediately.

They roll their eyes. "We're not here alone," Shane says. "Now go figure out the clues!"

"Okay," I say as my excitement mounts. I kiss both boys on the top of their heads and jog through the fair looking everywhere for a vendor cart that has cotton candy on it. And with every step, I look for and expect to find Colton and his impish grin waiting to surprise me.

But there's nothing.

I start to get panicked at the quiet calm of the grounds. After a bit of wandering I turn a corner and look up to see a lone funnel of cotton candy hanging from a stand. As I get closer I cry out when I see Ricky and Jackson standing in aprons and smiles.

"I can't wait any longer!" Ricky says, fidgeting behind the counter and handing me another box as both Jax and I laugh at his excitement to be a part of this.

I set the box down and open it to find an auction paddle that says: **Go back to where it all began. Where I learned defiance can be pretty damn sexy.**

I shake my head again, feeling like I'm having an out of body experience as I say goodbye to them. I walk as fast I can out to the parking lot, to where Haddie is sitting behind the wheel, eyebrows raised and fingers drumming in anticipation.

I slide into the car to her repeating "Tell me, tell me." Over and over. I tell her to drive where the date auction charity gala took place and then fill her in on the two clues I'd received at the carnival. She's bouncing in her seat with enthusiasm while I sit here wide-eyed and shocked at Colton's sweet surprise.

"Well shit, that bonk on the head at the race in Florida sure as fuck helped him in the romance department." She laughs. "I think it might become a mandatory thing for the penis-poking gender!"

I laugh with her. "You really didn't know about this part?" I ask Haddie several times.

"Ry, he told me he had a cool date planned for you and asked if I'd be your chauffeur for part of it. So I'm here, and I so can't wait to see what else he has in store for you!" she says, reaching over and running her hands over the words of the auction paddle. It's sitting on my thigh and I can't stop staring at it.

The stars must be aligned because we avoid Los Angeles traffic and make it to the old theater in record time. "I'll be waiting right here!" she yells as I climb out of the car with the paddle in my hand and jog to the grand front doors of the old theater to find one of them ajar.

I enter the familiar foyer and look around as I walk toward the door to the right of the stage like I did that night so many months ago. I start humming out of habit to Matchbox Twenty's *Overjoyed* playing softly on the speakers overhead. It has to be a complete coincidence because even Colton couldn't time my arrival this perfectly, but it makes me smile at how perfect it is that *my group* is playing. I blink back tears as the significance of this moment takes hold—Colton leading me back here after all this time where something I never really wanted to happen, actually started.

And look at us now.

I swallow the burn of tears in my throat as I push through the door and into the lit backstage hallway. And suddenly my tears are replaced with an uncontrollable fit of giggles when I see caution tape over the little alcove where Bailey tried to seduce him. And more hilarious than the caution tape is the little sign that says "Beware, piranhas lurking."

I'm still laughing as I turn the corner to see *the* storage closet door propped open and a light on inside. My heeled boots click on the linoleum as I try to figure out who is going to meet me this time. A part of me wants it to be Colton so I can kiss him and hug him and thank him for all of this, but at the same time I don't think I'm ready for this walk down memory lane to end just yet.

And the giggles return when I see Aiden and my co-counselor Austin sitting in chairs just inside the closet playing Uno. Aiden jumps up with a squeal when he sees me, and Austin and I laugh at his enthusiastic reaction.

"Hi, guys!"

"Rylee," he shouts out in excitement. "Here! This is for you!"

He fumbles as he hands an envelope and two boxes to me. One very small on top of a larger one. I look at both Aiden and Austin, their anticipatory grins matching mine as I set the boxes on the table and tear open the envelope. Colton's familiar penmanship greets me: **You were the first person to ever look at me and really see into my soul. And it scared the ever-loving shit out of me. Where did this happen? If you need a clue, it's in the top box. (Open the larger box once you leave the theater.)—C**

My heart is pounding and my hands are trembling with excitement. I know the answer. He's referring to the Penthouse where we had sex for the first time after the Merit Rum party, but nothing prepares me for what is inside the first box.

My breath catches and I instinctively lift a hand to cover my mouth before I reach out and lift the lone earring from it. The earring I couldn't find that night as I tried to gather my dignity and leave the hotel room. The earring I left, never caring if I saw it again or the man now giving it back to me.

Something about the sight of the earring and the fact that he kept it all this time, kept it when I walked out on him, causes so many emotions to surface I can barely speak as I thank Aiden and Austin before picking up the other box and hurrying back to Haddie and our next destination.

I climb in the car, stunned and bewildered, as I tell Haddie about the significance of the earring. She starts to drive to the hotel as I tear open the larger of the two boxes. And the air punches from my lungs from laughter as I look into a box of all the panties that have been ripped off me. Included in the box is another envelope that takes me a minute to open because I'm laughing so hard at the memories they evoke, and the fact that he actually kept them all.

"Geez, woman! You weren't kidding when you said the man put a dent in your drawers!" she teases as she nods her head, urging me to open the envelope.

I tear it open and a gift card falls out to La Perla for a ridiculous amount of money. The note wrapped around the gift card is worth ten times more to me though. It says: **You better buy a large supply, Ry, because I don't see my need to have you when, where, and how I want stopping any time soon.**

The blatant sensuality of his words causes an ache of desire to coil and spring to life between my thighs that I don't even bother to ignore.

"Wow!" Haddie drawls, breaking me from my less than pure thoughts as she looks over and reads the card while we're at a stoplight. "The man is that fucking hot *and* has a dirty, dominant mouth like that?" She draws in a shaky breath. "Shit, Ry ... I'd tell him to handcuff me to the bed and let me be his sex slave for life." She laughs.

I'm feeling a little blown away that this man is most definitely mine. "Who says I haven't?" I say with a smirk on my lips and a raise of eyebrows.

"Well hot damn!" she says, slapping my thigh. "That's my girl talking!"

We laugh together and try to figure out what the next clue at the hotel is going to be until she pulls up into the valet circle. "I'm assuming I'll be right back," I tell her as I climb out and jog into the lobby before I suddenly stop. I just can't go up to the Penthouse and knock on the door.

I head over to the front desk and when I approach, a woman eyes me up and down. "Ms. Thomas, I presume?"

"Yes ..." I reply, a little astounded she knows who I am.

"This way please," she says, leading me to a private elevator on the side of the lobby. She takes out a key card and presses it to the scanner causing the door to open. "There you go," she says, her stoicism breaking as she grins broadly at me before walking back to her desk.

"Thank you," I call out to her before stepping in. The familiar décor inside the car causes memories to flood back from our first time, my nerves heighten from the dark promise of the words Colton said to me as we made the same ascent in a different elevator. The car dings when I reach the top floor and I exit, unable to fight my smirk over the desperation-filled, clumsy exit we made that night.

I knock on the Penthouse door and hear a giggle from behind it as the knob starts to turn. Zander opens the door with Avery standing behind them, both have beaming smiles as they look at me. And the carefree giggle that falls from Zander's mouth warms my overflowing heart even more.

"Hi, guys! Let me guess, you have a clue for me?"

Zander nods his head frantically as he looks over at Avery to see if it's okay to give me what's in his hands.

"Hey, Rylee."

"Hi!"

"Okay, our clue is, what one word first comes to your mind when you see what Zander has?"

I look down as Zander produces a small black box from behind his back and holds it out to me. I look down at it, as perplexed as the look on Avery's face, until Zander flips it over.

And then I laugh.

The box contains a fire engine red pocket square for a tuxedo. My senses are suddenly assaulted with every sensation Colton evoked from me in the limo that night, when we were overdressed and underdressed. But that can't be the answer because that's two words. "Anticipation!" I almost shout when the word hits me like lightning, images of that more than memorable evening flashing through my mind.

"Bingo!" Avery cries out as Zander hops up and down.

"Good job, Ry!" he says as he holds out another box and envelope to me. I look at him with a furrowed brow that has him giggling again before I take it from him.

"This is for me?" I ask him.

"Uh-huh!" he says, nodding his head.

"You're sure?"

"Yes! Just open it!" he says with amused exasperation.

I slide my finger across the envelope and smile before I even know what it says because I know Colton's words are going to touch me.

Ry- I always knew you were different than the others ... but this is the night you became my checkered flag. Without a doubt. Here's to the night I knew the one thing I never wanted, I'd fight like hell to keep. Go where you first became familiar with the object in the box.—C

I cautiously open it and roll my eyes and shake my head when I see a scale model of a red F12 Ferrari. I know exactly where I'm going next because that night is most definitely one I'll never forget.

I say my goodbyes and vibrate with anticipation as I ride the elevator down to the lobby and hurry past a smirking hostess at the front desk and out to the car. I slide in and tell Haddie about the clue and laugh when she shakes her head as she drives the few blocks to the hotel where the other gala I attended with Colton is.

I direct her to drive to the top floor of the parking garage and instinctively suck in a breath when Sex comes into view. Images and emotions fill me and I don't even try to stifle the sigh they evoke in me.

"Damn that car is like a fucking visual orgasm," she says with a hum of appreciation.

"You have no idea," I drawl then whistle and am left blushing as I slide out and walk the short distance to its isolated spot in the garage. As I get closer I see a figure behind one of the columns beside the car and my heart leaps in my throat. I hope it's Colton. I've had enough of memory lane, and as much as I love this right now, I just want him. Desperately.

I laugh as Beckett steps out, a shit-eating grin spread wide across his handsome face. He looks over my shoulder at Haddie and nods his head subtly at her, his grin softening to a smolder that has my curiosity piqued, but my attention is diverted quickly when Becks talks.

"Well, I'm not sure what you've done to my man," he says, giving me a quick hug, "since his balls seem to have retracted, judging by this overt display, but fuck if I don't love it!"

"I'm sure you're giving him tons of shit," I tell him, and he just angles his head and looks at me for a second, a softness settling over his features.

"It's the happiest I've ever seen him," he says with a nod.

And before I even think of what I'm saying, the words are out of my mouth. "But why do you think that is?" I ask.

He just laughs that low chuckle of his and holds out a white plastic bag with humor in his eyes. I take the bag from him and look into it. It takes my mind a moment to figure out what I'm looking at. "Because I'm the whole alphabet," I whisper as I gaze at the plastic preschool letters.

"A to motherfucking Z, Ry," he says, causing my head to snap up so I catch the wink that he gives me mixed with a lazy, lopsided grin. I just look at him, a stupid smile on my face. "So, I am in charge of getting you to your next destination," he says.

I immediately look over my shoulder and am surprised to see Haddie's car gone. I was so caught up with Becks that I didn't even hear her leave. He motions for me to get in and I oblige. The minute that our seat belts are fastened and the engine roars to life, Becks looks over at me. "Where is the one place you proved to Colton that rookies can drive for the win?"

I laugh immediately, thinking of our intimate exchange about rookies and racing before realizing that Colton's referring to a more innocent time with the boys. "Go-kart track!" I shout as we head out of the parking garage and onto the side streets.

"Yes, ma'am," he tells me as we merge onto the freeway and lose the traffic behind us. We talk about this and that, but regardless of how hard I try, I can't get Becks to tell me what the rest of the clues are or the end game for this evening. He just smirks at me and shakes his head.

In no time, we arrive at the industrial park where Colton took the boys and me go-karting. "I'll be right here," Becks says as I hop out and enter through the glass door.

My smile widens as I see Dane and Scooter leaning against the counter. "Rylee!" Scooter yells and runs to hug me.

I squeeze him tight and kiss the top of his head before I arch an eyebrow at Dane. "You knew and didn't say anything to me!" I tell Dane, eliciting a belly-giggle from my sweet Scooter.

"Some things are worth being secretive about," he says with a shrug and a smirk before pushing off the counter to hand Scooter a bag.

I shake my head at him with a fake glare that makes him laugh. I don't say anything further because Scooter is basically bouncing out of his shoes with excitement. "Okay, Scoot ... you gonna help me figure this one out?"

"Can I?" he asks.

"Of course!" I tell him as I reach in the bag and lift out a plastic action figure of Spiderman. Tears immediately prick the back of my eyes, despite the soft smile forming on my lips.

"What's the answer? What does Spidey make you think of?"

And I think for a second because there are two possible answers, but given that Scooter's way of saying I love you was the catalyst that started all of this, I say, "I Spiderman you!" And I know immediately when his face falls that I got the answer wrong, but I don't care because I still got to tell him I love him. So then I try my other guess. "Spiderman. Batman. Superman. Ironman."

"Yay!" he shouts, jumping up and down before hugging me tightly as Dane and I laugh.

Dane looks up and meets my eyes as he holds out an envelope. "I guess things are as *perfect* as they seem."

"Imperfectly perfect," I tell him with a quiet smile as I open up the envelope.

Why the superheroes? Because after that night at the track, I'm not scared anymore. My childhood comfort isn't needed because I have you, Ry. It's your name I chant now, not theirs. The clue to your next location: "Welcome to the big leagues, Ace."

I laugh at the memory of him telling me this, of turning my lame attempt at seduction back around on me, all the while reeling from the other words that he's written. That he holds me in as high of a regard as he does his beloved superheroes. My heart is so swollen with love that it's bursting at the seams. When I look up to meet Dane's eyes through my tear blurred vision, he says nothing but his eyes say it all. *He's the one.*

I say my rushed goodbyes and hurry outside to the sexy purr of the F12. I slide into the seat and look over at a grinning Beckett. "Where to next, Ry?"

"The Surf Shack," I tell him with a shake of my head as we just stare at each other for a beat.

"*What?*" he asks as he angles his head at me.

I breathe in deeply and stare out the windshield for a moment, taking it all in. "Nothing, I'm just trying to process all this ... it's just overwhelming."

"Yeah well," he says, gunning the engine at the stoplight, "it appears Hell sure as fuck has frozen over." He laughs and I join in, laying my head back on the head rest. I'm thankful that Becks allows me the silence to collect my thoughts and reflect on everything Colton's told me so far today.

We pull into the parking lot and my mind immediately remembers taking Tanner here and Colton's near fight with him. Of the overabundance of testosterone and the shocked look on his face when I left him standing alone outside in rejection. I look over at Becks and the look on his face seems to be saying "*Well, go on then.*"

I climb out and enter the restaurant to find Rachel standing at the hostess podium. Her grin is huge and she immediately says, "Your table is waiting for you."

"Thanks, Rachel," I say as I hurry past her to see what my next surprise is. I assume it's Kyle since he's the one boy I haven't seen yet. I walk out onto the patio and think back on getting to know Colton during our first time here, learning about his past, his family, and how he likes me *laid-back*.

When I look up through the cloud of memories I see Quinlan and Kyle sitting at the table—our table—with grins as wide as the ocean at their back. "Hi, guys!"

"Hey, Ry," Quinlan says the same time Kyle greets me. "So ... we have another clue for you."

"Your brother is something else," I say affectionately.

"Yeah, I think so," she says with a laugh. "But then again, love will do that to you." Her eyes well with tears as they meet mine, and I see a softness there, an acceptance, a thank you.

Kyle interrupts our silent exchange by shoving another box toward me. "Open it, open it!" he says. "You have to give the right answer to get the next clue!"

I slide the lid off the box and start laughing when I see a set of sheets, sheets with the alphabet on them. Quin looks at me oddly and says, "I sure hope there's a good explanation for that one because it seems rather odd to us outsiders."

"Oh there is definitely a good explanation." I laugh, impressed that he didn't forget anything on this scavenger hunt. I look over at Kyle. "Nothing between us but sheets."

"Woohoo!" he says, jumping up and almost knocking over the table. Quinlan steadies the table and wraps an arm over his shoulders with a laugh. "She got it right!" he tells Quin. She responds with a nod and he hands an envelope over to me.

"Should I open this?" I ask, although my fingers are already itching to rip it apart.

"Yes!" he cries, startling other patrons in the restaurant.

I tear it open and read the note inside:

Ry- I knew more than ever when I couldn't have you, how much I couldn't live without you. I might not have said it with words, but I thought about it often. Where were we when we talked about "Nothing between us ever again except for sheets?"

I feel like I have a permanent smile plastered to my face as I say my goodbyes and make my way back out to Beckett in the waiting car. "Well?" he asks with a tilt of his head.

"Broadbeach Road!"

We head up the coast, and as we draw closer, my excitement rises. I'm certain Colton is waiting for me.

Chapter Forty-Three

As we drive down Broadbeach, I'm excited and nervous and every emotion in between. The gates open before we reach them, and I don't even give Beckett a chance to stop completely before I'm out of the car and running toward the front door where Sammy stands.

"Hi, Sammy!" I say almost out of breath as I wait for him to move away from the door.

"Don't you want your next clue?" His deep voice rumbles and I think my mouth falls lax and shoulders sag because I thought there were no more clues. I thought I was in the homestretch and on my way to see Colton.

"Sure," I force out. Without thinking, I suddenly cover my face to block it from whatever Sammy is throwing up into the air. For a minute it doesn't register with me. The tiny sparkles of silver reflecting against the sun's rays and then it hits me. Every part of my body stands at attention as goose bumps blanket my body. And it seems so funny really, that this strong, intimidating man is standing amid a rainfall of sparkle. It's priceless in more ways than one, because it's *glitter in the air.*

The sob strangles in my throat as a smile spreads across Sammy's face as he holds out a box to me. I take it from him, words robbed, and my heart tumbling fearlessly. When I open the box, the tears I have held don't stand a chance because inside is a coffee mug filled with sugar cubes.

And it may be corniness at its finest but the thought that Colton heard me that night, heard me tell him the significance of the bridge of Pink's song and is saying it back to me right now on top of all of the other gestures he's made tonight wrecks me.

Undoes me, lays me wide open, and completes me with a single, ugly pink coffee mug filled with sugar cubes.

"So?" Sammy asks, trying to suppress the grin on his face at my overemotional reaction to this tacky clue.

"*You called me sugar,*" I tell him with a wavering voice and a smile on my face.

"Attagirl!" He laughs and steps aside, opening the door behind him. "Last clue." My eyes flash up to his. "Go where you first heard this with Wood."

"Thanks, Sammy!" I yell over my shoulder as I run like a madwoman through the house and up the stairs. My heart is pounding and my hands are shaking and my mind is reeling, desperate to see him, touch him, kiss him, thank him, but when I reach the patio it's empty except for hundreds of lit candles sprinkled over every imaginable surface.

I gasp at the beauty of the soft lights twinkling amidst the darkening sky as I walk into the upstairs terrace. I run my finger over the top of a chaise lounge as I hear *Glitter in the Air* floating softly on the speakers above and laugh.

"Fuckin' Pink." It's his amused voice, that rasp that washes over me, holding me a willing hostage, and as much as it startles me, it makes me feel at home.

"Fuckin' Pink," I repeat as I turn to face Colton—the man I love with all of my heart—standing before me with the sunset at his back haloing his dark features in its soft light. So many emotions surge through me as he stands there, hands shoved deep in the pockets of his worn denim jeans, his favorite T-shirt covering his shoulders leaning casually against the doorjamb, and that half-shy smile that melts my heart gracing his lips.

"Did you have a good day?" he asks casually as his eyes rake up and down the length of my body, his tongue darting out to wet the lips he's fighting not to turn into a full blown smirk.

And God how I want to run into his arms and kiss him senseless, my body vibrating with both an emotional and physical need so strong that I squeeze my hands around the coffee mug to prevent myself from giving in. "I was kind of sent on a wild goose chase, but I'm pretty sure I'm right where I belong now."

"Hmm ..." He pushes off the wall and saunters slowly my way, sex personified and then some. "And where would that be?" he asks with an arch of his brow.

His nonchalance is killing me, burning a hole right through the fire raging inside of me. All I want to do is devour this man. This man who put thoughts and words and mementos of our time together and wrapped them up in one neat package for me to unravel piece by piece, allowing me to remember the significance of each and every one. And more importantly, he remembered each and every one. That they all matter to him as much as they do to me.

"Right here," I breathe. "I belong right here with you, Colton." I step toward him—my need, my fix, my eternal addiction—and reach out to place my hand on his cheek when all I really want is to pull him to me and hold on forever. "Thank you," I tell him, our bodies mere inches apart but our hearts undeniably connected. "I'm speechless."

He lets his smile spread and reaches out to play with a curl resting on my shoulder. I watch as his eyes follow his fingers. The fact that he seems nervous over my compliment, makes him that much sweeter, and this whole evening that much more meaningful.

After a beat, his eyes move slowly back to mine, crystal green swimming with emotion, a soft shrug of his shoulders. "You are the most selfless person I know. I just wanted to do something to show you how much it means to me. I wanted the boys to be a part of it all so they can show you how much it means to them too."

Tears well in my eyes for the hundredth time today, and I swallow down the lump in my throat as I look at this man so beautiful inside and out. A man I once thought arrogant, who only looked out for himself. A man that proved me wrong in spades.

Or I guess I should say in aces.

I rub my thumb back and forth on his cheek and smile at him. "I'm floored … overwhelmed really … by everything you put into this." I look down for a minute to try and steady the waver in my voice. "No one's ever done something like this for me before."

He leans in and brushes the sweetest of kisses against my lips. I try to deepen the kiss, ravenous for the rest of him, the sound of his sigh, the heat of his touch, but he pulls back, kisses the top of my nose, and then rests his forehead against mine. He brings his other hand up to match the first, fingertips tangled in my hair while palms cradle my jaw.

"So a first of sorts," he says, the heat of his breath warming my lips.

"Yes." I release a shaky breath, my heart pounding.

"Good, because, Ry, I want to be your first, your last, and every fucking thing in between." He emphasizes each word as if it almost pains him to say them.

My heart squeezes because the hopes and dreams I've wished for us are now a possibility, but before I can truly grasp the reality of this, he leans back and looks into my eyes. He stares at me with such intensity, that it's like he's seeing me for the first time, and then he asks me a question that I wasn't expecting. "Why do you love me, Rylee?"

I jostle my head and look back at him, so many things passing through my mind that I can't get the words out, so I just laugh. He looks at me oddly, and I take advantage of the break to catch him off guard and grab the back of his neck to pull him down to me.

My lips are on his in a heartbeat, my tongue slipping between his parted lips and melding with his. I can feel his surprise in the tightening of his lips, but it dissipates in seconds as his hands reach out to mimic mine and tangle in my curls as we slip into the gentle tenderness of the kiss. I show him why I love him with the caress of my tongue, the satisfied moan in my throat, my unrequited need to always have more from him.

And although it's not nearly enough for me, I pull back with his taste on my tongue and look him in the eyes. "I love you, Colton Donavan, for so many reasons." I have to stop because emotion overwhelms me and I want him to see my eyes when I say this to him so that he knows with certainty why I feel how I feel.

"I love you for who you are, for everything you aren't, for where you came from, and for where you want to go." I let a soft smile play over my lips as I look at him, the man I love so much, and allow myself to feel everything that I'm telling him. "I love your little boy smirk hidden beneath your bad boy sneer. I love you because you've let me in, handed me your heart, trusted me with your secrets, and let me see the side of you that no one else has gotten to … *you've let me be your first.*" My voice breaks on the last words and tears pool in my eyes as I stare at him, overcome with emotion.

"I love that you have an affection for cotton candy and sexy-ass cars. I love this dimple right here..." I lean up and lay a kiss where it's hiding "...and I love this right here," I say, running my hand over the stubble on his face. "And I love these right here when you're hovering over me, about to make love to me," I say, squeezing his biceps as he flexes them for me and flashes me a smile. "But more than anything, I love what's in here." I lean forward and press a kiss to his chest where his heart thunders beneath my lips. I keep them pressed there momentarily before I look up at him beneath my eyelashes and finish the most important reason of all. "Because what's in here, Colton, is pure and good and untouched and so incredibly beautiful it leaves me speechless, like it did today … like it is right now."

He stares at me, muscle pulsing in his jaw as he tries to accept everything that I've just said to him.

Our eyes are locked, our souls are bared, and our hearts are so accepting of everything the other is that we're lost in our unspoken words.

Within a heartbeat he pulls me into him, wraps his arms around me, and holds on tight. "*Fuck, I love you*," he says, his face is buried in the curve of my neck, and I can feel the unevenness of his heated breath as he tries to compose himself.

The desperation of his touch and in his words cements everything between us as we cling to each other.

"This is what I mean," he murmurs, pressing a kiss to the side of my neck, his mouth a whisper from my ear. "Tonight's supposed to be about you—completely about you—and yet you just gave me so much that I can barely fucking breathe right now."

He leans back and the emotion in his eyes is overpowering. Little boy, grown man, and rebellious rogue are all looking at me right now, all telling me they love me. He takes in a deep breath and forces a swallow.

"It's impossible to be around you, Ry, and not be moved by you somehow, someway. You leave me tongue-tied and make my goddamn stomach twist in knots half the time." He shakes his head and I smile at him, so touched by his compliments. He reaches out and moves a piece of hair from my face. "You loved me at my darkest," he whispers, and steals my breath.

The stark reality of his words cause goose bumps to dance over my flesh and I'm speechless. His eyes glisten with moisture as he bites his bottom lip, before finding the words he needs to finish expressing himself.

"You loved me when I hated myself. When I pushed you away and tried to hurt you so that you couldn't see … everything from my past. You accepted my fear and loved me because of it." He shakes his head. "And then you grabbed my balls and told me *non-negotiable*." We both laugh at his words, the levity of the comment allowing us to expel some of the pent up energy from this unexpectedly intense conversation.

"That still goes by the way," I say to him with a smirk, and he leans forward and brushes his lips against mine.

"I …" He sighs. "Ry, you have given me so fucking much and today I just wanted to let you know that I get it. That I accept it now and feel it in return." He shoves a hand through his hair and closes his eyes for a beat, followed by that shy smile I love returning to his lips.

He starts to speak and then stops to clear the emotion strangling his words before he looks back up and meets my eyes. "You gave me hope when I thought I was hopeless. You taught me that defiance is sexy as fuck, that curves are definitely my kryptonite, and that *fuck blondes*, because brunettes are way more fun." I laugh, enjoying the return of my arrogant bad boy as he scrubs his hands over his face, the scratch of stubble grating through the air. "I'm fucking rambling here … not making much sense, so bear with me."

"There's nowhere else I'd rather be, Colton," I tell him as he leads me to a chaise lounge. I sit down and he leans on his knees, on the ground in front of me, his body between the V of my thighs, his hands holding onto my waist.

"Ry, I asked you why you love me, but what I really wanted was to tell you all the reasons I love you. It's important for me to know you don't doubt my feelings for you … because fuck, Ry, you've knocked me on my ass. You were the one thing I never wanted—never, ever expected in my life—and fuck if I can live without you now." He laughs at his admission while my smile widens. "You test me and tempt me and make me look at the truths I don't want to face and are stubborn as hell, but God, baby, I wouldn't want you any other way. Wouldn't want *us* any other way." He places his hands on my shoulders, his thumbs caressing the hollow between my collarbones as he shakes his head and continues.

"I think I always knew you were so much *more* … but I knew I was in love with you the night of the Kids Now event … you stood in that garden and pushed me to take a chance … dared me to love you." His voice breaks with the emotion from remembering that night.

"And then we had sex on *Sex*," I add in with a laugh that earns me a sexy as hell groan from deep in his throat.

"Fuck, Ry, between stairwells and car hoods and cotton candy, I'll never be able to escape thinking about you," he drawls.

"That was my plan all along," I tease with a smirk.

"Oh really? You've been playing me this whole time?"

"Uh-huh," I say. "Hate the game and not the player, right?" I laugh. "Welcome to the big leagues, Ace." The comment is off my tongue in a flash, and my sarcasm is rewarded by the grin I love spreading wide on his lips. He shakes his head, leans in to tease my lips with his, and surprises me by deepening the kiss. His tongue tempts and tantalizes me, desire coiling and need clenching every muscle south of my waist before he pulls back.

"See," he whispers, "this is why I love you. It's not the big things you do but the million fucking little things that you don't even know you're doing. It's making me laugh because you know I'm uncomfortable talking about this kind of shit and being okay with it. It's for making me see the world in a different light, like ice cream for breakfast and pancakes for dinner type of light." He shakes his head and looks down momentarily.

"And this is why I love you," I tell him. "Because no matter how uncomfortable you are expressing yourself, you know I need to hear it and you're trying ... hell you knocked it out of the park today. It was—you are—perfect."

"I'm so far from perfect, Ry" he says with a self-deprecating laugh.

I reach out and touch him, run my hand over the line of his jaw. "You're my kind of perfect, Colton."

He smiles softly at me, his eyes suddenly becoming so intense and serious. "No, I don't think you get it, Ry, and I don't know how else to say it ..." He reaches out and cups my face again, holding my head with unsteady hands so that my eyes lock with his. "I want to be your motherfucking checkered flag, Rylee. Your pace car to lead you through tough times, your pit stop when you need a break, your start line, your finish line, *your goddamn victory lane.*"

His words have stolen mine and feed the need I've had since our first meeting. As much as I tried to fight the feeling that fateful night, I wanted to be his. Wanted so much more than a make-out session in a backstage hallway. I wanted the whole frickin' race with him.

"Your trophy," I muse with a soft smile, thinking back to our conversation the morning after our first time together, and I know he remembers, because he returns the same smiles back at me.

"No," he whispers as he leans forward and presses his lips to mine. "You're so much more than a trophy, Rylee. Trophies are inconsequential when all is said and done ... but you? *You could never be inconsequential.*" I can feel his lips curve up to a smile.

"No, you and me together ... *that would make you mine,*" I tell him with a smile of my own as I contribute a memorable moment from our past myself.

"Good one," he concedes, leaning back with a devilish smirk on his handsome face. "My turn," he says, licking his lips before his grin returns. "Is there anyone whose ass I have to kick before I can make it official?" he says with a laugh, his words challenging me to remember.

I shake my head, smiling as his fingers trail up my arms and his eyes dare me to recall my line. His touch is distracting, but I remember. I bat my eyelashes at him. "Make what official, Mr. Donavan?" I ask, and when I meet his eyes, I'm surprised by his intense gaze.

"*This, Rylee.*" He breathes. "Make *this* official," he says.

I gasp, my hand flying up to cover my mouth as I look down at the sparkling engagement ring. I'm so thankful I'm sitting because the world is moving around me in a blur. All I can focus on is the brilliance of the man in front of me, asking to make my world complete. A world I never thought would exist for me.

I remind myself to breathe, even though I still can't trust myself to form words properly, so I just stare at him, my body covered in goose bumps despite the warmth of his love pulsing through me. I stare at him through tear blurred eyes and nod subtly in shock. I don't move my eyes from his, because I can see this moment means as much to him as it does to me.

"Make this official with me, Rylee," he says, his voice certain but hands are unsteady. I love the fact that he's nervous, that I mean so much to him that he's worried I might say no.

"I told you once that if I couldn't say the words, I'd do anything I could to prove to you how I feel about you. Well I can say the words now, baby. You showed me how. I love you." His eyes hold mine but I can't help but look down at that shy smile of his that owns my heart. "I love who you are and what you make me. I love that your spark has stopped the blur. That you wanted to race with me. That I don't need the superheroes anymore because I need you instead." He shakes his head slightly and nervously laughs before he begins again.

"Shit, we've already done the *for better or worse* part and the *in sickness and health*, so let's do the *'til death do us part* too. Make a life with me, Ryles. Start with me. End with me. Complete me. Be my one and only first. Be my goddamn victory lane and my fucking checkered flag because God knows I'll be yours if you'll let me. Marry me, Ry?"

Tears are coursing down both of our faces, and I'm so overwhelmed by the beauty of his words and the outpouring of his soul that I can't speak, so I show him instead. I lean forward and press my lips to his, the taste of salt mingling on our lips as I pour myself into the kiss.

And then I start giggling as my lips are pressed against his, and emotions run rampant through me. I can't help it. I lean back and dash away my tears as he looks at me.

"You're killing me here, Ry…" His voice wavers, a mix of exasperation and anxiety. His eyes hold mine—beseeching, imploring, pleading—and I realize that I know the answer without a doubt, but never told him.

"Yes, Colton." I say, my voice escalating with excitement as more tears form. "Yes, I'll marry you."

"Thank Christ!" He sighs and shakes his head, total adoration in his eyes as he looks at me. My eyes are still locked with his, but his hand reaches out to take mine. He breaks our connection and looks down, drawing my eyes down to watch him slip the cushion cut canary diamond, framed by smaller diamonds, onto my ring finger.

We're silent as we stare at it, the enormity of the moment hitting us. The ring is beautiful and huge but a simple gold band would have done the trick, because when I look up, there's my real prize. Dark hair, green eyes, stubbled jaw, and a heart that owns me: mind, body, and soul.

"I love you," I whisper.

"I love you too," he says and presses a kiss to my lips and then throws his head back and laughs before yelling at the top of his lungs, "She said yes!"

I'm startled by his shout, but then I understand when I hear a roar of cheers and rush to the edge of the terrace. When I look down I'm shocked to see everyone looking up at us from the patio below. Everyone from today, including both sets of our parents.

They're all cheering and whistling and all I can do is shake my head and accept their happiness. I wave at them all, holding my hand out to show off my ring and celebrate with them.

I look over at Colton and the emotions swallow me whole. I love him with all my heart. No questions. No doubts. No fears.

"Hey, Ryles," he says, pulling me into him. "If they're gonna stare …" He raises an eyebrow and smiles when he sees the ring on my left hand resting on his bicep.

I throw my head back and laugh before completing the line for him. "Might as well give them something good to stare at."

He raises an eyebrow at me. "Fuck, I love you, soon-to-be-Mrs. Donavan," he drawls out, chills dancing on my spine and a smile spreading on my lips, as he leans forward and kisses me.

The cheers rise to a riotous level down below, but all I hear is Colton's soft groan. All I feel is every place our bodies are touching. All I know is that the warmth spreading inside of me, taking hold, is finding permanence.

Everything else fades away.

The crowd below.

The world beyond.

Because I have everything I need right here in my arms.

The one thing neither of us ever wanted turned out to be the one thing we don't ever want to live without.

Each other.

Chapter Forty-Three and 1/2 Bonus Scene

Mother's Day Post

Fucking Rylee.

I adjust myself some, morning wood flying full fucking staff, as I sit down on the foot of the bed and stare at her. Tanned skin against white sheets. She's on her side, the fabric is resting across her abdomen and is pinned between her thighs—right where I desperately want to be. My eyes devour her perfect tits—nipples pink and tight—then make the logical descent down to that sweet fucking V of her legs. Fucking perfection.

Nothing but sheets? Not anymore…more like nothing but Rylee.

Skin, sweat, and hot fucking damn.

I shake my head and fight my grin. The one that says how in the fuck did I get to the point where one woman and a lack of designer-ass sheets would make me happy as fuck?

I don't know and I don't care because hell if I don't want her right now. But having sex with her—waking her up by licking my way between her thighs until her hands are fisted in my hair and my name is a goddamn scream on her lips, would only take a little bit of the sting away of today's significance. The question is, what exactly can I do, can I say to make it right for her? Ease the pain in her heart and soul?

And then I see her diamond glint from the sun's rays. Sparkles of light around the room…of the one thing signifying the only thing that matters anymore, us. The one that says she's mine. It still punches the air from my lungs when I think about it, about the vows I'll be making in a few months. How this selfless saint can love an irredeemable sinner like me. But fuck if I'm going to question it anymore. I'm balls deep already, I might as well go all in.

I reach out to touch her, touch that spot on her hip, her mark telling me that we—us—are permanent. I don't want to wake her up, but I can't fight it anymore.

Never can when it comes to her.

I crawl my way up her body, and begin tugging on the sheet, sliding it softly from between her thighs. The friction just enough to draw that sigh from her that turns me rock hard faster than fuck. A soft moan falls from those bee-stung lips of hers as I run the sheet back and forth until her eyes startle awake and her breath hitches.

She looks at me, sleep-drugged violet irises locked to mine and a sluggish smile tugs up one of the corners of her mouth. My God. Fucking Kryptonite.

"Hey," she murmurs, her body stretching against mine. She turns onto her back, the sheet falling completely off of her now—her heat, my heaven and every fucking inch in between on display.

"Good morning." And that's all I can say. Tongue gets fucking tied in my mouth as I stare at her, the pang I wanted to ease from her, hitting me out of the blue. And fuck, the unexpected punch of emotion swamps me momentarily. I know she sees it, can see her eyes widen, register the look on my face, the occasion we'd planned on avoiding mentioning today.

I clench my jaw, my eyes unable to look away from her—my whole fucking alphabet—and I do the only thing I can think of. I know she'll be surprised later by the bonfire that the boys and I have planned… but right now, I need to tell her. Need to show her. Need to ease the fucking ache just beneath the surface.

Over what we lost.

For the unknown of if we'll ever get it back.

I hold her eyes as they narrow and try to ask questions I can't fucking put into words. I lean down and press a kiss to her bare abdomen. The smooth skin with the faint and jagged scars there reminding us both about how quick fate can change lives. For the worse. For the better. For us.

I keep my lips there, her stomach stills as she holds her breath. I look up to her, see the tears filling the eyes that hold my heart like a goddamn vice, and say, "It may not be today. It may not happen the old fashioned way…but fuck Ry, it's going to happen someday. If we can't have any, then we get a surrogate, or we adopt…I'll do anything to give you that dream of yours. Anything."

"Colton…" her voice drifts off, a sad smile on her lips, but her eyes never leave mine.

"When it happens…I know you'll be incredible. I know our child will be the luckiest kid in the world…" I press another kiss to just above her navel, my dick telling me to hurry the fuck up because the scent of her vanilla, the taste of her skin is dragging me under its addictive haze. "… and I think one day a year will never be enough to tell you how great you'll be…so I'll start now…and every year after…"

I slide up her body, her taut nipples dragging against my skin, scarring lines of straight up lust into me. I hold her chin still, my whole fucking world in my hands, and smile. "Happy Mother's Day, Ry."

Her breath catches and her eyes widen, surprised by my comment but when I press my lips to hers, when I take what's mine, fuck if I don't doubt we'll get there someday.

Somehow.

Someway.

Shit, she deserves nothing less, she's my checkered flag.

Chapter Forty-Four

1 year later

You're late. Who do you think you are, the bride or something?

It's all the text says and I laugh as I try to type a text back but can't because my hands are shaking. I can't steady them and yet I need to. If my mom walks in she's going to think I'm nervous. She's going to think I have doubts and that my feet are getting cold.

And that's the farthest thing from the truth.

Because I am so ready to dive in headfirst. So excited to see him, to kiss him, to become *officially* his, I'm bouncing up and down with excitement. My stomach churns because I can't wait to see his face—the best part of a wedding I think—when he'll see me for the first time.

I look down at my phone and reply. **I can be late if I want to. It's my wedding. Rule number one. The bride—the wife—is always right. Non-negotiable.**

I look out the window of our bedroom to the deck below and take in the tropical paradise the terrace has been transformed into. Our close family and friends are milling around, the boys are all dressed in matching tuxedos, ushering them to their seats.

I enjoy this quiet moment away from the frenzy that ruled my morning and the chaos I know will ensue shortly. *My last few moments as Rylee Thomas.* Dressed in white—every ounce of me ruched and inlayed and princessed to perfection—with one simple exception that I refused to budge on.

I look in the mirror at the black and white checkered sash that wraps around my waist and falls down the back of my dress. My little ode to Colton and our private joke.

My phone dings. **Already giving rules and we're not even married yet? A certain wife just might need to be fucked into submission later. My rule number one: You can have any rule you want, baby, but in the bedroom I'm the one making the rules.**

I laugh, my body already strung so tight with need that I know his simple touch will set me off. I smirk, thinking of the checkered flag theme that's carried over to my undergarments and the groan I'll hear when Colton discovers it later. And I'm so desperate for that part, considering I've not let him touch me for the past month, regardless of how much he begged and pleaded. But when I decided to screw my own rules—give in to my own desire of wanting him to make love to him, he rejected me. "*Welcome to the big leagues*" his preferred comment of choice.

Ace, you already dominate my mind, heart, and soul ... in the bedroom's just an added bonus. Besides, since when do you follow rules?

I hit send as I breathe in deeply and smile at my reflection. Hair swept up with loose curls falling haphazardly, eyes bright and without doubt, so ready to walk down the aisle to the man I want to spend the rest of my life with. My gaze catches the glimmer of the wedding traditions I'm wearing. And I pick my phone back up.

I love my gift. You didn't have to. Thank you. Can't wait to see you. I go to hit send and then stop myself, needing to tell him in *our way*. So I add to the text, ***Unconditionally*, Katy Perry**.

Tears blur my vision as I think of him and run my fingers over the bracelet around my wrist. The gift he left for me on my dresser. When I opened it my mom's brow furrowed, but I laughed at the alphabet letters linked together with alternating diamonds and sapphires.

My something blue and something new.

My eyes focus on the diamond studs in my ears that my mom wore when she married my dad and I hope we can have a marriage as successful and loving as theirs.

My something old.

My heart aches remembering the look on Had's face last night when she offered the simple tiara for me to wear. "You're the only sister I have left now. I'd like for you to wear it."

My something borrowed.

I close my eyes for a moment, emotions threatening to overwhelm me as I take this all in. As I etch in my brain what this feels like—life changing and yet so full of excitement all at once. And then my mind drifts toward the man I can't wait to spend my life with. The man who caught me that first day, and despite a few bumps, has never let me fall—except for more in love with him. Every single day.

What is Colton thinking and feeling right now? Is he jittery? Nervous? Does he feel as certain as I do?

My phone alerts me again.

Get used to being spoiled. Not too much longer now. You know how much I love you because I'm handing over my balls momentarily to type the next song title, but fuck if it's not true –*Halo*, Beyonce. Whew. Balls back in place now. And hey, there's a lot of dressed up women down here, how will I know which one is you?

The words to the song hit me the same time as his sarcasm, and I emit a sobbing laugh, my body unsure which emotion it should let rule. And I decide to let them all rule—every single one—because this is a once in a lifetime kind of day.

And because I allow myself to feel everything right now, all I want is him, desperately. I appreciate all of the guests being here, but I couldn't care less about all of the pomp and circumstance because what matters most is the man that's going to be waiting for me at the end of the aisle.

I pick up my phone one last time, a soft smile on my face and type, **I'll be the one in white.**

The knock on the door pulls me back from my thoughts. "Come in."

"You ready, sweetheart?"

My mom's voice tugs at all of the emotions rolling through me, and I have to fight the burn in the back of my throat. I keep telling myself not to cry—that I'll mess up my makeup—but I know it's futile. I've shed a lifetime of tears over the past three and a half years; I'm entitled to ruin my makeup with tears of joy now.

"Yeah, I am." I look over at my mom and my lips curve into a soft smile that reflects hers. She holds my gaze, the pride along with a tinge of sadness that she's letting me go, is evident in her blue eyes. "Don't start," I warn her, because I know if she begins crying, so will I.

"I know." She sniffles and then laughs as places her hands on both sides of my cheeks and stares into my eyes. "He's the one, Ry. A mother knows these things." She shakes her head, a soft smile on her face before she answers the question in my eyes. "*He dances in the rain with you.* That's how I know."

I swallow back the tears again as I recall her advice the day we left the hospital. About how life isn't how you survive the storm, but how you dance in the rain. And if I had any doubt about what I was about to do, it would have vanished in an instant with her simple comment.

Nothing like a mother's stamp of approval to make my moment that much sweeter.

I'm about to say something when Haddie comes barreling through the door. "Time to fly the flag, baby, because it's altar time!" she says with a whistle. "Hot damn, woman!"

"Thanks." I laugh as she and my mom start to gather my dress up and we move toward the staircase, the soft notes of *A Thousand Years* is being played on an acoustic guitar down below. The words reveal everything I feel about the man waiting for me.

Quinlan gives us the go-ahead from downstairs that signals Colton is in position and can't see me. My mom and Haddie help me walk down the stairs with my train so I don't trip and break my ankle. We reach the bottom floor and my mom pulls me into a tight hug before pulling back and smiling at me with so many emotions swimming in her eyes.

"I know," I whisper to her with a nod as Shane comes to escort her to her seat.

I feel a hand on my arm and turn to find the soft smile of my brother looking so handsome in his tux. Tanner locks eyes with me and just shakes his head. "It's definitely not dress up at Nana's house," he teases, love reflected in his eyes as he reaches out and grabs my hands. "You ready to do this, Bubs?"

I nod my head vigorously, emotion clogging my throat as I think back to when we were little and used to play wedding at our Nana's house. Gummy lifesavers for wedding rings and stuffed animals for guests. "Never been more ready," I tell him, kissing him on the cheek as my usually stoic brother's eyes well up with tears.

"You look stunning." He shakes his head in disbelief one more time, before placing a soft kiss on my cheek.

"Dad?" I ask, looking over his shoulder for our father.

"Trying to compose himself," he says with a wink. "It's not every day you give your baby girl away. He'll be here in a second." I nod to him and then he turns to go stand beside Quinlan who's already a blubbering mess. She meets my eyes and shakes her head, a silent acknowledgment that if we talk right now we'll both be crying so hard we won't recover.

"And there's the woman who's responsible for hundreds of females crying in their coffee today." I turn my head to find the man I've grown to love over the past year.

"Becks." It's all I can say, but the admiration in my tone tells him all he needs to know. I adore him in so many ways, least of all for pushing Colton and me together when all we wanted was to break apart.

"Hey, gorgeous," he says. "You've got time to skip out if you want. His ego's only going to get bigger after he claims the ultimate prize today."

My heart squeezes at his words. "Only if you're driving," I tease as I take in a deep breath to tame my emotions.

"Nah, he might actually kick my ass for that." He laughs softly as he pulls me into a hug. "He's waiting for you," he whispers into my ear before stepping back and nodding to me.

His words hit their mark as everything around me comes into crystal clear focus. The music. Haddie and Quinlan in their classic black dresses and vibrant bouquets. Tanner rocking on his heels, trying to be patient, but anxiously awaiting the reception so he can take off his bow tie. The strings of the guitar. The hum of everything swirling around me. My heart thundering with anticipation beyond words.

I am so ready for this.

Haddie steps closer, my kick-ass friend has tears in her eyes, and starts to fix my train around me. She finishes and looks at me with a smile. "Just remember, marriage is gonna be tough sometimes. When it is, wear a dress with a zipper up the back."

I laugh as I look at her like she's crazy.

"He'll have to touch you to help you undress and what's underneath will make him forget whatever it is he's pissed at." She raises her eyebrows. "Then will come the best part, *make-up sex*." She laughs causing me to roll my eyes.

"Thanks, Had," I tell her with a shake of my head, because even though I'm sure about what I'm about to do, my stomach's just dropped to my feet.

"I love you, Ry." She presses a kiss to my cheek as I bite my lip and nod. "One for luck," she whispers to me.

"And one for courage," I whisper back and kiss her cheek in turn, not needing the tequila this time because I'm high enough on emotion as it is.

She starts to walk toward Beckett as Quinlan and Tanner start their walk down the aisle, but stops and turns back. "Hey, Ry?"

"Yeah?"

"Today's going to go incredibly fast. Everything is going to hit you at a hundred miles an hour. Make sure you stop and take it all in so you can really remember the first day of the rest of your lives together."

I can't even breathe I'm trying so hard not to cry right now. I nod and blow out a loud breath, trying to compose myself. Our eyes hold, unspoken words passing between us, before she turns and loops her arms through Becks' and starts their walk.

I peek around the curtain, wanting to see everything, take it all in, but all my eyes do is search for him. And from where I stand, I can't see him. So I look over our family and friends. Colton's crew, my co-counselors, our families fill the chairs and watch as our best friends walk down the aisle together. I catch Dorothea's eyes, her smile widening as she mouths "gorgeous" to me before nudging Andy. He turns his head immediately and our gazes lock before he nods his head subtly, the expression on his face filled with awe and gratitude.

"You ready, kiddo?"

The voice of the man who I used to compare all men to is behind me, and I know I'm going to lose it. I turn around and stare at my father, so incredibly handsome, and my whole body trembles with the thought that I'll no longer be his little girl after today. I breathe out a shaky sigh as he looks at me, unable to hide the tears pooling in the corners of his eyes.

"You did good, Ry." He nods his head, strong chin quivering with emotion.

And my first tear slips down my cheek after I hear what every little girl wants from their daddy, approval—especially about the person I've chosen to spend the rest of my life with.

"Thank you, Dad." I can't manage much more without the floodgates opening and I know he feels the same way because we both look away.

Pachelbel's Canon begins and chills cover my body. That's my cue. My dad holds his elbow out to me, and I weave my hand through it, holding on one last time. He'll always be my hero and the one I look to for advice, but it's time to step toward the man whom I'll make new memories with.

My future.

My once upon a time.

My happily ever after.

"You've never looked more beautiful," he whispers to me as we step into the doorway and my eyes blur with unshed tears. "Your husband is waiting."

Those bittersweet words—a daddy letting his little girl go—nearly break me as I force a swallow down my throat to keep the waterworks at bay.

I draw in a deep breath and look at the colorful rose petals scattered on the white fabric aisle in front of me. I blink away the moisture from my eyes, because when I raise them to see Colton for the first time, I want this moment to be crystal clear. Unhindered. Perfect.

Just like the love I feel for him.

We take the first step. I hear the rustling of our guests as they strain to see me and hushed murmurs when they do. I hear the violin strings and the click of cameras. I feel my pulse thunder through my veins and feel the trembling in my dad's arm as we take this most important of walks together. I smell the flowers that litter the terrace mingled with the soft ocean breeze. I try to take it all in, take Haddie's advice and memorize every single detail.

And above all that, I hear Colton inhale as I come into view, and I can't wait any longer. Every part of my body is vibrating with anticipation.

I look up.

And my feet move.

But my heart stops. And beats again.

My breath is punched from my lungs as I lock eyes with Colton and take in the stunned look on his face. The man who is always so sure of himself looks like the world has stopped, tilted, and spun off course.

And the funny thing is ... *it has*, starting the minute he caught me in his arms.

Our eyes remain locked. Even when I kiss my dad on the cheek and he shakes Colton's hand before going to sit with my mom. Even when Colton takes my hands in his and shakes his head with a little chuckle and says, "Nice checkered flag."

"I was afraid you wouldn't know which one I was," I tease and I feel like I can breathe for the first time all day. My heart's pounding and my hands are shaking, but he's got me now.

"Baby, I'd know where you are even if I were blind." And that smile, the one that lights up his eyes and warms my soul, spreads across his lips. I get so lost in his eyes and the unspoken words they're communicating that I don't even realize our officiate has begun the ceremony until Colton looks over at her and then back at me. The green of his eyes glisten with emotion, and his smile softens as he stares at me.

"Rylee," he says, shaking his head subtly as he looks down at our hands and then back up to me. "I was a man racing through life, the idea of love never crossing my radar. It just wasn't for me. And then you *crashed* into my life. You saw good in me when I didn't. You saw possibility when I saw nothing. When I pushed you away, you pushed back ten times harder." He laughs softly. "You showed me your heart, time and again. You taught me checkered flags are so much more valuable off the track than on. You brought light to my darkness with your selflessness, your temerity ..." He reaches up and rubs a thumb over my cheek to wipe away the tears that are silently sliding down my cheeks now.

His personal vows signify the depth of his love for me—the man who swore he couldn't love, does whole-heartedly.

"You've given me a life I never even knew I wanted, Ry. And for that? I promise to give myself to you—the broken, the bent, and every piece in between—wholeheartedly, without deception, without outside influences. I promise to text you songs to make you hear me when you just won't listen. I promise to encourage your compassion because that's what makes you, you. I promise to push you to be spontaneous because breaking rules is what I do best," he says with a smirk as a lone tear slides down his face. "I promise to play lots and lots of baseball, making sure we touch each base. *Home run*!" He says the last word softly so only I can hear, and I laugh through my tears.

And I can't hold back anymore so I reach out and rub my hand over the side of his jaw, not caring one bit about the assumptions people might be making about that vow.

"And that right there ... that laugh? I promise to make you laugh like that every single day. *And sigh*. I like hearing your sighs too." He winks at me. "I promise nothing will be more valuable in my life than you. That you will never be inconsequential. That those you love, I'll love too," he says and then looks over to the row where all of the boys sit. "As I stand here promising to be yours, to give you all of me, I already know that a lifetime will never be long enough to love you. It's just not possible." He shrugs, my heart swelling as his voice wavers slightly. "But, baby, I've got forever to try, if you'll have me."

"Yes!" I choke out as Colton slips my ring on my finger, my body trembling, my heart never more steady, my head completely clear.

"I love you," he whispers.

My tears fall and I don't even try to stop them. He looks so conflicted, wanting to draw me in his arms and comfort me. He looks over to our officiate, silently asking for permission to touch me. And it's so cute that my man, who always disregards rules, is afraid to break them now.

I wipe my eyes with a Kleenex that Haddie hands me and draw in a deep breath to prepare myself for getting through my vows. "Colton, as much as I tried to fight it, I think I've been in love with you since I fell out of that storage closet and crashed into your arms. *A chance encounter*. You saw a spark in me when all I'd felt for so long was grief. You showed me romance when you swore it wasn't real. You taught me I deserve to feel when all I'd been for so long was numb." I shake my head and look down at our hands, before looking back up to meet his eyes.

"You showed me scars—inside and out—are beautiful and to own them without fear. You showed me the real you—*you let me in*—when you always shut others out. You showed me such fortitude and bravery that I had no choice but to love you. And even though you never knew it, you showed me your heart time and time again. Every bent piece of it." I breathe, my trembling hands holding his.

And the look in his eyes—filled with acceptance, adoration, reverence—is one I will never forget. Tears slide silently down his cheeks, in such stark contrast to the intensity on his face but I see his vulnerability. I feel the love.

"You say I brought light to your darkness, but I disagree. Your light was always there, I just showed you how to let it shine. You're giving me the life I've always wanted. And for that? I promise to give myself to you—the defiance, the selflessness, the whole damn alphabet—wholeheartedly, without deception, without outside influences."

And I can't help it, even though I know it's against the rules, I lean forward and press a soft kiss to his lips, and when I lean back, the look in his eyes and the lopsided smile on his face is one I'll remember for the rest of our lives.

"Rule breaker," he teases with a raise of his eyebrow as I prepare to finish my vows.

"I learned from the best." I shake my head and look back at him with clarity. "I promise to encourage your free spirit and rule breaking ways because that's what makes you, you. I promise to challenge you and push you so we can continue to grow into better versions of ourselves. I promise to be patient and hold your hand when you want it held the least, because that's what I do best. I promise to text you songs too so we can keep the lines of communication open between us. And I promise to wear dresses with zippers up the back," I throw in on a whim, prompting Colton to look over at Haddie who is laughing behind me. He shakes his head, before focusing back on me.

"I promise a lifetime of laughter, ice cream breakfasts and pancake dinners. And as much as I love waving that checkered flag? *Batter-up, baby*." My smile matches his as my love for him swells and soars to new heights. "I promise that nothing will be more valuable in my life than you—because everything else is inconsequential—and you, Colton, are most definitely not. I remember sitting in a Starbucks watching you and wondering what it would be like to get the chance to love you, and now I get a lifetime to find out. And I still don't think that will be enough time." I take his ring from Haddie, the band etched with a checkered design, and slip it on his finger.

Becks starts mocking and all the guests laugh. As much as I want to throttle him, I never could. This is my life now and he's a part of it.

"You're next, fucker," Colton mutters to him under his breath, causing him to choke more and me to laugh louder. It takes a minute for the laughter to abate and for everyone to settle down so that the focus is back on us.

"Colton, we've got forever to try, if you'll have me?"

"You know this is permanent, right?" he says softly, reminding me of the symbol forever marking my hip. I nod my head subtly as he looks at me, head angled, eyes dancing, lips smiling, and says, "I wouldn't have you any other way." He looks down at his hand, the new band on his ring finger and shakes his head for a moment as he accepts what's just happened. The look on his face is priceless. And with impatience rivaling that of one of my boys, his eyes dart over to the officiate.

"Yes, Colton." she chuckles, knowing exactly what he wants. "You may kiss your bride!"

Wonderment and love flow through me.

"Thank Christ!" He exhales as he steps into me and frames my face with his hands. "This is one checkered flag I'm forever claiming."

And then his lips are on mine, our connection irrefutable, as I hear the officiate announce, "Friends and family, may I present to you Mr. and Mrs. Colton Donavan."

Chapter Forty-Four

Colton—Raced

I look at myself in the mirror, my thoughts a jumble of shit but my pulse steady, body calm. I shake my head. Life is such a mindfuck sometimes.

The man I see looking back at me is not the same one I would have found a year or even six months ago.

It's like each fucking day with her makes me a better person. A better man. Erases some of the demons bit by bit, moment by moment.

I splash some water on my face, the disbelief still riding high that I'm about to get fucking married. Me? Colton fucking Donavan. The self-proclaimed bachelor for life. The man who thought no pussy is good enough to want for a lifetime.

Fuck! I laugh into the empty bathroom. Talk about underestimating the power of voodoo.

How naïve I was. Always needing to mask the pain and hide the scars on my soul by burying myself in the next willing piece of ass. Never—never—did I think this day would come. That I'd wake up wanting a woman in bed with me and not just beneath me.

Fucking Rylee.

The woman knocked me on my ass like a three hundred pound linebacker. Talk about blindsiding my way of fucking life filled with tits, ass, Jack and Jim, and thinking only about myself.

Because now all I can think about is her.

Even now.

Right fucking now I should be hung over, puking my guts out with nerves over the ball and chain about to get shackled to my ankle. But fuck if I feel any of that. All I want is to see her. Kiss her. Make her mine in every way.

Ride off into the proverbial motherfucking sunset.

And all of this because I got schooled by Becks into understanding why the *alphabet* is so damn important. A to fucking Z of it.

"Dude, you gonna finish getting ready or what?"

Becks's voice startles me. I glance down to my phone where Ry's last text is on the screen still—**I'll be the one in white**—to check the time and realize shit's about to get real.

"Hold your horses, Daniels." I lift my chin in acknowledgement to him through my reflection as I bring the tumbler of aged Macallan he bought for the occasion to my lips. "I'm just zipping up now."

"Don't pinch your dick. You just might need that tonight since she's been holding out on you." He chuckles as he pours himself a glass.

"No shit." I tuck my shirt in, my mind wandering to just what's going to be beneath her dress besides my voodoo pussy. Because fuck if it's not torture to sleep beside the woman you want more than the air you breathe when she won't let you touch her. "A month is a long fucking time, dude." I groan the words out, my dick already stirring for the action it's been missing.

He throws his head back and laughs at me. "For you that's like a lifetime."

"Fuck off." He just raises his eyebrows at me, then I can't help but laugh. "It's been brutal."

"Poor baby. You'll get no sympathy from me. Welcome to how the other half lives, where snapping your fingers doesn't result in any woman you want dropping to her knees."

I laugh. "Not anymore, brother. Not anymore." I'm on the please remain standing program now. I glance up from where I'm trying to put my checkered flag cuff links through the holes to meet his eyes.

"You really ready to do this?" He quirks his eyebrows up at me, like he's waiting for the about face. For me to freak the hell out because I'm about to get hitched.

He's fucking crazy if he thinks I'm walking away from Rylee. Not now. Not ever. That checkered flag's only ever going to wave for me.

"I should be nervous right? Pacing and shit. But I'm not. Fucking scary but true … *it's Rylee*," I tell him with a shrug as if that it explains it all. The thought unnerving even to me.

But fuck if I've been able to make sense of the truths she's allowed me to face, the man she's given me the room to become.

"It is indeed Rylee, and shit, man, I don't know what she sees in you," he teases, "but, she looks incredible."

What? "You've seen her?" So not fucking fair. So many things I want to ask him about her, but I keep my balls and retain my dignity. I'll see for myself soon enough if she's nervous or smiling or crying.

Being beautiful is a given.

"Had to talk to her, let her understand the big ass mistake she's about to make … give her a chance to ride off in the sunset with the more handsome of the two of us."

I snort out a laugh as I walk toward him. "Yep. We will be doing that in about six hours. Thanks for showing her the lesser so she knows she's getting the more."

"Cocky as fuck and you still end up with the girl."

"Always." I sit down on the edge of the chair across from him and flash him an arrogant-ass grin. And fuck if I know where it comes from but all of a sudden there are so many things I need to say to him and not enough words to say them with. We may fuck with each other, ride each other's asses when we can't see what's right in front of us, but I know the shove he gave me knocking my dick in the dirt is part of the reason I got my shit together. Is why I'm sitting here right now, about to marry the girl I sure as shit don't deserve.

Well him and the defiant as fuck woman who grabbed me by the balls and said non-negotiable.

"Hey, Becks?"

"What do you need?"

And that right there gets me. His unwavering friendship.

I look down for a moment and take a sip of the Macallan. "That's good shit. Thanks," I say, stalling.

"A rarity for a one-of-a-kind type of day."

Years of friendship come down to right now. Two young kids, now men, and the one that was fucked-up just might finally have it together. How the hell do I tell him that? Thanks for putting up with my bullshit and being my punching bag and wingman all at once?

"Thanks, man. *For everything.*" It's all I've got, but I think he knows what I'm saying because he meets my eyes for a moment, a slight smirk on his face, and nods his head in acknowledgement.

"Always." He sips his drink and then leans forward and taps it against mine. "And just remember to always end a fight with these two words: *yes dear*. Biting your tongue at the end of a fight will up the ante of her using hers later to make-up."

I laugh with him and his fucked-up logic that makes perfect sense before tossing back the rest of my drink.

"You ready, Son?" My dad's voice from the door interrupts us.

I sigh and fuck if I can't stop the smile that's on my face. "Yep, just putting my tie on," I say, rising to get it. I meet my dad's eyes and we had our father-son moment earlier but I still can't get over that look he gives me.

The pride mixed with attaboy. The look the fucked-up little boy I was would have killed to have as much as something to eat and yet here I am, twenty something years later, and it means more now than I ever thought it could.

Sweet Jesus. When people say weddings make you sappy, they weren't fucking kidding. But fuck anyone who tells me I don't deserve this. I've been to Hell and back, survived the darkest shit imaginable and I'm standing here with my old man and my best friend about to marry the woman who took the pieces the poison hadn't eaten through and made me whole again.

I think I need another drink.

Let's get this waiting shit over.

I'm restless. Antsy as fuck. I mean, I'm close to all of the people here but they seriously need to stop chatting and sit the hell down so I can see her.

"Cool your jets. You've waited this long, I don't think another couple of minutes will kill you."

Her voice startles me but I keep my eyes focused on all of the guests. "Easy for you to say," I tell my sister, knowing it's no use to bullshit her that the nerves are starting to kick in.

"Well it's about time," she says sarcastically, her hand dusting something off the shoulder of my jacket.

I glance over at her. "Exactly my point. It's about time for it to start."

"That's not what I meant." She snorts in amusement. "I meant it's about time you're finally acting normal about this. That your nerves are showing. You were freaking me out with the Mr. Cool-Calm-and-Collected routine. I wanted to ask who stole my brother."

I roll my eyes at her, my patience wearing out but for all the right reasons. When I meet her gaze I see the tears there, accept the love in them. I just sigh and shake my head, an unsteady grin on my face. "I'm getting married, Q."

A tear leaks over and she runs her hands up and down my lapels. "I know. It's surprising as hell but you deserve it. All of the happiness and love she brings you." She steps up on her toes and kisses my cheek. "Just treat her like you treated me, minus the nuggies and wedgies," she says with a wink, emotion breaking her voice, "and you'll be just fine."

I pull her into me and kiss the side of her cheek. She bats me away so I don't mess up her makeup or hair. "Thanks."

She just nods her head at me before shaking it. "I won't believe it until I see a ring on your finger." She laughs. "I guess now would be a good time to tell her parents that our family has a no return policy on you."

"Quinlan," I warn her, but the smile on my face gives away that I don't care if she tells them that or not because they won't need to return me. I'm in this for the long haul.

She's called from my mother upstairs and she kisses my cheek one last time before running up the steps.

Time passes slower than the pace car around the track. I'm amped up, ready to get the show on the road, and a new Mrs. Donavan into bed when all is said and done. The officiate leads me outside. I stand there and make eye contact with my mom who has been a wreck all day since we had breakfast until now.

The music starts. Some classical shit that I'm sure I'll never remember but at the same time will know every time I hear it what it means. Where I was. What she looked like.

Tanner and Quinlan walk down. Then Becks and Haddie. I don't even see them. I'm rocking on my heels. Clasping my hands in front of me. Telling myself to breathe.

Fuck. I'm really doing this. Really *want* to do this.

The wedding march starts. At least I know this song. Kind of hard to miss.

But when the music starts, I feel like the bottom drops out.

All of my insecurities, fears, worries begin to overtake me. I strain to find Rylee around the curve of the guests. I want to yell at them to sit the hell down so I can see her because I'm fucking suffocating and she's my air. My next breath.

My fucking everything.

And then life zooms in 3D fashion when I catch the first glimpse of her.

The blur around me stops.

All I see is white. Can't tell you a goddamn thing about the dress except for the color because all I'm focused on is her face.

Look up.

Look at me, Ryles.

I want to shout the words to her. Let her know I'm here, waiting. But then realize she can take all the time in the fucking world because I'm not going anywhere.

Yep. This man who loved to run is firmly rooted in place. Fuckin'A.

I can't hear my mom sobbing, can't feel the breeze of the ocean, can't hear the music anymore because Rylee looks up.

And I'm lost. Staggered. Found. Saved.

To her. To the moment. For the rest of my life.

My saint. The words run through my head as I lock eyes with her. Every demon left within leaves with the exhale of my breath I didn't realize I was holding.

Her smile is unwavering and eyes fill with tears as she walks so calmly toward me. And thank fuck for that. Thank God she never listened when I warned her off of me. Because it may have been a great view of her ass walking away, but that means I'd never have the chance to see this—accept this—know this feeling. The one that she's walking toward me, no secrets hidden, all slates wiped clean, and a future to build together.

I'm a lucky fucking bastard.

I breathe in, my chest aching, and when the oxygen hits my lungs I'm able to think a little clearer. My eyes obey the command to take in the whole package, take a chance to remember this one moment for the rest of my life.

And then I see it.

I laugh out loud—can't help myself—when I see the checkered flag wrapped around her waist. Only Rylee would do this for me. Add something as an ode to the significance of our checkered past and of her being my checkered flag.

I can't keep my eyes off of her. She's everything right now. Fucking everything.

I shake her dad's hand and vaguely hear his kind words because all I see is her.

"Nice checkered flag," I tell her with a laugh when all I want to do is kiss her. I feel like it's been weeks since we have, but it's been less than twenty-four hours. Pathetic but true as fuck.

"I was afraid you wouldn't know which one I was," she says, referring to her text as I take her hands in mine.

And now I feel like I can breathe again, feel like myself again because Rylee's right where she belongs. "Baby, I'd know where you are even if I were blind."

I smile at her, see so many things in those eyes of hers that I don't even realize the officiate has begun. And fuck if the nerves aren't beginning to hum now.

The vows I had planned to say all jumble in my head, crossing lines and not making any sense. I hear my cue and in the split second decide that this self-proclaimed player is going to do something a year ago I would have hidden from.

I decide to let it all out. Speak from the heart. Lay it on the line so she has no doubts.

"Rylee," I say, shaking my head and looking down at our hands, calling to my superheroes asking for help to not fuck this up, before looking back up at her. "I was a man racing through life, the idea of love never crossing my radar. It just wasn't for me. And then you *crashed* into my life. You saw good in me when I didn't. You saw possibility when I saw nothing. When I pushed you away, you pushed back ten times harder." I close my eyes momentarily, a nervous laugh falling from my lips as I hope she understands how important that is to me. How she never gave up on me. Ever.

I squeeze her hands as so many emotions fill me. I have to clear my throat to continue. "You showed me your heart, time and again. You taught me checkered flags are so much more valuable off the track than on. You brought light to my darkness with your selflessness, your temerity ..." The tears start falling down her cheeks and I know they're from joy but I have to brush them away.

"You've given me a life I never even knew I wanted, Ry. And for that? I promise to give myself to you—the broken, the bent, and every piece in between—wholeheartedly, without deception, without outside influences. I promise to text you songs to make you hear me when you just won't listen. I promise to encourage your compassion because that's what makes you, you. I promise to push you to be spontaneous because breaking rules is what I do best," I say, trying to smile at her as it all catches up with me—the moment, the meaning, the woman willing to accept me—and I can't help the tear that falls when I try to blink it away. I need something funny here, something to make her laugh so the sound of it will make me more at ease. "I promise to play lots and lots of baseball, making sure we touch each base. *Home run!*"

She laughs and I breathe a sigh of relief knowing I'll be able to make it through the rest of what I have to say and that I won't fuck them up. That I've got this.

"And that right there ... that laugh? I promise to make you laugh like that every single day. *And sigh.* I like hearing your sighs too." God that blush on her cheeks makes me want to take her upstairs and put it there from exertion. Soon, Donavan. Soon.

"I promise nothing will be more valuable in my life than you. That you will never be inconsequential. That those you love, I'll love too." I look over toward the boys, knowing how important it is to acknowledge them. To let them know that they are part of this package deal too. "As I stand here promising to be yours, to give you all of me, I already know that a lifetime will never be long enough to love you. It's just not possible. But, baby, I've got forever to try, if you'll have me."

My last words tumble out. Hope I said everything I'm supposed to say in a set of vows but don't really care if I didn't because Rylee heard. She gets me.

I pull the ring from my pocket and slide it on her trembling fingers. And the sight of my ring, the diamond band against her engagement ring, sends an adrenaline rush through me. Fills me with a pride I've never known and don't think I can explain.

She chokes out a yes and I think I say I love you. Scratch that. I know I did, but it's all a blur because I realize that it's my turn to listen. To be put on the hot spot because fuck if it's not easier to say the words than it is to hear them, accept them, believe them.

Earn them.

And then she touches my cheek and motherfucker ... her hand on my face makes every ounce of testosterone in my body beg to take her. I glance over at the person marrying us, giving her the *help a brother out* look, to see if I can kiss her but am met with a deadpan expression.

And as much as I want her lips on mine, I can wait. This moment means too much to me and I'll have the rest of my life to kiss Rylee.

Among other things. And hell if that's not a great fucking motivating thought to keep my hands to myself right now.

"Colton, as much as I tried to fight it, I think I've been in love with you since I fell out of that storage closet and crashed into your arms. *A chance encounter*. You saw a spark in me when all I'd felt for so long was grief. You showed me romance when you swore it wasn't real. You taught me I deserve to feel when all I'd been for so long was numb." Her voice is shaky at first and then she evens it out and it's so goddamn sexy—that rasp in it—that I fall under her spell like I did that first night. I squeeze her hands to let her know it's okay, I'm right here. That I can't wait to listen to the rest of what she has to tell me.

"You showed me scars—inside and out—are beautiful and to own them without fear. You showed me the real you—*you let me in*—when you always shut others out. You showed me such fortitude and bravery that I had no choice but to love you. And even though you never knew it, you showed me your heart time and time again. Every bent piece of it."

If I hadn't already known what being broken felt like, I'd say those words of hers would have just shattered me, but in a good way. Because I know the difference. I'll never break when I have her by my side because she'll bend with me, hold the chips that break off when times get tough and help me put them back.

She's opened me up for all to see and now I know why she only wanted close friends of ours here instead of the massive party I suggested. She wanted me comfortable, willing to accept the fact that she just laid me wide open with her words and be okay with that, with the tears sliding down my cheeks.

The woman knows me better than I know myself.

"You say I brought light to your darkness, but I disagree. Your light was always there, I just showed you how to let it shine. You're giving me the life I've always wanted. And for that? I promise to give myself to you—the defiance, the selflessness, the whole damn alphabet—wholeheartedly, without deception, without outside influences."

I force a swallow down my throat and before I can process everything, her lips are on mine. Yep, she knows exactly what I need.

"Rule breaker," I say, wanting so much more than the tease of her taste.

"I learned from the best," she says.

There's my girl, learning how to live on the edge.

"I promise to encourage your free spirit and rule-breaking ways because that's what makes you, you. I promise to challenge you and push you so we can continue to grow into better versions of ourselves. I promise to be patient and hold your hand when you want it held the least, because that's what I do best. I promise to text you songs too so we can keep the lines of communication open between us. And I promise to wear dresses with zippers up the back."

What? She throws me but when I hear Haddie laughing and look over to her I can only begin to guess what she's told Ry. But I'll take it because a zipper up the back means she needs my hands on her to help.

And hands on her naked curves are never a bad thing.

"I promise a lifetime of laughter, ice cream breakfasts, and pancake dinners. And as much as I love waving that checkered flag? *Batter-up, baby*."

Game on. Yes, she's taken ladies and gents. This woman is one hundred percent mine.

"I promise that nothing will be more valuable in my life than you—because everything else is inconsequential—and you, Colton, are most definitely not. I remember sitting in a Starbucks watching you and wondering what it would be like to get the chance to love you, and now I get a lifetime to find out. And I still don't think that will be enough time."

I watch as Rylee slides the ring on my finger and wait for the fear to take hold. For the *what the fuck am I doing* to fill my thoughts. But there's nothing. Fucking nothing but love.

And then Becks starts coughing.

"You're next, fucker." The words are out of my mouth before I can stop them. And when I look up to meet Ry's eyes as everyone is around us laughing and she's smiling wide at me, I realize just how right I got this. Letting her in. Letting her help heal me.

Letting her love me.

"Colton, we've got forever to try, if you'll have me?"

"You know this is permanent, right?" I stare into her eyes. The ones I know narrow and glare when she's pissed at me, the ones that close halfway before rolling up when she's about to come, the ones that widen in surprise or brim with tears when she's touched, and I realize I can't wait to wake up every morning of the rest of my life and learn how else they can look at me. Fuck I'm lucky.

"I wouldn't have you any other way." I hear her suck in a breath when I glance down at my new ring and then realization hits me.

I glance over to the officiate and I don't give a fuck if she says no; I'm kissing her this time because I know the important shit is over.

Vows are said.

Rings are on.

Rylee's mine.

"Yes, Colton." She laughs at me. "You may kiss your bride!"

"Thank Christ!" My body hums and all of the sudden my adrenaline hits me when I know we're official. That I get these lips for the rest of my life. "This is one checkered flag I'm forever claiming."

I kiss her. I pour all of the words I couldn't say to tell her how I feel into it. Fuck the peck on the lips shit because this man's going in for the kill. Gotta make sure she knows on the first kiss of our married life exactly how I feel.

My actions definitely speak louder than words.

"Friends and family, may I present to you Mr. and Mrs. Colton Donavan."

The words hit my ears while my mouth is on hers and I know I've never felt more whole.

Rylee fucking Donavan.

That has one hell of a ring to it.

I kiss her again before I release her to hear that laugh I love falling from her lips.

My wife.

My life.

Thank fuck I can drive like the wind because happily ever after is waiting for us to drive into its sunset.

Chapter Forty-Five Bonus Scene

2 months later

The house smells like a goddamn bakery. I've never had a sweet tooth, but the sight before me is making me crave some sugar. Well, more like a specific dessert that I know from experience tastes so good it can knock this grown man to his knees. I lean against the doorjamb as Rylee moves to the beat as she hums along to some seductive ass song. All I can do is watch her: the way she sways her curves in those killer jeans, tight in all the right places, the tank top that I'd bet my ass has no bra beneath it, and her hair pulled up.

Sweet Jesus. There may be a bag of sugar sitting on the counter beside her, but I sure as shit would prefer the sweetness between her thighs any fucking day of the week.

And that any day is going to start right about now. Long hours testing at the track make for a good day, but ending it like this? Talk about getting to claim a checkered flag when I'm not even in the race.

I watch her. How can I not? Shit, a year ago I would've called myself a pussy for thinking that I'd get turned on watching a woman bake Christmas cookies. But damn, that was BR: before Rylee.

There's something so goddamn sexy about the way she moves to the music. I'm not sure if it's because she doesn't know I'm here so she's letting loose, or if it's because my fingertips have memorized every inch of skin beneath those fine as fuck jeans. Regardless, it's worth taking a moment to appreciate.

But I think I need to appreciate it a little closer. Like with my fingers and mouth because I need all hands on deck when it comes to Ryles.

I walk forward, take note of the counters of my kitchen lined with cookies, some frosted, some not. It's a strange sight in what used to be my bachelor pad, but it makes me smile for some weird reason. It makes me think of a home and how fucking lucky I am that she actually said '*I do*' a few weeks ago.

We're married. Talk about crazy.

"Arrgh!" she yelps as I slip my arms around her waist, tug her back against me, and press a kiss to the addictive curve of her neck.

"Hmm, you smell better than the cookies," I murmur, lips against her skin, dick against the swell of her ass, and my head already filled with the things I want to do to her.

"Good day at the track?" She asks tilting her head to the side so it presses against mine. And there's something about the motion that just pulls on those dark parts remaining inside of me and tells them, *"See? I can be loved."*

"Yeah. Car's handling good. Needs a few tweaks yet, but it'll be ready to go." I rest my chin on her shoulder as she dips her paintbrush in the icing and spreads it over the unfrosted cookie. "What's all this for?"

"I'm playing Betty Crocker." She finishes painting a Christmas tree green and holds it up, "See?"

"Can you play her in just an apron and heels and nothing else?" The thought alone has me groaning. Heels and ruffles bent over the kitchen table. Game on, baby.

"And who, kind sir, are you going to play?" She teases, the smile on my lips automatic.

"A baseball player." She bursts out laughing at our long running joke that takes me back to that first date, cotton candy, and Ferris wheels. And then more cotton candy mixed with the taste of Rylee on my tongue. *Fuck.* What is it with this woman and sugar that makes me want to bury myself balls deep in her without a second thought? *"Wanna see my stick?"*

She wiggles her ass where my dick presses against it. The woman loves to test my restraint in every way possible. "Hmm, I can feel your stick all right. Too bad you're only getting to first base until I finish frosting these cookies."

Fuck that. Like she doesn't know she just issued me a challenge I'll take so much pleasure in winning. Sure as shit, I'll be sliding into home in no time, *frosting and all.* "We'll see about that," I chuckle into her ear and brush my lips against her neck in that place that she likes. Her body tenses momentarily as goose bumps chase over her skin. This is going to be a piece of cake.

Or I guess I should say a piece of cookie since they're about to be cleared to the floor so that I can play out my dining room table fantasy.

"Mmm-hmm," she murmurs. I reach out to dip a finger in the icing, and she bats my hand away. "Hands off, Ace."

"My hands do what they want," I say as I place them over her boobs, brush my thumbs over the hard tips of her nipples, and cause that sigh of hers that turns me rock hard to fall from her lips. "And you'll like it."

"I will, will I?" She asks and when she turns around to face me, the frosting paintbrush in her hand hits my chin with the natural motion of the action.

Her eyes flicker down to where green frosting is coating my chin and then back up to my eyes. She fights the smile on her lips when I raise my eyebrows in a silent warning. "You want to play dirty now, do you?"

The smirk she was fighting is now full blown as she keeps her eyes locked on mine when she leans forward to lick the frosting off of my chin. I swear to God the tip of her tongue is like an open ended live-wire because fuck if an electric shock doesn't mainline straight down to my dick and then streak back up to jumpstart my heart.

She finishes her tantilization by sucking gently on my chin. "There was some right there," she murmurs. "I'm just trying to play clean."

I laugh softly, my cock now thick and ready against her abdomen. Thoughts of wiping the counter clean in one fell swoop so I can have my way with her fill my head again. If she keeps this shit up, it's going to be more than just a thought.

"Sweetheart, that right there was playing dirty..." She starts to argue with me, but I cut the words off by kissing her again. The frosting on her tongue and the simple taste of her sears my goddamn memory and what feels like my balls from the ache it creates there. Just when I have her where I want her – sinking into me, lips taking, and tongue demanding – I pull back and reach for the paintbrush covered in frosting.

"What?" She feigns innocence as those pursed lips of hers fall open in the shape of an O. And hell if my dick isn't begging to put the space between them to good use right now.

Before she can comprehend what I'm doing, I have the neckline of her cami-tank pulled down, and sweet Jesus, I was right. *No bra.* The sight of her pink nipples has every part of my body begging to take her hard and fast. And then that sound - her shocked gasp when I take the brush and paint frosting around her nipple – only serves to intensify that slow, sweet ache I have to take her.

After admiring my handiwork, I flick my eyes back up to hers to find them wide and hazy with need. "See, you're dirty now too." I smirk. "Makes it a hell of a lot easier to slide into home plate when you don't mind a mess."

"Is that your master plan, huh? This woman has cookies that will burn if —oh God…" she moans as I close my lips over her nipple and gently suck on it, the frosting a nice addition to her already addictive flavor. She part moans, part sighs as I suck a little harder, causing her hands to grab my hair.

"Let the cookies burn," I say and fuck if the immediate nod of her head isn't more of a turn on than her tight peak in my mouth. The fact that she wants me just as badly as I do her fuels my desire.

She watches as I paint her other breast. This time I make a production of it despite my body being on edge – want and need crashing into each other. My tongue over frosting. Her fingers in my hair. The heat of her skin on my lips. Christmas cookies only come once a year so I might as well make the most of it.

The banging on the front door startles the hell out of us.

"What the fuck?" I bark as I stand up. Rylee pulls me in to her, tells me to ignore the distraction, and fuck, I'm more than game. No one's going to stop me from hitting this homerun. We dive back in to our addictive desire with mouths and tongues and her bare chest pressing against mine.

The pounding starts again. "Go away!" I shout in frustration just as Rylee releases me. "No," I groan against her ear, desperate for more.

"Dude, why's your door fucking locked?"

Rylee and I lock eyes when we hear Becks's muted voice. "Go away, Daniels. I'm trying to get laid!"

Rylee laughs and fists a hand in my shirt to pull me in for a chaste kiss before pushing me away. "See what he needs and then you better get your big stick ready because I'm expecting a grand slam, rookie." She raises her eyebrows in a silent taunt as she lifts her chin for me to get the door.

Rookie? Bullshit. I start to correct her, tell her I'm far from that, but the words get lost in the sight of her stuffing her tits back into her top. She can call me whatever the fuck she wants as long as she's moaning my name later.

"Yes ma'am," I say as I adjust my dick in my pants and then yank open the front door. "Dude, you really know how to kill a boner don't you? You better make this quick because we're playing baseball here."

Becks looks at me, confusion on his face, but the quick moment of silence allows me to realize that something's wrong. His usual smirk and smart ass greeting are missing.

"You look like shit. Must be a woman who has your panties in a bunch. Who is she?" I have to tease him. This is our thing, harassing the shit out each other instead of having some Kumbaya session.

His silence tells me I'm right. It's woman trouble. And now I'm even more curious. Who the hell has knocked Daniels on his ass while we were on our honeymoon?

Ignoring my question, he glances over my shoulder and nods his head at Ry. No smile. No quip. Something's definitely up. *Fuck*. The best friend in me wants to invite him in and the selfish, horny bastard in me doesn't want to. I glance over my shoulder to where Rylee's wet and frosted and waiting for me. She meets my gaze. I can see the concern in hers over Becks and that I should deal with him first. But shit, there's that smudge of green frosting on her collarbone calling to me. Sweet Christ. Am I really picking friend duty over sex?

"This better be good, Daniels, because you're causing a rain delay in my game," I say as I step back for him to come inside.

Rylee disappears from sight as we walk into the family room. "So what gives, man? Who's the woman who's fucking you up?" I ask, never expecting in a million years the answer he gives.

"Haddie Montgomery."

Chapter Forty-Six Bonus Scene

1 Year Later

"I'm so confused…intrigued…*turned on*," Colton says as I lead him by the hand through the tunnel. And the way he says it—half groan, half plea—causes that sweet pang of desire to stir in my core.

"Considering turning you on isn't very hard to do…" I let the words trail off as his chuckle fills the night around us. Anxiety over all of the details dissipates when I see the blanket laid out with the picnic basket on it. My contacts have done their jobs. Everything else is up to me.

"Don't you dare lift that blindfold, Ace!" I slap his hand away hoping that all of this was worth it: The surprise private flight, the blindfold I put on him before we landed so that he wouldn't recognize our location, the mindless chatter to distract him as we walked into the facility.

"So if I leave it on, do I get sexual favors for obeying?" he asks, hope laced with suggestion in his tone.

"You just might get all kinds of favors if you're lucky," I taunt. His hand is still in mine but my feet falter when they hit the asphalt track and take in this iconic facility. Even under the cover of night, its enormity looms all around us. Our only company is a single light tree turned on at the opposite end of the grandstand and Sammy keeping guard at the entrance.

I stare at the empty speedway and then back to Colton. For a split second I'm reminded of that night back at the track in Fontana a little over two years ago. When he relieved the burdens on his soul he'd spent a lifetime carrying and let me completely into his life. The poignancy is not lost on me that I'm taking him to a similar setting to celebrate our first wedding anniversary.

"Almost there," I murmur as I shake away visions from that night, grateful for the journey we've been on and the happiness we've found.

"I can tell we're outside, the ground is hard…all I'm going to say is that there better not be a hundred people in front of us waiting to shout *surprise*, sweetheart, because when I think of a blindfold and you in the same sentence, it brings certain activities or rather *positions*, to mind and I sure as hell don't think you'd appreciate having an audience while we play out that scenario. Then again…you might like having someone watch."

"Just come here and shush." *Men.* I roll my eyes and put my hands on his shoulders to position him perfectly: body squared to the asphalt stretch laid out in front of us and feet placed within the band of brick beneath us.

"Bossy, bossy," he mutters under his breath.

Hours of preparation, secrecy, and anticipation lead up to this moment. He's helped me find myself, lose myself again with him by my side, given me confidence, made me feel sexy…and whole—something I never thought I'd be again. My love surges as I lean forward and press a kiss to the back of his neck. When he doesn't flinch, a soft smile forms on my lips.

"I wanted to do something special for you for our first anniversary," I explain as all of a sudden my nerves begin to hum as I step to his side. I can't wait to see his reaction.

"Ry…" I love when that tender tone comes into his voice, the one reserved only for me.

"You can look now."

His trademark smirk returns and then falls into a shocked O as he lifts the blindfold. My heart skips over a beat in excitement as surprise flickers over his features.

"What? Is this…? Holy shit, Ry!" he exclaims as he takes in the sight around us: the famed Indianapolis speedway and its start/finish line delineated in bricks beneath us. I wonder how it looks through his eyes. Is the track still a place where he finds consolation to outrun the demons of his past or is it now a path to a brighter future where he can enjoy the wind in his face instead of worrying about the ghosts that linger?

"Surprise!" I hold my hands out to my sides and shrug, tears burning the back of my eyes. Colton swoops me up in his arms and spins me around, his laugh echoing around us.

His lips find mine causing that instant chemistry we always have to spark to life. I can tell he's torn between prolonging our kiss and stopping to ask questions. I don't make him choose. I pull back so that I can explain but he stops me.

"No. Not yet. Give me a minute," he murmurs against my lips as he rests his forehead against mine and pulls me in closer.

After a few moments of silence, he kisses my nose and then slowly releases me so that my body can slide down the length of his. That spark? It turns into a full-blown wildfire at the feel of his chest, hard and strong, against my breasts.

"Ry...?" he says, voice gruff, fingers lacing with mine.

"What's the one race you've yet to win?"

"The Indy 500," he states, eyebrows narrowing as he tries to figure out where I'm going with this.

I take a few steps away, the coy smirk on my face unmistakable. "You mean you've never claimed the checkered flag here?"

"No." He angles his head to the side and stares. I can tell he's working this all out, thinks he knows where I'm going with it, but doesn't believe I'd step outside of the box and do something like this.

Time to prove him wrong.

Taking another step toward the blanket, I begin to unbutton the top of my dress. His eyes widen. His breath hitches. His fingers fidget to reach out and touch. And even after a year of marriage, I love that offering myself to him still causes this reaction. It's powerful. Heady. Comforting.

"Well..." I bite my bottom lip and shrug out of my dress so it can slide down my body and pool at my feet. "I'm giving you an opportunity to claim it. *Right now.*"

His eyes scrape over the sultry combination of lace and leather I've been hiding beneath my dress. His lips part in disbelief before slowly spreading into that I'm-going-to-claim-that-checkered-flag smirk of his that makes my stomach somersault. When he steps toward me, I'm able to see so many things in his eyes through the darkness: surprise, amusement, acceptance, and desire.

But the one emotion I recognize more than any other is the one thing he thought he could never give anyone: love. And that warms me more than anything as the arrogant, bad boy I fell in love with walks toward me with a swagger that says he's going to claim what's his.

"Fuckin' A, Ry..." he groans as he takes another look at my ensemble before reaching out and yanking my body against his. Our lips are inches apart, our bodies breathing as one, and our hearts pound against each other's.

"You gonna claim this checkered flag, Ace?" I raise my eyebrows to taunt him all the while every nerve in my body is attuned to everything about him: his cologne, the hitch of his breath, the widening of his eyes as they grow hazy with desire, and the unmistakable feeling of his dick hardening against me.

"Baby, I was born to claim it." I catch a glimpse of his smirk a heartbeat before his mouth slants over mine. Our tongues intertwine in a savage union of lust and want, desire and greed, and I know there's no turning back. Hands roam like we are touching for the first time, fingertips digging possessively into flesh, and it's still not enough—will never be—because everything I feel for my husband intensifies with each passing day.

And by the way he's kissing me, I know he feels the same. He nips my lip and pulls on it softly as he leans back, need in his eyes and my name a strained sound on his lips when his fingers dip between my thighs to find out that my panties are crotchless.

"Happy first anniversary."

"*Fuck!*" he groans. "You trying to get me to rip these off of you?" He asks as his fingers slide along the seam of my sex. And now it's my turn for my breath to stutter from the expertise of his touch, and the anticipation that he knows what my body needs without having to say a single word.

"*Fucking* is the point. And the panties?" I say, my breath hitching when he slides his finders back and forth coating them with my own arousal, teasing my clit with a hint of touch before moving back down. "They save you from ripping them off of me." On the last slide up and down, he tucks his fingers into me. My fingernails score his shoulders as I hold tight and let the sensation swamp me when

We both groan. My muscles contract around him in response causing every interior nerve to engage. The night around us fills with the sounds of my moans and his hushed praise as he works his fingers in and out of me.

"You're so wet," he murmurs against the skin of my shoulder The warmth of his breath causes goose bumps to race over my skin despite the heated fever pitch he's working my body into. "I'm gonna make you come...then I'm gonna lay you down, fuck you hard and fast because you—this—right now—has me so fucking turned on...but after...later...I'll make it up to you. I'll slide my tongue in your pussy, flick it over your clit until you come so hard your muscles will be sore tomorrow from it."

His words, his actions, the here and now—all three of them drive me faster to the edge. "Colton," I pant as I buck my hips into his hands, taking what I want, getting what I need. And what I need is more.

"Almost there." He changes the angle, adjusts the pressure, and adds his thumb against my swollen clit. Within a minute that ball of white hot heat churning in my belly explodes into lightning bolts of pleasure, surging out to my limbs before retracing their steps right back to the apex of my thighs with a pleasure so intense it bears on painful.

Still lost in my post-orgasmic high, I don't realize he's supporting my sagging yet sated body until he withdraws his fingers from me and steps back. My legs are unsteady but I get lost in the devilish smirk on his lips when he brings his fingers to his mouth and sucks on them. There is something so damn hot about the action but it's the words he says next that are even sexier.

"My turn." He unfastens his pants, pulls down the zipper, and frees his dick. I lick my lips in reflex as he runs his hand up and back over its length. He's a striking picture standing there so devastatingly handsome with dark hair and broad shoulders looking so much like the bad boy I never wanted but now can't imagine living without. My heart swells in my chest. And then of course when he strokes himself and lets his head fall back so I can watch, I'm seriously turned on.

Like that's not hard to be when it comes to Colton.

He lifts his head back up, emerald eyes blazing through the darkness. "Get on all fours," he commands and my pussy clenches at the dominance in his tone. A part of me wants to challenge him, keep my control, but with my panties wet and body on fire for his touch, I obey. Ever so slowly, I turn my back to him, make a show of dropping to my knees, and crawl out onto my hands.

The carnal sound he emits deep in the back of his throat tells me he likes what he sees: my ass in the air, lace top stockings at mid thigh, and my face looking over my shoulder with a coy smile. Colton moves toward me, his teeth biting his bottom lip and his hungry eyes roam over the lines of my body as he drops to his knees.

His hands knead the flesh of my hips, fingers laced with intention and dick rubbing ever so softly at my opening. My lips fall lax at the sensation and I drop my head down to wait for the pleasure just within reach. I'm lost in that suspended state of anticipation when he surprises me by leaning over, his chest to my torso so he can scrape his stubbled chin against the bare curve of my shoulder.

"You blindfolded me, took the reins…mmm…it was fucking hot, Ry, but a man has to get his control back somehow...And I'm taking that control right now." The deep timbre of his voice is strained—the sound of a man about to lose restraint—and the knowledge that I can do this to him, *for him*, still surprises me and turns me on.

"You want control?" I ask

His chuckle resonates as he runs his chin down the bare skin of my back. With one hand on my hip, he takes the other and runs the crest of his cock up and down my pussy to make sure I'm ready for him.

"Then take it, Ace."

The words aren't even out of my mouth before he enters me in one slick thrust. We both cry out from the sensation. My hips buck from that pleasurable burn that tells me he's filling me to the edge of reason and from the knowledge of what's coming next. Because God yes, I love the soft and slow with Colton but damn if I don't like his hard and fast too. To know that I can push my husband to the brink, cause that animalistic urge to surface momentarily as he pistons into me is an extremely heady and satisfying feeling.

And no sooner than the thought passes through my desire laden mind, does he start the slow withdraw out before grinding back into me. That sweet ache of pleasure begins to simmer anew. The feel of his hands—one on my waist and the other on my shoulder holding me against him so that he can draw out every last sensation gives the whole act a sense of desperation.

Take. *Harder.* Sate. *Faster.* More. *Deeper.* The words flash in my mind but die in the fog of pleasure he's wrapping around me.

"Goddamn woman," he says drawing the words out. The slap of his body against mine and our harsh panting as he picks up the pace are the only sounds we make. Our bodies move in perfect synch, his action becomes my reaction, causing my knees to dig into the unforgiving asphalt beneath the blanket. But I welcome the pain with the pleasure because my body is riding that fine line of heightened sensation and it only enhances the intensity.

He changes the angle some, pushing himself deeper, faster, harder—unconsciously giving me all of the things I wanted to ask of him—until he cries out my name in a harsh growl. His hips buck, fingers bruise and soothe all at the same time as he loses his control to me once again.

After a moment, he loosens his hold just before I feel the brush of his lips against my bare shoulder. I can't help my soft moan that falls in protest as he slips out of me. He shifts to sit on the blanket beside me and we lock eyes. So many emotions surge within and pass between us without speaking a single word.

The moment is so real, so raw, so packed with feeling that I can't help but remember our first date and my thoughts as I looked in my rearview mirror at him standing beneath the street light.

"Most definitely an angel," I murmur, overwhelmed with how far we've come since that night.

Colton narrows his eyes and angles his head, "An angel? What are you talking about?"

The soft smile on my lips spreads. "Nothing," I say with a shake of my head. The man's ego doesn't need any more boosting. Colton doesn't need me to tell him that I know the answer to the question without a doubt. He was most definitely an angel fighting through the darkness. My angel.

Confusion flickers over his face momentarily before he leans forward and cups the side of my face, thumb brushing over my bottom lip still swollen from his kiss. The depth of emotion in his eyes causes a lump to form in my throat because I know I'm responsible for them. The man who never thought he could feel, now feels in spades.

And this should be humorous: him with his pants half down and me in lace and leather sitting on a blanket in the dark in the middle of an empty racetrack. But it's not. It's perfect. It's us.

It's perfectly imperfect.

"Happy anniversary," I whisper.

"Happy anniversary." He leans forward and kisses me tenderly. Our lips linger against each other's and I feel his mouth spread into a smile. "I can't believe you gave me the only checkered flag I've never claimed for our first anniversary." The awe in his voice warms my heart and makes all of the trouble I went through to do this worth it, a thousand times over.

"I had to make it memorable. Moments like this only happen once in a lifetime."

"Everything with you is memorable," he says winning my heart all over again, "because you're my once in a lifetime."

Epilogue One

10 Years Later

The vibration of the motor rumbles in my chest long before the car slings into turn four. I track the car, my eyes glued to it as he fights traffic on his second to last lap, and I wonder if it will always be this way. If I'll always be a nervous wreck when he's out there.

Definitely. Without a doubt.

I hear him shift gears as he enters into turn two, the only turn I can't see from my place in the box along pit row, so I turn to look at the monitor in front of me. I hear the announcer growing frantic as the end of the race nears, and I don't fight my pride or smile.

"Donavan's flying through turn three. One more to go and he's claiming the checkered flag here today, race fans, as well as taking the lead in the current points standings. Traffic moves aside as he enters turn four and now Donavan's on the homestretch with no one even challenging him." His excitement is contagious as I look up from the screen to watch the car fly toward the start/finish line.

And even though the outcome is unfolding in front of me, my rising anxiety won't be soothed until I can wrap my arms around him again.

"And it's Donavan across first! Donavan takes the checkered flag here today at the Indy Lights Grand Prix, ladies and gentleman! Another one in the bag for this talented driver I know we'll see so much more of in victory lane."

The box around me buzzes with excitement, but I don't even stop to chat because my headset's off and I'm jogging down the stairs. Everyone knows the drill by now, so I'm not worried about who's with whom or where we'll meet up again. I fight through the crowd just in time to see his car slowly enter the black and white checkered staging area of victory lane.

My body vibrates with excitement, and my heart is in my throat as I see the crew descend around him, reaching their hands into the open capsule of the car and squeeze his shoulders or pat the top of his helmet in congratulations. I stand back letting them have their team moment, anxious to congratulate him myself.

I see the steering wheel get passed out, and then I watch as he unfolds his body from the car. Hands help steady him as he climbs out and finds his legs after sitting for the past five hours.

The crew steps back as one man approaches. This has been the good luck routine for the past year. Love swells as I watch the man I fall in love with more and more every single day step forward and start to help unbuckle his helmet.

The media pushes their way around me to get closer, but I remain rooted and watch the moment that chokes me up every single time I see it. A moment that will never lose its impact.

The helmet and white balaclava comes off in one smooth stroke, allowing me to see Zander's eyes sparkle with the same pride and excitement I feel over his win. Colton takes his helmet from him and grabs *our son* in a quick embrace packed full of so many emotions. And I know what Colton is saying to him. The same thing he's told him countless times over the years. *"I'm proud of you, son. I love you."* These are the words he wants him to never forget, or ever be ashamed to say. I swallow the lump in my throat as Colton ruffles Zander's sweat-soaked hair and then steps back to let him have his moment in the sun.

Colton gets lost in the crowd as Becks steps forward and slings an arm around Zander to praise him before the media descends around them.

I stand in the crowd of people around me and wait, knowing he'll find me. It takes only minutes before I feel his hands slide around my waist and pull me back against him, my softness to his steel, at the same time I feel his mouth against my ear.

"Zander did good today, huh?" The rasp of his voice has me closing my eyes momentarily and wondering how over ten years later that sound can still get to me. Can still cause every feeling to flood back like the first night we met.

I angle my head sideways, his stubble tickling my skin as I move my mouth closer to his ear so he can hear me above the announcers and craziness around us. "He gets better with each race," I tell him as I press a kiss to the underside of his jaw and hold it there for a moment. "He has a great teacher," I say, my lips pressed against his skin. "It's your turn to take the checkered flag now." I lift my head up just in time to catch him raise an eyebrow and flash a roguish smirk, and I know he's most definitely not thinking about his race next week. I can't help the laugh that falls from my lips. "On the track, Ace! You already claimed this one!"

"Damn straight I did." He laughs before pressing another chaste kiss to the side of my head, leaving his lips there momentarily before murmuring, "I gotta get back to the team. See you in a bit?"

"Mmm-hmm. Tell everyone dinner's at six-thirty sharp tomorrow, okay?"

"Yep," he says as he turns me around in his arms to face him and then looks at me for a beat with that soft smile I love. The years have been kind to him, a few more lines around his eyes perhaps, but he still has the same Adonis-like looks that stop my heart.

He leans forward and presses a kiss to my lips, and it takes everything I have to not sink a little farther into it, into him. Because even after all this time, I simply can't get enough of him.

Like everything else about me, he senses my need for him and I can feel his smile on his lips before he brushes one last kiss against mine. He leans forward and whispers into my ear, "There'll be plenty of that later."

"Whatever happened to when I want, where I want, huh, Ace?" I challenge him.

I love the carefree sound that falls from his lips as he throws his head back in a full-bodied laugh. He shakes his head and just looks at me, his eyes darting over to a meeting room over my shoulder. "I believe I already proved that theory earlier this morning, Mrs. Donavan." His words cause the ache he'd sated earlier on the desk in that room to come back with a vengeance. He trails a finger down my cheek. "I'll be more than happy to prove that point to you again a little later tonight though."

"Oh no worries." I smirk. "Your *point* was more than proven."

"Baby, this point was most definitely more than proven," he murmurs suggestively as he splays his hand across my lower back and pulls me hard against him so I can feel every single inch of that point pressed against my lower belly. All I can do is breathe out as every part of my body craves him again. "Fuck, I love you," he says, pressing a chaste kiss to my lips before winking at me and walking back toward Zander and the race team.

And all I can do is watch his back as he walks away—strong shoulders, head held high, and still sexy as hell. I shake my head, reminded of when all those years ago as he walked away from me in a race suit. How he called out my name, found the courage to tell me he raced me, and changed more than just our lives, forever.

Epilogue Two

Colton

The house is buzzing with noise like a goddamn beehive.

Just how Ry likes it. Though fuck if I know why, because it's filled with high powered testosterone, overtaking her tiny bit of estrogen.

I glance out on the patio as I walk down the stairs to see Shane talking to Connor about how he's doing with his new job, his arm around his wife and a bottle of beer to his lips.

All of the boys are here for our once a month *family dinner* as Ry calls it, even though some of the boys—shit, men now—are starting families of their own.

"Hey, Shane," I call out to him through the open pocket doors. "I have a few more beers in here if you want them," I tease and he snorts and rolls his eyes in response.

"No thanks. I'm good with just one," he says, holding the bottle up to me in a mock toast with a wide smirk. I laugh, the memory of him green and hungover making me smile.

I walk through the hallway and take it all in. Aiden in his UCLA baseball jersey fresh from practice shooting the shit with Zander in his board shorts and backwards baseball hat, a relaxed grin on his face. Scooter sitting on the deck outside playing with Spiderman figurines with Shane's two year old son. *Shit.*

The sight makes me feel like I'm older than dirt.

Everyone's here but Kyle and Ricky. I feel sorry as fuck for the freshman girls at Stanford those two are currently unleashing their charm on. Or maybe it's their own type of voodoo. The women don't stand a chance against them. Hearts are gonna be breaking.

Fuck 'em and chuck 'em.

Thinking of those two has the old term hitting me like a ton of bricks as the memories of that first night flash back. I don't even fight my smile as I think of the hearts I used to break ... damn I was good—until a certain wavy haired vixen crashed into my damn life, grabbed hold, and never let go. Defiance and curves and my world got turned upside down when I opened up that damn storage closet.

And thank Christ for that.

My fucking Rylee.

And then I hear her voice in the kitchen, and my feet head toward her without a second thought. I clear the doorway and every ounce of love I never thought I could have, never thought a possibility, fucking sucker punches me like it does every goddamn time I see them like this.

Pots are boiling on the stove, the microwave is dinging, and the Goo Goo Dolls are playing overhead, but I don't notice any of that because my eyes are fixed on the sight before me, my heart beating like a damn freight train. They're sitting cross-legged on the floor, knees touching, giggling uncontrollably over some shared secret, flour coating their hair and faces, and complete adoration reflected back at one another.

I stand there and watch them, my soul aching in the best fucking way possible at how I'm the luckiest son of a bitch on the face of the earth. I've been to Hell and back, but it was worth every goddamn second for what I feel right now ... feelings that aren't so fucking foreign any more.

The ones I can't imagine living a lifetime without.

The giggles stop as a pair of green eyes look up at me from beneath dark lashes, freckles on his scrunched nose dusted with flour, and a lopsided smirk on his lips. He just looks at me, gauging if I'm going to get upset at the mess he obviously played a part in.

Then violet eyes look up at me, that soft smile, on those lips I love, directed straight at me. And I silently marvel at how that simple smile gets me every fucking time, no matter how many years have passed. It has me wanting to pull her into my arms, share all my secrets, and fuck her senseless simultaneously.

Her voodoo powers still in full fucking effect.

And fuck if I'd want it any other way.

I fight the smile creeping onto my lips because I'm the biggest fucking softie when it comes to him—a fact I deny regularly—and try to act tough. "What's going on here?" I ask, stepping into the room as Rylee pats her hands together and a plume of flour flies into the air like a dust cloud around her, causing them to erupt into another fit of giggles.

I walk over to them, flour coating the soles of my bare feet, and squat down beside them. My eyes dart back and forth over them before I reach out and place a dot of flour on his nose with my finger. "Looks like you guys made quite a mess," I say, trying to play the part of disciplinarian but failing miserably.

"Well thanks, *Captain Obvious*!" he giggles at me, sarcasm in full swing.

"*Ace Thomas*!" Ry reprimands our son, but his words have already knocked me on my ass.

I look at him, search his face over and over, studying it like a fucking road map to see if he has any clue, any goddamn inkling what he's just said to me, but there's nothing looking back at me but mischievous green eyes and a heart-breaking smile. My spitting image.

"*Hey?*"

That telephone-sex rasp of a voice pulls me back from flashes of plastic helicopters, superhero Band-aids covering an index finger, and the sound of thwacking. Thoughts I don't really remember but that seem clear as fucking day somehow. I shake my head and try to clear out the confusion before I look over to her. "Yeah?"

"You okay?" She reaches out, touches my cheek, and stares at me.

And then he starts giggling, breaking the thoughts holding me hostage. He points to the flour she's now transferred to my own cheek. "What?" I growl in a monster voice, causing the almost six year old to squeal like a little girl as my fingers reach out to tickle him.

"You're a flour monster too now!" he says between panted breaths as he tries to squirm away from me.

Our tickle fest lasts for a few more seconds as I let him escape, chase him, and then hug him. And he wiggles for a bit more before I feel his arms slide around my neck and hold on tight.

Those tiny arms pack the biggest punch of all because they hold everything I am in their fucking hands. I take a moment and breathe him in—little boy, flour, and a bit of Ry's vanilla all mixed in one—and close my eyes.

I guess it was *in the cards after all.*

Fuck me running.

He saved me.

Then. And now.

Just like his mother did.

I feel her hand on my back, feel her lips press against my shoulder, and open my eyes to look at her—*my whole fucking alphabet*—and smile.

"I think our flour monster here needs to take a quick bath before dinner," she says.

"Nah." I reach up to ruffle his hair, flour flying again. "Nothing a cannonball in the pool won't wash off, right, Ace?"

He shouts out a "Woohoo!" and gives me a high five before running out of the kitchen at full speed. I watch him run and jump into the pool, Zander yelping as the splash soaks him.

"He's got you wrapped around his little finger," she says as she walks over to the sink to wash the flour from her hands.

"And you don't?" I ask with a shake of my head as I walk up behind her and slide my arms around her waist, pulling her back into me. And fuck if that ass of hers pressed against my dick doesn't make me ache to take her, throw her over my shoulder, and haul her upstairs right now.

I press a kiss to that spot beneath her neck, and even after all this time, her body responds instantly to me. Goose bumps appear on her exposed skin, her breath hitches and the fucking sigh that turns me on, as if her hands are wrapping around my dick, falls from her lips. And if her beautiful body doesn't turn me hard as fucking steel, her responsiveness does without a fucking hesitation.

That and how much I know she loves me, faults and all.

How in the fuck did I get so lucky?

I shake my head as all of the shit that's happened in my life flashes through my mind. I chuckle, the things that hit me the hardest—that mean the most—all started with a damn storage closet and this defiant-as-fuck woman in my arms who called me to the carpet, grabbed me by the balls, and told me our outcome was non-negotiable.

And fuck me, we've still got a lifetime left for her to call all the shots she wants because my balls are still nestled exactly where they're supposed to be, right in her hands.

"What are you laughing about?" she asks.

"Just thinking of the look on your face when you found out I'd won the auction," I tell her, the memory clear as fucking day. "You were so pissed."

"What woman wouldn't have been when you came off as arrogant as you did?" She snorts out a laugh and then sighs softly.

And the sigh alone makes my dick start to get hard.

"Arrogant? Me? *Never*," I tell her.

"Whatever! I know you fixed that auction, Ace."

And I laugh. God, I love this woman. Ten years later and still feisty as fuck.

"Baby, that answer I'll hold on to forever," I tell her, pressing a kiss to the back of her head.

"That's not possible," she whispers, looking up to press a kiss to the underside of my jaw, "because you'll be busy holding on to me."

Fuckin' A straight I will.

I squeeze her a little tighter, not wanting to let her go just yet because, fuck, what racer doesn't want to hold on to their checkered flag a little longer?

At least I know mine waves only for me.

My kryptonite.

My alphabet, motherfucking A to Z.

My fucking Rylee.

The End

Aced

Find my hand in the darkness
And if we cannot find the light,
We will always make our own.
—*Tyler Knott Gregson*

Prologue

Colton

"Ry?" I call her name the minute I clear the top of the stairs. The little note she left me on the counter is in my hand. "Your nothing-but-sheets date night starts now," it reads. Curiosity rules my thoughts and fuels my actions.

Well, that and the image of her naked and waiting for me. My day's been for shit though, so I'm not going to push my luck and expect a miracle like that to turn it around. But a man can sure as fuck hope.

SoMo is playing as I walk onto the upper patio of the house where our original nothing-but-sheets date took place a long-ass time ago. *Sweet Christ*. My feet falter when I find Rylee. She's leaning back on the chaise lounge, dressed in some kind of black lacey thing that I don't pay much attention to because it's see-through enough for me to tell she's naked as sin beneath it. Her hair is piled on top of her head, her lips are bare, and her knees are spread so her feet are on either side of the chair. And I'm distracted momentarily—my eyes searching for a glimpse of the something more between those thighs of hers—before realizing sky-high heels complete the outfit.

Fuck me. I can already feel the spikes of those heels digging into my ass as her legs wrap around me. That's a pain any man can find pleasure in.

"Hey," she says in that raspy voice of hers that calls to my heart, my dick, and every nerve in between. A coy smile plays at the corners of her mouth as her eyes narrow, one foot taps, and eyebrows rise. "I see you got my note. Glad you knew where to find me."

"Baby, I could be deaf and blind and I'd still find you. No way in hell I could forget that night."

"Or that morning," she says, and damn, she's right. It was one helluva morning too. Sleepy sex. Just-woke-up sex. Sunrise sex. I think we tried all of those and then some. And I love the flush that crawls up her cheeks from the memory. My sex-kitten wife greeting me after work in lace and heels is embarrassed. The irony isn't lost on me. I love how she can be this way for me, when I know, despite her confidence, it still unnerves her.

"Definitely a good morning," I agree, as I stare at her. She's always drop-dead gorgeous but there's something new, something different about her tonight, and it has nothing to do with the lace. I can't tell what it is but it's knocked the breath right out of me.

Shit, what am I missing? Panic flickers inside me that I've missed something major. Could it be one of those dates guys have to put in their calendar with five alerts, so they don't forget it? I run through the usual suspects: It's not our anniversary. Not her birthday.

I move to the other shit a guy usually doesn't notice. Her hair's the same color. It must be new lingerie. Is it? Fuck if I know. If it is, can a scrap of lace really change her demeanor?

Damn. I know lingerie changes mine, but that's for a whole different reason.

What else can it be, Donavan? Bite the bullet and just ask. Save yourself the guessing game and the trouble you'll be in if you guess wrong and hurt her feelings. No need to get the hormones she just got back under control—after all those years of fertility shit—to get all out of whack again.

"Something's different about you . . ." I leave the comment open-ended so she can respond.

But of course she doesn't take the bait. I should have known my wife is smarter than that. She'll make me work for the answer, so we just stare at each other in a battle of wills before her smile slowly widens into a full grin.

Give me a clue, Ry.

Nope. She's not going to. I should've guessed as much. Might as well admire the view anyway: cleavage, lace, a whole lotta skin, and thighs I can't wait to be between. The smirk on her face tells me she knows exactly what I'm doing when I finally meet her gaze. When her eyes flicker to the table beside her, she *finally* gives me something to go off.

The table is covered in takeout boxes from our favorite Chinese restaurant. There's a galvanized bucket of ice with some bottlenecks sticking out of it and paper plates and chopsticks piled on the side. Truth be told, I was so busy looking at her, I hadn't even noticed the food.

But now, my stomach growls.

"I got your favorite," she says, fidgeting with the hem of the lace so my eyes are drawn back to the V of her thighs, where it's dark enough I can't see anything. But fuck if it's not from a lack of trying. "I hope you're in the mood for Chinese. I thought we could eat out."

I can't hide the lightning-quick grin that flashes across my face because the type of eating out I'm thinking of has nothing to do with chopsticks. And from the purse of her lips, she knows perfectly well what I'm thinking. And yes, I may be hungry, but I don't really give a flying fuck about food right now because there's the taste of something else I'd rather have on my tongue.

"I know you've been working hard, stressed about the race next week. Sonoma has always been a tough one for you . . . so I thought I'd treat you to a date night with your hot wife," she continues with a lift of her eyebrows, taunting and daring me all at once. Goddamn tease.

"Does my *hot wife* think that when she greets me on the patio in a getup like that, I'll give a rat's ass about the dinner, the cold beer, or the sunset we'll get to enjoy while eating it?" I ask as I cross the distance; the need to have my hands on her growing stronger with each passing second.

"For starters . . . yes."

"I like starters." I reach out and trace the line of her collarbone with my fingertip. After all this time, there is still something so damn sexy about her body moving ever so slightly into my touch, telling me she wants me as badly as I want her. "And I also like dessert . . ." I say, my voice trailing off. The air is thick with sexual tension as I drop to my knees on the chaise between hers. She's crazy if she thinks she's going to greet me like this and not get fucked good and hard before we leave this patio. "But you forgot one very important thing."

Her violet eyes widen as I lean in. "What's that?" she asks, her voice breathless. My every nerve is attuned to the sound of it.

"You forgot to kiss your husband hello." I catch a flash of a smile before she tilts her head back so our lips are in perfect alignment.

"Well, let me correct that right now, *sir*," she says, knowing damn well that term will only turn me on more. Shit. Like that's a hard thing for her to do. It's Rylee, isn't it?

Before I can finish thinking about what more I want her to do while calling me sir, she leans forward and closes the distance between us. And fuck yes, I want all of her right now, but I'll take what I can get. Besides, the way she kisses me is so damn sexy. It's that kind of kiss guys hate to admit they love: the soft and slow kind that causes that ache deep in my balls before it slowly spreads up my spine and tickles the base of my neck. It's the kiss that comes two steps before I lose control and panties are torn because the need to bury myself in her tight, hot pussy is the only desire I have.

When she pulls back to end the kiss, I groan in complaint and fist my hands to prevent myself from reaching out and yanking her against me. I'm ready to say screw the dinner, regardless of how hungry I am.

"Better?" she asks, sass on her lips and seduction in her eyes.

"Hmm . . . there are other parts of me that still need to be welcomed home properly." I fight the grin I want to give her because I love when she's like this. Feisty. Sexy. Mine. Shedding her reserved nature in the way she only does around me.

"What a poor, deprived husband you are," she says, her lips in a sexy pout while her fingers walk up my thigh. I watch the ascent of her hand, my dick definitely wanting those fingers to move faster. "And I promise to welcome all of those parts home properly, but first . . . *you need to eat*."

Buzzkill. *Seriously?* She thinks she can tempt me with her touch and then stuff an egg roll in my mouth? Does she not know me by now? That when it comes to her I have no restraint? Well, unless of course those restraints are tying her to a bed.

"You tease." I lock eyes on hers the same time I reach out and grab onto her hand. I place it exactly where I want it: my cock. "Why wait? We can have dessert first."

"Nice try, Ace, but dinner's going to get cold." She cups my balls, fingernails scraping ever so softly that the minute my head falls back and the moan falls from my lips, she tugs her hand from my grip. "Let's eat."

"Oh, now that's cold." I laugh. What else can I do? Like always, the woman has me by the balls. I stare at her, smirk on my lips and disbelief in my eyes, as I swing my legs over the edge of the lounge chair. "You can't greet me wearing that and expect me to focus on Kung Pao chicken."

"But it's your favorite," she says, voice playful. With determined actions, she starts to open containers.

I'm hungry all right, but not for Chinese.

I reach out and tug her against me, so her back is to my front, and the feel of her warm body against mine strengthens my resolve. I've decided Chinese food is much better reheated. And if I have any say in the matter, that's exactly what's going to happen to ours.

"I beg to differ. You're my favorite," I murmur against the curve of her shoulder as her curls tickle my cheek and her vanilla scent fills my nose. My let's-always-stick-to-the-schedule wife's body stiffens in resistance at first, but when I press a kiss just beneath her ear in that clothes-immediately-fall-off zone, her body melts into mine and she relaxes. "I want dessert first."

"Rule breaker," she sighs, lacing her fingers with mine on her chest. She's trying to figure out how to rein me in when she should know by now it won't do any good. I always get what I want when it comes to getting my fill of her.

"You wouldn't like me any other way."

"True."

"How about we compromise?"

"Compromise?" she asks, as if she's shocked to hear that word coming from my mouth when discussing sex.

"Yes, it means you give some and I give some."

"I have a feeling what you want to give and what I want to give are two entirely different things," she teases. "Don't forget that I know you, Donavan. I know you like to play dirty—"

"Damn straight I do, especially when it comes to having sex with you."

She just smiles and shakes her head at me. "But I have a plan."

"You always have a plan," I say with an exasperated laugh. "Bet my plan is better."

"Lay it on me," she deadpans and then realizes exactly what she's said. I can feel the laugh she tries to hide vibrate from her back into my chest.

"How about we have sex first and then eat?" I suggest, knowing I'm driving her crazy. Her laugh rings around us, but for the first time since I've been home, I hear something different in her tone. Before I can give it much thought, she continues.

"Nope. That's not the plan. And definitely not a compromise. Food first, then sex," Rylee says as she shifts away and moves to face me. She crosses her arms over her chest and nods, trying to take a hard line with me.

"I love when you get all demanding." I lean forward with a half-smile on my lips, knowing my comment will get her all riled up.

She narrows her eyes, and I can see her mind working to figure out a way to negotiate so she gets what she wants. And for the life of me, I can't figure out what that is. I've been so absorbed in work—the narrow lead I have in points over Luke Mason going into Sonoma and all of the other shit that goes with it—I've obviously missed something.

"It seems we're at an impasse," she finally says. Her prior confidence, which had momentarily wavered, is back, and I'm more than ready for action.

"Good thing I drive a hard bargain," I say with a quirk of my eyebrows as I glance down at her outfit.

I'll drive more than a bargain, sweetheart.

"Oh, I know you do, Ace, but I think we need to leave it up to the fortune cookies to decide what we do next." Her eyes light up with challenge while I start laughing at how ridiculous that sounds.

"The fortune cookies? What are you talking about?"

"Well . . . you said you wanted dessert first so I'm just trying to compromise," she says with a bat of her eyelashes.

"Not that kind of dessert," I state. There's nothing I can do but shake my head at her and her asinine suggestion, but fuck, I'll take any help I can get to speed up this process so I can slow it down with her. Come to think of it, I'm sure I can twist any of those stupid little fortunes to my benefit. So be it. *Game on, Ryles.* "It's ridiculous, but you planned this so you get to make the rules. Let's just hope those fortunes say you need to have hot monkey sex with your husband."

Her face lights up and her lips curve into a grin. She leans forward and grants me a great view of her cleavage as she starts rummaging through the plastic bag on the table. My eyes shift and focus on the dark pink of her nipples just beneath the sheer fabric, until she starts waving the cookies in front of my eyes with the smuggest of smiles.

She knows exactly what she's doing, and has no shame in playing it up as I work my tongue in my cheek, bide my time, and let her have this moment.

"Only three?" I ask when she sets them on the table in front of us. "How are we going to decide who gets the third one?"

"Since we're learning to compromise . . ." Her voice trails off as she elbows me in the ribs. And just as she starts to pull away, I grab her arm, pull her into me, and press a chaste kiss on her mouth. It's already been way too damn long since I kissed her. She swats me away when I try to slip my tongue between her lips. "Are you trying to sway me for the third cookie, Donavan?"

"Did it work?" A man can always hope.

"Here. You go first," she says, leaving me hanging without an answer as she holds the cookie in front of me by the cellophane. When I take it from her, she shifts so she sits square to me, her bent knee against my thigh, giving me a perfect view of her pussy. In a glance, I can make out the trim strip of her hair down there, and fuck if it doesn't turn me on even more.

Fortune cookie gods, please be kind. Sex is needed.

"Okay. Let's see," I say as I pull the cookie out of the bag and break it with a dramatic flair, praying it's a fortune I can work with. I pull the strip of paper out and shake my head as I read the words. *Really? How fucking perfect is this?*

"What does it say?" she asks as I laugh.

"It's been a long race, but you've finally crossed the finish line." I look up and she seems as amused as I am.

"I'd say that's a fitting fortune," she says, eyes narrowing as she contemplates the words. "I guess the real question is what race are they talking about?"

"Life?" I shrug. "Fuck if I know."

She laughs and fidgets with the cookie in her hand. Why does she seem so on edge all of a sudden?

"You're trying to figure out how that gets you sex, and I don't think that helps you out in any way, shape, or form."

Shit. She's right. There's no way to parlay this into me getting sex before food because if I've already crossed the proverbial finish line, it doesn't bode well for me.

"Damn it. That's a food-before-sex one. Don't get cocky, Donavan. I'm primed for a comeback," I say pushing her cookie toward her and taking a bite of mine, hoping this silly game will end soon, but am enjoying myself all at the same time. "Your turn."

The things I do for my wife.

"Okay," she says as she breaks the cookie and stares at her fortune. "It says *your lucky numbers are six, nine, and sixteen.*" She looks up from her fortune, eyes guarded, teeth worrying her bottom lip.

"That's random. Nothing else is on there?" I ask as I grab it from her. Yep. It says exactly that. Must be a misprinted fortune, but hell, I'll take it because I can use it. "Sweet! This is a sex-before-food one because it says your lucky number is six and nine . . . *sixty-nine*. And guess what? I happen to like doing certain things pertaining to that number too . . ."

"You're incorrigible," she says, playfully pushing against my chest, before uncharacteristically fisting her hand in my shirt and pulling me into her. Our faces are inches apart, the heat of her breath is on my lips, but there is something in her expression that stops me from kissing her.

And I never stop myself from kissing her.

"What is it?" I ask. She just shakes her head, trying to blink away the tears welling in her eyes despite the smile on her lips. "Talk to me, Ry. What's wrong?" My hands are cupping her face as I wait for her to explain. Tears make me fucking panic. How'd we get from sexy to flirty to funny to tears?

"I'm being stupid," she says, shaking her head as if that is going to help clear the tears from her eyes. She must sense I'm freaked the fuck out because she pushes against my hands holding her head, and presses her lips to mine. "I love you." Her voice is soft as her lips move against mine, and something about her tone makes my heart beat a bit faster. "Like head-over-heels, butterflies-in-my-stomach kind of love you . . . that's all."

Her words dig deep down into the places that rarely get paid attention to these days: the goddamn abyss where the demons from my childhood live. The ones that used to rule my life until Rylee came along using her fucking perfection and selfless love to help brighten that darkness, and chase away the doubt that occasionally rears its bitch of an ugly head.

I lean back to make sure this woman who means the whole goddamn world to me really is okay. Because if she isn't, I'll do whatever it takes to make sure she is. When she bites her bottom lip, smiles and nods she's fine, I smooth my thumb over the indent her teeth just left, before trying to lighten the suddenly serious moment. "You scared me for a minute. I thought you were upset about the prospect of sixty-nining, and that would mean I'd be in a whole world of hurt with this death-do-us-part thing since I kind of like when I get to do that with you."

"You perform that number exceptionally well, so no, that number stays in play," she says with a cute wink. She bites the inside of her cheek and eyes the third and final cookie in my hand before flicking her gaze back up to mine.

Thank fuck for that, but there is something most definitely off with her. "Here," I say as I hold out the last fortune cookie, hoping to make whatever wrong I've done, right.

"No. You open it." She shoves it back toward me, smile back in place. "It's the tie-breaker."

When I try to make her take the cookie, she just pushes it into my hands and scoots back. "Sex before food, sex before food," I chant and we both chuckle. But my laugh dies off when I read the fortune, and try to make sense of it. "*OVbunEN*."

What the fuck? I read it again before I look up to meet Ry's eyes. The sight of her—tears welling, that smile so goddamn big on those perfect lips—knocks the breath out of me. And, suddenly, it all clicks into place.

It's like everything is moving in slow motion—thoughts, breath, vision—everything except for my heart. Because it's pounding like a fucking freight train as I glance back down to the jumbled words on the paper, before looking back up to her.

There's no fucking way.

Can't be.

"*Really?*" I ask. I don't even recognize the awed disbelief in my voice as I ask about the one thing I thought we'd never get another chance at again.

The first tear slips over and slides down her cheek as we stare at each other, but this one doesn't make me panic like they usually do.

"*Really*," she whispers.

Disbelief turns into the best fucking reality. Ever.

OVbunEN.

Bun in the oven.

"You're pregnant?" I can't even believe the words I'm saying as I pull her toward me, and onto my lap.

She can't get the words out to tell me yes so she just nods her head as tears fall, and her arms cling to me. And fuck, her hands digging into my back feel incredible because I don't think I've ever felt closer to her. Not even when I'm in her.

I have one hand on her neck and the other on her lower back. Air's not even welcome in the space between us as we hold on to each other on this patio where so many firsts have happened for us. Telling me here of all places makes perfect fucking sense, now.

My face is buried in the curve of her neck. And if I thought my heart and soul had been lost to her before, I was so fucking wrong it's not even funny. Right now, in this moment, I've never felt more connected to her. My fucking Rylee.

My mind flickers back over the years of agonizing fertility treatments when emotions ran high, and hope always gave way to heartbreaking disappointment. When we finally acknowledged last year that having a baby the traditional way was never going to happen for us, Rylee lost herself for a bit. Fuck yes, it put a strain on our marriage, but it was more devastating for me to watch the woman I love more than my own soul slip away day by day, bit by bit, and not be able to do a goddamn thing about it.

The helpless feelings I had during that time can take a hike.

When I lean back and move my trembling hands to her face, I don't think she's ever been more beautiful than in this moment: eyes alive, lips in a glowing smile, and a tiny part of us growing inside her.

"We're gonna have a baby," she whispers. And although I already know it, hearing her say it causes my breath to catch and my heart to summersault. "June ninth."

Six. Nine.

Fuckin' A.

We finally crossed the finish line we thought we'd never reach.

Chapter One

Colton

Six months later

"I was a little worried when you told me to come over today that you'd lost control of your balls, but this?" Becks asks, as he takes a measured look at the empty beach around us. "This is just what the doctor ordered."

"Where's the faith, brother?" I slide a glance over to him behind my sunglasses. "Can you see me at a baby shower?" I ask. He snorts in response. "I assure you my balls are firmly attached. There is no way in hell I'm setting foot anywhere near the house right now." I mock-shiver at the thought of all those women who'd gladly leave lipstick on my cheek.

"A whole new definition for the estrogen vortex."

"Damn straight." I reach over and tap the neck of my beer against his. "And not in a good way."

"And for that reason alone, I think the baby's a girl," he says with a laugh, causing me to grunt at his logic. "Dude, you've played women for so damn long, it'd be funny as fuck and serve you right to watch one play you for the rest of your life." He holds up his pinkie telling me if we had a little girl, I'll be wrapped around her finger. Fucker's probably right, but I'm not telling him that. Besides, the smarmy grin on his face is wide enough to earn the bottle top I throw at him.

"No one is playing me. That you can be sure of." I tip my bottle to my lips, as Becks laughs long and hard at the words he knows are a lie.

"I don't think you have any idea what's about to hit you, brother."

He's right. I have no fucking clue. Zip. Zero. Zilch. All I know is the closer the due date gets the more I feel like I haven't had enough time to get ready for it. *It?* More like a complete overhaul of our life. Scary fucking shit.

"So, how are you doing with all of this?"

"Shit's getting real," I muse with a slow nod of my head.

"Considering there's a baby shower up at the house right now with women dressing themselves in toilet paper—in some ritual I pray I never understand—and talking about crowning that has nothing to do with the kind a king wears . . . and diapers . . . yeah, it's definitely real. But uh, nice try, Wood. You never answered my question."

"I'm good." *Back off, Daniels.*

"We've known each other how long?" he asks, and I know he's going in for the kill here. I just wish I knew what the fuck he's hunting for, so instead of giving him the answer he already knows, I just concentrate on peeling the label on my beer bottle.

"Pussy," he mutters under his breath. Baiting me. Fueling a fire I'd rather not light.

"What's your bag, Becks? You want to know that this whole baby thing scares the shit out of me? That it's fucking with my head?" I pick up a shell and huck it at a pile of seaweed to the right of me. "Feel better, now?"

I want to shove up and walk down to the water, get the hell away from him, and yet he knows me well enough that if I do, then he's gotten under my skin. Pressed the buttons he's been waiting to push.

How the fuck do I explain that everything already feels the same and so goddamn different, and yet I wouldn't want to change it even if I could? He'd be bringing out the damn straight jacket.

"Me feel better? No." He chuckles, grating on every nerve. "But I think you do." I glare at him from behind my lenses. "Wanna talk about it?"

"No," I snap. Leave the shit I don't want to talk about alone. But the silence eats at me, taunts me to speak. I can trust Becks; I know I can. Yet as the words form, I choke on them. *Man the fuck up, Donavan.* "Yes. Fuck. I don't know."

"Well, that simplifies things," he teases, trying to draw a laugh out of me.

I take my hat off, scrub a hand through my hair, and put it back on to buy some time. "I'm having a kid, Becks. And all of it's scary as shit. Diapers and futures and expectations and . . . I don't know what else, but I'm sure I'm missing a million other things. What the fuck qualifies me to be a dad? Not just any dad, but a good one? I mean, look at my fucked-up childhood. It's all I know. How in the hell do I know when I'm stressed and tired that I'm not going to revert to the only thing I've ever known?" I end the question, my voice almost a shout, and realize everything I just said.

Have another beer, Donavan. You sound like a sap.

Becks laughs. And not just any kind of laugh but a chiding chuckle that scrapes on my nerves like 60-grit sandpaper.

"Thank God! It's about damn time you start acting like you're freaking out because sure as shit I'd be too. Look, no one qualifies to be a good parent. You just kind of learn as you go, mistakes and all." He shrugs. "And as for the last one . . . dude, look how you are with the boys at The House. You'd never hurt them. It's not in your makeup regardless of the fucked-up shit you grew up with."

Hearing his words I nod my head, finding some relief that the shit that's been bouncing around in my head is normal. But my normal and Becks's normal growing up are polar opposites. So while I appreciate the sentiment, it doesn't stop the freight train of fear I'm going to fail epically at this parenting shit. That Rylee will be so head over heels in love with the baby she'll forget me. That I have the same blood running through my veins as my mother who'd had no regard for me. That I have the same blood running through my veins as my father who hadn't stuck around.

"Dude, it's totally normal to be freaked," he says, as I open the cooler and grab another beer to drink away my stupidity. "You'll fuck up sometimes, but that's how it is. There's no manual on how to be a good dad . . . you learn as you go. Kind of like the first time you had sex. Practice makes perfect type of thing."

I laugh. Fucking Becks. He's the only person I know who could compare parenting to sex, and I'd completely understand the parallel. He gets me.

"And sex? *Now that's something* I've practiced a lot."

"By the look of Rylee's belly, I think you finally mastered that skill. So, see? No need to worry. You've got this."

"Damn." The word falls from my mouth as images of earlier today flood my mind. I was supposed to be moving the couch in the great room to make space for the rental tables and chairs being delivered for the shower. Rather, I found myself looking down at Ry's cheeks hollowing out as she sucked me off. The look in her eyes and smirk on her lips as she ran my slick cock up through the V of her cleavage until it met the sweetness of her wet mouth. My balls tighten remembering how her lips looked stretched around me when she teased my tip before sliding it back down again.

"That good, huh?" Becks asks, dragging me from the images of my hot wife.

"Fucking perfection." It's futile to fight the smug grin on my lips.

"So, is it true then?" I glance over to Becks, my beer now stopped halfway to my lips as I wait for him to explain. "That pregnant women are really that horny?"

My eyes flicker back toward the house at our backs. Laughter from the estrogen invasion floats down to us and I nod my head. "Brother, let's just say that voodoo doesn't hold a fucking candle to pregnant pussy."

"No shit?"

"Nympho." I draw the word out.

The look on his face right now—the raised eyebrows, slow nod of his head, slack jaw—is classic. "Damn. Just damn."

"You have *no* idea," I say with a laugh. "Shit. All the guys were warning me about hormones and mood swings, and I'm sitting over here with a cat-ate-the-canary grin on my face because pussy is my friend. Dude, the only pregnancy craving she's having is for my cock, and I'm more than willing to help her out."

"You lucky bastard."

"Don't I know it."

"Aren't you afraid you're going to . . ." His voice trails off but I can hear the amusement in his tone. "Never mind . . ."

"Finish what you were going to say, Daniels."

"Well, I was going to say, aren't you afraid all that sex is going to hurt the baby—poke it in the head or something? But then I forgot you're only about three inches long so there's no need to worry about that." He stifles the chuckle.

"Fucker." It's my go-to comment with him and even with the dig, I can't help but laugh because I wouldn't expect anything less from him. Besides, I could use the distraction since I keep questioning whether I should have made the call to my private investigator, Kelly, this week.

Ball's already rolling. Too late to stop it now.

I know nothing good can come from it. No happy endings to be had in this situation. In fact, I'm sure it'll fuck me up before it makes me better. But maybe, just maybe, I can lay this one last thing to rest. Close this final circle before the baby comes and move on.

Full circles and shit.

At least once this one's linked together; the goddamn ghosts can just chase each other over and over like a hamster on a wheel while I'm putting the pedal to the metal one hundred miles per hour in the opposite direction.

"Dude," Becks says, pulling me from my thoughts, "you need to take advantage of the sex while you can because after the baby comes, you won't be getting any for a while."

"So I've heard," I groan. How I'm going to go from my wife being a nympho to a nun is not lost on me. "Changes, man. They just keep happening. One day I'm single, the next I'm getting married, and now I'm about to have a baby. How the fuck did that happen?" Despite my words, the smile is wide on my face.

"Not sure how you found a woman who's willing to put up with your crap but she deserves a damn medal for it."

"Thanks for the support." I tip my beer his way in a cheers motion.

"Always. That's what I'm here for . . . but with all of these changes happening, I need to ask you, what's gotten under your skin? Something's up with you and I know you well enough to know it's more than what you've just said."

Here we go again. *Let the Becks psych evaluation begin.*

I refuse to look at him, not wanting him to know I'm not okay. That this banter is all a front because my head feels like it's been put in a blender: too much, too goddamn fast, with too many doubts, and too many unknowns. My fucking past that never goes completely away.

Goddamn ghosts.

"Colton?" he goads.

My beer stops midway to my mouth as irritation fires anew and sarcasm becomes my friend. "Are you asking as my crew chief, my best friend, or my shrink?"

"I've got lifetime privileges for two of the three, so does it really matter?"

Fuck. He's got me there. Why is he pushing the goddamn issue? Does he really want to know the truth? Because I sure as fuck would rather stick my head in the sand. Ignorance is bliss and all that shit.

"I'll get the job done. No worries there," I say way too easily and immediately curse myself because Becks will see right through that response in a heartbeat. I just wonder if he's going to let sleeping dogs lie or if he's going to jingle the leash so they come out to play.

"Ah . . ." he says, drawing the sound out. "But you forget, I do worry. It's my job. You've got a lot of shit going on, and I need your head straight before you even board a plane to the Grand Prix."

"Jesus Christ, Becks. Always worried about the track. Well, there's other shit to life besides the goddamn track!" I snap at him, pissed he knows just what to say to set me off and at the same time hating that he's right.

Baited hook? Meet line and sinker.

Motherfucker. You'd think by now I'd be immune to Becks pushing buttons, and yet every damn time I react on cue like a puppet.

"No worries. My head will be just fine," I say, trying to gain some traction. "You satisfied?"

"You think I care about the fucking track, Donavan? You think racing rules my every thought? No. Not hardly. What does though is having to pick up a phone and call your wife who's nine months pregnant and tell her I put you in a car knowing you had a fucked-up head, that you crashed and died because you were distracted and couldn't focus on the task at hand. Now that? That's what I worry about . . . so you can take out whatever it is you don't want me to know and tell me I'm a selfish asshole for thinking about racing. What I really want to know is that your head is in the goddamn game enough that I don't have to watch some medic put you in a fucking body bag because you can't focus and won't tell anyone why. Call me selfish, call me whatever the fuck you want to . . . talk to me, don't talk to me . . . *Christ* . . . just make sure you're good to go so that doesn't happen." And then in perfect Beckett fashion, he ends his tirade as quick as he starts it.

Silence returns. Eats at me. Pulls from me the truth I don't want to confess.

"I'm trying to find my dad." Fuck. Where did that come from? I wasn't going to tell anyone until I had something solid—like concrete-barrier solid—and yet there I go spilling secrets like a leaky faucet.

Wanting to see his reaction, I glance his way from behind my mirrored lenses; he takes a deep breath and nods his head twice as he digests what I've just said.

"I'm not going to pretend I understand the why behind this . . . but man, aren't some things better left for dead?" There's understanding in his tone, but at the same time, there's no way he can understand. No one can. My shoes have walked through the proverbial Valley of Death more times than I care to count. Maybe I need to go there one more time to finally shake the shadow so I can move forward without it hanging over my head.

"That's just it though—he's always been a loose end. I need to tie it up, cut the strings for good, and never look back." I take a long tug on my beer and try to wash away the bitter taste thinking of him leaves. "It's a shot in the dark. Kelly probably won't find him. And if he does? Maybe just knowing where he is will be enough. Maybe not." I sigh. Feeling more stupid for calling Kelly now than I did before. "Fuck it. Forget I said anything."

"No can do. You said it. I heard it. At least that explains what's crawled up your ass lately. Does Ry know?"

"There's nothing to tell yet." I ignore the twinge of guilt. "She's already stressed about the new kid at work and the baby . . . The last thing I need is for her to worry about me."

"That's what you've got me for."

"Exactly," I say with a definitive nod of my head.

"And your pops? What does he say about all of this?"

Guilt: the gift that keeps on giving.

"Same thing. I'll tell him if something comes of it. Besides . . . he's my dad, if I need to do something, he always supports me." *And yet if that's the case, why aren't you telling him?*

"Exactly," Becks says, and the simple word validates my guilt.

Why in the world am I looking for the piece of shit who never wanted me when I have a man who took me in battered and broken and never looked back?

Exactly.

Thoughts. Doubts. Questions. All three circle the other. But only Kelly will be able to confirm if I'll ever find the answers.

"I promise my head will be clear when I hit the track." It's the only thing I can say to my best friend. My fucked-up way of apologizing.

He nods his head and adjusts the bill of his ball cap. "Well, I hope you find what you're looking for, brother, but I kind of think you already have." When I glance over to him, he tips the green neck of his bottle toward the deck over my shoulder. Confused, I follow his line of sight and look up to see Rylee standing at the railing talking to guests.

Our eyes lock. That goddamn sucker punch of emotion hits me like a battering ram, because for a man who thought he'd never feel anything, she makes me feel everything. The whole fucking gamut.

I remember to breathe. That pang of desire just as strong now as that first time I saw her. But there's so much more that goes with it now: needs, wants, tomorrows, yesterdays, and every fucking thing in between.

Becks is most definitely right.

My father's not the endgame. Just another ghost to exorcise from my soul.

I'm a lucky fucker because I *have* found what I never knew I was looking for. Thank fuck she's looking right back at me.

Chapter Two

Rylee

The fear still holds my heart hostage.

I try to push it down, not think about it, and go about my day to day with work, the boys, and Colton, but every once in a while it rules my thoughts. It doesn't matter that I'm seven months along now. The worry this will all be taken away from me like it has the two times before still sits in the back of my mind with each twinge of my belly or ache in my hips.

And so here I sit in the nursery amid piles of onesies, diapers, and receiving blankets afraid to open a single thing in fear I'll jinx this. That if I open one package of clothes, pre-wash one load of laundry, put sheets on the mattress of the bassinet, I'll cause my long-awaited dream of motherhood to come crashing down.

The rocking chair is safe though. I can sit here and close my eyes and feel the baby move, enjoy the ripples across my hardened belly that allow me to breathe a little easier each and every time I feel a kick. I can rest my hands on my abdomen and know that he or she is a fighter, is healthy, and can't wait for me to hold him or her in my arms. I can sit here and feel the love surging through me for this baby Colton and I made together, and know without a doubt, this perfect little being will only cement and make stronger the love we feel for one another.

And I try to maintain this feeling to will away the worry when I rise from the rocking chair and run my hand over the mattress on the crib. I can't believe this is really happening, that in less than three months' time, there will be this new addition to our life and everything and nothing will change all at once.

Moments in time. How easily we shift from one role to the next and never question the butterfly effect of these transitions. How will this one event segue into the next? Or will it?

A baby. *Our baby*. Even though the life is growing inside me, and I can feel him or her move every now and again, I'm still staggered by the reality of it.

Carefully, I sink to my knees to sort through the baby gifts stacked on the floor. By the looks of the stacks, our friends and family are excited to meet and spoil Baby Donavan. I reach out and pick up a fuzzy yellow blanket, my smile automatic as I hold it up to my cheek to feel its softness.

"Does a baby really need all this stuff?" Colton's voice startles me. He's leaning with his shoulder against the doorjamb, thumbs hooked in the pockets of his shorts. Every inch of his toned, tanned chest all the way down to that V of muscles, calls to the pregnancy hormones that have been ruling my sex drive these past few months.

And even without the hormones, I'm sure I'd still be staring because there is no shortage of want on my end when it comes to him. Just the sight of him gets my blood humming, my heart racing, and makes my soul content.

I take a moment to appreciate my handsome husband. My gaze scrapes over every inch of him before lifting to take in that cocky smirk on his lips that tells me he knows exactly what I'm thinking. And when I lock onto his emerald irises, the amusement I expect to be there isn't. Instead Colton's eyes are a mixture of guarded emotion I can't quite read. It's reminiscent of those first months of dating, when secrets were kept, and I hate the feeling of unease that tickles the back of my neck from its reappearance.

Forcing aside the innate need within me to ask and fix, I tell myself if something's wrong, he'll tell me when he's ready. I shrug off the niggling worry. It's probably just pre-baby jitters. He's been handling this all so much better than I thought he would, but at the same time the past few weeks he's withdrawn some. And while that concerns me, I know he's bound to have some fears and reservations like most impending parents.

"I'm not sure if it's all needed. It's definitely a lot of stuff for one little baby." I finally answer as I glance at the piles of gifts around me.

"You're gorgeous."

The unexpected comment has my eyes flashing up to meet his and love to swell in my chest. Disbelieving he can see me as beautiful when I feel like a beached whale, I let the soft laugh fall from my mouth as I shift onto my butt, brace my hands behind me for support, and stretch out my legs. "Thanks, but I don't really think that a huge stomach and toes swollen like sausages qualifies me for the *gorgeous* category."

"Well, in that case, maybe just the beautiful category," he teases with a flash of a grin as he enters the room. He looks around, picks up a checkered flag baby quilt that causes his eyebrows to lift in amusement before he moves to where I'm sitting.

"Hmm," I murmur, nowhere near agreeing with the beautiful consensus. But when I look back up to meet his gaze, I can see that when he looks at me, beautiful is what he sees, and I'll take it, because when a man sees you at what you feel is your worst and thinks you're at your best, you don't question it.

"You're working too hard, Ry," he says as he lowers himself to the floor in front of me. I force myself not to sigh at the refrain, but it's the one thing we've argued about lately, his want for me to take maternity leave. "You need to stop doing so much. Let others help you."

I look down to the blanket in my hands, hating he's right and that he can see how much I'm struggling with ceding control. "I know, but there's just so much to do before the baby comes that only I can do. With the new project coming online and Auggie struggling at The House and . . ." My voice trails off thinking of the newest addition to the brood and how much attention he needs that I'm not going to be able to give him. Everything on my invisible task list is screaming at me for it to be done—like yesterday, done—and there are not enough hours in the day. Becoming overwhelmed by the mere thought, I blow out a breath as tears sting the back of my eyes. My internal struggle about letting people down resurfaces; I already feel I'm dropping the ball, and I haven't even started maternity leave.

"Breathe, Ry. I know your type-A personality wants to have all your ducks in a row," he says, "but it's not possible. Other people can do things. It might not be just how you want it, but at least it's help. And if it doesn't get done, it will still be there after BIRT comes."

"Colton!"

"What's wrong with BIRT? Baby In Rylee's Tummy," he states innocently, knowing damn well he's just trying to irritate me. *Or make me smile.*

"Stop calling him that." I smack a hand on his leg as he laughs out loud, and he grabs my hand before I can pull it away.

"Him? Did you just say *him?*" Our long-running debate about the baby's unknown gender just became front and center. He pulls my arm, and I move forward at the same time as he leans in. He presses a tender kiss to my lips that sends a shockwave of desire way down to my core. I can feel his lips curve into a smile as they remain against mine.

"Yes, I said *he* . . . but that's just a pronoun," I murmur, loving being close to him. The past couple days he's felt so far away. I've just chalked it up to him feeling as overwhelmed as me but for different reasons: the points lead he's barely hanging onto with the Grand Prix coming up next month, the baby shower today with over fifty women filling his sole private place on earth, and the impending changes in general with the baby's birth. It's a lot for any man to adjust to, let alone a man who never expected to have most of them in his life.

Is he still okay with all this? Saying he's ready to have a baby and really meaning it are two completely different things. I know he has no regrets—wants our baby as much as I do—yet I can't seem to quell my concern about how he'll adjust to the inevitable changes to our lives.

He holds my hand idly in his lap. The need to connect with him and ease my worry rides shotgun beside my want and desire *for* him. And the impulse to sate both is just too great to not give in to, so I graze my fingertips across the fabric covering his dick and love his quick intake of air.

"Are you trying to distract me, Ryles?"

"Never," I tease, my mind now fixated on the temptation just beneath my fingers.

"We were talking about pronouns, remember? *He* is just a pronoun?" he asks trying to get back to the topic at hand. He swears I should know the gender because after all, I'm the one carrying the baby. *Men.*

And while I have a fifty-fifty chance of being right, I know it's a boy. Has to be. The little boy with dark hair and green eyes who has filled my recent dreams. A freckled nose that scrunches up when he causes mischief and melts my heart just like his daddy. But that's all an assumption, mother's intuition, and is not something I'm going to verbalize.

"Uh-uh." His fingers tighten on my arm as I try to cop another feel of him, distract him from becoming fixated on a pronoun that may or may not be right. "*Pronouns.*"

"Well, if you want to talk grammar . . . I seem to remember that wet and willing are adjectives," I murmur, knowing damn well he'll be able to read both mischief and desire in my eyes. *Two can play this distraction game, Ace.*

He throws his head back and laughs, and I know he has caught my reference to the words he teased me with the very first night we had sex on Sex. He pulls me even closer this time and doesn't hold back when his lips meet mine. We kiss like we haven't seen each other in weeks. Need mixes with greed. Passion collides with want. My body vibrates with desperation because how can it not when he can push every one of my libido buttons with such a simple connection?

His kiss is like gravity, pulling at every part of me until I want to cling to him and hold on so I'm never taken away. Our tongues meet, demanding at first, before the kiss morphs into a tender reflection of love and desire. His free hand comes up to cup the side of my face, his thumb running over my cheek as he ends the kiss despite my protests. And at first I take the look in his eyes as one of amusement over me wanting some form of physicality with him *yet again*, but when he speaks, I know it's because he is seeing right through my attempts.

Damn him. He knows me too well.

"Did you forget I'm the master of the game of distraction, Ryles?" He lifts his eyebrows and a cocky, lopsided grin pulls up one corner of his mouth. "I see what you're trying to do here."

"Are you turning down sex?"

"Oh baby, I'll never turn down sex with you . . . I just want to get back to pronouns." He grants me a lightning-fast grin as he cuffs both of my hands and laces our fingers, presumably to prevent mine from wandering and tempting him further. For a man who doesn't want to pick a name, he sure seems set on clarifying his parts of speech.

He wants pronouns? I'll give him pronouns, all right.

"Like stick *it* in *me*, type of pronouns?"

He shakes his head and chuckles. "Not those specifically, no."

"You'd rather talk grammar than please your wife?"

That flash of a grin is back. "No, I'd rather discuss why you hate the name BIRT."

"You're exasperating. And a tease," I say, knowing I'll get the sex eventually if the tenting of his shorts is any indication of his state of mind. He may be resisting now, but I know sex will win out in the end. It always does.

"So you think the baby is a boy?" he asks, eyes wide, voice excited. And the lighthearted tone tugs on my heartstrings.

"Does it matter what I think, considering you won't even discuss names with me? I mean we're getting close to the wire here, Donavan."

"I love when you *Donavan* me," he says then squeezes my hand when I try to pull away. "C'mon, Ryles, fly by the seat of your pants. Let the moment rule us. Live dangerously," says the racecar driver to the social worker. All I can do is sigh in exasperation.

"Our baby's name is permanent. It's not a decision to be made on the spur of the moment." I still can't believe he's sticking to his plan of naming the baby after we meet him or her. I thought this strategy was a joke the first time he brought it up but now know different.

"Look, you have names you like and I have names I like. Why don't we just wait and see what BIRT looks like when he or she is born and then we'll both say them and go from there?" I narrow my eyes at him, desperate to know the names he prefers or if he likes any of the ones I've thrown out at him over the past few months. His silence on the topic is killing me. "Live dangerously with me, Ry." He chuckles as I shake my head, trying to feign irritation and hide my own smile.

"I already do live dangerously. I married you, *remember?*"

"Oh baby, I remember. No man is going to forget the things you did to me this morning," he says with a wicked gleam in his eyes.

I blush immediately, momentarily embarrassed by my very needy *and very horny* self, that didn't resist him despite knowing the caterers would be arriving at any moment. And of course the thought of his eyes heavy with desire and his cock thick and hard in my mouth makes my body ache to have him *again*. This time for my pleasure though, and I don't think he'd have a problem delivering on that demand.

I have to force the image from my mind because I think he accomplished exactly what he was hoping for with the comment.

"Now look who's trying to distract whom. BIRT's name?" I arch an eyebrow as his laughter rings around us. The man is relentless. "What if I don't like any of the names you pick and you don't like any of the names I like?"

"Well, that's easy." He shrugs. "I'll distract you."

"That must be the word of the day. Nice try, but that's not easy to do when it comes to something this important . . . oh God, that feels good," I moan as he takes my foot into his lap and starts rubbing its instep. Everything I have been overdoing the past few days between work and getting ready for the shower has manifested in the size of my swollen feet, so this feels like absolute Heaven. I sag against the wall at my back, eyes closing as I welcome the pleasure he's giving me.

Screw chocolate, forget sex with Colton, and forgo paradise, because *this*, a foot rub after being on your feet all day when you're pregnant, is absolute nirvana. He uses his adept fingers to push and press and rub to put me in a pleasure coma.

I lift my head and open my eyes to find him looking at me with a huge grin on his face. "What?"

"See?" He shrugs. "Distraction. All it takes is changing the subject, shifting gears somehow, and I can get what I want."

He thinks he's so crafty that I'll fall for it every time, but when it comes to Colton Donavan, I learned a long time ago that he likes to play dirty to get what he wants. Good thing I've learned from the master because I know all his tricks and will put them to good use against him.

"Magic hands," I murmur breathlessly, as his thumb presses against a pressure point that feels like it mainlines an electric current to the delta of my thighs.

"Your feet are so swollen." His head is down as his fingers rub their way up to my calf bringing me much more joy than they should.

"There are other things on me that are swollen," I deadpan. And the reaction I want from him is almost instantaneous when his eyes flash up and hands still momentarily. That lopsided grin of his—part arrogant bad boy, part eager lover—graces his lips as he holds my gaze.

"That so?" He tries to feign nonchalance and yet his reaction already told me he's willing to play my game. Time to see how quick he will take the bait because this woman is desperate for more than just his touch on my instep.

"Mm-hmm. Swollen means super sensitive. And sensitive means intense." I run my hands over my breasts that are spilling out of the cami tank top. His eyes follow and take notice of my nipples hardening from my touch against the thin fabric. I may have a huge belly, can't see my ankles, and would never have thought in a million years I'd be seducing my husband at seven months pregnant, but the way he looks at me—with a predatory gleam, not to mention the hitch in his breath—tells me he doesn't care. He finds me sexy. He still wants me. And that provides the confidence I need to give me the wherewithal to keep going.

"Intense is good."

"Intense is incredible," I all but moan as our eyes lock in a playful war of wills over who is going to make the first move. "Swollen means tight. Responsive. Multi—"

"I think I need to inspect," he says as he shifts onto his knees, his gaze never leaving mine. His hands slide up my thighs, feather-light touches laced with intent, moving my loose knit skirt with them as they go.

"If you inspect, you must try out the goods," I taunt. His touch tests my resolve, the sight of his tanned chest and scent of cocoa butter in his sunscreen bending my restraint.

"Demanding, are we?" He stops and lifts his eyebrows, a smile playing at the corners of his mouth.

"Haven't had any complaints yet," I toss back at him as he leans forward and presses a whisper of a kiss to my mouth. When he starts to pull away, I move with him because I want more. Always do when it comes to him.

Mirth flashes through his eyes because he knows he's caught me in a catch-all: trying to be the seductress when all I want is him, in me, on me, doing something to me, and very soon.

"Do you want something?" he asks, as his fingers continue their tantalizing ascent to the apex of my thighs. I love the hiss he emits when his thumbs brush over the swollen flesh, discovering I'd taken my panties off when I changed into more comfy clothes after the shower. His touch falters, a small show of the desire and need to control warring within him before he moves his fingers back down toward my knees.

"You." Why beat around the bush when that sweet ache deep in my lower belly is already flashing with heat and the one and only person I know that can sate it is sitting before me?

"*Me?*" He dips his head down and presses a kiss to first my left and then my right thigh. From beneath his thick lashes, he looks up at me then slowly wets his bottom lip. "Is that why you're not wearing any panties? What specifically do you want from me?"

His hands begin to move again, seducing me with his contact and mesmerizing me with the knowledge of what he's withholding.

My laugh is low and laced with suggestion. "Well, it's not just what I want from you per se but more where exactly I want you that's important."

"Do you want me here?" he asks as the pads of his fingers graze ever so softly over the seam of my sex. Even though I try to stay still, I arch my hips in a nonverbal begging motion.

And then he removes his fingers.

"Don't tease me, Donavan." My body aches on the verge of pain for him to touch me again. His chuckle fills the silence of the room as he leans forward, his eyes on mine, and then uses his tongue to trace around the outline of my nipple through the fabric. Just enough to let me know what it feels like but not enough to let me succumb to the sensation of it.

"Oh, I'm not teasing, Donavan," he says back, mimicking me with mirth in his eyes and purpose in his touch. "I'm just getting the lay of the land."

"I'm pretty sure the lay of the land is that you need to fuck me soon."

I love the lightning-fast grin that flashes over his features and the slight stutter in his movement from hearing me demand like this. He tsk-tsks with a shake of his head and another taunting tease of his fingertips.

"Rest assured, I intend to fuck you, sweetheart, but I'm all about equal opportunity."

My muscles clench at the first part of his statement while I'm trying to figure out just what he means by the last part, because now is not the time to be witty. Now is the time to give the hormone-riddled woman exactly what she wants.

"Equal opportunity?" I sigh in frustration and then gasp in surprise when Colton uses his knees to press my legs a little farther apart and at the same slides his fingers between the lips of my sex. If it were physically possible, my body sags in relief and tenses at the same time because I've finally gotten his touch and now I just want more.

"Yep," he says as he lowers his head, the warm heat of his mouth closing over my clit his fingers have exposed. My head lolls back against the wall as a ripple of pleasure washes over my body. My hands are in his hair, fingers gripping, and hips lifting to tell him I want more from him. Cool air hits when his mouth releases the skin he's sucking on. My hands try to keep him in the cradle of my thighs and a chuckle falls from his mouth, the reverberation heightening the nerves he's just brought to the surface. "Equal parts pleasure here," he says, dipping his head down again so his tongue slides up and down the cleft of my sex . . . and here."

An incoherent moan falls from my mouth as Colton slides his fingers inside me and curves them to hit the nerves within. And my God . . . thoughts escape me and sensation overwhelms me as the combination of his fingers and tongue begin to satisfy my insatiable need for sex.

He creates a rhythm all his own: the slide of his tongue, the skillful movement of fingers inside me, the soft sucking on my clit. My body reacts: muscles clench, back arches, hands hold tight as he causes the ebb and flow of sensations needed to climax.

"C'mon, Ry," he murmurs. The heat of his breath against my slick skin makes me writhe and buck into his hand. "Come for me so I can fuck you when you're still coming. Coat my cock with your cum while its sweet taste is fresh on my tongue."

His words are like that last lick of gasoline thrown onto a smoldering fire. Incendiary. Provocative. Inevitable.

I give into the moment—the feeling, the *everything* with him—and crash over the edge into that free fall of white-hot heat. It sears up my spine, out to my fingers and toes to gain strength, before slamming back into my core where he's continuing to push my climax to beyond bearable. Intense is too tame of a word for what he's made me feel.

Every. Time. The simple thought flickers how he gives me nothing less than his best every single time.

My muscles are so damn tight—my mind so lost in that post-orgasmic wash of pleasure—and my nails are digging so hard into his shoulders that I'm not sure how he escapes the confine of my thighs. But when he does, with my arousal still glistening on his mouth and hunger burning in his eyes, I can't help but stare at him and thank every damn lucky star in the sky that he's mine.

Because Colton Donavan on any day is drop-dead handsome, but when his waist is framed between my thighs, his chest bared so every inch of bronzed skin is shadowed for effect, and the look in his eyes says he's going to take me as he sees fit—no holds barred—he's indescribable.

Rogue. Rebel. Reckless.

The words flit through my mind, memories colliding from another place, another time, but still so fitting all this time later as he undoes his shorts and pulls his dick out. It's thick and hard, ready to claim, and hell if my mouth doesn't water at the sight, my damn hormones kicking into overdrive again despite having just come.

"Colton." His name on my lips is a plea and a demand all at the same time that causes his arrogant smirk to return.

The crest of his dick presses against my pleasure. His tongue darts out to wet his bottom lip. His eyes flash to mine one last time before he looks to where he's slowly pushing into me.

"Fuck," he moans. "I love watching your pussy stretch around me. Love how it pulls tight when you take me in."

His words hit my ears but my body is completely focused on him filling me, stretching me, drawing pleasure with each and every tilt of his hips. So many sensations and emotions flush through my body. All I can do is close my eyes, lay my head back, and lose myself in the onslaught of desire I know is coming.

He's gentle yet demanding, drawing all the way out before taking his hand and guiding his cock so its head can rub right where I need it most. My nerves are so sensitized that when I shift my hips, my eyes open in shock at how damn good it feels.

And the look on his face tells me he knows my reaction well enough to know he's hit the spot perfectly. So much so he's determined to do it again. Pull me to the surface from my post-orgasmic state so I can momentarily catch my breath before he shifts into high gear and pulls me back under the next wave of pleasure.

He begins to do just that, picking up the pace, looking down at me with concentration in his eyes and pleasure etching the lines of his face. The muscles in his neck and shoulders are taut, and his mouth is pulled tight as he pushes us both beyond the edge of reason.

My pulse speeds up but my mind slows down. The sting of the carpet into my back. The press of his fingers into my thighs. The feeling of oblivion as he swells inside me. My name on his lips. The sight of him coming undone.

"Colton," I cry out, my back arching as I let his action dictate my every reaction. Anything else I say is incoherent because my second orgasm is always so much stronger. This one is no exception. I fumble for something to hold onto and instantly Colton's hands find mine, lacing our fingers as I succumb to the sensations he's drawn from me.

Now that he knows I've had mine, he begins to chase his own release. And even though I'm still coming down from my high, it's impossible to drag my eyes away from him: teeth biting into his bottom lip, hips bucking harder into me, and his head falling back, lost in his own bliss.

"Goddamn it, Ry . . ." he moans brokenly, the sexiest sound in the world to me because *I put it there*. When he empties himself into me, he stills—his hands, his hips, his breath—lost in the wash of pleasure. And then slowly he lifts his head up as he unlaces our fingers, and that satisfied grin turns up the corners of his mouth as his eyes meet mine. "Damn, woman."

"Mm," I murmur, groggy and sated and completely enamored with him.

"Intense enough for you?"

Like he has to ask. "I think I'll keep you."

He laughs, deep and rich, as he withdraws from me and crawls over my legs so he can lean over me on his hands. He looks at me long and hard, so many things in his eyes I can't decipher. The one I can is the one that's most important. It's the look that tells me I am his whole world and hell if I'm going to argue with that. What sane woman would? He's the total package: sexy, thoughtful, generous, mischievous, and most importantly, all mine. Love isn't a strong enough word for what I feel for him.

"I don't think you get a choice in that matter."

Chapter Three

Rylee

"Baxter's not going to be very happy with you."

I look up from the dog at my feet—lying on her back spread-eagle—with a smile on my face and know my dog is definitely not going to be happy when I come home with the scent of another on me.

"Hey bud. You're right," I say to Zander as he leads the charge of the middle school boys through the front door. "How was school today, guys?"

My question is greeted with an array of *fine, good, boring,* from the four of them as their attention shifts to Racer who has scrambled up from my feet to meet her boys. I love seeing how excited they all are to lavish attention on the newest member of the house.

Rubbing a hand over my belly, I lean against the counter and watch them sitting on the floor with the ball of fur. They've all enjoyed taking on the responsibility of having a pet better than I thought. Thankfully. I just hope she does her job as a therapy dog and helps out the latest boy, Auggie, assimilate into our madness.

I glance over to where he's coloring quietly at the table. His head is down, but I can see his eyes angling over to watch the boys and their camaraderie from beneath his shock of sandy-blond hair. He takes in their teasing, the elbowing of each other, their comfort, and I can see him desperate to make a connection. So many things hold him back. He wants to be a part of the crew, but the PTSD, along with a plethora of other issues living in a violent and abusive home ensued—things that skated just beneath the radar of social services for so very long—hasn't provided him the coping skills needed to assimilate. When your parents keep you locked in a dog crate for hours, if not days on end, as a punishment without any outside social interaction for year upon year, knowing how to fit in just isn't something you can do.

To say it breaks my heart is an understatement. The therapists suggested we bring in a therapy dog for comfort, with the hope Racer will eventually create the opening for him to have a connection with the other boys.

And of course, Auggie's part of the reason I'm so stressed about the lack of time before the baby is due. I desperately want to see him connect with someone here as much as he has with me before I go on maternity leave. If he doesn't, then I worry he'll feel as confined as he was in his parents' self-imposed prison at home.

The baby moves beneath my hand, my constant reminder of how lucky my child is going to be to never have to even remotely experience any of these horrors.

"Hey Auggie? Do you want a snack before I leave for the night?" He looks over to me, a ghost of a smile on his sweet lips as he nods ever so slightly. The sight of a smile, regardless of how faint, gives me an inch of hope in this marathon we're running together. "Oreos and milk?"

His smile becomes more surefooted at the same time Scooter pipes up, "Dude, I'm all over that!" *Perfect.* Just what I wanted to happen. A table of boys eating cookies and milk together. All different walks of life, making their own path together.

"Dude," I mimic him with a grin on my face, "put your backpacks away and it'll be waiting for you."

"Rad," one of them says as my phone alerts a text. As I reach into the pantry, I glance over to my cell sitting on the counter and see it's from Colton. I'm not sure what he needs but my shift ends in fifteen minutes and this opportunity with all the boys together is way too important to break up the moment.

"Okay," I say, as I pull out two packages of Oreos and cups. "Snacks get doled out in the order of who tells me something good about their day."

"Pit and the peak!" Ricky says with exasperation. He likes to pretend he's too old for this tradition we started a few years ago, but I secretly know he enjoys it.

"Yep." I start filling the plastic cups as Kyle passes out napkins.

"Auggie goes first," Zander says, surprising me. I think both Auggie and I startle at the comment but for completely different reasons. Zander slides me a glance that says he knows exactly what he's doing. It may be almost six years since he was in similar shoes, but he remembers the anxiety like it was yesterday and is trying to help Auggie in the only way he knows how.

My heart swells with pride at the kind heart he has, and I'm reminded of how very far he's come. And the knowledge that Zander could overcome and thrive encourages my hopes that Auggie will be able to have the same success.

"Z's right. Auggie gets to go first," I say.

And the best part about it is that in a house constantly full of bickering, they just showed it to be one weighted more heavily with love and compassion.

"Hello?" I answer the phone as I crawl along the highway, traffic moving at a snail's pace in the last few miles to the house. I'm so exhausted. Presuming it's Colton calling me back, I answer on the Bluetooth's first ring, not waiting for caller ID to pop up on the Range Rover's GPS screen. My calls have been going straight to his voicemail since I've left work so when I answer, I fully expect to hear the lecture right off the bat about how I need to take my maternity leave now. And I'm lucky because as vocal as he is on it, he understands the reasons behind why I haven't. I have a feeling the compassion is waning the more out of breath I am and the more swollen my feet become.

That's exactly why I've been telling him I'm perfectly fine to go to my checkups without him so he doesn't hear Dr. Steele tell me I need to start taking it easier. And maybe that's why I answer right away, so he thinks everything is okay instead of the actual throbbing in my rapidly swelling toes and ankles.

"Rylee Donavan?"

"Yes. Who's this?" I try to place the female voice on the other end of the line but come up empty.

"This is Casey at TMZ and—"

"How'd you get my number?" I ask, cutting off the tabloid reporter, my guard instantly up.

"We'd like to know if the tip we received is true and how you're dealing with it all?"

Curiosity and unease meld into a ball of discord. I stutter a response I know I shouldn't even ask. "Wh . . . what are you talking about?"

"The video proving your husband's infidelity."

And it's like my ears don't hear what she says over the roar of disbelief and flash of hurt that burns in my chest. "Video?" And I reiterate the word more to myself, lost in my own world of upset than to her.

"The sex tape."

I know it's not possible but I gasp and stop breathing all at the same time. I disconnect the call instantly. My heart drops into the pit of my stomach. I struggle to catch my breath. Luckily I'm turning off on Broadbeach because my thoughts are so scattered and the adrenaline is pumping so fast that my hands are shaking.

Normally I don't let bullshit like this get to me—after all I am married to a man who was once known as one of the racing world's top playboys.

Colton wouldn't do that to me. He loves me. He loves us. We're each other's world.

And yet despite knowing this, something about the phone call unnerves me. Staggers me. Resonates in my ears when it shouldn't.

How did they have my number? What video is she talking about?

I'm too close to the house to call and even if I wanted to, I don't think my fingers are steady enough to push the right buttons.

Calm down, Rylee. It's all I can tell myself because this isn't the first rumor that has been spread about Colton and whatever hot woman he's been in the same vicinity as. But it's the first time I've been sought out to give a response before I knew anything about the *scandal.*

When the gates on the driveway shut behind me, I sigh, equal parts relief and anxiety, and scramble out of the car as fast as my pregnant body can. When Sammy opens the front door before I even put my key in the lock, I know way more than a purported rumor from TMZ is going on.

Even worse, he just nods at me without saying a word and steps outside closing the door behind him so Colton and I are alone. Not a good sign at all.

"Colton?" I call his name as I drop my purse on the table before following the sound of his voice in the office. So many things run through my head as I cross the short distance and none of them are welcome. I'm ready to barrel into the room and demand answers regarding the rumored cheating that the *rational* part of my brain knows must be wrong.

"They're fucking crazy if they think I'm going to believe them," Colton asserts, fist pounding against the desk. My feet falter and my demands die on my lips when I see him: back to me, broad shoulders framed against the window, head hung down, body visibly tense. The scene beyond him of the ocean is serene but in just the instant I've been in the room, I know Colton is anything but.

The sight of him physically upset like this isn't normal. It throws me for a second and makes me fear the phone call I received might just be real. The uncertainty I felt in the car comes back with a vengeance, vibrating through my body in a flash of heat and wave of dizziness. The words I was determined to say when I saw Colton are lost to worry as I try to wrap my head around the sudden assault to my perfectly imperfect world.

"I don't care what you think you're seeing, CJ, it's not fucking possible. Zip. Zero. Zilch." Anger vibrates off him and slams around the room's walls as he listens to his lawyer on the other end of the line. Leaning against the doorjamb, I attempt to steady myself, my emotions caught in turmoil as I try to read into the conversation without knowing any additional information. "I don't need a fucking road map . . . What you don't get though is that I've never even put myself in the situation where someone could even imply such bullshit!"

He hangs his head and blows out a breath as CJ talks and as much as I want him to get off the phone and tell me what in the hell is going on, I also want him to carry on his conversation without him knowing I'm home. I *need* to hear the non-sugarcoated version I'm sure he'll give me. Hearing Colton without a filter will allow me to believe the extensive explanations I'm going to need to hear the minute he gets off the phone.

"You're not fucking listening to me," he grits out exasperated. "They can Photoshop it however they want. It's NOT true! Guys like me only get one chance at this shit. I got my chance. I got my Rylee. Why in the hell would I fuck that up?" His words are barked out with spite to prove whatever point he's making and yet they weave around my heart and squeeze tight because the way he says it—like it's the simplest truth in the world—only helps fortify so many things: my belief in how my husband feels about me, that the rumor is pure bullshit on a slow gossip news day, I'm going to have to thicken my skin to weather whatever storm is bearing down on us.

"Fuckin' A! Do you . . .?" Colton's words trail off as he turns around and sees me leaning against the doorjamb, one hand on my belly, the other covering my mouth. Our eyes lock, uncertainty passing between us as my name falls from his mouth in a hushed whisper. "Ry . . ." And even if I didn't know whatever was going on was bad, the etched lines on his face and taut carriage confirmed it. "I want to see the entire thing. Not just the ten-second snippet you have. If they want their money, CJ, they'll show me their bargaining chip now, won't they?" He walks toward me, gaze never wavering despite the worry it holds.

When he reaches me, he pulls me into him without saying another word and wraps his arms around my shoulders, burying his head in the curve of my neck despite the phone still at his ear.

And this show of emotion freaks me out. My heart thunders. My stomach churns. My eyes close as I absorb his familiarity and try to hold on to it as best as I can. Because if he's worried, then I know I'm going to be freaked.

"I'm at my computer. I'll be waiting for the email." I hear the clatter of his iPhone as he tosses it on the table beside us moments before he gathers me tighter into him. My hands are on his back, my lips against his neck, his all-familiar scent in my nose, and yet it suddenly feels like so very much is different.

We stand like this for several moments despite the anxiety rioting through my soul as I let him breathe me in because I fear what he's going to say when he lets go. Is he going to apologize? Confess to something I don't want to hear that will shatter our ideal little world?

"Just tell me," I finally breathe out, my chest aching with worry and fear. His body tenses as he grabs my shoulders and leans back to look at me, the reporter's words repeating in my mind.

"Ry . . ." My name falls from his mouth again and as much as I want to beg him to say something besides it, I'm also almost afraid to. I welcome the silence but hope for some noise. "Someone is claiming to have a video."

"So it's true," I state, trying to keep my voice void of emotion as tears immediately sting the backs of my eyes. And when I'm afraid they're going to leak over, I close my eyes and shake my head, as if I can rid my mind of the bad dream I feel is sucking us in its clutches.

"What's true?" he demands.

"The phone call." It's all I say, purposely trying to draw a reaction from him so he has to explain what's going on.

"Phone call? What in the fucking hell are you talking about, Ry?" He takes a step back and runs a hand through his hair as he leans a hip against the desk behind him.

"I think you need to be the one to start explaining, Colton, because I'm a little freaked out. Something's going on here and I should have found out from you . . . not from TMZ calling to ask me if I'd like to make a statement about the rumored video proving my husband cheated on me!" I yell, hands flailing, voice escalating. The disbelief I want to feel doesn't feel so certain anymore when his jaw falls lax and hands grip the edges of the desk.

He blinks his eyes a few times, hurt I don't understand flashing in them, as he digests what I've said before shaking his head. "Fucking Christ, Ry. You actually believed I'd cheat on you?" The shock on his face staggers me—unfettered disbelief I'd even consider his infidelity to be true—and knocks me from my momentary lapse. I can see the man in front of me, feel his love for me, and know I'm crazy for even considering it.

"I didn't know what to think," I whisper, my confession hanging in the air between us. And then his words to CJ hit my ears again, and I know I was wrong to even let the idea find any kind of purchase in my conscience. I shift so I can sit down, my body as tired as my head all of the sudden.

"Someone is trying to blackmail us."

"*What?*" I'd laugh at the ludicrous claim if I weren't sitting here right now, sick to my stomach. "Who?"

Colton shakes his head. "CJ doesn't know who for sure. He, she, they are hiding behind a lawyer right now." So many questions race through my mind as I wait for him to continue.

"Blackmail is illegal, isn't it?" I ask, wondering how someone could be hiding behind a lawyer and do this.

Colton emits a self-deprecating laugh that gives me no comfort and only results in making me feel stupid for asking. "Money in exchange for an item they claim is mine is considered a transaction," he states using his fingers to make quotation marks over the last word, which leads me to believe this is something he has argued about with CJ. Just as I'm about to ask more, he says something that makes my ears buzz and changes the direction of my thoughts. "They say they have a video of me having sex with another woman."

And even though I knew as much from my short-lived conversation with TMZ, I still suck in an audible breath when I hear him say the words and automatically start shaking my head as I try to reject them. Everything I know I should say or ask is stuck in my throat because as much as I believe him, why is dread sifting through my body weighing every part of me down?

Dread. Curiosity. Unease. All three swirl in an eddy of discord as I try to process this.

I can tell my lack of a response makes Colton worry. He steps forward and then steps back. Antsy and irritated. "Do you doubt me?" he asks, voice rising in pitch with each word. I don't answer him. I'm too inside my own head, too overwhelmed by every single thing about this.

"No." I mouth the word, unable to find my voice.

"Don't you ever doubt my love for you!" I jump as his voice thunders through the room; his palm hits the desk to reinforce the words. And I can see he immediately regrets the reaction by the fisting of his hands and how his head falls back to try and rein in his anger. When he lifts his head back up, he meets my eyes with a determination I've never seen before. "Ry, I swear on the life of this baby that I have not so much as touched, kissed, or anythinged another woman, let alone put myself in a position to be videotaped having sex with them."

I force a swallow down my throat. I believe him. Have no doubt. And yet . . . "I want to see it," I say with more certainty than I feel.

"You walked in just as the full video came across to CJ. He's emailing it to me." He scrunches his nose momentarily and in that instant I can see how worried he is about this. And not about the existence of a tape, but more so what this is going to do to me. To us. "You don't need to see it."

"Don't tell me what I need to do, Colton. If you didn't do anything, then it shouldn't be an issue, right?" I slowly stand and walk over to the desk so I can sit at the computer while Colton remains with his hips against the desk and head hung down, no doubt preparing himself for whatever we're about to watch.

I click alive the computer screen, and my breath hitches immediately when I see the email sitting in the inbox from CJ. The subject line of "Video" taunts me as I wait for Colton to come over.

"Please, Ry," he begs. "I don't know what's going to be on here . . . and you're not going to be able to unsee it once you do. I know for a fact it's not me but at the same time, whatever they have on tape, I don't even want that image in your head so you doubt me." He hangs his head down again before looking back up to me with determined clarity. "I would never cheat on you, Ry. *Never*."

I worry my wedding ring around my finger, knowing what he's saying to be true but at the same time, needing to see for myself. My only response is to move the cursor and open the email. The fortifying breath he draws in disrupts the silence in the room and rides shotgun to the sound of my own pulse thundering like a drum in my ears.

I double-click the file.

Snow fills the screen, gray, white, and black grain that holds my attention hostage. I will for it to clear and *not* want it to clear all at the same time. And when it finally does, it takes me a second to believe what I'm seeing.

"Oh fuck!" falls from Colton's mouth the exact same time as the thought flickers through my mind.

The image is dark, grainy, but *the what* and *the where* are unmistakable. The memory zooms back in high definition color in my mind as I watch the one person that is unmistakably clear in the video, Colton, unknowingly look up toward the camera as he holds a woman's hips and drives into her over and over.

Not just any woman though.

One in a dress, which is pulled up over her hips and bunched down around her waist, so she is completely exposed.

And even though the video is black and white, I know the dress is red. Fire-engine red to be exact.

Because the woman is me.

In the parking garage.

On the hood of Sex.

And in case I wasn't sure, the concrete wall of the parking garage is painted with the hotel's name. There is no mistaking the where or the what. *Or the whom.*

Both of us lean in closer out of reflex as we watch the video unfold, second by second, thrust after thrust, and I'm not sure if I'm more mesmerized or horrified at first before the realization sets in with what exactly this means. There is no audio on the security cam's footage so the office weighs heavy with the silence until the clip goes dark and the video ends.

We're both stunned, unsure what to say, not certain what to do. I feel like a thousand-pound weight has been lifted from my shoulders because Colton was right: he wasn't cheating on me.

That weight has been replaced with an anvil teetering on the edge of a cliff, waiting to fall off and harm anyone in its path.

And we're standing in that damn path.

Someone has footage of Colton and me having sex.

I think even if I watched the video replay one hundred times I still wouldn't believe it.

"They're on crack if they think I'm going to pay them three million dollars for that," Colton says, breaking the silence, voice resolute, and staggering me in more ways than just one. Dumbfounded with my hand over my mouth, I force myself to look away from the black square on the computer screen and over to him.

And if I thought he was angry before, he's livid now.

"What did you just say?" I finally stutter, not sure if I'm more shocked at the three million dollar figure or that he doesn't care that a video of us having sex has been made.

"You heard me," he growls at the walls. He shoves off from where he's sitting atop the desk and starts pacing the room. I need to understand what he means, but I'll wait him out . . . wait for him to temper his anger. There's no way in hell we're not paying this. That's me. And him. Naked. Having sex. For anyone to watch. Oh my God!

He doesn't answer me, just keeps muttering to himself as he paces, working something out in his head. I'd much rather he shares than remain silent. After a few minutes, he waltzes back to the computer and frames his body above mine as he reaches over the back of the chair. "Watch it again."

"Did you call the police? Did you—"

"That's futile," he snaps at me. "It's not our property. Wasn't stolen from us or our house so it's not ours to claim."

"But it's us!" I reiterate my voice breaking and eyes widening.

"Play it again," he demands, in a voice I've only ever heard when he's at work. It's the do-not-fuck-with-me tone that tells whoever he's dealing with to do as he says without question.

I hesitate, confused as to why he wants to watch it again, prompting him to move his hand over mine on the mouse and click the play button. Our images spring to life once more and again I'm transfixed. It's like a car accident: I know I need to look away and yet I'm mesmerized. As much as I'm appalled, there is something about watching the two of us together, stepping outside of the moment, and seeing how fluidly we move in sync. Undeniable proof we were meant to be together.

"CJ believes it," he murmurs, more talking to himself than to me. I try to follow his train of thought, but replaying it has caused deafening panic to strike again. Every single breath—each thought—takes an enormous amount of effort. *How are we going to fix this?* "So will everyone else."

Exactly, I want to scream at him. Everyone will believe it's us. How could they not?

Colton turns my chair around so I'm facing him. "Do you trust me?" he asks, and I'm already shaking my head no because *that* gleam in his eye means he's about to tell me something I don't want to hear. And God yes, I trust him, but this isn't a normal, "can you trust me?" type of question. "CJ watched this. He *believed* what they said."

"Huh?" I'm not following him.

"Don't you get it, Ry? They have no clue the woman is *you*. Your face . . . it's not identifiable in one single frame."

"But every other part of me is," I shriek, as the sudden knowledge of where he's going with this forms in my head. He can't be serious. My stomach knots, forcing me to focus on breathing for a moment as my eyes look deep into his and question what I see there.

"Watch it again."

"I don't want to watch it again," I shout, shrugging his hands off my shoulders and not liking what he's suggesting one bit. "And I refuse to entertain whatever idea is in your head." Panic returns with a vengeance.

"Hear me out, Ry," he says, getting down to eye level with me as I avert my eyes to where my hands are resting on my belly. "Please look at me." I take a moment before I raise my eyes and I'm glad that when I do, he seems as conflicted as I feel. "Do you really think that if we pay off whoever this person is they won't keep an extra tape for insurance? That they won't get their money and *accidentally* let the tape end up on the Internet?"

"Colton . . ."

"No, Ry. You just told me TMZ called you. They've already contacted media and planted a seed. Do you actually think they'd do that if they'd planned on taking the money and then disappearing with the video for good? Something is off here, and I can't figure out what the fuck it is."

His comments weigh down the atmosphere around us and it takes everything I have to blink, to breathe, to think, because this just can't be happening. He's right. The fact they've already contacted a tabloid tells me it's something more . . . and hell if I know what the more is or why the video is surfacing right now.

"I've been wracking my brain, have some ideas, but that's beside the point, right now. The point is they want money, want to make us panic . . . want to tear us apart right when we're about to be happiest we've ever been with the baby coming." His eyes soften momentarily as he looks down to where my hands rest before looking back up to me with more resolve than I want him to have. "Think about it, Ry," he urges, and I hate that he makes so much sense.

He can tell my mind is spinning and my ears are tuning him out. I grit my teeth and fight a wave of nausea. "What exactly are you thinking?"

His chest rises as he takes in a deep breath, and I fear he's preparing himself for the backlash from whatever he has to say. "It's not as bad as it looks."

"What's not? The video? The situation? The idea in your head?" My voice rises with each word.

"All of it," he states.

"Are you fucking kidding me?" I ask, eyes wide with disbelief. "There's a video of you screwing me on the hood of a Ferrari!"

"No. There's a video of me fucking *somebody* on the hood of the Ferrari. Your face is never shown. The only people who know that dress is red are you and me. The only people who know you hold your hands over your tits when you're about to come, or that you reach out and scratch your nails over my hip like that when I come, are you and me. No. One. Else."

I just keep shaking my head, eyes blinking, pulse pounding in my ears. "You're out of your goddamn mind." I throw my hands up, helpless and astounded. "So easy for you to suggest when the video is so dark you can barely see your dick but you sure as hell can see all of me, laid out and spread-eagle."

"Listen to me, Ry. I couldn't care less if my dick was on display or not."

"Stupid me. I forgot you're used to being seen by the masses. After all, you were the playboy once upon a time. You had your dick on display for more women than I care to count." I take a dig at him, wanting him to be as upset as I am over this whole thing.

"That's exactly my point. I'm the notorious playboy. The player. People expect this shit from me."

"But they're going to think you cheated on me," I say, completely dumbfounded by the turn of events. And while I may have learned not to care what people think, I do care about that.

"I don't give a fuck what people think about me . . . you know that. The only person that matters is you. You know I didn't cheat on you—"

"This is a bad idea, Colton."

"I'm not paying some bastard three mil so he or she can turn around and release the tape anyway. I don't bow down to threats, Ry. Never have. Never will." We stare at each other in silence and his words sink in, take hold, and as much as I want to reject the idea immediately, I fear that what he says is true.

"But what about your parents? My parents? The baby?" I say, each passing moment adding more panicked dread to my voice. "There's going to be a video out there, documented for them to google and know about." I have to stop. A gasp falls from my lips because as the baby moves into my ribs my breath doesn't come fast enough.

"Calm down, Ry. Please." He sits on his knees again and pulls me against him. I close my eyes, attempt to wish this all away, yet know there is no way that's possible. "We'll tell our family it's not what they think. That it's Photoshopped. We'll have Chase issue a press release to the media. It'll say something like we were sent this tape that's been tampered with. That we were being blackmailed for a ridiculous amount of money and we won't entertain paying for it because my image has been cut and pasted into it somehow, and it's not true."

I push him away and just stare at him, seeing the logic but at the same time, that's *us* on there. Him and me. "No one's going to believe it, Colton. You know better than anyone the press is going to run with the story and report it in the worst light possible. Sensationalize it. Try to document how distraught I am. Dig up old photos of you with other women, plaster them all over the pages to show that's how you are."

"Who cares?"

"I do," I scream, causing his head to startle while I stare at him with blank, disbelieving eyes. Surely it's not possible that what I'm thinking and what he's saying is the same thing. "I'd care that people think you are fucking around behind my back. I'd hate that people would think I'm this meek woman holding on to her famous husband because she has this new baby and can't get any better so she stays." The first tear falls over my cheek and I shove it away, hating that it fell and despising I just admitted that.

"No! All that matters is what you and I know," he emphasizes but it falls on deaf ears. "The press isn't going to—"

"That's what they do."

"Rylee—"

"Don't *Rylee* me! Do you want some sick fuck somewhere jacking off to images of you and me having sex? I mean, seriously? Doesn't that make your stomach turn, Colton? I'm your wife. Not some whore you slept with and discarded for God's sake." I push myself out of the chair needing to get away from him and get some perspective. He's talking crazy, and right now, I have enough crazy in my life.

I move through the house, his frustrated sigh behind me, and walk onto the patio overlooking the beach below. Alone, I can think without him clouding my thoughts. I can breathe without him and his logic that I fear is one hundred percent correct in how things will go if we do pay whomever it is off.

We're in a no-win situation. Damned if we do, damned if we don't.

I sink down into a chair on the edge of the patio and pet Baxter's head when he sidles up next to me. My mind flashes back to those images that are etched in my mind with crystal-clear precision. Good images. Personal images. Intimate images. The fight in the garden after hearing Tawny's comments in the bathroom. How I'd gone from thinking I was losing Colton to finding out he was willing to try and have a relationship with me. The exhilaration that had ruled my thoughts as we'd entered the elevator. The disbelief as we'd walked toward the red Ferrari and the knowledge of what Colton had wanted to do with me on it. My desire overwhelming my senses, giving into the emotion and having sex with Colton on the hood, cementing that bond we shared and feeling on top of the world.

All the while, a camera had been capturing our moment. And someone behind that camera had been watching.

My skin crawls. The ball of acid sits in my stomach, the acrid taste of incredulity on my tongue.

This is so screwed up I don't even know what to think, where to go, what to do. Of course, the one time I stepped out of my perfectly modest box look what happened. And as much as I want to be pissed at Colton because the whole sex on the hood of the car thing was his idea, I can't. I didn't say no. I went along with the idea, was persuaded by passion, got lost in the moment, and had loved every minute of it, simply because it was with Colton.

Who would have thought almost six years later, this would come back to haunt us?

"Hey," Colton says from behind me and I don't respond because I don't even know what to say or think anymore. "I'm sorry."

"Who would do this to us, Colton? Why all this time later? It doesn't make sense." And even after I say the words, the justified spite that's still within me after all of these years comes back with a vengeance when I think of the one person who would want to ruin our happiness. "Tawny."

Colton blinks his eyes slowly, telling me he already has considered this. "I don't think so."

"What?" My back's up, ire already boiling in my blood as he bites the inside of his cheek and holds my stare. "How dare you defend her," I accuse, even when I know he hasn't and that I'm being completely irrational.

"I'm not defending her," he says in that placating tone of his that is like oil to my water. "Tawny isn't stupid enough to cross that line. She may be a vindictive cunt, but she wouldn't cross me. Not after the paperwork I made her sign when I fired her. The consequences of fucking with us again were laid out quite candidly, and I assure you she's not that stupid . . ."

"Oh." It's all I can say. His eyes hold mine. I had no clue that he'd done that. "But she knew we were there that night, knew what we were doing. When we came back up I told her about . . ." My voice trails off as the memory flashes through my mind. My immediate thought when I saw her of *here comes the rain to fuck with my parade*, and how victorious I felt telling her that Colton and I had just fucked on the hood of Sex. How for the first time, I was confident in where we stood in our relationship.

Oh my God. Did I bring this upon us?

"No, Ry. This isn't on you. Please," he begs, because he knows me well enough to know what I'm thinking. "I've crossed a lot of people in my life. In racing. In dating. In business. *By surviving*. It could be any one of the many."

"Who else knew about that night then? Parking garage staff? Sammy?" I go through the names out loud and see the anger flicker in his eyes when I mention his most-trusted person.

"Sammy had to sign the same agreement Tawny did plus about twenty more. It wasn't him." And I know he hates the narrowing of my eyes because he explains, "Not him, Ry. If he wanted to blackmail me, he has much better dirt on me than that."

A flash of anger fires through me. It must be the volatile emotions and uncertainty weaving around us because I can't remember the last time Colton's past playboy status bugged me. Yet *that* simple comment causes me to more than bristle at the thought. "Charming," I say, sarcasm rich in my voice.

"It's no secret. I used to live a little, Rylee. I won't apologize for who I was but rather be thankful for the man you helped make me. *Understood?*" The bite in his tone hits me where intended, and I feel guilt for my snarky comment. Our gazes connect. So many emotions swim in his eyes and it hits me just how upset he is. He probably feels he brought all of this upon us somehow and yet his first thought was to protect me. How could I have doubted him? I worry my bottom lip through my teeth and answer him with a nod of my head.

"Who else then? The valet or parking staff? Security?"

"Mm. Not likely. Not after all this time. It feels too timed, you know?" I murmur in agreement. "My gut instinct says it's Eddie or someone connected to him. It's a long shot but there could be a possibility there . . . I just don't know." He blows out a breath and scrubs a hand over his face, and the sound of the chafe against his stubble fills the silence. "I've already called Kelly to try and sniff him out but I doubt we'll find anything."

His eyes will me to believe him but my heart says this is on me. Somehow, someway, Tawny told someone along the way and now, whether she knows it or not, she's going to get her one last dig. I can't look at him, can't face him, knowing that our one night of pleasure—the catalyst of so very much for us—is now going to come back and haunt us.

"Fuck me!" he says, eyes widening as he holds his finger up in the just-one-minute motion before jogging into the house. By the time I've followed him into the office, he already has the video replaying and is pointing at the screen. "Right there," he shouts, a strained smile spreading on his lips. "Give me my phone," he demands, his face lighting up while I'm left in the dark, handing him his cell.

I watch him as he flips through his phone for something, my eyes drawn to the screen to the frozen image of his hands gripping my hips in all their naked glory.

"Look at the date," he says, excitement woven in his tone as he looks down at the calendar app on his phone. I look at the timestamp on the video and realize it has been tampered with because the date is wrong. It says last year, not six years ago. I was so busy getting lost in the frantic feeling of watching our images on the screen that I never thought to look at the timestamp. "That's the date of the Iowa race last year."

"Okay." I draw the word out, ideas forming of where he's going with this line of thought.

"The exact date, Ry. If we don't pay him and the jackass releases the tape, we have proof the video was tampered with. There is no way I can be in that parking garage in Los Angeles on that date because I was *in* the goddamn race. And we will have proof at the office that we flew home the next day."

I put my hands on both sides of my head as I try to take this in. "But Colton . . . that is *US*," I say, incredulity in my voice.

"I know," he says, not realizing how much the thought bugs me. "But whoever has this tape, either tampered with it to make the dates more recent to try to cause problems, or this is the one they found . . . I don't know, but I know we have everything we need to prove that's not me if they were to release it to the press."

I drop down into a seat opposite him, my head spinning, my chest hurting, as I try to figure out the best plan of attack. It seems to me like this is an ambush with no way to escape. "There is no way out of this," I murmur.

"I'm trying to find one that doesn't affect you," he says, and I can hear the self-deprecation in his voice.

"I know . . . I'm just having a hard time wrapping my head around it all. I just need time to think this through without the shock warping my reason, you know?"

"I do," he says, walking over to stand in front of me, and leaning down so we're eye to eye.

"Did they give you a time frame in which to respond?" I ask, not even believing that question has to leave my mouth.

"Seventy-two hours."

Reaching up, I run my hands over the stubble of his jaw to weave in the hair at the base of his neck. I can't believe how much he has grown as a person over our time together. He's learned to make good choices, has great instincts, and has always kept my best interests in mind. Why should I doubt he's trying to do that right now as well?

Trust me, his eyes beg.

Trust him, my reason tells me.

"Let's see what Kelly finds out . . . then I'll trust your judgment on what you think we should do from there, but I've got to tell you that doing nothing doesn't sit well with me."

He nods his head and leans in, brushing a soft kiss to my lips. When he steps back, his eyes are serious and intense. "I'll never let anything happen to you."

I close my eyes and lean my forehead against his.

Every knight has a weak link in their armor.

I fear I just might be his.

Chapter Four

Rylee

"The baby's growth is on par. The heartbeat is strong and within normal range . . . but I'm a little concerned about your blood pressure, Rylee," Dr. Steele says, as she looks back down at the chart in her hand.

"I know. It's just . . . we had something unexpected happen last night and it's still kind of crazy and . . ." I stop and blow a breath out, trying to calm myself yet again and not worry about what Colton says he'll take care of, but know is futile. I can't rid my mind of the grainy images or the fear that this is all going to spiral out of control. "Sorry." I shake my head to blink away the threatening tears.

"It's okay. Sometimes things can be a bit overwhelming with your first baby coming. A lot of women get stressed over feeling their life is going to change so drastically and they can no longer do it all." She reaches out and squeezes my forearm. "I'm inclined to put you on modified bed rest at this point."

"No!" The word falls out in a shocked gasp, my eyes flying up to meet the concern in hers as my blood pressure starts to elevate again.

"Don't think I don't know that's why Colton hasn't been coming in. We both know he wants you off your feet, and you fear if he hears me suggest it, he'll pressure you." The stern warning in her voice is unmistakable. And there's no use denying it, so I just nod my head and worry my hands together. "I'll trust you'll use good judgment or I'll be forced to put you on bed rest for the remainder of your pregnancy. The longer the baby is in utero, the better all around for him or her. Delivering early because of preeclampsia isn't an option I want. Try to make Colton deal with whatever situation came up last night so you're not involved and your blood pressure can stay on an even keel."

"I will," I say, knowing I can't. Her intelligent eyes assess the truthfulness of my statement. She nods her head. I guess I was believable.

"Okay. We'll see you in two weeks then. Take care," she says as she pats me on the shoulder before walking out of the examination room.

My drive home is consumed by unwanted thoughts of last night, when I shouldn't be thinking about it. Doctor's orders. But the images of Colton and me in the garage keep coming back to mind. The real ones. The ones I remember. Not the cheapened black and white version, which seems so classless, but the ones that will forever be etched in my subconscious because they meant so very much to me. I blow out a breath, still not believing how a night that was the spark of so many good things for us has now come back in such a malevolent way.

Driving onto Broadbeach Road, I'm so preoccupied with what I'm going to tell Colton about the doctor's visit that when I turn the bend in the street leading to our driveway, I'm shocked to see the melee; the road clogged with paparazzi. As I pull closer I notice two of the big dogs—Laine Cartwright, Denton Massey—and I immediately know something is going on. Through closed windows I hear words like "video" and statements of "how does it feel?" The baseless hope I had that it was something completely different than the video vanishes instantly.

The assholes released the tape.

My first thought is that Colton told them to fuck off and die without telling me. My next thought is he wouldn't do that without telling me. He promised he'd see what Kelly learned before making any decisions.

My heart drops as I do my best to keep my head down while I drive through the gates. Memories flood back to the last time the entrance to our house looked like this. Tawny had been involved that time so doesn't it fit that she'd be involved this time too? But at the same time, it's been six years. Why now? Why this? What's the damn purpose behind it?

Nothing makes sense and the simple fact is driving me crazy.

My hands are shaking by the time I put the Range Rover in park. And as much as I want to bolt out of the car and find out what the hell is going on, I've learned to wait until the gates close at my back before I open the door so the vultures can't get a shot they can sell. Once they do and I'm protected from sight, Sammy is already at my door opening it.

"Sammy?"

"Rylee," he says with a nod of his head and an aversion of his eyes, ignoring my questioning look. My feet falter on the short distance to the front door when it hits me. If the video has been released, Sammy knows who is on that tape. He arranged the car to be where it was that night. He's seen me naked. And having sex.

Oh fuck.

And when I stop, he stops, only ratcheting up my embarrassment. When he places his hand softly on my lower back to help usher me to the door, I realize just how bad the situation is. He's shielding my body just in case someone has managed to get me in their long-range lens.

This time I'm glad when he opens the front door for me and then steps outside because I can't look him in the eyes. I'm mortified with embarrassment but at least he'll be the only person who will know. I drop my purse on the table and go in search of Colton.

He's not in the office or kitchen, and I'm surprised when I find him upstairs on the upper patio, elbows resting on his knees, glass of amber liquid in one hand, phone to his ear with the other, and his head hung down in concentration.

"We were obviously played, CJ. Fucking full-court press without a goddamn ball." The resignation in his voice causes the hair on my arms to stand on end because why does he sound so defeated when he figured this was going to happen in the first place? That the asshole was going to release the tape anyway? "I know, but . . . fuck this is a clusterfuck. I didn't see this coming. Not from a million miles away." He pauses as CJ says whatever he's saying. "There is no controlling it. Don't you get that?" he shouts. By the shake of his head, he obviously disagrees with what is being said. "This conversation is done before I say something I'm going to regret and that you don't deserve."

He drops the phone on the chair next to him and without even looking up, downs the rest of the alcohol, meeting my eyes in a fleeting glance before concentrating back on the glass he's just emptied. "I'm assuming you didn't get my zillion texts?" he asks, irritated and agitated.

"I was at the doctor." *Oh shit. I was so stressed about how I was going to relay Dr. Steele's warning to Colton, I completely forgot to turn my ringer back on.* "Sorry," I say, cautiously stepping onto the patio. "What's going on, Colton?" I ask, although by his conversation with CJ, I already know.

He scrubs a hand over his face and when I get a little closer to him, something about his movements tells me he's a little buzzed. And I hate that he can't look me in the eye.

"The fuckers released the video," he says, words mirroring the thoughts I had when I saw paparazzi outside. The grimace on his face only serves to heighten my sense of dread.

"Okay," I say with a slow nod. "Well, you were right then." What else can I say?

The low chuckle he emits is anything but amused, and I will him to look at me so I can see what he's thinking. But he won't. Instead he just purses his lips, eyes focused on the bottle of Jack next to him, and pours himself another drink.

"But I was so very wrong." The words hang between us as he slowly raises his eyes to meet mine. And the look in them—absolute and utter apology mixed with regret and concern—causes more than just feelings of dread. Something is so very wrong.

"What do you mean?"

"They never wanted the money." Another long pull on the whiskey and the fact he never even winces tells me he's had more than a few already. "Nope. Not even close." He shakes his head when all I want to do is shake the answer out of him as the silence stretches. "In fact," he says as he raises his glass toward me, "they one-upped us."

"What do you mean they one-upped us?" The teeter-totter of uncertainty we are standing on starts to crash without a stopping point.

"They reeled me in, Ry, like a fucking fish on a hook. Doctored the time stamp like they knew I'd notice it. Made me think that was the only video of that night . . ." His voice draws off as he finally meets my eyes. "But there was one more. Another angle."

And that simple statement hijacks my breath and makes my heart thunder. "Another angle?" My voice is barely a whisper.

"Fuckin' A straight," he barks out, his self-deprecating laugh back that sounds equal parts sinister and lost hope.

"What the fuck do you mean, Colton?" I ask, my own mind running a million miles per hour now. I'm scared, worried, uncertain, and it all comes through in the words. *Another angle?* What do paparazzi know out front that I don't?

"Sit down," he orders, as he reaches out to grab my hand and tries to make me.

"*Don't!*" I warn him as I shrug out of his grip, letting the single word mean so many things. Don't coddle me. Don't bullshit me. Don't tell me to calm down because I'm not an idiot. I know something is very wrong here.

His eyes hold mine while the silence that feels like hours stretches between us, unnerving me more and more with each and every second that passes. He starts to speak a few times and stops; the words he wants to use not coming to him.

"Just tell me," I implore.

He closes his eyes momentarily before running a hand through his hair and taking a long swallow of his drink. I wrack my brain to remember the last time I saw him this stressed. It's been so long that I feel completely out of practice in what to say or how to soothe him.

"They played me. Knew I was going to say 'fuck them' and not pay. They never wanted the money, Ry," he says. Even though I'm not completely following him, I'm also mentally begging him to get to the point because I need to know why he's this upset. "Nope. They wanted to prove what an arrogant son of a bitch I am. Prove that even when I do what I think is best for my family, I still can't fucking protect you."

"What's on the tape, Colton?"

"Close-ups. Your face. Your body. Us together. The correct date," he says so quietly, it takes me a second to realize what he is actually saying.

"No!" I shout. He reaches out for me but I step back. The pressure in my chest mounts and the buzzing in my head grows louder.

"Ry . . ." My name is a plea on his lips and even though I hear it, I can't respond. My discordant thoughts are colliding together like a kaleidoscope—fractured images of unfinished thoughts that overwhelm me and confuse me all at once. "How was I supposed to know?"

The emotion in his voice pulls on every single one inside me, and yet I'm not sure which one to hold on to for a reaction. I want to rage and scream while at the same time I want to run and hide and pretend I didn't hear a thing.

I brace my hands on the patio railing; my eyes focus on the tranquility of the beach below, but all I feel inside is a dissonant storm of turmoil. "There's no mistaking it's me?" I ask, hoping against hope he's going to tell me what I need to hear.

"There are close-ups of us getting off the elevator and walking toward the car. Of you during," he says, voice empty, because how else can he possibly sound, "of us leaving after."

I press the heel of my hand on my breastbone, the pressure mounting steadily as I try to fathom how the situation he swore to me was under control is more like a tornado about to touch down.

And then it hits me. I've been so dumbfounded listening to him and trying to get what is wrong out of him that it didn't compute to me the real reason paparazzi are outside. It's not just because it was a sex tape where they thought the Prince of Racing was cheating on his do-good wife. No. Not in the least. They are out there circling like sharks with chum in the water because they've seen the tape where the Prince is actually fucking said wife on the hood of a car.

Oh. My. God.

I have a sex tape. That's been made public.

Oh. Shit.

Even through his whiskey-fogged mind, Colton must sense it's all clicked for me because when I turn around to face him, a deep exhale falls from his mouth. He watches me warily, possibly wondering if I'm going to rage and scream or go into my no-nonsense, let's-fix-this business mode.

"How bad?" It's all I can say, the only question I can think to voice.

"I already have Chase on it."

"That's not what I asked." His response gives me all I need to know though. If his publicity rep is already responding, that means it's public. Like majorly public. Like it's beyond controlling, public. "How bad, Colton?" His chuckle returns in response. I start to pace one way then stop and forget what I was doing. I can't focus. "How is this even . . .?" I can hope, although the dread I feel already tells me what the answer is. The anger festers but is held at bay by disbelief. "Like viral bad?"

"The public loves their celebrity sex tapes," he says, sarcasm thick in his voice and the look I've learned to hate on his face. The one I've seen so many times during our fertility journey that says there's nothing he can do to make it better besides put one foot in front of the other and try to put this all behind us. And that's not what I want to see right now. This is the last thing I need.

I want to dig my heels in instead of putting one foot in front of the other.

His eyes, usually so full of life, are deadly serious. I just shake my head back and forth as he starts to speak because I don't want to listen any more and yet need to hear everything.

"I have our lawyers on this, Ry. We'll find out—"

"Does it matter, Colton? Does it?" I throw my hands up, my body vibrating with anger, my soul hiding in embarrassment. "It's not like CJ is going to be able to get it taken down from the Internet. Because that's what you're not telling me, right? That's why you won't answer me when I ask how bad it is because you're afraid to say that a video of us having sex is being uploaded left and right to computers all over the goddamn place and there's not a fucking thing we can do about it."

I feel violated in so many ways right now, and not just because I'm naked. But more so because someone took an intimate, meaningful moment between him and me and exploited it. Demeaned it. Made it sleazy.

Made us sleazy.

This is not some sex scandal. *It. Is. Us.* A married couple. We're not cheating on each other. We're not into some weird taboo sex. Loving each other to the point where the outside world faded away and we became caught up in each other was our only fault.

"Please calm down, Ry. It's not good for the baby."

"Calm down? Are you kidding me? *THIS* isn't good for the baby. Not in the goddamn least," I say as I try to control the anger that's raging out of control. "You're the revered playboy who has lived your life in the public eye. Shit like this is good for your popularity, right? I mean this may elevate you to rock-star status with your groupies. *But. Not. Me!*" I scream as the shock finally gives way to anger. And I know I'm being mean and irrational but I don't care because this isn't fair.

"Ry . . . C'mon. That's not—"

"Not fair?" I yell, finishing his words that mirror my thoughts. "You want to know what's not fair, Colton? What this is going to do to me. I'm the good girl who works for a non-profit with little boys who look up to me. How am I going to explain this to them? *Fuck.* I'm the face of a company who asks for donations to fund our projects. So when you want to talk about fair, think about how in the hell this is going to affect me."

I have to move to abate my anger, the fire in my veins reflected in the aimless and erratic direction of my feet as I move from the doorway to the railing and then back to the doorway. Colton stands there watching me without saying a word. "Oh look, Bob, let's give money to Rylee Donavan. She's the class act who spread her legs and taped it for the world to see. Maybe we can ask her to do a video for us while she's at it because that'd sure as fuck raise some money for the organization."

"Rylee!" Colton barks out my name, trying to get me to stop my misplaced rage, but I don't care because it's not his professionalism at stake. *It's mine.* One I've built with years of hard work and sweat and tears. "How will anyone ever look at me again without seeing the look on my face when I come with my legs spread wide?"

We stare at each other now, but I can't hold back the spite in my tone or the accusation in my glare any longer as the detailed visual of that night fills my mind. The one of him standing before me with his pants unzipped and every other part of him completely clothed while I looked up at him from the hood of the car, my dress bunched up around my waist, breasts exposed. "I was naked for the world to see. *All of me.* Do you know how that feels? Do you have any clue? Fuck, Colton! This is who *you* are. You live your life in front of the masses and—"

"And what? You think this doesn't bug me?" He steps into me, chest heaving, anger palpable. "That I'm not devastated that a special moment between you and me is now on display for everyone to see? You think I give a rat's ass about people seeing my dick? I don't, Rylee. Not in the fucking least. I feel violated, and it's not because of me but because of you. I care because it's YOU. I worry because it was my idea and you went along with it when I knew that wasn't your norm, and now what? Now you're going to blame me for this and do *I don't know what* to our relationship?" The muscle in his jaw pulses as he clenches his teeth, his hands fisting, and eyes begging me for forgiveness that isn't his to ask for. I went with him willingly. I let him fuck me on the hood of the car and now years later look what's happened.

"I don't know," I whisper. Too many emotions are overwhelming me and pulling me in so many directions. He stands, the glass clinking as he sets it next to the bottle of Jack Daniels, before taking a few steps away from me, running his hand through his hair, and then stepping back toward me.

"If we let this get to us, we're letting them win. Giving them exactly what they want," he says, an unspoken plea for me not to shut him out right now.

And as much as I know his words hold truth, when he reaches out to me, I step back. The pressure in my chest increases and my head starts to hurt. I feel vulnerable, and I hate that feeling.

"My dad," I murmur, my heart beginning to pound so fast I become dizzy. "My dad's going to know about this. And Tanner." I'm not sure why the idea is so very devastating to me when I know they'd never watch it when a public of voyeurs will, but it does all the same.

The tears well as I think how embarrassed my parents are going to be. When I think of how my mom is going to have to answer questions at work or how my dad's going to react when his buddies at his weekly poker match ask him if that's really his daughter on the tape.

The sharp pain comes out of nowhere and despite immediately knocking the breath from me, I gasp out in pain. Colton's at my side in an instant as I brace one hand on the back of the lounge chair while my other one holds onto the swell of my belly. The immediate thought of '*No, it's too early*,' fills my head . . . and terrifies me.

"Ry." The fear in his voice matches how I feel. "Please sit down."

I roll my shoulders to get his hands off me. As much as I want him to pull me close right now, I also don't want to be touched at all. Don't want to be coddled. Don't want to be soothed. My nerves are raw and abraded; my emotions have been raked over the coals. When I sit down and stare at my hands folded in my lap, I will the baby to move to tell me he's okay while I try to calm down the riot of instability inside me.

And of course as I slow down, I'm forced to think, to let reason seep through the disbelief, and I hate when I feel the tears begin to burn in the back of my throat.

"Who would do this, Colton?" I finally look up and meet his eyes. I hate seeing his suffering, but I can't find it within me to comfort him like he is me. I know that makes me a bitch, but all I can think about is my job. The boys. My parents.

Us.

I know we can survive this, know we've weathered storms before, but we are now in such a different place in our lives than the other times. We are on the cusp of bringing this new life into our world. How do we manage the chaos from the outside when our inner circle is shifting too? Even the smallest of storms can cause damage, but how can you repair it when you can't even see it coming?

He sits down on the table in front of me and the look on his face tells me he's waiting for me to tell him to leave me alone. We stare at each other for a few seconds, so many things pass between us in the gaze and yet I can't say a single one of them.

"I don't know. I'll find out and try to fix this." It's all he can say and yet I know there is no fixing this. There is only fallout and that in itself scares the crap out of me because there is no parachute to help us float above the chaos this video will create.

"I know," I say quietly. I shake my head trying to stop the imminent tears I don't want to shed.

"Are you okay?" he asks and I know he means about everything, but I don't have the wherewithal to lie to him.

"The baby kicked." I can't tell him I'm okay, because I'm not. I have too many things going on in my head, and I just need to process it all. He won't stop looking at me and right now I don't want to be stared at. Currently, too many people online are gawking at me, and yet the one who can see the deepest into me is the one I don't want looking. All I want to do is crawl in a hole and be left alone, and therein lies the problem.

My privacy is nonexistent.

"I just want to be by myself for a bit."

"Ry, please."

"No. I just need to wrap my head around this."

I can see him want to tell me not to go, to stay here and talk to him, but I can't. I don't even know what to say to myself. I can't comprehend where I go from here or how I can rebound from this to claim my life back.

The waves crash onto the beach below. I watch them, know the breeze is hitting my face by the way my hair moves with it, but I can't feel it. My thoughts run wild, images in my mind that were so meaningful now turned into someone else's sick, twisted pleasure. I'm nauseated to think that somewhere, someone might be getting off right now on a video of us having sex. Creating fantasies in their own mind, making their own sound effects to it.

My stomach churns as I imagine some dark, seedy room with a creepy guy and a box of Kleenex. I know I'm overreacting but the image keeps repeating in my mind.

Feeling so exposed, so vulnerable, I curl into a tighter ball on the lounge chair where I'm sitting on the lower patio. These feelings are so foreign to me that I'm struggling to accept that this situation is actually real. Since we've been married, vulnerability has been absent in my life. That feeling of helplessness is nonexistent. Colton has never made me feel that way. Besides the random articles here and there, we've been able to keep our life *ours*, unaffected by the outside world. I have never doubted in his ability to smooth things when they go awry. We've turned to each other, reassured each other, taken care of each other.

And I know that those three actions aren't going to fix things now.

We can't say it's a bullshit story—someone out to make a name for themselves—because their name is irrelevant when it comes to sex in the public eye. It's going to be *our* names splashed around, twisted into some sordid story so I'm made to be some whore because let's face it: the men usually get hero status while the women are left with the tarnished reputation.

Normally I'd be in auto-fix mode by now. That's what I do, who I am. If there's a problem, I attack it with a clear head and try to mitigate damages and get it taken care of. I don't think there is a single way to mitigate anything when it comes to this situation and that's what's staggering me. Even worse, I'm sitting here, wanting to sink into oblivion but have my phone in my hand, fighting the urge to see how bad things really are. I have a feeling the fact that I had to turn my ringer off an hour ago to get some peace and quiet is already telling me the answer.

"Hey," Haddie says. The cushion next to me dips when she sits down and puts her arm around me. I should be shocked she's here, but I'm not. She always seems to know what I need to hear. Whether Colton called her because he feels lost that I don't want to speak to him right now or because she came on her own accord, doesn't matter. And as much as I want to be alone, wallow in whatever pity I have for myself that is useless anyway, it also feels good to have her beside me. The one person who will know what I need or don't need to hear right now because she knows me inside and out.

Out of habit, she reaches out and rubs her hand over my belly and deep down, beyond my embarrassment, I know the baby is the real reason I'm lost in a fog. I can't even process the thought that one day our son or daughter is going to google their mom or dad and come across us having sex on the hood of a car. In a garage. In public. How do you explain that?

My whole body tenses at the thought, the burn of tears back with a vengeance. "How bad is it?" I ask for what feels like the tenth time today. Again, I don't really expect an answer as I reach up to wipe away the tear that escapes and slides down my cheek.

"Well . . ." she starts and trails off, trying to find the right words. "When I told you to have some wild, reckless sex with the man, I guess I should have added the caveat to have some wild, reckless sex where there weren't any cameras."

All I can do is sigh, thankful she's trying to infuse some humor into the situation but not really feeling it. "Not funny."

"C'mon. That was a little funny," she says, holding her thumb and forefinger an inch apart.

"There's nothing funny about this whatsoever. Just tell me," I say again, wanting to know how bad it is because I'm too chicken shit to look myself.

She blows out a breath, and I close my eyes wanting to crawl inside myself. "It's bad. Like Internet frenzy, social media everywhere, reporters will be at the gate for some time, type of bad."

"*Fuck.*" One word says it all for me.

"That's kind of what got you in this position so maybe we should choose a different word."

I turn my head to look at her, not amused at all despite the exasperated smile turning up the corners of my mouth. "How about *bullshit?*"

"That's a good one. You've definitely stepped in it."

"Did you watch it?" I ask, because she is the one person who's going to give me the truth and not sugarcoat things. She nods her head slowly, serious eyes holding mine. "And?"

"It's definitely you and Colton, if that's what you're asking," she says, cutting straight to the chase and causing my stomach to churn. I know she is holding back a flippant comment—"a damn, girl" or "a holy hotness"—and I appreciate her restraint.

"Did Colton tell you about the whole . . . everything yesterday?"

"Yes," she states matter-of-factly and looks back toward the ocean beyond.

"Why? Why would someone do this to us, Had?"

"If I had one guess, I'd say money," she muses, "but that's what I don't understand. If it was all about the money, wouldn't the person sell the tape to make a bazillion dollars? The only thing that makes sense is someone seriously wants to fuck with you guys."

I want to cry. I want to sob. To rage. However, I push the heels of my hands over my eyes and just press them there, hoping they miraculously hold back the tears. Because as screwed up as it is in my mind, I feel like if I cry—if one tear leaks over—then this is really real. This isn't a nightmare I'm going to wake from.

"This can't be happening," I say to no one and everyone.

"Colton's worried about you," she says softly. "Wants to talk to you."

"He should be," I snip and then wince. "Look." I sigh. "I know he is but I need to clear my head for a bit before I talk to him. I mean, I have my parents calling and Tanner, and God only knows who else is leaving one of the million messages on my phone. I don't want to talk to anyone right now."

"I get it," she says, as I rest my head back on her shoulder. "But you're going to need to talk to everyone at some point or else you're going to explode."

"I know," I murmur, closing my eyes and wondering how I'm going to face anyone again. Exploding sounds like a more viable option.

But I can't.

The baby. I have to focus on our little miracle and not let any of this affect my stress, my health, or my blood pressure because it's still too early for him or her to come. I have to keep it together. Bury the emotion. Hide from the embarrassment. Push down the pain. Do what it takes.

I have this baby depending on me.

I'm a mom now. My needs come second.

Chapter Five

Colton

"Who the fuck is it, Kelly?" I pinch the bridge of my nose as I stare at my computer screen. Fucking Google and its far-reaching fingers. Pictures upon pictures of Rylee stare back at me. Stills taken from the video. Her body on display for the world to see, and all I can see is red. Rage in my blood, revenge on my mind. Finding the bastard who did this is my only thought so I can plow my fist into his face and then ask why if he's still conscious.

"I'm on it."

"Well, while I wait a few thousand more downloads will occur. No biggie," I say, sarcasm front and center, even though I know this isn't *his* fault. Shit, it's only been hours since the video appeared and it's already everywhere: TMZ, Perez Hilton, YouTube, E!, fucking CNN. You name it; it's there. "I want this bastard found the fuck out."

"And then what, Colton? It's not like they stole it from your house and then uploaded it. It was a random video taken in a public place. It's fodder for public use."

"I don't give a fuck," I shout into the phone. It alerts another call, and I cringe when I look down to see who it is. Dad. *Fuck.* "I gotta go. Keep me up to speed." I stare at the phone for a fleeting second, not wanting to tackle this just yet, before I switch the call over. "Dad."

"Hey," my dad says. In that single word I can hear him searching out how I'm doing. He never fails. No matter what curveball my life has thrown, my dad has always had my back.

"I take it you've seen the big news." Sarcasm is my friend today. Well, that and fucking Jack Daniels, but I had to cut myself off to prevent getting plastered. I need a clear head so I can deal with this crap. And so I can be there for Ry, my only focus in this whole shitstorm.

Even with valid reasons to abstain clear as fucking day, my eyes veer from my empty glass over to the bottle sitting on the kitchen counter. The sight of the whiskey tempts me. Sings to me like a siren luring me to crash and burn.

"Just wanted to check and make sure you and Rylee were okay." Thank fuck he finally speaks, pulling me from the temptation to drown my problems away. I swivel so my back faces the kitchen—and the bottle—while I wait for him to say more, ask the questions I know are on his tongue. Yet I'm met with silence. Rolling my shoulders, I blow out a breath as I try to let in the one person who matters most when all I want to do is shut people out right now.

"I'm worried about her," I confess as I look out the window. She's still curled up on the chaise lounge where she's been since Haddie left. The food next to her untouched. It's fucking killing me to not go out there and talk to her, but I'm the reason she's hurting.

I'm not going to let her pull away. Don't think she will. But she asked for space, and I'm giving it to her. *For now.*

"It takes a lot to catch me off guard, Dad," I say finally as my mind runs faster than I can say the thoughts, "and this . . . fuck . . . this just blindsided us."

"I don't want an explanation, son. I've lived this life too long to know how people twist and manipulate things to hurt others. I'm just calling to let you know we're behind you. I'm here if you need to talk and to make sure you take care of her."

"She told me she trusted me to handle this, and now? Now, I don't even know what the fuck to say to her."

"How about you start by using her name."

My knee-jerk reaction is to yell at him for the comment, but it dies on my lips when I click another link with the mouse and more images of Ry fill the screen: close-ups of her face, her tits, her spread legs, her goddamn everything.

I'm sure my dad can hear the sound of my fist hitting the desk through the connection and yet he says nothing. The drywall calls to me. It's so much more tempting to hit—satisfying—because the destruction is there, visible, and yet helps fucking nothing.

"*Her name?* Easier said than done, Dad. I brought her into my public world, pushed her, and now this is what she gets for loving me?"

"I bet she gets a whole lot more than that, Colton, or she wouldn't be with you." His words hang on the connection as I struggle whether or not to believe him. Is *the more* worth enough for her to stick with me through all of this?

His words repeat in my head.

I sure as fuck hope he's right. Everything's been too perfect as of late. Is this the other shoe dropping to put me back in my place and remind me how cruel fate can be?

"Remember, son, marriage isn't about how madly in love you are through the good times, but how committed you are to each other in the bad times."

And as cheesy as my dad's advice sounds, I hear it. Hold on to it. And hope to fucking God it's the truth because the shit has most definitely hit the fan.

"She won't even speak to me." I chuckle in frustration and force myself to turn off the computer. If I see one more image I have a feeling the drywall will be too tempting to resist. Unclench your fists, Donavan. Shove down the urge to hit something.

"I probably wouldn't want to speak to you right now either," he says. "You grew up in this world. As much as your mom and I tried to shelter you from it, the cameras were always there. You're used to them, the intrusion. She's not. She's always been a private person and now the two worlds have collided in such an intrusive way. You need to give her some space, let her come to terms with feeling violated, and then you need to do something to remind her how very special that moment was to you two so you don't let the vultures take that away from you."

Yeah. Because once they take a part of your soul, they only want more. And fuck if I plan on letting them have another piece of it.

"Thanks, Dad."

"I'm always here if you need me. Let's hope a huge story will come along and brush this under the rug sooner rather than later." *One can hope.* "You can't control this, son. The only thing you can do is to turn your wounds into wisdom."

My phone beeps again as I glance back to Rylee and her unmoving figure so very close but who seems so far away. "Yeah. Thanks, Dad. I'll talk to you soon. Chase is on the other line."

"Chase."

"You need to make a statement, Colton." As much as I love my publicist's straight-to-the-point manner, right now I don't really want to hear a fucking thing she says.

"I shouldn't have picked up," I say drolly, the only warning to her of the mood I'm in.

"Or the both of you need to make a public appearance and show you aren't fazed by any of this. The Ivy or Chateau Marmont?" she asks, knowing me well enough to ignore my comment.

"You're reaching for pie in the goddamn sky if you think I'm going to let Rylee anywhere near a public place right now."

"I get it, but you need to face the chaos head-on."

"Out of the fucking question. Now tell me how bad it is on your scale."

"Well, no publicity is bad publicity," she says, causing every part of me to bristle with anger.

"I'm going to pretend you didn't say that."

"Look, I'm not going to sugarcoat it, but it's what you'd expect from the fickle, sex-starved masses. You look like some sex god where *attaboys* will be handed out, and Ry looks exactly the opposite."

"But we're married," I shout, pissed off they're treating her like a whore.

"That's how I'm spinning it. Intimate moment between husband and wife. You didn't know about the cameras. Sell the story that some sick fuck is taking advantage of you two caught in a passionate moment. Make him out to be the bad guy and that you are the victims."

But I'm not a victim.

Never again.

Baxter's collar jingles as he follows me through the darkened house. My eyes burn from staring at the computer. Keeping it turned off didn't last very long. So many images, so many comments, and every single one of them was like a personal attack on me because they were all about Rylee. And it's only been hours since the video has been released. I fear what the morning will bring.

Turn wounds into wisdom. My dad's words ring in my ears and yet right now I'm not quite sure how that's possible. Wisdom won't punish the fucker who did this. It won't let me sleep better at night. It won't suffice as an apology to Rylee.

When I enter the bedroom, my feet falter and my hand with my drink stops halfway to my mouth when I see her. She's lying on her left side, body pillow tucked under her big belly and between her legs, sound asleep. Every part of my body tenses and relaxes simultaneously at the sight of her: perfection I don't deserve in any way, shape, or form.

Fucking Rylee.

My breath.

My life.

My kryptonite.

And now I've brought whatever the fuck this is down on her.

I sit in the chair across from the bed in our little sitting area that overlooks the beach darkened by the night beyond. It takes all I have not to crawl into bed and pull her against me and reassure her that everything is going to be fine again when she wakes up. Because it isn't. Far fucking from it.

Silence is much better than bullshit.

So I sit in silence with my legs propped on the coffee table in front of me and pour myself another glass of whiskey. I can drown in it now—let it sing me to sleep—since it's way too fucking late at night for anyone to need me.

I take a sip and watch Baxter go plop down on his bed. Shit, if he had a doghouse, I'd be in it tonight. And for good reason.

The alcohol burns but doesn't dull the ache in my gut or take the edge off the unknown and worry. Only Rylee can do that, and she's still not speaking to me.

I've done this husband thing for almost six years now. Thought I was doing a pretty damn good job at it. But then something like this happens and I'm reminded how little I can actually control, especially when it comes to taking care of those around me. There's no stopping the crazy we are going to wake up to in the morning. In my heart of fucking hearts—the one she brought back to life again—I know this for a fact.

Just like I know we can withstand this tornado we're in the middle of. It won't be the first. I sure as fuck hope it will be the last. Such optimism when I'm used to living by the *hope for the best, expect the worst* approach.

Who the fuck did this to us? And why?

Thoughts, theories, speculation. All three circle in my head and none of them make sense.

Rylee. My goddamn perfection in this whirlwind of chaos and bullshit. She is the only thing still crystal clear to me. My spark. My light.

My chest constricts. *We're introducing a baby into this mix.*

That lick of panic that's been on standby is dulled by the Jack, but it's still there.

Still flickering.

Still telling me there's no turning back.

Chapter Six

Rylee

I wake with a start. It's more than just the baby resting on my bladder. It's that sudden awareness when I reach out to find cold sheets, realizing Colton's not beside me. And then before I can shift to see if he even came to bed, yesterday comes flooding back to me.

In full 3D effect.

My whole body tenses. I want to pull the pillow over my head and hide, and in fact, I do just that for a brief moment to collect my thoughts and try to find the me that's hiding underneath layer upon layer of humiliation and mortification. But I can't live like this—hiding in shame—so I allow myself a momentary pity party before I get up to face the feared chaos.

The phone call to my parents last night comes back to mind. How supportive they were amidst my apologies for the embarrassment caused, and the promise that this footage was not something Colton and I even knew about. How my mom kept reiterating they were sorry someone was trying to exploit us in the worst way, but that the most important thing was to take care of the baby and my health.

Who thinks they'd ever have to make *that* apology to their parents? Ugh.

The baby shifts and reminds me how very hungry I am and how full my bladder is. I rise slowly from the bed, take care of my morning business, and then set off to find Colton and food. We need to talk. I shut him out last night so I wouldn't take my disbelieving anger out on him when this whole thing is just as much my fault as his.

I prepare myself before I look out our bedroom window to the gates at the front of the house. Being on the second story allows me to see the street clearly and of course the minute I move the curtains, I wish I hadn't.

Paparazzi lurk there, milling around, waiting for any movement from our house. They're vultures waiting for the tiniest bit of flesh they can tear away and use to their liking: to sensationalize, to vilify, to exploit, and to manufacture lies.

And it's not like they haven't seen enough of my flesh already.

My stomach tightens at the sight. Too much. Too fast. I wince, worried what this is doing to my blood pressure. The room around me becomes foggy as dizziness overwhelms me momentarily. I fear what I'm going to find when I go downstairs to my laptop, which adds pressure to the constriction in my chest.

I sit on the edge of the bed and attempt to calm myself. The welfare of the baby my only thought as I try to regain the determination I felt ten minutes ago to face head-on whatever the day brings. A few deep breaths later, my cell on the nightstand vibrates. The name on the screen causes me to cringe. With quiet resolve, I have no choice but to answer him.

"Hello?"

"Are you okay, Rylee?" My sweet boy—now grown man in college—coming to the rescue.

"Hey, Shane. I'm okay. *I'm sorry*." The apology is off my tongue in an instant. Two words I feel like I'm going to be saying a lot in the coming days.

"Do you need me to come home?" The simple question has tears welling in my eyes. I'd like to blame it on the hormones but I can't. Yesterday showed me how cruel the masses could be to no one in particular and yet today, this moment, I'm shown once again how much good there is still in the world. That a boy once lost, who I spent a lifetime comforting and trying to help heal, has taken to me like I am his own. And there is something so very poignant about the thought that it's exactly what I needed to receive.

"You have no idea how much that simple question means to me, Shane. I appreciate the offer more than you know, but there's not much anyone can do. More than anything I'm mortified . . . It's just . . ." I exhale audibly into the connection because what exactly am I supposed to say? I know he's an adult now, that he understands as much as anyone the fishbowl world I now live in, but that doesn't take away any of the awkwardness.

"It's okay. You don't need to say anything. Colton and I talked last night. He explained everything." I breathe a slight sigh of relief because that saves me from having to take a step in this dance of discomfort. Well, at least when it comes to Shane.

I'll still have to address the boys at The House at some point. The thought causes me to roll my shoulders in unease.

"Are you sure you don't want me to drive down?" he asks again. "I can skip some classes tomorrow."

"No. Thank you, though. I don't want you skipping any classes. Just hearing your voice has made me feel better."

"Okay. If you're sure."

"Positive."

"Okay. Speaking of classes, I've got to get to one right now."

We say our goodbyes, and I sit on the bed with my phone clutched in my hand. All I can think about is Shane and the little ray of sunlight his call afforded me. How that little boy I took in at The House way back when has grown into this incredible man who worried enough about me to call Colton to make sure I was okay.

There is right in this world. And I helped make it. I hold on to that thought. I think I'm going to need it in the coming days.

I make my way down the stairs listening for sounds of Colton in the kitchen. That flutter of panic happens when dead silence greets me. When there is no response to my whistle for Baxter, I head toward the downstairs bedroom that houses our workout equipment to find the door shut, the beat of Colton's feet hitting the treadmill coming through it.

And as much as I need to talk to him, I also need to face the reality of what my world now looks like through the microscope of public scrutiny. Besides, by the way he's pounding the belt of the treadmill, I have a feeling Colton needs the release the exercise will bring.

I grab an apple on the way to the office but don't even bother to take a bite of it once the screen of the computer flickers to life. Images upon images of myself litter the monitor. Good images. Bad images. Violating images.

No wonder the treadmill sounded like it was going to break. Colton must have been surveying the damage before he ran.

The pictures suck the air from my lungs so it takes me a moment, my eyes wide with horror, before I can even my breathing. And as much as I know I should turn the computer off and not click on the links to see the public's perception, this is me. My life. I have to know what I'm facing.

With a reluctant hand, I click on the first Google link and am brought to a massive gossip news site. An image of some of the boys and me from a promotional event a few months back dominates the page, but it's the title that owns my mind. "Risky Business: Sex tape vixen leads our troubled youth."

My hands start shaking as I read the article and the comments that don't have merit gracing the pages. "Rylee Donavan surely knows how to land the racing world's most eligible bachelor. I wonder just what she'd do for you in exchange for a donation." Or "Is this how we fundraise nowadays? Is Corporate Cares struggling to fund their next project so their most prominent employee decides to take matters in her own hands to raise awareness? She's been known to say *anything for her boys*. We didn't realize this was her anything."

Link after link.

Comment after comment.

I don't want to believe what I'm reading and seeing so I keep clicking, keep reading, keep being shocked by the cruelty of others.

Oh. My. God. This isn't possible. It's just not. Can't be. I'm not *that person*. The media whore needing to further my career. Yet *that's* what they've made me out to be.

My eyes burn as I search and scrutinize and look for some kind of good in the links, but I'm fooling myself if I actually think I'm going to find some. And when I do, the positive and supportive stories are buried four pages in by the sensationalized crap that sells.

I'm horrified by the images I'm not yet familiar with. The ones from the new version of the tape. And yet I can't stop clicking the links and reading the bylines. I can't stop seeing all of my hard work and dedication to a worthy cause dragged through the mud because some asshole wants to prove a point none of us are privy to.

I replay it again. Paralyzed. Lost in the images. Mortified. Wondering for the first time if there is more to this than just an attack on Colton. The obvious go-to answer. *What if this is about me?* What if someone has a vendetta against me because I was the person taking care of their son?

It's a ridiculous thought. I shake my head to clear it from my mind. It's not possible. Even if it were, they'd have no clue this video even existed.

But the thought lingers. Worries around in my head. Draws my eyes back to the video on the monitor and the final image frozen on screen when the video ends. I close my eyes and sigh because the lasting image is more damaging than the sex itself. It's a close up of Colton and me as we leave the garage. He is looking over to me and I am looking ahead, almost as if I'm directing my face toward the camera. Like I knew it was there. The worst part is that I have the happiest of smiles on my face. Emotions I can still feel all these years later rush back to me, but this time they've been tainted. Because with the grainy quality of the video, the smile I have on my face can now be misread.

I look smug, calculating, manipulative. Like I knew exactly where the camera was, and was telling anyone watching, "*Look who I landed.*"

Lost in thought, I stare out the windows beyond and try to figure out what we need to do and where we need to go from here because my worst fear is that this will hurt the boys somehow. Boys that have had way too much happen in their short lifetimes to be affected by this too.

"Ry?" Colton calls to me from the doorway where he's standing with a towel draped around his neck, both hands pulling down on it. His chest is misted with sweat from his workout, and a cautious expression plays on his face. And there are so many questions in that single syllable. Are you all right? Are you going to speak to me yet? Do you know how much I missed you?

And just the sound of his voice quiets the turmoil within. Whereas last night all I wanted to do was lash out at him—blame him when it's not his fault—today I just want him to pull me into him and hold on tight.

"Hey," I say as I stare at him in a whole new light. This is the first real problem we've encountered since we've been married, and yet he was able to step back and give me the space I needed when I know it was killing him not to rush in and try to fix what can't be fixed. "Good run?"

He shrugs. "Just trying to work off some shit," he murmurs as he moves into the room behind the desk where I am, and clicks the computer screen off. "Please don't read any more."

"Look, I'm the good girl. I don't do things that get attention so this is . . ." I blow a breath out not sure what I'm trying to say. "I needed to know how bad it was," I explain quietly, as my eyes follow his when he leans a hip on the desk in front of me. We sit in silence for a moment, until I reach out and he meets my hand halfway, our fingers lacing in an unexpected show of unity that sounds stupid but feels so very significant.

Us against them.

"And . . ."

"It's bad," I say as I look up from our hands to meet the somber expression in his eyes. When I just purse my lips and nod my head because there is nothing else I can say, he just squeezes our fingers.

"I talked to my parents. To Tanner. To Shane." My voice fades off as the disbelief I have to take stock and let him know the damage control I've done takes hold. Unsure how to respond to me when he's always so sure, he just nods his head as our eyes hold steadfast. "Our baby is going to grow up knowing this is out there." My voice is so soft, it sounds so very different than the storm of anger that rages inside me, and yet I can't find it within me to show my emotions. I can feel his fingers tense from my comment, see his Adam's apple bob from the forced swallow, and notice the tick of muscle as he clenches his jaw.

"We'll get through this."

The condescending chuckle falls from my lips, the first break in my fraudulent façade because it's so damn easy for him to say. "I know." Voice back, emotion nonexistent, tone unsure.

Colton stares, willing me to say more but I don't. I just match him stare for hollow stare as images of myself from Google flicker through my mind. Finally he breaks our connection and reaches his fingers to pinch the bridge of his nose before blowing out a sigh.

"Scream at me, Ry. Yell. Rage. Take it out on me. Do anything but be silent because I can't handle when you're silent with me," he pleads. All I can do is shake my head, dig down within myself to will the emotion to come. When I can't find the words or the feeling behind them, it unnerves him, worries him. "I'm sorry, baby. Were we stupid that night? Maybe. Do I regret that night?" He shakes his head. "I regret all of this, yes, but that night in general? No. So many damn things happened that put you and me where we are now. So for that? I'm not sorry. You pushed me that night, made me question if I could give someone more of myself." He reaches his free hand up to brush a thumb over the line of my jaw. His touch reassuring, his words helping soothe the sting of our situation.

"It's not your fault," I say, trying to ease the concern in his eyes.

"Maybe not directly . . . but I made you color outside of your perfectly constructed lines . . . do something against your nature, and look what happened. I'm so sorry. I wish I could make this right," he says, dropping his head as he shakes his head in defeat. "All I can try to do is mitigate the damage. That's it." He throws his hands up. "It's killing me because I can't fix this." The break in his voice and the tension in his body would have told me everything I needed to know even if he hadn't uttered a sound.

I look at my achingly handsome husband, so distraught, so desperate to make wrongs right that aren't his to be held responsible for. And seeing him as upset as I am makes me feel a little better and allows me to dig into the deep well of emotion. I finally find the words I need and want to tell him. The decisions I came to last night when I sat on the deck and considered the life-altering situation we were in.

"Stop. Please quit beating yourself up over this. I don't blame you." I pause, my teeth worrying my bottom lip as I put words to my thoughts and wait for him to hear that last sentence. "Thank you for giving me space last night. At first I was pissed at you . . . just because you are the one here to lash out at. But the longer I sat and thought, I realized that more than anything, my fury is aimed at whoever did this. *They* took a moment between the two of us and made it something for others to judge and ridicule."

Colton pulls on our hands so the chair I'm sitting in rolls toward him. He leans forward, our faces inches apart, and looks into my eyes. "No one knows us. No one understands why our relationship works but us. I know the real you, Rylee Jade Thomas Donavan. They don't have a clue how fucking incredible you are. Only I get the privilege of knowing you like ice cream for breakfast and pancakes for dinner. I'm the only one who gets to know that when you scream and rage you get that little crease in your forehead that's so fucking adorable. I love that you love those boys like they are your life and would never do a goddamn thing to hurt them. I know you're disciplined and modest and hate coloring outside the lines, but that you do sometimes just for me. The fact that you do means the world to me. And more than anything, I love that you raced me even when I didn't have any wheels on the fucking track."

His words hit me and wrap around my heart like a bow on a package that's wrapping is tattered and torn. They crawl into my soul and take hold because they are exactly what I need to hear to reinforce the love I have for him. My gruff, arrogant husband can be the man I need him to be when I need it the most and that says volumes for what I mean to him.

He leans forward and presses a kiss to my lips so tender it makes me adore him more. When he leans back he rests his forehead against mine, our noses touch, his exhale my next breath, and I feel a bit steadier even though nothing's changed.

"We'll get through this, Ry. Just like we have before. Just like we always will. What we have between us," he says, voice thick with emotion as he pauses to find the words, "is a beautiful thing."

"A beautiful thing is never perfect," I murmur.

"You're right. We're far from perfect. We're *perfectly imperfect*."

If I wasn't already madly in love with my husband, that two-word description would win me over. It reinforces the arrow shot through my heart. Words I used once to describe him have now come back to represent exactly what we are as a couple. And the fact he realizes, accepts, and acknowledges it, makes it that much more meaningful.

"You're right," I say with a shaky voice. He presses a kiss to my nose and leans back, hands smoothing my messy hair out of my face before holding my face in his hands so I can see the intention in his eyes.

"I promise you, I will find out who did this and make them pay." His statement means a lot to me but I know even if he does find them, the damage is done. We'll never be able to get those images, the privacy of that moment back, and so I just nod my head in response.

"I need to talk to the older boys about this somehow." Although I'm at a loss for words of what exactly I'm going to say to them. Everyone but Auggie is a teenager. Teenagers and their long-reaching fingers into social media will find out about this. The thought makes my heart fall.

"No, you don't." He scrubs the towel through his hair and shakes his head like I'm crazy.

"Some of the pictures splashed all over the Internet are of them, Colton. Of course I have to." A tinge of hysteria laces the edges of my anger. "Kids at school are going to talk. They need to hear it from me. Have to. I can't let them think I'm some kind of . . ." My voice trails off as I try to figure out what exactly I think they are going to think of me now.

"Ry, listen to me. They love you. You don't have to say any—"

"Yes, I do."

"I'll speak to them," he states matter-of-factly, causing my head to whip up at the response since I know how uncomfortable he is with that kind of thing.

"You what?"

"You're not leaving the house right now with the press out there. I'm not letting them take pictures of you to have fodder for their lies. They can have me . . . let them vilify me. Not you. No way." I'm shocked by his words and yet shouldn't be. "Chase is issuing a statement to the press for us. Hopefully that will help all of this die down."

"Mm-hmm." I must look at him like a doe in the headlights because as much as I know this will die down, people will forever know what I look like naked. That's not an easy thing to swallow. Not now. Not ever.

And even when Chase issues that statement, it will do very little to dim the sparkle of the sensationalism.

"I've got to go take a shower. Then I'm going to work from home the rest of the week," he says as he rises from his seat, his comment causing my stomach to churn in anxiety.

"I have my shift tomorrow," I say, suddenly realizing reality needs to continue amid this storm of chaos. "Can you and Sammy figure out how to get me out of here so I can get there?"

The minute his body stills, I know a fight's coming. He doesn't disappoint but goes straight for the kill. "Dr. Steele called this morning." I'm immediately irritated and defensive before he even says another word. I feel like he's been waiting to make this point. Inwardly I groan because that means he knows about my blood pressure issues.

"Yes?" I say nonchalantly even though inside I'm already preparing for World War Donavan.

"The way I see it, you're staying home tomorrow."

"That's bullshit!" He just quirks an eyebrow to say *try me*.

"Well, seems to me she called to check on you. Said she was worried about your blood pressure . . . with all of this." I avert my eyes to my hands folded in my lap.

"I'm fine." I nod my head with a forced smile on my lips in hopeful reassurance.

"That's not what she said," he says, making said blood pressure feel as though it is rising.

"Colton, I'm going to work tomorrow, with or without your help. If you want my blood pressure to stay low, you'll help," I fire back, lips pursed, eyebrows raised. Two can play this game. We stare at each other, both daring the other to back down but neither budging.

"Exactly. I'll help. I'll go instead and talk to the boys about it," he lifts his eyebrows, "while you stay here."

"Don't push me on this," I warn.

His chuckle fills the room. "That's rich, Donavan," he says with a shake of his head as he walks toward the door. "I need to take a shower but this discussion is over."

I snort in response. He stops abruptly, back still to me when he speaks. "I love the boys, Rylee. More than you know. I said I'd never come between you and them . . . but you, and that baby of ours you're carrying, are my first priority. Numero Uno. You'd better start making both of them yours too, or we're going to have a huge fucking problem. End of discussion." And he doesn't even give me a chance to pick my jaw up off the floor to respond before he waltzes out of the office, tossing, "Don't look at the computer anymore either," over his shoulder.

Staring at the empty doorway, I'm not quite sure what to think so I lean back in the chair and blow out a slow and steady breath to calm myself. Colton's never said anything like that to me before, and while everything he just said holds serious merit, I'm still astounded he said it. And while a small part of me warms, knowing he wants to take care of me, a larger part is irritated he's laying down the law. The irony.

It doesn't mean I have to abide by it though.

I look toward the ceiling and close my eyes momentarily. The many things I need to do run through my head, but I can't do any of them because I can't leave my house, can't carry on my life like normal. I'm stuck here and that thought alone makes me feel claustrophobic.

I'm exposed to the world but trapped in my house.

Feeling defeated, my eyes flutter open to see the beach beyond the windows down below. And for the first time since we've met, I truly understand why Colton finds such refuge in his beloved beach—the crash of the waves, the feel of the sand beneath his feet, and the sense he's this tiny blip on Mother Nature's radar.

A soft chuckle falls from my lips as it hits me. On the beach, he feels *inconsequential*. How very fitting for a man who once told me I would never be that to him to have the need to feel that way at times.

My mind shifts back to that place and time. A ghost of a smile turns up my lips of the welcome memory of the Merit Rum party: dancing in the club followed by him chasing me into the hallway. Angry words. Contemptuous kisses. Hungry eyes. An elevator ride to the penthouse with a promised threat to decide. *Yes. Or. No.*

I find comfort in the memory. Without that night, there most likely wouldn't be this. No Colton. No baby on the way. No chaos to want to hide from.

My eyes are drawn back to the beach. To the temptation of Colton's place to escape. Sadly, right now,

I couldn't escape down there if I wanted to. At least he can get on his board and paddle out beyond the break to get some distance from the photographers. I'm not so lucky.

What I'd give to be inconsequential right now.

And yet deep down, no matter how hard I try, I know I will never be that to Colton. He'd never allow it. My handsome, complicated, and very stubborn husband takes too much pride in the two things he never thought he'd have—a wife and her love—to ever let me feel inconsequential again.

Chapter Seven

Colton

"Grab a beer, boys."

The looks on their faces? Fucking priceless as I motion to the cooler sitting beside the table. Aiden's mouth is hanging open, waiting to catch flies. Both Ricky and Kyle's eyes look like they are bugging out of their heads. Zander and Scooter shift uncomfortably on the bench, glance over their shoulders like they don't want Jax to walk in and get them in trouble.

"Go on," I encourage and lean over and open the lid myself.

Aiden sees it first. His laugh rings across the room. "It's root beer, guys." His voice is part relief, part disbelief as he shakes his head and passes down the silver cans of soda.

The others join in. Eyes flicker from the cans back to me, looks of curiosity over why I'm here and what's going on. The crack of the tops of the cans fill the room. I wait for them the take that first sip before looking back to me.

"I need to have a man-to-man talk with you guys so I figured you could handle having a beer or two while we chat." I nod my head to reinforce my point and get five more nods in return.

"Are we in trouble?" Ricky asks, hands fiddling with the tab on his can.

"No, but I need to talk to you guys about something." Fuck. Fuck. Fuck. Why am I nervous? I look down at my hands. *Buck the fuck up, Donavan.* They're all under fourteen. How am I going to do this? Crap.

"What?" Zander asks, eyebrows raised, voice innocent.

And shit. Innocent is the keyword here. Did I know what sex was at age thirteen? Hell yes, I did. Thought I did, anyway. A messy French kiss with Laura Parker was the extent of it. The sheets I'd balled up in the morning, mortified for my mom to find, had been my reality.

"So . . . you guys might start hearing some stuff at school or see stuff on TV or the Internet about Rylee and me." Brows furrow. Lips quirk. And my palms sweat. I clear my throat. "Sometimes adults do things in the heat of the moment that leads to . . . er . . . uh . . . consequences."

"Heat of the moment?" Aiden says with a snicker. I swear to God I blush for the first time in what feels like forever.

"You know sometimes you do something without thinking—"

"Like that time you climbed on the counter to get the cookies on top of the refrigerator and—"

"No. Not like that," I cut Kyle off. Sweet Jesus this is going to be difficult. "More like when two married people love each other they—"

"Do they have to be married?" Scooter asks.

Seriously? Do I have to go here? I feel like I'm sitting on hot coals. My balls are burning and I can't sit still.

"For the most part, *yes*." I'm going to be struck by lightning for saying that. For lying through my teeth.

Aiden snickers again. I guess at age fourteen he knows where I'm going with this. And is enjoying watching me struggle.

"Anyway, there is going to be some talk about us and I wanted to say that you know Rylee. You know the person she is. So please don't believe any of the crap you hear being said."

There. Maybe that will be enough.

"But why? What's on the Internet?"

I just fucked this up. If I were their age and someone said this to me, I'd immediately go and online and search for it. Curiosity and all that.

The snicker again from Aiden. The one that says he either already knows because someone said something at school today or is assuming.

Don't lose your cool, Donavan.

"Five Three X," he murmurs under his breath, confusing the fuck out of me but making perfect sense to the four of them by the way they whip their heads his way and their mouths fall open like they know perfectly well what he's saying.

"*What?*" I ask.

Five pairs of eyes look down at hands on soda cans and leave me lost in the goddamn dark.

"Someone going to explain what the hell five three X means?"

Snickers times five now.

"Aiden?"

He looks up, meets my eyes, and the look he gives me tells me he knows exactly what I'm here to tell them about. A single scathing look that tells me he's pissed at me for whatever it is he's read about Ry—like it's all my fault—and all I can do is sigh and run a hand through my hair. And try to figure out what the fuck he's talking about.

A part of me loves this glare he's giving me. He's pissed with me because he's protective of Ry, but at the same time . . . really? I'm being eye-scolded by a fourteen-year-old?

And then it hits me. The visual of what Five Three X looks like. 53X

SEX.

Jesus fucking Christ. When did I get so old I don't know that lingo and when did these kids get so old when they're not?

I jog my knee. Take a breath. What the hell am I supposed to say now? I wasn't really going to go into the sex part of it. Was I? I don't even know. I thought this was going to be a cinch. A little chat. Don't believe everything you see or hear on the Internet type of thing.

And now I'm stuck with birds and bees and son-of-a-bitch Aiden just threw a whole goddamn hornet's nest on me when I wasn't looking.

Can anyone say fish out of water?

"Dude. It's totally cool," Aiden says, taking point for the brood despite the two youngest, Zander and Scooter, blushing.

"No, it's not cool," I say, finding my footing. "Rylee's super concerned that you will be affected by this and she doesn't want you to—"

"Look, we're not going to click on anything, okay?" My eyes bug out of my head. "No one wants to see you bumping uglies . . . especially us."

That's one way to put it. My mouth goes dry as snickers fall, red creeps into cheeks, and eyes are averted from mine.

"Well . . . then . . ." Shit. *Great job, Donavan. You've got Aiden pissed at you but you still haven't made them understand that this is about more than just sex.* I scrub a hand over my face and try to figure out what the fuck I need to say to get the point across. "Listen, guys, you love Rylee like I do, right?" All heads nod and each pair of eyes narrow as they wait to see what else I'm going to say. "That's what I thought. So I need you to understand that there have been some mean, ugly things said about her because of the images out there of us. She's upset and really hurt by them. But more than anything, she's worried it's going to affect all of you. So when I ask you not to click on anything online, don't click on anything. When I ask you not to believe anything crappy said about her or her reasons for supporting The House, don't believe them. You guys are her world, and she'd hate herself if you were hurt in any way from this. So can you do that for me? Can you ignore all of this and pretend like it didn't happen so Rylee doesn't have to worry about you guys?"

For fuck's sake, please understand what I'm asking here.

Aiden's gaze meets mine. Gone is the immature smugness from moments before. It's been replaced with an understanding that seems to go well beyond his years. He nods his head once to me, eyes relaying his unspoken words: *we promise.*

I shift in my seat when all I really want to do is sag in relief. *Thank Christ.* I start to talk and then stop, unsure what to say next.

"Dodgers," Aiden says, recognizing my uncertainty and owning this conversation like nobody's business. "Let's talk about last night's Dodgers game."

All I can do is shake my head.

I'm not ready for this parenting shit.

Chapter Eight

Rylee

"What the fuck do you mean early parole?" Colton's voice ricochets off the stairwell and up into the room, shocking me from the case reports I'm trying to complete on my laptop and indicating he is home. Within an instant, I set my computer aside and move downstairs to find out what's going on.

"I know, CJ. I know," Colton says, one hand fisted at his side, posture tense, as I walk into the great room, his back to me framed against the open doors to the patio. "But it's too much of a goddamn coincidence, don't you think? The timing, his vindication . . . all of it adds up."

Colton must sense me and turns to meet my eyes, holding one finger up requesting I wait while he finishes the conversation. I watch the emotions play over his face as he listens to our lawyer. He moves to abate the restlessness of whatever CJ is telling him, my eyes following him pace, my mind trying to figure out what's going on. They say their goodbyes, and he turns again to face me.

"Eddie."

It's all he says as he smacks his hands together. That simple name—a blast from our past—and Colton's reflex reaction cause details from three years ago to flood back to me. The CD Enterprises patent for an innovative neck protection device being denied because someone else was already in the process of getting a very similar one approved. Almost identical in fact. Investigations to find out that the other patent applicant had CDE's same exact blueprints for the device, followed by digging into the layering of the corporation applying to find Eddie Kimball on the board of directors.

The same Eddie Kimball who Colton had fired for stealing said blueprints.

As I look at the fire lighting up Colton's eyes, I think of the two-year legal battle that ensued over the right of ownership and future revenues from the device the blueprints made. I'm reminded of the stress, the lies, the accusations, the mediation meetings, and offers of settlement to buy time on Eddie's part. After spending a fortune in legal counsel, the judge eventually ruled in our favor and convicted Eddie of numerous charges—fraud, perjury, false witness—and sentenced him to a four-year jail sentence.

"How?" I ask, making calculations about someone I mentally told myself was out of our lives. The trial ended three years ago. He had a four-year sentence.

"Early release. Good Behavior. Jails too crowded from the three-strikes statute." He answers my unspoken questions as he runs a hand through his hair, his head nodding, and I can see him trying to put the pieces of the puzzle together in his mind.

"Tawny knew where we were." It's all I say, voice quiet, gaze fixed on him. He looks up, narrows his eyes, and grits his teeth, not wanting to hear me say it again.

"I know," he says with a sigh, "but I'm trying to figure out how it all fits together. What? Did Tawny go up and get the video of us that night? If she had it way back when, then why keep it and release it all this time later?" He slumps down on the couch and puts his head in his hand while he tries to make sense of it.

I move and sit down next to him and rest my head on his shoulder.

"I can't give you the answers but it all seems too convenient for her not to have had a hand in this." My voice is calm but anger fires in my veins at the thought that either of them have had a hand in this. And yet I shouldn't expect any less from them.

Bitches can't change their stripes. Oh wait, that's *tigers*. Hmpf. Doesn't matter because I refuse to give her a second thought. If she did do this, then Lord have mercy on her when Colton gets done with her.

The idea doesn't take the sting out of our public humiliation any less, but at least with this newfound information about Eddie's release, we might have some place to start looking.

"Kelly is trying to track him down through his parole officer," Colton says, pulling me from my thoughts. He reaches out and squeezes my knee to show me he's present although I know mentally he's a million miles away.

"This is all just so fucked up," I murmur, speaking my thoughts aloud and garnering a sound of agreement from him. We sit like this for a few moments. The silence is comforting because we know outside this bubble we've surrounded ourselves with, there are people waiting to tear us apart.

My cell phone rings from the kitchen counter causing me to sigh because I'm sure it's some intrusive person from a tabloid. "I need to change my number," I groan.

"I'll handle this," he says, beating me to the punch and getting up from the couch. Besides, with the time it would take to get my pregnant self up, the call would probably go to voicemail.

I sink back into the couch and wait for Colton to answer and unleash his temper on whatever poor soul thinks they are calling me, so I'm surprised when I hear him greet the person warmly.

"Hey, good afternoon," Colton says. "She's right here, Teddy. Hold on."

And there is something in that split second of time that causes my brain—that has been so overwhelmed by everything today—to fire on all cylinders. I thought of my parents and the boys. I've read articles denouncing my motives and implying I released the tape for my own benefit. I called Jax and had him cover my shift at The House. And yet not once did I pick up the phone and call my boss. Not once did I think of damage control or how this man I greatly admire is going to look at me now.

Pregnancy brain.

Oh shit.

Scenarios flicker through my mind as I take the phone from Colton. Our eyes meet momentarily, and I can already see he's thinking the same thing I am.

"Hey Teddy," I say, my voice ten times more enthusiastic than I feel.

"How you doing, kiddo?" he asks cautiously.

"I'm sorry I haven't called you," I say, immediately using those two words again even though I technically haven't done anything wrong.

"No need to." It's all he says and the awkward silence hangs through the connection. I can sense he's trying to figure out how to approach this conversation, an awkward dance of unspoken words. "But we do need to talk."

And the angst I had shelved momentarily returns in a blaze of glory.

"What do you need from me, Teddy?" I feel the need to rise and walk, subdue the discord I already feel, but don't have the energy. Colton steps behind the couch and places his hands on my shoulders and begins to knead away the tension there.

My boss sighs into the line and it's the only sound I need to hear to know my fears about why he's calling are warranted. "Some benefactors are raising their hypocritical highbrow hands and protesting your lead on the project."

I take a deep breath, biting back the comments on my tongue. "I see. Well, take me off as the lead then. Let me have my shifts at The House, and I'll work behind the scenes on the upcoming project."

When he doesn't respond immediately, I bite my bottom lip. "I wish I could." And then silence. We sigh simultaneously, the singular sound a symphony of disquiet.

"What do you mean you wish you could?"

"Ry . . ."

And it hits me. It's not that he wants me to take a back seat on the project. He wants me off the project entirely. And out of The House.

"Oh," I say. Colton's fingers tense as he feeds off my physical reaction. Right now I'm so glad he can't see my face because he'll see how devastated I am. He already feels guilty enough for things he can't control. "I won't risk the project. The boys, the mission, everything means way too much to me. I've put my blood, sweat, tears, and heart into this and I can't risk it for the many more we are going to be able to help. I know this is hard for you and I won't make you ask me so I'll just say it. I'll take an early maternity leave. I'll hate it. It'll kill me to leave Auggie right now just as we're making progress and a breakthrough is on the horizon . . ." My voice trails off, ending my ramble as I struggle to articulate how hard this is for me. In the same breath, I know it was ten times harder for him to pick up the phone to call me and ask this of me.

"They want more than an early maternity leave, Rylee."

"What do you mean?"

"The Board wants me to place you on an indefinite leave of absence."

"Indefinite?" I stutter, voice unsteady, disbelief tingeing its edges as I prod him for the answer I want. "As in three-month type of indefinite?"

"You know I respect you. You know *I* know this project is a continued success because of you and that the boys are contributing members to society because of all the time and hard work you've put in." I hate that all of a sudden Teddy sounds like he's speaking to a room of stiff suits instead of me, the woman who has worked for him for over twelve years. However, I understand his protective wall of detachment more than he knows because I'm fortifying mine too right now. I have to. It's the only way I'll be able to get through this conversation when he tells me I am no longer mother to my boys. To my family. When I don't respond, he continues, trying to find his footing in a world where he is boss, mentor, and friend. "I swear to

God I went to bat for you, kid . . . but with the board vote coming up," he says, shame in his voice but I get where he's coming from. The annual vote to approve his position is next month and if he fights too hard, he might not get renewed.

Teddy losing his position would be a colossal mistake; the boys would lose both of us—their biggest advocates. I bite back the bitterness, the want to argue, because with him still in the mix, I know there will at least be one of us working with them.

"It's temporary. I promise you that. Just until the attention dies down."

Yeah. Temporary. The bitterness returns. Disbelief overwhelms me and shakes loose a new thought: what if his contract isn't renewed? Would *I* still have a place at Corporate Cares?

The fear replaces my rage, allows me to calm down and realize fighting him is like preaching to the choir. I just need to fade into the background regardless of the fact I feel like I'm bathed in a neon light. It will be hard as hell but I don't want to rock the boat for him any more than I already have.

"Okay," I respond softly, my voice anything but certain. And I want to ask him how he knows it's temporary—need some kind of concrete here—but know it's useless to ask. This is hard enough for both of us as it is, so why throw false promises in there too?

"I feel like I'm selling you out for the donations—"

"No—"

"But we need these funds," he murmurs.

Desperately. Non-profits always need funds. I've been doing this way too long to know there's never enough and always so many we can't help.

"I won't risk the project, Teddy." And I know he's having a hard time finding the right words to ask me to step down. And the fact it's hard for him shows just how much he believes in me, and that means the world to me. "I'll step down effective immediately." I choke on the words as tears clog in my throat and drown out all sound momentarily, my mind trying to wrap itself around what I just said. Colton's reaction is reflected in the tightening of his fingers on my shoulders, and I immediately shrug out of his grip, push myself up off the couch, and walk to the far side of the room. It is almost a reflex reaction to feel the need to come to terms with this on my own. Yet when I turn to look at Colton and the unwavering love in his eyes, I know I'm not alone. Know together we are a unified front.

"Ry . . ." The resigned sadness in Teddy's voice is like pinpricks in an already gaping wound.

"No. It's okay. It's fine. I'm just . . . it's okay," I reiterate, unsure whether I'm trying to assure him or myself. I know neither of us believes it.

"Quit telling me it's okay, Rylee, because it's not. This is *bullshit*," he swears into the phone, and I can hear how he feels in the single word that keeps coming up over and over.

"But you're handcuffed. The boys come first," I say, immediately hearing Colton's earlier words said in such a different way. "They always come first, Teddy."

"Thank you for understanding the situation I'm in."

I nod my head, unable to speak, and then I realize he can't see me. The problem is that I *don't* understand. I want to rage and scream, tell him this is a railroad because the video does not prevent me from doing my job whatsoever and yet, the die is cast. The video is viral. My job is not mine anymore.

Holy shit. The one constant in my life for as long as I can remember is gone. Talk about going from having a sense of purpose to feeling completely lost in a matter of moments.

How can one video—a single moment in our lives—cause this gigantic ripple effect?

"I need to see the boys one last time." It's the only thought I can process.

"I'm sorry, Rylee, but that's probably not a good idea right now with . . . with everything."

"Oh." My plans for them before I took maternity leave are now obsolete; the bond I was building with Auggie will be non-existent when I return.

If I get to return.

The thought hits me harder than anything else. With Teddy still on the line, I drop the phone and run to the bathroom where I empty the contents of my stomach into the toilet.

Within moments I feel Colton's hands on me: one holding my hair back and the other rubbing up and down the length of my spine in silent reassurance as dry heaves hit me with violent shudders.

"I'm so sorry, Rylee. I know your job and the boys mean the world to you," he murmurs, as I sit there with my forehead resting on the back of my hand atop the toilet seat.

The first tear slips out; the only show of emotion I allow. I can feel it slide ever so slowly down my cheek. With my eyes closed and the man I love behind me, I allow myself to consider the endless uncertainty.

Is this all about me? And if so, whoever did this just got exactly what they wanted. To devastate me. To take my heart and soul—my boys—away from me. To hand me a punishment capable of breaking me.

Taking Colton or the baby away from me would be the only thing worse they could do. And that sure as hell isn't going to happen.

I may be down, but I'm not out.

Chapter Nine

Colton

"Let's hope we never need it."

"It's strictly a precaution," I say about the restraining order Rylee just signed at the police station against Eddie Kimball. I flip on my blinker, eyes scanning the rearview mirror to make sure we are still paparazzi-free, as I turn onto the unfamiliar street.

"I still disagree though. You should have one too."

Nope. Not me. I hope the fucker comes face-to-face with me. Welcome the thought, actually. I'm jonesing for a chance to beat the truth out of him.

"I can more than handle myself," I state calmly.

Her huff of disapproval is noted and ignored. I drive slowly through the tree-lined streets occasionally leaning over the console toward the passenger seat so I can read the house numbers on her side of the car. And in doing so, I've drawn her attention to figure out where we're going and provided the perfect distraction to get her to drop the topic. For now, at least. I'm sure she'll bring it up again but for now she's diverted.

"Last stop," I say as I pull up when I've found the correct house.

"Where are we?" she asks, curiosity in her tone as she cranes her neck to look around us.

"Proving one of us right," I tell her. "Sit tight."

I open the door and get out, shutting it on her questions, and walk around the car to the sidewalk. She opens her door and I glance over to her before she can get out. "*Don't.*" A single word warning her to stay in the car. Our eyes lock, her temper flashing in hers, but my bite's bigger and she knows it. So after a moment she mutters something under her breath but shuts the door without getting out.

Fuck if I'm not being an asshole. Like that's something new. But at the same time, if I'm laying all my cards on the table, it has to be face-to-face. I can't have the catfight bullshit I'm sure Ry would initiate if she were at my side: a distraction when I'm trying to call Tawny's bluff.

I check the address once more as I walk up the concrete path, the daggers from Rylee's glare burning holes into the back of my shoulders. The house is nothing special—a little run-down, flowers in the planters, a red wagon on the porch—and I can't help but think it's a long-ass way from the high-rise condo she had the last time I visited her.

I knock on the door. A dog barks nearby. I shift my feet. Take my sunglasses off because I want there to be no mistaking what I'm saying and how I mean it. Let's get this done and fucking over with. Problem is when all's said and done, I have a feeling I might be eating a little crow for Rylee, and I've heard it tastes like shit.

I should know better by now. Ry's usually right when it comes to this kind of thing. Only one way to find out.

I knock again. Look over my shoulder to where Rylee sits in the car, window down, head tilted to the side as she tries to figure out what in the fuck I'm doing.

C'mon. Answer the damn door. I don't have time for this shit. Wasted minutes.

Did she or didn't she? That's the big fucking question of the hour.

Tawny.

I grit my teeth at the name. At the person who has been dead to me. She may have been one of my oldest friends, but she tried to play me for a fool, tie me to her with her bullshit lies, and more than anything, fucked with Rylee. End. Of. Story.

My hands fist. Memories return. Temper flares.

The door swings open. I jolt seeing someone I don't know at all anymore.

"Colton!" Her blue eyes widen in shock. The lines etched around them tell me life's been tough. Too bad, so fucking sad. The beauty queen's lost her crown. You fuck with people, you reap what you sow. Her hand immediately flies up to pat her hair and smooth down her shirt.

Don't worry sweetheart, I wouldn't even touch you with a ten-foot pole.

"What the fuck are you and Eddie trying to pull, Tawny?" I want to catch her off guard, see if I can glimpse a flicker in her eyes. Something. Anything. A goddamn clue whether she had a hand in this whole situation.

"What are you . . .?" Her voice fades as she shakes her head, eyes blinking as if she can't believe I'm standing here. The feeling is mutual.

Cat got your tongue, T?

"Colton . . . please, come in." She reaches out, puts her hand on my arm, and I yank it back in automatic reflex. Does she think I'm here for her? That maybe . . . fuck, I don't know what she could be thinking, but obviously from the hurt that flashed in her eyes she sure as shit didn't expect my rejection.

Good. At least the stage is set for this conversation. Her hopes dashed. All expectation out the damn door.

"No thanks. I've got better things waiting for me in the car," I say with a lift of my chin. I then step to the side so she can see Rylee.

And so Rylee can see her. Understand why we're here. That I listened to her, heard her, and am trying to get some answers. I just hope like hell Ry stays put so I can up the ante. Take the pot and finish this on my terms. Because I need to do that.

"Oh."

Yeah. *Oh*. Glad we got the fact I'm still married out of the way. *Happily*. Now, back to business.

"Tell me about the tape." Images flash in my head: Ry crying on the phone with Teddy, Ry on the patio all by herself, the vulgar comments made beneath the video on YouTube about what other sick fucks want to do to her.

"What tape?" She shakes her head back and forth, eyes narrowed in confusion.

"Cut the crap, T. I fell for your lies once upon a fucking time, and I'm a little short of change to buy them now." I cross my arms over my chest and raise my eyebrows.

"I'm sorry, Colton, but I have no idea what you're talking about."

I'm not buying the innocent routine. "Did you watch TV at all this week? Go to the store? Read People magazine? *Anything?*"

"My son's been sick for the past few days so unless you mean Scooby Doo on TV, no. Why? What's going on?" she asks, tone defensive, and I purposely don't answer. I want to use the silence as a way to make her nervous. She fidgets, shifts her feet, works her tongue in her cheek.

Goddamn it. *Ry was right*. She knows something. Fuckin' A.

"Shit, I haven't seen Eddie in over four years," she finally says.

I stare at her, eyes determined to find some kind of deception in her words but all I see is the woman I used to know, curves a little fuller, clothes messy, and eyes tired.

And I don't care how rough it seems life has been for her. Looks can be deceiving. I still don't trust her. Not one bit. Not after what she did to us way the fuck back when and what I'm pretty sure she had a hand in now.

"Video footage has surfaced of Ry and me from six years ago. You're the only one who knew where we were and what we did that night." I let the comment hang in the space between us. She tries to hide her reaction—a lick of her lips, a quick look to the car driving down the street—but once you've had a relationship with someone, you can read them like a clock. Tick fucking tock. And I know she has more to say. "The Kids Now event. When Ry and I had sex in the parking garage. Footage of us is plastered all over the media, Tawny. You're the only one who knew."

She forces a swallow down her throat. A glance behind her where there are Hot Wheels all over the floor. A shift of her feet. A bite into her bottom lip. All done before she finally has the courage to meet my eyes again.

"Care to change your answer, now?"

"Oh my God," she murmurs more to herself than to me. And something about the way she says it bugs me. It seems genuine, full of surprise, real. I call bullshit. She's just playing the part without dressing up for the cameras. "I completely forgot about that video."

"You forgot?" I sneer, sarcasm rich in my voice. "That's awfully convenient."

"No, really," she says, reaching out to touch me, and then stopping presumably when she remembers my reaction the last time she tried. Smart woman.

"I'm losing my patience," I say between gritted teeth.

"That night after I left the party, I met up with Eddie. We had some drinks. Too many. I told him about the charity event, seeing you and Rylee there, and what she had said about you guys on the hood of Sex. I was feeling angry, rejected, and didn't think twice about it until after he was fired. That's when he called me, livid and unhinged. Said he knew the perfect way to get back at you and that he had gotten hold of a video from that night. Had it in a safe place."

Bingo. Dots connected. A confirmation. Now let's try to complete the picture.

"And you never thought to tell me?" I shout. My hands flex as I resist the urge to grab her shoulders and shake her in frustration.

"It was a different time. You fired me shortly thereafter and I was furious, ashamed, disowned by my mother . . . so no, I'm sorry, Colton, I didn't. I was so busy worrying about myself, being selfish." She sighs, clasping and unclasping her hands in front of her. And I fucking hate when she looks up at me with clarity in her eyes I've never seen before. I don't want to see it but I can't ignore it either. "I was a different person back then. Time . . . things . . . kids, life, it changes you."

"Kids?" I snort out, holding my anger in front of me like a shield as I remember her shocking blindside all these years later. "You mean like the baby you lied about and tried to tell me was mine? Used as a pawn in your fucked-up games?" I take a step forward, fists clenched, anger owning me.

"Yes, as in that one," she says her voice barely audible. "I . . . I'm so—"

"Save the apologies, Tawny. Your bullshit lies and accusations almost made me lose the most important person in the world." The acrid taste of revulsion hits my tongue. "That's something that doesn't deserve forgiveness."

My words hit her like a one-two punch—hard, fast, and bruising. Does she think her quivering bottom lip will win me over? Make me forget the past?

Not hardly.

"I know," she says giving me whiplash. I expected denial and defiance, attitude and arrogance, and she gives me neither. Our eyes hold for a long moment and fuck, all of a sudden I feel like I'm seeing her for the first time in a different light. *Don't fall for her act, Donavan.* People like her don't change. Can't. It's not possible.

But you changed.

The voice in the back of my head so very quiet, barely audible, sounds like a scream, causing me to bite back the snide comments as the unwelcome tang of doubt replaces them.

The look on Rylee's face flashes in my mind from the day Tawny came waltzing in the house to tell me she was pregnant with my baby. A manipulative game by one of the masters. Too bad for her I was a master at it myself. Had no problem going up to the plate against her curveballs. But Rylee . . . she didn't even have a bat in her hand.

I hold onto that thought—Ry's tears, the nasty fight, the break we took—all of it, and tell the tiny ounce of pity I feel for Tawny to take a fucking hike. She brought this upon herself. Not me. Not Rylee. Just her.

Tawny starts to speak and then stops. "If I had known that Eddie really had a tape . . . or what he was going to do, I would have told you."

I stare at her, leery of the sudden decency that doesn't fit with the memory of the woman I used to know, and deliver a visual warning: *You better not be fucking with me.*

"Tell me what you know." My voice is gruff, incapable of believing her or that the years have changed her enough she'd actually look out for me. She'd have told me, my ass.

Would she have?

Does it really fucking matter, Donavan? Get as much info as you can, turn your back, and walk away. You don't need to know if she's changed, wonder if life has been rough for her, because the only thing that matters is the woman sitting in the car behind you.

"Honestly—"

"I'd like to believe that honesty is something you're capable of but you're not the one dealing with . . ." I let my words fall off, catch myself from letting her have a glimpse into my private life. Don't want her to know about the butterfly effect this video she knew about is having on everything in Rylee's life. Because if she's playing me and is behind this—somehow, someway—then she'll have gotten exactly what she was looking for: hurting Rylee, which hurts me. And while I may be sympathetic at times, it's only toward my wife, only with the boys, and only with those I care about. Tawny and I may have a past together, but she is most definitely not any of those people.

"Look, I know you don't want to hear it but I fucked up. Was in a bad place with pressures you have no idea about and I won't use as an excuse . . . but it was a long time ago. Like I said, I'm a different person now, Colton. I don't expect you to believe me . . . to know I'm sorry for the games I played, but I am." We hold each other's gaze, my jaw clenched tight, pulse pounding.

I expected to come here, fight with her, and threaten her to get some answers. Not in a million years did I expect her to be like this: apologetic, decent, sincere. And so the fuck what if she is? It changes nothing. Top priority is getting answers so I can try to make my wife whole again.

"At first I thought he was lying about the tape," she says, breaking through my warring thoughts. "I thought he was trying to get in my pants by feeding my spite over you choosing Rylee, because . . . well, because it was Eddie. You know how untrustworthy he was."

She leans her back against the doorjamb and I shift my feet, wanting to rush this, get the fuck away from here, but I need more. Seeing her causes the memories to resurface. The lies she told. Her manipulative ways. How I thought she'd been in cahoots with Eddie in stealing the blueprints way the fuck back when. Despite investigators and depositions, and every other legal means under the sun CJ couldn't find shit to prove she was involved. To say I had a hard time believing she was innocent is an understatement. But I did. Had no choice.

The question is, do I believe that now?

"Did you ever watch it?" And it's a stupid question, but the thought of her of all people watching Ry and me have sex seems ten more times intrusive than the other millions of people who have.

"No. Never," she says definitively, earning her a rise of my eyebrow in disbelief. "Really. That's why I never thought twice about it."

Great. Now I've given her the idea to go watch it. *Brilliant, Donavan*. Fucking brilliant. But then again, I had to ask. Had to know.

I blow out a breath, roll my shoulders, and ask the one question left that makes no fucking sense to me. "If he had the video though, why wait all this time?"

She angles her head as she stares at me, feet shifting, arms crossed over her chest. "I don't know, Colton. I just don't know."

Impatient, uncomfortable, and still a little thrown by this new woman in front of me that looks the same but sounds so very different, I just nod my head, turn my back, and stride down the walk to my car. I don't know what else to do. There is no good in goodbye here. There's just the closing of a door on another chapter of my past.

"Colton."

Every muscle in my body tenses—feet want to keep walking—yet curiosity stops me dead in my tracks. With my back to her, I wait for her to say whatever it is she wants to say.

"It's good to see you happy. It suits you. I know now that's because of Rylee."

I lift my eyes to meet Rylee's at the same time Tawny speaks. I hear her statement, take it for what it is, and don't try to find a hidden meaning or an underlying dig. With eyes locked on Rylee's, I nod my head in acknowledgement and walk toward the car.

Time can change people. The woman with violet eyes staring back at me? She's my living proof that I've done just that, *changed*.

Tawny might have changed too, yet I don't have the effort to care right now. I have a wife that is more important than the air I fucking breathe, and being this close to Tawny, I'm starting to suffocate.

I need my air.

Chapter Ten

Colton

"Talk about blindsiding her," Becks says.

"Which one?" I ask with a laugh followed by a hiss as I throw back the Macallan. The shit's smooth but burns like a motherfucker.

"I was talking about Tawny but you've got a point there," Becks says with a smirk. "I imagine Rylee got whiplash when she saw Tawny open the front door."

"I'm sure she did, but thank fuck she stayed in the car or who knows what would have happened."

"You're a brave fucker taking Ry there after everything she did to the two of you," he says as he lifts two fingers to our waitress for another round.

"Brave or stupid. But this right here," I say, holding my left hand in the air and pointing to my wedding ring, "means I didn't dare visit Tawny without her. That would have been *no bueno*. Besides, she had a right to know since she called it."

"Dude, I still can't get over the fact you saw Tawny after all this time."

"Yeah . . . well . . ." I shrug, thinking of all of the shit I said way back when about how I'd never step within a hundred yards of her again. "Sometimes the promises you make to yourself are the easiest to break. And shit, we were on the way back from the police station so I figured why not kill two birds with one stone since we'd dodged the vultures?"

"I can't believe the paps are still all over you. Is Ry okay after yesterday?"

I blow out a breath. Fucking assholes. "A little shaken but she's scrappy." I clench my fist on the table as I recall her phone call yesterday. How she tried to take a walk on the beach to get some fresh air but paparazzi shifted from the gate to the sand and swarmed her before she could even reach the waterline.

And I know how she felt—needing the fresh air—because I feel the same way. Isn't that why I'm here right now? Decompressing. Grabbing a few minutes while she's taking a nap after the excitement of my visit to Tawny today, to hang with Becks, shoot the shit, and get a change of scenery to make me a better man. Sitting in your own house day after day can wear on any man. Make you feel like an animal in the zoo: caged, pacing, and constantly toyed with by those on the outside looking in.

I grit my teeth and thank fuck the back entrance of Sully's pub was paparazzi-free so Sammy could drop me off and I could slide in and meet Becks without being mobbed. After yesterday and how they treated Ry, my fuse is short and ready to ignite at the slightest misstep.

"Was it strange seeing her again after all this time?" Becks asks as he lifts his beer to his lips.

"Is the sky blue? Fuck, man . . . it was weird. But she gave me what I needed to know so maybe she's changed some."

"Don't give her that much credit," he murmurs.

"I don't give her any."

"Smart," he says and slides the cardboard coaster around on the table. "Should have known Eddie would be the one to pull shit like this. Fucker."

"Fucker," I repeat because anything else would be a waste of breath. I glance at my phone to make sure Ry or Kelly hasn't texted since the noise in the bar is getting louder the longer we sit here.

"Everything okay?"

"After ten more of these it will be. Need to drink to forget," I say, rolling my shoulders and letting out a frustrated sigh. Too much shit, too damn fast. I want my happy, baby-crazed wife back. Her job back. Our life back. "It's not gonna help shit and I'll be sicker than a dog in the morning, but sometimes, it's just what the doctor ordered."

"Truth. And I've got just the prescription for us," Becks says as he motions to the waitress again to head over to our regular table tucked in the back.

"What can I get you boys?" she asks, smile wide and cleavage jiggling.

"Bottle of Patron Gold. Two shot glasses, please. We need to forget," Becks says.

"That'll sure do the job," she says with a lift of her eyebrows. "Looks like you're going to be stuck here for a while anyway with the way paparazzi are stacking up outside."

"Shit," I mutter under my breath.

"Sorry, hon. We find out who in here called, we're kicking their sorry asses to the curb," she says louder than normal so those around us can hear her. She starts to walk away and then stops and turns around. "And we'll stick 'em with your tab."

I throw my head back with a laugh. "I like the way you think."

She returns within minutes, our ongoing tab and prior large tips always earning us the best service. "Here you go, boys," she says, as she sets two full shot glasses in front of us, and the bottle in between us. "May God rest your souls."

"Amen to that," Becks says as he lifts his glass. "What's the first thing we need to forget?"

"Paparazzi."

"Cheers," he says as we tap our glasses against each other's. "Fuck you, paparazzi."

We toss the shots back. My throat burns as the warmth starts to flood through me. Becks lifts a lime from the bowl on the table and I mutter, "*Pussy*," under my breath, earning me a flip of his finger. "Umm." I think of what I want to forget next. "Fucking CJ."

"Okay," he draws the word out as he pours us another shot, "but if I'm drinking to forget something, I need to know what I'm supposed to forget since I sure as hell hope you're not fucking CJ."

"No. I'm not fucking CJ." I belt out a laugh. My mind is starting to spin as I glance around the bar. "Because my goddamn hands are cuffed and not in a good way. He called earlier, said that in the eyes of the law, the tape was public. Eddie didn't steal it from us per se. He uploaded it for free . . . isn't making any money off it and so we can't do shit about it. He gets his kicks fucking with us and we have no legal means to get back at him."

"Sure as shit there are other means though," he says with a smirk and a raise of his fist.

"Now that," I say as I hold up my shot, "I'll drink to. Cheers, brother."

"Cheers."

Our glasses clink. The tequila burns until it warms. Our laughter gets louder and our cheers get sloppier and take longer to come up with.

But I begin to forget.

About Eddie. The pressure to fix it all. And the thousands of men jacking off to the image of my wife holding her tits as she comes. And the rage over how she lost her job. And becoming a father. The need to win the next race. Being told to bite my tongue with the press.

And God does it feels good to forget.

I'm lost in thought, trying to figure out how many shots we've downed, when my phone rings. I fumble with my cell before answering.

"If it's good enough to make me sober, Kelly, I just might forgive you for ruining my buzz," I say into the phone with a laugh.

"You drunk?"

"Well on my way."

"Understandably," he says in his no nonsense tone. "Eddie checks in with his parole officer once a month."

"Mm," I say as visions fill my head of waiting for him outside the social services office and greeting him with a fist to the face.

"Don't even think about it, Donavan. You got the restraining order for Rylee. Leave it at that. Just like I've told you all week long, you touch him, he's going to sue you like he owns the Fluff and Fold and take you to the cleaners. It's not worth it."

Quit fucking telling me what to do.

"Let him try," I sneer, admitting to myself he's right but also knowing revenge gives its own special satisfaction. I begin to say something else when the thought hits me that I might be able to get him back and not lift a fucking finger. The problem is I want to lift more than a finger at him. I want a whole knock-out fist.

"Thanks, Kelly. Keep me up to speed." Thoughts try to connect through my fuzzy mind on how I can make this all work to my advantage. Fuck Eddie over. Redeem Rylee. Get back the happily ever after.

My plan could work.

"Everything okay?" Becks asks, as he looks up from his own phone.

Later, Donavan. Figure it out later. Right now? Drink.

"Fucking peachy," I say, copying one of his go-to sayings. "Kelly's got a line on Eddie."

"And that pisses you off, why?"

"Just thinking."

"That's scary," he teases and I slide my glass across the table so it clinks against his in response. "What is it?"

"Bad juju, man," I finally say, trying to put into words what I think's been bugging me the past few days. The drinking to forget didn't numb this. "I've got this feeling that won't go away."

"I'm not following you."

"Things have been too goddamn perfect for us. I have the fucking fairy tale, Becks. The princess, the castle, the—"

"Jackass," Becks snorts as he points my way, causing me to laugh. Asshole. "Sorry. I couldn't resist," he says, putting his hands up in a mock surrender. "Please, continue."

"Nah. Never mind." Shut it down, Donavan. You sound like an idiot. A drunk one at that.

"No. Seriously. Go on."

I concentrate on drawing lines in the ridges of the worn tabletop. "Shit in our life was just too good. Too perfect. And now with the tape and Ry's job and . . ." My voice fades as I try to explain the feeling I don't understand, but that all of a sudden feels like it's clinging to me like a second skin. "I just keep waiting for the other shoe to drop to make this fairy-tale life of ours come crashing down. It's a shitty feeling."

"Feelings are like waves, brother. You can't stop them from coming but you sure as fuck can decide which ones to let pass you by and which ones to surf."

"Yeah, well, let's just hope I don't wipe the fuck out by picking the wrong one."

Becks and I decide we're looped enough to brave the chaos.

We push open the back door of Sully's and are met with blinding flashes of light and a roar of sound. I wince. The alcohol makes the clicking shutters and shouts of my name sound like they're coming through a megaphone. They stagger me. Blind me.

Anger the fuck out of me.

Sammy's here. Pushing people back to let Becks and I inch toward the Rover. But each step, each push of the mob against me fuels my fire.

Take a step. A camera hits my shoulders. My fists clench.

"Colton, how does it feel to be the most downloaded video on YouTube in over five years?"

Another step. Questions shout. Sammy's hands moving people back.

"Colton, are you and Rylee thinking of making a porn soon?"

One more step. A single thought: Rylee dealt with this on her own yesterday on the beach. Motherfucker.

"Colton, how is Rylee handling all of this?"

Another step. The car within reach. Flash in my eyes. Fury in my veins.

Fuck Chase's *no comment* advice. Fuck everyone. *I'm done.* Shoved way too far one way, and now I'm coming back swinging.

"You want a comment?" I shout. Silence is almost automatic. "Well, I'll give you one." I glance over to where Becks is standing in the open car door, eyes full of pride, telling me I'm doing the right thing.

"The question is, do you really want to know how we feel or are you just interested in twisting your story because sex sells so much better than the truth? I get it. I do. And if you take the selfless do-gooder who's spent her life helping others and turn her into a whore who makes sex tapes in exchange for funding . . . well shit, that sells ten times more. But that's not who Rylee Donavan is." I take a breath. My body vibrates with anger. My thoughts slowly click together.

That revenge I was looking for just found the most perfect stage of all.

"How about I give you a better story? How about you focus on the sick bastard who released this video of a private moment between my wife and me? How about you go harass the bastard who did this rather than harass my wife? I'll even give you a head start. *Eddie Kimball,*" I say, putting my plan in motion. "Focus on why he tried to blackmail us, because I assure you, he definitely had an agenda releasing this video. Sex sells. I get it . . . but uncovering the story behind his bullshit attack on my wife's reputation would make much better copy."

Good luck hiding now, you fucking weasel.

The night erupts in sound. But they give me a wide berth because I gave them something. I nod my head in goodbye.

The cameras flash. Each one causes me to feel more and more sober. Makes me realize what I just did. Slide into the car beside Becks and catch his nod of approval. Rest my head back on the seat with a sigh.

Fuck. You. Eddie.

You want to play hardball? I've got your number, you spineless son of a bitch. Right now some little nosey reporter is digging for the story. They'll connect the dots with your early release from prison. They'll use your name in the press and it'll shine like a fucking neon sign, notifying the many you owe a shitload of money to.

Oh, and how they'll come. I have no doubt about that with the amount of money you owe people. Plus three years worth of interest. They'll flush you out of hiding and right into karma's long reaching arms.

The best part is if I don't want to, I won't have to lift a single finger to give you what you deserve, because I just did.

Social media can be a bitch when you have shit to hide. Good thing I don't. *Good thing you do.*

Revenge can be a mean, nasty fucker sometimes.

"You good?" Sammy asks as he pulls out of the alleyway, leaving the flashing cameras behind.

"Yup." I sigh, long and loud as I meet his eyes in the rearview mirror. *It's crazy how much I need Rylee, right now.* "Home please. I miss my wife."

Chapter Eleven

Rylee

"Damn it," I shout in frustration as the flour flies all over the kitchen because I forgot to put the guard around the mixer's blade. Tears sting the backs of my eyes as I look around at the mess. Normally I'd find this amusing, laugh it off, but not right now. Not with how this week has gone. Nothing can seem to pull me from this funk I'm in.

I squeeze my eyes shut and ignore the voices in my head telling me I'm going crazy because I fear that I am. The video's ripple effect just continues to knock me on my ass. Gone are the things I normally use to center myself: my boys, my freedom outside this house, my work. Even Colton's visit to Tawny derailed me momentarily. Yes, I felt validated Colton believed enough in my assumption that he went and talked to her, but at the same time, it still knocked me back a step seeing her again.

Shake it off, Rylee. It's temporary. Enjoy playing the domesticated role, take advantage of the quiet time now before the baby comes, and life is turned around with lack of sleep and two a.m. feedings.

I pick up the carton of eggs on the counter and blow the flour off them so I can put them away and start to clean up this disaster. Mind focused on the mess at hand, I don't notice Baxter on the floor behind me. When I step on his paw, he skitters up and away from me with a yip causing me to lose my balance. I catch myself from falling by grabbing the edge of the counter, but all nine eggs in the carton fly across the kitchen making a distinct symphony of splats as they land on the tile floor, counter, and against the refrigerator door.

"Fuck!" Adrenaline begins to rush through my body, and just as quickly as it hits me, it morphs and changes into a rush of so many emotions that I'm suddenly fighting back huge, gulping sobs. And it's no use to fight them because they already own my body, so I carefully lower my pregnant body to the flour-ridden floor beneath me. Leaning against the cabinet behind me, I let them come.

Wave after wave. Tear by tear. Sob by sob.

So many feelings—anger, humiliation, despair—come forth before being replaced by the next in line that have been waiting all week to get out. And I just don't have the wherewithal to fight them anymore.

"Rylee?" Colton's voice calls from the front door, and I just close my eyes and try to wipe the tears away but there's no way I'll be able to hide them from him. "What the . . .? Ry, are you okay?" he asks as he rushes to my side where I just shake my head, tears still falling, the agony all-consuming.

He drops to his knees beside me, and the concern etched in his face as he looks me over, ignites my irrational temper.

"Leave me alone," I say between sobs.

"What's wrong?" he pleads, reaching out to wipe flour from my cheek, causing me to cry harder.

"Don't," I tell him as I shake my head away from his hands, making him lean back on his haunches. And I can feel his eyes on me, assessing me, trying to figure me out, and for some reason that thought sets me off. I've had enough eyes on my body judging me this week—scrutinizing me—and the notion causes the distress to come to a head. "You want to know what's wrong with me?" I yell unexpectedly, startling him.

"Please," he says ever so calmly.

"That!" I yell, pointing at him. "You walking around this house like everything is all right when it's not. You treating me with kid gloves and avoiding me every time I get emotional because you feel guilty about the video when it's not your fault. I'm sick of trying to pick a fight with you because I'm going stir crazy in this goddamn house and you won't take the bait. You just nod your head and tell me to calm down and walk away. Fight me, damn it! Yell at me! Tell me to snap the fuck out of it!" My chest is heaving and my body is trembling again. I know I'm being irrational, know I'm letting the hormones within me take charge, but I don't care because it feels so good to get it all out.

"What do you want to fight about?"

"Anything. Nothing. I don't know," I say completely frustrated that now he's giving me the option to fight with him, I don't know what to fight about. "I'm mad at you because I'm worried about you racing next week. I'm freaked out that all of this is going to distract you and you're not going to be careful and . . . and—"

"Calm down, Rylee. I'm going to be fine." He reaches out to take my hand, and I yank it back.

"DON'T tell me to calm down," I scream when he does exactly what I told him I hated. Visions of the crash in St. Petersburg flash through my mind and cause my breath to hitch. I shove it away, but the hysteria starts to take over. "I miss the boys. I'm worried about Auggie and how he's doing. *I miss my normal.* Nothing is normal! Everything is up in the air and I can't handle up in the air, Colton. You know I can't." I ramble, and he no doubt tries to follow my schizophrenic train of thought.

"Let's make our own normal then. Why don't we start by getting the baby's room set up? That's one thing we can do, right?" he asks, eyes wide, face panicked. But his words cause fear to choke in my throat.

"Look at me," he says. "Putting BIRT's room together is not going to make something happen to him, okay? I know that's why you haven't done it yet . . . but it's time. Okay?"

With those words, the fight leaves me. Those body-wracking sobs I had moments ago are now quiet. Tears well in my eyes but I refuse to look up at him and acknowledge what he's saying is true. The nursery *is* incomplete because I'm frozen with fear that if I actually finish it, I'm jinxing it. That fate's cruel hand will tell me I'm taking the baby for granted, and reach out and take him or her away from me again.

When I can finally swallow over the lump in my throat, I look up to meet the crystalline green of his eyes and nod, just as the first silent tear slips over and slides slowly down my cheek.

"It's all going to be okay, baby," he says softly. I don't deserve his tenderness after how I just yelled at him. And then of course that sets me off even further and another tear falls over.

"You're absolutely beautiful," he murmurs reaching forward to move hair off of my cheek, and I squeeze my eyes shut.

"No, I'm not."

"I'm the husband, I make the rules," he says with a soft laugh.

"How can you say that? I'm covered in flour because I tried to make you cookies, which is normally simple, and I failed so epically at that including dropping nearly a whole carton of eggs. And my belly is so big I can't reach my toes to paint them and they look horrible and I hate when my toes look horrible. I tried to shave today and I can't even see between my legs to do that and I'm going to go into labor and have all this hair and look like I don't take care of myself and . . . and . . . we're having a baby and what if I'm a horrible mother?" I confess all of this as we sit on a flour-covered floor with a dog licking up broken eggs, but the way Colton looks at me? He only sees me.

I take comfort in the thought. That even amid all this chaos swirling around us, my husband only sees me. That I can still stop the blur for him. That I'm still his spark.

Be my spark, Ry.

We sit in silence for a moment, the memory of that night in St. Petersburg clear in my mind, his hand on my cheek, our eyes locked, and it hits me. With him by my side, everything is going to turn out how it's meant to be. It always has. He knows how to calm my crazy even amidst the wildest of storms.

Colton leans forward and presses a kiss to my belly before placing a soft one on my lips. "C'mon," he says, grabbing my hands and starting to pull me up when I'd rather just stay right where I am, wallowing in my own self-pity.

"Why?" I ask as I look up at him beneath my lashes, lips pouting.

"We're going to go make our own kind of normal." Between the comment and grin he flashes me, I can't resist him. *I never can.* He gently pulls me up and before I can process it, he has me cradled in his arms and is walking toward the stairs. "Colton!" I laugh.

"That, right there . . . I've missed the sound of that laugh," he murmurs into the top of my head when we clear the landing.

He carries me into the bedroom and sets me down on the edge of the bed, fluffs a bunch of pillows against the headboard, and then helps me lean back against them. Our eyes hold momentarily—violet to green—and I can tell he's trying to figure something out. My curiosity is definitely piqued.

"Red or pink?" he asks. I look at him like he's crazy.

"What?"

"Pick one."

"Red," I say with a definitive nod.

"Good choice," he says as he turns around and disappears into the bathroom. I hear a drawer open, the clank of glass against glass, and then the drawer shut again. Carrying a bath towel in one hand, what appears to be a bottle of nail polish in the other, and a huge grin on his face, he climbs up on the bed and sits at my feet. "At your service, madam."

I just stare—a little shocked, a lot in like—and absolutely head over heels in love with him and the completely lost look on his face over what in the hell he should do next. And while the Type A in me wants to tell him the answers, I don't. My husband is trying to take care of me regardless of how awkward he feels and that's a very special thing.

He lays the towel out over the comforter and then gently lifts my legs so my feet are positioned atop of it. And I stifle a laugh as Colton holds the bottle up of fire-engine red nail polish and reads the instructions on the back, his eyebrows furrowed and teeth biting his bottom lip as he concentrates. He chuckles and shakes his head as he grabs my foot.

"I must really love you because I've never done this for anyone before." His cheeks flush with pink and his dimple deepens. All I can do is lean back, smile wide, and appreciate him all the more.

"Not even for Quin when you were kids?" I ask, thinking back to how sometimes Tanner would help me with girly stuff as long as I'd help him with icky boy stuff first.

"Nope," he says as he concentrates on painting my big toe. He grimaces as I feel him wipe at the sides of my nail. I fight the grin pulling at my lips because I have a feeling I am going to have more polish on my skin than on my nails. But *that's* okay. It doesn't matter. He's trying and that's what matters most.

I stare at my husband—gorgeous, inside and out. He listened to my rant, and picked the thing he could do something about to try and help me. I've always known I'm a lucky woman to have found him, but never realized just how fortunate until right now.

I watch him concentrate as I try to let go of the chaos of the last week.

Angered shock: What I felt when I found out my picture was on the cover of People magazine. Inside, a blow-by-blow story about the video and a million other lies about my purported sexual preferences. Psychologists giving their two cents about the heightened arousal that some people get when they have sex in public with the risk of being caught. I wanted to scream—to rage—and tell them to stop telling lies. To explain it was a moment of heated passion that got carried away. Two people loving each other.

Two people who still love each other.

Confinement: How I felt when Dr. Steele made a house call—something she normally doesn't do—because I couldn't leave the house without paparazzi following me to her office. A doctor, whose clientele includes a high ratio of celebrities, is not too fond of photos being taken of her office as other patients come and go.

Exposed: Not being able to turn on the television, open my email, go onto Google without knowing there was a chance of seeing an image of myself.

Lonely: How I feel without seeing my boys daily. I miss their laughter, their bickering, and their smiles.

Validation: Watching Tawny come into view over Colton's shoulder. Knowing he'd considered my feelings, confronting her in my presence when he'd promised he'd never see her again.

Hurt and hope: Colton's unexpected speech last week as he left Sully's Pub. Using my name and whore in the same sentence stabbed deeply into my resolve and stung enough that I'd picked a fight over it. But at the same time, I appreciated the fact he was saying something, *doing something,* to try and expose Eddie.

So many things, all unexpected, have caused my head to be in a constant whirl and our lives in upheaval even though I've never left the confines of our property.

"I wonder if your little speech the other night caused reporters to start digging up info on Eddie?" I murmur as I watch the top of his head.

He looks up and meets my eyes. "Not now, Ry. I don't want to talk about any of that right now. I want to spend time with my wife, paint her toes, talk to her, and not let the outside world in, okay?" He nods his head to reinforce what he's saying. "It's just you and me and—"

"Nothing but sheets," I finish for him, causing a huge grin to spread on those lips of his.

"I haven't heard that phrase in a long time," he says with a reflective laugh as he screws the cap onto the nail polish. I notice how much red is on his fingers from trying to fix his overage. He looks back down and shakes his head. "Not as good as when you do it, but—"

"It's perfect," I tell him without even looking at my toes. The overage of paint on my skin is almost like an added badge reflecting how much he loves me. "Besides, the part on my skin will come off in the shower."

"It will?" he asks as he spreads his fingers out and looks at his own speckled with nail polish. My bad boy marked by the deeds of a good husband. "Thank Christ, because I was worried how I was going to get it off. I thought I was going to have to use carb cleaner."

A giggle falls from my mouth and it feels so good. All of this does: his effort, his softer side, seeing him look so out of place, and simply spending time together.

He blows gently on my toenails to help them dry, and I find so much comfort in the silence. I lean my head back on the pillow and close my eyes as he moves from one foot to the other.

"I know you'll do good at the race next week," I murmur eventually, not wanting him to think from my whirlwind of emotions earlier that I'm as worried as I let on.

"I promise I'll come home to you and the baby safe and whole," he says, eyes intense and heart on his sleeve like the tattoos on his flank. And I know that's a promise he really can't make. After all these years together I know he can't control what others do or don't do on the track, but I hold dearly to the fact he's cognizant of it because that's all I can ask. "And with apple pie a la mode."

The laughter comes again because that's my go-to craving right now. Well, besides sex with him. "You know a way to a woman's heart."

"Nope. Just my woman's." His eyes light up as he shifts off the bed, and I immediately become saddened because I fear our time together seems over. I know he has a lot of work to do since he's so behind staying home with me, so I won't ask him to keep me company any longer. Besides he's been more than sweet enough to me after how I acted in the kitchen.

So I'm taken by surprise when Colton reaches behind my back and under my knees and picks me up off the bed. He's seriously trying to throw his back out by carrying my pregnant ass again but the only protest I emit is a startled gasp as I look into his eyes to find a mischievous gleam.

"Hold tight."

"What are you . . .?" I ask, confused as he sets me down on the edge of the bathtub. I look longingly at the tub and think of what I'd do to climb in it and let the hot water swirl all around me. But no can do being pregnant so I just sit silently and wait to see what Colton is up to.

He steps over and into the tub and one by one picks my legs up so they swing into the oval haven. I stare at him, partially wanting him to tell me to break the doctor's orders and take a bath, but also surprised that my husband—the man who never follows rules except for when it comes to what the doctor tells me I can and can't do while pregnant—seems to be going rogue.

And of course I kind of like it.

"Stand up," he says as he grabs my hands and helps to pull me up so we are both standing barefoot and fully clothed in the empty tub. With his eyes locked on mine, he drops to his knees and very cautiously pulls my shorts down. His eyes light up and a smirk plays at the corners of his mouth as he carefully pulls each foot out of the leg holes to avoid messing up my polish. When he's done and I'm staring at him like he's crazy, he looks up at me and orders, "Scoot back on the edge with your shoulders against the wall."

I do as he says, my butt on the lip of the tub and my back pressed against the chilled wall behind, and watch with curiosity as he drops to his knees before me. With his tongue tucked in his cheek, he scoots closer, hands pressing my knees apart as he moves between them.

I suck in my breath, eyes flashing up to lock onto his. My need for him still stronger than ever, but hidden beneath the layers of emotion this week has brought upon us, resurfaces. My body reacts viscerally to the thought of his hands on me: a warmth floods through my veins, my nipples harden, my heart picks up its pace, and my breathing evens.

"Do you trust me?" he asks, snapping me from the visions in my head of his fingers parting me and his tongue pleasuring me.

"Always," I stutter, knowing the last time he asked me this, the video was released. I hold my breath as he moves the towel from the edge of the tub to uncover a razor blade and shaving balm. Well, maybe not so much. My eyes widen as I realize he's trying to fix the second problem I complained about in my childish rant downstairs.

I bite back the immediate recant of my instant agreement about trust, because

a razor blade on my nether regions should allow for a reconsideration of the question. And I know he can see my hesitation because his eyes ask me again.

He wants to shave me. I'm nervous but at the same time feel a rush of heat between my thighs at how hot the simple idea is. I nod my head ever so slightly, my eyes on his, because yes, I've been married to the man for six years, trust him with every part of me . . . but shaving me? That's a whole helluva lot of trust.

And the old me would be massively embarrassed about sitting on the lip of the bathtub spread-eagle in broad daylight while my husband squirts shaving lotion into his hand, but for some reason I'm not. The world has seen me naked like this by now. However, the idea is so damn intimate and personal that when I look down to watch his hand disappear below my belly seconds before the cool, moist lotion is spread into the crease of my thighs, I feel a new connection with him, a new intimacy that restores some of what was lost with the video.

He turns the faucet of the tub on and lets it run a bit as he warms the razor under its flow. He looks back at me with an encouraging smile in place and then slowly moves the blade below the swell of my belly. We both hold our breaths as he begins to shave me; the only sound in the room is the soft scrape of metal against flesh and the trickle of water into an empty tub.

After a few minutes I allow myself to relax, the inability to see what he's doing only serving to heighten both the intensity and the sensuality of the whole act. He continues to shave, face etched in concentration on areas I can't see but can sure as hell feel. And it's not the bite of pain I expected. Instead it's the soft press of his fingers as he pushes my skin this way and that way. It's the warm water as he cups it and lets it fall over my sex. It's the way his fingertips feather ever so lightly over my seam to wipe away the excess shaving cream that doesn't wash away with the trickle of water.

These things add together, build into an intense experience I never would have expected and yet don't want him to stop. We've been disconnected this week, so stressed about the video and the repercussions, that we haven't even paused to pay much attention to each other besides the verbal, *Are you all right?* And *How are you doing?*

He runs the pad of his finger back down the length of me. In reflex, I push my hips forward some, a nonverbal beg for him to dip his fingers between the lips of my sex so he can discover just how much I want and need him right now. I groan out in frustration when his fingers leave my skin, prompting him to chuckle.

"Is something funny?" I ask him between gritted teeth.

He just shakes his head. "Nope. Just making sure I made that little landing strip you like nice and straight," he says, tongue between his teeth as he concentrates, oblivious to the sexual torment he is putting me through. But then again, maybe that's his goal. He can't be this clueless. He knows my body all too well to know his touch is going to stoke my fires from embers to a wildfire.

"There." He hmpfs in triumph as he leans back and looks at his handiwork, a smug smirk on his face as he looks up at me. That smug smirk soon turns into a cocky grin once he recognizes the look of libidinous desperation on my face. "What's wrong?" he asks, feigning ignorance.

He's definitely toying with me. And hell, I'm all for being played by him. What better way to forget the world outside than lose myself to the skilled hands of my husband?

"Nothing," I murmur, right before he pulls the hand-held showerhead from its base and stretches the necking so the sprayer faces the delta of my thighs. He turns it on, the pressure of the water creating its own pleasurable friction that causes me to suppress a hiss of desire.

"I think I missed some shaving cream right here," he says with a concerned look before his fingers touch me again. But this time, they slip between the seam of my pussy and slide up and down the length of it, spreading me apart so the pulse of the water hits my clit. I groan from the sensation as I selfishly offer myself to him by widening my knees and trying to tilt my hips up.

"Good. Got it," he says as his finger takes a pass over my clit before all touch and water leaves me.

"What?" I yelp, catching that lightning-fast grin of his as he starts to stand up.

"All done," he says causally, picking up the extra towel on the tub's edge to pat me dry.

"No, you're not."

His amused laugh falls into the silence around us. "Your toes are painted, your pussy is trimmed," he says, ticking off the tasks on his fingers. "Whatever else could there be to do?" Our eyes lock and then mine slowly drag down the length of his torso as he pulls his shirt over his head and tosses it outside of the bathtub. He nonchalantly undoes his belt and pulls it through the loops, making a show of throwing it aside as well. When he slides his pants and underwear down his hips his dick stands at attention when he straightens up.

"I don't know," I say with a lift of my eyebrows and suggestion lacing my tone.

"Okay. I'm going to take a shower then," he says with a smirk as he starts to step out of the bathtub, making me laugh.

"No, you're not." His eyes are back on mine, hungry with desire, and for a split second I wonder why he's not taking what's laid out before him when his want is so blatantly plastered on his face—*and* his body for that matter.

"I'm not?"

"No."

For a few moments, we stare silently at each other with words unspoken but so much emotion exchanged. And finally I ask what keeps crossing my mind. "I miss you. I want you." Something flickers in his eyes I can't read, but I can tell he's struggling with. "What's wrong, Colton?"

And I figure there is no better time than right now to ask since we are both literally and figuratively stripped down. There will be nothing left but the truth between us.

"I started all of this by taking you on the hood that night. I asked you to step outside of that perfectly square box you lived in and look what happened. Fuck yes, I want you, Ry. Every second of every damn day. But with everything that happened . . . I don't know . . . I'm not touching you until you tell me you want me to," he admits. While I want to tell him he just was in fact touching me, quite easily turning me on, I also understand how hard this has been for my always "hands-on" husband to not touch and take when he wants to.

I angle my head and stare at him, a smile spreading on my lips as my chest constricts with love for him. "I believe the motto is *anytime, any place . . . right, sweetheart?*" I ask, imitating perfectly the way he says it.

His grin lights up his face, his posture changing instantly from cautious to predatory. Shoulders broaden, fingers rub together as if he's itching to touch, and the tip of his tongue wets his bottom lip. His eyes trail up and over every inch of my body; the look in them alone setting my nerve endings ablaze.

"That's a good motto," he quips. "Time to put it to use."

"Yes, please," I murmur. He bends at the waist and places both hands on the edge of the tub beside my hips. At an achingly slow pace, he leans in and brushes his lips unhurriedly against mine. The kiss is equal parts torment and tantalizing, liquefying the desire already mounting within me. A delicious ache pools in my lower belly.

"Ride me." Two words are all it takes. He says them with his lips pressed against mine, and it's all I need to hear. I place my hands on his shoulders so he can help me stand and make it to the bed.

He lies down, propping a pillow beneath his hips, as I crawl beside him. I pull my shirt over my head and take one more taste of his kiss before I do just exactly what he's asked. Asked? Who am I kidding? More like demanded, but this is one demand I have no problem complying with since I'm on the receiving end of its delirious outcome.

Our lips meet, and I can feel his desire for me in the way his hands run down my arms and over to my torso. His fingers dig into my hips as he helps me settle atop him, our bodies expressing what we need from each other without a single word uttered.

Eye contact is way more intimate than words can ever be.

Rising up on my knees astride his hips, I scoot back so the crest of his dick is just at my entrance. His hand grabs the base of his shaft and runs it back and forth to spread my arousal onto him. And when we're both slick with my desire, I sink down slowly, inch by perfect inch upon the length of his cock until he's completely sheathed root to tip. My head lolls back and a moan of appreciation falls from my lips the same time he groans out my name. It may have only been a week since we last connected like this, but in our relationship where we both use physical touch to help say the words we've left unspoken, that's a long time.

I wait a moment—revel in the feeling of him filling me. And there is something about his reaction that is even sexier than the sensation of his dick awakening every erogenous nerve within me. It's the arch of his head back into the pillow so all I can see from my viewpoint is the underside of his jaw and Adam's apple—that place I love to nuzzle into. It's watching the tendons in his neck go taut from the desire I've created. It's seeing the darkened stubble in such contrast to the bronzed skin around it. It's the feel of his hands still gripping my hips, so his biceps are flexed, and the darkened disks of his nipples are tight with arousal.

All of it—the whole package—is like a visual aphrodisiac that makes the sensation of me rocking my hips over his all that more intense. Then of course the guttural groan of, "Fuck, Ry," only adds to it.

So I begin to slide up and down on his cock, changing the angle every couple strokes to make sure his crest hits where I need it to so I can get off with him. My God, how I needed this with him. From him.

It's amazing how we can feel so very far apart, how I can feel at the end of my rope after so much pandemonium this past week, yet when we are like this I feel complete again within minutes. Connected. United. Indestructible.

One.

I rise up, let the crest of his dick hit right were I need it to, and pop my hips forward to add some intensity to my pleasure. The girth of his shaft causes my thighs to tense and tighten over his hips. My body slowly begins to swell with warmth as desire surges within me. Letting my head fall back, I reach behind me and scratch my fingers over the tops of his thighs causing his hips to jut up and fill me more deeply when I thought it impossible.

"Oh God," I moan, head lolling back, hands falling to my sides. My words spur Colton on, encourage him to grind his hips up to work his dick between the confines of my thighs. And I pull back as he thrusts causing the root of his shaft to slide up and against my clit. My eyes roll back. I moan incoherently as I ride the high of sensation from him rubbing over one hub of nerves before moving right back in to tantalize the other in a two-for-one knockout punch.

"Come on, baby. Your pussy feels so damn incredible. Fuck, I love when you ride me." His words end on a groan as I begin rocking over him again, filling me with a sense of power, knowing I can knock him breathless.

And we began to move in unison. A slow slide followed by a quick grind by both of us as we take our time moving up the ever-beckoning ascent to climax. Explicit words muttered into the comfortable quiet. Tense fingers press into the flesh of my hips. The veins in his neck taut with strain as he holds on to the control I can slowly sense is slipping from his grip. Eyes locked on each other's as we tell each other our feelings with actions. Then a quickening of pace. Our breaths begin to labor and our bodies become slick with sweat.

And yet despite that slow, sweet build, my orgasm hits me unexpectedly. The tingling in my center starts measured and steady, then explodes into a burst of electricity that pulses through my body with such intensity it knocks the breath from me. My body drowns under the orgasmic haze, causing every one of my senses to be magnified. I hear the catch of Colton's breath as my muscles contract around him, feel the sudden sensitivity my climax brings, and ride the wave of dizziness that assaults me.

And just as I'm about comatose from the bliss—my head light and heart full—Colton begins to move beneath me. His actions rouse me to respond and help pull him over the cusp and into oblivion with me. We move in sync, and when he bottoms out in me, I can feel the hair around the base of his shaft teasing my swollen clit once again to draw out the aftershocks still quivering through me.

"What I'd give to flip you over right now and fuck you senseless," he groans when I slide back up him again.

"Yes, please," I murmur. He lifts his eyebrows in a nonverbal question, and I know he's petrified he'll hurt the baby, but my comment is all the consent he needs to tell him all will be fine. Because I know as much as Colton loves the soft and slow, he does that for me. Gives me what I need to get mine.

And I know as his wife that this is what he needs. *What he loves.*

With his help, I climb off him and get on my hands and knees, ass in the air, and head looking over my shoulder to see him taking in the sight of me swollen, wet, and completely his. Our gazes meet and the carnal lust in his is so strong I'm glad I offered him this. After a week of feeling so out of control, he needed this ownership of my pussy to right *his* world. And after all this time, I know giving him complete control allows him to find it.

"Fuck, I love looking at you like this," he murmurs, as his finger traces down the line of my slit and then back up, circling over the tight rim of muscles just above it. My whole body tenses as a deep-seated ache burns bright from his touch where we've played occasionally when we want to change it up. "I love seeing how goddamn wet I make you. The pink of your pussy. The curve of your ass. The jolt of your skin as I slam into you from behind. How you arch your back and shift your hips so you can take me all the way in. Fucking addictive."

He places his hand on the back of my neck and runs it down the length of my spine. The singular touch sending my nerves, already on high alert, into a frenzy of vibrations that heighten the anticipation of *when* he is going to enter me. And yes, while I've already had an orgasm, with Colton, there is always that thrill of him being in me that never goes away. I know this tease of touch will be followed by the overwhelming onslaught of sensations. My whole body tenses as I wait with expectant breath.

His hand slides from my spine over to my hip and down the back of my thigh before tracing back up my inseam to my apex. This time though, his fingers part me, one finger sliding in and out to be replaced by the crest of his head.

His sigh fills the bedroom. His hands grip the sides of my hips and urge them backward and onto him while he stays completely still. The guttural groan that fills the room matches the internal war my body has over whether it wants to chase another orgasm or just take the pleasure as it comes and enjoy helping him get his.

And I don't get a chance to answer my own questions, because the moment Colton is in me, he starts to move. The pace he sets is so demanding, I know this is every man for himself, and I'm perfectly okay with it. Because there is something so damn heady about being taken by Colton with such authority. It's animalistic and raw and greedy and so very necessary to the dynamic of our relationship. I wouldn't want him any other way.

"Goddamn," he cries out as the sound of our bodies connecting echoes through the room. A symphony of sex.

"Fuck me," I shout as his dick swells within me, the telltale sign he is so very close. So I reach back and scratch my fingernails over the sides of his thighs as he slams into me again. The groan he emits from the sensation is the only sound I need to know he's a goner. Within seconds his grip tightens, his hips thrust harder, and his body goes completely taut as my name falls in a broken cry from his lips.

After a few moments a satisfactory sigh falls from his lips that is so very rewarding to me. Slipping out of me, he starts to laugh and it takes me a second to sit on my butt to see what is so funny. He's looking at the sheets and the little marks of red all over their light blue color.

"Just when I thought I couldn't have made your toes look any worse, I did."

I look up from the sheet to see the love, amusement, and satisfaction in his eyes and I smile. "Hmm. Good. That means we'll have to do some of this all over again."

"Just some of it?" he asks, eyes narrowed. When I nod my head, my favorite dimple appears alongside his playful smirk. "Which part might that be?"

"The find-our-own-kind-of-normal part."

"Just that part?" he asks, head angled to the side. His dick still glistens with our arousal as he grabs the towel used for my toes earlier and helps clean me up.

"The sex part. Definitely the sex part," I say with a more-than-satisfied smile. He leans forward and seals the comment with a kiss.

"Definitely the sex part," he agrees.

Chapter Twelve

Rylee

"Ry, coverage just started," Haddie yells from the family room. My nerves start to rattle as I waddle my way out from the kitchen. I'm not feeling too great today so at least I have a reason to be off my feet and not feel guilty about it.

Besides, this race will be the first one I haven't attended since we've been married, and it's killing me not to be there. But between how far along I am in my pregnancy and the buzz still out there over the video, the last thing I wanted was to make a public appearance on national television where I could be caught off guard and asked anything by anyone.

Two weeks out from the video's release and the frenzy has only died down a fraction. All outings are still limited and heavily guarded.

Can't some socialite do something stupid to gain attention to help me out?

"Do you have the scanner?" Haddie pours herself a glass of wine that calls to my cravings on every single level, but I avert my gaze to the bowl of Hershey Kisses she put on the table for me. Gotta love having a best friend who knows all your quirks.

"No. I think you left it in the office," she says. I motion for her to stay seated, and that I'll get the scanner that allows us to listen to Colton and Becks's radio interaction while he's on the track.

I grab the radio sitting beside my cell and just as I pick it up, my phone rings. The House's number flashes on the screen and happiness surges through me because the calls have been way too far and few between the boys and me since I've had to take my leave of absence. And of course I've battled feeling like I'm not needed in their lives since when we do talk, our conversations are filled with generic niceties from boys who'd much rather be playing outside or on the PlayStation.

And I won't lie that it stings a little. Not being the one they go to. Who am I kidding? It stings a whole helluva lot.

So when I see the familiar phone number I grab it and answer immediately, the connection I crave with the other part of my life just within reach.

"Hello?"

"Hi, Rylee."

"Hey, Zander. How's it go—what's wrong?" I'm so thrilled to hear from him that it takes me a second to hear the tinge of distress in his voice.

"I . . ." he begins and stops, his sigh heavy through the connection.

"What, buddy? I'm here. Talk to me." Concern washes over me as I listen as closely as I can to hear whatever it is he's not saying.

"I'm going to get in trouble for telling you but I know you'll make it better," he says in a rush of words that has so many parts of me startle to attention.

"What do you mean?" I ask but don't have to because it all clicks into place the second the last word is out. The basic conversations, the sense the boys don't want to talk to me, the constant run around when I ask anything too detailed about their cases. Someone has told them they're not supposed to give me any information. I've been so wrapped up in my own warped world that I've taken everything at face value, taken it all personally, and didn't delve deeper to see behind the mask of vagueness.

How stupid could I be?

The knife of absolute disbelief twists deeply between my shoulder blades as various emotions flame to life. I focus on the most important: Zander is upset and I need to help him. I can seethe later, call Teddy and express my displeasure after, but right now one of my boys needs me when I didn't think they needed me anymore.

"Never mind," I correct myself, not wanting to put him in a position he should never be in and get to what matters. "Tell me what you need, Zand."

"These people . . . they want to foster me," he says in the slightest of whispers with a tremor to his voice.

And the selfish part of me immediately wants to yell *no*, reject the idea, because Zander is mine in a sense, and yet at the same time this is exactly what I'm supposed to hope for. So I'm left in that catch-all of being way too attached to a little boy that came to me damaged and broken and is now turning into a damn fine young man.

"That's good news," I say, infusing enthusiasm into my voice when I don't feel it whatsoever.

"No, it's not."

"I know it's scary—"

"It's my uncle." All encouragement is eradicated as memories of way back when flicker to the surface. His case file comes to the forefront of my mind, and I contemplate Zander's only remaining family member.

How is this possible? My mind reels with this new piece of the puzzle, my abdomen clenching in a Braxton Hicks contraction that knocks the air out of my lungs momentarily. But I try to focus on Zander and not the flash of pain.

I stutter, trying to find the appropriate response and cringe because I don't have one other than to say *no way in hell* and that's not exactly something I can promise him. "Tell me what's happening," I say, needing to get a clearer picture of everything I've been shut out from.

"He . . . he saw my picture with yours in a magazine and on the news." My whole world drops out because *that* means I'm the cause of this. My job is to protect my boys, not hurt them, and that goddamn video has done just that. A picture of Zander and me taken at some event was in a national publication and now someone wants to claim him.

Or use him.

I swallow down the bile threatening to rise as my stomach twists in the knots it deserves to be tied in.

"Jax told me they—"

"Who are *they?*" I ask immediately as I pace the office and try to push away the last image in my mind of the uncle. The one I have of the man so strung out he couldn't even make it to his sister's funeral: track marks on his arms, greasy hair, dirt under his fingernails, and uncontrollable fidgeting as he tried to claim Zander for one and only one reason—the monthly subsidy for fostering a child. While it may not be much, it's still a treasure trove to a junkie. Because let's face it, the communal druggie house in the ghetto's Willow Court is the perfect place to take a traumatized seven-year-old boy and nurture him back to his new normal. *Not.*

My skin crawls, knowing he would even have the gall to come forward again and yet here we are, six years later, and Zander's new normal is having the foundation shaken out from beneath his feet.

"I guess he's married now and they saw a picture of me in People Magazine and decided they want to foster me because I'm the only family they have." His comment is followed by an incomprehensible sound that tugs at my heartstrings. I know he has to be freaked out, ready to run and at the same time too scared to stay. "My caseworker called Jax, told him they're going to give them some supervised visits to see how it goes." And even though he doesn't say it, I can hear the plea in his voice to help him and not make him go.

"I'll make some calls. See what's going on, okay?" I try to sound hopeful, but fear I have no control over what the machine does. All I can do is assert my one, hopefully still powerful and relevant, voice since I was his caretaker for longer than anyone.

"Please, Rylee. I can't . . ." The damaged little boy's voice rings through loud and clear, a sound I thought I was never going to have to hear again. One I worked so hard to overcome and get rid of.

"I know," I tell him as tears burn in the back of my throat. "I know."

"I couldn't not tell you," he says, and I smile at the double negative he's fond of using. It's comforting in an odd sense.

"You did the right thing. Now go watch the race, try not to worry about it, and I'll see what I can do on my end, okay?"

"I'm scared."

And there they are. Two simple words that weasel their way into my heart and create fissures.

"Don't let them take me."

"I will do everything in my power to stop them," I say. Just what that is, I'm not sure yet besides raising hell. "I promise. I soccer you, Z," I add to reinforce his place in my life and heart.

"Yeah. Me too." And the phone clicks without him saying what he always says back to me.

I stare out the window and fear this may be one promise I might not be able to uphold. Visions fill my head of the first time Zander came to me—a broken boy, lost and afraid. Of the sleepless nights I spent beside his bed, building his trust, creating that bond, and now in one fell swoop I've let him down by not being there when he needs me.

And yet someone, somewhere, has handcuffed me so I *couldn't* know.

I tap my cell against my chin, my mind lost in thought as I try to figure out why after all this time his uncle would actually step forward and why social services would even entertain the idea. Because there are just too many kids, not enough caseworkers, and when the unwanted become wanted, it's so damn easy to dust your hands of one and get them off your caseload.

I hate my bitterness. Know that not all caseworkers are this way but right now I have the voice of a scared boy ringing in my ears and doubt niggling in my psyche.

Dialing, I shove away the doubt whether I should call Teddy or not. I wouldn't have thought twice about it before and hate that I am now. Corporations and their board of directors and all of the bullshit can kiss my ass right now.

They are to blame for this. Forcing me to take a leave of absence. Handcuffing me so I can't take care of one of my boys. Letting Zander down when he needs me the most.

Anger riots within me. I'm primed for a fight when Teddy answers the phone.

"Rylee," he greets me, just as I start to worry my wedding ring around on my finger.

"Teddy. I know it's a Sunday but—"

"Colton's racing, right? Is everything okay?" he asks immediately, concern lacing his tone.

"Colton's fine," I state coldly, not wanting to warm to him because he's worried about Colton. I squeeze my eyes shut, pinch the bridge of my nose, and hold on to the disbelief that he's been keeping this from me. And I know it sounds stupid, but all of a sudden, my disoriented emotions latch on to the fact someone has ordered I be kept in the dark about Zander. And that someone is most likely Teddy. "Did you think it wasn't important to tell me what's going on with Zander?"

Silence fills the line. I visualize him picking his jaw up off the ground. Insubordinate Rylee is rare and yet he shouldn't doubt I'd go there instantly when it comes to my boys.

"Rylee." My name again said with detached frustration.

"After working for you for twelve years, you didn't think I was important enough to let know that—"

"I was protecting you."

"Protecting me?" I all but yell into the phone, temper boiling, and body trembling with disbelieving anger. "How about you do your job and start protecting those who matter the most? The boys? Zander?"

"I was," he says, his voice barely audible. "If I'd told you without all the information, you'd act in haste, rush to The House before all facts are straight . . . and then that leave of absence would be permanent, Rylee. And that would not only hurt you, but the boys too. You are their number-one advocate, their fighting force, and so I was protecting Zander by not telling you. If you get fired, you're not going to be there when he needs you the most."

His words knock the whipping winds from my otherwise stalwart sails. They should shock me from my funk but almost plummet me further into it because it makes me realize how much I miss my boys, and how lost I feel right now without being able to champion for them even when I know it's best all around with the baby coming sooner rather than later.

"Teddy," I finally say, a cross between disbelief and gratitude mixed in my tone because he's right.

"I wanted to talk to his caseworker at social services first, get the answers before I called you."

"Okay. I just . . ." My voice fades off as I shake my head and try to figure where to go with this conversation when I was so sure of my knee-jerk reaction two minutes ago. "Why step forward now?"

"Opportunity? Obligation?" He fishes for the right answer when I know deep down it's none other than a self-serving agenda.

"Zander called me, Teddy. He's scared to death." *And I am too.*

"I know he is, Rylee, but this is what we strive for. To find good homes for these boys and give them the life they deserve. I know you're close to him and worry but social services is doing their job and vetting this couple—"

"Not just any couple," I say, incredulity in my voice, "but his uncle who used to be a hardcore drug addict. They want money." There's no other reason in my mind that someone would ignore their own flesh and blood for almost seven years and then suddenly want him.

"We don't know that. People can change." The laugh I give in response is so full of disbelief that it doesn't even sound like my own. My stomach tightens and acid churns in my gut.

They don't love him. So many thoughts race and circle but that's the one I cling to the most.

"Perhaps, but I'm a little leery of accepting he wants more than just the monthly living subsidy that comes along with fostering Zander. It's been so long Teddy, and voila, he sees a picture on TV of Zander and me, and all of a sudden he feels this deep-seated need to be an uncle again? I don't buy it."

It's bullshit is what it is.

His audible sigh is heard through the line. I feel my stress levels rising, not great for the blood pressure, no doubt. "Let's just see what happens, shall we? They're going to have a monitored visitation, see how things fare, and go from there."

"But Zander doesn't want to," I shout.

"Of course not, Ry. It's scary for him, but this is our job. Get them back with a family unit, and have the most normal life possible."

"I still don't believe for a minute that Zander's best interest is on anyone's mind but mine."

"I take offense to that, Rylee, and am going to chalk it up to you being upset." The stern warning is noted and yet a part of me doesn't care. "Trust me to do my job."

"Yes, sir," I state, trying to contain the sneer in my voice that I feel in regard to the reprimand. "I'm upset, Teddy, because he's upset and I can't do a damn thing about it."

"I know, kiddo. And that's why you're their number-one advocate. I'll keep you abreast of the situation. Now I've got to go before Mallory gets in a tizzy that I'm working on a Sunday."

"I'm sorry for bugging you," I apologize, acknowledging that he has a life to lead beyond the boys. Just like I do. I recall Colton's words about how I need to start taking care of our family too.

I blow out a breath as I sink down into the chair behind the desk and try to process the past ten minutes.

And I don't think any amount of time will help any of it make sense.

If someone steps forward and wants him because they love him, wants to give him a traditional home life with the white picket fence and Zander falls in love with them back, I'll be all for it. One hundred percent. But the scared tone and the broken waver in his voice scream unease and fear. They tell me so much more than any words could ever express.

Everything is tumbling out of control so fast around me and there is absolutely nothing I can do short of take him as my own. And as appealing as that sounds, then that would mean I'd leave six other boys to feel like I chose him over them. And I'd never do that. I love them all.

I clutch my stomach as a sharp pain contracts around it and tell myself to breathe deeply and try to calm down. The problem is that I know calm is not a damn option anymore, because it seems lately, everyone is out for something.

And that makes me worry how exactly I'm going to bring a baby into this world, and be able to protect him or her as fiercely as I'd like.

"Ry? Are you coming?" Haddie's voice breaks through the haze of disbelief and concern that weigh down my every thought.

"Be right there," I say. I'd much rather sit here and try to figure out what I can do to make this all right again.

"And it seems Donavan can do no wrong on the track this season, Larry. Let's just hope all of his extra-curricular activity off it doesn't prevent him from finishing strong here today," the television broadcaster says as the camera pans to a wide shot of Colton's car on pit row with the crew standing around it. I blanch at the commentator's statement, but my skin is getting thicker and thicker with each passing day.

It doesn't make it any easier but rather more my new normal. And I'm not really sure I like this new normal at all.

In my periphery I see Haddie watching me to see my reaction to the comment on the TV. I don't want to talk about it so I concentrate on the images on the screen. I'm able to make out the back of Becks's head, Smitty's face tight with concentration as he adjusts something on the wing, and then I find Colton in the back, shooting the shit with another racer. The sight of him calms me instantly and has me reaching for my cell in anticipation of his promised pre-race phone call. His voice is exactly what I need to hear right now.

"Fuck them," Haddie says, holding her middle fingers up to the television, making me laugh. I can tell that was her intention with the comment when I look her way.

"You could have gone, you know. I would have been fine by myself," I say, knowing full well I'd rather have her here with me to help calm my nerves since I can't be at the race.

"What? And leave your pregnant ass behind? Nope. Not gonna happen." She smiles as she lifts her wine glass to her lips. "Besides, someone had to stay here and guard the wine cabinet."

"Guard it or deplete it?" I ask with a raise of my eyebrows that gets a laugh from her followed by a guilty shrug.

"What good is it if it's not consumed?"

"True," I muse, shifting on the couch when a sharp pain hits my lower back. As much as I try to hide the wince, it doesn't go unnoticed by Haddie. I grit my teeth and ride it out as my stomach rolls again and fight the wave of nausea that temporarily holds my body hostage.

"You okay?" Haddie asks. She shifts to get up and move over to me, but I stop her with a wave of my hand as I take a deep breath and plaster a fraudulent smile on my lips.

"Yeah. The baby's not too thrilled about something I ate, I think," I lie, talking myself into it when I know it's most likely the stress over everything: the tape, Zander, the race. Too many things at once.

"Uh-huh," she says in that way that tells me she's not buying my story. "It doesn't have anything to do with the phone call about Zander or the—"

The ring of my cell cuts her off and I scramble to answer it, fumbling my phone even though it's in my hand. I just really need to hear Colton's voice to quiet everything in my head.

"Colton?" I sound desperate but I don't care.

"Hey sweetheart. I'm just about to get strapped in but I wanted to call real quick and tell you I love you," he says, voice gruff, the sound of chaos all around him in the background.

"I love you too," I murmur into the phone followed by an audible sigh.

"You okay?" he asks. It sounds as though he is searching to understand the caution in my response.

The tears sting the backs of my eyes as I nod my head before I realize he can't see me. I swallow over the lump in my throat. "Yes. It's race day. You know how nervous I get." And technically I'm not lying to him. I do get nervous, but it's the other things about Zander I desperately need to share that I can't before he gets on the track.

Things I can't have mulling around in his head when he's supposed to be concentrating on the race.

"I'm going to be fine, Ry. In fact, I'm going to win and then rush home to get my victory kiss from you and claim my checkered flag."

My mind flashes to my cache of checkered-flag panties—my unofficial yet Colton-approved race day uniform. The underwear I have worn every race day since that first one in St. Petersburg so very long ago.

Just like the ones I'm wearing right now.

"Smooth one, Ace." I laugh, feeling a tad better even though his words do nothing to abate my unease when I see him on television going two hundred plus miles an hour, wedged between a concrete barrier and another mass of metal.

"You like that?" He chuckles. "You wearing them?"

"You better win and rush home so you can find out for yourself."

"Hot damn."

"Be safe," I reiterate as I hear Becks call his name in the background.

"Always." I know that cocky grin is on his face, and his certainty allows me to breathe a little easier.

"Okay."

"Hey Ryles?" he says just as I'm about to pull the phone away from my ear.

"Yeah?"

"I race you." And I can hear his laugh as he hangs up the phone, but the feeling those words evoke stay long after the line goes dead. I sit there with my phone clutched to my chest and send a little prayer into the universe to let him come back whole and safe to me.

"You okay?" Haddie asks softly.

"I'll tell him about Zander when he gets home," I say as if I need to justify my actions.

"Radio check, One. Two. Three." The radio comes to life as Colton's spotter calls out and immediately distracts us from our conversation.

"Radio check, A, B, C," Colton says, and for the first time in what feels like hours, a smile lights up my face.

But the low ache deep in my belly stays constant. The ball of tension sitting in my chest only increases as the familiar call is made on the television, "Gentlemen, start your engines."

Chapter Thirteen

Colton

Fuck, it's hot.

My fire suit is plastered to my skin. Sweat soaks my gloves. My hands cramp from gripping the wheel. My body aches from fatigue.

But victory is so damn close I can almost taste it.

Get out of the goddamn way, Mason!

His car is slower, his lap time slipping by a few tenths, and yet every time I try to swerve around him to move up from third place position, he moves to cut me off.

Fucking prick.

"Patience, Wood." Becks's voice comes through the radio loud and clear.

"Fuck that. He's slower. Needs to move," I say as the force of the backside of turn four exerts pressure into my voice.

I pass the start/finish line. Four more to go.

"He's low on fuel," Becks says, his way to try and calm me down, buy some time so I don't push the car too hard, too fast, and burn it up with the endgame in sight. And he knows I know this. Knows we both want the same fucking thing. But he also knows I'm getting amped up on the end of the race adrenaline and might lose sight of the specifics.

"We good?" I ask referring to our fuel supply.

"We're cutting it close but yeah, we're good."

I whip out to the right, try to slingshot past Mason but he blocks me and the ass end slides way too fucking close to the wall. "Asshole," I grit out as I fight to gain control back of the car.

"Watch the loose stuff," my spotter says into the mic. I bite back the smartass comment *I know it's there* because I'm busy fighting its pull on the wheel. Hitting the concrete barrier beside me at two hundred miles per hour because of loose debris on the top of the track isn't on the agenda today.

Three laps to go.

My arms burn as I fight the wheel into the next turn. My eyes flicker to the traffic ahead of me, to the car right in front of me, and to the ones on either side of me so I can find a sliver of space to try to pass.

I see it just as Becks yells into the mic. "He's out! He's out! Go. Go. Go. Wood!"

Split seconds of time. Luke Mason beside me. Luke Mason on the apron at the bottom of the track as I pass him.

Gotta have gas to go, asshole.

Fuck yeah. One car down. One car left to go. *C'mon, baby.* I press the throttle and check the gauges to make sure I push her to the brink because there's one lap left. I refuse to leave anything left in the car when I can lay it all out on the start/finish line.

Steady, Colton. Steady, I tell myself as the tach edges the red line just as I get up behind Stewart's ass end. Getting sucked into his draft helps conserve my gas. And thank fuck for that because I'm sure Becks is busting a nut on pit row questioning if I'm going to burn her up.

White flag. One lap left.

Turn and burn, baby. Turn and burn.

"Traffic is coming up in two," the spotter says as I come out of turn one and see the cluster of lapped traffic clogging the track. "Go low," he instructs, causing Becks to swear into the mic. Means I'll have to let up a little, and I can't let up when I'm chasing the one spot.

"You sure?" Becks asks. He never questions this kind of shit. I don't have time to wait for an answer because I'm already moving down to the white line of the apron praying to fuck this works since lapped traffic usually stays low to make way for the lead cars.

And just as I start to question him a hole opens up between the top of the track and the middle in front of me and it's only big enough for one car: Stewart or me. I slingshot around the car I'm behind, use the conserved energy from the draft to help give me the boost. Our tires rub. Stewart from the top line. Me from the bottom line.

It's like a game of fucking chicken. Split-second reactions. Who's going to back off? Who's going to keep their foot on it? And I've faced a whole shitload of fear in my life so I'm not letting it own me right now. No way. No how.

I hear the squeal of tires as the car begins to get loose again when we connect. Forearms straight and hands gripping, I fight to keep the wheel straight as we fly an unheard of four wide out of turn two.

And I know it's crazy. Has to look like a suicide mission to those watching, because there are four of us and not enough track to keep this up, and yet no one backs off. Something's gotta give and it sure as fuck isn't going to be me if I can help it. Fear is temporary. Regret lasts forever. And another press on the gas pedal ensures I'll have neither.

We barrel into turn three as the two outside cars fall off. It's Stewart and me, nose to nose, coming into the track's final turn.

And the final stretch to clinch the win.

I slingshot out of the turn and give her all she's got: throw the car into the red and pray it pays off. I can't tell who's ahead, our noses seem even, our cars testing the barriers of machine's ability against man's will.

C'mon, one three. C'mon, baby.

The checkered flag waves one hundred yards out. Keep the car straight, Donavan. Out of the wall. Away from Stewart. Don't touch. If we touch, it's over for both of us.

"C'mon, Wood!" Becks shouts into the mic as the checkered flag waves and a whelp comes through the radio. I have no idea which one of us won. Split seconds pass that feel like hours.

"Goddamn right we won!" Becks yells. Elation soars through my tired body, reviving it, and bringing it back to life as I pump a fist in the air.

"Fuckin' A straight!"

Victory lane. People and cameras are everywhere as I pull the car into it. Becks and the rest of the crew greet me. Funny thing is I'm still searching for the one face I want to see the most and know isn't there.

And I don't think I realized how much that would fuck with my head—how much it mattered she was there every race—but pulling into the checkered victory lane without seeing her feels a little less complete. She's so much more than just my wife. She's my goddamn everything.

And then I laugh when I look up as I take the pin out of the wheel to see Becks standing there. "Motherfucking victory, Wood," he says. He takes my helmet and balaclava, handing them off to someone else as he helps me stand from the car. My legs are wobbly and I'm hotter than fuck, but when my best friend pulls me in for a quick hug, it sets in that I've finally won the elusive title on this track I've been chasing for so damn long.

"Great job, brother," I tell him as I grab a baseball hat Smitty hands me and put it on, body dead tired but fueled on the adrenaline of victory.

The next minutes pass in a blur: confetti raining down, speeches thanking sponsors, interviews, the cold Gatorade that has never tasted better, the spray of champagne onto the crew. I'm riding that high, so goddamn glad to have this monkey off my back in winning this race. I do my proper dog and pony show, thank the sponsors, talk well of the competitors, thank the fans, but all I really want to do is get back to the pits, call Ry, take a shower, and sit back with Becks and have a stiff drink before facing more media circus.

Interview number five finished. I roll my shoulders, take a sip of Gatorade, and prepare myself to answer the same questions again for the next in line.

But when I look up and see the look on my dad's face, the next in line is forgotten. The victory not so sweet. My heart leaps in my throat. My mind spins. My feet move on autopilot as I make my way to him.

"Dad," I say. The dread and worry in my tone match the expression on his face.

"It's Rylee."

Chapter Fourteen

Rylee

I'm lost to dreams.

To darkness and warmth and a little girl with cherubic curls and a heart-shaped mouth. To her pudgy hand holding my pinky on my left hand. My eyes are mesmerized by her as she giggles, the sound warming my soul, filling my heart, and making them ache all at the same time.

There's a tug on my right hand that startles me. I'm so transfixed on my lost baby girl I never realized someone else was beside me. I look down to the top of a dark head of hair just as he looks up to me. I'm greeted with a row of freckles, a lopsided grin, and green eyes that look so familiar.

"Are you lost?"

"Nope," he says as he swings our joined hands back and forth some, a dimple flashing as his grin widens. "Not anymore."

Arms slip around my waist. The welcome warmth of a body pulling me from the dream I already can't remember. I snuggle into him, the scent of my husband unmistakable—a mixture of soap and cologne—and a calm falls back over me.

Then I hear the monitor beep, the whoosh of the baby's heartbeat filling the room, and I'm shocked awake to the here and now. I'm in a hospital bed being monitored rather than in the comfort of our home.

"It's just me," he murmurs into the back of my head. My hair heats from his breath as he pulls me tighter against him. Our bodies spoon and our hearts beat against each other's in a lazy rhythm.

"You're here," I say, voice groggy.

"Special delivery," he says, and I can hear the smile in his voice. "All the way from victory lane."

"Congratulations. I'm so proud of you and so sorry you had to leave your celebration." All those years chasing the win at the Grand Prix and of course, because of me, the one time he does, he doesn't get to revel in the glory of it all.

"Hmm." He presses another kiss to my head as his fingers lace with mine. "I'd rather be here. It wasn't the same without you. I missed you, Ryles."

How easy it is for him to make me smile and chase away the fear.

"I missed you too . . ." I wait for him to start the questions and as if on cue, the sigh falls from his mouth in resignation of ruining this moment.

"You two trying to give me a heart attack?" he asks, so many emotions overlapping in his voice in the single sentence.

"No. Everything is fine now. Just a few contractions they were able to stop. An ultrasound. Some fetal monitors. All routine things to make sure everything is okay," I explain, attempting to hide how freaked out I was when being hooked up to machines to monitor the two of us. How the room was filled with a sea of scrubs, and even though Haddie held my hand and kept my anxiety at bay, all I wanted was Colton.

"Common things?" he asks, skepticism in his voice. "You're still having issues with your blood pressure. That's far from fucking common when we're talking about you and the baby."

Shit. I close my eyes momentarily, sucking up my cowardice, and prepare to tell him the truth.

"Want to fill me in here, Ry?"

My mind flickers to the many warnings we've been given about my pregnancy: The high risk, the damaged arteries from the accident and the miscarriage that could pose a problem with heavy bleeding during labor, the stress on my uterus that will increase the bigger the baby gets.

"You have every right to be mad at me," I whisper, because for some reason it's easier to say it that way. "I had the stress under control, attempting to keep my blood pressure in the range it's supposed to be in . . . and then between the race and . . ." My words fall off as I replace them with a sigh representative of the heaviness in my heart about Zander.

"And what?" he prompts. "What else happened to push you too far?" The minute the words are out of his mouth I know he regrets them by the quick tensing of his body against mine.

Should I count the ways multiple things are causing stress right now?

"Zander called before the race started. He was scared, confused. A wreck. His uncle is trying to foster him." My words are so quiet. I try to keep my emotions in check since the constant rhythm of my heartbeat is visible on the monitor beside us.

"Okay," he says slowly, and I can sense his mind working, trying to figure out where I'm going with this. "You gotta give me more than that to make me understand why it put you in the hospital."

"It's his uncle." I swallow over the anger in my throat and continue. "The druggie asshole who wanted nothing to do with him when he first came to us."

"Why come forward now?" His simple question, and the confusion in which he says it, expresses exactly how I feel. I breathe a sigh of relief, thankful for his identical response, because it adds validation to my gut reaction over this.

"Why do you think?" Disgust laces my tone and even though it's not directed at him, I know he takes it that way.

"The video. Your work promo pictures splashed all over the fucking place," he says as everything clearly clicks into place for him.

"Mm-hmm." Because there is nothing else I can say without making it sound like I blame him in part for this turn of events.

"Money?" he asks.

"The monthly foster stipend isn't a ton but—"

"But it's enough to support your habit should you have one," he muses.

"Or better yet," I say as the thought hits me—staggers me even though I'd prefer to not even entertain the idea, "sell an interview with Zander to spill all kinds of juicy details on the woman helping run Corporate Cares who just so happens to be currently on leave from her job due to the release of a sex tape."

"That could explain the sudden urgency."

"Could." I shrug, closing my eyes and concentrating on the feel of security I have with his arms wrapped around me.

"People will do anything for money."

"And some people don't even need money as a motivator." The comment falls out without thought, but I know Colton knows I'm referring to Eddie. That damn video has become the catalyst to cause all of this: invasion of privacy, loss of normal freedoms, embarrassment, losing my job, Zander's situation, me in the hospital, our life unraveling. *Too. Many. Ripples.*

"Ry . . ." My name comes out in a resigned sigh as he rubs the stubble of his chin against the back of my neck, causing my entire body to stand at attention. "You need to put you and the baby first."

"I know. I do need to. I'm trying to . . ." And Colton is one hundred percent right . . . but in a sense, Zander is my child too. "But you didn't hear him, Colton. He was terrified. Scared. Lost. *And I didn't know*." I take a deep breath and focus on the whir of the machine monitoring the baby's movements. I focus on that and feel centered. "Teddy gave me some kind of explanation—the corporate song and dance that this is what we strive for. It's all bullshit. He doesn't have the connection with the boys I do . . . doesn't know the ins and outs of their stories like I do."

"He'll fight for them though if it comes down to it," Colton says softly, a quiet reassurance and an unintentional slap in the face to me all at once. But I don't feel the slap's sting. I know Colton's comment comes from a place of love.

Those are my boys. My heart. No one will fight as hard for them as I will. I know this much to be true.

"It should be me," I murmur, my heart hurting, my body exhausted. "But I don't think it will do an ounce of good. If the system does the half-ass job they usually do and don't vet them properly, then they'll get him."

"Unless he's adopted," Colton states plainly. He pulls me in tighter and I nod my head.

We settle in the silence of the sterile room that is now so much more bearable with Colton's presence. The heat of his breath, the scent of his cologne, the feel of his body against mine—all three things center me from that out-of-control feeling of fear I entered this hospital with.

The baby's movements I can and can't feel are broadcast through the room, my own reminder of priorities and unconditional love. Lulled by the sound and Colton being here, I slowly begin to drift off.

"We could adopt, Zander."

Colton's words snap me awake. My breath hitches, my body jolts, my heart hopes momentarily before the reality of the situation sets in. Tears prick the backs of my eyes over the enormity of the heart of the man behind me. One who swore he couldn't love, and yet day after day the capacity and way in which he does, makes me fall more in love with him.

"The fact you've said that means the world to me but . . . but I can't just choose one boy to adopt," I say with a conflicted heart because yes, it would fix everything, but doing that would tell the other boys I love Zander more than them and that's not the case. "But thank you for saying it. The fact you'd even consider it means the world to me."

"I think we should do more than consider it." I just nod at his comment, the resolve in his voice so strong there's no point in arguing since I know he's speaking from the experience of what it's like to be an orphaned little boy. "Don't count it out, Rylee."

"I won't," I say for good measure, "but I can't do that to the others who want to belong to someone just as much as Zander does."

"They belong to each other," he says, "and that's what matters most."

His words throw me. They're unexpected and yet so very true. And contradictory. How would adopting one not ruin that bond?

"Turn your mind off, Ryles. Shut it down for a bit. For me. For the baby. For you." He rubs a hand up and down my arm, sliding it over my belly between the two monitors resting there. I'm sure it's pure coincidence but within seconds the sound of the baby moving beneath his hand fills the room. Hearing the hitch in Colton's breath in reaction makes my heart swell.

"I'm sorry I took you away from your victory celebration," I murmur, "but at the same time I'm not because I'm glad you're here."

"There's nowhere else I'd rather be," he says as he rests his chin on my shoulder and presses a kiss to my cheek. "I lie. There's definitely somewhere else I'd like to be." Suggestion laces his voice and since sex is my only pregnancy craving, I groan.

"I have a feeling this victory lane is closed for business for a while," I say.

"Good thing I just claimed it in Alabama."

"You better be talking about a trophy, Ace."

"Nah. That's right here in my arms."

Chapter Fourteen

Colton

Not this time. No fucking way.

That's the only thought that runs through my head on constant goddamn repeat as I stand in the doorway and push away images burned in my mind from that night so very long ago: the blood everywhere, the baby we lost, finding Rylee lifeless like a Raggedy Ann doll.

Not this time, I repeat as I step into the room and release the breath I feel like I have been holding since I hopped on the chartered plane after the race to get back here when I see Rylee. She's asleep in the bed, bands are around her belly, the baby's heartbeat owning the silence of the room in the most comforting of sounds.

Everything that is important to me is in that bed and yet I did this to her. The race. The video. The stress of it all has put them both in jeopardy.

I don't want to disturb her, wake her from the rest I know she desperately needs, and yet I can't resist—never can when it comes to her—so I move to the side of the bed and just stare. The curls of her hair on the pillow. Her dark lashes against her pale skin. The rise and fall of her chest. The glitter of my ring on her finger. The shine on the skin on her abdomen from being stretched with life beneath it.

Damn it, she still scares me. Unnerves me. Every damn hour of every day and yet there's a part of me that needs that. Fear drives a man to go places he'll never venture, to push himself beyond his reason, and here I stand scared shitless with a woman I can't live without and a baby soon to be born when I swore those were two things I was never capable of.

Goddamn fear. I love it and I hate and yet I wouldn't change a damn thing about it because I'm looking at the result of it right in front of me.

I shake away to overage of emotion that I'm still not good with. I'm just tired, worn the fuck out from the race and the sleep I should have got on the plane but couldn't because I was too damn busy looking out the window hoping the scar tissue holding my heart together would hold fast until I was able to see her again and know she is okay.

And here she is, whole and strong and so beautiful and my fingers itch to touch her, but I hesitate even though she's so much stronger than I ever give her credit for. It's me I worry about now as I lift my eyes to watch the baby's heart monitor on the opposite side of the bed.

My mind flashes back to a father I've never known. Doubts creep into my resolve and make me question if I'm going to be able to handle this. A little fucking late to ask myself, I know, and yet did he stand next to my mom at some point and wonder the same thing? Did he start out wanting to be a good man and then not make the connection with me so he left without a second thought? Or did he not know I existed at all?

The notion sticks with me as I stare at my whole goddamn world lying on the bed in front of me and that fear takes hold again. I just hope the fear will continue to make me more of a man this time around because I'm petrified I'm going to fuck this up.

I need to call Kelly and decide whether I want him to continue the search for my biological dad or not. The jury's out on that one. I have enough shit churned up right now that I don't need to muddy the already murky waters.

Drawing in a deep breath I know the only way to silence the disquiet in my head is to hold onto the one person in my life who never seems to doubt me, Rylee. Giving into the urge as inherent as breathing, I sit gently on the bed beside her making sure not to disturb any of the wires she's plugged into. When she doesn't stir, I shift so that I can lie down behind her, my front to her back. I breathe her in as she snuggles her back against me in her sleep like she knows I'm here.

We lay like this for a few minutes, the scent of her vanilla in my nose and so many thoughts, so many emotions, flood through me and yet I can't put concretes to any of them. How can I even concentrate on them when she's like this with me: Finding comfort when I'm the reason she's so stressed out in the first place.

But I'm here now and I'm not going to let anything happen to her.

I hold tight to that truth with her body against mine, calming my nerves. I'm about to drift off, the ease of being right where I need to be pulling me into sleep, when her arm reaches back to grab my hand and pull my arm around her. Our fingers lace together and we sit in the silent comfort for a few moments.

"Hey," I say, pressing a kiss into the back of her head, my voice thick with emotion.

"I'm sorry for worrying you," she murmurs drowsily when I feel like the same words should be falling from my mouth.

"You two scared me," I say, trying to put words the fear that lodged in my throat when my dad told me she was having contractions.

"Everything is fine now," she explains. Her words do nothing to abate the fear that held me hostage as I was suspended on a plane in the air, helpless with only the warnings Dr. Steele has given us over the course of the pregnancy to occupy my thoughts. The high risk. The damaged arteries from the accident. The scar tissue from the miscarriage that could cause heavy bleeding during labor. The pressure on her fragile uterus that will increase the bigger the baby gets.

But I shake them away right now because I'm here and she's okay and the baby seems content to not meet us just yet.

"Why was your blood pressure through the roof?" I ask although I already feel like I know the answer.

Because of me…

"There's a lot going on," she states softly and there's something in her tone that makes me think I'm missing something, but I can't see her face to know for sure.

"What haven't you told me?" I ask hating the vague answers she keeps giving me.

"They gave me some type of steroids for the baby to help lung development," she says, avoiding my question and fueling my temper.

"Rylee." Her name is a stern warning not to fuck with me because I'm tired and worried and now I definitely know something is going on. "Whatever it is, let me help. Please. I'll fix…" and my words fade off because the last time I said I'd fix it, I failed epically so why would she trust me now?

The silence stretches between us and I hate that it feels uncomfortable when we are body to body, our heart beating as one. I wait for the other shoe to drop when I had no idea there was one dangling by a shoelace.

"Someone wants to foster Zander," she says causing my body to freeze in a war of emotions. The unwanted kid still lingering inside of me stands at attention knowing the worth that this must be instilling in Zander right now. And yet at the same time a part of me knows that as much as Rylee's life mission is to give her boys a home and better life, she has to be dying inside with the fear she's going to lose a boy that really never was hers to keep.

The stiffness in her posture confirms my assumption without her saying a word. "It's his uncle. Ex-con. Druggie," she states evenly when all of my senses revolt at the very idea that some piece of shit like that gets to even have the honor to know a kid like Zander.

"Money." It's my only response, and yet I know it's the right one because I hear the uneven rattle as she draws in a breath.

"Zander called me, upset, scared…asking me to help him and I had no clue what was going on." I can sense her getting riled up and pull her tighter against me.

"C'mon. Calm—" I stop myself from telling her to calm down since last time it was followed by a melt down worthy of global warming. And then I hear that damn hitch in her breath the same time I feel her body shudder and I know I'll do whatever it takes to make her happy, keep the baby safe, and make sure that Zander is taken care of regardless of what that might be.

"How can I calm down?" she says as I hear the sounds on the monitors begin to pick up their pace in the room around us. "Teddy didn't tell me and Zander is scared and there's nothing I can—"

"We'll adopt him," I blurt out, my own comment surprising me because while adoption is something we had spoken about before, it had never been in this context.

"No, we can't." Her voice breaks and the sound pulls at every chord within me. "I couldn't pick just one boy. That's just…But thank you for saying it. The fact that you'd even consider it means the world to me."

The sound of the baby's movement on the monitor refocuses my mind to the here and the now. To what it might take to make sure Rylee and the baby remain safe and healthy. But as the sound of Rylee's heartbeat slowing fills the room, I wonder just how I'm going to accomplish that without taking care of things for Zander too.

Her boys are her heart.

And she is mine.

So how do I prevent either of them from breaking?

At least in the hospital I can hear it beating, know it's healthy. I hold onto that thought as the gentle staccato of her heart soothes the still erratic one within me.

"I shouldn't have called and worried you…taken you away from your victory celebration," she confesses, "but I was scared."

Me too.

"As long as you promise to take it easy and listen to the damn doctor then we'll get you home and have our own celebration," I tell her, the notion not lost on me that as always she is thinking about me when she should be thinking about her.

"Ha. And you expect me to keep my blood pressure down with how you like to celebrate," she teases as she wiggles her ass against my dick causing me to muffle a laugh into the back of her head. "I have a feeling this victory lane is closed for business for a while."

"Good thing I just claimed it in Indy."

"You better be talking about a trophy, Ace."

Chpater Fifteen

Rylee

"I need your help, Shane," I say, sounding desperate and not caring a single bit that I do.

"Rylee." He chuckles, sounding so much like a grown man rather than the awkward teenager that once came to me alone and traumatized. The irony I'm now turning to him for help is not lost on me. "Colton said you were going to call and try to bribe me to help you escape your house."

Damn it! He's thought of everything to keep me stuck at home where the walls of this house feel like they are closing in on me more and more every day. Sure paparazzi have died down but they are still present, still perpetuating the sensationalism. They might not all be sitting outside, but the covers of the rags still show the grainy image of me in the garage. However, now it's next to one of me leaving the hospital in a wheelchair two days ago with titles that are equivalent to the conversation Colton and I had on our first date: Chupacabras and three-headed aliens.

"I'm not trying to bribe you to escape. I'll sit here, not be stubborn, and listen to doctor's orders so long as I know Zander's okay," I confess. "I've talked to him and he seems fine, and Colton and Jax are telling me he's fine, but Shane, he'll talk to you." The last words are emphasized so he understands I'm referring to the brotherly bond they've formed over the years. The connection between two battered souls that have healed together, shared experiences no one should ever have to, and came through it on the other side, is something that has allowed them to be the odd couple of closeness in The House.

And I'm hoping I can call on that bond right now to help find out how he's doing.

"On one condition," he says, throwing me for a loop.

"Mm-hmm?" I respond, curious if Colton has anything to do with this one condition.

"That you let me handle this. I don't want you stressed out and back in the hospital. I'll tell you everything I find out as long as I know you're going to put you and the baby first." I hear his words, and as much as I'm irritated with the ultimatum, pride overrides it and allows me to listen to what he's saying. To the concern in his voice, the compassion in his words, the remarkable man he's become.

It tells me I've done my job. And I hold tight to that idea since right now I can't continue to care for them. I have to trust in the time I've invested thus far with both of these boys and that their bond will remain steadfast when one needs the other the most.

"Can I trust you to do that, Rylee?" he asks, breaking through the emotion clouding my mind and clogging my throat.

"Yes," I say, feeling like a scolded child and yet it's hard to feel anything but love for him.

"He's struggling. He's scared and worried. We're the only good he knows. He fears going back to that constant life of not knowing what's next . . . and I can understand that," he murmurs, no doubt lost in his own memories.

He tells me exactly what I assumed but what no one else would confirm.

"Thank you for telling me." My mind races, wanting to rush over and see Zander face to face to reassure him, and wanting to beg Teddy to get back to me even though I know he's waiting on the caseworker to get back to him.

"I'm coming home next week for a few days. I'm going to stay at The House, already talked to Jax about it, and hang with Zand to make sure he's okay."

"Thank you," I say softly into the phone with my eyes closed and my heart full of love. "That's a really cool thing for you to do. He'll like hanging with you."

"He's family," Shane says. In my mind's eye, I can see that boyish smile on his face and the casual shrug that's typical of him. All I can do is smile and acknowledge that, yes, I've done a good job.

"He's family."

It seems so surreal to be folding baby clothes. Yes, my belly is so big I can't see my toes and a mountain of yellow clothes surrounds me, but with everything going on, it still feels so very far off and just around the corner simultaneously.

"While the idea of you being tied to the bed is rather hot, I'd prefer to do it with you as a willing candidate and not because you won't listen to the doctor," Colton says from the doorway. I turn to find a smirk on his face but the warning loud and clear in his eyes.

"Cute. Very cute," I say drolly.

"Well, you'd be even cuter flat on your back in our bed." We stand, a visual battle of wills war between us, and when he finally breaks eye contact and looks around, I notice his startled expression. "You put stuff away?"

"I figured it was about time," I murmur, slightly embarrassed at how long I've let my anxiety hold this process up. "It's safe enough that if he's born now, she should be okay."

"Nice change of pronouns there," he says with a laugh as he walks up to me and wraps his arms around me from behind, resting his chin on the curve of my shoulder.

"I couldn't let you think I knew BIRT's sex."

His laugh rings out, the vibration of it going from his chest into mine as I finish folding some of the receiving blankets I had pre-washed. "BIRT, huh? You've come over to my dark side and are calling him that now?"

"I've always liked your dark side," I say, intending one thing but when I feel his hands that have slid over my belly falter in their movement, I realize he took it in a completely different way. We stand there in silence momentarily as I let him shake the ghosts off his back that my comment caused to resurface.

"Did you feel that?" I ask, my hands flying to land on top of his so I can direct them to where the baby has moved beneath his palms.

"It's so bizarre," he murmurs. There's a sense of awe in his voice that tells me the darkness in his thoughts has passed for now. He presses his hands against my belly to try and will the baby to move again.

"BIRT likes his daddy's voice," I say softly, absorbing this moment we'll never get back once he's born. He presses his lips to the side of my neck and holds them there. It's almost as if he knows what I'm thinking and feels the same way, so he is trying to suspend time to make the here and now last as well.

"I have something for you. Will you come with me?" he asks.

"Is that something handcuffs and restraints?" I tease.

"Not unless you want them to be." With a laugh, he takes my hands and leads me down the hallway and into our bedroom.

I give him a look as he pats the bed for me to hop up. "And I fell for it," I say as he helps me up onto the mattress, my mind already wondering what exactly is going on since Dr. Steele said to hold off on sex for a bit. And as strict as Colton's been following her rules, he's either going to force me to rest or plan to exert himself.

I vote for the exertion.

"It's not what you think, you nympho," he says as he props pillows behind my back and under my knees before leaning in and brushing a kiss to my lips. And of course, because I can never resist him, I bring my hand up to the back of his neck and hold him there so I can steal one more from him.

"A girl can hope," I murmur against his lips. When he pulls back, a smile lights up his face and a mischievous glimmer is in his eyes.

"Not until this girl gets clearance from the doctor," he says. He walks around the edge of the bed and grabs something off his nightstand, holding it behind his back so I can't see it. And the cutest part about the action is that in the sequence of movements, I've watched my confident, demanding husband morph with discomfort so I know whatever is behind his back pushes his comfort zone.

"So I have something for you," he says and then stops with a shake of his head that's reminiscent of when one of the boys is embarrassed. It tugs at my heartstrings and gives me an exact picture of what BIRT will look like if he is a boy. He looks down at a crudely wrapped rectangular box in brown paper as he reaches it out to me. I close my hand over his and don't let go until he looks at me.

"Thank you, but I don't need anything."

"I thought it was a good idea at the time . . . but now I feel like it's lame so you can laugh at me all you—"

"I'm going to love it," I say with complete conviction, because if this present is making him this unsure then I know he's the one coloring outside of his already messy lines.

With the weight of his stare, I slowly unwrap the gift to find a picture frame made of thick rustic wood void of a photo in it. I stare at it for a moment because while it is actually quite beautiful, I sense there is a deeper meaning here than just a gift so try to figure out what it is that Colton's telling me.

"It's empty," he states, drawing my eyes up to his while my hands run over the texture of the wood. It's weathered but refined, rough but smooth, kind of like the two of us. The idea brings a smile to my lips.

"I see that."

"It's been a rough couple of weeks for us," he says as he climbs on the bed beside me. He lies on his side, head propped on his hand as I nod and try to figure how this all fits together. "Kelly is trying to find my dad." My mind slams on the brakes at that because I'm so confused and lost how we got from a frame to a person Colton has never spoken about before.

"*What?*" I look at him while he concentrates on his hand on my stomach. My mouth is opening and closing like a guppy because I don't know what to say or how we got from point A to point B in this conversation. I can tell he's just as confused as I am so I rein in my need to know and let him find the words to explain everything.

"I'm scared about being a dad," he says and continues the confession. And it's not like I don't get the fear, because I have it too, but I'm starting to connect the dots in the sense that he fears he is going to be like the father he never knew somehow. "And I thought maybe if I knew about my sperm donor then it would ease the fear that I'll be like him."

As much as I want to shift to take his face in my hands so he's forced to look in my eyes, I allow him the space he needs. "You will be *nothing* like him, Colton. There's not a doubt in my mind."

I've seen him with the boys at The House. I've watched him help them overcome adversity only he could understand. Does he not have any clue how important that is? How that interaction more than just hints at the incredible father I know he will be? I wish he could see the same man I see every single day when he looks in the mirror.

He just nods his head yet doesn't say anything for a moment. I wish there was something I could say or do to reassure him further when only time will prove the truth in my statement.

"I don't know," I say with a shake of my head. "I think it's a bad idea . . . I don't see how finding him is going to help you at all." And I probably should keep my opinions to myself, let him deal with his past how he needs to, but at the same time we've had so many things crash into our reality recently, I don't know how much more we can take. "What are you hoping to achieve if you find him?"

"A clean slate." He then clears the emotion from his throat. "This frame is empty because I want to start this next chapter of our life with a completely clean slate. Our family deserves this. It's . . ." His voice fades off. I reach out and link my fingers through his. His words—his thoughtfulness—are so damn overwhelming that I can't find the words to speak just yet. "Never mind," he says again.

"No. Please, finish. I'm quiet because I'm touched and stunned you thought of this and did this for us . . . especially after everything that has happened this month."

"I sound like a fucking chick here but this empty frame is also my promise to you that from today forward I don't want to just take pictures with you, I want to make memories. Good ones more than bad ones. Funny ones. Memorable ones. Precious ones. They will shift and change over time, each stage of our life together dictating what goes here, but more than anything, this empty frame with be filled with our new normal . . ." His voice trails off. Tears flood my eyes. The depth of emotion in this incredible gift from a man who thinks of himself as unromantic—despite the grand sweeping gestures he shows me time and again—is so very poignant and fitting.

"I love it," I whisper, my eyes meeting his as I look at him through a kaleidoscope of tears. "It's absolutely perfect." I hug the frame, my empty treasure box in a sense, and revel in how much Colton has grown since we've met.

I shift so I'm on my left side, facing him, our bodies mirroring one another's. We stare at each for a few moments, our visual connection so very intense as feelings are exchanged without any words being spoken.

"I don't have anything to give you," I finally say.

A shy smile turns up the corners of his mouth. "You've given me more than I've ever wanted."

It's silly that even after all this time I still react viscerally to praise from him, but it's undeniable. As I draw in a shaky breath, his eyes narrow and my fingers trace over the grooves in the frame lying between us.

"Sometimes I play the 'I'm game' with the boys . . . want to play with me?" His grin grows, and I realize the innuendo.

"You know I'd never turn down the chance to play with you," he says, nodding his head for me to continue. "How do you play?"

"I tell you something that starts with 'I'm' and then you go. You don't get to ask questions though . . . That way you're forced to listen to what you think the person is saying. It's an I go, you go, type thing." I'm shocked that in all our time together, I've never explained this to him, but I feel this is an absolutely perfect moment. "I'll go first. *I'm scared too*," I say in a whisper, as if the lower voice will help my confession somehow seem less.

He starts to say something that doesn't begin with "I'm" and I shush him and bring a finger to his lips. "No reassurances. Sometimes that makes you feel like your fears are invalid. Your turn."

I watch him struggle finding the words to express whatever it is weighing heavily on his mind. He takes a deep breath, looks over my shoulder for a few moments, and his fingers pluck at the sheet. In the last five years, he's grown leaps and bounds in not only identifying but in the ability to articulate his emotions. And yet right now I can tell he's at a loss on how to phrase them.

The silence stretches. My concern over what has him so tongue-tied grows.

"I'm afraid you'll never forgive me for the video and that I couldn't fix it." He won't look at me.

I close my eyes momentarily, letting the apology in his voice be the balm to the open wounds that video has caused and nod my head to let him know I heard him. Given the number of times he has apologized, I shouldn't be surprised this was his first confession. At the same time, I appreciate his need to tell me it again.

"I'm worried that when people see us now, all they'll be able to think of is the video. I can only hope it will die down and go away at some point." Colton closes his eyes momentarily and gives a subtle nod. His reaction is all I need to know he feels the same way.

"I'm hopeful Eddie will get what he deserves," Colton says, disgust and spite lacing his tone.

"I'm in agreement," I say with a laugh, because I didn't give a confession but I didn't exactly break the rules either.

"Rule breaker," he murmurs with a shy smile on his lips.

"Not hardly," I say. "Your turn."

"I'm worried you're going to be so focused on Zander that it's going to put you back in the hospital again," he says with a lift of his eyebrows and a glance down to my belly.

"I'm concerned I'm going to let him down and not be able to help him when he needs me the most." I fight the unease my confession brings, and try to staunch its very real side effects. I worry it will end up doing just what Colton fears, too.

"I'm certain that somehow we'll make everything right for him," he says, shaking his head to stop me before I even open my mouth. He knows me so well.

"I'm positive my husband likes this game because it prevents me from saying too much and arguing with him," I confess matter-of-factly, causing him to bark out a laugh in agreement. The sound of it puts a smile on my lips before the quiet falls back around us as Colton figures out what to say next.

"I'm afraid I'm not going to be man enough to give you what you need when you need it most." He licks his lips and forces a swallow down his throat. His eyes never waver from mine despite the absolute swell of emotion riding its way through them.

Wow. Well I guess he's bringing out the deep confessions now. I so did not expect that comment from him. It knocks me back a second while I wrap my head around it. Does he mean in all aspects of life or just with the baby coming? I wonder what it is he thinks I need that he's not giving me.

Doubt is the chisel that causes the fissures to drive a solid relationship apart, and I hate he feels like I have any when it comes to him.

"Colton," I begin to say, breaking my own rules, because I have to tell him he's more than man enough in all aspects for me, but he reaches out and puts a finger to my lips.

"Uh-uh." He shakes his head. "Your turn."

And I just stare, desperately wanting to tell him he's so very off base to worry about that and yet I don't. Can't. I need to allow him to say what he needs to say. I blow out a breath in frustration and discomfort because we may know each other inside and out, yet this is more soul-bearing than anything we have done in such a long time, and as cathartic as it may be, it's also scary as hell.

"I'm afraid you won't find me sexy anymore after I have the baby."

He may not speak, but his head shakes back and forth to tell me I'm crazy. "I'm afraid that every time you look at me, you think you've made a mistake in marrying me."

Is he crazy? His words stab my heart. It's so unbelievable the world sees Colton as an arrogant, self-assured man. Yet with me—*especially* right here, right now—he reveals the insecurity all people have but keep close to the vest.

"I'm afraid you are going to pull away when the baby is born," I say without thinking and realize that my deepest fear has been spoken out loud. The quick hitch in Colton's breath tells me without him saying a word that he fears the same thing. I panic momentarily, fear lodging in my throat. I know I need to fix this somehow so I keep talking like I was going to finish the sentence, ". . . but need you to know that I can't do this without you."

Silence settles between us. Our eyes lock. My heart hopes he really hears what I'm saying. "I'm afraid that I'm going to panic in the delivery room, see things I can't unsee, or not be able to handle watching you in pain."

And hearing him say something so many men fear makes me feel better. Like we're normal in a sense when our relationship and everything surrounding us is far from it.

"I'm afraid of labor." *Who wouldn't be?* The unknown pain and the absolute unexpected followed by the beautiful ending. Colton just raises his eyebrows and nods his head.

"I'm afraid I'm going to be like *them*," he says, the term *them* unmistakable in its meaning: his mother and father. His eyes burn into mine, and it kills me that he has even put himself in the same category as them. Yes, their genes run through him but that doesn't mean his heart isn't different.

Blood makes the body, not the man.

"I'm scared I'm going to make too many mistakes as a mother."

Colton rolls his eyes, prompting me to reach out and wipe his hair off his forehead. He grabs my wrist and brings the palm of my hand to his lips and presses a sweet kiss to the center of it before bringing it down to rest over his heart. "I'm sure I'm going to make way more mistakes as a father but I know that with you by my side, our baby will grow into an incredible human being . . . just like his mother." He whispers the last words, causing tears to sting my eyes, which is in complete contradiction to the soft smile on my lips from the way he changed his confession to make it a positive.

I should have known he'd find a way to make me feel better about my fears by skating under the radar and breaking the rules without actually breaking them.

"I'm sure BIRT will have your green eyes, your stubborn streak, and your incredible capacity to love," I say as Colton clears his throat. His fingers tighten over mine on his chest. I know he wants to refute my comment, the one I put out there to try to lessen his fear about him being like his biological parents, but he doesn't.

And that's a good sign because hopefully if I say it enough, he'll eventually start to believe it.

"I'm afraid that everything was going so well for us. But first it was the video . . . and now . . ." he blows out a breath and I try to figure out what's eating at him, "now . . . the other shoe is going to drop."

I stare at him, so perfectly imperfect and full of fear just like I am, and yet he walked in here tonight and gave me a gift most husbands would never even think of. Yet he still doubts us, still worries the other shit will affect us when all we need is each other.

All we've ever needed is each other.

"I'm certain that even if the other shoe drops, it'll be off an octopus with a lot of shoes so we'll be able to handle it, because I married the only man ever meant for me. We can handle anything that comes our way, shoe by dropping shoe."

Colton just falls onto his back and starts laughing, deep and long. I can tell he needed something humorous to release the stress clawing him apart from the inside out. I find comfort I can use a game I invented for little boys and still affect the grown man in my life.

Then again, boys, men, they're really no different from the other.

After a moment he rolls back onto his side and scoots up against me so my belly hits his. He cradles my face in his hands. "Octopus shoes?" He laughs again with a lift of his eyebrows and a flash of that irresistible dimple.

"Yep. They've got eight feet. Lots of shoes to drop," I tease, wanting to keep the moment now that our hearts are a bit lighter.

Colton just shakes his head with a soft smile on his lips, love in his eyes, and tenderness in his touch. How in the hell did I get to be so lucky to be the one sharing my life with this contradiction of a man?

"God, I fucking race you, Ryles," he says, sealing the sentiment with a kiss and stealing my heart once again.

With my eyes closed, our lips touching, and hearts beating as one, I think back to our wedding day, to the vows we made, and the promises we made and have kept. The "You know that's permanent, right?" and I know there's nothing I would ever change because he's here, he's mine, and no matter what life throws at us, he'll be here for me. He's protected me. Put me first. Made me consequential. Made me whole.

With every beautifully scarred, bent piece of him.

Chapter Sixteen

Colton

"Did you beat the shit out of him?"

I look up from the stacks on my desk just as Becks takes a seat in front of me, propping his feet up on its edge. "Please. Make yourself at home."

"Don't mind if I do," he says in that slow even drawl of his that's equal parts irritating and comforting to me. "So?"

"He didn't show," I explain with a shake of my head. "I sat outside the damn office for an hour before and an hour after his appointed meeting with his parole officer and the fucker never showed."

Such a waste of time. Staking out the probation office during the two hours around Eddie's appointment time. Watching drug deals go down and a hooker giving a guy head in his car, while I waited to have my moment with Eddie. Draw him out to give him a little payback of my own.

"Can't you get in trouble seeking him out with the restraining order?" he asks.

"Restraining order was filed on Ry's behalf. Not mine," I say with a smirk. I want him nowhere fucking near her. Now me on the other hand? I have no problem coming face to face with him. In fact, there's nothing I'd like more.

"So you can approach him, kick his ass, and . . ."

"And no one's worse for wear," I say with a shrug. "Well, besides him that is."

"Can take the man out of the trouble but can't stop the boy in him from looking for it," he says with a shake of his head.

"Damn straight."

"But wait. He didn't show, so now what? Will he be hauled back to jail for violation or some shit?" He laces his fingers and brings his hands behind his head.

"No clue. Possibly . . . but I have a feeling he's a helluva lot more scared of the loan sharks and their thugs than missing a parole appointment. Getting put back in jail might be the safest place for him, considering the amount of phone calls I've received asking me if I know his whereabouts."

"Well played, brother," he says with a shake of his head. "Giving his name up like that to the press."

"It hit me that night at the bar. The loan sharks came knocking when we fired him. Then he fucked us by stealing the blueprints to sell so he could pay them back. So why not fuck him over by using them to pay me back?"

Full circles. They're everywhere I look.

"Scary fucking shit, dude," he muses. I glance to the garage down below. "So . . . how are things? Ry good?"

"Yeah. Good."

"That doesn't sound convincing."

I lean back in my chair and prop my feet on my desk like he did, lace my fingers behind my head, and look at the ceiling. "What if I told you I was looking into adopting Zander?"

Becks doesn't say a goddamn word, yet I can tell by the jerk of his body to attention in my peripheral vision that he heard me. "Subtlety isn't something you know how to do, is it?" he coughs out.

"Nope. So?"

"I'd ask you if you're fucking crazy on many fronts. Especially since you're using the term *I* and not *we*."

Fucking pronouns.

I roll my eyes. "Semantics."

"You don't sound so sure about that," Becks says as he pokes holes through my story.

"Rylee said she wouldn't think of it. That she can't choose one boy over the others. I get it, but I told her I was looking into it anyway. The whole Zander thing is really eating her up."

"Eating her up or you up?" he asks, eyes daring me to lie to him.

Shit. He's calling me on the carpet and there's no way I can deny it since he knows my history. Because fuck yes, a part of me wants to give Zander the opportunity I had. Save him like I was saved.

And yet at the same time, I understand Ry's stance because I couldn't pick him and not the other boys.

"You told me once, fight or flight. I chose to fight," I say, thinking of that night a long time ago after Ry lost the baby. Becks had snapped me to attention, and forced me to be the man I feared being and of truths about myself I had to face. The ones that made me realize Ry was worth the goddamn effort and then some. "Well, I'm fighting."

"For what though, Wood? What exactly is it you're fighting for now?" He leans forward, puts his hands on his knees, and looks me in the eye.

I shove up out of my chair and walk over to the wall of windows that looks down to the shop below. It's easier to watch the guys than deal with this shit.

Memories I thought I'd forgotten hit me out of nowhere: The fear with each knock on the front door that my mom was coming to take me away from Dorothea and Andy. Hands that high-fived and didn't hit. Lights left on in the hallway because horrible things happened in the dark. Superhero posters on the walls I'd stare at when the nightmares hit. Fear turned to hope. Hope gave me life.

That life gave me love: Rylee.

"I'm fighting because like you said, she's the goddamn alphabet, Becks." I turn around to face him, hands out to my sides and a shrug of my shoulders. "Those boys are her life, and she's mine."

This conversation, this confession, and these feelings, all make me anxious. Uncomfortable. Vulnerable.

Add feelings on top of feelings when I don't want them to.

My cell phone rings and thank fuck for that because shit's getting heavy. And the only kind of heavy I like is Ry's weight on top of me.

"Kelly."

"I've found your father." I freeze. Mind misfires thoughts. Hand stops midway in the air and then drops.

What the fuck did I do this for? Doubt rears its ugly stepsister of a head to let me know she's still there. Still waiting for me to fuck all of this up.

I can't speak. All I can do is clear my throat.

"Confirmation should come within the hour. When it does I'll shoot you over his address in an email."

"Yeah. Thanks." I let the phone slip from my hand and land with a thud on my desk. I stare at it for a minute. Deciding. Wondering. Avoiding.

You got what you wanted, Donavan.

What are you going to do about it?

Chapter Seventeen

Rylee

Heading to The House. Zander is meeting with his uncle. Just found out and am speeding to get there in time.

Shane's text replays in my head over and over as I search my purse for my car keys before moving to the laundry room that connects to the garage to see if they are hanging on the rack of keys. They're not. My body vibrates with anguish and my heart lodges into my throat over the need to get to Zander so I can walk him through this.

And to pick apart every one of his uncle's nuances so I can make the claims I want to make about why he can't be approved to foster.

I know I'm breaking my promise to Shane about not reacting off the information he feeds me when it comes to Zander, but . . . it's one of my boys. I need to be there. If it were Shane in distress I'd do the same thing.

"Sammy!" I yell, not sure if he's in his office off the main floor or outside doing any of the various things he does that continually remain a mystery to me. I'm smart enough to know Colton has conveniently had him staying around the house lately to keep an eye on me. That doesn't sit well with me. "Sammy. Do you know where my keys are?" I try to keep the panic out of my voice but it's no use because I need to get to The House ASAP.

"Everything okay?" he asks as he jogs down the hallway toward me, the concern in his tone matching the look on his face. And I realize he thinks I'm in labor, hence the slightly panicked widening of his eyes.

"Yes. I'm looking for my keys."

"Do you need me to run to the store for you?" he asks, his eyes narrowing.

"No, thank you. I need to get to The House," I tell him as I cross my arms over my chest and just stare.

"Sorry. You're not supposed to be going anywhere. Colton sa—"

"Did he hide my car keys?" I ask, voice becoming shriller with each word. Reality sets in that I'm not being forgetful with pregnancy brain like I thought when I couldn't find my keys, but Colton actually hid them. "Are you fucking kidding me?" I yell, throwing my hands up, my misdirected anger aimed at Sammy.

"He wanted to make sure you stayed safe," he states quietly, knowing not to cross my temper.

I start to walk away from him, mentally trying to figure out how to get there, when I turn back around. "Drive me then."

Sammy startles at my directive, considering I have never asked him for anything let alone demanded him to do something since Colton and I have been married. "Let me call Colton," he says as he goes to step away.

"*No*." He stops and turns to look at me like I've lost it. The funny part is I have and can't bother to care that I have. "I'm as much your boss as he is. I'll take the blame, Sammy, but one of my boys needs me." I know I'm putting him in a horrible position—piss off the husband or face the wrath of the pregnant wife—but at this point, I don't care. All I can think about is Zander.

"Rylee," he says, my name a resigned sigh.

"Never mind," I say as the idea hits me and I start to walk past him to where Colton keeps his stash of extra keys. "I'll just take Sex then." By the way he sucks in his breath I know I've just delivered the coup de grace by threatening to take Colton's baby. My husband may be a generous man, but when it comes to his beloved Ferrari, that's another story.

My mind flickers back to the last time I asked to get behind the wheel. *Nice try, sweetheart, but the only place you're allowed to drive me is out of breath on the hood.* I can still see his telltale smirk and the salacious look in his eyes, before I begrudgingly moved away from the door of the driver's seat.

That was three years ago. I'm smart enough not to come between a man and his car, but I sure as hell know how to use it as leverage to get what I want.

With the weight of Sammy's presence at my back, I open the middle drawer of the desk and make a show of rifling through it to prove my point.

"I promised Colton I'd make sure you stayed here."

"I'll deal with him if you drive me, Sammy. Not taking me is ten times worse for my health and the baby than taking me. *Happy wife, happy life*," I say with false enthusiasm. "And if not, voila!" I turn around with the key dangling between my fingers.

Our eyes meet momentarily before his dart back to the key fob. "Fuck," he mutters under his breath through gritted teeth. That single word can mean so many things, but right now for me it means I've won.

Power to the pregnant woman!

I enter The House with my key, not caring if I'm going to be in trouble or not, because judging by the strange cars in the driveway, someone is here already. I feel thankful seeing Jax's and Kellan's cars on the street. I know they are more than capable of handling the situation, but *it's Zander. My Zander*. The boy I've spent endless hours with to heal his broken heart. The boy who *soccers* me.

When I clear the great room, I hear startled gasps. The boys look up from doing their homework at the table and run over to me with Racer following excitedly on their heels. Auggie sits back with a soft smile on his lips as I'm greeted with desperately missed hugs and a mind-spinning spew of words as they all try to tell me what's been going on with them at the same time. Tiny hands run over my belly and tell me how much bigger it seems, and ask when is the baby going to come because they can't wait to meet him. Because in a house full of boys, they know the baby *has* to be a boy. A girl is not an option. My heart swells and hurts simultaneously because although it's only been a few weeks, it feels like I've missed years of their lives.

I bite back my anger toward Eddie for taking this away from me. The incessant chatter, the sticky hands, and the dirt-smudged smiles. The things that make my world go round and my heart happy. Hell yes, I'm pissed at him, but right now I'm with my boys and don't want his vindictiveness to tarnish the small amount of time I'll get with them.

Later I can stew. Later I can I punch my pillow in anger. But right now, I'm going to soak this up and ignore that I'm going to miss every single thing the minute I have to leave again.

"Rylee?" Kellan says as he clears the hallway, eyes wide, and grin welcoming.

"Hey. Sorry I didn't call but—"

"You're here for the same reason as Shane, who keeps calling, saying he's going to be here any second, yeah?" His voice is deceptive in tone—not letting the boys on what his eyes are telling me—but it's clear he's concerned about Zander too. At the mention of Shane, the noise starts up around us again from the boys, excitement that their older brother is on his way to roughhouse and tell them stories about how cool college is.

"Yes." I nod. "He needs me," I mouth to him above the fray and he motions with his chin toward the back patio that I can't see through the angled blinds.

"Okay guys, how about you finish your homework," I say, stepping right back into the role I was born to play, knowing Kellan won't take offense to me taking over momentarily. "I need to go check on Zander and when I come back in, if your homework is done, I'll stay for dinner."

Cheers fill the air around me followed by the scraping of chairs and elbowing of boy against boy as the fight to regain their position at the table begins so they can finish.

Kellan meets my eyes again now that the boys aren't watching, and I can tell he's just as upset by all of this as I am. "How long have they been here?" I ask as I reach down to scratch Racer behind the ears.

"Jax is out there with them, watching. The caseworker, the uncle and aunt, and Zander," he adds, answering the questions I would ask next.

"Thanks." Our eyes hold momentarily and suddenly it hits me how nervous I was to come face to face with him and Jax. They are the ones feeling the effects of my dismissal—extra shifts, upset boys, curious questions. And yet instead of shaking his head and walking away at the mess I've created for all of us, he gives me a gentle but sincere smile. I don't see the resentment or pity I feared. Rather I see camaraderie, as if he knows I'd move heaven and earth to fix the situation if I could because I'm not oblivious to the toll it's taken on not only me, but everyone involved.

I smile in return, my thank you for not passing judgment. He nods his head as I slowly slide open the door to the backyard and step out before closing it behind me. I see Zander and my heart breaks instantly. I'm transported back to six years ago when he first came to us, broken and traumatized. His knees are pulled up to his chest as he sits on a chair with his side to me, his arms wrapped around them, his face looking blankly toward the wood panel fence. From what I *can* see, there is a look of complete detachment on his face. All that's missing is the stuffed dog he used to tote around for comfort, which now sits up in the closet somewhere.

In a single afternoon, the two people sitting opposite him—his uncle and aunt—have potentially erased the crucial years of work, the countless, grueling hours gaining his trust, helping ease the nightmares that had owned his psyche. *Have I lost the hopeful, sweet boy I love so much?*

Zander lifts his head and vacant eyes meet mine, crushing my cautious hope about anything positive coming from this situation. It takes everything I have to force a smile on my lips and nod my head in encouragement for him to talk to them. He stares at me, the look of betrayal blatant on his face, but it's necessary for the caseworker to see I'm trying to help facilitate this connection. When I approach him after the meeting to tell him he can't let this happen, then I won't look so unprofessional.

I shift my eyes from Zander to the uncle and aunt. The uncle glances over to me. *Fuck.* I see recognition in his eyes before they suggestively slide up and down the length of my body in a not-so-subtle show that says he knows exactly what I look like naked.

My skin crawls and stomach churns with revulsion and the little smirk he gives me—just a hint of the curl of his lip—tells me he knows how it's making me feel and is enjoying it. He tucks his tongue in his cheek before giving me a slight nod of the head and looking back toward his wife.

I watch them try to interact with Zander. They attempt to talk about things he has no interest in. Because he's a thirteen-year-old boy now, not the seven-year-old they once might have known. SpongeBob isn't cool and Xbox is no longer the coveted game system I want to scream at them. He loves soccer and building Halo Lego sets and reading Harry Potter and Percy Jackson.

You don't know a thing about him! All you want is the money that comes with him.

I can see beneath their brushed hair and best clothes. I can see the wolves in sheep's clothing. I'm certain they have no concern for Zander or his best interest. And it all becomes more than obvious the longer Zander remains silent and unresponsive, because the two of them shift their fidgeting and attention toward each other with raised eyebrows and shrugged shoulders, silently asking each other what to do now that he's not answering them.

I glance over to the caseworker sitting on the other side of the yard with his legs crossed, ankle resting on opposite knee, and a clipboard balanced on his leg. And while he may have a pen in hand and paper he's supposed to be taking notes on, his phone sits atop the paper. He's so busy texting someone he hasn't once looked up to watch the interaction—or rather lack thereof—nor notice the ever-disappearing presence of Zander losing himself to the safe world he created in his mind so very long ago. That same world I spent months pulling him out of, showing him not everyone is bad and evil—out to hurt those they love—and that it was safe to step outside.

My body vibrates with anger, my teeth bites into my tongue because all I want to do is go to him, pull him into my arms, and reiterate the promise I made him all those years ago: I'm never going to let anything bad happen to him ever again.

Lost in my observation, I forget Jax is there until he motions with his hands to silently get my attention. And when I look at him, his eyes express the same thing as Kellan's, indicating he feels the same disbelief.

No way in hell are they taking Zander from us.

Now I just have to figure out how to prevent that.

"Zander?" I call as I enter his room. The shades are pulled closed and the light remains off, but through the light of the open doorway I can see him curled up on his side in his bed.

When he doesn't respond, the sense of dread that has been tickling the back of my neck and making my stomach churn exacerbates. I glance over to Shane opposite me in the hallway and the concern in his eyes mirrors how I feel.

We move into the room together. Shane lived here long enough to know the drill, so he stands against the wall to observe while I step forward to engage Zander. And my immediate worry is that Zander has closed off even more. Jax and I spent five minutes with the caseworker, providing valid reasons why the uncle is not a good fit to foster Zander. I feel like our arguments fell on deaf ears. Now, looking at Zander rocking on his bed with his beloved stuffed dog held tight to his chest, I'm more worried than ever. I can't remember the last time he climbed up to the top shelf of his closet and pulled the sacred dog from its box. The only tangible reminder of his old life.

I sit on the chair next to the bed and feel a whisper of hope when he scoots back as if to make room for me. "May I?" I ask, as I reach out to touch him, hating feeling like we are back to square one. When he nods his head, I breathe a little sigh of relief. He isn't closing himself off from me completely. Silence weighs heavily around us. The smell of his fear almost palpable, and unfortunately one I know all too well when it comes to my boys.

God, how I've missed them.

I use my touch to soothe because I know words won't do anything for him right now. And then the idea comes to me.

"I have an idea." I scoot off the chair and very slowly lower to my knees. I rest my arms on the comforter with my chin atop my hands so we are face to face. I take in his downturned mouth and wait for him to look up to me so he can see I'm here and not going anywhere.

"I think we should play the 'I'm' game," I say, hoping he goes along with it, as it would afford me a glimpse into how far he has relapsed.

His eyes flash up to meet mine, and I see something flicker in them but wait him out, knowing that patience is so very important right now. I reach out and put his hand in mine, needing to ease some of the loneliness I can feel emanating from him.

He opens his mouth and then closes it a few times before finally speaking, his voice a whisper. "I'm scared."

Two words. *I'm scared.* They're all it takes to make me close my eyes and take a deep breath, because in that moment, I'm reminded of Colton's confessions a few nights ago. I realize that no matter how old they are, the fear will always be there. It will morph and change over time, but the invisible scars of their youth have left an indelible mark and will always have a profound effect on how they process emotion and deal with changes.

"I'm scared too," I tell him, causing his eyes to widen and prompt me to explain further. "I'm scared you're going to pull away and not realize how much I'll fight to keep you safe and sound."

"I'm worried that it won't matter to them, because I'm just a number in a broken system and they're going to want to tick me off as done," he confesses, and it amazes me how very intuitive he is with regard to the systematic process we have worked so very hard to shield him from.

"I'm positive you're so much more than just a number, and in fact are a smart, funny, compassionate teenager as well as an incredible soccer player," I say, hoping the positive might break through and help the negative. A ghost of a smile plays at the corners of his lips as his eyes hold mine, tears glistening in them that he blinks away.

"I'm . . ." He pauses as he tries to figure out the rest of his thoughts. "I'm sure that my uncle cares more about the monthly payment he'd get for fostering me than he does having a thirteen-year-old boy in his house." He breathes out long and even. I scour my mind to decide what to tell him next that might help to draw out more of his feelings and get him to talk, so I'm startled when he continues without any prompting.

"I remember his house," he murmurs. "The cigarette smoke, the bent spoons, lighters, and tin foil on the coffee table next to the needles I was forbidden to touch. The couch that was supposed to be brown, but was almost white on the seams, and stained everywhere else that I could see even when all the shades were drawn. I remember sitting in the corner while my dad and him would slap the inside of their elbows before turning their backs to me . . . and then they'd sit back on the couch with their heads looking at the ceiling and creepy smiles on their faces." His eyes focus on our hands where I'm rubbing my thumb back and forth over the top of his. And yes, he broke the rules, didn't start his confession with "I'm", but he's talking and that's ten times more than I ever thought I was going to get when I knelt down beside him.

"I'm sorry you had to go through that." I try to add strength to my voice so he doesn't realize how much his words have affected me. "And I'm so very proud of the person you've become in spite of all of that."

His eyes flash up to mine again on those last words, his head shaking back and forth a few times like he wants to reject them as my statement sinks in. "You did two 'I'ms,'" he says.

"So I did." I shift, feeling a tight pang as my stomach twists with worry. I suddenly feel like I'm going to be sick. I try to take a deep breath and push it down. "You can go again if you want."

"I'm going to run away if I'm told I have to go live with them." My mouth shocks open and I immediately start to refute him, but when he shakes his head to tell me I can't speak. I bite my tongue, which is laced with so many pleas for him to have faith.

"I'm going to do everything in my power to ensure neither of those things happen." The sadness and resignation returns to his eyes. Tears well in my eyes and my chest constricts. This is one promise I *have to* follow through on.

"I'm certain that..." he says, and then shakes his head. "Never mind."

"No. Please tell me," I urge, because the break in his voice worries me. *Shit.* Another painful twinge. Zander's eyes are closed and his lips are pulled tight in thought.

After some time he draws in a long, uneven breath, and when somewhere in the house laughter erupts, he opens his eyes to find mine again. "I'm certain that if they're allowed to foster me, I'll die."

And yes, he's a thirteen-year-old boy and most people would write the statement off as melodramatic, but he's not one to say something for attention. So as his statement hangs in the air and suffocates us, I struggle with a response so he knows I hear him and haven't disregarded him. And yet I have no clue what to say because his comment can have so many connotations, and I'm not sure which one he means by it.

"Zander . . ." A sharp pain knocks the rest of the thoughts from my head and has me doubling over instantly. I try to hide the grimace on my face and fight the immediate need to curl up in the fetal position. Another pang hits me, causing my whole body to tense and my fingers to grip the comforter beneath them. I cringe when I feel the wetness between my legs; Full bladder, baby resting upon it, and a tense body is not a good mixture.

Seconds pass as I try to register the pain, and how I'm going to explain to a bunch of boys—who are obsessed with bodily functions—what just happened. Then I realize that the wetness keeps spreading.

Another sharp pain hits, this time drawing a gasp from my mouth. My mind spins as elation mixed with fear vibrates through my body on a crash course of adrenaline-laced hormones.

"Rylee?" Shane is at my side in an instant. Zander shifts to sit up, his face a picture of panic, and his eyes ask Shane for help. *His* face looks just as freaked out.

"My water broke," I say with a laugh tinged with hysteria.

"*What?*" Shane exclaims, eyes wide with panic. "You can't be—it's not—oh shit. What do you need?" He walks to one side of the room and then back unsure what to do as I breathe deeply and slowly push myself up from the ground. And then he stops abruptly, eyes lighting up and mouth shocking open. "This is because I brought you here, isn't it? The stress. Zander. Holy shit!"

"No." I shake my head, trying to hide my own fear.

"Yes, it is. You promised," he shouts, worry controlling his thoughts. "Oh my God. Oh my God!" His hands are in his hair; his feet are walking the floor. "Colton's going to kill me. Frickin' kill me."

"Shane," I say softly. "Shane!" He stops and turns to look at me. "No. He's not."

"It's too early," he whispers, eyes wild with fear.

"Go get Sammy." Oh shit.

It's too early.

The thought runs through my head, paralyzing me with a mixture of anxiety, fear, and worry, until a sniffle behind me snaps me to the here and now.

The baby's not full term yet. In a pregnancy that has left me in a constant state of worry and fear, the thought is downright unnerving.

"I'm okay, Zand," I say, hoping it's the truth, fearing it's not.

I look back to meet eyes welled with tears. "This is my fault," he whispers.

No. No, that's not true.

But for the first time in my life, I reach back and put my hand on top of his and don't say a word to assuage his fears.

Because mine are greater right now.

And when I squeeze his hand, I'm not sure who I'm reassuring more, him or me.

Chapter Eighteen

Colton

Swing. Watch. Walk. Scratch your head and contemplate. Repeat.

Why anyone plays golf on a weekly basis beats the shit out of me. I'm so bored that watching paint dry would be more fucking interesting.

There's a reason I race for a living. Adrenaline. Speed. Excitement. Too bad I can't take the golf cart and open that baby up. Lay down some rubber on this boring green. Now *that* would be fun.

But sponsorships call. The dog and pony show must be performed. The ass-kissing must commence.

I slide a glance to Becks standing behind the head of Pennzoil and notice him giving me a lopsided smirk that says, "Quit being such a little bitch." And he's right. I need to, but I have so much shit to do and not enough time to do it in. Using my middle finger, I scratch the side of my head and give him the bird on the sly, causing his smirk to widen and his head to shake, obviously enjoying my misery.

The shrill sound of my cell disrupts the silence just as the Pennzoil rep is mid swing. He shanks the ball into the rough and immediately shoots me a glare for committing the cardinal sin of not silencing my cell on the green.

Fuck. Guess I screwed the pooch on that one.

I mumble an apology as Becks walks over to smooth over my error, and I pick up to see what Sammy needs.

"Sammy."

"It's time!" Rylee's voice fills the line. Confused, I hold the phone out so I can look at the screen. Yep. Sam's number all right.

"Time for . . . WHAT?" I shout, disturbing the silence on the green once again and not giving a fuck because my head is spinning and my heart is pounding.

"The baby," she whispers, her voice a mixture of so many emotions I can't place any of them.

"You sure?" I ask like a dumbfuck. Of course she's sure.

"My water broke."

Can't get any more sure than that. *Oh fuck*. This is like real, real. "I'm on my way."

I start to walk one way off the green and then stop and head the other way, hands shaking, mind reeling, and absolutely clueless about what to do now. The adrenaline I was begging for just moments ago is now coursing through me like jet fuel to the point I can't focus on anything and yet need to do everything.

"Wood. You okay?" Becks asks, as I look like a goddamn ostrich walking back and forth with my head stuck up my ass.

"I gotta go." I put my phone in my pocket. Take it out. Grab my club. Put it in my golf bag upside down. Start looking for my glove and can't find it only to see it's on my hand.

"Colton." Becks's stern voice breaks through the mosh pit of chaos in my head so that I stop pacing aimlessly.

"The baby . . . Ry's in labor. I gotta go," I say again as Becks throws his head back and starts laughing.

"Not so calm and collected now, are you?" He chuckles.

If looks could kill he'd be in a body bag right now as I start rifling through my golf bag for my keys before realizing we're on the back nine and way too fucking far from the country club's parking lot.

"Chill, dude." He puts his hand on my shoulder and squeezes it. "I'll drive you to the clubhouse and then come back and deal with the suits," he says, reading my crazed actions to know what I'm thinking. "Just promise me you're stable enough to drive."

That comment isn't even worthy of a response.

Push the up button. Push it again. Pace three steps. Grumble. Push it again.

I'm not nervous. Not at all.

Door dings. Enter the elevator. Push the number three button. Smile politely to the man in the car, but keep my head down.

Scratch that. I'm freaking the fuck out now.

A stop on the first floor. The man walks off. Push close door. Push close door. Close the fucking door!

A baby. Holy shit.

Door closes.

I'm coming, Ryles.

Doors open just as my cell rings. I answer as I walk toward the nurses station.

"I don't have much time, Shane. What's up?"

"Is she okay?" he asks.

"Not sure yet. I'm almost there. I'll text—"

"I'm so sorry. It's all my fault."

Come again? "What's your fault?"

"I told Rylee I'd take care of Zander and then I called her and told her I was going there because the foster douchebag was meeting him and she was there. Zander told her lots of things and said he'd die if he went and that made her go into labor and now I'm worried I caused all of this—"

"Whoa! Slow down," I say to stop his word vomit. What the fuck is he talking about? His words irritate my temper like an itch. How? Why?

Missing pieces fit together in my mind. Ry was at The House. Sammy was driving her to the hospital. Goddammit! Sammy drove her to The House to begin with. Against. My. Orders.

That itch turns into a full-blown scratch. I'll be having words with Sammy. No doubt there.

"Colton?" I can hear the fear in his voice that I'm angry.

My mind is scattered as I make a wrong turn and get lost down the wrong hallway in this monster of a hospital. "I'm not mad," I lie through gritted teeth because, hell yes, I'm pissed but it's not at him. It's at my wife.

"She was just trying to help Zander," he says quietly, and my heart goes out to the kid. Kid? Shit. He's a man now. *When the fuck did that happen?* I'm still trying to wrap my head around the notion—around the fact I'm here for her to have our baby—but it's not lost on me Shane's trying to protect Rylee from my anger.

Even now, when I'm frazzled and lost in this goddamn hospital trying to get to her, it's impossible not to recognize the incredible job my wife has done to instill compassion for others in her boys.

Our baby's going to be one lucky kid to have her as a mom.

"Colton?" Shane's voice pulls me back from my thoughts just in time to prevent me from going the wrong way down a hallway.

Get a grip, Donavan. Pay attention. Get to Ry.

"Is he okay?" I finally digest his words from a minute ago about what Zander had said. My shoes squeak on the polished floor as I rush down the hallway and look for signs to direct me.

"I'm with him. Yes. But Ry was so upset and—"

"Look. I'll fix it somehow, okay?" I then pass what feels like the same exact place for a second time. I'm anxious. Worried. Need to get to Rylee and yet couldn't find my way out of a wet paper bag right now if I had to.

"There is no fixing it," he says with resignation.

"There is if we adopt him," I say off the cuff, distracted, overwhelmed, trying to get to Rylee, navigate this place, and carry a conversation that I shouldn't be having right now.

"Oh."

And then it hits me what I've said and who I've said it to. Fuck! Ry's concerns flood my head and yet I just went and opened by big fucking mouth and did exactly what she didn't want to do—hurt one of her boys. Let them think we'd pick one over the others.

"Shit!" I say through gritted teeth as I make myself stop and pinch the bridge of my nose. I need to figure out how to make this right. I've been there. Unwanted. Feeling slighted. Jealous. On the wrong end of the schoolyard pick. *Fix this, Donavan.* "That's not what I meant. I'm doing too many things at once: talking, walking, and trying to get to Ry. I suggested the idea just to fix the situation but we'd never really do it because there's no way we could just adopt one of you and not all of you. And social services—"

"Would never allow you to adopt all of us," he says, finishing my sentence for me. But then nothing else.

Silence hangs on the line as I grimace at what I just said. At talking without thinking. Fuck. Fuck. Fuck. Talk to me, Shane. *Cuz, dude, as much as I want to make sure this is right, I also have somewhere else I need to be like ten damn minutes ago.*

"Shane?"

"Of course. Makes sense," he says. And goddammit, I'm torn between making sure I believe he's not upset and getting to where I need to be. I look up and fucking kick myself when I see the nurses station to my left.

"I'm here. I gotta go. We'll talk later. I'll keep you up to date, yeah?"

"Yeah." I don't hear anything else because I hang up as I impatiently wait for the nurse to look up. And when she does I get the usual response: wide eyes, big gasp, flushed cheeks.

"Hi. Wh . . . How . . . What can I help you with?" she stutters as her hand automatically goes to pat down her hair in a move I've seen more times in my life than I care to count.

"Room number for Rylee Donavan, please." My smile is forced, my patience nil. Because now that I'm here I need to see her, touch her, know she's not in pain.

That's brilliant, Donavan. Labor. The word means it's not going to be easy. Pain is inevitable.

"Three eleven is the room, and you'll need this," she says as she pulls out a visitor's badge from a stack sitting on the ledge next to her. "What name do you want?" She winks. "Your secret is safe with me."

"Ace Thomas." The name is off my tongue without thought. *Where'd that come from?*

"Ace Thomas, it is," she says writing it out and handing me the badge. "Good luck, Mr. Donav—Thomas."

I flash her a smile and jog down the hall to where Sammy sits in a chair outside the door to her room. He lifts his eyes and locks them on mine. He knows I know, knows I'm pissed, and stiffens his spine.

"Her. Safety. Comes. First," I say through gritted teeth. "Always. Understood?"

The words he wants to say as my friend are written clearly in his eyes, but his obligation as my employee and lead security keep them from coming out of his mouth. "Understood."

It's all he says. All I need to hear from him. Discussion over. Point made.

I push through the door and into the room anxious about what awaits me. *No turning back now. This is real as real can be.*

Ry's back is to me and Dr. Steele is just walking out. She smiles when she sees me. "Everything looks good, Colton. Be prepared to be a daddy within the next twenty-four hours," she says, then shakes my hand.

"Colton!" Relief. I can hear it in her voice and breathe a little easier now that I'm here.

"I guess we didn't have time to repaint those toes," I say as I walk to her side of the bed and press a kiss to her lips. That's what I needed. A little bit of Ry to calm me.

"Or do other things," she murmurs with a smile.

"I got here as fast as I could."

"Ace Thomas, huh?" she says, her eyes flickering down to my nametag and then back to mine with amusement. "I seem to have heard that somewhere before."

"Hmm. I'm not sure what you're talking about." I feign ignorance.

"Just don't tell my husband you're here. He's got a mean right hook."

I laugh. *God, I fucking love this woman.* Framing her face with my hands, I take in the feel of her skin beneath mine and breathe in a huge sigh of relief. "You okay?" She nods her head, her eyes searching mine, and I know what she's looking for, knows I've connected the dots. "Yes, I'm mad at you . . ."

Furious. Livid.

But I love you more.

"Don't be mad at Sammy. I made him drive me," she says with a cringe, and I hold back the snort I want to give because Sammy's a badass motherfucker. I doubt she *made him* do anything but at the same time, I know how Rylee gets when it comes to her boys.

"Have you talked to Zander? I need to make sure he's okay."

The saint. In a moment that's all about her, she's thinking about them.

"Rylee," I say with a sigh but know she won't give up or relax until she knows they are okay. "I just talked to Shane."

"What did he say about Zander?"

"We talked. Shane's still there with him. I'm sure he's fine. Let's worry about—"

"No. He's not. He was scared and said some things that—"

"I'll call him, okay? Make sure he's all right. If I promise to do that, will you stop worrying about everyone else and start thinking about yourself right now?" Her huge violet eyes look up at me, searching to see if I'll really make sure, and when she likes what she sees, she worries her bottom lip with her teeth and nods reluctantly. "Good, because I wasn't taking no for an answer." I flash her what she calls my panty-dropping smile. She rolls her eyes.

"Did you forget that this is my show, Ace?" She laughs as she reaches out and fists a hand in my shirt to pull my lips back to hers for another kiss. By all means. Kiss away. "No need to give me that smile, considering I'm not wearing any panties to drop in the first place."

I laugh long and hard over that. The hospital gown, the monitors on her belly, the rubber gloves. They all scream sexy. *Not.* "So there's no chance—"

"No chance in hell," she says, pushing against my chest and as silly as it seems, this banter makes me feel a bit more relaxed about what it is that's about to happen to us.

"You in pain?" I ask, unsure exactly what to ask or do.

"Only when I have contractions," she says with a smirk. Smartass.

"So we sit and wait?"

"We sit and wait," she agrees. I link my hand with hers and sit in the chair beside her bed.

Hours pass.

Minutes tick. Seconds lag.

Anticipation riots. Boredom reins. Doubt lingers.

I'm excited. Can't wait to meet this little person.

Contractions come.

What am I doing? Fuck. Fuck. Fuck. I'm not ready to be a dad yet.

Contractions go.

Suck it up.

I'm brash and moody and selfish and I say *fuck* way too much.

Quit being such a pussy.

Contractions come.

I've never changed a diaper. Never even held a newborn. *God, what am I doing?* I'm completely clueless. Inept. How could I think I could do this?

Contractions go.

It's a little too fucking late to turn back now, Donavan.

Panic claws at my throat. Fear tightens around my windpipe. I stand, pace the room to abate my nerves while Ry sleeps.

Breathe, Donavan. Fucking breathe. Ry's the one in labor and you're the one nervous? Think of her. Worry about her.

The after part you're worried about will just happen.

Relax.

Chill the fuck out.

I call Shane to eat up time. Try to right my wrongs and make sure he's cool. Make sure Zander's better. Hang up. Send Sammy to get some decent coffee downstairs. Wait some more.

I look out the window to the city beyond just as night begins to eat the daylight. Deep breath in. Exhale all the bullshit out. I glance up, surprised to see Ry awake in the window's reflection.

Our eyes meet as a sleepy smile forms on her lips and my world clicks back into its place. How could I doubt this? Our connection? Our love? Our future? She's my Midas. Everything she's ever touched in my life has been made better, fucking golden, including me as a man.

I turn back around. Ready to do this.

Wheels on the track.

Hands on the wheel.

It's time to add our first memory to the frame.

Chapter Nineteen

Rylee

"You're doing great, baby," Colton murmurs in my ear. My head's back on the pillow, eyes closed. He brushes my hair from my forehead, kisses the top of my hand clasped in his.

"I'm tired," I whisper, my body feeling exhaustion like I've never felt before. Bone-deep. Dead-tired. And yet there is this underlying current like a livewire buzzing through me. Fueling me.

"I know, but you're almost there," he says, words laced with encouragement. He feels helpless. I know he does. My big bad husband who can't rush in to save the day for me. Who can't do anything really but hold my hand.

I open my eyes and meet his green ones. "Are you okay?" I ask, noting the guarded emotion in his eyes and figuring he's a little freaked out.

"Shush. I'm fine. Don't worry about me. Let's meet BIRT," he says with a reassuring smile that gives me just what I need.

A laugh. A moment to relax, albeit brief. This man who is so full of contradictions and owns every piece of my heart. "You're relentless."

"And you're beautiful."

Tears well. I'm sure it's the hormones surging through my body or just the connection I feel with him right now in the midst of bringing this life we've created into the world, but all of a sudden the tears are there. He reaches out, thumbs on my cheeks, and holds my face in his hands, shaking his head very slowly.

"Thank you," he says. That shy smile I love ghosts his lips as his emerald eyes swell with unfathomable emotion. And I'm not sure what it is he's thanking me for—those simple words could mean so many things—so I just nod my head ever so subtly because he has no idea how much those two words and the intention behind them mean to me.

"Another contraction is coming, Rylee. I need you to be strong. A couple more pushes and I think we are going to meet your new little miracle," Dr. Steele says, interrupting the moment and reinvigorating my depleted energy.

"Okay." I nod my head as Colton's hand squeezes mine.

"Give me a good push," she says.

A deep breath in. My whole body taut as I hold my breath and push. Dizziness hits as the ten-second count slowly comes to an end. The world fading to black as every part of my body is exhausted.

"There's the head," she says, pulling me from the darkness and making this all more real, more urgent than I ever could have imagined. "Lots of dark hair."

And when I open my eyes, Colton has shifted so he can look down to see the baby. His expression when he looks back at me? Fear and inexplicable emotion in his tear-filled eyes. His jaw is slack and awe is written all over his face. Our connection is brief but intense before the mesmerizing sight of our baby pulls his eyes away from mine once again.

And as envious as I am that he gets to see our miracle first, I also know I'll never forget his expression. The pride and astonishment etched in the lines of his face have forever imprinted in the space of my heart.

Chapter Twenty

Colton

My hand is squeezed in a goddamn vise-like grip.

My heart is too but for a completely different reason.

The sight in front of me. Incredible. Indescribable. Grounding in a way I never thought possible.

"This is the hard one, Ry. Last push and you're done," Dr. Steele says, as she looks up at her and then back down to where my eyes are glued. "And go."

My hand is squeezed. Rylee's moan fills the room. Her body tenses. "*Spiderman. Batman. Superman. Ironman.*" The words come from out of nowhere. I'm not even sure if I whisper them aloud or just in my head. But the only other thought that flickers is that they belong here.

Full circles.

And then all thoughts are lost. Emotion rules. Pride swells. A tiny pair of shoulders emerge followed quickly by a little body.

Snapshots of time pass. Seconds that feel like hours.

My breath is stolen. Hijacked. Robbed. And so is my goddamn heart because there's no other way to describe what I feel as Dr. Steele says, "Congratulations, it's a boy!"

"Oh shit." My whole world picks up, moves, flips upside down, and reverses on its axis. And I couldn't be happier about it.

Soft cries. Dark hair. Cutting the cord. A blur of disbelief as my eyes lock on the baby. My son.

Holy motherfucking shit.

My son.

I'm a dad.

The moment hits me like a goddamn sucker punch—every part of me reacting to the impact—as Dr. Steele places him on Rylee's belly. Nurses wipe him off as Ry's sobs fill the room when she gets to see him for the first time.

I'm looking at fingers and toes and ears and eyes and trying to figure out how this completely perfect little person is a part of me.

How is it even possible?

Swimming in emotion, I lean down and press a kiss to Rylee's forehead. Her eyes are as focused as mine on our son. "I love you," I murmur with my lips still pressed against her skin.

His crying stops instantly the minute Ry cradles him in her arms. *He knows.* How simple is that? And if I thought I was sucker-punched before, the sight of her holding our son is the knockout punch. I'm looking down at his little face and hers next to each other, and shit I never expected to feel in my life surges through me, wraps around my heart, and fills it in a way I never thought was possible.

My whole fucking world.

My Rylee. My son. My everything.

"He's beautiful," she says, awe in her voice and tears sliding down her cheeks. She presses a kiss to the top of his head, and for some reason the visual hits me hard.

The future flashes: first steps, skinned knees, first homerun, first kiss, first love.

Tears sting. My chest constricts. All I can think is that this little boy may get kissed by a lot of women during his lifetime but this first kiss is the most important.

He's taken from her. Cries fill the room. He's measured and weighed. Tested and looked over. I can't take my eyes off him for a single second.

I glance back and find Ry. Her eyes match mine—both so overwhelmed with everything that we don't have words. I feel like such a sap—the tears in my eyes, the inability to speak—like I should be the arrogant bastard I normally am. It seems even assholes like me have a soft spot. Yeah. Ry's always been that to me, but I have a feeling I just found another that aces all the rest.

If it's in the cards.

My heart stumbles in my chest. The memory flickers and dies in seconds. One I can't place, can't remember, and yet somehow know it means something. And I don't give it a second thought when the nurse holds him out to me, wrapped tightly in a blanket.

I freeze. Like arctic-chill freeze because all of the sudden I'm afraid I'm going to hurt him. Thank fuck the nurse sees my reaction because she shows me how to hold him and then places him in my arms.

And then he looks up. And this time I freeze for a completely different reason.

I'm mesmerized, lost, and found again. By bright blue eyes, little lips, and a soft cry. By dark hair and perfect ears. By his untouched innocence, unconditional trust, and love: all three given without asking the first time I look into his eyes.

I go to speak. To reassure my son I won't let him down. I open my mouth. I close it. I can't lie to him right off the bat. Can't tell him that when I know I'm going to screw up sometimes.

But I sure as fuck am going to do everything in my power to be what he needs.

Chapter Twenty-One

Rylee

Pinch me.

This can't be real. This beautiful baby boy in my arms can't possibly be mine.

But if this is a dream it's so incredibly real I never want to wake from it. Sure my body is exhausted, and despite my legs still being slightly numb, I ache all over the place. But the one ache I don't think will ever go away is the one in my chest from my heart overflowing with love.

I can't stop looking at him as he sleeps soundly against my chest. The nurses suggested putting him in his bassinet but I can't bear to part with him just yet. I've waited way too long for this moment. I'm fixated on every single thing about him and can't get over how much he looks like what I think Colton would have looked like as a baby.

When I look across the dimly lit room toward Colton, his phone is up and he is taking another picture in an endless line of photos of us. It's adorable how he wants to document every moment. His need for his son to have tangible memories of being a baby since he has absolutely none is both moving and bittersweet.

I smile softly as the flash goes off and then raise my eyebrows and wait for him to lower the phone. When he does, our gazes meet, and there's the slightest flicker of something I can't quite read. He blinks it away as quickly as it comes and grants me an exhausted smile in exchange.

"Is he sleeping?" he asks, leaning forward so he can see for himself.

"No. Do you want to hold him?" I ask, knowing damn well I don't want to give him up, and yet also feel I've been hogging him. It's only been two hours since we moved into the maternity suite and between trying to get the baby to latch on and the nurses coming in and out constantly, Colton hasn't had another chance to hold him.

"No." He shakes his head. "Leave him be." He stands and comes to sit on the edge of my bed and leans forward to press a gentle kiss to our son's head before granting me one as well. Our lips linger momentarily before he leans back, a large sigh falling as he shakes his head again. I get it though, because I keep shaking mine too, trying to wrap my head around the fact the one thing I never thought I'd ever get to experience has just happened.

And I was able to share it with him.

"Well, I guess I can't stall any longer on the name thing unless we want to make BIRT the official one on the birth certificate."

"No," I whisper, harshly contradicting the smile on my lips. "So we're really going to say our first choice at the same time and go that route?" The whole idea makes me nervous. And I hate that such a lasting, important decision is going to be made on the fly.

"Yep. Perfect plan."

"No." He's going to give me hives if he keeps this up. And he knows it. I can see it in the little smirk on his face and gleam in his eyes. Damn, Donavan.

"Or we could just call him Ace Thomas Donavan and call it a day," he murmurs, head cocked to the side, lips pursed as he waits for my reaction. My eyes flicker down to his visitor's badge, where the two names are spelled out, and for a moment I'm hit with utter clarity amidst the haze of drugs and fog of fatigue.

Ace Thomas.

Looking down at my sweet baby boy, I roll the name on my tongue as it repeats over and over in my mind. It's nowhere close to the unique and trendy names I'd narrowed down on my numerous lists, and yet as I stare at his tiny fingers curled around my pinkie, I can't believe I didn't think of the name myself because it couldn't be more perfect.

Those two names hold so much significance in our relationship so why not put them together? My nickname for Colton and his endless attempts to know what ACE stood for. Allowing my son to have a part of my identity by giving him my family's last name as his middle name. Our first date at the carnival when Colton used the name as his alias and confessed he used it because he wanted me all to himself. And of course, Colton's own definition of the acronym that fits so poignantly now: A chance encounter.

And look what we have now as a result of that chance encounter.

"Ace Thomas," I murmur softly, liking the sound of it more and more with each passing second.

"I had other names in mind but as I was sitting watching you sleep between contractions, I couldn't get it out of my head. It fits, doesn't it?"

"It does," I say hesitantly. When I look from our son to Colton and then back to our son, I know it makes absolute perfect sense. "Hey Ace," I say to the snuggling baby in my arms. My heart skips a beat as I feel like all the stars have aligned and our little world we've created becomes complete.

The soft suction of his mouth on my breast is strangely the most comforting feeling I've ever experienced. Almost as if my body knows this was meant to be. And as I look down at him it hits me that this little being depends on Colton and me for absolutely everything. It's a humbling and overwhelming feeling, but one that warms me completely.

"Are you two going to catch any sleep?" the nurse asks as she checks my vitals yet again on what feels like the ever-constant rotation through our room. And it always seems like the interruption is immediately after I fall asleep.

"We're trying to," I murmur softly as I look down at Ace as he eats.

"I know it's hard with nurses coming in and out constantly but you should consider putting him in the nursery so you can get some sleep."

"Absolutely not." Colton's voice is resolute when he speaks from the recliner in the corner of the room making both the nurse and my head turn to look at him. "There's a reason Sammy's sitting outside on a chair. The last thing we need is paparazzi snapping pictures of him, selling it to the highest bidder, and then plastering it all over the place. No. End of discussion."

I stare at him, eyes blinking over and over as I come to terms with what he's just said. After the clusterfuck of the past month with the media's intrusion on our lives, how could I be so ensconced in our little bubble that the thought never crossed my mind? That people will be clamoring to get pictures of Ace to sell and make money from?

"He's right," I say, caught off guard as I look at the nurse staring at us like we're crazy.

"Okay," she says with a sympathetic smile, "if you change your mind, let me know. We do deal with this fear quite a lot here so I assure you we have safety measures in effect to prevent that from happening. If you end up needing some sleep, just buzz me at the nurses station."

"Thanks," Colton says, the muscle in his jaw clenching and unclenching as he stares at her.

She finishes checking my vitals and then reaches to check Ace out since he's fallen asleep and is no longer latched on. She looks at her temporal thermometer and frowns some. "His body temp is a little cold. It's normal for a newborn to have trouble keeping their body heat but let's help him a bit and get him skin on skin with you." She starts unbundling him and taking his white T-shirt off so I'm left with a tiny ball of pink who's dwarfed by the white diaper.

I know this is normal but it's a little different when it's your baby. She hands Ace to me, lifts down the shoulder of my hospital gown so I can slide Ace inside, and his smooth skin is resting against my bare chest.

"We'll let him be like this for a bit and see if that helps or else we'll have to bring a warmer in, okay?"

"Okay," I say as she collects her things. I don't even pay attention because the feeling of him against me is all-consuming. He tries to suckle my collarbone and I laugh quietly at the sensation and how very surreal this feels.

When I look up, Colton's eyes are locked onto the two of us, expression completely stoic. "What are you thinking about?" I ask, knowing damn well it could be a loaded question but needing to ask it nonetheless.

"Nothing. Everything." He shrugs. "Everything has changed and yet nothing is different. I don't know how to explain it."

I nod my head ever so slowly understanding and not understanding what he's saying and needing so much more of an explanation from him but having a feeling I'm not going to get one. Ace moves and I'm drawn back to watch him for a bit as I fight the exhaustion and the fear of hurting him if I fall asleep while he's lying on my chest.

"I feel like I'm hogging him," I murmur, my lips kissing the crown of his head, reveling in that scent of a newborn baby, before looking over to Colton as I scrunch my nose up in an apology.

"No. You're good," he says with a gesture to reinforce his words before he leans back in his reclining chair and closes his eyes, effectively changing the subject.

"You sure you don't want to hold him?"

"No," he says, eyes still closed. "The nurse said he needs skin to skin with you to help his body temperature."

"He can be skin to skin with you and get the same thing," I explain, my tired mind trying to understand how on earth Colton could say no when I don't feel like I ever want to let him go.

"No. No. I'm okay." He rejects the idea quickly with eyes still closed and arms crossing over his chest.

He's afraid of Ace. Big man. Teeny baby. Lack of experience. Fears of inadequacy. The notion flickers and fades through my mind: his history, his staunch refusal, the way he's seemed busy when I've needed him to hold Ace, add validation to my assumption.

I'm scared. Colton's confession from the 'I'm game' float through my mind.

"He needs you too," I whisper softly, my voice breaking with enough emotion to cause his head to lift so our eyes meet. "Your son needs you too, Colton."

"I know," he says with a slow nod of his head. And even though there is guarded trepidation in his eyes, I don't back down this time from our visual connection. Instead I let my eyes ask him everything I can't say aloud or push him on further. "You two look so peaceful and perfect together. I just don't want to disturb you."

And as much as I know he's being honest in his response, I also know he's using it to distract me from delving deeper into his nonchalance.

Talk to me, Colton. Tell me what's going on in that wonderful, complicated, scarred, scared, beautiful mind of yours.

I want to reassure him, tell him he's not going to drop Ace, harm him, or taint his innocence, and yet I don't think there is anything I can say that will lessen his unease.

Give him time, Rylee.

Chapter Twenty-Two

Colton

This can't be real. I know it can't be.

She's dead.

Kelly proved it to me. So why is she calling to me from inside that *room? The one that fills me with such a vile, visceral reaction. Bile's in my throat. My mouth feels like the morning after I've drunk a fifth of Jack. My stomach a bath of acid.*

Run, Colton. *Put one foot in front of the fucking other and escape while you can.*

"Colty, Colty. Sweet little Colty," she says in a singsong voice. One I've never heard her use before. It calls to me. Draws me in. Makes me want to see and fear to know.

Goddamn ghosts. Even sound asleep they come back to haunt me.

I clear the doorway, the smell of mildew and must hits my nose and pulls the nightmares I thought were dead and gone from my mind. The problem: they're not nightmares. They were reality. My reality.

And when I look up I'm knocked back a step to see the woman in the rocking chair. I know her but don't remember her looking like this at all: dark hair pulled back, a pink tank top on, and the softest expression on her face as she looks down at the baby cradled in her arms. She's sitting in the stream of moonlight, a smile on her face, and the baby's hand is wrapped around one of her fingers.

"Colty, Colty. Sweet little Colty," she sings again and all I can do is blink and wonder if what I'm seeing is really real, if it really happened, or is just a figment of my imagination.

That's not me. Can't be.

This is me.

I pat my chest. See the glint of my wedding ring against the light. And yet I can't help but stare at my mother looking so real and normal and . . . nice. *Not the strung-out, crazy-haired, high monster who used to trick me, trade me, and starve me for her own benefit.*

"Stop calling him that. He'll get a complex." A deep voice to my right startles me. I catch a glimpse of the man in the shadows: tall, broad-shouldered, dark hair, jeans hanging low on a shirtless torso.

But I can't see his face.

My heart races. Is it my dad or the monster?

Is he one and the same?

The bile comes up—fast and furious—and I throw up all over the carpet as the thought rips me apart in a way I never thought possible. Was the monster my dad?

I throw up again. My body rejecting the idea over and over, dry heaves of disbelief, but no one in the room moves or notices me.

It's a dream, Colton. *A goddamn fucking dream. It's not real. It is not.*

And yet when I look up again, the man coming out of the shadows seems different, more familiar than moments ago, but it's my mother's voice that whips my head her way.

"Acey, Acey. Sweet little Acey."

No! *I scream but no sound comes out as she looks up at me. Her eyes are bloodshot and ragged now. Her mouth painted red like a twisted clown. She starts to lift the baby,* my son, *up and out to the man in the room.*

"No!" I yell again. I can't move, can't save him. My feet are stuck to the floor. The darkness of the room is slowly swallowing me whole.

"Yes," the man growls as his meaty fingers reach out to take Ace from her.

The hands. Those hands. *The ones that fill my fucking nightmares. The ones that stained my soul.*

I fight against the invisible hands holding me in place. Need to get to him. Have to save him.

And then he steps out of the darkness and into the light. My shout fills the room and hurts my ears. But no one looks. No one stops. It's the monster from my childhood's life taking my son, but he has my face.

My face.

My hands.

I'm going to abuse my son.

Spiderman. Batman. Superman. Ironman.

I'm shocked awake from my struggle when my ass hits the floor as I fall out of the hospital recliner.

I lie where I am for a few seconds in the room's silence. My breathing harsh. My mind fucked. My heart racing out of control.

Fucking Christ.

I close my eyes and let my head fall back onto the floor. My body tense, mind reeling. Thoughts, images, emotions crash together like the rubber debris scattered on the topside of the track: always where you're afraid to touch them for fear you'll spin out of control.

But this time I need to touch them. Need to know what has scared the fuck out of me more than the normal nightmare.

It doesn't matter because I'm already spun. Crazed. There's only one thing I remember and it's the one I wish I could forget: I'm the one who hurt Ace.

Or rather, I'm the one who will hurt Ace.

Get a fucking grip, Donavan.

Shake it off.

It was just a dream.

Then why does the fear feel more real than anything I've ever felt before in my life?

Chapter Twenty-Three

Rylee

"Can you take him for a second?" I ask Colton. He's busy on his iPad in the corner of the hospital room. "I want to brush my teeth before everyone gets here."

Colton's eyes flicker over to me and then to the bassinet the nurse moved across the room and out of the way beyond my reach. I wince as I try to scoot up a little, and he slowly gets up and approaches the bed. I'm not one for games but I know the longer Colton fears Ace, the harder this transition of having a child will be for him. And while my body aches all over, the dramatic grimace on my face was for good measure.

He reaches out hesitantly and I place Ace in the cradle of his arms. I hear him suck in a breath.

"Thanks. I'll be just a sec," I say as I push myself off the bed and slowly make my way to the sink area. I take my time, brushing my hair and teeth, and apply a little makeup while watching father and son out of the corner of my eye.

Colton stands there looking down at Ace, his features softening as he takes in his spitting image and I wonder what's going through his head. Is the connection stronger than the fear or is he still just trying to come to terms with this life-changing moment?

I glance in the mirror's reflection to see Colton slowly sit down with Ace cradled in his arms, and I swear to God my heart can't swell any more with love at the sight of the two of them together. And he's completely focused on Ace so I'm afforded the moment to watch the two of them together unhindered.

There must be something about the sight that makes my mind recall what I thought I heard him say yesterday. When I was slowly blacking out in one of my final pushes, I thought I heard Colton quietly say the names of his beloved superheroes.

The longer I watch this awkward dance between new father and baby, I know he did. But the question is *why?*

Moving into the room, I purposefully sit back on the bed without taking Ace from him. And the funny thing is, he's so absorbed in our son, he doesn't notice.

"Why did you say the superheroes before he was born?" I ask softly. He may be looking down, but I can see his body tense and know there's a reason behind it.

Silence stretches and either he didn't hear me, or he doesn't want to answer. Regardless, he's still holding Ace and that's what matters. I lay my head back and just as I close my eyes he speaks.

"Because I figured if I called to them then, he might never have to call to them himself. And I wanted to welcome our baby into the world with the strength of those who gave me hope—kept me alive—on his side."

His words, the raw grit in his tone, tell me he still has so many fears I don't know about yet. When I open my eyes to meet his, I hate the lingering shadow of a past I thought we had put behind us. It hasn't been there in so very long.

"Colton . . ." His name is a plea, an apology, an endearment simultaneously, and before I can say another thing, there is a knock at the maternity suite's door and the moment is gone.

"Come in," I say.

Within seconds the room is a whirlwind of sound, people, balloons, and oohs and aahs as our family and friends descend upon us.

"Let me see my grandbaby," Colton's mom, Dorothea, says as she leads the charge into the room, her hands outstretched and smile wide as she reaches out to take Ace from her son.

"You'd think you were royalty or something with all the press outside," Haddie says above the fray, and even though I can't see her yet, I can hear her.

I look over and meet Colton's glance, and give him a nod in acknowledgement. He was right in making the call to keep the boys away from here and out of paparazzi's lenses' crosshairs. And God yes, I want to see them all. Look Zander in the eye to really make sure he's okay like he told me he was on the phone, and thank Shane for staying with him last night. Have them come here to the hospital—a place most of them still associate with where they had to lie to doctors about why they were hurt—and see it's not always a bad place. So they could meet the newest brother in their family, and see for themselves that I'm perfectly fine.

The last thing I want to happen though is to deliberately put them in the public eye. That should be avoided for Zander at all costs. Besides, Teddy might have turned a blind eye to my visit to The House and interference in Zander's visitation there yesterday so the board doesn't know, but I don't think he'd be able to do the same if pictures of the boys at the hospital were plastered on the Internet.

"Oh my God, he's adorable," Dorothea says, pulling me from my thoughts. I glance to Colton and back to where Andy, my mom, and dad gather around her as she holds the newest member of the family. I watch them all for a second, enamored by how my always-regal mother-in-law has been reduced to a bunch of expressions and sounds as she revels in her first moments as a grandmother.

"We figured we'd all bombard you at once so you could get this all over with in one shot," Quinlan says as she leans forward and gives me a tight hug. And for some reason—probably the hormones running in overdrive right now—I hold on a little longer than necessary and just breathe her in.

"Thanks," I say as she pulls back and looks at me closely.

"You doing okay?" she asks, prompting a nod from me as emotion forms into a lump in my throat and lodges the words there.

"Yeah," I say with a soft smile. "I'm just tired." She reaches out and squeezes my hands, my thumb running over the tiny pink heart tattooed on the inside of her wrist.

"Congrats!" Her rockstar boyfriend Hawke says from behind her before he steps forward and presses a kiss to the top of my head. "We can't wait to spoil him rotten."

"Don't get him started," Quin says with a roll of her eyes. "He already has a mini guitar for him. And microphone. And—" Hawke's hand covers her mouth in a mock attempt to shut her up and save him the embarrassment, but I think it's a little too late.

"Outta the way." I know there's no ignoring that voice nor do I want to. "I need to see my girl."

Hawke and Quin step back so Haddie can barrel through and launch herself at me. Within seconds I find myself squeezed so tight I can barely breathe.

"You're a mom," she says into my ear with such love and affection that tears sting the backs of my eyes. I don't care either because we've been through a lifetime of ups and downs together so I love being able to experience this up with her. "Do you know how hard it is for me not to push the grandparents away so I can hog him all to myself?"

"I think you'll lose that fight," I say, pulling back and looking at the smile on her face and the tears in her eyes.

"And Ace, huh?" she says with a quirk of her eyebrows, earning her a smirk of mine in return, considering she is the one who started the whole acronym with me way back when.

"What am I, chopped liver?" Becks asks as he squeezes into the room and along the wall toward me, since everyone else is focused on where my mom is now holding Ace at the foot of the bed.

"No . . . but I'd easily trade you for the warm chocolate chip cookie and milk this hospital gives you," I tease, causing him to laugh and shake his head.

"I see how you are, Donavan," he says as he leans in and presses a kiss to my cheek. "You did good, Ry. We're so damn happy for you."

"Thanks, Becks." My God. Where are all the emotion and tears coming from right now? You'd think things were sad the way I'm leaking like a faucet instead of being the exact opposite: perfect.

"And of course he looks just like his Uncle Becks. Damn handsome." Haddie rolls her eyes beside him and then gives him the "I'm innocent" face when he looks at her and that makes me laugh.

"Nope. I'm pretty sure his good looks take after his Uncle Tanner," my brother says, stepping beside Becks and shaking his hand with a good-natured squeeze, kissing Haddie on the cheek in greeting before looking at me. "Hey Bubs. How're you handling all of this?"

"It's indescribable," I say softly because there really are no words to accurately describe the feelings, emotions, and sensations that are a constant high in my body and mind right now.

"You look gorgeous." I roll my eyes at the comment. "And he definitely does take after me."

"Bullshit, Thomas," Colton says, as he steps to the other side of the bed and reaches out to shake his hand. "I get to claim this one."

Tanner gives him the hands up motion like it's no contest and Colton laughs. Colton glances down at me and squeezes my hand. I can see the pride in his eyes over Ace and that gives me more hope than I thought I was even looking for that he'll overcome his fear. Look at what those few moments of holding Ace did already.

"Where's your better half?" I ask my brother.

"She had an event to work and is super bummed but she's going to try to drive up tomorrow to meet him." He leans in and gives me a hug that brims with love and whispers in my ear, "Mom's in fricking heaven having a new little baby to spoil. She's already telling Dad she's not sure how she's going to live so far away from him, so be prepared for her wanting to spend the night a lot."

"Thanks for the warning, but I might just need the help."

"Ha. You needing it and accepting it are two different things," he says with a doubtful lift of his eyebrows. He's so very right but I can't let him know that. I glance over to where Ace is nestled gently in my mother's arms and the need to hold him is so strong right now I have to tell myself he's okay. And of course he is. I trust every single person in this room but when you have something be a part of you for nearly nine months, it's a little hard to not need that connection.

My eyes shift to the sight of Andy and Colton in a quick but heartfelt embrace. I watch as Andy steps back, one hand still on the side of Colton's cheek, and his eyes searching his son's in that way he always does to make sure he's okay. It's the look of unconditional love, and I hope that when people watch me interact with Ace, they see the same thing.

Their connection captivates me. As I watch Colton accept love from his dad, my concern over Colton's lack of engagement dissipates. By demonstration, Andy has given Colton all the tools he needs to know how to be a good father. My fears fade as a vivid picture forms in my head of how Colton will love Ace: absolute, unequivocal devotion.

Just as he has loved me.

Andy glances my way. "And there's the woman of the hour!" His voice booms through the room and then he immediately winces when he realizes how loud he was.

"Andy . . ."

He swoops down and gathers me up in one of his bear hugs you can usually feel all the way to your toes, but at least he's a little gentler this time around. "Rylee-girl, you've made me so damn happy. All over again. You are such a blessing to this family," he says. He pulls back and does the same thing I was just admiring with Colton to me—hand on my cheek, eyes searching mine—and I feel blessed to be completely loved by my in-laws.

"You good?" he asks, eyes double-checking to make sure the smile on my face is real.

"I'm incredible," I whisper back with the smile spreading on my lips. How lucky was Colton to have sat on this amazing man's doorstep? A patient man capable of teaching him what it means to love so completely. For that, I will forever be grateful to him. "Congratulations, Grandpa."

He throws his head back and laughs that full-body laugh of his that reminds me so much of Colton's, even though he is adopted, that I squeeze his hands and wonder if Ace will have the same mannerism when he laughs like that when he's older.

"Move out of the way, Andy, I need to hug this new momma who just gave me my first grandchild," Dorothea says. She all but pushes her husband out of the way so she can hold my cheeks in her hands and kiss both of them.

"Hi." Surprise flickers through me when I see tears in her eyes.

"Thank you," she whispers, her usually resonating voice unsteady and laden with emotion. "He's absolutely adorable. You must be over the moon."

"No need to thank me—"

"Yes, there is," she says with a nod of her head to tell me not to argue. I'm smart enough to know by now when to pick my battles with her and this is not one of them. She leans in and gives me what feels like the hundredth hug in as many seconds before standing back with a soft smile on her lips and adoration in her eyes.

My gaze shifts over her shoulder to my dad. I'll never forget the look on his face: awe, pride—discomfort at being packed like sardines in the room—but more than anything, love.

"Hi, sweetie." He steps forward and presses a kiss to my head. But I don't let him off that easily because I wrap my arms around him and hug him tight.

"Hiya, Daddy. What do you think?"

"I think I couldn't be more proud of you and in love with him and I haven't even gotten to hold him yet," he says with a laugh. "You're going to be a fantastic mother."

And this time I don't fight the tears but let one slip over and down my cheek, because that's a huge compliment coming from a man I've idolized my whole life.

"Your turn," my mom says, softly nudging my dad from the side as she holds out Ace for him to take for the first time. I watch the transition from one of my parents to the other and instantly know I'm going to enjoy watching them be grandparents to my son. And not that Dorothea and Andy won't either, but it's *my* parents, so the notion hits home a little more, knowing the same arms that rocked me as a newborn are going to rock him too.

I look to the right and notice Colton also watching them and realize he will never be able to have that same thought, and a part of me hurts for him because of it. And for the first time, I truly understand his hesitation, feeling like he's on the outside here because not a single person in this room shares the same blood running through them with him like I do. It's a humbling thought that opens my eyes all at the same time.

My dad looks up from Ace in his arms and asks Colton something, so my mom's attention shifts to me. "Hey baby girl," she says as she sits on the edge of the bed and reaches out with her fingers to move the strands of hair from my face. "You look tired. You in a lot of pain?"

"Just sore, but the pain was definitely worth it," I say as she leans forward and presses a kiss to my forehead.

"Yes, he is most definitely worth it. You two sure know how to make a beautiful baby."

"It's in the genes," I say.

The conversation continues on around us as my mom asks me to retell everything I've already told her about on the phone: how my water broke, the labor, how Ace is eating, about his health, about my recovery. At some point I scoot over and she sits in the bed beside me. I put my head on her shoulder, and she plays with my hair like she used to when I was a kid and was sick. It's comforting and soothing and just the right person I need right now to bridge that gap for me from pregnant to now being a mother. She knows I don't need words, just her silent support, and it means the world to me as I look around this room crammed full of our friends and family.

There's barely any room for anyone to move and everyone is watching Ace get passed from person to person and complimenting on what an easy baby he is to not be scared by all of this. And suddenly I'm overwhelmed with the thought that as many heartbreaking lows as I've been through trying to have a baby, it couldn't have turned out more perfectly.

My heart is absolutely the fullest it has ever been in my life.

Time passes, the chatter subsides, and at some point Ace begins to cry. My body reacts to the sound of him. Panic sets in as Tanner tries to soothe him by bringing him up to his shoulder. And it's not that I don't want my brother to hold him but rather I *need* to hold him more. My body vibrates to hold my son again with a strange new mix of maternal instinct and hysteria.

"I can take him, Tanner," I say, trying to subtly let him know.

"I can handle it, Ry," he says. As I meet Haddie's eyes she knows I'm starting to freak out.

"Tanner," my mom's voice rings above the chatter in a warning, "we've got a new momma here who is a bit overwhelmed by all of us swooping in on her at once. She hasn't held Ace in a bit, and I'm sure she's getting a little frantic, so why don't you hand him over?" And even though I can't see her face, I know the exact look she gives him from my own experience.

He responds immediately but by the time he gets Ace to me I'm sweating and heading toward a full-blown panic attack. "Here you go," Tanner says as he slips him into my arms and plants a kiss on both of our heads. "He really is beautiful."

And I can breathe again. He's crying and I have no clue if it's because of all of the stimuli or if he's actually hungry, but I don't care because he's back in my arms. I look up to find Colton through the crowd of people, and he can tell I'm flustered and overwhelmed. When he mouths *I love you*, it puts a little more right in my world.

"Okay, guys," he says after winking at me, "it's feeding time and not for me." Laughter rings through the room. "Thanks for coming to meet Ace, but it's time to say goodbye and head out."

The room explodes in a hurried frenzy of hugs and congratulations and promises to stop by the house later in the week or phone calls to check in before Colton ushers them all out. The women linger a little longer, asking the questions they couldn't with the guys around before they begrudgingly leave the room with just my mom left.

"Thank you," I whisper to her with a sigh as I unbutton my hospital gown and let Ace latch on. That instant surge of calming hits me. *All better*.

"It may have been a long time ago for me, but I remember that feeling of panic and *give me my baby back* and being overwhelmed."

"You've got that right," I murmur, both of our heads angled downward as we watch Ace fall into bliss.

"Just remember that your hormones are going to be out of whack for a while so expect the sudden hot flashes and mood swings—"

"Great," I say with a laugh.

"How's Colton doing with all of this?" she asks.

"He's fine," I say hesitantly, and I'm not sure if I'm trying to fool her or want her to delve deeper into my comment. But being my mother, I'm pretty sure it's the latter.

"Fine can mean a lot of things," she murmurs as she leans her head on top of my head resting on her shoulder.

I'm quiet for a few moments. As involved in our lives as our families are, I usually don't relay the details of every issue. Part of me feels kind of alone right now. Part of me also needs the reassurance that what I think I should do about it is the right thing.

"Fine as in, he's present, but I know he's scared for so many reasons. Afraid to do too much, not enough, to drop him, that he might not connect with him, that he might be like his parents . . . I don't know." So much for keeping my thoughts private. But at least I've said them to the one person I know won't judge me and won't repeat them elsewhere. Thank God for our mother-daughter bond.

"Men are fickle creatures," she murmurs. "Of course he has fears. And his are probably a little more justified after all he's been through. Give him time. He looks at his hands and sees how big they are against Ace's head and thinks how he might accidentally hurt him somehow." I murmur a sound of understanding. The soothing feeling of Ace nursing and my lack of sleep, cause my exhaustion to catch up with me. "Your body was made to do this, to be this . . . It has gone through all sorts of changes over the past nine months. Plus you've raised the boys so you're more comfortable with kids than he is."

"True," I say softly.

"This is all new to him. A shock to the way he's lived his life. The one thing he never wanted or expected until he met you. Men have a hard time adjusting to change when they have no control over it. He'll come around, sweetie. He has no choice."

But he does, I think to myself. I know the old Colton who used to close himself off with impenetrable steel walls. He wouldn't do that to his son, though. There's no way he would. Because that would make him too much like his birth parents.

"I know. I just don't want him to pull away."

"He might for a bit, but here's the thing, Rylee: the connection between you and Ace, and Colton and Ace is completely different. Perfect example is what just happened. You don't want to part from Ace. He's the air you breathe right now. It's rarely the same for men."

"I never thought of it that way."

"I know the idea of having to be apart from him causes your heart to race. And if you had to, you wouldn't give a second thought to driving onto sidewalks, over people if need be, to get home to him as quick as you can. That's normal," she says with a chuckle. "I used to feel the same way with you guys. I'd need a break . . . but the minute I had it I needed to be with you as soon as possible. But for Colton? It's a different type of feeling for him. There's this huge change in his life right now. A bonus, yes, but at the same time it's scary as hell for him. Not to mention he worries he's being replaced in your life by the one man that's probably more handsome than he is."

I snort a laugh at the comment but her words of wisdom hit home more than I thought they would. "Thanks, Mom. You always know what to say."

"Hardly, but thank you."

The door to the room opens with perfect timing and Colton walks in at the same time my mom rises from beside me on the bed. "There's my cue," she says as she leans over and presses another kiss to Ace's head before looking up into my eyes. "I'm always here for you. Always. Any time."

"Thank you. I love you."

"Love you too," she says as she gives Ace one last glance and turns to face Colton. "I'll leave you with your family now, Colton. Take good care of my babies." She steps forward and gives him a long hug before kissing his cheek.

"I will. Let me walk you out."

They leave the room and the comforting silence surrounds Ace and me once again.

Chapter Twenty-Four

Rylee

I'm switching Ace from my left side to my right side when the door swings open into the room. "Thanks for walking her out," I say distractedly. When Colton says nothing back I look up and let out a little yelp at the man standing near the foot of the bed.

"I'm sorry. You scared me." I do a double take and notice the blue scrubs, the top of a surgical cap covering his hair as he looks down at the clipboard in one hand and a pen poised to write with the other.

"Shift change paperwork check," he mumbles, keeping his head down and even though I can't see his face, I suddenly have an uneasy feeling begin to crawl over my skin that burns its way up my throat. "How's that sweet little baby of yours?" His voice and the question cause the hairs on the back of my neck to stand up.

Where are you, Colton? Did Sammy go with you?

"What do you need?" My voice is even and calm despite the alarm bells sounding in my head as I subtly try to look at his nametag that is flipped upside down.

"Now that you have him," he says, lifting his head a little to indicate Ace resting against my breast, "could you imagine if you lost him?"

Discord vibrates within me at the extremely odd question and yet when I stare at him, he seems completely normal and focused on what he's writing on the chart in his hand. I try to move Ace to cover my exposed breast, while I slowly inch my hand down toward the nurse call button. And of course it's located on the bedrail right near where he is standing, so I try to be ever so discrete as uncertainty overtakes me.

"No. Never," I finally answer.

"I lost everything. My wife. My kids. All by the hands of someone else," he says, his voice hollow and even. I stare at him now, wanting him to lift his face from where he's focused. I realize he's scribbling furiously but hasn't asked me a single question to take notes on.

My finger hovers over the call button, not wanting to make a scene, and yet my gut instinct is telling me something's off here. My mom's words flicker in my mind about how crazy a new mom can feel, and I wonder if that's what is going on here: hormones surging and taking over my rational mind.

Ace must sense my discomfort because he starts crying. "I'm so sorry," I finally respond, distracted, trying to watch what he's doing while trying to tend to my son. "How horrible."

"I thought it was only fair he knows how it feels. To feel vulnerable. To be exposed. To think he might lose it all. Jeopardize his happiness."

I shake my head. That eddy of unease returns for one more whirl as I try to figure out what in the hell he's talking about as Ace's wails escalate in pitch. "I'm sorry. I'm not following you, and you're making me uncomfortable. I'd appreciate it if you'd leave my room."

He looks up for the first time and meets me with crystalline blue eyes that hold a hint of humor oddly matching the slight smirk on his lips. "Of course. I just need your autograph on this form I have to turn in, and I'll be out of your hair," he says as he walks forward and places the manila folder on the table beside me. And as much as he makes me uncomfortable, I glance up one more time to look at him, trying to place why he looks familiar, but his head is already back down and focused on what he's fumbling with in his pocket.

"Sure." Anything. Just get the hell out of here. I set Ace down in the dip between my thighs as I grab the pen he hands me.

And then I open the folder.

My mouth drops open.

My mind is shocked.

My privacy invaded.

My little bubble popped.

Everything clicks all at the same time when I see the still photo of me from the video, spread-eagled, and every part of me unmistakable.

I look back up. His hair's a little longer and there's a goatee covering his facial scar that would have given him away instantly. But there is no doubt this is the man who has turned our world upside down in the past month.

Eddie Kimball.

I think I hear a click. I'm not sure. I force my eyes from his face to the phone he's holding up and just before the flash goes off, I bend my body over, hiding my face and exposed breast and start screaming. My finger jabbing at the call button over and over as Ace's cries rise with my burgeoning panic.

"Help!" I scream. Ace's wails escalate. "Help!"

"*Why so camera-shy now?* Donavan stole everything from me. Revenge is a bitch." He runs from the room just as the nurse comes through on the intercom.

"Everything okay, Mrs. Donavan?"

"Security!" I shout into the room. I pick Ace up and hold him tightly to my chest, rocking him as my body shakes, and my mind tries to process the fear that's clouding my judgment.

The door flings open as my nurse runs in the same exact time as a loud crash is heard in the hallway followed by a fire alarm of some sort that shrieks through the hallway of the hospital wing. "Are you okay?"

"Yes. Yes. We're fine." I keep rocking. "It's okay," I repeat to Ace over and over, as I try to reassure myself I am okay. But I'm not.

Far from it.

The nurse picks up the phone in the room and starts speaking words I don't hear because my pulse is thundering in my ears. And the minute she lowers the phone the wailing alarm stops.

But the one in my head and heart screams even louder. I'm afraid it will never shut up now.

Fear like I've only known a few times in my life—the accidents that made me lose one man and almost another—owns my soul right now. We're supposed to be safe. Supposed to be happy. And yet the man who has wreaked so much havoc in our lives just caused it to implode again.

"Tell me what happened," the nurse says at the same time Colton comes barging into the room completely out of breath, his posture defensive, and eyes wild with fear as they scour over Ace and me to make sure we are okay.

"Rylee? They were shouting for security to the room."

"*Eddie*." It's the only word I need to say for him to understand why I'm crying tears I didn't even know were coursing down my cheeks, and holding Ace to me so tightly, that if it weren't for his crying, I'd think I was smothering him.

"You're okay?" he asks through gritted teeth. The muscle in his jaw pulses as he waits for my response. A quick nod of my head and he charges out of the room.

The old me would have yelled at him to come back. Tell him I need him more. *Which is still partially true.*

But I don't say a word.

I. *Am*. Okay. *For now.*

Eddie Kimball just fucked with my son.

I hope my husband fucks with him.

Chapter Twenty-Five

Colton

"The police have it under control."

"Like hell they do!" I growl into the phone at CJ and Kelly as I pace the hallway of the hospital like a caged fucking animal. "He was in HER room. ALONE. The fucking bastard was within a foot of her and Ace. Taunting her. That is a huge goddamn problem!"

"Did he get a picture?" CJ asks, prodding the sleeping dragon within.

"Do you think I fucking know?" I grit through clenched teeth. "She doesn't know. Doesn't think so, but isn't sure. It all happened so quickly." My skin crawls, thinking how fucking close he was to her. To Ace.

The heavy sigh on the connection grates even more on my nerves because I feel like I'm not being told something. "What are you not telling me?"

Anger eats at me. Ire like I've never known before scratching through my resolve and testing my restraint to not go take that eye for an eye right now because he's already taken way too fucking much from me.

"Nothing," CJ says and before I can question him further, he continues, "the hospital security—"

"Is for shit," I finish for him. "They let a random man dressed in scrubs and a surgical cap, which he probably bought at Scrubs-R-Us or some shit, lift an I.D. off the nurses station, and waltz into her fucking room the moment Sammy helped me manage the vultures outside when I walked our family out. He had to have been hiding if Sammy didn't see him. Probably watched and waited for me to leave. *Fucking bastard.*" My hands fist. The urge to punch a fucking wall so goddamn strong I have to stand in the middle of the hall so there's nothing within reach I can destroy. "They'll be lucky I don't sue their asses for—"

"Calm down—"

"Don't tell me to calm the fuck down!"

"I'm already filing grievances with Cedars, and Kelly has notified the police of the violation of the restraining order that—"

"It's not going to do a fucking lick of good, but go right ahead. Just be ready to have bail money to post when I come face to face with him because you're going to need it." I glance over to the door of Rylee's room, knowing I need to get this rage out before I can face her and not scare her.

"Colton. Let the legal system—"

"I'm getting Rylee out of here right now." I don't need to hear his pacifying bullshit that's not going to do a damn bit of good. Not like my fist hitting Eddie's face will. "I'll hire a nurse if I have to, but we're leaving within the hour. Fuck their protocol with discharge papers. I'll have Sammy wait if need be, but I'm not putting them at risk out in the goddamn open like this."

"Understandable," Kelly speaks for the first time.

"Find him or you're fired."

I end the call. The urge to throw my phone so intense that I squat down on my haunches for a second with my head in my hands and force myself to breathe. To do exactly what I told CJ not to tell me to do: calm down and be rational. But rational went out the goddamn window the moment that bastard went after my wife.

Rational is way the fuck overrated.

God, I wish I had found him. Caught up with him somewhere in the hospital grounds and beat the shit out of him until he lost consciousness.

But nothing. He disappeared into the goddamn wind. *Fuck.*

Just like the ghosts of the nightmares that are sitting in the back of my mind laughing at this. Chiding me and telling me this is proof I can't take care of my own wife and son. That I'm no better than my mother. That I let the same man threaten my wife and now my son as I sit on the other side of the fucking door, wrists handcuffed, unable to do a goddamn thing to stop him.

Acey, Acey. Sweet little Acey.

I scrub my hands over my face as I rise to my feet and tell myself the mixture of rage and exhaustion are playing tricks on me. I need to shut out the voices in my head. I need to tell the doubt to fuck off and die.

What I need is the crunch of his nose against my knuckles.

I sigh and head toward the hospital room. Five minutes ago I couldn't wait to get out of the room so I wouldn't have to look her in the eyes and see the fear there, or look at Ace and know I already let him down within the first thirty hours of his life. And yet now all I can think about is getting to them, packing our shit up, getting the fuck out of here, and going home to our own little world.

Chapter Twenty-Six

Rylee

My body breaks out in a sweat. It's a different kind than I've ever experienced before. This kind is that whole-body heat that causes your limbs to tremble, heart to race, and head to become dizzy. I swallow over the unease as Sammy drives us out from the protected cover of the hospital's parking garage into the driveway where paparazzi swarm us instantly.

All in a shoving match to try to get their lenses to see through the dark tinted windows of the Rover and get the first picture of Ace. The coveted shot they could sell and make a year's salary with a single frame.

Fists bang on the windows. My body jumps. I lean over the baby carrier buckled in between Colton and me. With my back to the window to block the view of Ace and my eyes closed, I fight back the threatening tears.

"Don't, Ry. Please don't," Colton murmurs as he reaches out to take my hand with one hand and smooth over my hair with the other. I clear my throat and blink the tears away and stare at Ace—this sweet, innocent baby who doesn't deserve any of this.

I chose to step into this lifestyle because I love Colton, and yet now I've brought this baby into it. I know it's too late but I don't like it. Eddie waltzed into that room to make a point and to taint this perfect moment in our lives just like he did with the video.

"We'll never get this back," I whisper. Hands thump the rear window as Sammy turns into the traffic and away from the vultures looking for scraps.

"What do you mean?"

"This moment. Our time in the hospital where we get to bond before everyday life gets in the way. He took that from us. He took that feeling away. We'll never get that back."

"Yes, we will," Colton answers immediately. He releases my hand and frames my face so I'm forced to look up and meet his gaze filled with so much concern and guilt over what happened. "Remember that empty picture frame? This was the first memory we put in there. No one will ever be able to take that away from us, baby. It's just you, Ace, and me. Our first memory slid into that frame without us ever doing it. Eddie was there for a split second of time. I'm so sorry I fucked up and wasn't there. But this—this moment, this memory, this life-changing event—overshadows it by miles."

He runs his thumb over my bottom lip as if he's trying to reinforce his words with his touch. And it does work. His whispered words and reassuring touch calms me so I'm able to shut out the external factors and focus on what matters most: *us*.

Solidifying this notion further, he presses a kiss to my nose and then to my lips before resting his forehead against mine. "Thank you for the greatest gift I've ever been given besides you. This memory doesn't even need a frame though because the look on your face when you held Ace for the first time will forever be burned in my mind."

His words anchor my tumultuous psyche and the foundation that's been shifted beneath my feet. His touch reinforces our undeniable connection and irrevocable love. The baby sleeping peacefully in the carrier between us the greatest proof of that love.

"I don't blame you. Never. I'm just . . . we just have more than us to worry about, and it scares me because I feel like we have no control over anything."

"No one has control of life, Rylee. That's the beauty and fear in living it. We take each day as it comes, try to maintain our little piece of it, and enjoy every goddamn moment we're given."

"I just want our little piece to have peace."

The gates at home are just as crazy with paparazzi as the hospital. Probably even more so because they all knew where we'd be going when we left, and so we go through the routine again of thumping on the windows and shouting through the glass for us to give a statement.

Desperate to regain some kind of privacy and keep our son free from this absolute madness, I demand Sammy pull into the garage to let us out, which means he first has to move Sex out while I sit in the car so he can pull the Range Rover in.

I know I am being ridiculous and yet every part of my life and body has been exposed to the public beyond—my nonexistent privacy ever so easily invaded as shown by Eddie's demonstration today—that I desperately need to keep Ace as ours before sharing him with the world.

Screw the offers to our publicist, Chase, from People Magazine and US and Star offering ridiculous amounts of money for the first pictures with Ace. This isn't a matter of money to me, but rather the gaining back of some of our privacy. Our normalcy. Not feeling so goddamn exposed. The vulnerability that comes with living in a fishbowl surrounded by prying eyes.

I need our burst bubble back to whole again. Colton and I worked so hard to keep that bubble around us—cocoon our marriage and us in its early days. The one that told the press to back the hell off because no matter how hard they tried, we weren't going to bend to their gossip or tricks.

And we haven't.

Even with the release of the video, we didn't. And yet I still feel like they stole something from us. The part of us that makes us feel like every other couple in America, trying to make their marriage work and live their day-to-day life. It's not the anonymity so much but rather the constant state of being bared and vulnerable to the prying eyes and public scrutiny that caused me to lose my job, put Zander at risk, and took a special moment in our lives and turned it into Internet ecstasy.

It's just too much. All at once. So much so I'm hoping Ace helps us find that peace again. The piece of peace I told Colton I need.

My nerves are frayed. My body beyond exhausted. My mind in a mental overload so much so that everything I try to focus on becomes harder to concentrate on instead of easier. It's been such a long time since I've felt this way, Mrs. Always-in-Control. Yet right now I'm so drained I don't have the strength to care.

We walk into the house and as tired as I am, I feel restless, antsy, wanting to close myself off in a room with my two men and let the world fall away. Instead, I pull Ace against my chest and pace, letting the unsettled feeling rule my movement.

"Ry, you need to sit down," Colton says as he comes down the stairs from putting the bags and gifts away. All I can do is shake my head and try to figure out why I'm feeling so restless even in our own house. "You just had a baby. You promised me you'd take it easy until you heal more. This," he says motioning to my pacing, "is not resting."

"I know. I will," I murmur softly, my mind distracted elsewhere and locked on an idea.

"What is it, Ry? I can see your mind working. What's going on?"

"Do you ever wish we could just shut the world out? Make this our own little space and ignore everyone else?" I stop moving as I utter the final words, but my mind keeps going.

Colton angles his head and stares at me, trying to decipher what it is I'm getting at. "Yeah. All the time." He smiles softly. "But I kind of think you'd get sick of me if I was your only company."

I force a swallow down my throat as the huge pocket sliding glass doors behind him loom larger than life, my eyes flicker to the expanse of them that never bugged me before but now all of the sudden seem like this huge beacon advertising our life and allowing people to see in.

"No one can see in here, Rylee. In the fifteen years I've lived here, not a single photo has been taken from the beach." His tone is serious, eyes full of concern. I should love that he can read me so well. Appreciate that he immediately tries to assuage my anxiety before I even express it.

But I can't. I'm too focused on the large windows and thoughts of long-range lenses that might somehow be able to see us through the tinted glass.

"What about rogue reporters? Or drones? Drones are the newest thing," I say, risking sounding like a crazy woman, but the need to keep this space in lockdown is more important.

"You know the windows are tinted. We can see out but no one can see in, unless they are open, okay?" He has a placating tone in his voice that pisses me off at first and then snaps me out of the moment of hysteria, bringing me back to myself.

"Sorry." I shake my head and press a soft kiss to the top of Ace's forehead. "Today rattled me. I don't mean to sound crazy. I'm just tired and—"

"Today rattled me too, Ry. It makes me thank God I overhauled the security system last year." He walks toward me and pulls Ace and me into my safe space, his arms, and presses a kiss to both of our foreheads. "You guys are my everything. There's not a thing in the world I wouldn't do to make sure the two of you are safe."

The next twelve hours pass in bouts of sleep followed by blurry-eyed moments of shoveling food in, changing diapers, and trying to stay awake while Ace nurses so I don't hurt him somehow. It's a brutal cycle I'm sure I'm doing all wrong. I can't for the life of me bear to hear Ace cry, so when he does, I try to nurse him or lie on the couch with him on my chest so I can sleep when he does. The minute I set him down in his bassinet, he wakes right back up.

I'm mid-slumber, blissfully so, and yet sleeping so lightly out of partial fear I won't hear Ace if he wakes up and needs me. So when I startle awake with my heart in my throat and with a body full of aches, what scares me most is the reality I've fallen asleep on my side with Ace beside me nursing.

That panicked feeling doubles as I immediately put my hand on Ace's chest to make sure he's breathing and that I didn't roll over on him in my sleep. Just as my mind is back at ease, Colton thrashes beside me, yelling out in a voice sounding hollow and scared. Was this why I woke up in the first place?

"Colton!" I gasp out to try and wake him. At the same time I hurriedly gather Ace into me so somehow, some way, Colton doesn't hurt him while in the throes of his nightmare. "Colton!" I try to push myself up against the headboard with Ace pressed against my chest when Colton's protests and harsh grunts fill the silence of the room around us.

"No!" he shouts again, but this time shocks himself awake. Without seeing his eyes through the moonlit room, I know whatever he dreamt about has left him shaken. I can smell the fear in his sweat, hear the grate of his voice, and sense how disoriented he is.

"It's okay, Colton," I say, jarring him again as he startles at the sound of my voice. It unnerves me, considering I can't remember the last time he had a dream like this. When I reach out to touch him he jumps, and I just keep my hand on his arm to let him know he's with me and not in the dark room with the musty-smelling mattress that still controls his dreams from time to time.

Or maybe more often than that and he hasn't told me.

"Fuckin' A," he grits out as he shoves himself off the mattress and starts to walk back and forth at the foot of the bed, trying to work off some of the discord rioting through his system. He rolls his shoulders to come to grips with whatever it was that marred his dreams.

After a few moments with his fingers laced behind his head in a complete inward focus he stops at my side of the bed and rests his hips against the mattress. "I'm sorry."

"Nothing to be sorry for," I say, eyeing him cautiously as I study his body language to figure out his state of mind. If he's freaked, moody, scared . . .

"Goddamn fucking dreams." He makes the statement more to himself than to me. Since I can't remember how long it's been since Ace last nursed, I let him latch on as Colton sifts through his emotions.

"You want to talk about it?"

"No!" he barks into the room before sighing when he realizes the bite in his voice. "Sorry . . . I'm just in a bad spot. Okay?"

All I can do is nod my head and hope he'll talk to me, get out whatever it is into the open so it doesn't eat at him like I know his past sometimes does. He doesn't know I can see when the ghosts move in, how the demons of his past try to ruin his happiness, haunt his eyes, and etch lines in his face.

As much as I hate asking this question, I need to. "Is it Ace?" I ask in the softest of tones almost fearful of the answer.

"No." He sighs deeply. "Yes," he says even softer than I did. And as much as I'm internally freaking out over this, as much as it's supporting the theory I thought was happening in the hospital, I also know Colton well enough that I need to sit back and listen because he deserves a minute to explain. "It's not him, Ry. It's not you . . . it's just me being a dad is stirring shit up I thought I'd come to terms with."

"That's understandable."

"No, it's not. It's fucking bullshit. You can sit there and carry our son for nine months, go through all that labor pain like a goddamn champ, looking no worse for wear, and hell if I'm not the asshole so fucked up with nightmares, I'm afraid to sleep in the bed in case you have Ace in here." His words hang in the silence as it expands angrily in the space between us.

"Kelly found your dad, didn't he?"

Colton looks over at me and even though it's dark, I can see his jaw clench and the intensity in his eyes, and know the answer before he nods ever so slowly in response. Everything clicks into place for me.

"Yeah, and between that and the dreams, my head's one goddamn patchwork quilt of bullshit." The pain in his voice is raw, the turmoil within him almost palpable, and while I rarely press him to talk about things, this time I am.

"How so?"

"*How so?*" he mocks me, sarcasm lacing the laugh he emits after it.

"Tell me about your dreams."

"No." The quick response unnerves me and tells me they are worse than the normal ones he usually has no problem sharing. And that in itself worries me.

"Do you plan on going to see your dad?" I ask, knowing full well what happened the last time I made a suggestion like this to him. How he'd sought out his mom and that night at the track where he'd bared his past, let go of the demons that had spent a lifetime weighing him down. It had allowed him to begin the journey forward. When he doesn't answer, I respond in a way completely contradictory to the way I did when he first told me about this. "I think you should."

Colton startles at my comment, confusion over my about-face written all over his handsome features. "Come again?"

"Maybe you need to look him in the eyes, see that you are absolutely nothing like him. Maybe you'll find out he knew nothing about you or—"

"Or maybe I'll find out my dad was my abuser and not only is *her* blood running through me but so is his." His anger causes my mind to spin in a direction I'd never considered before.

"What are you saying, Colton?" I push gently for more because I hadn't expected *that* response.

"My dreams," he begins and then stops momentarily as he shakes his head. He reaches out to hold Ace's tiny hand that has escaped from the blanket. "I've been having this dream that I walk in that room and my mom is there. She's younger, prettier, not at all how I remember her, and she's holding a baby. I think it's me. She sings to me and there's a man in the corner I can't see. I think he's my dad. When I look back to her she's how I remember—strung out, used up . . . It's so real. I can smell her, the stale cigarettes. I can hear the drips from the apartment faucet I used to count. See the superheroes I tried to draw in crayon on the wall so I could focus on them when . . ." His words break my heart for the horror he endured and survived and is now reliving due to circumstances beyond my control.

I wish there was something I could do to help him, comfort him, anything to help take this pain and conflict from him. *But I can't.* All I can do is stand beside him, listen to him, and be here for him when or if he decides to face this ghost head-on.

"Fuck," he curses as he shoves up from the bed again. Baxter lifts his head to see if it's time to go out as Colton walks to the wall of windows looking into the darkness of the night to his beloved beach down below. "The fucking problem is *it's me* in the dream. His body. His hands. His stench. But my goddamn hands reaching out to take Ace and do God knows fucking what to our son." My stomach rolls as I look down at Ace's angelic face. I can't even fathom how much I'm going to hurt for him when he gets his first set of shots, so I can in no way comprehend the horrors Colton's mom made him endure for a five-minute high.

"Oh, Colton," I murmur to his back, needing him to come closer so I can wrap my arms around him and reassure him. But I know even my touch won't calm the stormy waves crashing against each other inside him.

"You know . . . I asked Kelly to find my dad so I could come full circle with my history and put it to bed. I sure as hell don't want a Kumbaya session with him that's for sure. Wasn't even sure I'd speak to him, but deep down I think I wanted to see if we were alike in any way. Stupid, I know, but a part of me needs to know." He turns to face me now and in a sense I get he's asking for me to understand something he doesn't even understand.

"And now?" I prompt in the hopes he'll keep talking, that voicing aloud his fears will allow him to overcome them.

"Now it's like," he sighs and runs a hand through his hair, such a striking silhouette against the moonlight coming through the windows at his back, "now I wonder if the dreams are true. Was that fucker my dad?" he asks, voice full of distraught disbelief. "I never once thought that as a kid. Never once made that connection. I knew I had *her* tainted blood in me, have dealt with that, knowing the other half of me was at least okay . . . but what if he's just as bad? Even worse? What if I go to see my dad and it's true? Then what, Ry?"

The look on his face and sound in his voice tears me apart because all I can offer are words right now and words won't help. They won't take away fear or mitigate the unknown. But I offer them anyway. "Then we deal with it. You and I. Together." I reach out for his hand and link my fingers with his. He blows out a breath. "Parents give you their genes but don't make the person you become."

Will he ever be free of this torment? See the amazing man inside of him that we all see?

"Still, Ry. If it's true, every time I hold Ace will I . . .? I don't know." His voice fades off as he looks down at our linked hands, the silence heavy in the air around us. "Since I've been eight years old, there hasn't been a single person in my life I have had a blood connection with. That's what being adopted is like. And it's not like Andy, Dorothea, or Quin made me feel any less because they were related and I wasn't . . . but a part of me wanted to have that connection with someone. *Desperately*. I used to watch Andy, memorize everything about him so I could learn to laugh like him, talk like him, gesture like him. Just so I could be *like* somebody. So people might see us together and from our mannerisms alone think I was his son."

"Colton." It's all I can say as pain radiates in my heart, digs into my soul, and brings tears to my eyes for the little boy hoping to belong *and* for the grown man still affected by the memories.

Still conflicted by the memories.

"Do you know what it's like to know that for the first time in almost thirty years I'm connected to someone? Blood. Genes. Mannerisms. All inherited. That Ace is a part of me?" The incredulity in his voice resonates louder than the words.

"You're not alone anymore." I squeeze his hand, a silent affirmation.

"You're right. I'm not," he says. I watch his posture change—spine stiffens, shoulders straighten—to be more defensive. A man's vulnerability only lasts for so long after all. "But at the same time I was naïve in thinking that this—the blood connection with Ace—would override the rest of this shit."

I narrow my eyebrows. "What shit?" I ask, trying to figure out which one of the myriad of things can be considered as *shit*.

"Nothing. Never mind," he says as he stands back up and presses a kiss to my forehead and Ace's. "Just some things I need to work through on my own. I promise I'll try to be quick."

Our eyes connect under the cover of night, and I worry about what the darkness is hiding that I'd normally be able to see. I thought it was just the idea of becoming a dad but now I worry it's more.

I've been so absorbed in my own world with everything that's happened over the past few weeks that now I feel like an ass. I can worry about Zander, be upset over my job, and yet not once did I stop to look at the man beside me, my rock, to ask him what other shit he was dealing with.

I want to tell him, just not now. Can't he deal with this all in a bit? Hell yes, it's a selfish thought but at the same time, when I look down at Ace he trumps all of this. He is the perfect moment in our lives and we need to stay just like this, all together, as a unit. Colton promised me this moment and now we've found it, all I want to do is hold on to it for as long as I can.

But when I look back up to Colton and see the stress in his posture, I know that while the moment is perfect for me, he's just taking a little bit longer to find his.

"Get some sleep. I'm going to go sit out on the patio for a bit and clear my head," he says. I know that means the nightmare is still there, still lingering in the fringes of his mind and he's not ready to go back to sleep again for fear it will return.

I bite back what I really want to say. *Don't go. It's lonely in bed without you. Talk to me.* Instead I say, "Okay. I'm here when you need me." *Because we do need you.* But I also know Ace and I need the him that is one hundred percent and if he needs some time to get there, then I'm resigned to give it to him.

For him. Anything for him.

And for *us*.

This is marriage; being who you are while being what your partner needs when they need it the most. Stepping up while they need to step out.

"Night," he says as he heads toward the door.

"Colton?" His name is part plea, part question because I know he is shutting down and possibly shutting me out.

He stops in the doorway and turns to face me. "It's going to be fine, Ryles. All of it."

Chapter Twenty-Seven

Colton

The motherfucker is dead.

My feet pound the sand. One after the other. My cadence: *Fuck. You. Eddie.*

Angry strides eating up distance but doing absofuckinglutely nothing to lessen the rage. All they do is put more distance between paparazzi sitting at the public entrance to the beach and me.

My lungs burn. My legs ache. My eyes sting as sweat drips into them. I pick up the pace. Needing the exhaustion, the sand, the space to clear my head before I turn around and head back.

Fuck. You. Eddie.

I push myself to the brink of exhaustion. As far north as I can go before I'm bent over, hands on my knees, gasping for air. And even fatigued the image doesn't go away. Won't go away.

The picture he took.

Ry's face is in the corner, mouth open in protest, one hand reaching to cover her breast, and the other reaching out to cover the camera lens. But the joke's on us. It wasn't Ry he was taking a shot of. Nope. She was just the frame around what Eddie wanted more: Ace sitting between the dent of her thighs. White diaper. A mess of dark hair. Mouth open crying. Face beat red.

One day old and already thrown into the goddamn inferno of chaos that is my life. Used. For money. For revenge. To hurt us. Take the purest thing in my life and use it to hurt me.

Not fucking cool. That's sleazy. Unacceptable.

Fuck. You. Eddie.

I turn back south. My feet move again. Arms pump. My leave from reality only temporary.

I sure hope that cool half a million he just pocketed was worth it. When I get done with him, he'll realize that damn photo cost him so much more.

Now I have to face Rylee. Tell her the man who took our moment, our piece of peace, has stolen from us again. Took the control to introduce our son to the world in our own way. Made Ace a pawn in this fucked-up game of his.

Fuck. You. Eddie.

Rylee's face fills my mind: eyes wide with panic, voice wavering, paranoia over the windows consuming her. And now I have to go add a little more crazy to her chaos.

On top of everything else I've already heaped there.

Too much. Just too goddamn much. Open ends. Unexpected surprises. Forced hands. Uncontrollable situations. The never-ending unknown.

Fuck. You. Eddie.

CJ's words were gasoline added to a wildfire already out of control. What had his answer been when I asked him how that little fucker keeps getting the upper hand in this goddamn game of payback? *The only power Eddie has over you is the reaction you give him.* My response? A curt *Fuck you.*

He holds no power over me. *None.* I'll let him think he does, but his hand's been dealt. Cards are on the table. He may have the wild card.

But I'm carrying all the aces.

Chapter Twenty-Eight

Rylee

"Shh! Don't be so loud. You're going to scare him," Aiden shouts in a whispered voice to the rest of the boys gathered around him. Or more like gathered around Ace.

Seven heads—blond, brown, and one red—form a phalanx of overeager boys all vying to watch him sleep in Shane's arms. All but one.

Zander sits on the couch, just outside of the circle and watches from afar. A slight smile is on his face but there is a distance in his eyes I recognize and detest. I watch him observe but make no move to get closer. And instinct tells me he's doing what he knows, putting up a wall around him, distancing himself from his brothers, so if he's fostered out, the blow won't be as hard to take.

Defense mechanism 101.

Why do I suddenly feel the need to take this course?

I look up from watching Zander to find Shane's eyes above the heads of the other boys. Our gazes hold and I can't read the look in his. He's getting so old now, graduating from college next semester, and has gotten so much better at guarding the emotions in his eyes. I can't read what they say, and it's not like this is the time or place to ask him what he's not telling me.

An elbow is traded between Auggie and Scooter. The interaction surprises me, and even though my reprimand is automatic, a small part of me smiles at this small step in Auggie's marathon journey to fitting in. And then the other part of me is saddened I haven't been there to know of this progress.

"Easy, boys," Colton warns from where he's talking to Jax in the kitchen when elbows bump again.

Questions ring out left and right. Does he sleep all the time? Is it my turn to hold him yet? Are his diapers nasty? Is it my turn to hold him yet? Does he really come out of your belly button? Is it my turn to hold him yet? Is it true he eats milk from your boobies?

That one earns some snickers and a few pairs of blushed cheeks.

"Zander, you want to come sit next to me?" I ask, needing to draw him out of his shell some.

"Okay," he mumbles as he rises from the couch and shuffles over. He sits next to me, and I put my arm around him and pull him in close. Needing and trying to offer some comfort, and pull some from him even in his silence.

"I missed you," I murmur as I press a kiss to the top of his head that I'm sure embarrasses him, but I don't care. Affection is something that never goes to waste no matter how much the other person thinks they don't need or want it.

"Me too," he says. I rest my cheek on the top of his head and just hold him there as the boys continue to stare at Ace, mesmerized by how little he is.

And a part of me is slightly surprised I'm not as freaked out as I imagined I would be watching all of these typically not-so-gentle boys crowding around him. But I shouldn't be; these are my boys—my family—and I trust them because I know they'd never hurt something so dear to me.

Then again, I'm so exhausted I think the only thing that pulls me wide-awake instantly is the sound of Ace's cry. Other than that I feel like I'm walking through a fog.

I'm talking to Zander, asking about school and simple things, trying to draw him out of his shell, when out of the blue a flash goes off.

Something in me snaps and takes over me.

"No!" I shout, flying off the couch as fast as my sore body can go. Heads turn to look at me as shock silences the room. "No pictures!" My voice is shaky but firm. My heart races and fingers tremble, as anxiety owns my body. I'm on panic-riddled autopilot as I jerk Connor's phone from his hand and delete the picture he took of Ace immediately.

I see the shock in his eyes, the lax jaw, the shake of his head, and yet all I can think of is Ace. All I can feel is the rage I've kept in check after losing my shit yesterday when Colton told me about Eddie's ultimate invasion of our privacy. How it's eaten at me bit by bit. Made me feel like our life is spinning out of control and will never get our bubble back.

I need our bubble back. Desperately.

I'm standing in the middle of the family room, Connor's phone grasped in one hand, and the boys looking at me, unsure what to do. My body begins to shiver as a hot flash of dizziness engulfs me. Sweat beads on my skin. My stomach turns. I look from boy to boy, unable to explain, and worried because I know I just scared them and yet I can't help it.

The panic attack hits me like a flash flood—instant and yanking me under its pull—magnifying everything I was feeling and then some. But just as my knees start to buckle, Colton's arms wrap around me from behind and pull me against him.

"Breathe, Ry," he murmurs into my ear, his warm breath on my flushed skin, a grounding sound when all of a sudden I feel like I'm losing it. And when I can focus again, the looks on the faces around me tell me as much. "You're okay. Just a little panic attack. I've got you."

His words and the feel of his body against mine calm the anxiety seizing me, limb by limb, nerve by nerve to the point it's hard to focus or catch my breath. My clothes stick to me as I break out in a cold sweat.

"I've got you," he says again, his voice the only thing I can focus on. The one thing I need. I can see the concern on the boys' faces but my emotions are paralyzed. I can't feel, can't bother to care to explain I'm okay, that they shouldn't worry. I have a momentary ability to focus. The fact I'm not thinking of the boys first means something is off with me. That's not me at all.

And that realization—that snippet of reality—causes a second wave of anxiety to hit me harder than the first.

"Something's wrong," I whisper so softly I don't even know if Colton hears me.

"Ry's okay," I hear Jax say as he steps forward and reassures the boys like I should. But I can't. Words are locked in my throat. "Just a panic attack."

"Let's go upstairs," Colton murmurs. His body is still behind mine, and just as he turns us, I lock eyes with Shane. I can see the fear in his eyes, his own panic written all over his face, and yet Colton pushes me to walk toward the hallway before I can unlock the apology in my throat.

"I can't," I murmur, lost in a daze. "I'm sorry. I don't know . . ."

"C'mon, baby." His voice is soothing as he gently lifts me into his arms once we clear the boys' line of sight. "I've got you." I start to wriggle, unsure, uneasy, un-everything. "I'm not gonna let you fall, Rylee. I'll never let you fall," he murmurs against the side of my face.

I sink into him, hear his words and let him take the reins. Knowing he's right but don't want to admit I'm having a hard time dealing with everything right now. Each step he takes is like the hammer reinforcing everything that's been piled onto my buckling back.

"It's just all too much, too fast," he murmurs.

Step.

The video release. Invasion of privacy. Exposed. Embarrassed. Violated. Helpless.

Step.

Taking a forced leave of absence from my job. Lost. My purpose gone. Betrayed.

Step.

Zander's uncle stepping forward. Handcuffed. Inadequate. Taken advantage of.

Step.

Ace's birth. Emotional overload. Intense joy. Unconditional love.

Step.

Eddie in the hospital room. Fear. Panic. Betrayed.

Step.

First night home as a new mom. Overwhelmed. Exhausted. Changed.

Step.

The reappearance of Colton's nightmares. Unsettling. Disruptive. A wild card.

Step.

Eddie selling Ace's picture. Violated. Used. Exploited. Helpless.

Step.

Zander today. Distant. Scared. Reticent.

Step.

The flash of Connor's camera. Out of control. Protective. Scared.

Too much, too fast. Colton's words keep repeating in my head.

"Stop thinking, baby," Colton says. "You keep tensing up. Just shut it all out for a while."

I close my eyes as he clears the landing, my pulse racing and body still trembling, but I feel a bit calmer with the staccato of his heartbeat against my ear. He lays me gently on the bed, the softness of the mattress beneath me nowhere as calming as the warmth of his body against mine.

"A little better?" he asks as he brushes my hair off my face.

I nod my head, hating the sting of tears and the burn in my throat. "I'm sorry." It's the only thing I can manage to say as I attempt to find myself through this panic-laced fog.

"No . . . don't be sorry," he says, pressing a kiss to my forehead. "You're exhausted. I know you're used to being so strong but stop fighting it. Allow yourself a couple hours not to be. Okay?"

I open my eyes and look into the crystalline green of his. I see love, concern, compassion, and more than anything I see *his* need to take care of me. So as much as I'm feeling a little less shaky, I sigh and nod my head. "I need to apolo—"

"I've got everything under control." He presses a finger to my lips to quiet me. "Just close your eyes and rest."

And I do. I close my eyes as I hear his footsteps retreat down the hallway. Follow them down the stairs and onto the tiled floor below. I force myself to relax, to try and quiet my head.

For some reason I don't think it's going to happen.

Ace is crying.

I just shut my eyes.

The crying is getting closer.

Then why is it dark outside?

And it's getting louder.

How long have I been asleep?

And louder.

Please leave me alone.

I squeeze my eyes shut tighter. Roll on my side away from the doorway. I just need to sleep. Don't want to think. Just want to drift back into the blackness of slumber and shut everything out.

"Ry? Ry?" Colton's hand pushes gently on my shoulder. Ace's cries hit a fever pitch.

"Yeah," I murmur, eyes still closed, but my breasts tingle with the burn of milk coming in as my body reacts instinctively to the sound of my baby.

"Ace is hungry," he says, pushing my shoulder again.

And even though he says the words and I can hear Ace cry, that innate instinct isn't there. There's cotton in my mouth. I can't tell him no. I'm not sure that I want to either. But at the same time the only word I can use to describe how I feel is listless.

You're just tired. You got an hour's sleep when you really need twelve. Your body is sore, changing, working overtime to produce milk and heal, and is making you more groggy than ever.

That's all.

"'Kay." It's all I say as I roll on my side and lift up my shirt on autopilot. My breasts ache they are so heavy with milk. Colton lies Ace down beside me in the middle of our bed as I guide my nipple into his mouth.

Ace latches on, and I wait for that feeling to consume me. The one I've gotten every other time we've connected like this in the most natural of actions. There's usually this soothing calm that spreads throughout me, like endorphins on speed. And this time when Ace latches on, all I want to do is close my eyes and crawl back into sleep I desperately need.

"I'll be right back," Colton says, causing panic I don't quite understand.

Don't go! I shout the words in my head and yet my lips make no sound. My throat feels like it is slowly filling with sand. My chest feels tight. Sweat beads on my upper lip.

Get it together, Ry. It's just your hormones. It's the adjustment period. Mixed with exhaustion. And feeling like I don't know what in the hell I'm doing even when I do.

Tomorrow will be better.

And the day after that even more.

Chapter Twenty-Nine

Colton

"You want to tell me what we're doing here, son?"

I glance over to my dad and then back to the garage across the street from us. I don't say a word. And even if I wanted to tell him, I'm not sure exactly what to say. My body vibrates with uncertainty. Head and heart an ocean apart on this decision. My leg jogs up and down where I sit in the passenger seat. Jet Black Heart conveniently plays on the radio and all I can do is hum the words that hit too close to fucking home.

My dad's car stands out like a sore thumb in this neighborhood. Sleek and red, subtle as far as my standards, but flashy for this rundown part of town. Guess I should have thought about that when I called him up and said, "I need you to drive me somewhere."

No other details given.

And of course within an hour he was at my house, passenger door open for me to scoot in. No questions asked. Almost as if he knew I needed time to work through all the shit going on in my head.

No small talk. No bullshitting. Just a turn of his steering wheel when I indicated to take a right or a left as we drove.

So why am I here? Why am I chasing this goddamn ghost when the man beside me is all I've ever needed?

It all comes back to full circles. Eventually everything connects. Now I just need to see the connection for myself before I leave it there and walk away for good.

My elbow rests on the doorjamb, my hand rubbing back and forth on my forehead as I stare at the dilapidated storefront. The mechanic's bay is open on the side, a late model sedan up on a lift, rusted parts just to the outside of the door, but it's the pair of boots I can see standing on the other side of the car that holds my attention.

Buck the fuck up, Donavan. It's now or never.

"Be right back," I say as I open the door, realizing I never answered his question. With my heart in my throat and a pocketful of confusion, I walk across the sidewalk and up to the open bay, wondering if I'm about to come face to face with my worst nightmare or a man who has no clue I even exist.

Flashbacks hit me like a car head-on into the wall: fast as fuck, out of the blue, and knocking the wind out of me. Memories so strong I feel like I'm back there in *that room*, full of shame, shaking with fear, and fighting the pain.

My feet falter. My pulse pounds. My conscience questions me. My stomach rolls over.

And just as I'm about to turn around and retreat, the man comes walking around the front of the car. I freeze.

"Get the fuck out of here!" he growls. And at first I think he's talking to me but then I see him kick the flank of a mutt standing just inside the door. Its yelp echoes through the garage and fades but tells me so much about this man in the few seconds I've been in his presence.

Only assholes kick an animal.

He sees me the same time I see him. Our eyes meet, green to green. Just like mine. Curiosity sparks. His greedy eyes flicker to the expensive car behind me, to my watch, and over my clothes

My first thought: *It's not him.* He's not the fucker who haunts my dreams and stole my childhood. The exhale I thought I'd give doesn't come. Relief mixed with confusion adds to the pressure in my chest.

We stare at each other like caged animals trying to gauge the situation. Figuring out why it feels like there is a threat when none has been made.

I take in every detail about him: hair slicked back, cracked hands stained with grease, a cigarette dangling from his lips, a teardrop tattoo at the corner of his left eye, and the unmistakable stench of alcohol. A sneer is on his lips and a chip weighs visibly on his shoulder.

My second thought: *I know your type.* Your lot in life is everyone else's fault. Bad luck. Hard time. Never your fault. Entitled when you don't deserve shit.

I stare at him—jaw clenched, eyes searching—and wait for a reaction. Anything. Something. The little boy in me figuring that in some fucked-up way he'd know I was his son. Some kind of recognition. A sixth sense.

But there is nothing. Not even a flicker in his dead eyes.

Seconds pass. But the emotions rioting within me make it feel like an hour. And I'm not sure why all of a sudden my temper is there. Fuse snapped. Confusion rising.

But it is. My temper is front and fucking center. Anger is alive.

He takes a step forward, gaze still flicking back to the car and my watch, mind still figuring how much he can take me for in bogus repairs. Because that's what he sees: rich guy, expensive car, and a chance to fuck me over. Nothing else even computes. He looks down at the red rag he's wiping his hand on before meeting my eyes again. Cocky bastard of a smirk on his lips.

"Can I help you with something? Car having some trouble?" His voice sounds like years of cigarettes ground into the gravel.

I can't tear my gaze from him. Hate that I keep waiting for something to spark in his eyes when I don't want it to. Just something to tell me I mattered at some point. A flash of a thought. A pang of regret. A question of what-if over time.

There's absolutely nothing, just his words hanging in the air. He narrows his eyes, broadens his shoulders.

I shift my feet. Swallow. Decide.

"No. I need absolutely *nothing* from you."

One last look. A first and last goodbye. Circle completed.

Fuck this shit.

I turn on my heel and walk away without another look. With my hands shaking and my heart conflicted, I slide into the passenger seat. I can't bring myself to look at my dad. *My real dad.* The only dad I have.

"Just drive."

The car starts. The world zooms by as I move back into the comfort of the blur. The place I haven't returned to in so very long. My dad doesn't say a word, doesn't ask a thing. He just drives and leaves me alone with the motherfucking freight train of noise in my head.

Regret. Doubt. Confusion. Anger. Hurt. Uncertainty. Guilt. Each one takes their time in the limelight as we drive. *Shut it down, Colton.* Lock it up. Push it away.

The car pulls to a stop. The blur fades to clear. The beach stretches before us off Highway 101. *It's my spot.* The place I go when I need to think.

Of course he'd know to bring me here. That *this* is what I needed.

I sit for a moment, quiet, unmoving, before the guilt eats up the air in the car until I can't breathe anymore. I shove the door open and stumble from it, needing the fresh air, the space to think, and the time to grieve when there's nothing really dead to grieve over.

And that's the goddamn problem, isn't it? Why in the fuck am I upset? What did I expect? A reunion? An *attaboy?* Fuck no. I didn't want one either. And yet that teeny, tiny piece of me wanted to know I mattered. Wanted to know that the blood we shared tied us together somehow.

But it doesn't. Not in the fucking least. I'm nothing like him. I know that from the two minutes I came face to face with him, looked him in the eyes, and felt only indifference.

Does he even know I exist? The thought comes out of nowhere, and I don't know if it makes the situation worse or better. Ignorance over abandonment.

Fuck if I know. Hell if I care.

But I do.

My chest hurts. It's hard to breathe. I sit down on the seawall separating the asphalt from the sand and tell myself this is exactly what I wanted. To prove he's nothing to me. To close the circle. And walk away.

So what in the hell is wrong with me?

It's the man in the car behind me. That's who. How could I betray him? How could I let him drive me there? Would he think I didn't believe he was enough for me when he's given me *everything?*

I'm such a selfish prick. To think I was looking for more when I've had it right in front of me since the day he found me on his steps.

The ocean crashes on the beach and I lose myself in the sight. Find comfort in the sound. Use the one place I've always escaped to, to quiet the shitstorm in my head.

I hear him before I see him. The fall of footsteps. The scent of the same soap he's used since I was little. The shuffle as he swings his legs over the wall to sit beside me. The sounds of his thoughts scream in the silence.

"You okay, son?"

His words are like poison lacing the guilt I already own. All I can do is blow out a breath and nod my head, eyes staring straight at the water.

"Was that your father, Colton?"

I take a moment to answer. Not because I have to think about it but because how I respond is important. Was he my father? By blood, yes. And yet when I hold Ace, even though I'm scared shitless and don't know what the fuck I'm doing and still fear I'm not going to be the man he needs me to be, I still feel connected with him. An indescribable, unbreakable bond.

I didn't feel it with the man at the garage.

But I do feel it with Andy.

I look over to him. Our eyes hold, grey to green, father to son, superhero to saved, man to man, and I answer without a single fucking ounce of hesitation.

"No. *You are.*"

Chapter Thirty

Rylee

"Are you sure you're all right and don't need any help?"

No. Yes.

Silence fills the space where my answers should be. "Yes. We're all fine, Mom. I'm just . . . I'm just trying to get him on a schedule and want to do that before people start coming over."

I grit my teeth. The lie sounds so foreign coming from my mouth. Like an echo down a tunnel that I recognize but can't place as my own voice when it comes back to me.

"Because it would be perfectly normal for you to need help, sweetheart. There is no shame in needing your mom when you become a mom."

"I know." My voice is barely above a whisper. The only response I can give her.

"You know I'm here for you. Any time. Day or night. To be there with you to help or just to sit on the other end of the phone line."

"I know." The emotion in her voice—the swell of love in it as she searches if I'm being truthful—almost undoes me.

Almost.

"Okay, then. I'll let you get back to my handsome grandson now."

Silence.

"Mom?" Fear. Hope. Worry. All three crash into each other and manifest in the desperate break in my voice.

Tell her something's wrong with you. That you don't feel right.

"Ry?" Searching. Asking. Wanting to know.

No. You're perfectly fine. You can handle this. Your hormones are just out of whack. This is normal.

"You still there, Rylee? Are you okay?"

"Yes. I'm fine." A quick response to mask the unease I feel. "I was going to . . . I forgot what I was going to ask. Bye, Mom. I love you."

"Love you, too."

Silence again.

The music from the baby swing where Ace sits floats in from the family room. He begins to cry and yet I sit and stare out to the beach beyond, lost in thought. Convincing myself that I'm fine. Telling myself that empty void I suddenly feel is normal. Wondering if I'm not hardwired correctly to be a mother.

That maybe, just maybe, there was a bigger reason as to why I lost my other two babies.

That's crap and you know it.

But maybe . . .

"Ry?" Colton calls out to me as the front door slams.

Ace's cries pick up a pitch at the sound of his dad's voice, and all I can do is close my eyes from where I'm still sitting, lost in staring at the clouds out the window. I open my mouth to tell him I'm in the living room but nothing comes out.

"Rylee?" Colton's voice is a little more insistent this time, concern lacing the edges, and it's just enough to break through the fog that seems to have a hold over me. I put my hands on the arm of the chair to stand but can't seem to get up.

There is a change in Ace's cry. It's garbled at first and then muffled, and I sag in an unnatural relief, knowing Colton has given him his pacifier. And the relief is quickly followed by an intense wave of self-loathing. Why couldn't I have done that? Pick up Ace. Why did I have to wait for Colton to walk in the front door to take care of him? That's my job. Why couldn't I make my legs walk over there to do it myself? I'm failing miserably at the one thing I've always wanted and always knew I was born to be: a mother.

The tears well in my eyes and my throat burns as I shake my head to clear it from thoughts I know are ridiculous but feel nonetheless. *Snap out of it, Ry.* You're a good mom. You just need a little more time to recover. It's your hormones. It's the exhaustion. Possibly a touch of the baby blues. It's the need to do every little thing for Ace yourself because you don't think Colton can at this point with everything he's going through. You're just trying to step up to the plate and do it all when you can't and that's driving your type A, controlling personality batty.

"Rylee?" Colton shouts my name this time, panic pitching his voice.

"Coming," I say as I force myself to stand up and swallow over the bile rising in my throat. I close the fifty or so feet to the family room to find Colton awkwardly holding Ace, trying to keep the pacifier in his mouth so he stops crying.

I look at the two of them together and know I should feel completely overwhelmed with love but for some reason all I want to do is sit down and close my eyes. So I do just that. And even with them closed, I can feel the weight of Colton's stare. The silence that is usually comforting between us is suddenly awkward and uneasy. Almost as if he's passing judgment on me because . . . because I don't know why but I feel it anyway.

"Everything okay, Ry?"

Is it okay? I open my eyes and stare at him, not certain how to answer him because it sure doesn't feel okay right now.

"Yes. Yeah. I was just . . . uh . . ." I don't think even if I could put into words how I feel, he'd understand me. I fumble for something to say as I watch him try to figure out how to undo the onesie to change Ace's diaper.

Has he even changed a diaper yet? Or have I always jumped up and taken care of it, needing to be the supermom I think is expected of me and I expect of myself? I can't remember. Five days worth of sleepless nights and endless diaper changes and feedings run together. It's like my mind and body have been thrown into the washing machine on spin cycle and when the door opens everything is upside down and inside out.

When I come back to myself, his hands have stopped fooling with the snaps between Ace's legs and his eyes are locked on mine, waiting for me to finish my answer. "Ry?" I hate the sound in his voice—love his concern but hate the question in it. *Am I all right? Is everything okay?*

NO, IT'S NOT! I want to yell to make him see something feels so off. And yet I say nothing.

And then it hits me. Lost in this haze of hormones and exhaustion, I totally forgot about where he went, what he did today. The whole reason I was lost in thought in the first place was because I was worried about not having heard from him yet.

I cringe at my selfishness. At sitting here feeling sorry for myself when I know the courage it just took for him to come face to face with his dad.

"Sorry. I'm here. Just . . . I was in the office, worried because you hadn't answered my texts. I was . . ." This time when he looks up from Ace, I can see the stress etched in the lines of his handsome face and know without him saying a word that he did in fact find his biological dad. "You found him?"

He sighs as he looks back down to a fussy Ace with a slow nod of his head. I give him time to find the words to express what he needs to say, watch him reach out and run the back of his hand over Ace's cheek. The sight of him connecting to Ace like that tugs at my heartstrings. That feeling I felt like I had been missing moments ago—of utter love seeing my two men together—fills me with such a sense of joy that I cling to it, suddenly realizing how absent it was before.

And the thought alone makes me choke back a sob, feel like I'm losing my mind. *Keep it together, Ry. Keep. It. Together.* Colton needs you right now. It's not the time to need him because he needs you.

"Did you?" I ask, trying to regain my schizophrenic focus.

"He's hungry," he says abruptly as he lifts him off the floor and carries him to me. We've been together long enough that I know avoidance when I see it and yet for the life of me when he places Ace in my arms for me to nurse, I blank for a second. My mind and body not clicking together on what I need to do.

And as loud as Ace is crying, the last thing I want to do is nurse so in a move I register as callous but don't quite understand, I tune Ace out and focus on Colton as he walks across the room and into the kitchen. I hear the cupboard open, close, the clink of glass to glass, and know he's poured himself a drink. Jack Daniels.

Crap. It must have been really bad.

I wish he had let me go with him today. I wish we didn't have Ace so I wouldn't fear leaving my own goddamn house because of the cameras and never-ending intrusion into our privacy. Both of those things prevented me from being there for my husband on a day he needed me the most. Guilt stabs sharply, consumes my state of mind, as I wait for him to return and hopefully talk to me.

Out of nowhere and without a trigger, a sudden wave of sadness bears down on me in a way I've never felt before. Oppressive. Suffocating. So stifling it's significantly worse than the darkest of days after losing Max and both of my babies. And just as my shock ebbs from the onslaught I feel, a ghost of a thought becomes stronger and knocks the wind out of me: I just want our life back to when it was Colton and me and no one else.

Oh my God. *Ace*.

The unspeakable thought staggers me. Its ludicrousness takes my breath momentarily but is gone as quick as it comes. The acrid taste of it still lingers though but thankfully the rising pitch of Ace's cries breaks its hold on my psyche.

I try to get a grip on myself, remorse and confusion fueling my actions as I gather him closer to me and kiss his head over and over, begging him to forgive me for a thought he will never even know I had.

But I will remember.

With shaky hands, I go through the motions of getting him latched onto my breast as quickly as possible, needing this moment of bonding to quiet the turmoil I feel within me. When his cries fade as he starts to suckle, I close my eyes and wait for the rush of endorphins to come. I hope for it, beg for it, but before I feel it I hear Colton enter the room and stop in front of me.

I open my eyes to find his and have to fight the urge to look away, fearful if he looks close enough, he'll see into me and realize the horrible thought I just had. Panic strikes, my nerves sensitive like bare flesh on hot coals. I just need something to ground me right now—either the soothing rush from nursing or to be wrapped in the arms of my husband—to prevent me from feeling like I'm slowly spiraling out of control.

And just as my breath becomes shallow and my pulse starts to race, it hits me. That slow rush of delayed hormones spreads their warmth through my body and dulls the erratic and out-of-control emotions. All of a sudden I have a bit of clarity, can focus, and the person I need to focus on most is right in front of me.

Our eyes hold in the silence of the room, the intensity and confusion in the green of his makes my heart twist from the unmistakable pain I see in their depths. His eyes flicker down to Ace at my breast and hold there for a moment before lifting back up to meet mine with a touch more softness in them, but the hurt still plain as day.

"Do you want to talk about it?"

Colton clears his throat and swallows, his Adam's apple bobbing. "I saw what I needed to see, know what I need to know. Curiosity satisfied," he says as he sits down on the coffee table in front of me.

And I know that sound in his voice—guarded, protective, unaffected. There is a whole storm brewing behind the haunted look in his eyes, yet I'm not sure if I should draw it out of him or leave it be and wait for the eye to pass on its own.

My own curiosity gets the best of me. My innate need to fix and soothe and help him when he's hurting controls my actions. "Did you get to—?"

"He's a piece of shit, okay?" he explodes, startling both Ace and myself. "He didn't give a goddamn flying fuck who I was. All he saw was a nice car, nice clothes, and was totaling up dollar signs in his eyes for how much he could take me for. He reeked of alcohol, had the tats to show he'd earned his prison cred . . ." The words come out in a complete rush of air, the hurricane within him needing to churn. The muscle in his jaw pulses with anger, his muscles visibly taut as he lifts the glass of amber liquid to his lips. He pushes the alcohol around the inside of his mouth trying to figure out what to say next before he swallows it. "I am nothing like him. I will never be anything like him." He grits the words out with poisoned resolution.

"I never thought you were or would be." Still unsure of the right thing to say, I take the direct approach with him. He doesn't need to be coddled right now or treated with kid gloves. That would only diminish the validity of his feelings and what he's going through.

"Don't, Ry," he warns as he shoves up from the table, his anger eating at him. "Don't give me one of your speeches about what a good man I am because *I'm not*. I'm the furthest fucking thing from it right now, so thanks . . . but no thanks."

He turns to face me, eyes daring me to say more, the defensive shield he carries at the ready, up and armed. Our gaze locks, mine asking for more, needing to understand what happened to rock the solid foundation he's been standing on for so very long.

"You know I went there today with no expectations whatsoever. But a small part of me . . . the fucked-up part obviously," he says with a condescending chuckle, "thought he'd see me and shit, I don't know . . . that he'd just know who I was. Like because we shared blood it would be an automatic thing.

And even more fucked up than wanting to know I was a blip on his fucking radar, was at the same time, I didn't want him to realize it at all." His voice rises and he throws his hands out to his sides. "So yeah . . . tell me how I'm supposed to explain that."

The anger is raw in his voice and there's nothing I can say to take away the sting of what he went through. I just wish I'd been there with him.

"You don't owe an explanation to anyone," I state softly. His legs eat up the length of the living room and he moves like a caged animal. "Everyone wants to feel like they belong to someone . . . are connected to another. You have every right to be confused and hurt and anything else you feel."

"Anything else I feel?" he asks, that self-deprecating laugh back and longer this time around. "Like what a fucking prick I am for asking Andy to go with me? For asking the only dad I've ever known, the only man who has ever given a rat's ass about me, to drive me to find a man who hasn't given me a second thought his entire life? Yeah . . . because that screams son-of-the-fucking-year now, doesn't it?"

His verbal diatribe stops just as abruptly as it starts, but his restraint from saying more manifests itself in his fisted hands at his sides. And I can see his internal struggle, know he feels guilty over needing to close this last door to his past at the expense of possibly making Andy feel less in all senses of the word in his life.

I want to shake him though and assure him Andy wouldn't see this as betrayal. Find a way to make him see that he'd see it as his son taking the final step to lay the demons to rest. Find peace in the one constant that has been his whole life.

"Your dad has always supported you, Colton." His feet stop, back still to me, but I know I've gotten his attention. "He encouraged you to find out about your mom. You're his son." He hangs his head forward at the term, the weight of his guilt obvious in his posture. "He's proven he'll do anything for you . . . I imagine he's glad he was the one with you when you faced the final unknown of your past."

I hope he really hears my words and realizes that as a parent all you want is your child to be whole, healthy, and happy, and that was exactly what Andy wanted for him today. I thought I understood that concept. Now I have Ace—albeit for a brief five days of motherhood—I know I'd move heaven and earth for him to have those same exact things.

He walks toward me without saying anything and sits back down in front of me. He reaches out and tickles the inside of Ace's palm so he closes his hand around Colton's pinky. There is something about the sight—huge hand, tiny fingers holding tight—that hits me hard and reinforces the notion that Ace depends on us for absolutely every single thing. That we are his lifeline in a sense. I wonder if a baby senses when one half of that connection is absent.

"I look at Ace," he says, his voice calmer, more even, "and I feel this instant connection. I figured it was because I have blood ties to someone for the first time in my life. That it was an automatic thing you feel when you're related to someone. I can't tell you how many times over the years I've felt like a fucking outsider, cheated out of having this feeling." He pauses for a moment, runs a hand through his hair and clears his throat, the grate in his voice the only sign of the emotion wreaking havoc inside him. "But today I was standing there looking at this bitter man with eyes just like mine, who couldn't be bothered to give a shit about me, and I felt *absolutely nothing*. No click. No connection. No anything. *And his blood runs through me*." His voice breaks some, but his confession causes every part of me to bristle with guilt for my feelings moments ago. The ironic parallel of how I desperately needed the connection with Ace when he latched on to nurse to make me feel whole and centered again.

"It freaked me the fuck out, Ry," he confesses, pulling me from my thoughts. "That connection I thought I was missing for most of my life, I've had all along with my dad. *Andy*. Today, I realized that blood ties mean shit if you don't put in the time to make them worth it. So yeah, I'm connected by blood to Ace . . . but in a sense, I've been no better than that sperm donor was to me."

I start to argue with him, my back up instantly, but he just shakes his head for me to stop. When he lifts his gaze from Ace to meet mine, there are so many emotions swimming in them, but it's the regret in them I take notice of.

"Look, I know I haven't been very hands-on with Ace. I'm still petrified of hurting him or doing the wrong thing because I'm absolutely fucking clueless. But standing in that driveway, looking at that piece of shit, I realized Ace doesn't care if I'm perfect . . . all he cares is that I'm there with him every step of the way. Just like Andy has been for me. Shit, Ry, I've been so busy trying to figure out what kind of dad he needs me to be that I'm not really being one at all."

My tears are instant as I look at the little boy become entirely eclipsed by the grown man I've loved all along.

"You're going to be an excellent father, Colton."

We both lean forward at the same time, our lips meeting in a tender kiss packed with a subtle punch of every emotion we share between us: acceptance, appreciation, love, and pride.

"You are nothing like him. We've known that all along. Now you finally know it, too. I'm so proud of you, Colton Donavan," I murmur against his lips. He brushes one more kiss to my mouth before pressing his signature one to the tip of my nose.

We sit there for some time in silence. The three of us. My new little family.

I fight fiercely against that undertow of discord that seems like a constant so I can revel in this moment. Memorize the feel of it and the sense of completeness I have with them by my side.

And all I keep thinking is that the storm has finally passed.

I just hope there are no new clouds on the horizon.

Chapter Thirty-One

Rylee

I stare at the open email from CJ on the screen. At the five magazines listed down the page with ridiculous dollar figures next to them. Their offers for the first photos of the new Donavan family. The tamed ex-bad boy racing superstar, his sex-crazed wife, and their little piece of perfect between them.

My muscles tense. My eyes blur. My mouth goes dry at the thought of anyone getting his or her sights on Ace. The mere thought of taking him out of the house causes me to break out in a panic attack. Thankfully Colton was able to get the pediatrician to make a house call for his first check up or else I'm not sure what I would have done.

I close the email. No way. No how. Publicity pictures are not even an option.

Any pictures for that matter.

Because even though the public got Eddie's picture of Ace—scrunched-up red face, mouth open, hands blurred in movement—to obsess over, it wasn't enough. Not even close. It almost gave the reverse effect. They are now hungry for more. Staking out the house, trying to bribe Grace to sneak a picture while she's cleaning the house. You name it, nothing's off limits.

And I refuse to give it to them. They've taken enough from me, so I refuse to give them any more.

My phone vibrates again from where it sits on the desk beside me. I glance at the screen. This time a text from Haddie instead of the five I've received from my mom today, telling me that pretty soon she's not going to take no for an answer. That she's going to come over without asking so she can see her grandson and help me in any way possible.

I clear the text from the screen and send it to the vortex of the bazillion other texts from family and close friends asking when they can come over, if they can bring us dinner, or if I need them to stop at the store for diapers.

Take the offer, Rylee.

The last time someone came over—the boys—I had a breakdown. And I've had plenty more on my own in the silence of this house; the last thing I need is to show everyone else how unstable I am.

Just tell her to come.

No, because then she'll know how much I'm struggling. I can't let everyone know the lie I'm living. That the woman they all said would be such a natural mother can't even look at her son some moments without wanting to run and hide in the back of the closet. How more and more I cringe when he cries, have to force myself to go get him when I'd rather just lie in bed with my hands over my ears and tears running down my cheeks.

Type the words, Ry. Ask her to get here.

I have the baby blues. That's all this is. A goddamn roller coaster of emotion, extreme joy interlaced with moments of soul-bottoming lows, all controlled by the flick of the hormonal switch.

She wouldn't understand. These feelings are normal. Every new mother goes through it, but no one else understands it unless they're in the midst of it.

I can get through this on my own. It's just my need to control everything that makes it feel like it's uncontrollable: the outside world, my emotions, our everything. I can prove I can handle this, that I'm good at this. It's only been seven days. I can handle this on my own.

Take the break she'll give you. It's exactly what you need.

How can I let someone else watch Ace, when I'm having a hard enough time allowing Colton? I know I'm the only one who can nurse him, but there are still diapers and burping and rocking left for others to help with. And it's not because I don't think Colton can handle it, but if I get there first, prove to myself I've got a handle on this, then maybe it will help me feel less haywire.

Get a few minutes to yourself. Let her come over. Take a shower without rushing. Brush your teeth without staring to see if his chest is moving. Eat some food without a baby attached to you.

I pick my phone up, hands trembling as I stare at Haddie's text. Every part of me is conflicted over what to write.

We're good. Thanks. Just settling in. Maybe next week when we're in a better routine.

I hit send. Will she see through that response? Will she come over anyway and in five minutes know something is wrong with me?

Maybe that's what I want.

I don't know.

I close my eyes and lean back in the chair. Lost in my thoughts, I try to find some quiet in my head since Ace is asleep in the swing right now while Colton is outside the walls of my self-imposed prison.

The first tear falls and slides silently down my cheek. Thoughts come and fade with each tear that drops, but for some reason my mind fixates on the empty picture frame on the bookcase beside me. The one that's supposed to be filled with the new memories we make together as a family and yet when I open my eyes to look at it, its emptiness is all I see.

Just like I feel.

I came in here with the intent to do so many things and now for the life of me, I can't remember what they were. I swear that pregnancy brain has turned into postpartum brain with how groggy and forgetful I feel when I'm wide awake.

Check on Zander. Take a shower. Reassure Shane I'm all right after the other night. Pump breast milk. Ask Colton if the police have gotten any closer to finding Eddie. Eat. Must remember to eat something. Email Teddy about status of Zander's caseworker. Respond to the texts on my phone.

It all makes my head hurt. Every single item. And as important as each item is, I don't want to do any of them. All I want to do is pull the blankets over my head and sleep. The only place I can escape my thoughts and feelings that don't feel like mine.

I go to close Outlook on the computer when an email closer to the bottom of the screen catches my eye that I didn't notice before. It's from CJ and has the subject: LADCFS process started.

What the hell? What process was started with the Los Angeles Department of Child and Family Services? Colton's comments flicker back into my mind from a few weeks ago but I refuse to listen to them. Refuse to believe he did what I think he did.

I open the email and read:

Colton,

As per your instruction, I have started the initial legwork to qualify you and Rylee as suitable candidates to adopt Zander Sullivan. I'd like to reiterate that this can be a tedious and often cumbersome process and might not end in your favor. Attached you will find the completed forms submitted on Rylee's and your behalf to get the ball rolling.

I reread the email, emotions on a merry-go-round in my mind: shock, disbelief, pride, and anger on a constant circle.

How could he do this without telling me? How could he force my hand and make me choose one boy over the others?

For some reason I can't grasp onto the positive side of it. I can see it, realize it, but I can't hold on to the thought long enough that one of my boys means enough to Colton to want to do this. All I can see is that he acted without me.

This is not even an option.

Can't be.

It may help save one but it would alienate the others.

I lose my grip on the edges of the rabbit hole I felt I was slowly clawing my way out of and slide back down into its darkness. It's sudden and all-consuming. The feelings are so intense, so inescapable, that the next time I come up for air, the shadows in the room have shifted. Time has passed.

I'm freaked. Ace is screaming. Blood curdling screams that call to my maternal instincts and aching breasts overfull with milk. And yet all I want to do is escape to the beach down below where the wind will whip in my ears and take the sound away. Give me an excuse not to hear him.

"Goddammit, Ry! Where the fuck are you?" Colton's voice bellows through the house, disapproval and anger tingeing the echo when it hits me.

Is that what snapped me out of my trance? Colton calling me?

Déjà vu hits. Same place, same situation as yesterday, and yet this time the tone in Colton's voice speaks way louder than the words he says. And before I even set foot into the family room, I'm primed and ready for a fight.

I walk into the room just as Colton's lifting an absolutely livid Ace out of his swing and pulling him to his chest to try and soothe him. He lifts his eyes when he hears my footsteps and the look he gives me paralyzes me.

"That's twice I've walked in the front door in two days to find Ace screaming and you nowhere to be found. What the fuck is going on, Rylee?" His voice is quiet steel and ice when he speaks, spite and confusion front and center.

I stare at him dumbfounded. I know I deserve the reprimand, that he has every right to ask the question, and yet I don't have the words to explain to him the why behind it.

"Answer me," he demands, causing Ace's cries to start again, his pacifier falling from his mouth.

"I . . . I . . . I can't . . ." I fumble for the words to express what's going on when I don't even know myself. So I change gears. Use my emotions to throw the whole kitchen sink into the argument I can see brewing and do so knowing this is going to be nasty. He's on edge from the emotional overload of seeing his dad yesterday and I'm overwhelmed with the constant free fall of my emotions. "How dare you submit adoption paperwork on our behalf for Zander and keep it from me! I told you I couldn't pick one boy and not the others!" I yell at the top of my lungs, combining two completely unrelated topics—and it feels so damn good. So damn cleansing when I've been holding so much in for so long. And yes, I'm fighting a battle to distract him from the truth, but I can't stop myself once I start. "You went behind my back, Colton. How dare you? How dare you think for one goddamn second you know what I want or what Zander needs?"

Colton stands there, slightly stunned, eyes wide and jaw clenched—our baby on his shoulder—and just stares at me with absolute insolence. "*I don't know what Zander needs?*" he asks, voice escalating with each word. "You want to fight, sweetheart, you better come at me with something stronger than that because you and I both know the truth on that one." Hurt flashes in his eyes and as much as I hate myself for it, it does nothing to stop the tsunami of anger taking over me.

"You. Hid. It. From. Me," I grit out in a barely audible voice.

"I did?" he says incredulously, taking a few steps in my direction as Ace continues to cry, feeding off the room's atmosphere. "I told you I was going to look into it. The email is sitting on the fucking computer clear as goddamn day. If I was hiding it from you, don't you think I would have deleted it? Or better yet, tell CJ to send it to my work email so you wouldn't see it? I was just getting our names in the system, trying to show interest in Z to maybe fuck with the social worker and have him stop the process. Get a grip, Ry—"

"Don't you dare say that to me," I scream, hysteria unhinging at the simple statement because I don't want to see the truth in it. Can't. "Don't you waltz in here like you have a fucking clue what's going on and treat me like I'm your goddamn nanny."

He startles his head from the whiplash in my change of topic. "What in the fuck are you talking about? I've told you twenty fucking times to let me help and you won't. It's like you're on some goddamn mission to prove you're supermom. Last I checked this isn't a competition, so stop making it one. *Nanny?* Jesus Christ, have you lost your mind?" He looks at me, chest heaving, head shaking, like he doesn't even know me and the sad thing is, I don't even know me right now.

I despise this woman who picked a fight with her husband because she's scared and confused and not sure what is going on inside her. However, I can't seem to stop for the life of me. We stand ten feet apart but there is nothing but animosity vibrating in the air between us.

There's so much I want to say to him. So many things I need to try to explain and yet I can't find the words, and Ace's constant crying is like rubbing gravel in an open wound that just seems to agitate me more.

Colton closes the distance between us, his eyes searching my face for answers I can't give him. "When you want to fight about something worth fighting about, Rylee, you know where to find me." His eyes dare me to come back at him, press those buttons of his he wants me to push. When I don't say a word, he holds a crying Ace out for me to take. "Until then, your son is hungry and has been for who knows how long before I walked in the fucking door."

I look down at Ace and then back to Colton as my body freezes and words fall out of my mouth I can't even believe I'm saying. "Feed him yourself."

No. I don't mean that.

"What?" Confusion like I've never seen before blankets his face.

Help me snap out of this, Colton. Please help me.

"Feed him formula." My voice doesn't even sound like my own.

Something's wrong with me. Can't you see it?

"Rylee . . ." Ace's cries escalate as Colton holds him in that space suspended between the two of us. I know Ace can smell the milk on me, know he's hungry, but that goddamn veil of listlessness falls like a lead curtain around me to the point that it's taking everything I have not to turn and run. And at the same time to *not* fight to the death on this single point I am still shocked I'm even fighting over.

Take my shoulders and shake me. Tell me to snap out of this funk.

My thoughts, my breath, my soul all feel like they are being suffocated to the point that the room starts to spin and my body starts to feel like I've stepped into an oven. The air is hot, thick as I suck it in, making it hard to breathe and my head to be fuzzy.

He eyes me, frantic flickers from Ace to me as he tries to figure out what's going on. He's scared. Worried. Freaked.

I am too.

"I thought you wanted to only nurse for the first two months, that—"

"I'm not producing milk," I lie, as I struggle to wade through this viscous veil of darkness that feels like it's taking hold of me, seeping from my feet up my legs.

No. No. No. Fight, Rylee. Fight its pull on you.

"Quit lying to me."

"I'm not lying." He points to my shirt. I look down to see two wet patches staining my red shirt dark where my breasts have leaked through my nursing pads from Ace's continual crying.

This is not you. Ace. Think of Ace. He needs you.

My mind is utterly exhausted and depleted from this civil war inside me that continues to rage regardless of whether I want to step on the battlefield or not.

"Give him to me," I sob. Suddenly, the tears come harder than before as I reach out to take Ace. And the thing that affects me even more than my own thoughts is the look on Colton's face and the slight way he pulls Ace back, searching my eyes to make sure I'm okay, before handing him over to me.

I turn my back to him and sit down on the couch, grabbing my nursing pillow and within seconds Ace is latching on, greedy hands kneading, and little mouth frantic for food. My sobs continue uncontrollably, but I refuse to look up and meet Colton's eyes. I can't. I need to do my job. Be the best mom I can be to Ace while fighting this invisible anchor slowly weighing me down and pulling me under.

"Rylee?" Colton says calmly, restraint audible in his even tone as he tries to figure out what in the hell just happened.

It takes me a second to stop crying long enough to be able to speak. "Can you please run to the store and get some formula. I just really need formula." My voice is so quiet I'm surprised he hears it. But I need him to go so I can have a moment to pull myself together so he doesn't think I'm losing it, although I really feel like I am.

"Talk to me, please."

"I'm fine. Everything's fine. I just have a little case of the baby blues and what would really help me is if you went to the store right now and got me some formula so when I feel like this you can help me by feeding Ace." I try to gain back my business-as-usual attitude with slow and measured words asking for help the only way I'm capable of right now.

Please just go and give me a few minutes to have this breakdown so when you come back I'm better.

I can sense his hesitation to leave by the way he starts to move and stops a couple times before blowing out a loud sigh. "Are you sure that—?"

"Please, Colton. I'll be right here feeding Ace the ten minutes you're gone."

"Okay. I'll hurry." And the fact he hesitates again is almost too much for me to bear. The tears burn my throat again.

But he goes and the minute he's gone, I welcome the unsteady silence that wraps itself around me like a warm blanket fresh out of the dryer. I want to snuggle in it and pull it over my head until I can't see or think or feel. Lose myself to the nothingness around me.

I look down at Ace and hate myself immediately. I have this beautiful, healthy baby I know I love very much, but I can't seem to muster up that feeling when I look at him. This love is the most natural of instincts, the most simplest and complex form of love—from mother to child—and yet somehow something is so broken in me. When I look at him, all I feel is the ghost of it, instead of that all-encompassing rush I felt just days ago.

And knowing it and losing it is incomparably worse than never knowing it at all.

"Now that you have him, could you imagine if you lost him?" Eddie's taunt flickers through my mind. It haunts me. Make me question myself.

He did this to you, Rylee. He's responsible.

How is that possible? He can't be the cause of this.

It has to be me. Something has to be wrong with me.

My mom told me most new moms would drive on sidewalks to get home to their newborn. What does that say about me if I just want to drive the other way?

All I want is that connection to be back. For it to not feel so damn forced, because that's exactly how I feel right now, sitting in this empty house. I'm nursing him because he needs to be fed, not because I want to. *I'm just going through the motions.* I'm watching my life from behind a two-way mirror, and no one knows I'm hiding there.

I close my eyes, a contradiction in all ways, and try to quiet my head. And the minute I feel relaxed for the first time in what feels like forever, I'm scrambling up as fast as I can, Ace still latched on, and running for the office. I grab my phone and frantically dial Colton as that black veil of doom and gloom slips over my sanity.

Ring.

Images of Colton lying dead on the side of the road somewhere fill my head. Car smashed. Thrown from the car because he was in such a rush to help me he forgot to put his seatbelt on.

Ring.

Colton lying shot dead on the floor of the local minimart just up the road where he walked in and interrupted a robbery in progress.

Ring.

Tears are burning. My mind like a horror slide show telling me that Colton isn't coming home again. Panic claws at my throat, claustrophobia in wide-open space.

Ring.

"Pick up the phone. Pick up the phone!" I scream into the receiver, hysteria taking over as I move back into the family room, one hand still cradling Ace, the other on the phone.

Beep. Colton's voice fills the line as his voicemail begins.

No. Please no.

I pace the floor, nerves colliding with anxiety, panic crashing into fear. Working myself into a frenzy as I wait for the knock on the door from the police telling me something has happened to Colton.

The problem this time though is I can't step outside the emotions holding my thoughts hostage and realize I'm losing my mind like I was able to a few days ago. No, this time I'm in such a state of agitation that when Colton opens the door from the garage into the house I almost tackle him with Ace in my arms. "Oh my God, you're okay." I sob, wrapping my free arm around him, needing to feel the heat of his body against mine so I can believe it's true.

"Whoa!" he says, thrown off guard by my sudden attack. He drops the bag holding the can of formula and tries to comfort me as best as he can without smashing Ace between us. "I'm okay, Ry. Just went to the store for formula." I can hear the placating tone in his voice, the confusion woven in it, and I don't really care because he is here and whole and came back to me.

"I was so worried. I had this horrible feeling that something happened to you and when you didn't pick up your phone, I thought that—"

"Shh. Shh," he says, using his free hand to smooth over my cheek as he looks into my eyes. "I'm okay. I'm right here. I'm sorry about my phone. I've had it on do not disturb so if it rings it doesn't wake Ace up if he's napping."

I use the clarity in his eyes to soothe the uncertainty in me. "I'm gonna go put Ace in his swing, can you give him to me?" he asks, eyes alarmed as he looks down to where Ace is asleep in my arms and then looks back up to meet my gaze. I force myself to take a deep breath, hand him over, and then watch as Colton buckles him in the swing's bucket seat and turns it on.

Within seconds he's back in front of me, pulling me against his chest and wrapping his arms around me tightly. I breathe him in. Try to use everything familiar about him to quiet the riot within me: that place under the curve of his neck that smells of cologne, the rhythm of his heartbeat against my cheek, the scratch of his stubble against my bare skin, the weight of his chin resting on my head.

I sag, letting him hold up the weight that's been bearing down on my shoulders. "Ry . . . you're scaring the shit out of me. Please talk to me. Let me do something . . . anything to give you what you need. Helpless doesn't look good on any man, least of all me," he pleads, his arms only holding me tighter as his words make me want to pull away and dig my hands into his back simultaneously.

"Something's wrong with me, Colton. *I'm broken.*" My voice is barely a whisper, but I know he hears it because within a second his hands are on my face guiding it up to look at the concern heavy in his.

"No. Never. You're not broken, just a little bent," he says with a soft smile, trying to replicate that moment so very long ago. Bring back a piece of our past to try and fix the current situation, but this time I'm not too sure it's going to help.

"I feel like I'm going crazy." The words are so difficult to say. Like I'm pulling them one by one from the pit of my stomach. When they are finally out, I feel instant regret and relief concurrently. The continual contradictions seem to be the only thing my mind can keep consistent.

His head moves back and forth in reflex, immediately rejecting my comment as his hands run over my cheeks, eyes looking deeply into mine. "What can I do? Do you want me to call Dr. Steele?" I can tell he's panicked, lost in my minefield of hormones, unsure what to do to help me.

"No." I reject the idea immediately, shame and obstinacy ruling my response. "It's just the baby blues. It's just going to take me a few days to get over it." I hope he's fooled by the resolution in my voice because I sure as hell am not.

"Then why don't we get some help? Your mom or my mom or Haddie—"

"No!" The thought of someone else knowing is almost as suffocating as the emotion. Even my own mom. That would mean I've failed. That I'm not good enough. The thought causes more panic. "I don't want anyone to know."

An admission I can't believe I've made.

"Then a nanny. Someone who—"

"I'm not trusting Ace with anyone." This is a non-negotiable option for me. My body starts trembling at the thought, panic vibrating through every inch of my body at just the thought of someone we don't know touching him.

"Rylee," Colton says, exasperated. "I want to help you but you're not giving me any way that I can."

"I just need time," I whisper. *I hope*. My head shaking in his hands, my eyes blurring with tears, and my heart racing, as another swell of panic hits me and takes me for its ride. "Just hold me, please?" I ask.

"There's nothing I want to do more," he says as we sit on the couch and he cradles me across his lap so my head is on his shoulder, legs falling over his thighs.

I use his touch to calm me. Need it to. Let the warmth of his body and the feel of his thumb rubbing back and forth on my arm assuage the wrong inside me that I can't seem to make right or fight my way out from.

Snuggling into him, I realize how much I depend on this tie between the two of us. That connection we feel when we make love—the one we haven't been able to have since I've been on bed rest and know won't have again for several more weeks—has been lost. It makes me feel farther away when more than anything, what I really need is to feel close to *him*.

My heart aches in a way I can't explain. Almost as if it's in mourning. There has been no loss. Just a gain. A huge one. Ace.

I start to apologize again but stop myself. Apologies are only good if you can stop doing what you're sorry for. The problem is I don't know if I can.

But I've got two huge reasons to fight like hell.

Hopefully, they'll be enough.

Chapter Thirty-Two

Colton

"I'm all out of patience." That and a lot of other fucking shit but Kelly doesn't need to know that.

"I know you are. I've got two lines on him. I'm staking out one place—sitting in my car in front of it right now—and I've got Dean on the other. Twenty-four, forty-eight hours tops . . . But I've gotta tell you, Colton, if a man wants to get lost in a city, Los Angeles is a good place to do it." He pauses, unspoken words clogging up the line. "Are you sure, though? I mean—"

"Don't question me, Kelly. If you want out, walk now. I'll get Sammy to do what I need if you can't." There is no mistaking the threat in my tone.

"Relax, Donavan." Those words are like nails on a chalkboard to me. Piss me off. The irony since I think I said something similar to Ry to set her off. "I'll set everything up. Get it all in place but I still think you need to let the police handle this."

My laugh is low and rich. And lacking any amusement. "Eddie is a blip on their radar. Not mine. He's done enough to my family. I'm done fucking around with this. Get. It. Done."

"Understood. Just remember you can lead a horse to water but you can't make him drink."

"This horse is thirsty for revenge. I'm sure he'll drink."

"I'll call when I have him. Now go spend time with that hot wife and cute baby of yours." I know he's trying to cheer me up with the comment but it does anything but.

I murmur an incoherent goodbye because I'd love to do just that—spend time with my hot wife. But I can't. She's hidden beneath who knows what, and I can't do a goddamn thing to help her.

Give her time, she said earlier. Time my ass. Each hour she slips farther away from me.

Even now as I walk into our bedroom and see her on the bed with Ace, I can see her struggling—eyes scrunched tight, crease in her forehead—as she tries to feel that connection with him while he's nursing. She says it's the only time she doesn't feel completely numb. And thank fuck she's keeping her head above water. *Barely*. But luckily it's above the surface enough to nurse Ace because trying to get him to drink from a bottle has been a goddamn nightmare.

Useless seems to be my new middle name.

It's just the baby blues. That's it. *About ten days to two weeks*. That's how long Google tells me it can last. A topic that's a long fucking way from my typical search history of good porn sites, Indy Weekly Magazine, and surf reports.

We're eight days in. *Halfway through*.

This wasn't supposed to be this hard. We were supposed to have Ace—the baby we never thought we'd ever have—and be blissfully happy. Get the unexpected cherry on top of our happily-ever-after sundae.

Not this bullshit.

I thought the hard part would be coming face to face with my dad. That would be our biggest challenge. That I would be the one to fuck this all up. I had no clue that while I was closing the damn door on the skeletons in my closet, Ry would slowly come undone.

The other shoe most definitely has dropped.

Humpty fuckin' dumpty. The thought's there instantly of another time, another place when I felt this goddamn helpless. This time though . . . man, I'm not sure what it's going to take to put things back together again.

I walk over to the bed, to my whole fucking world, and hate that it doesn't feel so whole. I press a kiss to the side of her shoulder and just leave my lips pressed there for a second as I breathe her in. *Fight, Ry. We need you. I need you.* I'm not sure if she's asleep or not because she doesn't react, and man, how I want her to react. I know she's doing everything she can to keep herself together right now—for all of us—when it seems all she wants to do is fade away.

My scrappy fighter, who is so goddamn beautiful even now with circles beneath her eyes, will find her way. I just can't pressure her regardless of how much I want to.

Or at least that's what Google says. *Her mind is betraying her.*

Reaching down, I scoop up Ace, who thank fuck is completely content with his full belly, and carry him out of the room.

What the hell do I do with him now?

My hands feel like clubs when I change diapers.

My lullaby game is non-existent.

The blanket thing? How in the hell do you get it to look like a burrito? It's not that fucking easy. So what if I used a four-inch piece of duct tape to keep it closed? Call me resourceful.

Or an idiot.

It's taking everything I have not to cry uncle and call in the cavalry: our moms, Quinlan, Haddie. But then that's admitting defeat and fuck if I want to admit that. Plus I can't do that to Ry. She's already so fragile. Asking others for help without her consent would be a slap to her face. Push her farther under water when she's already drowning. Prove to her that I don't think she's capable of handling this.

And that's not what my intention would be. But with Ry right now? Shit, I know that's just how she'd take it.

Yet my cell sits on the counter and looks so damn tempting.

I'm a fish out of water. It's not pretty. I've paced, I've rocked, I've swayed, and no goddamn dice. Ace won't have any of it.

Just go to sleep!

"Look, little man," I say, holding him up so I can look in his eyes as he continues to fuss. "I'm new at this. Have no clue what the fu—er, heck I'm doing here. Can you give a guy a break and go easy on me? Please?"

I can't believe I'm pleading with a newborn—that I've been reduced to this—but desperate times call for desperate measures.

"It's just you and me, dude. *Boys club*. Your momma's having a tough time so you're stuck with me. I know I suck . . . don't have boobs like she does. Believe me, I miss them too. One day you'll understand. But for now . . . you have to man up. I'll show you how. First step, go to sleep for me."

Please. I close my eyes for a moment, unsure what to do now. My mom's not too far away and could get here quickly at this ungodly hour of night. When I open them back up, his eyes are closed.

Thank fuck for that.

Chapter Thirty-Three

Rylee

The darkness calls to me. Pulls me. Drowns me in its welcome warmth. It's like a lover's kiss, addictive, all-consuming, and irresistible.

I don't want to leave it.

But I have to.

I'm going to be better today. I'm going to look at Ace and want to wrap my arms around him and pull him in close to me, breathe him in, love him till it hurts.

Connect with him.

Be a mother to him.

My sweet Ace. My miracle baby. My everything.

The constant merry-go-round continues. Colton brings Ace in. He nurses. My head hurts, my heart aches, and my soul tries tirelessly to be what I need to be for him. For them.

It kills me when I can't.

Colton watches, gauges if I'm better today. Or worse. If he should leave Ace with me a little longer. If it's helping or hurting. There are lines etched on his face. Concern. Worry. Disbelief.

My mom. Short texts. Avoided phone calls. Unanswered messages. I know she's worried. I know I can talk to her. But I can't bring myself to pick up the phone.

Colton talks to me. Spends endless hours trying to pull me toward his light.

"I think I'm going to skip the next race or two. Denny deserves a shot at driving the car. Besides, I'll miss Ace too much if I'm gone."

You're lying. You're afraid to leave me here alone with him.

And yet I don't respond. Can't. Because I'm afraid of being alone with Ace too.

The silences screams around us.

"I talked to Zander today." He tries again.

My Zander.

"He sounds better."

If I could feel relief, I would. But I won't believe it until I see it for myself.

"I told him when you're feeling better you're going to have him come back over. He misses you. The boys miss you." I can see the look in his eyes that says, *I miss you.*

I miss you, too.

But Colton doesn't stop, doesn't dwell on the fact I don't respond to his unspoken words. He just walks slowly back and forth with Ace on his shoulder and rambles on about nothing and everything until his cell phone rings or our son falls asleep.

Or Ace needs to nurse again.

The endless cycle. One I abhor and crave desperately. Because it means he hasn't given up on me.

Guilt eats at me. Niggles in the back of my mind. Confuses me. I try. I really do. I fight the pull of the water over my head, drowning in the numbness that ebbs and flows before I can resurface from its hold. I fight to come up for air for my burning lungs, before plunging back down into its depths.

A text from Colton even though he's just downstairs:

Remember this one? It still holds true. I'm here. Keep fighting. I'll wait. All of Me by John Legend.

A flashback of our earlier times. An attempt to lift me up. A challenge for me to remember the feeling. The love. *Myself.* But I'm so buried I can't even lift my head. Or take a breath.

I'm so sorry, Colton. I'm so sorry, Ace.

I'm trying.

I'm fighting.

Don't give up on me.

I really do love you. I just can't feel it. Or show it.

But I will.

It's just the baby blues. I'm stronger than this. Than it. I just need a bit more time.

Tomorrow will be better.

Chapter Thirty-Four

Colton

"I can't wait to get my hands on this little guy." Haddie rubs her hands together as she leans forward and hugs me distractedly, already reaching out to grab Ace from me.

"Thanks for getting here so quickly. I didn't know who else to call." Who Rylee wouldn't freak out over, I add silently, because she sure as fuck is going to go ballistic when she wakes up to find Haddie here.

"Anytime. Besides I should be thanking you," she says, lacing kisses on Ace's head. "Ry's been so set on getting his routine down before having visitors that I thought I'd never get to see him."

"About that . . ." I say, taking a deep breath, knowing I'm crossing some kind of marital boundary I shouldn't be, but am past caring. "She's struggling a bit. Baby blues." I nod my head to reinforce my words, to try and relay the rest of what Rylee has forbid me to say. Haddie narrows her eyes at me.

"Oh, that's normal. Everyone I know goes through it a bit. No worries, Donavan, I'll cheer her up," she says with a wink.

I know I need to move. Get to Kelly ASAP but fuck is it hard to leave Ry when she's like this. This could go so wrong on so many fronts. Ry is going to kill me. She's not going to be able to hide from Haddie what's going on. And a tiny little piece of me feels relieved because I don't know what to do anymore.

I'm lost. Like on-a-deserted-island lost and don't have a clue how to help her.

This could push her over the edge or help reel her back. I hope to hell it's the latter.

"Now go. Get. I know you're in a rush. I've got it covered here," Haddie says, interrupting my thoughts.

"She's napping upstairs. I didn't tell her I was going."

"GO! I've got it under control. You're starting to eat into my auntie and Ace time." She starts to shut the front door, and I walk toward the car where Sammy is waiting in the passenger seat when she calls to me. "Hey, Colton?"

I turn, my hand resting with the car door handle, anticipation humming in my blood. "Yeah?"

"Kick Eddie extra hard in the nuts for me, will ya? He deserves it for fucking with my bestie."

"Only if he's still standing when I'm done with him." I slide into the driver's seat. Sammy's chuckle fills the car, and my mind races.

"We're good to go?" I ask, my eyes flickering back and forth from Kelly to Sammy to make sure we're all on the same page.

"Yep. Dean's got him inside. Everything else is in place." Our eyes meet, his unspoken warning I don't want to see is loud and fucking clear within them: cool my jets, my temper, and let the plan work.

And as much as I know he's right, I turn my back to him and start up the walk without acknowledging I saw it.

No one's going to tell me how to run my own show. I know the fallout for my actions. They're clear as fucking day. But I also know Eddie's fucked with my wife and my son, and if a man doesn't stand up for his family, he shouldn't be standing at all.

Going to jail isn't an option. And not because I care about having a record or the media frenzy it would cause. I just can't do that to Ry with how she is or to Ace with how little and helpless he is. But it sure as fuck doesn't mean I'll toe the line.

Bring it, fucker. I'm ready for you. Pumped and primed. Push my buttons. *Pretty please*.

Without knocking, I open the door to the rundown apartment. Kelly's cohort, Dean, is standing just inside. Our eyes meet. A mutual understanding is passed between us—my *thanks*, his *take your time*—before he steps out without another sound.

I take three steps in. I don't hear the door shut. I don't notice that Sammy's back is pressed against it, because my eyes are focused on the man sitting on the ripped couch in front of me: elbows on knees, head hanging down, leg anxiously jogging up and down.

Rage like I've felt very few times in my life roars through me. A fucking freight train of fury I need to keep on track before I let it derail.

I clear my throat. When Eddie realizes someone else is in the apartment, he whips his head up with eyes wide as saucers and mouth open. He looks like shit. *Good.*

"What the . . .?" he asks at first, looking startled, eyes blinking as he shoves up from the couch to stare at me again. And then he belts out a long, low condescending laugh that does nothing but confuse me and piss me off further.

"Something funny?" I ask, fists clenched, curiosity piqued why this is so amusing to him.

"I should have known," he says with a shake of his head, his body visibly relaxing.

Give me a reason, you fucker. Just one.

"Were you expecting somebody else?" I know my threat is nothing compared to the others he will face. That unexpectedly works in my favor.

"Yes. No." That taunting smirk is back front and center. "Your pretty little wife, perhaps."

Bingo.

I'm across the room in two seconds. Arm cocked. Fist flying. The give of flesh against my knuckles. The thud of bone connecting against bone. The crunch that is nowhere near satisfying enough after what he's done to my family.

The sound of glass shattering as his arm hits the lamp and knocks it over breaks through my silent rage, brings me back to the here and now. Reminds me that I want some answers before I finish what he started.

I don't worry about the neighbors hearing us and calling the cops. In places like this no one pays attention. They all keep their head down and stay in their own trouble. I should know. I grew up in a place just like this. No one came to the rescue of the little boy screaming in pain on the other side of the wall.

The thought fuels my anger. Adds strength to my resolve to not be that person. To not stoop to the level of the man in front of me.

But God, how I want to stoop.

"Look at me," I yell. My voice fills the room. He lifts his head up from where he's landed askew on the couch, a red welt swelling on his cheek. "Don't talk about my wife, again. This is between you and me, you fucking bastard."

That chuckle of his is louder, and it takes every ounce of restraint I have to not unleash the fury I feel.

Because I want what I came here for. Answers first. Vindication second. And, oh how sweet that last one will be. He doesn't have a clue what's about to hit him.

"You want to settle a score? Go right ahead. You think you scare me, Donavan? Think again. *You. Can't. Touch. Me.* You're such a pussy you have to bring your goddamn henchman over there," he says, pointing to Sammy standing silently at the door, "to do your dirty work for you."

"I think your black eye will prove I can do my own dirty work just fine." I look over my shoulder and lift my chin to Sammy to tell him to leave. It's better this way. No witnesses. No *he said, she said.* Just my word against Eddie's. Kelly's so damn convinced that Eddie'll sue if I touch him anyway.

Oops. Guess I already broke that rule. My bad.

"Is everyone in your life that tight on your string? One pull on it and they dance?" He raises his eyebrows as his eyes follow Sammy out the door. I glare at him. Bide my time. He's so fucking arrogant I can see him itching to gloat about how he pulled this all off.

"You don't know shit about my life, Eddie."

"I know I won't dance. So how does it feel to pull a string and get back a big giant *fuck you,* huh?"

"Is that what this was all about? Proving you're better than me?" I ask, feigning indifference when I'm anything but.

Take the bait, Eddie. Feed your ego. Prove. Me. Wrong.

He rises from the couch and steps toward me with eerie calm. "I *am* better than you," he says as he steps right into my wheelhouse. Tempting me like never before. "And I'm not stupid either. Lift your shirt up. I bet your pansy ass is wearing a wire. Trying to hook me on something I didn't do."

Is he fucking crazy? Like I'd let the police be in on this little get together we're having. Shit, he's going to wish I went with a wiretap.

"Prison was that good to you, huh?" I taunt as I lift my shirt up and turn around for him to see I'm not wired. "You into guys now?

"Fuck you," he spits.

"No thanks," I say, taking a step closer. "I want nothing more from you than answers. Everything else you've got coming to you is of your own making."

He quirks his head, arrogant smirk spreading wide. "Thanks to your son, nothing else is coming to me. Sold that picture of him to the tabloids." He sneers. "Made a mint and paid off old debts. *Thanks to Ace*, I'm free and clear."

Fucking pompous bastard. Joke's on him though. That's the only reason I'm not throwing another fist into his face.

"Bravo," I say as I clap my hands slow and deliberately. His eyes narrow, his jaw clenches. Good. I'm pissing him off. "You could have made more money with the video though." The lie flows off my tongue, but I have to force the words out. "Bet you didn't think of that now, did you?"

There's the hook, fucker. Take a big bite so I can set it.

"Prison has a way of putting things on hold." He glares at me. "But it also allowed me a lot of time to plan, to figure out how to get the fucker back who put me there."

"Get me back? *For what?* Because I didn't let you waltz out of my office with the blueprints, sell them to someone else as your own, collect the royalties, and get away with it? Are you out of your fucking mind? Did you think I was going to let you take what was mine and use it?"

"Seems like I took what was yours and did it anyway."

The quiet comment's double meaning—the stolen blueprints and exposure of Rylee on the video—calls to me like a goddamn moth to a flame. This time I can't resist.

He sees my punch coming and gets a quick one into my rib cage before my knuckles meet his jaw. His head snaps back. His body slams into the wall behind him. The sound of him grunting overrides my quick sting of pain from where he landed his.

My body vibrates with anger. Pure unfettered rage as I stare at the waste of space and talk myself out of finishing this right now. And of course because he's a cocky fucker, when he lifts his head back up, that curl to his lips tests my restraint.

Jesus Christ. This is so much fucking harder than I thought it would be. To keep my shit together when all I want to do is show him the rage I feel. Throw punch after punch. Relieve the stress and pain he has caused us.

But that won't solve anything.

"You're a useless piece of shit. Deserve everything you get."

"What I get? Like I said, Donavan. You can't touch me. I did nothing illegal. The video wasn't yours. I didn't steal it. It was in a safety deposit box while I served my time. Shit, it gained in value."

"Did that eat at you, Eddie?" I ask, stepping back into his personal space. "Taunt you every fucking day while you sat in a six-by-ten cell? You felt entitled to fuck with my family because you're a useless piece of shit who can't control his own gambling habits, so to save his own ass, has to rob Peter to pay Paul? It's so much easier to place the blame somewhere else than realize you did this to yourself." I poke my finger in his chest as I laugh under my breath. Taunt him. "Talk about being a pussy."

Dangle the carrot.

"A pussy?" he asks, voice louder as he stands taller. Little-man complex front and center as he puffs his chest out. "You cost me everything!" His voice thunders into the empty apartment, spittle flying from his mouth, as he slowly becomes unhinged. "My wife. My kids. *Everything*!"

"Cheaters never prosper," I say in a singsong voice. He starts to come after me, nostrils flared, fists clenched, but stops when I just raise my eyebrows at him. My empathy is nil. "You. Can't. Touch. Me," I whisper back to him in the same voice he used with me.

"Fuck you!" he screams, rage winding with each and every word. "You're the one who caused all of this. Not me. You want to point a finger? Point it at yourself, you arrogant son of a bitch."

"I caused this? You're out of your goddamn mind!" *Come at me. Please.* Give me a fucking reason to go against my promise to myself. *Motherfucker.* My fists are clenched, my blood is on fire, and it is taking every ounce of restraint I have to not knock his teeth out. But I don't. He's baiting me. Doing a damn fine job of it. But a black eye is one thing. Knocking his teeth out is another.

But damn is it tempting.

His jaw clenches. Hands fist. His body physically bristles at my criticism. His ego so large he's dying to correct me. "You're such an arrogant asshole. I knew you wouldn't part with your money. Even planted some seeds with the tabloids to put pressure on you. But fuck, you're the goddamn golden boy so you figured you'd take the hit in stride. Get an ego boost from the attention it sure as fuck was going to get you. But not once did you think about that precious wife of yours, did you?" His words serve their purpose. Dig at me. Carve into the guilt. "Threw her to the goddamn wolves rather than pay me the money. You proved me right. You're all about you and could give a fuck less about Rylee or her reputation—"

"Don't you fucking say her name again," I yell. I connect with him, forearm against his throat as I pin him against the wall behind him. And he doesn't resist. Knows damn well he's pushing my buttons and he's having way too much fun doing it because he thinks I can't touch him. His lack of reaction a non-verbal, *fuck you*.

"Why? Does it bug you, Donavan, that I called it right? That when I knew you weren't going to pay, I chose to fuck your wife over anyway. Prove to her what a piece of shit her husband is. That he chose money over her?" I press my arm harder into him, needing to shut him up yet wanting the torture of hearing more. "How did it feel when she pushed away from you? When she blamed you for losing her job? I hoped it ripped you apart inside. Fucked with your head because it's nowhere close to how I felt when you took my wife from me."

"Go to hell," I grit out, unable to move because I know if I do, I'm not going to be able to stop myself. My fury has a mind of its own and all it's waiting for is any little thing to set it off. "I'm not playing into your mind games. Because you're leaving out that you're the one who fucked up. You were so goddamn thirsty for revenge that you forgot about the loan sharks waiting to crawl up your ass. You let your temper get the best of you, uploaded the video without even negotiating, and were shit out of luck because your bargaining chip just went out the goddamn window. You lost your money and knew the bill collectors were coming." I let the smirk play the corners of my mouth as my fists beg to finish the talking for us.

"I get the last laugh though, don't I?" he taunts in his calm, even voice despite the pressure on his chest. "That little video made you the 'it couple' for the media. Caused a frenzy. Frenzy means more money. Upped the price of the photo of your son to a pretty penny. Killed two birds with one stone: paid off my debts and got a final 'fuck you' in with your kid." He leans his head forward as far as he can so his face is inches from mine. He whispers but I can hear it clear as fucking day. "You're not such a badass when every man in America is watching that wife of yours come and fantasizing it was them with her, now are you?"

Restraint snapped.

Promise to myself reneged.

The fucker deserves it.

This one's for Rylee

My fist flies. The impact is bittersweet as his head snaps to the side, blood spurting from his nose, a groan falling out as he brings his hands to his face and slides down the wall. I'm only allowing myself one.

Fuck it's going to be hard to walk away. *So I don't*. I step closer, rein in the fury and take the high road when all I want to do is crawl in the gutter with him. I reach out and yank his hair so his head snaps up to look at me.

"Don't *ever* come near my family again." My threat is plain as day. I let go of his hair, shoving his head back. "What is it they say about revenge? Before you try to get it, make sure to dig two graves?" I grate out, voice shaking, body amped up on adrenaline. "Maybe you should have taken the advice." He looks up, confusion flickering in his eyes as to what I mean. His mind only focused on the grave he dug for me, and not the one he should have dug for himself.

Well, if he doesn't get it now, he sure as fuck is going to understand in about two minutes.

"Fuck you," he says as I walk toward the door.

I stop and hang my head down as a chuckle falls from my mouth that clearly says the same thing back to him. I let the silence eat up the room. Allow him to think this is all there is going to be.

And then I drop the hammer.

"You may have paid your debts back. But I think you forgot about the interest you owe them. I guess I'll let someone else do my dirty work for me after all."

I open the door and walk out of the apartment, a part of me wishing I could see the expression on his face, the other part of me never wanting to see him again. Holding my hand up, I ask the guys standing a few feet away to give me a minute. A goddamn second to catch my breath and figure out how the fuck I feel about getting but not getting what I wanted.

Because yes, I got my answers. Got them tied up with a nice little bow that normally I'd question the ease in which he confessed them. But I know that fucker inside out. I worked with him for years, watched him across the table from me in mediation and on the stand during the trial, can read him like a fucking road map. Do I question the answers' validity? Not enough to care because he was so itching to one-up me. Desperate to prove he stuck it to me in the end—got me back—that he was so amped up on the high of it, there was no way in hell he'd be able to spin the truth.

So yes, I'm good with his explanations. But fuck if I'm not struggling with giving him what he deserves by my own hand. *Rylee*. The reason. The answer. The goddamn everything. *That's why* I have to be okay with this outcome. With someone else doing my dirty work to reach the same endgame.

And when I look up, they are there, ready and willing to do it for me. And for them. Three fuckers solid as tree stumps. Scary shit to owe money to these guys.

"You have five minutes to collect your interest before Kelly calls the cops. Make sure he's alive when they get here. He seems to be in violation of a restraining order."

Fucker has no idea what's about to hit him. Fairly sure it'll wipe the smarmy smirk off his face.

I think he'll welcome going back to jail after they get done with him.

I meet Sammy's eyes. I see the question there. *You've wanted a piece of Eddie for so damn long, why are you walking away now?*

But Sammy knows why. Probably can still hear the fury in my voice from the hospital all these days later. *Her. Safety. Comes. First.*

And if not, it doesn't matter. I don't need to justify shit to anyone. I have two perfectly good reasons at home. They're what matters. My end all, be all.

The reason I'll never stop trying to be the man deserving of *them*.

I just shake my head and slide into the waiting car. I've wasted enough time on Eddie fucking Kimball.

Eddie will not be bugging you again. He's in custody.

My feet stop as I look at the text. I need a minute.

Fuck, I need more than a minute. I need to drown myself in a fifth and take a whole goddamn evening to swim in it. So I can brood. Be that cocky asshole I used to be and not give a fuck about anything or anyone.

But I can't.

So I sit down on the step to the front door and sigh, close my eyes, hang my head, and give myself sixty seconds I can't afford to take. Because once I walk in the door, I need to be the same man who just walked away from Eddie without throwing another punch. Responsible. Mature. Selfless.

Right now I want to be anything but.

Or is it that I'm a pussy and fear what I'm walking in on? A goddamn powder keg of unknown. Will my wife be here? Because I miss her so fucking much. Or just that shell of her that I've grown to despise?

Yeah, you've been pussified, Donavan. Needing a woman to complete you when you used to not need shit. My, how the player has fallen.

I chuckle. Not for relief but because I need something to take the edge off all this pent-up emotion. And because I know what else I need to do when I go inside, what I need to tell Ry is going to happen, and I just hope the news about Eddie helps take the sting out of it.

The door opens behind me. It closes. And I wait for it. Know it's coming.

"You okay?" Haddie asks as she sits down beside me and holds out a beer and a bag of ice to me. I look over to her, wondering how she knew I needed both. "Call it a lucky guess."

"Thanks." I take them and hiss when I put the ice on my knuckles. We sit in silence for a few moments.

"Shane stopped by unexpectedly. He's in with Ace right now," she says, surprising me. But I shouldn't be. Shane's one of Ry's boys. He knows something is wrong just like I do. "Ry's out on the upstairs patio. I talked her into getting some fresh air."

"She is?" Hope tinges my voice. She must be feeling better. I knew she'd come around.

"Colton?" By the way Haddie says my name, I know: Rylee isn't better at all. In fact, it reinforces what I have to do even more.

"I'm calling the doctor in the morning." I answer the unspoken question she left hanging out there, bring the beer to my lips, and take a long pull on it. And I hate myself for saying it because now I've put it out there, I have to admit there is something wrong with Rylee.

And I don't want there to be something wrong with her.

"At first I was pissed at you, at her . . . You didn't tell me and I'm her bestie. I should know this. But

I get it. I understand how proud Ry is. How she thinks she can handle everything and if she admits she can't then it makes it even worse. But, Colton, this is about her getting better. Not about her being weak." She leans her head on my shoulder and sighs.

I shake my head. Emotions fucked. Head more so. "I thought that dealing with Eddie today would help. I could come back and tell her he won't bother us anymore. Maybe knowing that worry was gone might be what she needed to help her break through . . ." I stop when I realize how fucking stupid that sounds.

"It might help some," Haddie says softly, "but it's not going to fix her. We're back to Matchbox Twenty on repeat again but there's no music this time. *In fact, there's no sound at all.* She needs help, Colton."

I scrub my hands over my face. "I know, Had. I know."

"She tried to keep it together for a while but I know her well enough to know better," she says as I stand up.

"Thank you . . . for everything." Our hug is brief, my need to see Ry ruling my thoughts.

"Always," Haddie says as I open the door and walk into my house.

I hear voices, my hopes rising to be dashed once again when I see Shane on the couch talking to Ace. And fuck, for some reason seeing Ace hits me hard, validates the reasons why I walked away from Eddie.

My end all, be all.

Shane looks up when he notices me. "Hey," he says as he stands immediately, eyes locked on mine. I know a threat when I see one but for the fucking life of me can't figure out why Shane's the one giving it to me.

"What's wrong, Shane?" I ask, mind spinning as he hands Ace off to Haddie without letting me see him first.

"Can we talk?"

And if he wasn't so dead serious, I might laugh at the sudden growl to his voice and stiffening of his spine. "Sure," I say as I fire a look at Haddie and get a shrug in response. "Why don't we head into the office?"

I lead the way, let him walk in first, and then shut the door. We take seats on opposite sides of the desk, and this time when he looks at me I see so much more than the threat from a moment ago. I see a scared kid trying to be a brave man and I'm not sure of the footwork of how to go about this.

Well, I'm scared too. For different reasons. But scared nonetheless.

"What'd you want to talk about, Shane?"

He shifts in his seat, fidgets his hands, and before he even speaks, I can see we need to spend some more time together so I can help him look controlled when he's not feeling it. That's a must for a man and I've dropped the ball in teaching him that.

"You're supposed to be the one who takes care of her," he accuses with more certainty than his eyes reflect, suddenly nervous now that he's actually standing his ground. "I mean, you can see something's wrong with her, right?"

I bite back the flippant comment I'd normally give—how I sure as shit know how to take care of my fucking wife. The exhaustion and the shit with Eddie make it so goddamn tempting, but I'm able to find my restraint. To realize this is Shane in front of me trying to make sure Ry's okay.

I lean back in the chair and roll my shoulders, put myself in his shoes. "She's having a tough go of it, isn't she?" I meet his gaze. I don't shy away from it, because I want him to see I understand Rylee needs help.

"If you're not going to get her a doctor, then I will," he states, voice resolute but then throws me for a fucking loop when his eyes well up with tears before he quickly looks down.

"I'm calling one tomorrow. She asked me for time to try and get through it," I explain with more patience than I feel. But it's one of her boys, a part of her family. "But she's not getting any better so I'm going to get her some help. She's going to be okay, Shane."

"Don't say that," he says between clenched teeth. He squeezes his eyes closed and his face transforms. "That's what they said about my mom. And look what happened to her." His voice breaks as he delivers the words.

Fuck. How could I have not seen this coming? How could I have not realized Shane would compare Rylee's postpartum depression to his mother's depression? The illness that caused her to take her own life in an overdose of pills. Or the fact he is the one who found her and is forever scarred by the memory.

"Look at me, Shane." I pause, waiting for him to lift his head and meet my eyes. The courageous man who walked in here is gone. The broken boy who lost his world when his mom died has replaced him. I scramble to fix it. Him. Use words that won't do shit but will sound like it. "She will get better." And I'm not sure if the strong resolve in my voice is to convince him or me. "I am going to have a doctor see her tomorrow. It might take some time, but we'll get our Rylee back, okay?"

He stares at me no doubt deciding if he believes me or not. He nods his head slowly as he begins to speak. "Rylee is the only mom I have. I'll do whatever it takes to make sure she gets better."

I nod my head, the words he doesn't say are reflected in his eyes: *I can't lose another person.*

I understand that more than you know, kid.

"That makes two of us."

Chapter Thirty-Five

Rylee

"Ry?" Colton's voice shocks me from the darkness of my mind into the blinding light of the patio.

Everything wars inside me: relief against spite, fear against hope, numbness against pain.

He stands in the doorway. Vitriol-laced accusations scream in my head but don't form into words. Can't. It's too much effort.

"You left me." My voice sounds hollow, unaffected. Numb.

I missed you like a drowning person misses the air.

The baby monitor clicks as he sets it on the table. The cushion whooshes as he sits beside me. His eyes give an apology I don't want to accept.

"I had to take care of some things, Ry." He sounds tired. Rough. Something's going on and yet I can't find enough energy to care.

My body begins to hum. The ghost of the panic attack I had when I found out he had left comes back to haunt me. I wring my hands. Try to hold on to my control even though I can feel it slowly slipping away from me.

I can't breathe.

"I went to see Eddie."

Air feels like water, slowly filling my lungs with each inhale. Closing over my head and pulling me under.

"It was the first time he'd surfaced so I had to go."

The deeper I fall the more my body begins to burn with heat from the inside out.

"He won't be bugging us ever again."

I fight back. Break the surface. My lungs heaving for the air his words bring me.

My eyes open wide and meet his, a moment of clarity amidst this haze.

"Thank you," I say, voice hoarse as I try to elicit the emotion to match my words. *But I can't feel.* When I don't want to it's all I can do, and when I do want to, I can't.

I keep my eyes locked on his. Hope they'll be the lifeline I need to keep me afloat, and sustain this feeling of normalcy for a little longer. The span of time seems to be less and less as the days go on.

Colton reaches out and runs the back of his hand down the side of my cheek. Tears well. I fight them back. I open my mouth to speak, but the words don't come out.

I need help.

He moves to sit next to me, pulls me in close to him. I try to find comfort, try to use that hum of our bodies touching to tell me I'm still alive. And if I'm alive I can keep treading water until I can get to the edge.

I close my eyes. A tear slides over. A little piece of me leaving with it.

"Shane is really worried about you."

I saw it in his eyes: the fear, the memories of his mom, the worry. I couldn't stop them. I couldn't reassure him. He saw right through it.

Guilt. The one constant I feel is back, swims in my head.

"Your mom. I'm not going to be able to keep her away much longer, Ry. She's worried." *I am too.* I can hear the unspoken words in his voice but don't have the wherewithal to respond. "I've kept her happy with pictures and videos. Telling her you're sleeping when she calls. She's going to come up this weekend."

"No!" It's the only show of emotion I can give. The need to keep this under wraps from those who would be disappointed in my failure the most.

"I'm going to call Dr. Steele then." His voice is soft but slams into my ears like the harshest of noises.

"No!" My voice cracks with panic—the word on repeat in my head—as I try to shove away from him. Struggle as he pulls me hard into him to stop my resistance against the idea.

I fight because I can handle this.

No, I can't.

And because I'm scared. What if I can't ever find my way back?

Yes, I can.

The darkness is so much more tempting than the fight. Less work. Less struggle. But Ace and Colton are worth fighting for. I'm so sick of the dark. So sick of its loneliness. I do the only thing I can: cling onto Colton, my light.

"I'm holding tight so you can let go, Ryles," he says into the crown of my head, the heat from his breath warming the cold lingering inside me. "Let go, baby. Deal with what you need to. And just know that Ace and I are here for you when you come back to us. Then we'll get our little piece of peace."

He still loves me.

He still wants us.

He's fighting the fight for me.

Even when I can't.

Chapter Thirty-Six

Colton

"Haddie must have called in the troops."

My mother's laugh is deep and rich through the phone. The concern is there though. I can hear her hiding it.

But it's okay. I am too.

I glance to the extra bedroom where the door is shut and wonder what is taking them so long.

"You have no idea. She only means well." Then silence. *Fuck.* Here we go. "You should have told us, Colton. It's nothing to be ashamed of. We're here to help you." I can hear the hurt in her voice, get that she thinks I didn't trust her coming into our private life enough to tell her what was going on. And if my own mother feels this way, I'm going to have to steel myself for how Ry's mom is going to handle this.

I clear my throat, unsure what to say. "It's not like that, Mom. It's complicated." Tread lightly, Donavan. She's not intruding; she just wants to be a mom.

Just like Rylee does.

"I know it is." Her voice is softer. Her hurt feelings back in check. Being a mom again—pushing away her hurt to help me deal with mine. "Has the doctor finished talking to her yet?"

I glance at the door again. "No."

"I'm sure she's just reassuring Rylee. Sometimes when you hear things you don't want to hear and they're spoken by someone else, you actually listen to them."

"I miss her, Mom."

God, I sound like such a pussy. You can't miss someone who is right in fucking front of you twenty-four/seven.

"Of course you do. You've all had a lot of changes over the past few months."

"Changes?" I snort and then press a kiss to the top of Ace's head. Use him to calm me. "I feel like we've had the shit beat out of us so much in the past month I'm surprised we're not black and blue." Sarcasm she doesn't deserve is thick in my voice.

"You're only alive if you bruise," she says softly.

Then I must be thriving.

"Yeah." I sigh. My eyes are back on the door but her comment sticks in my mind.

"You can't do this all yourself, son. Let all of us help you. We're setting up a schedule so we can come and—"

"I don't know about that, Mom. I appreciate it, but Rylee—"

"Sorry. This is what family does. We rally the troops and take care of our own," she says, the no-nonsense tone in her voice taking me back twenty years to when I was a punk kid getting reprimanded. "You don't have a choice. Ry's mom, Quinlan, Haddie, and I will take shifts if need be. Anything it takes. And you'll take the help and not argue. Understood?"

Yep. Right back there to being ten and getting caught trying to light firecrackers in the backyard.

"Yes, ma'am."

"And you need the break too. You'll burn yourself out. A proud man is a good man. But he can also be a stupid one."

I can't help the laugh that falls from my mouth. My blunt mother telling me like it is. One of very few women who can.

"Mom, I have to go," I say as the door opens.

"Let me know what she says so I can let everyone know and—"

I hang up the phone. Cut her off. I need to know.

"Dr. Steele?"

"Walk me out, please?" she asks.

"Sure." We head to the front door. This doesn't sound good. My dread builds with each footstep. My heart is in my throat by the time we walk outside and shut the door behind us.

"He is an adorable little guy, isn't he?" she says as she focuses on Ace when all I want her to do is tell me about Rylee.

"Doc?" I finally ask, hoping she'll have pity on me.

"You were right to call me, Colton." The breath I'm holding burns in my lungs. "She's definitely struggling with more than the typical baby blues."

I feel a flicker of relief. I don't know why. She hasn't said she's going to be okay, but at least I'll know the beast we're facing.

"Okay, so what do I need to do for her?" Something. Anything. I'm a guy. I need to fix things and this not being able to fix Rylee is fucking me up.

She smiles softly at me. "To be honest, there's no clear-cut answer here. I talked with Rylee. Explained how she's not alone. That a lot of women go through this and that getting help does not mean she's failing as a mother." She reaches out and plays with Ace's hand as she continues. "Sometimes, postpartum depression is triggered by a sequence of events that seems out of the person's control. Add in the rush of hormones. Then there's the pressure of trying to get a newborn—who couldn't care less about a schedule—to be on a schedule because every book you've read says that's what you should be doing or you're not doing it right. All of those combined are like the perfect storm of uncontrolled chaos. In Rylee's case, her mind has internalized it all and has fallen into a little downward dip of depression."

I blow out a breath, hear her words and know it's not my fault. But I'm a guy so I blame myself nonetheless. "Is she going to be okay?"

She nods. "I've written a prescription for some anti-depressants and—"

"Can she still nurse?" I ask, knowing that nursing is the only time she feels somewhat connected to Ace.

"Yes. There is much debate on this. In my opinion the trade-off is worth it: getting Rylee on the road to recovery versus a trace of the drugs passed on through the milk."

"Okay."

"She's a fighter, Colton. Get her out in the fresh air. A walk on the beach. A drive in the car. Anything you can think of doing to get her up and about without triggering her panic attacks."

I chuckle. She does realize who we are, right? Did she forget there's a reason she's making a house call and we're not going to her office?

"I know. It's difficult in . . . your situation, but the more stimuli, the better."

"Thanks," I say quietly. "I appreciate you making the house call."

"She's going to be fine, Colton. She just needs a little time. It's not going to happen overnight. The drugs take some time to take effect, so be patient like you've been so far, and soon enough you'll have your wife back."

The words cause my heart to pound. Fucking stupid since she's been here all along. And yet my pulse is racing at the mere thought of getting my best friend back. Hearing her laughter. Watching her eyes light up with joy over staring at Ace. Listening to her sing off key to her beloved Matchbox Twenty. It's the little things I miss. The day-to-day. The insignificant.

Desperate may not be something a man should wear but fuck if I'm not swathed in it wanting her to come back to me.

After the gates close behind Dr. Steele, I head inside, uncertain which Rylee I'm going to find: The fighter I've grown to admire or the lost woman I can't even recognize.

"Let's go, little man. Let's see if we can make your momma smile."

Chapter Thirty-Seven

Rylee

Fading in.

My moments with Ace, the ones I can feel, I try to hold tight to them. Try to use them to keep me afloat. Soak them in.

A text from Colton: **Photograph by Ed Sheeran.**

A rush of warmth. A flash of happy. The recollection of that night. Of sweetness. A picture frame waiting to be filled. Memories to make.

Panic I won't be able to make it. A struggle to hold on to the good from the song, and not the bad. Please help me hold on to the good.

Falling out.

Thoughts come. Thoughts go.

The house a constant revolving door: my mom, Haddie, Dorothea, Quinlan. Frustrating me. Reviving me. Holding me up so I can fall, but not be alone when I do.

My mom. Opening blinds. Zipping through the house like Mary Poppins infusing her cheer to try and make me smile. Except I can't smile. I can't feel anything. Watching her hold Ace, coo over him, connecting with him should make me happy, jealous—anything—and yet I feel absolutely nothing.

The clock ticks. Time in Ace's life I can't get back.

My Colton. I watch him with Ace. Day after day. Night after night. Moments I capture, file away, and pray can keep. Colton asleep with Ace on his chest, tiny fingers curled against his muscles. Made-up lullabies that dig into the fog and make me feel something . . . lighter. A flicker of warmth. A strand of hope. A moment I can embrace.

Before the lead curtain falls again.

Seconds spent.

A tug of war of inner wills.

Hours gone.

And every night, Colton pulls me against him as we lie in bed and murmurs in my ear the wonderful memories we still have to make to put in our picture frame. The warmth of his body against mine is his subtle reminder to his wife, who is still lost in her own mind, that she's not alone.

Days lost.

"Teddy called today," Colton says. The ocean breeze is cool. The soothing surge from Ace nursing a little stronger today. The fog a little lighter.

"Hmm?" Afraid to hope. Wanting to know but fearing the worst.

"The board voted to keep him on as director." An unexpected flutter. A tinge of excitement. "You'll be reinstated if you choose to go back to work after your maternity leave."

A deep breath in. Exhale out.

"Mm-hmm." A bit of inflection.

Colton's smile at my response. *I love his smile.* The feel of Ace's hand kneading my breast. *I love his little hands*. A glimpse of hope.

A pile of jumbled jigsaw pieces. Two finally fitting together.

A text from Colton: **I'll Follow You by Jon McLaughlin**

He tries so hard to keep me above the fray. To do anything to help me hold on a little longer than last time. A message to tell me I'm not alone. That it's okay.

A pinprick of light at the end of the tunnel.

You can do this.

Change is never easy.

Fight to hold on.

Fight to let go.

Fight because they're your whole world.

Chapter Thirty-Eight

COLTON

"I still can't get over it."

"Get over what?" I ask as I look from where Ace is passed out on my chest—mouth open, hands up, legs apart. Content as fuck. And thankfully asleep since he's been running me ragged.

"You. A dad." Becks chuckles with a shake of his head.

"Yeah well, he looks sweet right now . . . but don't let him fool you. He's a stubborn little cuss. He had me up to my elbows in shit earlier. Not a pretty sight." Fucking disgusting. But shit, I'd do it a hundred more times if I could be rewarded by the soft smile on Rylee's face when I looked up and saw her standing in the doorway watching us.

Becks throws his head back and laughs. "Fuck. I would have paid to see that."

"No. You wouldn't," I deadpan, "but you do what you have to do."

Becks nods his head and lifts his chin toward the pool deck where Rylee is reading. Baby steps. Tiny bits of her returning to me. "Haddie says she's doing better?"

"One step forward. Three back." I shrug. "But at least we're moving, right? Just trying to figure out our new kind of normal or some shit like that."

"And you're hanging in there?"

"Most days," I say with a laugh. "But God I'd kill to get on the track. I need some speed to clear my head and give me a chance to not think for a bit."

"Not thinking is what you do best. You don't need to hit the track for that."

"Fuck off," I say with a laugh. And regardless of my response, I welcome the dig. Need a bit of our typical banter to get a little part of my normal.

"Dude, you better watch your mouth or else Ace's first word is going to be fuck. And while it would be funny as fuck," he says, raising his eyebrows at the intended pun, "I think that might earn you a spot in the doghouse."

"True . . . but fuck—"

"There you go again." He laughs, causing me to just shake my head and sigh.

"This is going to be harder than I thought."

"Most good things in life are," he says with a lift of his eyebrows. And I stare at him for a beat, hearing what he's saying. That shit's tough right now but it's all worth it.

Damn straight it is.

"Like I said, just say when and I'll get the track time reserved for you," he says as he stands. His unspoken, *I've got your back*, comes through loud and clear.

"Thanks . . . for everything."

"No problem, brother. That's what I'm here for."

They're gone.

I'm thankful the vultures have packed up shop and gotten the hell out of Dodge, but I still can't believe it's true. I check the live feed on my phone from the security camera mounted on the front gate one more time. The street's still free and clear of paparazzi scum who had been camping out there for what felt like for-fucking-ever.

Thank God they listened for once. Chased the story I hand-fed them about Eddie. Uncovered truths behind his actions: his desperate and fucked-up act to exact revenge on my wife because he was found guilty. Paparazzi's apologies mean shit to me. They're just covering their asses from getting sued for slander. Besides, I know it won't stop them from doing the same thing with their next story, their next lead, their next chance to fuck up someone else's life.

Of course, I'm not blind to the fact they're all playing nice in the hopes of getting first crack at pictures of Ace if we ever decide to go that route and sell the rights. So I'll take their printed retractions. Use their hope to clear our street and rid our lives of their constant presence. But more than anything I'll hold tight to the fact that their apologies have helped restore Rylee's reputation.

Too bad she's so lost in her depression she doesn't know it.

Because while their apologies may have restored calm outside the gates, they've done nothing to quiet the storm still brewing inside them.

From my chair on the patio, I set my cell down and watch the set of waves roll in, immediately itching to grab my board and get lost in the ocean. My mind wanders. Thoughts run. Will Ace want me to teach him to surf some day? Will he be interested in racing?

Or will I just be the authority he resists until he gets old enough to understand the why behind my rules? *Like father, like son.*

The baby monitor crackles on the table beside me. I give him a sec, wait to see if he's awake, but nothing. I lean back in my chair and get lost in thoughts about the next race. My everyday world that feels so fucking far away from the one I'm currently living in.

"Shh. Shh." Ry's voice comes through the monitor and startles me. My heart races. My eyes burn with emotion I don't want to feel but can't stop as I bring it to my ear to hear more.

Silence. Nothing else. Should I go upstairs or stay here and see what happens? If I'm there, does it add more pressure on her as she takes a step forward when so many we've taken have been backward?

And then those dark thoughts in the back of my mind take hold. The ones I haven't wanted to acknowledge but linger nonetheless. The ones that make the evening news headlines about what mothers with postpartum depression have done to their children.

I'm up and on my feet in a second. A war of emotions battle over what to think and what to do. I stand in the hallway, frozen in indecision with what feels like the weight of the world on my shoulders.

Hope surges through me. I hate it and love it at the same time.

I choose to love it. Need to.

C'mon, Ry. Give me something to tell me I'm right.

"My sweet boy. You hungry?" I exhale the breath I didn't realize I was holding, pissed at myself for doubting her but knowing I have every right to.

Joy, relief, fear, concern, caution. Too many fucking feelings hit me at once. The biggest of all of them is relief that I can see the light at the end of this long-ass tunnel. Our life has been put on hold for what feels like forever, and it's time to get it back.

She's not better yet. We still have a long way to go. Hell yes, this moment is a baby step, but fuck if I won't take it because we weren't even crawling a few days ago. This step may be on wobbly legs, but it's a step all the same.

When I enter the bedroom, Rylee is lying on the middle of the bed, and Ace is nursing beside her. It's the first time I haven't had to bring him to her. The thought sinks in and takes hold as I watch the two of them together. A visual sucker punch of love.

Leave her be, Colton.

Good in theory, but not in my reality. I don't know why I resist the pull when I know in the end it's futile. It always is when it comes to Rylee.

I cross the room, pull my shirt over my head, and slide into bed behind her without saying a word. Careful of disturbing Ace, I put my arm around her hip, and line our bodies up. And just breathe her in.

God, I've missed her.

"Sorry. I didn't hear him wake up. I didn't mean for you to have to get him." I give her the lip service, soft words that won't upset her, when I'm not sorry at all.

Silence greets me. I hold back the sigh I want to breathe out. Push down the disappointment she's lost again. Accept that the power of her own mind is ten times more powerful than any love I can give her. Fight the fear I won't be able to pull her back again.

So I begin the routine. My nightly process. My way of telling her I'm not giving up on her. I tell her about a memory I can't wait to make with her.

"I thought of another one today. Memory two hundred thirteen that I can't wait to put in our picture frame. We should rent a private island. Or a secluded beach somewhere. Sand, sun, and our family left all alone to do as we please. Silly, right?" My own voice rings in my ears but her body relaxes against mine and I know she's listening. "It's not though. Because the island rules are that you're required to wear very skimpy bikinis. Or go topless. Topless is preferable. And yes, to make it fair, I'd have to wear that loincloth thingy so we have clothing equality on the island. Oh shit," I murmur as I press a kiss into the back of her hair. "I'm still getting used to this baby thing. I forgot topless doesn't bode well with a kid. So I guess topless would only be allowed when Ace is napping. I'm sure we could find a few ways to occupy our time during those hours anyway."

I lose my train of thought. Get lost in the feel of her body against mine, and how much I miss physical intimacy between us. Because physical is my barometer. Makes me feel closer to her and at the same time tells me we're okay. And without it, I hate not knowing if we're okay.

"Sorry," I say, pulling myself from my thoughts. "I was daydreaming about being on the beach with you."

"Thank you."

Her voice is so faint but I hear it immediately. I squeeze my eyes shut, overwhelmed from those two simple words.

Gathering her a little tighter, I rest my chin on the curve of her shoulder. I look down in front of her where Ace has fallen asleep, and I know I need to put him in his bassinet but I don't. Not yet. This feels a little too normal when we've had anything but, so I want to make it last a little bit longer. Just the three of us.

There are so many things I want to say to her, so many reasons why she doesn't need to thank me, but I don't. I was given two glimpses of my wife tonight. That's enough to tell me more is coming soon.

So I do what I think is best. I continue on. "Don't thank me yet, Ryles. This island doesn't have any indoor plumbing. Or Diet Coke. And I know how you love your Diet Coke. But they do have . . ." I continue on. My rambling evening entertainment.

Anything for my Ry.

Chapter Thirty-Nine

Rylee

Hi sweetheart. Just checking in to see how you're doing. I love you. I'm here for you. I'll be up later this week.

The text from my mom sits on my phone. The screen is lit up. My insides are still so very dark.

I miss the outside world.

Lazy walks on the beach. Trips to the farmers market in town where I get to laugh at Colton with his hat pulled low to avoid attention. The roar of the racetrack and vibration of the engine in my chest as I sit in the infield and answer emails while Colton tests the car. The incessant chatter, sound of kitchen chairs scooting over worn linoleum, complaints about homework, and sly smiles given behind one another's back that are a constant at The House from my boys.

I miss everything that makes me feel alive.

But I'm not ready yet. I miss the idea of everything but not the reality. Because with the reality comes the chaos. The intrusive cameras and judging eyes. The scrutiny and the exposure. The lack of any control or privacy. The never-ending sense of vulnerability.

Besides, how can I begin to want any of *those* things when I can't even look at my beautiful baby boy and feel that soul-shifting love I should for him? Sure it's there, hidden deep down and buried beneath the haze. I know it is. I've felt it before. And that almost makes it worse. To want something and never have it is one thing but to have something, lose it, and know what you're missing is brutal.

And I'm missing Ace. Not him, per se, because he's here and I feed him, but rather the emotion. Brief moments of intense joy and overwhelming love peek through every now and again. The want to have them return consumes me to the point they drive me back into the warped and silent comfort of the darkness.

And then when I resurface, there is Colton. The songs he texts to help me remember. And to help me forget.

It's when the sky is the darkest that you can tell which stars are the brightest. There's only one star I see: Colton's light shines the brightest to me. Maybe because he's the one saving me.

I wish I could feel the amusement I know is beneath the surface when I watch him deal with Ace in his adorably awkward way. The made-up lullabies about car parts and superheroes he sings to stop Ace from crying are so sweet. I try to dredge it up, hold on to my smile, but it's a constant battle between the darkness and light.

Then there's the night. When he pulls me into him and tells me about the silly places he is going to take me, the memories we are going to make, and lifts that lead curtain for a bit so I can lose myself in his voice and humor. I can look down to Ace at my breast and have Colton's body against my back and know I can beat this.

And so I fight, winning little pieces of myself back day by day. Moment by moment. Because it's the things we love most that destroy us. Break us down. Tear us apart. But they are also the things that build us back up. Heal us. Make us complete again.

"Hey, man!" Colton's voice rings down the hallway, interrupting my thoughts. I immediately start to rise from the couch, bothered I was actually enjoying sitting beside Ace in the bouncer, and start to head upstairs because the unexpected usually triggers uncontrollable anxiety. And that anxiety inevitably leads to another trip down the rabbit hole.

"I'm sorry I didn't call first, but I was driving back to school and needed to stop by. Can I speak to you and Ry for a moment?"

Shane's voice echoes down the foyer and makes me falter. And it's not what he says that stops me from standing but rather the tone in his voice—formal, businesslike, and anxious—that makes me sit at attention.

"Not a problem. Let me go tell Ry that you're here first," Colton says, followed by the lowering of their voices. They say something I can't hear but can assume it is the typical question of how I am doing that gets asked when they arrive. "Be right back." Footsteps. "Hey, Ry?"

"Yeah?" My voice is shaky as I answer, and I hate that the anxiety surges within me when it's just Shane. He's the boy who has been with me the longest. The one I have watched grow into a man.

"Shane stopped by. Okay?" Colton's eyes hold mine. They're telling me that Shane's coming in and to prepare for it. My two-minute warning. I force a swallow down my throat as I try to reason with myself that this is Shane; he poses no threat to Ace or me, or my little world.

I nod my head.

"Come on in," Colton yells as he stands there with eyes locked on mine and waits for Shane to close the distance.

C'mon, Ry. You scared him last time. Show him that you're not his mother. That this beast can be conquered. Be the you he knows. Try, baby. Please.

And as much as I prepare myself, when Shane walks into the living room, my heart races out of control and body breaks out in a cold sweat. And I detest that I can't muster up more than a forced smile when our eyes meet. I open my mouth to say hi, but the word doesn't come out.

I see concern in his expression, and he glances over to Colton, blatantly telling him he lied, that I'm not better like he'd said moments before at the door. Colton nods to trust him.

"So you're heading back to campus?" Colton says, saving me from having to speak as he leads the way into the living room and motions for him to sit down.

"Yes. Yeah. I spent the night at The House with the gang." His eyes flicker back and forth between the two of us as he sits down on the edge of the chair before landing on Ace sleeping contently in the bouncer. "He's getting so big."

"Yeah. It's crazy," Colton says. He stares at Shane as he watches Ace, and I can see him narrow his eyes to try and figure out the same thing I am: why does Shane seem so nervous?

I want to ask so many things: how is school, how is Zander, is Auggie hanging in there? Do you miss me? But my restlessness only adds to the awkward silence filling the room. Colton finally speaks. "That was cool of you to hang out with the boys. I was thinking maybe in a week or two when Ry is feeling a little better, we'll have all you guys over for a barbecue."

And as much as I know Colton is trying to make Shane feel more comfortable, it feels like hands are squeezing my lungs at the mere thought of so many people being in my space at once. He said a few weeks, though. Maybe by then . . .

"Yeah, uh . . ." Shane shifts and rubs his palms down the thighs of his pants. "Well, I stayed with the boys because we had a little house meeting and um, I came here because I wanted to let you know about it."

I vaguely hear him over the roar of my heartbeat. My curiosity is piqued and internal instinct overrides the depression's pull trying to yank me back from the edge and protect me from whatever it is that is making him so nervous. Colton's eyes meet mine and something flashes in them—a moment of unexpected clarity—that worries me.

"Go on," Colton says cautiously.

"I've been thinking about what you said, Colton, and after looking at Zander's situation from all sides, I think you're right." Shane wrings his hands and keeps his eyes focused on them as Colton sighs loudly.

"*What thing did I say*, Shane?" he asks, voice searching, body language pensive as if he fears he already knows.

"About Zander."

Colton scrunches up his nose in a show of regret and I'm completely lost. My body wants to shut down but my mind fights the allure to find out what's going on. I look back to Shane, trying to find the words to ask an explanation when I catch Colton mouth out of the words, "Not now," with a shake of his head.

Panic, my one constant, returns, jolting through my system as I look back and forth from Colton to Shane, both of them realizing I saw the exchanged warning. Something's going on, and it's about Zander. I need to know now or else I'm going to go crazier than I already feel. I open my mouth, shut it, then open it again, willing my frenzied thoughts to find the voice that's been silent for so very long.

"No," Shane says, standing up to Colton, causing us both to snap our heads to him. "She deserves to know that we've voted, and we're okay with it."

I blink my eyes rapidly as I try to understand his cryptic comment. I feel like I've just walked into a movie halfway through and I'm lost in the plot. As much as I want to be angry at Colton, he obviously fears that whatever Shane has to say is going to knock me back a few of the steps I've gained these past few days.

"What?" My voice breaks. It sounds foreign to my ears. My eyes widen as I search their faces for answers. Now it's their turn to both look at me.

"I'm just trying to fix everything I started," he says, and I don't understand what he means. He looks at me with little boy's eyes in a grown man's body, begging me to let him help me. "It's my fault."

"*What* are you talking about?" Colton asks, voice demanding yet sounding just as confused as I am.

"I told you about Zander's meeting with his uncle at The House that day when I shouldn't have. I should have known better. But how was I to know Zander was going to say things that would cause you to get so upset you'd go into labor? And then we came here to meet Ace. You were fine one minute and then you talked to Z and . . ." His voice drifts off, and I strain to remember bits and pieces from when the boys came. But I can't—just flashes of wide eyes and scared faces—and I know I obviously frightened them somehow. "I just want you to get better, Rylee. And I want Zander to stay in our family where he's safe. *We all want these things*. And I kept thinking if you knew Zander was safe then maybe you'd get better."

A part of me awakens when I hear his words. I want to tell him it's so much more than that but the love and concern lacing his tone somehow weave into and wrap around me, warming up the places this postpartum depression has left so very cold. It's scary and foreign and exciting to feel these things even if it's just a fraction of what is normal.

"Then I remembered the comment you made, Colton. The one about how you'd adopt Zander if it would fix the situation and—"

"No!" I shout, standing up in protest. Both of them stare at me as I struggle to make my point and understand why that sudden flicker of warmth I felt moments ago is now gone. In seconds, my mind spins in a tornado of thoughts with clarity sharper than I've felt in weeks.

Shane's not nervous; he's upset. Upset and hurt that in his darkest hour I never thought to adopt him, *choose him*, and now all of a sudden Zander's in this situation and Colton obviously told him his suggestion when never in a million years would I even consider it.

The twister spins out of control. Anger, betrayal, compassion, despair, love. They all whirl inside me. I can't catch my breath. I can't speak. And yet the feelings within me are so violent, crashing into one another without recourse, that I can't process them. I begin to shut down. Crawl with my tail between my legs into the darkness because obviously I thought I was stronger when I'm not.

I need my bed. To pull the covers over me and to try and quiet the riot in my head, but I don't move. Instead I start to hyperventilate, my lungs convulsing as panic takes over my body, so all I can do is sag back down into the couch to try and catch my breath.

Colton's at my side in an instant. His eyes are alarmed, but hands are gentle as he rubs my back and tells me he's there. My body burns for oxygen, my blood on fire, and my head starts to become dizzy. I clutch my head in my hands, desperate for some kind of control.

"No peeking, Scooter!" Shane's voice sounds off. How can it be in front of me when he's beside me? Regardless, the sound of it pulls me to the present. I open my eyes and he's holding his cell phone so I can see a video playing on the screen. The camera pans across the room and six heads are bowed down: Connor, Aiden, Ricky, Kyle, Scooter, and Auggie. Curiosity pulls my head above water; the sight of my boys keeps it there as my breathing slowly evens.

"Okay. You ready?" It's Shane's voice on the phone, his hand recording, as an array of yeses sound. "We all know that Zander was told today his uncle has been approved to foster him."

"*What?*" Colton says in shock, hand stilling on my back, the same time the breath I just got back catches in my chest. My eyes, mesmerized by the sight of my boys again, sting with unwanted tears. Disbelief courses right alongside the panic.

Spiral. Twist. Slide. Back down into the dark.

"Just listen," Shane urges, his voice giving me a focal point to cling to.

The video continues. "Who is in favor and completely okay and know that it has nothing to do with playing favorites—"

"Jesus. We got it, dude!" Aiden says. "We all know we're Donavans. We don't need a formal adoption process or the official name change to tell us that. It's a given. Just take the vote, Shane."

Colton sucks in a breath beside me. My pulse starts to race again. A little at first. Then a lot. But this time it's not from anxiety. The lack of panic and the presence of disbelieved hope pull me a little closer toward the surface.

"Shut it, Aid!"

"Always the boss," Aiden says, eyes rolling, as Connor elbows him.

"Who is in favor of Rylee and Colton filing a petition to adopt Zander?" Six arms rise in the air without a moment's hesitation. Shane flips the camera lens onto him to show his hand in the air. "And it's a landslide," he says, angling it back to my crew where they've all raised their heads, smiles on their faces, and patience gone.

I'm transfixed with the images as a few of them give a shout out to me until a scuffle ensues over hogging the spotlight and then the video stops. But when Shane goes to pull his hand holding the phone away, I reach out in reflex and grab it, my eyes lifting up to meet his.

I don't know what to say. All I know is how I feel. And how I feel is that I actually feel *something* when there's been nothing in so long. A sudden rainstorm in an arid desert.

My hand squeezes his wrist as I scramble to mouth the words backing up like a dam in my mind. Nothing comes out but I can't let go of him. And I can't look away.

Colton runs his hand up and down the length of my spine in reassurance as Shane lowers to his knees in front of me and puts his free hand on top of mine, holding steadfast to his. Eyes laced with concern and swimming with love meet mine.

"We know you're not choosing Zander over us. You're doing what you've always done. You're trying to save him just like you have done for each one of us." His voice breaks and tears well, despite him trying to hold it together. "We didn't tell Zander about the vote, didn't want to get his hopes up if you guys decide not to pursue it . . . but we also didn't want you to throw the idea out because you thought it would upset us."

"I don't even know what to say," Colton says, his voice thick with emotion.

"There's nothing to say." He shrugs, bringing back thoughts of the little boy I first met. "I'll admit when you first told me about it, I was a little shocked. Surprised. But at the same time, it's what you said *after* telling me you'd adopt Zander that I heard the loudest."

Colton looks back and forth between us and shakes his head as he tries to recall what Shane's talking about.

"You told me Ry nixed the idea because it would make the rest of us feel bad. That spoke louder to me than anything. She was willing to hurt him to spare our feelings. It didn't sit right with me. Ry, you raised us to look out for one another, take care of each other. Be a family. Well, Zander's our family. So I mentioned it to Aiden. Played it down. Pretended I'd had a dream about it happening to see what he'd say. He thought it was brilliant. Didn't have a problem with it. We went from there." His voice fades off, but I hear hope in his tone and see optimism in his eyes.

"Shane." It's the sound of Colton's stilted voice that causes the first tear to slide over.

"I just wanted to try to make things right."

The curtain lifts. Huge body-wracking sobs take over my body as the curtain lifts to the highest it's been since my mind fell into this depression. And I still can't speak. All I can do is show them that the smile on my face is not forced anymore—a break in the black clouds. A ray of light flooding me with the knowledge there is still good in the world. That I've raised seven boys who came to me damaged and beyond hope—with all odds stacked against them—and have turned them into compassionate, loving individuals who have formed a family.

My family. Their family.

"Ry? Baby, look at me." It's Colton's voice that pulls me out of this storm of emotion. I actually want to stay in it though, because it feels so damn good to feel something other than the weight of sadness. But I look at him anyway. I want him to see the glimpse of the real me peeking through because I know as good as this feels, as long as it has lasted, it will probably be gone soon. In my compromised psyche, I know you don't snap out of postpartum depression so easily.

But it gives me hope. Tells me I can do this. That the glimpse will turn into more. Baby steps as Colton says.

"These are happy tears, right?" he asks as I glance over to Shane and then back to him. Both of their eyes hold a cautious optimism.

"Yes."

I might not be broken after all.

Chapter Forty

Colton

Fuckin' Beckett.

He knows just how to push my buttons. Get me where I need to be. Even if it takes a few *fibs* as he calls them. More like bald-faced lies.

But who's the fool? I fell for them. I'm right where he wants me. On the track. In the car and just hitting my stride on my thirtieth lap after some new adjustments.

God, I needed this. Everything about it: the routine, the camaraderie with the crew, the vibration of the car all around me, the control and response when everything else has felt so chaotic.

The freedom.

I shift, coming into turn one. Let my car own the track since I'm alone on it, getting a feel if the last adjustment was right or wrong.

"Wood?" No other words need to be said to know what he's asking me.

"Feels good. Ass end's not sliding as I come outta the bank." I take a sip of water from the tube. It's piss-warm. Fuck.

"Okay. Open her up then for a few laps once you hit the line. Push to pass. Let me see what the gauges say when we do that."

"Open her up? You get some last night, Daniels? I don't think I've ever heard you say those words." Hands grip the wheel, body braced for the force as I come out of turn four toward the start/finish line.

"Wouldn't you like to know?" He chuckles. That's an affirmative on getting laid. "Let's see what she can do."

I drop the hammer. Race the motherfucking wind. Let the vibration of the car and the fight of the wheel own my mind and body: escape from the worry about Rylee—the constant responsibility of Ace, the *everything* that feels like it has been on my shoulders—and just be.

The car and me. Machine and man. Speed against skill. Chaos versus control.

Each lap peels away the world around me a little bit more. Pulls me into the blur. Lets me become a part of the car, hear each rattle, feel every vibration, and listen to what she's saying to me.

If she's going to be a whore or a wife for the next race: let me use her, abuse her until I get mine at the start/finish line, or if I need to praise her, stroke her with foreplay, and hope she gets off by the time the checkered flag is waved.

"Gauges are looking good. How's she feel?"

"A good mix." He knows I mean she's a little bit of both—whore and wife—the perfect mix to win a race.

"We need a little more whore for the next race. Push her harder. See if she sucks or swallows."

I laugh into the open mic as I head into turn three. Routine entry, down shift, gaze drops down to the gauges one last time before the track and car own them with the concentration the turn takes.

The ass end slides high, fishtails at the topside of the curve. Rubber tires hit a rash of pellets. I hydroplane across them, slick tires over balls of rubber.

FUCK!

Split seconds of time. Increments of thoughts. Routine of movements.

The nose end turn turns high. Arms tense fighting the wheel. A flash of concrete wall.

Ace. An image of him flashes before my eyes. A slideshow of frames. His cry is in the whine of the engine.

Releasing the wheel. Crossing my arms so I can hold onto the harness.

Ryles. Soft smile. Big heart. Incredible strength. Just when she's coming back to me.

Shoulders shoving into the seat. The car spins. Nosecone hits the wall. Metal sparking as it shreds.

"Wood!"

Spinning. Hands grip seatbelts tight. Waiting for the second impact.

Nothing.

C'mon. C'mon. C'mon

Spinning.

Slipping down the track.

Spinning.

Grass flying as I hit the infield.

Coming to a stop.

Taking a breath.

Hands stiff from holding tight to the seatbelts.

"Goddammit, Colton! Answer me."

Sound comes back. Adrenaline takes over. My heart pounds. My mouth is dry.

But I'm fine.

"I'm good. Fine," I rasp as my body starts to tremble from the aftereffects. "Fucked up the nosecone and front right side."

"You're good?" His voice is shaky.

"I'm good." *Well, I will be*. After I have a stiff drink.

"Fuck, Colton! I told you to open her up, not tear her up and slam her into the goddamn wall!" he yells through the mic as I unpin the wheel to get out.

My chuckle fills the connection—the tinge of hysteria in it clear as fucking day.

I'm grateful for his comment. For getting me back to the norm when a part of me is so lost in my own head over shit I never allow myself to think about.

And yet sometimes when you're forced to close your eyes, everything else becomes so much clearer.

"Colton?"

"Can I come in?" I look at my dad. There are so many things I want to say. No, *need* to say to him.

My mind hasn't stopped since I left the track. The wreck made my mortality front and fucking center like never before. I have a kid now. Responsibilities. People that matter to me when before the only person I cared about besides my parents, Quin, and Becks was me, myself, and I.

I got out of the car needing to call Ry. Talk to her. Hear her voice. Get home so I could hold Ace. But know I can't.

It was just another day at the track. I spun out. A job hazard. I couldn't call her because even though she's making huge strides, she's still not one hundred percent, and I didn't want to do anything to trigger her to pull away.

So I drove. *Aimlessly*. Ended up at the beach. Then drove some more. Checked in with Haddie to make sure Ry was good and ended up here. Fucking full circles.

"Come in. Everything okay? Ry and Ace?" he asks as I follow him into the house I grew up in.

"Yes. Yeah." *Shit*. He's worried. "Sorry. They're fine. It's all good." We walk past the stairs I used to slide down on cardboard, and the liquor cabinet I used to sneak bottles from in high school. I focus on that shit because all of a sudden I'm antsy, nervous. Feel stupid for coming here but need to tell him nonetheless.

"It's good to see you out and about," he says.

"Haddie's with Ry," I explain when he doesn't ask. "I had to get some time at the track."

"How'd it go?"

"Good. Fine. Hit the wall."

Fight or flight time, Colton. Say what you need to say.

"Colton?"

I snap from my thoughts. The shit that I'm here to say but have now lost the words for. "Sorry." I sigh, lift my hat and run a hand through my hair.

"I said hitting the wall doesn't sound like it went well. Are you okay?" His grey eyes look at me in that way he has since I was a kid. Checking for ghosts he's not going to find.

"Yes. No." I shake my head. "Fuck if I know." I laugh and can hear the nerves in it as I watch him sit down and lean back on the couch, expression guarded, eyes an open fucking door that say, "*Talk to me, son*."

I shove up out of the seat I've just sat in and walk toward the mantle where it is littered with picture frames of Q and me as kids. A house that has been featured in every style magazine known to man, and my mom keeps our homemade frames sitting on the mantle like they fit right in with the Louis whatever chair I was never allowed to sit on. I'm restless, fidgety, and just need to get this the fuck over with so I can stop thinking about it and get home.

"I had no right to ask you to go with me the other day." That wasn't what I was expecting to say but, fuck it, might as well go with it. He stares at me, father to son, body and eyes warring between asking for more and letting it come to me.

"I'm not following you."

Of course you're not going to make this easy on me, are you? *Fuck.* I sigh. Move. Pace. Hand through hair again.

"When I asked you to drive me so I could see my . . . uh . . ." Fuck. I can't say the word. Can't use the same term for that piece of shit as I do for this man in front of me, my endgame superhero.

"*Dad.* You can say it, Colton. I'm confident with my place in your life."

"I know but it was a slap in your face, and it's been eating at me. I shouldn't have asked you to go," I say as I turn around and meet his eyes again. "Or I should have told you where we were going. Given you a choice."

"It's never a slap in my face when you want to spend time with me, son. The fact you wanted me there with you tells me more than you'll ever know."

I stare at him, jaw clenched, and head a mess. I don't deserve him. Never have. But sure as shit, I'm not letting him go.

"It was chickenshit of me." It's all I can say.

"It's only natural for you to wonder. What you need to ask yourself is, did you get what you wanted out of it?"

"Yes. No. Fuckin'A straight I'm so angry but I don't know *why.*" I pace again. Pissed I'm still bugged by it all.

"Why? Because you wanted him to see you, pull you into a hug, and start a relationship?" he goads, knowing damn well that wasn't what I wanted. "Have a get-to-know-you session?"

"No," I shout, hand banging down on the table beside me. The sound echoes around the room while I rein in my temper. I don't want to have emotion over the loser. None. So why do I feel so fucked up when I thought I had it all under wraps? "I didn't want shit from him other than to see him so I could look at the fucking reflection of what I never want to be to Ace. *You happy?*"

"Perfectly," he says with a ghost of a smile that taunts me. I've punched guys for less. But I force myself to breathe. Unclench my fists. Redirect my anger. *Try to at least.*

"Really? My fucked-up head makes you happy?" I grate out between gritted teeth.

"Nope. But you've been through a lot of shit this month, Colton. Taken on a lot of responsibilities and haven't really gotten to deal with any of this, so here I am. Scream and yell. That vase right next to you? *Throw it.* Watch it break against the wall. I'll cover for you with your mom. Tell her I fell or something." He pauses and lifts his eyebrows.

"What? She'd kill you. That's like some antique-ey thing we were never allowed to touch."

"Even better. Expensive shit sounds better when it breaks."

"You're fucking crazy." I laugh, not really sure what else to say because he looks dead serious. What is going on here?

"Yeah, well, you have to be crazy to be a good parent." His lips curl up, eyes flash with something, and I know I'm about to get schooled. Too bad I have no idea what the lesson covers. So I just stare at him and wait, knowing from experience that something else is coming. The difference is that as a kid, I'd let it go in one ear and out the other. This time, I'm fairly certain I won't be so blasé.

"Connect the dots here, Dad, because I'm lost." White flag is waving. Help me out.

"Being a parent is the hardest thing I've ever done. It's made me question my sanity more times than you can imagine," he says dryly, and I know many of those times were because of me. "And there are times that you have to bite your tongue so hard you're not sure if it's going to be in one or two pieces when you open your mouth. It's exhausting and you're constantly doubting yourself, wondering if you're doing the right thing, saying the right thing, being the right thing."

I look at him like he's crazy and yet every single thing he says is gold. So damn true I can't argue a single point.

"But then there are those moments, Colton, when you watch your child do something and are so damn proud of them you are left speechless. And those moments take every single doubt and fear and heartache and moment of insanity you've ever had and wipe the slate clean. That's how I felt watching you go to see your dad. That's how I feel knowing you and Ry are going to adopt Zander. That's how I feel watching you be a father. Hell, son, when you stepped up to the plate after Rylee got sick and swung it out of the goddamn park by taking care of Ace? I've never been prouder."

My eyes sting with tears I don't want to shed from the praise I never like to receive. Yet at the same time understand completely now that I'm a father.

"I've never been more proud to be your father than I am right now. *That man*," he says, pointing over his shoulder to tell me he's referring to my biological father, "doesn't deserve to get to know the incredible person you are."

The lump in my throat feels like it is the size of a football. "Thank you." I feel like a shy little kid, unworthy of the no-holds-barred love he's given me my whole life when I haven't always been easy. Fuck. Who am I kidding? I've been a nightmare. And yet the quip that's on my tongue dies when I look back to his eyes. I see love and approval and pride and shit that makes me uncomfortable to see. I know Ace needs to see it every day of his life so he can know exactly what I feel right now.

"No need to thank me, son." We stare at each other for a moment, years of unspoken words traded in the span of silence. "Now . . . I'm sure you didn't stop by to hear me blather on. What can I do for you?"

Just like him to lay down the law and then act like we're not even in court.

"Believe it or not, you gave me the answer anyway."

And he did. Tons of answers, in fact. *He* turned wounds into wisdom.

The most important thing is that he let me be who I needed to be, guided me when I needed it, and let me figure shit out on my own when I was too stubborn to ask for help. Regardless, he let me grow, let me experience, let me chase the goddamn wind as I raced, and the fact he was by my side without judgment the whole time, made me the man I am today.

Now I can't wait to be that exact same man for Ace.

Chapter Forty-One

Rylee

I startle awake.

Colton's arms have fallen off me in sleep, and I struggle to remember the last time I slept this deeply. The last thing I remember was memory number who knows what that had to do with zip-lining through the forests of Costa Rica.

Naked.

I seem to think every one of his memories had to do with me being naked. It's kind of funny. Kind of not.

I sit up and look at Ace asleep in the bassinet. His hands are up over his head, lips are suckling even in his sleep. I stare and wonder what type of person he'll be. What will his future hold? Images that are so crystal clear slide through my head: first smiles, first steps, first day of school, first date. So many of them have this little boy with dark hair and green eyes and freckles over the bridge of his nose it's almost as if I've seen a picture of what he's going to look like before.

But the one thing I don't expect, don't even notice until it hits me like a lightning strike, is that the oppressive weight of dread and doom doesn't come. It doesn't drop one single time to darken my thoughts or steal my calm.

I wait for it. Hope for the best, expect the worst for a while. But the panic, the sweat, the fingers clawing at my throat and squeezing my heart, don't come.

All that does is a soft smile on my lips. Not one forced or laced with guilt that comes because I need to show I'm improving, but rather because I really feel it.

Tears well. Big fat tears slide down my cheeks. And the funny thing is the taste of the salt as it hits my lips is like a smelling salt waking me up from passing out. And I'm not sure how long this is going to last but for the first time in the six weeks since Ace's birth, I feel optimistic, hopeful . . . *like me.*

So I sit in this mass of a bed with my sweet baby boy beside me—who I desperately want to pick up but was fussy and difficult for Colton to put down tonight. I want to pull him tight to my chest and tell him he's been my heartbeat throughout this mess. Apologize to him. Say words about events he's never going to even know or remember but that will make me feel a little better.

I'm transfixed by him, feeling like I'm looking at him for the first time and in a sense I am, because he's already grown and changed so much. I feel like I have to make up for lost time, although I know I have a whole lifetime to do that with him. Hesitantly, I reach out to touch him and then pull back when he squirms, smelling the milk on me.

And even though I shift back onto the bed, I can't take my eyes off him. He's so beautiful. Everything I've ever wanted. My ace in a loaded deck of cards.

The thought makes me smile. Memories colliding of that first encounter between Colton and me—jammed closets and first kisses and fear over how strong the chemistry was between the player and this good girl—when I first called him Ace.

A chance encounter that lead to this moment. Right here. Right now. Where so much love fills me that I'm swamped by it. And I'll take being swamped by love because I've been drowning in sadness for what feels like forever.

I look at him now. My achingly handsome husband. His dark hair is a little longer than normal, falling over his forehead. Dark lashes fan on bronze skin. That perfectly imperfect nose of his. And those lips that have murmured memories he wants to make with me every single night over the past five-plus weeks.

Rogue, rebel, reckless. Those words still apply to him. As do so many others that would make him blush, roll his eyes, and play them off because they make this stoic man uncomfortable. My *rock* is the one I can't seem to get out of my head. Because that's exactly what he has been to me.

My everything.

Just like with Ace, I reach out my hand and pull it back. He deserves a good night's sleep. Some peace and quiet since he has been the one handling all of my noise. And yet I can't resist. Never can when it comes to him.

I lean forward and press a soft kiss to his lips, wanting nothing more than this connection with him.

My body is still recovering, and the thought of sex is the furthest thing from my battered mind, and yet this simple touch, lips to lips, completes the sensation that something is still missing.

It's probably bogus, my mind still playing tricks on me, and yet the spark that hits when I kiss him jumpstarts every part of my body drugged by the postpartum depression back to life.

My hands frame his cheeks as I brush my lips to his again, need becoming want, want becoming all-consuming. The desire to feel his touch in a way that's not to soothe but rather to sate a need.

A gasp of breath. A flash open of startled eyes. A reach of his hands to grab onto mine holding him.

"Rylee." His voice. That sexy, sleep-drugged voice that calls to me as he says my name and owns my soul.

"Yeah. It's me." And I mean it in every sense of the word. His emerald eyes widen and lips part in shock as he pulls me into him. One arm wraps around my back and the other cradles the back of my head as he presses me into his chest.

Our hearts connect. His feels like it wants to jump out of his chest and collide with mine as it beats an erratic yet familiar rhythm that is one hundred percent ours.

His hands hold me tight and don't let go. He's already lost me once, and I love the knowledge he's going to make damn sure I'm not going to leave again.

The scrape of his stubble as he rubs his cheek against mine, a subtle sting of coarse to soft tells me this is real, this is him, and I am loved. Irrevocably.

The scent of soap and shampoo still lingers from his shower. The smell of home, of comfort . . . of safety as I breathe him in.

Everything seems so new and yet so familiar all at the same time. Whoever said the only way to find yourself is to get completely lost, knew exactly what they were talking about.

His hand fists my hair and pulls my head back. Emerald eyes own my soul when they meet mine. They ask if this is a dream, if I'm really here, and I do the only thing I can. I lean forward and take a sip from his lips—the taste of his kiss is seared into my soul, one I'll never forget—and it reawakens my senses the minute it hits my tongue.

We move in the darkness.

Two soulmates reuniting.

Two best friends grateful to have their other half.

Two lovers rediscovering each other in an intimate dance of tongues and the slide of fingertips over thirst-starved flesh.

Two parts of a puzzle finally realizing their piece of peace they've been missing has been found.

Once again.

Epilogue

PART 1
COLTON

Eight months later

The turbulence jolts me awake.

Well, that's what I'll tell the twenty or so people on the other side of the door. Because it sure as shit isn't the turbulence that wakes me up. No. It's Ry's hand sliding into my pants, fingernails tickling my nuts, and soft-as-fuck lips, kissing the underside of my jaw.

"Ry . . ." I sigh.

"Be quiet," she warns against my skin, my body already fully alert at this unexpected wake-up call. Her other hand slides up beneath my shirt. Nails against bare skin. Teeth nipping my earlobe. Hot breath against my neck. "Your mom has Ace. You were asleep. And I was horny."

Well, damn.

I glance at the cabin door, visually make sure the latch is set to lock before I lay my head back and close my eyes. Her tongue then does something to me that sends a jolt of electricity straight down my spine connecting to where her fingers are slowly stroking me.

"Horny is good." Her lips meet mine as she climbs astride me. Tongues and teeth. Greed and need. Wet against hard. Goddamn she's hot. Sexy fucking hot. "But it's going to take a whole helluva lot more to get me to tell you where we are going."

The stutter in her movement tells me I'm right, know her angle: confession by orgasm. Not a bad way to be tortured but my lips are sealed.

Maybe I'll wait to tell her though. I've been to a lot of places with her, but the mile-high club isn't one of them.

Maybe it's time to venture there.

She sits up, a taunt in her eye and determination on her face. But that pout on her lips tells me she's game to change my mind.

Change away, Ryles.

"Guess I'll just have to take care of myself then."

Don't you dare. My eyes say it but lips don't. I'm too goddamn focused on her hands traveling over her tits, hard nipples visible through the thin cotton, down to where her fingers pull up her loose skirt inch by fucking inch. And then they disappear beneath the flowy fabric so I can't see shit.

But I sure as fuck see her head fall back, lips fall open, and hear the sigh fall from her lips as her hands begin to move in a motion I know all too well. Quick strokes of her finger to add friction to her clit.

Motherfucker.

Another quiet moan. Her back arches. Tits push forward. Hands move quicker, harder. Her skirt inches up farther so I can see the slick arousal on her fingers.

She's playing me and I don't even have a ball in her court. Playing with fire when I want to be the only one striking the goddamn matchstick.

My stick's out all right. Now I just need to light the flame.

Within a beat I have Rylee flipped over, hands cuffed beside her head, and our faces inches apart. "You're playing with fire, sweetheart," I tease between teeth gritted in restraint.

The scent of her arousal on her fingers fills my nose. Temptation at its fucking finest. *Two can play this game, sweetheart.* I lower my mouth, take the tips of her fingers between my lips and suck. Tongue laving over them, savoring her addictive taste. Her body squirms beneath me. A moan hums in the back of her throat.

"Don't make a sound," I whisper around her fingers.

One final suck. One last taste. One last hit. I look down at her beneath me. Her lips are parted, cheeks are flushed, and her eyes are heavy with desire. Goddamn sex personified.

And thank fuck for that because I'm digging in and taking what's mine. Her orgasm. Her moans. Her scratch marks. And every damn thing in between.

"Burn, baby, burn," she taunts with a gleam in her eyes as I release her hands so I can free my dick. And before I can pull my pants down far enough to free my thighs, her hand is pulling up her skirt, and bringing herself back to the brink of climax.

It's such a turn-on. Watching her own her sexuality. Getting herself off. But it's too damn much—the need to have, to take, to claim—and so I do just that.

With one hand on her throat and my dick in her pussy, I dive head first into the addiction that is everything about her. And at thirty-eight thousand feet above the middle of nowhere, she comes quickly—legs tensed, eyes locked on mine, and lips pulled tight—with my hand over her mouth to muffle her moans. The look on her face and her pussy pulsing around my dick pulls me over the edge so I can chase her.

When I catch my breath and look down at her all I can do is shake my head. "That's one hell of an effort," I whisper, leaning down to press my lips to hers, "but even your voodoo pussy isn't magic enough to get me to tell you."

She laughs. That's all she can do.

Goddamn, I'm a lucky man.

Epilogue

PART 2

Rylee

The airport was a thatch hut. We walked straight from the private jet to the awaiting cars, and the road we're on is rutted dirt that requires serious suspension. Ben Montague plays on the radio as I take in the foliage, thick and green around us, causing my curiosity to grow with each passing bump along the road.

Where in the hell is he taking me?

I think back to the look on our boys' faces when we deplaned on the tarmac. Their incessant chatter filled the air. My parents' laughter as they became caught up in Colton's mysterious family vacation. The knowing glance between Becks and Colton, and Haddie's squeeze of my hand before we all loaded into our waiting vehicles. The shower of kisses rained down upon Ace by his adopted brother and his six other brothers—who claim him simply because we unceremoniously claim them—before we separate in three separate car arrangements. The happiness in my heart when Zander looked up and met my eyes. Unspoken words passed between us. *Thank yous* to Colton and I for saving him and at the same time allowing him to still be a part of the family he'd made with the boys. The slight smile on his lips and lift of his head to ask if it's okay to ride with them instead of us was all I needed to know we made the right choice. That we didn't harm the others by saving Zander.

And off we went.

Two vans: one driven by Becks and Haddie with the boys, and the other driven by Andy with the rest of our family. A whole lot of smiles as the doors closed and not much explanation by Colton on the two-way radios other than "we're almost there."

And then there's the three of us in our Jeep. The SUV jostles in the terrain and pulls me back to the sights around us, all the while reminding me how fortunate I am to have everyone here. My boys. My family. My husband.

My everything.

Well, everything except for not knowing where we are, why we've been divided, or where we're headed.

I glance over to Colton. I know it's useless to ask again because he's not going to give me an answer.

Live dangerously with me, Ry.

His words to me flicker through my memory, and I can't help but smile. I want to tell him I'll live dangerously a million times over so long as he never gives up on me. But I know I don't have to worry about that happening. He's already proven he won't. So I do the only thing I can. I shake my head in disbelief and accept how full of love my heart is for him.

We've been through so much in the last year. Things I never thought we'd have to face hit us head-on, blindsided us, and knocked us flat on our asses. Yet here we are, stronger because of it. And I'm not oblivious to the fact we survived when so many other couples wouldn't have.

How could we not have? *It's permanent, right?*

And I glance back to check on Ace, the reason we fought so hard to find our piece of peace again. He seems completely unfazed by this rough ride. I take in his dark hair with a bit of a wave at the ends—the perfect combination of Colton's color and my texture—and my smile is automatic. Green eyes look up and steal my heart like they do every single time they meet mine. Just like his father's.

He babbles something incoherently, chubby cheeks bulging and hands waving in emphasis. I may have no idea where we are going, but I know he's going to be in heaven having all of his brothers, his grandparents, and aunts and uncles here to play with and give him nonstop attention.

"We've lost them," I say, as alarm moves through me when I glance up from Ace and notice the vans aren't behind us.

"Becks knows where he's going. They're fine." It's all he says. Nothing else. I'd love to wrap my hands around that sexy neck of his and force him to tell me where we are and where he's taking me.

"You sure?"

"Yep."

Gah! I tried sex on the plane, sweet-talking, and just about anything else I could imagine but nope, the man won't budge. I just hope wherever the hell we are, my clothes are suitable, because it's not like he gave me a chance to pack. Who knew Colton would surprise us all after the first race of the season by flying us from St. Petersburg to wherever we are now?

Definitely not me.

I look back at Ace to see his eyes closing. The rocking of the car has lulled him to sleep. When I turn around, the view out the windshield hijacks my breath: white sand, palm trees swaying in the breeze, and a small hut on stilts stretched out over the crystal clear water.

"Colton!" I glance over to him and then back to the sight before me, and then back to him. A slow, shy smile turns up one corner of his mouth—dimple winking—but it's the look in his eyes that holds me rapt.

And something fires in my mind, covered somewhere in cobwebs but I must be crazy trying to figure it out when all of this is in front of me.

Colton opens the door and I glance back, deciding to leave Ace sleeping for a moment while I admire the view. I get out of the car as Colton comes around the front, a knowing smile still on his lips, and love in his eyes.

"Do you know this place?" he asks, head angled, hands reaching out to pull me against him.

"What? Colton! This is just . . ." I'm shocked, curious, floored, and grateful as I look up at him with confusion in my eyes.

"I wanted to take a family vacation. We all deserve it after this year, don't you think?" he asks. I know him well enough to know he's holding something back. What it is though, I don't know.

"This place is incredible." I'm still in his arms but my head swivels from side to side to take it all in.

"And secluded," he adds, causing my focus to turn back on him.

"I like secluded," I murmur.

"And bathing suits are optional."

The laugh comes freely. "I'm sure they are," I respond as my mind fires again, but this time it all comes back to me. Knocks me flat on my ass. Takes hold of my heart and squeezes so damn tight my chest hurts from love.

My eyes flash up to his—violet to green—and the words fall from my mouth in a whisper. "This . . . this is from . . ." He nods his head, smile spreading, and waits as my words pause and mind recalls. "When I was sick. This is one of the memories you said you wanted to make with me." Awe owns my voice as I try to comprehend that he did this for me.

"Yes," he whispers and brushes his lips against mine in the most tender of kisses. The kind that owns your soul and completes your heart. "It's the first of many of those memories I plan to make come true for you. We're going to have to buy a lot more frames to put them in."

"Colton . . ." Tears well in my eyes as I pull him closer, the moment so poignant I'm at a loss for words.

"And yes, there is a very skimpy bikini on the bed in there for you that is for my eyes only. Or you can skip it and just run around naked."

"Run around naked?" I say as I look back toward the car where Ace sleeps.

"And that's why our family is at a huge house about three miles down the road. Babysitters," he says with a quirk of his eyebrows.

"You've thought of everything," I murmur against his lips.

"Mm-hmm," he says as he presses a kiss to my nose.

"I can't wait to see you in that loincloth."

He throws his head back and laughs, the vibrations of it echoing in my chest, and all I can do is stare at him. And then laugh with him. Because if we've learned one thing in our marriage it's that we need to laugh as much as we breathe and love like we are the air that allows us to do both.

I stare at him—stubbled cheeks, emerald eyes, and dark hair—and all I see is happiness. All I feel is love. All I know is completeness. All I want is forever with him.

My husband.

My rock.

My piece of peace.

My memory maker.

My happily ever after.

THE END

Slow Burn Bonus Chapter

Haddie and Becks in Las Vegas

The bass of the club's music hits hard as I scan the nearly naked women surrounding us—every single one of them ripe for the picking. A bat of fake lashes. An accidental lean over the bar, tits on display, and painted lips offering up what is literally and figuratively on the table.

So why am I not finding some hot piece, offering to take her up to our room? Shit, I could use a little release after the stress of a long week.

It's Wood's fault. That's my go-to answer. *It's always his fault*. And hell if I'll tell my best friend he was right when he said, "She's got a hot friend."

Hot friend, *my ass*. Haddie Montgomery's more like molten fucking lava.

I sweep my eyes across the crowded dance floor and try to move past her, but it's no goddamn use. *Don't kid yourself. Daniels, you've been looking at her all night*. I toss back the rest of my drink, but my damn eyes remain fixed as she throws her arms up in the air and swivels her hips. Those long, shapely legs move to the beat and hell if I can't get the thought of them and those sexy as fuck heels wrapped around me somehow, someway, out of my damn head.

I avert my gaze, try to distract myself with one of the many easy targets in the club but no one else calls to every part of me like Haddie does. And of course my eyes shift back to the floor just in time to see her dress sneak up some, every toned inch of those thighs is on display as she grinds her hips to the beat. I groan. And I don't even care that I do, because hell if a sane, red-blooded American male would look away from that perfection.

"Hey." I hear to my right as his hand bumps against my arm holding my fresh drink.

"Thanks," I say, forcing myself to pull my eyes from the sight of her, and focus on the man who's like a second brother to me. But when I meet his eyes, they're studying me, amusement mixed with confusion. *Here we go again*. I hate when Colton gets this damn look. "What? What the fuck is that look for?"

"Seriously? You have the two point five look on your face, dude," he says taking a sip of his beer and shaking his head as if he's ashamed.

"*Two point five?*" I sputter, completely shocked that he of all people would say that after the revelation he dropped on me earlier. The one where he admitted that he, the man who's the king of condoms, is sliding skin on skin with his girlfriend, Rylee. Taking that giant leap of trust for the first time ever to bareback with a woman. The confession still staggers me even after more than a few cocktails.

And he's accusing me of the two point five look? I don't think he has any room to throw stones in the fucking glass house he built. "Two point five?" I repeat. "This coming from the barebacking cowboy, himself? *Whatever*. You have no idea what you're talking about. Have another."

"Which one is she?" he asks slinging an arm over my shoulder and pointing toward the dance floor.

"No one." I try to deflect. "Just a whole lot of flesh on display and fuck if it's not something to look at while I get nice and drunk. I've got an asshole for a boss so this buzz," I say with a laugh when he tightens his arm around my neck in a headlock for my dig at him, "and that woman over there are—"

"Hot damn!" he says catching my slip of the tongue. And hell if I wouldn't want to be slipping my tongue into her, but shit if I didn't just give ammunition to the king of antagonization to start taking making his own digs in retaliation. He slaps my back harder than necessary. "I knew just by the sappy-ass look on your face you were looking at some woman on the floor, imagining wedded bliss, and the two point five kids you're going to have with her."

"Shut-up dude. You are so far from—"

"So which one is she?" he goads and I know he's only just getting started. He'll keep at it until I give him something to be smug about.

I look back out to the floor with him scrutinizing my every damn move—trying to figure out which woman has caught the eye of a picky son-of-a-bitch like me. And when I look, a part of me is relieved that Haddie and her best friend, Colton's date Rylee, are no longer on the dance floor...and then another part of me is pissed because I sure as hell was enjoying the show.

"Hot blonde, red dress, two o'clock?" Colton asks, drawing my eyes to the woman on the floor shaking her shit like she should be on a pole. She's definitely hot, all the right curves in all the right places, but nah, not my thing. Owning your sexuality is one thing, but putting it on display? I'll pass.

I look over at Colton and roll my eyes. "Seriously?"

"With those moves?" he says, eyes flicking back out to her. "*Damn.*"

"Dude I'm all for moves like that in bed," I say causing him to snort out that laugh of his that makes me smile regardless of the mood I'm in. "but if I wanted to screw a mannequin, I'll go to Macy's. Besides, isn't eating out of plastic hazardous to your health? BPA or some shit like that?"

He throws his head back and laughs while I take a long drink of my Merit Rum and Coke. And of course I feel bad for talking shit about the unsuspecting woman.

"Sounds like an STD to me, but fuck dude, live on the wild side." He bumps my shoulder with his. "One taste won't kill you."

"This coming from Mr. Discriminate himself? I assure you, it most definitely is not all the same."

"Yeah, you got me there." He shivers in mock disgust, and I can't help but laugh. He looks back out toward the dance area and nods his chin towards where Red Dress is still bumping and grinding. "Not even just for the night?"

"Nah, you know me. Not my thing."

I hear their laughter float over the music before I see them, grateful for the interruption. I lean my elbow on the railing and turn to watch them walk up, pretending not to care. Colton turns too when he hears Rylee so I'm able to watch their approach without him noticing. I take in Haddie's more than handful size tits that bounce a bit with that walk of hers. The combination of blonde hair against her tanned skin begs me to run my eyes down the length of her svelte figure. When my gaze makes its way back up, her mouth is spread wide in a grin and fuck if I don't want something else spread wide on her with me in between them. I get lost in the thought and when I refocus, she is staring right back at me, lips pursed, eyes curious.

"*Yes?*" Those chocolate colored eyes of hers hold mine. Tempt me. Dare me. Question me.

"Sorry." I shake my head, sheepish smile in place. "I was just thinking." *Smooth Becks*. Brilliant response to why you were staring at her like you want to eat her for dinner. Shit, might as well be breakfast since I'm sure it'd be an all night affair, with her body sure as hell being the main course.

"Thinking?" She asks as she reaches out and takes my drink from my hand and tips it up to me, silently asking if it's okay. I nod my head and she lifts it to her lips, taking a sip before handing it back to me. "Thanks. Don't you know Country that you're in a club, in Vegas of all places, so thinking's not allowed?" She sidles up next to me, her body brushing against mine, and snapping my every nerve to attention.

"*Country?*" Where the hell did that nickname come from?

"Yeah," she says with a smirk before shaking her head to get her hair out of her face. "Laid back. Polite. Good guy. Slow and steady wins the race." She raises her eyebrows, challenging me to argue with her assessment.

And fuck if she's not right, so why am I sensing that "country" is a bad thing for her? And why the hell do I care? "Nothing's wrong with slow and steady," I tell her, enjoying how she angles her head to the side and just watches me. "... a man shouldn't be faulted for drawing things out just to make sure the end game is that much sweeter."

And I feel like I've scored a touchdown when I see her eyes widen, take note of the quick intake of breath. Interesting. Playing field seems to be wide open. Good thing I'm a patient man because this woman most definitely does not sit on the sidelines.

"Sweet is good," she leans in and says in my ear, her words a whisper. "But some girls like a little spice added in." She leans back and flashes me a smartass grin, tossing the ball back in my court. Goddamn if it's not hot that her comebacks are as witty as her tits are perfect.

"*City*, I assure you I have talents that can't be put on a resume." I take a drink and raise an eyebrow, failing miserably to hide my smirk. "Besides, it's not the sugar or the spice that matters but rather the man that's mixing it."

We stare at each other for a moment, in silent standoff, as we try to figure out what the other is saying. Is there interest here? Would it be worth it? Damn, who cares because she most definitely would be one helluva wild ride.

A slow, knowing smirk curls up one corner of her mouth, the music changes and becomes more seductive as she shakes her head ever so subtly. "*City?*" She asks and then runs her tongue over her top lip as her eyes taunt me.

My mind goes blank as I focus on her mouth. Shit, I need to play this safe. For all I know, this is just how she is with everyone, a little flirty and a whole lot of fun. After all, it can't get more complicated than going after the best friend of my best friend's girl.

I look out at the floor again, bodies grinding, connections being made even if only for the night, before I look back at Haddie, her eyebrows raised and body so on fire that my dick begs to fly full staff. It's probably just me. And the alcohol. And the influence of the club around me.

It's probably nothing.

But then again, *damn*.

Just damn.

I can't resist. If I can't reach out and touch, I might as well leave a mark with my words. Let her think about how slow and steady might not be such a bad thing after all. "Yeah, City," I repeat. "Classy, non-stop, and always wanting to be in the thick of it all." I take a drink, my eyes locked on hers while she watches, contemplating what I've said.

"The thick of it, huh?" She takes my drink from my hand again and smirks as she sucks ever so slowly from the straw.

And once again, my eyes are drawn to those lip-glossed lips of hers and notice how they are sucking on my straw. *So that's why they put straws in men's drinks*. I have a whole new appreciation for those annoying little fuckers now. I watch her tongue play with it momentarily and realize that part of the reason she's so damn sexy is because she's not purposefully trying to be.

Something catches her eye and I follow her head as she turns to watch Colton lead Rylee up the stairs toward the mezzanine. At least I don't have to worry about him sticking his nose in where it doesn't belong now. When I look back toward Haddie, she's moved toward me, her face closer to mine. I can smell the scent of the alcohol from my drink on her breath, and hell if I can understand why that makes me want her that much more.

"Yep. Always wanting to be in the middle of the action," I say, lifting the straw out of my drink and taking a sip.

Haddie twists her lips until the smirk breaks its way through. "Action's always good. Being in the middle of it's even better." She arches an eyebrow at me as I try and figure out what her next words are going to be but remain silent. It's time to let her wonder what I'm thinking for a change. I hold her gaze, the swirling lights overhead changing color and reflecting in her blonde hair. "And I think I'm wanting some right now."

I force a swallow, those taunting yet innocent words of hers causing a visceral reaction that I try to ignore. "What kind of action are you looking for?" There. Let her figure out if I'm flirting or if that's just how I am, because I can't tell shit with her. And fuck, I can always figure everyone out. So what's so different about her?

She doesn't answer. Instead, she turns and looks over her shoulder. "You coming?"

And fuck...there are so many ways my mind answers that question that I groan. I swallow over the ache that our flirting and her damn, fine ass in perfect view creates. "You know what they say?"

"What?" she asks, stopping momentarily, "Every good man's place is behind a woman?"

I chuckle. That most definitely was not where I was going with this conversation, but there she goes again, wanting me to take the bait. "The only reason for a man to be behind a woman is because he's checking out her very fine ass." And hell if that's not the truth right now.

She licks her lips and I have a hard time looking away from her tongue as it darts out and then back in. "Haven't had any complaints so far, Country," she says with a shake of her head, her hair swaying all the way down her back. "And uh, there are many more places I'd prefer a man to be," she says with a wink before turning and walking into the crowd, without even checking to see if I'm following.

Yeah, on top of you. Or under. Or...shit, my mind reels with the possibilities.

She may think I'm slow and steady but hell if I'm stupid.

Time to dance.

Sweet Ache Christmas Scene

"Q?" Hawke's voice floats down the hall, a mixed melody of curiosity and excitement in that velvet rasp of his. I shift in anticipation. My body already on fire for his touch.

It's been eight long weeks. Fifty-six days worth of Skype chats, dirty talking over the buzz of my vibrator and his strained voice panting my name. One thousand three hundred forty four hours of missing him, wanting him, waiting for him to come home to me.

"In here," I say at the same time the sounds of his boots stop outside the bedroom door.

I've envisioned the next few seconds in my head - how it's going to play out, what his reaction will be—and as much as I want it to be absolutely perfect, I'm having a ridiculously hard time not running to the door, throwing it open, and jumping into his arms.

The handle turns. I hold my breath. The door swings open. My body stills as my bad boy rocker with the good guy heart slowly comes into view. I take in the black combat boots, the Eagles' T-shirt, leather wrist cuffs—my body vibrating with excitement. And then I meet his eyes. Storm colored irises stare back with so many emotions swimming in them—happiness, relief, longing, and desire.

The moment holds. Two lovers kept apart by distance, now reconnecting yet savoring those final last seconds before libidinous hunger gives way to the clothes ripping, teeth nipping, hands digging kind of sex my body instantly craves at the sight of him.

"Hi." My voice is breathless. Desperate. Needy.

And then his eyes leave mine and take in the rest of me. His quick intake of breath fills the room and even though he doesn't speak, that singular sound is all I need to hear to know he feels the same way.

I watch his eyes scrape up the high heels, fishnet stockings, and leather cupless bustier before meeting my eyes. A slow, cocky grin pulls up one corner of his mouth the same time he drops bags with a thud to the floor.

"Hi." A bob of his Adam's apple. A twitch of his fingers as if he's itching to touch. A quirk of his eyebrow. All a slow seduction themselves when I don't need anything but him and me. Right here. Right now.

"Welcome home. Merry Christmas. Get undressed." All three of my demands are equally important. Only one is urgent.

That tug of a smirk turns into a full-blown grin as Hawke casually makes his way toward me, drawing out his reaction in painstakingly slow fashion. "Welcome home. Merry Christmas. Get undressed," he repeats with a raise of one eyebrow. "It's time to unwrap my present." The comment takes me back to that first time I drove him home three years ago.

You're like unwrapping a present. So many surprises to discover.

He stops in front of me, our bodies a whisper apart, our breaths feathering over each others, and desire ricocheting in the space between us. His cologne, his energy, everything I've missed over the past few months assaults my senses and makes me want to take and ravage but I know he likes his foreplay. And his *sugar*.

Let's see how long it takes him to find it.

With eyes intense, his hands come up to frame my face. Every part of me that wasn't already standing to attention, sparks instantly to life. Unspoken words pass between us as his mouth slowly descends to meet mine. A soft brush of a kiss. A gentle touching of tongues. My hands sliding beneath the hem of his shirt to touch the corded muscle beneath. His fingers tensing on my jaw as he draws out this first meeting of lips in a tantalizing temptation of everything I want to devour but love that he's savoring.

God, I missed him. Missed this. Can't wait to drown myself in more than just the taste of his lips over the next three weeks he's home and off tour. And completely mine.

"Now that's a welcome home if I've ever seen one," he murmurs as the kiss ends but our lips remain brushing against each others.

"There's a lot more where that comes from." Suggestion laces my tone but desire tinges the edges.

"I can see that," he says as he runs his hands down my bare arms to link his hands with mine. He steps back and holds our arms out so that he can look at me once again. And the minute he sees it, I can tell. The dart of his tongue to wet his lips. The stutter in movement. The flash of gray up to meet my eyes. "My two biggest vices—you and sugar—all wrapped into one stellar package."

I love the grate in his voice. The audible sound of his desire. It turns me on. Causes that sweet ache he always creates to intensify.

"Unwrap me, rocker boy."

A strained chuckle falls from his lips. With eyes still on mine, he pushes me to sit back on the bed behind me as he drops to his knees on the floor before me. The spread of my legs apart is an instant reaction, my own reflection of need for him as he moves between them. His eyes flick down to my nipples and an appreciative groan rumbles deep in his throat before his gaze lifts back to mine.

He lifts a brow in question. "For me, sweetness?"

It takes everything I have to not throw my head back and laugh. Who else does he think I'd wet my nipples and dip them in pixie stick sugar for?

"You use instruments. *I use sugar.*" My last word falls off into a gasp when his lips close over the sugared peak of my breast. My head falls back, my legs fall open, and my body eases into the bliss of his tongue sweeping circles over the sensitive skin.

One of his hands finds its way between my thighs as his tongue continues its welcome assault on my senses. His other hand grabs my ass and scoots it closer to the edge of the bed and farther into the adept skill of his fingers waiting and wanting there.

"Hawke." His name is on my lips while my taste is on his tongue as he switches from side to the other with a satisfied sigh. And when his lips close around my nipple this time, his guitar hardened fingers part the lips of my pussy and dip into my wetness.

"Fucking perfection," he murmurs, the vibration of his voice, warmth of his mouth, and skill of his fingertips give me everything I've been missing, craving, and desperate for. With his thumb on my clit, he begins to slide his fingers in and out of me, scraping over right where I need it to me.

And while my vibrator may have taken care of business while he's been gone, there is nothing—absolutely nothing—that equals the feeling of his hands on me. In me. Pleasuring me into that riotous orgasmic frenzy that only he can.

His teeth scrape over my nipple. My hands thread through his hair. His fingertips curve against my hub of nerves. My body tenses. He quickens the pace of his fingers, driving me harder and faster. Our breaths pant. Our hearts race. His absence has made my orgasm so much easier to summon.

A moan falls from my lips as I tighten around his fingers, my tell tale sign I'm so very close. He lifts his face to watch me: eyes locked, teeth biting into his bottom lip, sex personified.

"I'm coming," I moan just as my body goes tight, the orgasm slamming into me with reckless abandon. My fingernails dig into his arms as he draws out the sensations: softer strokes, incendiary words, intense eyes.

"Goddamn. I've missed watching you come. Making you come," he murmurs as he leans in and kisses me long and thoroughly, sugar and need a potent combination on his tongue. He withdraws his fingers, the sounds and smell of my desire fill the room, an aphrodisiac that only makes me want more of him.

When Hawke rises from the floor, his knees still between mine, he pulls his shirt over his head and balls it with one hand before tossing it aside. I take the moment to appreciate every single inch of him but stop to watch his hands, still glistening from my arousal, undo the buttons on his jeans.

Damn.

"My turn, sweetness."

My eyes flash up to his, sass on my lips and reignited desire in my eyes. "Play me, Hawkin."

Hard Beat—Chapter One

Beaux

Tanner Thomas is a household name on the foreign beat. I've heard he's a strict professional who is returning to the field after a tough blow with the loss of his partner. The unfortunate turn of events is admittedly horrible but it makes him a perfect match for me. Someone who probably doesn't want to team up with anyone new and by the laws of human nature won't want to get close to anyone right now.

Laughter erupts on the other side of the room causing me to glance over to where I last caught a glimpse of Tanner's back. As always on a mission, disinterest is my best friend. It allows me to slip below the radar, slide seamlessly into the flow of things, and always remain in the periphery.

But as I observe the various reporters, producers, and photojournalists working their way toward him, it strikes me there is something different in the atmosphere tonight. The general mood in the room is lighter, energetic, and in some inexplicable way feels hopeful in a sense.

I don't want to attribute it to the presence of Tanner Thomas. It's ludicrous to believe that a single person can breathe life into a community like has happened tonight.

But there's no denying it either.

And it's not just the alcohol flowing more freely than normal. There's a current in the room that's indescribable. It's like they know he's here so things are going to start happening again instead of the day after day monotony that has the norm since I arrived over two weeks ago.

"C'mon T-squared!" Someone yells with a slap of his hand on the bar, and I start craning my head back and forth to see between the crowd of bodies from my spot on the other side of the bar.

"I'm game if you're game!" A voice booms before I can catch a glimpse of what's going on. I don't need to see whose lips are moving to know it was Tanner speaking because chill raced over my skin at the sound of the familiar baritone I know from watching his broadcasts. It's likely just the knowledge that I'm so close to pulling my boots up and wading straight into the thick of my cover that causes the goose bumps to come. That undeniable thrill of anticipation.

That has to be the cause of the sudden fluttery feeling in my stomach.

Another reporter I've spoken to on a few occasions, Gus, I believe is his name, hands me a shot with a whoop of a laugh and before I can even ask why, a hush falls over the room.

"Shh. Shh. Shh." Pauly, a fellow reporter, climbs atop a chair, a shot glass filled with amber liquid in one hand and his other motioning for the lot of us to quiet down. He looks down to his right and for the first time I catch a fleeting glimpse of Tanner's face before the crowd shifts and I lose sight of him again. "Tanner Thomas . . . we are so glad to see your ugly ass back in this shithole. I'm sure once you hand our asses to us time and again by getting the story first, we'll want you to leave, but for now we're glad you're here. Slainte!"

"Slainte!" I say back in unison with the rest of the crowd, then the sound of swearing fills my ears as the burn of the alcohol hits everyone's throats.

Needing to appear to be a part of the group, I take a sip but I know well enough that a drunk woman in a city like this is just asking for trouble. And I get in enough trouble on my own, thank you.

When I glance back through the crowd again, I'm startled when I lock eyes with Tanner. It's only a split second of time, just long enough for me to tip my shot glass to him before someone moves and blocks our connection, but it's enough to have me holding my breath and that fluttering to return in my belly.

I sit there in complete indecision for a second, since that momentary connection unarmed me for some reason when I'm hard to rattle. *Jesus, Beaux, it's not like you've never met a mark before.* Exhaling slowly, I tell myself that I need to keep my wits. It was stupid for me to search him out since I don't plan on meeting him face to face until our assigned meeting at ten tomorrow morning. Besides, my new boss, Rafe, might not have even told him about me yet. He warned me Tanner was going to resist the idea of a new partner, that he might be tough on me. Little did Rafe know that in my line of work, tough is an everyday norm.

So if I don't plan on meeting Tanner until tomorrow, why do I keep looking back to where he's sitting? What am I going to gain with one more glimpse of him?

Absolutely nothing.

And yet I look again. This time there is a complete break in the crowd and I catch Pauly's eyes. By the way he smirks at me, then looks over to Tanner and throws his head back with a laugh I know they are talking about me. Call it woman's intuition or just plain curiosity but I know. And now I definitely can't look away.

The problem, though, is that not looking away means that my gaze moves from Pauly to Tanner and this time I'm afforded more than just a glimpse of him. I'm granted the whole entire package.

Dark hair frames his tanned face and there's something intriguing about his eyes that I can't quite put my finger on across the distance. I don't have a chance to consider it for very long because when he shifts his gaze and his eyes lock on mine, I freeze in place: lips shocked open, heart skipping a beat, and a flash of something I want to deny as being attraction flickers through me.

But this time I recover quickly and turn my lips up into a slow, knowing smile as we hold each other's gaze. In contrast to the flash of hunger I catch in his eyes, he nods his head nonchalantly with an arrogant curl to his mouth before looking away.

But I keep staring.

And there's something about the whole exchange that infuriates me.

I need to remember he's just my cover, the man I need to partner up with to protect my ass. So there's no reason to be irritated that he just reeled me in with those eyes and then disregarded me without so much as a second look. Ironically it's the exact same thing I had planned on doing to him - use my looks right off the bat if I sensed any attraction in order to catch him off guard enough to use my brain and intuition to do my job.

I may be an agent, but first and foremost I'm a woman, and no woman likes to be made to feel like they are inconsequential. For the first time in forever I am pissed about someone not noticing me.

Agitated and irritated, I'm suddenly tossing back the shot I had no intention of drinking,. The burn comes fast and I hope my sense follows suit because no man has ever thrown me off my game when it comes to work, romantically or otherwise--and yet with a single glance, Tanner Thomas has done just that.

I turn the glass around in circles on the scarred table top as I try to figure out what exactly it was about the exchange that instantly had him getting beneath my skin. It was ten seconds tops and yet those ten seconds packed a punch I never expected.

It had to be the look he gave me. While I've seen him a hundred times filing live reports—and I've both appreciated his looks and admired his skills--yet nothing prepared me for the absolute intensity in his eyes. Not to mention the flash fire of heat that surged in my lower belly when our gazes met.

And with that last thought, I'm immediately shoving my chair back. All my best laid plans have gone out the window: the play it cool, we'll meet face to face for the first time tomorrow, fly under the radar. I've made a living on being able to read people and in that brief meeting of our eyes, he was able to get a visceral reaction out of me. That in itself is rare. Even more unheard of is for me to take the bait and say fuck it to my rules, which is exactly what I'm doing by walking across the bar to face this head on.

There's something about the contradiction between the look in his eyes and his rigid posture that tells me he doesn't like to be handled. Wants all of the control. And God yes in a lover that's sexy as hell, but in a man I have to work with under difficult circumstances, it's not so appealing. I need to get the upper hand here so I can control the situation before it even starts.

Fate has to be on my side because the barstool next to Tanner is vacant when I approach. So I slide into the seat, face him and wait for him to look my way. I know he senses my presence, can see the stiffening of his posture, the fleeting tension in his fingers, but he doesn't lift his eyes from where he's tracing lines over the grooves on the scarred wood bar top.

He's attractive in an odd combination of rugged mixed with preppy pretty boy. Camera worthy looks but with a hint of edge to the lines giving character to his face.

The seconds pass as I wait him out, questioning my decision to come over here but I won't back down now. I'm not wishy washy. Hate women that are. I didn't get where I am professionally by being a damn doormat. But standing here waiting for him to glance my way suddenly unnerves me.

"Whatever you're looking for, I'm not him," he says without looking up.

The part of me that felt uncertainty sags in relief and welcomes his hostility. I can definitely work with his lack of warmth, hold onto it, and use it to my advantage to find my footing. He has no clue that we're about to enter into a partnership.

"I don't believe I'm looking for anything." I feign nonchalance, don't want to give him any more than he is giving me and yet at the same time hope it brings a reaction out of him. Something. Anything.

"Good."

Well, that wasn't exactly what I was looking for but at least he hasn't gotten up and left. I glance up to the bartender and then back toward Tanner. "Whiskey sour," I order from the bartender, and notice a slight startle of Tanner's head in my periphery. I smirk, his reaction giving me the perfect in to get his full attention. "And put it on his tab."

Bingo. Tanner snaps his head up and immediately meets my gaze. If I thought the intensity in his eyes was powerful before, it's tenfold now. The problem is that it's not just the intensity that pins me immobile, but also the unique amethyst color of his eyes mixed with his undeniable good looks. Proximity to him might not have been a good idea because I find myself captivated by him.

A completely foreign and unwelcome feeling hits me so fast that I shove away from the bartop. I maintain my smirking expression and the challenging look I'm giving him even as my insides somersault into nothingness and that quick ache of lust hits me head on. The flash of intrigue comingled with amusement in his eyes tells me that he'd love nothing more for me to be the typical female I'm sure he's used to dealing with: compliant, star-struck, fumbling over her words.

He's got another thing coming if that's what he's expecting.

"I don't believe I offered to buy you one." He leans back and angles his head, eyes assessing and daring me all at once.

"Well, I don't believe I asked you to be an asshole either, so the drink's on you." The comment is off my tongue before I can think it through. We stare at each other like two caged animals circling, trying to figure the other one out, and knowing regardless of our indifference, there is definitely a game of some sort being played between us. Good thing I know what that game is.

"Then I guess you should steer clear of me and neither of us will have to worry about me being an asshole." He grunts the words out, and I don't know whether I should be glad or upset about his response.

On one hand his lack of interest could make this whole mission easier. He'll leave me alone, let me do my thing, so long as I get my work done when he needs it. On the other hand, he's damn attractive and it could be extremely beneficial to use sex appeal to my advantage. Reel him in, keep him under my wing, and get my job done quicker by playing the innocent female card.

The problem with using sex appeal though is that I've watched other female agents play theirs up, draw lines, erase them, redraw them, and in the end get hurt by becoming too emotionally invested.

All my training has warned me that there will be one person that will make me cross that line. *No way. Not me*. The job, the mission, the objective, all three mean way too much to cross any lines, regardless of the sexual chemistry I feel licking at my heels as I stand here and hold his stare.

I wait for the comment I can see forming on his lips to come but just as unexpected as this conversation has been, he breaks our eye contact without saying another word and refocuses on the glass in his hand.

"So you're the one, huh?" My thoughts turn to words before I realize what I'm saying and disbelief robs me from saying anything else as Tanner turns to look at me again, glass stopped midway to his lips, and that way he has of staring straight into you and seeing every single thing you want to hide.

"The one?"

And without any pertinent words being exchanged or even so much as an introduction being made, I know without a doubt that Tanner Thomas is the one person who's going to make me question crossing that damn line. Call it a gut reaction or a psychotic episode, but I have a feeling that this mission is going to be anything but the easy get in, get out, get done type that I had planned on it being.

And it will have nothing to do with the mission but rather everything to do with the attractive man before me and his inquisitive eyes.

Once I process the thought, try to laugh it off, and ferret it away to worry about and obsess over later, I scramble to answer his question hanging heavy in the air between us. Make the comment relevant somehow, some way.

"Yep, the one that every reporter in this room hates and wants to be all at the same time," I explain, speaking nothing but the truth I've come to learn while waiting for him to arrive.

Skepticism causes him to narrow his eyes and amusement has him pursing his lips as he tries to figure out if he believes me or not. I'm not sure if he does or not because he breaks our stare and motions to the bartender for a bottle of whiskey. The exchange of money for the bottle happens quickly. Tanner scoots his chair back, grabs the neck of the fifth of alcohol and gives me a half-cocked, arrogant smirk.

"Yep, I'm the one." He turns his back to me and strides away.

Cocky son of a bitch. And he most definitely is, yet I still watch him leave the bar, lifting the bottle up to the protests of the other journalists gathered to welcome him back.

And even when he's cleared the doorway and I can no longer see him, I'm still watching. There's just something about him when I most definitely don't want there to be.

He's the one all right.

Hopefully he's the one I can avoid.

About the Author

New York Times Bestselling author K. Bromberg writes contemporary romance novels that contain a mixture of sweet, emotional, a whole lot of sexy, and a little bit of real. She likes to write strong heroines and damaged heroes who we love to hate but can't help to love.

A mom of three, she plots her novels in between school runs and soccer practices, more often than not with her laptop in tow and her mind scattered in too many different directions.

Since publishing her first book on a whim in 2013, Kristy has sold over one and a half million copies of her books across eighteen different countries and has landed on the *New York Times*, *USA Today*, and *Wall Street Journal* Bestsellers lists over thirty times. Her Driven trilogy (*Driven*, *Fueled*, and *Crashed*) is currently being adapted for film by the streaming platform, Passionflix, with the first movie (*Driven*) out now.

With her imagination always in overdrive, she is currently scheming, plotting, and swooning over her latest hero. You can find out more about him or chat with Kristy on any of her social media accounts. The easiest way to stay up to date on new releases and upcoming novels is to s to sign up for her newsletter or follow her on Bookbub.

Made in the USA
Las Vegas, NV
12 February 2022

43786964R00442